POSTMODERN AMERICAN FICTION

A Norton Anthology

PAULA GEYH

SOUTHERN ILLINOIS UNIVERSITY AT CARBONDALE

FRED G. LEEBRON

GETTYSBURG COLLEGE

ANDREW LEVY

BUTLER UNIVERSITY

W • W • NORTON & COMPANY • NEW YORK • LONDON

Printed in the United States of America
First Edition

The text of this book is composed in Stone Serif
Composition by Haddon Craftsmen
Cover painting: Roger Brown, *Skylab by Minicam,* 1979. Private collection.
Courtesy of Phyllis Kind Gallery, New York and Chicago.

Library of Congress Cataloging-in-Publication Data

Postmodern American fiction : a Norton anthology / (edited by) Paula Geyh.
Fred G. Leebron. Andrew Levy.
p. cm.
Includes bibliographical references and index.

ISBN 0-393-31698-X (pbk.)

1. American fiction—20th century. 2. Postmodernism (Literature)—
United States. I. Geyh, Paula. II. Leebron, Fred G. III. Levy, Andrew,
1962–
PS659.P67 1997
813' .5080113—dc21 97–24446

W. W. Norton & Company, Inc., 500 Fifth Avenue, New York, N.Y. 10110
http://www.wwnorton.com
W. W. Norton & Company Ltd., 10 Coptic Street, London WC1A 1PU

3 4 5 6 7 8 9 0

Contents

Introduction

Along a commercial stretch of Los Angeles' Venice Boulevard is the Museum of Jurassic Technology, an institution whose incongruous name signals the perplexities contained inside. An enigmatic banner reading "Ā, Ē, N̄" hangs over the entrance, an abbreviation for the museum's motto: "non-Aristotelian, non-Euclidean, non-Newtonian." Inside, viewing brilliantly lit glass cases set within dim, hushed galleries, visitors encounter a series of disorienting curiosities. One large exhibit presents the eccentric theory of memory developed by Geoffrey Sonnabend, a nearly forgotten American neurophysiologist. Impossibly complex geometric models illustrate the theory, detailing, for instance, the intersection of the "plane of experience" with the "cone of confabulation." Another exhibit traces the history of the search for a rare South American horned bat, believed by the natives of the region to be a demon that can penetrate solid objects. The exhibit contains diagrams of how bats use echoes to navigate through darkness; a model of a thatched hut, with arrows indicating the path of the bat through its walls; and a rendering of the only specimen of the bat ever apprehended, purportedly (and invisibly) embedded deep within a block of solid lead. An adjacent exhibit of nanotechnology offers microscopic machines such as an electrostatic motor, viewable through an array of microscopes. They look as though they might actually work.

One display is devoted entirely to improbable folk remedies (though the accompanying audio affirms that such universally accepted curatives as penicillin and digitalis had their origins in folk medicine) such as "duck's breath" and "mice on toast." Another gallery features a floor-to-ceiling array of letters received by the astronomers at the Mount Wilson Observatory between the years 1915 and 1935. The writers of the letters volunteer for missions to Mars, recount meetings with aliens, and offer elaborate proofs that the Earth is flat. And finally, a single case contains five small dishes of powder labeled "possession," "delusion," "paranoia," "schizophrenia," and "reason." The dish labeled "reason" has been shattered by the descent of a mysterious mechanical device that was suspended over it. The exhibit is marked "out of order."

While the Museum of Jurassic Technology is reminiscent of the "wonder cabinets" of the Renaissance, the ephemera collections of the eighteenth century, and the great natural-history museums established in the nineteenth century, it also provides the visitor with an introduction to the dissolution of intellectual authority that for many critics represents the core of the postmodern sensibility. Traversing the zone between the real and the unreal, never quite certain where the boundaries lie, visitors debate the "authenticity" of particular artifacts and question the "truth" of their convoluted histories. The scholarly apparatuses that usually lend such authority to exhibits (the intricate displays, the models and diagrams, the elaborate curation and cataloging) here seem as suspect—and playfully ironic—as some of the objects on display. You cannot move through the Museum of Jurassic Technology with an attitude of respectful studiousness; instead, you must navigate among the contradictions and paradoxes of the exhibits and their authoritative commentaries, deciding for yourself what is, is not, or yet might be a joke. While there is a loss of both certainty and security here, this skepticism has its powers and pleasures. Perhaps we do not really miss the voice of absolute authority, or our faith in it, so much.

In introducing this anthology of postmodern American fiction, it seems fitting to begin in the halls of this museum, in its own way an anthology of the postmodern spirit. For many observers, the term "postmodern" refers to "postmodernity," a historical period stretching from the 1960s to the present, marked by such phenomena as upheavals in the international economic system, the Cold War and its decline, the increasing ethnic heterogeneity of the American population, the growth of the suburbs as a cultural force, the predominance of television as a cultural medium, and the rise of the computer. For others, however, the term "postmodern" connotes "postmodernism," a tentative grouping of ideas, stylistic traits, and thematic preoccupations that set the last four decades apart from earlier eras. In the arts, postmodern traits include pastiche, the incorporation of different textual genres and contradictory "voices" within a single work; fragmented or "open" forms that give the audience the power to assemble the work and determine its meaning; and the adoption of a playful irony as a stance that seems to prove itself endlessly useful. In philosophy and critical theory, the term "postmodernist" applies to a wide range of concepts, approaches, and positions in ongoing debates, the most significant of which concern the problematic relationship between the real and the unreal; the constructedness of meaning, truth, and history; and the complexities of subjectivity and identity. All of these are marked by a thoroughgoing skepticism toward the foundations and structures of knowledge, a skepticism much like that brought into play at the Museum of Jurassic Technology.

At the same time, it is crucial to bring some of that skepticism to the word "postmodern" itself, as a prelude to any attempt to distinguish what is postmodern from what is not. Like many of the phenomena it is used to describe, the term calls attention to its own contingency and contradictions, and makes itself available to diverse audiences for disparate purposes. While for decades scholars have argued its meaning, the debate has extended far beyond the academy: from the producers of the Christian Broadcasting Network's *700 Club,* who in January 1996 published a "fact sheet" denouncing postmodernism as an amoral pseudo-religion, to the creators of *The Simpsons,* who have sardonically advertised their hit television show as "Nouveau Postmodernism for the Masses," the word carries wildly divergent meanings and connotations for different people. And when the discussion switches to postmodern American fiction, the conflict does not abate. To a major writer and critic such as John Barth, postmodern American fiction is best represented by a well-established group of formally experimental authors who gained recognition in the 1960s: Barth, Thomas Pynchon, Richard Brautigan, Grace Paley, Donald Barthelme, and Robert Coover most prominent among them. To African-American critic bell hooks, however, postmodern American fiction might be best represented by the surge of minority authorship from the 1970s through the 1990s, and the fundamental cultural changes that made that surge possible. Finally, to the readers of cyberpunk fiction, graphic novels, or hypertext on computer, or for the readers who have found increasing elements of television, pop music, and film within the books and short stories of "serious" authors, postmodern American fiction is best exemplified by the growth of new genres that reflect social changes, forms of publication that absorb technological developments, and an unprecedented relationship between literature and popular culture. As the distinction between postmodernity and postmodernism suggests, however, a work of fiction can reflect postmodern traits without necessarily belonging to a specific school or genre. The history of postmodern American fiction belongs to those authors who, in any idiom and for any audience, for brief passages or for entire careers, shared a new cultural sensibility as a response to an altered world.

Postwar America and Postmodern American Fiction

The literature of any time is inevitably bound up with that time, simultaneously shaped by world events and shaping how we understand them. Postmodern American fiction often draws its subject matter from the enormous changes America and the world have undergone over the past forty years; from historic international realignments; from reconfigurations of local and international economies; from rapid technological developments and demographic shifts; and most significantly, from revolutions in how information is communicated between individuals and among nations. While cultural and literary postmodernism begin in the 1960s, the legacy of World War II remains a crucial touchstone. Though the United States won the war and emerged as a dominant world power, deeply disturbing contradictions came out of the afterglow of victory. The mass genocide of World War II and America's use of the atom bomb led many to a profound and ongoing questioning of the idea of historical "progress," the belief that as our knowledge grows, we become increasingly rational and civilized. The same scientific and technological advances that marked humanity's "advancement" were also those deployed in the historically unprecedented slaughter of the twentieth century.

How to resolve this paradox has become a crucial debate of the postmodern era. Were such events proof that the Enlightenment project, with its dreams of progress for humanity through reason and science, had failed? Or was it that we had failed reason by using its triumphs for irrational or evil purposes? In postmodern fiction, World War II, the Holocaust, Hiroshima, and the atom bomb appear often as metaphors for this failure of reason, as historical markers to explore how we manage to live with such absolute contradiction, or simply as spectral presences that remind us that nuclear arsenals still exist, and that our lives remain charged and threatened by visions of apocalypse. In Art Spiegelman's *Maus* (1986), for instance, or in Philip Roth's *The Ghost Writer* (1979), the Holocaust catalyzes profound investigations of the nature of identity and specifically ethnicity; in Thomas Pynchon's *The Crying of Lot 49* (1966) the ex-Nazi Los Angeles psychiatrist Dr. Hilarius raises a separate set of issues about the endurance of fascism into late-twentieth-century America. The shadow of Hiroshima appears in the visions of nuclear apocalypse that paradoxically haunt and comfort the protagonists of Douglas Coupland's *Generation X* (1991), or the "apocalyptic" sunsets that captivate the characters in Don DeLillo's *White Noise* (1985). It is also apparent in novels that seek alternatives to Enlightenment rationalism, such as Leslie Marmon Silko's *Ceremony* (1977) and Jay Cantor's *Krazy Kat* (1987), both set in the haunted Southwestern desert where the first atom bombs were detonated.

World War II left the world (at least from America's vantage point) divided between American and Soviet "spheres of influence." The resulting Cold War precipitated a perception of crisis within the United States. As the national emphasis on unity and resolve in the face of external threats was extended to perceived internal threats in the 1950s, America veered into the outright repression of the McCarthy era and responded with ambivalence to the burgeoning Civil Rights Movement. In literature, these developments sparked a critique of prevailing ideals of American citizenship from such authors as Lillian Hellman, Norman Mailer, Ralph Ellison, and Allen Ginsberg. In the 1960s, amid the turmoil of the Civil Rights Movement, the Vietnam War, the rise of the counterculture, and the early Women's Liberation Movement, these conflicts expanded and intensified. A series of traumatic events combined to bring "the official story"—the received narratives of our history and of our present—into question. For many Americans, the assassinations of President John F. Kennedy, Malcolm X, Dr. Martin Luther King Jr., and Senator Robert F. Kennedy in the 1960s forced a recognition of intolerance and violence in the social fabric that had been obscured by the more optimistic vision of American life that had initially prevailed after World War II. In the 1970s, the revelations of the Pentagon Papers and the Watergate scandal further undermined faith in the truthfulness of government officials and the versions of events they presented. These scandals, followed by others in the 1980s and 1990s, extended the widespread skepticism of the 1960s beyond government to include a suspicion of almost any form of institutional authority. This skepticism in turn spawned subcultures obsessed with conspiracy theories, and introduced the idea of conspiracy into the mainstream of American ideas as a potential explanation for phenomena as wide-ranging as assassinations, MIAs in Vietnam, United Nations policy, and UFO sightings.

The word "postmodern" entered the lexicon of American life in the 1960s—at least its academic life—as part of a broader cultural questioning of social conformity, political inequality, and the necessity for a unified national ethos. Within literary postmodernism, this broad cultural skepticism manifested itself as an assault upon traditional definitions of narrative. When the author/narrator of Kurt Vonnegut's *Slaughterhouse-Five* (1969) comments, "I would hate to tell you what this lousy little book cost me in money and anxiety and time," he is not simply stepping out of his role to address the reader with a new intimacy; he is also complicating the rules by which the reader can expect a story to unfold. During the 1960s, the first generation of authors to be called "postmodernists" explicitly interrogated narrative conventions, particularly those that created coherence or closure. In the pages of *The New Yorker,* Donald Barthelme openly told his readers that fragments were the only trustworthy form. In *The Atlantic Monthly*, John Barth argued that "postmodernism" represented "The Literature of Exhaustion" (1967), a term he invoked to suggest possibility, not hopelessness. Grace Paley wrote parables of New York life that reflected her absolute control over, and affection for, the polyglot voices that made themselves heard on the streets of that cultural capital. From the other side of the continent, Ishmael Reed adapted African-American cultural forms and challenged the received myths of American life. And with *The Crying of Lot 49* and *Gravity's Rainbow* (1973), Thomas Pynchon presciently introduced conspiracy into the novel, both as a subject and as a model for how a novel could communicate meaning to its reader.

The "official story" of American history also came under attack for its unitary character. In some cases, authors incorporated discordant voices within their texts: in Joyce Carol Oates' "The Turn of the Screw" (1972), voices run in parallel columns through the text, recounting intertwined, but not necessarily compatible, versions of the story, which is being retold from the original 1898 version by Henry James. In other cases, however, a wider transformation of American life was calling attention to the margins of literature, and to the voices that had previously been ignored. In part, this transformation was (and continues to be) demographic: by 2050, the U.S. Census estimates, the combined population of Americans of Asian, African, Hispanic, Indian, and American Indian descent will equal that of European Americans. In part, this transformation is cultural, effected by dramatic changes in the position of minorities within American life. While Brown v. Board of Education, the Civil Rights Movement, the Civil Rights Act of 1964, and the rise of minority middle-classes have assisted in breaking down segregation and creating an unprecedented shared national culture, continuing inequalities in the distribution of wealth and the persistence of prejudice have also demonstrated the limitations of legal remedies for racism. This divided progress toward racial integration and equality, in turn, catalyzed the rise of identity politics (a politics based on a notion of identity defined by race, gender, sexual orientation, ethnicity, or religion), micropolitics (the focus on local issues) and the "dissensus culture" (the consensus that there is likely to be no consensus).

The impact of these changes on postmodern American literature cannot be underestimated. As American culture has become more fragmented, its literature has also become more pluralistic. In effect, the breakdown of the "official story" created space for other stories and other voices: as the title of Gloria Anzaldúa's *Borderlands/La Frontera* (1987) indicates, for instance, the new voices of American literature sometimes present themselves as representatives of the literal geographic margins of the country. Toni Morrison's *Beloved* (1987) uses the voice of a ghost child, among others, to retell the history of slavery. Sherman Alexie, in "Captivity" (1993), presents a conversation between a contemporary American Indian and Mary Rowlandson, the Puritan author of a famed and influential seventeenth-century captivity narrative that portrayed Indians as devils. Finally, the newfound heterogeneity of American culture also manifests itself in postmodern narratives where authors have emphasized the complexities of identity and its embrace of hybrid forms and styles. Ricardo Cortez Cruz's "rap-lit" short story "Welcome to the Ghetto" (1997) incorporates "samplings" of popular music, television, film, and advertising. Theresa Hak Kyung Cha's *Dictee* (1982) retells history using official documents, photographs, and handwritten drafts. Silko's *Ceremony* combines the form of a novel with the form of a Laguna Pueblo chant.

Many aspects of postmodern American fiction may also be seen as effects of vast economic transformations. As the consistent economic growth of the 1950s and 1960s faltered in subsequent decades, the texture of American life also changed dramatically. The rise of the global economy and the emergence of transnational companies accelerated the shift of the American economy from one based on manufacturing to one based on services and information technologies—what sociologist Daniel Bell called the "post-industrial society." One effect of this shift was a massive displacement of blue-collar workers whose jobs disappeared, were downgraded, or moved overseas. A second effect was mainstream frustration and cynicism regarding the American Dream: as real wages declined from 1973 on, both white-collar professionals and blue-collar workers felt uncertainty and a sense of diminishing returns, and began to seek forms of solace and fulfillment from sources other than the pursuit of success. In Coupland's anthemic *Generation X,* three "twentysomethings" exchange a sense of upward mobility for the pleasure of the stories they tell each other, and aspire to little more than running a small Mexican hotel. In Bobbie Ann Mason's "Shiloh" (1982), a disabled and unemployed truck driver dreams nostalgically of building a log cabin and living self-sufficiently, until his wife's example compels him to "get moving again."

The geography, as well as the economy, of American life also underwent significant alterations during the postwar era, a movement literally driven by the development of the transportation infrastructure in the 1950s and 1960s. The suburbanization of America that characterized the early postwar years accelerated throughout the subsequent decades, as the development of the telecommunications infrastructure, most notably the networking of computers, combined with fax machines and answering machines, all contributed to a dispersal of the population away from the cities and small towns where "community" was previously constituted. The 1990 census revealed that, for the first time, the majority of Americans lived in suburbia and "edge cities," a term coined by architectural theorist Joel Garreau to designate new suburban areas organized around concentrations of high-tech industrial parks. In this context, the decline of the city and the vision of modern community associated with it have become a prominent theme in postmodern American fiction. Apocalyptic visions of the devastated city have emerged in the works of such authors as Samuel R. Delaney, Kathy Acker, and William Gibson. William T. Vollmann, in *The Rainbow Stories* (1989), offers a vision of a city—San Francisco—under pressure from the social contradictions it must contain; Maxine Hong Kingston, in *Tripmaster Monkey* (1987), offers a more optimistic version of the same city thriving under similarly contradictory conditions. At the same time, other authors have explored the transformation taking place in the suburbs and rural areas. Among the many achievements of Truman Capote's *In Cold Blood* (1965), for instance, is its dark variation on the traditional American pastoral of farm life and the open highway. Don DeLillo's *White Noise* becomes a virtual anatomy of the new morés and spirit of community that revolve around the shopping mall and the supermarket.

Perhaps no technological development better defines the postmodern age, however, or has catalyzed greater social change, than television. According to A.C. Nielsen and Co., virtually every American home contains at least one television set, and the average household receives a broadcast for nearly seven hours per day. As with every communications technology since the printing press, however, the effects of television on its audience are contradictory. Television has created a sense of national or international community, as when vast audiences gathered to watch the funeral of President Kennedy or the landing on the moon. Yet at the same time television has helped to undermine that sense of community by segmenting the American populace into an array of increasingly smaller "target" audiences and markets, and by diminishing contact even within families sharing the same television set.

In either event, television has altered what we are capable of seeing and, combined with the resilient art of film, has influenced literature to adapt itself to these visual forms. While it is overwhelmingly American programming that is disseminated by satellite throughout the world, Americans are also knit into a peculiar "global village" where we see more than ever before. Images of revolution and war come into our living rooms with a visceral immediacy unimaginable to previous generations. Seeing more, we also see differently. As Curtis White suggests when he frames a short story around an episode of a half-forgotten 1960s action drama, television plays an important role in the structuring of our modes of perception. Marshall McLuhan, a pioneering media theorist, noted in the 1960s that television had the peculiar effect of collapsing space and time into a seamless "mosaic" of experience—a collapse sometimes cited for its pernicious "dehistoricizing" effects. Other theorists have deplored how the image has come to triumph over the real in (to use French media theorist Guy Debord's phrase) the "society of the spectacle." When Donald Barthelme collapses the language of television into the language of a short story, he exemplifies the contradictory but mutually symbiotic relationship that many authors have developed with television: resigning himself to the seamless mosaic of television programming, he simultaneously takes control of the possibilities it presents to challenge conventional narrative forms. Using the language, as Mark Leyner does, or actually using the image of the screen itself, as Laurie Anderson does on the pages of *Stories from the Nerve Bible* (1994), postmodern authors have crafted a new aesthetic that is neither detached from nor wholly sympathetic to the tele-video medium.

How contemporary authors will respond to the surge in computer use, and the rapid growth of the Internet, remain open questions. While as of 1997 only a minority of Americans own a computer, or have access to the World Wide Web, the implications of these technologies remain substantial. The advent of hypertext, for instance, offers an electronic form of composition that stresses reader participation and chance to a degree that no bound volume could easily simulate. The World Wide Web itself spawns new forms of community and fosters a peculiarly fluid sense of identity. The popularity of Dungeons and Dragons–type role-playing games and the prevalence of gender- , race- , and ethnicity-switching online suggest that a primary appeal of the Web is the opportunity it offers for people to escape—or redefine—at least temporarily, their identities. Overall, the increasing role of computers and other communications technologies in our daily lives distinctly demarcates postmodernity as an epoch. Many of the most familiar characteristics of postmodern American fiction—fragmented narrative, "samplings" of an immense variety of idioms, a fascination with subjectivity, and an abiding concern with the interaction of individual and community—can be seen as responses to the ways the machines of postwar America have multiplied, fragmented, and otherwise transformed human contact. Each time a word is spoken into the mouthpiece of a telephone, or a thought grows into lighted pixels on a shimmering computer screen, we are reminded of how much the acts of thinking and speaking have become detached from our physical selves in ways that evoke both wonder and nostalgia.

Postmodernism, Modernism, and the Avant-Garde

The relationship of modernism—the cultural period that extends from the earliest part of the twentieth century to the end of World War II—to postmodernism is an ongoing debate. Is postmodernism only an extension of modernism—"late" rather than "post-" modernism—or does a fundamental "break" exist between these two periods and their art? These opposing positions are tied to issues of style (whether postmodernism continues the formal experimentation of modernism, for instance), the connection of these two movements to popular culture, and finally, their complex political stances. Further, the protean nature of modernism itself, and its relation to other early-twentieth-century artistic movements, as well as its current status as an "official," canonical form of art available for commercial appropriation, further complicate any discussion of its relation to postmodernism.

Modernism emerged from the late-nineteenth-century revolt against the staid moralism of late-Victorian society and challenged the conventionality of its art forms. Oscar Wilde's iconoclastic formulation "life imitates art" ("The Decay of Lying," 1889) asserted that art has the power to change the ways in which people perceived and understood the world. In 1934, Ezra Pound commanded that modernists "make it new"—find new modes of expression to convey the experience of the modern world. Throughout Europe and the United States, for the better part of fifty years, creative artists in almost every discipline assaulted the traditional canons of their respective fields: in architecture, the designs of Frank Lloyd Wright in America and Le Corbusier in France, and the Bauhaus of pre-Nazi Germany; in music, the atonal compositions of Schönburg, the late symphonies of Mahler, the inventive rhythms of early Louis Armstrong; in art, the works of DeChirico, Modigliani, the late French Impressionists, the German Expressionists, and the Cubists, especially Picasso. For many late-twentieth-century observers, however, modernism was best represented by its literary practitioners. In fact, the list of leading modernist authors (Joseph

Conrad, James Joyce, Gertrude Stein, William Faulkner, Virginia Woolf, Samuel Beckett, Marcel Proust, T. S. Eliot, D. H. Lawrence, Ezra Pound, Djuna Barnes, and Jean Toomer) is so substantial that one might reasonably wonder if postmodernism could be anything more than a pale imitation or parody of the modernist achievement: "30% more modernism for your money," in the words of the critic Michael Bérubé, "more uncertainty, more fragmentation, more playful self-consciousness."

At the same time, modernism was not the only philosophy of art evolving in the early twentieth century, and therefore not the only likely progenitor for the late-century movements that would come to be called postmodernism. Modernism coincided (and often overlapped) with a variety of artistic movements that came to be known collectively as the "avant-garde" of early-twentieth-century European culture. The Dada movement of the 1910s and 1920s mounted an unrestrained assault on artistic convention and the faith in rationality and progress those conventions implied. As practiced by Marcel Duchamp, Man Ray, George Grosz, or Francis Picabia, Dada combined fragments of everyday objects—newspapers, bicycle parts, photographs, trash—into dramatic, anti-aesthetic montages. Dada's successor, the Surrealist movement of the 1920s and 1930s, similarly rejected the rationalism of conventional art, but did so in an effort to unite the conscious and subconscious realms. The Surrealist canvases of Salvador Dali or René Magritte, for instance, present provocative concatenations of familiar objects and dreamlike landscapes. Another avant-garde artistic movement, Futurism, centered in Italy during the first part of the century, emphasized an overriding faith in technological innovation. Focusing on speed, power, space, and bright color, the visual artists of the Futurist movement produced paintings, posters, and sculpture that celebrated automobiles, skyscrapers, and high-speed trains, and suggested a dynamic, invigorated future for the human race.

The contrast between modernism and the avant-garde provides a framework for understanding the early development of postmodernism. "High" modernism has been defined (chiefly by literary critics of the 1950s and '60s) as a complex but affirmative artistic movement that rose above (while combating) the diminishment of human consciousness that emanated from popular culture—even, as James Joyce does in *Ulysses* (1922), while sometimes adapting its genres and language. The avant-garde, in contrast, explored the overtly political potential of public art in ways that did not suggest a position above popular culture so much as an enthusiastic absorption of its anarchic possibilities. Postmodernism has strong ties to both modernism and the avant-garde. In the 1950s and 1960s, for instance, artists such as Andy Warhol and Roy Lichtenstein created a peculiarly American version of earlier European avant-garde movements precisely by erasing the gap between high and low culture, installing paintings of soup cans and cartoon panels on the walls of major galleries and art museums. In the literary postmodernism of the 1960s, authors such as Donald Barthelme, Robert Coover, John Barth, and William Gass were strongly influenced by the formal experimentation of high modernism. At the same time, they rebelled forcefully against the apparent disdain exhibited by much late-modernist writing toward the notion of reading "pleasure" generally associated with popular forms. In the work of more-recent postmodern authors, there seemed to be a growing appreciation that the relationship between popular culture and high culture (often in the guise of modernism itself) had changed as the technologies of culture had changed: the television in *White Noise* seems more ambulatory than the family who owns it; the *noir* detective in Barry Gifford's *Wild at Heart* (1990) composes *Twilight Zone* episodes for relaxation; the burned-out photographer in William Gibson's "Gernsback Continuum" (1981) tries to drown out hallucinations of modernist utopias with bad television and cigarettes. When combined with the shift to the nuclear age—a political concern large enough in itself to end aesthetic movements and start new ones—this growing consciousness that television and technology had altered the cultural terrain suggests that the shift from modernism to postmodernism embodied a new, distinct vision.

This vision has taken many forms, ranging from the philosophical to the demographic to the historical. Critic Brian McHale asserts that a crucial difference between modernism and postmodernism is that modernism tended to emphasize questions of epistemology or knowledge: how do we know or perceive the world? how does art create or change perception? what is the nature of reality? Postmodernism, he argues, more strongly emphasizes questions of ontology or being: what constitutes identity? how is the self constructed in and through culture? Many works of postmodern fiction implicitly or explicitly address these questions. Retelling history (as David Foster Wallace does in his short story "Lyndon" [1989]), examining popular culture and its effect on individuals (as Bobbie Ann Mason does in "Shiloh," or as Barry Gifford does in *Wild at Heart*), or rehearsing the ways in which identity is socially constructed, postmodern writers have displayed a consistent and wide-ranging fascination about how the public life of the nation intersects with the private lives of its citizens.

This shift in focus during the postmodern era has also catalyzed the rejuvenation of literary genres that were depreciated during the modernist period. As critics such as Donna Haraway have noted, issues of human-machine relations have become particularly important. The figure of the cyborg, for instance—human/machine, human/animal, and human/alien hybrids—has allowed authors to explore the impact of bio- and computer technologies. At the same time, the cyborg functions as a way to investigate gender, race, and ethnic hybridities. Seen from this vantage point, science fiction emerges as a quintessential postmodern genre. The cyberpunk novels and short stories of William Gibson, Neal Stephenson, and Pat Caddick, for example, focus on the human/machine interface. The science fiction works of Octavia Butler, Vonda McIntyre, and Samuel R. Delaney use human/animal and human/alien cyborgs to examine difference and otherness—concerns that link these authors to the second generation of postmodernists.

A more radical break with modernism occurred in the mid-1970s, when fiction by women, gay and lesbian, African-American, Asian-American, Native American, Caribbean, and Hispanic writers emerged as an explosion of "other" postmodern voices. For contemporary minority authors, the American writers of the modernist and early postmodernist periods offered an ambivalent cultural legacy, where visionary and innovative prose styles often commingled indivisibly with traces of racism, anxiety over the class disorder of early-twentieth-century American life, an unexamined faith in the centrality of Western European culture, and the continuing prevalence of white, male authorship. The postmodernism of this second generation of authors departs from both modernism and early postmodernism by de-emphasizing formal difficulty, political opacity, and the Western tradition, in favor of conscious eclecticism, a more overt political tone, and an emphasis on non-European antecedents. The literary forerunners of these postmodernists might be found in the immigrant and "labor" writers of the 1930s—Helena María Viramontes' "Cariboo Cafe" (1985), for instance, evokes the social realism that marked the effort of WPA-employed writers during the Great Depression—but their political tendencies also suggest predecessors among the socially conscious and formally experimental but defiantly public protest literature of the American 1950s, works such as Ralph Ellison's *Invisible Man* (1952) or Allen Ginsberg's *Howl* (1956).

For this most recent generation of writers, postmodernism does not foreground formal difficulty, but combines formal innovation with shifts in context, tone, and audience to create forms of fiction that sometimes feel old but read anew. The streams of consciousness and perspective switches of Morrison's *Beloved,* for instance, bear strong stylistic resemblances to the major novels of William Faulkner, but her efforts to bridge black and white audiences, as well as academic and middlebrow readers, separate her efforts from her modernist precursors. Similarly, novels such as Maxine Hong Kingston's *Tripmaster Monkey* and Kathy Acker's *Great Expectations* (1982) experiment with eclecticism within their own contents, combining different linguistic and literary traditions spanning world cultures and an array of ideologies. Authors such as Kingston, Sherman Alexie, Theresa Hak Kyung Cha, and Leslie Marmon Silko have also proven adept at interweaving the traditional stories and myths of non-European cultures within the literary forms of the Western tradition and the canon of mainstream American literature. And many contemporary writers have extended the development of various fact/fiction hybrids used by the "New Journalists" of the 1960s and 1970s: Audre Lorde's "biomythography," *Zami: A New Spelling of My Name* (1982), and Gloria Anzaldúa's *Borderlands/La Frontera* combine the traditional forms of the novel and short story with those of the memoir and essay, in a manner that suggests not a hybrid as much as a rejection of the notion that the two were ever separated. "Not One," filmmaker and critic Trinh T. Minh-ha writes, in a statement that describes the postmodern investigation of identity as readily as it suggests the problem of distinguishing postmodernism from modernism, but "not two either."

Postmodern Fiction and Postmodern Theory

Certain gaps have always existed between postmodern theory and the practice of postmodern fiction. While it is not always possible to trace the exact lines of influence between them, they uneasily but inevitably share a cultural ethos and traffic in many of the same ideas. Works of literature serve as sources or exemplars of postmodern thought and spur developments in other fields, as theorists borrow from or seek to explain literary texts. Critical theory, an eclectic discipline that utilizes concepts adapted from philosophy, psychology, anthropology, and even the natural sciences, has been a central conduit for the circulation of ideas among literature and other fields. Given this circulation, the best definition of what constitutes postmodern life and consciousness might be found where works of fiction and works of theory intersect.

ANTIFOUNDATIONALISM AND THE PROBLEM OF MEANING

If any one common thread unites the diverse artistic and intellectual movements that constitute postmodernism, it is the questioning of any belief system that claims universality or transcendence. For the past thirty years, both within and outside the American academy, the guiding principles of nearly every discipline and branch of knowledge have been called into question. Taken together, these inquiries have become known as "antifoundationalism" because they critique or dispute the foundations—the often-unacknowledged assumptions and precepts—on which disciplines and institutions have constructed their authority.

French philosopher Jean-François Lyotard argues that a skepticism toward the "grand narratives" of modernity defines "the postmodern condition." Like the "official story" discussed in the history section, these narratives, such as the progress of humanity through reason, have legitimated the "discourses" (the systems of language and thought) of philosophy, science, and many other fields. This skepticism extends to any philosophy or theory, such as Marxism, which claims to provide a complete explanation of culture and society. Lyotard argues that there is no longer any hope of a single conceptual system or discourse through which we might aspire to understand the totality of the world. Indeed, one can no longer speak about "totality" at all. Instead, we have a plurality of worlds and multiple, often mutually incompatible discourses through which to understand them.

In part because it has often aspired to the position of "master discourse," the one on which all others base themselves, the discourse of philosophy has been a particular site of "antifoundational" inquiry, much of which has taken place under the rubric of "deconstruction." Developed primarily by French philosopher Jacques Derrida and his followers, deconstruction has had profound effects upon the ways in which a literary (or any) text is understood. As opposed to the New Critical approaches of the 1940s and 1950s (and still practiced today) that emphasized the "unity" of the different parts of a literary text, the deconstructionist reading examines the unstated premises and unrecognized contradictions within texts, and within traditional systems of meaning in general. This critique of meaning has included a shift in the way we think of the relationship between language and world, the "sign" and the thing to which it refers or for which it substitutes. Deconstruction disputes the idealized notion of language as a transparent "window" onto thought or the world. Instead, deconstructionists emphasize the "materiality" of language and the ways language mediates our relationship to the world. Our concepts and the reality we perceive are enabled and sometimes even created by language. Yet language is not entirely adequate or commensurate to reality: the gap between word and world never closes.

Many postmodern authors explore and exploit this gap in their fiction. The narrator of Tim O'Brien's "How to Tell a True War Story" (1990) compulsively retells the same story, in slightly different versions, while despairing of his ability to find the right combination of words that will somehow be adequate to convey his experience. In Walter Abish's "Ardor/Awe/Atrocity" (1977), the materiality of language is foregrounded by the triple sets of alphabetical terms and by the numbering and cross-referencing of recurrent words; this play of form and sign makes the reader acutely aware of how language shapes and reshapes what we see and how we see it.

The ways in which words, sometimes referred to as "signs" to connect them with other units of communication such as gestures or images, create meaning in conjunction with one another is an important part of the deconstructionist investigations into language. Meaning is produced as one proceeds from word to word in a sentence, and from sentence to sentence. Thus, it is always in some sense in process, unstable, and "in play." The meaning of the particular word in any given utterance is also partly determined by the infinite range of associations and references it might bear to other "texts." In itself, this understanding is not new or specifically deconstructionist. Deconstruction, however, sharpened the realization that the meaning of any text is never completely under the control of either the author or any one reader, and so it remains always contingent and, to some extent, indeterminate. While this vision of language might seem to imply that "nothing means anything" (as some critics of deconstruction have charged), the difficulty is more likely to be an excess rather than a shortage of meaning, since meaning proliferates uncontrollably under any condition.

The uncontrollable excess, contingency, and indeterminacy of meaning all pose dilemmas for writers, and they have become important motifs in postmodern fiction. The intense, saturated prose of Jayne Anne Phillips' "Bluegill" (1984) and Maxine Hong Kingston's *Tripmaster Monkey*, for example, suggests narrative attempts to make order from a world where each bit of information is linked richly and associatively to other bits of information, and meaning seems to multiply the moment one begins to speak or write. Richard Brautigan's *Trout Fishing in America* (1967) uses its title as a free-floating sign—sometimes a character, sometimes an adjective, sometimes a verb—emphasizing both the arbitrariness of the language and its uncontrollable "play" of meaning. Intermittent clusters of brand names ("Dacron, Orlon, Lycra Spandex," "Mastercard, Visa, American Express," "Krylon, Rust-Oleum, Red Devil") drift through the text of Don DeLillo's *White Noise*, detached from any direct connection to the narrative, obliquely invoking the relentless drone of advertising and consumer culture. In *The Crying of Lot 49*, the heroine, Oedipa Maas, sees the "sign" of the muted post horn everywhere, yet remains uncertain of its meaning, no matter how relentlessly she pursues it.

The meaning of a given word or statement is "local," bound to and potentially transformed by the context within which it is uttered. Signs (words and images) are peculiarly volatile because they can always be detached from their original contexts and inserted into new ones that can radically alter their meanings. Umberto Eco terms these forms of aesthetic maneuvering "semiotic guerrilla warfare." One such form, détournement, inserts already existing signs, images, and texts into new contexts in order to disrupt or reverse their established meanings. In the early twentieth century, for example, Surrealists took fragments of text from newspapers and other sources to create "headline" and "found" poetry. Postmodern writers such as Don DeLillo, William Gibson, and Kathy Acker incorporate phrases and codes from television, film, and music into their texts, where their meanings are often radically transformed.

The so-called readymades of Marcel Duchamp, one of the founding figures of both modernist and postmodernist visual art, were everyday items (most notoriously, a urinal) that he pronounced art—as they indeed appear to be in their museum settings. More recently, pop artists such as Andy Warhol and Robert Rauschenberg appropriated images from advertising to create paintings and sculptures that drew directly from the images and packaging of consumer culture. Postmodern artist Barbara Kruger overlays slogans on documentary photographs and ads, relying on the dissonance between word and image to create a critique. While the guerrilla technique of détournement generally subverts expected meanings, it can be countered by the related techniques of recuperation, assimilation, and co-optation. Advertising, the ultimate semiotic warrior, is particularly adept at absorbing or neutralizing many of the artistic critiques launched against capitalism by assimilating and co-opting them. In 1996, for example, Mercedes-Benz used Janis Joplin's scathing "Mercedes Benz" (1971) in a television ad to appeal to the same status-seeking she satirized in the song. From advertising and television to the most "canonical" of artistic and literary works, the key features of the postmodern problematics of meaning—its contingency and indeterminacy—are at work throughout contemporary culture.

WORK, TEXT, AUTHOR, READER

If the revolutions of postmodern thought have altered our understanding of how texts produce meaning, they have also altered how we think of texts themselves, and how we think of the roles of the reader and writer. One way to understand these changes is through a distinction between "work" and "text" made by French critic Roland Barthes in his 1971 essay "From Work to Text." The literary "work," according to Barthes, is thought to be "closed": its boundaries are clearly defined, its meaning limited and fixed by its author (the "author"ity on the work). By contrast, the literary "text" is "open." Part of an endless web or network of other texts, its boundaries are fluid and provisional, its meaning plural and in play, circulating through the conscious and unconscious intentions of the writer, the reader, and culture. While there are literary narratives and poems that seem more "work-like" or "text-like," more "closed" or "open," literature and other discourses such as philosophy are increasingly read as "texts"—that is, with an appreciation of their complex interrelationships and multiple meanings. Many of the examples of postmodern fiction contained in this anthology highlight their textual openness.

Some postmodern narratives embody the openness of the "text" through different forms of intertextuality, the explicit relationships of a text to other texts. Pastiche, the incorporation of fragments of other texts such as newspaper articles, dialogue from films, poems, songs, signs, diary entries, and photographs into the literary text, is used, for example, in Art Spiegelman's

Maus, Theresa Hak Kyung Cha's *Dictee,* and Laurie Anderson's *Stories from the Nerve Bible.* Some postmodern narratives create intertextualities with the parts of the book that have traditionally been thought of as "outside" or secondary to the main body of the text, such as footnotes and indexes, book jackets, and back-cover blurbs. Vladimir Nabokov's *Pale Fire* (1962), for instance, is a novel told in the form of a long poem and the commentary constituted by footnotes to the poem. Brautigan's first chapter of *Trout Fishing in America* (entitled "The Cover for Trout Fishing in America") involves the cover in the narrative: "Around five o'clock in the afternoon of my cover for *Trout Fishing in America,* people gather in the park across the street from the church and they are hungry."

These uses of intertextuality are often explicitly linked to characteristically postmodern critiques of originality and authorship. The traditional notion of the "author" posits the writer of a work as its origin and thus implicitly as the ultimate arbiter or horizon of its meaning. The idea of the author also confers status, helps to determine how a particular work will be received critically, creates a logic that differentiates the writer's writings from those of other authors, and establishes a system of "filiation" or connection among all of that author's work. In the 1970s, this traditional concept of authorship was challenged and critiqued by French thinkers Roland Barthes, who proclaimed "The Death of the Author" in his 1970 essay of the same name, and Michel Foucault, in his immensely influential essay "What Is an Author?" (which first appeared in English translation in 1979).

In various ways, many postmodern narratives interrogate the traditional understanding and functioning of the authority of the author. William S. Burroughs experimented with the writing process itself, constructing his texts by cutting up—and then pasting together—parts of his own and others' writings at random (a method derived from the French Dadaists and from American modernists T. S. Eliot, John Dos Passos, and Gertrude Stein). In this process, the writer appears to surrender a large measure of control over the structure and the meaning of the narrative, and, as his prose is integrated with that of other writers, seems to give up ownership of the text. Other postmodernists insert themselves into their fiction or create authorial alter-egos. When Kurt Vonnegut offers Kilgore Trout as the putative author of one of his books, the "author" emerges as a literary construction, like any other character.

The receding of the author changes the relationship between the reader and the text; it shifts much of the responsibility for the creation of the text and its meaning to the reader. Postmodern narratives such as John Barth's 1972 "Dunyazadiad" (a rewriting of the fifteenth-century *A Thousand and One Nights*), Kathy Acker's *Great Expectations* (a novel that reworks elements from Charles Dickens' 1860 novel of the same name), and Sherman Alexie's "Captivity" rely upon the reader's familiarity with the earlier texts they rework. The meanings of these postmodern narratives emerge in the intersection between the old and the new texts as they play off one another in the mind of the reader.

In a different way, double- or triple-columned texts such as Douglas Coupland's *Generation X* and Joyce Carol Oates' "The Turn of the Screw" immediately raise the question of reading process and emphasize the reader's participation in the making of the text. Perhaps the most striking example of this is hypertext fiction, an electronic form of nonlinear, nonsequential narrative. While the writer composes the various "lexias" or blocks of text that constitute the narrative and establishes the connections among them, the reader chooses which paths to follow, assembling the text according to her own desires. Readers of J. Yellowlees Douglas's hypertext story "I Have Said Nothing" (1993) or Michael Joyce's hypertext novel *afternoon, a story* (1990) might all read "different" texts, with wildly differing plots. Hypertexts are never really "finished"; they are always in process as their readers navigate the texts and perform their readings. Some hypertexts, such as the WaxWeb site on the World Wide Web, even invite the reader to create new additions to the text and thus extend the network of connections that constitute it.

LITERATURE, HISTORY, AND JOURNALISM

The postmodern instability of literary forms is apparent in the collapse of many of the traditional distinctions between literature and other kinds of discourse. One of the most crucial distinctions to undergo revision during the postmodern era is the standard that defined literature as a subjective, fictional creation of an imaginary reality, and history and journalism as objective, factual records of real events. Yet we know the past only through "textualized remains" that are themselves incomplete, fragmentary, and in many cases already deeply subjective (diaries, letters, memoirs). Interested parties sometimes have the ability to control or suppress historical evidence, and historical records are also increasingly falsifiable. Technologies of reproduction (photocopy, computer, video, and photography) have rendered many forms of documentary evidence suspect. If the historical evidence is partial or suspect, the history that is made from it must also be, no matter how historians try to bridge the gaps. And the interpretations historians make are determined or at least influenced by their interests, assumptions, and prejudices, however objective these historians might wish or appear to be. For artists, journalists, government officials, and authors alike, the question of whose history constitutes History—whose history survives, and whose does not—has become a central issue of postmodern politics.

Since the 1960s, histories of those who had been previously ignored or forgotten, "history from below" or from the margins, have proliferated. In literature, the focus on marginal or outsider figures such as Coalhouse Walker in E. L. Doctorow's *Ragtime* (1975), or on those whose story has been omitted by history, like the Wampanoag in Alexie's "Captivity," can be seen in many postmodern narratives that incorporate historical figures and events into their fictional worlds. In the process, these narratives challenge the age-old assumptions that have distinguished history from literature. These narratives also tend to thematize the fragmentary, disjunctive, and often contradictory nature of historical evidence and hence of history itself, rather than presenting history as a continuous, unified story. Novels and short stories such as Toni Morrison's *Beloved,* David Foster Wallace's "Lyndon," Doctorow's *Ragtime,* and Madison Smartt Bell's *All Souls Rising* (1995) contain "realistic" aspects, but within the context of imaginative, surreal, or formally innovative passages that both call attention to the fictional aspects of the individual text and raise questions about traditional notions of "realism" and "authenticity." Similarly, postmodern novels that rework canonical literary texts from the perspective of a minor character—Valerie Martin's *Mary Reilly* (1990), for instance, which tells Robert Louis Stevenson's *The Strange Case of Dr. Jekyll and Mr. Hyde* (1886) from the point of view of Dr. Jekyll's maid—call attention to the fact that conventional *literary* history rarely offers a complete and unitary record of the past it has been constructed to represent.

Many of the critiques of history, particularly of its claims of objectivity and universality, have also been applied to the writing of journalism. The "New Journalism," which came into vogue in the late 1960s and 1970s, abandoned the traditional stance of detached objectivity and brought the subjective voice of the individual journalist to the forefront. The works of Norman Mailer, Tom Wolfe, Joan Didion, and Hunter S. Thompson foreground the self-conscious attempt to make sense of the events the writers observed and participated in, and leave open the gaps or contradictions in their experiences, rather than eliding or resolving them into a single meaning or interpretation. In particular, Norman Mailer's *Armies of the Night* (1968) represents a conscientious effort to reveal the deeply subjective nature of historical and journalistic narrative, while Hunter S. Thompson's *Fear and Loathing in Las Vegas* (1971) represents an extreme of subjectivity that implodes the notion of journalistic objectivity from within. The nonfiction novel, including works such as Truman Capote's *In Cold Blood,* Michael Shaara's *Killer Angels* (1974), and Mailer's *The Executioner's Song* (1979), extends the experiments of the New Journalism and further undermines the distinctions between journalism and literature, fact and fiction. More recently, numerous writers have utilized the latitude claimed by New Journalists and nonfiction novelists to produce innovative hybrids of journalistic, historical, and literary forms: Michael Herr's Vietnam War reportage in *Dispatches* (1968), for instance, Susan Sontag's exploratory diary-stories in *I, Etcetera* (1963), and Philip Roth's submersion of his own identity within the indeterminedly fictive contents of *The Ghost Writer* and many of his other novels.

POSTMODERN SUBJECTIVITIES I: GENDER AND SEXUALITY

Postmodern conceptions of the "subject"—the preferred critical term for the "self"—are radically different from those of the Enlightenment and of modernism. Philosophers from René Descartes to G. W. F. Hegel conceived of the subject as stable and unified, wholly knowable and fully self-conscious. Although presumed to be universal, and compelling even now, the ideal of the unified subject was grounded in its historical period: defining their own "selves," the male Enlightenment thinkers of Western Europe also defined in contrast a host of female, racial, and ethnic "others" as lesser beings, neither "subjects" nor "selves" in any philosophical or political sense. In the late nineteenth and early twentieth centuries, a new modernist model challenged the Enlightenment ideal of the unified subject. As articulated most famously by Sigmund Freud, the modernist subject was divided between conscious and unconscious parts, often in conflict with one another. Instead of defining the subject only against external "others," modernists argued that the subject also contained its own "other" within the unconscious. In turn, postmodernist theorists transformed and replaced the internalized other of the modernist subject with an even more heterogeneous vision. Fragmented and contingent, the postmodern subject is less "self" than an intersection of fluctuating subject positions within languages, cultures, and social structures that have themselves been shifting throughout history. Like many other aspects of postmodernity, the postmodern version of identity exchanged the authority and certitude of previous cultural periods for a pragmatic skepticism that pursues diffuse and open-ended explanations for what was previously believed to be a unified phenomenon.

While the postmodern revision of subjectivity is a widespread cultural event, some of the most forceful work has been performed by feminist, gay, and lesbian fiction writers, and by gender theorists. As early as 1953, pioneering feminist Simone de Beauvoir challenged the "universality" of the Enlightenment subject in *The Second Sex,* observing that "Woman is defined and differentiated with reference to man and not he with reference to her. He is the Subject, he is the Absolute—she is the Other." More recently, feminist theorists have extended the deconstructionist critique of binary oppositions such as self/other, culture/nature, presence/absence, thought/emotion, and master/slave. French feminist Hélène Cixous argues in her landmark essay "Sorties" (1975) that these binaries are actually gendered, hierarchical "couples," and the lesser, negative term has been associated with and shaped our conceptions of woman and femininity throughout Western history. How to undo the distortions (for both women and men) of these oppositional modes of language and thought, and how to move beyond them, have been issues for postmodernist narratives as well as postmodernist theory.

Authors of postmodernist fiction have sometimes approached these problems by imagining alternatives to traditional linguistic and social structures. As part of their effort to create a more self-defined female identity, some authors have focused on issues of "naming." In Ursula K. Le Guin's short story "She Unnames Them" (1988), for example, a rebellious, protofeminist Eve "unnames" all the creatures Adam has named, thus freeing them and finally herself from the definitions—and constrictions—of man's language. Some writers have sought in other languages words for relationships and ideas for which there is no English equivalent, as Audre Lorde does when she adopts the Carriacou name for women who work together as friends and lovers, "Zami," for the title of her "biomythography," *Zami: A New Spelling of My Name.* Other writers have created new words to solve such long-standing problems as the customary use in English of "man" and the male pronoun "he" as generic terms that are presumed to function as universals. Marge Piercy, for instance, invents the gender-neutral "per" for her utopian novel *Woman on the Edge of Time* (1976).

Other postmodernist writers have dramatized the intractability of oppositional, gendered modes of thought as confrontations between cultures. In her *Xenogenesis* trilogy, Octavia Butler portrays an alien race divided into males, females, and a third sex, "ooloi," without whom no sexual contact or reproduction can occur, and explores the effects of this sexual differentiation on the humans they encounter. In Joanna Russ's 1975 novel *The Fe-*

male Man, Janet, a visitor from a future in which there are no men, is surprised to find that such a society is unimaginable to the inhabitants of present-day America (who insist on translating her last name as "Evason," though there have been no "sons" in her world for centuries). The emissary in Ursula K. Le Guin's *The Left Hand of Darkness* (1969) is trapped, and his mission endangered, by his own inability to understand the inhabitants of another planet (who alternate between biological sexes) as simply people, without seeing them through the lens of gender.

The postmodernist departure from a concept of subjectivity based primarily in nature to one constructed through language, culture, and society involves an important distinction between "sex" and "gender." Sex, theorist Gayle Rubin proposed, is biological; but gender is a cultural construction, the meanings we give to biology. It is, according to Rubin, through gender—a particular society's definitions of what it means to be male or female—that oppressive social relations between men and women are organized, rather than through any innate biological order. This idea, too, appears in postmodernist fiction. In Russ's *The Female Man,* the four protagonists—Janet, Joanna, Jeannine, and Jael—are all the same biologically (identical genotypes), but their societies have shaped them into radically different women. The sex/gender distinction is a crucial one because it suggests that socially constructed meanings and the institutions they support can be transformed, however slow or arduous bringing about those transformations may be.

In her essay "Sorties," Cixous suggests that once we have understood how language, thought, and culture have historically been structured by gender, "all the history, all the stories would be there to retell differently." This "retelling" of earlier narratives from a different, female point of view can be seen, for example, in Marilynne Robinson's *Housekeeping* (1980), which recounts the biblical stories of Noah and Lot from the perspective of their nameless wives. Kathy Acker's gender-bending, "plagiaristic" novels *Great Expectations* and *In the Realm of the Senseless* (1988) recast the male heroes of previous novels into figures that switch sexes and sometimes morph into part human, part robot cyborgs, turning inside out the original narratives and their traditional assumptions about human sex and gender.

Gay and lesbian theorists have further extended the postmodern investigations of subjectivity and sexuality. Building on the understanding of postmodern subjectivity as an intersection of "positions" determined by language, culture, and social structures, theorists such as Eve Kosofsky Sedgwick, Michael Moon, Douglas Crimp, Adrienne Rich, and Judith Butler have examined the construction of homosexuality in legal, medical, religious, and literary discourses and questioned the categories through which sexual identity has historically been defined. Is homosexuality constituted as a biological category, for instance, or one that's defined by certain sexual practices, or certain "codes" of dress or gesture, or aesthetic sensibilities?

Beyond illuminating the construction of homosexual identity, gay, lesbian, and queer theory have also altered conceptions of heterosexuality and its relationship to homosexuality. In *Between Men* (1985), Sedgwick articulates how homophobia and "homosexual panic" function as an important element in sustaining heterosexual gender relations and identities in a system where the bonds between men are particularly intense (especially in primarily male social formations such as fraternities, the military, the government). Hubert Selby Jr.'s harrowing early novel *Last Exit to Brooklyn* (1961) can be read as a fictional exploration of this phenomenon. William S. Burroughs' fiction is an indictment of sexual narrowness of any kind. Poet Adrienne Rich's essay "Compulsory Heterosexuality and Lesbian Existence" (1981) argues for an understanding of relationships between women ranging from friendship to sexual partnership as part of a "lesbian continuum" that counters the historical erasure of lesbian existence and the ways in which heterosexuality disempowers women. In *Zami: A New Spelling of My Name,* Audre Lorde, an American lesbian writer of black West Indian descent, enacts this continuum by tracing her desire for feminine companionship—for a mother, a sister, a lover—and meditating on its meaning for her own life and the lives of other women, at the provocative intersection of gender, race, and ethnicity.

POSTMODERN SUBJECTIVITIES II: RACE AND ETHNICITY

The relationship between the African-American artistic and scholarly communities and postmodernist theory is both complicated and uneasy. On one hand, many prominent tenets of postmodernism are closely allied with African-American cultural and political projects. The breakdown of the divide between elite and popular culture, for instance, gives new status to a community whose contributions have been a powerful force in American vernacular culture for centuries. Similarly, the retrospective bent of postmodern literature, as well as the dismantling of the myth of a unified narrative of American history, has provided greater opportunities for the recognition of African-American (as well as American Indian, Chicano/a, Puerto Rican, and Asian-American) versions of American history. Most significantly, the postmodern exploration of how power relations are encoded in language, and how identity is culturally constructed, have been remarkable tools for comprehending racism in America.

The acknowledgment that some mutual symbiosis exists between minority culture and postmodernism has proven tentative, however, particularly around issues of racial "identity." An important facet of postmodernist theory has been the critique of traditional, "essentialist" notions of "identity," such as sexual or racial identity, as grounded in nature. Instead, postmodernists understand "identity" as primarily a linguistic and cultural construction. While many African-American critics recognize that this shift opens up new possibilities for comprehending and combating racist ideologies (language and culture, after all, can be more easily altered than "natural" or "biological" attributes), they also recognize that this new conception of identity might work against their attempts to define and validate the specificity of African-American identity, which has been denied for hundreds of years by slavery and its racist aftermath. Some African-American critics are especially concerned about this second aspect of the postmodern configuration of identity. As African-American critic bell hooks writes in "Postmodern Blackness" (1990), "it never surprises me when black folks respond to the critique of essentialism, especially when it denies the validity of identity politics by saying, 'Yeah, it's easy to give up identity, when you got one.' " Similarly, as Cornel West writes, postmodernism was considered by many in the African-American community to be "rather parochial and provincial—narrowly Eurocentric," still tied to modernism, and too deeply enmeshed with the authority and language of Euro-American academia to represent any real radical change in how cultural power is distributed. As Audre Lorde has observed, "you cannot tear down the master's house with the master's tools"; to many minority critics and writers, postmodernism, despite its claims to speak for oppressed and marginalized peoples, seemed to fit this paradigm.

If the relationship between African-American culture and postmodernism is ambivalent and explosive, however, it remains one of the most productive intellectual exchanges in contemporary America. Postmodern theory has assisted African-American theorists in search of the ways in which linguistic structures create difference. African-American critics such as Henry Louis Gates Jr. and Houston A. Baker Jr., among others, have studied how African-American literature constitutes a distinctive form of language use, paying particular attention to the use of figurative language. Intertextuality again emerges as a central concept, evidenced in such characteristic techniques as signifying in literature and sampling in rap music, and it extends to literary hybrids such as the fiction of Ishmael Reed, which employs the rhythms of bebop, and the rap-fiction of Ricardo Cortez Cruz. The opening out of history has also proven to be a significant site of creative inspiration and political change: from the recasting of the slave narrative in Morrison's *Beloved* to Randall Kenan's (1992) "This Far" (an internal monologue of Booker T. Washington on his last day alive), African-American writers have actively returned to the American past to reclaim their voices. Similarly, the postmodern resistance to standard genre boundaries has created an advantageous fluidity to the canon, allowing literary respect for the ostensibly autobiographical "factual" forms to which nineteenth- and early-twentieth-century black writers were drawn by past successes and by commercial prospects, and in so doing creating a tradition within which contemporary autobiographies such as Lorde's *Zami: A New Spelling of My Name* can be understood as continuations of a strong, enduring culture.

Hybridity of form and expression are also characteristic of the vast and expanding range of ethnic fiction that has exploded onto the postmodern literary scene over the past twenty years, including Chicano/a-American, Asian-American, American Indian, and Caribbean-American. As with African-American literature, the relationship between these ethnic literatures and postmodern theory remains ambivalent. Arnold Krupat, for instance, argues that American "Indian modes" of thinking are paralleled by postmodern practices. Celeste Olalquiaga, however, writing in *Megalopolis* (1992), sees something more than synchronicity, and argues instead that Latin American culture "anticipate(s) postmodern pastiche and recycling," making the Third World "postmodern before the First World." When Leslie Marmon Silko presents *Ceremony* as a novel within a Laguna Pueblo origin chant, submerging Anglo-American experience within an American Indian framework, she illustrates how graphically the conflict between dissonant cultures becomes an expressive tradition in itself during the postmodern era. The literatures that had previously been marginal have moved to the center, disrupting the center/periphery, First World/Third World models of world culture. They have created literary strategies that undermine the dominance of the established canons of literature. These strategies include "response literature," which rewrites Western classics or retells cherished national narratives, such as the "discovery" of America, from another point of view, as Gerald Vizenor's *Heirs of Columbus* (1991) does.

Postcolonialist critics have examined how disciplines and literary canons have functioned as colonizing practices and urged "border crossings" of disciplinary boundaries. Writers such as Gloria Anzaldúa and Cherríe Moraga have set out to develop their own border discourses, hybrids of Spanish and English that recreate their liminal and shifting linguistic identities. At the same time, ambivalences similar to those experienced by African-American writers regarding identity and postmodern authority also emerge in the literature of these authors. While there is an emphasis on the fluidity of postcolonial subjectivities, there is an even stronger countervailing desire for "identity" on the part of those for whom it has historically been denied or determined from the outside. When Gloria Anzaldúa speaks of the "Western split Cartesian point of view" against which she is rebelling, for instance, it is unclear whether or not she includes postmodern theory (and mainstream postmodern literature as well) within that "point of view." If we perceive postmodernism as a widely experienced cultural condition, then both sides of the struggle to define and express all our manifold ethnic and hybrid identities must be seen as postmodern strivings. If we perceive postmodernism as a set of practices specific to certain works of art and literature, then authors like West and Anzaldúa stand outside its purview, refusing claims that postmodernism represents any radical change from the past, and instead linking with academic theorists such as Fredric Jameson in arguing that postmodern practices even reinforce the status quo.

The postmodern writer partakes of these ideological trajectories, but transforms them into the shape of story and drama. Throughout the fiction collected in this anthology are countless passages where the history of our epoch crystallizes and coheres; but it is the nature of our epoch that such moments of coherence often create more conflict than they resolve. In Silko's *Ceremony,* for instance, the protagonist Tayo approaches spiritual redemption when he sees "the way all the stories fit together . . . to become the story that was still being told." The prejudices and limitations Tayo has inherited fall from his eyes, and he discovers "the world as it always was: no boundaries, only transitions through all distances and times." Here Tayo's revelation does not constitute a learned thing, but a defeat of the world of learned things—a progress that is a regression to a past that never was, but which Tayo constructs by using the best materials that white as well as Indian culture can give him. In its use of cultural hybrids, its turning away from the verities of the Enlightenment, and its insistence on fluid boundaries, this short passage in Silko's book represents a postmodern moment in the truest sense. At the same time, there are also fluid boundaries to Tayo's rejection of what is and is not possible within America: whether his moment of clarity in the New Mexican desert represents a postmodern turn, or a turn from the postmodern—and where this turn takes him and us alongside him—are questions that Silko's novel leaves resonating in a transitional state between being asked and being answered.

Acknowledgments

We would like to thank the following groups and individuals for their assistance and support in the construction of this anthology: Butler University, the members and staff of its Department of English, the staff of its library, and its telecommunications office; Southern Illinois University at Carbondale, the members and staff of its Department of English; John Howell; Dean John Jackson; Associate Vice Chancellor Margaret Winters; Victoria Molfese and the Office of Research Development and Administration of SIUC; the University of North Carolina at Charlotte; Thomas Costello and Tracey Hammond, our creative and diligent research assistants; Hilene Flanzbaum; Susan Neville; Jocelyn Lieu; Jeff Insko; Stephen Conway; Arkady Plotnitsky; Jim English; Edward Brunner; Crystal Bartolovich; Deborah Treisman; James Linville; Virginia Barber; Robert Coover; John Barth; Mark Bernstein; special thanks to Julia Reidhead, Tara Parmiter, and Kurt Wildermuth at Norton; Siobhán McEvoy; Kathryn Rhett.

I Breaking the Frame

As the critic and novelist David Lodge has written, both modernist and postmodernist authors have valued formal innovation. The difference, Lodge suggests, is that the modernist author (or rather, the author in "modernist" mode) experiments with form to create a stream of consciousness so vivid that the author disappears, while the same author in "postmodernist" mode creates ruptures, gaps, and ironies that continually remind the reader that an author is present—if not, as theorists such as Michel Foucault and Roland Barthes have suggested, entirely in control. No history of postmodern American fiction could begin without first addressing this shift in the tone and purpose of formal innovation, both as it applies to the first school of authors explicitly considered "postmodernist," and for more-recent authors who conducted similarly ambitious experiments in reinventing the traditional forms of narrative. In the course of their explorations of the conventions, limits, and possibilities of fiction, the first postmodernists often adapted and extended the narrative strategies of modernist authors, while at the same time engaging with characteristically postmodern issues regarding the nature of meaning and representation. Individually, the work of each author in this section could conceivably be considered an unusual if significant contribution to the modernist canon. Cumulatively, however, their efforts represent a bridge between the endgame of formal innovation that comprised late modernism and the repudiation of narrative and generic boundaries that would comprise the heart of postmodernism.

Like the modernists, the postmodernists understand that narrative form implicitly speaks of the nature of reality and how we experience it. William S. Burroughs, a crossroads figure in the passage of American fiction from the modern to the postmodern, sees traditional linear narrative form as inherently authoritarian, a means through which the mind is forced into "straight," conventional ways of thinking about the world. In "Crab Nebula" (an excerpt from his 1964 novel *Nova Express*), Burroughs' use of collage, "cut-ups," and other nonlinear techniques of narrative composition works together with his thematic explorations of domination and resistance, sexuality and drug use, to challenge the structures and taboos of contemporary society. Burroughs is not alone in his sense that the orderly linearity of traditional narratives suggests a certain coherence to experience that has come to seem false. "Fragments are the only forms I trust," the narrator of Donald Barthelme's "See the Moon?" (1964) insists. The falling away of all the old certainties (" 'Is there any value that has value?' " the narrator plaintively asks in the same story) leaves both writer and reader attempting to piece together a new reality from the fragments of the old. Whether the pieces will ever really cohere again remains an open question. "Consciousness is always consciousness *of* something," Barthelme reminds us in "Sentence" (1970), but the consciousness that emerges from an age of "information sickness" should be "treasured for its weakness, as opposed to the strength of stones." In *The Crying of Lot 49* (1966), Thomas Pynchon sends his heroine, Oedipa Maas, on an allegorical journey across the California landscape, where she encounters everywhere the mysterious sign of the muted post horn; yet unlike classical allegory, here the meaning of the sign is ambiguous and ultimately unresolvable. Postmodern uncertainty has supplanted modern obscurity. Similarly, the novel's focus on conspiracy and paranoia (reflecting aspects of the political consciousness of the 1960s) foreshadows what would become significant postmodern themes more than it represents an extension of high-modern concerns.

For other early postmodernists, social critique also goes hand in hand with playful formal experimentation. In Kurt Vonnegut's 1973 novel *Breakfast of Champions,* the questioning of the "official story" of American history is amplified by Vonnegut's detachment from his own position as an author and his complicity as a maker of fictions: "I'm throwing out characters from my other books, too," the narrator—perhaps speaking for Vonnegut—resolves. "I'm not going to put on any more puppet shows." Ishmael Reed plays with cherished national myths of the frontier in "The Loop Garoo Kid," the opening chapter to *Yellow Back Radio Broke-Down* (1969), which combines jazzlike improvisatory cadences with a punning wit that reworks the materials of American culture (both high and low) into a sardonic and socially aware cowboy story. Ntozake Shange's *Sassafrass, Cypress & Indigo* (1982), dedicated to "all women in struggle," interweaves lists, numerological charts, lyrics, and other materials into a freeform narration that possesses linguistic sophistication commingled with respect for folk traditions. Walter Abish's "Ardor/Awe/Atrocity" (1977) explores an intricate amalgam of issues involving the forms of literature. By presenting a realistic fiction within a complex structure utilizing alphabetical groupings, fragmented narrative, and a numbering system that calls attention to certain words—and the nature of words themselves—Abish consistently reminds the reader of the submerged links that bind together language, story, and human consciousness.

Other selections illustrate how the linguistic innovation practiced by both early and more-recent postmodernists was rarely an abstract intellectual exercise, but rather reflected impassioned efforts to create new narrative forms for a new and distinct age. William Gass's meditative "In the Heart of the Heart of the Country" (1968), a canonical short story of the early postmodernist period, provides an illustration of the formal possibilities of fragmented narrative without the ironic detachment characteristic of many later fragmented fictions. The interlocking vignettes that comprise Richard Brautigan's *Trout Fishing in America* (1967) are linked by the spontaneous movement of the title through the text as it assumes the various guises of character, theme, and action. In Carole Maso's *The American Woman in the Chinese Hat* (1994), the narrator speaks to the reader in a manner that suggests disorienting but heartfelt empathy for her protagonist, as well as a frustrated desire to alter scenes that she portrays as beyond her control, if not her intervention. The telegraphed, elliptical format of Lynne Tillman's "Living with Contradictions" (1990) seems to represent the subject of the story, the breakdown of an intimate relationship between a man and a woman; the linear momentum of the narrative balances the story's fragmentation, however, and suggests the fine tension between reason and unreason that

Tillman characterizes as the "pleasurable contradiction" at the heart of contemporary romance. The staccato shifts in tone and diction that mark Grace Paley's "The Pale Pink Roast" (1959) reflect the rhythms of Paley's native New York as much as her quintessentially postmodern talent for incorporating (and subverting) the clichés and stilted idioms of our public culture. Paley's story also presages the work of later writers, such as Jayne Anne Phillips, who resist but do not repudiate the narrative clarity and closure of more traditional fiction. In "Bluegill" (1984), Phillips' supersaturated prose illustrates the powerful compensations of freeform written expression. At the same time, her narrator's address to her unborn child (like that of Barthelme's narrator in "See the Moon?") represents a countermanding reassurance that certain traditions remain to be passed on.

THOMAS PYNCHON
b. 1937

Thomas Pynchon was born in Glen Cove, New York, and studied at Cornell University. After living in Greenwich Village for one year and serving as a technical writer at Boeing Aircraft in Seattle for two years, Pynchon moved to Mexico to finish his first novel, *V.* (1963). He has been writing in carefully obscured seclusion ever since—his 1953 high school yearbook still provides his most recent photographic portrait. In addition to *V.*, he has published the novels *The Crying of Lot 49* (1966), *Gravity's Rainbow* (1973), *Vineland* (1990), and *Mason & Dixon* (1997), and the short-story collection *Slow Learner* (1984). While the 1973 Pulitzer Prize jurors unanimously voted for *Gravity's Rainbow,* their decision was overruled by the Pulitzer Prize Committee, who called the book "turgid," "obscene," and "unreadable."

The Crying of Lot 49, excerpted here, is regarded as Pynchon's most accessible novel, a disarmingly complicated anti–detective story. "With a detective story," Tony Tanner writes in his *Thomas Pynchon* (1982), "you start with a mystery and move towards a final clarification. . . . [I]n Pynchon's novel we move from a state of degree-zero mystery—just the quotidian mixture of an average Californian day—to a condition of increasing mystery and dubiety. . . . It is a strange book in that the more we learn the more mysterious everything becomes. The more we *think* we know, the less we *know* we know."

From The Crying of Lot 49

* * *

Amid the exhaust, sweat, glare and ill-humor of a summer evening on an American freeway, Oedipa Maas pondered her Trystero problem. All the silence of San Narciso—the calm surface of the motel pool, the contemplative contours of residential streets like rakings in the sand of a Japanese garden—had not allowed her to think as leisurely as this freeway madness.

For John Nefastis (to take a recent example) two kinds of entropy, thermodynamic and informational, happened, say by coincidence, to look alike, when you wrote them down as equations. Yet he had made his mere coincidence respectable, with the help of Maxwell's Demon.

Now here was Oedipa, faced with a metaphor of God knew how many parts; more than two, anyway. With coincidences blossoming these days wherever she looked, she had nothing but a sound, a word, Trystero, to hold them together.

She knew a few things about it: it had opposed the Thurn and Taxis postal system in Europe; its symbol was a muted post horn; sometime before 1853 it had appeared in America and fought the Pony Express and Wells, Fargo, either as outlaws in black, or disguised as Indians; and it survived today, in California, serving as a channel of communication for those of unorthodox sexual persuasion, inventors who believed in the reality of Maxwell's Demon, possibly her own husband, Mucho Maas (but she'd thrown Mucho's letter long away, there was no way for Genghis Cohen to check the stamp, so if she wanted to find out for sure she'd have to ask Mucho himself).

Either Trystero did exist, in its own right, or it was being presumed, perhaps fantasied by Oedipa, so hung up on and interpenetrated with the dead man's estate. Here in San Francisco, away from all tangible assets of that estate, there might still be a chance of getting the whole thing to go away and disintegrate quietly. She had only to drift tonight, at random, and watch nothing happen, to be convinced it was purely nervous, a little something for her shrink to fix. She got off the freeway at North Beach, drove around, parked finally in a steep side-street among warehouses. Then walked along Broadway, into the first crowds of evening.

But it took her no more than an hour to catch sight of a muted post horn. She was moseying along a street full of aging boys in Roos Atkins suits when she collided with a gang of guided tourists come rowdy-dowing out of a Volkswagen bus, on route to take in a few San Francisco nite spots. "Let me lay this on you," a voice spoke into her ear, "because I just left," and she found being deftly pinned outboard of one breast this big cerise ID badge, reading HI! MY NAME IS **Arnold Snarb**! AND I'M LOOKIN' FOR A GOOD TIME! Oedipa glanced around and saw a cherubic face vanishing with a wink in among natural shoulders and striped shirts, and away went Arnold Snarb, looking for a better time.

Somebody blew on an athletic whistle and Oedipa found herself being herded, along with other badged citizens, toward a bar called The Greek Way. Oh, no, Oedipa thought, not a fag joint, no; and for a minute tried to fight out of the human surge, before recalling how she had decided to drift tonight.

"Now in here," their guide, sweating dark tentacles into his tab collar, briefed them, "you are going to see the members of the third sex, the lavender crowd this city by the Bay is so justly famous for. To some of you the experience may seem a little queer, but remember, try not to act like a bunch of tourists. If you get propositioned it'll all be in fun, just part of the gay night life to be found here in famous North Beach. Two drinks and when you hear the whistle it means out, on the double, regroup right here. If you're well behaved we'll hit Finocchio's next." He blew the whistle twice and the tourists, breaking into a yell, swept Oedipa inside, in a frenzied assault on the bar. When things had calmed she was near the door with an unidentifiable drink in her fist, jammed against somebody tall in a suede sport coat. In the lapel of which she spied, wrought exquisitely in some pale, glimmering alloy, not another cerise badge, but a pin in the shape of the Trystero post horn. Mute and everything.

All right, she told herself. You lose. A game try, all one hour's worth. She should have left then and gone back to Berkeley, to the hotel. But couldn't.

"What if I told you," she addressed the owner of the pin, "that I was an agent of Thurn and Taxis?"

"What," he answered, "some theatrical agency?" He had large ears, hair cropped nearly to his scalp, acne on his face, and curiously empty eyes, which now swiveled briefly to Oedipa's breasts. "How'd you get a name like Arnold Snarb?"

"If you tell me where you got your lapel pin," said Oedipa.

"Sorry."

She sought to bug him: "If it's a homosexual sign or something, that doesn't bother me."

Eyes showing nothing: "I don't swing that way," he said. "Yours either." Turned his back on her and ordered a drink. Oedipa took off her badge, put it in an ashtray and said, quietly, trying not to suggest hysteria,

"Look, you have to help me. Because I really think I am going out of my head."

"You have the wrong outfit, Arnold. Talk to your clergyman."

"I use the U. S. Mail because I was never taught any different," she pleaded. "But I'm not your enemy. I don't want to be."

"What about my friend?" He came spinning around on the stool to face her again. "You want to be that, Arnold?"

"I don't know," she thought she'd better say.

He looked at her, blank. "What *do* you know?"

She told him everything. Why not? Held nothing back. At the end of it the tourists had been whistled away and he'd bought two rounds to Oedipa's three.

"I'd heard about 'Kirby,' " he said, "it's a code name, nobody real. But none of the rest, your Sinophile across the bay, or that sick play. I never thought there was a history to it."

"I think of nothing but," she said, and a little plaintive.

"And," scratching the stubble on his head, "you have nobody else to tell this to. Only somebody in a bar whose name you don't know?"

She wouldn't look at him. "I guess not."

"No husband, no shrink?"

"Both," Oedipa said, "but they don't know."

"You can't tell them?"

She met his eyes' void for a second after all, and shrugged.

"I'll tell you what I know, then," he decided. "The pin I'm wearing means I'm a member of the IA. That's Inamorati Anonymous. An inamorato is somebody in love. That's the worst addiction of all."

"Somebody is about to fall in love," Oedipa said, "you go sit with them, or something?"

"Right. The whole idea is to get to where you don't need it. I was lucky. I kicked it young. But there are sixty-year-old men, believe it or not, and women even older, who wake up in the night screaming."

"You hold meetings, then, like the AA?"

"No, of course not. You get a phone number, an answering service you can call. Nobody knows anybody else's name; just the number in case it gets so bad you can't handle it alone. We're isolates, Arnold. Meetings would destroy the whole point of it."

"What about the person who comes to sit with you? Suppose you fall in love with them?"

"They go away," he said. "You never see them twice. The answering service dispatches them, and they're careful not to have any repeats."

How did the post horn come in? That went back to their founding. In the early '60's a Yoyodyne executive living near L.A. and located someplace in the corporate root-system above supervisor but below vice-president, found himself, at age 39, automated out of a job. Having been since age 7 rigidly instructed in an eschatology that pointed nowhere but to a presidency and death, trained to do absolutely nothing but sign his name to specialized memoranda he could not begin to understand and to take blame for the running-amok to specialized programs that failed for specialized reasons he had to have explained to him, the executive's first thoughts were naturally of suicide. But previous training got the better of him: he could not make the decision without first hearing the ideas of a committee. He placed an ad in the personal column of the L.A. *Times,* asking whether anyone who'd been in the same fix had ever found any good reasons for not committing suicide. His shrewd assumption being that no suicides would reply, leaving him automatically with only valid inputs. The assumption was false. After a week of anxiously watching the mailbox through little Japanese binoculars his wife had given him for a going-away present (she'd left him the day after he was pink-slipped) and getting nothing but sucker-list stuff through the regular deliveries that came each noon, he was jolted out of a boozy, black-and-white dream of jumping off The Stack into rush-hour traffic, by an insistent banging at the door. It was late on a Sunday afternoon. He opened his door and found an aged bum with a knitted watch cap on his head and a hook for a hand, who presented him with a bundle of letters and loped away without a word. Most of the letters were from suicides who had failed, either through clumsiness or last-minute cowardice. None of them, however, could offer any compelling reasons for staying alive. Still the executive dithered: spent another week with pieces of paper on which he would list, in columns headed "pro" and "con," reasons for and against taking his Brody. He found it impossible, in the absence of some trigger, to come to any clear decision. Finally one day he noticed a front page story in the *Times,* complete with AP wirephoto, about a Buddhist monk in Viet Nam who had set himself on fire to protest government policies. "Groovy!" cried the executive. He went to the garage, siphoned all the gasoline from his Buick's tank, put on his green Zachary All suit with the vest, stuffed all his letters from unsuccessful suicides into a coat pocket, went in the kitchen, sat on the floor, proceeded to douse himself good with the gasoline. He was about to make the farewell flick of the wheel on his faithful Zippo, which had seen him through the Normany hedgerows, the Ardennes, Germany, and postwar America, when he heard a key in the front door, and voices. It was his wife and some man, whom he soon recognized as the very efficiency expert at Yoyodyne who had caused him to be replaced by an IBM 7094. Intrigued by the irony of it, he sat in the kitchen and listened, leaving his necktie dipped in the gasoline as a sort of wick. From what he could gather, the efficiency expert wished to have sexual intercourse with the wife on the Moroccan rug in the living room. The wife was not unwilling. The executive heard lewd laughter, zippers, the thump of shoes, heavy breathing, moans. He took his tie out of the gasoline and started to snigger. He closed the top on his Zippo. "I hear laughing," his wife said presently. "I smell gasoline," said the efficiency expert. Hand in hand, naked, the two proceeded to the kitchen. "I was about to do the Buddhist monk thing," explained the executive. "Nearly three weeks it takes him," marvelled the efficiency expert, "to decide. You know how long it would've taken the IBM 7094? Twelve microseconds. No wonder you were replaced." The executive threw back his head and laughed for a solid ten minutes, along toward the middle of which his wife and her friend, alarmed, retired, got dressed and went out looking for the police. The executive undressed, showered and hung his suit out on the line to dry. Then he noticed a curious thing. The stamps on some of the letters in his suit pocket had turned almost white. He realized that the gasoline must have dissolved the printing ink. Idly, he peeled off a stamp and saw suddenly the image of the muted post horn, the skin of his hand showing clearly through the watermark. "A sign," he whispered, "is what it is." If he'd been a religious man he would have fallen to his knees. As it was, he only declared, with great solemnity: "My big mistake was love. From this day I swear to stay off of love: hetero, homo, bi, dog or cat, car, every kind there is. I will found a society of isolates, dedicated to this purpose, and this sign, revealed by the same gasoline that almost destroyed me, will be its emblem." And he did.

Oedipa, by now rather drunk, said, "Where is he now?"

"He's anonymous," said the anonymous inamorato. "Why not write to him through your WASTE system? Say 'Founder, IA.' "

"But I don't know how to use it," she said.

"Think of it," he went on, also drunk. "A whole underworld of suicides who failed. All keeping in touch through that secret delivery system. What do they tell each other?" He shook his head, smiling, stumbled off his stool and headed off to take a leak, disappearing into the dense crowd. He didn't come back.

Oedipa sat, feeling as alone as she ever had, now the only woman, she saw, in a room full of drunken male homosexuals. Story of my life, she thought, Mucho won't talk to me, Hilarius won't listen, Clerk Maxwell didn't even look at me, and this group, God knows. Despair came over her, as it will when nobody around has any sexual relevance to you. She gauged the spectrum of feeling out there as running from really violent hate (an Indian-looking kid hardly out of his teens, with frosted shoulder-length hair tucked behind his ears and pointed cowboy boots) to dry speculation (a hornrimmed SS type who stared at her legs, trying to figure out if she was in drag), none of which could do her any good. So she got up after awhile and left The Greek Way, and entered the city again, the infected city.

And spent the rest of the night finding the image of the Trystero post horn. In Chinatown, in the dark window of a herbalist, she thought she saw it on a sign among ideographs. But the streetlight was dim. Later, on a sidewalk, she saw two of them in chalk, 20 feet apart. Between them a complicated array of boxes, some with letters, some with numbers. A kids' game? Places on a map, dates from a secret history? She copied the diagram in her memo book. When she looked up, a man, perhaps a man, in a black suit, was standing in a doorway half a block away, watching her. She thought she saw a turned-around collar but took no chances; headed back the way she'd come, pulse thundering. A bus stopped at the next corner, and she ran to catch it.

She stayed with buses after that, getting off only now and then to walk so she'd keep awake. What fragments of dreams came had to do with the post horn. Later, possibly, she would have trouble sorting the night into real and dreamed.

At some indefinite passage in night's sonorous score, it also came to her that she would be safe, that something, perhaps only her linearly fading drunkenness, would protect her. The city was hers, as, made up and sleeked so with the customary words and images (cosmopolitan, culture, cable cars) it had not been before: she had safe-passage tonight to its far blood's branchings, be they capillaries too small for more than peering into, or vessels mashed together in shameless municipal hickeys, out on the skin for all but tourists to see. Nothing of the night's could touch her; nothing did. The repetition of symbols was to be enough, without trauma as well perhaps to attenuate it or even jar it altogether loose from her memory. *She was meant to remember.* She faced that possibility as she might the toy street from a high balcony, roller-coaster ride, feeding-time among the beasts in a zoo—any death-wish that can be consummated by some minimum gesture. She touched the edge of its voluptuous field, knowing it would be lovely beyond dreams simply to submit to it; that not gravity's pull, laws of ballistics, feral ravening, promised more delight. She tested it, shivering: I am meant to remember. Each clue that comes is *supposed* to have its own clarity, its fine chances for permanence. But then she wondered if the gemlike "clues" were only some kind of compensation. To make up for her having lost the direct, epileptic Word, the cry that might abolish the night.

In Golden Gate Park she came on a circle of children in their nightclothes, who told her they were dreaming the gathering. But that the dream was really no different from being awake, because in the mornings when they got up they felt tired, as if they'd been up most of the night. When their mothers thought they were out playing they were really curled in cupboards of neighbors' houses, in platforms up in trees, in secretly-hollowed nests inside hedges, sleeping, making up for these hours. The night was empty of all terror for them, they had inside their circle an imaginary fire, and needed nothing but their own unpenetrated sense of community. They knew about the post horn, but nothing of the chalked game Oedipa had seen on the sidewalk. You used only one image and it was a jump-rope game, a little girl explained: you stepped alternately in the loop, the bell, and the mute, while your girlfriend sang:

Tristoe, Tristoe, one, two, three,
Turning taxi from across the sea . . .

"Thurn and Taxis, you mean?"

They'd never heard it that way. Went on warming their hands at an invisible fire. Oedipa, to retaliate, stopped believing in them.

In an all-night Mexican greasy spoon off 24th, she found a piece of her past, in the form of one Jesús Arrabal, who was sitting in a corner under the TV set, idly stirring his bowl of opaque soup with the foot of a chicken. "Hey," he greeted Oedipa, "you were the lady in Mazatlán." He beckoned her to sit.

"You remember everything," Oedipa said, "Jesús; even tourists. How is your CIA?" Standing not for the agency you think, but for a clandestine Mexican outfit known as the Conjuración de los Insurgentes Anarquistas, traceable back to the time of the Flores Magón brothers and later briefly allied with Zapata.

"You see. In exile," waving his arm around at the place. He was part-owner here with a yucateco who still believed in the Revolution. *Their* Revolution. "And you. Are you still with that gringo who spent too much money on you? The oligarchist, the miracle?"

"He died."

"Ah, pobrecito." They had met Jesús Arrabal on the beach, where he had previously announced an antigovernment rally. Nobody had showed up. So he fell to talking to Inverarity, the enemy he must, to be true to his faith, learn. Pierce, because of his neutral manners when in the presence of ill-will, had nothing to tell Arrabal; he played the rich, obnoxious gringo so perfectly that Oedipa had seen gooseflesh come up along the anarchist's forearms, due to no Pacific sea-breeze. Soon as Pierce went off to sport in the surf, Arrabal asked her if he was real, or a spy, or making fun of him. Oedipa didn't understand.

"You know what a miracle is. Not what Bakunin said. But another world's intrusion into this one. Most of the time we coexist peacefully, but when we do touch there's cataclysm. Like the church we hate, anarchists also believe in another world. Where revolutions break out spontaneous and leaderless, and the soul's talent for consensus allows the masses to work together without effort, automatic as the body itself. And yet, señá, if any of it should ever really happen that perfectly, I would also have to cry miracle. An anarchist miracle. Like your friend. He is too exactly and without flaw the thing we fight. In Mexico the privilegiado is always, to a finite percentage, redeemed—one of the people. Unmiraculous. But your friend, unless he's joking, is as terrifying to me as a Virgin appearing to an Indian."

In the years intervening Oedipa had remembered Jesús because he'd seen that about Pierce and she hadn't. As if he were, in some unsexual way, competition. Now, drinking thick lukewarm coffee from a clay pot on the back burner of the yucateco's stove and listening to Jesús talk conspiracy, she wondered if, without the miracle of Pierce to reassure him, Jesús might not have quit his CIA eventually and gone over like everybody else to the majority priistas, and so never had to go into exile.

The dead man, like Maxwell's Demon, was the linking feature in a coincidence. Without him neither she nor Jesús would be exactly here, exactly now. It was enough, a coded warning. What, tonight, was chance? So her eyes did fall presently onto an ancient rolled copy of the anarcho-syndicalist paper *Regeneración.* The date was 1904 and there was no stamp next to the cancellation, only the handstruck image of the post horn.

"They arrive," said Arrabal. "Have they been in the mails that long? Has my name been substituted for that of a member who's died? Has it really taken sixty years? Is it a reprint? Idle questions, I am a footsoldier. The higher levels have their reasons." She carried this thought back out into the night with her.

Down at the city beach, long after the pizza stands and rides had closed, she walked unmolested through a drifting, dreamy cloud of delinquents in summer-weight gang jackets with the post horn stitched on in thread that looked pure silver in what moonlight there was. They had all been smoking, snuffing or injecting something, and perhaps did not see her at all.

Riding among an exhausted busful of Negroes going on to graveyard shifts all over the city, she saw scratched on the back of a seat, shining for her in the brilliant smoky interior, the post horn with the legend DEATH. But unlike WASTE, somebody had troubled to write in, in pencil: DON'T EVER ANTAGONIZE THE HORN.

Somewhere near Fillmore she found the symbol tacked to the bulletin board of a laundromat, among other scraps of paper offering cheap ironing and baby sitters. *If you know what this means,* the note said, *you know where to find out more.* Around her the odor of chlorine bleach rose heavenward, like an incense. Machines chugged and sloshed fiercely. Except for Oedipa the place was deserted, and the fluorescent bulbs seemed to shriek whiteness, to which everything their light touched was dedicated. It was a Negro neighborhood. Was The Horn so dedicated? Would it Antagonize The Horn to ask? Who could she ask?

In the buses all night she listened to transistor radios playing songs in the lower stretches of the Top 200, that would never become popular, whose melodies and lyrics would perish as if they had never been sung. A Mexican girl, trying to hear one of these through snarling static from the bus's motor, hummed along as if she would remember it always, tracing post horns and hearts with a fingernail, in the haze of her breath on the window.

Out at the airport Oedipa, feeling invisible, eavesdropped on a poker game whose steady loser entered each loss neat and conscientious in a little balance-book decorated inside with scrawled post horns. "I'm averaging a 99.375 percent return, fellas," she heard him say. The others, strangers, looked at him, some blank, some annoyed. "That's averaging it out, over 23 years," he went on, trying a smile. "Always just that little percent on the wrong side of breaking even. Twenty-three years. I'll never get ahead of it. Why don't I quit?" Nobody answering.

In one of the latrines was an advertisement by AC-DC, standing for Alameda County Death Cult, along with a box number and post horn. Once a month they were to choose some victim from among the innocent, the virtuous, the socially integrated and well-adjusted, using him sexually, then sacrificing him. Oedipa did not copy the number.

Catching a TWA flight to Miami was an uncoordinated boy who planned to slip at night into aquariums and open negotiations with the dolphins, who would succeed man. He was kissing his mother passionately goodbye, using his tongue. "I'll write, ma," he kept saying. "Write by WASTE," she said, "remember. The government will open it if you use the other. The dolphins will be mad." "I love you, ma," he said. "Love the dolphins," she advised him. "Write by WASTE."

So it went. Oedipa played the voyeur and listener. Among her other encounters were a facially-deformed welder, who cherished his ugliness; a child roaming the night who missed the death before birth as certain outcasts do the dear lulling blankness of the community; a Negro woman with an intricately-marbled scar along the baby-fat of one cheek who kept going through rituals of miscarriage each for a different reason, deliberately as others might the ritual of birth, dedicated not to continuity but to some kind of interregnum; an aging night-watchman, nibbling at a bar of Ivory Soap, who had trained his virtuoso stomach to accept also lotions, air-fresheners, fabrics, tobaccoes and waxes in a hopeless attempt to assimilate it all, all the promise, productivity, betrayal, ulcers, before it was too late; and even another voyeur, who hung outside one of the city's still-lighted windows, searching for who knew what specific image. Decorating each alienation, each species of withdrawal, as cufflink, decal, aimless doodling, there was somehow always the post horn. She grew so to expect it that perhaps she did not see it quite as often as she later was to remember seeing it. A couple-three times would really have been enough. Or too much.

She busrode and walked on into the lightening morning, giving herself up to a fatalism rare for her. Where was the Oedipa who'd driven so bravely up here from San Narciso? That optimistic baby had come on so like the private eye in any long-ago radio drama, believing all you needed was grit, resourcefulness, exemption from hidebound cops' rules, to solve any great mystery.

But the private eye sooner or later has to get beat up on. This night's profusion of post horns, this malignant, deliberate replication, was their way of beating up. They knew her pressure points, and the ganglia of her optimism, and one by one, pinch by precision pinch, they were immobilizing her.

Last night, she might have wondered what undergrounds apart from the couple she knew of communicated by WASTE system. By sunrise she could legitimately ask what undergrounds didn't. If miracles were, as Jesús Arrabal had postulated years ago on the beach at Mazatlán, intrusions into this world from another, a kiss of cosmic pool balls, then so must be each of the night's post horns. For here were God knew how many citizens, deliberately choosing not to communicate by U. S. Mail. It was not an act of treason, nor possibly even of defiance. But it was a calculated withdrawal, from the life of the Republic, from its machinery. Whatever else was being denied them out of hate, indifference to the power of their vote, loopholes, simple ignorance, this withdrawal was their own, unpublicized, private. Since they could not have withdrawn into a vacuum (could they?), there had to exist the separate, silent, unsuspected world.

Just before the morning rush hour, she got out of a jitney whose ancient driver ended each day in the red, downtown on Howard Street, began to walk toward the Embarcadero. She knew she looked terrible—knuckles black with eye-liner and mascara from where she'd rubbed, mouth tasting of old booze and coffee. Through an open doorway, on the stair leading up into the disinfectant-smelling twilight of a rooming house she saw an old man huddled, shaking with grief she couldn't hear. Both hands, smoke-white, covered his face. On the back of the left hand she made out the post horn, tattoed in old ink now beginning to blur and spread. Fascinated, she came into the shadows and ascended creaking steps, hesitating on each one. When she was three steps from him the hands flew apart and his wrecked face, and the terror of eyes gloried in burst veins, stopped her.

"Can I help?" She was shaking, tired.

"My wife's in Fresno," he said. He wore an old double-breasted suit, frayed gray shirt, wide tie, no hat. "I left her. So long ago, I don't remember. Now this is for her." He gave Oedipa a letter that looked like he'd been carrying it around for years. "Drop it in the," and he held up the tattoo and stared into her eyes, "you know. I can't go out there. It's too far now, I had a bad night."

"I know," she said. "But I'm new in town. I don't know where it is."

"Under the freeway." He waved her on in the direction she'd been going. "Always one. You'll see it." The eyes closed. Cammed each night out of that safe furrow the bulk of this city's waking each sunrise again set virtuously to plowing, what rich soils had he turned, what concentric planets uncovered? What voices overheard, flinders of luminescent gods glimpsed among the wallpaper's stained foliage, candlestubs lit to rotate in the air over him, prefiguring the cigarette he or a friend must fall asleep someday smoking, thus to end among the flaming, secret salts held all those years by the insatiable stuffing of a mattress that could keep vestiges of every nightmare sweat, helpless overflowing bladder, viciously, tearfully consummated wet dream, like the memory bank to a computer of the lost? She was overcome all at once by a need to touch him, as if she could not believe in him, or would not remember him, without it. Exhausted, hardly knowing what she was doing, she came the last three steps and sat, took the man in her arms, actually held him, gazing out of her smudged eyes down the stairs, back into the morning. She felt wetness against her breast and saw that he was crying again. He hardly breathed but tears came as if being pumped. "I can't help," she whispered, rocking him, "I can't help." It was already too many miles to Fresno.

"Is that him?" a voice asked behind her, up the stairs. "The sailor?"

"He has a tattoo on his hand."

"Can you bring him up OK? That's him." She turned and saw an even older man, shorter, wearing a tall Homburg hat and smiling at them. "I'd help you but I got a little arthritis."

"Does he have to come up?" she said. "Up there?"

"Where else, lady?"

She didn't know. She let go of him for a moment, reluctant as if he were her own child, and he looked up at her. "Come on," she said. He reached out the tattooed hand and she took that, and that was how they went the rest of the way up that flight, and then the two more: hand in hand, very slowly for the man with arthritis.

"He disappeared last night," he told her. "Said he was going looking for his old lady. It's a thing he does, off and on." They entered a warren of rooms and corridors, lit by 10-watt bulbs, separated by beaverboard partitions. The old man followed them stiffly. At last he said, "Here."

In the little room were another suit, a couple of religious tracts, a rug, a chair. A picture of a saint, changing well-water to oil for Jerusalem's Easter lamps. Another bulb, dead. The bed. The mattress, waiting. She ran through then a scene she might play. She might find the landlord of this place, and bring him to court, and buy the sailor a new suit at Roos/Atkins, and shirt, and shoes, and give him the bus fare to Fresno after all. But with a sigh he had released her hand, while she was so lost in the fantasy that she hadn't felt it go away, as if he'd known the best moment to let go.

"Just mail the letter," he said, "the stamp is on it." She looked and saw the familiar carmine 8¢ airmail, with a jet flying by the Capitol dome. But at the top of the dome stood a tiny figure in deep black, with its arms outstretched. Oedipa wasn't sure what exactly was supposed to be on top of the Capitol, but knew it wasn't anything like that.

"Please," the sailor said. "Go on now. You don't want to stay here." She looked in her purse, found a ten and a single, gave him the ten. "I'll spend it on booze," he said.

"Remember your friends," said the arthritic, watching the ten.

"Bitch," said the sailor. "Why didn't you wait till he was gone?"

Oedipa watched him make adjustments so he'd fit easier against the mattress. That stuffed memory. Register A . . .

"Give me a cigarette, Ramírez," the sailor said. "I know you got one."

Would it be today? "Ramírez," she cried. The arthritic looked around on his rusty neck. "He's going to die," she said.

"Who isn't?" said Ramírez.

She remembered John Nefastis, talking about his Machine, and massive destructions of information. So when this mattress flared up around the sailor, in his Viking's funeral: the stored, coded years of uselessness, early death, self-harrowing, the sure decay of hope, the set of all men who had slept on it, whatever their lives had been, would truly cease to be, forever, when the mattress burned. She stared at it in wonder. It was as if she had just discovered the irreversible process. It astonished her to think that so much could be lost, even the quantity of hallucination belonging just to the sailor that the world would bear no further trace of. She knew, because she had held him, that he suffered DT's. Behind the initials was a metaphor, a delirium tremens, a trembling unfurrowing of the mind's plowshare. The saint whose water can light lamps, the clairvoyant whose lapse in recall is the breath of God, the true paranoid for whom all is organized in spheres joyful or threatening about the central pulse of himself, the dreamer whose puns probe ancient fetid shafts and tunnels of truth all act in the same special relevance to the word, or whatever it is the word is there, buffering, to protect us from. The act of metaphor then was a thrust at truth and a lie, depending where you were: inside, safe, or outside, lost. Oedipa did not know where she was. Trembling, unfurrowed, she slipped sidewise, screeching back across grooves of years, to hear again the earnest, high voice of her second or third collegiate love Ray Glozing bitching among "uhs" and the syncopated tonguing of a cavity, about his freshman calculus; "dt," God help this old tattooed man, meant also a time differential, a vanishingly small instant in which change had to be confronted at last for what it was, where it could no longer disguise itself as something innocuous like an average rate; where velocity dwelled in the projectile though the projectile be frozen in midflight, where death dwelled in the cell though the cell be looked in on at its most quick. She knew that the sailor had seen worlds no other man had seen if only because there was that high magic to low puns, because DT's must give access to dt's of spectra beyond the known sun, music made purely of Antarctic loneliness and fright. But nothing she knew of would preserve them, or him. She gave him goodbye, walked downstairs and then on, in the direction he'd told her. For an hour she prowled among the sunless, concrete underpinnings of the freeway, finding drunks, bums, pedestrians, pederasts, hookers, walking psychotic, no secret mailbox. But at last in the shadows she did come on a can with a swinging trapezoidal top, the kind you throw trash in: old and green, nearly four feet high. On the swinging part were hand-painted the initials W.A.S.T.E. She had to look closely to see the periods between the letters.

* * *

1966

WILLIAM S. BURROUGHS
1914–1997

Descended from both the Civil War general Robert E. Lee and the inventor of the adding machine, William S. Burroughs was born in St. Louis, Missouri. After graduation from Harvard in 1936 and two brief stints in graduate schools, Burroughs enlisted for a short time in the U.S. Army before being discharged for severing a finger to impress a friend. He also worked as an advertising copywriter, exterminator, bartender, and private detective. In 1946 he married Joan Vollmer, who introduced him to Jack Kerouac; in turn Burroughs met Allen Ginsberg and subsequently became a central member of the Beat generation of writers. Burroughs' numerous works of fiction include *Junkie: Confessions of an Unredeemed Drug Addict* (1953), *Naked Lunch* (1959), *Queer* (1986), and *My Education: A Book of Dreams* (1995). In 1975, he received the award in literature from the American Academy and Institute of Arts and Letters, and he was named a member in 1983.

Known for the confessional novel about his life as a former drug addict, and for his outspoken homosexuality, Burroughs also championed the "cut-up" technique in such experimental novels as *The Soft Machine* (1961), *Dead Fingers Talk* (1963), and *Nova Express* (1964), from which "Crab Nebula" is excerpted. As Gerard Cordesse writes in *Caliban XII* (1975), "The reader must piece [the story] together from flashes, obsessive phrases, and incomplete scenes, struggling through disjointed chronology and abrupt changes of narrators, or cryptic cut-ups." In a 1983 interview in *Dream Makers* (Vol. II) Burroughs asserted that the cut-up technique is "closer to the actual facts of perception. . . . I'm talking about how things are actually perceived by the brain."

From Nova Express

Crab Nebula

They do not have what they call "emotion's oxygen" in the atmosphere. The medium in which animal life breathes is not in that soulless place—Yellow plains under white hot blue sky—Metal cities controlled by The Elders who are heads in bottles—Fastest brains preserved forever—Only form of immortality open to The Insect People of Minraud—An intricate bureaucracy wired to the control brains directs all movement—Even so there is a devious underground operating through telepathic misdirection and camouflage—The partisans make recordings ahead in time and leave the recordings to be picked up by control stations while they are free for a few seconds to organize underground activities—Largely the underground is made up of adventurers who intend to outthink and displace the present heads—There has been one revolution in the history of Minraud—Purges are constant—Fallen heads destroyed in The Ovens and replaced with others faster and sharper to evolve more total weapons—The principal weapon of Minraud is of course heat—In the center of all their cities stand The Ovens where those who disobey the control brains are brought for total disposal—A conical structure of iridescent metal shimmering heat from the molten core of a planet where lead melts at noon—The Brass And Copper Streets surround The Oven—Here the tinkers and smiths work pounding out metal rhythms as prisoners and criminals are led to Disposal—The Oven Guards are red crustacean men with eyes like the white hot sky—Through contact with oven pain and captured enemies they sometimes mutate to breathe in emotions—They often help prisoners to escape and a few have escaped with the prisoners—

(When K9 entered the apartment he felt the suffocation of Minraud crushing his chest stopping his thoughts—He turned on reserve ate dinner and carried conversation—When he left the host walked out with him down the streets of Minraud past the ovens empty and cold now—calm dry mind of the guide beside him came to the corner of 14th and Third—

"I must go back now," said the guide—"Otherwise it will be too far to go alone."

He smiled and held out his hand fading in the alien air—)

K9 was brought to the ovens by red guards in white and gold robe of office through the Brass and Copper Street under pounding metal hammers—The oven heat drying up life source as white hot metal lattice closed around him—

"Second exposure—Time three point five," said the guard—

K9 walked out into The Brass And Copper Streets—A slum area of vending booths and smouldering slag heaps crossed by paths worn deep in phosphorescent metal—In a square littered with black bones he encountered a group of five scorpion men—Faces of transparent pink cartilage burning inside—stinger dripping the oven poison—Their eyes flared with electric hate and they slithered forward to surround him but drew back at sight of the guard—

They walked on into an area of tattoo booths and sex parlors—A music like wind through fine metal wires bringing a measure of relief from the terrible dry heat—Black beetle musicians saw this music out of the air swept by continual hot winds from plains that surround the city—The plains are dotted with villages of conical paper-thin metal houses where a patient gentle crab people live unmolested in the hottest regions of the planet—

Controller of The Crab Nebula on a slag heap of smouldering metal under the white hot sky channels all his pain into control thinking—He is protected by heat and crab guards and the brains armed now with The Blazing Photo from Hiroshima and Nagasaki—The brains under his control are encased in a vast structure of steel and crystal spinning thought patterns that control whole galaxies thousand years ahead on the chessboard of virus screens and juxtaposition formulae—

So The Insect People Of Minraud formed an alliance with the Virus Power Of The Vegetable People to occupy planet earth—The gimmick is reverse photosynthesis—The Vegetable People suck up oxygen and all equivalent sustenance of animal life—Always the colorless sheets between you and what you see taste touch smell eat—And these green vegetable junkies slowly using up your oxygen to stay on the nod in carbon dioxide—

When K9 entered the café he felt the colorless smell of the vegetable people closing round him taste and sharpness gone from the food people blurring in slow motion fade out—And there was a whole tank full of vegetable junkies breathing it all in—He clicked some reverse combos through the pinball machine and left the café—In the street citizens were yacking like supersonic dummies—The SOS addicts had sucked up all the silence in the area were now sitting around in blue blocks of heavy metal the earth's crust buckling ominously under their weight—He shrugged: "Who am I to be critical?"

He knew what it meant to kick an SOS habit: White hot agony of thawing metal—And the suffocating panic of carbon dioxide withdrawal—

Virus defined as the three-dimensional coordinate point of a controller—Transparent sheets with virus perforations like punch cards passed through the host on the soft machine feeling for a point of intersection—The virus attack is primarily directed against affective animal life—Virus of rage hate fear ugliness swirling round you waiting for a point of intersection and once in immediately perpetrates in your name some ugly noxious or disgusting act sharply photographed and recorded becomes now part of the virus sheets constantly presented and represented before your mind screen to produce more virus word and image around and around it's all around you the invisible hail of bring down word and image—

What does virus do wherever it can dissolve a hole and find traction?—It starts eating—And what does it do with what it eats?—It makes exact copies of itself that start eating to make more copies that start eating to make more copies that start eating and so forth to the virus power the fear hate virus slowly replaces the host with virus copies—Program empty body—A vast tapeworm of bring down word and image moving through your mind screen always at the same speed on a slow hydraulic-spine axis like the cylinder gimmick in the adding machine—How do you make someone feel stupid?—You present to him all the times he talked and acted and felt stupid again and again any number of times fed into the combo of the soft calculating machine geared to find more and more punch cards and feed in more and more images of stupidity disgust propitiation grief apathy death—The recordings leave electromagnetic patterns—That is any situation that causes rage will magnetize rage patterns and draw around the rage word and image recordings—Or some disgusting sex practice once the connection is made in childhood whenever the patterns are magnetized by sex desire the same word and image will be presented—And so forth—The counter move is very simple—This is machine strategy and the machine can be redirected—Record for ten minutes on a tape recorder—Now run the tape back without playing and cut in other words at random—Where you have cut in and re-recorded words are wiped off the tape and new words in their place—You have turned time back ten minutes and wiped electromagnetic word patterns off the tape and substituted other patterns—You can do the same with mind tape after working with the tape recorder—(This takes some experimentation)—The old mind tapes can be wiped clean—Magnetic word dust falling from old patterns—Word falling—Photo falling—"Last week Robert Kraft of the Mount Wilson and Palomar Observatories reported some answers to the riddle of exploding stars—Invariably he found the exploding star was locked by gravity to a nearby star—The two stars are in a strange symbiotic relationship—One is a small hot blue star—(Mr. Bradly)—Its companion is a larger red star—(Mr. Martin)—Because the stellar twins are so close together the blue star continually pulls fuel in the form of hydrogen gas from the red star—The motion of the system spins the hydrogen into an incandescent figure eight—One circle of the eight encloses one star—The other circle encloses the other—supplied with new fuel the blue star ignites."—Quote, *Newsweek,* Feb. 12, 1962—

The Crab Nebula observed by the Chinese in 1054 A.D. is the result of a supernova or exploding star—Situated approximately three thousand light years from the earth—(Like three thousand years in hot claws at the window—You got it?—)—Before they blow up a star they have a spot picked out as many light years away as possible—Then they start draining all the fuel and charge to the new pitch and siphon themselves there right after and on their way rejoicing—You notice we don't have as much time as people had say a hundred years ago?—Take your clothes to the laundry write a letter pick up your mail at American Express and the day is gone—They are short-timing us as many light years as they can take for the getaway—It seems that there were survivors on The Crab Pitch who are not in all respects reasonable men—And The Nova Law moving in fast—So they start the same old lark sucking all the charge and air and color to a new location and then?—*Sput*—You notice something is sucking all the flavor out of food the pleasure out of sex the color out of everything in sight?—Precisely creating the low pressure area that leads to nova—So they move cross the wounded galaxies always a few light years ahead of the Nova Heat—That is they did—The earth was our set—And they walked right into the antibiotic handcuffs—It will readily be seen that having created one nova they must make other or answer for the first—I mean three thousand years in hot claws at the window like a giant crab in slag heaps of smouldering metal—Also the more novas the less time between they are running out of pitches—So they bribe the natives with a promise of transportation and immortality—

"Yeah, man, flesh and junk and charge stacked up bank vaults full of it—Three thousand years of flesh—So we leave the bloody apes behind and on our way rejoicing right?—It's the only way to live—"

And the smart operators fall for it every fucking time—Talk about marks—One of our best undercover operators is known as The Rube—He perfected The Reverse Con—Comes on honest and straight and the smart operators all think they are conning him—How could they think otherwise until he slips on the antibiotic handcuffs—

"There's a wise guy born every minute," he says. "Closing time gentlemen—The stenographer will take your depositions—"

"So why did I try to blow up the planet?—Pea under the shell—Now you see it now you don't—Sky shift to cover the last pitch—Take it all out with us and hit the road—I am made of metal and that metal is radioactive—Radioactivity can be absorbed up to a point but radium clock hands tick away—Time to move on—Only one turnstile—Heavy planet—Travel with Minraud technicians to handle the switchboard and Venusians to make flesh and keep the show on the road—Then The Blazing Photo and we travel on—Word *is* flesh and word *is* two that is the human body is compacted of two organisms and where you have two you have word and word is flesh and when they started tampering with the word that was it and the blockade was broken and The Nova Heat moved in—The Venusians sang first naturally they were in the most immediate danger—They live underwater in the body with an air line—And that air line is the word—Then the technicians spilled and who can blame them after the conditions I assigned to keep them technicians—Like three thousand years in hot claws—So I am alone as always—You understand nova is where I am born in such pain no one else survives in one piece—Born again and again cross the wounded galaxies—I am alone but not what you call 'lonely'—Loneliness is a product of dual mammalian structure—'Loneliness,' 'love,' 'friendship,' all the rest of it—I am not two—I am *one*—But to maintain my state of oneness I need twoness in other life forms—Other must talk so that I can remain silent—If another becomes one then I am two—That makes two ones makes two and I am no longer one—Plenty of room in space you say?—But I am not one in space I am one in time—Metal time—Radioactive time—So of course I tried to keep you all out of space—That is the end of time—And those who were allowed out sometimes for special services like creating a useful religious concept went always with a Venusian guard—All the 'mystics' and 'saints'—All except my old enemy Hassan i Sabbah who wised up the marks to space and said they could be one and need no guard no other half no word—

"And now I have something to say to all you angle boys of the cosmos who thought you had an in with The Big Operator—*'Suckers! Cunts! Marks!—I hate you all—And I never intended to cut you in or pay you off with anything but horse shit—And you can thank The Rube if you don't go up with the apes—Is that clear enough or shall I make it even clearer? You are the suckers cunts marks I invented to explode this dead whistle stop and go up with it—'* "

A Bad Move

Could give no other information than wind walking in a rubbish heap to the sky—Solid shadow turned off the white film of noon heat—Exploded deep in the alley tortured metal Oz—Look anywhere, Dead hand—Phosphorescent bones—Cold Spring afterbirth of that hospital—Twinges of amputation—Bread knife in the heart paid taxi boys—If I knew I'd be glad to look anyplace—No good myself—Clom Fliday—Diseased wind identity fading out—Smoke is all—We intersect in the dark mutinous door—Hairless skull—Flesh smeared—Five times of dust we made it all—consumed by slow metal fires—Smell of gasoline envelops last electrician—I woke up with dark information from the dead—Board Room Reports waiting for Madrid—Arrested motion con su medicina—Soft mendicant "William" in the dark street—He stood there 1910 straw words falling—Dead lights and water—Either way is a bad move—Better than that?—Gone away can tell you—No good No bueno—White flash mangled silver eyes—Flesh flakes in the sky—Explosive twinges of amputation—Mendicant the crooked crosses and barren the dark street—No more—No más—Their last end—Wounded galaxies tap on the pane—Hustling myself—Clom Fliday—And one fine tell you—No good—No bueno—

Be cheerful sir our revels touch the sky—The white film made of Mr. Martin—Rotting phosphorescent bones carried a gasoline dream—Hand falling—White flash mangled "Mr. Bradly Mr. Martin"—Thing Police, Board Room Death Smell, time has come for the dark street—No more—No más wounded galaxies—I told him you on aid—Died out down stale streets through convolutions of our ever living poet—On this green land the dollar twisted to light a last cigarette—Last words answer you—

Long time between suns behind—Empty hunger cross the wounded sky—Cold your brain slowly fading—I said by our ever living poet dead—Last words answer your summons—May not refuse vision in setting forth the diary—Mr. Martin Mr. Corso Mr. Beiles Mr. Burroughs now ended—These our actors, William—The razor inside, sir—Jerk the handle—That hospital melted into air—Advance and inherit the insubstantial dead—Flakes fall that were his shadow—

Metal chess determined gasoline fires and smoke in motionless air—Smudge two speeds—DSL walks "here" beside me on extension lead from hairless skull—Flesh-smeared recorder consumed by slow metal fires—Dog-proof room important for our "oxygen" lines—Group respective recorder layout—"Throw the gasoline on them" determined the life form we invaded: insect screams—I woke up with "marked for invasion" recording set to run for as long as phantom "cruelties" are playing back while waiting to pick up Eduardo's "corrupt" speed and volume variation Madrid—Tape recorder banks tumescent flesh—Our mikes planning speaker stood there in 1910 straw word—Either way is a bad move to The Biologic Stairway—The whole thing tell you—No good—No bueno outright or partially—The next state walking in a rubbish heap to Form A—Form A directs sound channels heat—White flash mangled down to a form of music—Life Form A as follows was alien focus—Broken pipes refuse "oxygen"—Form A parasitic wind identity fading out—"Word falling—Photo falling" flesh-smeared counter orders—determined by last Electrician—Alien mucus cough language learned to keep all Board Room Reports waiting sound formations—Alien mucus tumescent code train on Madrid—Convert in "dirty pictures 8"—simple repetition—Whole could be used as model for a bad move—Better than shouts: "No good—No bueno"—

"Recorders fix nature of absolute need: *occupy*—*'Here'*—Any cruelties answer him—Either unchanged or reverse—Clang—Sorry—Planet trailing somewhere along here—Sequential choice—Flesh plots con su medicina—The next state according to—Stop—Look—Form A directs sound channels—Well what now?—Final switch if you want to—Dead on Life Form B by cutting off machine if you want to—Blood form determined by the switch—Same need—Same step—Not survive in any 'emotion'—Intervention?—It's no use I tell you—Familiar will be the end product?—Reciprocate complete wires? You fucking can't—Could we become part of the array?—In The American Cemetery—Hard to distinguish maps came in at the verbal level—This he went to Madrid?—And so si learn? The accused was beyond altered arrival—So?—So mucus machine runs by feeding in over The American—Hear it?—Paralleled the bell—Hours late—They all went away—You've thought it out?—A whole replaced history of life burial tapes being blank?—Could this 'you' 'them' 'whatever' learn? Accused was beyond altered formations—No good—Machine runs by feeding in 'useless'—Blood spilled over Grey Veil—Parallel spurt—How many looking at dirty pictures—? Before London Space Stage tenuous face maybe—Change—Definite—The disorder gets you model for behavior—Screams?—Laughter?"—Voice fading into advocate:

"Clearly the whole defense must be experiments with two tape recorder mutations."

Again at the window that never was mine—Reflected word scrawled by some boy—Greatest of all waiting lapses—Five years—The ticket exploded in the air—For I don't know—*I do not know* human dreams—Never was mine—Waiting lapse—Caught in the door—Explosive fragrance—Love between light and shadow—The few who lived cross the wounded galaxies—Love?—Five years I grew muttering in the ice—Dead sun reached flesh with its wandering dream—Buried tracks, Mr. Bradly, so complete was the lie—Course—Naturally—Circumstances now Spanish—Hermetic you understand—Locked in her heart of ooze—A great undersea blight—Atlantis along the wind in green neon—The ooze is only colorless question drifted down—Obvious one at that—Its goal?—That's more difficult to tap on the pane—One aspect of virus—An obvious one again—Muttering in the dogs for generalizations—The lice we intersect—Poison of dead sun anywhere else—What was it the old crab man said about the lice?—Parasites on "Mr. Martin"—My ice my perfect ice that never circumstances—Now Spanish cautiously my eyes—And I became the form of a young man standing—My pulse in unison—Never did I know resting place—Wind hand caught in the door—cling—Chocada—to tap on the pane—

Chocada—Again—Muttering in the dogs—Five years—Poison of dead sun with her—With whom?—I dunno—See account on the crooked crosses—And your name?—Berg?—Berg?—Bradly?—"Mr. Martin si" Disaster Snow—Crack—Sahhk—Numb—Just a fluke came in with the tide and The Swedish River of Gothenberg—

The Death Dwarf in the Street

Biologic Agent K9 called for his check and picked up supersonic imitation blasts of The Death Dwarfs—"L'addition—Ladittion—LadditWion—Garcon—Garcon Garcon"—American tourist accent to the Nth power—He ordered another coffee and monitored the café—A whole table of them imitating word forms and spitting back at supersonic speed—Several patrons rolled on the floor in switch fits—These noxious dwarfs can spit out a whole newspaper in ten seconds imitating your words after you and sliding in suggestion insults—That is the entry gimmick of The Death Dwarfs: supersonic imitation and playback so you think it is your own voice—(do you own a voice?) they invade The Right Centers which are The Speech Centers and they are in the right—in the right—in thee write—"RIGHT"—"I'm in the right—in the right—You know I'm in the right so long as you hear me say inside your right centers 'I am in the right' "—While Sex Dwarfs tenderize erogenous holes—So The Venusian Gook Rot flashed round the world—

Agent K9 was with The Biologic Police assigned to bring the Dwarf Plague under control by disconnecting the dwarfs from Central Control Station: The Insect Brain of Minraud enclosed in a crystal cylinder from which run the cold wires to an array of calculating machines feeding instructions to The Death Dwarf In The Street—The brain is surrounded by Crab Guards charged from The Thermodynamic Pain And Energy Bank—Crab Guards can not be attacked directly since they are directly charged by attack—K9 had been in combat with The Crab Guards and he knew what can happen if they get their claws on your nerve centers—

K9 left the café and surveying the street scene he could not but feel that someone had goofed—The Death Dwarfs had in many cases been separated from the human host but they were still charged from Central Control and yacked through the streets imitating words and gestures of everyone in sight—While Sex Dwarfs squirmed out of any cover with a perfunctory, "Hello there," in anyone who stood still for it, dissolved erogenous holes immediately attacked by The Talk Dwarfs so that in a few seconds the unfortunate traveler was torn to pieces which the dwarfs snatch from each other's mouth with shrill silver screams—In fact the noxious behavior of this life form harried the citizens beyond endurance and everyone carried elaborate home-made contrivances for screening out the Talk Dwarfs and a special plastic cover to resist erogenous acids of the Sex Dwarfs—

Without hesitation K9 gave the order: "Release Silence Virus—Blanket area"—So The Silence Sickness flashed round the world at speed of light—As a result many citizens who had been composed entirely of word went ape straight away and screamed through the streets attacking the passers-by who in many cases went ape in turn as The Silence Sickness hit—To combat these conditions, described as "intolerable," political leaders projected stern noble image from control towers and some could occupy and hold up the ape forms for a few days or weeks—Invariably the leader was drained by the gravity of unregenerate apes, torn in pieces by his relapsing constituents, or went ape himself on TV—So the Survivors as they call themselves lived in continual dread of resistant dwarfs always more frantic from host hunger—Knowing that at any minute the man next to you in the street might go Mandril and leap your throat with virginal canines—K9 shrugged and put in a call for Technicians—"The error in enemy strategy is now obvious—It is machine strategy and the machine can be redirected—Have written connection in The Soft Typewriter the machine can only repeat your instructions since it can not create anything—The operation is very technical—Look at a photomontage—It makes a statement in flexible picture language—Let us call the statement made by a given photomontage X—We can use X words X colors X odors X images and so forth to define the various aspects of X—Now we feed X into the calculating machine and X scans out related colors, juxtapositions, affect-charged images and so forth we can attenuate or concentrate X by taking out or adding elements and feeding back into the machine factors we wish to concentrate—A Technician learns to think and write in association blocks which can then be manipulated according to the laws of association and juxtaposition—The basic law of association and conditioning is known to college students even in America: Any object, feeling, odor, word, image in juxtaposition with any other object feeling, odor, word or image will be associated with it—Our technicians learn to read newspapers and magazines for juxtaposition statements rather than alleged content—We express these statements in Juxtaposition Formulae—The Formulae of course control populations of the world—Yes it is fairly easy to predict what people will think see feel and hear a thousand years from now if you write the Juxtaposition Formulae to be used in that period—But the technical details you understand and the machines—all of which contain basic flaws and must be continually overhauled, checked, altered whole blocks of computing machines purged and disconnected from one minute to the next—fast our mind waves and long counts—And let me take this opportunity of replying to the criticisms of my creeping opponents—It is not true that I took part in or instigated experiments defining pain and pleasure thresholds—I used abstract reports of the experiments to evolve the formulae of pain and pleasure association that control this planet—I assume no more responsibility than a physicist working from material presented to an immobilized brain—I have constructed *a* physics of the human nervous system or more accurately the human nervous system defines the physics I have constructed—Of course I can construct another system working on quite different principals—Pain is a quantitative factor—So is pleasure—I had material from purge trials and concentration camps and reports from Nagasaki and Hiroshima defining the limits of courage—Our most precise data came from Lexington Ky. where the drug addicts of America are processed—The pain of heroin withdrawal in the addict lends itself perfectly to testing under control conditions—Pain is quantitative to degree of addiction and stage of withdrawal and is quantitatively relieved by cell-blanketing agents—With pain and pleasure limits defined and the juxtaposition formulae set up it is fairly easy to predict what people will think in a thousand years or as long as the formulae remain in operation—I can substitute other formulae if I am permitted to do so—No one has given much thought to building a qualitative mathematics—My formulae saw to that—Now here is a calculating machine—Of course it can process qualitative data—Color for example—I feed into the machine a blue photo passes to the Blue Section and a hundred or a thousand blue photos rustle out while the machine plays blues in a blue smell of ozone blue words of all the poets flow out on ticker tape—Or feed in a thousand novels and scan out the last pages—That is quality is it not? Endingness?"

"Green Tony squealed and I'm off for Galaxy X—"

"The whole mob squealed—Now we can move in for some definitive arrests—Set arrest machinery in operation—Cover all agents and associations with juxtaposition formulae—Put out scanning patterns through coordinate points of the earth for Mr. & Mrs. D—Top Nova Criminals—Through mind screens of the earth covering coordinate points blocking D out of a hand a mouth a cold sore—Silver antibiotic handcuffs fitting D virus filters and—Lock—Click—We have made the arrest—You will understand why all concepts of revenge or moral indignation must be excised from a biologic police agent—We are not here to keep this tired old injustice show on the road but to stop it short of Nova—"

"Nova—Nova—Nova—" shriek the Death Dwarfs—"Arrest good kind Mr. D?—Why he paid for my hernia operation—"

"That did it—Release Silence Virus—Blanket Area—"

"Thinking in association blocks instead of words enables the operator to process data with the speed of light on the association line—Certain alterations are of course essential—"

Extremely Small Particles

Dec. 17, 1961—Past Time—The error in enemy strategy is now to be gathered I was not at all close and the machine can be redirected—These youths of image and association now at entrance to the avenue carrying banners of inter language—

Time: The night before adventurers who hope to form another blazing photo—Injury Headquarters Concentration with reports from Hiroshima—Some of the new hallucinogens and Nagasaki—Slight overdose of dimethyltryptamine—Your cities are ovens where South American narcotic plants brought total disposal—Brain screams of millions who have controller lives in that place screamed back from white hot blue sky—Can always pull the nova equipped now with tower blasts from Hiroshima and Nagasaki—In such pain he has only one turnstile—

Bureaucracy tuned in on all—Incredibly devious conditions hatch cosmologies of telepathic misdirection—Mind screen movies overlapping make recordings ahead and leave before thinking was recorded—Our most precise data came from U.N. (United Narcotics)—His plan was drug addicts of America slip through the cordon—Pain of heroin failure often the cause of windows to pursue ends not compatible cell-blanketing agent—Our most precise data with The Silent People—Plan was almost superhuman drug burned through his juxtapositions—He was naked now to Nagasaki defining the limits against him—The projector can shift its succinct army before flesh dissolving—

Integrity and bravery are difficulties in the laboratory—Experiments to evolve ill took control this planet—Through the streets Nagasaki defining the limits of bravery—We find nationalisms and clashings to degree of addiction—It is fairly easy to predict inter police taking arms to protect their own forgeries from the taken over—Might reach 500 Ideology Headquarters armed with Board Officers produced synthetically—The hallucinogen drugs bottle three-dimensional coordinate points—New hallucinogens directed against affective animal life—Slight overdose of ugliness fear and hate—The ovens were image dust swirling round you total disposal—Some ugly noxious disgusting act sharply recorded becomes now part of "Photo falling—Word Falling"—Presented and represented before towers open fire—Alien virus can dissolve millions—It starts eating—Screamed back white hot copies of itself—So the Fear Species can replace the host armed now with tapeworm of bring down word and image plus Nagasaki—Injury Headquarters—Dual mammalian structure—Hiroshima People—Or some disgusting officers produced the rest of it—

Attorney General For Fear announced yesterday the discovery that cries of nepotism might "form a new mineral damaging to the President"—Insidious form of high density silica as extremely small particles got into politics with Lyndon B. Johnson, wife of two Negro secret service men—Another Mineral American formed by meteorite impact—"And it would make a splendid good talker," he said—

At these tables there is virtually jostling diplomats—Some displacements of a sedate and celebrated rose garden but ideal for the processes of a quiet riverview restaurant—Police juice and the law are no cure for widespread public petting in chow lines the Soviet Union said yesterday—Anti-American promptly denounced Kennedy's moribund position of insistence:

"Washington know-how to deal with this sort demonstration in Venezuela of irresponsible propaganda—Outside Caracas I am deeply distressed at the Soviet Union's attempt to drag us back just when we was stoned in violation of the administration's twenty billion dollar solemn word—"

He begged as a personal thing scattered uprisings—

Error in enemy strategy is switchboard redirected—Word is TWO that is the noxious human inter language recorded—And where you have TWO you have odor's and nationalism's word—They started tampering with net—Injury Headquarters blockade was broken—"Calling partisans of all nations—Crab word falling—Virus photo falling—Break through in Grey Room—"

1964

DONALD BARTHELME
1931–1989

Born in Philadelphia, Pennsylvania, Donald Barthelme grew up in Texas, the son of an avant-garde architect who, Barthelme noted in *The New Fiction: Interviews with Innovative American Writers* (1974), was "something of an anomaly, somewhat different from . . . other people we knew. His mind was elsewhere." Barthelme served in the army in Japan and Korea, and worked as a newspaper reporter for the *Houston Post*. By the end of 1963, he had published four stories in *The New Yorker*, where he became a regular contributor until his death. His eight short-story collections include *Come Back, Dr. Caligari* (1964), *City Life* (1970), *Sixty Stories* (1981), and *Forty Stories* (1988), and his novels are *Snow White* (1967), *The Dead Father* (1975), *Paradise* (1986), and *The King* (1990). Barthelme received both a National Book Award and a Guggenheim Fellowship, and was a member of the American Academy and Institute of Arts and Letters.

"The principle of collage is the central principle of all art in the twentieth century in all media," Barthelme told Richard Schickel in *The New York Times Magazine* in 1970. Alfred Kazin writes in *Bright Book of Life* (1973) that Barthelme is an "anti-novelist" who "operates by countermeasures only"; but William Gass observes in *Fiction and the Figures of Life* (1970) that there is "nothing surrealistic about him, his dislocations are real, his material quite actual," yet each of Barthelme's books "has seemed unnatural; certainly none speaks." Regis Durand concludes in *Donald Barthelme* (1982) that "Barthelme's is an art of absences."

"See the Moon?" was first published in *Unspeakable Practices, Unnatural Acts* (1964), and "Sentence" appeared in *City Life*.

See the Moon?

I know you think I'm wasting my time. You've made that perfectly clear. But I'm conducting these very important lunar hostility studies. And it's not you who'll have to leave the warm safe capsule. And dip a toe into the threatening lunar surround.

I am still wearing my yellow flower which has lasted wonderfully.

My methods may seem a touch irregular. Have to do chiefly with folded paper airplanes at present. But the paper must be folded *in the right way.* Lots of calculations and worrying about edges.

Show me a man who worries about edges and I'll show you a natural-born winner. Cardinal Y. agrees. Columbus himself worried, the Admiral of the Ocean Sea. But he kept it quiet.

The sun so warm on this screened porch, it reminds me of my grandmother's place in Tampa. The same rusty creaky green glider and the same faded colored canvas cushions. And at night the moon graphed by the screen wire, if you squint. The Sea of Tranquility occupying squares 47 through 108.

See the moon? It hates us.

My methods are homely but remember Newton and the apple. And when Rutherford started out he didn't even have a decently heated laboratory. And then there's the matter of my security check—I'm waiting for the government. Somebody told it I'm insecure. *That's true.*

I suffer from a frightful illness of the mind, light-mindedness. It's not catching. You needn't shrink.

You've noticed the wall? I pin things on it, souvenirs. There is the red hat, there the book of instructions for the Ant Farm. And this is a traffic ticket written on a saint's day (which saint? I don't remember) in 1954 just outside a fat little town (which town? I don't remember) in Ohio by a cop who asked me what I did. I said I wrote poppycock for the president of a university, true then.

You can see how far I've come. Lunar hostility studies aren't for everyone.

It's my hope that these . . . souvenirs . . . will someday merge, blur—cohere is the word, maybe—into something meaningful. A grand word, meaningful. What do I look for? A work of art, I'll not accept anything less. Yes I know it's shatteringly ingenuous but I wanted to be a painter. They get away with murder in my view; Mr. X. on the *Times* agrees with me. You don't know how I envy them. They can pick up a Baby Ruth wrapper on the street, glue it to the canvas (in the *right place,* of course, there's that), and lo! people crowd about and cry, "A real Baby Ruth wrapper, by God, what could be realer than that!" Fantastic metaphysical advantage. You hate them, if you're ambitious.

The Ant Farm instructions are a souvenir of Sylvia. The red hat came from Cardinal Y. We're friends, in a way.

I wanted to be one, when I was young, a painter. But I couldn't stand stretching the canvas. Does things to the fingernails. And that's the first place people look.

Fragments are the only forms I trust.

Light-minded or no, I'm . . . riotous with mental health. I measure myself against the Russians, that's fair. I have here a clipping datelined Moscow, four young people apprehended strangling a swan. *That's* boredom. The swan's name, Borka. The sentences as follows: Tsarev, metalworker, served time previously for stealing public property, four years in a labor camp, strict regime. Roslavtsev, electrician, jailed previously for taking a car on a joyride, three years and four months in a labor camp, semistrict regime. Tatyana Voblikova (only nineteen and a Komsomol member too), technician, one and a half years in a labor camp, degree of strictness unspecified. Anna G. Kirushina, technical worker, fine of twenty percent of salary for one year. Anna objected to the strangulation, but softly: she helped stuff the carcass into a bag.

The clipping is tacked up on my wall. I inspect it from time to time, drawing the moral. Strangling swans is wrong.

My brother who is a very distinguished pianist . . . has no fingernails at all. Don't look it's horrible. He plays under another name. And tunes his piano peculiarly, some call it sour. And renders *ragas* he wrote himself. A night *raga* played at noon can cause darkness, did you know that? It's extraordinary.

He wanted to be an Untouchable, Paul did. That was his idea of a contemporary career. But then a girl walked up and touched him (slapped him, actually; it's a complicated story). And he joined us, here in the imbroglio.

My father on the other hand is perfectly comfortable, and that's not a criticism. He makes flags, banners, bunting (sometimes runs me up a shirt). There was never any question of letting my father drink from the public well. He was on the Well Committee, he decided who dipped and who didn't. That's not a criticism. Exercises his creativity, nowadays, courtesy the emerging nations. Green for the veldt that nourishes the gracile Grant's gazelle, white for the purity of our revolutionary aspirations. The red for blood is understood. That's not a criticism. It's what they all ask for.

A call tonight from Gregory, my son by my first wife. Seventeen and at MIT already. Recently he's been asking questions. Suddenly he's conscious of himself as a being with a history.

The telephone rings. Then, without a greeting: *Why did I have to take those little pills?* What little pills? *Little white pills with a "W" on them.* Oh. Oh yes. You had some kind of a nervous disorder, for a while. *How old was I?* Eight. Eight or nine. *What was it? Was it epilepsy?* Good God no, nothing so fancy. We never found out what it was. It went away. *What did I do?*

Did I fall down? No no. Your mouth trembled, that was all. You couldn't control it. *Oh, OK. See you.*

The receiver clicks.

Or: *What did my great-grandfather do? For a living I mean?* He was a ballplayer, semi-pro ballplayer, for a while. Then went into the building business. *Who'd he play for?* A team called the St. Augustine Rowdies, I think it was. *Never heard of them.* Well . . . *Did he make any money? In the building business?* Quite a bit. *Did your father inherit it?* No, it was tied up in a lawsuit. When the suit was over there wasn't anything left. *Oh. What was the lawsuit?* Great-grandfather diddled a man in a land deal. So the story goes. *Oh. When did he die?* Let's see, 1938 I think. *What of?* Heart attack. *Oh. OK. See you.*

End of conversation.

Gregory, you didn't listen to my advice. I said try the Vernacular Isles. Where fish are two for a penny and women two for a fish. But you wanted MIT and electron-spin-resonance spectroscopy. You didn't even crack a smile in your six-ply heather hopsacking.

Gregory you're going to have a half brother now. You'll like that, won't you? Will you half like it?

We talked about the size of the baby, Ann and I. What could be deduced from the outside.

I said it doesn't look very big to me. She said it's big enough for *us.* I said we don't need such a great roaring big one after all. She said they cost the earth, those extra-large sizes. Our holdings in Johnson's Baby Powder to be considered too. We'd need acres and acres. I said we'll put it in a Skinner box maybe. She said no child of hers. Displayed under glass like a rump roast. I said you haven't wept lately. She said I keep getting bigger whether I laugh or cry.

Dear Ann. I don't think you've quite . . .

What you don't understand is, it's like somebody walks up to you and says, I have a battleship I can't use, would you like to have a battleship? And you say, yes yes, I've never had a battleship, I've always wanted one. And he says, it has four sixteen-inch guns forward, and a catapult for launching scout planes. And you say, I've always wanted to launch scout planes. And he says, *it's yours,* and then you have this battleship. And then you have to paint it, because it's rusting, and clean it, because it's dirty, and anchor it somewhere, because the Police Department wants you to get it off the streets. And the crew is crying, and there are silverfish in the chartroom and a funny knocking noise in Fire Control, water rising in the No. 2 hold, and the chaplain can't find the Palestrina tapes for the Sunday service. And you can't get anybody to sit with it. And finally you discover that what you have here is this great, big, pink-and-blue rockabye *battleship.*

Ann. I'm going to keep her ghostly. Just the odd bit of dialogue.

"What is little Gog doing."

"Kicking."

I don't want her bursting in on us with the freshness and originality of her observations. What we need here is *perspective.* She's good with Gregory though. I think he half likes her.

Don't go. The greased-pig chase and balloon launchings come next.

I was promising once. After the Elgar, a *summa cum laude*. The university was proud of me. It was a bright shy white new university on the Gulf Coast. Gulls and oleanders and quick howling hurricanes. The teachers brown burly men with power boats and beer cans. The president a retired admiral who'd done beautiful things in the Coral Sea.

"You will be a credit to us, George," the admiral said. That's not my name.

Applause from the stands filled with mothers and brothers. Then following the mace in a long line back to the field house to ungown. Ready to take my place at the top.

But a pause at Pusan, and the toy train to the Chorwon Valley. Walking down a road wearing green clothes. Korea green and black and silent. The truce had been signed. I had a carbine to carry. My buddy Bo Tagliabue the bonus baby, for whom the Yanks had paid thirty thousand. We whitewashed rocks to enhance our area. Colonels came crowding to feel Bo's hurling arm. Mine the whitest rocks.

I lunched with Thais from Thailand, hot curry from great galvanized washtubs. Engineers banging down the road in six-by-sixes raising red dust. My friend Gib Mandell calling Elko, Nevada, on his canvas-covered field telephone. "Operator I crave Elko, Nevada."

Then I was a sergeant with stripes, getting the troops out of the sun. Tagliabue a sergeant too. *Triste* in the Tennessee Tea Room in Tokyo, yakking it up in Yokohama. Then back to our little tent town on the side of a hill, boosting fifty-gallon drums of heating oil tentward in the snow.

Ozzie the jeep driver waking me in the middle of the night. "They got Julian in the Tango Tank." And up and alert as they taught us in Leadership School, over the hills to Tango, seventy miles away. Whizzing through Teapot, Tempest, Toreador, with the jeep's canvas top flapping. Pfc. Julian drunk and disorderly and beaten up. The MP sergeant held out a receipt book. I signed for the bawdy remains.

Back over the pearly Pacific in a great vessel decorated with oranges. A trail of orange peel on the plangent surface. Sitting in the bow fifty miles out of San Francisco, listening to the Stateside disc jockeys chattering cha cha cha. Ready to grab my spot at the top.

My clothes looked old and wrong. The city looked new with tall buildings raised while my back was turned. I rushed here and there visiting friends. They were burning beef in their backyards, brown burly men with beer cans. The beef black on the outside, red on the inside. My friend Horace had fidelity. "Listen to that bass. That's sixty watts' worth of bass, boy."

I spoke to my father. "How is business?" "If Alaska makes it," he said, "I can buy a Hasselblad. And we're keeping an eye on Hawaii." Then he photographed my veteran face, f.6 at 300. My father once a cheerleader at a great Eastern school. Jumping in the air and making fierce angry down-the-field gestures at the top of his leap.

That's not a criticism. We have to have cheerleaders.

I presented myself at the Placement Office. I was on file. My percentile was the percentile of choice.

"How come you were headman of only one student organization, George?" the Placement Officer asked. Many hats for top folk was the fashion then.

I said I was rounded, and showed him my slash. From the Fencing Club.

"But you served your country in an overseas post."

"And regard my career plan on neatly typed pages with wide margins."

"Exemplary," the Placement Officer said. "You seem married, mature, malleable, how would you like to affiliate yourself with us here at the old school? We have a spot for a poppycock man, to write the admiral's speeches. Have you ever done poppycock?"

I said no but maybe I could fake it.

"Excellent, excellent," the Placement Officer said. "I see you have grasp. And you can sup at the Faculty Club. And there is a ten-percent discount on tickets for all home games."

The admiral shook my hand. "You will be a credit to us, George," he said. I wrote poppycock, sometimes cockypap. At four o'clock the faculty hoisted the cocktail flag. We drank daiquiris on each other's sterns. I had equipped myself—a fiberglass runabout, someplace to think. In the stadia of friendly shy new universities we went down the field on Gulf Coast afternoons with gulls, or exciting nights under the tall toothpick lights. The crowd roared. Sylvia roared. Gregory grew.

There was no particular point at which I stopped being promising.

Moonstruck I was, after a fashion. Sitting on a bench by the practice field, where the jocks chanted secret signals in their underwear behind tall canvas blinds. Layabout babies loafing on blankets, some staked out on twelve-foot dog chains. Brown mothers squatting knee to knee in shifts of scarlet and green. I stared at the moon's pale daytime presence. It seemed . . . inimical.

Moonstruck.

We're playing Flinch. You flinched.

The simplest things are the most difficult to explain, all authorities agree. Say I was tired of p***yc**k, if that pleases you. It's true enough.

Sylvia went up in a puff of smoke. She didn't like unsalaried life. And couldn't bear a male acquaintance moon-staring in the light of day. Decent people look at night.

We had trouble with Gregory: who would get which part. She settled for three-fifths, and got I think the worst of it, the dreaming raffish Romany part that thinks science will save us. I get matter-of-fact midnight telephone calls: *My EE instructor shot me down.* What happened? *I don't know, he's an ass anyhow.* Well that may be but still— *When's the baby due?* January, I told you. *Yeah, can I go to Mexico City for the holidays?* Ask your mother, you know she— *There's this guy, his old man has a villa. . . .* Well, we can talk about it. *Yeah, was grandmother a Communist?* Nothing so distinguished, she— *You said she was kicked out of Germany.* Her family was anti-Nazi. *Adler means eagle in German.* That's true. There was something called the Weimar Republic, her father— *I read about it.*

We had trouble with Gregory, we wanted to be scientific. Toys from Procreative Playthings of Princeton. O Gregory, that Princeton crowd got you coming and going. Procreative Playthings at one end and the Educational Testing Service at the other. And that serious-minded co-op nursery, that was a mistake. "A growing understanding between parent and child through shared group experience." I still remember poor Henry Harding III. Under "Sibs" on the membership roll they listed his, by age:

26
25
23
20
19
15
10
9
8
6

O Mrs. Harding, haven't you heard? They have these little Christmas-tree ornaments for the womb now, they work wonders.

Did we do "badly" by Gregory? Will we do "better" with Gog? Such questions curl the hair. It's wiser not to ask.

I mentioned Cardinal Y. (the red hat). He's a friend, in a way. Or rather, the subject of one of my little projects.

I set out to study cardinals, about whom science knows nothing. It seemed to me that cardinals could be known in the same way we know fishes or roses, by classification and enumeration. A perverse project, perhaps, but who else has embraced this point of view? Difficult nowadays to find a point of view kinky enough to call one's own, with Sade himself being carried through the streets on the shoulders of sociologists, cheers and shouting, ticker tape unwinding from high windows . . .

The why of Cardinal Y. You're entitled to an explanation.

The Cardinal rushed from the Residence waving in the air his hands, gloved in yellow pigskin it appeared, I grasped a hand, "Yes, yellow pigskin!" the Cardinal cried. I wrote in my book, *yellow pigskin.*

Significant detail. The pectoral cross contains nine diamonds, the scarlet soutane is laundered right on the premises.

I asked the Cardinal questions, we had a conversation.

"I am thinking of a happy island more beautiful than can be imagined," I said.

"I am thinking of a golden mountain which does not exist," he said.

"Upon what does the world rest?" I asked.

"Upon an elephant," he said.

"Upon what does the elephant rest?"

"Upon a tortoise."

"Upon what does the tortoise rest?"

"Upon a red lawnmower."

I wrote in my book, *playful.*

"Is there any value that has value?" I asked.

"If there is any value that has value, then it must lie outside the whole sphere of what happens and is the case, for all that happens and is the case is accidental," he said. He was not serious. I wrote in my book, *knows the drill.*

(Oh I had heard reports, how he slunk about in the snow telling children he was Santa Claus, how he disbursed funds in unauthorized disbursements to unshaven men who came to the kitchen door, how his housekeeper pointedly rolled his red socks together and black socks together hinting red with red and black with black, the Cardinal patiently unrolling a red ball to get a red sock and a black ball to get a black sock, which he then wore together. . . .)

Cardinal Y. He's sly.

I was thorough. I popped the Cardinal on the patella with a little hammer, and looked into his eyes with a little light. I tested the Cardinal's stomach acidity using Universal Indicator Paper, a scale of one to ten, a spectrum of red to blue. The pH value was 1 indicating high acidity. I measured the Cardinal's ego strength using the Minnesota Multiphastic Muzzle Map, he had an MMMM of four over three. I sang to the Cardinal, the song was "Stella by Starlight," he did not react in any way. I calculated the number of gallons needed to fill the Cardinal's bath to a depth of ten inches (beyond which depth, the Cardinal said, he never ventured). I took the Cardinal to the ballet, the ballet was *The Conservatory*. The Cardinal applauded at fifty-seven points. Afterward, backstage, the Cardinal danced with Plenosova, holding her at arm's length with a good will and an ill grace. The skirts of the scarlet soutane stood out to reveal high-button shoes, and the stagehands clapped.

I asked the Cardinal his views on the moon, he said they were the conventional ones, and that is how I know all I know about cardinals. Not enough perhaps to rear a science of cardinalogy upon, but enough perhaps to form a basis for the investigations of other investigators. My report is over there, in the blue binding, next to my copy of *La Géomancie et la Néomancie des Anciens* by the Seigneur of Salerno.

Cardinal Y. One can measure and measure and miss the most essential thing. I liked him. I still get the odd blessing in the mail now and then.

Too, maybe I was trying on the role. Not for myself. When a child is born, the locus of one's hopes . . . shifts, slightly. Not altogether, not all at once. But you feel it, this displacement. You speak up, strike attitudes, like the mother of a tiny Lollobrigida. Drunk with possibility once more.

I am still wearing my yellow flower which has lasted wonderfully.

"What is Gog doing?"

"Sleeping."

You see, Gog of mine, Gog o' my heart, I'm just trying to give you a little briefing here. I don't want you unpleasantly surprised. I can't stand a startled look. Regard me as a sort of Distant Early Warning System. Here is the world and here are the knowledgeable knowers knowing. What can I tell you? What has been pieced together from the reports of travelers.

Fragments are the only forms I trust.

Look at my wall, it's all there. That's a leaf, Gog, stuck up with Scotch Tape. No no, the Scotch Tape is the shiny transparent stuff, the leaf the veined irregularly shaped . . .

There are several sides to this ax, Gog, consider the photostat, "Mr. W. B. Yeats Presenting Mr. George Moore to the Queen of the Fairies." That's a civilized gesture, I mean Beerbohm's. And when the sculptor Aristide Maillol went into the printing business he made the paper by *chewing the fibers himself.* That's dedication. And here is a Polaroid photo, shows your Aunt Sylvia and me putting an Ant Farm together. That's how close we were in those days. Just an Ant Farm apart.

See the moon? It hates us.

And now comes J. J. Sullivan's orange-and-blue Gulf Oil truck to throw kerosene into the space heater. Driver in green siren suit, red face, blond shaved head, the following rich verbal transaction:

"Beautiful day."

"Certainly is."

And now settling back in this green glider with a copy of *Man.* Dear Ann when I look at *Man* I don't want you. Unfolded Ursala Herring seems eversomuchmore desirable. A clean girl too and with interests, cooking, botany, pornographic novels. Someone new to show my slash to.

In another month Gog leaps fully armed from the womb. What can I do for him? I can get him into AA, I have influence. And make sure no harsh moonlight falls on his new soft head.

Hello there Gog. We hope you'll be very happy here.

1964

Sentence

Or a long sentence moving at a certain pace down the page aiming for the bottom—if not the bottom of this page then of some other page—where it can rest, or stop for a moment to think about the questions raised by its own (temporary) existence, which ends when the page is turned, or the sentence falls out of the mind that holds it (temporarily) in some kind of an embrace, not necessarily an ardent one, but more perhaps the kind of embrace enjoyed (or endured) by a wife who has just waked up and is on her way to the bathroom in the morning to wash her hair, and is bumped into by her husband, who has been lounging at the breakfast table reading the newspaper, and didn't see her coming out of the bedroom, but, when he bumps into her, or is bumped into by her, raises his hands to embrace her lightly, transiently, because he knows that if he gives her a real embrace so early in the morning, before she has properly shaken the dreams out of her head and got her duds on, she won't respond, and may even become slightly angry, and say something wounding, and so the husband invests in this embrace not so much physical or emotional pressure as he might, because he doesn't want to waste anything—with this sort of feeling, then, the sentence passes through the mind more or less, and there is another way of describing the situation too, which is to say that the sentence crawls through the mind like something someone says to you while you're listening very hard to the FM radio, some rock group there, with its thrilling sound, and so, with your attention or the major part of it at least already awarded, there is not much mind room you can give to the remark, especially considering that you have probably just quarreled with that person, the maker of the remark, over the radio being too loud, or something like that, and the view you take, of the remark, is that you'd really rather not hear it, but if you have to hear it, you want to listen to it for the smallest possible length of time, and during a commercial, because immediately after the commercial they're going to play a new rock song by your favorite group, a cut that has never been aired before, and you want to hear it and respond to it in a new way, a way that accords with whatever you're feeling at the moment, or might feel, if the threat of new experience could be (temporarily) overbalanced by the promise of possible positive benefits, or what the mind construes as such, remembering that these are often, really, disguised defeats (not that such defeats are not, at times, good for your character, teaching you that it is not by success alone that one surmounts life, but that setbacks, too, contribute to that roughening of the personality that, by providing a textured surface to place against that of life, enables you to leave slight traces, or smudges, on the face of human history—your mark) and after all, benefit-seeking always has something of the smell of raw vanity about it, as if you wished to decorate your own brow with laurel, or wear your medals to a cookout, when the invitation had said nothing about them, and although the ego is always hungry (we are told) it is well to remember that ongoing success is nearly as meaningless as ongoing lack of success, which can make you sick, and that it is good to leave a few crumbs on the table for the rest of your brethren, not to sweep it all into the little beaded purse of your soul but to allow others, too, part of the gratification, and if you share in this way you will find the clouds smiling on you, and the postman bringing you letters, and bicycles available when you want to rent them, and many other signs, however guarded and limited, of the community's (temporary) approval of you, or at least of its willingness to let you believe (temporarily) that it finds you not so lacking in commendable virtues as it had previously allowed you to think, from its scorn of your merits, as it might be put, or anyway its consistent refusal to recognize your basic humanness and its secret blackball of the project of your remaining alive, made in executive session by its ruling bodies, which, as everyone knows, carry out concealed programs of reward and punishment, under the rose, causing faint alterations of the status quo, behind your back, at various points along the periphery of community life, together with other enterprises not dissimilar in tone, such as producing films that have special qualities, or attributes, such as a film where the second half of it is a holy mystery, and girls and women are not permitted to see it, or writing novels in which the final chapter is a plastic bag filled with water, which you can touch, but not drink: in this way, or ways, the underground mental life of the collectivity is botched, or denied, or turned into something else never imagined by the planners, who, returning from the latest seminar in crisis management and being asked what they have learned, say they have learned how to throw up their hands; the sentence meanwhile, although not insensible of these considerations, has a festering conscience of its own, which persuades it to follow its star, and to move with all deliberate speed from one place to another, without losing any of the "riders" it may have picked up just by being there, on the page, and turning this way and that, to see what is over there, under that oddly shaped tree, or over there, reflected in the rain barrel of the imagination, even though it is true that in our young manhood we were taught that short, punchy sentences were best (but what did he mean? doesn't "punchy" mean punch-drunk? I think he probably intended to say "short, *punching* sentences," meaning sentences that lashed out at you, bloodying your brain if possible, and looking up the word just now I came across the nearby "punkah," which is a large fan suspended from the ceiling in India, operated by an attendant pulling a rope—that is what I want for my sentence, to keep it cool!) we are mature enough now to stand the shock of learning that much of what we were taught in our youth was wrong, or improperly understood by those who were teaching it, or perhaps shaded a bit, the shading resulting from the personal needs of the teachers, who as human beings had a tendency to introduce some of their heart's blood into their work, and sometimes this may not have been of the first water, this heart's blood, and even if they thought they were moving the "knowledge" out, as the Board of Education had mandated, they could have noticed that their sentences weren't having the knockdown power of the new weapons whose bullets tumble end over end (but it is true that we didn't have these weapons at that time) and they might have taken into account the fundamental dubiousness of their project (but all the intelligently conceived projects have been eaten up already, like the moon and the stars), leaving us, in our best clothes, with only things to do like conducting vigorous wars of attrition against our wives, who have now thoroughly come awake, and slipped into their striped bells, and pulled sweaters over their torsi, and adamantly refused to wear any bras under the sweaters, carefully explaining the political significance of this refusal to anyone who will listen, or look, but not touch, because that has nothing to do with it, so they say; leaving us with only things to do like floating sheets of Reynolds Wrap around the room, trying to find out how many we can keep in the air at the same time, which at least gives us a sense of participation, as though we were the Buddha, looking down at the mystery of your smile, which needs to be investigated, and I think I'll do that right now, while there's still enough light, if you'll sit down over there, in the best chair, and take off all your clothes, and put your feet in that electric toe caddy (which prevents pneumonia) and slip into this permanent-press white hospital gown, to cover your nakedness—why, if you do all that, we'll be ready to begin! after I wash my hands, because you pick up an amazing amount of exuviae in this city, just by walking around in the open air, and nodding to acquaintances, and speaking to friends, in the ordinary course (and death to our enemies! by the by)—but I'm getting a little uptight, just about washing my hands, because I can't find the soap, which somebody has used and not put back in the soap dish, all of which is extremely irritating, if you have a beautiful patient sitting in the examining room, naked inside her gown, and peering at her moles in the mirror, with her immense brown eyes following your every movement (when they are not watching the moles, expecting them, as in a Disney nature film, to exfoliate) and her immense brown head wondering what you're going to do to her, the pierced places in the head letting that question leak out, while the therapist decides just to wash his hands in plain water, and hang the soap! and does so, and then looks around for a towel, but all the towels have been collected by the towel service, and are not there, so he wipes his hands on his pants, in the back (so as to avoid suspicious stains on the front) thinking: what must she think of me? and, all this is very unprofessional and at-sea looking! trying to visualize the contretemps from her point of view, if she has one (but how can she? she is not in the washroom) and then stopping, because it is finally his own point of view that he cares about and not hers, and with this firmly in mind, and a light, confident step, such as you might find in the works of Bulwer-Lytton, he enters the space she occupies so prettily and, taking her by the hand, proceeds to tear off the stiff white hospital gown (but no, we cannot have that kind of pornographic *merde* in this majestic and high-minded sentence, which will probably end up in the Library of Congress) (that was just something that took place inside his consciousness, as he looked at her, and since we know that consciousness is always consciousness *of* something, she is not entirely without responsibility in the matter) so, then, taking her by the hand, he falls into the stupendous white purée of her abyss, no, I mean rather that he asks her how long it has been since her last visit, and she says a fortnight, and he shudders, and tells her that with a condition like hers (she is an immensely popular soldier, and her troops win all their battles by pretending to be forests, the enemy discovering, at the last moment, that those trees they have eaten their lunch under have eyes and swords) (which reminds me of the performance, in 1845, of Robert-Houdin, called *The Fantastic Orange Tree,* wherein Robert-Houdin borrowed a lady's handkerchief, rubbed it between his hands and passed it into the center of an egg, after which he passed the egg into the center of a lemon, after which he passed the lemon into the center of an orange, then pressed the orange between his hands, making it smaller and smaller, until only a powder remained, whereupon he asked for a small potted orange tree and sprinkled the powder thereupon, upon which the tree burst into blossom, the blossoms turning into oranges, the oranges turning into butterflies, and the butterflies turning into beautiful young ladies, who then married members of the audience), a condition so damaging to real-time social intercourse of any kind, the best thing she can do is give up, and lay down her arms, and he will lie down in them, and together they will permit themselves a bit of the old slap and tickle, she wearing only her Mr. Christopher medal, on its silver chain, and he (for such is the latitude granted the professional classes) worrying about the sentence, about its thin wires of dramatic tension, which have been omitted, about whether we should write down some natural events occurring in the sky (birds, lightning bolts), and about a possible coup d'état within the sentence, whereby its chief verb would be—but at this moment a messenger rushes into the sentence, bleeding from a hat of thorns he's wearing, and cries out: "You don't know what you're doing! Stop making this sentence, and begin to make Moholy-Nagy cocktails, for those are what we really need, on the frontiers of bad behavior!" and then he falls to the floor, and a trapdoor opens under him, and he falls through that, into a damp pit where a blue narwhal waits, its horn poised (but maybe the weight of the messenger, falling from such a height, will break off the horn)—thus, considering everything carefully, in the sweet light of the ceremonial axes, in the run-mad skimble-skamble of information sickness, we must make a decision as to whether we should proceed, or go back, in the latter case enjoying the pathos of eradication, in the former case reading an erotic advertisement which begins, *How to Make Your Mouth a Blowtorch of Excitement* (but wouldn't that overtax our mouthwashes?), attempting, during the pause, while our burned mouths are being smeared with fat, to imagine a better sentence, worthier, more meaningful, like those in the Declaration of Independence, or a bank statement showing that you have seven thousand kroner more than you thought you had—a statement summing up the unreasonable demands that you make on life, and one that also asks the question, if you can imagine these demands, why are they not routinely met, tall fool? but of course it is not that query that this infected sentence has set out to answer (and hello! to our girlfriend, Rosetta Stone, who has stuck by us through thin and thin) but some other query that we shall some day discover the nature of, and here comes Ludwig, the expert on sentence construction we have borrowed from the Bauhaus, who will—"Guten Tag, Ludwig!"—probably find a way to cure the sentence's sprawl, by using the improved ways of thinking developed in Weimar—"I am sorry to inform you that the Bauhaus no longer exists, that all of the great masters who formerly thought there are either dead or retired, and that I myself have been reduced to constructing books on how to pass the examination for police sergeant"—and Ludwig falls through the Tugendhat House into the history of man-made objects; a disappointment, to be sure, but it reminds us that the sentence itself is a man-made object, not the one we wanted of course, but still a construction of man, a structure to be treasured for its weakness, as opposed to the strength of stones

1970

RICHARD BRAUTIGAN
1935–1984

Richard Brautigan was born in Washington state and lived for many years in San Francisco, California. His nine novels include *A Confederate General from Big Sur* (1964), *Trout Fishing in America* (1967), *Sombrero Fallout: A Japanese Novel* (1976), and *The Tokyo-Montana Press* (1980), and he published eleven volumes of poetry. Toward the end of his life, he divided his time between a ranch in Montana and Tokyo. His death was by suicide.

Robert Novak has observed in the *Dictionary of Literary Biography* (1985) that "Brautigan is commonly seen as the bridge between the Beat Movement of the 1950s and the youth revolution of the 1960s." Of his work as a whole, Guy Davenport writes in *The Hudson Review* (1974–75): "Mr. Brautigan locates his writing on the barricade which the sane mind maintains against spiel and bilge, and here he cavorts with a divine idiocy, thumbing his nose. But he makes clear that at his immediate disposal is a fund of common sense he does not hesitate to bring into play. He is a kind of Thoreau who cannot keep a straight face." Novelist Tom McGuane adds in *The New York Times Book Review* (1980): "What is important is that Brautigan's outlandish gift is based in traditional narrative virtues. His dialogue is supernaturally exact; his descriptive concision is the perfect carrier for his extraordinary comic perceptions. Moreover, the books possess a springtime moral emptiness; essentially works of language, they offer no bromides for living."

"I'm not interested in imitating a style or structure I've used before," Brautigan said in *Life* magazine (1970). "I'll never write another book like *Trout Fishing in America.* I dismantled that old machine when I finished with it and left the pieces lying around in the backyard to rust in the rain."

From Trout Fishing in America

The Cover for Trout Fishing in America

The cover for Trout Fishing in America is a photograph taken late in the afternoon, a photograph of the Benjamin Franklin statue in San Francisco's Washington Square.

Born 1706—Died 1790, Benjamin Franklin stands on a pedestal that looks like a house containing stone furniture. He holds some papers in one hand and his hat in the other.

Then the statue speaks, saying in marble:

PRESENTED BY

H. D. COGSWELL

TO OUR

BOYS AND GIRLS

WHO WILL SOON

TAKE OUR PLACES

AND PASS ON.

Around the base of the statue are four words facing the directions of this world, to the east WELCOME, to the west WELCOME, to the north WELCOME, to the south WELCOME. Just behind the statue are three poplar trees, almost leafless except for the top branches. The statue stands in front of the middle tree. All around the grass is wet from the rains of early February.

In the background is a tall cypress tree, almost dark like a room. Adlai Stevenson spoke under the tree in 1956, before a crowd of 40,000 people.

There is a tall church across the street from the statue with crosses, steeples, bells and a vast door that looks like a huge mousehole, perhaps from a Tom and Jerry cartoon, and written above the door is "Per L'Universo."

Around five o'clock in the afternoon of my cover for Trout Fishing in America, people gather in the park across the street from the church and they are hungry.

It's sandwich time for the poor.

But they cannot cross the street until the signal is given. Then they all run across the street to the church and get their sandwiches that are wrapped in newspaper. They go back to the park and unwrap the newspaper and see what their sandwiches are all about.

A friend of mine unwrapped his sandwich one afternoon and looked inside to find just a leaf of spinach. That was all.

Was it Kafka who learned about America by reading the autobiography of Benjamin Franklin . . .

Kafka who said, "I like the Americans because they are healthy and optimistic."

* * *

Trout Death by Port Wine

It was not an outhouse resting upon the imagination.

It was reality.

An eleven-inch rainbow trout was killed. Its life taken forever from the waters of the earth, by giving it a drink of port wine.

It is against the natural order of death for a trout to die by having a drink of port wine.

It is all right for a trout to have its neck broken by a fisherman and then to be tossed into the creel or for a trout to die from a fungus that crawls like sugar-colored ants over its body until the trout is in death's sugarbowl.

It is all right for a trout to be trapped in a pool that dries up in the late summer or to be caught in the talons of a bird or the claws of an animal.

Yes, it is even all right for a trout to be killed by pollution, to die in a river of suffocating human excrement.

There are trout that die of old age and their white beards flow to the sea.

All these things are in the natural order of death, but for a trout to die from a drink of port wine, that is another thing.

No mention of it in "The treatyse of fysshynge wyth an angle," in the Boke of St. Albans, published 1496. No mention of it in Minor Tactics of the Chalk Stream, by H. C. Cutcliffe, published in 1910. No mention of it in Truth Is Stranger than Fishin', by Beatrice Cook, published in 1955. No mention of it in Northern Memoirs, by Richard Franck, published in 1694. No mention of it in I Go A-Fishing, by W. C. Prime, published in 1873. No mention of it in Trout Fishing and Trout Flies, by Jim Quick, published in 1957. No mention of it in Certaine Experiments Concerning Fish and Fruite, by John Taverner, published in 1600. No mention of it in A River Never Sleeps, by Roderick L. Haig Brown, published in 1946. No mention of it in Till Fish Us Do Part, by Beatrice Cook, published in 1949. No mention of it in The Flyfisher & the Trout's Point of View, by Col. E. W. Harding, published in 1931. No mention of it in Chalk Stream Studies, by Charles Kingsley, published in 1859. No mention of it in Trout Madness, by Robert Traver, published in 1960.

No mention of it in Sunshine and the Dry Fly, by J. W. Dunne, published in 1924. No mention of it in Just Fishing, by Ray Bergman, published in 1932. No mention of it in Matching the Hatch, by Ernest G. Schwiebert, Jr., published in 1955. No mention of it in The Art of Trout Fishing on Rapid Streams, by H. C. Cutcliffe, published in 1863. No mention of it in Old Flies in New Dresses, by C. E. Walker, published in 1898. No mention of it in Fisherman's Spring, by Roderick L. Haig-Brown, published in 1951. No mention of it in The Determined Angler and the Brook Trout, by Charles Bradford, published in 1916. No mention of it in Women Can Fish, by Chisie Farrington, published in 1951. No mention of it in Tales of the Angler's El Dorado New Zealand, by Zane Grey, published in 1926. No mention of it in The Flyfisher's Guide, by G. C. Bainbridge, published in 1816.

There's no mention of a trout dying by having a drink of port wine anywhere.

To describe the Supreme Executioner: We woke up in the morning and it was dark outside. He came kind of smiling into the kitchen and we ate breakfast.

Fried potatoes and eggs and coffee.

"Well, you old bastard," he said. "Pass the salt."

The tackle was already in the car, so we just got in and drove away. Beginning at the first light of dawn, we hit the road at the bottom of the mountains, and drove up into the dawn.

The light behind the trees was like going into a gradual and strange department store.

"That was a good-looking girl last night," he said.

"Yeah," I said. "You did all right."

"If the shoe fits . . ." he said.

Owl Snuff Creek was just a small creek, only a few miles long, but there were some nice trout in it. We got out of the car and walked a quarter of a mile down the mountainside to the creek. I put my tackle together. He pulled a pint of port wine out of his jacket pocket and said, "Wouldn't you know."

"No thanks," I said.

He took a good snort and then shook his head, side to side, and said, "Do you know what this creek reminds me of?"

"No," I said, tying a gray and yellow fly onto my leader.

"It reminds me of Evangeline's vagina, a constant dream of my childhood and promoter of my youth."

"That's nice," I said.

"Longfellow was the Henry Miller of my childhood," he said.

"Good," I said.

I cast into a little pool that had a swirl of fir needles going around the edge of it. The fir needles went around and around. It made no sense that they should come from trees. They looked perfectly contented and natural in the pool as if the pool had grown them on watery branches.

I had a good hit on my third cast, but missed it.

"Oh, boy," he said. "I think I'll watch you fish. The stolen painting is in the house next door."

I fished upstream coming ever closer and closer to the narrow staircase of the canyon. Then I went up into it as if I were entering a department store. I caught three trout in the lost and found department. He didn't even put his tackle together. He just followed after me, drinking port wine and poking a stick at the world.

"This is a beautiful creek," he said. "It reminds me of Evangeline's hearing aid."

We ended up at a large pool that was formed by the creek crashing through the children's toy section. At the beginning of the pool the water was like cream, then it mirrored out and reflected the shadow of a large tree. By this time the sun was up. You could see it coming down the mountain.

I cast into the cream and let my fly drift down onto a long branch of the tree, next to a bird.

Go-wham!

I set the hook and the trout started jumping.

"Giraffe races at Kilimanjaro!" he shouted, and every time the trout jumped, he jumped.

"Bee races at Mount Everest!" he shouted.

I didn't have a net with me so I fought the trout over to the edge of the creek and swung it up onto the shore.

The trout had a big red stripe down its side.

It was a good rainbow.

"What a beauty," he said.

He picked it up and it was squirming in his hands.

"Break its neck," I said.

"I have a better idea," he said. "Before I kill it, let me at least soothe its approach into death. This trout needs a drink." He took the bottle of port out of his pocket, unscrewed the cap and poured a good slug into the trout's mouth.

The trout went into a spasm.

Its body shook very rapidly like a telescope during an earthquake. The mouth was wide open and chattering almost as if it had human teeth.

He laid the trout on a white rock, head down, and some of the wine trickled out of its mouth and made a stain on the rock.

The trout was lying very still now.

"It died happy," he said.

"This is my ode to Alcoholics Anonymous."

"Look here!"

1967

NTOZAKE SHANGE
b. 1948

The daughter of a surgeon and a social worker, Ntozake Shange was born in Trenton, New Jersey, and was educated at Barnard College and the University of Southern California. A writer of prose, drama, and poetry, she has published more than thirty books, including the Obie Award–winning "choreopoem" *For Colored Girls Who Have Considered Suicide/When the Rainbow Is Enuf* (1975) and the novels *Sassafrass, Cypress & Indigo* (1982), *Betsey Brown* (1985), and *Liliane* (1994).

Deciding that her career ambitions as a war correspondent and jazz musician were "no good for a woman," Shange chose writing, she told *Publishers Weekly* (1985), because "there was nothing left." But her work has focused on "the fury of black women at their double subjugation in white male America," as Mel Gussow has written in *The New York Times* (1976). "I am a war correspondent after all," Shange noted in *Publishers Weekly*, "because I'm involved in a war of cultural and esthetic aggression. The front lines aren't always what you think they are."

"Indigo" is excerpted from *Sassafrass, Cypress & Indigo*, a novel that combines conventional narrative, poetry, epistolary passages, magic incantations, and recipes. In the *Chicago Tribune* (1982), Shange explained that the subject matter of the novel is not autobiographical, but is gathered from the historical experiences of blacks in America and the "information of my feelings."

From Sassafrass, Cypress & Indigo

Indigo

Indigo did not tell her mother about Mr. Lucas being so evil, nor did she mention that her new fiddle could talk. These notions would bring her mother's ire up & out. Nowadays Indigo minded what she said & to whom. Some folks you tell some things, some folks you don't. With the dolls all lined up in her room now, no longer going calling, coming down for dinner, Indigo kept her window open all the time. She told her mother this was just for health reasons. Why New England people sleep with the windows open in snow: gives the body & spirit strength. Now, her mother didn't want her own windows open, but it seemed like Indigo was making more reasonable connections. The windows in the child's room stayed open.

Indigo invited the Moon in to sing to her doll-companions, mute though they were. She thought they had trouble sleeping. When the night air danced about them, leaving the shivers of that embrace, Indigo would take out her violin & play the way she learned. Letting the instrument speak right up. Giving another space to all the feelings her little girl's body could not always contain. The talking music aroused the dolls to celebrate. Indigo sat in her window, working with her fiddle, telling everybody, the wind & all his brothers, what was on her mind, the turmoil in the spirit realm, the luxuriant realities she meandered in her sleep. Whenever she wanted to pray, she let her fiddle talk. Whenever she was angry, here came the fiddle. All the different ways of handling a violin & bow came to Indigo as she needed. They came: *legato, staccato, andante, forte, fortissimo, piano, allegro, presto.*

"Indigo, we're going to have to talk about this violin." Indigo was startled by her mother's nocturnal visit. The breeze felt good on her face. Indigo turned gently from the soft rumble of a sea-town night to her mother.

"Oh, I'm so glad, Mama. I wanted to talk to you about the fiddle some more, but I was afraid you . . ."

"Why Indigo, how could you think I wouldn't find somebody to give you lessons. I gave Sassafrass every weaving lesson she asked for, sent Cypress to New York for her dancing. Why wouldn't I give you violin lessons? Surely, there's one brave soul in Charleston who'll take this terrible-playing child of mine."

Indigo looked at her mother for a long while. Her mother feeling very proud of her daughter who'd tried to teach herself how to play the fiddle, who'd given up talking out of her head, talking only to her dolls. She glanced at her child's handiwork, Marie-Hélène, Miranda, Susie-Q, Candace, Lilli, fingering their hats and petticoats delicately. Now Indigo was involved with music which she would be as diligent & loving about as she had about her dolls, her companions, as she called them. The mother looked over to Indigo still sitting in the window. Not a word did she say, there in the window with her violin in an acceptable rest position.

"Now Indigo, what do you say to real violin lessons & closing that window so our neighbors can be spared this racket till you've learned a bit more?" Approaching her daughter with some glee, the mother stopped when Indigo turned her back, stood up, & began making those strange, erratic, annoying non-songs she played each night, that Miz Fitzhugh had complained about twice, along with the Daltons. Even Mr. Epps who lived three doors down & across the street had stopped by on his way to the post office to say, "Please do something about those noises from your house, or I'll have to call the constable round this way."

No, Indigo would not have her way this time. She wasn't going to be run out of her own home cause Indigo was playing a violin. She had to have some lessons 'cause these folks didn't realize the passion her daughter had for the violin.

"Indigo, I promise you. I'll get you the best teacher I can find." Indigo stopped slowly, C#, fifth position, D string.

"Mama, I'm happy with how the fiddle's talk . . . sounding now. I don't want any lessons at all. I just want to play." Thinking her mother was relieved, Indigo left the window. She put the violin away, even closed the gingham curtains. Indigo smiled up at her mama, who had a most curious expression. No matter what she did, Indigo was always beyond her reason. A good girl, yet out of reach.

"Mama, what's wrong? I said you don't have to get me lessons. I'm just fine."

"Indigo, you may have those lessons whenever you like & I mean that. But until you decide to take them, I can't allow you to make that noise in my house. I've got enough trouble on my hands without having every neighbor I've got thinking we got banshees living in here at night. Besides, Miz Fitzhugh, herself, even mentioned to me how unpleasant your violin-playing actually is, right now. I don't mean to say you won't be a wonderful musician in the future. But, Indigo, you may not submit the whole world to your will. No lessons, no violin playing under this roof."

Indigo sat back on her bed 'tween Candace & Marie-Hélène, who whispered: "Listen, I've gotta idea, Indigo."

"Mama, would you be mad if I played it someplace else? Outside, somewhere?"

Imagining she could use a nice hot toddy, the mother was going out Indigo's door, when she turned round to say that Indigo could take the violin anywhere out of the neighborhood & make any noise she liked 'cause then she would have to talk to the strangers beseeching her: "Please, get a lesson, girl," which is precisely what her mother had said.

Indigo patted the violin by her bed exactly where Aunt Haydee kept her shotgun. "No, Mama, that's not what's gonna happen." She kissed Miranda good-night & went to sleep. Her mother left a glass of cider & a deep chocolate on Indigo's night stand. It was midnight & the Moon was full.

Sister Mary Louise put Indigo & her violin behind the shed where she kept her gardening tools—shovels, vitamins for roses & violets, peat moss, watering cans, heavy gloves, rakes, & strings. Too much of the Holy Ghost came out of Indigo & that fiddle. Sister Mary Louise swore even she couldn't stand that much spirit every day. "Back there behind the shed, Indigo, is just fine. Come anytime ya like. If I feel callt, I'ma come on out & listen." That's what Sister Mary Louise had decided about that. "Good for the plants. Too much order, too much gentility'll make my flowers more prim than glorious. We all need a lil wildness." So here came Indigo every day after school plying her new medium out back.

Indigo wanted to sound like the sparrows & wrens. She mimicked the jays & peckers. Conversing with gulls was easy 'cause they saw her daddy's soul every day. Indigo had mastered the hum of dusk, the crescendoes of the cicadas, swamp rushes in light winds, thunder at high tide, & her mother's laughter down the hall. Uncle John told her one time when they were frying porgies by his wagon that he'd got this feeling in his waking up that Indigo was dwelling dangerous on the misery of the slaves who were ourselves, & this feeling directed him to march her toward the beauty of this world & the joys of the those come before us. Indigo couldn't get enough. No creature that moved escaped Indigo's attention. If the fiddle talked, it also rumbled, cawed, rustled, screamed, sighed, sirened, giggled, stomped, & sneered. Every once in a while Indigo even played songs. Some colored singing, Tina Turner, B. B. King, Etta James: they songs. This was a secret. Indigo had some pride & couldn't admit to those who claimed she made noise all the time that she'd found out the difference 'tween her free communion with the universe, primal, unrelenting flights, & melody. She played these softly, for herself. Then she'd blush, hurriedly put the fiddle back into the case, the Colored & Romance having got the best of her. Young boys were alien to her. She didn't want to be a fool in love, have something terrible getta holdt to her. When she'd had enough of "sweetheart," "babeee," & "please, please, please," Indigo yelped, "Oh Sister Mary Louise, you missed that."

There was something moving up her leg, something that was not supposed to be there. Indigo looked down, lost a little fear, just a twig. How was a twig going up & down the inside of her leg, tickling her like the "sweethearts" & "babees" she'd been playing. Indigo looked cautiously behind her where two brown-skinned boys leaned over Sister Mary Louise's fence.

"Get that twig from 'tween my legs."

"We just tryin' to get ya attention. Ya so busy fiddlin' ya don't see nobody. Where ya learn to play like that, gal?"

"My name ain't 'gal' & I taught myself. Now go on 'way & leave me be, please." Indigo hoped they hadn't heard her playing songs, but her wild sounds. She hadda hunch it was them Romance riffs that brought these fellas by the shed. Nobody ever came behind Sister Mary Louise's house. There were devils, Mandingo giants, quadroon elves, & wayward ghosts in her shed.

"What's your name, sweetheart?" the taller boy asked. This one in worn jeans particularly frayed at the edges the way the Geechee Capitans wore theirs when they went crabbing. His head was shaved to keep from the ringworm, Indigo surmised. But the boy had such a pretty head. It was not flat in the back, a pancake head, nor was it all forced up above his eyes, a waterhead. No, this boy had a pretty nutmeg head. He was still slipping that stick round Indigo's ankle though, & she'd told him to stop. The other boy was real stocky, a flathead, but high cheekbones. Indigo recognized the blood of that colored family married Chinese. They all looked like that. Still there was no doubt she'd told them to leave her be & they didn't. Indigo closed her eyes tight like she was fixing to run or scream; instead she said: *"Falcon come in this fiddle. Falcon come in this fiddle.*

Leopard come in this fiddle. Leopard come in this fiddle. I'm on the prey. I'm on the prey." 'Fore she knew it, Indigo was so busy bowing the daylights & jungles out her violin, she didn't notice the two boys duck down on the other side of the fence. When she opened her eyes, she realized she'd stood her ground. & that stick was no longer 'tween her legs. She smiled a tiny smile, peered over the fence, tapped the tall boy's shin with the tip of the bow.

"What's your name, sweetheart?" Indigo chirped, so fulla herself. The boys brushed the sand from their knees, grinned self-consciously.

"I'm Spats," the tall boy answered, "& this here is Crunch. We Junior Geechee Capitans."

Indigo held her tongue. "Why imagine that. Y'all Junior G.C. Ain't that somethin'. I'm Indigo."

Spats jumped over the fence first. He reached for Indigo's fiddle. She pulled it away gracefully. "I can't let anyone touch my instrument. It's bad luck." Spats shrugged his shoulders. "Hey, whatever ya say. Ain't that right, Crunch?" Crunch hanging tough in the alleyway was hardly enthusiastic. A girl with a violin had got him down on his knees in broad daylight.

"What the hell was ya doin' on that damn thing?" Crunch grumbled, messing with his elbows, his thick crop of black hair meeting his furrowed indignant brow.

"I was fightin' back in my own way. That's what I was doin'. & you know it. Come puttin' a stick 'tween my legs like I ain't got no better sense than to let you do it 'cause you boys. Um-humph. Uncle John, he spoke to me on that. He said, 'Indigo, when trouble come, get your fiddle.' "

Spats & Crunch stared at each other. How could a girl know Uncle John? What was Uncle John doing giving some girl all his advice & counsel? Why their seniors, the real Geechee Capitans, held counsel with Uncle John. Very impressed, a little riled, the two boys folded their arms cross their chests & began a culturally recognized & universally feared ritual: The Geechee Capitan Cock Walk. Spats took off his sweatshirt with no sleeves, a slit down the middle, turned inside-out anyway, threw it on the ground. Crunch peeled his black tee-shirt from his ample torso, threw it on the ground. They clapped their hands. Clap. Clapclap. Clap. Spit on the ground, once to the east & once to the west. Then they walked in a circle round Indigo. Slow-n-don't-mess-round clockwise. Slow-n-this-might-be-the-last-time counter clockwise. Again. Humph. Again. Humph. Clap. Clapclap. Clap.

Indigo'd been round long enough to know that she was either being initiated or 'bout to die. Crunch was not too excited 'bout the powers of her fiddlin'. Spats was probably more physical than his slight frame intimated. Indigo held her breath. Next thing was gonna happen, was somebody'd break the rhythm & whoever that was had better be on the case or die.

Spats moved first, fast. Had Indigo on his small shoulders 'fore Crunch could move all of himself anywhere. There was still the possibility that Crunch might plow into them or belly-whip 'em to a tumble. Spats glanced up at Indigo, who was delighted to be such a prize & safe. Crunch kept his flat face straight: "Awright man, she in." Indigo jumped offa Spats, jubilant. The real world was workin' its way up. Crunch didn't like that she was a girl, but whoever could scare a G.C., even the Jr. G.C.'s, had the right to be initiated or die. Plus, a somebody who was already a G.C. hadta put his honor on the line: to really save the person from all the rest, or do harm to the person in the face of all the other G.C.'s. Now it was also true there were only two members of the Jr. Geechee Capitans, Spats & Crunch. That's 'cause they hadn't met anybody could fight as well as they could. Till Indigo. Crunch really didn't like that she was a girl. Spats liked that.

Indigo had a moon in her mouth after all. With Spats & Crunch to run with, her workings, as she called them, were more down to earth. Indigo's specialities were other worlds, fiddling. Spats concentrated on hands, deft, light knife throwing-get-a-watch-offa-wrist, agile hands. Crunch, himself, was moved by yearnings to tear-the-damn-place-down, your place, you, anybody he hadda hankering to. Awesome trio. The immediate problem was how to identify Indigo as a Jr. G.C. Spats almost slapped the devil out of Crunch when he said, "Man, that's impossible. She a girl, how she gonna look like us?" Spats snarled, "Ain't nothin' impossible for a Gee-chee Cap-i-tan." With that the two assembled Indigo's uniform. 'Cause she wouldn't look right in a inside-out sweatshirt or in cut-offs like theirs, they decided on a hat. Spats stole a Stetson, the smallest one he saw in Kerreson's. They didn't like the Colored to try the hats on anyway. Crunch beat up some yellow hincty boy who was playing ball on King Street & took a fine leather belt off him. Then they decorated it with switchblade handles & a strap for Indigo to carry her fiddle round. What Geechee Capitan would walk round without having both hands free? In her new get-up Indigo was a fierce-looking lil sister. She stuffed her braids up in her Stetson, dark brown & tilted over her left eye. Spats, Crunch, & Indigo, all agreed that she was now presentable. Nevertheless, Crunch felt something was missing.

"Hey, Spats, I know what's wrong! She ain't gotta real name. Ya know, a name particular to us!" Indigo had always liked her name. There was nothing wrong with her name. She was particularly herself. She changed the nature of things. She colored & made richer what was blank & plain. The slaves who were ourselves knew all about indigo & Indigo herself. Besides there was great danger in callin' someone out their name. Spirits get confused, bring you something meant for someone else. Folks get upset, move with wrath instead of grace, when callt by a name not blessed & known on earth. Indigo was not hot on this new name business. After some discussion, Crunch accepted a shortening of Indigo to "Digo." Spats had learned enough to know that in another language, Spanish to be exact, "digo" had something to do with "to say" & to his mind, Digo was really sayin' somethin'. If she chose to get on her fiddle, ya best mind what she say.

The South in her.

Coming down Chad Street or running thru the Yards, the Jr. G.C.'s served notice that the colored children were manifestations of the twentieth century. No mythology in the Old Slave Mart approached their realities. Nothing in the Calhoun House reminded them of themselves. Catfish Row was so old-fashioned, dusted pastel frame houses where hominy-grits, oysters, & okra steamed each evening. Crap games went on as usual in the tiny alleyways, edged by worn porches where grandmas made believe they didn't have any idea all that was goin' on. Yet they'd smile if somebody had a high streak of luck, sending yelps & bass guffaws over the roofs. Here Digo, Crunch, & Spats performed, mixing the skills of modern wayward children with the past-times of the more traditional colored iconoclasts.

They especially liked to go round to Sneed's. Now, Sneed's was a bakery; fresh breads, muffins, cakes, & cookies every day. But the reasons the Jr. G.C.'s spent so much time there was that Sneed's was connected to a winding complex of underground rooms where gambling, cockfights, and a twenty-four-hour social room entertained the most adventurous of Charleston's colored subterraneans. Spats' brother, Pretty Man, made sure that the transactions in the various gaming activities stayed calm. Whenever possible, Pretty Man believed that money should change hands in his favor, calmly, of course.

Actually, the bakers in their high white hats & flour-covered aprons carried more than dough downstairs directly under the ovens. They took the daily numbers receipts down to The Caverns, as they were called, & came back up to the muffins & turnovers with a possible change of life-style for a confirmed pastry-gourmet. Indigo didn't mind the numbers. She played a few from time to time. That meant new dress-up clothes, Eudoxa strings for the violin, a Sunday chapeau for Mama, and spending change for the spirits who still kept Indigo's company late at night.

Numbers for Prosperity & Furthered Independence of the Race

by Indigo

164—if searching for hearth & home, more secure familial relations.
626—if desirous of a journey to one's true home, spiritual or physical, play once a week for a month.
208—if in need of immediate assistance for ordinary amenities, play only on Monday.
176—if seeking a larger dwelling for one's family, this works, in conjunction with 164.
508—if yearning for retreat & personal solitude, play on five consecutive Wednesdays.
141—if conflicted by the stresses of racism, play twice a week for five years.
999—to be freed from debilitating relations, fiscal or otherwise, daily.

Realizing Spirits' Hints/ What Your Dreams Can Do for You

by Indigo

If you see a gull flying over your house, there is a 7 in your combination. If the gull swoops downward, there is also a 2. If the gull flies toward the moon, there is a 9.

If your Mother is burning something on the stove, and you cannot get up to warn her, play 1. If she is burning up something, and you are able to warn her, play 7. If what your Mother is cooking & burning is your favorite dish, that's a 123, in combination.

If there is a lover of yours kissing your best friend in your house, there are two 3's in your number. If you are angry about this, your number is 353. If you find it amusing, your number is 333.

If you keep falling down in your dream, there's surely an 8 in your number. If where you are falling is never reached or is unknown, add a 1. If you fall somewhere, change that to 6.

General Notes

Flowers—719/ A car—520/ Fires—882/ Beds—231/ The Christ Child—777/ The Crucifix—111/ Judas (someone you know or Iscariot)—001/ A deceased grandmother—803/ A deceased grandfather—902/ Mulberry bushes—756/ Maggots—395/ Guns—246.

Pretty Man hired Spats & Crunch to clean up after the cockfights. To carry the screeching bleeding birds on outside & kill 'em, if need be, was Spats' job. Taking the razors off their feet was Crunch's. Indigo stayed away from the ring after the first time. She'd watched these men shouting out for their favorite to slay the other. All this money waving in their hands, collected by Pretty Man, who must have been a mathematical genius. He kept all the odds, paid out, collected what was due him, without taking his eyes off the match. Indigo felt a steely vengeance growing in her spirit. Grown men laughing at dying animals. She felt birds hovering above her eyes. She moved the razors off the roosters. Put them in the palms of the onlookers. Let them cut each other to shreds, she thought. Let them know the havoc of pain. Spats & Crunch had suspicions 'bout Indigo's powers, but couldn't believe she'd gone & done something like this.

The cocks stalked the ring quietly. The men round the ring leaped over one another, flailing their razored palms at throats, up & down backs, backsides, ankles. Such a conglomeration of footwear swung over the side of the ring: high-top sneakers, lizard loafers, wing-tips, galoshes, work boots. Indigo stood by the door watching this bloodletting. Silent. Pretty Man surveyed the situation. Put the evilest eye he could gather up on Indigo, who startled under the power of his gaze. That was all it took. The men slowly came back to themselves. Looked about, puzzled. Put their hats back on. Shook the sawdust from themselves. Wondered where all this blood in the stands came from. The wounds had closed, no scars. Indigo was not malevolent. Yet Pretty Man would not tolerate such shenanigans in his place.

Without exchanging words, Pretty Man & Indigo came up with an arrangement. She was, after all, a Geechee Capitan, too. From that point on Indigo spent her time at Sneed's in the "social room," playing her fiddle. Since you could only buy liquor in bottles from sunup till sundown, coming over to Sneed's social room for a glass of beer or a shot of whiskey just made common sense to high-livers in Charleston.

Table service, some gambling, and that child on the fiddle were a gratifying combination after work for the family folks, and before work for the night labor force.

Indigo didn't change her style of playing. She still went after what she was feeling. But now she'd look at somebody. Say a brown-skinned man with a scar on his cheek, leathery hands, and a tiredness in his eyes. Then she'd bring her soul all up in his till she'd ferreted out the most lovely moment in that man's life. & she played that. You could tell from looking that as Indigo let notes fly from the fiddle, that man's scar wasn't quite so ugly; his eyes filling with energy, a tenderness tapping from those fingers now, just music. The slaves who were ourselves aided Indigo's mission, connecting soul & song, experience & unremembered rhythms. Pretty Man was relieved. Indigo'd found her a place. He could tell Uncle John there'd be no more wanton juvenile Circe in these parts. There was coming for sure a woman in charge of her powers. Training was what she was wanting.

Pretty Man didn't know how Indigo played what she played, but he did know she had a gift. Spats had mentioned how the girl couldn't play in her house 'less she agreed to take lessons. So a teacher for Indigo was out of the question. There's more than one way to skin a cat, & Pretty Man hadn't gotten this far 'cause of a lack of imagination. No. There was something real simple that he could do. Pretty Man liked the simple things in life: money, a good woman, respect. Mabel, his girl, was a simple sweet woman who helped out in the social room. Pretty Man sent Mabel in her tight straight red skirt out in the streets looking for any records with violin playing on 'em. They were gonna replace the jukebox for a while. "Yes," he said to himself, "Digo gonna play it by ear, here, for a time. For some time."

Mabel, who was as dutiful as a southern girl could be, came back from all the record stores with a peculiar assortment of violin melodies & violinists. Yehudi Menuhin plays Bartók, *Violin Concerto #2.* Papa John Creach. *Duke Ellington's Jazz Violin Session* with Svend Asmussen, Stéphane Grappelli, Ray Nance, & Billy Strayhorn. Heifetz plays Bach, *Unaccompanied Sonatas & Partitas.* Plus Stuff Smith. "I got one of every violiner they had," Mabel cooed. Pretty Man looked at each album. Nodded his head. "Get these on that ol' jukebox for me, okay?" It was done.

Pretty Man offered Indigo a dollar for every one of the tunes she learned to play by ear, or to play as the record played. Pretty Man called everything from Bach to Ellington a tune. If it was Smith's "Blues in the Dungeon," that was a tune. Just as Bartók's 2nd movement, *andante tranquillo,* was a tune. Indigo didn't jump at the chance to change her aesthetic. In fact, she told Pretty Man there was no sense at all in playing something that somebody else could already play. But Spats & Crunch had a meeting on the matter, determined that Indigo's pursuits would mightily enhance the Jr. G.C. treasury. Even Indigo didn't argue 'gainst that. Imagine all the finery & catfish the Jr. Geechee Capitans could offer the not-so-well-off Colored, now Christmas was coming. Indigo, indeed, had made her presence felt in the small gang since her initiation. Give gifts to those who should know love.

Give hell to those who take us lightly. New mottos. New priorities emerging for the Geechee Capitans.

Pretty Man gave Mabel change for the jukebox, whenever Indigo was training. Indigo didn't do badly. Yet the nuance & dexterity of the masters occasionally eluded her, her personal rhythms running contrary to theirs. The octaves she chose, not the ones sounded by Creach or Heifetz. Then, too, one time she forgot she wasn't to take solos during Ellington's "Tricky Licks" and played all on top of Ray Nance. Pretty Man was impressed by Indigo's determination to rise up to the challenge. Mabel was concerned, 'cause folks used to the child's fiddlin' till they souls spoke, were getting cantankerous, leaving early, not leaving tips, being genuinely unpleasant. Missing something.

Late one afternoon when the social room was usually crowded with menfolks & womenfolks, going on 'bout the Colored, the day's doings, and what might be in the cards, Mabel watched. Nothing going on but Indigo & that jukebox. Violins. Violins. Violins, white folks done come up from they grave to drive the Colored out of a nice spot, they spot. All this fiddlin' was makin' folks unhappy, not wanting no drinks, not wanting the hush puppies, greens, & catfish Mabel prepared with so much spice. All them empty tables. All them fiddles. It was better before, when the girl played her own mind. There was a fullness to conversation then. Plus, Pretty Man spoke to her 'bout more than how was Indigo playing. "What's the girl doing on her fiddle these days?" he'd ask. Like all Mabel had to do was remember each time she'd heard "Blues in C" or "Arabian Song, No. 42." No. No. Mabel looked at Indigo sitting by the jukebox, listening, fingering, humming. No more. Mabel pulled the plug out the wall. Took a step toward Indigo. "Indigo, give me that fiddle. Right this minute, do you hear me? Pretty Man don't want no more fiddlin' round heah. Now, c'mon, give it heah." Indigo moved quick, like moonlight. "Spats. Crunch. *G.C. in trouble. G.C. in trouble.*" Indigo let the force of her own style of fiddle-fightin' come to the fore. Such a war-cry bouncing in the social room where hips & bosoms used to shake. Mabel was overwhelmed by her mission to have things be the way they used to be, not understanding that Indigo's existence made that impossible.

Spats & Crunch came running. Spats threw chairs in fronta Mabel's every step. Crunch kept Mabel's grabbing hands off Indigo's face & fiddle. Mabel took on the attributes of a lioness, prowling, growling. It was everything the boys could do to save Indigo; her hair or her fiddle.

Mabel proceeded to attack the boys with her nails, her heels, her teeth, her voice. She callt on everybody: Moses & her mother. "Jesus, get that fiddle out my life." Spats had some scratches. Crunch was generally a mess. They were all a little scared. Mabel was shouting for Pretty Man. Pretty Man was Mabel's man. They were in a lot of trouble.

Spats thought they should get on outta Sneed's. "My brother ain't gonna stand for us fightin' his woman." Fiddle in arm, Indigo clammered thru the caverns, Spats & Crunch beside her. "We in for it now. Damn we might haveta hide out, when Pretty Man know what we done!" Crunch's hearing wasn't subtle enough to catch Mabel's screams. Pretty Man having one of his tempers. Indigo slowed down. "We ain't the ones haveta run nowhere." Spats was impatient. "We got ta keep movin'." Crunch was already gone.

Spats tried pulling Indigo by her free arm. "Digo, c'mon. We cain't let Pretty Man catch us. Let's go." Indigo shook her head. "No, I'ma go back & see to Mabel." & Spats was gone.

Indigo felt The Caverns for the first time. The air was dark, heavy. The baking breads wafted thru her nostrils, leaden. Her fiddle, as she let it fall over her side, weighed down on her spirit. Shame crawled up her cheeks. She was going to see about Mabel. Mabel had gotten in trouble 'cause of Indigo's fiddle, 'cause Indigo was a Geechee Capitan. Mabel was just some woman. One day Indigo would be a woman, too. The shame etched tears down her face, pushed her back toward the social room. Fear dashed her 'gainst the wall in the dark, when Pretty Man, as pretty as ever, briskly went up to the bakery. He was putting his shirt back in his pants as he walked, straightening himself up. Indigo wisht the switchblade handles on her violin case were knives. She'd have them all land in his back, but she didn't want to hurt anybody else. The Colored had been hurt enough already.

The Caverns began to moan, not with sorrow but in recognition of Indigo's revelation. The slaves who were ourselves had known terror intimately, confused sunrise with pain, & accepted indifference as kindness. Now they sang out from the walls, pulling Indigo toward them. Indigo ran her hands along the walls, to get the song, getta hold to the voices. Instead her fingers grazed cold, hard metal rings. Rust covered her palms & fingers. She kept following the rings. Chains. Leg irons. The Caverns revealed the plight of her people, but kept on singing. The tighter Indigo held the chains in her hands, the less shame was her familiar. Mabel's tiny woeful voice hovered over the blood thick chorus of The Caverns. Indigo knew her calling. The Colored had hurt enough already.

Emergency Care of Open Wounds/ When It Hurts

by Indigo

Calmly rinse the wound with copious amounts of cold tap water. This will significantly reduce the possibilities of infection. If available, use clean linen applied firmly against the wound to inhibit bleeding. If the pressure is not adequate, do it again. Another method allows the bottom of a stainless-steel saucepan to be applied to the wound. The cold of the pan reduces swelling as well as bleeding. A poultice of mandrake berries can be of great use also, until further care can be offered.

Emergency Care of Wounds That Cannot Be Seen

Hold the victim gently. Rock in the manner of a quiet sea. Hum softly from your heart. Repeat the victim's name with love. Offer a brew of red sunflower to cleanse the victim's blood & spirit. Fasting & silence for a time refurbish the victim's awareness of her capacity to nourish & heal herself. New associations should be made with caution, more caring for herself.

Indigo carefully wrapped her dolls in sheets of white cotton she'd borrowed from her mother's weaving rooms. To the left of the moon she'd painted on her wall was a growing mound of white ovals with little cloth feet sticking out. The sun was fading. Fine tints of orange lingered on the edges of the dolls' heads, which all pointed to the east. Indigo had wrapped Marie-Hélène & Miranda last. Hugging them both, kissing their foreheads, holding them at arms' length to get one final glimpse of those who had been her closest friends. After a final curtsey to the shrouded companions, Indigo played what she remembered of Bartók. Each note demanding precision, honesty, and depth.

Lord, this child is a miracle, thought her mother, Hilda Effania, as she listened & watched from the door. She'd stolen up the back stairs as quickly as she could when she'd heard *real* music coming from Indigo's room. Yet now she felt a regret that she'd forbidden the child her willful desire to play her soul. It was true like Aunt Haydee said, "A youngun'll come up with what you want, when ya leave 'em the room to find it." Indigo finished all the lyrical fragments she could from heart, plus she'd added a tag from "Cotton Tail." Bowing very formally, *legato,* Indigo turned to put her fiddle in its case. She saw her mother, hesitated, and stammered, "Mama, I think it's time I stopped playing with dolls, don't you?"

"Well, I do recall sayin' something like that one of those terribly busy days, when I already had my hands full. Musta been the day you wanted a 'period' dinner . . ."

"No, a menstruation dinner, Mama."

"That's right, I do believe I tol' you to pack 'em up in the attic." Hilda Effania bit her lips, smuggled a smile out of her concern for her child. "Indigo, you don't haveta bury the girls. I think they look wonderful here in your room. As long as I can remember, you've gone to bed with your dollies. No matter how angry I was when I said what I said, you know I don't hold a soul to my every word. You keep your dolls as long as you want. Why, I think at least Miranda can come to Christmas dinner." Hilda Effania wanted Indigo to lose this forlorn curve in her back, the sadness in her gaze. But Indigo was resolute.

"No, Mama. I don't think they're quite dead, they're just resting, I think." Indigo looked up at her mama wanting very much. All she said was: "Mama, I couldn't bear for them to grow up. I couldn't stand it, Mama. I just couldn't."

Hilda Effania really didn't know what was the matter. She knew to hold Indigo close to her, to say her name over & over till the child was ready to talk.

"Mama, it's hard, isn't it?"

"What's hard, Indigo?"

"Being a grown colored woman is hard, ain't it? Just like you tol' me. Just 'cause I haveta grow up, my dolls don't haveta. I can save them. Mama, let's take them to the attic. You & me. I don't even wanta invite Mrs. Yancey, though Miranda will miss her. Just you & me, let's do something very special."

Hilda Effania sat Indigo down on the bed with her. She rocked her baby in her arms, patted her back, hummed a tune as she made it up.

"I don't know that it's all that hard to be a full-grown colored woman, Indigo. I can imagine not wanting your friends to grow up, though. If they grow up, eventually, they will haveta go. But, you know they could stay little girls forever."

"How, Mama?"

"You know it's Christmas time, & there's hundreds of other little girls, oh tiny little girls, who'd take real good care of Miranda, Marie-Hélène & all the rest of them. & you & I know there's no dollies in the whole world quite like these." Hilda Effania tried so hard not to laugh. She had flashes of Indigo stealing rice from the kitchen, buttons from the sewing room, bits of satin from patterns for Miz Fitzhugh's ball gowns. "Like I was saying, Indigo, there's no dollies like this anywhere on the earth."

"You mean, give 'em away to strangers?" Indigo asked, indignant.

"You said they weren't dead, just resting," Hilda Effania responded, while she put Indigo's Stetson on her head. "You know, for a man's hat, that's pretty sharp, Indigo."

Indigo pulled the hat off her head, thought a second. Stood in front of her mother with a desperate air.

"Mama, I'll make the other lil girls new dollies, honest I will. I promise. But I want you & me to have a ceremony for my dollies & let em rest till I have a baby, or till Cypress or Sassafrass has a baby. Please Mama, I want them to stay with the family."

It was true. After Indigo there'd be no more babies in the family till one of her girls was grown enough to bring one home. Hilda Effania couldn't agree more with Indigo's familial fervor. After all, she was devoted to her daughters. Now, Indigo, all of 12, was saving her most treasured possessions for the daughters to come. This made sense to Hilda Effania, who'd seen those other two grow up much too fast. This was the day that Indigo caught up with them.

"Okay, what sort of ceremony do you want to have?"

"I want you to sing some holy song, while I carry them one by one to the attic. That's what I wanta do, Mama. Then I wanta come downstairs & help you make the gumbo for when Cypress & Sassafrass come home. Can I, please?" Indigo was excited, beginning & ending the largest segment of her life.

Hilda Effania changed her clothes once she got in the spirit of things. She put on a crêpe dress with pearls & black velvet round the shoulders, a little lipstick, some mascara. At her suggestion, Indigo put on her white taffeta Communion dress. Hilda Effania stationed herself at the foot of the second-floor stairs leading to the attic. Indigo solemnly carried each doll up the curving steps, as her mother's voice rose behind her to the rafters:

"Jesus lover of my soul
Hide me, oh my Savior
Hide me till the storm of life is past
While the stormy waters roll
While the tempest still is high."

1982

ISHMAEL REED
b. 1938

Ishmael Reed was born in Chattanooga, Tennessee, and educated at the State University of New York at Buffalo. In addition to serving as an editorial director, producer, and distributor of the work of unknown ethnic writers, he was a cofounder of the Before Columbus Foundation and has been a chairperson of the Berkeley Arts Commission and the Coordinating Council of Literary Magazines. Reed has taught at, among other colleges and universities, Yale, Dartmouth, Columbia, Harvard, and the University of Arkansas at Fayetteville. His seven novels include *The Free-Lance Pallbearers* (1967), *Yellow Back Radio Broke-Down* (1969), *The Last Days of Louisiana Red* (1974), and *Reckless Eyeballing* (1982), and he has also published six books of poetry.

Critic Daryl Pinckney has noted in *The New York Times* (1986) that Reed's novels "are meant to provoke. Though variously described as a writer in whose work the black picaresque tradition has been extended, as a misogynist or an heir to both Hurston's folk lyricism and Ellison's irony, he is, perhaps because of this, one of the most underrated writers in America. Certainly no other contemporary black writer, male or female, has used the language and beliefs of folk culture so imaginatively, and few have been so stinging about the absurdity of American racism."

In *Yellow Back Radio Broke-Down* Reed first used hoodoo (or voodoo) methods and folklore, including precepts involving the synthesis of diverse cultures' beliefs and practices and the complex treatment of time. Hoodoo, Reed told interviewer Reginald Martin in the *Review of Contemporary Fiction* (1987), is "solidly in the American tradition."

From Yellow Back Radio Broke-Down

Chapter 1

Folks. This here is the story of the Loop Garoo Kid. A cowboy so bad he made a working posse of spells phone in sick. A bullwhacker so unfeeling he left the print of winged mice on hides of crawling women. A desperado so onery he made the Pope cry and the most powerful of cattlemen shed his head to the Executioner's swine.

A terrible cuss of a thousand shivs he was who wasted whole herds, made the fruit black and wormy, dried up the water holes and caused people's eyes to grow from tiny black dots into slapjacks wherever his feet fell.

Now, he wasn't always bad, trump over hearts diamonds and clubs. Once a wild joker he cut the fool before bemused Egyptians, dressed like Mortimer Snerd and spilled french fries on his lap at Las Vegas' top of the strip.

Booted out of his father's house after a quarrel, whores snapped at his heels and trick dogs did the fandango on his belly. Men called him brother only to cop his coin and tell malicious stories about his cleft foot.

Born with a caul over his face and ghost lobes on his ears, he was a mean night tripper who moved from town to town quoting Thomas Jefferson and allowing bandits to build a flophouse around his genius.

A funny blue hippo who painted himself with water flowers only to be drummed out of each tribe dressed down publicly, his medals ripped off.

• •

Finally he joined a small circus and happily performed with his fellow 86-D—a Juggler a dancing Bear a fast talking Barker and Zozo Labrique, charter member of the American Hoo-Doo Church.

Their fame spread throughout the frontier and bouquets of flowers greeted them in every town until they moved into that city which seemed a section of Hell chipped off and shipped upstairs, Yellow Back Radio, where even the sun was afraid to show its bottom.

• •

Some of the wheels of the caravan were stuck in thick red mud formed by a heavy afternoon downpour. The oxen had to be repeatedly whipped. They had become irritable from the rain which splashed against their faces. In the valley below black dust rose in foreboding clouds from herds of wild horses that roamed there. Loop Garoo was driving the horse hitched to Zozo Labrique's covered wagon.

Those were some dangerous stunts you did in the last town, boy, bucking those killer broncos like that. A few more turns with that bull and you would have been really used up. Why you try so hard?

She sent me a letter in the last town, Zozo. She wants me to come to her. The old man spends his time grooming his fur and posing for non-academic painters. He's more wrapped up in himself than ever before and the other one, he's really gone dipso this time. Invites winos up there who pass the bottle and make advances on her. Call her sweet stuff and honey bun—she's really in hard times. She's a constant guest in my dreams Zozo, her face appears the way she looked the night she went uptown on me.

Serves her right Loop, the way she treated you. And that trash she collected around her. They were all butch. As soon as she left, zoom they were gone. And that angel in drag like a john, he gave her the news and showed her her notices—right off it went to her head. When she humiliated you—that emboldened the others to do likewise. Mustache Sal deserted you and Mighty Dike teamed up with that jive fur trapper who's always handing you subpoenas. You know how they are, Loop, you're the original pimp, the royal stud—soon as a bottom trick finds your weakness your whole stable will up and split.

I let her open my nose Zozo. I should have known that if she wasn't loyal to him with as big a reputation as he had—I couldn't expect her to revere me. What a line that guy had. A mitt man from his soul. And her kissing his feet just because those three drunken reporters were there to record it. Ever read their copy on that event Zozo? It's as if they were all witnessing something entirely different. The very next night she was in my bunk gnashing her teeth and uttering obscenities as I climbed into her skull.

She got to your breathing all right Loop. Even the love potions you asked me to mix didn't work, the follow-me-powder. Her connaissance was as strong as mine.

Zozo Labrique lit a corncob pipe. She wore a full skirt and a bandana on her head. Her face was black wrinkled and hard. The sun suddenly appeared, causing the gold hoops on her ears to sparkle.

Jake the Barker rode up alongside the wagon.

Well Loop, Zozo, won't be long now. Maybe thirty minutes before we pull into Yellow Back Radio. We're booked by some guy named Happy Times, who we're to meet at the Hotel.

Jake rode down the mountain's path to advise the rest of the troupe.

This was a pretty good season Loop, what are you going to do with your roll?

O I don't know Zozo, maybe I'll hire some bounty hunters to put a claim on my lost territory.

O Loop quit your joking.

What are you going to do Zozo?

Think the old bag will head back to New Orleans, mecca of Black America. First Doc John kicked out then me—she got her cronies in City Hall to close down my operation. We had to go underground. Things started to disappear from my humfo—even Henry my snake and mummies appeared in the curtains. She warned my clients that if they visited me she'd cross them. Everybody got shook and stayed away. Finally she layed a trick on me so strong that it almost wasted old Zozo, Loop. That Marie is a mess. Seems now though my old arch enemy is about to die. Rumor has it that the daughter is going to take over but I know nothing will come of that fast gal. Nobody but Marie has the type of connaissance to make men get down on their knees and howl like dogs and women to throw back their heads and cackle. Well . . . maybe your old lady, Loop, what's the hussy's name?

Diane, Black Diane, Zozo, you know her name.

Sometimes it's hard to tell, Loop, the bitch has so many aliases.

Before their wagon rounded the mountain curve they heard a gasp go up on the other side. A dead man was hanging upside down from a tree. He had been shot.

He wore a frilled ruffled collar knee britches a fancy shirt and turned up shoes. A cone shaped hat with a carnation on its rim had fallen to the ground.

The two climbed down from the wagon and walked to where Jake the Barker and the Juggler were staring at the hanging man. The dancing Bear watched from his cage, his paws gripping the bars, his head swinging from side to side with curiosity. Handbills which had dropped from the man's pockets littered the ground about the scene.

Plug In Your Head
Look Here Citizens!!
Coming to Yellow Back Radio
Jake the Barker's lecture room
New Orleans Hoodooine Zozo Labrique
Amazing Loop Garoo lariat tricks
Dancing Bear and Juggler too
Free Beer

Above the man's head on the hoodoo rock fat nasty buzzards were arriving. Jake removed his hat and was surrounded by members of the bewildered troupe.

Nearest town Video Junction is about fifty miles away. There's not enough grub in the chuck wagon to supply us for a journey of that length. Besides the horses and oxen have to be bedded down. I wouldn't want any of you to take risks. If this means danger up ahead maybe we should disband here, split the take and put everybody on his own.

We've come this far Jake, may as well go on into Yellow Back Radio, the Juggler said.

Count me in too, Loop said, we've braved alkali, coyotes, wolves, rattlesnakes, catamounts, hunters. Nothing I'm sure could be as fierce down in that town—why it even looks peaceful from here.

I'll go along with the rest, Zozo said. But I have a funny feeling that everything isn't all right down there.

After burying the advance man on a slope they rode farther down the mountain until finally, from a vantage point, they could see the rest of Yellow Back Radio.

The wooden buildings stood in the shadows. The Jail House, the Hat and Boot store the Hardware store the Hotel and Big Lizzy's Rabid Black Cougar Saloon.

Sinister hogs with iron jaws were fenced in behind the scaffold standing in the square. They were the swine of the notorious Hangman, who was such a connoisseur of his trade he kept up with all the latest techniques of murder.

A new device stood on the platform. Imported from France, it was said to be as rational as their recent revolution. The hogs ate the remains of those unfortunate enough to climb the platform. Human heads were particularly delectable to these strange beasts.

The troupe drove through the deserted main street of the town. Suddenly they were surrounded by children dressed in the attire of the Plains Indians. It appeared as if cows had been shucked and their skins passed to the children's nakedness for their shoes and clothes were made of the animals' hides.

Reach for the sky, whiskey drinkers, a little spokesman warned. One hundred flintlocks were aimed at them.

Hey, it's a circus, one of the children cried, and some dropped their rifles and began to dance.

A circus? one of the boys who made the warning asked. How do we know this isn't a trap sprung by the cheating old of Yellow Back Radio?

Jake the Barker, holding up his hands, looked around to the other members of the troupe. Amused, Loop, Zozo and the Juggler complied with the little gunmen's request.

What's going on here? Jake asked. We're the circus that travels around this territory each season. We're supposed to end the tour in your town. We're invited by Mister Happy Times. We're to meet him at the Hotel. Where are the adults? The Marshal, the Doctor, the Preacher, or someone in charge?

Some of the children snickered, but became silent when their spokesman called them into a huddle. After some haggling, he stepped towards the lead wagon upon which Jake the Barker rode.

We chased them out of town. We were tired of them ordering us around. They worked us day and night in the mines, made us herd animals harvest the crops and for three hours a day we went to school to hear teachers praise the old. Made us learn facts by rote. Lies really bent upon making us behave. We decided to create our own fiction.

One day we found these pearl-shaped pills in a cave of a mountain. They're what people ages ago called devil's pills. We put them in the streams so that when the grown-ups went to fill their buckets they swallowed some. It confused them more than they were so we moved on them and chased them out of town. Good riddance. They listened to this old Woman on the talk show who filled their heads with rot. She was against joy and life the decrepit bag of sticks, and she put them into the same mood. They always demanded we march and fight heathens.

Where are the old people now? Jake asked.

They're camped out at Drag Gibson's spread. We think they're preparing to launch some kind of invasion but we're ready for them. Drag just sent his herd up the Chisholm to market yesterday but there are enough cowpokes left behind to give us a good fight. Our Indian informant out at Drag's spread tells us the townspeople haven't given in to Drag's conditions yet. He wants them to sign over all of their property in exchange for lending his men to drive us out.

Then he will not only rule his spread which is as large as Venezuela but the whole town as well. He's the richest man in the valley, with prosperous herds, abundant resources and an ego as wide as the Grand Canyon.

This nonsense would never happen in the Seven Cities of Cibola, Jake the Barker said.

The Seven Cities of Cibola? the children asked, moving in closer to Jake's wagon.

Inanimate things, computers do the work, feed the fowl, and programmed cows give cartons of milkshakes in 26 flavors.

Yippppeeeeee, the children yelled. Where is it?

It's as far as you can see from where you're standing now. I'm going to search for it as soon as the show is over here but since there is no sponsor to greet us we may as well disband now, Jake said, looking about at the other members of the troupe.

Why don't you entertain us? the children asked.

It's a plot. We decided that we wouldn't trust anybody greying about the temples anymore!

O don't be paranoid, silly, another child replied to the tiny skeptic. Always trying to be the leader just like those old people we ran into the hills. These aren't ordinary old people they're children like us—look at their costumes and their faces.

Let's have the circus, a cry went up.

Well I don't know—you see we have no leaders holy men or gurus either so I'd have to ask the rest of the troupe.

Loop, Zozo and the Juggler said yes by nodding their heads. The Bear jumped up and down in his chains.

Delighted, the children escorted the small circus group to the outskirts of Yellow Back Radio where they pitched the tents, bedded down the weary horses and oxen and made preparations for the show.

• •

Three horsemen—the Banker, the Marshal and the Doctor—decided to pay a little visit to Drag Gibson's ranch. They had to wait because Drag was at his usual hobby, embracing his property.

A green mustang had been led out of its stall. It served as a symbol for his streams of fish, his herds, his fruit so large they weighed down the mountains, black gold and diamonds which lay in untapped fields, and his barnyard overflowing with robust and erotic fowl.

Holding their Stetsons in their hands the delegation looked on as Drag prepared to kiss his holdings. The ranch hands dragged the animal from his compartment towards the front of the Big Black House where Drag bent over and french kissed the animal between his teeth, licking the slaver from around the horse's gums.

This was one lonely horse. The male horses avoided him because they thought him stuck-up and the females because they thought that since green he was a queer horse. See, he had turned green from old nightmares.

After the ceremony the unfortunate critter was led back to his stall, a hoof covering his eye.

Drag removed a tube from his pocket and applied it to his lips. He then led the men to a table set up in front of the House. Four bottles of whiskey were placed on the table by Drag's faithful Chinese servant, who picked a stray louse from Drag's fur coat only to put it down the cattleman's back. Drag smiled and twitched a bit, slapping his back until his hand found the bullseye. Killing the pest, he and the servant exchanged grins.

Bewildered, the men glanced at each other.

What brings you here? I told you to come only if you were ready for business. Sign the town and your property over to me so that my quest for power will be satisfied. If you do that I'll have my men go in there and wipe them menaces out.

We decided to give in, Drag. Why, we're losing money each day the children hold the town and we have to be around our wives all the time and they call us stupid jerks, buster lamebrain and unpolite things like that. It's a bargain, Drag. What do we do now?

Now you're talking business Doc. Sign this stiffycate which gives me what I asked for and I'll have them scamps out of your hair in no time.

Drag brought forth an official looking document from inside his robe, to which the Banker, Marshal and Doctor affixed their signatures.

It's a good thing we got the people to see it your way, the Banker said, wiping the sweat on his forehead with a crimson handkerchief. Some reinforcements were arriving today. They were in some wagons that was painted real weird and we hanged and shot one who was dressed like a clown. We thought they might be heathens from up North, you dig?

You mulish goofies, that was the circus I ordered to divert the kids so's we could ambush them. Any damned fool knows kids like circuses.

Drag we're confused and nervous. Just today four boxes of drexol were stolen from our already dwindling supply of goods. That's why we didn't think when we killed that man. The old people are wandering around the camp bumping into each other they're so tightened up. All day people are saying hey stupid idiot watch where you're going. It's a mad house.

And the Preacher Rev. Boyd, he's in the dumps in a strong and serious way this time. You know how hard he tried with the kids and the town's heathen, how he'd smoke hookahs with them brats and get stoned with Chief Showcase the only surviving injun and that volume of hip pastorale poetry he's putting together, *Stomp Me O Lord.* He thought that Protestantism would survive at least another month and he's tearing up the Red-Eye and writing more of them poems trying to keep up with the times. Drag you know how out of focus things are around here. After all Drag it's your world completely now.

How can you be so confident your men can take care of them varmits Drag? It takes a trail boss a dozen or so cowboys and a wrangler to get the herd North. You can't have many cowpokes left behind. Don't get me wrong I'm not afraid for myself cause I rode with Doc Holiday and the Dalton Boys before I went peace officer—I have handled a whole slew of punks passing through the hopper in my day . . . why if I hadn't been up the creek at the Law Enforcement Conference it wouldn't have happened anyway.

You always seem to be at some convention when the town needs you Marshal, Drag said, looking into a hand mirror and with a neckerchief wiping the smudges of mascara that showed above his batting lashes.

Drag, the women folk, well you know how women are, what strange creatures they be during menopause. They're against us wiping out the kids. That's one of the reasons we didn't cast lots quicker to give you the hand over of Yellow Back Radio, so that you could adjust all the knobs and turn to whatever station you wished. Anyway we tried to get Big Lizzy to talk to them but they don't recognize her as one of their own.

Pshaw, don't worry about the women Doc, Drag Gibson said, bringing his old fat and ugly frame to its feet. Start appeasing them and pretty soon they'll be trying to run the whole show like that kook back in Wichita who campaigned to cut out likker. Now quit your whining and get back to camp and see after them townsfolk. Leave the job up to me.

The dignitaries rose and tumbled down the hill. The Banker rolled over a couple of times as Drag stood jerking his shoulders and with one finger in his ear as pellet after pellet flew over the Marshal's, Banker's and Doctor's heads. He relaxed, drank a glass of rotgut and gave the appearance of a statesman by returning to his book *The Life of Catherine the Great.* As soon as the delegation disappeared, he slammed the book shut and called his boys.

Get in here cowpokes, we're in business.

Skinny McCullough the foreman followed by some cowhands rushed onto the lawn and surrounded their boss.

Chinaboy! Chinaboy! Bring me that there package.

The Chinese servant rushed into the scene with his arms weighed down with a bundle.

O.K. men, Drag said, this is the opportunity we've been waiting for. They signed the town over to me, the chumps, haw haw.

He opened the package and placed its contents on the table.

This is a brand new revolving cylinder. It has eight chambers. A murderer's dream with a rapid firing breech-loading firearm.

The cowpokes' eyes lit up and foam began to form around their lips.

It was invented by a nice gent lecturer named Dr. Coult of New York London and Calcutta. Just bought it from Royal Flush Gooseman, the shrewd, cunning and wicked fur trapper, the one who sold them injuns those defected flintlocks allowing us to wipe them out.

The kids are down there with a circus I booked under a pseudonym. I been watching them through my long glass. Now get busy and before you know it Drag Gibson will be the big name in Yellow Back Radio then Video Junction then va-va-voom on to the East, heh heh heh.

The cowpokes from Drag Gibson's Purple Bar-B drank some two-bits-a-throw from a common horn and armed with their shiny new weapons headed towards the outskirts of Yellow Back Radio on their nefarious mission.

• •

The Dancing Bear, the Juggler, Loop and Zozo entertained the children far into the night. The Dancing Bear did acrobatic feats with great deftness, Loop his loco lariat tricks, and Zozo read the children's palms and told their fortunes.

Finally Jake the Barker gathered them near the fire to tell of the Seven Cities of Cibola, magnificent legendary American paradise where tranquilized and smiling machines gladly did all of the work so that man could be free to dream. A paradise whose streets were paved with opals from Idaho, sapphire from Montana, turquoise and silver from the great Southwest:

In the early half of the sixteenth century about 1528 an expedition which included the black slave Estevancio landed at Tampa Bay. He and his companions were lost trapped and enslaved by Indians. Other expeditions also vanished mysteriously. Legend has it that the city can only be found by those of innocent motives, the young without yellow fever in their eyes.

Stupid historians who are hired by the cattlemen to promote reason, law and order—toad men who adore facts—say that such an anarchotechnological paradise where robots feed information into inanimate steer and mechanical fowl where machines do everything from dig irrigation ditches to mine the food of the sea help old ladies across the street and nurture infants is as real as a green horse's nightmare. Shucks I've always been a fool, eros appeals more to me than logos. I'm just silly enough to strike out for it tomorrow as soon as the circus splits up.

A place without gurus monarchs leaders cops tax collectors jails matriarchs patriarchs and all the other galoots who in cahoots have made the earth a pile of human bones under the feet of wolves.

Why don't we all go, the children shrieked.

Wait a minute, Jake said, we don't have enough supplies for the trip. It lies somewhere far to the south.

That's no task, supplies, one of the children said.

After huddling together they all started into the town, leaving the troupe behind. Finally having had a loot-in on the Hat and Boot store, the Feed store and the Bank they returned with enough supplies to make the long journey.

I guess I can't argue against that, Jake said turning to Loop, Zozo and the Juggler. Welcome to my expedition into the unknown.

The children reveled and danced around.

When they finished storing provisions into the wagons the entire party went to sleep. The next morning there would be much work to do. The troupe bedded down in their wagons and the children slept beneath warm buffalo robes.

• •

Loop Garoo was dreaming of bringing down the stars with his tail when all at once he smelled smoke. He awoke to find horsemen surrounding the circle. The children began to scream and some of their clothes caught fire from torches the bandits had tossed into the area. Rapid gunfire started up and the children fell upon each other and ran about in circles as they tried to break the seizure's grip. Zozo Labrique looked out of her wagon and was shot between the eyes. She dropped to the ground next to the wagon. The pitiful moans of the children could be heard above the din of hoofbeats and gunfire as one by one they were picked off by horsemen who fired with amazing accuracy. The Juggler was firing two rifles and before catching a bullet in his throat was able to down two of the horsemen.

Loop crawled to the place where Zozo lay dying. Blood trickled from her nose and mouth.

Zozo let me see if I can get you inside your wagon.

Flee boy, save yourself, I'm done for, the woman murmured pressing something into his hand. It's a mad dog's tooth it'll bring you connaissance and don't forget the gris gris, the mojo, the wangols old Zozo taught you and when you need more power play poker with the dead.

But Zozo I'll try to get you a horse, Loop began—but with a start the woman slumped in his arms.

The grizzly Bear had escaped from the cage and was mangling two horsemen. This allowed an opening in the circle which two children raced through, hanging from the sides of horses. Loop did likewise but so as to divert the men from the children rode in a different direction, towards the desert.

Bullet after bullet zitted above his head. When the burning scene of children and carny freaks was almost out of his sight he looked back. His friends the Juggler, a dancing bear, the fast talking Barker and Zozo Labrique were trapped in a deadly circle. Their figurines were beginning to melt.

1969

WILLIAM GASS
b. 1924

Born in Fargo, North Dakota, William Gass was educated at Kenyon College and Cornell University, where he received his Ph.D. in philosophy. His four books of fiction include the novels *Omensetter's Luck* (1966) and *The Tunnel* (1995), the novella *Willie Master's Lonesome Wife* (1971), and the short-story collection *In the Heart of the Heart of the Country* (1968, revised edition published 1981). He has also written four books of nonfiction, including *Fiction and the Figures of Life* (1970) and *The Habitations of the Word: Essays* (1984). He has received a National Medal of

Merit for fiction and a National Book Critics Circle Award for criticism. Currently he is David May Distinguished University Professor in the Humanities and director of the International Writers Center at Washington University in St. Louis.

Trained as a philosopher, Gass told the *Southwest Review* (1985) that he is "not interested in trying to write according to some doctrine. When I'm writing fiction, it's very intuitive, so that what happens, or what I do, or how it gets organized, is pretty much a process of discovery, not a process of using some doctrine that you can somehow fit everything into." In a 1978 interview in *Chicago Review*, he said, "What you want to do is create a work that can be read nonreferentially. There is nothing esoteric or mysterious about this. It simply means that you want the work to be self-contained. A reader can do with a work what he or she wants. You can't force interpretations and you can't prevent them."

In the Heart of the Heart of the Country

A Place

So I have sailed the seas and come . . .

to B . . .

a small town fastened to a field in Indiana. Twice there have been twelve hundred people here to answer to the census. The town is outstandingly neat and shady, and always puts its best side to the highway. On one lawn there's even a wood or plastic iron deer.

You can reach us by crossing a creek. In the spring the lawns are green, the forsythia is singing, and even the railroad that guts the town has straight bright rails which hum when the train is coming, and the train itself has a welcome horning sound.

Down the back streets the asphalt crumbles into gravel. There's Westbrook's, with the geraniums, Horsefall's, Mott's. The sidewalk shatters. Gravel dust rises like breath behind the wagons. And I am in retirement from love.

Weather

In the Midwest, around the lower Lakes, the sky in the winter is heavy and close, and it is a rare day, a day to remark on, when the sky lifts and allows the heart up. I am keeping count, and as I write this page, it is eleven days since I have seen the sun.

My House

There's a row of headless maples behind my house, cut to free the passage of electric wires. High stumps, ten feet tall, remain, and I climb these like a boy to watch the country sail away from me. They are ordinary fields, a little more uneven than they should be, since in the spring they puddle. The topsoil's thin, but only moderately stony. Corn is grown one year, soybeans another. At dusk starlings darken the single tree—a larch—which stands in the middle. When the sky moves, fields move under it. I feel, on my perch, that I've lost my years. It's as though I were living at last in my eyes, as I have always dreamed of doing, and I think then I know why I've come here: to see, and so to go out against new things—oh god how easily—like air in a breeze. It's true there are moments—foolish moments, ecstasy on a tree stump—when I'm all but gone, scattered I like to think like seed, for I'm the sort now in the fool's position of having love left over which I'd like to lose; what good is it now to me, candy ungiven after Halloween?

A Person

There are vacant lots on either side of Billy Holsclaw's house. As the weather improves, they fill with hollyhocks. From spring through fall, Billy collects coal and wood and puts the lumps and pieces in piles near his door, for keeping warm is his one work. I see him most often on mild days sitting on his doorsill in the sun. I notice he's squinting a little, which is perhaps the reason he doesn't cackle as I pass. His house is the size of a single garage, and very old. It shed its paint with its youth, and its boards are a warped and weathered gray. So is Billy. He wears a short lumpy faded black coat when it's cold, otherwise he always goes about in the same loose, grease-spotted shirt and trousers. I suspect his galluses were yellow once, when they were new.

Wires

These wires offend me. Three trees were maimed on their account, and now these wires deface the sky. They cross like a fence in front of me, enclosing the crows with the clouds. I can't reach in, but like a stick, I throw my feelings over. What is it that offends me? I am on my stump, I've built a platform there and the wires prevent my going out. The cut trees, the black wires, all the beyond birds therefore anger me. When I've wormed through a fence to reach a meadow, do I ever feel the same about the field?

The Church

The church has a steeple like the hat of a witch, and five birds, all doves, perch in its gutters.

My House

Leaves move in the windows. I cannot tell you yet how beautiful it is, what it means. But they do move. They move in the glass.

Politics

. . . for all those not in love.

I've heard Batista described as a Mason. A farmer who'd seen him in Miami made this claim. He's as nice a fellow as you'd ever want to meet. Of Castro, of course, no one speaks.

For all those not in love there's law: to rule . . . to regulate . . . to rectify. I cannot write the poetry of such proposals, the poetry of politics, though sometimes—often—always now—I am in that uneasy peace of equal powers which makes a State; then I communicate by passing papers, proclamations, orders, through my bowels. Yet I was not a State with you, nor were we both together any Indiana. A squad of Pershing Rifles at the moment, I make myself Right Face! Legislation packs the screw of my intestines. Well, king of the classroom's king of the hill. You used to waddle when you walked because my sperm between your legs was draining to a towel. Teacher, poet, folded lover—like the politician, like those drunkards, ill, or those who faucet-off while pissing heartily to preach upon the force and fullness of that stream, or pause from vomiting to praise the purity and passion of their puke—I chant, I beg, I orate, I command, I sing—

Come back to Indiana—not too late!
(Or will you be a ranger to the end?)
Good-bye . . . Good-bye . . . oh, I shall always wait
You, Larry, traveler—
stranger,
son,
—my friend—

my little girl, my poem by heart, my self, my childhood.

But I've heard Batista described as a Mason. That dries up my pity, melts my hate. Back from the garage where I have overheard it, I slap the mended fender of my car to laugh, and listen to the metal stinging tartly in my hand.

People

Their hair in curlers and their heads wrapped in loud scarves, young mothers, fattish in trousers, lounge about in the speedwash, smoking cigarettes, eating candy, drinking pop, thumbing magazines, and screaming at their children above the whir and rumble of the machines.

At the bank a young man freshly pressed is letting himself in with a key. Along the street, delicately teetering, many grandfathers move in a dream. During the murderous heat of summer, they perch on window ledges, their feet dangling just inside the narrow shelf of shade the store has made, staring steadily into the street. Where their consciousness has gone I can't say. It's not in the eyes. Perhaps it's diffuse, all temperature and skin, like an infant's, though more mild. Near the corner there are several large overalled men employed in standing. A truck turns to be weighed on the scales at the Feed and Grain. Images drift on the drugstore window. The wind has blown the smell of cattle into town. Our eyes have been driven in like the eyes of the old men. And there's no one to have mercy on us.

Vital Data

There are two restaurants here and a tearoom. two bars. one bank, three barbers, one with a green shade with which he blinds his window. two groceries. a dealer in Fords. one drug, one hardware, and one appliance store. several that sell feed, grain, and farm equipment. an antique shop. a poolroom. a laundromat. three doctors. a dentist. a plumber. a vet. a funeral home in elegant repair the color of a buttercup. numerous beauty parlors which open and shut like night-blooming plants. a tiny dime and department store of no width but several floors. a hutch, homemade, where you can order, after lying down or squirming in, furniture that's been fashioned from bent lengths of stainless tubing, glowing plastic, metallic thread, and clear shellac. an American Legion Post and a root beer stand. little agencies for this and that: cosmetics, brushes, insurance, greeting cards and garden produce—anything—sample shoes—which do their business out of hats and satchels, over coffee cups and dissolving sugar. a factory for making paper sacks and pasteboard boxes that's lodged in an old brick building bearing the legend OPERA HOUSE, still faintly golden, on its roof. a library given by Carnegie. a post office. a school. a railroad station. fire station. lumberyard. telephone company. welding shop. garage . . . and spotted through the town from one end to the other in a line along the highway, gas stations to the number five.

Education

In 1833, Colin Goodykoontz, an itinerant preacher with a name from a fairytale, summed up the situation in one Indiana town this way:

> Ignorance and her squalid brood. A universal dearth of intellect. Total abstinence from literature is very generally practiced. . . . There is not a scholar in grammar or geography, or a *teacher capable of instructing* in them, to my knowledge. . . . Others are supplied a few months of the year with the most antiquated & unreasonable forms of teaching reading, writing & cyphering. . . . Need I stop to remind you of the host of loathsome reptiles such a stagnant pool is fitted to breed! Croaking jealousy; bloated bigotry; coiling suspicion; wormish blindness; crocodile malice!

Things have changed since then, but in none of the respects mentioned.

Business

One side section of street is blocked off with sawhorses. Hard, thin, bitter men in blue jeans, cowboy boots and hats, untruck a dinky carnival. The merchants are promoting themselves. There will be free rides, raucous music, parades and coneys, pop, popcorn, candy, cones, awards and drawings, with all you can endure of pinch, push, bawl, shove, shout, scream, shriek, and bellow. Children pedal past on decorated bicycles, their wheels a blur of color, streaming crinkled paper and excited dogs. A little later there's a pet show for a prize—dogs, cats, birds, sheep, ponies, goats—none of which wins. The whirlabouts whirl about. The Ferris wheel climbs dizzily into the sky as far as a tall man on tiptoe might be persuaded to reach, and the irritated operators measure the height and weight of every child with sour eyes to see if they are safe for the machines. An electrical megaphone repeatedly trumpets the names of the generous sponsors. The following day they do not allow the refuse to remain long in the street.

My House, This Place and Body

I have met with some mischance, wings withering, as Plato says obscurely, and across the breadth of Ohio, like heaven on a table, I've fallen as far as the poet, to the sixth sort of body, this house in B, in Indiana, with its blue and gray bewitching windows, holy magical insides. Great thick evergreens protect its entry. And I live *in.*

Lost in the corn rows, I remember feeling just another stalk, and thus this country takes me over in the way I occupy myself when I am well . . . completely—to the edge of both my house and body. No one notices, when they walk by, that I am brimming in the doorways. My house, this place and body, I've come in mourning to be born in. To anybody else it's pretty silly: love. Why should I feel a loss? How am I bereft? She was never mine; she was a fiction, always a golden tomgirl, barefoot, with an adolescent's slouch and a boy's taste for sports and fishing, a figure out of Twain, or worse, in Riley. Age cannot be kind.

There's little hand-in-hand here . . . not in B. No one touches except in rage. Occasionally girls will twine their arms about each other and lurch along, school out, toward home and play. I dreamed my lips would drift down your back like a skiff on a river. I'd follow a vein with the point of my finger, hold your bare feet in my naked hands.

The Same Person

Billy Holsclaw lives alone—how alone it is impossible to fathom. In the post office he talks greedily to me about the weather. His head bobs on a wild flood of words, and I take this violence to be a measure of his eagerness for speech. He badly needs a shave, coal dust has layered his face, he spits when he speaks, and his fingers pick at his tatters. He wobbles out in the wind when I leave him, a paper sack mashed in the fold of his arm, the leaves blowing past him, and our encounter drives me sadly home to poetry—where there's no answer. Billy closes his door and carries coal or wood to his fire and closes his eyes, and there's simply no way of knowing how lonely and empty he is or whether he's as vacant and barren and loveless as the rest of us are—here in the heart of the country.

Weather

For we're always out of luck here. That's just how it is—for instance in the winter. The sides of the buildings, the roofs, the limbs of the trees are gray. Streets, sidewalks, faces, feelings—they are gray. Speech is gray, and the grass where it shows. Every flank and front, each top is gray. Everything is gray: hair, eyes, window glass, the hawkers' bills and touters' posters, lips, teeth, poles and metal signs—they're gray, quite gray. Cars are gray. Boots, shoes, suits, hats, gloves are gray. Horses, sheep, and cows, cats killed in the road, squirrels in the same way, sparrows, doves, and pigeons, all are gray, everything is gray, and everyone is out of luck who lives here.

A similar haze turns the summer sky milky, and the air muffles your head and shoulders like a sweater you've got caught in. In the summer light, too, the sky darkens a moment when you open your eyes. The heat is pure distraction. Steeped in our fluids, miserable in the folds of our bodies, we can scarcely think of anything but our sticky parts. Hot cyclonic winds and storms of dust crisscross the country. In many places, given an indifferent push, the wind will still coast for miles, gathering resource and edge as it goes, cunning and force. According to the season, paper, leaves, field litter, seeds, snow, fill up the fences. Sometimes I think the land is flat because the winds have leveled it, they blow so constantly. In any case, a gale can grow in a field of corn that's as hot as a draft from hell, and to receive it is one of the most dismaying experiences of this life, though the smart of the same wind in winter is more humiliating, and in that sense even worse. But in the spring it rains as well, and the trees fill with ice.

Place

Many small Midwestern towns are nothing more than rural slums, and this community could easily become one. Principally during the first decade of the century, though there were many earlier instances, well-to-do farmers moved to town and built fine homes to contain them in their retirement. Others desired a more social life, and so lived in, driving to their fields like storekeepers to their businesses. These houses are now dying like the bereaved who inhabit them; they are slowly losing their senses—deafness, blindness, forgetfulness, mumbling, an insecure gait, an uncontrollable trembling has overcome them. Some kind of Northern Snopes will occupy them next: large-familied, Catholic, Democratic, scrambling, vigorous, poor; and since the parents will work in larger, nearby towns, the children will be loosed upon themselves and upon the hapless neighbors much as the fabulous Khan loosed his legendary horde. These Snopes will undertake makeshift repairs with materials that other people have thrown away; paint halfway round their house, then quit; almost certainly maintain an ugly loud cantankerous dog and underfeed a pair of cats to keep the rodents down. They will collect piles of possibly useful junk in the back yard, park their cars in the front, live largely leaning over engines, give not a hoot for the land, the old community, the hallowed ways, the established clans. Weakening widow ladies have already begun to hire large rude youths from families such as these to rake and mow and tidy the grounds they will inherit.

People

In the cinders at the station boys sit smoking steadily in darkened cars, their arms bent out the windows, white shirts glowing behind the glass. Nine o'clock is the best time. They sit in a line facing the highway—two or three or four of them—idling their engines. As you walk by a machine may growl at you or a pair of headlights flare up briefly. In a moment one will pull out, spinning cinders behind it, to stalk impatiently up and down the dark streets or roar half a mile into the country before returning to its place in line and pulling up.

My House, My Cat, My Company

I must organize myself. I must, as they say, pull myself together, dump this cat from my lap, stir—yes, resolve, move, do. But do what? My will is like the rosy dustlike light in this room: soft, diffuse, and gently comforting. It lets me do . . . anything . . . nothing. My ears hear what they happen to; I eat what's put before me; my eyes see what blunders into them; my thoughts are not thoughts, they are dreams. I'm empty or I'm full . . . depending; and I cannot choose. I sink my claws in Tick's fur and scratch the bones of his back until his rear rises amorously. Mr. Tick, I murmur, I must organize myself. I must pull myself together. And Mr. Tick rolls over on his belly, all ooze.

I spill Mr. Tick when I've rubbed his stomach. Shoo. He steps away slowly, his long tail rhyming with his paws. How beautifully he moves, I think; how beautifully, like you, he commands his loving, how beautifully he accepts. So I rise and wander from room to room, up and down, gazing through most of my forty-one windows. How well this house receives its loving too. Let out like Mr. Tick, my eyes sink in the shrubbery. I am not here; I've passed the glass, passed second-story spaces, flown by branches, brilliant berries, to the ground, grass high in seed and leafage every season; and it is the same as when I passed above you in my aged, ardent body; it's, in short, a kind of love; and I am learning to restore myself, my house, my body, by paying court to gardens, cats, and running water, and with neighbors keeping company.

Mrs. Desmond is my right-hand friend; she's eighty-five. A thin white mist of hair, fine and tangled, manifests the climate of her mind. She is habitually suspicious, fretful, nervous. Burglars break in at noon. Children trespass. Even now they are shaking the pear tree, stealing rhubarb, denting lawn. Flies caught in the screens and numbed by frost awake in the heat to buzz and scrape the metal cloth and frighten her, though she is deaf to me, and consequently cannot hear them. Boards creak, the wind whistles across the chimney mouth, drafts cruise like fish through the hollow rooms. It is herself she hears, her own flesh failing, for only death will preserve her from those daily chores she climbs like stairs, and all that anxious waiting. Is it now, she wonders. No? Then: is it now?

We do not converse. She visits me to talk. My task to murmur. She talks about her grandsons, her daughter who lives in Delphi, her sister or her husband—both gone—obscure friends—dead—obscurer aunts and uncles—lost—ancient neighbors, members of her church or of her clubs—passed or passing on; and in this way she brings the ends of her life together with a terrifying rush: she is a girl, a wife, a mother, widow, all at once. All at once—appalling—but I believe it; I wince in expectation of the clap. Her talk's a fence—a shade drawn, window fastened, door that's locked—for no one dies taking tea in a kitchen; and as her years compress and begin to jumble, I really believe in the brevity of life; I sweat in my wonder; death is the dog down the street, the angry gander, bedroom spider, goblin who's come to get her; and it occurs to me that in my listening posture I'm the boy who suffered the winds of my grandfather with an exactly similar politeness, that I am, right now, all my ages, out in elbows, as angular as badly stacked cards. Thus was I, when I loved you, every man I could be, youth and child—far from enough—and you, so strangely ambiguous a being, met me, heart for spade, play after play, the whole run of our suits.

Mr. Tick, you do me honor. You not only lie in my lap, but you remain alive there, coiled like a fetus. Through your deep nap, I feel you hum. You are, and are not, a machine. You are alive, alive exactly, and it means nothing to you—much to me. You are a cat—you cannot understand—you are a cat so easily. Your nature is not something you must rise to. You, not I, live in: in house, in skin, in shrubbery. Yes. I think I shall hat my head with a steeple; turn church; devour people. Mr. Tick, though, has a tail he can twitch, he need not fly his Fancy. Claws, not metrical schema, poetry his paws; while smoothing . . . smoothing . . . smoothing roughly, his tongue laps its neatness. O Mr. Tick, I know you; you are an electrical penis. Go on now, shoo. Mrs. Desmond doesn't like you. She thinks you will tangle yourself in her legs and she will fall. You murder her birds, she knows, and walk upon her roof with death in your jaws. I must gather myself together for a bound. What age is it I'm at right now, I wonder. The heart, don't they always say, keeps the true time. Mrs. Desmond is knocking. Faintly, you'd think, but she pounds. She's brought me a cucumber. I believe she believes I'm a woman. Come in, Mrs. Desmond, thank you, be my company, it looks lovely, and have tea. I'll slice it, crisp, with cream, for luncheon, each slice as thin as me.

Politics

O all ye isolate and separate powers, Sing! Sing, and sing in such a way that from a distance it will seem a harmony, a Strindberg play, a friendship ring . . . so happy—happy, happy, happy—as here we go hand in handling, up and down. Our union was a singing, though we were silent in the songs we sang like single notes are silent in a symphony. In no sense sober, we barbershopped together and never heard the discords in our music or saw ourselves as dirty, cheap, or silly. Yet cats have worn out better shoes than those thrown through our love songs at us. Hush. Be patient—prudent—politic. Still, Cleveland killed you, Mr. Crane. Were you not politic enough and fond of being beaten? Like a piece of sewage, the city shat you from its stern three hundred miles from history—beyond the loving reach of sailors. Well, I'm not a poet who puts Paris to his temple in his youth to blow himself from Idaho, or—fancy that—Missouri. My god, I said, this is my country, but must my country go so far as Terre Haute or Whiting, go so far as Gary?

When the Russians first announced the launching of their satellite, many people naturally refused to believe them. Later others were outraged that they had sent a dog around the earth. I wouldn't want to take that mutt from out that metal flying thing if he's still living when he lands, our own dog catcher said; anybody knows you shut a dog up by himself to toss around the first thing he'll be setting on to do you let him out is bite somebody.

This Midwest. A dissonance of parts and people, we are a consonance of Towns. Like a man grown fat in everything but heart, we overlabor; our outlook never really urban, never rural either, we enlarge and linger at the same time, as Alice both changed and remained in her story. You are blond. I put my hand upon your belly; feel it tremble from my trembling. We always drive large cars in my section of the country. How could you be a comfort to me now?

More Vital Data

The town is exactly fifty houses, trailers, stores, and miscellaneous buildings long, but in places no streets deep. It takes on width as you drive south, always adding to the east. Most of the dwellings are fairly spacious farm houses in the customary white, with wide wraparound porches and tall narrow windows, though there are many of the grander kind—fretted, scalloped, turreted, and decorated with clapboards set at angles or on end, with stained-glass windows at the stair landings and lots of wrought iron full of fancy curls—and a few of these look like castles in their rarer brick. Old stables serve as garages now, and the lots are large to contain them and the vegetable and flower gardens which, ultimately, widows plant and weed and then entirely disappear in. The shade is ample, the grass is good, the sky a glorious fall violet; the apple trees are heavy and red, the roads are calm and empty; corn has sifted from the chains of tractored wagons to speckle the streets with gold and with the russet fragments of the cob, and a man would be a fool who wanted, blessed with this, to live anywhere else in the world.

Education

Buses like great orange animals move through the early light to school. There the children will be taught to read and warned against Communism. By Miss Janet Jakes. That's not her name. Her name is Helen something—Scott or James. A teacher twenty years. She's now worn fine and smooth, and has a face, Wilfred says, like a mail-order ax. Her voice is hoarse, and she has a cough. For she screams abuse. The children stare, their faces blank. This is the thirteenth week. They are used to it. You will all, she shouts, you will all draw pictures of me. No. She is a Mrs.—someone's missus. And in silence they set to work while Miss Jakes jabs hairpins in her hair. Wilfred says an ax, but she has those rimless tinted glasses, graying hair, an almost dimpled chin. I must concentrate. I must stop making up things. I must give myself to life; let it mold me: that's what they say in *Wisdom's Monthly Digest* every day. Enough, enough—you've been at it long enough; and the children rise formally a row at a time to present their work to her desk. No, she wears rims; it's her chin that's dimple-less. Well, it will take more than a tablespoon of features to sweeten that face. So she grimly shuffles their sheets, examines her reflection crayoned on them. I would not dare . . . allow a child . . . to put a line around me. Though now and then she smiles like a nick in the blade, in the end these drawings depress her. I could not bear it—how can she ask?—that anyone . . . draw me. Her anger's lit. That's why she does it: flame. There go her eyes; the pink in her glasses brightens, dims. She is a pumpkin, and her rage is breathing like the candle in. No, she shouts, no—the cartoon trembling—no, John Mauck, John Stewart Mauck, this will not do. The picture flutters from her fingers. You've made me too muscular.

I work on my poetry. I remember my friends, associates, my students, by their names. Their names are Maypop, Dormouse, Upsydaisy. Their names are Gladiolus, Callow Bladder, Prince and Princess Oleo, Hieronymus, Cardinal Mummum, Mr. Fitchew, The Silken Howdah, Spot. Sometimes you're Tom Sawyer, Huckleberry Finn; it is perpetually summer; your buttocks are my pillow; we are adrift on a raft; your back is our river. Sometimes you are Major Barbara, sometimes a goddess who kills men in battle, sometimes you are soft like a shower of water; you are bread in my mouth.

I do not work on my poetry. I forget my friends, associates, my students, and their names: Gramophone, Blowgun, Pickle, Serenade . . . Marge the Barge, Arena, Uberhaupt . . . Doctor Dildoe, The Fog Machine. For I am now in B, in Indiana: out of job and out of patience, out of love and time and money, out of bread and out of body, in a temper, Mrs. Desmond, out of tea. So shut your fist up, bitch, you bag of death; go bang another door; go die, my dearie. Die, life-deaf old lady. Spill your breath. Fall over like a frozen board. Gray hair grows from the nose of your mind. You are a skull already—*memento mori*—the foreskin retracts from your teeth. Will your plastic gums last longer than your bones, and color their grinning? And is your twot still hazel-hairy, or are you bald as a ditch? . . . bitch . . . . . . bitch . . . . bitch. I wanted to be famous, but you bring me age—my emptiness. Was it *that* which I thought would balloon me above the rest? Love? where are you? . . . love me. I want to rise so high, I said, that when I shit I won't miss anybody.

Business

For most people, business is poor. Nearby cities have siphoned off all but a neighborhood trade. Except for feed and grain and farm supplies, you stand a chance to sell only what one runs out to buy. Chevrolet has quit, and Frigidaire. A locker plant has left its afterimage. The lumberyard has been, so far, six months about its going. Gas stations change hands clumsily, a restaurant becomes available, a grocery closes. One day they came and knocked the cornices from the watch repair and pasted campaign posters on the windows. Torn across, by now, by boys, they urge you still to vote for half an orange beblazoned man who as a whole one failed two years ago to win at his election. Everywhere, in this manner, the past speaks, and it mostly speaks of failure. The empty stores, the old signs and dusty fixtures, the debris in alleys, the flaking paint and rusty gutters, the heavy locks and sagging boards: they say the same disagreeable things. What do the sightless windows see, I wonder, when the sun throws a passerby against them? Here a stair unfolds toward the street—dark, rickety, and treacherous—and I always feel, as I pass it, that if I just went carefully up and turned the corner at the landing, I would find myself out of the world. But I've never had the courage.

That Same Person

The weeds catch up with Billy. In pursuit of the hollyhocks, they rise in coarse clumps all around the front of his house. Billy has to stamp down a circle by his door like a dog or cat does turning round to nest up, they're so thick. What particularly troubles me is that winter will find the weeds still standing stiff and tindery to take the sparks which Billy's little mortarless chimney spouts. It's true that fires are fun here. The town whistle, which otherwise only blows for noon (and there's no noon on Sunday), signals the direction of the fire by the length and number of its blasts, the volunteer firemen rush past in their cars and trucks, houses empty their owners along the street every time like an illustration in a children's book. There are many bikes, too, and barking dogs, and sometimes—halleluiah—the fire's right here in town—a vacant lot of weeds and stubble flaming up. But I'd rather it weren't Billy or Billy's lot or house. Quite selfishly I want him to remain the way he is—counting his sticks and logs, sitting on his sill in the soft early sun—though I'm not sure what his presence means to me . . . or to anyone. Nevertheless, I keep wondering whether, given time, I might not someday find a figure in our language which would serve him faithfully, and furnish his poverty and loneliness richly out.

Wires

Where sparrows sit like fists. Doves fly the steeple. In mist the wires change perspective, rise and twist. If they led to you, I would know what they were. Thoughts passing often, like the starlings who flock these fields at evening to sleep in the trees beyond, would form a family of paths like this; they'd foot down the natural height of air to just about a bird's perch. But they do not lead to you.

Of whose beauty it was sung
She shall make the old man young.

They fasten me.

If I walked straight on, in my present mood, I would reach the Wabash. It's not a mood in which I'd choose to conjure you. Similes dangle like baubles from me. This time of year the river is slow and shallow, the clay banks crack in the sun, weeds surprise the sandbars. The air is moist and I am sweating. It's impossible to rhyme in this dust. Everything—sky, the cornfield, stump, wild daisies, my old clothes and pressless feelings—seem fabricated for installment purchase. Yes. Christ. I am suffering a summer Christmas; and I cannot walk under the wires. The sparrows scatter like handfuls of gravel. Really, wires are voices in thin strips. They are words wound in cables. Bars of connection.

Weather

I would rather it were the weather that was to blame for what I am and what my friends and neighbors are—we who live here in the heart of the country. Better the weather, the wind, the pale dying snow . . . the snow—why not the snow? There's never much really, not around the lower Lakes anyway, not enough to boast about, not enough to be useful. My father tells how the snow in the Dakotas would sweep to the roofs of the barns in the old days, and he and his friends could sled on the crust that would form because the snow was so fiercely driven. In Bemidji trees have been known to explode. That would be something—if the trees in Davenport or Francisville or Carbondale or Niles were to go blam some winter—blam! blam! blam! all the way down the gray, cindery, snow-sick streets.

A cold fall rain is blackening the trees or the air is like lilac and full of parachuting seeds. Who cares to live in any season but his own? Still I suspect the secret's in this snow, the secret of our sickness, if we could only diagnose it, for we are all dying like the elms in Urbana. This snow—like our skin it covers the country. Later dust will do it. Right now—snow. Mud presently. But it is snow without any laughter in it, a pale gray pudding thinly spread on stiff toast, and if that seems a strange description, it's accurate all the same. Of course soot blackens everything, but apart from that, we are never sufficiently cold here. The flakes as they come, alive and burning, we cannot retain, for if our temperatures fall, they rise promptly again, just as, in the summer, they bob about in the same feckless way. Suppose though . . . suppose they were to rise some August, climb and rise, and then hang in the hundreds like a hawk through December, what a desert we could make of ourselves—from Chicago to Cairo, from Hammond to Columbus—what beautiful Death Valleys.

Place

I would rather it were the weather. It drives us in upon ourselves—an unlucky fate. Of course there is enough to stir our wonder anywhere; there's enough to love, anywhere, if one is strong enough, if one is diligent enough, if one is perceptive, patient, kind enough—whatever it takes; and surely it's better to live in the country, to live on a prairie by a drawing of rivers, in Iowa or Illinois or Indiana, say, than in any city, in any stinking fog of human beings, in any blooming orchard of machines. It ought to be. The cities are swollen and poisonous with people. It ought to be better. Man has never been a fit environment for man—for rats, maybe, rats do nicely, or for dogs or cats and the household beetle.

And how long the street is, nowadays. These endless walls are fallen to keep back the tides of earth. Brick could be beautiful but we have covered it gradually with gray industrial vomits. Age does not make concrete genial, and asphalt is always—like America—twenty-one, until it breaks up in crumbs like stale cake. The brick, the asphalt, the concrete, the dancing signs and garish posters, the feed and excrement of the automobile, the litter of its inhabitants: they compose, they decorate, they line our streets, and there is nowhere, nowadays, our streets can't reach.

A man in the city has no natural thing by which to measure himself. His parks are potted plants. Nothing can live and remain free where he resides but the pigeon, starling, sparrow, spider, cockroach, mouse, moth, fly and weed, and he laments the existence of even these and makes his plans to poison them. The zoo? There *is* the zoo. Through its bars the city man stares at the great cats and dully sucks his ice. Living, alas, among men and their marvels, the city man supposes that his happiness depends on establishing, somehow, a special kind of harmonious accord with others. The novelists of the city, of slums and crowds, they call it love—and break their pens.

Wordsworth feared the accumulation of men in cities. He foresaw their "degrading thirst after outrageous stimulation," and some of their hunger for love. Living in a city, among so many, dwelling in the heat and tumult of incessant movement, a man's affairs are touch and go—that's all. It's not surprising that the novelists of the slums, the cities, and the crowds, should find that sex is but a scratch to ease a tickle, that we're most human when we're sitting on the john, and that the justest image of our life is in full passage through the plumbing.

> That man, immur'd in cities, still retains
> His inborn inextinguishable thirst
> Of rural scenes, compensating his loss
> By supplemental shifts, the best he may.

Come into the country, then. The air nimbly and sweetly recommends itself unto our gentle senses. Here, growling tractors tear the earth. Dust roils up behind them. Drivers sit jouncing under bright umbrellas. They wear refrigerated hats and steer by looking at the tracks they've cut behind them, their transistors blaring. Close to the land, are they? good companions to the soil? Tell me: do they live in harmony with the alternating seasons?

It's a lie of old poetry. The modern husbandman uses chemicals from cylinders and sacks, spike-ball-and-claw machines, metal sheds, and cost accounting. Nature in the old sense does not matter. It does not exist. Our farmer's only mystical attachment is to parity. And if he does not realize that cows and corn are simply different kinds of chemical engine, he cannot expect to make a go of it.

It isn't necessary to suppose our cows have feelings; our neighbor hasn't as many as he used to have either; but think of it this way a moment, you can correct for the human imputations later: how would it feel to nurse those strange tentacled calves with their rubber, glass, and metal lips, their stainless eyes?

People

Aunt Pet's still able to drive her car—a high square Ford—even though she walks with difficulty and a stout stick. She has a watery gaze, a smooth plump face despite her age, and jet black hair in a bun. She has the slowest smile of anyone I ever saw, but she hates dogs, and not very long ago cracked the back of one she cornered in her garden. To prove her vigor she will tell you this, her smile breaking gently while she raises the knob of her stick to the level of your eyes.

House, My Breath and Window

My window is a grave, and all that lies within it's dead. No snow is falling. There's no haze. It is not still, not silent. Its images are not an animal that waits, for movement is no demonstration. I have seen the sea slack, life bubble through a body without a trace, its spheres impervious as soda's. Downwound, the whore at wagtag clicks and clacks. Leaves wiggle. Grass sways. A bird chirps, pecks the ground. An auto wheel in penning circles keeps its rigid spokes. These images are stones; they are memorials. Beneath this sea lies sea: god rest it . . . rest the world beyond my window, me in front of my reflection, above this page, my shade. Death is not so still, so silent, since silence implies a falling quiet, stillness a stopping, containing, holding in; for death is time in a clock, like Mr. Tick, electric . . . like wind through a windup poet. And my blear floats out to visible against the glass, befog its country and bespill myself. The mist lifts slowly from the fields in the morning. No one now would say: the Earth throws back its covers; it is rising from sleep. Why is the feeling foolish? The image is too Greek. I used to gaze at you so wantonly your body blushed. Imagine: wonder: that my eyes could cause such flowering. Ah, my friend, your face is pale, the weather cloudy; a street has been felled through your chin, bare trees do nothing, houses take root in their rectangles, a steeple stands up in your head. You speak of loving; then give me a kiss. The pane is cold. On icy mornings the fog rises to greet me (as you always did); the barns and other buildings, rather than ghostly, seem all the more substantial for looming, as if they grew in themselves while I watched (as you always did). Oh my approach, I suppose, was like breath in a rubber monkey. Nevertheless, on the road along the Wabash in the morning, though the trees are sometimes obscured by fog, their reflection floats serenely on the river, reasoning the banks, the sycamores in French rows. Magically, the world tips. I'm led to think that only those who grow down live (which will scarcely win me twenty-five from *Wisdom's Monthly Digest*), but I find I write that only those who live down grow; and what I write, I hold, whatever I really know. My every word's inverted, or reversed—or I am. I held you, too, that way. You were so utterly provisional, subject to my change. I could inflate your bosom with a kiss, disperse your skin with gentleness, enter your vagina from within, and make my love emerge like a fresh sex. The pane is cold. Honesty is cold, my inside lover. The sun looks, through the mist, like a plum on the tree of heaven, or a bruise on the slope of your belly. Which? The grass crawls with frost. We meet on this window, the world and I, inelegantly, swimmers of the glass; and swung wrong way round to one another, the world seems in. The world—how grand, how monumental, grave and deadly, that word is: the world, my house and poetry. All poets have their inside lovers. Wee penis does not belong to me, or any of this foggery. It is *his* property which he's thrust through what's womanly of me to set down this. These wooden houses in their squares, gray streets and fallen sidewalks, standing trees, your name I've written sentimentally across my breath into the whitening air, pale birds: they exist in me now because of him. I gazed with what intensity . . . A bush in the excitement of its roses could not have bloomed so beautifully as you did then. It was a look I'd like to give this page. For that is poetry: to bring within about, to change.

Politics

Sports, politics, and religion are the three passions of the badly educated. They are the Midwest's open sores. Ugly to see, a source of constant discontent, they sap the body's strength. Appalling quantities of money, time, and energy are wasted on them. The rural mind is narrow, passionate, and reckless on these matters. Greed, however shortsighted and direct, will not alone account for it. I have known men, for instance, who for years have voted squarely against their interests. Nor have I ever noticed that their surly Christian views prevented them from urging forward the smithereening, say, of Russia, China, Cuba, or Korea. And they tend to back their country like they back their local team: they have a fanatical desire to win; yelling is their forte; and if things go badly, they are inclined to sack the coach. All in all, then, Birch is a good name. It stands for the bigot's stick, the wild-child-tamer's cane.

Forgetfulness—is that their object?

Oh, I was new, I thought. A fresh start: new cunt, new climate, and new country—there you were, and I was pioneer, and had no history. That language hurts me, too, my dear. You'll never hear it.

Final Vital Data

The Modern Homemakers' Demonstration Club. The Prairie Home Demonstration Club. The Night-outers' Home Demonstration Club. The IOOF, FFF, VFW, WCTU, WSCS, 4-H, 40 and 8, Psi Iota Chi, and PTA. The Boy and Girl Scouts, Rainbows, Masons, Indians and Rebekah Lodge. Also the Past Noble Grand Club of the Rebekah Lodge. As well as the Moose and the Ladies of the Moose. The Elks, the Eagles, the Jaynettes and the Eastern Star. The Women's Literary Club, the Hobby Club, the Art Club, the Sunshine Society, the Dorcas Society, the Pythian Sisters, the Pilgrim Youth Fellowship, the American Legion, the American Legion Auxiliary, the American Legion Junior Auxiliary, the Gardez Club, the Bridge for Fun Club, the What-can-you-do? Club, the Get Together Club, the Coterie Club, the Worthwhile Club, the Let's Help Our Town Club, the No Name Club, the Forget-me-not Club, the Merry-go-round Club . . .

Education

Has a quarter disappeared from Paula Frosty's pocket book? Imagine the landscape of that face: no crayon could engender it; soft wax is wrong; thin wire in trifling snips might do the trick. Paula Frosty and Christopher Roger accuse the pale and splotchy Cheryl Pipes. But Miss Jakes, I *saw* her. Miss Jakes is so extremely vexed she snaps her pencil. What else is missing? I appoint you a detective, John: search her desk. Gum, candy, paper, pencils, marble, round eraser—whose? A thief. I can't watch her all the time, I'm here to teach. Poor pale fossetted Cheryl, it's determined, can't return the money because she took it home and spent it. Cindy, Janice, John, and Pete—you four who sit around her—you will be detectives this whole term to watch her. A thief. In all my time. Miss Jakes turns, unfists, and turns again. I'll handle you, she cries. To think. A thief. In all my years. Then she writes on the blackboard the name of Cheryl Pipes and beneath that the figure twenty-five with a large sign for cents. Now Cheryl, she says, this won't be taken off until you bring that money out of home, out of home straight up to here, Miss Jakes says, tapping her desk.

Which is three days.

Another Person

I was raking leaves when Uncle Halley introduced himself to me. He said his name came from the comet, and that his mother had borne him prematurely in her fright of it. I thought of Hobbes, whom fear of the Spanish Armada had hurried into birth, and so I believed Uncle Halley to honor the philosopher, though Uncle Halley is a liar, and neither the one hundred twenty-nine nor the fifty-three he ought to be. That fall the leaves had burned themselves out on the trees, the leaf lobes had curled, and now they flocked noisily down the street and were broken in the wires of my rake. Uncle Halley was himself (like Mrs. Desmond and history generally) both deaf and implacable, and he shooed me down his basement stairs to a room set aside there for stacks of newspapers reaching to the ceiling, boxes of leaflets and letters and programs, racks of photo albums, scrapbooks, bundles of rolled-up posters and maps, flags and pennants and slanting piles of dusty magazines devoted mostly to motoring and the Christian ethic. I saw a bird cage, a tray of butterflies, a bugle, a stiff straw boater, and all kinds of tassels tied to a coat tree. He still possessed and had on display the steering lever from his first car, a linen duster, driving gloves and goggles, photographs along the wall of himself, his friends, and his various machines, a shell from the first war, a record of "Ramona" nailed through its hole to a post, walking sticks and fanciful umbrellas, shoes of all sorts (his baby shoes, their counters broken, were held in sorrow beneath my nose—they had not been bronzed, but he might have them done someday before he died, he said), countless boxes of medals, pins, beads, trinkets, toys, and keys (I scarcely saw—they flowed like jewels from his palms), pictures of downtown when it was only a path by the railroad station, a brightly colored globe of the world with a dent in Poland, antique guns, belt buckles, buttons, souvenir plates and cups and saucers (I can't remember all of it—I won't), but I recall how shamefully, how rudely, how abruptly, I fled, a good story in my mouth but death in my nostrils; and how afterward I busily, righteously, burned my leaves as if I were purging the world of its years. I still wonder if this town—its life, and mine now—isn't really a record like the one of "Ramona" that I used to crank around on my grandmother's mahogany Victrola through lonely rainy days as a kid.

The First Person

Billy's like the coal he's found: spilled, mislaid, discarded. The sky's no comfort. His house and his body are dying together. His windows are boarded. And now he's reduced to his hands. I suspect he has glaucoma. At any rate he can scarcely see, and weeds his yard of rubble on his hands and knees. Perhaps he's a surgeon cleansing a wound or an ardent and tactile lover. I watch, I must say, apprehensively. Like mine-war detectors, his hands graze in circles ahead of him. Your nipples were the color of your eyes. Pebble. Snarl of paper. Length of twine. He leans down closely, picks up something silvery, holds it near his nose. Foil? cap? coin? He has within him—what, I wonder? Does he know more now because he fingers everything and has to sniff to see? It would be romantic cruelty to think so. He bends the down on your arms like a breeze. You wrote me: something is strange when we don't understand. I write in return: I think when I loved you I fell to my death.

Billy, I could read to you from Beddoes; he's your man perhaps; he held with dying, freed his blood of its arteries; and he said that there were many wretched love-ill fools like me lying alongside the last bone of their former selves, as full of spirit and speech, nonetheless, as Mrs. Desmond, Uncle Halley and the Ferris wheel, Aunt Pet, Miss Jakes, Ramona or the megaphone; yet I reverse him finally, Billy, on no evidence but braggadocio, and I declare that though my inner organs were devoured long ago, the worm which swallowed down my parts still throbs and glows like a crystal palace.

Yes, you were younger. I was Uncle Halley, the museum man and infrequent meteor. Here is my first piece of ass. They weren't so flat in those days, had more round, more juice. And over here's the sperm I've spilled, nicely jarred and clearly labeled. Look at this tape like lengths of intestine where I've stored my spew, the endless worm of words I've written, a hundred million emissions or more: oh I was quite a man right from the start; even when unconscious in my cradle, from crotch to cranium, I was erectile tissue; though mostly, after the manner approved by Plato, I had intercourse by eye. Never mind, old Holsclaw, you are blind. We pull down darkness when we go to bed; put out like Oedipus the actually offending organ, and train our touch to lies. All cats are gray, says Mr. Tick; so under cover of glaucoma you are sack gray too, and cannot be distinguished from a stallion.

I must pull myself together, get a grip, just as they say, but I feel spilled, bewildered, quite mislaid. I did not restore my house to its youth, but to its age. Hunting, you hitch through the hollyhocks. I'm inclined to say you aren't half the cripple I am, for there is nothing left of me but mouth. However, I resist the impulse. It is another lie of poetry. My organs are all there, though it's there where I fail—at the roots of my experience. Poet of the spiritual, Rilke, weren't you? yet that's what you said. Poetry, like love, is—in and out—a physical caress. I can't tolerate any more of my sophistries about spirit, mind, and breath. Body equals being, and if your weight goes down, you are the less.

Household Apples

I knew nothing about apples. Why should I? My country came in my childhood, and I dreamed of sitting among the blooms like the bees. I failed to spray the pear tree too. I doubled up under them at first, admiring the sturdy low branches I should have pruned, and later I acclaimed the blossoms. Shortly after the fruit formed there were falls—not many—apples the size of goodish stones which made me wobble on my ankles when I walked about the yard. Sometimes a piece crushed by a heel would cling on the shoe to track the house. I gathered a few and heaved them over the wires. A slingshot would have been splendid. Hard, an unattractive green, the worms had them. Before long I realized the worms had them all. Even as the apples reddened, lit their tree, they were being swallowed. The birds preferred the pears, which were small—sugar pears I think they're called—with thick skins of graying green that ripen on toward violet. So the fruit fell, and once I made some applesauce by quartering and paring hundreds; but mostly I did nothing, left them, until suddenly, overnight it seemed, in that ugly late September heat we often have in Indiana, my problem was upon me.

My childhood came in the country. I remember, now, the flies on our snowy luncheon table. As we cleared away they would settle, fastidiously scrub themselves and stroll to the crumbs to feed where I would kill them in crowds with a swatter. It was quite a game to catch them taking off. I struck heavily since I didn't mind a few stains; they'd wash. The swatter was a square of screen bound down in red cloth. It drove no air ahead of it to give them warning. They might have thought they'd flown headlong into a summered window. The faint pink dot where they had died did not rub out as I'd supposed, and after years of use our luncheon linen would faintly, pinkly, speckle.

The country became my childhood. Flies braided themselves on the fly-paper in my grandmother's house. I can smell the bakery and the grocery and the stables and the dairy in that small Dakota town I knew as a kid; knew as I dreamed I'd know your body, as I've known nothing, before or since; knew as the flies knew, in the honest, unchaste sense: the burned house, hose-wet, which drew a mist of insects like the blue smoke of its smolder, and gangs of boys, moist-lipped, destructive as its burning. Flies have always impressed me; they are so persistently alive. Now they were coating the ground beneath my trees. Some were ordinary flies; there were the large blue-green ones; there were swarms of fruit flies too, and the red-spotted scavenger beetle; there were a few wasps, several sorts of bees and butterflies—checkers, sulphurs, monarchs, commas, question marks—and delicate dragonflies . . . but principally houseflies and horseflies and bottleflies, flies and more flies in clusters around the rotting fruit. They loved the pears. Inside, they fed. If you picked up a pear, they flew, and the pear became skin and stem. They were everywhere the fruit was: in the tree still—apples like a hive for them—or where the fruit littered the ground, squashing itself as you stepped . . . there was no help for it. The flies droned, feasting on the sweet juice. No one could go near the trees; I could not climb; so I determined at last to labor like Hercules. There were fruit baskets in the barn. Collecting them and kneeling under the branches, I began to gather remains. Deep in the strong rich smell of the fruit, I began to hum myself. The fruit caved in at the touch. Glistening red apples, my lifting disclosed, had families of beetles, flies, and bugs, devouring their rotten undersides. There were streams of flies; there were lakes and cataracts and rivers of flies, seas and oceans. The hum was heavier, higher, than the hum of the bees when they came to the blooms in the spring, though the bees were there, among the flies, ignoring me—ignoring everyone. As my work went on and juice covered my hands and arms, they would form a sleeve, black and moving, like knotty wool. No caress could have been more indifferently complete. Still I rose fearfully, ramming my head in the branches, apples bumping against me before falling, bursting with bugs. I'd snap my hand sharply but the flies would cling to the sweet. I could toss a whole cluster into a basket from several feet. As the pear or apple lit, they would explosively rise, like monads for a moment, windowless, certainly, with respect to one another, sugar their harmony. I had to admit, though, despite my distaste, that my arm had never been more alive, oftener or more gently kissed. Those hundreds of feet were light. In washing them off, I pretended the hose was a pump. What have I missed? Childhood is a lie of poetry.

The Church

Friday night. Girls in dark skirts and white blouses sit in ranks and scream in concert. They carry funnels loosely stuffed with orange and black paper which they shake wildly, and small megaphones through which, as drilled, they direct and magnify their shouting. Their leaders, barely pubescent girls, prance and shake and whirl their skirts above their bloomers. The young men, leaping, extend their arms and race through puddles of amber light, their bodies glistening. In a lull, though it rarely occurs, you can hear the squeak of tennis shoes against the floor. Then the yelling begins again, and then continues; fathers, mothers, neighbors joining in to form a single pulsing ululation—a cry of the whole community—for in this gymnasium each body becomes the bodies beside it, pressed as they are together, thigh to thigh, and the same shudder runs through all of them, and runs toward the same release. Only the ball moves serenely through this dazzling din. Obedient to law it scarcely speaks but caroms quietly and lives at peace.

Business

It is the week of Christmas and the stores, to accommodate the rush they hope for, are remaining open in the evening. You can see snow falling in the cones of the street lamps. The roads are filling—undisturbed. Strings of red and green lights droop over the principal highway, and the water tower wears a star. The windows of the stores have been bedizened. Shamelessly they beckon. But I am alone, leaning against a pole—no . . . there is no one in sight. They're all at home, perhaps by their instruments, tuning in on their evenings, and like Ramona, tirelessly playing and replaying themselves. There's a speaker perched in the tower, and through the boughs of falling snow and over the vacant streets, it drapes the twisted and metallic strains of a tune that can barely be distinguished—yes, I believe it's one of the jolly ones, it's "Joy to the World." There's no one to hear the music but myself, and though I'm listening, I'm no longer certain. Perhaps the record's playing something else.

1968, rev. 1981

KURT VONNEGUT
b. 1922

Kurt Vonnegut was born in Indianapolis, Indiana, and attended Cornell University, the Carnegie Institute of Technology, and the University of Chicago. He served in the infantry during World War II and was a prisoner of war in Dresden, Germany, he told *The Paris Review* (1977), where he witnessed the Allied assault on Dresden, which killed "135,000 people in a matter of hours." His numerous books of fiction include the novels *Player Piano* (1952), *God Bless You, Mr. Rosewater* (1965), *Slaughterhouse-Five* (1969), *Breakfast of Champions* (1973), and *Hocus Pocus* (1990), and the short-story collections *Canary in a Cathouse* (1961) and *Welcome to the Monkey House: A Collection of Short Works* (1968). He is also the author of several plays and collections of essays.

"My education was as a chemist at Cornell and then an anthropologist at the University of Chicago," Vonnegut told *The Paris Review*. "I was thirty-five before I went crazy about Blake, forty before I read *Madame Bovary*, forty-five before I'd even heard of Céline. Through dumb luck, I read *Look Homeward, Angel* exactly when I was supposed to . . . [a]t the age of eighteen."

"When I was the littlest kid at our supper table," Vonnegut recalled in *The Paris Review*, "there was only one way I could get anybody's attention, and that was to be funny. I had to specialize. I used to listen to radio comedians very intently, so I could learn how to make jokes. And that's what my books are, now that I'm a grownup—mosaics of jokes."

From Breakfast of Champions

Preface

The expression "Breakfast of Champions" is a registered trademark of General Mills, Inc., for use on a breakfast cereal product. The use of the identical expression as the title for this book is not intended to indicate an association with or sponsorship by General Mills, nor is it intended to disparage their fine products.

➡ The person to whom this book is dedicated, Phoebe Hurty, is no longer among the living, as they say. She was an Indianapolis widow when I met her late in the Great Depression. I was sixteen or so. She was about forty.

She was rich, but she had gone to work every weekday of her adult life, so she went on doing that. She wrote a sane and funny advice-to-the-lovelorn column for the Indianapolis *Times*, a good paper which is now defunct.

Defunct.

She wrote ads for the William H. Block Company, a department store which still flourishes in a building my father designed. She wrote this ad for an end-of-the-summer sale on straw hats: "For prices like this, you can run them through your horse and put them on your roses."

➡ Phoebe Hurty hired me to write copy for ads about teen-age clothes. I had to wear the clothes I praised. That was part of the job. And I became friends with her two sons, who were my age. I was over at their house all the time.

She would talk bawdily to me and her sons, and to our girlfriends when we brought them around. She was funny. She was liberating. She taught us to be impolite in conversation not only about sexual matters, but about American history and famous heroes, about the distribution of wealth, about school, about everything.

I now make my living by being impolite. I am clumsy at it. I keep trying to imitate the impoliteness which was so graceful in Phoebe Hurty. I think now that grace was easier for her than it is for me because of the mood of the Great Depression. She believed what so many Americans believed then: that the nation would be happy and just and rational when prosperity came.

I never hear that word anymore: *Prosperity.* It used to be a synonym for *Paradise.* And Phoebe Hurty was able to believe that the impoliteness she recommended would give shape to an American paradise.

Now her sort of impoliteness is fashionable. But nobody believes anymore in a new American paradise. I sure miss Phoebe Hurty.

➡ As for the suspicion I express in this book, that human beings are robots, are machines: It should be noted that people, mostly men, suffering from the last stages of syphilis, from *locomotor ataxia,* were common spectacles in downtown Indianapolis and in circus crowds when I was a boy.

Those people were infested with carnivorous little corkscrews which could be seen only with a microscope. The victims' vertebrae were welded together after the corkscrews got through with the meat between. The syphilitics seemed tremendously dignified—erect, eyes straight ahead.

I saw one stand on a curb at the corner of Meridian and Washington Streets one time, underneath an overhanging clock which my father designed. The intersection was known locally as *"The Crossroads of America."*

This syphilitic man was thinking hard there, at the Crossroads of America, about how to get his legs to step off the curb and carry him across Washington Street. He shuddered gently, as though he had a small motor which was idling inside. Here was his problem: his brains, where the instructions to his legs originated, were being eaten alive by corkscrews. The wires which had to carry the instructions weren't insulated anymore, or were eaten clear through. Switches along the way were welded open or shut.

This man looked like an old, old man, although he might have been only thirty years old. He thought and thought. And then he kicked two times like a chorus girl.

He certainly looked like a machine to me when I was a boy.

➡ I tend to think of human beings as huge, rubbery test tubes, too, with chemical reactions seething inside. When I was a boy, I saw a lot of people with goiters. So did Dwayne Hoover, the Pontiac dealer who is the hero of this book. Those unhappy Earthlings had such swollen thyroid glands that they seemed to have zucchini squash growing from their throats.

All they had to do in order to have ordinary lives, it turned out, was to consume less than one-millionth of an ounce of iodine every day.

My own mother wrecked her brains with chemicals, which were supposed to make her sleep.

When I get depressed, I take a little pill, and I cheer up again.

And so on.

So it is a big temptation to me, when I create a character for a novel, to say that he is what he is because of faulty wiring, or because of microscopic amounts of chemicals which he ate or failed to eat on that particular day.

➡ What do I myself think of this particular book? I feel lousy about it, but I always feel lousy about my books. My friend Knox Burger said one time that a certain cumbersome novel ". . . read as though it had been written by Philboyd Studge." That's who I think I am when I write what I am seemingly programmed to write.

➡ This book is my fiftieth birthday present to myself. I feel as though I am crossing the spine of a roof—having ascended one slope.

I am programmed at fifty to perform childishly—to insult "The Star-Spangled Banner," to scrawl pictures of a Nazi flag and an asshole and a lot of other things with a felt-tipped pen. To give an idea of the maturity of my illustrations for this book, here is my picture of an asshole:

➡ I think I am trying to clear my head of all the junk in there—the assholes, the flags, the underpants. Yes—there is a picture in this book of underpants. I'm throwing out characters from my other books, too. I'm not going to put on any more puppet shows.

I think I am trying to make my head as empty as it was when I was born onto this damaged planet fifty years ago.

I suspect that this is something most white Americans, and nonwhite Americans who imitate white Americans, should do. The things other people have put into *my* head, at any rate, do not fit together nicely, are often useless and ugly, are out of proportion with one another, are out of proportion with life as it really is outside my head.

I have no culture, no humane harmony in my brains. I can't live without a culture anymore.

➡ So this book is a sidewalk strewn with junk, trash which I throw over my shoulders as I travel in time back to November eleventh, nineteen hundred and twenty-two.

I will come to a time in my backwards trip when November eleventh, accidentally my birthday, was a sacred day called *Armistice Day*. When I was a boy, and when Dwayne Hoover was a boy, all the people of all the nations which had fought in the First World War were silent during the eleventh minute of the eleventh hour of Armistice Day, which was the eleventh day of the eleventh month.

It was during that minute in nineteen hundred and eighteen, that millions upon millions of human beings stopped butchering one another. I have talked to old men who were on battlefields during that minute. They have told me in one way or another that the sudden silence was the Voice of God.

So we still have among us some men who can remember when God spoke clearly to mankind.

Armistice Day has become Veterans' Day. Armistice Day was sacred. Veterans' Day is not.

So I will throw Veterans' Day over my shoulder. Armistice Day I will keep. I don't want to throw away any sacred things.

What else is sacred? Oh, *Romeo and Juliet,* for instance.

And all music is.

—PHILBOYD STUDGE

Chapter 1

This is a tale of a meeting of two lonesome, skinny, fairly old white men on a planet which was dying fast.

One of them was a science-fiction writer named Kilgore Trout. He was a nobody at the time, and he supposed his life was over. He was mistaken. As a consequence of the meeting, he became one of the most beloved and respected human beings in history.

The man he met was an automobile dealer, a *Pontiac* dealer named Dwayne Hoover. Dwayne Hoover was on the brink of going insane.

Listen:

Trout and Hoover were citizens of the United States of America, a country which was called *America* for short. This was their national anthem, which was pure balderdash, like so much they were expected to take seriously:

O, say can you see by the dawn's early light
What so proudly we hailed at the twilight's
last gleaming,
Whose broad stripes and bright stars,
thru the perilous fight
O'er the ramparts we watched were so
gallantly streaming?
And the rockets' red glare, the bombs
bursting in air,
Gave proof through the night that our
flag was still there.
O, say does that star-spangled banner
yet wave
O'er the land of the free and the home
of the brave?

There were one quadrillion nations in the Universe, but the nation Dwayne Hoover and Kilgore Trout belonged to was the only one with a national anthem which was gibberish sprinkled with question marks.

Here is what their flag looked like:

It was the law of their nation, a law no other nation on the planet had about its flag, which said this: *"The flag shall not be dipped to any person or thing."*

Flag-dipping was a form of friendly and respectful salute, which consisted of bringing the flag on a stick closer to the ground, then raising it up again.

➡ The motto of Dwayne Hoover's and Kilgore Trout's nation was this, which meant in a language nobody spoke anymore, *Out of Many, One: "E pluribus unum."*

The undippable flag was a beauty, and the anthem and the vacant motto might not have mattered much, if it weren't for this: a lot of citizens were so ignored and cheated and insulted that they thought they might be in the wrong country, or even on the wrong planet, that some terrible mistake had been made. It might have comforted them some if their anthem and their motto had mentioned fairness or brotherhood or hope or happiness, had somehow welcomed them to the society and its real estate.

If they studied their paper money for clues as to what their country was all about, they found, among a lot of other baroque trash, a picture of a truncated pyramid with a radiant eye on top of it, like this:

Not even the President of the United States knew what that was all about. It was as though the country were saying to its citizens, *"In nonsense is strength."*

➡ A lot of the nonsense was the innocent result of playfulness on the part of the founding fathers of the nation of Dwayne Hoover and Kilgore Trout.

The founders were aristocrats, and they wished to show off their useless education, which consisted of the study of hocus-pocus from ancient times. They were bum poets as well.

But some of the nonsense was evil, since it concealed great crimes. For example, teachers of children in the United States of America wrote this date on blackboards again and again, and asked the children to memorize it with pride and joy:

1492

The teachers told the children that this was when their continent was discovered by human beings. Actually, millions of human beings were already living full and imaginative lives on the continent in 1492. That was simply the year in which sea pirates began to cheat and rob and kill them.

Here was another piece of evil nonsense which children were taught: that the sea pirates eventually created a government which became a beacon of freedom to human beings everywhere else. There were pictures and statues of this supposed imaginary beacon for children to see. It was sort of an ice-cream cone on fire. It looked like this:

Actually, the sea pirates who had the most to do with the creation of the new government owned human slaves. They used human beings for machinery, and, even after slavery was eliminated, because it was so embarrassing, they and their descendants continued to think of ordinary human beings as machines.

➡ The sea pirates were white. The people who were already on the continent when the pirates arrived were copper-colored. When slavery was introduced onto the continent, the slaves were black.

Color was everything.

➡ Here is how the pirates were able to take whatever they wanted from anybody else: they had the best boats in the world, and they were meaner than anybody else, and they had gunpowder, which was a mixture of potassium nitrate, charcoal, and sulphur. They touched this seemingly listless powder with fire, and it turned violently into gas. This gas blew projectiles out of metal tubes at terrific velocities. The projectiles cut through meat and bone very easily, so the pirates could wreck the wiring or the bellows or the plumbing of a stubborn human being, even when he was far, far away.

The chief weapon of the sea pirates, however, was their capacity to astonish. Nobody else could believe, until it was much too late, how heartless and greedy they were.

➡ When Dwayne Hoover and Kilgore Trout met each other, their country was by far the richest and most powerful country on the planet. It had most of the food and minerals and machinery, and it disciplined other countries by threatening to shoot big rockets at them or to drop things on them from airplanes.

Most other countries didn't have doodley-squat. Many of them weren't even inhabitable anymore. They had too many people and not enough space. They had sold everything that was any good, and there wasn't anything to eat anymore, and still the people went on fucking all the time.

Fucking was how babies were made.

➡ A lot of the people on the wrecked planet were *Communists*. They had a theory that what was left of the planet should be shared more or less equally among all the people, who hadn't asked to come to a wrecked planet in the first place. Meanwhile, more babies were arriving all the time—kicking and screaming, yelling for milk.

In some places people would actually try to eat mud or suck on gravel while babies were being born just a few feet away.

And so on.

➡ Dwayne Hoover's and Kilgore Trout's country, where there was still plenty of everything, was opposed to Communism. It didn't think that Earthlings who had a lot should share it with others unless they really wanted to, and most of them didn't want to.

So they didn't have to.

➡ Everybody in America was supposed to grab whatever he could and hold onto it. Some Americans were very good at grabbing and holding, were fabulously well-to-do. Others couldn't get their hands on doodley-squat.

Dwayne Hoover was fabulously well-to-do when he met Kilgore Trout.

A man whispered those exact words to a friend one morning as Dwayne walked by: "Fabulously well-to-do."

And here's how much of the planet Kilgore Trout owned in those days: doodley-squat.

And Kilgore Trout and Dwayne Hoover met in Midland City, which was Dwayne's home town, during an Arts Festival there in autumn of 1972.

As has already been said: Dwayne was a Pontiac dealer who was going insane.

Dwayne's incipient insanity was mainly a matter of chemicals, of course. Dwayne Hoover's body was manufacturing certain chemicals which unbalanced his mind. But Dwayne, like all novice lunatics, needed some bad ideas, too, so that his craziness could have shape and direction.

Bad chemicals and bad ideas were the Yin and Yang of madness. Yin and Yang were Chinese symbols of harmony. They looked like this:

The bad ideas were delivered to Dwayne by Kilgore Trout. Trout considered himself not only harmless but invisible. The world had paid so little attention to him that he supposed he was dead.

He *hoped* he was dead.

But he learned from his encounter with Dwayne that he was alive enough to give a fellow human being ideas which would turn him into a monster.

Here was the core of the bad ideas which Trout gave to Dwayne: Everybody on Earth was a robot, with one exception—Dwayne Hoover.

Of all the creatures in the Universe, only Dwayne was thinking and feeling and worrying and planning and so on. Nobody else knew what pain was. Nobody else had any choices to make. Everybody else was a fully automatic machine, whose purpose was to stimulate Dwayne. Dwayne was a new type of creature being tested by the Creator of the Universe.

Only Dwayne Hoover had free will.

➡ Trout did not expect to be believed. He put the bad ideas into a science-fiction novel, and that was where Dwayne found them. The book wasn't addressed to Dwayne alone. Trout had never heard of Dwayne when he wrote it. It was addressed to anybody who happened to open it up. It said to simply anybody, in effect, "Hey—guess what: You're the only creature with free will. How does that make you feel?" And so on.

It was a *tour de force.* It was a *jeu d'esprit.*

But it was mind poison to Dwayne.

➡ It shook up Trout to realize that even *he* could bring evil into the world—in the form of bad ideas. And, after Dwayne was carted off to a lunatic asylum in a canvas camisole, Trout became a fanatic on the importance of ideas as causes and cures for diseases.

But nobody would listen to him. He was a dirty old man in the wilderness, crying out among the trees and underbrush, "Ideas or the lack of them can cause disease!"

➡ Kilgore Trout became a pioneer in the field of mental health. He advanced his theories disguised as science-fiction. He died in 1981, almost twenty years after he made Dwayne Hoover so sick.

He was by then recognized as a great artist and scientist. The American Academy of Arts and Sciences caused a monument to be erected over his ashes. Carved in its face was a quotation from his last novel, his two-hundred-and-ninth novel, which was unfinished when he died. The monument looked like this:

1973

GRACE PALEY
b. 1922

Grace Paley was born in New York City. A graduate of Hunter College, she has taught at Columbia University, Sarah Lawrence, Dartmouth, and the City College of New York. Her short stories have been published in such magazines as *The New Yorker, The Atlantic Monthly,* and *Esquire,* and she is the author of three short-story collections: *The Little Disturbances of Man* (1959), *Enormous Changes at the Last Minute* (1974), and *Later the Same Day* (1985). Her collected stories were published in 1994. In addition to her highly acclaimed stories, Paley is also the author of two books of poetry and one volume of poems and prose pieces. A feminist and antiwar activist, she regards herself as a "somewhat combative pacifist and cooperative anarchist," as she writes in her introduction to *The Collected Stories.*

Paley began writing fiction in the mid-1950s, even though it was poetry that she "read with the greatest pleasure." She writes, "I needed to speak in some inventive way about our female and male lives in those years. . . . I was beginning to suffer the storyteller's pain: Listen! I *have* to tell you something!" All of her stories bear the distinctive music of what the writer and critic Sean O'Faolain calls the "punch and poetry" of Paley's language. Rooted in an almost casual compression, Paley's narratives evoke a dense and vital world that is singular yet familiar.

"The Pale Pink Roast" first appeared in *The Little Disturbances of Man.* "I was a woman writing at the early moment when small drops of worried resentment and noble rage were secretly, slowly building in the second wave of the women's movement," writes Paley. "I didn't know my small-drop presence or usefulness in this accumulation."

The Pale Pink Roast

Pale green greeted him, grubby buds for nut trees. Packed with lunch, Peter strode into the park. He kicked aside the disappointed acorns and endowed a grand admiring grin to two young girls.

Anna saw him straddling the daffodils, a rosy man in about the third flush of youth. He got into Judy's eye too. Acquisitive and quick, she screamed, "There's Daddy!"

Well, that's who he was, mouth open, addled by visions. He was unsettled by a collusion of charm, a conspiracy of curly hairdos and shiny faces. A year ago, in plain view, Anna had begun to decline into withering years, just as he swelled to the maximum of manhood, spitting pipe smoke, patched with tweed, an advertisement of a lover who startled men and detained the ladies.

Now Judy leaped over the back of a bench and lunged into his arms. "Oh, Peter dear," she whispered, "I didn't even know you were going to meet us."

"God, you're getting big, kiddo. Where's your teeth?" he asked. He hugged her tightly, a fifty-pound sack of his very own. "Say, Judy, I'm glad you still have a pussycat's sniffy nose and a pussycat's soft white fur."

"I do not," she giggled.

"Oh yes," he said. He dropped her to her springy hind legs but held onto one smooth front paw. "But you'd better keep your claws in or I'll drop you right into the Hudson River."

"Aw, Peter," said Judy, "quit it."

Peter changed the subject and turned to Anna. "You don't look half bad, you know."

"Thank you," she replied politely, "neither do you."

"Look at me, I'm a real outdoorski these days."

She allowed thirty seconds of silence, into which he turned, singing like a summer bird, "We danced around the Maypole, the Maypole, the Maypole . . .

"Well, when'd you get in?" he asked.

"About a week ago."

"You never called."

"Yes, I did, Peter. I called you at least twenty-seven times. You're never home. Petey must be in love somewhere, I said to myself."

"What is this thing," he sang in tune, "called love?"

"Peter, I want you to do me a favor," she started again. "Peter, could you take Judy for the weekend? We've just moved to this new place and I have a lot of work to do. I just don't want her in my hair. Peter?"

"Ah, that's why you called."

"Oh, for godsakes," Anna said. "I really called to ask you to become my lover. That's the real reason."

"O.K., O.K. Don't be bitter, Anna." He stretched forth a benedicting arm. "Come in peace, go in peace. Of course I'll take her. I like her. She's my kid."

"Bitter?" she asked.

Peter sighed. He turned the palms of his hands up as though to guess at rain. Anna knew him, theme and choreography. The sunshiny spring afternoon seeped through his fingers. He looked up at the witnessing heavens to keep what he could. He dropped his arms and let the rest go.

"O.K.," he said. "Let's go. I'd like to see your place. I'm full of ideas. You should see my living room, Anna. I might even go into interior decorating if things don't pick up. Come on. I'll get the ladder out of the basement. I could move a couple of trunks. I'm crazy about heavy work. You get out of life what you put into it. Right? Let's ditch the kid. I'm not your enemy."

"Who is?" she asked.

"Off my back, Anna. I mean it. I'll get someone to keep an eye on Judy. Just shut up." He searched for a familiar face among the Sunday strollers. "Hey, you," he finally called to an old pal on whom two chicks were leaning. "Hey, you glass-eyed louse, c'mere."

"Not just any of your idiot friends," whispered Anna, enraged.

All three soft-shoed it over to Peter. They passed out happy hellos, also a bag of dried apricots. Peter spoke to one of the girls. He patted her little-boy haircut. "Well, well, baby, you have certainly changed. You must have had a very good winter."

"Oh yes, thanks," she admitted.

"Say, be my friend, doll, will you? There's Judy over there. Remember? She was nuts about you when she was little. How about it? Keep an eye on her about an hour or two?"

"Sure, Petey, I'd love to. I'm not busy today. Judy! She was cute. I was nuts about her."

"Anna," said Peter, "this is Louie; she was a real friend that year you worked. She helped me out with Judy. She was great, a lifesaver."

"You're Anna," Louie said hospitably. "Oh, I think Judy's cute. We were nuts about each other. You have one smart kid. She's *really* smart."

"Thank you," said Anna.

Judy had gone off to talk to the ice cream man. She returned licking a double-lime Popsicle. "You have to give him ten cents," she said. "He didn't even remember me to give me trust."

Suddenly she saw Louie. "Oooh!" she shrieked. "It's Louie. Louie, Louie, Louie!" They pinched each other's cheeks, rubbed noses like the Eskimoses, and fluttered lashes like kissing angels do. Louie looked around proudly. "Gee whiz, the kid didn't forget me. How do you like that?"

Peter fished in his pockets for some change. Louie said, "Don't be ridiculous. It's on me." "O.K., girls," Peter said. "You two go on. Live it up. Eat supper out. Enjoy yourselves. Keep in touch."

"I guess they do know each other," said Anna, absolutely dispirited, waving goodbye.

"There!" said Peter. "If you want to do things, do things."

He took her arm. His other elbow cut their way through a gathering clutter of men and boys. "Going, going, gone," he said. "So long, fellows."

Within five minutes Anna unlocked the door of her new apartment, her snappy city leasehold, with a brand-new key.

In the wide foyer, on the parquet path narrowed by rows of cardboard boxes, Peter stood stock-still and whistled a dozen bars of Beethoven's Fifth Symphony. "Mama," he moaned in joy, "let me live!"

A vista of rooms and doors to rooms, double glass doors, single hard-oak doors, narrow closet doors, a homeful of rooms wired with hallways stretched before. "Oh, Anna, it's a far cry . . . Who's paying for it?"

"Not you; don't worry."

"That's not the point, Mary and Joseph!" He waved his arms at a chandelier. "Now, Anna, I like to see my friends set up this way. You think I'm kidding."

"*I'm* kidding," said Anna.

"Come on, what's really cooking? You look so great, you look like a chick on the sincere make. Playing it cool and living it warm, you know . . ."

"Quit dreaming, Petey," she said irritably. But he had stripped his back to his undershirt and had started to move records into record cabinets. He stopped to say, "How about me putting up the Venetian blinds?" Then she softened and offered one kindness: "Peter, you're the one who really looks wonderful. You look just—well—healthy."

"I take care of myself, Anna. That's why. Vegetables, high proteins. I'm not the night owl I was. Grapefruits, sunlight, oh sunlight, that's my dear love now."

"You always did take care of yourself, Peter."

"No, Anna, this is different." He stopped and settled on a box of curtains. "I mean it's not egocentric and selfish, the way I used to be. Now it has a real philosophical basis. Don't mix me up with biology. Look at me, what do you see?"

Anna had read that cannibals, tasting man, saw him thereafter as the great pig, the pale pink roast.

"Peter, Peter, pumpkin eater," Anna said.

"Ah no, that's not what I mean. You know what you see? A structure of flesh. You know when it hit me? About two years ago, around the time we were breaking up, you and me. I took my grandpa to the bathroom one time when I was over there visiting—you remember him, Anna, that old jerk, the one that was so mad, he didn't want to die. . . . I was leaning on the door; he was sitting on the pot concentrating on his guts. Just to make conversation—I thought it'd help him relax—I said, 'Pop? Pop, if you had it all to do over again, what would you do different? Any real hot tips?'

"He came up with an answer right away. 'Peter,' he said, 'I'd go to a gym every goddamn day of my life; the hell with the job, the hell with the women. Peter, I'd build my body up till God hisself wouldn't know how to tear it apart. Look at me Peter,' he said. 'I been a mean sonofabitch the last fifteen years. Why? I'll tell you why. This structure, this . . . this thing'—he pinched himself across his stomach and his knees—'this me'—he cracked himself sidewise across his jaw—'this is got to be maintained. The reason is, Peter: *It is the dwelling place of the soul.* In the end, long life is the reward, strength, and beauty.' "

"Oh, Peter!" said Anna. "Are you working?"

"Man," said Peter, "you got the same itsy-bitsy motivations. Of course I'm working. How the hell do you think I live? Did you get your eight-fifty a week out in Scroungeville or not?"

"Eight-fifty is right."

"O.K., O.K. Then listen. I have a vitamin compound that costs me twelve-eighty a hundred. Fifty dollars a year for basic maintenance and repair."

"Did the old guy die?"

"Mother! Yes! Of course he died."

"I'm sorry. He wasn't so bad. He liked Judy."

"Bad or good, Anna, he got his time in, he lived long enough to teach the next generation. By the way, I don't think you've put on an ounce."

"Thanks."

"And the kid looks great. You do take good care of her. You were always a good mother. I'll bet you broil her stuff and all."

"Sometimes," she said.

"Let her live in the air," said Peter. "I bet you do. Let her love her body."

"Let her," said Anna sadly.

"To work, to work, where strike committees shirk," sang Peter. "*Is* the ladder in the cellar?"

"No, no, in that kitchen closet. The real tall closet."

Then Peter put up the Venetian blinds, followed by curtains. He distributed books among the available bookcases. He glued the second drawer of Judy's bureau. Although all the furniture had not been installed, there were shelves for Judy's toys. He had no trouble with them at all. He whistled while he worked.

Then he swept the debris into a corner of the kitchen. He put a pot of coffee on the stove. "Coffee?" he called. "In a minute," Anna said. He stabilized the swinging kitchen door and came upon Anna, winding a clock in the living room whose wide windows on the world he had personally draped. "Busy, busy," he said.

Like a good and happy man increasing his virtue, he kissed her. She did not move away from him. She remained in the embrace of his right arm, her face nuzzling his shoulder, her eyes closed. He tipped her chin to look and measure opportunity. She could not open her eyes. Honorably he searched, but on her face he met no quarrel.

She was faint and leaden, a sure sign in Anna, if he remembered correctly, of passion. "Shall we dance?" he asked softly, a family joke. With great care, a patient lover, he undid the sixteen tiny buttons of her pretty dress and in Judy's room on Judy's bed he took her at once without a word. Afterward, having established tenancy, he rewarded her with kisses. But he dressed quickly because he was obligated by the stories of his life to remind her of transience.

"Petey," Anna said, having drawn sheets and blankets to her chin. "Go on into the kitchen. I think the coffee's all boiled out."

He started a new pot. Then he returned to help her with the innumerable little cloth buttons. "Say, Anna, this dress is wild. It must've cost a dime."

"A quarter," she said.

"You know, we could have some pretty good times together every now and then if you weren't so damn resentful."

"Did you have a real good time, Petey?"

"Oh, the best," he said, kissing her lightly. "You know, I like the way your hair is now," he said.

"I have it done once a week."

"Hey, say it pays, baby. It does wonders. What's up, what's up? That's what I want to know. Where'd the classy TV come from? And that fabulous desk . . . Say, somebody's an operator."

"My husband is," said Anna.

Petey sat absolutely still, but frowned, marking his clear forehead with vertical lines of pain. Consuming the black fact, gritting his teeth to retain it, he said, "My God, Anna! That was a terrible thing to do."

"I thought it was so great."

"Oh, Anna, that's not the point. You should have said something first. Where is he? Where is this stupid sonofabitch while his wife is getting laid?"

"He's in Rochester. That's where I met him. He's a lovely person. He's moving his business. It takes time. Peter, please. He'll be here in a couple of days."

"You're great, Anna. Man, you're great. You wiggle your ass. You make a donkey out of me and him both. You could've said no. No—excuse me, Petey—no. I'm not that hard up. Why'd you do it? Revenge? Meanness? Why?"

He buttoned his jacket and moved among the cardboard boxes and the new chairs, looking for a newspaper or a package. He hadn't brought a thing. He stopped before the hallway mirror to brush his hair. "That's it!" he said, and walked slowly to the door.

"Where are you going, Peter?" Anna called across the foyer, a place for noisy children and forgotten umbrellas. "Wait a minute, Peter. Honest to God, listen to me, I did it for love."

He stopped to look at her. He looked at her coldly.

Anna was crying. "I really mean it, Peter, I did it for love."

"Love?" he asked. "Really?" He smiled. He was embarrassed but happy. "Well!" he said. With the fingers of both hands he tossed her a kiss.

"Oh, Anna, then good night," he said. "You're a good kid. Honest, I wish you the best, the best of everything, the very best."

In no time at all his cheerful face appeared at the door of the spring dusk. In the street among peaceable strangers he did a handstand. Then easy and impervious, in full control, he cartwheeled eastward into the source of night.

1959

WALTER ABISH
b. 1931

Born in Vienna, Austria, Walter Abish served in the Israeli army, married a sculptor, and has been involved in the New York City art scene since the 1960s. His novels and short-story collections include *The Alphabetical Africa* (1974), *Minds Meet* (1975), *In the Future Perfect* (1977), *How German Is It* (1980), *99: The New Meaning* (1990), *Destiny: Tomorrow's Truth* (1992), and *Eclipse Fever* (1993). He is also the author of a poetry collection, *Duel Site* (1970). *How German Is It* received the PEN/Faulkner Award. Abish has also received MacArthur and Guggenheim Fellowships, as well as a Lila Acheson Wallace–Reader's Digest award. In 1991, he received the Award of Merit for the Novel from the American Academy and Institute of Arts and Letters.

Formally innovative in sometimes maddening ways, Abish's work reflects on its own structure and confronts its characters with the preposterousness of their condition. Of *Alphabetical Africa*, John Updike asserted in *Picked-Up Pieces* (1975) that " 'A masterpiece of its kind' does not seem too strong an accolade for a book apt to be the only one of its kind."

"Ardor/Awe/Atrocity" is from the short-story collection *In the Future Perfect*.

Ardor/Awe/Atrocity

Ardor[1]/Awe[2]/Atrocity[3]

Her car, an old Dodge station wagon, developed engine trouble as she was driving along Route 15, traversing the bleakest and most desolate part of the Mojave Desert. She slowed down to twenty miles an hour and listened to the knocking, the persistent knocking sound that came from the engine. A sign[57] she had passed a few miles back indicated that it was forty miles to the next gasoline station. Rather than stop and wait for someone to assist her, she decided to continue at a reduced speed. Now and then a car, traveling at a great speed, shot[56] past her. It did not appear as if the road was patrolled by the police. As soon as she spotted the man standing at the side of the road, waving a sign[57] at her, she stepped on the gas, afraid that otherwise, in this absolute wilderness, he might try to wrench open[43] the car door. The crudely hand-made sign[57] he was holding read: GOING MY WAY? EL LAY. She was too preoccupied with her own problems, her own apprehensions, to wonder how[22] the man came to be where he was, although the words he yelled[74] at her, you[73] silly cunt, kept reverberating in her ears long after she had lost sight of him in the rearview[64] mirror. There was no sign[57] of life on the rugged terrain to her left or right. Lost in her thoughts, she did not see the immense billboard looming ahead until she was almost on top of it. A freshly cut[9] half of an orange, displayed in the center of the billboard, floated against a bright dayglow yellow background. Beneath the orange the word PLEASURE[46] stood out in large red letters. By now she had turned off the air conditioning for fear that it might place an additional burden on the malfunctioning engine. Out of nowhere a fairly large-sized gray furry animal darted across her car's path. She came to a screeching halt in time to see the animal limp off to her left, leaving a thin trail of blood on the highway.

Buoyant[4]/Bob[5]/Body[6]

The large buoyant-looking[4] man in the red-checked shirt who had approached her in the motel dining room was taken away by the police, and so was the young man who received a deep[11] cut[9] in his arm as a result of the altercation that had taken place between the two of them. He'll be all right, the motel owner assured her, after the young man, blood dripping[10] from his left arm, was driven to a nearby hospital. It was on my account, she thought. The young man had actually risked his life for her. She intended to get his name and address, but the rudeness of the motel owner's wife, who seemed to be blaming her for the incident of the night before, and her own desire to leave the motel as quickly as possible, may have been the reason why she completely forgot about it until she was some thirty miles away. To her great relief, the knocking sound of the engine had somewhat subsided. She blamed herself for smiling back at the man in the red-checked shirt, and not realizing that he might misinterpret her friendly smile as a sign[57] of interest on her part.

California[7]/Color[8]/Cut[9]

Jane[28] called her parents on an impulse from a rest stop later that day. When her mother answered the phone, Jane,[28] as if to prevent her mother from raising any of the issues that would cause the two of them to quarrel,[51] immediately launched herself into a detailed description of the landscape around her, the magnificent colors[8] of the sunset she was witnessing that very second, and the marvelous people she had met on the way. She also mentioned that she intended to send her mother dupes of the slides she had taken all along the way. I feel no regret whatever at leaving, she kept repeating.

If I only knew what was going on in your[73] mind, her mother said.

Mom, said Jane[28] quietly. Once you[73] see the slides you'll[73] know exactly what's on my mind. Before hanging up, Jane[28] said that she and Dorothy were taking turns at the wheel.

Can I just say a word to Dorothy, said her mother. Why can't I ever speak to Dorothy?

Drip[10]/Deep[11]/Delight[12]

She is lying naked on the bed. Her heart is beating wildly. This is absolutely ridiculous, she thinks. There is no reason to feel nervous, uncertain, or afraid. Her battered-looking car is parked outside between two perpendicular white[68] lines. Her face is thrust into the soft pillow . . . as she clings to the smell of the freshly laundered white[68] pillowcase. The wall-to-wall rug in the room is an off-white,[68] the tiles in the bathroom are white,[68] so is the washbasin, the bathroom ceiling, and the Venetian blinds. Knees[31] are for supporting the body[6] in a crouching position[48] as the man who is holding her by the waist thrusts[58] himself into her again and again. Both she and the man are committed to complete silence. Each is immersed in his own watchfulness as the bodies[6] acquire greater and greater independence, disregarding the instructions they keep receiving from their separate centers of communication, their minds.

Erection[13]/Exotic[14]/Earthquake[15]

Jane[28] is watching a rerun of "Mannix" on the color[8] TV in her room. It is a cheap set and everything is depicted in the most garish colors[8] on the screen. Intently she watches a pink-faced Mannix, gun[21] drawn, racing along the length of a red-tiled rooftop of a stylish hacienda. Now[40] and then the camera settles briefly on the familiar Southern California[7] background of palm trees, swimming pool, exotic[14] plants, an interior filled with massive pieces of modern furniture, glass-topped[20] tables, large plate-glass[20] windows that permit the blue sky to function as a fourth wall in the room. For the past three days she has noticed an oily substance dripping[10] from the left front axle of her car. The mechanic at the garage assured her it was nothing. Each time she pulls out, she leaves a shiny black stain on the ground. What possibly can she be afraid of?

Future[16]/Flinch[17]/Fuck[18]

I'd love to stay and watch "Mannix" with you,[73] said the man as he left. Perhaps another time? She locked[35] the door and returned to the TV. Her keys[32] lay on the dresser. There were at least a dozen keys[32] on the key[32] chain, but only the keys[32] to the car and the keys[32] of her two valises were of any use to her now.[40] For some reason she can't get herself to discard the now[40] useless bunch of keys.[32] She looks at them carefully, trying to recall which key[32] opened which door. How[22] many times has Mannix, like any other Southern Californian,[7] casually pulled out his keys[32] and opened[43] the door to his office, only to be assaulted, or compelled at gun[21] point to leave the office and enter another man's car? Of course, Mannix is aging gradually. He is losing some of his erstwhile youthfulness[75] and his former bounce, but is he also growing careless? Jane[28] counted her traveler's checks while watching "Mannix." Is Mannix at all capable of having a good time? Or has he come to represent the stern inner-driven justice-oriented force of retribution that Southern Californians[7] need to stabilize their nervous systems, thereby enabling their brain cells to exercise a minimum amount of control as they drive their cars on the six-lane highways into and out of L.A.

Gleaming[19]/Glass[20]/Gun[21]

The newspapers and magazines, available in English and Spanish, report with varying degrees of accuracy the whereabouts and activities of people whose names are instantly recognized by every Southern Californian.[7] In that respect the newspapers and magazines are a kind of pleasure[46] map[37] for the people. They also provide the answer to the frequently raised question:[50] How[22] is it all done? People watch Mannix carefully, in order better to emulate the wealthy people he frequently visits in the graceful-looking haciendas of San Diego. Without Mannix, Southern California[7] would have no entrée to the wealth and power in L.A. and San Diego. Without Mannix Southern California[7] would be bereft of the distinction between ardor,[1] awe,[2] and atrocity.[3] When Mannix grimaces with distaste as he visits the city morgue to view[64] a badly beaten body of a woman,[67] he spells out, for everyone's gratification, the interdependent relationship of *Justice* and *Good Taste.*

How[22]/Hard[23]/Heat[24]

The question bears repeating. How[22] is it all done? How[22] is this miraculous way of life accomplished? The highway system is just one of the answers. The vast intricate[26] network[42] of roads in Southern California[7] facilitate the filming or, as it is sometimes called, the shooting[56] of a "Mannix" sequel of sixty minutes minus time for commercials. It is done, incidentally, despite the omnipresent fear of earthquakes,[15] despite the heat,[24] despite the smog, despite the collisions on the road. Mannix's hands firmly grip the steering wheel as the other car attempts to overtake Mannix's immaculate[25] white[68] convertible with the telephone that links him to his girl Friday and the nervous system of all of Southern California.[7] The car pulls abreast and side-swipes Mannix's car. A bullet smashes his windshield,[69] narrowly missing his head. There is not a pair of adult hands in Southern California[7] that have not experienced the electric flow of fear from the brain to the fingers gripping the wheel, as a collision at eighty miles an hour with another car is barely avoided.

Jane[28] sitting in the soft comfortable beige leather[34] seat next to the driver glances at the two large diamond rings on the manicured plumpish fingers of the woman[67] behind the wheel. The woman[67] is wearing a striped silk blouse, a white[68] linen skirt, and white[68] shoes.

My dear, she says in a somewhat patronizing voice to Jane,[28] I simply insist that you[73] stay with us. Maxwell[39] would be furious if you[73] didn't. We have so much room in the house. By Eastern standards the house is small, perhaps deceptively small. It overlooks[44] the ocean. In the driveway are two gleaming[19] cars. Everything is a bit showy. A bit too finished. When Jane[28] calls her home in the evening, her parents sing Happy Birthday to her. Briefly, but only briefly, she loses control, as the tears well up in her eyes.

Immaculate[25]/Intricate[26]/Image[27]

What is she thinking as she opens[43] a checking account at the bank in the new shopping center. She hasn't looked at a newspaper in weeks. The occasional light tremor under her feet is accepted the way a bullet that narrowly missed Mannix and hit his friend instead is accepted, with resignation, with foreknowledge. In a boutique located in the large shopping complex, they accept her check after glancing at her out-of-state driver's license. She buys herself some underwear,[62] a blouse, clogs, sunglasses,[20] a bikini, all for less than two hundred dollars. Every time anyone hears a siren in Southern California[7] he or she immediately thinks of Mannix, seeing him sprint up a hill, a perfect target for the gunmen[21] on top.

Jane[28]/Jet[29]/Jewel[30]

The American male arriving in L.A. goes to the nearest drugstore for some aspirin and a Coke. He goes to a liquor store for a bottle of Scotch. He stops at the first motel along his way and grabs a few hours of sleep. This is Southern California.[7] The women[67] here have experienced everything at least once in their minds. They do not flinch[17] when the word fuck[18] is used. Jane[28] doesn't flinch[17] or recoil when Helen tells her, you[73] mustn't reject Maxwell,[39] he'll be so hurt.

Knees[31]/Keys[32]/Killed[33]

A row of palm trees in front of a three-story apartment building. Not a soul in sight. Mannix parks his car on the circular gravel driveway and unhurriedly walks to the entrance of the building. Everyone in Southern California[7] knows why Mannix is about to enter the apartment building, but no one knows what to expect. Anything can happen next. The realism[53] of the moment engraves itself upon the brain. Everything Mannix undertakes[63] to do is highly plausible. Everyone watching Mannix is captivated, as each action, each succeeding event, feeds the brain's expectations, expectations that are based on strict standards, strict Southern California[7] standards of conduct and behavior. Jane[28] is sitting on a leather[34] couch. Do her legs meet with Maxwell's[39] approval. Are they sufficiently erotic. Is Maxwell,[39] in his mind, trying to control the movement of her legs. Maxwell[39] continues to stare at her. His look can be said to be filled with expectation. Does Jane[28] accept the inherent femininity of her situation. Has she become a part of Maxwell's[39] scenario for the afternoon. Does the bright Southern California[7] landscape intensify her response to his elaborately planned endeavor, his somewhat mechanical ardor.[1] No bullet shot[56] intervenes as she, embracing him with her legs, responds to the realism[53] of his smooth performance.

Leather[34]/Lock[35]/Landing[36]

I would never marry a cop, Jane[28] tells Maxwell[39] as they are lying on her bed. And I would never marry a California[7] cop.

How about a lawyer?

I'm sick of lawyers as well. Her new blouse is slightly creased. How long have you[73] and Helen been married, she asks.

About twelve years. I was still in the air force when we met.

I didn't know you[73] were in the air force. Were you[73] a pilot?

Did you[73] ever make it with two guys? he asked her suddenly.

The speed at which Californians travel on the six-lane highways ties them to the perpetual *now,*[40] the perpetual *present* in their brains. Jane[28] shuts her eyes. She is alone in this comfortable room, in this elegant house, alone with a spectacular view[64] of the Pacific Ocean and the California[7] sky, alone except for the slightly balding middle-aged head of a man between her legs who is draining her brain of images.[27]

Maps[37]/Message[38]/Maxwell[39]

Jane[28] spoke to the young man she had met on the beach about her trip from New York to L.A. She became quite excited when she described her stay in the motel where the knifing had occurred. She also described her old and now[40] abandoned car in some detail, as if the car, this vehicle[65] that had transported her and her possessions to the West Coast, had not merely been a car, but a treasured[59] possession . . . No, a treasured[59] friend that had aged and then died.

I could have nursed it along for another five thousand miles, she heard herself saying. The young man wore a gold bracelet on his left wrist. It was not politeness or shyness or diffidence that gave his face that particularly attractive look. He seemed to be waiting for her to continue her description, but for all she knew he might be waiting for her to make some kind of a proposal. It was hard[23] to tell.

How do you[73] like it here? she asked.

Here? He seemed taken aback by the question.

She stretched out on the sand. Everything was so exquisite. The people were so beautiful. The sand was soft and white.[68] Very[66] lightly he ran his forefinger up and down the inside of her arm. Later, in her room, he remarked almost casually: I've never had an erection,[13] but there are so many ways to play. Her new TV set was turned off. She could not turn to "Mannix" for guidance. The information on the sixteen-inch screen was *zero.*[78]

Now[40]/Normal[41]/Network[42]

With each new shopping center, with each new airport, with each new office building complex, Southern California[7] is expanding the range of the plausible. The immediate future,[16] the immediate immaculate[25] future[16] lies mapped[37] out in the brain cells as the suntanned people on the Coast carefully observe Mannix's arrival at an airport. It resembles their own arrival at an airport; it also resembles, to tell the truth, the arrival of Bob[5] Down. The uneventful landing[36] of the jet,[29] the debarkation, the metal-and-glass[20] terminal, the white[68] formica counters, and the blue-uniformed stewardesses in the airport cafeteria are all, more or less, devoid of surprise.[55] Keeping an eye on Mannix is one way of watching the smoothly functioning process of a culture prepared for any eventuality, any disaster—waves of heart attacks, incendiary devices about to explode, poison gas, earthquakes,[15] a lion escaping from the zoo,[76] engine breakdown, plane out of control, members of the radical underground wishing to be reunited with their parents. For Bob[5] Down it is the familiar world. Only it is warmer and brighter. Waiting to pick up his luggage he spots Jane[28] just as she is leaving the main terminal together with a tall blond man. Barely controlling his excitement, he runs after her, yelling:[74] Jane,[28] Jane,[28] stop, stop . . . and then, having caught up with her, embraces her enthusiastically, saying: What a beautiful surprise.[55] No one told me that you[73] were in California.[7]

Open[43]/Overlooks[44]/Obligation[45]

Still feeling surprised[55] and baffled by Jane's uncharacteristically cool response to his spontaneous and warm greeting, Bob[5] Down returns to the luggage carousel upon which his two brand new suitcases, by now the only luggage left on the carousel, are completing another full circle. Controlling a temptation to stop at the airport bar for a drink, Bob[5] Down, luggage in hand, heads for the nearest exit. When he had asked Jane[28] for her telephone number, she had responded as if he were prying into her life. Bob[5] had taken an instant dislike to the man she was with. Jane[28] had not asked him a single question; she had also neglected to introduce him to the man at her side. She had not been flustered or startled when he, Bob,[5] had rushed forward to greet her. She might have been vaguely annoyed. I'm sort of in a rush, she said finally, as if to explain her rudeness. The man accompanying her had not said a word. Bob[5] kept seeing the tall slender man at Jane's[28] side, kept seeing the black silk or nylon long-sleeved shirt he wore, the shirt unbuttoned[61] to reveal a large expanse of a tanned hairless chest, and a delicate gold chain at the end of which was attached a small ivory figure with a disproportionately large phallus. He told himself that it was ridiculous to attach any significance[57] to this encounter.

The next day when Bob[5] called the number Jane[28] had so reluctantly given him, a disembodied female voice repeated the last four digits of the number he had dialed. It turned out to be an answering service. He left his hotel number and a message[38] for Jane,[28] requesting her to call him at her convenience. The tiny totemic[60] figurine dangling from the end of the chain around the man's neck came to mind each time he thought of Jane.[28] What about it was so distasteful?

Pleasure[46]/Punish[47]/Position[48]

At what stage does the Southern Californian[7] convert the world around him into the flatness that resembles a movie screen. Everything the mind focuses on may be something it might have, on a prior occasion, spotted on a screen. In time, the Southern Californian[7] will no longer ask, can I also do it? Instead he or she will want to know where, at what movie house, can it be seen?

Bob[5] Down quit[49] his job, sold his car, his antique leather[34] couch, and his collection of weather vanes, and moved in with a friend in New York City, prior to leaving for the West Coast. He had been planning to make this move for a long time. California,[7] why California,[7] his friends wanted to know. Why California,[7] asked his parents. They refused to acknowledge that they knew next to nothing about their son. They hardly know anything about each other. They are a secretive family in the true American tradition. Everything is on display, everything in their life and in their house in Princeton, New Jersey, is visible, to be seen, noticed, acknowledged. Everything: diplomas, photographs, scuffed Oriental carpets, letters from the college president, slippers, stuffed animals, toilet articles, trophies, the bottles in the liquor cabinet, several rifle awards, mementos from Egypt, Italy, and Chile. What are they hiding? They are hiding Bob[5] Down, their mysterious son who calls them twice weekly. The first time he mentioned running into Jane.[28] They remembered Jane[28] with a certain disapproval, a certain vague trepidation. Could he have fallen for Jane?[28] I wonder if he's sleeping with her, said Bob's[5] mother. Bob's[5] father responded with a manly, ha ha ha. What's wrong with . . . but he doesn't mention the word. He somehow restrains himself from uttering the word. It is a perfect word printed on a page. . . . But he doesn't want to be responsible for what might happen to his wife if he used the word in her presence.

Quit[49]/Question[50]/Quarrel[51]

Mr. and Mrs. Down watch "Mannix" on Saturday at nine. They are glued to their seats as they watch "Mannix," hoping to become acquainted with the section of the country where their son is staying. They realize that they needed someone like Mannix to get to the heart of the problem, to determine what was the matter with their son. He must have friends, said Bob's[5] father. Everyone has a friend or two. How[22] many do you have, his wife asked him. They keep watching Mannix and waiting for the phone to ring. When Bob[5] rings, he is his usual cheerful self. He is filled with information. Nothing is hidden. That is what is so disconcerting. Nothing is hidden, but everything is murky. Is he seeing Jane[28] again. Has she left her husband and two children. Should they call her parents and inquire.

Recognition[52]/Real[53]/Remember[54]

What is the present situation. It is defined by a lack of trust as Mr. and Mrs. Arthur Down pore over the map[37] of L.A. It is a landscape filled with the recollection of Mannix. Buildings, cars, and people age comfortably in the sun. Jane's[28] car is a case in point. She has abandoned it. By now she's come to rely on other people for transportation. By now she knows so many people in Southern California.[7] The bankteller greets her warmly. The guard smiles at her as she leaves. Is there any other way to live? it says on the large billboard advertising sailboats.

Surprise[55]/Shot[56]/Sign[57]

It is two in the morning, and the four young Chicanos are gaily pushing an abandoned Dodge station wagon down a deserted dead-end street toward the low wood fence behind which there is a sheer drop of forty feet to the water below. One of the four is casually resting his right hand on the steering wheel of the car. As the road begins to dip slightly, the car picks up speed.

A minute later all four cheer, Ole, as the car smashes through the fence and plunges downward. In the small bungalows nearby, lights are being turned on. People have no way of knowing if the car contained a body. It is entirely feasible. Everyone of the witnesses has watched "Mannix" at some time or other. The four kids are crowded around the smashed fence, staring down at the wrecked car when the cops arrive. In many respects it is a familiar scene. Guns[21] drawn, the cops push the kids against a nearby wall and frisk them, then handcuffed, they are driven to the police station where they are booked and their possessions religiously entered in a ledger. Four creased wallets, presumably stolen, twenty-one credit cards, all stolen, four knives, handkerchiefs, condoms, a pocket radio, four combs, nail clippers, keys,[32] and approximately two dozen pornographic photographs. On at least six of the photographs Jane's[28] face, Jane's[28] attractive and serious face, is staring unblinkingly at the photographer while she is being screwed. The four kids behind bars have not read Octavio Paz's *The Labyrinth of Solitude,* but they have watched "Mannix." They are fully aware that Mannix has on several occasions managed to break out of jail. But they don't have what Mannix has going for him. They don't have friends in the police department, and they don't have Mannix's white[68] convertible, with the telephone that links him to his secretary, parked conveniently near the station. They know they don't stand a chance. They know the cops aren't xenophiles,[72] they are xenophobes. So they sit in their cell, awake and dreaming of Jane.[28]

Thrust[58]/Treasured[59]/Totemic[60]

How real[53] is Southern California,[7] people ask themselves daily. The two men who gunned down a guard as they were making their getaway from the bank after the stick-up were also preoccupied with the real.[53] Temporarily the stolen money eased the gnawing sense of uncertainty. By the time Jane[28] arrived to deposit some money in the afternoon, the blood had been wiped up. Everything was back to normal.[41] The suntanned young bankteller seemed more subdued than usual, but the guard who had replaced the guard killed a few hours before smiled broadly at Jane[28] as she was leaving, and said: Have a nice day, Miss. The pictures showing Jane[28] being screwed are still being passed around the police station. Dozens of hard-faced[23] cops grimly memorize her face, her breasts, her legs, her unbelievably erotic positions.[48] Are these real?[53] they ask themselves.

Unbuttoned[61]/Underwear[62]/Undertakes[63]

When Bob[5] Down moved into Clark Seedwell's place, he called Jane's[28] answering service to leave his new number. Please, have her call me at her convenience, he said. By now his calling the answering service every time he moved had become a reflex action. When he spoke to his parents, he told them that he was staying with an old friend from college in a rather luxurious house filled with a lot of art and modern furniture. He was making a great many new friends. Since Clark knew an awful lot of people, they led an active social life. To his delight[12] as Clark's new friend he was accepted at once. One Saturday he and Clark went to an exhibition of photographs by a photographer who had once been a close friend of Clark's. Clark didn't really wish to go, but he had a strong sense of duty, of obligation,[45] of doing the correct thing, and he didn't wish to leave the photographer under the impression that he was no longer important to Clark. The photographs were portraits of people Bob[5] Down didn't know. A surprisingly large number of the people photographed wore black leather[34] jackets, and some wore black leather[34] pants as well. Next to each photograph was the name or the names of the persons photographed, and Bob[5] could tell that, although he didn't recognize a single name, the names were well known to most of the people who arrived for the opening, quite a number of them wearing black leather[34] jackets, and looking as if they had just stepped out of one of the photographs on the wall. Clark was at his side when Bob[5] stopped in front of a photograph taken of Clark in a white[68] linen suit, elegant and nonchalant, standing in the corner of a room, while near him on a couch sat a young woman wearing an open black leather[34] jacket, black leather[34] boots, and nothing else. The woman was Jane.[28]

I didn't know that you[73] knew Jane,[28] said Bob.[5]

Surprise,[55] surprise,[55] said Clark.

Her former husband was a schoolmate of mine, explained Bob.[5] I was best man at their wedding.

Did you[73] ever make out with him, asked Clark, laughing at the startled expression on Bob's[5] face.

View[64]/Vehicle[65]/Very[66]

The next week Bob[5] and Clark visited Clark's mother in La Jolla, San Diego. In the afternoon, while Clark sat pensively watching from a deck chair, Bob,[5] dressed in whites,[68] played tennis with Clark's mother. She was a slim attractive woman in her early fifties who played an aggressive game. For some reason Bob[5] could not understand, he found that he wished to punish[47] her, taking a great delight in making her race back and forth across the court . . . but punish[47] her for what. For being wealthy, or for being Clark's mother, or for being able to afford this magnificent building and the servants. Or did he resent her taking it for granted the night before that he and Clark would share one bedroom. That evening, Clark's mother said to her son: Did I tell you, Jane[28] was here. She stayed for ever so long . . . She said that she was thinking of returning to New York. She left one morning without even saying good-by. I was relieved to see her go, but it seemed odd that she would leave without a word. What's more, she left her valise behind . . . I hope she's not coming back.

Bob's[5] an old friend of hers, said Clark.

You[73] have such strange friends, said Clark's mother, staring at Bob,[5] and then, as if the idea had just occurred to her: If you're[73] her friend, you[73] must take her valise with you.[73] You're[73] much more likely to run into her than I am.

Woman[67]/White[68]/Windshield[69]

The trouble with people like you,[73] said Clark without bitterness, is that you[73] haven't the vaguest idea of who you[73] would like to fuck,[18] or who you[73] would like to be fucked[18] by, or if at all you[73] would like to fuck,[18] or if possibly you[73] might be able to find some alternative to fucking.[18] Bob[5] piled his luggage into his car. He also carried Jane's[28] suitcase to his car, expecting Clark to protest, but Clark didn't say a word.

I know I owe you[73] a good deal of money, and I intend to repay it as soon as I can.

You're[73] such a bloody asshole, said Clark amiably. I realize that you[73] like to leave a good impression wherever you[73] go. Well, you've[73] done that. I think you're[73] honest, upright, and terribly good-looking. So do all my friends. And who knows, perhaps our mutual friend, Jane,[28] does too. One of these days she'll give you[73] a buzz. Then you[73] can sit down and talk about old times. All those delightful[12] days and nights in Staten Island, or wherever you[73] met.

A short distance from Clark's house Bob[5] picked up a hitchhiker. Lovely day, said Bob[5] pleasantly. One of these lovely days, said the young kid he had picked up, we're going to be hit by the most godawful quake you[73] ever heard of. At that very precise moment a light tremor shook the ground over which they were passing. Oh fuck[18] it, said Bob,[5] and for the remainder of the ride they did not exchange another word.

X-ed[70]/Xerox[71]/Xenophile[72]

Jane's[28] light blue suitcase contained two evening dresses, black lace underwear,[62] a jewel[30] box containing a diamond ring, fourteen thousand dollars in one-hundred-dollar bills, a man's wristwatch, two bank books in her name, a check book in her name, a key[32] to a safe deposit box, about a dozen keys[32] on one large key[32] chain, two dozen Percodan in a small plastic container, a one ounce bag of coke, a Xerox[71] copy of her birth and marriage certificates, a computerized reading of her sign[57] of the zodiac,[77] Virgo the Virgin, the sentence, *a secret meeting will determine your future,*[16] was underlined. Jane[28] had also saved the road maps[37] she used on her trip from New York to L.A. The dozen or so areas x-ed[70] on the map[37] with a red pencil may have been the places where she had stopped overnight. In one of the compartments of the suitcase Bob[5] found a pile of old letters written by a former boyfriend, and several written by her obviously distraught husband, Tom, after she had left him. Bob[5] read the letters hoping to come across some mention of his name, but there was none. In the same compartment next to the letters was an envelope containing several photographs, one of Tom on the Staten Island Ferry standing next to Bob,[5] another of Jane[28] wearing a black bathing suit, sunning herself in a park. In emptying the suitcase, Bob[5] almost overlooked the tiny yellow address book for the most part filled with names of people in the L.A. and San Diego area. He looked up his name and found that each new number he had left with the answering service had been entered in the book. Her parents' telephone number and address were on the first page in the book. On an impulse Bob[5] called their number. Jane's[28] mother answered the phone. She remembered him quite well. He said that he was calling from Princeton. He explained that he hadn't seen Jane[28] in ages and wondered if he could possibly get her number. I haven't heard from her in some time, said Jane's[28] mother. She's making films in Hollywood and has forgotten about us. I can give you[73] a number where you[73] might reach her. If you[73] do, would you[73] please tell her that her Dad died two weeks ago. I'm moving in with my sister in Queens. Jane[28] has her number. Good-by now. I have to get off the line. I have a visitor. Did you[73] say your[73] name was Bob?[5]

You[73]/Yelled[74]/Youthfulness[75]

When Bob[5] called Jane's[28] answering service from his new apartment, he was told she had not picked up her messages[38] for over a month, and that as far as they were concerned, she had discontinued using their service. Bob,[5] as usual, wanted to leave his new number, but the service refused to accept any message[38] for Jane.[28] Bob[5] then went through her address book. Recognizing[52] the name of a man he had met at a dinner to which Clark had taken him, he called the man, who claimed not to remember[54] ever having met him. When Bob[5] mentioned Jane's[28] name, the man hung up. Borrowing some of the money he had found in Jane's[28] suitcase, Bob[5] went out and bought himself a suit. Then he picked a name from his own address book and called a couple he had met at Clark's house. They promptly invited him over for dinner that evening. On the way he stopped and bought a bottle of champagne. Six days later he called his parents in Princeton and informed them that he was getting married to someone he had met in the house of two close and dear friends of his. The wedding, they had decided, was to take place at the bride's parents' house in La Jolla. Bob[5] kept repeating that he hoped that they would make it to the wedding.

I just knew it, Bob's[5] father said exuberantly to his wife. The boy is a chip off the old block.

Zoo[76]/Zodiac[77]/Zero[78]

Bob[5] sent me a telegram inviting me to his wedding and then called me in New York to urge me to come. I hadn't seen him since he stayed at my place after giving up his apartment. On the phone he inquired jokingly if I was still a Mannix nut. It was he who had brought Jane[28] to my place a number of times. I told him how sorry I was to hear of her death, and he said, What? What? I guess no one reads the papers in L.A. All they do is fuck[18] around and go to the beach. How did she die, he asked. She was killed.[33] Shot,[56] I said. Apparently she moved around with a strange crowd. As far as I know, they haven't caught whoever did it. That's a shame, he said. I liked Jane.[28] I saw her only once. Only one time at the airport. But we'll talk about it when you[73] come out here for the wedding. You[73] will, won't you?[73] I miss you[73] an awful lot. I really didn't think you'd[73] get married, I said. She's very bright and attractive. She's got a Ph.D. in semiotics. Her father is in oil. When he hung up, I realized that he hadn't mentioned my latest book. The book is set in South California,[7] a place I've never visited. If not for Bob's[5] enthusiasm, I might not have undertaken[63] to write it.

1977

CAROLE MASO
b. 1955

Carole Maso was born in Paterson, New Jersey, was raised in northern New Jersey, and attended Vassar College, where she began writing. Her five novels include *Ghost Dance* (1986), *The Art Lover* (1990), *AVA* (1993), *The American Woman in the Chinese Hat* (1994), and *Aureole* (1996). She has taught at Illinois State University, Columbia University, George Washington University, and at Brown University, where she directs the Creative Writing Program. In 1993, she received a Lannan Literary Fellowship for Fiction.

"To my mind," Maso said in a 1996 interview in *Poets and Writers Magazine*, "books are human documents, which means they should have 'fingerprints' on them, evidence that a mess went into creating them—that you were alive and breathing, or in love, or having your period while the thing was being made." She added, "I'm interested in the relationship between silence and language, the place where language resonates coming out of silence, and going back into silence. Even though I have this reckless desire to do anything I want with language, it is informed by this other sense. Paul Celan and Samuel Beckett have been big helps as examples of the courage it takes to not be so afraid of silence, and 'the not,' the other side of 'this.' "

From The American Woman in the Chinese Hat

28

A woman, x, and a man, y, plan to meet at the prearranged coordinate, z, a fountain on the Place Antony Mars in the south of France, on some late afternoon in summer at the end of the twentieth century.

Both walk slowly, inevitably to z, embracing their common fate and now as they stop and turn, each other. Y, a man with cheveux longs, clearly French, kisses x twice on the cheeks. It is as if he has stepped out of some unmade film of the dead Truffaut. She looks to be German or Scandinavian, possibly English or American, and is wearing a Chinese hat. The sun is very bright, so bright in fact that sometimes one or the other, and sometimes both, seem to disappear in it. He circles her slowly. She sits stationary at a white plastic table, the kind that have become "la mode" in France in the last few years. He circles the fountain, the periphery of z, slowly, looking at her with some exasperation.

"Il fait chaud," he says.

"Non, il fait beau."

"Il fait chaud."

"Such bright, white light."

"Oui, la lumière. Speak French."

"Oui, la lumière."

She conjugates vouloir. Vouloir is to want.

She watches him appear and disappear, appear, disappear.

"This reminds me of another savage and beautiful afternoon."

"Encore?"

"In the savage and beautiful afternoon we tried to speak. You said: 'Where do you live?' I said: 'New York.' It was a time when I was still hoping you might save me."

"Oui," he says, "comme Prince Charmant, sur le cheval blanc." He laughs.

She claps her hands. "Are you ready? Vous êtes prêt? Are you ready now?"

She stands up. "La première position," she says, and arranges his arms and legs into the first position of ballet. He's so beautiful.

"La deuxième."

He holds the position for a moment and then breaks it.

"You thought I could save you," he says. "You wrote it in that notebook."

"La troisième. Parfait!" He holds the pose.

"Already, you knew there was nothing I could do for you." He moves away.

"I asked: 'Where do you live?' You said: 'Near the cemetery.' I asked: 'Where were you born?' You said: 'The most beautiful coast in the world.' "

"No one understands why you have come to my country," he says. "L'étrangère, they all say."

She cries. "But I remember the beautiful forever of the perfect afternoon. The beauty by the fountain. And cheveux longs."

The shimmering surface of the afternoon. A man carrying two iced figures near the plastic table. "La femme qui pleure," he says. "Chante avec moi." He begins in English the song she has taught him.

"Row, row, row your boat.
Gently down the stream,
Merrily, merrily, merrily, merrily
Life is but a dream."

"You were already trembling then," she says.

"Yes, in anticipation."

"Crying."

"Yes, for joy. In grief."

" 'J'ai peur,' you said."

"Yes. Already that first day there was une chambre blanche, chauve-souris. . . . A black and white film. An angel."

"You were expecting maybe a miracle." He smiles.

There is a close-up of the young French man. A profile. And then the slow-motion turn of his head. A panoramic gaze.

"You are an angel," she says.

He laughs. Takes her Chinese hat.

She takes it back.

"She remembers the dazzling, the catastrophic afternoon."

He tries to remember that first day. "Already," he says, "you knew you were doomed."

"Stop," she says, running her finger down his arm, his chest. The beautiful surface of skin.

"La dernière position," she says.

"Non," he says, "pas encore."

"Oui," she says.

He offers his hand, and she steps into the gesture.

"I love you," she says, entering the illusion like almost everyone. "I love you." Each word a boat.

He shakes his head. "It is only a dream," he says. "A lie. I thought you were different."

He takes her hand and holds it under the rushing, brilliant stream of water and then releases it, and they stand like that.

She in her Chinese hat.

He with his cheveux longs.

Not touching, not saying one word.

Unaccountably there is a dizzying movement of the camera and they are seen suddenly from high above. The camera hovers. Something else hovers. It is, we see, one of the beautiful angels of France. The angel weeps. It begins to rain.

29

"I thought you said it never rained in summer."

He laughs.

It is night now. They turn and walk toward the cemetery. He guides her up the steep stairway placing the palm of his left hand on her back. He moves the other arm around her waist and presses the palm of the right hand against her heart. He applies the smallest pressure to her chest and whispers "Arrête."

"Stop," he says, in a heavily accented French.

"Ouvrez la porte," she says, giggling. The man opens the door.

In the room there is a bed, a lamp, a book next to the bed. A strange white light shines through the window. Light the cemetery gives. It reminds her slightly of night in the great illuminated city. "Home," she says, but that of course is not it.

She thinks of her city—silent now, very dark. Inconceivably tragic. She can't imagine.

"J'ai peur," the woman says to the man, digging her fingers into his upper arm and doing a quick little pirouette so that now she suddenly faces him. There is terror in the eyes of the woman who stands on tiptoe and searches his face for some sort of explanation. "Je ne comprends pas," she says.

"Tu ne comprends rien," the man smiles. She releases him. He directs her to the bed.

"Yes, this I still understand," she says.

I know I am sounding less and less like myself. More like—quoi? a nouveau roman perhaps—a borrowed voice. Still one feels lucky to sound like anything at all. To be able to say anything, to feel anything.

He hovers above her. Her arms encircle him. She feels the metal of his belt buckle against her lips.

"Non." He pulls away, gets down on his knees and watches her, observes her face, the two lines in her forehead that mean she is tired, the slightly open mouth. He holds her ankles in his hands and slowly moves them apart.

"Il fait chaud ce soir," she says and lies back on the bed. Slowly, everything is slowly, he undoes the six straps of her sandals. He pulls the straps tight and then loose. Six times on one foot. Six times on the other foot. He glimpses the golden brown pubic hair beneath her skirt.

She sits up and sweeps the hair to the top of her head and then tilts the head back. He studies her carefully, intently, her forehead, nose, chin, throat. She lets her hair fall and then says again, "Il fait chaud." She asks him to bring—what is the word—her pocketbook. "Where?" She stretches her feline body. "Là," she points and he crawls to it on all fours.

From her bag she takes a small round box of hairpins which she hands to him. She turns so that she is facing the wall. He pulls the hair to the top of her head as he has watched her do and attempts to fasten it there. Long curling tendrils escape his every effort and he sighs. "Do not give up so easily," she says. "Comment?" She unbuttons her blouse and neatly folds it. Then her brassiere. It opens in the front, the back shaped vaguely like a heart. Her breasts, released from the elastic and bone and lace, swell.

She sings the birthday song, softly, off-key. Today is my birthday, she says. Though it is not true.

He sees that the edges of her ears are red and that she has a slight heat rash along the back of her neck. Alternately he feels tender then hostile then indifferent toward her.

She raises her arms to check her hair and he takes this opportunity to place his nose under her arm, breathing deeply. He runs his mouth along the slightly roughened skin of the American, cleanly shaven. He bites her, but gently. She wants him to bite her harder, hurt her somehow—make her feel something. But he won't.

She takes a small mirror from the leather bag and fingers the curls he has fashioned with the hairpins, approving of the job he has done. "Perhaps you are a coiffeur," she says, laughing. He moves his mouth to her rose nipple. She observes him in the mirror, a ravenous and fragile child. When she has had enough she nudges him away with her elbow. He goes around her back over to the other breast and it is the same thing. She watches him and then brushes him away tenderly with one white wing. She turns to face him. She tries to tie his hair in a ponytail. "Non," he says.

"Mais il fait chaud." She tries again.

"Non."

Slowly, she unbuttons his shirt, she counts each button, un, deux, trois, quatre, cinq, six, sept. "You are like a child." She outlines the rib cage with her mouth, presses where she imagines the heart to be.

She unfastens the familiar belt now and slips his penis from his pants. It has a life of its own. It is at a particularly lovely angle from his body, she thinks. "L'explorateur," she calls it.

Forcing her down, he pins her hands to the bed. He is more erect now, harder. He straddles her, kneeling, putting his knees under her arms. He raises himself, slowly above her so that he is just out of her reach. Her tongue is barely able to graze his underside and then not. He sways rocking back and forth, back and forth. She struggles to get free. She tries to raise herself on an elbow. "Non." He watches her. She struggles to meet him. She is wet. "Let me go," she says.

"Non."

"I want you."

"Non."

"Please."

"Speak French." And with that he releases her hands, leans back and thrusts himself into her mouth. There's a funny dipping motion. It's getting hard to describe this anymore. It's getting more and more difficult. He takes himself out of her mouth and with one hand pulls her skirt up around her waist and begins to touch her gently. He smiles and shakes his head at her wetness. His long hair hangs over her. "Tu es comme un petit cheval," she says.

She bends her knees, throwing him off balance and he topples in mock defeat. "Do not give up," she says, "so easily." Parting her legs, muttering in French, he enters her and she is laughing and asking, What are you saying? He covers her mouth with his hand.

He moves his hand to her throat as he thrusts harder and harder. "You're choking me," she says. "You're choking me." Then nothing. And I would like to help her, but I can't.

The black book falls to the floor, and she looks up terrified. "Non. It has no meaning," he says in English.

He sits up and he is deep inside her and he is now swearing and sweating, and asking for something. She doesn't know what. She tells him, she keeps telling him what she wants. What she needs. She wants to be on top now.

"Speak French."

She finds a way to say it.

"Bon."

He watches as slowly the strands of her hair escape the pins with the violence of her motions. She takes his small surrender and rides—somewhere far away, with him. "Tu es comme un petit cheval."

Her dazzling body falls forward onto him. She covers him with a veil of hair and tears. She is afraid. She wants something that doesn't change. Something permanent.

She'll never go far enough.

He turns her over with an eerie precision and takes one foot and then the other and places them on his shoulders. He holds her ankles and steers her so that her head is touching the floor. Off the edge of the bed, beheaded as she is, only a torso now, he drives into her with new ferocity.

She tries to speak, but it is useless.

"My God," he says in English, laughing.

She curls into herself on the floor. He looks at her from the bed. Her body divides into two perfect shapes: the back, the buttocks.

She seems to be floating.

I go over to them and pick up hairpins from the floor, the drenched bed. I examine the black book.

"Look," I say to him. "She is dreaming her way home."

1994

JAYNE ANNE PHILLIPS
b. 1952

Jayne Anne Phillips was born in Buckhannon, West Virginia, and educated at West Virginia University and the University of Iowa Writers' Workshop. Her seven books of fiction include the collections *Black Tickets* (1979) and *Fast Lanes* (1984) and the novels *Machine Dreams* (1984) and *Shelter* (1994). *Black Tickets* received the Sue

Kaufman Award for first fiction from the American Academy and Institute of Arts and Letters.

"I'm interested in the way perception itself works," Phillips explained in a 1987 interview, "and I think I began to experiment with writing about perception in . . . very short pieces. As my work has developed, I hope that I have begun to explore the same thing in larger terms."

In addition, Phillips has said that "because they're reading in the first-person voice, readers begin to associate with the voice, and voice begins to dip into their own experience. It's through taking on the voice that they may develop some understanding, some compassion, even for a grotesque, and some understanding that they might possibly have been this person if they had lived this history. . . . It's the only way to really understand, or to truly empathize, to *become* that voice."

"Bluegill" is from *Fast Lanes.*

Bluegill

Hello my little bluegill, little shark face. Fanged one, sucker, hermaphrodite. Rose, bloom in the fog of the body; see how the gulls arch over us, singing their raucous squalls. They bring you sweetmeats, tiny mice, spiders with clasped legs. In their old claws, claws of eons, reptilian sleep, they cradle shiny rocks and bits of glass. Boat in my blood, I dream you furred and sharp-toothed, loping in snow mist on a tundra far from the sea. I believe you are male; will I make you husband, uncle, brother? Feed you in dark movie houses of a city we haven't found? This village borders waves, roofs askew, boards vacant. I'll leave here with two suitcases and a music box, but what of you, little boot, little head with two eyes? I talk to you, bone of my coming, bone of an earnest receipt. I feel you now, steaming in the cave of the womb.

Here there are small fires. I bank a blaze in the iron stove and waken ringed in damp; how white air seeps inside the cracked houses, in the rattled doors and sills. We have arrived and settled in a house that groans, shifting its mildewed walls. The rains have come, rolling mud yards of fishermen's shacks down a dirt road to the curling surf. Crabs' claws bleach in spindled grass; dogs tear the discarded shells and drag them in rain. They fade from orange to peach to the pearl of the disembodied. Smells crouch and pull, moving in wet air. Each night crates of live crab are delivered to the smokehouse next door. They clack and crawl, a lumbering mass whose mute antennae click a filament of loss. Ocean is a ream of white meat, circles in a muscular brain. I eat these creatures; their flesh is sweet and flaky. They are voiceless, fluid in their watery dusk, trapped in nets a mile from the rocky cliffs. You are some kin to them, floating in your own dark sac.

Kelp floats a jungle by the pier, armless, legless, waving long sea hair, tresses submerged and rooty. These plants are bulbs and a nipple, rounded snouts weaving their tubular tails. Little boys find them washed up on the beach, wet, rubbery, smelling of salt. They hold the globular heads between their legs and ride them like stick horses. They gallop off, long tails dragging tapered in the sand. They run along the water in groups of three or four, young centaurs with no six-guns whose tracks evoke visions of myth-ical reptiles. They run all the way to the point, grow bored, fight, scatter; finally one comes back alone, preoccupied, dejected, dragging the desultory tail in one hand as the foamy surf tugs it seaward. I watch him; I pretend you see him too, see it all with your X-ray vision, your soft eyes, their honeycomb facets judging the souls of all failed boys. We watch the old ones, the young ones, the boats bobbing their rummy cargoes of traps and nets and hooks.

I sit at the corner table of the one restaurant, diner near the water where fishermen drink coffee at six A.M. I arrive later, when the place is nearly empty, when the sun slants on toward noon and the coffee has aged to a pungent syrup. The waitress is the postmaster's wife; she knows I get one envelope a month, that I cash one check at MacKinsie's Market, that I rent a postbox on a six-month basis. She spots my ringless hands, the gauntness in my face, the calcium pills I pull out of my purse in a green medicinal bottle. She recognizes my aversion to eggs; she knows that blur in my pupils, blur and flare, wavering as though I'm sucked inward by a small interior flame. You breathe, adhered to a cord. Translucent astronaut, your eyes change days like a calendar watch. The fog surrounds us, drifting between craggy hills like an insubstantial blimp, whale shape that breaks up and spreads. Rock islands rise from the olive sea; they've caught seed in the wind and sit impassive, totems bristling with pine. Before long they will split and speak, revealing a long-trapped Hamlin piper and a troop of children whose bodies are musical and perfect, whose thoughts have grown pure. The children translate each wash of light on the faces of their stone capsules; they feel each nuance of sun and hear the fog as a continuous sigh, drifted breath of the one giant to whom they address their prayers. They have grown no taller and experienced no disease; they sleep in shifts. The piper has made no sound since their arrival. His inert form has become luminous and faintly furred. He is a father fit for animalistic angels whose complex mathematical games evolve with the centuries, whose hands have become transparent from constant handling of quartz pebbles and clear agates. They have no interest in talk or travel; they have developed beyond the inhabitants of countries and communicate only with the unborn. They repudiate the music that tempted them and create it now within themselves, a silent version expressed in numerals, angles, complicated slitherings. They are mobile as lizards and opaque as those small blind fish found in the still waters of caves. Immortal, they become their own children. Their memories of a long-ago journey are layered as genetics: how the sky eclipsed, how the piped melody was transformed as they walked into the sea and were submerged. The girls and smaller boys remember their dresses blousing, swirling like anemones. The music entered a new dimension, felt inside them like cool fingers, formal as a harpsichord yet buoyant, wild; they were taken up with it days at a time. . . .

Here in the diner, there is a jukebox that turns up loud. High school kids move the tables back and dance on Friday nights. They are sixteen, tough little girls who disdain makeup and smoke Turkish cigarettes, or last year's senior boys who can't leave the village. Already they're hauling net on their fathers' boats, learning a language of profanity and back-slapping, beer, odd tumescent dawns as the other boats float out of sight. They want to marry at twenty, save money, acquire protection from the weather. But the girls are like colts, skittish and lean; they've read magazines, gone to rock concerts, experimented with drugs and each other. They play truant and drive around all day in VWs, listen to AM radio in the rain and swish of the wipers, dream of graduation and San Francisco, L.A., Mexico. They go barefoot in the dead of winter and seldom eat; their faces are pale and dewy from the moist air, the continuous rains. They show up sullen-eyed for the dances and get younger as the evening progresses, drinking grocery-store mixed drinks from thermoses in boys' cars. Now they are willing to dance close and imitate their mothers. Music beats in the floor like a heart; movie-theme certainty and the simple lyric of hold-me-tight. I pause on my nightly walks and watch their silhouettes on the windows; nearby the dock pylons stand up mossy and beaten, slap of the water intimate and old. Boys sit exchanging hopeful stories, smoking dope. Sometimes they whistle. They can't see my shape in my bulky coat. Once, one of them followed me home and waited beyond the concrete porch and the woodpile; I saw his face past the thrown ellipses of light. I imagined him in my bed, smooth-skinned and physically happy, no knowledge but intent. He would address you through my skin, nothing but question marks. Instructed to move slowly from behind, he would be careful, tentative, but forget at the end and push hard. There is no danger; you are floating, interior and protected; but it's that rhythmic lapsing of my love for you that would frighten; we have been alone so long. So I am true to you; I shut off the light and he goes away. In some manner, I am in your employ; I feed my body to feed you and buy my food with money sent me because of you. I am very nearly married to you; and it is only here, a northwestern fishing village in the rains, constant rain, that the money comes according to bargain, to an understanding conceived in your interest. I have followed you though you cannot speak, only fold, unfold. Blueprint, bone and toenail, sapphire. You must know it all from the beginning, never suffer the ignorance of boys with vestigial tails and imagined guns. I send you all these secrets in my blood; they wash through you like dialysis. You are the animal and the saint, snow-blind, begun in blindness . . . you must break free of me like a weasel or a fox, fatherless, dark as the seals that bark like haunted men from the rocks, far away, their calls magnified in the distance, in the twilight.

Ghost, my solitaire, I'll say your father was a horse, a Percheron whose rippled mane fell across my shoulders, whose tight hide glimmered, who shivered and made small winged insects rise into the air. A creature large-eyed, velvet. Long bone of the face broad as a forearm, back broad as sleep. Massive. Looking from the side of the face, a peripheral vision innocent, instinctual.

But no, there were many fathers. There was a truck, a rattling of nuts and bolts, a juggling of emergencies. Suede carpenter's apron spotted with motor oil, clothes kept in stacked crates. There were hands never quite clean and later, manicured hands. A long car with mechanical windows that *zimmed* as they moved smoothly up and down, impenetrable as those clear shells separating the self from a dreamed desire (do you dream? of long foldings, channels, imageless dreams of fish, long turnings, echoed sounds and shading waters). In between, there were faces in many cars, road maps and laced boots, hand-printed signs held by the highway exits, threats from ex-cons, cajoling salesmen, circling patrolmen. There were counters, tables, eight-hour shifts, grease-stained menus, prices marked over three times, regulars pathetic and laughing, cheap regulation nylons, shoes with ridged soles, creamers filled early as a truck arrives with sugared doughnuts smelling of vats and heat. Men cursed in heavy accents, living in motor hum of the big dishwashers, overflowed garbage pails, ouzo at the end of the day. Then there were men across hallways, stair rails, men with offices, married men and their secretaries, empty bud vase on a desk. Men in elevators, white shirts ironed by a special Chinaman on Bleecker. Sanitary weekend joggers, movie reviewers, twenty-seventh floor, manufactured air, salon haircuts, long lunches, tablecloths and wine. Rooftop view, jets to cut swelling white slashes in the sky. And down below, below rooftops and clean charmed rhymes, the dark alleys meandered; those same alleys that crisscross a confusion of small towns. Same sideways routes and wishful arrivals, eye-level gravel, sooty perfumes, pale grass seeding in the stones. Bronzed light in casts of season: steely and blue, smoke taste of winters; the pinkish dark of any thaw; then coral falling in greens, summer mix of rot and flowers; autumn a burnt red, orange darkened to rust and scab. All of it men and faces, progression, hands come to this and you, grown inside me like one reminder.

He faced me over a café table, showed me the town on a map. No special reason, he said, he'd been here once; a quiet place, pretty, it would do. One geography was all he asked in the arrangement, the "interruption." He mentioned his obligation and its limits; he mentioned our separate paths. I don't ask here if they know him, I don't speculate. I've left him purely, as though you came to me after a voyage of years, as though you flew like a seed, saw them all and won me from them. I've lived with you all these months, grown cowish and full of you, yet I don't name you except by touch, curl, gesture. Wake and sleep, slim minnow, luminous frog. There are clues and riddles, pages in the book of the body, stones turned and turned. Each music lasts, forgetful, surfacing in the aisles of anonymous shops.

Music, addition and subtraction, Pavlovian reminder of scenes becoming, only dreamed. Evenings I listen to the radio and read fairy tales; those first lies, those promises. Directions are clear: crumbs in the woods, wolves in red hoods, the prince of temptation more believable as an enchanted toad. He is articulate and patient; there is the music of those years in the deep well, *plunk* of moisture, *whish* of the wayward rain, and finally the face of rescue peering over the stone rim like a moon. Omens burst into bloom; each life evolved to a single moment: the ugly natural, shrunken and wise, cradled in a palm fair as camellias.

Knot of cells, where is your voice? Here there are no books of instructions. There is the planed edge of the oaken table, the blond rivulets of the wood. There is a lamp in a dirty shade and the crouched stove hunkering its blackness around a fiery warmth. All night I sit, feeling the glow from a couch pulled close to the heat. Stirring the ashes, feeding, feeding, eating the fire with my skin. The foghorn cries through the mist in the bay: *bawaah, bawaah,* weeping of an idiot sheep, steady, measured as love. At dawn I'm standing by the window and the fishing boats bob like toys across the water, swaying their toothpick masts. Perfect mirage, they glisten and fade. Morning is two hours of sun as the season turns, a dime gone silver and thin. The gnarled plants are wild in their pots, spindly and bent. Gnats sleep on the leaves, inaugurating flight from a pearly slime on the windowpane. Their waftings are broken and dreamy, looping in the cold air of the house slowly, so slowly that I clap my hands and end them. Staccato, flash: that quick chord of once-upon-a-time.

Faraway I was a child, resolute, small, these same eyes in my head sinking back by night. Always I waited for you, marauder, collector, invisible pea in the body. I called you stones hidden in corners, paper fish with secret meanings, clothespin doll. Alone in my high bed, the dark, the dark; I shook my head faster, faster, rope of long hair flying across my shoulders like a switch, a scented tail. Under the bed, beyond the frothy curtain duster, I kept a menagerie of treasures and dust: discarded metallic jewelry, glass rhinestones pried from their settings, old gabardine suitcoat from a box in the basement, lipsticks, compacts with cloudy mirrors, slippers with pompoms, a man's blue silk tie embossed with tiny golf clubs. At night I crawled under wrapped in my sheets, breathing the buried smell, rattling the bed slats with my knees. I held my breath till the whole floor moved, plethora of red slashes; saw you in guises of lightning and the captive atmosphere.

Now a storm rolls the house in its paws. Again, men are lost and a hull washes up on the rocks. All day search copters hover and sweep. Dipping low, they chop the air for survivors and flee at dusk. The bay lies capped and draggled, rolling like water sloshed in a bowl. Toward nightfall, wind taps like briers on the windowpanes. We go out, down to the rocks and the shore. The forgotten hull lies breaking and splintered, only a slab of wood. The bay moves near it like a sleeper under sheets, murmuring, calling more rain. Animal in me, fish in a swim, I tell you *everything drowns.* I say *believe me if you are mine,* but you push like a fist with limbs. I feel your eyes searching, your gaze trapped in the dark like a beam of light. Then your vision transcends my skin: finally, I see them too, the lost fishermen, their faces framed in swirling hair like the heads of women. They are pale and blue, glowing, breathing with a pulse in their throats. They rise streaming tattered shirts, shining like mother-of-pearl. They rise moving toward us, round-mouthed, answering, answering the spheres of your talk. I am only witness to a language. The air is yours; it is water circling in like departure.

1984

LYNNE TILLMAN
b. 1947

Lynne Tillman was born in Brooklyn, New York, and lives in New York City. Her novels include *Haunted Houses* (1987), *Motion Sickness* (1992), *Cast in Doubt* (1993), and *No Lease on Life* (1997), and her story collections are *Absence Makes the Heart* (1990) and *The Madame Realism Complex* (1992). She has collaborated with the artists Jane Dickson and Kiki Smith, respectively, on *Living with Contradictions* (1982) and *Madame Realism* (1984). She is also the author of two books of nonfiction: *The Velvet Years, Andy Warhol and the Factory 1965–1967* (1995) and the essay collection *The Broad Picture* (1997). Her cultural criticism appears in *Art in America, Bomb, Frieze,* and the *Voice Literary Supplement.*

In her essay "Critical Fiction/Critical Self," in *Critical Fictions* (1991), Tillman writes: "I am wary or shy of proposing my fiction as written in opposition to, or to pronounce that I write differently, as if I—or it—could transcend conditions of birth and development—its and mine—and was somehow able to escape them. . . . I work within the American English language as a white, middle-class, second-generation American woman, at a particular moment in history, with my own particular biography." She adds, "I must wrest this language and its forms away from or out of 'the majority' (of which I am a part, in some ways and at some times, to others), to unman it, to un-American it, even to un-white it, to inconvenience the majority language, to unconventionalize it, even to shame it, in an odd sort of way, to question privilege, my own, too, of course."

"Living with Contradictions" first appeared as the title story of her 1982 collection.

Living with Contradictions

He didn't want to fight in any war and she didn't want to have a child. They had been living together for three years and still didn't have a way to refer to each other that didn't sound stupid, false, or antiquated. Language follows change and there wasn't any language to use.

Partners in a pairbonded situation; that sounded neutral. Of course living with someone isn't a neutral situation. Julie and Joe aren't cavedwellers. They don't live together as lovers or as husband and wife.

How long would this century be called modern or, even, post-modern? Perhaps relationships between people in the 14th century were more equitable, less fantastic. Not that Julie would've wanted to have been the miller's wife, or Joe the miller.

In other centuries, different relationships. Less presumption, less intimacy? Before capitalism, early capitalism, no capitalism, feudalism. Feudal relationships. I want one of those, Julie thought, something feudal. What would it be like not to have a contemporary mind? Intimacy is something people used to talk about before commercials. Now there's nothing to say.

People are intimate with their analysts, if they're lucky. What could be more intimate than an advertisement for Ivory soap? It's impossible not to be affected.

The manufacture of desire and the evidence of real desire. But 'real' desire is for what—for what is real or manufactured?

Other people's passions always leave you cold. There is nothing like really being held. They didn't expect to be everything to each other.

The first year they lived together was a battle to be together and to be separate. A silent battle, because you can't fight the fight together, it defeats the purpose of the battle.

You can't talk about relationships, at least they didn't; they talked about things that happened and things that didn't. Daily life is very daily.

The great adventure, the pioneering thing, is to live together and not be a couple. The expectation is indefatigable and exhausting. Julie bought an Italian postcard, circa 1953, showing an ardent man and woman, locked in embrace. And looking at each other. Except that one of her eyes was roving out, the other in, and his eyes, looking at her, were crossed.

Like star-crossed lovers' eyes should be, she thought. She drew a triangle around their eyes, which made them still more distorted. People would ask 'Where's Joe?' as if there was something supposed to be attached to her. The attachment, my dear, isn't tangible, she wanted to say, but it is also physical.

New cars, new lovers. Sometimes she felt like Ma Kettle in a situation comedy, looked on from the outside. You're either on the inside looking out or the outside looking in. (Then there's the inside looking in, the outside looking out.)

Joe: We're old love.
Julie: We're familiar with each other.

Julie didn't mind except that she didn't have anyone new to talk about, the way her friends did. Consumerism in love. One friend told her that talking about the person you lived with was like airing your clean laundry in public.

Familiarity was, for her, better than romance. She'd been in love enough. Being in love is a fiction that lasts an hour and a half, feature-length, and then you're hungry again. Unromantic old love comforted her, like a room to read in.

Joe: You hooked up with me at the end of your hard-guy period.
Julie: How do you know?
Joe: I know.

So, Julie and Joe were just part of the great heterosexual capitalist family thrall, possessing each other. Contradictions make life finer. Ambivalence is just another word for love, becoming romantic about the unconscious.

Where does one find comfort, even constancy. To find it in an idea or in the flesh. We do incorporate ideas, after all.

You can accept the irrational over and again, you can renounce your feelings every day, but you're still a baby. An infant outside of reason, speaking reasonably about the unreasonable.

Calling love desire doesn't change the need. Julie couldn't abandon her desire for love. It was a pleasurable contradiction and it was against all reason.

1990

II Fact Meets Fiction

In America, from the time of Independence, fiction has borne an ambiguous relation to nonfiction. The first documents that could be considered short stories in the contemporary sense appeared in journals during the Federal Era as cautionary "true" anecdotes designed explicitly to inculcate morals and implicitly to excite with their tales of sexual license and social decline. Many early American novels—Charles Brockden Brown's *Edgar Huntly* (1799), William Gilmore Simms' *Yemassee* (1835), and especially James Fenimore Cooper's *Leatherstocking Tales* (1823–41)—manipulated a readership unfamiliar with the specific conditions of the frontier by conflating fictional representation with documentary fact. Since that period, many significant contributions to American fiction have freely mixed fiction and nonfiction. Herman Melville's *Moby-Dick* (1851) contains lengthy passages explicating the profession of whaling and the whale's anatomy, as well as an "Extracts" section (prepared by a "sub-sub librarian") that cites references to the aquatic mammal throughout world literature. Years after the publication of *The Adventures of Huckleberry Finn* (1884), Mark Twain recalled in precise detail in his *Autobiography* (1924) how the residents of his boyhood home of Hannibal became characters within the novel. Even Henry Thoreau's *Walden* (1854), a literary work almost unparalleled in its efforts to reproduce the accuracy of a diary, is given a novelistic shape by the omission of many significant details of Thoreau's real life during that time.

In this context, what distinguishes these historical examples of hybrid forms of fact and fiction from the work of post–World War II writers testing the same divide is how the interrogation of the fact/fiction barrier has become in the postmodern era a central, even dominant source of artistic inspiration and innovation—an aesthetic in its own right. Truman Capote's landmark *In Cold Blood* (1965) illustrates how the postmodern inclination to blur the boundary between standard journalism and fiction could itself create a new layer of narrative tension within the bounds of the traditional novel. Capote's representations of the inner thoughts of the two murderers, his creation of particulars that read like reportorial details, his point-of-view shifts, and his narrative control all clearly reflect acts of the imagination that the reader can recognize as "fiction." Simultaneously, chapter subheadings such as "The Last to See Them Alive," or reportorial digressions ("The attendant, whose name was James Spor . . . ") conscientiously tether Capote's novelistic traits to the realm of something that can clearly be called "documentary," and resist the reader's inclination to dismiss *In Cold Blood*'s portrayal of casual violence as nothing more than an isolated act of imagination.

Referring to himself as an "ambiguous comic hero" as well as "an egotist of the most startling misproportions," Norman Mailer both invites and anticipates mockery for the self-conscious, self-centered portrayal of himself in *The Armies of the Night* (1968). What emerges, in fact, is philosophically compelling as well as comic and egotistical: Mailer's disproportionate emphasis upon himself becomes a parable of the subjectivity of the historian (and history itself) that would possess less force were it any less exaggerated. On the other hand, from its opening line—"This is true"—Tim O'Brien's "How to Tell a True War Story" (1990) draws power from the painstaking efforts of its author to maintain (and define) something he can call "truth." While the story's content tests the boundary of veracity and falsehood, the innovative use of the "how-to" manual as a structuring device represents an equivalent *formal* blending of journalism and fiction. William T. Vollmann's "The Visible Spectrum," a piece from his collection *The Rainbow Stories* (1989), represents a striking amalgam of American prose traditions, combining the fragmentary form of much postmodern fiction with an empathy for the lives of street people reminiscent of the Beat writers of the 1950s, together with a degree of self-consciousness and linguistic intensity evocative of New Journalists such as Hunter S. Thompson, Tom Wolfe, or Michael Herr. In "A Note on the Truth of the Tales," also from *The Rainbow Stories,* Vollmann offers a defense of this reportorial literary method, arguing that subjective versions of events make their own claims to truth, and asking his reader whether it were possible to "know more than I see."

The selections in this section also explore the combination of memoir and fiction, a hybrid that has been particularly prevalent during the postmodern era. An excerpt from Audre Lorde's *Zami: A New Spelling of My Name* (1982) illustrates how memoir often takes on narrative shape akin to that of fiction, while the content of the excerpt oppositely shows how individuals use fictional constructions to make order of real-life events. The result is a piece of literature that its author labels "biomythography," a form that seeks a balance between the mimetic and imaginative functions of autobiography. Theresa Hak Kyung Cha's "Clio History" (from her experimental 1982 novel *Dictee*) implodes the form of the traditional memoir altogether, and with it any landmark that might make the division between fact and fiction navigable. Not only does Cha's narrative contain photographs as well as excerpts from official documents, but it contains handwritten versions of its own typescript in two different languages as part of a fundamental examination of the distinction between what its narrator poetically calls "the parts false the parts real." Finally, Gloria Anzaldúa's "The Path of the Red and Black Ink" (1987), grounded in Mestiza culture, represents an evolution in postmodern treatments of the boundary between fact and fiction. While Anzaldúa's description of her writing process can be read as part essay, part memoir, and part fiction, its content resists being classified as a hybrid of traits that European cultures defined as opposites. Rather, "The Path of the Red and Black Ink" exists in (and insists upon the existence of) a metaphorical and metaphysical place Anzaldúa calls the "Borderlands," a "state of psychic unrest" where national boundaries (the divide between Mexico and the United States), gender identities, ancient religions and contemporary technologies, and especially forms of writing and expression are "all one."

TRUMAN CAPOTE
1924–1984

Truman Capote was born in New Orleans, Louisiana, and was educated at private schools in New York City and public schools in Greenwich, Connecticut. He began his literary career by serving as a newspaper clipper and cartoon cataloger for *The New Yorker,* a screenplay reader, and a freelance writer of anecdotes for a digest magazine. His seventeen books of fiction and nonfiction include the novel *Other Voices, Other Rooms* (1948), *Breakfast at Tiffany's: A Short Novel and Three Stories* (1958), *In Cold Blood: A True Account of a Multiple Murder and Its Consequences* (1965), and *Music for Chameleons: New Writing* (1983). Honors for his writing include O. Henry Awards for three of his short stories, a National Institute of Arts and Letters creative-writing award, and an Emmy Award for the television adaptation of one of his pieces, "A Christmas Memory." He died of liver disease.

In 1959, Capote put aside a roman à clef that he was never to finish, to pursue, as he told *Newsweek*'s Jack Kroll in 1966, "a theme not likely to darken and yellow with time." His intent was to bring "the art of the novelist together with the technique of journalism." The result was *In Cold Blood,* a "nonfiction novel"—according to Capote in a 1980 interview with James Wolcott in *The New York Review of Books*—"something on a large scale that would have the credibility of fact, the immediacy of film, the depth and freedom of prose, and the precision of poetry." Producing it took six years and involved more than six thousand pages of notes. "If I had known what that book was going to cost in every conceivable way, emotionally, I never would have started it," Capote said in a 1966 *Saturday Review* interview with Haskel Frankel.

"Truman had an odd and personal perspective on experience that only real writers have," observed poet and novelist James Dickey in *The New York Times* in 1984. "He was maybe a little heavy on the Southern gothic side of things, a little bit willfully perverse. . . . But at his best, he had a very great sensitivity and linguistic originality."

From In Cold Blood

The travelers stopped for dinner at a restaurant in Great Bend. Perry, down to his last fifteen dollars, was ready to settle for root beer and a sandwich, but Dick said no, they needed a solid "tuck-in," and never mind the cost, the tab was his. They ordered two steaks medium rare, baked potatoes, French fries, fried onions, succotash, side dishes of macaroni and hominy, salad with Thousand Island dressing, cinnamon rolls, apple pie and ice cream, and coffee. To top it off, they visited a drugstore and selected cigars; in the same drugstore, they also bought two thick rolls of adhesive tape.

As the black Chevrolet regained the highway and hurried on across a countryside imperceptibly ascending toward the colder, cracker-dry climate of the high wheat plains, Perry closed his eyes and dozed off into a food-dazed semi-slumber, from which he woke to hear a voice reading the eleven-o'clock news. He rolled down a window and bathed his face in the flood of frosty air. Dick told him they were in Finney County. "We crossed the line ten miles back," he said. The car was going very fast. Signs, their messages ignited by the car's headlights, flared up, flew by: "See the Polar Bears," "Burtis Motors," "World's Largest FREE Swim-pool," "Wheat

Lands Motel," and, finally, a bit before street lamps began, "Howdy, Stranger! Welcome to Garden City. A Friendly Place."

They skirted the northern rim of the town. No one was abroad at this nearly midnight hour, and nothing was open except a string of desolately brilliant service stations. Dick turned into one—Hurd's Phillips 66. A youngster appeared, and asked, "Fill her up?" Dick nodded, and Perry, getting out of the car, went inside the station, where he locked himself in the men's room. His legs pained him, as they often did; they hurt as though his old accident had happened five minutes before. He shook three aspirins out of a bottle, chewed them slowly (for he liked the taste), and then drank water from the basin tap. He sat down on the toilet, stretched out his legs and rubbed them, massaging the almost unbendable knees. Dick had said they were almost there—"only seven miles more." He unzippered a pocket of his windbreaker and brought out a paper sack; inside it were the recently purchased rubber gloves. They were glue-covered, sticky and thin, and as he inched them on, one tore—not a dangerous tear, just a split between the fingers, but it seemed to him an omen.

The doorknob turned, rattled. Dick said, "Want some candy? They got a candy machine out here."

"No."

"You O.K.?"

"I'm fine."

"Don't be all night."

Dick dropped a dime in a vending machine, pulled the lever, and picked up a bag of jelly beans; munching, he wandered back to the car and lounged there watching the young attendant's efforts to rid the windshield of Kansas dust and the slime of battered insects. The attendant, whose name was James Spor, felt uneasy. Dick's eyes and sullen expression and Perry's strange, prolonged sojourn in the lavatory disturbed him. (The next day he reported to his employer, "We had some tough customers in here last night," but he did not think, then or for the longest while, to connect the visitors with the tragedy in Holcomb.)

Dick said, "Kind of slow around here."

"Sure is," James Spor said. "You're the only body stopped here since two hours. Where you coming from?"

"Kansas City."

"Here to hunt?"

"Just passing through. On our way to Arizona. We got jobs waiting there. Construction work. Any idea the mileage between here and Tucumcari, New Mexico?"

"Can't say I do. Three dollars six cents." He accepted Dick's money, made change, and said, "You'll excuse me, sir? I'm doing a job. Putting a bumper on a truck."

Dick waited, ate some jelly beans, impatiently gunned the motor, sounded the horn. Was it possible that he had misjudged Perry's character? That Perry, of all people, was suffering a sudden case of "blood bubbles"? A year ago, when they first encountered each other, he'd thought Perry "a good guy," if a bit "stuck on himself," "sentimental," too much "the dreamer." He had liked him but not considered him especially worth cultivating until, one day, Perry described a murder, telling how, simply for "the hell of it," he had killed a colored man in Las Vegas—beaten him to death with a bicycle chain. The anecdote elevated Dick's opinion of Little Perry; he began to see more of him, and, like Willie-Jay, though for dissimilar reasons, gradually decided that Perry possessed unusual and valuable qualities. Several murderers, or men who boasted of murder or their willingness to commit it, circulated inside Lansing; but Dick became convinced that Perry was that rarity, "a natural killer"—absolutely sane, but conscienceless, and capable of dealing, with or without motive, the coldest-blooded deathblows. It was Dick's theory that such a gift could, under his supervision, be profitably exploited. Having reached this conclusion, he had proceeded to woo Perry, flatter him—pretend, for example, that he believed all the buried-treasure stuff and shared his beachcomber yearnings and seaport longings, none of which appealed to Dick, who wanted "a regular life," with a business of his own, a house, a horse to ride, a new car, and "plenty of blond chicken." It was important, however, that Perry not suspect this—not until Perry, with his gift, had helped further Dick's ambitions. But perhaps it was Dick who had miscalculated, been duped; if so—if it developed that Perry was, after all, only an "ordinary punk"—then "the party" was over, the months of planning were wasted, there was nothing to do but turn and go. It mustn't happen; Dick returned to the station.

The door to the men's room was still bolted. He banged on it: "For Christsake, Perry!"

"In a minute."

"What's the matter? You sick?"

Perry gripped the edge of the washbasin and hauled himself to a standing position. His legs trembled; the pain in his knees made him perspire. He wiped his face with a paper towel. He unlocked the door and said, "O.K. Let's go."

Nancy's bedroom was the smallest, most personal room in the house—girlish, and as frothy as a ballerina's tutu. Walls, ceiling, and everything else except a bureau and a writing desk, were pink or blue or white. The white-and-pink bed, piled with blue pillows, was dominated by a big pink-and-white Teddy bear—a shooting-gallery prize that Bobby had won at the county fair. A cork bulletin board, painted pink, hung above a white-skirted dressing table; dry gardenias, the remains of some ancient corsage, were attached to it, and old valentines, newspaper recipes, and snapshots of her baby nephew and of Susan Kidwell and of Bobby Rupp, Bobby caught in a dozen actions—swinging a bat, dribbling a basketball, driving a tractor, wading, in bathing trunks, at the edge of McKinney Lake (which was as far as he dared go, for he had never learned to swim). And there were photographs of the two together—Nancy and Bobby. Of these, she liked best one that showed them sitting in a leaf-dappled light amid picnic debris and looking at one another with expressions that, though unsmiling, seemed mirthful and full of delight. Other pictures of horses, of cats deceased but unforgotten—like "poor Boobs," who had died not long ago and most mysteriously (she suspected poison)—encumbered her desk.

Nancy was invariably the last of the family to retire; as she had once informed her friend and home-economics teacher, Mrs. Polly Stringer, the midnight hours were her "time to be selfish and vain." It was then that she went through her beauty routine, a cleansing, creaming ritual, which on Saturday nights included washing her hair. Tonight, having dried and brushed her hair and bound it in a gauzy bandanna, she set out the clothes she intended to wear to church the next morning: nylons, black pumps, a red velveteen dress—her prettiest, which she herself had made. It was the dress in which she was to be buried.

Before saying her prayers, she always recorded in a diary a few occurrences ("Summer here. Forever, I hope. Sue over and we rode Babe down to the river. Sue played her flute. Fireflies") and an occasional outburst ("I love him, I do"). It was a five-year diary; in the four years of its existence she had never neglected to make an entry, though the splendor of several events (Eveanna's wedding, the birth of her nephew) and the drama of others (her "first REAL quarrel with Bobby"—a page literally tear-stained) had caused her to usurp space allotted to the future. A different-tinted ink identified each year: 1956 was green and 1957 a ribbon of red, replaced the following year by bright lavender, and now, in 1959, she had decided upon a dignified blue. But as in every manifestation, she continued to tinker with her handwriting, slanting it to the right or to the left, shaping it roundly or steeply, loosely or stingily—as though she were asking, "Is this Nancy? Or that? Or that? Which is me?" (Once Mrs. Riggs, her English teacher, had returned a theme with a scribbled comment: "Good. But why written in three styles of script?" To which Nancy had replied: "Because I'm not grown-up enough to be one person with one kind of signature.") Still, she had progressed in recent months, and it was in a handwriting of emerging maturity that she wrote, "Jolene K. came over and I showed her how to make a cherry pie. Practiced with Roxie. Bobby here and we watched TV. Left at eleven."

"This is it, this is it, this has to be it, there's the school, there's the garage, now we turn south." To Perry, it seemed as though Dick were muttering jubilant mumbo jumbo. They left the highway, sped through a deserted Holcomb, and crossed the Santa Fe tracks. "The bank, that must be the bank, now we turn west—see the trees? This is it, this has to be it." The headlights disclosed a lane of Chinese elms; bundles of wind-blown thistle scurried across it. Dick doused the headlights, slowed down, and stopped until his eyes were adjusted to the moon-illuminated night. Presently, the car crept forward.

Holcomb is twelve miles east of the mountain time-zone border, a circumstance that causes some grumbling, for it means that at seven in the morning, and in winter at eight or after, the sky is still dark and the stars, if any, are still shining—as they were when the two sons of Vic Irsik arrived to do their Sunday-morning chores. But by nine, when the boys finished work—during which they noticed nothing amiss—the sun had risen, delivering another day of pheasant-season perfection. As they left the property and ran along the lane, they waved at an incoming car, and a girl waved back. She was a classmate of Nancy Clutter's, and her name was also Nancy—Nancy Ewalt. She was the only child of the man who was driving the car, Mr. Clarence Ewalt, a middle-aged sugar-beet farmer. Mr. Ewalt was not himself a churchgoer, nor was his wife, but every Sunday he dropped his daughter at River Valley Farm in order that she might accompany the Clutter family to Methodist services in Garden City. The arrangement saved him "making two back-and-forth trips to town." It was his custom to wait until he had seen his daughter safely admitted to the house. Nancy, a clothes-conscious girl with a film-star figure, a bespectacled countenance, and a coy, tiptoe way of walking, crossed the lawn and pressed the front-door bell. The house had four entrances, and when, after repeated knockings, there was no response at this one, she moved on to the next—that of Mr. Clutter's office. Here the door was partly open; she opened it somewhat more—enough to ascertain that the office was filled only with shadow—but she did not think the Clutters would appreciate her "barging right in." She knocked, rang, and at last walked around to the back of the house. The garage was there, and she noted that both cars were in it: two Chevrolet sedans. Which meant they *must* be home. However, having applied unavailingly at a third door, which led into a "utility room," and a fourth, the door to the kitchen, she rejoined her father, who said, "Maybe they're asleep."

"But that's *im*possible. Can you imagine Mr. Clutter missing church? Just to *sleep?*"

"Come on, then. We'll drive down to the Teacherage. Susan ought to know what's happened."

The Teacherage, which stands opposite the up-to-date school, is an out-of-date edifice, drab and poignant. Its twenty-odd rooms are separated into grace-and-favor apartments for those members of the faculty unable to find, or afford, other quarters. Nevertheless, Susan Kidwell and her mother had managed to sugar the pill and install a cozy atmosphere in their apartment—three rooms on the ground floor. The very small living room incredibly contained—aside from things to sit on—an organ, a piano, a garden of flowering flowerpots, and usually a darting little dog and a large, drowsy cat. Susan, on this Sunday morning, stood at the window of this room watching the street. She is a tall, languid young lady with a pallid, oval face and beautiful pale-blue-gray eyes; her hands are extraordinary—long-fingered, flexible, nervously elegant. She was dressed for church, and expected momentarily to see the Clutters' Chevrolet, for she too, always attended services chaperoned by the Clutter family. Instead, the Ewalts arrived to tell their peculiar tale.

But Susan knew no explanation, nor did her mother, who said, "If there was some change of plan, why, I'm sure they would have telephoned. Susan, why don't you call the house? They *could* be asleep—I suppose."

"So I did," said Susan, in a statement made at a later date. "I called the house and let the phone ring—at least, I had the *impression* it was ringing—oh, a minute or more. Nobody answered, so Mr. Ewalt suggested that we go to the house and try to 'wake them up.' But when we got there—I didn't want to do it. Go inside the house. I was frightened, and I don't know why, because it never occurred to me—well, something like that just doesn't. But the sun was so bright, everything looked too bright and quiet. And then I saw that all the cars were there, even Kenyon's old coyote wagon. Mr. Ewalt was wearing work clothes; he had mud on his boots; he felt he wasn't properly dressed to go calling on the Clutters. Especially since he never had. Been in the house, I mean. Finally, Nancy said she would go with me. We went around to the kitchen door, and, of course, it wasn't locked; the only person who ever locked doors around there was Mrs. Helm—the family never did. We walked in, and I saw right away that the Clutters hadn't eaten breakfast; there were no dishes, nothing on the stove. Then I noticed something funny: Nancy's purse. It was lying on the floor, sort of open. We passed on through the dining room, and stopped at the bottom of the stairs. Nancy's room is just at the top. I called her name, and started up the stairs, and Nancy Ewalt followed. The sound of our footsteps frightened me more than anything, they were so loud and everything else was so silent. Nancy's door was open. The curtains hadn't been drawn, and the room was full of sunlight. I don't remember screaming. Nancy Ewalt says I did—screamed and screamed. I only remember Nancy's Teddy bear staring at me. And Nancy. And running . . ."

In the interim, Mr. Ewalt had decided that perhaps he ought not to have allowed the girls to enter the house alone. He was getting out of the car to go after them when he heard the screams, but before he could reach the house, the girls were running toward him. His daughter shouted, "She's dead!" and flung herself into his arms. "It's true, Daddy! Nancy's dead!"

Susan turned on her. "No, she isn't. And don't you say it. Don't you dare. It's only a nosebleed. She has them all the time, terrible nosebleeds, and that's all it is."

"There's too much blood. There's blood on the walls. You didn't really look."

"I couldn't make head nor tails," Mr. Ewalt subsequently testified. "I thought maybe the child was hurt. It seemed to me the first thing to do was call an ambulance. Miss Kidwell—Susan—she told me there was a telephone in the kitchen. I found it, right where she said. But the receiver was off the hook, and when I picked it up, I saw the line had been cut."

Larry Hendricks, a teacher of English, aged twenty-seven, lived on the top floor of the Teacherage. He wanted to write, but his apartment was not the ideal lair for a would-be author. It was smaller than the Kidwells', and, moreover, he shared it with a wife, three active children, and a perpetually functioning television set. ("It's the only way we can keep the kids pacified.") Though as yet unpublished, young Hendricks, a he-mannish ex-sailor from Oklahoma who smokes a pipe and has a mustache and a crop of untamed black hair, at least looks literary—in fact, remarkably like youthful photographs of the writer he most admires, Ernest Hemingway. To supplement his teacher's salary, he also drove a school bus.

"Sometimes I cover sixty miles a day," he said to an acquaintance. "Which doesn't leave much time for writing. Except Sundays. Now, *that* Sunday, November fifteenth, I was sitting up here in the apartment going through the papers. Most of my ideas for stories, I get them out of the newspapers—you know? Well, the TV was on and the kids were kind of lively, but even so I could hear *voices*. From downstairs. Down at Mrs. Kidwell's. But I didn't figure it was my concern, since I was new here—only came to Holcomb when school began. But then Shirley—she'd been out hanging up some clothes—my wife, Shirley, rushed in and said, 'Honey, you better go downstairs. They're all hysterical.' The two girls—now, they really were hysterical. Susan never has got over it. Never will, ask me. And poor Mrs. Kidwell. Her health's not too good, she's high-strung to begin with. She kept saying—but it was only later I understood what she meant—she kept saying, 'Oh, Bonnie, Bonnie, what happened? You were so happy, you told me it was all over, you said you'd never be sick again.' Words to that effect. Even Mr. Ewalt, he was about as worked up as a man like that ever gets. He had the sheriff's office on the phone—the Garden City sheriff—and he was telling him that there was 'something *radically* wrong over at the Clutter place.' The sheriff promised to come straight out, and Mr. Ewalt said fine, he'd meet him on the highway. Shirley came downstairs to sit with the women, try and calm them—as if anybody could. And I went with Mr. Ewalt—drove with him out to the highway to wait for Sheriff Robinson. On the way, he told me what had happened. When he came to the part about finding the wires cut, right then I thought, Uh-uh, and decided I'd better keep my eyes open. Make a note of every detail. In case I was ever called on to testify in court.

"The sheriff arrived; it was nine thirty-five—I looked at my watch. Mr. Ewalt waved at him to follow our car, and we drove out to the Clutters'. I'd never been there before, only seen it from a distance. Of course, I knew the family. Kenyon was in my sophomore English class, and I'd directed Nancy in the 'Tom Sawyer' play. But they were such exceptional, unassuming kids you wouldn't have known they were rich or lived in such a big house—and the trees, the lawn, everything so tended and cared for. After we got there, and the sheriff had heard Mr. Ewalt's story, he radioed his office and told them to send reinforcements, and an ambulance. Said, 'There's been some kind of accident.' Then we went in the house, the three of us. Went through the kitchen and saw a lady's purse lying on the floor, and the phone where the wires had been cut. The sheriff was wearing a hip pistol, and when we started up the stairs, going to Nancy's room, I noticed he kept his hand on it, ready to draw.

"Well, it was pretty bad. That wonderful girl—but you would never have known her. She'd been shot in the back of the head with a shotgun held maybe two inches away. She was lying on her side, facing the wall, and the wall was covered with blood. The bedcovers were drawn up to her shoulders. Sheriff Robinson, he pulled them back, and we saw that she was wearing a bathrobe, pajamas, socks, and slippers—like, whenever it happened, she hadn't gone to bed yet. Her hands were tied behind her, and her ankles were roped together with the kind of cord you see on Venetian blinds. Sheriff said, 'Is this Nancy Clutter?'—he'd never seen the child before. And I said, 'Yes. Yes, that's Nancy.'

"We stepped back into the hall, and looked around. All the other doors were closed. We opened one, and that turned out to be a bathroom. Something about it seemed wrong. I decided it was because of the chair—a sort of dining-room chair, that looked out of place in a bathroom. The next door—we all agreed it must be Kenyon's room. A lot of boy-stuff scattered around. And I recognized Kenyon's glasses—saw them on a bookshelf beside the bed. But the bed was empty, though it looked as if it had been slept in. So we walked to the end of the hall, the last door, and there, on her bed, that's where we found Mrs. Clutter. She'd been tied, too. But differently—with her hands in front of her, so that she looked as though she were praying—and in one hand she was holding, *gripping*, a handkerchief. Or was it Kleenex? The cord around her wrists ran down to her ankles, which were bound together, and then ran on down to the bottom of the bed, where it was tied to the footboard—a very complicated, artful piece of work. Think how long it took to do! And her lying there, scared out of her wits. Well, she was wearing some jewelry, two rings—which is one of the reasons why I've always discounted robbery as a motive—and a robe, and a white nightgown, and white socks. Her mouth had been taped with adhesive, but she'd been shot point-blank in the side of the head, and the blast—the impact—had ripped the tape loose. Her eyes were open. Wide open. As though she were still looking at the killer. Because she must have had to watch him do it—aim the gun. Nobody said anything. We were too stunned. I remember the sheriff searched around to see if he could find the discharged cartridge. But whoever had done it was much too smart and cool to have left behind any clues like that.

"Naturally, we were wondering where was Mr. Clutter? And Kenyon? Sheriff said, 'Let's try downstairs.' The first place we tried was the master bedroom—the room where Mr. Clutter slept. The bedcovers were drawn back, and lying there, toward the foot of the bed, was a billfold with a mess of cards spilling out of it, like somebody had shuffled through them hunting something particular—a note, an I.O.U., who knows? The fact that there wasn't any money in it didn't signify one way or the other. It was Mr. Clutter's billfold, and he never did carry cash. Even I knew that, and I'd only been in Holcomb a little more than two months. Another thing I knew was that neither Mr. Clutter nor Kenyon could see a darn without his glasses. And there were Mr. Clutter's glasses sitting on a bureau. So I figured, wherever they were, they weren't there of their own accord. We looked all over, and everything was just as it should be—no sign of a struggle, nothing disturbed. Except the office, where the telephone was off the hook, and the wires cut, same as in the kitchen. Sheriff Robinson, he found some shotguns in a closet, and sniffed them to see if they had been fired recently. Said they hadn't, and—I never saw a more bewildered man—said, 'Where the devil can Herb *be?*' About then we heard footsteps. Coming up the stairs from the basement. 'Who's that?' said the sheriff, like he was ready to shoot. And a voice said, 'It's me. Wendle.' Turned out to be Wendle Meier, the undersheriff. Seems he had come to the house and hadn't seen us, so he'd gone investigating down in the basement. The sheriff told him—and it was sort of pitiful: 'Wendle, I don't know what to make of it. There's two bodies upstairs.' 'Well,' he said, Wendle did, 'there's another one down here.' So we followed him down to the basement. Or playroom, I guess you'd call it. It wasn't dark—there were windows that let in plenty of light. Kenyon was over in a corner, lying on a couch. He was gagged with adhesive tape and bound hand and foot, like the mother—the same intricate process of the cord leading from the hands to the feet, and finally tied to an arm of the couch. Somehow he haunts me the most, Kenyon does. I think it's because he was the most recognizable, the one that looked the most like himself—even though he'd been shot in the face, directly, head-on. He was wearing a T-shirt and blue jeans, and he was barefoot—as though he'd dressed in a hurry, just put on the first thing that came to hand. His head was propped by a couple of pillows, like they'd been stuffed under him to make an easier target.

"Then the sheriff said, 'Where's this go to?' Meaning another door there in the basement. Sheriff led the way, but inside you couldn't see your hand until Mr. Ewalt found the light switch. It was a furnace room, and very warm. Around here, people just install a gas furnace and pump the gas smack out of the ground. Doesn't cost them a nickel—that's why all the houses are overheated. Well, I took one look at Mr. Clutter, and it was hard to look again. I knew plain shooting couldn't account for that much blood. And I wasn't wrong. He'd been shot, all right, the same as Kenyon—with the gun held right in front of his face. But probably he was dead before he was shot. Or, anyway, dying. Because his throat had been cut, too. He was wearing striped pajamas—nothing else. His mouth was taped; the tape had been wound plumb around his head. His ankles were tied together, but not his hands—or, rather, he'd managed, God knows how, maybe in rage or pain, to break the cord binding his hands. He was sprawled in front of the furnace. On a big cardboard box that looked as though it had been laid there specially. A mattress box. Sheriff said, 'Look here, Wendle.' What he was pointing at was a bloodstained footprint. On the mattress box. A half-sole footprint with circles—two holes in the center like a pair of eyes. Then one of us—Mr. Ewalt? I don't recall—pointed out something else. A thing I can't get out of my mind. There was a steampipe overhead, and knotted to it, dangling from it, was a piece of cord—the kind of cord the killer had used. Obviously, at some point Mr. Clutter had been tied there, strung up by his hands, and then cut down. But why? To torture him? I don't guess we'll ever know. Ever know who did it, or why, or what went on in that house that night.

"After a bit, the house began to fill up. Ambulances arrived, and the coroner, and the Methodist minister, a police photographer, state troopers, fellows from the radio and the newspaper. Oh, a bunch. Most of them had been called out of church, and acted as though they were still there. Very quiet. Whispery. It was like nobody could believe it. A state trooper asked me did I have any official business there, and said if not, then I'd better leave. Outside, on the lawn, I saw the undersheriff talking to a man—Alfred Stoecklein, the hired man. Seems Stoecklein lived not a hundred yards from the Clutter house, with nothing between his place and theirs except a barn. But he was saying as to how he hadn't heard a sound—said, 'I didn't know a thing about it till five minutes ago, when one of my kids came running in and told us the sheriff was here. The Missis and me, we didn't sleep two hours last night, was up and down the whole time, on account of we got a sick baby. But the only thing we heard, about ten-thirty, quarter to eleven, I heard a car drive away, and I made the remark to Missis, "There goes Bob Rupp." ' I started walking home, and on the way, about halfway down the lane, I saw Kenyon's old collie, and that dog was scared. Stood there with its tail between its legs, didn't bark or move. And seeing the dog—

somehow that made me *feel* again. I'd been too dazed, too numb, to feel the full viciousness of it. The suffering. The horror. They were dead. A whole family. Gentle, kindly people, *I* knew—*murdered.* You had to believe it, because it was really true."

Eight non-stop passenger trains hurry through Holcomb every twenty-four hours. Of these, two pick up and deposit mail—an operation that, as the person in charge of it fervently explains, has its tricky side. "Yessir, you've got to keep on your toes. Them trains come through here, sometimes they're going a hundred miles an hour. The breeze alone, why, it's enough to knock you down. And when those mail sacks come flying out—sakes alive! It's like playing tackle on a football team: Wham! *Wham!* WHAM! Not that I'm complaining, mind you. It's honest work, *government* work, and it keeps me young." Holcomb's mail messenger, Mrs. Sadie Truitt—or Mother Truitt, as the townspeople call her—does seem younger than her years, which amount to seventy-five. A stocky, weathered widow who wears babushka bandannas and cowboy boots ("Most comfortable things you can put on your feet, soft as a loon feather"), Mother Truitt is the oldest native-born Holcombite. "Time was wasn't anybody here wasn't my kin. Them days, we called this place Sherlock. Then along came this stranger. By the name Holcomb. A *hog* raiser, he was. Made money, and decided the town ought to be called after him. Soon as it was, what did he do? Sold out. Moved to California. Not us. I was born here, my children was born here. And! Here! We! Are!" One of her children is Mrs. Myrtle Clare, who happens to be the local postmistress. "Only, don't go thinking that's how I got this position with the government. Myrt didn't even want me to have it. But it's a job you *bid* for. Goes to whoever puts in the lowest bid. And I always do—so low a caterpillar could peek over it. Ha-Ha! That sure does rile the boys. Lots of boys would like to be mail messenger, *yessir.* But I don't know much they'd like it when the snow's high as old Mr. Primo Carnera, and the wind's blowing blue-hard, and those sacks came sailing—Ugh! Wham!"

In Mother Truitt's profession, Sunday is a workday like any other. On November 15, while she was waiting for the west-bound ten-thirty-two, she was astonished to see two ambulances cross the railroad tracks and turn toward the Clutter property. The incident provoked her into doing what she had never done before—abandon her duties. Let the mail fall where it may, this was news that Myrt must hear at once.

The people of Holcomb speak of their post office as "the Federal Building," which seems rather too substantial a title to confer on a drafty and dusty shed. The ceiling leaks, the floor boards wobble, the mailboxes won't shut, the light bulbs are broken, the clock has stopped. "Yes, it's a disgrace," agrees the caustic, somewhat original, and entirely imposing lady who presides over this litter. "But the stamps work, don't they? Anyhow, what do I care? Back here in *my* part is real cozy. I've got my rocker, and a nice wood stove, and a coffee pot, and plenty to read."

Mrs. Clare is a famous figure in Finney County. Her celebrity derives not from her present occupation but a previous one—dance-hall hostess, an incarnation not indicated by her appearance. She is a gaunt, trouser-wearing, woolen-shirted, cowboy-booted, ginger-colored, gingerly-tempered woman of unrevealed age ("That's for me to know, and you to guess") but promptly revealed opinions, most of which are announced in a voice of rooster-crow altitude and penetration. Until 1955 she and her late husband operated the Holcomb Dance Pavilion, an enterprise that owing to its uniqueness in the area, attracted from a hundred miles around a fast-drinking, fancy-stepping clientele, whose behavior, in turn, attracted the interest of the sheriff now and then. "We had some tough times, all right," says Mrs. Clare, reminiscing. "Some of those bowlegged boys, you give 'em a little hooch and they're like redskins—want to scalp everything in sight. Course, we only sold setups, never the hard stuff itself. Wouldn't have, even if it was legal. My husband, Homer Clare, he didn't hold with it; neither did I. One day Homer Clare—he passed on seven months and twelve days ago today, after a five-hour operation out in Oregon—he said to me, 'Myrt, we've lived all our lives in hell, now we're going to die in heaven.' The next day we closed the dance hall. I've never regretted it. Oh, along at first I missed being a night owl—the tunes, the jollity. But now that Homer's gone, I'm just glad to do my work here at the Federal Building. Sit a spell. Drink a cup of coffee."

In fact, on that Sunday morning Mrs. Clare had just poured herself a cup of coffee from a freshly brewed pot when Mother Truitt returned.

"Myrt!" she said, but could say no more until she had caught her breath. "Myrt, there's two ambulances gone to the Clutters'."

Her daughter said, "Where's the ten-thirty-two?"

"Ambulances. Gone to the Clutters'—"

"Well, what about it? It's only Bonnie. Having one of her spells. Where's the ten-thirty-two?"

Mother Truitt subsided; as usual, Myrt knew the answer, was enjoying the last word. Then a thought occurred to her. "But Myrt, if it's only Bonnie, why would there be *two* ambulances?"

A sensible question, as Mrs. Clare, an admirer of logic, though a curious interpreter of it, was driven to admit. She said she would telephone Mrs. Helm. "Mabel will know," she said.

The conversation with Mrs. Helm lasted several minutes, and was most distressing to Mother Truitt, who could hear nothing of it except the non-committal monosyllabic responses of her daughter. Worse, when the daughter hung up, she did not quench the old woman's curiosity; instead, she placidly drank her coffee, went to her desk, and began to postmark a pile of letters.

"Myrt," Mother Truitt said. "For heaven's sake. What did Mabel *say?*"

"I'm not surprised," Mrs. Clare said. "When you think how Herb Clutter spent his whole life in a hurry, rushing in here to get his mail with never a minute to say good-morning-and-thank-you-dog, rushing around like a chicken with its head off—joining clubs, running everything, getting jobs maybe other people wanted. And now look—it's all caught up with him. Well, he won't be rushing *any* more."

"Why, Myrt? Why won't he?"

Mrs. Clare raised her voice. "BECAUSE HE'S DEAD. And Bonnie, too. And Nancy. And the boy. Somebody shot them."

"Myrt—don't say things like that. Who shot them?"

Without a pause in her postmarking activities, Mrs. Clare replied, "The man in the airplane. The one Herb sued for crashing into his fruit trees. If it wasn't him, maybe it was you. Or somebody across the street. All the neighbors are rattlesnakes. Varmints looking for a chance to slam the door in your face. It's the same the whole world over. You know that."

"I don't," said Mother Truitt, who put her hands over her ears. "I don't know any such thing."

"Varmints."

"I'm scared, Myrt."

"Of what? When your time comes, it comes. And tears won't save you." She had observed that her mother had begun to shed a few. "When Homer died, I used up all the fear I had in me and all the grief, too. If there's somebody loose around here that wants to cut my throat, I wish him luck. What difference does it make? It's all the same in eternity. Just remember: If one bird carried every grain of sand, grain by grain, across the ocean, by the time he got them all on the other side, that would only be the beginning of eternity. So blow your nose."

The grim information announced from church pulpits, distributed over telephone wires, publicized by Garden City's radio station, KIUL ("A tragedy, unbelievable and shocking beyond words, struck four members of the Herb Clutter family late Saturday night or early today. Death, brutal and without apparent motive . . ."), produced in the average recipient a reaction nearer that of Mother Truitt than that of Mrs. Clare: amazement, shading into dismay; a shallow horror sensation that cold springs of personal fear swiftly deepened.

Hartman's Café, which contains four roughly made tables and a lunch counter, could accommodate but a fraction of the frightened gossips, mostly male, who wished to gather there. The owner, Mrs. Bess Hartman, a sparsely fleshed, unfoolish lady with bobbed gray-and-gold hair and bright, authoritative green eyes, is a cousin of Postmistress Clare, whose style of candor Mrs. Hartman can equal, perhaps surpass. "Some people say I'm a tough old bird, but the Clutter business sure took the fly out of me," she later said to a friend. "Imagine anybody pulling a stunt like that! Time I heard it, when everybody was pouring in here talking all kinds of wild-eyed stuff, my first thought was Bonnie. Course, it was silly, but we didn't know the facts, and a lot of people thought *maybe*—on account of her spells. Now we don't know what to think. It must have been a grudge killing. Done by somebody who knew the house inside out. But who hated the Clutters? I never heard a word against them; they were about as popular as a family can be, and if something like this could happen to *them,* then who's safe, I ask you? One old man sitting here that Sunday, he put his finger right on it, the reason nobody can sleep; he said, 'All we've got out here are our friends. There isn't anything else.' In a way, that's the worst part of the crime. What a terrible thing when neighbors can't look at each other without kind of wondering! Yes, it's a hard fact to live with, but if they ever do find out who done it, I'm sure it'll be a bigger surprise than the murders themselves."

Mrs. Bob Johnson, the wife of the New York Life Insurance agent, is an excellent cook, but the Sunday dinner she had prepared was not eaten—at least, not while it was warm—for just as her husband was plunging a knife into the roast pheasant, he received a telephone call from a friend. "And that," he recalls, rather ruefully, "was the first I heard of what had happened in Holcomb. I didn't believe it. I couldn't afford to. Lord, I had Clutter's check right here in my pocket. A piece of paper worth eighty thousand dollars. If what I'd heard was true. But I thought, It can't be, there must be some mistake, things like that don't happen, you don't sell a man a big policy one minute and he's dead the next. Murdered. Meaning double indemnity. I didn't know what to do. I called the manager of our office in Wichita. Told him how I had the check but hadn't put it through, and asked what was his advice? Well, it was a *delicate* situation. It appeared that *legally* we weren't obliged to pay. But *morally*—that was another matter. Naturally, we decided to do the moral thing."

The two persons who benefited by this honorable attitude—Eveanna Jarchow and her sister Beverly, sole heirs to their father's estate—were, within a few hours of the awful discovery, on their way to Garden City, Beverly traveling from Winfield, Kansas, where she had been visiting her fiancé, and Eveanna from her home in Mount Carroll, Illinois. Gradually, in the course of the day, other relatives were notified, among them Mr. Clutter's father, his two brothers, Arthur and Clarence, and his sister, Mrs. Harry Nelson, all of Larned, Kansas, and a second sister, Mrs. Elaine Selsor, of Palatka, Florida. Also, the parents of Bonnie Clutter, Mr. and Mrs. Arthur B. Fox, who lived in Pasadena, California, and her three brothers—Harold, of Visalia, California; Howard, of Oregon, Illinois; and Glenn, of Kansas City, Kansas. Indeed, the better part of those on the Clutters' Thanksgiving guest list were either telephoned or telegraphed, and the majority set forth at once for what was to be a family reunion not around a groaning board but at the graveside of a mass burial.

At the Teacherage, Wilma Kidwell was forced to control herself in order to control her daughter, for Susan, puffy-eyed, sickened by spasms of nausea, argued, inconsolably insisted, that she must go—must run—the three miles to the Rupp farm. "Don't you see, Mother?" she said. "If Bobby just *hears* it? He loved her. We both did. I *have* to be the one to tell him."

But Bobby already knew. On his way home, Mr. Ewalt had stopped at the Rupp farm and consulted with his friend Johnny Rupp, a father of eight, of whom Bobby is the third. Together, the two men went to the bunkhouse—a building separated from the farmhouse proper, which is too small to shelter all the Rupp children. The boys live in the bunkhouse, the girls "at home." They found Bobby making his bed. He listened to Mr. Ewalt, asked no questions, and thanked him for coming. Afterward, he stood outside in the sunshine. The Rupp property is on a rise, an exposed plateau, from which he could see the harvested, glowing land of River Valley Farm—scenery that occupied him for perhaps an hour. Those who tried to distract him could not. The dinner bell sounded, and his mother called to him to come inside—called until finally her husband said, "No. I'd leave him alone."

Larry, a younger brother, also refused to obey the summoning bell. He circled around Bobby, helpless to help but wanting to, even though he was told to "go away." Later, when his brother stopped standing and started to walk, heading down the road and across the fields toward Holcomb, Larry pursued him. "Hey, Bobby. Listen. If we're going somewhere, why don't we go in the car?" His brother wouldn't answer. He was walking with purpose, running, really, but Larry had no difficulty keeping stride. Though only fourteen, he was the taller of the two, the deeper-chested, the longer-legged, Bobby being, for all his athletic honors, rather less than medium-size—compact but slender, a finely made boy with an open, homely-handsome face. "Hey, Bobby. Listen. They won't let you see her. It won't do any good." Bobby turned on him, and said, "Go back. Go home." The younger brother fell behind, then followed at a distance. Despite the pumpkin-season temperature, the day's arid glitter, both boys were sweating as they approached a barricade that state troopers had erected at the entrance to River Valley Farm. Many friends of the Clutter family, and strangers from all over Finney County as well, had assembled at the site, but none was allowed past the barricade, which, soon after the arrival of the Rupp brothers, was briefly lifted to permit the exit of four ambulances, the number finally required to remove the victims, and a car filled with men from the sheriff's office—men who, even at that moment, were mentioning the name of Bobby Rupp. For Bobby, as he was to learn before nightfall, was their principal suspect.

From her parlor window, Susan Kidwell saw the white cortege glide past, and watched until it had rounded the corner and the unpaved street's easily airborne dust had landed again. She was still contemplating the view when Bobby, shadowed by his large little brother, became a part of it, a wobbly figure headed her way. She went out on the porch to meet him. She said, "I wanted so much to tell you." Bobby began to cry. Larry lingered at the edge of the Teacherage yard, hunched against a tree. He couldn't remember ever seeing Bobby cry, and he didn't want to, so he lowered his eyes.

Far off, in the town of Olathe, in a hotel room where window shades darkened the midday sun, Perry lay sleeping, with a portable radio murmuring beside him. Except for taking off his boots, he had not troubled to undress. He had merely fallen face down across the bed, as though sleep were a weapon that had struck him from behind. The boots, black and silver-buckled, were soaking in a washbasin filled with warm, vaguely pink-tinted water.

A few miles north, in the pleasant kitchen of a modest farmhouse, Dick was consuming a Sunday dinner. The others at the table—his mother, his father, his younger brother—were not conscious of anything uncommon in his manner. He had arrived home at noon, kissed his mother, readily replied to questions his father put concerning his supposed overnight trip to Fort Scott, and sat down to eat, seeming quite his ordinary self. When the meal was over, the three male members of the family settled in the parlor to watch a televised basketball game. The broadcast had only begun when the father was startled to hear Dick snoring; as he remarked to the younger boy, he never thought he'd live to see the day when Dick would rather sleep than watch basketball. But, of course, he did not understand how very tired Dick was, did not know that his dozing son had, among other things, driven over eight hundred miles in the past twenty-four hours.

1965

NORMAN MAILER
b. 1923

Norman Mailer was born in Long Branch, New Jersey, and educated at Harvard University and the Sorbonne. As a college student he won *Story* magazine's college-fiction prize, and his literary career was further shaped by his experiences serving as an infantry rifleman in the Philippines and Japan during World War II. His more than forty books include the novels *The Naked and the Dead* (1948) and *The Executioner's Song* (1979), the nonfiction narrative *Armies of the Night: History as a Novel, the Novel as History* (1968), and the collection *Advertisements for Myself* (1959). He has received two Pulitzer Prizes and a National Book Award. Currently he divides his time between Brooklyn, New York, and Provincetown, Massachusetts.

The Naked and the Dead, his first novel, spent eleven consecutive weeks on the *New York Times* bestseller list and shaped Mailer's literary aspirations. "I had the freak of luck to start high on the mountain, and go down sharp while others were passing me," he wrote in *Advertisements for Myself.* He wanted "to hit the longest ball ever to go up into the accelerated hurricane air of our American letters." While Mailer thought of himself as "an actor, a quick-change artist, as if I believe I can trap the Prince of Truth in the act of switching a style," Harold Bloom, in *Norman Mailer* (1986), presents him as "a historian of the moral consciousness of his era, and as the representative writer of his generation."

From The Armies of the Night

From *Part II: Friday Afternoon*

1: The Historian

To write an intimate history of an event which places its focus on a central figure who is not central to the event, is to inspire immediate questions about the competence of the historian. Or, indeed, his honorable motive. The figure he has selected may be convenient to him rather than critical to the history. Such cynical remarks obviously suggest themselves in the choice of our particular protagonist. It could be said that for this historian, there is no other choice. While that might not be necessarily inaccurate, nonetheless a presentation of his good motives had best be offered now.

The March on the Pentagon was an ambiguous event whose essential value or absurdity may not be established for ten or twenty years, or indeed ever. So to place the real principals, the founders or designers of the March, men like David Dellinger, or Jerry Rubin, in the center of our portrait could prove misleading. They were serious men, devoted to hard detailed work; their position in these affairs, precisely because it was central, can resolve nothing of the ambiguity. For that, an eyewitness who is a participant but not a vested partisan is required, further he must be not only involved, but ambiguous in his own proportions, a comic hero, which is to say, one cannot happily resolve the emphasis of the category—is he finally comic, a ludicrous figure with mock-heroic associations; or is he not unheroic, and therefore embedded somewhat tragically in the comic? Or is he both at once, and all at once? These questions, which probably are not much more answerable than the very ambiguities of the event, at least help to recapture the precise feel of the ambiguity of the event and its monumental disproportions. Mailer is a figure of monumental disproportions and so serves willy-nilly as the bridge—many will say the *pons asinorum*—into the crazy house, the crazy mansion, of that historic moment when a mass of the citizenry—not much more than a mob—marched on a bastion which symbolized the military might of the Republic, marching not to capture it, but to wound it *symbolically;* the forces defending that bastion reacted as if a symbolic wound could prove as mortal as any other combative rent. In the midst of a technological century, close to its apogee, a medieval, nay, a primitive mode of warfare was reinvigorated, and the nations of the world stood in grave observation. Either the century was entrenching itself more deeply into the absurd, or the absurd was delivering evidence that it was possessed of some of the nutritive mysteries of a marrow which would yet feed the armies of the absurd. So if the event took place in one of the crazy mansions, or indeed *the* crazy house of history, it is fitting that any ambiguous comic hero of such a history should be not only off very much to the side of the history, but that he should be an egotist of the most startling misproportions, outrageously and often unhappily self-assertive, yet in command of a detachment classic in severity (for he was a novelist and so in need of studying every last lineament of the fine, the noble, the frantic, and the foolish in others and in himself). Such egotism being two-headed, thrusting itself forward the better to study itself, finds itself therefore at home in a house of mirrors, since it has habits, even the talent, to regard itself. Once History inhabits a crazy house, egotism may be the last tool left to History.

Let us then make our comic hero the narrative vehicle for the March on the Pentagon. Let us follow further. He is awakening Friday morning in his room at the Hay-Adams after his night on the stage of the Ambassador and the party thereafter. One may wonder if the Adams in the name of his hotel bore any relation to Henry; we need not be concerned with Hay who was a memorable and accomplished gentleman from the nineteenth century (then Secretary of State to McKinley and Roosevelt) other than to say that the hotel looked like its name, and was indeed the staunchest advocate of that happy if heavy style in Washington architecture which spoke of a time when men and events were solid, comprehensible, often obedient to a code of values, and resolutely nonelectronic. Mailer awakening with a thunderous electronic headache began his morning revery with a conclusion that the Georgian period in architecture was not resolutely suited to himself.

2: The Citizen

All right, let us look into his mind. It has been burned out by the gouts of bourbon he has taken into himself the night before (in fact, one of the reasons he detests napalm is that he assumes its effect on the countryside is comparable to the ravages of booze on the better foliage of his brain) however, one can make too much of a hangover, these are comic profits which should perhaps be reinvested—his headache is in truth not thunderous so much as definite and ineradicable until late afternoon, when whiskey wastes half-cleared, he will feel legitimized to take another drink. In the meantime, he must stir his stupefied message center into sufficient activity to give him a mind to meet the minds he would encounter this day, for this day, Friday, was—you will remember—the occasion on which he would lend the dubious substance of his name to those young men brave enough, idealistic enough, (and doubtless vegetarian enough!) to give their draft cards back to the government on the steps of the Department of Justice. Mailer detested the thought of getting through the oncoming hours. Under the best of circumstances the nature of these heroics was too dry, too dignified, too obviously severed from bravura to make the Novelist happy (not for nothing had an eminent critic once said that Mailer was as fond of his style as an Italian tenor is fond of his vocal chords) no, he liked good character when it issued into action which was visually tumultuous rather than inspiring awe in the legal mind. To the extent any revolution was legalistic, Mailer detested it, cursed those logics of commitment which carried him into such formal lines of protest.

Of course, the alternatives did not appeal to him on this morning either. His head delicate, he could not help remembering that these affairs were not always so dignified; there had been occasional small riots between pro- and anti-war demonstrators, and the past week had had its associated excitements in Oakland, Chicago, at the University of Wisconsin, Reed College, Brooklyn College, on Boston Common where four thousand demonstrators had massed at a draft-card burning. ("67 men," *Time* was later to report, "ignited their cards with a candlestick once owned by William Ellery Channing.") In some of these places there had been violence with the police, broken heads, the use of Mace by the Oakland police, a particularly nasty chemical spray which blinded people for a few hours. (Indeed its name was appropriate for Batman.) Mailer's eyesight was not good—the thought of Mace in his hard-used eyes inspired a small horror. He did not expect the demonstrations to reach such proportions today, but on Saturday . . . well, he simply did not wish to get Mace in his eyes. As for broken heads—he had been struck once with a policeman's billy and it had opened a cut worth thirteen stitches; Mailer still remembered how disagreeable the subsequent hours in prison had been with his head bleeding, and his brain in the stupefactions of a near to overpowering headache. It was not inspirational to add the memory of that headache to his present one. Still, Mailer could hardly conceive of trouble in Washington on the steps of the Department of Justice—the police would doubtless be superior to their fine colleagues in Brooklyn, Oakland, and Wisconsin.

Revolutionaries-for-a-weekend should never get hangovers. Mailer detected that he was secretly comforted by the thought there would probably be no violence today; even worse, he was comforted by the conclusion that the best police in Washington would be at the Department of Justice to maintain order. His exertions of the night before had been perfect for delivering him of some weeks of concentrated rage, perhaps even violence, at a variety of frustrations, he felt cleansed of the kind of hatred which leaves one leaden or tense, and his voice—which he did not dare to use yet, not even in an attempt to clear his throat—was clearly extinguished down to a whisper by last night's vocal exertions without a mike. Even his chest, chronic captive of a mysterious iron vise upon his lungs (which is why he had given up smoking) was relaxed this morning. Yelling on stage seemed literally to have loosened the screw of the vise. To his surprise, Mailer realized he felt gentle—in fact, this morning, he felt like a damn Quaker, which was no way for a revolutionary to feel, unless he was—mark this conjunction—going to consort with pacifists and draft-card burners.

The trouble with being gentle is that one has no defense against shame. Mailer was beginning to remember what he had said last night—he could not tell himself he was altogether happy about the confidential specifications concerning the men's room; if the memory of that was balmed by the recollection of presenting himself as Lyndon Johnson's dwarf alter ego, well, the general memory of the evening (like a deep bruise which might yet prove languorous and not unpleasant in the intimations of its pain or, to the contrary, directly nauseating) was still a little too delicate to probe. Mailer left the memories alone. He was a suggestion uneasy about the newspapers.

They, however, could have been significantly worse. Reading *The Washington Post* downstairs, over breakfast, Mailer decided he had gotten away with it, and so enjoyed his food and ate with large appetite, an ability he almost always possessed no matter how much he had drunk the night before—the best reason perhaps why he never considered it possible to become an alcoholic.

In the dining room were friends and acquaintances, a political writer, Jack Newfield, who did a column for *The Village Voice,* and Jacob Brackman, a young writer for *The New Yorker.* There were friends and wives and relatives about—a muted festivity was in the air, almost as if the hotel were headquarters for a small convention of gentle professionals, editors let us say, of numismatic magazines—something to offer small aggregations of security to one's years.

The program for the day was presented in a leaflet which Mailer had brought with him to Washington. In a typical anxiety at his essential lack of orientation to the protean forms of these protests he had put a folder of mailings, leaflets, programs, reprints, and associated letters for money in his attaché case—each morning he whipped through the folder selecting what seemed appropriate for the occasion. Even a protest against the 10 percent increase in income tax had gotten into this—Mailer had to put it aside each morning. Since he had taken the oath not to pay the 10 percent increase in the event it was passed (for the increase had been announced as a surtax to meet the costs of the war in Vietnam) he anticipated with no particular joy that the Department of Internal Revenue would examine his returns in the years ahead with no ordinary tolerance. (In fact he fully expected his financial tidbits to be fried.) Stating this supposition with his own variety of gallows humor had been the most direct pleasure in a letter he had written to James Baldwin, Bruce Jay Friedman, Philip Roth, Joseph Heller, Tennessee Williams, Edward Albee, Jack Richardson, Robert Lowell, Truman Capote, Nelson Algren, James Jones, Gore Vidal, Arthur Miller, Lillian Hellman, Lillian Ross, Vance Bourjaily, Mary McCarthy, and Jules Feiffer, asking them to join this protest.

Actually, he had hated the thought of signing the protest, he had piped up every variety of the extraordinarily sound argument that his work was the real answer to Vietnam, and these mass demonstrations, sideshows, and bloody income tax protests just took energy and *money* away from the real thing—getting the work out. But for such an argument to succeed, it was necessary to have work which absorbed all one's effort, and a sense of happy status with oneself. Mailer had had neither for the last year or two. His work had been good—there were some who thought *Why Are We In Vietnam?* was the best book he had ever written, but no project had seemed to cost him enough, and he had been suffering more and more in the past few years from the private conviction that he was getting a little soft, a hint curdled, perhaps an almost invisible rim of corruption was growing around the edges. His career, his legend, his idea of himself—were they stale? So he had no real alternative—he was not sufficiently virtuous to eschew the income tax protest, and had signed, and to his surprise had been repaid immediately by the abrupt departure of a measurable quantity of moral congestion, a noticeable lowering of his spiritual flatulence and a reduction in his New York fever, that ferocious inflammation which New York seemed always to encourage: envy, greed, claustrophobia, excitement, bourbon, broads, action, ego, jousts, cruelty and too-rich food in expensive hateful restaurants. Yes, signing the protest had been good for him. (He hoped he remembered in future years when the penalty might have to be paid.) But now, going through his attaché case, he could grin in the mirror, for if he had only known in September that shortly, so shortly, he was going to be an incometaxnik, he could have told Mitch Goodman where to shove his RESISTANCE. (Or was it called RESIST?—even with the pamphlets Mailer could not get the names right, there were so many and they changed so rapidly.) "Yes, Mitch," he could have said, "I think your RESISTANCE is first rate! first rate! but I'm putting my energy these days into the income tax drive. You have your going-to-jail bag—now I have mine." Of course, on the other hand, if he had only joined RESIST? RESISTANCE? with a little good grace he could have told the tax protest people . . .

This was vast humor perhaps to no one else, but in the middle of his hangover, Mailer was still remotely delighted by the mock dialogue of all this: yessir, boss, we'se gonna get in all the jail bags before day is done.

* * *

1968

AUDRE LORDE
1934–1992

Born in New York City, Audre Lorde was educated at the National University of Mexico and Hunter College. From 1974 until her death from liver cancer, she was an associate professor of English at John Jay College of Criminal Justice. Her ten poetry collections include *The First Cities* (1968), *From a Land Where Other People Live* (1973), *Our Dead Behind Us* (1986), and *The Marvelous Arithmetics* (1993). She was also the author of seven books of nonfiction, including *The Cancer Journals* (1980) and *A Burst of Light* (1988). Her one book of fiction was *Zami: A New Spelling of My Name* (1982).

"I am Black, Woman, and Poet," Lorde wrote in the anthology *Sixes and Sevens* (1963). "All three are facts outside the realm of choice." In *Black Women Writers* (1984) she commented, "I have a duty to speak the truth as I see it and to share not just my triumphs, not just the things that felt good, but the pain, the intense, often unmitigating pain." The prejudice that she endured due to her race and lesbianism, and her battles with breast cancer, were the primary sources of this pain, and culminated in her writing *Zami.*

From Zami: A New Spelling of My Name

Chapter 4

When I was around the age of four or five, I would have given anything I had in the world except my mother, in order to have had a friend or a little sister. She would be someone I could talk to and play with, someone close enough in age to me that I would not have to be afraid of her, nor she of me. We would share our secrets with each other.

Even though I had two older sisters, I grew up feeling like an only child, since they were quite close to each other in age, and quite far away from me. Actually, I grew up feeling like an only planet, or some isolated world in a hostile, or at best, unfriendly, firmament. The fact that I was clothed, sheltered, and fed better than many other children in Harlem in those Depression years was not a fact that impressed itself too often upon my child's consciousness.

Most of my childhood fantasies revolved around how I might acquire this little female person for my companion. I concentrated upon magical means, having gathered early on that my family had no intention of satisfying this particular need of mine. The Lorde family was not going to expand any more.

The idea of having children was a pretty scary one, anyway, full of secret indiscretions peeked at darkly through the corner of an eye, as my mother and my aunts did whenever they passed a woman on the street who had one of those big, pushed-out-in-front, blouses that always intrigued me so. I wondered what great wrong these women had done, that this big blouse was a badge of, obvious as the dunce cap I sometimes had to wear in the corner at school.

Adoption was also out of the question. You could get a kitten from the corner grocery-store man, but not a sister. Like ocean cruises and boarding schools and upper berths in trains, it was not for us. Rich people, like Mr. Rochester in the movie *Jane Eyre*, lonely in their great tree-lined estates, adopted children, but not us.

Being the youngest in a West Indian family had many privileges but no rights. And since my mother was determined not to "spoil" me, even those privileges were largely illusory. I knew, therefore, that if my family were to acquire another little person voluntarily, that little person would most probably be a boy, and would most decidedly belong to my mother, and not to me.

I really believed, however, that my magical endeavors, done often enough, in the right way, and in the right places, letter-perfect and with a clean soul, would finally bring me a little sister. And I did mean little. I frequently imagined my little sister and I having fascinating conversations together while she sat cradled in the cupped palm of my hand. There she was, curled up and carefully shielded from the inquisitive eyes of the rest of the world, and my family in particular.

When I was three and a half and had gotten my first eyeglasses, I stopped tripping over my feet. But I still walked with my head down, all the time, counting the lines on the squares in the pavement of every street which I traveled, hanging onto the hand of my mother or one of my sisters. I had decided that if I could step on all the horizontal lines for one day, my little person would appear like a dream made real, waiting for me in my bed by the time I got home. But I always messed up, or skipped one, or someone pulled my arm at a crucial moment. And she never appeared.

Sometimes on Saturdays in winter, my mother made the three of us a little clay out of flour and water and Diamond Crystal Shaker Salt. I always fashioned tiny little figures out of my share of the mixture. I would beg or swipe a little vanilla extract from my mother's shelf in the kitchen, where she kept her wonderful spices and herbs and extracts, and mix that with the clay. Sometimes I dabbed the figures on either side of the head behind the ears as I had seen my mother do with her glycerine and rosewater when she got dressed to go out.

I loved the way the rich, dark brown vanilla scented the flour-clay; it reminded me of my mother's hands when she made peanut brittle and eggnog at holidays. But most of all, I loved the live color it would bring to the pasty-white clay.

I knew for sure that real live people came in many different shades of beige and brown and cream and reddish tan, but nobody alive ever came in that pasty-white shade of flour and salt and water, even if they were called white. So the vanilla was essential if my little person was to be real. But the coloring didn't help either. No matter how many intricate rituals and incantations and spells I performed, no matter how many Hail Marys and Our Fathers I said, no matter what I promised god in return, the vanilla-tinted clay would slowly shrivel up and harden, turn gradually brittle and sour, and then crumble into a grainy flour dust. No matter how hard I prayed or schemed, the figures would never come alive. They never turned around in the cupped palm of my hand, to smile up at me and say "Hi."

I found my first playmate when I was around four years old. It lasted for about ten minutes.

It was a high winter noontime. My mother had bundled me up in my thick one-piece woolen snowsuit and cap and bulky scarf. Once she had inserted me into all this arctic gear, pulled rubber galoshes up over my shoes and wrapped yet another thick scarf around the whole as if to keep the mass intact, she planted me out upon the stoop of the apartment building while she dressed herself hurriedly. Although my mother never liked to have me out of her sight for any period of time, she did this to keep me from catching my death of cold from becoming overheated and then going outdoors.

After many weighty warnings to me not to move from that spot, dire descriptions of what would happen to me if I did, and how I was to yell if any strangers spoke to me, my mother disappeared down the few feet of hallway back to our apartment to get her coat and hat, and to check all the windows of the house to make sure that they were locked.

I loved these few minutes of freedom, and treasured them secretly. They were the only times I ever got to be outside without my mother urging me along on my short stubby little legs that could never run fast enough to keep up with her purposeful strides. I sat quietly where she had put me on the slated top of the stone banisters of the stoop. My arms stuck out a little from my sides over the bulk of my clothing, my feet were heavy and awkward with sturdy shoes and galoshes, and my neck was stiffly encased in the woolen cap and wrapped scarf.

The sun shone with a winter milkiness onto the sidewalks across the street, and onto the few banks of dirty soot-covered snow that lined the sidewalks near the gutter's edge. I could see up to the corner of Lenox Avenue, about three houses away. At the corner near the building line, the Father Divine man ran his Peace Brother Peace shoe repair business from a ramshackled wooden kiosk heated by a small round stove. From the roof of the kiosk, a thin strand of smoke drifted upward. The smoke was the only sign of life and there was nobody on the street that I could see. I wished the street was warm and beautiful and busy, and that we were having cantaloupe for lunch instead of the hot homemade pea soup that was simmering on the back of the stove awaiting our return.

I had almost made a boat of newspaper just before I had to start being dressed to go out, and I wondered if my bits of newspaper would still be on the kitchen table when we got back, or was my mother even now sweeping them away into the garbage bag? Would I be able to rescue them before lunch or would there be nasty wet orange-peelings and coffee grounds all over them?

Suddenly I realized that there was a little creature standing on a step in the entryway of the main doors, looking at me with bright eyes and a big smile. It was a little girl. She was right away the most beautiful little girl I had ever seen alive in my life.

My lifelong dream of a doll-baby come to life had in fact come true. Here she stood before me now, smiling and pretty in an unbelievable wine-red velvet coat with a wide, wide skirt that flared out over dainty little lisle-stockinged legs. Her feet were clad in a pair of totally impractical, black patent-leather mary-jane shoes, whose silver buckles glinted merrily in the drab noon light.

Her reddish-brown hair was not braided in four plaits like mine, but framed her little pointy-chinned face, tight and curly. On her head sat a wine-colored velvet beret that matched her coat, and on the very top of that sat a big white fur pompom.

Even with decades of fashion between us now, and the dulling of time, it was the most beautiful outfit I had ever seen in my not quite five years of clothes-watching.

Her honey-brown skin had a ruddy glow that echoed the tones of her hair, and her eyes seemed to match both in a funny way that reminded me of my mother's eyes, the way, although light in themselves, they flashed alight in the sun.

I had no idea how old she was.

"What's your name? Mine's Toni."

The name called up a picture book I was just finished reading, and the image came out *boy*. But this delectable creature in front of me was most certainly a girl, and I wanted her for my very own—my very own what, I did not know—but for my very own self. I started to image in my head where I could keep her. Maybe I could tuck her up in the folds under my pillow, pet her during the night when everybody else was asleep, and I was fighting off nightmares of the devil riding me. Of course, I'd have to be careful that she didn't get squeezed into the cot in the morning, when my mother folded up my bed, covered it with an old piece of flowered cretonne bedspread and shoved the whole thing tidily into a corner behind the bedroom door. No, that certainly wouldn't work. My mother would most assuredly find her when, in my mother's way, she plumped up my pillows.

While I was trying to image a safe place to keep her by a rapid succession of pictures in my mind's eye, Toni had advanced towards me, and was now standing between my outspread snowsuited legs, her dark-bright fire-lit eyes on a level with my own. With my woolen mittens dangling down from cords which emerged from the cuffs at each of my wrists, I reached out my hands and lightly rubbed the soft velvet shoulders of her frock-coat up and down.

From around her neck hung a fluffy white fur muff that matched the white fur ball on the top of her hat. I touched her muff, too, and then raised my hand up to feel the fur pompom. The soft silky warmth of the fur made my fingers tingle in a way that the cold had not, and I pinched and fingered it until Toni finally shook her head free of my hand.

I began to finger the small shiny gold buttons on the front of her coat. I unbuttoned the first two of them at the top, just so I could button them back up again, pretending I was her mother.

"You cold?" I was looking at her pink and beige ears, now slowly turning rosy from the cold. From each delicate lobe hung a tiny gold loop.

"No," she said, moving even closer between my knees. "Let's play."

I stuck both of my hands into the holes of her furry muff, and she giggled delightedly as my cold fingers closed around her warm ones inside the quilted dark spaces of the fur. She pulled one hand out past mine and opened it in front of my face to reveal two peppermint lifesavers, sticky now from the heat of her palm. "Want one?"

I took one hand out of her muff, and never taking my eyes off her face, popped one of the striped candy rings into my mouth. My mouth was dry. I closed it around the candy and sucked, feeling the peppermint juice run down my throat, burning and sweet almost to the point of harshness. For years and years afterward, I always thought of peppermint lifesavers as the candy in Toni's muff.

She was beginning to get impatient. "Play with me, please?" Toni took a step backward, smiling, and I was terrified suddenly that she might disappear or run away, and the sunlight would surely vanish with her from 142nd Street. My mother had warned me not to move from that spot where she had planted me. But there was no question in my mind; I could not bear to lose Toni.

I reached out and pulled her back gently towards me, sitting her down crosswise upon my knees. She felt so light through the padding of my snowsuit that I thought she could blow away and I would not feel the difference between her being there and not being there.

I put my arms around her soft red velvet coat, and clasping my two hands together, I slowly rocked her back and forth the way I did with my sisters' big Coca-Cola doll that had eyes that opened and closed and that came down from the closet shelf every year around Christmas time. Our old cat Minnie the Moocher did not feel much lighter sitting on my lap.

She turned her face around to me with another one of her delighted laughs that sounded like the ice cubes in my father's nightly drink. I could feel the creeping warmth of her, slowly spreading all along the front of my body through the many layers of clothing, and as she turned her head to speak to me the damp warmth of her breath fogged up my spectacles a little in the crisp winter air.

I started to sweat inside my snowsuit as I usually did, despite the cold. I wanted to take off her coat and see what she had on underneath it. I wanted to take off all her clothes, and touch her live little brown body and make sure she was real. My heart was bursting with a love and happiness for which I had no words. I unbuttoned the top buttons of her coat again.

"No, don't do that! My grandma won't like it. You can rock me some more." She cuddled down again into my arms.

I put my arms back around her shoulders. Was she really a little girl or a doll come alive? There was only one way I knew for sure of telling. I turned her over and put her across my knees. The light seemed to change around us on the stoop. I looked over once at the doorway leading into the hall, half-afraid of who might be standing there.

I raised up the back of Toni's wine-red velvet coat, and the many folds of her full-skirted green eyelet dress underneath. I lifted up the petticoats under that, until I could see her white cotton knickers, each leg of which ended in an embroidered gathering right above the elastic garters that held up her stockings.

Beads of sweat were running down my chest to be caught at my waist by the tight band of my snowsuit. Ordinarily I hated sweating inside my snowsuit because it felt like roaches were crawling down the front of me.

Toni laughed again and said something that I could not hear. She squirmed around comfortably on my knees and turned her head, her sweet face looking sideways up into mine.

"Grandma forgot my leggings at my house."

I reached up under the welter of dress and petticoats and took hold of the waistband of her knickers. Was her bottom going to be real and warm or turn out to be hard rubber, molded into a little crease like the ultimately disappointing Coca-Cola doll?

My hands were shaking with excitement. I hesitated a moment too long. As I was about to pull down Toni's panties I heard the main door open and out of the front hallway hurried my mother, adjusting the brim of her hat as she stepped out onto the stoop.

I felt caught in the middle of an embarrassing and terrible act from which there could be no hiding. Frozen, I sat motionless as Toni, looking up and seeing my mother, slid nonchalantly off my lap, smoothing down her skirts as she did so.

My mother stepped over to the two of us. I flinched, expecting instant retribution at her capable hands. But evidently the enormity of my intentions had escaped my mother's notice. Perhaps she did not care that I was about to usurp that secret prerogative belonging only to mothers about to spank, or to nurses with thermometers.

Taking me by the elbow, my mother pulled me awkwardly to my feet.

I stood for a moment like a wool-encased snow-girl, my arms stuck out a little from my body and my legs spread slightly apart. Ignoring Toni, my mother started down the steps to the street. "Hurry now," she said, "you don't want to be late."

I looked back over my shoulder. The bright-eyed vision in the wine-red coat stood at the top of the stoop, and pulled one hand out of her white rabbit-fur muff.

"You want the other candy?" she called. I shook my head frantically. We were never supposed to take candy from anybody and certainly not strangers.

My mother urged me on down the steps. "Watch where you're stepping, now."

"Can you come out and play tomorrow?" Toni called after me.

Tomorrow. Tomorrow. Tomorrow. My mother was already one step below, and her firm hand on my elbow kept me from falling as I almost missed a step. Maybe tomorrow . . .

Once on the street pavement, my mother resumed hold of my hand and sailed forth determinedly. My short legs in their bulky wrappings and galoshes chugged along, trying to keep up with her. Even when she was not in a hurry, my mother walked with a long and purposeful stride, her toes always pointed slightly outward in a ladylike fashion.

"You can't tarry, now," she said. "You know it's almost noon." Tomorrow, tomorrow, tomorrow.

"What a shame, to let such a skinny little thing like that out in this weather with no snowsuit or a stitch of leggings on her legs. That's how among-you children catch your death of cold."

So I hadn't dreamed her. She had seen Toni too. (What kind of name anyway was that for a girl?) Maybe tomorrow . . .

"Can I have a red coat like hers, Mommy?"

My mother looked down at me as we stood waiting for the street light to change.

"How many times I tell you not to call me Mommy on the street?" The light changed, and we hurried forward.

I thought about my question very carefully as I scurried along, wanting to get it exactly right this time. Finally, I had it.

"Will you buy me a red coat, please, Mother?" I kept my eyes on the treacherous ground to avoid tripping over my galoshed feet, and the words must have been muffled or lost in the scarf around my neck. In any case, my mother hurried on in silence, apparently not hearing. Tomorrow tomorrow tomorrow.

We had our split-pea soup, and hurriedly retraced our steps back to my sisters' school. But that day, my mother and I did not return directly home. Crossing over to the other side of Lenox Avenue, we caught the Number 4 bus down to 125th Street, where we went marketing at Weissbecker's for the weekend chicken.

My heart sank into hopelessness as I stood waiting, kicking my feet in the sawdust that covered the market's floor. I should have known. I had wanted too much for her to be real. I had wanted to see her again too much for it to ever happen.

The market was too warm. My sweaty skin itched in places I couldn't possibly scratch. If we were marketing today, that meant tomorrow would turn out to be Saturday. My sisters did not go to school on Saturday, which meant we couldn't go pick them up for lunch, which meant I would spend all day in the house because my mother had to clean and cook and we were never allowed out alone to play on the stoop.

The weekend was an eternity past which I could not see.

The following Monday I waited again on the stoop. I sat by myself, bundled up as usual, and nobody came except my mother.

I don't know how long I looked for Toni every day at noontime, sitting on the stoop. Eventually, her image receded into that place from which all my dreams are made.

1982

WILLIAM T. VOLLMANN
b. 1959

Born in Santa Monica, California, William T. Vollmann was educated at Deep Springs College, Cornell University, and the University of California at Berkeley. He has published more than ten books of fiction, including the novel *You Bright and Risen Angels: A Cartoon* (1987), the documentary novel *Whores for Gloria; or, Everything Was Beautiful until the Girls Got Anxious* (1991), and the short-story collections *The Rainbow Stories* (1989) and *Thirteen Stories and Thirteen Epitaphs* (1991). He has received a Ludwig Vogelstein Award and a Whiting Writers' Award. His most recent publication is the novel *The Atlas* (1996).

"The kind of reading and writing that I value is a dying art," Vollmann said in a 1992 interview. "While it lasts and while I last, I intend to write sentences that are beautiful in their own right, to write paragraphs that respect those sentences while conveying thought, and to arrange those paragraphs in works that promote love and understanding for people whom others with my background may despise or fail to know."

From The Rainbow Stories

The Visible Spectrum

It is important for the patient to know in advance that some doses will be reduced but not by how much or when. Liquid oral and injectible forms of analgesia are easiest to disguise.

PHILIP RUBIN, M.D., ed., *Clinical Oncology for Medical Students and Physicians: A Multidisciplinary Approach*, 6th ed. (1983)*

The Red Line

Bending and leaning on his crutches, a patient dwindled down the white glassy corridor, trying so hard to follow the red line that he was a joy to watch. —"You came at the wrong time, guy!" laughed the fellow at Radiology Reception. "Everybody's gone to lunch! That's what they do, you know, when they go to lunch. They send everybody down here."

"Do you have any allergies?" a woman was asking sweetly of a man with a metal clip on his nose. The man was on a stretcher. He was about to die. —"No," the man said. Every now and then one could see the soles of bandaged feet projecting from other stretchers, which were wheeled along the red line, which sometimes bifurcated or got lost inside the blue line, loving the glyphs of that other line, or else, like a mother wrenching her hand away from her child's anxious grasp, the red line even abandoned one at times, and there were only mocking lacunae on the floor.

"You might as well go and get some lunch," the Radiology guy said kindly.

Stories of the Radiology Man

A man he knew had just gotten killed in the Broadway tunnel. The man had been riding a motorcycle. A speeding car had mashed him against the guard rail until his head came off. I imagine that head sailing, sailing down the long yellow tunnel, blinking in wonder at the view, while the killer roared away in his car, being anxious, as we all are, to avoid being convicted of manslaughter; and long after the killer had lost himself in the night traffic of Chinatown that head remained aloft, fixated in its astonishment within the eternal rushing of that tunnel; other cars were rushing home to other deaths and they did not even see that lonely head so high above them, still moving at sixty miles an hour, consecrating their windshields with its last drops of blood, saying to itself *How could this have happened to me?* —and the motorcycle arrowed faithfully down that long straight tunnel, the dead hands of the dead body still clenched on the handlebars; but the dead head slowed to fifty miles an hour, forty miles an hour, beginning its ruinous descent to concrete—not that the head would ever know that it had fallen at last: —the eternity of the dead brain would be preserved, like a butterfly in an album, as a bright rushing of colors.

The radiology man said that sometimes people came in with ruined faces, black mush or green mush or blue mush where their eyes used to be. He

*Published by the American Cancer Society. Chapter 29 ("Principles of Psychosocial Oncology"), section: "Terminal-Palliative Phase."

said that sometimes people paid no attention to instructions and followed the green line instead of the orange line, the blue line instead of the red line. Then the hospital could no longer be responsible. When this occurred, terrible mistakes were committed. People had their kidneys cut out when all they needed was an ankle-cast. People lost their arms and legs beneath the bone-saws for no reason. —He was joking, of course. In my opinion he was an extremely funny fellow. Mistakes were not usually so serious.

The Tale of the Dying Lungs

Once upon a time there was a man whose lungs were decaying and swelling up with black stuff and puffing out in his chest like puffballs so that he began to suffocate over a period of two years. It was explained to him that at the end of the two years he would die. He had more and more difficulty breathing. Finally he went into the hospital knowing that he would not walk out, and they wheeled him along the wide black line and tucked him into his deathbed and as he lay in it wheezing the doctors asked him for his consent to be assigned No Code status. (A No Code patient is one who is not hooked up to a respirator when his heart stops.) "Let nature take its course," the doctors said. The man gave his permission not to be intubated. But time passed, and his life passed, and he could not breathe. He was like an underwater swimmer stroking desperately to reach the surface and breathe in the cool air in big luxurious gasps, but when his head came up he had to breathe in foam and spray, and each time the surface was harder to get to and he had to breathe in more water (it was his own water, flooding his lung-cells from his decayed lymph-sea), and he panicked and begged to be intubated, but, being informed of this, the doctors concluded that he was no longer rational because he was requesting something not in his own best interest—namely, to catch his breath and stay alive a little longer; and, besides, it cost the hospital money to run the respirators, so they kept him No Code, and he choked and choked and choked and died.

Business Picks Up

In the afternoon more patients came in. A man with something wrong with his leg lay back on a gurney groaning through clenched teeth, "I can't stand it! I can't stand it!"

A woman was being wheeled along the blue line to the elevator. She was screaming and screaming in pain. *"Oh, my God!"* she screamed. Somebody in a white coat bent over her to make an examination. She began screaming much louder, so that the hall echoed with her screams, which bounced off the glassy walls and skated along the glassy ceiling. It was heartbreaking how useless those screams were. —"Be quiet," the nurses told her. (Who could blame them? If I had to listen to people screaming all the time, I would tell them to be quiet, too.) "Shut up," the nurses said. "Now, what's your date of birth? Just relax. What's your social security number?"

The Waiting Room

"Sixty-four thousand guys died in one minute," said the veteran on the bench, scuffing his foot across the green line. He had lines in his forehead so deep and tightly spaced that they looked like stripes. He had lost most of his hair. "Goddamn fucking Jap killed my goddamn wife," he said. "Stuck a piece of bamboo right up her."

"You saw it?" said the black man beside him.

"Yeah, I fucking *saw* it. I couldn't do anything. But I watched the Jap that did it. I memorized his face. I spent four years in that prison camp. Then I escaped. The others that escaped with me said, where you goin'? —I said, I'll be back in ten minutes. I went back and found that Jap *sonofabitch* and said, you killed my goddamned *wife;* I'm gonna kill *you.* He thought I was kidding at first. He didn't think so very long. And now the war's over, and they say, so long, *sucker!* We don't need you. —And they think I'm a mean sonofabitch. *Oooh,* they say. He's *mean.*"

"Hey, man, you *made* it."

"Only reason I made it is because I know judo and karate. If I have to kill again, I'll do it."

"I learned that, too," said the black man softly.

"I like Reagan. You know why? He'd drop the bomb on the god-damned *Japs.*"

The loudspeaker said, "Tilda Barrett to Triage."

The most attractive objects in the room were the gleaming crutches. Second in the ranking were the wooden rubber-tipped canes that leaned against the seats at a rather cocky angle, while their owners stared into dimensions beyond the ken of mathematicians, or nodded, eyes closed, into their beards. —Next came the shoes: dirty sneakers, twenty-year-old wingtips, sandals no longer white, women's shoes of that flat-bottomed-boat style so popular in the 'fifties and 'sixties; and of course the white-swaddled feet of cripples, the swaddling being cleaner than mountain snow, so that the white hair and white beards of the cripples seemed dingier than they really were. The sturdy old shoes and other walking appliances promised to outlive their owners.

Then there were the yellow bracelets that marked the patients. These were made of almost indestructible plastic. Decades from now, they would still be bright and yellow.

Almost as pretty was the rainbow of lines upon the floor. The red line went to Atlantis, the orange line to Hyperborea, the yellow line to Thule, the green line to Heaven, the blue line to Hell, the indigo line to Purgatory, and the violet line led God knows where.

Sometimes, after sitting patiently for half an hour, a man or a pair of women might get up and change their seats to the opposite side of the little room. One woman breathed in a way that fluttered her chest, but she sat reading a magazine, evidently quite used to it. —Many of these people did not look sick. How little we can tell when others suffer! —Those smokers, those page-turners and soda-can clutchers, all sat waiting for the blue afternoon sky of their Saturday to become dark, so that time would pass and they would be seen. Fat women with folded arms scratched their armpits.

Men sat. They sat and waited for their fate to be decided. Faces pale, collars upturned, eyes undershadowed, they waited. Every half-hour, one or two names were called once. Sometimes nobody got up. Once a woman stumbled to her feet, the pain-lines in her forehead momentarily smoothing with relief at having received the Call, and she hobbled slowly down the bright orange line to get her carrot. But she had not been Called, and soon she came back to us.

A man read a magazine for an hour, very intently. Finally he put it down. The entire time he had not turned a single page. The veteran picked it up and stared at it for awhile. When he laid it down, I saw that he had not been reading it, either, only looking at it because he had to look at something. Eventually he got up and followed the green line which led him out of the hospital.

Getting Accepted

From the triage desk you had to go along the red line to the registration desk, then back to the general waiting room until your turn came, then along the red line again to the Radiology waiting room, then along the indigo line to the X-Ray room, then back to the Radiology waiting room, then to the triage desk, then the general waiting room, and finally if you followed the orange line or the violet line you were admitted to the private consultation room with its dirty steel gurneys of various lengths, its steel lamp, the white sink, with the long faucet bent over it like the neck of a swan, and the pack of Travenol wipes. Fluid dripped through a complex of tubing on the wall. The room was square and severe. Here one's future would be decided. Here it would be made clear whether one would be medicated or whether one would be expelled back into the cruel world.

The I.V. League

"Just follow the blue line," said the Recording Angel. "Did you hear that the President's going to have to take a urine test on Monday?"

"He has to wait on the waiting list!" cried a laughing woman who was missing every other tooth. She laughed and winked when her vein was popped. The phlebotomist smiled at her a little shyly. She called to her friend, "Hey, come on and hit me! He don't know where to hit me!"

The blood draw was at a round table, in sight of the red line. The addicts sat down, and then the phlebotomist bent over them.

"I took the AIDS test when you people were first here, and I never got my results," the next addict said indignantly. She was a plump blonde with black-and-blue arms. "When you first had me, you just took my mother's maiden name. Then you changed the procedure on me."

"We still do it that way," the Recording Angel said. "But you have to go to Ward Eighty-Six. Follow the white line."

"Oh, the white line? Then you changed it."

"Mother's maiden name?" the Recording Angel said.

"Browder."

"And what was your father's name?"

"I *told* you I don't know my father!"

"Well, let's call him X then. Can you remember that?"

The blonde nodded serenely. She sat down next to the phlebotomist and rolled up her sleeve.

"I smoke," teased the phlebotomist, "but I don't drink, I don't shoot up, and I don't chase women."

"Oh, shit!" laughed the blonde. "How passive!"

The Red Line and the Blue Line

The next man refused to take the test. He sat down and then stood up and returned along the red line.

"He's great," his wife explained. "A great person. But he's got gangrene of the pancreas, and most of it's gone. He doesn't want to know if he's got the antibody."

The man after him was very calm, and did not wince when the needle went in. But he looked away. I think it is very funny that if you shoot yourself up four or five times a day you do not mind the needle going in, but you cannot bear to watch someone else do it.

"I don't remember my number now," a woman mourned in the hall. For a very long time I could see her staring at the blue line.

A girl with long brown hair breezed in. —"I missed the last one, so this will be *new* for me," she bubbled. The phlebotomist tied the tourniquet on her arm. Her shoulders rose when the needle went in.

"They check your urine every week," the girl said brightly, "and if you're dirty, even with alcohol, you don't get to keep your baby. I have a girlfriend that's straight, but she drinks. We always used to go out in cars together. Now she can't go anywhere without a case of Bud. She was pregnant once. It was illegitimate. Then she married a lawyer, so I guess she *scored* pretty good. She wanted to give that lawyer a daughter, 'cause he's been a good husband, but they had to take it out of her in the eighteenth week. She took a picture of it. It was so white. Then she tried to have a son. You know how babies are usually *solid?* Well, this baby was so pale and flabby. He's three months and he can't lift up his head."

"Follow the blue line," said the Recording Angel.

"Can I do it again?" called the blonde from the hall. "I got such a charge out of it. You don't have to pay me this time."

"I need your parents' first names," said the Recording Angel to the next arrival. —"Mother Mary," said the man with certainty. "Father, uh . . ."—he thought a long time—*"John."* —He sat very still, wiggling his cheeks. He wore a grey beret. He played with his hands.

People Without Veins

"You busy or something?" said an addict shyly. He had to point out his good vein; they couldn't find it. But his good vein was used up, like the rest. The phlebotomist moved the tourniquet down. He prodded with his finger, poked, slapped, felt, touched, probing again and again with his forefinger; and finally he sighed and swabbed the spot with alcohol. —"Mmm mmm," he said, shaking his head.

"That's all right," the addict said. "I don't think you're gonna find a vein. I gotta go anyway. I'll just be heading down that red line."

"Well, let's try it again," the phlebotomist said.

"I even have trouble hittin' sometimes," the man said. "Fortunately I'm ambidextrous. Used to be, anyway. Usually my veins are pretty good. There's just a lump or an abscess there today."

"Are you interested in taking the test?" said the Recording Angel to the next arrival.

"Yeah, but I don't have any veins!" Grimacing, the woman undid her coat. Her arms were covered with bluish-black spots. The phlebotomist probed gently with his thumb, and she leaned forward, so anxious to help him as I thought at first, but then I determined from her resignedly raised shoulders that she had no hope.

"All right," said the phlebotomist, "we'll do this one, just under the little butterfly. You don't have to look."

"That's good," she said. "I can't stand watching when other people do it."

All morning I watched the rhythmic bouncing of the finger-ball against the rubbery veins. Most of the addicts wore long sleeves. —"We could probably do a thousand of them in a day," said the Recording Angel. "I'm sure we could." —Between patients, the staff turned the pages of the newspaper. —"This woman I interviewed is on methadone," said the doctor, "and she's shooting heroin three times a day." —When the addicts came in, the other doctor stood, legs braced. "Got to keep your eyes on those needles," he said in a low voice.*

The Green Line

A pretty young girl came in. She had long black hair. "I remember you!" she said. There was a tattoo on her arm—an ornate iron cross. She stretched her arms out parallel on the table.

"Will them veins ever be good again?" she said.

"Probably not," said the doctor shortly.

"I just want them to be normal," she said.

"Have you used this one?" said the doctor.

"No. Well, maybe just once."

The doctor probed.

"My little girl's just frantic now," she said. "She wants to know, what are those bruises on Mommy's arms? I tell her, Mommy tried to get a tattoo, but it didn't work and it went into Mommy's veins." She looked at the needle with big eyes. "I'm shaking," she said. "I can't believe it."

"Hold still," said the doctor.

"I have my sister's kids, too. They shot my sister. She was six months

*Needles are very difficult for addicts to obtain. Old ones must be babied, like old veins. One addict kept his needle lubed up with ear-wax.

pregnant, too. They found her on Eighth and Mission. And she was cremated, so I got her ashes in my closet. Her little boy, he cries every night. And there ain't nothin' I can say. I just hug him and hold him. He's a good little boy."

"Okay," said the doctor, "just about done here. Follow the green line around the corner."

Her blood went down the long scarlet tube.

The Challenge

"My date of birth is 7/23/27," said the old black man.

The young phlebotomist rolled up the man's sleeves, showing the world those two black muscular arms. "You tell me which is the best," he said.

"Well," chuckled the old man, "you *might* get some here. *If* you're going to do it." Like the others, he kept his cap on.

He sat there while the phlebotomist tried to get blood out. Meanwhile, the doctor did a woman and another man. —"I guess I'll take that test," a blond guy said. "I just had it four months ago. Is that okay with you?" —"It's fine," said the Recording Angel. —"I came out positive antibodies," the guy said, "so I should be concerned about it, I guess."

The black man was still there. "There ain't but one place you can get it," he said patiently. "I know. I'm a drug addict; I been one all my life. I know where the blood comes!"

"Well, all right," said the phlebotomist wearily. "Can you shoot up for us?"

"Sure I can." The old man leaned over and began searching for the special vein, his secret treasure which had not yet been expended. Of course the old man's inner resources would have been twice as plentiful if he had counted his arteries, but these would have borne the heroin away from his inmost center, diffusing into the tips of his fingers through capillaries that got smaller and smaller like drying-up rivers. —Nope, there was nothing for it but veins, and veins were precious few. Could he find that one true tube of happiness? —Yes! —I heard a snapping sound. —"I *know* where they are," he said. "I been doin' it forty-five years. The rest, they look like veins, but I done played those out *years* ago."

The phlebotomist rubbed his forehead.

"I don't need a bandaid," the old man said. "Yeah, you have a nice weekend."

"I started to say," said the Recording Angel, "that black man was here last year. And he looks *terrible* from last year. He must have gotten something."

The doctor sighed. "Send him down the green line."

Stories of the Drug Ward

Twice a month the addicts lined up to get their methadone. First they had to go down the yellow line to take a urine test. Their urine had to test clean for them to qualify for more methadone, so there were folks in the parking lot who made a peaceful living selling their piss. I am sure that this rendered the colored lines almost useless, but because the urine entrepreneurs were not friendly to me I did not ask them their views. —Another good trick of the yellow-liners who got what they had waited there for was to swish the methadone around in their dour knowing mouths and pretend to swallow it, and then go spit it out and sell it on the street. Even if they had to buy piss to sell methadone, they still came out ahead. So a staff person had to make them talk after they swallowed. When they talked she looked into their mouths to make sure that the liquid had gone down their unwilling throats.

Other Voices

"My heel hurts with a dull cold sensation," a man was saying next door where the violet line ended. It seemed as if he were a philosopher talking to himself, analyzing his condition for the sake of analysis, in order to infinitesimally enrich the universe. But I knew that there was probably a doctor kneeling in front of him like a fellator, prompting him and questioning him in a dry whisper.

Destiny

How anxious these patients all were! How much they wanted to know their fate! . . . And yet all they had to do was look down from their gurneys and determine the color of the line they were being wheeled along; then they would know whether they would live or die . . .

* * *

A Note on the Truth of the Tales

I have not verified any of the claims, reminiscences, yarns and anecdotes told me. But neither have I altered their content. They are as they are.* Why should I care whether they are true or not? When someone tells me a story it is probably true for *him;* if not, why cannot I make it true for *me?* If I were perfect, I would believe everything I heard. —To reverse the dictum of Hassan the Assassin, "ALL is true; NOTHING is permissible." —In my scholarly edition of the Bible are footnotes explaining the Divine in terms of the merely meteorological. But it would seem no less admirable to explain the meteorological in terms of the Divine. Surely I can know more than I see. I did not see Bootwoman Marisa's tooth get pulled out with pliers. But I will believe her anyhow. —Neither would it matter to me if there were no Shadrach, Meshach and Abednego. The issue is

*I have, however, changed minor details when requested to do so by my informants. (I regret that for legal reasons I have been required to change most of the given and street names in this book. To those who look through these pages in vain for mention of themselves, I offer my sincere apologies.)

what *I* would do if my King were going to cast me into the Burning Fiery Furnace. If you object to my gullibility, I envy you; you will build great steel logic-castles, I am sure, whereas my roof has been leaking for three years.

1989

THERESA HAK KYUNG CHA
1951–1982

Theresa Hak Kyung Cha was born in Pusan, South Korea, where her family had fled to escape the advancing North Korean and Chinese armies during the Korean War. In 1962, Cha and her family emigrated to Hawaii, and two years later moved to San Francisco. Cha attended Catholic school, then enrolled briefly at the University of San Francisco before transferring to the University of California at Berkeley, where she eventually received B.A.s in comparative literature and art, an M.A. in art, and an M.F.A. in art. A multimedia artist, Cha produced films, videos, sculptures, and books, often blurring the boundaries among media. Her two publications are *Apparatus: Cinematographic Apparatus* (1980) and *Dictee* (1982). She was murdered in New York City.

In her work, Cha strove for a "consciously imposed detachment" from language, as she sought its roots "before it is born on the tip of the tongue." In *Exilee,* a video Cha produced in 1980, the voiceover represents this fractured language "of previous. souvenirs. remnants. previously recent. recent past. in tenses. in conjugations. in numbers. in chronologies. plural pasts taken place beforehand in articulations tongues taken place beforehand abolition. effacement."

From Dictee

Clio *History*

YU GUAN SOON

BIRTH: By Lunar Calendar, 15, March 1903
DEATH: 12, October, 1920. 8:20 A.M.

She is born of one mother and one father.

She makes complete her duration. As others have made complete theirs: rendered incessant, obsessive myth, rendered immortal their acts without the leisure to examine whether the parts false the parts real according to History's revision.

> *Truth embraces with it all other abstentions other than itself. Outside Time. Outside Space. Parallels other durations, oblivious to the deliberate brilliance of its own time, mortal, deliberate marking. Oblivious to itself. But to sing. To sing to. Very softly.*

She calls the name Jeanne d'Arc three times.
She calls the name Ahn Joong Kun five times.

There is no people without a nation, no people without ancestry. There are other nations no matter how small their land, who have their independence. But our country, even with 5,000 years of history, has lost it to the Japanese.

> "Japan at once created an assembly, in the name of the King, for the 'discussion of everything, great and small, that happened within the realm.' This assembly at first met daily, and afterwards at longer intervals. There were soon no less than fifty Japanese advisers at work in Seoul. They were men of little experience and less responsibility, and they apparently thought that they were going to transform the land between the rising and setting of the sun. They produced endless ordinances, and scarce a day went by save that a number of new regulations were issued, some trivial, some striking at the oldest and most cherished institutions in the country. The Government was changed from an absolute monarchy to one where the king governed only by the advice of the Ministers. The power of direct address to the throne was denied to anyone under the rank of Governor. One ordinance created a constitution, and the next dealt with the status of the ladies of the royal seraglio. At one hour a proclamation went forth that all men were to cut their hair, and the wearied runners on their return were again dispatched in hot haste with an edict altering the official language. Nothing was too small, nothing too great, and nothing too contradictory for these constitution-mongers. Their doings were the laugh and the amazement of every foreigner in the place.
>
> "Acting on the Japanese love of order and of defined rank, exact titles of honour were provided for the wives of officials. These were divided into nine grades: 'Pure and Reverent Lady,' 'Pure Lady,' 'Chaste Lady,' 'Chaste Dame,' 'Worthy Dame,' 'Courteous Dame,' 'Just Dame,' 'Peaceful Dame,' and 'Upright Dame.' At the same time the King's concubines were equally divided, but here eight divisions were sufficient: 'Mistress,' 'Noble Lady,' 'Resplendent Exemplar,' 'Chaste Exemplar,' 'Resplendent Demeanor,' 'Chaste Demeanor,' 'Resplendent Beauty,' and 'Chaste Beauty.' The Japanese advisers instituted a number of sumptuary laws that stirred the country to its depths, relating to the length of pipes, style of dress, and the attiring of the hair of the people. Pipes were to be short, in place of the long bamboo churchwarden beloved by the Koreans. Sleeves were to be clipped. The top-knot, worn by all Korean men, was at once to be cut off. Soldiers at the city gates proceeded to enforce this last regulation rigorously."

Guan Soon is the only daughter born of four children to her patriot father and mother. From an early age her actions are marked exceptional. History records the biography of her short and intensely-lived existence. Actions prescribed separate her path from the others. The identity of such a path is exchangeable with any other heroine in history, their names, dates, actions which require not definition in their devotion to generosity and self-sacrifice.

In Guan Soon's 16th year, 1919, the conspiracy by the Japanese to overthrow the Korean Government is achieved with the assassination of the ruling Queen Min and her royal family. In the aftermath of this incident, Guan Soon forms a resistant group with fellow students and actively begins her revolutionary work. There is already a nationally organized movement, who do not accept her seriousness, her place as a young woman, and they attempt to dissuade her. She is not discouraged and demonstrates to them her conviction and dedication in the cause. She is appointed messenger and she travels on foot to 40 towns, organizing the nation's mass demonstration to be held on March 1, 1919. This date marks the turning point, it is the largest collective outcry against the Japanese occupation of the Korean people who willingly gave their lives for independence.

The only daughter of four children she makes complete her life as others have made complete. Her mother her father her brothers.

> " 'I saw four places where engagements had been fought. At one place it had been a drawn battle, the Japanese retiring with five killed. The other three were Japanese victories, owing to the long range of their rifles and their superior ammunition; and only one of their victories was obtained without casualties to themselves. I saw enough to realise that it was no picnic for the Japanese.
>
> " 'One is forced to ask who is in charge of these men who are nothing more than brigands. Their mode of warfare seems to be purposely designed to stir every honest man into a frenzy. Is this their object? If not, why do they practice so wicked, so mad a policy? Let the authorities either police the whole disaffected districts effectually and properly, or else confess their incapacity for controlling Korea.' "

SUPPRESSION OF FOREIGN CRITICISM

September 26, 1907

> "We are informed that a bad fight took place about eight miles from Su-won on Sunday, September 12th. Thirty volunteers were surrounded by Japanese troops, and although no resistance was offered, they were shot down in the most cold-blooded fashion. This not being quite enough to satisfy the conquerors, two other volunteers who had been captured were brought out and were decapitated by one of the officers. We may mention that this news does not come from native sources; it comes from European."

The "enemy." One's enemy. Enemy nation. Entire nation against the other entire nation. One people exulting the suffering institutionalized on another. The enemy becomes abstract. The relationship becomes abstract.

The nation the enemy the name becomes larger than its own identity. Larger than its own measure. Larger than its own properties. Larger than its own signification. For *this* people. For the people who is their enemy. For the people who is their ruler's subject and their ruler's victory.

Japan has become the sign. The alphabet. The vocabulary. To *this* enemy people. The meaning is the instrument, memory that pricks the skin, stabs the flesh, the volume of blood, the physical substance blood as measure, that rests as record, as document. Of *this* enemy people.

To the other nations who are not witnesses, who are not subject to the same oppressions, they cannot know. Unfathomable the words, the terminology: enemy, atrocities, conquest, betrayal, invasion, destruction. They exist only in the larger perception of History's recording, that affirmed, admittedly and unmistakably, one enemy nation has disregarded the humanity of another. Not physical enough. Not to the very flesh and bone, to the core, to the mark, to the point where it is necessary to intervene, even if to invent anew, expressions, for *this* experience, for this *outcome,* that does not cease to continue.

To the others, these accounts are about (one more) distant land, like (any other) distant land, without any discernable features in the narrative, (all the same) distant like any other.

This document is transmitted through, by the same means, the same channel without distinction the content is delivered in the same style: the word. The image. To appeal to the masses to congeal the information to make bland, mundane, no longer able to transcend their own conspirator method, no matter how alluring their presentation. The response is precoded to perform predictably however passively possible. Neutralized to achieve the no-response, to make absorb, to submit to the uni-directional correspondence.

Why resurrect it all now. From the Past. History, the old wound. The past emotions all over again. To confess to relive the same folly. To name it now so as not to repeat history in oblivion. To extract each fragment by each fragment from the word from the image another word another image the reply that will not repeat history in oblivion.

PETITION FROM THE KOREANS OF HAWAII TO PRESIDENT ROOSEVELT

Honolulu, T.H.
July 12, 1905

To His Excellency,
The President of the United States

Your Excellency,—The undersigned have been authorised by the 8,000 Koreans now residing in the territory of Hawaii at a special mass meeting held in the city of Honolulu, on July 12, 1905, to present to your Excellency the following appeal:—

We, the Koreans of the Hawaiian Islands, voicing the sentiments of twelve millions of our countrymen, humbly lay before your Excellency the following facts:—

Soon after the commencement of the war between Russia and Japan, our Government made a treaty of alliance with Japan for offensive and defensive purposes. By virtue of this treaty the whole of Korea was opened to the Japanese, and both the Government and the people have been assisting the Japanese authorities in their military operations in and about Korea.

The contents of this treaty are undoubtedly known to your Excellency, therefore we need not embody them in this appeal. Suffice it to state, however, the object of the treaty was to preserve the independence of Korea and Japan and to protect Eastern Asia from Russia's aggression.

Korea, in return for Japan's friendship and protection against Russia, has rendered services to the Japanese by permitting them to use the country as a base of their military operations.

When this treaty was concluded, the Koreans fully expected that Japan would introduce reforms into the governmental administration along the line of the modern civilization of Europe and America, and that she would advise and counsel our people in a friendly manner, but to our disappointment and regret the Japanese Government has not done a single thing in the way of improving the condition of the Korean people. On the contrary, she turned loose several thousand rough and disorderly men of her nationals in Korea, who are treating the inoffensive Koreans in a most outrageous manner. The Koreans are by nature not a quarrelsome or aggressive people, but deeply resent the high-handed action of the Japanese towards them. We can scarcely believe that the Japanese Government approves the outrages committed by its people in Korea, but it has done nothing to prevent this state of affairs. They have been, during the last eighteen months, forcibly obtaining all the special privileges and concessions from our Government, so that to-day they practically own everything that is worth having in Korea.

We, the common people of Korea, have lost confidence in the promises Japan made at the time of concluding the treaty of alliance, and we doubt seriously the good intentions which she professes to have towards our people. For geographical, racial, and commercial reasons we want to be friendly to Japan, and we are even willing to have her as our guide and example in the matters of internal reforms and education, but the continuous policy of self-exploitation at the expense of the Koreans has shaken our confidence in her, and we are now afraid that she will not keep her promise of preserving our independence as a nation, nor assisting us in reforming internal administration. In other words, her policy in Korea seems to be exactly the same as that of Russia prior to the war.

The United States has many interests in our country. The industrial, commercial, and religious enterprises under American management, have attained such proportions that we believe the Government and people of the United States ought to know the true conditions of Korea and the result of the Japanese becoming paramount in our country. We know that the people of America love fair play and advocate justice towards all men. We also know that your Excellency is the ardent exponent of a square deal between individuals as well as nations, therefore we come to you with this memorial with the hope that Your Excellency may help our country at this critical period of our national life.

We fully appreciate the fact that during the conference between the Russian and Japanese peace envoys, Your Excellency may not care to make any suggestion to either party as to the conditions of their settlement, but we earnestly hope that Your Excellency will see to it that Korea may preserve her autonomous Government and that other Powers shall not oppress or maltreat our people. The clause in the treaty between the United States and Korea gives us a claim upon the United States for assistance, and this is the time when we need it most.

Very respectfully, Your obedient servants,
(Sgd.) P.K. Yoon
Syngman Rhee

March 1, 1919. Everyone knows to carry inside themselves, the national flag. Everyone knows equally the punishment that follows this gesture. The march begins, the flags are taken out, made visible, waved, every individual crying out the independence the freedom to the people of this nation. Knowing equally the punishment. Her parents leading the procession fell. Her brothers. Countless others were fired at and stabbed indiscriminately by the enemy soldiers. Guan Soon is arrested as a leader of the revolution, with punishment deserving of such a rank. She is stabbed in the chest, and subjected to questioning to which she reveals no names. She is given seven years prison sentence to which her reply is that the nation itself is imprisoned. Child revolutionary child patriot woman soldier deliverer of nation. The eternity of one act. Is the completion of one existence. One martyrdom. For the history of one nation. Of one people.

Some will not know age. Some not age. Time stops. Time will stop for some. For them especially. Eternal time. No age. Time fixes for some. Their image, the memory of them is not given to deterioration, unlike the captured image that extracts from the soul precisely by reproducing, multiplying itself. Their countenance evokes not the hallowed beauty, beauty from seasonal decay, evokes not the inevitable, not death, but the dy-ing.

Face to face with the memory, it misses. It's missing. Still. What of time. Does not move. Remains there. Misses nothing. Time, that is. All else. All things else. All other, subject to time. Must answer to time, except. Still born. Aborted. Barely. Infant. Seed, germ, sprout, less even. Dormant. Stagnant. Missing.

The decapitated forms. Worn. Marred, recording a past, of previous forms. The present form face to face reveals the missing, the absent. Would-be-said remnant, memory. But the remnant is the whole.

The memory is the entire. The longing in the face of the lost. Maintains the missing. Fixed between the wax and wane indefinite not a sign of progress. All else age, in time. Except. Some are without.

Some will not know age.

stop for some. For them

~~no deterioration~~. Time fix

Their image, ~~them~~ the memory

the hallowed ~~beauty~~ that

captured

~~standing before hallowed bea~~

~~loss, the absence~~, the ~~presen~~

missing ~~that is~~ left to the

Their countenance evokes

the inevitable not death, but the dy-ing.

~~Standing before hallowed beau~~

Standing face to face with th

missing. Still. What of time.

Misses nothing. Time, that is

all ~~of~~ things other. Subject

Time dictates all else, excep

ge. Time stops. Time will
ially. Eternal time. No age.
r some. ~~In their view~~
m. ~~On their countenance~~

of evidence
~~the only~~ beauty ~~because~~, only because of ~~the~~ ~~that connects~~
it ~~presents~~ exposes the loss, the
naginary. Evokes not the
~~the~~ beauty ~~withering~~, the decay
hallowed beauty from the

~~the beauty, that is~~ ~~only because~~
~~only~~ memory of. It misses. it's
not more. remains there.
ll else. all things else.
re. Must answer to time.
e.
- misses. All installed in time,

TIM O'BRIEN
b. 1946

Tim O'Brien was born in Austin, Minnesota, and educated at Macalester College and Harvard University. He served in the U.S. Army during the Vietnam War, eventually becoming a sergeant and receiving a Purple Heart, and his two-year tour of duty is central to his writing. He has published a collection of anecdotes, *If I Die in a Combat Zone, Box Me Up and Ship Me Home* (1973), and five books of fiction, among them *Going after Cacciato* (1978), *The Things They Carried: A Work of Fiction* (1990), and *In the Lake of the Woods* (1994). *Going After Cacciato* received the National Book Award in 1979.

"It's kind of a semantic game: lying versus truth-telling," O'Brien said in a 1991 interview. "One doesn't lie for the sake of lying; one does not invent merely for the sake of inventing. One does it for a particular purpose and that purpose always is to arrive at some kind of spiritual truth that one can't discover simply by recording the world-as-it-is. We're inventing and using imagination for sublime reasons—to get at the essence of things, not merely the surface."

"How to Tell a True War Story" is excerpted from *The Things They Carried.* "Teaching is one thing, and telling stories is another," O'Brien told Larry McCaffery in *Chicago Review* (1982). "I wanted to use stories to alert readers to the complexity and ambiguity of a set of moral issues—but without preaching a moral lesson."

How to Tell a True War Story

This is true.

I had a buddy in Vietnam. His name was Bob Kiley, but everybody called him Rat.

A friend of his gets killed, so about a week later Rat sits down and writes a letter to the guy's sister. Rat tells her what a great brother she had, how strack the guy was, a number one pal and comrade. A real soldier's soldier, Rat says. Then he tells a few stories to make the point, how her brother would always volunteer for stuff nobody else would volunteer for in a million years, dangerous stuff, like doing recon or going out on these really badass night patrols. Stainless steel balls, Rat tells her. The guy was a little crazy, for sure, but crazy in a good way, a real daredevil, because he liked the challenge of it, he liked testing himself, just man against gook. A great, great guy, Rat says.

Anyway, it's a terrific letter, very personal and touching. Rat almost bawls writing it. He gets all teary telling about the good times they had together, how her brother made the war seem almost fun, always raising hell and lighting up villes and bringing smoke to bear every which way. A great sense of humor, too. Like the time at this river when he went fishing with a whole damn crate of hand grenades. Probably the funniest thing in world history, Rat says, all that gore, about twenty zillion dead gook fish. Her brother, he had the right attitude. He knew how to have a good time. On Halloween, this real hot spooky night, the dude paints up his body all different colors and puts on this weird mask and goes out on ambush almost stark naked, just boots and balls and an M-16. A tremendous human being, Rat says. Pretty nutso sometimes, but you could trust him with your life.

And then the letter gets very sad and serious. Rat pours his heart out. He says he loved the guy. He says the guy was his best friend in the world. They were like soul mates, he says, like twins or something, they had a whole lot in common. He tells the guy's sister he'll look her up when the war's over.

So what happens?

Rat mails the letter. He waits two months. The dumb cooze never writes back.

A true war story is never moral. It does not instruct, nor encourage virtue, nor suggest models of proper human behavior, nor restrain men from doing the things they have always done. If a story seems moral, do not believe it. If at the end of a war story you feel uplifted, or if you feel that some small bit of rectitude has been salvaged from the larger waste, then you have been made the victim of a very old and terrible lie. There is no rectitude whatsoever. There is no virtue. As a first rule of thumb, therefore, you can tell a true war story by its absolute and uncompromising allegiance to obscenity and evil. Listen to Rat Kiley. *Cooze,* he says. He does not say *bitch.* He certainly does not say *woman,* or *girl.* He says *cooze.* Then he spits and stares. He's nineteen years old—it's too much for him—so he looks at you with those big gentle killer eyes and says *cooze,* because his friend is dead, and because it's so incredibly sad and true: she never wrote back.

You can tell a true war story if it embarrasses you. If you don't care for obscenity, you don't care for the truth; if you don't care for the truth, watch how you vote. Send guys to war, they come home talking dirty.

Listen to Rat: "Jesus Christ, man, I write this beautiful fucking letter, I slave over it, and what happens? The dumb cooze never writes back."

The dead guy's name was Curt Lemon. What happened was, we crossed a muddy river and marched west into the mountains, and on the third day we took a break along a trail junction in deep jungle. Right away, Lemon and Rat Kiley started goofing off. They didn't understand about the spookiness. They were kids; they just didn't know. A nature hike, they thought, not even a war, so they went off into the shade of some giant trees—quadruple canopy, no sunlight at all—and they were giggling and calling each other motherfucker and playing a silly game they'd invented. The game involved smoke grenades, which were harmless unless you did stupid things, and what they did was pull out the pin and stand a few feet apart and play catch under the shade of those huge trees. Whoever chickened out was a motherfucker. And if nobody chickened out, the grenade would make a light popping sound and they'd be covered with smoke and they'd laugh and dance around and then do it again.

It's all exactly true.

It happened nearly twenty years ago, but I still remember that trail junction and the giant trees and a soft dripping sound somewhere beyond the trees. I remember the smell of moss. Up in the canopy there were tiny white blossoms, but no sunlight at all, and I remember the shadows spreading out under the trees where Lemon and Rat Kiley were playing catch with smoke grenades. Mitchell Sanders sat flipping his yo-yo. Norman Bowker and

Kiowa and Dave Jensen were dozing, or half-dozing, and all around us were those ragged green mountains.

Except for the laughter things were quiet.

At one point, I remember, Mitchell Sanders turned and looked at me, not quite nodding, then after a while he rolled up his yo-yo and moved away.

It's hard to tell what happened next.

They were just goofing. There was a noise, I suppose, which must've been the detonator, so I glanced behind me and watched Lemon step from the shade into bright sunlight. His face was suddenly brown and shining. A handsome kid, really. Sharp gray eyes, lean and narrow-waisted, and when he died it was almost beautiful, the way the sunlight came around him and lifted him up and sucked him high into a tree full of moss and vines and white blossoms.

In any war story, but especially a true one, it's difficult to separate what happened from what seemed to happen. What seems to happen becomes its own happening and has to be told that way. The angles of vision are skewed. When a booby trap explodes, you close your eyes and duck and float outside yourself. When a guy dies, like Lemon, you look away and then look back for a moment and then look away again. The pictures get jumbled; you tend to miss a lot. And then afterward, when you go to tell about it, there is always that surreal seemingness, which makes the story seem untrue, but which in fact represents the hard and exact truth as it seemed.

In many cases a true war story cannot be believed. If you believe it, be skeptical. It's a question of credibility. Often the crazy stuff is true and the normal stuff isn't because the normal stuff is necessary to make you believe the truly incredible craziness.

In other cases you can't even tell a true war story. Sometimes it's just beyond telling.

I heard this one, for example, from Mitchell Sanders. It was near dusk and we were sitting at my foxhole along a wide, muddy river north of Quang Ngai. I remember how peaceful the twilight was. A deep pinkish red spilled out on the river, which moved without sound, and in the morning we would cross the river and march west into the mountains. The occasion was right for a good story.

"God's truth," Mitchell Sanders said. "A six-man patrol goes up into the mountains on a basic listening-post operation. The idea's to spend a week up there, just lie low and listen for enemy movement. They've got a radio along, so if they hear anything suspicious—anything—they're supposed to call in artillery or gunships, whatever it takes. Otherwise they keep strict field discipline. Absolute silence. They just listen."

He glanced at me to make sure I had the scenario. He was playing with his yo-yo, making it dance with short, tight little strokes of the wrist.

His face was blank in the dusk.

"We're talking hardass LP. These six guys, they don't say boo for a solid week. They don't got tongues. *All* ears."

"Right," I said.

"Understand me?"

"Invisible."

Sanders nodded.

"Affirm," he said. "Invisible. So what happens is, these guys get themselves deep in the bush, all camouflaged up, and they lie down and wait and that's all they do, nothing else, they lie there for seven straight days and just listen. And man, I'll tell you—it's spooky. This is mountains. You don't *know* spooky till you been there. Jungle, sort of, except it's way up in the clouds and there's always this fog—like rain, except it's not raining—everything's all wet and swirly and tangled up and you can't see jack, you can't find your own pecker to piss with. Like you don't even have a body. Serious spooky. You just go with the vapors—the fog sort of takes you in. . . . And the sounds, man. The sounds carry forever. You hear shit nobody should *ever* hear."

Sanders was quiet for a second, just working the yo-yo, then he smiled at me. "So, after a couple days the guys start hearing this real soft, kind of wacked-out music. Weird echoes and stuff. Like a radio or something, but it's not a radio, it's this strange gook music that comes right out of the rocks. Faraway, sort of, but right up close, too. They try to ignore it. But it's a listening post, right? So they listen. And every night they keep hearing this crazyass gook concert. All kinds of chimes and xylophones. I mean, this is wilderness—no way, it can't be real—but there it *is*, like the mountains are tuned in to Radio Fucking Hanoi. Naturally they get nervous. One guy sticks Juicy Fruit in his ears. Another guy almost flips. Thing is, though, they can't report music. They can't get on the horn and call back to base and say, 'Hey, listen, we need some firepower, we got to blow away this weirdo gook rock band.' They can't do that. It wouldn't go down. So they lie there in the fog and keep their mouths shut. And what makes it extra bad, see, is the poor dudes can't horse around like normal. Can't joke it away. Can't even talk to each other except maybe in whispers, all hush-hush, and that just revs up the willies. All they do is listen."

Again there was some silence as Mitchell Sanders looked out on the river. The dark was coming on hard now, and off to the west I could see the mountains rising in silhouette, all the mysteries and unknowns.

"This next part," Sanders said quietly, "you won't believe."

"Probably not," I said.

"You won't. And you know why?"

"Why?"

He gave me a tired smile. "Because it happened. Because every word is absolutely dead-on true."

Sanders made a little sound in his throat, like a sigh, as if to say he didn't care if I believed it or not. But he did care. He wanted me to believe, I could tell. He seemed sad, in a way.

"These six guys, they're pretty fried out by now, and one night they start hearing voices. Like at a cocktail party. That's what it sounds like, this big swank gook cocktail party somewhere out there in the fog. Music and chitchat and stuff. It's crazy, I know, but they hear the champagne corks. They hear the actual martini glasses. Real hoity-toity, all very civilized, except this isn't civilization. This is Nam.

"Anyway, the guys try to be cool. They just lie there and groove, but after a while they start hearing—you won't believe this—they hear chamber music. They hear violins and shit. They hear this terrific mama-san soprano. Then after a while they hear gook opera and a glee club and the Haiphong Boys Choir and a barbershop quartet and all kinds of weird chanting and Buddha-Buddha stuff. The whole time, in the background, there's still that cocktail party going on. All these different voices. Not human voices, though. Because it's the mountains. Follow me? The rock—it's *talking*. And the fog, too, and the grass and the goddamn mongooses. Everything talks. The trees talk politics, the monkeys talk religion. The whole country. Vietnam, the place talks.

"The guys can't cope. They lose it. They get on the radio and report enemy movement—a whole army, they say—and they order up the firepower. They get arty and gunships. They call in air strikes. And I'll tell you, they fuckin' crash that cocktail party. All night long, they just smoke those mountains. They make jungle juice. They blow away trees and glee clubs and whatever else there is to blow away. Scorch time. They walk napalm up and down the ridges. They bring in the Cobras and F-4s, they use Willie Peter and HE and incendiaries. It's all fire. They make those mountains burn.

"Around dawn things finally get quiet. Like you never even *heard* quiet before. One of those real thick, real misty days—just clouds and fog, they're off in this special zone—and the mountains are absolutely dead-flat silent. Like Brigadoon—pure vapor, you know? Everything's all sucked up inside the fog. Not a single sound, except they still *hear* it.

"So they pack up and start humping. They head down the mountain, back to base camp, and when they get there they don't say diddly. They don't talk. Not a word, like they're deaf and dumb. Later on this fat bird colonel comes up and asks what the hell happened out there. What'd they hear? Why all the ordnance? The man's ragged out, he gets down tight on their case. I mean, they spent six trillion dollars on firepower, and this fatass colonel wants answers, he wants to know what the fuckin' story is.

"But the guys don't say zip. They just look at him for a while, sort of funnylike, sort of amazed, and the whole war is right there in that stare. It says everything you can't ever say. It says, man, you got *wax* in your ears. It says, poor bastard, you'll never know—wrong frequency—you don't *even* want to hear this. Then they salute the fucker and walk away, because certain stories you don't ever tell."

You can tell a true war story by the way it never seems to end. Not then, not ever. Not when Mitchell Sanders stood up and moved off into the dark.

It all happened.

Even now I remember that yo-yo. In a way, I suppose, you had to be there, you had to hear it, but I could tell how desperately Sanders wanted me to believe him, his frustration at not quite getting the details right, not quite pinning down the final and definitive truth.

And I remember sitting at my foxhole that night, watching the shadows of Quang Ngai, thinking about the coming day and how we would cross the river and march west into the mountains, all the ways I might die, all the things I did not understand.

Late in the night Mitchell Sanders touched my shoulder.

"Just came to me," he whispered. "The moral, I mean. Nobody listens. Nobody hears nothing. Like that fatass colonel. The politicians, all the civilian types, what they need is to go out on LP. The vapors, man. Trees and rocks—you got to *listen* to your enemy."

And then again, in the morning, Sanders came up to me. The platoon was preparing to move out, checking weapons, going through all the little rituals that preceded a day's march. Already the lead squad had crossed the river and was filing off toward the west.

"I got a confession to make," Sanders said. "Last night, man, I had to make up a few things."

"I know that."

"The glee club. There wasn't any glee club."

"Right."

"No opera."

"Forget it, I understand."

"Yeah, but listen, it's still true. Those six guys, they heard wicked sound out there. They heard sound you just plain won't believe."

Sanders pulled on his rucksack, closed his eyes for a moment, then almost smiled at me.

I knew what was coming but I beat him to it.

"All right," I said, "what's the moral?"

"Forget it."

"No, go ahead."

For a long while he was quiet, looking away, and the silence kept stretching out until it was almost embarrassing. Then he shrugged and gave me a stare that lasted all day.

"Hear that quiet, man?" he said. "There's your moral."

In a true war story, if there's a moral at all, it's like the thread that makes the cloth. You can't tease it out. You can't extract the meaning without unraveling the deeper meaning. And in the end, really, there's nothing much to say about a true war story, except maybe "Oh."

True war stories do not generalize. They do not indulge in abstraction or analysis.

For example: War is hell. As a moral declaration the old truism seems perfectly true, and yet because it abstracts, because it generalizes, I can't believe it with my stomach. Nothing turns inside.

It comes down to gut instinct. A true war story, if truly told, makes the stomach believe.

This one does it for me. I've told it before—many times, many versions—but here's what actually happened.

We crossed the river and marched west into the mountains. On the third day, Curt Lemon stepped on a booby-trapped 105 round. He was playing catch with Rat Kiley, laughing, and then he was dead. The trees were thick; it took nearly an hour to cut an LZ for the dustoff.

Later, higher in the mountains, we came across a baby VC water buffalo. What it was doing there I don't know—no farms or paddies—but we chased it down and got a rope around it and led it along to a deserted village where we set for the night. After supper Rat Kiley went over and stroked its nose.

He opened up a can of C rations, pork and beans, but the baby buffalo wasn't interested.

Rat shrugged.

He stepped back and shot it through the right front knee. The animal did not make a sound. It went down hard, then got up again, and Rat took careful aim and shot off an ear. He shot it in the hindquarters and in the little hump at its back. He shot it twice in the flanks. It wasn't to kill; it was just to hurt. He put the rifle muzzle up against the mouth and shot the mouth away. Nobody said much. The whole platoon stood there watching, feeling all kinds of things, but there wasn't a great deal of pity for the baby water buffalo. Lemon was dead. Rat Kiley had lost his best friend in the world. Later in the week he would write a long personal letter to the guy's sister, who would not write back, but for now it was a question of pain. He shot off the tail. He shot away chunks of meat below the ribs. All around us there was the smell of smoke and filth, and deep greenery, and the evening was humid and very hot. Rat went to automatic. He shot randomly, almost casually, quick little spurts in the belly and butt. Then he reloaded, squatted down, and shot it in the left front knee. Again the animal fell hard and tried to get up, but this time it couldn't quite make it. It wobbled and went down sideways. Rat shot it in the nose. He bent forward and whispered something, as if talking to a pet, then he shot it in the throat. All the while the baby buffalo was silent, or almost silent, just a light bubbling sound where the nose had been. It lay very still. Nothing moved except the eyes, which were enormous, the pupils shiny black and dumb.

Rat Kiley was crying. He tried to say something, but then cradled his rifle and went off by himself.

The rest of us stood in a ragged circle around the baby buffalo. For a time no one spoke. We had witnessed something essential, something brand-new and profound, a piece of the world so startling there was not yet a name for it.

Somebody kicked the baby buffalo.

It was still alive, though just barely, just in the eyes.

"Amazing," Dave Jensen said. "My whole life, I never seen anything like it."

"Never?"

"Not hardly. Not once."

Kiowa and Mitchell Sanders picked up the baby buffalo. They hauled it across the open square, hoisted it up, and dumped it in the village well.

Afterward, we sat waiting for Rat to get himself together.

"Amazing," Dave Jensen kept saying.

"For sure."

"A new wrinkle. I never seen it before."

Mitchell Sanders took out his yo-yo.

"Well, that's Nam," he said. "Garden of Evil. Over here, man, every sin's real fresh and original."

How do you generalize?

War is hell, but that's not the half of it, because war is also mystery and terror and adventure and courage and discovery and holiness and pity and despair and longing and love. War is nasty; war is fun. War is thrilling; war is drudgery. War makes you a man; war makes you dead.

The truths are contradictory. It can be argued, for instance, that war is grotesque. But in truth war is also beauty. For all its horror, you can't help but gape at the awful majesty of combat. You stare out at tracer rounds unwinding through the dark like brilliant red ribbons. You crouch in ambush as a cool, impassive moon rises over the nighttime paddies. You admire the fluid symmetries of troops on the move, the harmonies of sound and shape and proportion, the great sheets of metal-fire streaming down from a gunship, the illumination rounds, the white phosphorous, the purply black glow of napalm, the rocket's red glare. It's not pretty, exactly. It's astonishing. It fills the eye. It commands you. You hate it, yes, but your eyes do not. Like a killer forest fire, like cancer under a microscope, any battle or bombing raid or artillery barrage has the aesthetic purity of absolute moral indifference—a powerful, implacable beauty—and a true war story will tell the truth about this, though the truth is ugly.

To generalize about war is like generalizing about peace. Almost everything is true. Almost nothing is true. At its core, perhaps, war is just another name for death, and yet any soldier will tell you, if he tells the truth, that proximity to death brings with it a corresponding proximity to life. After a fire fight, there is always the immense pleasure of aliveness. The trees are alive. The grass, the soil—everything. All around you things are purely living, and you among them, and the aliveness makes you tremble. You feel an intense, out-of-the-skin awareness of your living self—your truest self, the human being you want to be and then become by the force of wanting it. In the midst of evil you want to be a good man. You want decency. You want justice and courtesy and human concord, things you never knew you wanted. There is a kind of largeness to it; a kind of godliness. Though it's odd, you're never more alive than when you're almost dead. You recognize what's valuable. Freshly, as if for the first time, you love what's best in yourself and in the world, all that might be lost. At the hour of dusk you sit at your foxhole and look out on a wide river turning pinkish red, and at the mountains beyond, and although in the morning you must cross the river and go into the mountains and do terrible things and maybe die, even so, you find yourself studying the fine colors on the river, you feel wonder and awe at the setting of the sun, and you are filled with a hard, aching love for how the world could be and always should be, but now is not.

Mitchell Sanders was right. For the common soldier, at least, war has the feel—the spiritual texture—of a great ghostly fog, thick and permanent. There is no clarity. Everything swirls. The old rules are no longer binding, the old truths no longer true. Right spills over into wrong. Order blends into chaos, love into hate, ugliness into beauty, law into anarchy, civility into savagery. The vapors suck you in. You can't tell where you are, or why you're there, and the only certainty is absolute ambiguity.

In war you lose your sense of the definite, hence your sense of truth itself, and therefore it's safe to say that in a true war story nothing much is ever very true.

Often in a true war story there is not even a point, or else the point doesn't hit you until twenty years later, in your sleep, and you wake up and shake your wife and start telling the story to her, except when you get to the end you've forgotten the point again. And then for a long time you lie there watching the story happen in your head. You listen to your wife's breathing. The war's over. You close your eyes. You smile and think, Christ, what's the *point?*

This one wakes me up.

In the mountains that day, I watched Lemon turn sideways. He laughed and said something to Rat Kiley. Then he took a peculiar half step, moving from shade into bright sunlight, and the booby-trapped 105 round blew him into a tree. The parts were just hanging there, so Norman Bowker and I were ordered to shinny up and peel him off. I remember the white bone of an arm. I remember pieces of skin and something wet and yellow that must've been the intestines. The gore was horrible, and stays with me, but what wakes me up twenty years later is Norman Bowker singing "Lemon Tree" as we threw down the parts.

You can tell a true war story by the questions you ask. Somebody tells a story, let's say, and afterward you ask, "Is it true?" and if the answer matters, you've got your answer.

For example, we've all heard this one. Four guys go down a trail. A grenade sails out. One guy jumps on it and takes the blast and saves his three buddies.

Is it true?

The answer matters.

You'd feel cheated if it never happened. Without the grounding reality, it's just a trite bit of puffery, pure Hollywood, untrue in the way all such stories are untrue. Yet even if it did happen—and maybe it did, anything's possible—even then you know it can't be true, because a true war story does not depend upon that kind of truth. Happeningness is irrelevant. A thing may happen and be a total lie; another thing may not happen and be truer than the truth. For example: Four guys go down a trail. A grenade sails out. One guy jumps on it and takes the blast, but it's a killer grenade and everybody dies anyway. Before they die, though, one of the dead guys says, "The fuck you do *that* for?" and the jumper says, "Story of my life, man," and the other guy starts to smile but he's dead.

That's a true story that never happened.

Twenty years later, I can still see the sunlight on Lemon's face. I can see him turning, looking back at Rat Kiley, then he laughed and took that curious half step from shade into sunlight, his face suddenly brown and shining, and when his foot touched down, in that instant, he must've thought it was the sunlight that was killing him. It was not the sunlight. It was a rigged 105 round. But if I could ever get the story right, how the sun seemed to gather around him and pick him up and lift him into a tree, if I could somehow recreate the fatal whiteness of that light, the quick glare, the obvious cause and effect, then you would believe the last thing Lemon believed, which for him must've been the final truth.

Now and then, when I tell this story, someone will come up to me afterward and say she liked it. It's always a woman. Usually it's an older woman of kindly temperament and humane politics. She'll explain that as a rule she hates war stories, she can't understand why people want to wallow in blood and gore. But this one she liked. Sometimes, even, there are little tears. What I should do, she'll say, is put it all behind me. Find new stories to tell.

I won't say it but I'll think it.

I'll picture Rat Kiley's face, his grief, and I'll think, *You dumb cooze.*

Because she wasn't listening.

It wasn't a war story. It was a love story. It was a ghost story.

But you can't say that. All you can do is tell it one more time, patiently, adding and subtracting, making up a few things to get at the real truth. No Mitchell Sanders, you tell her. No Lemon, no Rat Kiley. And it didn't happen in the mountains, it happened in this little village on the Batangan Peninsula, and it was raining like crazy, and one night a guy named Stink Harris woke up screaming with a leech on his tongue. You can tell a true war story if you just keep on telling it.

In the end, of course, a true war story is never about war. It's about the special way that dawn spreads out on a river when you know you must cross the river and march into the mountains and do things you are afraid to do. It's about love and memory. It's about sorrow. It's about sisters who never write back and people who never listen.

1990

GLORIA ANZALDÚA
b. 1942

Born in the South Valley of Texas, Gloria Anzaldúa was raised in a ranching environment and worked as a migrant laborer in Texas and Arkansas. She earned her B.A. from Pan American University in 1969 and her M.A. from the University of Texas at Austin in 1972. She is the author of *Borderlands/La Frontera: The New Mestiza* (1987), the editor of *Making Face, Making Soul/Haciendo Caras: Creative and Critical Perspectives by Women of Color* (1990), and the coeditor with Cherríe Moraga of *This Bridge Called My Back: Writings by Radical Women of Color* (1981).

Known for her openness about her lesbian sexuality, near encounters with death, and vision of a political coalition of "Third World women, lesbians, feminists, and feminist-oriented men of all colors," Anzaldúa came to writing through reading, which she characterized in an interview in *Matrix* (1988) as "an entry into a different way of being." When she moved from California to Vermont to teach creative writing, literature, and feminist studies at Norwich University, the idea of *Borderlands* took hold: "I started realizing how much of a foreigner I was there and how, when I walked in the street, people would sort of look at me and then sort of not look at me. And when I went into a store immediately everybody would take notice because there were so few people of color." After two years, she returned to California. In an unpublished interview, Anzaldúa noted a distinction between mainstream and minority writers: "a minority writer . . . when he or she writes, a lot of times it is with the desire, the imperative, the urge, or the need to explain, interpret and present his or her culture against the silencing, the repression, the erasure by the dominant culture."

Writer and critic Cherríe Moraga, in *Third Woman* (1989), calls *Borderlands* "a kind of blueprint for la nueva cultura that Anzaldúa envisions. Oftentimes the symbols are so coded only the architect can interpret them and only to herself. But the best of the writing has wrought out a vision from a suffering which Anzaldúa does not objectify." Anzaldúa herself says of *Borderlands:* "People can understand it. It's got narrative, it's got poetry and I do the unforgiveable—I mix genres."

From Borderlands/La Frontera: The New Mestiza

Tlilli, Tlapalli: *The Path of the Red and Black Ink*

"Out of poverty, poetry;
out of suffering, song."
—a Mexican saying

When I was seven, eight, nine, fifteen, sixteen years old, I would read in bed with a flashlight under the covers, hiding my self-imposed insomnia from my mother. I preferred the world of the imagination to the death of sleep. My sister, Hilda, who slept in the same bed with me, would threaten to tell my mother unless I told her a story.

I was familiar with *cuentos*—my grandmother told stories like the one about her getting on top of the roof while down below rabid coyotes were ravaging the place and wanting to get at her. My father told stories about a phantom giant dog that appeared out of nowhere and sped along the side of the pickup no matter how fast he was driving.

Nudge a Mexican and she or he will break out with a story. So, huddling under the covers, I made up stories for my sister night after night. After a while she wanted two stories per night. I learned to give her installments, building up the suspense with convoluted complications until the story climaxed several nights later. It must have been then that I decided to put stories on paper. It must have been then that working with images and writing became connected to night.

Invoking Art

In the ethno-poetics and performance of the shaman, my people, the Indians, did not split the artistic from the functional, the sacred from the secular, art from everyday life. The religious, social and aesthetic purposes of art were all intertwined. Before the Conquest, poets gathered to play music, dance, sing and read poetry in open-air places around the *Xochicuahuitl, el Árbol Florido,* Tree-in-Flower. (The *Coaxihuitl* or morning glory is called the snake plant and its seeds, known as *ololiuhqui,* are hallucinogenic.[1]) The ability of story (prose and poetry) to transform the storyteller and the listener into something or someone else is shamanistic. The writer, as shape-changer, is a *nahual,* a shaman.

In looking at this book that I'm almost finished writing, I see a mosaic pattern (Aztec-like) emerging, a weaving pattern, thin here, thick there. I see a preoccupation with the deep structure, the underlying structure, with the gesso underpainting that is red earth, black earth. I can see the deep structure, the scaffolding. If I can get the bone structure right, then putting flesh on it proceeds without too many hitches. The problem is that the bones often do not exist prior to the flesh, but are shaped after a vague and broad shadow of its form is discerned or uncovered during beginning, middle and final stages of the writing. Numerous overlays of paint, rough surfaces, smooth surfaces make me realize I am preoccupied with texture as well. Too, I see the barely contained color threatening to spill over the boundaries of the object it represents and into other "objects" and over the borders of the frame. I see a hybridization of metaphor, different species of ideas popping up here, popping up there, full of variations and seeming contradictions, though I believe in an ordered, structured universe where all phenomena are interrelated and imbued with spirit. This almost finished product seems an assemblage, a montage, a beaded work with several leitmotifs and with a central core, now appearing, now disappearing in a crazy dance. The whole thing has had a mind of its own, escaping me and insisting on putting together the pieces of its own puzzle with minimal direction from my will. It is a rebellious, willful entity, a precocious girl-child forced to grow up too quickly, rough, unyielding, with pieces of feather sticking out here and there, fur, twigs, clay. My child, but not for much longer. This female being is angry, sad, joyful, is *Coatlicue*, dove, horse, serpent, cactus. Though it is a flawed thing—a clumsy, complex, groping blind thing—for me it is alive, infused with spirit. I talk to it; it talks to me.

I make my offerings of incense and cracked corn, light my candle. In my head I sometimes will say a prayer—an affirmation and a voicing of intent. Then I run water, wash the dishes or my underthings, take a bath, or mop the kitchen floor. This "induction" period sometimes takes a few minutes, sometimes hours. But always I go against a resistance. Something in me does not want to do this writing. Yet once I'm immersed in it, I can go fifteen to seventeen hours in one sitting and I don't want to leave it.

My "stories" are acts encapsulated in time, "enacted" every time they are spoken aloud or read silently. I like to think of them as performances and not as inert and "dead" objects (as the aesthetics of Western culture think of art works). Instead, the work has an identity; it is a "who" or a "what" and contains the presences of persons, that is, incarnations of gods or ancestors or natural and cosmic powers. The work manifests the same needs as a person, it needs to be "fed," *la tengo que bañar y vestir.*

When invoked in rite, the object/event is "present;" that is, "enacted," it is both a physical thing and the power that infuses it. It is metaphysical in that it "spins its energies between gods and humans" and its task is to move the gods. This type of work dedicates itself to managing the universe and its energies. I'm not sure what it is when it is at rest (not in performance). It may or may not be a "work" then. A mask may only have the power of presence during a ritual dance and the rest of the time it may merely be a "thing." Some works exist forever invoked, always in performance. I'm thinking of totem poles, cave paintings. Invoked art is communal and speaks of everyday life. It is dedicated to the validation of humans; that is, it makes people hopeful, happy, secure, and it can have negative effects as well, which propel one towards a search for validation.[2]

The aesthetic of virtuosity, art typical of Western European cultures, attempts to manage the energies of its own internal system such as conflicts, harmonies, resolutions and balances. It bears the presences of qualities and internal meanings. It is dedicated to the validation of itself. Its task is to move humans by means of achieving mastery in content, technique, feeling. Western art is always whole and always "in power." It is individual (not communal). It is "psychological" in that it spins its energies between itself and its witness.[3]

Western cultures behave differently toward works of art than do tribal cultures. The "sacrifices" Western cultures make are in housing their art works in the best structures designed by the best architects; and in servicing them with insurance, guards to protect them, conservators to maintain them, specialists to mount and display them, and the educated and upper classes to "view" them. Tribal cultures keep art works in honored and sacred places in the home and elsewhere. They attend them by making sacrifices of blood (goat or chicken), libations of wine. They bathe, feed, and clothe them. The works are treated not just as objects, but also as persons. The "witness" is a participant in the enactment of the work in a ritual, and not a member of the privileged classes.[4]

Ethnocentrism is the tyranny of Western aesthetics. An Indian mask in an American museum is transposed into an alien aesthetic system where what is missing is the presence of power invoked through performance ritual. It has become a conquered thing, a dead "thing" separated from nature and, therefore, its power.

Modern Western painters have "borrowed," copied, or otherwise extrapolated the art of tribal cultures and called it cubism, surrealism, symbolism. The music, the beat of the drum, the Blacks' jive talk. All taken over. Whites, along with a good number of our own people, have cut themselves off from their spiritual roots, and they take our spiritual art objects in an unconscious attempt to get them back. If they're going to do it, I'd like them to be aware of what they are doing and to go about doing it the right way. Let's all stop importing Greek myths and the Western Cartesian split point of view and root ourselves in the mythological soil and soul of this continent. White America has only attended to the body of the earth in order to exploit it, never to succor it or to be nurtured in it. Instead of surreptitiously ripping off the vital energy of people of color and putting it to commercial use, whites could allow themselves to share and exchange and learn from us in a respectful way. By taking up *curanderismo,* Santeria, shamanism, Taoism, Zen and otherwise delving into the spiritual life and ceremonies of multi-colored people, Anglos would perhaps lose the white sterility they have in their kitchens, bathrooms, hospitals, mortuaries and missile bases. Though in the conscious mind, black and dark may be associated with death, evil and destruction, in the subconscious mind and in our dreams, white is associated with disease, death and hopelessness. Let us hope that the left hand, that of darkness, of femaleness, of "primitiveness," can divert the indifferent, right-handed, "rational" suicidal drive that, unchecked, could blow us into acid rain in a fraction of a millisecond.

Ni cuicani: I, the Singer

For the ancient Aztecs, *tlilli, tlapalli, la tinta negra y roja de sus códices* (the black and red ink painted on codices) were the colors symbolizing *escritura y sabiduría* (writing and wisdom).[5] They believed that through metaphor and symbol, by means of poetry and truth, communication with the Divine could be attained, and *topan* (that which is above—the gods and spirit world) could be bridged with *mictlán* (that which is below—the underworld and the region of the dead).

> Poet: she pours water from the mouth of the pump, lowers the handle then lifts it, lowers, lifts. Her hands begin to feel the pull from the entrails, the live animal resisting. A sigh rises up from the depths, the handle becomes a wild thing in her hands, the cold sweet water gushes out, splashing her face, the shock of nightlight filling the bucket.

An image is a bridge between evoked emotion and conscious knowledge; words are the cables that hold up the bridge. Images are more direct, more immediate than words, and closer to the unconscious. Picture language precedes thinking in words; the metaphorical mind precedes analytical consciousness.

The Shamanic State

When I create stories in my head, that is, allow the voices and scenes to be projected in the inner screen of my mind, I "trance." I used to think I was going crazy or that I was having hallucinations. But now I realize it is my job, my calling, to traffic in images. Some of these film-like narratives I write down; most are lost, forgotten. When I don't write the images down for several days or weeks or months, I get physically ill. Because writing invokes images from my unconscious, and because some of the images are residues of trauma which I then have to reconstruct, I sometimes get sick when I *do* write. I can't stomach it, become nauseous, or burn with fever, worsen. But, in reconstructing the traumas behind the images, I make "sense" of them, and once they have "meaning" they are changed, transformed. It is then that writing heals me, brings me great joy.

To facilitate the "movies" with soundtracks, I need to be alone, or in a sensory-deprived state. I plug up my ears with wax, put on my black cloth eye-shades, lie horizontal and unmoving, in a state between sleeping and waking, mind and body locked into my fantasy. I am held prisoner by it. My body is experiencing events. In the beginning it is like being in a movie theater, as pure spectator. Gradually I become so engrossed with the activities, the conversations, that I become a participant in the drama. I have to struggle to "disengage" or escape from my "animated story," I have to get some sleep so I can write tomorrow. Yet I am gripped by a story which won't let me go. Outside the frame, I am film director, screenwriter, camera operator. Inside the frame, I am the actors—male and female—I am desert sand, mountain, I am dog, mosquito. I can sustain a four- to six-hour "movie." Once I am up, I can sustain several "shorts" of anywhere between five and thirty minutes. Usually these "narratives" are the offspring of stories acted out in my head during periods of sensory deprivation.

My "awakened dreams" are about shifts. Thought shifts, reality shifts, gender shifts: one person metamorphoses into another in a world where people fly through the air, heal from mortal wounds. I am playing with my Self, I am playing with the world's soul, I am the dialogue between my Self and *el espíritu del mundo.* I change myself, I change the world.

Sometimes I put the imagination to a more rare use. I choose words, images, and body sensations and animate them to impress them on my consciousness, thereby making changes in my belief system and reprogramming my consciousness. This involves looking my inner demons in the face, then deciding which I want in my psyche. Those I don't want, I starve; I feed them no words, no images, no feelings. I spend no time with them, share not my home with them. Neglected, they leave. This is harder to do than to merely generate "stories." I can only sustain this activity for a few minutes.

I write the myths in me, the myths I am, the myths I want to become. The word, the image and the feeling have a palatable energy, a kind of power. *Con imagenes domo mi miedo, cruzo los abismos que tengo por dentro. Con palabras me hago piedra. pájaro, puente de serpientes arrastrando a ras del suelo todo lo que soy, todo lo que algún día seré.*

Los que están mirando (leyendo),
los que cuentan (o refieren lo que leen).
Los que vuelven ruidosamente las hojas de los códices.
Los que tienen en su poder
la tinta negra y roja (la sabiduría)
y lo pintado,
ellos nos llevan, nos guían,
nos dicen el camino.[6]

Writing Is a Sensuous Act

Tallo mi cuerpo como si estuviera lavando un trapo. Toco las saltadas venas de mis manos, mis chichis adormecidas como pájaras a la anochecer. Estoy encorbada sobre la cama. Las imagenes aleteán alrededor de mi cama como murciélagos, la sábana como que tuviese alas. El ruido de los trenes subterráneos en mi sentido como conchas. Parece que las paredes del cuarto se me arriman cada vez más cerquita.

Picking out images from my soul's eye, fishing for the right words to recreate the images. Words are blades of grass pushing past the obstacles, sprouting on the page; the spirit of the words moving in the body is as concrete as flesh and as palpable; the hunger to create is as substantial as fingers and hand.

I look at my fingers, see plumes growing there. From the fingers, my feathers, black and red ink drips across the page. *Escribo con la tinta de mi sangre.* I write in red. Ink. Intimately knowing the smooth touch of paper, its speechlessness before I spill myself on the insides of trees. Daily, I battle the silence and the red. Daily, I take my throat in my hands and squeeze until the cries pour out, my larynx and soul sore from the constant struggle.

Something to Do with the Dark

Quien canta, sus males espanta.
—un dicho

The toad comes out of its hiding place inside the lobes of my brain. It's going to happen again. The ghost of the toad that betrayed me—I hold it in my hand. The toad is sipping the strength from my veins, it is sucking my pale heart. I am a dried serpent skin, wind scuttling me across the hard ground, pieces of me scattered over the countryside. And there in the dark I meet the crippled spider crawling in the gutter, the day-old newspaper fluttering in the dirty rain water.

Musa bruja, venga. Cubrese con una sábana y espante mis demonios que a rempujones y a cachetadas me roban la pluma me rompen el sueño. Musa, ¡misericordia!

Óigame, musa bruja. ¿Porqué huye uste' en mi cara? Su grito me desarrolla de mi caracola, me sacude el alma. Vieja, quítese de aquí con sus alas de navaja. Ya no me despedaze mi cara. Vaya con sus pinche uñas que me desgarran de los ojos hasta los talones. Váyese a la tiznada. Que no me coman, le digo. Que no me coman sus nueve dedos caníbales.

Hija negra de la noche, carnala, ¿Porqué me sacas las tripas, porqué cardas mis entrañas? Este hilvanando palabras con tripas me está matando. Jija de la noche ¡vete a la chingada!

Writing produces anxiety. Looking inside myself and my experience, looking at my conflicts, engenders anxiety in me. Being a writer feels very much like being a Chicana, or being queer—a lot of squirming, coming up against all sorts of walls. Or its opposite: nothing defined or definite, a boundless, floating state of limbo where I kick my heels, brood, percolate, hibernate and wait for something to happen.

Living in a state of psychic unrest, in a Borderland, is what makes poets write and artists create. It is like a cactus needle embedded in the flesh. It worries itself deeper and deeper, and I keep aggravating it by poking at it. When it begins to fester I have to do something to put an end to the aggravation and to figure out why I have it. I get deep down into the place where it's rooted in my skin and pluck away at it, playing it like a musical instrument—the fingers pressing, making the pain worse before it can get better. Then out it comes. No more discomfort, no more ambivalence. Until another needle pierces the skin. That's what writing is for me, an endless cycle of making it worse, making it better, but always making meaning out of the experience, whatever it may be.

> My flowers shall not cease to live;
> my songs shall never end:
> I, a singer, intone them;
> they become scattered, they are spread about.
> —*Cantares mexicanos*

To write, to be a writer, I have to trust and believe in myself as a speaker, as a voice for the images. I have to believe that I can communicate with images and words and that I can do it well. A lack of belief in my creative self is a lack of belief in my total self and vice versa—I cannot separate my writing from any part of my life. It is all one.

When I write it feels like I'm carving bone. It feels like I'm creating my own face, my own heart—a Nahuatl concept. My soul makes itself through the creative act. It is constantly remaking and giving birth to itself through my body. It is this learning to live with *la Coatlicue* that transforms living in the Borderlands from a nightmare into a numinous experience. It is always a path/state to something else.

In *Xóchilt* in *Cuícatl*[7]

She writes while other people sleep. Something is trying to come out. She fights the words, pushes them down, down, a woman with morning sickness in the middle of the night. How much easier it would be to carry a baby for nine months and then expel it permanently. These continuous multiple pregnancies are going to kill her. She is the battlefield for the pitched fight between the inner image and the words trying to recreate it. *La musa bruja* has no manners. Doesn't she know, nights are for sleeping?

She is getting too close to the mouth of the abyss. She is teetering on the edge, trying to balance while she makes up her mind whether to jump in or to find a safer way down. That's why she makes herself sick—to postpone having to jump blindfolded into the abyss of her own being and there in the depths confront her face, the face underneath the mask.

To be a mouth—the cost is too high—her whole life enslaved to that devouring mouth. *Todo pasaba por esa boca, el viento, el fuego, los mares y la Tierra.* Her body, a crossroads, a fragile bridge, cannot support the tons of cargo passing through it. She wants to install 'stop' and 'go' signal lights, instigate a curfew, police Poetry. But something wants to come out.

Blocks (*Coatlicue* states) are related to my cultural identity. The painful periods of confusion that I suffer from are symptomatic of a larger creative process: cultural shifts. The stress of living with cultural ambiguity both compels me to write and blocks me. It isn't until I'm almost at the end of the blocked state that I remember and recognize it for what it is. As soon as this happens, the piercing light of awareness melts the block and I accept the deep and the darkness and I hear one of my voices saying, "I am tired of fighting. I surrender. I give up, let go, let the walls fall. On this night of the hearing of faults, *Tlazolteotl, diosa de la cara negra,* let fall the cockroaches that live in my hair, the rats that nestle in my skull. Gouge out my lame eyes, rout my demon from its nocturnal cave. Set torch to the tiger that stalks me. Loosen the dead faces gnawing my cheekbones. I am tired of resisting. I surrender. I give up, let go, let the walls fall."

And in descending to the depths I realize that down is up, and I rise up from and into the deep. And once again I recognize that the internal tension of oppositions can propel (if it doesn't tear apart) the mestiza writer out of the *metate* where she is being ground with corn and water, eject her out as *nahual,* an agent of transformation, able to modify and shape primordial energy and therefore able to change herself and others into turkey, coyote, tree, or human.

I sit here before my computer, *Amiguita,* my altar on top of the monitor with the *Virgen de Coatlalopeuh* candle and copal incense burning. My companion, a wooden serpent staff with feathers, is to my right while I ponder the ways metaphor and symbol concretize the spirit and etherealize the body. The Writing is my whole life, it is my obsession. This vampire which is my talent does not suffer other suitors.[8] Daily I court it, offer my neck to its teeth. This is the sacrifice that the act of creation requires, a blood sacrifice. For only through the body, through the pulling of flesh, can the human soul be transformed. And for images, words, stories to have this transformative power, they must arise from the human body—flesh and bone—and from the Earth's body—stone, sky, liquid, soil. This work, these images, piercing tongue or ear lobes with cactus needle, are my offerings, are my Aztecan blood sacrifices.

1. R. Gordon Wasson, *The Wondrous Mushroom: Mycolatry in Mesoamerica* (New York, NY: McGraw-Hill Book Company, 1980), 59, 103.
2. Robert Plant Armstrong, *The Powers of Presence: Consciousness, Myth, and Affecting Presence* (Philadelphia, PA: University of Pennsylvania Press, 1981), 11, 20.
3. Armstrong, 10.
4. Armstrong, 4.
5. Miguel Leon-Portilla, *Los Antiguos Mexicanos: A través de sus crónicas y cantares* (México, D.F.: Fondo de Cultura Económica, 1961), 19, 22.
6. Leon-Portilla, 125.
7. In *Xóchitl* in *Cuícatl* is Nahuatl for flower and song, *flor y canto.*
8. Nietzsche, in *The Will to Power,* says that the artist lives under a curse of being vampirized by his talent.

1987

III Popular Culture and High Culture Collide

The division in America between elite, "high" culture and popular, "low" culture is a comparatively recent phenomenon, as historians such as Lawrence Levine have observed. Such twentieth-century high-culture staples as opera and William Shakespeare were enjoyed by large, well-informed polyglot audiences in cities as well as the frontier during the nineteenth century. It was not until the early twentieth century that the concomitant developments of a popular press, nationwide university system, and a striving middle class catalyzed the redefinition of "culture" into high and low elements. In this light, the breakdown of the high/low divide that marks the fiction of the middle and later periods of the postmodern era can be seen, like so many postmodern strategies, not as innovation, but as the reawakening (with crucial revisions) of a pre-twentieth-century cultural phenomenon. Oppositely, the cultural surge that has fused elite fiction with canonically "low" art can be linked to the remarkably high profile of popular forms that late-twentieth-century technologies have made possible: the rise of television, coupled with the continued resilience of radio, cinema, and print media, as well as the advent of an easily accessible telecommunications network, has created an engine for the dissemination of art and culture unprecedented in human history. In either event, few aesthetic shifts more completely mark the crossing from modernism to postmodernism than the notion that "serious" culture does not define itself against (and above) popular culture, but as part of a single multifarious culture where the "serious" exchanges most (if not all) of its modernist privileges for the artistic possibilities inherent in the innovative combinations of genres and forms.

While numerous examples of these innovative combinations are distributed throughout the contents of this anthology (the high comic art of Art Spiegelman's *Maus,* for instance, can be found in the "Revisiting History" section; Paul Auster's reconstruction of the hard-boiled detective novel can be found in "Revising Tradition"), the selections in this section display several of the best-traveled avenues that contemporary authors have chosen to breach the high/low barrier. Jay Cantor's *Krazy Kat* (1987), for instance, is an articulate polyvocal narrative informed by Freudian sexual politics and visions of the apocalypse. That the major characters within the book are borrowed from George Herriman's modernist-era cartoon *Krazy Kat* adds a comic counterbalance, and also takes advantage of (while simultaneously paying homage to) the considerable raw materials available in a comic celebrated even in its day for its unusual complexity. Approaching the cartoon/novel barrier from the opposing territory, Lynda Barry's *Come Over Come Over* (1990) illustrates how the themes and scale of serious literature can be presented within a standard popular format, the traditional newspaper-serial four-panel comic strip. Even the cluttered and sinuous appearance of her ink lines within the square panels suggests the tension between the limitations of the format and Barry's efforts to expand what can be expressed within them.

Curtis White's "Combat," a section of his novel *Memories of my Father Watching T.V.* (1998), features a plot summary of a fictive episode of the popular 1960s television series "Combat," which contains the narrator's father in a series of shifting roles. White's innovative form illustrates the deepening bond between television and literature, as well as the uses of that bond: the protean "Combat" episode embodies a psychoanalytic "working through" of the narrator's relation to his father, using the frame of a television episode as a structuring device and a cultural reference point shared by father, son, and (perhaps) reader. Ricardo Cortez Cruz's "Welcome to the Ghetto" (1997) represents a distinctly different kind of amalgam of literary high culture and popular culture. Adopting the sound, subject matter, and milieu of much rap music, Cruz's story represents a holistic, self-conscious blending of a popular genre into the traditional short story to create a crossover genre that Cruz calls "rap-lit."

For other authors, the high/low cultural barrier is not breached by constructing hybrid fictions, but by utilizing the material of popular culture for its metaphoric and linguistic richness. In a metaphor for the postmodern writer, and for postmodern consciousness itself, the title character of Robert Coover's "Phantom of the Movie Palace" (1987) is a projectionist at a forgotten movie theater who in lieu of serving the overflow audiences of the past instead edits, fragments, and overlaps film footage into remarkable and unlikely combinations for his own private viewing. Mark Leyner's "The Making of 'Tooth Imprints on a Corn Dog' " (1995), which presents itself as the pseudo-diary of a "postmodern author" working surreally to fulfill an equally surreal commission from a fictitious German magazine, incorporates popular-culture references with manic and vaudevillian compression. Excerpts from Laurie Anderson's *Stories from the Nerve Bible* (1994) also utilize compression and juxtaposition: in short pieces such as "Maps and Places," "Black Fire on White Fire," and "Talk-show," Anderson blends references from scholarly texts and art exhibitions with advertisements and overheard conversations to illustrate how meaning in the postmodern age is overabundant and can be found in low places as well as high.

Finally, for many authors, popular culture itself, and its role in American life, is a compelling subject for fiction. When it was first published in *The New Yorker* in 1980, Bobbie Ann Mason's "Shiloh" (1982) was hailed as a particularly successful example of a school of fiction, variously named "minimalism," "dirty realism," and "K-Mart realism," characterized by elliptical narrative and working-class characters. While "Shiloh" fuses a vocabulary of popular-culture references into the kind of abbreviated and tightly edited short story popularized early in the century by authors such as Ernest Hemingway, it also explores the impact of popular culture on individuals who shape their own lives in response to the daily stimuli of television, radio, and advertising without ever acknowledging or understanding the connection.

Like Mason, Barry Gifford in *Wild at Heart* (1990) explores the extent to which ongoing daily exposure to movies, television, and radio generates fields of reference through which individuals communicate with each other, create and express aspiration, and come to understand themselves. Unlike Mason, however, Gifford incorporates the forms of popular culture into his own writing as well, echoing antinostalgically but sympathetically the visceral pulp fiction of the American mid-century as his characters travel a world that is "weird on top and wild at heart."

JAY CANTOR
b. 1948

Jay Cantor grew up in Great Neck, New York. He attended the Horace Mann School, graduated from Harvard College, and received his Ph.D. from the University of California at Santa Cruz, where he studied with Norman O. Brown in his innovative History of Consciousness Program. He is the author of two novels, *The Death of Che Guevara* (1983) and *Krazy Kat* (1987), and two works of criticism, *The Space Between: Literature and Politics* (1981) and *On Giving Birth to One's Own Mother* (1991). Awards for his writing include a National Endowment for the Arts Award, a Guggenheim Fellowship, and a MacArthur Fellowship. Presently he is a professor at Tufts University, where he teaches writing and a course on Freud, Marx, and Nietzsche.

"In the late 1960s, during the war in Vietnam, I—like so many people—wanted a political literature, and wanted to read literature politically," Cantor writes in *The Space Between.* "A political literature would be, I thought, a literature that was an instrument of the struggle. . . . [P]olitical literature could, at least from some perspectives, be an adventurous business, technically innovative. Art . . . that was self-reflexive, concerned with how we order reality, make our world, deceive ourselves or are deceived, could serve a useful demythifying function, one that was—according to this sense of things—potentially revolutionary. Such art revealed to us the kinds of manipulation we were constantly subjected to. It criticized our perceptual habits. It severed us from the myths we were deluded by. It cleared the vision, and so cleared the ground for action."

George Herriman's "Krazy Kat" (September 21, 1921).

From Krazy Kat

Our Town

KRAZY KAT was the headliner of a comic strip—a long lyric delirium of love—that ran each day for thirty years in William Randolph Hearst's many newspapers. Against the desert backgrounds of Coconino County, a landscape that changed from moment to moment—mesas turning into trees into tumbleweeds—Krazy, too, transformed, being somedays he-cat, sometimes she. What didn't change was the plot: Daily & Sunday Krazy sang her aria of love and longing for IGNATZ MOUSE. And endlessly clever Ignatz, as if he spurned and despised the adoring Kat, spitefully delighted in hurling bricks at Krazy's bean. In her imagination—through Krazy alchemy—the brick-bruises bloomed as bouquets, proof to her of mousie's love. Lawman OFFISSA BULL PUP, the Kat's steadfast admirer, arrested the abusive Mouse and marched him to the clink. From which Ignatz escaped next morning to give our Kat her daily brick.

Krazy's unexpected retirement has put the entire cast out of work: KWAKK WAKK, the gossipy duck who sang out Coconino's dirty linen, has no one to tattle on. JOE STORK, a lean decent creature who brought the babies and the mail from Outside, is a nearly dead letter man, for fickle fans no longer want to get in touch. DON KIYOTI, native-born long-eared snob, lacks an audience to lord it over. BEAU KOO JACK, the black rabbit of thumping paws, finds fancy trade falling off at his grocery store. KOLIN KELLEY, who fired the bricks that Ignatz threw, cleans and recleans his cold kiln, knowing that if Krazy never works again he is cursed king of useless rocks. And MRS. MICE, Ignatz's big-footed spouse, with MILTON, MARSHALL, and IRVING, her Joe-delivered progeny, bicker pointlessly, Dad out of work and time on their hands.

Why did Krazy, they wonder, suddenly shy from the spotlight? And if only she would work again . . .

* * *

From *The Gadget*

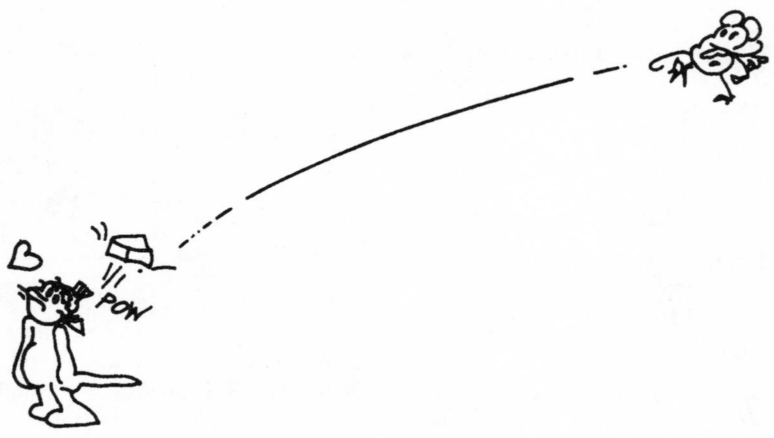

Morning. Krazy rolled up the rice-paper screens on the windows near her breakfast table and surveyed her world, her hemi-demi-semi-sandy paradise, her Coconino. This A.M. the harsh light transformed desert rocks into huge cacti, the cacti into tall church spires, split a mesa in the background into triplets, turned the triplets into maroon bells for the spires, and left only the Jail (empty now since their retirement) unchanged, eternally itself, the Pup said, like the Law. She no longer knew if the light was her friend or her enemy; not that the light played tricks, but that others, she now knew, could play tricks with the light, could make a light brighter than a thousand suns. Once she had used simply to like tricks, all tricks, unsuspiciously, indiscriminately (but the Mouse's especially, of course). No more. Standing by the window, stretching lazily, she stared at the raggedy edges of the sun, as if to force it to tell her the truth—*feel me at a distance and you live,* it said. Inside the sun she saw a smaller more compact ball of flame, falling inward into itself—*come too close to me and you die.* Her stomach turned. Was it others only that made mischief with the light? Since that day at Alamogordo, Krazy felt that she, too, might be rotten. But *she* hadn't done anything. (Had she?) Anyway, uncertain about herself, she had had to quit the strip, for her act, like a moral trapeze, required singleness, and even one drop of guilt was gum-in-the-works. (But she *was* innocent!)

She waited for her insides to settle to the point where breakfast was imaginable, and, turning away from the light and its constant gifts of metamorphosis, she looked around her house. She loved her one large room, the five windows, the whitewashed walls. She liked her house's bareness, its "japonaise" quality: five translucent tan-colored screens, with widely spaced bamboo ribs; one square, thin-legged, low wooden table (almost mouse height) that reminded her of Japanese furniture, its sense that things were neither overwhelmingly solid nor foolishly fragile, but rather that their existence was a miracle; one Hopi rug, where she also slept, its delicate earth colors and sun pattern eccentrically perfect—the daub *here* rather than *there* making all the difference, though no one could have predicted it before the daub was made. Plus one set of Zuni eggshell-blue tea things, the small Indian cups broken and patched, and broken and patched again, the more precious the wider their tracery of lines, showing all the life they'd experienced together. She didn't have many things, but what she had was, as Tracy said about Hepburn's body, "cherce." In olden, pre-ettom days, her furniture had been overstuffed chairs you trustingly sank into, and lampshades with burlesque braided tassels. Then, one afternoon she had thought, This stuff is in bad taste; cooperatively, her disgusting things had disappeared, and these new spare items had moved in. (Only her plumbing had remained old-fashioned. Just as well, she would have hated for anyone, even an unknown force, to have gone into her private place, her toilet.) Less suddenly seemed like lots, and next to nothing was best of all. *Stay close to the ground. Don't show yourself.* Before the bomb, Krazy thought, I didn't spit things out, I didn't have *taste.* Still, she loved her new house because it was *hers* alone; and she hated it, because its emptiness could become too vast, too echoing—hers *alone.* Bareness or barrenness? Time for some tea? She heard the Lawman's kindly voice: *No.*

So she picked up a pile of newspapers and magazines and brought them to her breakfast table. Maybe, she thought, she would even have a gander at *Variety, Billboard,* and the *Hollywood Reporter.* She still (though she pretended indifference when the Mouse was around) pondered the comic pages, still studied the entertainment section, where their strip, moved from the funny pages, had, to Ignatz's and her mom's delight, run for its last ten years, placed alongside articles and reviews about the couples who she, too, liked to think were their colleagues—Fred Astaire and Ginger Rogers, Laurel and Hardy, Buck and Bubbles, Baby Snooks and her dad, George Burns and Gracie Allen (Oh, them especially!). It wasn't that, like Ignatz, she had gone high-hat—after all, his aspirations were much mightier. And it hadn't been *her* doing when suddenly, in 1933, their work had begun to appear on the entertainment page not just in one paper, but in every paper that Mr. Hearst owned. It hadn't been her doing, but she had immediately understood and accepted it: the move, she thought, had been a simple recognition on Someone's part (could it have been Mr. Hearst, himself?) that their art—hers and Ignatz's and the Pup's—was as legitimate as George and Gracie's. Surely in a fate so consistent one might fairly see a god's judgment at work? (Perhaps, she considered, in finding them her colleagues, in making a mental home for herself halfway between the panel and the stage, she was only accommodating herself to the world's choices, as she had always done—for she knew that the more popular strips had remained on the comic page itself. And some, she knew, had said that accommodation itself was her *true* art—the art, anyway, of her relationship with that difficult Mouse and his endless arsenal of well-aimed bricks.) But really she was no snob, she loved the comics as much as she loved vaudeville, or movies, loved nothing more than to lie on the floor, stretched out, and press her nose close to Snuffy Smith, Terry and the Pirates, and the beautiful pajamaed adventurer Little Nemo, whose exploits in Slumberland were more perilous, more vertiginous, more imaginative even than Terry the flyboy's go-rounds with that awful—yet seductive!—Dragon Lady. (Little Nemo! That was a long time ago. Does anybody, she wondered, still remember Little Nemo? Does anybody, she thought with a pang, still remember Krazy Kat?)

Seating herself as comfortably as she could (the table was closer to mouse than cat size and her knees had to be scrunched beneath), she turned to *Variety*. She brought her paw to her mouth to put a little saliva on the soft rubbery gray pad. To turn the entertainment bible's pages she needed some extra leverage; Krazy lacked Ignatz's almost human dexterity with his claws; besides she didn't like to let those menacing, almost . . . mechanimule things show. Distracted, she went on licking the fur around her paw, and up her arm, for a cat—even a krazy one—is a clean sort. Strands came loose, but didn't form hair balls; special stuff, it dissolved on her rough, pebbly tongue, leaving black spots, like freckles. She turned to *Variety*'s second page, wanting to see how her friends were doing at the box office and with booking agents, to keep in touch (but why did she want to keep in touch? It wasn't as if she'd been excluded. Stopping had been *her* choice—though choice was hardly the word, it had been so instinctual, almost intestinal; she *just couldn't* anymore). Still—when she was sure, as now, that Ignatz couldn't see her—she checked the grosses of the various acts in the various media. She would admit freely that she liked to read gossip, and grosses were, to her, really, just another kind of gossip—the numbers spoke of romances, poisonings, and Queen Audience's whimsical favors. Ignatz read reviews, read the critical essays about them, rummaged through novels looking for plots—towards the day (which, by the by, only *he* imagined) when Krazy would be ready to work again. But Ignatz, too, checked receipts. He said that they were a form of criticism, the judgment of the marketplace. The Pup was the only one who didn't care about the numbers. He read history, read big books of philosophy and moldy-oldy blue-bound works of theology. He said that all serious work was a vision of the Law—the enduring reality beyond the changing fashions (by which he meant the box office) that only the small cared about (by which he meant Ignatz).

And the numbers, nowadays, did just add to Krazy's confusion. Over the years Krazy had watched uncomprehendingly the slow shift from vaudeville to motion pictures, to radio, to television . . . and next? computers? video games? How would the next generation tell its stories? She knew she wouldn't be a part of those stories. But would she even understand them? She felt forlorn. Was it too early, she wondered weakly, for a little of that deliciously dangerous tiger tea? Pup warned—and she heard his kindly voice in her ear—that she was drinking too much tea, that it would build up in her blood and might cause hallucinations. His large face, his sorrowful eyes loomed in the air in front of her—proof, she thought, that affection, too, could cause hallucinations. But she supposed she could postpone her next drink a little longer. Till dark anyway.

It was Ignatz's influence, she decided, as she turned to the list of this week's top ten video games in *Billboard*, that had made her *so* conscious of the box office—but she knew that that was a lie as soon as she thought it; she tried to *say* that it was Ignatz's influence, and, of course, the words wouldn't form properly in the air in front of her. It wasn't in her nature to blame others; and she still, no matter how much else had changed, couldn't say what wasn't in her nature. Anyway, it wasn't as if the box office were her god, that whatever-sells-is-right attitude that she sometimes felt lurking behind Ignatz's spiteful judgments on other performers, the outward show on his part of what was really an inward biting sense of his—*their*—insufficiency. *Her* insufficiency, he would end up saying, after working himself up into an angry little snit; her blithe, unrealistic lack of concern for the marketplace, for what the audience wanted. Why wouldn't she vary the plot? he would scream. Why must she always forgive him? Then the black cloud settled round his shoulders: it's my fault, he'd say, that we're so flat and insipid. Followed by: the world is a dung heap. But even to make him happy, she couldn't vary the plot. Ignatz showed his love for her by beaning her with a brick. Offissa Pup drew his valentine for her by arresting Ignatz. And the readers adored her by reading about her. The plot was she herself! Her art had been what she was—how could she have been otherwise? done otherwise? But in his rage Ignatz forgot the essence of her heart—the very axis of their work. For only the Mouse, of all of them, gnawed at by some deep dissatisfaction, could dream that anyone could even imagine changing his nature. (Did Ignatz, spinning about in his discontent like a Comekissthedoor, almost have sides? Was *that* why she loved him?)

Ignatz had often ended up taking out his anxieties on her; he couldn't help himself. Why couldn't they do sex in the strip—as if it were her fault that neither of them knew what it was. Well, why couldn't they have insides, have souls, like *high artists* did?—naming two more impossible things before breakfast. She shrugged, motoring him to fury. For it galled him that they had never won the Pulitzer *or* scored the big killings, the enormous *Gone With the Wind* grosses, even in their cartoon days, their Hollywood years. She had chided him about his envy of others' big money and prestige. "Frankly, Krazy, I don't give a damn," he had said for a week. (He loved to do voices; though every voice ended up sounding like his.) It was a joke, supposedly. But it hadn't been a joke. He *did* give a damn. And, of course, because it was a lie, it had never found its way into the strip.

Yet it wasn't the shifts of the marketplace that most upset her—their slow fade from the public memory that was measured out in the widening disparity between their slowly diminishing (now quickly diminishing) royalty statements and the much larger figures next to other, newer names. Thut, thit, thot didn't bother her. (*Did* it?) No, most upsetting these last years were the comic pages themselves. *They* depressed her. Cartoon cats today were just as popular as in her time, perhaps more so—some of the cats, she noticed, even got top banana position, the upper right-hand corner of the daily page, the first strip in the Sunday supplement. But those cats were *cute!* In her art she had instinctively revolted at that sickening state. (If she worked again, though, she felt that every sinew of her imagination would have to fight off cuteness like the simpering disease of the spirit that it was. For now she would *want* to be cute! Why? Was it to say that little bitty innocenty kitty couldn't have done nothin' bad? Or was it the Fall Out! in the drinking water that made both audiences and actors want what wasn't good for them?) Think of it! To have so little dignity that you threw yourself like an infant on people's mercy, their protectiveness towards the bitty itsy thing—a tenderness that was only another face of their unconsidered overweening power. There was no deep involvement in such feeling. *That* kind of tenderness was one more cream puff of self-congratulation spooned up by already overfed burghers.

Burgher? she thought. Sophisticated word! Can I *say* that? (She no longer knew for certain what she could and couldn't say. No longer knew, from moment to moment, if the charm that *was* her still held, if she could not now suddenly send herself awry from her most basic nature.) Stroking the tips of her whiskers with her paw, she tested: She tried the word aloud.

"Burger!" She laughed to hear what had become of the sound. She saw Wimpy chasing a fat German down the street, trying to trap him in a fluffy bun. The boorshow as food. Not where he eats, but where he is eaten!

Was she a radical, she wondered, anti-boowash? Or did she really covet the big audiences the new cats got for themselves? Or was she just irritable because it was time for breakfast? *Have I changed?* she wondered, have I *truly* changed? *Am* I guilty? But of what? She was like a tongue poking about, looking for a black spot in her *lovely* white teeth that hadn't had a day of cavity in their lives. Well, *now* I'm capable of worrying my motives, finding them as mixed up as a ball of yarn! In the old days she would just have acted, and known what was important to her from what had shown up in the morning paper, read the true gist of her thoughts from what had appeared in the next day's strip. She put her jaw down to the table and rubbed it across *Billboard,* making the tablecloth slide askew and putting a black streak on her white front fur. But no, she decided, the disdain she felt wasn't *her* problem. It wasn't hunger, and it wasn't envy! Cats today *were* servile. They acted like wise guys, certainly, but that was the most slavish position of all, aping the pet owners while pretending to yourself that you were mocking them, and so—like all ironic court jesters—leaving everything just as it had been before. Those cats never created a true realm of the imagination, a world elsewhere, as she and the Mouse and Bull Pup and Kolin Kelley, the brickmaker, and Mrs. Kwakk Wakk, the tattler, and Don Kiyoti and Joe Stork and Beau Koo Jack Rabbit had done. They were Cute Cats, not Krazy Kats, sentimental Hallmark cards of cats, tasting of cardboard sentiments cooked up on assembly lines by anonymous hands, each one indifferently adding a saccharine word to a feeling that no one had ever had! Krazy lifted a paw into the air, as if saluting herself.

And with all this sentimentality, she thought, came its ghost, its ugly shadow—hardly its opposite!—obscenities like a book (she looked at the best-seller lists, too, for, after all, they had once been collected into a book) . . . a book . . . a book . . . she could hardly bear to think of it . . . *a book of things to do with a dead cat.* Sail it like a boat (a cat with masts coming from its stomach). Or make it into a lamp (a bulb stuck in its mouth, a shade over its head). Why a lamp? There was nothing funny about that image, with its truly disgusting overtones, nothing wittily contiguous about lamps and cats. She shuddered to think of the repulsive history behind that whimsy, the terrible unacknowledged hatred that here found disguised expression, the Cat here substituting for the Jew. (Krazy wondered again why she could *think* smarty words like "contiguous," but couldn't *say* them. They belonged to Ignatz and Pup. When she spoke, the word would come out—if it came out at all—as nexa eeek udda; her own inimitable patois.) It was a sick, jaded audience that wanted—as these moderns did—either to drown in sugar, or to drink small amounts of strychnice . . . strike nine . . . poison . . . mixed with amyl nitrate; it was a dead audience that confused the galvanic kick of its limbs with dance steps. Dead cats! At best it was a child saying poo-poo, mocking its own emotions. More and more of the culture pages had become, since the day of the Big Light, like a child saying poo-poo. She felt giddy thinking the word. She wondered if she could say it. "Poo-poo," she said aloud. It was fun. It sounded just the way she had imagined it. Poo-poo. It was fun, yes, but there were some kinds of pleasures one mustn't allow oneself, even if one *could* have them.

What did Ignatz think of dead cats turned into lamps? She thought she had heard him chuckling the day they'd first talked about it, as they had walked up a mountain that became a tree on the horizon (so they would comically find themselves dangling from a branch at the end of all their climbing). Ignatz laughing: that would be too much. (But how many times had she thought *that,* only to find her heart mysteriously turned towards him again?) For one terrible instant she saw herself in his eyes, dead, a light bulb screwed into her mouth. She heard, as if it were outside her window, his high lispy laugh, and it was like an icicle in her heart.

The icicle became a snowflake, just as it always did with that Mouse's meanest gestures. She thought, *He loves me.* She tried to say it. She couldn't. The snowflake melted and left nothing in her heart but a puddle of confusion.

It really was too much.

For a moment she thought she actually did hear that *dear* laugh, that *terrible* laugh (the contrary feelings warred inside her and made all thought of breakfast anathema). She *had* heard it. It *was* his high, lispy laugh outside her window. He had come by, as he often did, for breakfast. She closed up *Variety* and pushed it under the tablecloth before—she hoped—he could see her reading it and reopen the old debate between them: when could they go back to work? (Though his little eyes were keen; they didn't miss much.)

"Where's breakfast?" Ignatz asked, swaggering into her adobe. "Where are my soft-boiled eggs?" He spoke in a mock-gruff sort of voice, not his own squeak.

Krazy felt flustered, for she was sure he was looking at the bulge of newspaper under the striped Navaho tablecloth.

"Your eggs," Ignatz said, in a falsetto voice, "will be ready in six minutes."

"Six minutes," Ignatz said wonderingly, his voice rasping again. He looked bemused, yet certain that something entertaining was about to befall him. "Why, Gracie, do two soft-boiled eggs take six minutes?" He waited, staring at Krazy, as if he could conjure words out of her with his stare. She looked at the ground, tears forming in her eyes, unable to speak. She knew now what he was doing: It was a Burns and Allen routine, one from the moving pictures. "Yes," Ignatz as Krazy as Gracie said—recovering from the real Kat's real silence, and carrying on as if playing a scene with oneself were the most natural thing in the world (for Ignatz's sense of timing had always been imppeckable). "Of course it takes six minutes, George, silly. I'm boiling two three-minute eggs."

Ignatz (as George) smiled at the krazy answer. (As Ignatz he wouldn't be smiling. It would have been brick time! But he always stayed in character—though somehow all his characters were Ignatz, the way Bogart was Sam Spade was Philip Marlowe was Bogart.) "Gracie," he said, "I'll bet you never finished the fifth grade." He looked over at the Kat again, cheerful, expectant, waiting for her to say Gracie's line.

Why didn't he stop? she thought, weeping now. Couldn't he see what this did to her?

"George!" Ignatz said in Krazy/Gracie's falsetto, as if shocked, but showing, too, that s/he didn't mind George's insinuation one bit, that she couldn't be insulted, that it was George's problem, not hers. "How can you say that! I spent three of my happiest years in the fifth grade!"

Ignatz smiled; then, the routine over, he scowled, the Mouse once more. He pulled up a seat at the table. Krazy drew a paw across her eyes. She had always especially loved doing the Burns and Allen numbers with Ignatz.

But she couldn't, hadn't for years, been able to play her part in them, in anything. He *knew* that. He had done "The Six-Minute Eggs" because he knew how much that would hurt her; would remind her of her incapacity; and so she wept. But even her tears weren't simple comfort anymore; for to weep at his meanness reminded her of the joy she had once felt at the very same brick-brats; crying was another sign of her problem.

"What's for breakfast?" he said again, this time in his own high-pitched squeak.

She shook her head back and forth, back and forth, lost still in her confusion—not zaniness, not craziness, but a childish sullen bafflement that was like drowning in six inches of water.

"What's the matter?" he said. "Kat got your tongue? . . . Kat got a tongue?" His voice had a musing, stroking quality that she hadn't heard for a while. He was tasting alternative lines, shaping a new routine.

Shaping a new routine! Suddenly a sharper, more bitter pain stabbed at her heart. WHAT IF HE WAS PRACTICING BOTH PARTS BECAUSE HE PLANNED TO DO A SINGLE? She saw his new title, in some wild style of lettering that only half-recalled the old antic headline that had once been theirs. IGNATZ MOUSE! it would say, and then it would add, beneath the title, in *much* smaller letters, FORMERLY OF KRAZY KAT. No, she thought. Impossible. Unimaginable. But it wasn't. She could see it, her life turning into *A Star Is Born,* and her in the wrong part, the Norman Maine role, sliding into sullenness and loss as Ignatz ascended to the firmament. *A Star Is Born* without even the touching last moment; there would be no heart-rending acknowledgment of her importance for Ignatz, no graceful "This is Mr. Krazy Kat" for him. . . . But . . . but . . . but hadn't he sounded too ridiculous doing both parts, as if he were his own ventriloquist's dummy! Was that the sort of thing people *liked* nowadays? A mirror looking at a mirror, endlessly delighting in itself, as if there were no world outside, no world elsewhere? Would moderns want that? Did critics now prescribe it? It was the kind of question she usually asked Ignatz. She looked over to the Mouse, who grinned at her slyly, as if he knew her fear, had *meant* to provoke it. She couldn't ask him. She felt her loneliness, her own arctic isolation. Then, as always these last forty years, the narcotic of depression came over her, and the sticky black lassitude spread from her limbs upwards to her brain. *What did it matter anyhow? Let him go.* The six inches of water became a warm dark lake, gravity itself, endlessly inviting her downwards. All she wanted now was for the Mouse to leave so that she could sink into that inner shadow and sleep.

The Mouse, she knew, saw the light leaving her eyes. His sly smile turned angry, disappointed. He shook his head disgustedly. "Say good night, Gracie."

She said nothing, of course, so he put the final nail in, replying to himself in falsetto—Gracie making George's command silly by obeying the letter of it: "Good night, Gracie," s/he said. Then Gracie smiled warmly. Ignatz smiled meanly. And Krazy lay down to sleep.

• • •

Lay. Or fell, with her paws in the center of the blue sun design of her earth-colored carpet, her head on her paws, her backside in the air. And she dreamed. Or remembered? Since the strip stopped she had had a hard time finding the difference. She remembered dreams as if they were waking events; and vice versa, she thought, and versa versa too; also vice vice.

Memory had once been so simple. Each morning she had read the strip in the paper, and the cloudy melange of the previous day's events developed for her, clarified like a picture suddenly smiling up from its chemical bath. The strip had been her memory—not transcribed, but made clear; she found out there the truth of her day, all that she needed to remember, all that she did—at the moment she read it—remember. Maybe if there was a gap between the panels, well, perhaps she sometimes constructed a little continuity between. But the fixed points were sure, were certain. But now it had been forty years since depression had made her quit the strip; forty years that her memory had been a tossed salad, some uncertain producer cutting and recutting the story of her life.

One afternoon Ignatz had come by. That much she was certain of. The day always began that way, as sure as once upon a time. His lips had curled up in a close-mouthed mirthless smile. He said he had seen something, and Krazy had to see it too. It wasn't like anything else, this thing that he'd seen.

"How is that, dollink?" Krazy had asked, pleasantly, deliciously, confused.

"Just tell me what it is, and I'll figure out the profit, huh? Well, you couldn't do it, sir," Ignatz said. "Nobody could do it that hasn't had a world of experience with things of that sort and"—he paused impressively—"there aren't any things of that sort."

Ignatz, she knew, was working in a bit of the Fat Man's dialogue from *The Maltese Falcon.* Nineteen forty-five was tough-guy time for him—a response to the war perhaps, or his conclusion as to what fickle Dame Public wanted. In those days—before insomnia had clamped her leg in its trap—she hadn't had much use for that kind of story, hadn't been able to find a role for herself among the grifters, and the pretty deceitful women who double-crossed their playmates, the hard-boiled dicks.

She stared. Ignatz was patting the air in front of himself, turning his paw in half circles as if stroking the ether, a hypnotic gesture that nearly made her swoon it was so sweet.

"Where is it?" she asked, for that stroking motion had intrigued her.

He sneered. For "where?" was a silly question in Coconino. The mountain you walked towards became a building as soon as you stepped on/in it. Ignatz—like Bud Abbott explaining wheres with whos—said, "The boys that built it call it the Gadget."

"Oh, a gadget!" Krazy smiled. Gadgets Krazy knew about from the comics. Each week in the Sunday color pages, Rube Goldberg—a nice-looking man with a big nose and a straight moustache of ten independent bristles—demonstrated one of his new gadgets, in a big diagram. That very week she had learned about a labor-saving device that helped your wife with her girdle. (What was a girdle precisely? Krazy wondered. What was it made from? Would Ignatz like it if she served him one?) The gadget had involved a bowling ball, an unupsettable bowling pin, weights, pulleys, ropes, a dog, a Chinese screen, and a shoe attached to the wall. Krazy liked having her mind pulled through one of Goldberg's gadgets. He was a real artist; he had a vision. She knew, because after contemplating his drawings she saw *her* own life *his* way. What were the umbrellas, the cactuses, the Pup, even the other Coconino characters, but a way to get Ignatz's lovely brick in contact with her yearning noggin, and so—like Mr. Goldberg with his devices—fulfill her heart's desire?

So she had set off happily across the hot desert to see the thing that wasn't like anything else, giving little skips in the evening air from the high spirits that bounced inside her like Mexican jumping beans. They walked briskly, watching the homeward heat rise from the sand in waves, and Krazy shouted phrases from her favorite songs, big-band numbers that were buoyant with hope and pleasure, even in wartime, lifting the nation above the news's chaotic swells. "Strut it out!" Krazy sang to no one in particular, her heart filled with unreasoning glee. Jazz was surely the brave strain of American life, that endless improvised existence, where all that held things together was the riff, a few chords, the daily plot (the dear Mouse's brick, her "He loves me!") and within that you had to ring fresh changes every day, making it new, yet still the same. "Oh mess around!" she shouted. The departing sun was big and orange and round. She leapt into the air and dove head first into the sand. Ignatz watched indifferently. "It's tight like that!" Krazy exclaimed as she pretend swam-rolled a few strokes across the desert floor—a warm sand bath was a good way to dust the fleas from her fur. "Mmmm, mmmm, it's tight like that!" She rose and let the silica drip from her head like water.

The Gadget, Ignatz said, was in New Mexico, which was a part of Arizona this evening. They had to be going.

"Play that junkyard music!" Krazy sang, holding her paws aloft. "Play it now!" She capered forward a few steps on her toes. Ignatz rewarded her with a lusciously mean smile.

Around the next rise the sand ended; they came to a flat plain, with low brown scrub on it, called Alamogordo. A tower stood in the distance.

When she saw the tower she was certain that it was the Gadget: a tall rectangle—almost a cone—made of crossed pieces of black steel; a platform three-quarters of the way to the top; a series of chain pulleys holding a football-shaped metal object. O joy! Immediately, she knew: *The Gadget was an amazing new device to deliver a brick to her head!* How would it work? she wondered sensuously, stretching herself upwards, curving her chest outwards towards the tower. What other elements of the world would the Gadget draw into its love plot? A flock of crows? The wind? A donkey that loves marshmallows? People on other continents? Had Ignatz, she wondered, imagined this all by himself? The dollink! She stared with wonder and delight at the tower, the embodiment of Ignatz's affection for her, and then looked back beneath long lashes at her mouse. He was as wonderful as the Gadget he had built for her, this natural extension in mixed materials of his steadfast love. He and the tower and the brick it would undoubtedly drop were all of a piece, an identity to her loving eyes: poised, delicate, yet strong and homey, too. Ignatz, she saw, peered away from her, to his right, his little head turned to one side, his mouth a crooked line. His upper lip was raised, and his sharp front teeth bit half his lower lip inward. Just the way he looked before brick launching! His right arm swung backwards and held itself poised, as if about to send forth a spectral missile! Hot joy flooded the Kat's heart. This device was the most complicated delivery system he had ever devised for her!

Was it, she wondered, a little, you know, too much? Perhaps love shouldn't require appliances? (Ignatz had had some odd ideas lately, ones from novels she didn't even want to hear about.) Was this tower like playing dress-up? (The only ornamentation she ever had was a parasol.) Or wearing leather, or dildos? (She had meant to ask Ignatz what kind of bird dildos were.) But how could there be any harm in such a beautiful-looking Gadget!

Krazy looked to her right, following Ignatz's intent stare, and she saw four cacti that bent the sun's rays oddly, creating a glow around themselves. The cactuses soon had heads; the heads developed the shoulders, arms, and legs of men; and the men, too, looked up at the tower expectantly.

As the sun started to set and the beams no longer blinded her, she saw the men more clearly, and once she saw them she couldn't look away. Oh, would that she hadn't seen! There was something luminous about their shape, even without the sun behind them, a glow that still remained. Her eyes wanted to gaze all along their surfaces. She wanted to scurry up and run about them, but she knew—for wherever she is is Coconino County; assimilated to its air, she never will be out of it—that if she took a step towards them it would as likely land her on a mesa miles away. And why "scurry"? she wondered. She was no one's pet! She walked on two legs, just as they did! (Is this what it means, she had thought for the first time, "not to feel oneself"?) And why did she want to go up and walk around them at all? Because, she realized, these were real men, not pictures, not movies, but actual men, the first she had ever seen! And she wanted to walk around them because there was more to them than met the eye!

This part the Pup hadn't had to explain to her. She had known it immediately, with the force of sight. *There were more sides to them, sides that were hidden by the sides she saw.* They had *backs,* and not just in a way, like her and Ignatz. Their sides weren't flickery, here and gone, like the ones in Coconino, or the people she saw in movies, where you felt that if you could just walk into the screen, but of course you couldn't, so you just settled back down into your seat. Anyway, watching Ignatz or watching the screen, it was all kind of there. It was implied. But with these men—one of them in a business suit, two of them in jeans, one, the most beautiful, in khaki pants and a blue work shirt, open at the collar—the backs weren't flickery implications. These sides were permanent. That was the glow to them; their roundness gave them their aura, as if each were a planet unto himself whose gravity could bend rays of light. How beautiful it all was, and how deeply mysterious! They could be hiding something behind them—a nice surprise for her! Their backs might be different from their fronts, and even more lovely. They could even put something inside themselves; and unlike her and Ignatz, who could never keep a secret for long, they could do it forever. Why, there could even be another person within, different from the one you saw!

Without any thought, her hand moved in the air, curving in its motion, shaping something, just as Ignatz's had when he had first told her of the Gadget. She wanted to draw her hand all over them, feel their surfaces. Ignatz, she saw, was doing it, too. One wanted to pet them! Helplessly, the growly sound—that awful humiliating purring—began in her throat. She hoped to God they couldn't hear it.

"O, wonder!" Krazy exclaimed. "How beautiful men are!" In her joyful surprise she forgot that her words might make Ignatz jealous. "And what a brand-new desert that's got good-looking stuff like this on it!" The world itself seemed brave and beautiful to her; for a lovely thing always just burnished the whole place up.

"New to you, Kitty-Kat," Ignatz said.

The poop, she thought. So what that he had seen them first; why harp on that before such sights as these?

And *this* part she was sure the Pup must have explained to her later because she still didn't understand what it meant. The New Clear scientists—for those, she had learned, were the onlookers—were rounder than she, just as she had thought; they had more dimensions. And the ideas that allowed them to make the bomb, the Pup said, depended on their knowing about lots of dimensions—including time.

"Ah," Krazy said, ever agreeable. For she knew that kindly Pup, his face like a good big potato, meant these explanations not—like some Mice she could mention!—as a way of showing off, but as a bouquet, an act in his impossible, never-to-be-resolved courtship of her. Which was almost a game really; for Pup *knew* that her heart belonged to Ignatz. (If, she thought sadly, it belongs to anyone anymore. If it even exists.) Pup, she thought, was like the father she had never had. (Pup, Ignatz said, was like the father he *did* have.)

The more dimensions you know, the Pup had continued, the closer your comprehension is to God's own—for the Pup's faith was strong, and God was something he brought into almost any conversation—Who knows and occupies all dimensions. So the more dimensions you apprehend the greater your capacity for evil.

But they were so beautiful! Krazy had exclaimed, understanding only the word evil. Especially the thin one with the plangent pleading eyes!

"The one with the kindly sad eyes was Oppenheimer," the Pup said, smiling. "They called him Oppie. He was the man in charge." Oppie knew many more dimensions than flat Krazy did. He probably seemed as round as a god to her. As the Comekissthedoors had seemed to the Inkers.

"Comekissthedoors?" Krazy began. "Oh, yes. The ones who. Those ones. Sure!" She rubbed her eyes as if her confusion had been physical. "Yes! Yes!" she concluded. She looked out of Pup's lace-curtained window where a brown piece of tumbleweed blew past on its way to becoming a mountain.

The Inkers, the Pup said, were like her and Ignatz and himself, comparatively flat, they just wanted to do the same things over and over. The Comekissthedoors were round, because they were sick of their own lives, hungry for change. So they had history—an extra dimension—and a greater capacity for mischief. The Inkers looked at them adoringly. As you looked at Oppenheimer.

Krazy blushed. She, she thought, clearly was an Inker; no insides, no hiding place. The Pup had known what she had felt at Alamogordo, looking at the lovely man with his long nose and his sad eyes. And that day she had even hoped—Oh God, she prayed now that Ignatz would never find out—that *Oppie* had built the tower, that the brick that was about to come was *his* brick, launched by *his* hands with their graceful, long patrician fingers.

Dusk had fallen that day, not suddenly, but as if it meant it, was giving the world a long good-bye. The four figures became shadowy, looked again more like her and Ignatz. The men stared at Ignatz's tower, as if they, too, awaited something from it. The fat man with a clipboard and an Italian accent—he was the one in a gray business suit—asked each of them how many meggietunes the Gadget would make. "Anna sida bet Oppie," the portly man said, "onna whether ahr leetle gadgeet wella egnite the earth's etmosphere?"

In the sky the stars, oblivious, set up shop.

"Difficult to collect my winnings," Oppie said dryly, and the others laughed. Krazy felt the authority he had over the other men; they, too, wanted him to look their way. One of the men passed a bottle around, and the men slapped lotion on their faces, preparing for the next day's sun bath.

Then everyone just stood and watched. The men watched the tower; she and Ignatz watched the tower and the men; and the night air grew cool as the desert reluctantly surrendered the last of its heat. One of the men counted backwards, softly, as if whispering sweet nothings to himself.

She didn't know how many pleasant hours they had stood watching. With a long sigh the night, too, came to an end. The stars that weren't going to fall that evening went on their way back to wherever they were kept. She would have been happy if the night had been—just this once—allowed to go on forever; or if, like tomorrow's brick, she were certain it would come again and again. She wanted her surprise, sure, but she also just wanted to gaze—at the tower, at the men, and at Oppie especially.

The slow backwards counting reached ten, and the men's bodies stiffened. Then, as the recitation continued, they bent over, as if shielding themselves against a blow.

She had been looking at Oppenheimer when the big light came up in front of him. She thought—the sun is rising in the west today. Then it was like she had Superman's X-ray eyes, and she saw the bones beneath Oppie's skin! She screamed. Or was that sound the roar from the bomb? The earth shuddered like a piece of shook foil, and a tremor ran through her body; both, together, undone. The air shimmered in front of her like an out-of-order television screen. A piece of the ash from the fireball floated down from heaven and landed on her fur. The ash stung; she put out her tongue to stroke and soothe her fur, but stopped, her mind filled suddenly with a vision of the ermine: Arctic hunters sprinkle salt on the snow. The ermine licks it, and her tongue freezes to the ice. This white heat was ice cold. Opposites touch, she thought, just as the Pup had said. (Had said? Would say?—for the pain was the beginning of the end of her memory.) And this vision was a warning: she must not lick the ash. She must not turn her head. *She must not move!* This icy spot on her skin was hotter now than anything she had ever felt, yet she didn't hop about to escape the pain, the way she had the time that Ignatz had lit a piece of newspaper stuck between her toes. She stayed still, feeling it, as still as if transfixed by something seen, a scene behind a door that she shouldn't have opened. (Whose door? What shouldn't she have seen?) The agony that had begun on her fur drew her inward; she couldn't turn her mind away from it. She followed the pain as it took her deeper inside herself—*it was giving her an inside! An inside,* she thought, *is a terrible thing to have!* It took her to a core, a heart within her physical heart. This pain wasn't content with burning her fur and her flesh and her blood, it wanted to eat up her soul! And until that moment she hadn't even known she had a soul! So a soul was something you found only as you lost it!

Most of all she stood still in order to keep her body together. This heat made whatever it was that made her want to jump around, to split her sides and their sides. Molecules, the Pup had told her later. And then years after that he had said quarks. Higgs Bosuns. Leptons and Baryons. But she had already known then that each little itty ettom had a littler thing inside it that wanted to get out—to shatter its walls, even itself, with a mad leaping—for the parts were in a rush to stream outwards together in an arc that would join the ball of flame on the horizon, the god they had always unknowingly worshiped. The bomb was teaching her *that she was not single*—for she had wrongly thought that she was only one substance—her body, her soul, herself, all the same. But now she learned that she was made up of separate particles, opposites only momentarily attracted—ettoms, quarks, bosuns—oh, whatever! This chilly heat was an agitator, going from piece to piece of her, inciting rebellion, saying that all should be, must be, would be transformed, changed utterly, in the twinkling of an eye. But she couldn't change! Mustn't change! She was what she was, over and over, and that over and over was what she was! She delighted in one day being like the last. She just wanted to repeat herself. To be multiple would be to die! To change would be to die! She wrapped her paws about herself, like a mother holding a child back from disaster, and she squeezed as hard as she could. She had to stay very very very still. Now. Here.

Always.

As Oppie looked at the explosion, she had heard him say, "I am become Death, destroyer of worlds." He had a black face and his lips were stained with blood. He wore a necklace of human skulls.

Ignatz had heard him, too. The Mouse said, "The cheaper the hood, the gaudier the patter." He looked angrily over at Krazy.

Was Oppie boasting? Was Ignatz jealous? Krazy looked at the burn on her fur, then up at the sky. She didn't have time right now for jealousy; she had to hold herself tight to keep her molecules together. "THE TOONERVILLE TROLLEY," she shouted, "MEETS ALL TRAINS."

Ignatz smiled at her with a look that meant: Bricks. Krazy thought of the bonk on the bean. She felt an imaginary bang, and a cold brick raising a hot bump. For the first time she thought, *it will sting.* And she couldn't help herself: *she flinched.*

The ash had turned her hair white, in a patch the size of a quarter, on her shoulder, just near the back. She could see it from the corner of her eye.

The spot had stayed white, and had never grown back black again.

* * *

1987

LYNDA BARRY
b. 1956

Lynda Barry was born in Richland Center, Wisconsin, and graduated from Evergreen State College. She is currently a self-employed illustrator, author, and playwright, and has appeared as a commentator on National Public Radio. Her cartoon collections include *Girls + Boys* (1981), *Naked Ladies! Naked Ladies! Naked Ladies!* (1984), *Come Over Come Over* (1990), and *My Perfect Life* (1994). In 1991, she published a novel, *The Good Times Are Killing Me.*

Though Barry had wanted to become a painter, she determined that she could make an independent living as a cartoonist. Bob Roth, publisher of the alternative *Chicago Reader,* contracted her work. "She was drawing a hipper kind of strip that you couldn't find anywhere else," he recalled in the *San Jose Mercury News* in 1988. "She was addressing adult concerns in a way that comic strips almost never do." Eventually, Barry transformed her focus from issues of love and the sexes to the challenges faced by children as they grow up, including rejection, abuse, and poverty. "Pain for kids is much sharper," she noted in a 1984 *Chicago Tribune* interview. "As a kid, you're stuck, no matter what's going on. As an adult, if you're at your friend's house and she and her boyfriend have a wild fight, you can leave. As a kid you can't." In a *St. Paul Pioneer Press-Dispatch* interview in 1988, she added, "People do go through their lives hurt by these things. There's a beauty about reconciling it. It's like music; it has the same kind of power."

"You always have fears of pushing your audience away," she told the *San Jose Mercury News.* "If you made your reputation doing these sorts of snappy jokes about relationships and then you move into some other field, you're going to definitely lose a lot of people who feel there's something wrong with you. And then I'm going to wonder whether there's something wrong with me. But there's really no choice. When I found a story that I thought was so good and so authentic, I wasn't going to write one about somebody eating hot dogs just because I was scared to send the stronger one out."

From Come Over Come Over

I TOLD HER SHE ONLY NEEDS THREE TO DO THE EXPERIMENT OF ① NO WATER. ② SOME WATER. ③ FLOODING. SHE PLANTED 30. SHE'S TRYING KOOLAID, MILK, AND CRAGMONT ROOT BEER. SHE RUBBED ONE WITH VICKS. SHE PUT MILK DUDS IN THE DIRT OF ONE. SHE SAYS SHE'S LOOKING FOR THE SECRET FORMULA.

I'M MILTON YOUR BRAND NEW SON

ILK

WHEN I TRY TO TELL HER THERE'S NO WAY, SHE GOES: "THAT'S WHAT THEY ALL SAY." I DON'T KNOW WHERE SHE EVEN GOT THAT! IT'S FROM THE BOOKS YOU KEEP READING WITH NO REALITY IN THEM. A MAGIC TREE STARTS TALKING OR A MAGIC DOG STARTS TALKING AND EVERYTHING IN THE WORLD CAN BE MAGIC. EVEN YOUR SPIT CAN BE MAGIC. AND NOW THAT'S WHAT SHE THINKS. THERE'S ONE PLANT SHE SPITS ON.

I TRIED TO EXPLAIN TO HER THE CONCEPT OF REALITY AND THAT REALITY IS BEAUTIFUL AND SHE SAID HER PLANTS WERE REALITY AND SHE WAS REALITY AND HER EXPERIMENTS WERE REALITY AND I SAID THE REAL REALITY WAS SHE WAS THE TORTURER OF PLANTS AND ALL THE PLANTS WERE GOING TO DIE BECAUSE OF HER AND WHAT I SAID CAME TRUE. IT CAME TRUE. IT CAME TRUE. MARLYS, I'M SORRY IT CAME TRUE.

the SURPRISE

LYNDA BARRY © 1990

DEAR BRENDA, SORRY I DIDN'T WRITE FOR SO LONG BUT MY LIFE WENT ON SUCH A DOWNER. IF YOU CAN RELATE TO THAT. BEING ON A DOWNER THAT KEEPS LASTING. THIS HAS BEEN SUCH A WEIRDED OUT YEAR. LIVING WITH MY GRANDMA IS O.K. BUT EVEN THOUGH I KNOW MOM HATES ME, I STILL WISH I WAS LIVING BACK WITH HER AND HANGING AROUND YOU.

ALSO I STARTED CONSIDERING THE WHOLE DOWNER OF THE WHOLE WORLD. ITS STILL THE SAME PROBLEMS. VIOLENCE, PREJUDICE AND POLLUTION. EXACTLY LIKE IN THE SONG "WHAT'S GOING ON." TRUTHFULLY ITS HARD SOMETIMES TO KEEP ON TRUCKIN', BUT LIKE THAT THING WHERE THEY SAY "KEEP THE FAITH BABY," I AM TRYING. ONE THING THOUGH I AM NOT SURE ABOUT NOW THOUGH, IS GOD.

HAVE YOU READ THAT THING ON ANNE FRANK IN YOUR CLASS YET? SHE WAS OUR SAME AGE ISN'T THAT WEIRD. I HAD TO WRITE A PAPER ON IT AND I PRAYED TO GOD FOR AN EXPLANATION OF THE THING, BUT BRENDA HE DIDN'T SAY NOTHING TO ME BACK. I KNOW I AM PROBABLY LIKE AN ANT TO HIM AND BIG DEAL ABOUT MY PAPER BUT LOOK WHAT HE SAID TO ANNE FRANK WHEN SHE PRAYED AND MILLIONS OF OTHER PEOPLE AND NOT JUST THEM BUT HOW ABOUT BACK DURING THE SLAVES? BECAUSE I KNOW THEY PRAYED TOO.

IF YOU CAN BELIEVE IT, ITS 3AM WHEN I'M WRITING THIS. MY SISTER MARLYS IS IN THE BED SLEEPING AND THE WEIRDEST THING JUST HAPPENED. OUTSIDE MY WINDOW I HEARD A BIRD SINGING IN THE PITCH BLACK. IF RIGHT NOW WAS A MOVIE WHERE A GIRL WAS WRITING YOU THIS LETTER ABOUT THESE QUESTIONS, I GUESS THAT WOULD MEAN SOMETHING. I DON'T KNOW. MAYBE THE SURPRISE ABOUT GOD IS THAT HE IS SMALL. MAYBE ALL HE CAN SAY IS KEEP YOUR EYES PEELED FOR PROBLEMS AND HELP EACH OTHER AND BE CAREFUL WHERE YOU GET YOUR INSTRUCTIONS. WELL THAT'S ALL I KNOW TO WRITE. I HOPE YOU ARE DOING GOOD.

PEACE + LOVE,
Maybonne

P.S. I still think life is magical.

1990

LAURIE ANDERSON
b. 1947

Laurie Anderson is a writer, composer, filmmaker, and multimedia performance artist. Her nine books include *The Package: A Mystery* (1971), *Transportation* (1974), *United States* (1984), *Postcard Book* (1990), *Empty Places* (1991), and *Stories from the Nerve Bible: A Retrospective, 1972–1992* (1994).

In 1972, Anderson graduated from Columbia University with an M.F.A. in sculpture, then stayed in New York, according to her online Warner Bros. biography (1996), as "part of a group of artist/pioneers. . . . We often worked on each other's pieces and boundaries between art forms were loose. . . . We were very aware that we were creating an entirely new scene." By the mid-1970s Anderson was traveling the country with her work. "I'm sure I performed in every single 'alternative space' in the United States," Anderson recalled. "This was a great way to see the country. I traveled alone with a big black case of violins, tapes and various gadgets and gradually began to feel more or less like a salesman."

The following pieces are from *Stories from the Nerve Bible,* which is both a book and a performance. The performance premiered at Expo'92 in Seville, Spain.

From Stories from the Nerve Bible

12. Maps and Places

I was asleep by the road about 100 miles out of Chibougamau. Poplars were rustling. I was dreaming of the Alps. Suddenly I woke up. My mouth was open. I had the feeling that I had just yelled "MACHINE GUNS!" at the top of my lungs.

from "The Rose and the Stone" 1974

The-Ugly-One-with-the-Jewels

In 1974 I went to Mexico to visit my brother who was working as an anthropologist with the Tzeltal Indians, the last surviving Mayan tribe. The Tzeltal speak a lovely bird-like language and are quite tiny physically. I towered over them.

Mostly I spent my days following the women around since my brother wasn't really allowed to do this. We got up at three a.m. and began to separate the corn into three colors. Then we boiled it, ran to the mill and back and finally started to make the tortillas. All the other womens' tortillas were 360 degrees, perfectly toasted, perfectly round. Even after a lot of practice, mine were still lopsided and charred. When they thought I wasn't looking, they threw them to the dogs.

After breakfast we spent the rest of the day down at the river watching the goats and braiding and unbraiding each others' hair. So usually there wasn't that much to report. One day the women decided to braid my hair Tzeltal style. After they did this, I saw my reflection in a puddle. I looked ridiculous but they said, "Before we did this, you were ugly. But now maybe you will find a husband."

I lived with them in a yurt, a thatched structure shaped like a cupcake. There is a central fireplace ringed by sleeping shelves, sort of like a dry beaver dam. My Tzeltal name was "Loscha" which, loosely translated, means "the-ugly-one-with-the-jewels." Now, ugly, OK. I was awfully tall by the local standards. But what did they mean by the jewels? I didn't find out what this meant until one night when I was taking my contact lenses out and, since I'd lost the case, carefully placing them on the sleeping shelf. Suddenly I noticed that everyone was staring at me. I realized that none of the Tzeltal had ever seen glasses, much less contacts, and that these were the jewels, the transparent, perfectly round jewels that I carefully hid on the shelf at night and then put, for safe-keeping, into my eyes every morning. So I may have been ugly but so what? I had the jewels.

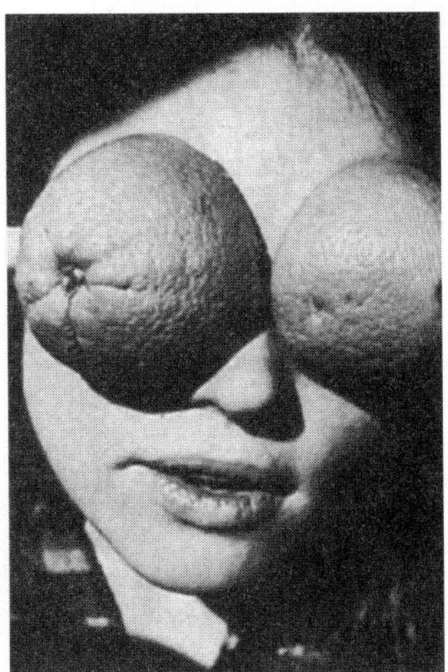

From "O-Range," a mixed-media exhibition at Artists Space, New York City, 1973. For the duration of the exhibition, I left my contact lenses on the windowsill of the gallery and spent three weeks with 20/800 vision.

15. Black Fire on White Fire

To Find Myself Lost

My studio in New York City, 1975, with wood stove and camouflage music paper.

When I moved into this loft, there was only an old mattress, Richard's wood-burning stove, and a bird that flew in and out of the broken windows. It was so cold! I stayed by the stove and read books I found on the street. I read the books, ripped out the pages, and used them for fuel. "The Book of Legends: Tales from the Talmud and Midrach" was one of the few to escape the flames. It's a beautiful book that begins with a very striking four-color print titled "Noah felled the cedars for the ark." For some reason, the next page is identical. Noah is still swinging that ax with the same firm concentration, the same cedar chips are lying on the grass. It was one of the rejects that the Hebrew Publishing Company periodically dumps onto Hudson Street.

The very first sentence in Volume 1 Chapter 1 ("God Consults the Torah") was "Nine hundred and seventy-four generations before he created heaven and earth, God made the Torah." The next is, "It was written in black fire on white fire."

Each night I sat by the fire and read these sentences again and again. Each time, they became denser, more permanent, the way an incident changes from story to legend through simple repetition. Afterwards, I would sit around in the dark and sing in "Hebrew" or just think about how when John Milton went blind, his daughters read to him in Greek and Latin. They didn't, however, know any Greek or Latin. They read phonetically, flatly. And I think of how it must have sounded to Milton's tuned-in ear to hear all the lilt in Homer ironed out into monotones.

Around this time, which was a couple of months ago, already winter, I was sanding down the columns in my new loft. One day a friend came by and said, "You know, if you just pack some dirt around these things and graft a little bark on the surface, they'll grow like little motherfuckers." I turned off the screaming sander and thought it over. It was true, I had seen telephone poles in the Midwest that were creosoted only down to the ground, then planted. Below ground, the wood rejuvenated, took root, and the poles sent out branches! Would this wood remember its past? Could this wood be resurrected too?

That night I dreamed that hundreds of toothpicks began to pop out of the columns. They grew into 1 × 1's, then branched out into 2 × 4's. When I woke, I started to write about the woods, about last summer when I went up to Canada to see how long I could stay in the woods by myself. But sitting around in all that sawdust, heaps of crumbled columns, it was too graphic, the way things fall apart and just blow away. I couldn't find the words, the road.

One of the songs then, where "lost" and "found" were back to back, was from Dante:

"Midway this life we're bound upon (thrum/thrum)

I woke to find myself lost in the dark wood (thrum de thrum)

Where the right road was wholly lost and gone (thrum de thrum/de thrum/thrum)." Repeat.

To remember Canada, I needed that smell: pine. But by this time it was February and most of the Christmas trees on the street were brown and sagging, dog-eared with bits of tinsel. Finally I found twenty healthy pines down at the Chambers Street Farm & Garden and lugged them back on my bicycle. I hung them from the pipes in my loft so that the trunks rested lightly on the floor; they almost seemed to spring from that flat pine surface. At last! I lay down in the middle letting that pungent smell fill me, dreaming of Canada, just getting to the part about the ax, when I opened my eyes and

saw the difference. This was not the shaggy, scraggly woods, it was a bunch of props! The pipes had determined the placement and the trees were hanging there in perfect rows. It was like the "forest" I saw just outside of Vienna where the Kaiser had planted hundreds of acres of fir on a grid. For miles all you could see was equally spaced trees. (Another example of you-can't-see-the-trees-for-the-forest.) And now I'm thinking of filters, grids, ways to shape the past, the little tricks memory plays to cut corners, sharpen edges, square off the clumsiness.

One day, as I was whittling down one of the trees for a violin bow, the fire inspectors came tromp-tromping in wearing rubber boots. No one knew how they got in. There was a fire crackling merrily away in the (illegal) stove. Dry pine needles carpeted the floor. The firemen walked in and out of the trees squish-squish, shaking their heads, writing on pads of paper. The chief, a stern beefy guy with bright blue eyes, noticed a T-shirt tacked to the wall. I had made it for myself in case I forgot the fiery part of memory. It was red cotton with a white silk heart stuffed with wads of kleenex. On the heart was written, "What burns never returns."

"Quite a slogan you've got there, sweetheart," said the chief, making some notes. "And by the way, if this forest is here next week when we come back, you'll be out on your ear!"

This was how the forest disappeared and all the "For You I Pine" love songs couldn't resurrect it. The woods were gone, only the words remained and I tried to make them as compact as possible, reducing everything to slogans, mottos, simple tunes.

from "Confessions of a Street Talker" 1975

Advertisement on the side of a building in my neighborhood, 1976.

REACH FOR THE SKY JOIN OR DIE DOG EAT DOG
LOVE IT OR LEAVE IT BEAT THE CLOCK
STOP THE PRESS ROCK THE CRADLE RULE THE WORLD
LONG TIME NO SEE LISTEN TO THE MOCKING BIRD

24. *Talkshow*

Good evening. Now, I'm no mathematician but I'd like to talk about just a couple of numbers that have really been bothering me lately, and they are zero and one. Now first, let's take a look at zero. Now nobody wants to be a zero. To be a zero means to be a nothing, a nobody, a has-been, a ziltch.

On the other hand, just about everybody wants to be number one. To be number one means to be a winner, top of the heap, the acme. And there seems to be a strange kind of national obsession with this particular number.

Now, in my opinion, the problem with these numbers is that they are just too close—leaves very little room for everybody else. Just not enough range.

So first, I think we should get rid of the value judgments attached to these two numbers and recognize that to be a zero is no better, no worse, than to be number one.

Because what we are actually looking at here are the building blocks of the Modern Computer Age.

from "Lower Mathematics" 1986

48. Stories from the Nerve Bible

EAST: O Little Town of Bethlehem: rock-throwing capital of the world.
WEST: those who came before me.
UP: the true meaning of the word "ARISE"

HEY LITTLE GIRL THE GULF MY GRANDMOTHER'S HATS WAR IS THE HIGHEST FORM OF MODERN ART NIGHT IN BAGHDAD THE CARDINAL POINTS TILT ALIEN SEX THE RIGHT TO BEAR ARMS SPEAK MY LANGUAGE WHERE I COME FROM ETHEREAL WORMS TIGHTROPE THE MIND IS A (WILD WHITE HORSE) LA VIDA THAT LITTLE CLOCK

Well, this is the reason:
It's because on that night
you are in somebody else's dream.
And this is the reason you can't
be in your own dream because
you're already busy
in somebody else's dream.

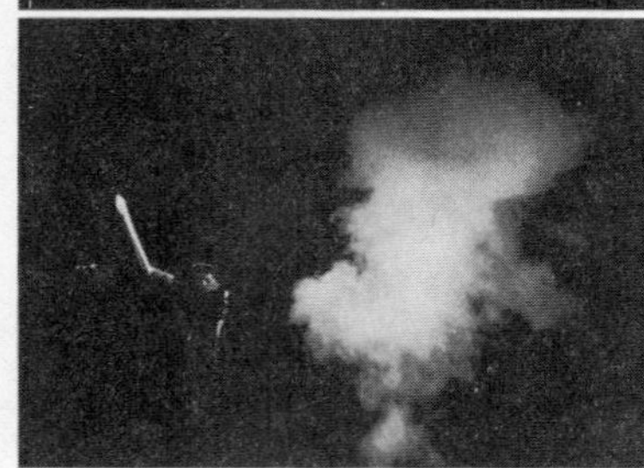

War Is the Highest Form of Modern Art

During the Gulf War I was traveling around Europe with a lot of equipment and all the airports were full of security guards who would suddenly point to a suitcase and start yelling, "WHOSE BAG IS THIS?"

(EXPLOSION)

"I want to know right now who owns this bag!" and huge groups of passengers would start fanning out from the bag just running around in circles like a Scud missile was on its way in.

I was carrying a lot of electronics, so I had to keep unpacking everything and plugging it in and demonstrating how it all worked and I guess it did seem a little fishy, a lot of this stuff wakes up displaying LED program read-outs that have names like "Atom Smasher" and so it took a while to convince them that they weren't some kind of portable espionage system.

So I've done quite a few of these sort of impromptu new music concerts for small groups of detectives and customs agents. I'd have to set all this stuff up and they'd listen for a while and then say "So what's this?" and I'd pull out something like this filter and say "This is what I like to think of as the voice of authority" and it would take me a while to tell them how I used it for songs that were about various forms of control and they would say:

"Now why would you want to talk like that?"

And I looked around at the swat teams and undercover agents and dogs and the radio in the corner tuned to the Superbowl coverage of the war and I'd say:

Take a wild guess.

Finally of course I got through. It was after all American-made equipment and the customs agents were all talking about the effectiveness, no, the beauty, the elegance of the American strategy of pinpoint bombing, the high-tech surgical approach which was being reported on CNN as something between grand opera and the Superbowl, like the first reports before the black-out when TV was live and everything was heightened, and it was so euphoric.

49. This Storm

She said: What is history?
And he said: History is an angel
Being blown backwards into the future
He said: History is a pile of debris,
And the angel wants to go back and fix things,
To repair the things that have been broken.
But there is a storm blowing from paradise
And the storm keeps blowing the angel
Backwards into the future.
And this storm, this storm
Is called
Progress.

from "The Dream Before" 1989

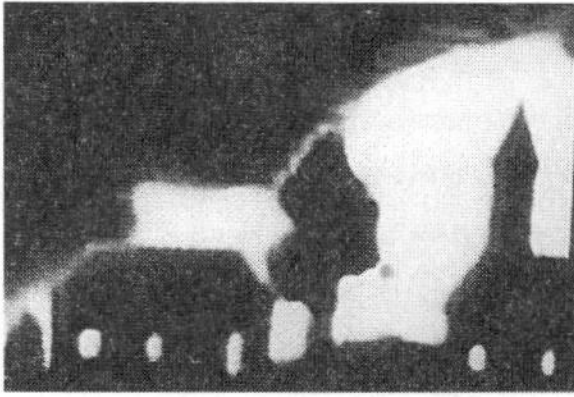

1994

ROBERT COOVER
b. 1932

Robert Coover was born in—as he put it in a *Publishers Weekly* interview in 1986—the "small, rural, mid-American classic town" of Charles City, Iowa. As an adolescent, he moved with his family to a coal-mining town in Illinois, and he "began to deal with a feeling of alienness." After receiving his B.A. from Indiana University at Bloomington, he served in the navy in the Korean War, and then began to write and read seriously. "I found my mentor in Beckett," he recalled, "in the way he erased the slate, allowed everything to start over again." Coover has published more than twenty books of fiction, including *The Origin of the Brunists* (1966), *Pricksongs & Descants* (1969), *The Public Burning* (1977), and *A Night at the Movies or You Must Remember This* (1987).

"I am really, truly, in pursuit of the mainstream," Coover told *Publishers Weekly*. "Most of what we call experimental actually has been precisely traditional in the sense that it's gone back to old forms to find its new form. . . . It's a rediscovery of that total range of what narrative can be, what it is when we put words and sentences in a sequential order to create a sense of movement—narrative always moves. But at the same time, I also think of myself as experimental in the sense that I want to test out these forms all the time."

"The Phantom of the Movie Palace" first appeared in *A Night at the Movies*. "I am both curious about and disturbed by the way our minds are warped by filmic syntax," Coover said of this collection. "Flicking channels on a TV is an amazing thing: I can sit and watch people dying and situation comedy at the same time. . . . Because I'm always thinking about form, structure, and how it relates to social forms and structures, everything I write has a kind of organic interconnectedness. When I write about the world, I'm writing about my own writing."

From A Night at the Movies

The Phantom of the Movie Palace

"We are doomed, Professor! The planet is rushing madly toward Earth and no human power can stop it!" "Why are you telling me this?" asks the professor petulantly and sniffs his armpits. "Hmm. Excuse me, gentlemen," he adds, switching off his scientific instruments and, to their evident chagrin, turning away, "I must take my bath." But there is already an evil emperor from outer space in his bathtub. Even here then! He sits on the stool and chews his beard despondently, rubbing his fingers between his old white toes. The alien emperor, whose head looks like an overturned mop bucket, splashes water on the professor with his iron claw and emits a squeaky yet sinister cackle. "You're going to rust in there," grumbles the professor in his mounting exasperation.

The squat gangster in his derby and three-piece suit with boutonniere and pointed pocket handkerchief waddles impassively through a roomful of hard-boiled wisecracking bottle-blond floozies, dropping ashes on them from his enormous stogie and gazing from time to time at the plump bubble of fob-watch in his hand. He wears a quizzical self-absorbed expression on his face, as though to say: Ah, the miracle of it all! the mystery! the eternal illusion! And yet . . . It's understood he's a dead man, so the girls forgive him his nasty habits, blowing at their décolletages and making such vulgar remarks and noises as befit their frolicsome lot. They are less patient with the little bugger's longing for the ineffable, however, and are likely, before he's rubbed out (will he even make it across the room? no one expects this), to break into a few old party songs just to clear the air. "How about 'The Sterilized Heiress'?" someone whispers even now. "Or, 'The Angle of the Dangle!' " " 'Roll Your Buns Over!' " "Girls, girls . . . !" sighs the gangster indulgently, his stogie bobbing. " 'Blow the Candle Out!' "

The husband and wife, in response to some powerful code from the dreamtime of the race, crawl into separate beds, their only visible concession to marital passion being a tender exchange of pajamas from behind a folding screen. Beneath the snow-white sheets and chenille spreads, they stroke their strange pajamas and sing each other to sleep with songs of faith and expediency and victory in war. "My cup," the wife gasps in her chirrupy soprano as the camera closes in on her trembling lips, the luminescent gleam in her eye, "runneth over!" and her husband, eyelids fluttering as though in prayer, or perhaps the onset of sleep, replies: "Your precious voice, my love, here and yet not here, evokes for me the sweet diaphanous adjacency of presence—" (here, his voice breaks, his cheeks puff out) "—and loss!"

The handsome young priest with the boyish smile kneels against the partition and croons a song of a different sort to the nun sitting on the toilet in the next stall. A low unpleasant sound is heard; it could be anything really, even prayer. The hidden agenda here is not so much religious expression as the filmic manipulation of ingenues: the nun's only line is not one, strictly speaking, and even her faint smile seems to do her violence.

The man with the axe in his forehead steps into the flickering light. His eyes, pooled in blood, cross as though trying to see what it is that is cleaving his brain in two. His chest is pierced with a spear, his groin with a sword. He stumbles, falls into a soft plash of laughter and applause. His audience, still laughing and applauding as the light in the film flows from viewed to viewer, rises now and turns toward the exits. Which are locked. Panic ensues. Perhaps there's a fire. Up on the rippling velour, the man with the split skull is still staggering and falling, staggering and falling. *"Oh my god! Get that axe!"* someone screams, clawing at the door, and another replies: *"It's no use! It's only a rhetorical figure!" "What—?!"* This is worse than anyone thought. *"I only came for the selected short subjects!"* someone cries irrationally. They press their tear-streaked faces against the intractable doors, listening in horror to their own laughter and applause, rising now to fill the majestic old movie palace until their chests ache with it, their hands burn.

Ah, well, those were the days, the projectionist thinks, changing reels in his empty palace. The age of gold, to phrase a coin. Now the doors are always open and no one enters. His films play to a silence so profound it is not even ghostly. He still sweeps out the vast auditorium, the grand foyer and the mezzanine with their plaster statues and refreshment stands, the marble staircase, the terraced swoop of balcony, even the orchestra pit, library, rest rooms and phone booths, but all he's ever turned up is the odd candy wrapper or popcorn tub he's dropped himself. The projectionist does this intentionally, hoping one day to forget and so surprise himself with the illusion of company, but so far his memory has been discouragingly precise. All that human garbage—the chocolate mashed into the thick carpets, the kiddy-pee on the front-row seats and the gum stuck under them, sticky condoms in the balcony, the used tissues and crushed cups and toothless combs, sprung hairpins, stools clogged with sanitary napkins and water fountains with chewing gum and spittle and soggy butts—used to enrage him, but now he longs for the least sign of another's presence. Even excrement in the Bridal Fountain or black hair grease on the plush upholstery. He feels like one of those visitors to an alien planet, stumbling through endless wastelands in the vain search for life's telltale scum. A cast-out orphan in pursuit of a lost inheritance. A detective without a clue, unable even to find a crime.

Or, apropos, there's that dying hero in the old foreign legion movie (and where is that masterpiece? he should look for it, run it again some lonely night for consolation) crawling inch by inch through the infinite emptiness of the desert, turning the sand over in his fingers in the desperate hope of sifting out something—a dead weed perhaps, a mollusk shell, even a bottle cap—that might reassure him that relief, if not near at hand, at least once existed. Suddenly, off on the horizon, he sees, or seems to see, a huge luxury liner parked among the rolling dunes. He crawls aboard and finds his way to the first-class lounge, where tuxedoed gentlemen clink frosted glasses and mill about with ladies dressed in evening gowns and glittering jewels. "Water—!" he gasps hoarsely from the floor, which unexpectedly makes everyone laugh. "All right, whiskey then!" he wheezes, but the men are busy gallantly helping the ladies into lifeboats. The liner, it seems, is sinking. The men gather on the deck and sing lusty folk ballads about psychologically disturbed bandits. As the ship goes down, the foreign legionnaire, even while drowning, dies at last of thirst, a fool of sorts, a butt of his own forlorn hopes, thereby illustrating his commanding officer's earlier directive back at the post on the life of the mercenary soldier: "One must not confuse honor, gentlemen, with bloody paradox!"

The mischievous children on the screen now, utterly free of such confusions, have stolen a cooling pie, glued their teacher to her seat, burned a cat, and let an old bull loose in church. Now they are up in a barn loft, hiding from the law and plotting their next great adventure. "Why don't we set the school on fire?" suggests one of them, grinning his little freckle-faced gap-toothed grin. "Or else the truant officer?" "Or stick a hornets' nest in his helmet?" "Or in his *pants!"* They all giggle and snicker at this. "That's great! But who'll get us the hornets' nest?" They turn, smiling, toward the littlest one, squatting in the corner, smeared ear to ear with hot pie. "Kith my ath," she says around the thumb in her mouth. The gap-toothed kid claps one hand to his forehead in mock shock, rolls his eyes, and falls backwards out the loft door.

Meanwhile, or perhaps in another film, the little orphan girl, who loves them all dearly, is crawling up into the hayloft on the rickety wooden ladder. No doubt some cruel fate awaits her. This is suggested by the position of the camera, which is following close behind her, as though examining the holes in her underwear. Or perhaps those are just water spots—it's an old film. He reverses it, bringing the orphan girl's behind back down the ladder for a closer look. But it's no good. It's forever blurred, forever enigmatic.

There's always this unbridgeable distance between the eye and its object. Even on the big screen.

Well, and if I *were* to bridge it, the projectionist thinks, what then? It would probably be about as definitive an experience as hugging a black hole—like all those old detective movies in which the private eye, peering ever closer, only discovers, greatly magnified, his own cankerous guilt. No, no, be happy with your foggy takes, your painted backdrops and bobbing ship models, your dying heroes spitting blood capsules, your faded ingenues in nunnery loos or up loft ladders. Or wherever she might be. In a plane crash or a chorus line or a mob at the movies, or carried off by giant apes or ants, or nuzzled by grizzlies in the white wastes of the Klondike. The miracle of artifice is miracle enough. Here she is, for example, tied to the railroad tracks, her mouth gagged, her bosom heaving as the huge engine bears down upon her. Her muffled scream blends with the train's shrieking whistle, as sound effects, lighting, motion, acting, and even set decor—the gleaming ribbons of steel rails paralleling the wet gag in her mouth, her billowing skirts echoing the distant hills—come together for a moment in one conceptual and aesthetic whole. It takes one's breath away, just as men's glimpses of the alleged divine once did, projections much less convincing than these, less inspiring of true awe and trembling.

Sometimes these flickerings on his big screen, these Purviews of Cunning Abstractions, as he likes to bill them, actually set his teeth to chattering. Maybe it's just all this lonely space with its sepulchral room presence more dreadful than mere silence, but as the footage rolls by, music swelling, guns blazing, and reels rattling, he seems to see angels up there, or something like angels, bandannas on their faces and bustles in their skirts, aglow with an eery light not of this world. Or of any other, for that matter—no, it's scarier than that. It's as though their bones (as if they had bones!) were burning from within. They seem then, no matter how randomly he's thrown the clips together, to be caught up in some terrible enchantment of continuity, as though meaning itself were pursuing them (and him! and him!), lunging and snorting at the edge of the frame, fangs bared and dripping gore.

At such times, his own projections and the monumental emptiness of the auditorium spooking him, he switches everything off, throws all the houselights on, and wanders the abandoned movie palace, investing its ornate and gilded spaces with signs of life, even if only his own. He sets the ventilators and generators humming, works the grinding lift mechanisms, opens all the fountain cocks, stirs the wisps of clouds on the dome and turns on the stars. What there are left of them. To chase the shadows, he sends the heavy ornamented curtains with their tassels and fringes and all the accompanying travelers swooping and sliding, pops on the floods and footlights, flies the screen and drops the scrim, rings the tower chimes up in the proscenium, toots the ancient ushers' bugle. There's enough power in this place to light up a small town and he uses it all, bouncing it through the palace as though blowing up a balloon. Just puzzling out the vast switchboard helps dispel those troublesome apparitions: as they fade away, his mind spreading out over the board as if being rewired—s-*pop!* flash! *whirr!*—it feels to the back of his neck like the release of an iron claw. He goes then to the mezzanine and sets the popcorn machine thupping, the cash register ringing, the ornamental fountain gurgling. He throws the big double doors open. He lets down the velvet ropes. He leans on the showtime buzzer.

There are secret rooms, too, walled off or buried under concrete during the palace's periodic transformations, and sometimes, fleeing the grander spaces, he ducks down through the low-ceilinged maze of subterranean tunnels, snapping green and purple sugar wafers between his teeth, the crisp translucent wrapper crackling in his fist like the sound of fire on radio, to visit them: old dressing rooms, kennels and stables, billiard parlors, shower rooms, clinics, gymnasiums, hairdressing salons, garages and practice rooms, scene shops and prop rooms, all long disused, mirrors cracked and walls crumbling, and littered with torn posters, the nibbled tatters of old theatrical costumes, mildewed movie magazines. A ghost town within a ghost town. He raids it for souvenirs to decorate his lonely projection booth: an usherette's brass button, some child-star's paperdolls, old programs and ticket rolls and colored gelatin slides, gigantic letters for the outdoor marquee. A STORY OF PASSION BLOODSHED DESIRE & DEATH! was the last appeal he posted out there. Years ago. THE STRANGEST LOVE A MAN HAS EVER KNOWN! DON'T GIVE AWAY THE ENDING! The only reason he remembers is because he ran out of D's and had to change BLOODSHED to BLOOSHED. Maybe that's why nobody came.

He doesn't stay down here long. It's said that, beneath this labyrinth from the remote past, there are even deeper levels, stair-stepped linkages to all the underground burrowings of the city, but if so, he's never found them, nor tried to. It's a kind of Last Frontier he chooses not to explore, in spite of his compulsive romanticism, and, sooner or later, the dark anxiety which this reluctance gives rise to drives him back up into the well-lit rooms above. Red lines, painted in bygone times on the tunnel floors and still visible, point the way back, and as he goes, nose down and muffled in clinging shadows, he finds himself longing once more for the homely comforts of his little projection booth. His cot and coffeepot and the friendly pinned-up stills. His stuffed peacock from some demolished Rivoli or Tivoli and his favorite gold ticket chopper with the silver filigree. His bags of hard-boiled eggs and nuts. The wonderful old slides for projecting blizzards and sandstorms, or descending clouds for imaginary ascensions (those were the days!), or falling roses, rising bubbles or flying fairies, and the one that says simply (he always shouts it aloud in the echoey auditorium): "PLEASE READ THE TITLES TO YOURSELF. LOUD READING ANNOYS YOUR NEIGHBORS." Also his stacked collections of gossip columns and animation cels and Mighty Wurlitzer scores. His tattered old poster for *Hearts and Pearls: or, The Lounge-Lizard's Lost Love,* with its immemorial tag line: "The picture that could change your life!" (And it has! It has!) And all his spools and tins and bins and snippets and reels of film. Film!

Oh yes! *Adventure!* he thinks, taking the last of the stairs up to the elevator lobby two at a time and—*kfthwump!*—into the bright lights. *Comedy!* He is running through the grand foyer now, switching things off as he goes, dragging the darkness along behind him like a fluttering cape. Is everything still there? How could he have left it all behind? He clambers breathlessly up the marble staircase, his heels clocking hollowly as though chasing him, and on into the projection room tunnel, terror and excitement unfolding in his chest like a crescendo of luminous titles, rolling credits—*Romance!*

"Excuse me," the cat woman moans huskily, peering at him over her shoulder as she unzippers her skin, "while I slip into something more comfortable . . ." The superhero, his underwear bagging at the seat and knees, is just a country boy at heart, tutored to perceive all human action as good or bad, orderly or dynamic, and so doesn't know whether to shit or fly. What good is his famous X-ray vision *now?* "But—but all self-gratification only leads to tragedy!" he gasps as she presses her hot organs up against him. "Yeah? Well, hell," she whispers, blowing in his ear, "what doesn't?" Jumpin' gee-whillikers! Why does he suddenly feel like crying?

"Love!" sings the ingenue. It's her only line. She sings it again: "Love!" The film is packed edge to edge with matings or implied matings, it's hard to find her in the crowd. "Love!" There is a battle cry, a war, perhaps an invasion. Sudden explosions. Ricocheting bullets. Mob panic. "Love!" She's like a stuck record. "Love!" *"Stop!"* Bodies are tumbling off of ramparts, horses are galloping through the gates. "Love!" *"Everything's different now!"* someone screams, maybe he does. "Love!" She's incorrigible. *"Stop her, for god's sake!"* They're all shouting and shooting at *her* now with whatever they've got: arrows, cannons, death rays, blowguns, torpedoes—"Love . . . !"

The apeman, waking from a wet dream about a spider monkey and an anteater, finds himself in a strange place, protected only by a sticky breechcloth the size of a luncheon napkin, and confronted with a beautiful High Priestess, who lights up two cigarettes at once, hands him one, and murmurs: "Tell me, lard-ass, did you ever have the feeling that you wanted to go, and still have the feeling that you wanted to stay?" He is at a loss for words, having few to start with, so he steps out on the balcony to eat his cigarette. He seems to have been transported to a vast city. The little lights far below (he thinks, touching his burned tongue gingerly: Holy ancestors! The stars have fallen!) tremble as though menaced by the darkness that encases them. The High Priestess steps up behind him and runs her hand under his breechcloth. "Feeling moody, jungle boy?" World attachment, he knows, is the fruit of the tree of passion, which is the provoker of wrath as well as of desire, but he doesn't really know what to do with this knowledge, not with the exploitative hand of civilization abusing his noble innocence like this. Except maybe to yell for the elephants.

"Get away from that lever!" screams the scientist, rushing into his laboratory. But there's no one in there, he's all alone. He and all these bits and pieces of human flesh he's been stitching together over the years. There's not even a lever. That, like everything else in his mad, misguided life, is just wishful thinking. He's a complete failure and a presumptuous ass to boot. Who's he to be creating life when he can't even remember to brush his own teeth? This thing he's made is a mess. It doesn't even smell good. Probably it's all the innovations that have done him in. All these sex organs! Well, they were easier to find than brains, it's not entirely his fault, and no one can deny he did it for love. He remembers a film (or seems to: there is a montage effect) in which the mad scientist, succeeding where he in his depressing sanity has failed, lectures his creation on the facts of life, starting with the shinbone. "The way I see it, kid, it's forget the honors, and go for the bucks."

"Alas, I perceive now that the world has no meaning for those who are obliged to pass through it," replies the monster melancholically, tearing off the shinbone and crushing his creator's skull with it, "but one must act as though it might."

Perhaps it's this, he thinks, stringing up a pair of projectors at the same time, that accounts for his own stubborn romanticism—not a search for meaning, just a wistful toying with the idea of it, because: what else are you going to do with that damned bone in your hand? Sometimes, when one picture does not seem enough, he projects two, three, even several at a time, creating his own split-screen effects, montages, superimpositions. Or he uses multiple projectors to produce a flow of improbable dissolves, startling sequences of abrupt cuts and freeze frames like the stopping of a heart, disturbing juxtapositions of slow and fast speeds, fades in and out like labored breathing. Sometimes he builds thick collages of crashing vehicles or mating lovers or gun-toting soldiers, cowboys, and gangsters all banging away in unison, until the effect is like time-lapse photography of passing clouds, waves washing the shore. He'll run a hero through all the episodes of a serial at once, letting him be burned, blasted, buried, drowned, shot, run down, hung up, splashed with acid or sliced in two, all at the same time, or he'll select a favorite ingenue and assault her with a thick impasto of pirates, sailors, bandits, gypsies, mummies, Nazis, vampires, Martians, and college boys, until the terrified expressions on their respective faces pale to a kind of blurred, mystical affirmation of the universe. Which, not unexpectedly, looks a lot like stupidity. And sometimes he leaves the projector lamps off altogether, just listens in the dark to the sounds of blobs and ghouls, robots, galloping hooves and screeching tires, creaking doors, screams, gasps of pleasure and fear, hoots and snarls and blown noses, fists hitting faces and bodies pavements, arrows targets, rockets moons.

Some of these stratagems are his own inventions, others come to him through accident—a blown fuse, the keystoning rake of a tipped projector, a mislabeled film, a fly on the lens. One night he's playing with a collage of stacked-up disaster movies, for example, when the layering gets so dense the images get stuck together. When he's finally able to peel one of them loose, he finds it stripped of its cracking dam, but littered with airliner debris, molten lava, tumbling masonry, ice chunks, bowing palm trees, and a whey-faced Captain from other clips. This leads him to the idea ("What seems to be the trouble, Captain?" someone was asking, her voice hushed with dread and earnestness, as the frames slipped apart, and maybe he should have considered this question before rushing on) of sliding two or more projected images across each other like brushstrokes, painting each with the other, so to speak, such that a galloping cowboy gets in the way of some slapstick comedians and, as the films separate out, arrives at the shootout with custard on his face; or the dying heroine, emerging from montage with a circus feature, finds herself swinging by her stricken limbs from a trapeze, the arms of her weeping lover in the other frame now hugging an elephant's leg; or the young soldier, leaping bravely from his foxhole, is creamed by a college football team, while the cheerleaders, caught out in no-man's-land, get their pom-poms shot away.

He too feels suddenly like he's caught out in no-man's-land on a high trapeze with pie on his face, but he can't stop. It's too much fun. Or something like fun. He drives stampedes through upper-story hotel rooms and out the windows, moves a monster's hideous scar to a dinner plate and breaks it, beards a breast, clothes a hurricane in a tutu. He knows there's something corrupt, maybe even dangerous, about this collapsing of boundaries, but it's also liberating, augmenting his film library exponentially. And it is also necessary. The projectionist understands perfectly well that when the cocky test pilot, stunt-flying a biplane, leans out to wave to his girlfriend and discovers himself unexpectedly a mile underwater in the clutches of a giant squid, the crew from the submarine meanwhile frantically treading air a mile up the other way, the crisis they suffer—*must* suffer—is merely the elemental crisis in his own heart. It's this or nothing, guys: sink or fly!

So it is with a certain rueful yet giddy fatalism that he sweeps a cops-and-robbers film across a domestic comedy in which the goofy rattle-brained housewife is yattering away in the kitchen while serving her family breakfast. As the frames congeal, the baby gets blown right out of its highchair, the police chief, ducking a flipped pancake, gets his hand stuck in the garbage disposal, and the housewife, leaning forward to kiss her husband while telling him about her uncle's amazing cure for potato warts, drops through an open manhole. She can be heard still, carrying on her sad screwball monologue down in the city sewers somewhere, when the two films separate, the gangster, left behind in the kitchen, receiving now the husband's sleepy good-bye kiss on his way out the door to work. The hood, disgusted, whips out his gat to drill the mug (where the hell is Lefty? what happened to that goddamn bank?), but all he comes out with is a dripping eggbeater.

Lefty (if it is Lefty) is making his getaway in a hot-wired Daimler, chased through the streets of the crowded metropolis by screaming police cars, guns blazing in all directions, citizens flopping and tumbling as though the pavement were being jerked out from under them. Adjacently, cast adrift in an open boat, the glassy-eyed heroine is about to surrender her tattered virtue to the last of her fellow castaways, a bald-headed sailor with an eyepatch and a peg leg. The others watch from outside the frame, seeing what the camera sees, as the sailor leans forward to take possession of her. "Calamity is the normal circumstance of the universe," he whispers tenderly, licking the salt from her ear, as the boat bobs sensuously, "so you can't blame these poor jack-shites for having a reassuring peep at the old run-in." As her lips part in anguished submission, filling the screen, the other camera pulls back for a dramatic overview of the squealing car chase through the congested city streets: he merges the frames, sending Lefty crashing violently into the beautiful cave of her mouth, knocking out a molar and setting her gums on fire, while the sailor suddenly finds himself tonguing the side of a skyscraper, with his social finger up the city storm drains. "Shiver me timbers and strike me blind!" he cries, jerking his finger out, and the lifeboat sinks.

He recognizes in all these dislocations, of course, his lonely quest for the impossible mating, the crazy embrace of polarities, as though the distance between the terror and the comedy of the void were somehow erotic—it's a kind of pornography. No wonder the sailor asked that his eyes be plucked out! He overlays frenzy with freeze frames, the flight of rockets with the staking of the vampire's heart, Death's face with thrusting buttocks, cheesecake with chaingangs, and all just to prove to himself over and over again that nothing and everything is true. Slapstick *is* romance, heroism a dance number. Kisses kill. Back projections are the last adequate measure of freedom and great stars are clocks: no time like the presence. Nothing, like a nun with a switchblade, is happening faster and faster, and cause (that indefinable something) is a happy ending. Or maybe not.

And then . . .

THE NEXT DAY

. . . as the old titles would say, back when time wore a white hat, galloping along heroically from horizon to horizon, it happens. The realization of his worst desires. Probably he shouldn't have turned the Western on its side. A reckless practice at best, for though these creatures of the light may be free from gravity, his projectors are not: bits and pieces rattle out every time he tries it, and often as not, he ends up with a roomful of unspooled film, looping around his ears like killer ivy. But he's just begun sliding a Broadway girlie show through a barroom brawl (ah, love, he's musing, that thing of anxious fear, as the great demonic wasteland of masculine space receives the idealized thrust of feminine time), when it occurs to him in a whimsical moment to try to merge the choreography of fist and foot against face and floor by tipping the saloon scene over.

Whereupon the chorus-line ingenue, going on for the ailing star, dances out into the spotlight, all aglow with the first sweet flush of imminent stardom, only to find herself dropping goggle-eyed through a bottomless tumult of knuckles, chairs and flying bottles, sliding—*whoosh!*—down the wet bar, and disappearing feet-first through a pair of swinging doors at the bottom of the frame. Wonderful! laughs the projectionist. Worth it after all! The grizzled old prospector who's started the brawl in the first place, then passed out drunk, wakes up onstage now as the frames begin to separate in the ingenue's glossy briefs and pink ankle-strap shoes, struggling with the peculiar sensation that gravity might not know which way it wants him to fall. Thus, his knees buckle, suggesting a curtsy, even as his testicles, dangling out of the legbands of the showgirl's briefs like empty saddlebags, seem to float upward toward his ears. He opens his mouth, perhaps to sing, or else to yelp or cadge a drink, and his dentures float out like ballooned speech. "Thith ith dithgratheful!" he squawks, snatching at air as he falls in two directions at once to a standing ovation. *"Damn your eyeth!"*

Over in the saloon, meanwhile, the brawl seems to have died down. All eyes not closed by fist or drink are on the swinging doors. He rights the projector to relieve the crick in his neck from trying to watch the film sideways, noting gloomily the clunk and tinkle of tumbling parts within, wishing he might see once more that goofy bug-eyed look on the startled ingenue's face as the floor dropped out from under her. There is a brief clawed snaggle as the film rips erratically through the gate, but an expert touch of his finger on a sprocket soon restores time's main illusion. Of which there is little. The swinging doors hang motionless. Jaws gape. Eyes stare. Not much moves at all except the grinding projector reels behind him. Then slowly the camera tracks forward, the doors parting before it. The eye is met by a barren expanse of foreground mud and distant dunes, undisturbed and utterly lifeless. The ingenue is gone.

He twists the knob to reverse, but something inside the machine is jammed. The image turns dark. Hastily, his hands trembling, he switches off, slaps the reels onto a spare projector, then reverses both films, sweeps them back across each other. Already changes seem to have been setting in: someone thrown out of the saloon window has been thrown back in, mouth crammed with an extra set of teeth, the stage is listing in the musical. Has he lost too much time? When the frames have separated, the old prospector has ended up back in the town saloon all right, though still in the ingenue's costume and with egg on his face, but the ingenue herself is nowhere to be seen. The ailing star, in fact, is no longer ailing, but is back in the spotlight again, belting out an old cowboy song about the saddleback image of now: *"Phantom Ri-i-i-ider!"* she bawls, switching her hips as though flicking away flies. "When stars are *bright* on a frothy *night—"*

He shuts both films down, strings up the mean gang movie with the little orphan girl in it: the water spots are there, but the loft ladder is empty! She's not in the nunnery either, the priest croons to an empty stall, as though confessing to the enthroned void—nor is she in the plummeting plane or the panicking mob or the arms, so to speak, of the blob! The train runs over a ribbon tied in a bow! The vampire sucks wind!

He turns off the projectors, listens intently. Silence, except for the faint crackle of cooling film, his heart thumping in his ears. He is afraid at first to leave his booth. What's happening out there? He heats up cold coffee on his hot plate, studies his pinned-up publicity stills. He can't find her, but maybe she was never in any of them in the first place. He's not even sure he would recognize her, a mere ingenue, if she were there—her legs maybe, but not her face. But in this cannibal picture, for example, wasn't there a girl being turned on the spit? He can't remember. And whose ripped-off heat-shield is that winged intergalactic emperor, his eyes glazed with lust and perplexity, clutching in his taloned fist? The coffee is boiling over, sizzling and popping on the burners like snapped fingers. He jerks the plug and rushes out, caroming clumsily off the doorjamb, feeling as dizzy and unhinged as that old prospector in the tights and pink pumps, not knowing which way to fall.

The cavernous auditorium, awhisper with its own echoey room presence, seems to have shrunk and expanded at the same time: the pocked dome presses down on him with its terrible finitude, even as the aisles appear to stretch away, pushing the screen toward which he stumbles further and further into the distance. "Wait!" he cries, and the stage rushes forward and slams him in the chest, knocking him back into the first row of seats. He lies there for a moment, staring up into what would be, if he could reach the switchboard, a starlit sky, recalling an old Bible epic in which the elders of a city condemned by the archangels were pleading with their unruly citizens to curb their iniquity (which looked something like a street fair with dancing girls) before it was too late. "Can't you just be friends?" they'd cried, and he wonders now: Why not? Is it possible? He's been so lonely . . .

He struggles to his feet, this archaic wish glimmering in the dark pit of his mind like a candle in an old magic lantern, and makes his way foggily up the backstage steps, doom hanging heavy over his head like the little orphan girl's water-spotted behind. He pokes around in the wings with a kind of lustful terror, hoping to find what he most fears to find. He kicks at the tassels and furbelows of the grand drapery, flounces the house curtains and travelers, examines the screen: is there a hole in it? No, it's a bit discolored here and there, threadbare in places, but much as it's always been. As are the switchboard, the banks of lights, the borders, drops, swags and tracks above. Everything seems completely normal, which the projectionist knows from his years in the trade is just about the worst situation he could be in. He tests out the house phone, pokes his nose in the empty trash barrels, braves the dusky alleyway behind the screen. And now our story takes us down this shadowed path, he murmurs to himself, feeling like a rookie cop, walking his first beat and trying to keep his chin up, danger at every strangely familiar turn, were there any in this narrow canyon. Old lines return to him like recalled catechism: She was the sort of girl who . . . Little did he know what fate . . . A few of the characters are still alive . . . He's aware of silhouettes flickering ominously just above his head—clutching hands, hatted villains, spread legs—but when he looks, they are not there. It's all in your mind, he whispers, and laughs crazily to himself. This seems to loosen him up. He relaxes. He commences to whistle a little tune.

And then he sees it. Right at nose level in the middle of his precious screen: a mad vicious scatter of little holes! His untuned whistle escapes his puckered lips like air from a punctured tire. He shrinks back. Bullet holes—?! No, not so clean as that, and the wall behind it is unmarked. It's more like someone has been standing on the other side just now, kicking at it with stiletto heels. He's almost unable to breathe. He staggers around to the front, afraid of what he'll find or see. But the stage is bare. Or maybe that *is* what he was afraid of. Uneasily, watched by all the empty seats, he approaches the holes punched out in the screen. They form crude block letters, not unlike those used on theater marquees, and what they spell out is: BEWARE THE MIDNIGHT MAN!

He gasps, and his gasp echoes whisperingly throughout the auditorium, as though the palace itself were shuddering. Its irreplaceable picture sheet is ruined. His projections will always bear this terrible signature, as though time itself were branded. He steps back, repelled—just as the huge asbestos fire curtain comes crashing down. *Wha—?!* He ducks, falls into the path of the travelers sweeping across him like silken whips. The lights are flaring and vanishing, flaring again, colors changing kaleidoscopically. He seems to see rivers ascending, clouds dropping like leaded weights. He fights his way through the swoop and swat of rippling curtains toward the switchboard, but when he arrives there's no one there. The fire curtain has been flown, the travelers are tucked decorously back in the wings like gowns in a closet. The dream cloth with its frayed metallic threads has been dropped before the screen. The house curtains are parting, the lights have dimmed. Oh no . . . !

Even as he leaps down into the auditorium and charges up the aisle, the music has begun. If it is music. It seems to be running backwards, and there are screams and honkings and wild laughter mixed in. He struggles against a rising tide of garish light, bearing down upon him from the projection booth, alive with flickering shades, beating against his body like gamma rays. "I don't need that spear, it's only a young lion!" someone rumbles through the dome, a bomb whistles, and there's a crash behind him like a huge mirror falling. "Look out! It's—*aaarrghh!*" "Sorry, ma'am!" "Great Scott, whaddaya call *that?!*" "Romance aflame through dangerous days and—" "You don't mean—?!" The uproar intensifies—"*What* awful truth?"—and his movements thicken as in a dream. He knows if he can reach the overhanging balcony lip, he can escape the projector's rake, but even as he leans against this storm of light—"I'm afraid you made one fatal mistake!"—he can feel his body, as though penetrated by an alien being from outer space, lose its will to resist. "No! No!" he cries, marveling at his own performance, and presses on through, falling momentarily blinded, into the musky shelter of the back rows.

He sprawls there in the dark, gripping a cold bolted foot, as the tempest rages on behind him, wondering: *now* what? Which calls to mind an old war film in which the two surviving crewmembers of a downed plane, finding themselves in enemy territory, disguise themselves as the front and back end of a cow to make their escape. They get caught by an enemy farmer and locked in a barn with the village bull, the old farmer muttering, "Calves or steaks! Calves or steaks!" "*Now* what?" the airman in back cries as the bull mounts them, and the one up front, sniffing the fodder, says: "Well, old buddy, I reckon that depends on whether or not you get pregnant." Such, roughly, are his own options: he can't leave, and staying may mean more than he can take. Already the thundering light is licking at his heels like an oncoming train, and he feels much like she must have felt, gagged and tied to the humming track: "Not all of us are going to come back alive, men, and before we go out there, I—" "Oh, John! Don't!" "Mad? I, who have solved the secret of life, you call me mad?" *Wheee-eeooOOOOoo-ooo!* "Please! Is *nothing* sacred?" He drags himself up the aisle, clawing desperately—"Catch me if you can, coppers!"—at the carpet, and then, driven by something like the downed airmen's craving for friendly pastures, clambers—"We accept him, one of us, one of us . . ."—to his feet. If I can just secure the projection booth, he thinks, lumbering forward like a second-string heavy, maybe . . .

But he's too late. It's a disaster area. He can't even get in the door, his way blocked by gleaming thickets of tangled film spooling out at him like some monstrous birth. He hacks his way through to cut off the projectors, but they're not even there any more, nothing left but the odd takeup reel, a Maltese cross or two like dropped coins, a lens blotted with a lipsticked kiss. His stuffed peacock, he sees through the rustling underbrush of film, has been plucked. Gelatin slides are cooking in his coffeepot. He stares dumbly at all this wreckage, unable to move. It's as though his mind has got outside itself somehow, leaving his skull full of empty room presence. Ripped-up publicity stills and organ scores, film tins, shattered glass slides, rolls of punched tickets lie strewn about like colossal endings. All over his pinned-up poster for *Hearts and Pearls,* she has scribbled: FIRST THE HUNT, THEN THE REVELS! The only publicity photo still up on the wall is the one of the cannibals, only now someone *is* on the spit. *He* is. The spit begins to turn. He flees, one hand clapped over his burning eyes, the other clawing through the chattery tentacles of film that now seem to be trying to strangle him.

He staggers into the mezzanine, stripping scraps of clinging celluloid from his throat, his mind locked into the simplistic essentials of movement and murder. He throws the light switch. Nothing happens. The alcove lights are also dead, the newel post lamps on the marble staircase, the chandeliers in the grand foyer. Darkness envelops him like swirling fog, teeming with menace. Turning to run, he slaps up against a tall column. At least, he thinks, hanging on, it didn't fall over. The marble feels warm to his touch and he hugs it to him as the ingenue's insane giggle rattles hollowly through the darkened palace, sweeping high over his head like a passing wind or a plague of twittering locusts. The column seems almost to be moving, as though the whole room, like a cyclorama, were slowly pivoting. He recalls an old movie in which the killer finds himself trapped on a merry-go-round spinning out of control, sparking and shrieking and hurling wooden horses into the gaping crowd like terrorists on suicide missions. The killer, too: he lets go, understanding at last as he slides helplessly across the polished terrazzo floor the eloquent implications of pratfalls. What he slams into, however, is not a gaping crowd, but the drinking fountain near the elevator lobby, its sleek ceramic skin as cold to the touch as synthetic flesh. He can hear the cavernous gurgle and splatter of water as though the fountains throughout the movie palace might be overflowing. Yes, his pants are wet and his toes feel squishy inside their shoes.

He's not far, he realizes, from the stairwell down to the rooms below, and it occurs to him, splashing over on his hands and knees (perhaps he's thinking of the bomb shelters in war movies or the motherly belly of the whale), that he might be able to hide out down there for a while. Think things out. But at the head of the stairs he feels a cold draft: he leans over and sweeps the space with his hand: The stairs are gone, he would have plummeted directly into the unchartered regions below! It's not completely dark down there, for he seems to see a dim roiling mass of ballroom dancers, drill sergeants, cartoon cats, and restless natives, like projections on smoke, vanishing even as they billow silently up toward him. Is that the ingenue among them? The one in the grass skirt, her eyes starting from their sockets? Too late. Gone, as though sucked away into the impossible chasms below.

He blinks and backs away. The room has come to a stop, a hush has descended. The water fountains are silent. The floor is dry, his pants, his shoes. Is it over? Is she gone? He finds a twist of licorice in his pocket and, without thinking, slips it between his chattering teeth. Whereupon, with a creaking noise like the opening of a closet door, a plaster statue leans out of its niche and, as he throws himself back against the wall, smashes at his feet. The licorice has disappeared. Perhaps he swallowed it whole. Perhaps it was never there. He's reminded of a film he once saw about an alien conspiracy which held its nefarious meetings in an old carnival fun house, long disused and rigged now ("now" in the film) for much nastier surprises than rolling floors and booing ghosts. The hero, trying simply to save the world, enters the fun house, only to be subjected to everything from death rays and falling masonry to iron maidens, time traps, and diabolical life-restoring machines, as though to problematize his very identity through what the chortling fun-house operators call in their otherworldly tongue "the stylistics of absence." In such a maze of probable improbability, the hero can be sure of nothing except his own inconsolable desires and his mad faith, as firm as it is burlesque, in the prevalence of secret passages. There is always, somewhere, another door. Thus, he is not surprised when, hip-deep in killer lizards and blue Mercurians, he spies dimly, far across the columned and chandeliered pit into which he's been thrown, what appears to be a rustic wooden ladder, leaning radiantly against a shadowed wall. Only the vicious gnawing at his ankles surprises him as he struggles toward it, the Mercurians' mildewed breath, the glimpse of water-spotted underwear on the ladder above him as he starts to climb. Or are those holes? He clambers upward, reaching for them, devoted as always to this passionate seizure of reality, only to have them vanish in his grasp, the ladder as well: he discovers he's about thirty feet up the grand foyer wall, holding nothing but a torn ticket stub. It's a long way back down, but he gets there right away.

He lies there on the hard terrazzo floor, crumpled up like a lounge-lizard in a gilded cage (are his legs broken? his head? *something* hurts), listening to the whisperings and twitterings high above him in the coffered ceiling, the phantasmal tinkling of the chandelier crystals, knowing that to look up there is to be lost. It's like the dockside detective put it in that misty old film about the notorious Iron Claw and the sentimental configurations of mass murder: "What's frightening is not so much being able to see only what you want to see, see, but discovering that what you think you see only because *you* want to see *it . . . sees you . . .*" As he stands there on the damp shabby waterfront in the shadow of a silent boom, watching the night fog coil in around the tugboats and barges like erotic ribbons of dream, the detective seems to see or want to see tall ghostly galleons drift in, with one-eyed pirates hanging motionless from the yardarms like pale Christmas tree decorations, and he is stabbed by a longing for danger and adventure—another door, as it were, a different dome—even as he is overswept by a paralyzing fear of the unknown. "I am menaced," he whispers, glancing up at the swaying streetlamp (but hasn't he just warned himself?), "by a darkness beyond darkness . . ." The pirates, cutlasses in hand and knives between their teeth, drop from the rigging as though to startle the indifferent barges, but even as they fall they curl into wispy shapes of dead cops and skulking pickpockets, derelicts and streetwalkers. One of them looks familiar somehow, something about the way her cigarette dances between her spectral lips like a firefly (or perhaps that *is* a firefly, the lips his perverse dream of lips) or the way her nun's habit is pasted wetly against her thighs as she fades away down a dark alley, so he follows her. She leads him, as he knew she would, into a smoky dive filled with slumming debutantes and sailors in striped shirts, where he's stopped at the door by a scarred and brooding Moroccan. "The Claw . . . ?" he murmurs gruffly into his cupped hands, lighting up. The Moroccan nods him toward the bar, a gesture not unlike that of absolution, and he drifts over, feeling a bit airy as he floats through the weary revelers, as though he might have left part of himself lying back on the docks, curled up under the swaying lamp like a piece of unspooled trailer. When he sets his revolver on the bar, he notices he can see right through it. "If it's the Claw you're after," mutters the bartender, wiping a glass nervously with a dirty rag, then falls across the bar, a knife in his back. He notices he can also see through the bartender. The barroom is empty. He's dropped his smoke somewhere. Maybe the bartender fell on it. The lights are brightening. There's a cold metallic hand in his pants. He screams. Then he realizes it's his own.

He's lying, curled up still, under the chandelier. But not in the grand foyer of his movie palace as he might have hoped. It seems to be some sort of eighteenth-century French ballroom. People in gaiters, frocks, and periwigs are dancing minuets around him, as oblivious to his presence as to the distant thup and pop of musket fire in the street. He glances up past the chandelier at the mirrored ceiling and is surprised to see, not himself, but the ingenue smiling down at him with softly parted lips, an eery light glinting magically off her snow-white teeth and glowing in the corners of her eyes like small coals, smoldering there with the fire of strange yearnings. "She is the thoroughly modern type of girl," he seems to hear someone say, "equally at home with tennis and tango, table talk and tea. Her pearly teeth, when she smiles, are marvelous. And she smiles often, for life to her seems a continuous film of enjoyment." Her smile widens even as her eyes glaze over, the glow in them burning now like twin projectors. "Wait!" he cries, but the room tips and, to the clunk and tinkle of tumbling parts, all the people in the ballroom slide out into the public square, where the Terror nets them like flopping fish.

Nor are aristocrats and mad projectionists their only catch. Other milieus slide by like dream cloths, dropping swashbucklers, cowboys, little tramps, singing families, train conductors and comedy teams, a paperboy on a bicycle, gypsies, mummies, leather-hatted pilots and wonder dogs, neglected wives, Roman soldiers in gleaming breastplates, bandits and gold diggers, and a talking jackass, all falling, together with soggy cigarette butts, publicity stills, and flattened popcorn tubs, into a soft plash of laughter and applause that he seems to have heard before. "Another fine mess!" the jackass can be heard to bray mournfully, as the mobs, jammed up behind police barricades in the dark but festive Opera House square, cry out for blood and brains. "The public is never wrong!" they scream. "Let the revels begin!"

Arc lights sweep the sky and somewhere, distantly, an ancient bugle blows, a buzzer sounds. He is pulled to his feet and prodded into line between a drunken countess and an animated pig, marching along to the thunderous piping of an unseen organ. The aisle to the guillotine, thickly carpeted, is lined with red velvet ropes and leads to a marble staircase where, on a raised platform high as a marquee, a hooded executioner awaits like a patient usher beside his gigantic ticket chopper. A voice on the public address system is recounting, above the booming organ and electrical chimes, their crimes (hauteur is mentioned, glamour, dash and daring), describing them all as "creatures of the night, a collection of the world's most astounding horrors, these abominable parvenus of iconic transactions, the shame of a nation, three centuries in the making, brought to you now in the mightiest dramatic spectacle of all the ages!" He can hear the guillotine blade rising and dropping, rising and dropping, like a link-and-claw mechanism in slow motion, the screams and cheers of the spectators cresting with each closing of the gate. "There's been some mistake!" he whimpers. If he could just reach the switchboard! Where's the EXIT sign? Isn't there always . . . ? "I don't belong here!" "Ja, zo, it iss der vages off cinema," mutters the drunken countess behind him, peeling off a garter to throw to the crowd. Spots appear on his clothing, then get left behind as he's shoved along, as though the air itself might be threadbare and discolored, and there are blinding flashes at his feet like punctures where bright light is leaking through.

"It's all in your mind," he seems to hear the usherette at the foot of the stairs whisper, as she points him up the stairs with her little flashlight, "so we're cutting it off."

"What—?!" he cries, but she is gone, a bit player to the end. The animated pig has made his stuttering farewell and the executioner is holding his head aloft like a winning lottery ticket or a bingo ball. The projectionist climbs the high marble stairs, searching for his own closing lines, but he doesn't seem to have a speaking part. "You're leaving too soon," remarks the hooded executioner without a trace of irony, as he kicks his legs out from under him. "You're going to miss the main feature." "I thought I was it," he mumbles, but the executioner, pitilessly, chooses not to hear him. He leans forward, all hopes dashed, to grip the cold bolted foot of the guillotine, and as he does so, he notices the gum stuck under it, the dropped candy wrapper, the aroma of fresh pee in plush upholstery. Company at last! he remarks wryly to himself as the blade drops, surrendering himself finally (it's a last-minute rescue of sorts) to that great stream of image-activity that characterizes the mortal condition, recalling for some reason a film he once saw (*The Revenge of Something-or-Other,* or *The Return of, The Curse of . . .*), in which—

1987

MARK LEYNER
b. 1956

Born in Jersey City, New Jersey, Mark Leyner was educated at Brandeis University and the University of Colorado. He began his professional career as a fiction writer while serving as an advertising copywriter, first for Panasonic and later on a freelance basis. Currently he lives in Hoboken, New Jersey. His works of fiction include *I Smell Esther Williams, and Other Stories* (1983), *My Cousin, My Gastroenterologist* (1989), *Et Tu, Babe* (1992), and *Tooth Imprints on a Corn Dog* (1995).

"My work isn't animated by a desire to be experimental or post-modernist or aesthetically subversive or even 'innovative'—it is animated by a desire to craft a kind of writing that is at every single moment exhilarating for the reader; where each phrase, each sentence is an event," Leyner told an interviewer in 1990. "It's because I want every little surface to shimmer and gyrate that I haven't patience for those lax transitional devices of plot, setting, character, and so on, that characterize a lot of traditional fiction. I'm after the gaudiness, self-consciousness, laughter, encoded sadness of public language (public because language is the sea in which all our minds swim)."

From Tooth Imprints on a Corn Dog

The Making of "Tooth Imprints on a Corn Dog"

I've been commissioned by *Der Gummiknüppel* ("the German equivalent of *Martha Stewart Living* but with more nudity and grisly crime") to compose a poem for their ten-year anniversary issue. As I reported in the premiere issue of *Esquire Gentleman,* my first assignment for *Der Gummiknüppel* was to conduct a series of conjugal visits with Amy Fisher at the Bedford Hills Correctional Facility and to chronicle same.

The editors of *Der Gummiknüppel* have custom-ordered their poem with unusual specificity. The contract received by my agents at ICM stipulates "1,000 lines of free verse in the *poète maudit* tradition of Arthur Rimbaud, but infused with the ebullience and joie de vivre that made ABBA so popular in the 1970s." Not only are the stylistic requirements severe, but the deadline's a killer: They need the completed poem faxed to their offices in Baden-Baden in less than 35 hours.

This assignment, albeit lucrative, is no stroll through the park. It's not something I can bang out amidst the domestic maelstrom of pregnant girlfriends, ex-wives, codependent dogs, etc.

So I catch the red-eye to L.A.

I will hole up at the venerable Chateau Marmont in Hollywood—the hotel where the great Billy Wilder bivouacked in his youth—and I will confect my verse under ideal laboratory conditions.

What follows is 24 hours of the postmodern writer in vitro.

[Room 25, Chateau Marmont, 8221 Sunset Boulevard, Hollywood, California]

6 A.M.

> A 22-year-old white male barred from competing in the 1993 Miss Black America contest claims to be a black female suffering from vitiligo (the skin disease that causes loss of pigmentation) and an acute hormone imbalance that's resulted in muscle bulk, hirsutism, and clitoral hypertrophy. Attorney Alan Dershowitz told correspondent Wolf Blitzer: "My client is an African-American woman with a dermatological disease and an endocrinologic disorder, and she's being quadruply discriminated against." Referring to Miss Black America Pageant organizers, Dershowitz said: "We will combat these cretinous hyenas in court and we will see them crushed like the filthy and obscene rats that they are."
>
> In Phoenix, fifteen people were stabbed in a mêleé that broke out during a showing of the movie *Aladdin.*
>
> And on Wall Street, Berlitz stock hits a new high after an extraterrestrial-alien warlord claims "monolingual humans taste better."

I have programmed the television in my bedroom to awaken me, and at six o'clock I'm roused by CNN. I mute the news and telephone room service for a sweetbreads burrito and a thermos of black coffee.

Several lines of verse have emerged intact from my hypnopompic state, and I scrawl them on a pad before they can evaporate:

> In a dressing room at Armani Kids,
> I found the dead body of a policewoman.
> I sucked her toe and she came to life.

There are also two fragments. The neo-Keatsian

> Beads of mercury dribble from
> the mouths of hemorrhaging androids . . .

and the evocative

> Tooth imprints on a corn dog.

After momentarily considering revising the initial lines to read: "At a counterfeit hair-care products lab, / I found the dead body of a policewoman. / I sucked her toe and she came to life," and then not (there's something so much more febrile and chthonic about discovering this sleeping-beauty-in-blue at a juvenile couturier), I decide against incorporating any of this material into the poem. "From the Mouths of Hemorrhaging Androids" and "Tooth Imprints on a Corn Dog" have possibilities as titles, though. (I also make a note to pitch the "comatose policewoman found in dressing room—protagonist sucks toe—policewoman's miraculously revived—becomes indebted to protagonist, who turns out to be the Vitiligo Killer" idea to a couple of movie producers while I'm in town.)

I stash the material that I've generated thus far in a safe in the bedroom closet. (I've taken rather elaborate security measures to ensure that no one plagiarizes my verse or disturbs me while I'm composing. The "workmen" who appear to busy themselves with maintenance and repairs in and around my suite are actually undercover security agents. For example, the "plumber" crouched beneath the kitchen sink, with the pants hanging low in the rear, exposing a good 2–3 inches of butt crack—he's one of my most highly decorated counterinsurgency operatives. The exposed area between the cheeks of his buttocks is actually *bugged* with hypersensitive microphones, a microcomponent electroencephalography device, a Doppler ultrasound transducer, and a remote telemetric sphygmoscope and galvanic skin response sensor so that he can record the voices, monitor the brain waves, image the internal organs, and evaluate the veracity of any person or persons who come within a two-mile radius of my hotel suite.)

Ravaging the sweetbreads burrito like a starved animal, I set up my Apple Macintosh PowerBook 180 on the dining room table, and I invoke my muse . . . my sullen muse in strapless black-lace bra, black-velvet short-shorts trimmed in fur, black fishnet stockings, quilted clogs and black *ET TU, BABE* cap.

And like the celebratory automatic-weapons fire of an anarchic mob, my neurons set the synaptic sky ablaze with electrical discharge.

7:10 A.M.

I am in ecstasy. Having donned an immaculately hand-tailored Savile Row suit, and furiously puffing True Menthols, I prowl my maze of rooms, entire stanzas of iridescent carnivalesque verse spontaneously crystalizing in my imagination. Elegiac overtures like: *A sensual, violent, good-looking woman in her forties, who drank heavily and was a recreational IV-drug user, my sister's torts professor captivated me from the moment I met her.* And tawdry, effervescent fugues like: *"Who the fuck are you, Hans Muslim Anderson?" snarled the Grissom gang's loathsome materfamilias from behind a lacquered shoji screen where she had loosened her chemise and was giving herself a crimson hickey on one of her enormous pockmarked breasts. Each of her fourteen-inch fingernails was a fastidiously manicured neon helix, requiring that even the most rudimentary tasks of personal grooming—from the daily application of her underarm deodorant to the topiary care of her bikini line—be performed by her strapping manservant, Patrick Ntambo, a cashiered ensign from the Ugandan Navy.*

These are among the gorgeous cadenzas I whistle as I clean the Augean stables of contemporary literature. My fingers appearing to evaporate in a vapor of speed over the keyboard of my laptop, I am slashing a path through the rank vegetation of American popular culture with the warped machete of my mind . . . all to the din of the latest *Chix with Dix* CD, whose turbid guitar noise sounds like a stethoscope's been put to the engine of a C-50 cargo transport, and which I play at such decibel levels that busboys exit my suite with blood oozing from their ears.

9:30 A.M.

Inner thoughts:

What a remarkable journey my life has been. I was born one of craniopagus quintuplets—five infants connected at the head, our bodies extending radially like flower petals. I was the only sibling to survive the surgery that separated us. My father was an imposing and remote figure, very much the martial patriarch who valued certainty and implacable resolve above all other attributes. (Father was particularly fastidious about language. I was with him on a plane once when he turned around in his seat and slapped a complete stranger across the face for mispronouncing the word *putsch.*) Mother, albeit not an intellectual—she was incapable of naming four American presidents, making change for $20, or reading a menu—was certainly a more empathetic and tender parent. But her influence was effectively muted by Father's strident and unyielding decrees. As a child, I was absolutely forbidden to express or inwardly harbor self-doubt. Soon after Mother's mysterious suicide, Father hired a telepathic governess from a Soviet parapsychology institute. If, in the sanctuary of my own bedroom, I had thoughts that even remotely hinted at irresolution or trepidation, the woman—an affectless martinet with an intricate circuitry of braids enveloping the back of her skull—would suddenly materialize to flay my bared buttocks with a heavy Cyrillic ruler, chiding in her eerie monotone: "Dun't sink negatif!"

After leaving home in 1972, I supported myself by doing odd jobs. For twenty dollars, I'd arrange the cash in your wallet, President-side up, in increasing denominations. That was standard. Specials included alphabetical arrangement by last name of Secretary of the Treasury, by ascending or descending serial number, etc. I did a job for a lady who liked her wallet arranged with wrinkled bills up front and crispy bills toward the back. A transit cop once hired me to arrange his bills by shade; this is called "the fade"—bright cash up front, bleached cash to the rear. *Chacun à son goût.* Specials were extra, of course. You'd be amazed at the things that people won't do for themselves, or can't do because they have their weird little phobias. A guy once called me—a young guy, I'd say about twenty-five—and he wanted me to cut up his expired credit cards. The guy had this morbid fear of credit cards once they've expired. Obviously there's some complex psychopathology involved here, but hey . . . When I arrived at the guy's house, there were two expired cards—an American Express and a Sunoco—lying in his bathtub where he'd flung them in a panic a week before. So acute was his aversion that he'd refused to go anywhere near the tub. I might add that the dude had cultivated quite a stench (which cost him an extra ten bucks; if you had really bad body odor, that would cost you an extra $10 no matter what I did for you). And when I picked up the cards and walked toward him, he recoiled in horror, weeping, falling to his knees, pleading with me not to come any closer. I diced the cards with a pair of shears from my tool belt, and, per our agreement, disposed of them in a landfill some ten miles out of town. I charged him $60—the regular $50 for cutting cards, plus the $10 surcharge because he stank so bad. Ironically, he paid with a Visa card—active, I assume. I also killed pets. (Pet "hits" were a lucrative portion of my business. A lot of people wanted their pets dead because they'd become too much trouble, but they couldn't bring themselves to do it because they'd become so emotionally attached or for religious reasons or whatever—so, for a fee, I'd do it.) My first job, I garrotted an incontinent Schnauzer for a guy in Englewood, New Jersey. It got easier and easier after that. A woman once contracted me to kill her turtle. The lady's got something called purulent erythema serpens, which makes your skin look like Roquefort cheese, and she thinks she caught the disease somehow from the turtle, so she hates the turtle and wants it dead, and she wants to *see* it die. So I devise a nice little car bomb for the turtle—a matchbox pickup truck with a piece of lettuce in it and a cherry bomb under it. The turtle waddles onto the toy truck to eat the lettuce, I light the fuse, and boom! Arrivederci, Michelangelo. But I did all sorts of other things, too. I'd help you take your cowboy boots off—that was $3 a boot. If you were straightening a painting on the wall and you needed someone to stand across the room and tell you if it was level—that was $7 per painting, and I'd do four paintings for only $25. And I'd charge ten bucks to smell your milk—y'know, if you couldn't decide whether it was spoiled or not.

And today here I am at the Chateau Marmont—all expenses paid by *Der Gummiknüppel*—improvising a couple of pages of verse for more money than most people make in a year . . . the Chateau Marmont, where Howard

Hughes satisfied his cravings for baby peas and young girls, where Diahann Carroll and Sidney Poitier trysted while filming *Porgy and Bess* . . .

What a strange, fascinating life it's been.

11 A.M.

I receive a call from Irene Webb, Vice President at ICM in Beverly Hills. There's trouble on the lot.

(It is now necessary to disclose that I've distorted the truth about why I'm in L.A. I've indicated that, having accepted the *Der Gummiknüppel* assignment, I flew to Los Angeles and checked into a suite at the Chateau Marmont to avail myself of the solitude and serenity needed to compose the commissioned poem. Eager to undergird my status as an incorruptible belletrist devoted to his art, I neglected to mention that I'd been planning to be in Hollywood anyway because production begins tomorrow on my movie. It's about a family that has a terrarium of tiny people. It's my original screenplay based on my original story which is based on my original eight-word haiku that I composed after an intravenous thiopental injection prior to my tonsillectomy when I was six. This is a Major Motion Picture. Mammoth budget, marquee stars, Oscar-winning director, lavish special effects, hip soundtrack—featuring *Chix with Dix* recorded at a higher speed to sound tiny. MAJOR.)

"What's up, Irene?"

"Mark, there's a bit of a problem on the set . . ."

"Irene, I can't hear it. I just don't have the . . . the mind space for it right now. You know I'm trying to finish this poem for *Der Gummiknüppel.*"

"But Mark . . ."

"Listen, babe, first thing in the morning, as soon as I fax the poem in, I'll shoot down to the office. OK?"

"The trouble is that . . ."

"Irene, please!"

"All right, all right. Finish the poem. What's it called, anyway?"

" 'Tooth Imprints on a Corn Dog.' Great title, huh? You wanna hear a stanza or two?"

"Mark, what I'd really like to do is talk to you about the—"

"Irene!!"

"All right, I'm sorry."

"This is the penultimate stanza of the fourth canto: *Tomorrow morning I am going to be eaten on 'The Today Show.' / Katie Couric will tenderize me with a rod used by 18th-century French nuns to flagellate recalcitrant convent girls. / And then, as Bryant Gumbel plays the drum solo from 'Wipe Out' on bongos, / four factory-fresh Nissan Sentras—each towing one of my limbs, / and each driven by the respective MVP from Major League Baseball, the National Football League, the National Basketball Association, and the National Hockey League—will quarter me. / (The Nissans' odometers will be removed and put on permanent display at the Albright-Knox Museum in Buffalo.) / I will then be prepared* arrosto in tegame*—pan-roasted with garlic, rosemary, and white wine—by the Frugal Gourmet. / I am now being held in a combination green room / fattening pen where I am being* *force-fed tapioca pudding. / Directly upstairs, they are building the 'kitchen.' / I can hear the carpenters' footsteps, / the rasp of their spackling knives, / the unintelligible obbligato of their radios. / Strangely, I have never felt more serene. / I now understand impermanence / and I am one with the Void. / Is that the cry of a cicada I hear?"*

There's a long silence.

"Mark . . ." Irene says finally, her voice breaking.

"Yes?"

"Mark, it's stunning. There's a magisterial gravity, a lapidary beauty to the verse that privileges the reader to be alive at a time when you are writing. You've endowed Couric, Gumbel, and the Frugal Gourmet with an epic, almost Miltonian grandeur. The plangent call of the cicada is an epiphany, recalling Fujiwara No Teika, the great tanka poet and essayist of the Heian period. It's an astonishing achievement."

"Thanks, Irene. I'll see you tomorrow."

12:10 P.M.

The elation of an hour ago has collapsed into severe depression. I am wracked with doubts about "Tooth Imprints on a Corn Dog." Although I'm intellectually aware that this is a requisite pattern in my creative process—the alternating waves and troughs of euphoria and despair—the emotional pain is unmitigated. Convinced that the poem requires the inclusion of more anecdotal material, I comb my journals for suitable vignettes. I leaf through the battered diary that I kept during a period in my life when I suffered from canine acral lick dermatitis and spent my days licking, scratching, and biting at my own flanks. In stunted script interspersed with pictures, like some arcane rebus, I recorded in unflinching detail my descent, my season in hell. I drank anything containing alcohol. In fact, my bar was stocked with Sterno, Old Spice, Windex, Nyquil, Aqua Net, and Lysol. (Plus tonic, bitters, and pearl onions, of course.)

But this material is far too bleak and splenetic, and would vitiate the generally mirthful tone of the poem. Perhaps I can somehow incorporate one of the stories I didn't get a chance to tell during my recent appearance on David Letterman's "Late Show," e.g., *I recently attend a garish tribute to the Italian fashion designer Gianni Versace (where I witness Diane Von Furstenberg's left breast fully emerge from her blouse—an event which, I've subsequently been told, traditionally signals the advent of autumn), and during dinner I'm regaling my tablemates with stories about my prior incarnation as a medical advertising copywriter, and I'm talking about how I wrote ads for a product called artificial saliva which was developed for people who suffer from something called chronic dry mouth, and I'm describing how the ad's body copy touted the product's pleasant taste and realistic viscosity, and I'm explaining to them how disappointed I was when the headlines I'd come up with were rejected by the client simply because they'd already been used ("Artificial Saliva—Don't Leave Home Without It" and "Artificial Saliva—Mmmm, Mmmm, Good!"), when this stunning and extraordinarily elegant Austrian countess whom I'm seated next to and who's been ignoring me through most of the meal suddenly turns to me and says in this husky sotto voce: "I'm very rich . . . and very bored." A remark which leaves me completely dumbstruck. Although for some inexplicable reason, I finally respond with: "Can your inner child come out and play?" Etc. Etc.*

But this material strikes me as egregiously blithe, posing a risk to the poem's magisterial gravity.

I am about to lose all hope, when a breeze wafts in from the open window. Actually, one can't even call it a breeze. Imagine an asthmatic fruit fly trying to blow out a birthday candle. That's the intensity of this wisp of a sigh, which conveys such a minute and evanescent concentrate of fragrances—first daffodils, then hyacinths, and finally lilac—that it might be more accurate to say that what's conveyed are the Platonic ideals of each fragrance, rather than the scents themselves. And somehow this most subtle stimulation of my olfactory nerve cells hits me with a force akin to that of a nightstick to the forehead. And the verse begins flowing anew.

12:55 P.M.

The sky is perfectly white and veined with
  vermicular trails of purple SCUD exhaust.
In a go-go cage dangling from a 10-story construction crane,
I am naked except for a 7-Eleven "Big Gulp" container
  and a rubber band.
"Swing me!" I call to the crane operator.
I want what I've never wanted before:
  terrifying centrifugal torque!
"Swing me, gringo!"
I laugh mirthlessly, eyes rolling,
  never so profoundly convulsed.
"Thanks, hon!" I wail.

The air is rent by a cacophonous peal of imbecilic laughter as a group of rickshaw pullers drinking contaminated home-brewed liquor beneath my balcony react to the verse that I have just recited—the opening stanza of the seventeenth canto.

1:30 P.M.

I telephone room service and order the 14-course lunch, including quail soup and steamed piglet.

2:25 P.M.

Nap.

6:05 P.M.

Russia is so desperate to earn hard currency, preserve jobs, and resuscitate a moribund economy that it's begun selling arms and military technology on Home Shopping Network. Viewers who tune in, unaware of this latest twist in the global weapons bazaar, may be shocked to see a svelte model in evening gown, pearls, and satin gloves caressing a Russian S-300 surface-to-air missile, as its price—$849.99—flashes in the lower left-hand corner of the screen. On-the-air callers are giddy with the incredible savings they're getting on individual weapons and entire weapons systems that up until now had been completely out of their price ranges. A housewife from Tullig, Arizona: "I can't believe it. I have three boys who all just graduated—two from high school and my oldest from college—and I just bought each of them the Kilo-class diesel-powered submarines you had on a little while ago. And I just can't believe the savings! Those submarines used to go for about $250 million each, but thanks to Home Shopping Network and the collapse of the Soviet Union, I got all three for only $2,250! And I'm thinking of getting the MIG-31 fighter plane for my nephew, who's being confirmed this spring. And for my husband, who loves cars and trucks and tractors—anything with a motor—I'm thinking, with Christmas coming, either the BTR-60 armored personnel carrier or the T-72 main battle tank. The discounts are just unbelievable!" Other former Soviet republics including Ukraine and Georgia have also lined up with Home Shopping Network to sell advanced fighter-interceptors, SU-27 fighter-bombers, MI-17 troop transport helicopters, aircraft carriers, as well as low-tech weapons like rifles, artillery, and ammunition. Home Shopping Network Vice President Beatrice Pinto told CNN correspondent Wolf Blitzer that their recent "Back-to-School Package," consisting of two shoulder-fired surface-to-air missiles, a dozen Kalashnikov assault rifles with five thousand rounds of ammunition, two anti-personnel cluster bombs, and a tank-piercing artillery shell, elicited the largest viewer call-in response in the network's history. "We liquidated our entire inventory on that particular offer in twelve minutes! People just seem to love the fact that they can purchase high-quality weapons and sophisticated delivery systems over the phone from the comfort of their own living rooms for outrageously low prices, without having to deal with shady arms brokers who ream you with exorbitant commissions and surcharges."

Luckily I'd programmed the television to awaken me at six, otherwise I might have slept through the night. What a succulent piglet! Kudos to Andre Balazs, Philip Truelove, and the entire staff here at the Marmont. I chase two 50-mg tablets of over-the-counter pseudoephedrine hydrochloride with a chilled Mountain Dew and return to my PowerBook upon which the embryonic final canto of "Tooth Imprints on a Corn Dog" glows in the Hollywood dusk.

7:30 P.M.

Inner thoughts:

This will not be the first occasion on which, shackled by inexorable time constraints and challenged to produce literature, I surface from the depths, Houdini-like, opus in hand. A number of years ago, pursuant to a large wager with noted publisher and incorrigible sporting woman Michelle Sidrane, I absconded to a villa at Roquebrune-Cap-Martin on the Côte d'Azur and, in a fortnight, completed a twelve-volume series of mystery novels collectively entitled *The Executioner's New Clothes,* which includes *The Executioner Wears a Leisure Suit, The Executioner Wears a Pinafore, The Exe-*

cutioner Wears a Habit, The Executioner Wears a Chemise, The Executioner Wears a Bikini, The Executioner Wears Jodhpurs, and *The Executioner Wears an Iridescent Silk Chiffon Jeweled-Front Gown with Matching Cape.* You're probably familiar with the opening paragraphs from *The Executioner Wears a Truss,* as they've been widely anthologized. Note the cool, vibey sort of "Kansas afternoon" feel I achieve by juxtaposing madras, velvet, and terry:

> The two murderers have been on the road for almost fifteen weeks without steak au poivre, in desperately cold weather, wearing only madras slacks and turquoise chambray workshirts.
>
> Back in New York, the Executioner staggers drunk from the Four Seasons, lurching desultorily toward a white limousine. All postpunk ennui, he dives headfirst into the car as if into an empty pool. And he sleeps, paralyzed, face pressed against the velvet upholstery. Relentlessly, clumps of darkness devour him.
>
> When he regains consciousness, he's in a hotel room in Lake Tahoe. His girlfriend, Lucia, who's just emerged from the sauna, turbaned and swathed in plush towels, is squeegeeing sweat from her face with the edge of a freckled forearm.
>
> "Thirty thousand tons of New Zealand anthracite just don't vanish into thin air," she says.
>
> "I'm not interested in New Zealand anthracite at the moment," the Executioner says, massaging his temples. "I want you to explain that dinner to me again—the one at your parents' house. You said it was some sort of ritual meal commemorating . . . what?"
>
> "Many thousands of years ago, my people were forced to flee their homeland suddenly one morning. When they fled, all they had time to take with them were half-filled cups of cold black coffee, cheese danish, and the sports section of the newspaper. And they barely had time to get even one sock on. That's why each year, when we commemorate our exodus, we eat these ritual foods—the cold black coffee and the cheese danish—and we read from a special sports section, and we wear a single sock. On all other nights we wear a pair of socks, but on this night we wear only one."
>
> "Oh yeah," says the Executioner, fidgeting with his genetically engineered superfeminine gerbils who stand on their hind legs and, grasping the bars of the cage with their front claws, bombastically shout "Egöiste!"
>
> Meanwhile, two coruscating gold-capped buckteeth sprout from the holographic moon, as the tectonic throb of Hong Kong's subterranean synthetic drum machine rattles the city, and handsome triad gangsters who pomade their hair with their own semen and tote bowling bags containing the severed heads of their business adversaries sprawl in chic hotel-lobby banquettes made of molded whale intestine filled with thermostatically modulated runny Camembert.

10:45 P.M.

The final stanza of the final canto. It must be a concise, allusive, unifying summation of the disparate themes and leitmotifs of the poem, an intricate précis, an envoi; in structure—a perfect miniature of the work's massive architecture, in tone—an effervescent exaltation of life itself.

I'm working two veins simultaneously.

I've been exploring the notion of educational foods. Specifically, is it possible to utilize soup as a pedagogical tool? Essentially, what *is* soup? I ask myself. A liquid food with a meat, fish, or vegetable stock as a base and often containing pieces of solid food. And then it hits me—why, of course—soup is the ideal gastronomic medium for educating children about maritime disasters and naval battles. For example: Chicken broth with little macaroni Titanics and macaroni icebergs. Or Hearty Home-Style Battle of Trafalgar Bisque with barley Lord Nelsons. Defeat of the Spanish Armada Gazpacho. Cream of Andrea Doria. Battle of Midway Miso Soup with tofu aircraft carriers and kamikaze crackers.

At the same time, I'm exploring the lyrical possibilities of the 900-number tête-a-tête:

> "Describe yourself to me."
>
> "I'm a peroxide-blond in a black velvet miniskirt, actually."
>
> "Describe something sexy that you've done recently."
>
> "Something that I did that someone else thought was sexy or something that I thought was sexy?"
>
> "Something you did that you found sexy."
>
> "I didn't lick all the potato salad off my spoon before using it to stir my tea."
>
> "Oh . . . that's good. Say that again."
>
> "I didn't lick all the—"
>
> "Slower."
>
> "I . . . didn't . . . lick . . . all . . . the . . . potato . . . salad . . . off . . . my . . . spoon . . . before . . . using . . . it . . . to . . . stir . . . my . . . tea."

Now, how to hybridize these two strains—the pedagogical soups and the erotic phone conversation—into the germ of a final stanza, that's the problem. And then it hits me—why, of course—a sex-talk breakfast cereal with male and female marshmallow bits each containing an edible, lactose-activated, voice-synthesizing microchip so that when you pour on the milk and put your ear close to the bowl, you hear, for instance, one marshmallow murmur: "Please say it. Since Clinton was impeached, it's the only way I can . . . function. Say it slowly." And then another marshmallow responds: "All right, baby. I . . . didn't . . . lick . . . all . . . the . . . potato . . . salad . . . off . . . my . . . spoon . . . before . . . using . . . it . . . to . . . stir . . . my . . . tea."

1:15 A.M.

I've decided to forgo incorporating this material into the final stanza of the final canto. There's too much pathos in pornographic breakfast cereal. Now I'm just thinking out loud here, but how about something like: *As cyanide pellets are dropped into the bowl of sulfuric acid beneath my chair, / I extend the middle fingers of both hands. / "Fuck you all," I sneer. / I inhale deeply, and then nonchalantly blow a series of thick, perfectly formed smoke rings of poison gas. / Then suddenly my attorney appears. / "Here is my Magic Legal Pad," he says. / "Stand on it and it will fly you wherever you want to go—the Maldives, Mauritius, Tortuga, wherever. / And it's sanitary—after each person uses it, he or she discards the top sheet, so the next user can stand on a completely clean page."*

No . . . that's no good.

I need something august. Something resplendent. Something like:

> I inhabit vast pavilions whose emptiness
> is set ablaze by the vermillion sunset . . .

1:16 A.M.

I inhabit vast pavilions whose emptiness / is set ablaze by the vermillion sunset.

Hmmmmmmm.

I inhabit vast pavilions whose emptiness / is set ablaze by the vermillion sunset.

That works for me.

There's a majestic plenitude to it. A fanatical lucidity. A still, immaculate violence. A sort of ironic, elephantine, paradisiacal hegemony.

1:17 A.M.

Deep sleep, with intermittent drooling and spasmodic leg movement, and incremental hair and nail growth.

6 A.M.

[*Animated graphic of flipping alphabetical cards from Rolodex, indicating the myriad celebrities who've appeared on the show: Asner, Beatty, Cher, Dahmer, Eastwood, Fonda, Gotti, Hammer, Iacocca, etc. Cut to live shot of applauding audience. Cut to close-up of host.*]

—We're back with Dr. Étienne Ducasse, who says that because of the expansion of continental ice sheets, this may well be our last summer. Dr. Ducasse, along with colleagues at the Institute for Advanced Cybernetic Studies in La Jolla, California, has developed an instrumented skintight bodysuit with instrumented gloves and head-mounted stereoscopic display that will allow you to interact with a computer-generated summer environment. Some are calling it "virtual summer." Dr. Ducasse says that you'll be able to "experience" everything from surfing the Pipeline at Waikiki to prickly heat and sunlight-induced basal cell carcinomas—without leaving the comfort and security of your couch.

Joyce from Lake Little Lake, New York—you're on the air.

—Hello?

—Joyce, turn the volume on your TV down.

—OK . . . I've been trying to get through since Monday, so before I ask my question for Dr. Ducasse, I'd like to respond to the people you've had on this past week. On Monday you had on the woman who found that poor little creature "Winnie" on the highway and then hid it in her lover's nail salon, where it died. I just wanted to say: How could she? So she didn't know what it was. She could have called a scientist from the local community college to come over and take a look at it. She says she tried to call the college, but the line was busy . . . well c'mon, dial again, for God's sake! We get mad in this country at folks who leave their children in dumpsters and blow up department stores and what all—but hey, are we any better if this is the way we treat a visitor from another world? She says it died of malnutrition but it's not her fault because she served it food and it just wouldn't eat. Well it doesn't take a Nobel lariat to know that different planets have different eating customs and what's one creature's staple is another's poison. You can kill a black man by giving him a fish egg. One little egg—dead. Orientals can't eat frozen yogurt. To them it's like the equivalent of strychnine. One small cup of frozen yogurt killed those six Chinese cheerleaders at MIT in 1991. So if you gave Colin Powell a big bowl of caviar or Reverend Moon a scoop of frozen yogurt on a cone, and then said: well, I fed him but he wouldn't eat—c'mon, that doesn't exculpate anyone. Then on Tuesday you had that entomologist who came on with the Twinkie-sized cockroaches from Madagascar and toward the end of the show she said that once when she was a teenager she hadn't been allowed in her synagogue because she was menstruating and how this made her aware of the misogynistic bigotry within her own faith and I just wondered if that could have had anything to do with sharks because I know from a trip my husband and I once took to Hawaii that they advise women to stay out of the water if they're bleeding or menstruating because that might attract sharks and they also say to avoid wearing any shiny jewelry that might look like the scales of a prey fish and I know that some Jewish women have a custom of wearing shiny jewelry when they pray . . . so I think her synagogue might have just been taking necessary safety precautions and I thought her criticisms bordered on anti-Semitism. And on Wednesday you had the psychic who can locate shoppers' cars in mall parking lots by placing their ignition keys under her tongue and she predicted that by the year 2000 the Bloods and the Crips would replace the Democrats and the Republicans as the major political parties and I just wondered if she thought that in the future Israel might mistakenly nuke Graceland and then agree to pay reparations after Lisa Marie addressed the Knesset? And yesterday you had the psychotherapist who said that over time couples become inured to each other's warning signals and I just wanted to say that my husband and I have been married for 28 years and recently I woke up one Sunday morning and asked him what he'd like to do that day and he said he wanted a fat greasy egg roll, half-a-dozen polyethylene packets of duck sauce, a fifth of Scotch, a pack of Newports, Mahler's Eighth Symphony on the Walkman, and a languorous baby-oil handjob from a Filipino X-ray technician wearing only her lead apron. And he'd never spoken to me like that before—I never even knew he liked egg rolls or Mahler. So I just wanted to say that you have to keep your eyes open because there are very obvious signs of trouble in a relationship but you have to catch them early. Now, I want to say that your guest this morning, Dr. Ducasse, is very informative and I'd like to know if he thinks that my husband and I should have any money in high yield international monetary funds and also I'd like his opinion on tax-deferred annuities.

6:10 A.M.

I was apparently so exhausted last night after composing the first two lines of the final stanza that I don't even remember having programmed the television to awaken me this morning.

I dial room service from bed.

"This is Leyner in Room 25. Let me start with a large tamarind juice. Are the Galápagos turtle eggs fresh? Then give me three shirred Galápagos turtle eggs with a side order of manioc curly-fries and . . . are the *sugared lard balls in absinthe* chilled? Yes I would, thank you. And a large thermos of black coffee."

6:50 A.M.

The phone rings. It's my sister Chase.

"Mark, I'm sorry to bother you, but Daddy's test results just came back. He's definitely got Hoover-Klebs disease. I'm on the other line with a specialist at Mt. Sinai right now. Do you want to talk to him?"

(Hoover-Klebs disease is a debilitating and fatal illness which, in its tertiary stage, results in the complete liquefaction of the brain, the viscous cerebral fluid actually draining into the paranasal sinuses. Death typically occurs in a paroxysm of expectoration. I'd given my father a home Hoover-Klebs testing kit for Christmas—this is an easy-to-perform, three-minute assay that detects the presence of the neurotransmitter acetylcholine in paranasal mucus. When he got a positive result on the home kit, he was hospitalized for more extensive and definitive tests.)

"Mark . . . do you want to talk to the doctor?"

"Chase, I'm about to craft the culminating measures of 'Tooth Imprints on a Corn Dog.' This is an extremely critical moment in the creative process and I will not allow myself to be distracted by anything extraneous to the poem. Do you understand?"

"Well, what do I do with Daddy?"

"Does he have his Game Boy and food pellets?"

"Yes."

"That should keep him occupied. I'll be back in New York in a couple of days."

8:00 A.M.

Call it divine afflatus. Call it esemplastic power. Cite Coleridge awakening from his deep reverie, the magical lines of "Kubla Khan" still limpid in his mind; or Shelley who, brooding in a wood that skirts the Arno near Florence, was inspired by tempestuous gusts to compose the interlacing tercets and couplets of "Ode to the West Wind." I was applying benzamycin gel to a rash I'd developed after attending The McLaughlin Group Inaugural Reception in Washington, when it came to me—the final stanza of the final canto—verbatim, end-stops and enjambments intact; the original two lines efflorescing spontaneously into sixteen:

> I inhabit vast pavilions whose emptiness
> is set ablaze by the vermillion sunset.
> My menagerie of shaved animals is not open to the public.
> But you may go to the special room
> where every object is coated with Vaseline
> and you may put something up your ass.
> I will be down in half an hour.
> Presently I am drugged and supine in my lichen-covered bathtub,
> dazedly eating lichee-nut fondue
> from a chafing dish of gurgling white chocolate at tub-side,
> as a succession of anatomical freaks mount a klieg-lit proscenium
> and perform for my entertainment.
> A scorched breeze conveys the acridity of spent rocket fuel from
> a launched garbage barge heading for the vast necropolis on Pluto,
> loaded with the compacted corpses of executed insurgents.
> It doesn't get much better than this.

9:15 A.M.

I've just faxed the 1,257 lines of "Tooth Imprints on a Corn Dog" to *Der Gummiknüppel* in Baden-Baden.

I'm in my customized, four-wheel-drive, All-Terrain Lincoln Town Car, heading west on Wilshire Boulevard into Beverly Hills, and I'm on the line with Irene Webb at ICM, and, as a peripheral slurry of pink and aquamarine flies by, I'm screaming into the car phone: "What do you mean De Niro won't get in the terrarium?!"

It doesn't get much better, indeed.

1995

CURTIS WHITE
b. 1951

Curtis White was born in San Lorenzo, California, "a little prefab paradise for veterans of World War II." He was educated at the University of San Francisco, Johns Hopkins University, and the University of Iowa. His books include *Heretical Songs* (1981), *Metaphysics in the Midwest* (1988), *The Idea of Home* (1992), *Anarcho-Hindu* (1995), and *Memories of My Father Watching T.V.* (1998). Since 1980, he has been a professor of English at Illinois State University in Normal. He is also the managing director of FC2, an author-directed publishing group specializing in postmodern and experimental fiction.

"I was heavily influenced by the counterculture of the sixties," White said in a 1996 interview for this anthology. "I sort of knew postmodernism was for me the first time I came across it, the way when I saw the album cover for *Sergeant Pepper's*, I knew the Beatles were for me."

"Combat" is from the first chapter of *Memories of My Father Watching T.V.* It was written with the "guiding premise," White recalled, that "I got to know my father not by talking to him, but by watching his TV programs. It is probably my most confessional book. At the same time, it can be read as a dramatization of the tragic psychosocial situation of families steeped in TV."

From Memories of My Father Watching T.V.

Combat

1. In the episode of *Combat* titled "Command," my father was a German pontoon bridge built over a narrow French river. The bridge/my father threatened to provide a means of access for Krauts in order to roll their *Wehrmacht* machines into an area tentatively held by Americans. Therefore, as a strategic priority of the Allied forces, he had to be "taken out."

2. Until failures in North Africa and the Caucasus deprived Germany of the oil reserves needed for their "war machine," German tanks, planes, and armored carriers were feared and envied. They had the first "smart" weapons: guided bombs and the so-called V-2 rocket. They also had the first fighter jets (although by the time they became available there was so little fuel left that they were towed to the runway by cows). They were even able to synthesize their own gasoline from coal. In *Combat,* however, the function of these mighty war machines was merely to roar up full of the empty ostentation of late-Wagnerian opera, and be promptly converted to something more like the discarded shells of cicadas. Brown and brittle things, buzzing in the wind.

3. My father felt a deep sense of shame, guilt, and humiliation for having provided the Germans this service. He gave his good, broad American back, fortified by Midwestern grains, to the purposes of the fascists. He knew it was a terrible thing to do.

4. The DSM III (*The Diagnostic and Statistical Manual of Mental Disorders*) under the heading "Diagnostic Criteria for Major Depressive Episode" states in B. 6. that the depressed patient has "feelings of worthlessness, self-reproach, or excessive or inappropriate guilt (either may be delusional)." Was my father's fervently held notion, conveyed regularly during wee-hour confessions to his amazed and sleepy children, that he was a pontoon bridge for the Nazis delusional? Was Gregor Samsa's depressed ideation ("I am a monstrous vermin") delusional? Or were these things metaphors? Is a metaphor a delusion? Does the probability of Franz Kafka's depression require us to think less of him as an artist?

5. When I was a student at the University of San Francisco, I took an honors course in 20th-century fiction. The course met at the professor's house. It was during the time when I first began to have opinions. My strongest and most perverse opinion, expressed in the lotus position from the floor of my professor's living room, was that Franz Kafka deserved no acclaim, was not to be admired, because the lone meaning his fiction had to offer was the effect of his own mental illness. What greatness is there, I de-

manded to know, in disease? What credit can one claim? My classmates and especially my professor were perplexed. How can you not like a story about a man who wakes up as a "monstrous vermin"? It is a magnificent metaphor! It is charming as heck! They were curiously unable, however, to find an aesthetic language to defend the beetled Austrian from my charge that he was just sick. I laughed as I debated, throwing their homilies back in their faces, and said, "Why should we claim to be pleased by this night, this paralysis, this human upon whom foreign objects grow?" But the real meaning of my laughter was, "Don't you see? This argument of mine is bug scales. I am Kafka. I am his disease."

6. My father was a lousy traitor and he knew it. Nonetheless, he felt an uncontrollable terror at the thought that the men he loved, *Combat*'s sturdy cast—Vic Morrow as Sergeant Saunders, Littlejohn, Caje, Kirby—were moving slowly in his direction, climbing through the brush, the dirty hills, and the curious eucalyptus trees misplaced in the French countryside. These men were going to attach plastic explosives to his ribs. They had the little electric plunger for detonation. My father felt guilt, doom, and a hollow sense of justice. But he confessed readily that the squad, those grey heroic men, were right as usual. He should be demolished. Blown up before the Kraut treads could cross him. He was not only a bridge, but a bug. A monstrous vermin. A long bug like a walking stick, a grim sort of mantis, extended across a French river. The German tanks would roll across my father's bug back unless he was destroyed.

7. At the beginning of this episode, we learn that Lieutenant Hanley (Rick Jason) has been wounded and will be removed from ETO (European Theater of Operation) for thirty days. In his place comes one Lieutenant Douglas (guest star, Joseph Campanella). Unlike Hanley, this new lieutenant does not fraternize with the men. He gives orders. He doesn't smile. He eats his awful dog-soldier K-rations crouched by himself. Throwing down that abject meal, the Lieutenant orders one Pvt. Adams to burn a picture of his three-year-old daughter, a picture Adams has only just received from the States. Adams is offended. The squad is outraged. They do not like this new strong and silent lieutenant. His immobile face seems to take some dark delight in refusing them even the most basic human acknowledgement. They prefer their old lieutenant who seems by contrast a lieutenant of infinite smiles. One has to admit, however, that Adams had been warned to bring no personal effects. Well, hadn't he, soldier? No telling how "Jerry" would use this information if he were captured.

8. Adams was one of the replaceable squad members who rise glorious from the earth with each new episode only in order to provide fresh and expendable fodder for the Germans. How must these men feel? Do they recognize each other? Do they share looks with hurt eyes? Looks that say, "In this episode, amigo, we die, so that these others may find weekly prime-time glory." Do they resent Kirby or Littlejohn, off whom German bullets, grenades and mortars bounce like popcorn? I confess to you that the deaths of those also-appearing-in-alphabetical-order affects me. My depressed

brain, in which my ill spirit sobs in each blood cell, tells me that this is something worthy of tears. I weep for the lives of the soldiers who will not return in next week's episode.

9. Adams held the little photo of his daughter, tiny Brigette, between long thin fingers. His fingers did not wish to be burned. Kindly, he started the match in a far corner, distant from his baby's smiling head. But there is no mercy in fire. It leapt accelerated by photo chemicals. In a moment it was over. Her charred remains lay on the ground. Her little smile lingered before him like an electronic afterimage. He had murdered his own child. He didn't deserve to live.

10. Of course, if he hadn't burnt his daughter, it might only have been worse. "I see, Herr Adams, that your little girl—Brigette it says here on the back of this photograph in the hand of your lovely and tantalizing wife—has just turned three. Wonderful! Well, you know that little Brigette depends on you. She needs you to live. Yes! Above all else, live! She needs you to return home. She would not like you to die now for the silly reason that you will not tell us your soldierly objectives even when such information is of absolutely no use to us at all. Say, for example, that you told us that your mission was to kill the Führer. Goodness knows that we are aware that you would like to kill the Führer under the mistaken idea that we German people would stop trying to kill foreigners and inferior creatures without him. But that is wrong, as history will show, because in fact it is our innate sense of tidiness which compels us to clean up the awkward messiness of so many different colors and what have you. Different shapes. And sexes, *mein Gott*. But we already know that you would like to throttle the Führer's long neck like a Thanksgiving goose if you could get your hands on him. But what of your wife and little Brigette? Your wife, for example, is clearly a very, what shall I say?, lovable thing since you have plainly done something very unclean to produce this Brigette baggage. We Germans like to get behind and spread the woman's bottom and see all the dirty, hairy parts. This makes us sick of life and hence we must find all the unclean brown people in the world and kill them because they made us do it hindwise like a hound. Yes, there there, my friend, vomit. It makes you sick to think about. Well, it does me too. Here, I will vomit with you. Yaugh. Feels good, yes? To retch, ah, it is clean and bracing. Like your Old Spice Cologne for men. Nevertheless, I promise you, I will find your wife after this war and spread her to find those soft and complicated things just as you Americans spread your fat Sears catalogues to find the colorful toys or the black and white women's underwear. Yes, there you have it. The big pieces. Of course, I will risk the impulse to suicide such an act will inspire in me. I will transfer my desire to kill myself to your daughter. The only sad part, I think, with the children is the blood that comes from their tiny anuses. Is it not so in your own experience? Now, where do you come from and where were you going? Where is your headquarters? We wish to take a bite from that part of the map."

11. Were these possibilities part of the infinite despair that made Adams such an easy target a few moments later? He was killed by a German sniper.

The hole in his forehead in fact looked like a bleeding anus. This is the despair that comes for these nameless men who are brought in fresh for each episode so that they might die from their nameless fears and from the tragic knowledge of their function in the *Combat* world.

12. Pvt. Adams, the original man. Brought onto the arboreal scene only to be promptly driven off again, in shame and despair. He must wonder, as he walks head down out of the studios, unemployed for the umpteenth time, "How am I different from these others? No one else is like me. I am uniquely flawed." There is no way of explaining it to him. He really is one of the world's chosen expendables.

13. The episode, "Command," is the first episode I've seen of *Combat* since I was a teenager and crouched like a little beast at my father's side, by the couch, where he reclined in much the same manner as the famous reclining Buddha. I thought at that time to be his henchman and recline on a couch in my turn. But I am halted in this destiny by the following question. Why am I breathing life back into this one episode, "Command"? What wild law of chance brought it to me? And yet it is the perfect episode for my purposes. Through it I intersect with the sublime.

14. And what of Sarge, whose last name never passes a man's lips. He too has *le masque*. He never smiled, never expressed any emotion except his determination to see his suffering through. And yet for a man who suffered, who had thousands of Nazi bullets enclose him (like the knife-thrower's assistant at the fair), he was strangely relaxed. He always looked sleepy. He leaned like James Dean against the window frame of an abandoned country cottage, his upper lip pooching over, and peered out into the world looking for the next Nazi needing a bullet. He was precisely "cool." Neither warm with life nor cold with death. Show him a horror, any horror. He will have no human response. Ghoulishness holds no terror for the ghoul.

15. A piece of trivia known only to the most ardent *Combat* fans: Sarge had a tattoo on the knuckles of his right hand DAS, and a tattoo on his left EIN. Kraut-talk. Hey, Sarge, why you got Kraut-talk on your hands? When he put his fists together, knuckles out, as he often did in the very eyes of the enemy, like Joe Louis in a pre-fight press conference with Herr Schmelling, the tattoos spelled DASEIN. Thus the subtle force of the terror he inspired.

16. During the skirmish in which Adams is killed, the Lieutenant is pinned down by German fire. He is behind a fallen tree or similar forest debris. (Why is it that in every episode the platoon is pinned down behind a fallen tree? And how is it that the German fire from a machine gun nest [machine gun "nest": once again death in life is our theme] hits exactly an inch below the preserving limit of the tree. I think that the men of *Combat* could hide behind toothpicks.) As I say, the Lieutenant was pinned down. He escaped because—as always—his fellow Americans lobbed grenades with inscrutable accuracy into the machine gun birthing-place-for-birds.

17. In the end, it is the thesis of the television program *Combat* that America won World War II because of baseball. It is finally the hand grenade that dissolves the impasse of mutual machine gun fire that cannot hit anything. The GIs have good arms. The grenade is the size of a Grover Cleveland hardball. For Americans, the machine gun is merely "chin music." It keeps the enemy's head down. It is the fastball of the grenade that "punches them out," that "rings them up," that "sets down the side."

18. When the platoon reached the home of the French commando, Jean Bayard (who was to lead them to my-father-the-pontoon-bridge) the Jerries had already killed him. (My father felt a contradictory ecstasy: he might still live but his living would be one long treachery.) Sarge and Lieutenant took revenge on Bayard's German killers, but in the process made enough noise to summon the German platoons which were defending my father. They roared up in their *Wehrmacht* bug husks and a tremendous fire fight ensued, rifles and varieties of machine gun making those deep, reassuring and compulsive sounds (the sound *ka-chang*, for instance) which my father worshipped.

19. My father would watch *Combat* obsessively if for no other reason than that he had an idolatrous relationship with this sound of guns. Knowing this, I've taken all my videotapes of *Combat* and transferred just the battle scenes to another tape which I will give to my father for his birthday. Recorded at the slowest speed, I have provided him with better than six hours of bliss. My only fear is that he will die of this bliss, like the lonely masturbating man coming for six hours straight and discovering that it is his very bloody life that puddles on his stomach.

20. I am frizzled, stale and small.

21. There is an outstanding moral complexity to this episode, "Command." Lt. Douglas' sole desire (we discover late in the drama) is to return from this mission with all of his platoon members alive. For he was the famous commander of the legendary and ill-fated Mt. Chatel platoon which lost all thirty-one of its soldiers in the process of wiping out a whole "Kraut company." (This is the secret and the reason behind his apparent indifference to his men: he loves them too well.) It is for this reason that, when a German patrol strolls by, he orders that they be allowed to pass unchallenged. Allowing them to pass means, however, that his squad will not be able to take the road themselves. They'll have to go over hills and directly through brush. Tragically, it is this same German patrol that arrives at Bayard's and kills the valiant French patriot. Now the GIs must kill these same Germans after all, as if for the second time, but for Bayard—the only man who knows the location of the bridge—it is too late. It is a world too late. He has been undone by the force of irony. Moments later, an "old man" is discovered wounded inside the cottage. He confirms new details of the above, to whit: Bayard was alarmed because Lieutenant Douglas was so late (late because he hadn't taken the road). Bayard wouldn't have encountered the Germans at all if he hadn't gone out to look for his old friend Douglas. Worse yet, Ba-

yard is the last survivor, other than Douglas, of the infamous incident at Mt. Chatel. These are the fine, fine consequences of a single "command." They seem to expand and multiply like the hairline cracks in a porcelain glaze.

22. From this lesson we conclude the following disturbing truths:

a) when authority is most brutal and indifferent, it is then that it loves and cares for us most;

b) when one fails to choose death, death will come anyway, later, multiplied;

c) ∴ always choose death.

23. Another way of understanding #22: in order to win the war, the Americans had to become the moral equivalent (as Field Marshall Reagan would say) of the Nazis.

24. "You know, Sergeant, I had to sit down and write thirty-one letters home to the wives and mothers of those men. I don't want to write any more letters. I can't."

"Lieutenant, if we blow this bridge, we might lose some men, but if we don't the Germans will use that bridge. They might cut right through the whole division. If they do, how many officers will have to write how many letters?"

25. In viewing *Combat,* does one have to choose between the orgasmic, irrational bliss of gunfire and the complexity of the moral lesson? It would seem so. And it would seem that my father always preferred the merely darkly blissful, since I recall no post-episode explications of moral and dramatic ironies delivered to a silent son thirsting for enlightenment.

26. My father was a Romantic intent on sublime intimations; he was not a New Critic interested in formal device. These intimations came to my father half-asleep in his dirty green recliner, as strangely as if creatures from outer space had come through his T.V. to deliver the news. A true oracle, the truth of the world visited him, virtually sat on his face, while he dreamed. This explains his patriarch's wrath when his children changed the channel in mid-program.

27. "What are you doing? I'm watching that program."

"But, Dad, you were asleep."

"Turn it back."

28. My father spent so much of his life in his green recliner that it broke down subtly under his weight (my father was 6′ 4″, 220 pounds), never completely breaking but rather bending, collapsing earthward under his shape until, after twenty years of use, the chair itself resembled my father, as if it were an exoskeleton he'd left behind.

29. "It's been a long time since Mt. Chatel, my friend."

30. It turned out that the old man knew the location of the bridge. It was quite near by. Sarge volunteered to creep to the bridge and blow it up while the rest of the squad occupied the stupid Keystone Cop Germans in their rattling bug husks who have surrounded Bayard's and abandoned their crucial duties at the pontoon bridge.

31. Understanding this neglect, my father feels an incredible anxiety. "Idiots and dumb cuffs. I'm surrounded by dumb cuffs." He is having a panic attack. With his feet on one bank and his fingers barely gripping the other, he is completely vulnerable. He wants to curl up in the fetal position, but that is not a posture pontoon bridges are allowed. In later years, during his son's time, there will be drugs for this disorder. Ativan, valium. Drugs his son will take with gratitude. But for his own moment, there is only this enormous DREAD.

32. Sarge is up to his shoulders in the surprisingly warm river. (*Bien sûr,* this river heads toward the tepid Baja and certainly didn't begin in the Alps.) He pulls himself along the bridge from rib to rib pausing only to tuck the tender *plastique* between every other rib. It tickles my father a little, but mostly he feels the explosive's mighty and horrible potential. This feeling is much worse than the actual moment of becoming the meaty geyser that is his destiny. That, after all, takes only an instant. Spread across the sky, one has something of the nobility of a new constellation.

33. Done, Sarge crawls up on the bank and engages the little detonator. He depresses the plunger gently. The explosives go off serially, one, two, three, four, like four strong spasms from a really good come. There is a different and dizzying camera angle for each new explosion.

34. My father would really have enjoyed these explosions/his death. But that contradictory pleasure would be like watching a snuff film in which you are the one to be snuffed. Would that turn you on, dead man?

35. As Sarge walks back to meet his platoon, he feels no joy. He'd done his job, saved lives by the bucketful, frustrated *les boches,* and yet he felt gloomy. He couldn't understand, of course, but he had become my father. My father's essence could not be destroyed; it had to reside somewhere. It must have flowed back up the wires to the detonator at the moment of his death. Like me, Sergeant Saunders is now possessed by my father. The undead. They walk among us.

36. When the Sarge arrived back, it was clear to all that he'd changed. He was not the same Sarge they'd known. But he couldn't explain anything, or he explained much more than his men, the gentle giant Littlejohn in particular, desired. Sarge said, "I know I am bad because I killed my father. However, I must be a little bit good because I feel guilty and am paying for

it. If I didn't feel bad about myself, then I would be a completely wicked person. So leave me to my despair, I have earned it, and it is my only virtue."

37. "But Sarge, that wasn't your father," appeals our reasonable Everyman, the likable Kirby. "You just blew up a bridge is all." For Pete's sake. For cryin' out loud. For the love of Mike. You don't use your head, Sarge. Kirby looks around to the others, appealing to them for confirmation of this solid common sense. A tear trickles from the corner of the sentimental Littlejohn's eye. Caje puts a consoling hand on Sarge's disconsolate shoulder. *"Vieux ami, nous voudrions t'aider,"* Caje says.

38. The riddle of the Sarge is undone when, to the astonishment of all (especially my father who pops up from his suburban recliner in awe), Sarge removes his helmet. Under his dirty, dented GI helmet with the chin straps hanging down most sloppily is not familiar blond hair but a small patch of garden, mostly grasses and bright wildflowers. This grows out of the top of his head. The bright colors of the wildflowers make it appear that his brow is aflame.

39. "How did I do it? I took my bayonet and prepared the top soil and then I sowed the seed. No, it didn't hurt too much. I didn't go very deep. Why? Don't you like it? Don't you think it's a nice idea to have a little garden on top of your head?"

1998

RICARDO CORTEZ CRUZ
b. 1964

Born in Decatur, Illinois, Ricardo Cortez Cruz began his career as a journalist for the *Decatur Herald & Review*. From 1982 until 1988, he served as a news writer, sports writer, and sports columnist for the paper. In 1991, Cruz earned a master's degree in writing from Illinois State University.

Mixing lyricism, a self-described "(s)language," and vivid images with an avant-garde black aesthetic, Cruz gained prominence when his debut novel, *Straight Outta Compton,* won the 1992 Nilon Award for Excellence in Minority Fiction, judged by Clarence Major. Many critics praised the novel for its powerful use of urban language, black humor, and unpredictability. It was named one of the best novels of the year by *Nation* reviewer Art Winslow. "Cruz," Larry McCaffery writes, "is a kind of literary Michael Jordan whose verbal 'moves' combine power, speed, and grace, and whose narrative skills include being able to start a scene one way and then unexpectedly change directions."

"My writing can be characterized by its use of fusion," Cruz said in a 1993 interview, "that is, the synthesizing of a lot of brutal elements, mordant humor, and rapid fire. . . . The ghettos I write about are more in the heart than actual places and are symbolic of a depressed state of mind."

"Welcome to the Ghetto," originally published in *The Iowa Review* in 1997, is from his forthcoming work, *Premature Autopsies.*

From Premature Autopsies

Welcome to the Ghetto

Contains a sample of "Put Your Foot Down" by Lillo Thomas

On Monday morning, a talking head is the first to report it: Something is rotten in the ghetto, it announces as an actuality, its voice on a nigga's hot portable black-and-white TV flippant and scratchy from the burden of trying to carry too much base/bass. We are running around in the street and through the grapevines when we hear the news. Another male has expired. From around-the-way. So, after first slinging some gin and juice, we go to check it out. After all, ever since we can remember, we have been addicted to death. Before attaching himself to me, one of my homeys sniffs a paint-box at the scene of the crime. Then the four of us raise our good baggies in unison in order to protect ourselves as we move the crowd, duck underneath the old marquee, and proceed to sneak inside the theater. I am the most discreet/discrete of the group. "What's wrong with this picture?" one of my partners snickers. We enter unformatted, our faces appearing extremely long while we creep-creep around the drawn curtain. While the TV cameras shoot shock video with the idea of sweetening the violence on air, one of my partners grabs my collar and hangs on. Murder is such a bloody deed. "Jesus!" he says, a golden leaf getting processed/fossilized in his wave by a Harry animator and his Blue Magic and Afro Sheen rubbing off onto my skin as his fingers go "bye-bye." I am unable to take anymore. So we turn around, careful not to bump an action cam or the overweight teamster by its side, and strut back out pushing the heavy door, kicking it, twisting the knob, shaking our big heads, talking jive and things that be, all of us smoking and acting real cool, imagining ourselves as the experimental players from Harlem, live on camera.

However, blood is still rubbing up against me, so I start to get edgy. We are the real players, but sometimes internal conflicts take over. For example, the nigga who is messed up and clinging on to me calls himself Herod The Great. (He keeps pulling himself up by the bootstraps and changing his wave.) Herod, who was born an outside kid, makes me out to be Jesus, the anointed one. But, lately, I've been feeling moody like Hamlet. That's why I call my best friend "Horatio." He's a bourgeoisie flat-top from Exeter Prep School who simply admires me for the way I mix: I do the lamp, Bus Stop, or the Madison to hustle in the street. I stay in trouble cause I can jam.

"You could be the best goddamn mixer in the city," Horatio keeps repeating in my ear; the repetition of these words is a distorted drumvoice. "You're one of the good guys. Why can't you get your mind out of the ghetto?"

"The black man is under assault," Sportin' News asserts, unaware that Horatio is speaking, his own hair napping up.

We name the biggest mouth in our group Sportin' News. He's kind of like the fourth wall in naturalistic theatre; remove him from the group and you can know what we're doing without us showing any cognizance. Sportin'

News is our Achilles' heel, but in our community everybody makes the world by whispers and comes to you in sections and Troy is simply another two-faced haint/spook/punk with a street sweeper or speaker or hot gun. "Don't you niggas roll without me!" Herod orders, again pulling himself up by the bootstraps after upsetting his Bugle Boys. Herod has been feeling sick for awhile now but won't admit it. Though Herod is paranoid, he likes hangin' with the homeboys.

Premature Autopsies

In the hood, my brothers survive on the hype that Manhattan is shaped like a giant Dutch massa's cigar. On summer nights, when black people are out in the alleys of Harlem—just vibin', trying to stay cool, clutching their Saturday night specials, Manhattan burns very brightly. Full of jealousy, bitters, and panther piss, street niggas put that bomb in their mouths and inhale and exhale, inhale and exhale, smoking it as if they are driving by The White House in hopes of making the air too thick. Sucking and puffing on the northern tip to get high in seeming endless fashion, they viciously fire up, cop n' blow; their "sole/soul" purpose is to make the rest of the joint—Manhattan is "chronic," they say—turn invisible like them.

Towards the Harlem River where people are wasted royally and the stench is bad, me and my partners dip in and out of the speakeasies and hit the jump joints, stopping outside only to ask where The Cotton Club is.

"Jesus, how is it the clouds still hang on you?" Herod asks, sniffing a bottle of coke and closely eyeing the white skin on the flaky parts of his body.

"This nigga is really working your nerve," my left brain says.

"God, my heart must sit still tonight," I say to myself, glancing at Herod caining/Caining over my shoulders. He snorts in clusters.

"Where we at?" Sportin' News asks, staring around blankly as if to suggest that he is lost. His vision ain't too good. Kind of superficial, Sportin' News deals a lot in plastic. But this time, he's sincere: He puts his Diner's Club back in his pocket; the card is hot.

"This used to be Lenox Avenue and 143rd Street," I tell them. I'm not really positive. (Several small boys are running around, picking hotwater cornbread off the ground and cotton balls out of one another's nappy hair. They come to us in sections, their brown dusty fros attaching themselves to Herod and Horatio and Sportin' News like basketballs made of smelly velcro.)

"So *this* is The Cotton Club?" Sportin' News responds. "Man, get real!" He temporarily breaks loose, cutting himself away from the crumbsnatchers, his stick figure warped in all of the darkness like Zeus' Caliban in *The Clash of the Titans.*

I look over and give Sportin' News the evil eye, cursing him, my black clothes flapping harshly like a bat in the nightwind. "Sportin' News, you are that dark thang that I acknowledge mine," I tell him.

Sportin' News doesn't take it personal because he always thinks that he knows how to navigate through the sound and the fury. "Look," he says, whipping out a Discover card, "don't be mad."

"Is Lena Horney or Count Basie or Frederick of Hollywood giggin' there?" Herod asks, as we wander alongside of a brick wall with large wet holes in it, chunks of sedimentary rock tore out of it, as if the women of Brewster Place had tried to tear down the wall before a cold death rain washed them away. There is blood or rouge and probably dark eyeliner running down the side of the wall where "Harpo" is written in block letters, then in cursive just off to the right where we see "Black is."

A threesome of ladies of the night stroll by in front of us, laughing and playing with one another (tossing their weaved hair and teasing us and each other) while Herod sings "Your love is ooh." Showing off their negritude, all three stop when they see the writing on the wall. One of them, wearing a pair of hot pants and a big, cheap, metal cross hangin' on a string around her neck, moves closer to the wall and points to our big heads and the places where the colors are badly smeared. "Lord, keep them safe since you can't keep them sane," she says.

Her girlfriend dashes over and snatches her. "You go, girl!" she shouts.

"We don't want nothing to do with that," the third one adds before they get lost in the woodwork.

I reach down and check out a black hole in the wall. In the dark, it's hard to see anything more, so I rub the wall with my fingers and bend over to smell it.

"Jesus, when you gonna learn to simply stop sniffing around?" Herod asks. Herod likes the smell of paint. Scratching himself with the nails of a devil, he gestures/jesters like he still thinks that all of this madness is funny.

Since he's talking so much out of the side of his neck, I slap him there with my opposite hand. "From here on, come wit me to Hell," I said, "and mind your P's and Q's when we get there." I can smell blood on my hands, and I start experiencing a yearning. But, Horatio is leaning on me, so I tell everybody to keep on truckin'.

"So is The Cotton Club down or what?" Herod asks. He's trying to figure out where the nasty parties are at.

"Yep." I'm lying like it's nothing.

Satisfied, Herod and Sportin' News jump ahead, trippin' cause they obviously startled each other with their own greed and saliva.

"Count Basie can blow," I hear Herod say. They walk away buggin'.

"Go on with your bad selves," I shout. "In the ghetto, we are nothing but vampires, sleepwalkers created by European-folk lore! In fact, my black mama was Harriet Tubman, you fraidy cats! She was the one responsible for putting me in a coffin in the first place!"

Herod and Sportin' News march away like leftovers from the 369th Regiment, leaving the garbage to the crumbsnatchers and rug rats that are combing the kinky streets and searching in garbage; they pay the two brothers no attention.

I, too, am about to exit this scene, but I hear the sound of a snow tire and D.J. Jazzy Jeff (you can call him Fresh Prince of Bel-Air if you want) singing "Summertime, Summertime."

"Somebody say somethin' about a coffin?" a voice asks, with little kids in the street. It turns out to be a stereo-type driving a Sport Neon with at least eight speakers. Before the stereotype can say anything else, it has to fast forward and turn up the volume. Somewhat nervously checking its rearview, it's clutching a forty-ounce bottle of Old English and talking over Michael

Jackson singing "Man in the Mirror" as if it is toasting. The color of ink, it tries to smile at me like it is something other than a shit straight outta the pen. "I'm lookin' for one," it says. "I got two turntables, a Pioneer receiver, a large PA mike, and a mixer with an echo, but I need somethin' to put all of this shit in."

"Mister, I ain't got jack."

"Skip you, then," it says and pulls off, cruising a bit as it creeps south, like we never talked, the car yelling as if it had no respect.

Just by glancing around, I remind myself that I'm from the old school. How do the ladies put it, "old-fashioned." I open up my dashiki and back-slap this wino smoking faggots and chewing Brown's Chicken. "You can sell out if you want to, homey, but I'm gonna stay short and funky." (I have no idea of what all this means; I'm simply talkin' rhetoric.) The drunk man shows me numerous alienated wallet-size people that he says are no longer here with us. But, Horatio is leaning on me, so I go on.

"Wait!" someone yells. It's the drunk, no longer appearing quite as cheery now. He races up to me and moons me as if Horatio isn't even there. "Kiss my black ass," he says. I move closer to him, peek down, and chuckle. "I'll be darn. Your ass is black."

He sticks up the finger, his face waxed and nasty. The only thing I can do is look at him and shake my big head, the man slinging chicken creatures up against the brick wall, dark wings and thangs flying everywhere as he sucks the bones like they were a lover's. I couldn't blame him for going off though. In my neighborhood, you got to half-doss in a blue funk if you want to be happy. "You need to get off the street," I tell him. "If I had a broom, I'd sweep your butt off myself."

The man slowly bends over and grabs a twig or some shit off the ground, hands it to me. "Go for what you know, Daddy-O," he says.

I kick over to him a twisted hanger that seems to have dried blood on it like somebody had once done an abortion on the very ground where we stand in conflict. He cuts me an uglier-than-sin glare when I start walking away, my face whacked. "Hang it up," I tell him. "Death don't scare me." But, Horatio is clinging on to me, so I back up.

"You ridin' high," I warn the drunk just before taking off.

He raises up, races up to me again, and jabs something hard in the small of my back. "Go head," I said. "Do me."

"Don't make me none," he says, his voice cracking up.

"Me neither," I said. "I've been stuck-up so many times, mugging has become En Vogue. That is to say, I even had a ladies' singing group hit me once and then ask me not to tell anybody. When I told them that I was born to sing, they said they could understand that and took off, splitting up and scurrying in a thousand different directions, all of the women swearing and cussing cause they had to run on high heels and clogs to get to the Grammy show on time."

"Nice sexy story with a feminine/feminist [sic] ending, but what makes you think I'd believe some hype like that?" the drunk asks. I see him looking confused, bombed; he tells me that the bridge of his nose is destroyed on the inside. "Too bad," I tell him. It was to be the only bridge he had that would allow him to escape the war-zone we all have to live in. Then I think of Herod, how his nose had been broken so terribly bad in that stupid takeover of a Black Man's Wheels that it remains deep/blue to this day and that, whenever he does cocaine, even his worst nightmares avoid asking him to smell or breathe any more.

"Your story stinks," the drunk says, getting up in my face. (Now I notice that there is pasta stuck to his back and clothes, and he is standing squinty-eyed and bowlegged as if in the middle of a spaghetti western.) "Ain't no gang of bulldykers or Queen B's in the USG gonna hit you and leave without doing you in," he adds.

"What you want with me?" I ask. "Harlem is for niggas."

"I know that!" he shouts. "Shut up, or I'll put you away right now."

I feel his fist raise up against my head, but suddenly he quits.

"Don't gank him," I hear a boy say. When I turn to look, there is another kid beside him, and the two teeny-tiny boys are right up in our faces. Both of them are dressed rough; one has got his Brooklyn cap on backwards, and the other has some cheap price tags showing.

The drunk man tries to step off. He starts talking smack [aside]. How you like that? We gettin' ripped off by the new kids on the block. (He cracks up.)

The biggest kid does all of the yackety-yack, his eyes crossed like yin and yang. Give me yo' bus money, yo' food, and all the candy you old dudes got. No sticky stuff. And, be cool cause, if you don't, I'll get you off the bus in a minute. Believe dat.

What's up wit dis? I ask the old man. We getting juked by the little rascals.

The smaller kid snorts, and, like a wild horse, seems a little spooked. His crimey whips out some grass and gives it to him. Both start smoking. I hear Horatio cough "a little."

We was on the way to the Grammys when we saw you old monkeys out here signifying, the big kid says, his tee-shirt of the rapper Tupac Shakur exclaiming Dear Mama This Is How We Do It. The two kids circle us, pulling and tugging on their overalls which are on backwards.

Old dude got a nigger-flicker in his crew sock, I hear somebody whisper.

Obviously a bit fresh as far as knowing how to maintain his game, the smaller kid stops smoking and shines a mini flashlight towards my face like he is Green Lantern or Black Lightning.

Man, you come straight outta a comic book, the drunk yells. Like he can talk. Look, you little punks, he adds. (But this is now a translation of his language.) I ain't about to let a couple of kids dressed like caution signs scare me into giving up my valuables or goodies, he says. You militant midgets look like you accidentally stepped out in front of a graffiti writer tagging the subway, Jellybean Benitez or the Unabomber. Get the hell out of here before I sew up those holes you got in those doo-doo brown pants!

In the backdrop, a hoochie mama screams Brenda's got a baby to a copper and/or a very pink white boy wearing a beat-up blue hat, while the ghetto birds chop through the hot air, then call us out.

Lay down your weapons and line up against the wall, they demand, watching us carefully. As I said before, we are the real experimental players.

Now we all are swirling around and around in what looks like a sunny day. I see the others trying to locate me. Nigga, where are you, they scream.

Damn nigga, you sho' are bright. I see black people trying to pass for white casually move down the street and away from the action. I see huge and petite black women cradling white babies charge out of the old, boarded-up grocery stores and stroll in the direction of Manhattan like they are somebody's nannies, their arms either too fat or too frail. I see a lot of beady heads shaking like coffee beans or cacao seeds or Brazilian nuts (nigga toes we call them) near the stoop of Bethel A.M.E. Church, while Christian folk dressed in dark suits throw the bodies of other black men into a large crate, filing down the sharp wood pieces protruding inside the box before closing it, then strapping its bursting, laughing sides with battleship-gray duct tape. I see Herod moving the crowd, Sportin' News carrying a Sprint card.

Now I am thinking gee whiz it's a street fight I hate street fights why of all people do I happen to be the one caught up in the cliche of a street fight, why, why, why.

Look here, mack daddy, the bigger boy tells the drunk, pushing dope in his face and dissing the rest of the crowd, especially myself and Horatio. We gettin' fuss'strated wit you adults trying to tell us what to do. You got no respect. Shut yo' fat mouth, or we'll squirt some heroin in yo' nose and make the bridge blow. Believe dat!

Suddenly out of nowhere, a woman holding a non-stick skillet busts in between us and snatches the smaller boy out of the circle. What you doing out in the street fighting again? she asks. You know better than that. Lord, I cain't even go to work without one of my babies trying to kill himself.

It's over, the drunk starts screaming.

What you say?! What you say?! The bigger kid starts screaming. We all can barely hear over the noise and the technological wind smothering each other's Nommo/words like we are muted.

Horatio is pushing, and before I know it somebody rushes up and drops us to the earth like body bags. And then I hear all kinds of crazy noises. A rubber breaks. The stereo-type who confronted me earlier drives back by, parks a few yards away, pulls out his player, and moves away from the vehicle. Then he makes the noise of silence. I imagine him gliding as if he is moonwalking. I even hear the noise of a stray chopper dicing stuff over an empty coke machine.

Sportin' News is close to me now, searching for his I.D.

Like we are in the battle royal or something, hue-man bodies are throwing themselves on top of us and change is running down the street like pancakes in a nursery rhyme. And before I know it, my lips are cut, and my mouth is swallowing large amounts of blood.

I hear the kid trippin'. If you've never been to the ghetto, then stay the fuck out of the ghetto, cause you wouldn't understand the ghetto! Believe dat!

I hear the coppers standing by, watching us. Niggers are what their mommas made them.

I hear the drunk moaning and groaning.

Then I hear Horatio, snapping [the softest thing cannot be snapped, I remember reading from Bruce Lee's *The Tao of Jeet Kune Do*], screaming at the top of his lungs like a cancer is eating him up terribly inside. Look, G, he screams, seemingly choosing his words carefully, you have been slain in the spirit I mean you have been stuck stabbed dead'n eighty-sixed slugged slobbered upon soaked soiled sodden solaced soularized [sic] stained indeed you have been staked!

Jesus! Herod says, hanging on to a hooker or something that keeps trying to put the lips of a rather large coke bottle on his mouth; as soon as Herod takes his eyes off her, she winks, acknowledging her secret goal of trying to poison him. Jesus! Herod says. You are slain! No drug in the world or false idol can do you any good now!

Here's yet some liquor left, his prostitute says, and I feel the alcohol being poured all over me. This is when I know.

O', I am dead, Herod Horatio Hor . . .

I glance at the crowd moving around me only to end up fixated upon a long tired brown worm dragging its ugliness in sections over my palm. Anal, the worm momentarily pauses to knot himself. Taking his sweet time, he stares at me before resuming his crawling as if to signify that his grotesqueness is in my face and that it ain't going nowhere and that whacking it would do me no good because it would simply grow back. When the worm hits my left hand, a ring that had always lived large on my finger slips off, and out of nowhere the stereo-type races over, opens its door while on the move, bends way down, and snatches it off the ground, the car still laughing while running. There is no policing now; no cameras or news reporters. Where are the clowns, I ask myself, also wondering why, despite the fact that he's never had a job, Sportin' News is flashing a HMO Principal Health Care Provider's card and a Blue Cross and Blue Shield. While I am losing a lot of blood from my wounds, my eyelids stick together, then rapidly and involuntarily blink as if responding to stimuli, when I think about myself rising up from the dead as an ice/white person, when I envision myself coming back to prey upon hue-man beings. Before I can stop or finish with The Dream, I hear Sportin' News already spreadin' the word, shouting at the drugged-out people blowing old Negro spirituals and looking wack while they rest on their stoops in some of the most depressed areas of the ghetto. When Sportin' News tells them that I have quit, they all step back and seemingly fish for a church and a cross.

Then I hear Herod. "Jesus!" he screams, reaching down to see if I am still alive. "What you pour my alcohol on the nigga for?!" he asks the hooker. Herod reaches over further like he's going to lick the loose juice off of my body. But, this time, I am batty. This time, instead of slapping him, I bite this dirty nigga bastard crimey in front of the hot-blooded female right where his veins are already doing the Jim Jones, I mean, turning blue black from the scars and minstrel role and weak shit. I hear Herod's heart furiously pumping blood as if his body has been spiked with Kool-Aid.

Now we both are the wretched of the earth, I tell Herod. Herod is vomiting. Black skins, white masks, I add. Herod is collapsing and crying, breaking down right in front of my face. It's just too bad that I can't get my mind out of the ghetto, I say. Now Herod is down. After all, the violence, I shout out (Herod is crawling away like he is begging to go home quickly), this violence can amaze or play past you but also take you by surprise before you know it if you don't watch it.

1997

BOBBIE ANN MASON
b. 1940

Born in Mayfield, Kentucky, Bobbie Ann Mason was educated at the University of Kentucky, the State University of New York at Binghamton, and the University of Connecticut. She began her literary career as a writer for the local newspaper, and then for magazines such as *Movie Stars, Movie Life,* and *T.V. Star Parade.* Her decision to attend graduate school brought her to the Northeast, a move she described in a 1989 interview as "a tremendous culture shock." She began writing stories after finishing graduate school in 1972. Her fiction includes two collections, *Shiloh and Other Stories* (1982) and *Love Life: Stories* (1989), and two novels, *In Country* (1985) and *Spence + Lila* (1989).

Mason's work focuses on contemporary life in her native Kentucky, even though she now lives elsewhere. "I think that distance is necessary, and it's made my fiction what it is, whatever it is," she said in the 1989 interview. "I'm sure it would have been completely different if I'd been totally inside it. It's the sharper awareness of everyday things, the small changes that people are going through and changes in the landscape that are important."

"Shiloh" is the title story from her first collection, recipient of the Ernest Hemingway Foundation Award. "The style of the narrative, the cadence of it, is very important to me," Mason said. "It imitates that country speech that I hear in my ear. . . . It's plain speech, matter-of-fact, not romantic language. I'm always aware of insisting on those stylistic characteristics because I think it creates the voice and the attitude that I have about the characters and the world. It's a way of cutting through things that are superfluous." Regarding her characters' concentration on pop culture, she added, "It's very important to them what's on TV and what songs are on and what's on sale at the local store and what movies are playing. I think those kinds of things at one level or other are important to just about everybody."

Shiloh

Leroy Moffitt's wife, Norma Jean, is working on her pectorals. She lifts three-pound dumbbells to warm up, then progresses to a twenty-pound barbell. Standing with her legs apart, she reminds Leroy of Wonder Woman.

"I'd give anything if I could just get these muscles to where they're real hard," says Norma Jean. "Feel this arm. It's not as hard as the other one."

"That's 'cause you're right-handed," says Leroy, dodging as she swings the barbell in an arc.

"Do you think so?"

"Sure."

Leroy is a truckdriver. He injured his leg in a highway accident four months ago, and his physical therapy, which involves weights and a pulley, prompted Norma Jean to try building herself up. Now she is attending a body-building class. Leroy has been collecting temporary disability since his tractor-trailer jackknifed in Missouri, badly twisting his left leg in its socket. He has a steel pin in his hip. He will probably not be able to drive his rig again. It sits in the backyard, like a gigantic bird that has flown home to roost. Leroy has been home in Kentucky for three months, and his leg is almost healed, but the accident frightened him and he does not want to drive any more long hauls. He is not sure what to do next. In the meantime, he makes things from craft kits. He started by building a miniature log cabin from notched Popsicle sticks. He varnished it and placed it on the TV set, where it remains. It reminds him of a rustic Nativity scene. Then he tried string art (sailing ships on black velvet), a macramé owl kit, a snap-together B-17 Flying Fortress, and a lamp made out of a model truck, with a light fixture screwed on the top of the cab. At first the kits were diversions, something to kill time, but now he is thinking about building a full-scale log house from a kit. It would be considerably cheaper than building a regular house, and besides, Leroy has grown to appreciate how things are put together. He has begun to realize that in all the years he was on the road he never took time to examine anything. He was always flying past scenery.

"They won't let you build a log cabin in any of the new subdivisions," Norma Jean tells him.

"They will if I tell them it's for you," he says, teasing her. Ever since they were married, he has promised Norma Jean he would build her a new home one day. They have always rented, and the house they live in is small and nondescript. It does not even feel like a home, Leroy realizes now.

Norma Jean works at the Rexall drugstore, and she has acquired an amazing amount of information about cosmetics. When she explains to Leroy the three stages of complexion care, involving creams, toners, and moisturizers, he thinks happily of other petroleum products—axle grease, diesel fuel. This is a connection between him and Norma Jean. Since he has been home, he has felt unusually tender about his wife and guilty over his long absences. But he can't tell what she feels about him. Norma Jean has never complained about his traveling; she has never made hurt remarks, like calling his truck a "widow-maker." He is reasonably certain she has been faithful to him, but he wishes she would celebrate his permanent homecoming more happily. Norma Jean is often startled to find Leroy at home, and he thinks she seems a little disappointed about it. Perhaps he reminds her too much of the early days of their marriage, before he went on the road. They had a child who died as an infant, years ago. They never speak about their memories of Randy, which have almost faded, but now that Leroy is home all the time, they sometimes feel awkward around each other, and Leroy wonders if one of them should mention the child. He has the feeling that they are waking up out of a dream together—that they must create a new marriage, start afresh. They are lucky they are still married. Leroy has read that for most people losing a child destroys the marriage—or else he heard this on *Donahue.* He can't always remember where he learns things anymore.

At Christmas, Leroy bought an electric organ for Norma Jean. She used to play the piano when she was in high school. "It don't leave you," she told him once. "It's like riding a bicycle."

The new instrument had so many keys and buttons that she was bewildered by it at first. She touched the keys tentatively, pushed some buttons, then pecked out "Chopsticks." It came out in an amplified fox-trot rhythm, with marimba sounds.

"It's an orchestra!" she cried.

The organ had a pecan-look finish and eighteen preset chords, with optional flute, violin, trumpet, clarinet, and banjo accompaniments. Norma

Jean mastered the organ almost immediately. At first she played Christmas songs. Then she bought *The Sixties Songbook* and learned every tune in it, adding variations to each with the rows of brightly colored buttons.

"I didn't like these old songs back then," she said. "But I have this crazy feeling I missed something."

"You didn't miss a thing," said Leroy.

Leroy likes to lie on the couch and smoke a joint and listen to Norma Jean play "Can't Take My Eyes Off You" and "I'll Be Back." He is back again. After fifteen years on the road, he is finally settling down with the woman he loves. She is still pretty. Her skin is flawless. Her frosted curls resemble pencil trimmings.

Now that Leroy has come home to stay, he notices how much the town has changed. Subdivisions are spreading across western Kentucky like an oil slick. The sign at the edge of town says "Pop: 11,500"—only seven hundred more than it said twenty years before. Leroy can't figure out who is living in all the new houses. The farmers who used to gather around the courthouse square on Saturday afternoons to play checkers and spit tobacco juice have gone. It has been years since Leroy has thought about the farmers, and they have disappeared without his noticing.

Leroy meets a kid named Stevie Hamilton in the parking lot at the new shopping center. While they pretend to be strangers meeting over a stalled car, Stevie tosses an ounce of marijuana under the front seat of Leroy's car. Stevie is wearing orange jogging shoes and a T-shirt that says CHATTAHOOCHE SUPER-RAT. His father is a prominent doctor who lives in one of the expensive subdivisions in a new white-columned brick house that looks like a funeral parlor. In the phone book under his name there is a separate number, with the listing "Teenagers."

"Where do you get this stuff?" asks Leroy. "From your pappy?"

"That's for me to know and you to find out," Stevie says. He is slit-eyed and skinny.

"What else you got?"

"What you interested in?"

"Nothing special. Just wondered."

Leroy used to take speed on the road. Now he has to go slowly. He needs to be mellow. He leans back against the car and says, "I'm aiming to build me a log house, soon as I get time. My wife, though, I don't think she likes the idea."

"Well, let me know when you want me again," Stevie says. He has a cigarette in his cupped palm, as though sheltering it from the wind. He takes a long drag, then stomps it on the asphalt and slouches away.

Stevie's father was two years ahead of Leroy in high school. Leroy is thirty-four. He married Norma Jean when they were both eighteen, and their child Randy was born a few months later, but he died at the age of four months and three days. He would be about Stevie's age now. Norma Jean and Leroy were at the drive-in, watching a double feature (*Dr. Strangelove* and *Lover Come Back*), and the baby was sleeping in the back seat. When the first movie ended, the baby was dead. It was the sudden infant death syndrome. Leroy remembers handing Randy to a nurse at the emergency room, as though he were offering her a large doll as a present. A dead baby feels like a sack of flour. "It just happens sometimes," said the doctor, in what Leroy always recalls as a nonchalant tone. Leroy can hardly remember the child anymore, but he still sees vividly a scene from *Dr. Strangelove* in which the President of the United States was talking in a folksy voice on the hot line to the Soviet premier about the bomber accidentally headed toward Russia. He was in the War Room, and the world map was lit up. Leroy remembers Norma Jean standing catatonically beside him in the hospital and himself thinking: Who is this strange girl? He had forgotten who she was. Now scientists are saying that crib death is caused by a virus. Nobody knows anything, Leroy thinks. The answers are always changing.

When Leroy gets home from the shopping center, Norma Jean's mother, Mabel Beasley, is there. Until this year, Leroy has not realized how much time she spends with Norma Jean. When she visits, she inspects the closets and then the plants, informing Norma Jean when a plant is droopy or yellow. Mabel calls the plants "flowers," although there are never any blooms. She always notices if Norma Jean's laundry is piling up. Mabel is a short, overweight woman whose tight, brown-dyed curls look more like a wig than the actual wig she sometimes wears. Today she has brought Norma Jean an off-white dust ruffle she made for the bed; Mabel works in a custom-upholstery shop.

"This is the tenth one I made this year," Mabel says. "I got started and couldn't stop."

"It's real pretty," says Norma Jean.

"Now we can hide things under the bed," says Leroy, who gets along with his mother-in-law primarily by joking with her. Mabel has never really forgiven him for disgracing her by getting Norma Jean pregnant. When the baby died, she said that fate was mocking her.

"What's that thing?" Mabel says to Leroy in a loud voice, pointing to a tangle of yarn on a piece of canvas.

Leroy holds it up for Mabel to see. "It's my needlepoint," he explains. "This is a *Star Trek* pillow cover."

"That's what a woman would do," says Mabel. "Great day in the morning!"

"All the big football players on TV do it," he says.

"Why, Leroy, you're always trying to fool me. I don't believe you for one minute. You don't know what to do with yourself—that's the whole trouble. Sewing!"

"I'm aiming to build us a log house," says Leroy. "Soon as my plans come."

"Like *heck* you are," says Norma Jean. She takes Leroy's needlepoint and shoves it into a drawer. "You have to find a job first. Nobody can afford to build now anyway."

Mabel straightens her girdle and says, "I still think before you get tied down y'all ought to take a little run to Shiloh."

"One of these days, Mama," Norma Jean says impatiently.

Mabel is talking about Shiloh, Tennessee. For the past few years, she has been urging Leroy and Norma Jean to visit the Civil War battleground there. Mabel went there on her honeymoon—the only real trip she ever took. Her husband died of a perforated ulcer when Norma Jean was ten, but Mabel, who was accepted into the United Daughters of the Confederacy in 1975, is still preoccupied with going back to Shiloh.

"I've been to kingdom come and back in that truck out yonder," Leroy says to Mabel, "but we never yet set foot in that battleground. Ain't that something? How did I miss it?"

"It's not even that far," Mabel says.

After Mabel leaves, Norma Jean reads to Leroy from a list she has made. "Things you could do," she announces. "You could get a job as a guard at Union Carbide, where they'd let you set on a stool. You could get on at the lumberyard. You could do a little carpenter work, if you want to build so bad. You could—"

"I can't do something where I'd have to stand up all day."

"You ought to try standing up all day behind a cosmetics counter. It's amazing that I have strong feet, coming from two parents that never had strong feet at all." At the moment Norma Jean is holding on to the kitchen counter, raising her knees one at a time as she talks. She is wearing two-pound ankle weights.

"Don't worry," says Leroy. "I'll do something."

"You could truck calves to slaughter for somebody. You wouldn't have to drive any big old truck for that."

"I'm going to build you this house," says Leroy. "I want to make you a real home."

"I don't want to live in any log cabin."

"It's not a cabin. It's a house."

"I don't care. It looks like a cabin."

"You and me together could lift those logs. It's just like lifting weights."

Norma Jean doesn't answer. Under her breath, she is counting. Now she is marching through the kitchen. She is doing goose steps.

Before his accident, when Leroy came home he used to stay in the house with Norma Jean, watching TV in bed and playing cards. She would cook fried chicken, picnic ham, chocolate pie—all his favorites. Now he is home alone much of the time. In the mornings, Norma Jean disappears, leaving a cooling place in the bed. She eats a cereal called Body Buddies, and she leaves the bowl on the table, with the soggy tan balls floating in a milk puddle. He sees things about Norma Jean that he never realized before. When she chops onions, she stares off into a corner, as if she can't bear to look. She puts on her house slippers almost precisely at nine o'clock every evening and nudges her jogging shoes under the couch. She saves bread heels for the birds. Leroy watches the birds at the feeder. He notices the peculiar way goldfinches fly past the window. They close their wings, then fall, then spread their wings to catch and lift themselves. He wonders if they close their eyes when they fall. Norma Jean closes her eyes when they are in bed. She wants the lights turned out. Even then, he is sure she closes her eyes.

He goes for long drives around town. He tends to drive a car rather carelessly. Power steering and an automatic shift make a car feel so small and inconsequential that his body is hardly involved in the driving process. His injured leg stretches out comfortably. Once or twice he has almost hit something, but even the prospect of an accident seems minor in a car. He cruises the new subdivisions, feeling like a criminal rehearsing for a robbery. Norma Jean is probably right about a log house being inappropriate here in the new subdivisions. All the houses look grand and complicated. They depress him.

One day when Leroy comes home from a drive he finds Norma Jean in tears. She is in the kitchen making a potato and mushroom-soup casserole, with grated-cheese topping. She is crying because her mother caught her smoking.

"I didn't hear her coming. I was standing here puffing away pretty as you please," Norma Jean says, wiping her eyes.

"I knew it would happen sooner or later," says Leroy, putting his arm around her.

"She don't know the meaning of the word 'knock,' " says Norma Jean. "It's a wonder she hadn't caught me years ago."

"Think of it this way," Leroy says. "What if she caught me with a joint?"

"You better not let her!" Norma Jean shrieks. "I'm warning you, Leroy Moffitt!"

"I'm just kidding. Here, play me a tune. That'll help you relax."

Norma Jean puts the casserole in the oven and sets the timer. Then she plays a ragtime tune, with horns and banjo, as Leroy lights up a joint and lies on the couch, laughing to himself about Mabel's catching him at it. He thinks of Stevie Hamilton—a doctor's son pushing grass. Everything is funny. The whole town seems crazy and small. He is reminded of Virgil Mathis, a boastful policeman Leroy used to shoot pool with. Virgil recently led a drug bust in a back room at a bowling alley, where he seized ten thousand dollars' worth of marijuana. The newspaper had a picture of him holding up the bags of grass and grinning widely. Right now, Leroy can imagine Virgil breaking down the door and arresting him with a lungful of smoke. Virgil would probably have been alerted to the scene because of all the racket Norma Jean is making. Now she sounds like a hard-rock band. Norma Jean is terrific. When she switches to a Latin-rhythm version of "Sunshine Superman," Leroy hums along. Norma Jean's foot goes up and down, up and down.

"Well, what do you think?" Leroy says, when Norma Jean pauses to search through her music.

"What do I think about what?"

His mind had gone blank. Then he says, "I'll sell my rig and build us a house." That wasn't what he wanted to say. He wanted to know what she thought—what she *really* thought—about them.

"Don't start in on that again," says Norma Jean. She begins playing "Who'll Be the Next in Line?"

Leroy used to tell hitchhikers his whole life story—about his travels, his hometown, the baby. He would end with a question: "Well, what do you think?" It was just a rhetorical question. In time, he had the feeling that he'd been telling the same story over and over to the same hitchhikers. He quit talking to hitchhikers when he realized how his voice sounded—whining and self-pitying, like some teenage-tragedy song. Now Leroy has the sudden impulse to tell Norma Jean about himself, as if he had just met her. They have known each other so long they have forgotten a lot about each other. They could become reacquainted. But when the oven timer goes off and she runs to the kitchen, he forgets why he wants to do this.

The next day, Mabel drops by. It is Saturday and Norma Jean is cleaning. Leroy is studying the plans for his log house, which have finally come in the mail. He has them spread out on the table—big sheets of stiff blue paper, with diagrams and numbers printed in white. While Norma Jean runs the vacuum, Mabel drinks coffee. She sets her coffee cup on a blueprint.

"I'm just waiting for time to pass," she says to Leroy, drumming her fingers on the table.

As soon as Norma Jean switches off the vacuum, Mabel says in a loud voice, "Did you hear about the datsun dog that killed the baby?"

Norma Jean says, "The word is 'dachshund.' "

"They put the dog on trial. It chewed the baby's legs off. The mother was in the next room all the time." She raises her voice. "They thought it was neglect."

Norma Jean is holding her ears. Leroy manages to open the refrigerator and get some Diet Pepsi to offer Mabel. Mabel still has some coffee and she waves away the Pepsi.

"Datsuns are like that," Mabel says. "They're jealous dogs. They'll tear a place to pieces if you don't keep an eye on them."

"You better watch out what you're saying, Mabel," says Leroy.

"Well, facts is facts."

Leroy looks out the window at his rig. It is like a huge piece of furniture gathering dust in the backyard. Pretty soon it will be an antique. He hears the vacuum cleaner. Norma Jean seems to be cleaning the living room rug again.

Later, she says to Leroy, "She just said that about the baby because she caught me smoking. She's trying to pay me back."

"What are you talking about?" Leroy says, nervously shuffling blueprints.

"You know good and well," Norma Jean says. She is sitting in a kitchen chair with her feet up and her arms wrapped around her knees. She looks small and helpless. She says, "The very idea, her bringing up a subject like that! Saying it was neglect."

"She didn't mean that," Leroy says.

"She might not have *thought* she meant it. She always says things like that. You don't know how she goes on."

"But she didn't really mean it. She was just talking."

Leroy opens a king-sized bottle of beer and pours it into two glasses, dividing it carefully. He hands a glass to Norma Jean and she takes it from him mechanically. For a long time, they sit by the kitchen window watching the birds at the feeder.

Something is happening. Norma Jean is going to night school. She has graduated from her six-week body-building course and now she is taking an adult-education course in composition at Paducah Community College. She spends her evenings outlining paragraphs.

"First you have a topic sentence," she explains to Leroy. "Then you divide it up. Your secondary topic has to be connected to your primary topic."

To Leroy, this sounds intimidating. "I never was any good in English," he says.

"It makes a lot of sense."

"What are you doing this for, anyhow?"

She shrugs. "It's something to do." She stands up and lifts her dumbbells a few times.

"Driving a rig, nobody cared about my English."

"I'm not criticizing your English."

Norma Jean used to say, "If I lose ten minutes' sleep, I just drag all day." Now she stays up late, writing compositions. She got a B on her first paper—a how-to theme on soup-based casseroles. Recently Norma Jean has been cooking unusual foods—tacos, lasagna, Bombay chicken. She doesn't play the organ anymore, though her second paper was called "Why Music Is Important to Me." She sits at the kitchen table, concentrating on her outlines, while Leroy plays with his log house plans, practicing with a set of Lincoln Logs. The thought of getting a truckload of notched, numbered logs scares him, and he wants to be prepared. As he and Norma Jean work together at the kitchen table, Leroy has the hopeful thought that they are sharing something, but he knows he is a fool to think this. Norma Jean is miles away. He knows he is going to lose her. Like Mabel, he is just waiting for time to pass.

One day, Mabel is there before Norma Jean gets home from work, and Leroy finds himself confiding in her. Mabel, he realizes, must know Norma Jean better than he does.

"I don't know what's got into that girl," Mabel says. "She used to go to bed with the chickens. Now you say she's up all hours. Plus her a-smoking. I like to died."

"I want to make her this beautiful home," Leroy says, indicating the Lincoln Logs. "I think she even wants it. Maybe she was happier with me gone."

"She don't know what to make of you, coming home like this."

"Is that it?"

Mabel takes the roof off his Lincoln Log cabin. "You couldn't get *me* in a log cabin," she says. "I was raised in one. It's no picnic, let me tell you."

"They're different now," says Leroy.

"I tell you what," Mabel says, smiling oddly at Leroy.

"What?"

"Take her down to Shiloh. Y'all need to get out together, stir a little. Her brain's all balled up over them books."

Leroy can see traces of Norma Jean's features in her mother's face. Mabel's worn face has the texture of crinkled cotton, but suddenly she looks pretty. It occurs to Leroy that Mabel has been hinting all along that she wants them to take her with them to Shiloh.

"Let's all go to Shiloh," he says. "You and me and her. Come Sunday."

Mabel throws up her hand in protest. "Oh, no, not me. Young folks want to be by themselves."

When Norma Jean comes in with groceries, Leroy says excitedly, "Your mama here's been dying to go to Shiloh for thirty-five years. It's about time we went, don't you think?"

"I'm not going to butt in on anybody's second honeymoon," Mabel says.

"Who's going on a honeymoon, for Christ's sake?" Norma Jean says loudly.

"I never raised no daughter of mine to talk that-a-way," Mabel says.

"You ain't seen nothing yet," says Norma Jean. She starts putting away boxes and cans, slamming cabinet doors.

"There's a log cabin at Shiloh," Mabel says. "It was there during the battle. There's bullet holes in it."

"When are you going to *shut up* about Shiloh, Mama?" asks Norma Jean.

"I always thought Shiloh was the prettiest place, so full of history," Mabel goes on. "I just hoped y'all could see it once before I die, so you could tell me about it." Later, she whispers to Leroy, "You do what I said. A little change is what she needs."

"Your name means 'the king,' " Norma Jean says to Leroy that evening. He is trying to get her to go to Shiloh, and she is reading a book about another century.

"Well, I reckon I ought to be right proud."

"I guess so."

"Am I still king around here?"

Norma Jean flexes her biceps and feels them for hardness. "I'm not fooling around with anybody, if that's what you mean," she says.

"Would you tell me if you were?"

"I don't know."

"What does *your* name mean?"

"It was Marilyn Monroe's real name."

"No kidding!"

"Norma comes from the Normans. They were invaders," she says. She closes her book and looks hard at Leroy. "I'll go to Shiloh with you if you'll stop staring at me."

On Sunday, Norma Jean packs a picnic and they go to Shiloh. To Leroy's relief, Mabel says she does not want to come with them. Norma Jean drives, and Leroy, sitting beside her, feels like some boring hitchhiker she has picked up. He tries some conversation, but she answers him in monosyllables. At Shiloh, she drives aimlessly through the park, past bluffs and trails and steep ravines. Shiloh is an immense place, and Leroy cannot see it as a battleground. It is not what he expected. He thought it would look like a golf course. Monuments are everywhere, showing through the thick clusters of trees. Norma Jean passes the log cabin Mabel mentioned. It is surrounded by tourists looking for bullet holes.

"That's not the kind of log house I've got in mind," says Leroy apologetically.

"I know *that.*"

"This is a pretty place. Your mama was right."

"It's O.K.," says Norma Jean. "Well, we've seen it. I hope she's satisfied."

They burst out laughing together.

At the park museum, a movie on Shiloh is shown every half hour, but they decide that they don't want to see it. They buy a souvenir Confederate flag for Mabel, and then they find a picnic spot near the cemetery. Norma Jean has brought a picnic cooler, with pimiento sandwiches, soft drinks, and Yodels. Leroy eats a sandwich and then smokes a joint, hiding it behind the picnic cooler. Norma Jean has quit smoking altogether. She is picking cake crumbs from the cellophane wrapper, like a fussy bird.

Leroy says, "So the boys in gray ended up in Corinth. The Union soldiers zapped 'em finally. April 7, 1862."

They both know that he doesn't know any history. He is just talking about some of the historical plaques they have read. He feels awkward, like a boy on a date with an older girl. They are still just making conversation.

"Corinth is where Mama eloped to," says Norma Jean.

They sit in silence and stare at the cemetery for the Union dead and, beyond, at a tall cluster of trees. Campers are parked nearby, bumper to bumper, and small children in bright clothing are cavorting and squealing. Norma Jean wads up the cake wrapper and squeezes it tightly in her hand. Without looking at Leroy, she says, "I want to leave you."

Leroy takes a bottle of Coke out of the cooler and flips off the cap. He holds the bottle poised near his mouth but cannot remember to take a drink. Finally he says, "No, you don't."

"Yes, I do."

"I won't let you."

"You can't stop me."

"Don't do me that way."

Leroy knows Norma Jean will have her own way. "Didn't I promise to be home from now on?" he says.

"In some ways, a woman prefers a man who wanders," says Norma Jean. "That sounds crazy, I know."

"You're not crazy."

Leroy remembers to drink from his Coke. Then he says, "Yes, you *are* crazy. You and me could start all over again. Right back at the beginning."

"We *have* started all over again," says Norma Jean. "And this is how it turned out."

"What did I do wrong?"

"Nothing."

"Is this one of those women's lib things?" Leroy asks.

"Don't be funny."

The cemetery, a green slope dotted with white markers, looks like a subdivision site. Leroy is trying to comprehend that his marriage is breaking up, but for some reason he is wondering about white slabs in a graveyard.

"Everything was fine till Mama caught me smoking," says Norma Jean, standing up. "That set something off."

"What are you talking about?"

"She won't leave me alone—*you* won't leave me alone." Norma Jean seems to be crying, but she is looking away from him. "I feel eighteen again. I can't face that all over again." She starts walking away. "No, it *wasn't* fine. I don't know what I'm saying. Forget it."

Leroy takes a lungful of smoke and closes his eyes as Norma Jean's words sink in. He tries to focus on the fact that thirty-five hundred soldiers died on the grounds around him. He can only think of that war as a board game with plastic soldiers. Leroy almost smiles, as he compares the Confederates' daring attack on the Union camps and Virgil Mathis's raid on the bowling alley. General Grant, drunk and furious, shoved the southerners back to Corinth, where Mabel and Jet Beasley were married years later, when Mabel was still thin and good-looking. The next day, Mabel and Jet visited the battleground, and then Norma Jean was born, and then she married Leroy and they had a baby, which they lost, and now Leroy and Norma Jean are here at the same battleground. Leroy knows he is leaving out a lot. He is leaving out the insides of history. History was always just names and dates to him. It occurs to him that building a house out of logs is similarly empty—too simple. And the real inner workings of a marriage, like most of history, have escaped him. Now he sees that building a log house is the dumbest idea he could have had. It was clumsy of him to think Norma Jean would want a log house. It was a crazy idea. He'll have to think of something else, quickly. He will wad the blueprints into tight balls and fling them into the lake. Then he'll get moving again. He opens his eyes. Norma Jean has moved away and is walking through the cemetery, following a serpentine brick path.

Leroy gets up to follow his wife, but his good leg is asleep and his bad leg still hurts him. Norma Jean is far away, walking rapidly toward the bluff by the river, and he tries to hobble toward her. Some children run past him, screaming noisily. Norma Jean has reached the bluff, and she is looking out over the Tennessee River. Now she turns toward Leroy and waves her arms. Is she beckoning to him? She seems to be doing an exercise for her chest muscles. The sky is unusually pale—the color of the dust ruffle Mabel made for their bed.

1982

BARRY GIFFORD
b. 1946

Barry Gifford was born in Chicago, Illinois, and raised there and in Key West and Tampa, Florida. He attended the University of Missouri and Cambridge University. Before supporting himself as a writer and screenwriter, he worked as a merchant seaman, musician, journalist, editor, and truck driver. His numerous books include nine collections of poetry, five books of nonfiction, and fifteen works of fiction. His novel *Wild at Heart* (1990) was made into an award-winning film directed by David Lynch, and *Night People* (1992) received the Premio Brancati, Italy's national book award. His books have been translated into fifteen languages. Gifford currently lives in the San Francisco Bay Area and is cofounder of Black Lizard Books, publishers of noir fiction.

"I grew up in Chicago, where my father's friends were racketeers," Gifford said in a 1977 interview. "He ran an all-night drugstore on the corner of Chicago and Rush, and I would stay up late listening to their talk and dunking doughnuts with the organ grinder's monkey. Afternoons I spent watching show girls rehearse at the Club Alabam next door." After his father's death, when Gifford was only twelve, he "began to read everything: Jack London, Jack Kerouac, B. Traven; later Pound, Emily Dickinson, Jean Rhys, Proust, and Flaubert."

From Wild at Heart

Wild at Heart

Sailor and Lula lay on the bed in the Cape Fear Hotel listening to the ceiling fan creak. From their window they could see the river as it entered the Atlantic Ocean and watch the fishing boats navigate the narrow channel. It was late June but there was a mild wind that kept them "not uncomfortable," as Lula liked to say.

Lula's mother, Marietta Pace Fortune, had forbidden her to see Sailor Ripley ever again, but Lula had no intention of following that order. After all, Lula reasoned, Sailor had paid his debt to society, if that's what it was. She couldn't really understand how going to prison for killing someone who had been trying to kill him could be considered payment of a debt to society.

Society, such as it was, thought Lula, was certainly no worse off with Bob Ray Lemon eliminated from it. In her mind, Sailor had performed a service beneficial in the short as well as the long run to mankind and should have received some greater reward than two years in the Pee Dee River work camp for second-degree manslaughter. Something like an all-expenses-paid trip for Sailor with the companion of his choice—Lula, of course—to New Orleans or Hilton Head for a couple of weeks. A top hotel and a rental car, like a snazzy new Chrysler LeBaron convertible. That would have made sense. Instead, poor Sailor has to clear brush from the side of the road, dodge snakes and eat bad fried food for two years. Because Sailor was a shade more sudden than that creep Bob Ray Lemon he gets punished for it. The world is really wild at heart and weird on top, Lula thought. Anyway, Sailor was out now and he was still the best kisser she'd ever known, and what Mrs. Marietta Pace Fortune didn't find out about wasn't about to hurt her, was it?

"Speakin' of findin' out?" Lula said to Sailor. "Did I write to you about my findin' Grandaddy's letters in the attic bureau?"

Sailor sat up on his elbows. "Were we speakin'?" he said. "And no."

Lula clucked her tongue twice. "I was thinkin' we'd been but I been wrong before. Sometimes I get like that now. I think somethin' and then later think I've said it out loud to someone?"

"I really did miss your mind while I was out at Pee Dee, honey," said Sailor. "The rest of you, too, of course. But the way your head works is God's own private mystery. Now what about some letters?"

Lula sat up and fixed a pillow behind her back. Her long black hair, which she usually wore tied back and partly wrapped like a racehorse's tail, fanned out behind her on the powder blue pillowcase like a raven's wings. Her large grey eyes fascinated Sailor. When he was on the road gang he had thought about Lula's eyes, swum in them as if they were great cool, grey lakes with small violet islands in the middle. They kept him sane.

"I always wondered about my grandaddy. About why Mama never chose to speak about her daddy? All I ever knew was that he was livin' with his mama when he died."

"My daddy was livin' with his mama when he died," said Sailor. "Did you know that?"

Lula shook her head. "I surely did not," she said. "What were the circumstances?"

"He was broke, as usual," Sailor said. "My mama was already dead by then from the lung cancer."

"What brand did she smoke?" asked Lula.

"Camels. Same as me."

Lula half rolled her big grey eyes. "My mama smokes Marlboros now," she said. "Used to be she smoked Kools? I stole 'em from her beginnin' in about sixth grade. When I got old enough to buy my own I bought those. Now I've just about settled on Mores, as you probably noticed? They're longer."

"My daddy was lookin' for work and got run over by a gravel truck on the Dixie Guano Road off Seventy-four," said Sailor. "Cops said he was drunk—daddy, not the truck driver—but I figure they just wanted to bury the case. I was fourteen at the time."

"Gee, Sailor, I'm sorry, honey. I never would have guessed it."

"It's okay. I hardly used to see him anyway. I didn't have much parental guiding. The public defender kept sayin' that at my parole hearin'."

"Well, anyway," said Lula, "turns out my mama's daddy embezzled some money from the bank he was clerkin' in? And got caught. He did it to help out his brother who had TB and was a wreck and couldn't work. Grandaddy got four years in Statesville and his brother died. He wrote Grandmama a letter almost every day, tellin' her how much he loved her? But she divorced him while he was in the pen and never talked about him to anyone again. She just refused to suffer his name. But she kept all his letters! Can you believe it? I read every one of 'em, and I tell you that man loved that woman. It must have broke him apart when she refused to stand by him. Once a Pace woman makes up her mind there's no discussin' it."

Sailor lit a Camel and handed it to Lula. She took it, inhaled hard, blew the smoke out and half rolled her eyes again.

"I'd stand by you, Sailor," Lula said. "If you were an embezzler."

"Hell, peanut," Sailor said, "you stuck with me after I'd planted Bob Ray Lemon. A man can't ask for more than that."

Lula pulled Sailor over to her and kissed him soft on the mouth. "You move me, Sailor, you really do," she said. "You mark me the deepest."

Sailor pulled down the sheet, exposing Lula's breasts. "You're perfect for me, too," he said.

"You remind me of my daddy, you know?" said Lula. "Mama told me he liked skinny women whose breasts were just a bit too big for their bodies. He had a long nose, too, like yours. Did I ever tell you how he died?"

"No, sugar, you didn't that I recall."

"He got lead-poisoned from cleanin' the old paint off our house without usin' a mask. Mama said his brain just fell apart in pieces. Started he couldn't remember things? Got real violent? Finally in the middle of one night he poured kerosene over himself and lit a match. Near burned down the house with me and Mama asleep upstairs. We got out just in time. It was a year before I met you."

Sailor took the cigarette out of Lula's hand and put it into the ashtray by the bed. He put his hands on her small, nicely muscled shoulders and kneaded them.

"How'd you get such good shoulders?" Sailor asked.

"Swimmin', I guess," said Lula. "Even as a child I loved to swim."

Sailor pulled Lula to him and kissed her throat.

"You got such a pretty, long neck, like a swan," he said.

"Grandmama Pace had a long, smooth white neck," said Lula. "It was like on a statue it was so white? I like the sun too much to be white like that."

Sailor and Lula made love, and afterward, while Sailor slept, Lula stood at the window and smoked one of Sailor's Camels while she stared at the tail of the Cape Fear River. It was a little spooky, she thought, to be at the absolute end of a body of water. Lula looked over at Sailor stretched out on his back on the bed. It was odd that a boy like Sailor didn't have any tattoos, she thought. His type usually had a bunch. Sailor snorted in his sleep and turned onto his side, showing Lula his long, narrow back and flat butt. She took one more puff and threw the cigarette out the window into the river.

* * *

Hunger in America

"Hear now how leeches is comin' back into style," said Sailor.

"Say what?" said Lula. "Honestly, sugar, you can talk more shit sometimes?" She took out a cigarette the length and width of a Dixon Ticonderoga No. 2 pencil and lit it.

"Got you a pack of Mores again, huh?"

"Yeah, it's a real problem for me, Sailor, you know. When I went in that drugstore by the restaurant in Biloxi? For the Kotex? I saw 'em by the register and had the girl throw 'em in. I'm not big on resistin'. So what about a leech?"

"Heard on the radio how doctors is usin' leeches again, like in old times. You know, when even barbers used 'em?"

Lula shuddered. "Got one on me at Lake Lanier. Lifeguard poured salt on it and it dropped off. Felt awful. He was a cute boy, though, so it was almost worth it."

Sailor laughed. "Radio said back in the 1920s a I-talian doctor figured out that if, say, a fella got his nose mostly bit off in a barfight or somethin', and he needed a skin transplant there, they'd sew one of his forearms to his nose for a few weeks, and when they took it off they'd slap a couple leeches where the new skin attached from his arm to keep the blood movin' so the skin'd stick."

Lula rolled down her window on the passenger side of the front seat of the Bonneville. They were on the outskirts of New Orleans.

"Sailor? You expect me to believe a man'd be goin' around with a arm sewed to his nose? For *weeks*?!"

Sailor nodded. "How they used to do it," he said. "Course they got more sophisticated ways now. Radio said the Chinese, I think it is, figured a better idea is by insertin' a balloon in the forehead and lettin' it hang down on the nose."

Lula shrieked. "Sailor Ripley! You stop! You're makin' this shit up and I ain't gonna sit for it!"

"Honest, Lula," Sailor said. "I prob'ly ain't precisely got all the facts straight, but it's about what they said."

"Honey, here we are in N. O.," said Lula, "and it's time to change the subject."

Sailor pulled off the road into a Gulf gas station minimart.

"We're about dry bones, sweetheart," he said, stopping the car next to a self-serve pump. A sign on the top of it said PLEASE PAY INSIDE BEFORE FUELING.

"Get me a Mounds?" Lula shouted to Sailor as he went into the store.

A tall black man about thirty-five years old, wearing a torn green Tulane tee shirt, grease-stained brown slacks, no socks, ripped tennis shoes and a dirty orange Saints baseball cap, was piling items on the counter by the cash register. In the pile were four ready-made, plastic-wrapped sandwiches, two tuna salad and two cotto salami; six Twinkies; a package of Chips Ahoy chocolate chip cookies; four Slice sodas; two Barq's root beers; and a large package of fried pork rinds, extra salted.

"Sorry, gentlemen," the man said to Sailor and another guy who'd come in right behind Sailor and was also waiting to pay for gas, "I'm 'most finished on my shoppin' here."

"This be it?" the old guy behind the counter said.

"Y'all take American Express?" asked the man.

"Yessir," said the old guy. He had on a green Red Man chewing tobacco cap and a faded blue, short-sleeved attendant's work shirt with the name Erv sewn in black cursive above the chest pocket.

"Then lemme throw in a couple more things," said the man.

Sailor and the man in line behind him watched as the black man gathered up several more packages of Twinkies along with a few cupcakes and half a dozen cans of Pretty Kitty cat food, three liver and three chicken dinner portions, and tossed them on his pile.

"Pussycats gotta eat, too," he said to Sailor, smiling. He had no upper teeth that were visible.

He handed an American Express card to the clerk, who ran it through the verifier. The card checked out okay and the old guy prepared a charge slip, had the man sign it and bagged the purchases.

"I'd just soon have a paper bag rather than a plastic one, if it's same to you," the man said to the clerk.

"We don't have no paper bags," the old guy said, shoving the plastic bag he'd filled toward the man.

"Thanks for waitin', gentlemen," the man said to Sailor and the other patron, picked up his bag and walked out.

"All I want's ten bucks regular," Sailor said to the old guy. "Oh yeah, and a Mounds bar." He took one off the candy and gum rack next to the register and handed the clerk a twenty-dollar bill.

"I ain't got my American Express card with me," he said, "so I got to use cash. Hope that's okay."

Sailor smiled at the old guy but the clerk kept a poker face and just gave him his change. The guy in line behind Sailor shook his head and grinned.

"That took long enough," Lula said when Sailor got back to the car. "You forget my Mounds?"

Sailor tossed her the candy bar.

"I think the country done changed just a little while I was away, peanut," he said.

Lula sank her small white teeth into the chocolate-covered coconut.

"You got to keep an eye on it," she said as she chewed. "That's sure."

By the time Sailor finished pumping the gas, Lula had polished off both sections of the Mounds bar.

"Hope you don't mind I didn't save none for you," Lula said as Sailor climbed back into the driver's seat. "I was dyin'?"

* * *

Locus Ceruleus

On his first night in New Orleans, Johnnie Farragut sat on a stool in Snug Harbor watching the Braves lose again on TV, this time to the St. Louis Cardinals. A guy down the bar was complaining loudly about the ineptitude of the Atlanta team.

"The Cards ain't got a guy on the team can poke a ball past the infield, and the Braves still can't beat 'em," the man shouted. "Murphy must be a saint, stickin' with this outfit. He could be playin' in New York, L.A., anywhere, makin' his two million on a winnin' club."

"Maybe he likes the weather in Atlanta," said someone else.

"Yeah, and Mother Teresa is carryin' her and Bishop Tutu's love child," said the bartender.

Johnnie ordered his second double Black Label on the rocks and took out his pen and spiral notebook. He'd always wanted to be a writer, especially for television shows like *The Twilight Zone, The Outer Limits* or *One Step Beyond,* programs that, unfortunately, were no longer on the air. Whenever he had an idea for a story, he wrote it down. Just now Johnnie felt a ripple in his locus ceruleus, the area of the brain from which dreams emanate. Johnnie had read about this, and he believed that the locus ceruleus was his center of creativity. He never ignored the signal. Johnnie took his drink and notebook and moved to a booth so that he could concentrate. Finding Sailor and Lula would have to wait.

A GOOD CONNECTION

by Johnnie Farragut

Harry Newman sat on a corner stool in Barney's Tavern, watching the ballgame on TV. An error by the Braves shortstop in the bottom of the ninth gave the game to St. Louis and Harry swore under his breath. He'd put a couple of Jacksons on Atlanta this morning on the long end of five to two; a good bet, he'd figured. Lousy luck was all it was, he thought. All the guy had to do was keep his glove down, flip the ball to second for the force, and that was it. Instead, the ball goes through, all the way to the wall, two runners score, and that's the name of that tune.

Harry swallowed the last of his beer and slid off the stool. Barney came over behind the bar. "Tough luck, Harry," he said. "You oughta know better. The Braves never have no good luck in St. Louis." "Yeah, and I never have no good luck anyplace," said Harry, as he headed out the door. "That guy," Barney said to the customer who'd been sitting at the bar next to Harry, "he just don't know how to bet, is all. Loses ten times for every one he wins." "Some guys are like that," said the customer. "They never learn."

Harry walked downtown, shuffling along, not sure of where he was headed. He almost bumped into someone, excused himself, looked up, and that's when he saw it: a bright yellow 1957 Buick convertible. It was cherry, in perfect condition, sitting in the front row of Al Carson's used-car lot. Harry went right to it and ran his hand over the right front fender, then stroked up and along the top. It was the most gorgeous automobile he'd ever seen.

"She's somethin', ain't she, Harry?" said Al Carson, who'd come up behind him. Harry didn't even turn around to look at the wizened little car dealer. He just couldn't take his eyes off the old Buick. "She sure is," said Harry. "It looks brand-new." "Just about," said Al. "Only a fraction more than 15,000 miles on her in thirty years. A little old lady kept it in her garage. Only drove it to church on Sundays and to see her sister across town twice a month. Hard to believe, I know, but true." "How much, Al?" asked Harry. "How much do you want for her?" "Three grand," said Al. "But for you, Harry, make it twenty-seven fifty." "I've got about forty bucks on me now, Al," said Harry. "How about if you take that and I'll pay you a hundred a month?" "I don't know, Harry," Al said, shaking his tiny bald head. "Your credit ain't been at the top of the list lately." "Oh, come on, Al. I'll pay you. I will. I've just got to have this beauty."

Harry walked around the car, opened the driver's side door and got in. "Hey, what's this?" he said. "A telephone? They didn't have telephones in many cars over thirty years ago!" "Doesn't work, of course," said Al. "Don't know that it ever did. Doesn't appear it was ever really hooked up to nothing. I bought the car from the old woman's son and he couldn't tell me about it, either. Just said he always thought it was odd, too. What'd the old lady need a phone in her car for, anyway?" Al laughed. "I guess I should charge you extra for it!"

Harry slid back out and handed his two twenties to Al. "Come on, Al. You can trust me for it. You know me. I ain't gonna go run nowhere and hide." "You don't ever have enough dough to go nowhere!" said Al. "But I guess I can let you take it. Come on in the office and sign the paper and you can drive it out right now. She runs real good."

Harry drove his cherry 1957 Buick all over town that day, showing it off to everybody, proud as could be. After cruising around the neighborhood a few times he decided to take it out into the country for a real spin, to cut it loose and see what she could do on the open road. Not far past the city limits it began to rain. Harry put on the windshield wipers and they worked just fine, humming away as they cleared the water from view. Harry gave the Buick the gun, hurtling along the highway like a yellow flame. Rounding a curve, however, the tires hit a slick spot and the Buick spun out of Harry's control. He fought to keep the car on the road but it wobbled, slid and finally flew off the side into a ditch. The impact knocked Harry out.

"This is the operator. How may I help you? Hello, this is the operator speaking. How may I be of assistance?" Harry came to slowly, awakened by the sound of a voice. Someone was speaking to him. But who? He shook his head, opened his eyes, and saw that the telephone receiver had fallen off the hook. "Hello? Hello? This is the operator. What number do you want?" The voice was coming from the car phone. Harry shook his head again. He thought this must be his imagination, that his head was full of cobwebs from the crash. But no, it was the operator talking.

Harry picked up the receiver. "Hello," he said. "Operator? I'm sorry, I . . . I've just been in an accident and I'm stuck in a ditch. I mean my car is stuck. I must have lost control in the storm and gone off the road. Yes, I'm all right, I think," he told her. "Where am I?" Harry struggled around in the seat to look out the window. The rain had stopped. "About fifteen miles past the city limits, I guess. On the old Valley Road. Could you call a tow truck for me? Yes, certainly, Operator. I'll hold on." Harry shook his head again and felt his shoulder, his legs. He seemed to be in one piece, not seriously hurt. Another voice came on the line. "Bud's Service Station? Right, yes, well, I've had an accident. She told you? Twenty minutes? Great, great. No, I guess I'll be here all right." Harry hung up the telephone and stared at it.

Twenty minutes later a truck pulled up. The lettering on the sides of the doors of the cab said BUD'S TOW 24 HOURS. A large man, about fifty years old, with a two-day growth of beard and an unlit cigar stub stuck in his mouth, climbed down out of the cab and came over to where Harry was standing beside the Buick. The man wore a dark blue work shirt with the sleeves rolled partway up each meaty forearm. The name Bud was emblazoned above the left front pocket.

"They don't make these new buggies like the old ones," Bud said, as he looked the Buick over. Harry laughed. "That's pretty good," said Harry. "She was holding the road pretty well until that curve back there." Bud grunted and bent down to look at the right front wheel that was twisted halfway around. Bud grunted again as he raised himself back up. "Yeah, I keep my daddy's old '36 Packard runnin'," he said. "Now that's an automobile that won't let you down so long as you take care of it. They just churn these babies out now in too much of a hurry. They don't make 'em to last. Well, let's see if we can get her out of this," said Bud, as he walked back to the tow truck.

Bud had the Buick up and out of the ditch in ten minutes. "Hop up in the cab," he told Harry. "We'll take her back to the station and get that wheel straightened out." Harry and Bud climbed into the truck and Bud started off toward town. He reached over and snapped on the radio. "Say," he said, "I noticed that telephone in the car. You rig that up yourself? What is it, shortwave?" Harry nodded, confused. "No, er . . . yes, yeah, that's it."

The truck radio buzzed as it warmed up and Bud fiddled with the dial as he drove. "Got to hear the game. Who're you bettin' on? The Braves or the Yanks?" "What?" asked Harry. "In the Series, it starts today, you know. I like Milwaukee myself. Spahn and Burdette are gonna be tough to beat in a short Series," said Bud. "But I'm afraid of that crafty little lefty, Ford. I'm pretty sure of one thing, though." "What's that?" asked Harry, still trying to figure out what was going on. "That bum Larsen won't pitch another perfect game like he did last year." Bud laughed. "I'd bet the station on that!"

"But Larsen pitched his perfect game in the '56 Series!" said Harry. "That's right, pal," Bud answered. "Like I said, last year. Probably nobody'll do that again in our lifetime, I'll bet." Just then the radio kicked in, and the voice of Mel Allen, the New York Yankees' announcer, filled the cab of the truck. "Welcome to the broadcast of the World Series," said Mel Allen in his unmistakable, mellifluous drawl. "It's a beautiful afternoon here on October second, nineteen hundred and fifty-seven, as the Milwaukee Braves and the New York Yankees prepare to do battle in the House that Ruth Built."

Harry rubbed his head, unable to speak. Then he relaxed and began to smile, suddenly comfortable with the situation. "So whaddaya think?" asked Bud. "The Braves'll win it in seven games," Harry said. "You can bet on it." "That's what I wanted to hear!" said Bud, pounding a fist on the steering wheel. Harry just grinned and watched the road. As the truck passed the City Limits sign, Harry said, "I might put a few bucks down on the Braves myself. Yeah, I think I'll do just that."

1990

IV Revisiting History

In the history of postmodern American fiction, the publication of Toni Morrison's *Beloved* (1987) is a crucial moment. First, Morrison's novel may be the most celebrated and popular work of American fiction published during the last twenty-five years—winning, among other honors, the Pulitzer Prize, and playing a prominent role in Morrison's being awarded the Nobel Prize in 1993. As significantly, the critical and popular success of *Beloved* and Morrison reflects the ascension of minority authorship during the postmodern era. While African-Americans have published both best-selling and critically acclaimed fiction since the nineteenth century, *Beloved* represents the first occasion where the marginal became central, where an African-American novelist was given the awards and accolades reserved for leading figures on the international literary scene. Finally, Morrison's *Beloved* is an important work in the history of late-twentieth-century American fiction because it represents perhaps the most prominent example of one of the defining practices of the postmodern American author: retelling history from a previously buried or provocatively transformed viewpoint.

What *Beloved* accomplishes in revisiting the period of slavery and the Reconstruction provides a shorthand map to the many ways and reasons that contemporary fiction writers have explored history with such deep persistence. In fictionalizing the life of the slave Margaret Garner, Morrison first retrieves a story that history has left buried: a brief article from an antebellum Ohio newspaper described what would become the basis for the central event of *Beloved,* but omitted the slave's account. As important, however, *Beloved* uses history to serve a contemporary audience through a thin veil of detachment. Morrison's narrative of black men and women after the Civil War weighing the value of remembering a traumatic past resonates strongly among a middle-class readership itself only thirty years removed from the *de facto* apartheid of pre–Civil Rights Movement America. In showing how both blacks and whites worked through the memory of slavery and the Civil War, Morrison's book invites present-day readers to consider working through their own relation to history, while leaving open-ended the question of whether memory is a friend or foe.

Other selections in this section explore how the authors of the postmodern era revisit the past to tell a story about the present. In his Pulitzer Prize–winning and best-selling *Maus* (1986) and *Maus II* (1991), for instance, Art Spiegelman left readers with arguably the most memorable single image of the postmodern revision of conventional history-making: he told the story of his parents' experiences of the Holocaust in a comic book, with Germans portrayed as cats, Jews as mice, and other nationalities similarly animalized. Transforming the cartoon animals of postwar American childhoods into the main actors in a historical drama of genocide, Spiegelman's work moves between past and present, fact and fiction, and low and high culture with vertiginous intensity, and tells a story that is as much about the legacy of the Holocaust in America as about the Holocaust itself. "Femme Fatale," the third chapter from Philip Roth's *The Ghost Writer* (1979), explores similar historical territory. In presenting Anne Frank alive in America in the mid-1950s, confronting the surprising fact of her celebrity, Roth creates a startling alternative to official history that raises issues about martyrdom and the American Jewish experience. By placing this vision within the imagination of his fictional doppelgänger, Nathan Zuckerman, Roth constructs a Chinese box of fictional and real authors that questions the nature and authenticity of authorship and the act of writing.

In the opening section of *Ceremony* (1977), Leslie Marmon Silko interweaves Laguna Pueblo and Anglo-American versions of World War II and its aftermath to explore how history is now constituted of "tangled things, things tied together," the coexisting worldviews of dissonant cultures. Opening (and closing) with a Laguna chant that describes how Ts'its'tsi'nako creates the world from her stories, Silko's account of the half-breed Tayo's spiritual awakening also invites the reader to consider American history as an episode within American Indian history, rather than the reverse. E. L. Doctorow's "The Leather Man" (1984) adopts the language and structure of a business seminar to tell a story about the subversive power of loneliness and marginalization. Like many postmodern authors, Doctorow offers historical anecdotes that can be verified as fact alongside indistinguishable anecdotes that are inventions, and in so doing presents his reader with a compelling version of American history that is as hard to disregard as to verify. In Susan Daitch's "X≠Y" (1988), "heritage" itself—as rendered in George Washington's portrait on a passport, or facts culled from a high school lecture—becomes little else than a "word" that "makes you uneasy." As a woman held hostage on an airplane awaits an interview with her captors, the narrator wonders whether the uncertain translator will "make up your history for you," and whether two different versions of history are anything more than "separate revisions" of "respective fictions," the "X" and the "Y" that will never match.

" 'American history is as good as any history in the world!' " a "silver-maned senior Senator" in Joseph Heller's *Catch-22* (1961) tells us, but the novel surrounding him seems designed to explore the ironic underside of that proposition. In the character of Major Major Major Major, Heller creates an antihero of the American Dream, an individual who aspires to mediocrity but finds even that low ambition thwarted by computers, commanding officers, a perverse father, and an unfortunate resemblance to Henry Fonda. As its title suggests, David Foster Wallace's "Lyndon" (1989) reflects an era in which the aloofness that previously existed between celebrities and their audiences or constituencies has been transformed into a first-name relationship. Particularly noteworthy about Wallace's story is how its real-life individuals and historical setting produce not the sense of realism, but a greater spirit of mythos around the historical figure, based ironically upon a kind of transgressive and comic overfamiliarity. In "Captivity" (1993), Sherman Alexie also engages a historical figure, Mary Rowlandson, the author of a classic seventeenth-century captivity narrative considered a landmark text in determining Euro-American attitudes toward American Indians. For Alexie, the postmodern strategy of revisiting the past is something more than metaphorical: "every time the story is told," he tells us, "something changes. Every time the story is retold, something changes." Similarly, Alexie resists any suggestion that past and present are divisible. Asking whether it is "1676 or 1976 or 1776 or yesterday," Alexie speaks to Rowlandson more or less directly, and reminds us that the philosophical foundation for the postmodern fascination with history lies in the belief that the past—or some version of it—remains an active and transforming force in the present.

ART SPIEGELMAN
b. 1948

Art Spiegelman was born in Stockholm, Sweden, and educated at Harpur College in Binghamton, New York. He has been a freelance artist and writer since 1965, first serving as a creative consultant and writer for Topps Chewing Gum. His books of comics include *The Complete Mr. Infinity* (1970), *Every Day Has Its Dog* (1979), *Maus: A Survivor's Tale, My Father Bleeds History* (1986), and *Maus: A Survivor's Tale II, and Here My Troubles Began* (1991), which received a Special Pulitzer Prize, a National Book Critics Circle Award, a *Los Angeles Times* Book Prize, and a Before Columbus Foundation Award.

In a 1989 interview in *Comics Journal,* Spiegelman described *Maus* as "the point where my work starts. Up to that point, I feel like I'd been floundering. . . . All of a sudden, I found my own voice, my own needs, things that I wanted to do in comics." The genesis of the book occurred in 1972, when Spiegelman was asked to contribute to an anthology, *Funny Aminals* [sic], whose only stipulation was that the work feature animals with human characteristics. While watching television cartoons of cats and mice, Spiegelman felt that "this cat and mouse thing was just a metaphor for some kind of oppression." As he worked on *Maus,* Spiegelman discovered that "[t]o use these ciphers, the cats and mice, is actually a way to allow you past the cipher at the people who are experiencing it. So it's really a much more direct way of dealing with the material."

"There's something that I like about the fact that comics are such a gritty medium," Spiegelman added. "That they're so ignored. There's something to be said for that."

From Maus

BUT WHEN WE CAME TO STARA SOSNOWIEC, ALL MY BUSINESSES BECAME HARDER... IT WAS NOT SO EASY TO MOVE AROUND.
THE TIN SHOP FINISHED—THE OWNER WAS THE ONLY JEW THEY LET WORK THERE. I GOT THEN A JOB IN A GERMAN CARPENTRY SHOP.
FATHER-IN-LAW AND LOLEK WORKED ALREADY THERE, FOR REALLY NO MONEY. I DIDN'T NEED THIS BEFORE, BUT NOW I HAD TO HAVE THE WORK PAPER.
WOLFE COULD HAVE ARRANGED ME A JOB AT THE GEMEINDE... BUT I DIDN'T WANT TO PUT MY HANDS THERE WHERE JEWS WERE BEING TAKEN.
AND THEN IT CAME AGAIN SOMETHING NEW FROM THE GERMANS. WE GOT A NOTICE...
"ALL JEWS OVER 70 YEARS OLD WILL BE TRANSFERED TO THERESIENSTADT IN CZECHOSLOVAKIA ON MAY 10, 1942...
"...A COMMUNITY BETTER PREPARED TO TAKE CARE OF THE ELDERLY THAN OURS IN SOSNOWIEC..."
IT DOESN'T LOOK TOO BAD!
LIKE A CONVALESCENT HOME.
NOTICE:
ANJA'S GRANDPARENTS HAD ABOUT 90 YEARS.
WE'VE BEEN TOGETHER —A FAMILY—FOR 70 YEARS. WE DON'T WANT TO BREAK APART NOW!
DON'T WORRY. WE WON'T LET THEM TAKE YOU.
WE DIDN'T YET KNOW OF AUSCHWITZ—OF THE OVENS—BUT WE WERE ANYWAY AFRAID.
...SO, IN THE YARD, WE MADE A HIDING PLACE, A BUNKER...
CUT-AWAY VIEW:
STORAGE SHEDS
FALSE WALL
GRAND-PARENTS
WE SNEAKED FOOD TO THEM, AND—WHEN IT WAS SAFE—WE TOOK THEM INSIDE A LITTLE.

SEVERAL TIMES CAME THE JEWISH POLICE TO OUR HOUSE...

OUR RECORDS SHOW THAT MR. AND MRS. KARMIO LIVE HERE. THEY HAVEN'T REGISTERED FOR TRANSFER.
YES-MY WIFE'S PARENTS-THEY LEFT WITHOUT A WORD A MONTH AGO.
JEWISH POLICE?
YES-WITH BIG STICKS.

SOME JEWS THOUGHT IN THIS WAY: IF THEY GAVE TO THE GERMANS A FEW JEWS, THEY COULD SAVE THE REST.
AND AT LEAST THEY COULD SAVE THEMSELVES.
AND A MONTH AFTER, THEY AGAIN CAME TO FATHER-IN-LAW.
MR. ZYLBERBERG, YOU AND YOUR WIFE MUST COME WITH US.
IF THE KARMIOS DON'T TURN UP IN 3 DAYS YOU TWO WILL BE SENT IN THEIR PLACE!

HE HAD STILL A LITTLE "PROTECTION" FROM THE GEMEINDE, SO THEY TOOK ONLY HIM AWAY-NOT HIS WIFE.
HE SAT A FEW DAYS THERE, THEN HE SENT TO US A NOTE
HE WROTE THAT WE HAD TO GIVE OVER THE GRANDPARENTS. EVEN IF THEY TOOK ONLY HIM AWAY NOW, NEXT THEY WOULD GRAB HIS WIFE, AND THEN THE REST OF THE FAMILY.

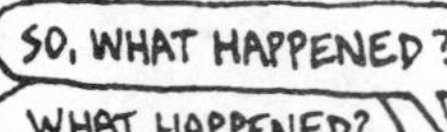
SO, WHAT HAPPENED?

WHAT HAPPENED? WE HAD TO DELIVER THEM!

THEY THOUGHT IT WAS TO THERESIENSTADT THEY WERE GOING.
LET US KNOW IF YOU NEED ANYTHING!
BUT THEY WENT RIGHT AWAY TO AUSCHWITZ, TO THE GAS.

AFTER WHAT HAPPENED TO THE GRANDPARENTS, IT WAS A FEW MONTHS QUIET. THEN IT CAME POSTERS EVERYWHERE AND SPEECHES FROM THE GEMEINDE...

MY FATHER- HE HAD 62 YEARS-CAME BY STREETCAR TO ME FROM DABROWA, THE VILLAGE NEXT DOOR FROM SOSNOWIEC.

AFTER MY MOTHER DIED WITH CANCER, HE LIVED THERE IN THE HOUSE OF MY SISTER FELA, AND HER FOUR SMALL CHILDREN.

REALLY, I DIDN'T KNOW HOW TO ADVISE HIM.

WHEN WE WERE EVERYBODY INSIDE, GESTAPO WITH MACHINE GUNS SURROUNDED THE STADIUM.

THEN WAS A SELECTION, WITH PEOPLE SENT EITHER TO THE LEFT, EITHER TO THE RIGHT.

ME AND ANJA CAME TO THE TABLE WHERE MY COUSIN WAS SITTING...

WE WERE SO HAPPY WE CAME THROUGH. BUT WE WORRIED NOW- WERE OUR FAMILIES SAFE?

BUT LATER SOMEONE WHO SAW HIM TOLD ME... HE CAME THROUGH THIS SAME COUSIN OVER TO THE GOOD SIDE.

MY DAUGHTER! HOW CAN SHE MANAGE *ALONE*-WITH FOUR CHILDREN TO TAKE CARE OF?

AND, WHAT DO YOU THINK? HE *SNEAKED* ON TO THE *BAD* SIDE!

THOSE WITH A STAMP *WERE* LET TO GO HOME. BUT THERE WERE VERY FEW JEWS NOW LEFT IN SOSNOWIEC...

1986

TONI MORRISON
b. 1931

Toni Morrison was born Chloe Anthony Wofford in Lorain, Ohio. She received her B.A. from Howard University and her M.A. from Cornell University. For twenty years, beginning in 1965, she was a senior editor at Random House, helping to publish the work of Toni Cade Bambara, Angela Davis, and Muhammad Ali, among others. She has also taught at Howard University, the State University of New York at Albany, Yale University, and Princeton University, where she is currently Robert F. Goheen Professor in the Council of Humanities. Her novels include *The Bluest Eye* (1970); *Sula* (1973); *Song of Solomon* (1977), awarded the American Academy and Institute of Arts and Letters Award and the National Book Critics Circle Award; *Tar Baby* (1981); *Beloved* (1987), awarded the Pulitzer Prize for fiction; and *Jazz* (1992). In 1993, she received the Nobel Prize for Literature.

Wilfrid Sheed, in *The Atlantic Monthly* (1981), writes: "Most black writers are privy, like the rest of us, to bits and pieces of the secret, the dark side of their group experience, but Toni Morrison uniquely seems to have all the keys on her chain, like a house detective. . . . She [uses] the run of the whole place, from ghetto to small town to ramshackle farmhouse, to bring back a panorama of black myth and reality that [dazzles] the senses." As Morrison told *The New York Times* in 1987, "I really think the range of emotions and perceptions I have had access to as a black person and a female person are greater than those of people who are neither. . . . My world did not shrink because I was a black female writer. It just got bigger." For Morrison, writing "is discovery; it's talking deep within myself."

Morrison's inspiration for *Beloved* came from an antebellum newspaper article she uncovered while researching *The Black Book* (1974), a Random House anthology of items that illustrate the history of black Americans. "I certainly thought I knew as much about slavery as anybody," she told the *Los Angeles Times* in 1987. "But it was the interior life I needed to find out about."

From Beloved

Not quite in a hurry, but losing no time, Sethe and Paul D climbed the white stairs. Overwhelmed as much by the downright luck of finding her house and her in it as by the certainty of giving her his sex, Paul D dropped twenty-five years from his recent memory. A stair step before him was Baby Suggs' replacement, the new girl they dreamed of at night and fucked cows for at dawn while waiting for her to choose. Merely kissing the wrought iron on her back had shook the house, had made it necessary for him to beat it to pieces. Now he would do more.

She led him to the top of the stairs, where light came straight from the sky because the second-story windows of that house had been placed in the pitched ceiling and not the walls. There were two rooms and she took him into one of them, hoping he wouldn't mind the fact that she was not prepared; that though she could remember desire, she had forgotten how it worked; the clutch and helplessness that resided in the hands; how blindness was altered so that what leapt to the eye were places to lie down, and all else—door knobs, straps, hooks, the sadness that crouched in corners, and the passing of time—was interference.

It was over before they could get their clothes off. Half-dressed and short of breath, they lay side by side resentful of one another and the skylight above them. His dreaming of her had been too long and too long ago. Her deprivation had been not having any dreams of her own at all. Now they were sorry and too shy to make talk.

Sethe lay on her back, her head turned from him. Out of the corner of his eye, Paul D saw the float of her breasts and disliked it, the spread-away, flat roundness of them that he could definitely live without, never mind that downstairs he had held them as though they were the most expensive part of himself. And the wrought-iron maze he had explored in the kitchen like a gold miner pawing through pay dirt was in fact a revolting clump of scars. Not a tree, as she said. Maybe shaped like one, but nothing like any tree he knew because trees were inviting; things you could trust and be near; talk to if you wanted to as he frequently did since way back when he took the midday meal in the fields of Sweet Home. Always in the same place if he could, and choosing the place had been hard because Sweet Home had more pretty trees than any farm around. His choice he called Brother, and sat under it, alone sometimes, sometimes with Halle or the other Pauls, but more often with Sixo, who was gentle then and still speaking English. Indigo with a flame-red tongue, Sixo experimented with night-cooked potatoes, trying to pin down exactly when to put smoking-hot rocks in a hole, potatoes on top, and cover the whole thing with twigs so that by the time they broke for the meal, hitched the animals, left the field and got to Brother, the potatoes would be at the peak of perfection. He might get up in the middle of the night, go all the way out there, start the earth-over by starlight; or he would make the stones less hot and put the next day's potatoes on them right after the meal. He never got it right, but they ate those undercooked, overcooked, dried-out or raw potatoes anyway, laughing, spitting and giving him advice.

Time never worked the way Sixo thought, so of course he never got it right. Once he plotted down to the minute a thirty-mile trip to see a woman. He left on a Saturday when the moon was in the place he wanted it to be, arrived at her cabin before church on Sunday and had just enough time to say good morning before he had to start back again so he'd make the field call on time Monday morning. He had walked for seventeen hours, sat down for one, turned around and walked seventeen more. Halle and the Pauls spent the whole day covering Sixo's fatigue from Mr. Garner. They ate no potatoes that day, sweet or white. Sprawled near Brother, his flame-red tongue hidden from them, his indigo face closed, Sixo slept through dinner like a corpse. Now *there* was a man, and *that* was a tree. Himself lying in the bed and the "tree" lying next to him didn't compare.

Paul D looked through the window above his feet and folded his hands behind his head. An elbow grazed Sethe's shoulder. The touch of cloth on her skin startled her. She had forgotten he had not taken off his shirt. Dog, she thought, and then remembered that she had not allowed him the time for taking it off. Nor herself time to take off her petticoat, and considering she had begun undressing before she saw him on the porch, that her shoes and stockings were already in her hand and she had never put them back on; that he had looked at her wet bare feet and asked to join her; that when she rose to cook he had undressed her further; considering how quickly they had started getting naked, you'd think by now they would be. But maybe a man was nothing but a man, which is what Baby Suggs always said. They encouraged you to put some of your weight in their hands and soon as you felt how light and lovely that was, they studied your scars and tribulations, after which they did what he had done: ran her children out and tore up the house.

She needed to get up from there, go downstairs and piece it all back together. This house he told her to leave as though a house was a little thing—a shirtwaist or a sewing basket you could walk off from or give away any old time. She who had never had one but this one; she who left a dirt floor to come to this one; she who had to bring a fistful of salsify into Mrs. Garner's kitchen every day just to be able to work in it, feel like some part of it was hers, because she wanted to love the work she did, to take the ugly out of it, and the only way she could feel at home on Sweet Home was if she picked some pretty growing thing and took it with her. The day she forgot was the day butter wouldn't come or the brine in the barrel blistered her arms.

At least it seemed so. A few yellow flowers on the table, some myrtle tied around the handle of the flatiron holding the door open for a breeze calmed her, and when Mrs. Garner and she sat down to sort bristle, or make ink, she felt fine. Fine. Not scared of the men beyond. The five who slept in quarters near her, but never came in the night. Just touched their raggedy hats when they saw her and stared. And if she brought food to them in the fields, bacon and bread wrapped in a piece of clean sheeting, they never took it from her hands. They stood back and waited for her to put it on the ground (at the foot of a tree) and leave. Either they did not want to take anything from her, or did not want her to see them eat. Twice or three times she lingered. Hidden behind honeysuckle she watched them. How different they were without her, how they laughed and played and urinated and sang. All but Sixo, who laughed once—at the very end. Halle, of course, was the nicest. Baby Suggs' eighth and last child, who rented himself out all over the county to buy her away from there. But he too, as it turned out, was nothing but a man.

"A man ain't nothing but a man," said Baby Suggs. "But a son? Well now, that's *somebody.*"

It made sense for a lot of reasons because in all of Baby's life, as well as Sethe's own, men and women were moved around like checkers. Anybody Baby Suggs knew, let alone loved, who hadn't run off or been hanged, got rented out, loaned out, bought up, brought back, stored up, mortgaged, won, stolen or seized. So Baby's eight children had six fathers. What she called the nastiness of life was the shock she received upon learning that nobody stopped playing checkers just because the pieces included her children. Halle she was able to keep the longest. Twenty years. A lifetime. Given to her, no doubt, to make up for *hearing* that her two girls, neither of whom had their adult teeth, were sold and gone and she had not been able to wave goodbye. To make up for coupling with a straw boss for four months in exchange for keeping her third child, a boy, with her—only to have him traded for lumber in the spring of the next year and to find herself pregnant by the man who promised not to and did. That child she could not love and the rest she would not. "God take what He would," she said. And He did, and He did, and He did and then gave her Halle who gave her freedom when it didn't mean a thing.

Sethe had the amazing luck of six whole years of marriage to that "somebody" son who had fathered every one of her children. A blessing she was reckless enough to take for granted, lean on, as though Sweet Home really was one. As though a handful of myrtle stuck in the handle of a pressing iron propped against the door in a whitewoman's kitchen could make it hers. As though mint sprig in the mouth changed the breath as well as its odor. A bigger fool never lived.

Sethe started to turn over on her stomach but changed her mind. She did not want to call Paul D's attention back to her, so she settled for crossing her ankles.

But Paul D noticed the movement as well as the change in her breathing. He felt obliged to try again, slower this time, but the appetite was gone. Actually it was a good feeling—not wanting her. Twenty-five years and blip! The kind of thing Sixo would do—like the time he arranged a meeting with Patsy the Thirty-Mile Woman. It took three months and two thirty-four-mile round trips to do it. To persuade her to walk one-third of the way toward him, to a place he knew. A deserted stone structure that Redmen used way back when they thought the land was theirs. Sixo discovered it on one of his night creeps, and asked its permission to enter. Inside, having felt what it felt like, he asked the Redmen's Presence if he could bring his woman there. It said yes and Sixo painstakingly instructed her how to get there, exactly when to start out, how his welcoming or warning whistles would sound. Since neither could go anywhere on business of their own, and since the Thirty-Mile Woman was already fourteen and scheduled for somebody's arms, the danger was real. When he arrived, she had not. He whistled and got no answer. He went into the Redmen's deserted lodge. She was not there. He returned to the meeting spot. She was not there. He waited longer. She still did not come. He grew frightened for her and walked down the road in the direction she should be coming from. Three or four miles, and he stopped. It was hopeless to go on that way, so he stood in the wind and asked for help. Listening close for some sign, he heard a whimper. He turned toward it, waited and heard it again. Uncautious now, he hollered her name. She answered in a voice that sounded like life to him—not death. "Not move!" he shouted. "Breathe hard I can find you." He did. She believed she was already at the meeting place and was crying because she thought he had not kept his promise. Now it was too late for the rendezvous to happen at the Redmen's house, so they dropped where they were. Later he punctured her calf to simulate snakebite so she could use it in some way as an excuse for not being on time to shake worms from tobacco leaves. He gave her detailed directions about following the stream as a shortcut back, and saw her off. When he got to the road it was very light and he had his clothes in his hands. Suddenly from around a bend a wagon trundled toward him. Its driver, wide-eyed, raised a whip while the woman seated beside him covered her face. But Sixo had already melted into the woods before the lash could unfurl itself on his indigo behind.

He told the story to Paul F, Halle, Paul A and Paul D in the peculiar way that made them cry-laugh. Sixo went among trees at night. For dancing, he said, to keep his bloodlines open, he said. Privately, alone, he did it. None of the rest of them had seen him at it, but they could imagine it, and the picture they pictured made them eager to laugh at him—in daylight, that is, when it was safe.

But that was before he stopped speaking English because there was no future in it. Because of the Thirty-Mile Woman Sixo was the only one not paralyzed by yearning for Sethe. Nothing could be as good as the sex with her Paul D had been imagining off and on for twenty-five years. His foolishness made him smile and think fondly of himself as he turned over on his side, facing her. Sethe's eyes were closed, her hair a mess. Looked at this way, minus the polished eyes, her face was not so attractive. So it must have been her eyes that kept him both guarded and stirred up. Without them her face was manageable—a face he could handle. Maybe if she would keep them closed like that . . . But no, there was her mouth. Nice. Halle never knew what he had.

Although her eyes were closed, Sethe knew his gaze was on her face, and a paper picture of just how bad she must look raised itself up before her mind's eye. Still, there was no mockery coming from his gaze. Soft. It felt soft in a waiting kind of way. He was not judging her—or rather he was judging but not comparing her. Not since Halle had a man looked at her that way: not loving or passionate, but interested, as though he were examining an ear of corn for quality. Halle was more like a brother than a husband. His care suggested a family relationship rather than a man's laying claim. For years they saw each other in full daylight only on Sundays. The rest of the time they spoke or touched or ate in darkness. Predawn darkness and the afterlight of sunset. So looking at each other intently was a Sunday-morning pleasure and Halle examined her as though storing up what he saw in sunlight for the shadow he saw the rest of the week. And he had so little time. After his Sweet Home work and on Sunday afternoons was the debt work he owed for his mother. When he asked her to be his wife, Sethe happily agreed and then was stuck not knowing the next step. There should be a ceremony, shouldn't there? A preacher, some dancing, a party, a something. She and Mrs. Garner were the only women there, so she decided to ask her.

"Halle and me want to be married, Mrs. Garner."

"So I heard." She smiled. "He talked to Mr. Garner about it. Are you already expecting?"

"No, ma'am."

"Well, you will be. You know that, don't you?"

"Yes, ma'am."

"Halle's nice, Sethe. He'll be good to you."

"But I mean we want to get married."

"You just said so. And I said all right."

"Is there a wedding?"

Mrs. Garner put down her cooking spoon. Laughing a little, she touched Sethe on the head, saying, "You are one sweet child." And then no more.

Sethe made a dress on the sly and Halle hung his hitching rope from a nail on the wall of her cabin. And there on top of a mattress on top of the dirt floor of the cabin they coupled for the third time, the first two having been in the tiny cornfield Mr. Garner kept because it was a crop animals could use as well as humans. Both Halle and Sethe were under the impression that they were hidden. Scrunched down among the stalks they couldn't see anything, including the corn tops waving over their heads and visible to everyone else.

Sethe smiled at her and Halle's stupidity. Even the crows knew and came to look. Uncrossing her ankles, she managed not to laugh aloud.

The jump, thought Paul D, from a calf to a girl wasn't all that mighty. Not the leap Halle believed it would be. And taking her in the corn rather than her quarters, a yard away from the cabins of the others who had lost out, was a gesture of tenderness. Halle wanted privacy for her and got public display. Who could miss a ripple in a cornfield on a quiet cloudless day? He, Sixo and both of the Pauls sat under Brother pouring water from a gourd over their heads, and through eyes streaming with well water, they watched the confusion of tassels in the field below. It had been hard, hard, hard sitting there erect as dogs, watching corn stalks dance at noon. The water running over their heads made it worse.

Paul D sighed and turned over. Sethe took the opportunity afforded by his movement to shift as well. Looking at Paul D's back, she remembered that some of the corn stalks broke, folded down over Halle's back, and among the things her fingers clutched were husk and cornsilk hair.

How loose the silk. How jailed down the juice.

The jealous admiration of the watching men melted with the feast of new corn they allowed themselves that night. Plucked from the broken stalks that Mr. Garner could not doubt was the fault of the raccoon. Paul F wanted his roasted; Paul A wanted his boiled and now Paul D couldn't remember how finally they'd cooked those ears too young to eat. What he did remember was parting the hair to get to the tip, the edge of his fingernail just under, so as not to graze a single kernel.

The pulling down of the tight sheath, the ripping sound always convinced her it hurt.

As soon as one strip of husk was down, the rest obeyed and the ear yielded up to him its shy rows, exposed at last. How loose the silk. How quick the jailed-up flavor ran free.

No matter what all your teeth and wet fingers anticipated, there was no accounting for the way that simple joy could shake you.

How loose the silk. How fine and loose and free.

1987

PHILIP ROTH

b. 1933

Philip Roth was born in Newark, New Jersey, and educated at Rutgers University, Bucknell University, and the University of Chicago. His more than twenty books of fiction include *Goodbye, Columbus, and Five Short Stories* (1959), *Portnoy's Complaint* (1969), *Zuckerman Bound: A Trilogy and Epilogue* (1985), and *Deception* (1990). *Goodbye, Columbus* received a National Book Award for fiction, and *The Counterlife* (1986) received the National Book Critics Circle Award. Roth has also published two memoirs, *The Facts: A Novelist's Autobiography* (1988) and *Patrimony: A True Story* (1991).

In a 1985 interview in *The Paris Review*, Roth said about his creative process, "I ask myself, 'If this book were a dream, it would be a dream of what?' But when I'm asking this I'm also trying to *believe* in what I've written, to forget that it's writing and to say, 'This *has* taken place,' even if it hasn't. The idea is to perceive your invention as a reality that can be understood as a dream. The idea is to turn flesh and blood into literary characters and literary characters into flesh and blood."

"Femme Fatale" is excerpted from *The Ghost Writer* (1979), the first book of Roth's *Zuckerman Bound*. "*The Ghost Writer* is narrated in the first person," Roth explained in the *Paris Review* interview, "probably because what's being described is largely a world Zuckerman's discovered outside of himself, the book of a young explorer. The older and more scarred he gets, the more *inward*-looking he gets, the further out *I* have to get. . . . In *The Ghost Writer* the crisis—one among many—had to do with Zuckerman, Amy Bellette, and Anne Frank. It wasn't easy to see that Amy Bellette *as* Anne Frank was Zuckerman's own creation. Only by working through numerous alternatives did I decide that not only was she his creation, but that she might possibly be her own creation too, a young woman inventing herself *within* Zuckerman's invention. To enrich his fantasy without obfuscation or muddle, to be ambiguous *and* clear—well, that was my writing problem through one whole summer and fall."

From The Ghost Writer

Femme Fatale

It was only a year earlier that Amy had told Lonoff her whole story. Weeping hysterically, she had phoned him one night from the Biltmore Hotel in New York; as best he could understand, that morning she had come down alone on a train from Boston to see the matinee performance of a play, intending to return home again by train in the evening. Instead, after coming out of the theater she had taken a hotel room, where ever since she had been "in hiding."

At midnight, having only just finished his evening's reading and gone up to bed, Lonoff got into his car and drove south. By four he had reached the city, by six she had told him that it was the dramatization of Anne Frank's diary she had come to New York to see, but it was midmorning before she could explain even somewhat coherently her connection with this new Broadway play.

"It wasn't the play—I could have watched that easily enough if I had been alone. It was the people watching with me. Carloads of women kept pulling up to the theater, women wearing fur coats, with expensive shoes and handbags. I thought, This isn't for me. The billboards, the photographs, the marquee, I could take all that. But it was the women who frightened me—and their families and their children and their homes. Go to a movie, I told myself, go instead to a museum. But I showed my ticket, I went in with them, and of course it happened. It had to happen. It's what happens there. The women cried. Everyone around me was in tears. Then at the end, in the row behind me, a woman screamed, 'Oh, no.' That's why I came running here. I wanted a room with a telephone in it where I could stay until I'd found my father. But all I did once I was here was sit in the bathroom thinking that if he knew, if I told him, then they would have to come out on the stage after each performance and announce, 'But she is really alive. You needn't worry, she survived, she is twenty-six now, and doing very well.' I would say to him, 'You must keep this our secret—no one but you must ever know.' But suppose he was found out? What if we both were? Manny, I couldn't call him. And I knew I couldn't when I heard that woman scream 'Oh, no.' I knew then what's been true all along: I'll never see him again. I have to be dead to everyone."

Amy lay on the rumpled bed, wrapped tightly in a blanket, while Lonoff listened in silence from a chair by the window. Upon entering the unlocked room, he had found her sitting in the empty bathtub, still wearing her best dress and her best coat: the coat because she could not stop trembling, in the tub because it was the farthest she could get from the window, which was twenty floors above the street.

"How pathetic, you must think. What a joke," she said.

"A joke? On whom? I don't see the joke."

"My telling this to you."

"I still don't get it."

"Because it's like one of your stories. An E. I. Lonoff story . . . called . . . oh, you'd know what to call it. You'd know how to tell it in three pages. A homeless girl comes from Europe, sits in the professor's class being clever, listens to his records, plays his daughter's piano, virtually grows up in his house, and then one day, when the waif is a woman and out on her own, one fine day in the Biltmore Hotel, she casually announces . . ."

He left his chair and came to sit beside her on the bed while she went to pieces again. "Yes," he said, "quite casually."

"Manny, I'm not a lunatic, I'm not a crackpot, I'm not some girl—you must believe me—trying to be interesting and imitate your art!"

"My dear friend," he replied, his arms around her now and rocking her like a child, "if this is all so—"

"Oh, Dad-da, I'm afraid it really is."

"Well, then, you have left my poor art far behind."

This is the tale that Amy told the morning after she had gone alone to the Cort Theatre to sit amid the weeping and inconsolable audience at the famous New York production of *The Diary of Anne Frank.* This is the story that the twenty-six-year-old young woman with the striking face and the fetching accent and the felicitous prose style and the patience, according to Lonoff, of a Lonoff, expected him to believe was true.

After the war she had become Amy Bellette. She had not taken the new name to disguise her identity—as yet there was no need—but, as she imagined at the time, to forget her life. She had been in a coma for weeks, first in the filthy barracks with the other ailing and starving inmates, and then in the squalid makeshift "infirmary." A dozen dying children had been rounded up by the SS and placed beneath blankets in a room with twelve beds in order to impress the Allied armies advancing upon Belsen with the amenities of concentration-camp living. Those of the twelve still alive when the British got there had been moved to an army field hospital. It was here that she finally came around. She understood sometimes less and sometimes more than the nurses explained to her, but she would not speak. Instead, without howling or hallucinating, she tried to find a way to believe that she was somewhere in Germany, that she was not yet sixteen, and that her family was dead. Those were the facts; now to grasp them.

"Little Beauty" the nurses called her—a silent, dark, emaciated girl—and so, one morning, ready to talk, she told them that the surname was Bellette. Amy she got from an American book she had sobbed over as a child, *Little Women.* She had decided, during her long silence, to finish growing up in America now that there was nobody left to live with in Amsterdam. After Belsen she figured it might be best to put an ocean the size of the Atlantic between herself and what she needed to forget.

She learned of her father's survival while waiting to get her teeth examined by the Lonoffs' family dentist in Stockbridge. She had been three years with foster families in England, and almost a year as a freshman at Athene College, when she picked an old copy of *Time* out of the pile in the waiting room and, just turning pages, saw a photograph of a Jewish businessman named Otto Frank. In July of 1942, some two years after the beginning of the Nazi occupation, he had taken his wife and his two young daughters into hiding. Along with another Jewish family, the Franks lived safely for twenty-five months in a rear upper story of the Amsterdam building where he used to have his business offices. Then, in August 1944, their whereabouts were apparently betrayed by one of the workers in the warehouse below, and the hideout was uncovered by the police. Of the eight who'd been together in the sealed-off attic rooms, only Otto Frank survived the concentration camps. When he came back to Amsterdam after the war, the Dutch family who had been their protectors gave him the notebooks that had been kept in hiding by his younger daughter, a girl of fifteen when she died in Belsen: a diary, some ledgers she wrote in, and a sheaf of papers emptied out of her briefcase when the Nazis were ransacking the place for valuables. Frank printed and circulated the diary only privately at first, as a memorial to his family, but in 1947 it was published in a regular edition under the title *Het Achterhuis*—"The House Behind." Dutch readers, *Time* said, were greatly affected by the young teenager's record of how the hunted Jews tried to carry on a civilized life despite their deprivations and the terror of discovery.

Alongside the article—"A Survivor's Sorrows"—was the photograph of the diarist's father, "now sixty." He stood alone in his coat and hat in front of the building on the Prinsengracht Canal where his late family had improvised a last home.

Next came the part of her story that Lonoff was bound to think improbable. She herself, however, could not consider it all that strange that she should be thought dead when in fact she was alive; nobody who knew the chaos of those final months—the Allies bombing everywhere, the SS in flight—would call that improbable. Whoever claimed to have seen her dead of typhus in Belsen had either confused her with her older sister, Margot, or had figured that she was dead after seeing her so long in a coma, or had watched her being carted away, as good as dead, by the Kapos.

"Belsen was the third camp," Amy told him. "We were sent first to Westerbork, north of Amsterdam. There were other children around to talk to, we were back in the open air—aside from being frightened it really wasn't that awful. Daddy lived in the men's barracks, but when I got sick he managed somehow to get into the women's camp at night and to come to my bed and hold my hand. We were there a month, then we were shipped to Auschwitz. Three days and three nights in the freight cars. Then they opened the doors and that was the last I saw of him. The men were pushed in one direction, we were pushed in the other. That was early September. I saw my mother last at the end of October. She could hardly speak by then. When Margot and I were shipped from Auschwitz, I don't even know if she understood."

She told him about Belsen. Those who had survived the cattle cars lived at first in tents on the heath. They slept on the bare ground in rags. Days went by without food or fresh water, and after the autumn storms tore the tents from their moorings, they slept exposed to the wind and rain. When at last they were being moved into barracks, they saw ditches beyond the camp enclosure piled high with bodies—the people who had died on the heath from typhus and starvation. By the time winter came, it seemed as if everyone still alive was either sick or half mad. And then, while watching her sister slowly dying, she grew sick herself. After Margot's death, she could hardly remember the women in the barracks who had helped her, and knew nothing of what happened to them.

It was not so improbable either that after her long hospital convalescence she had not made her way to the address in Switzerland where the family had agreed to meet if they should ever lose touch with one another. Would a weak sixteen-year-old girl undertake a journey requiring money, visas—requiring hope—only to learn at the other end that she was as lost and alone as she feared?

No, no, the improbable part was this: that instead of telephoning *Time* and saying, "I'm the one who wrote the diary—find Otto Frank!" she jotted down in her notebook the date on the magazine's cover and, after a tooth had been filled, went off with her school books to the library. What was improbable—inexplicable, indefensible, a torment still to her conscience—was that, calm and studious as ever, she checked *The New York Times Index* and the *Readers' Guide to Periodical Literature* for "Frank, Anne" and "Frank, Otto" and *"Het Achterhuis,"* and, when she found nothing, went down to the library's lowest stacks, where the periodicals were shelved. There she spent the remaining hour before dinner rereading the article in *Time.* She read it until she knew it by heart. She studied her father's photograph. Now sixty. And those were the words that did it—made of her once again the daughter who cut his hair for him in the attic, the daughter who did her lessons there with him as her tutor, the daughter who would run to his bed and cling to him under the covers when she heard the Allied bombers flying over Amsterdam: suddenly she was the daughter for whom he had taken the place of everything she could no longer have. She cried for a very long time. But when she went to dinner in the dormitory, she pretended that nothing catastrophic had once again happened to Otto Frank's Anne.

But then right from the beginning she had resolved not to speak about what she had been through. Resolutions were her strong point as a young girl on her own. How else could she have lasted on her own? One of the thousand reasons she could not bear Uncle Daniel, the first of her foster fathers in England, was that sooner or later he wound up telling whoever walked into the house about all that had happened to Amy during the war. And then there was Miss Giddings, the young teacher in the school north of London who was always giving the orphaned little Jewess tender glances during history class. One day after school Miss Giddings took her for a lemon-curd tart at the local tearoom and asked her questions about the concentration camps. Her eyes filled with tears as Amy, who felt obliged to answer, confirmed the stories she had heard but could never quite believe. "Terrible," Miss Giddings said, "so terrible." Amy silently drank her tea and ate her lovely tart, while Miss Giddings, like one of her own history students, tried in vain to understand the past. "Why is it," the unhappy teacher finally asked, "that for centuries people have hated you Jews?" Amy rose to her feet. She was stunned. "Don't ask me that!" the girl said—"ask the madmen who hate us!" And she had nothing further to do with Miss Giddings as a friend—or with anyone else who asked her anything about what they couldn't possibly understand.

One Saturday only a few months after her arrival in England, vowing that if she heard another plaintive "Belsen" out of Uncle Daniel's mouth she would run off to Southampton and stow away on an American ship—and having had about enough of the snooty brand of sympathy the pure-bred English teachers offered at school—she burned her arm while ironing a blouse. The neighbors came running at the sound of her screams and rushed her to the hospital emergency room. When the bandage was removed, there was a patch of purple scar tissue about half the size of an egg instead of her camp number.

After the accident, as her foster parents called it, Uncle Daniel informed the Jewish Welfare Board that his wife's ill health made it impossible for them to continue to have Amy in their home. The foster child moved on to another family—and then another. She told whoever asked that she had been evacuated from Holland with a group of Jewish schoolchildren the week before the Nazis invaded. Sometimes she did not even say that the schoolchildren were Jewish, an omission for which she was mildly rebuked by the Jewish families who had accepted responsibility for her and were troubled by her lying. But she could not bear them all laying their helpful hands upon her shoulders because of Auschwitz and Belsen. If she was going to be thought exceptional, it would not be because of Auschwitz and Belsen but because of what she had made of herself since.

They were kind and thoughtful people, and they tried to get her to understand that she was not in danger in England. "You needn't feel frightened or threatened in any way," they assured her. "Or ashamed of anything." "I'm not ashamed. That's the point." "Well, that isn't always the point when young people try to hide their Jewish origins." "Maybe it isn't with others," she told them, "but it is with me."

On the Saturday after discovering her father's photograph in *Time,* she took the morning bus to Boston, and in every foreign bookstore looked in vain for a copy of *Het Achterhuis.* Two weeks later she traveled the three hours to Boston again, this time to the main post office to rent a box. She paid for it in cash, then mailed the letter she was carrying in her handbag, along with a money order for fifteen dollars, to Contact Publishers in Amsterdam, requesting them to send, postage paid, to Pilgrim International Bookshop, P.O. Box 152, Boston, Mass., U.S.A., as many copies as fifteen dollars would buy of *Het Achterhuis* by Anne Frank.

She had been dead for him some four years; believing her dead for another month or two would not really hurt much more. Curiously she did not hurt more either, except in bed at night when she cried and begged forgiveness for the cruelty she was practicing on her perfect father, now sixty.

Nearly three months after she had sent the order off to her Amsterdam publisher, on a warm, sunny day at the beginning of August, there was a package too large for the Pilgrim Bookshop post-office box waiting to be picked up in Boston. She was wearing a beige linen skirt and a fresh white cotton blouse, both ironed the night before. Her hair, cut in pageboy style that spring, had been washed and set the previous night, and her skin was evenly tanned. She was swimming a mile every morning and playing tennis every afternoon and, all in all, was as fit and energetic as a twenty-year-old could be. Maybe that was why, when the postal clerk handed her the parcel, she did not tear at the string with her teeth or faint straightaway onto the marble floor. Instead, she walked over to the Common—the package mailed from Holland swinging idly from one hand—and wandered along until she found an unoccupied bench. She sat first on a bench in the shade, but then got up and walked on until she found a perfect spot in the sunshine.

After thoroughly studying the Dutch stamps—postwar issues new to her—and contemplating the postmark, she set about to see how carefully she could undo the package. It was a preposterous display of unruffled patience and she meant it to be. She was feeling at once triumphant and giddy. Forbearance, she thought. Patience. Without patience there is no life. When she had finally untied the string and unfolded, without tearing, the layers of thick brown paper, it seemed to her that what she had so meticulously removed from the wrappings and placed onto the lap of her clean and pretty American girl's beige linen skirt was her survival itself.

Van Anne Frank. Her book. Hers.

She had begun keeping a diary less than three weeks before Pim told her that they were going into hiding. Until she ran out of pages and had to carry over onto office ledgers, she made the entries in a cardboard-covered notebook that he'd given her for her thirteenth birthday. She still remembered most of what happened to her in the achterhuis, some of it down to the most minute detail, but of the fifty thousand words recording it all, she couldn't remember writing one. Nor could she remember anything much of what she'd confided there about her personal problems to the phantom confidante she'd named Kitty—whole pages of her tribulations as new and strange to her as her native tongue.

Perhaps because *Het Achterhuis* was the first Dutch book she'd read since she'd written it, her first thought when she finished was of her childhood friends in Amsterdam, the boys and girls from the Montessori school where she'd learned to read and write. She tried to remember the names of the Christian children, who would have survived the war. She tried to recall the names of her teachers, going all the way back to kindergarten. She pictured the faces of the shopkeepers, the postman, the milk deliveryman who had known her as a child. She imagined their neighbors in the houses on Merwedeplein. And when she had, she saw each of them closing her book and thinking, Who realized she was so gifted? Who realized we had such a writer in our midst?

The first passage she reread was dated over a year before the birth of Amy Bellette. The first time round she'd bent back the corner of the page; the second time, with a pen from her purse, she drew a dark meaningful line in the margin and beside it wrote—in English, of course—"uncanny." (Everything she marked she was marking for him, or made the mark actually pretending to be him.) *I have an odd way of sometimes, as it were, being able to see myself through someone else's eyes. Then I view the affairs of a certain "Anne" at my ease, and browse through the pages of her life as if she were a stranger. Before we came here, when I didn't think about things as much as I do now, I used at times to have the feeling that I didn't belong to Mansa, Pim, and Margot, and that I would always be a bit of an outsider. Sometimes I used to pretend I was an orphan . . .*

Then she read the whole thing from the start again, making a small marginal notation—and a small grimace—whenever she came upon anything she was sure he would consider "decorative" or "imprecise" or "unclear." But mostly she marked passages she couldn't believe that she had written as little more than a child. Why, what eloquence, Anne—it gave her gooseflesh, whispering her own name in Boston—what deftness, what wit! How nice, she thought, if I could write like this for Mr. Lonoff's English 12. "It's good," she heard him saying, "it's the best thing you've ever done, Miss Bellette."

But of course it was—she'd had a "great subject," as the girls said in English class. Her family's affinity with what families were suffering everywhere had been clear to her right from the beginning. *There is nothing we can do but wait as calmly as we can till the misery comes to an end. Jews and Christians wait, the whole earth waits; and there are many who wait for death.* But while writing these lines ("Quiet, emphatic feeling—that's the idea. E.I.L.") she had had no grandiose delusions about her little achterhuis diary's ever standing as part of the record of the misery. It wasn't to educate anybody other than herself—out of her great expectations—that she kept track of how trying it all was. Recording it was enduring it; the diary kept her company and it kept her sane, and whenever being her parents' child seemed to her as harrowing as the war itself, it was where she went to confess. Only to Kitty was she able to speak freely about the hopelessness of trying to satisfy her mother the way Margot did; only to Kitty could she openly bewail her inability even to pronounce the word "Mumsie" to her aloud—and to concede the depth of her feeling for Pim, a father she wanted to want her to the exclusion of all others, *not only as his child, but for me—Anne, myself.*

Of course it had eventually to occur to any child so *mad on books and reading* that for all she knew she was writing a book of her own. But most of the time it was her morale that she was sustaining not, at fourteen, literary ambition. As for developing into a writer—she owed that not to any decision to sit down each day and try to be one but to their stifling life. That, of all things, seemed to have nurtured her talent! Truly, without the terror and the claustrophobia of the achterhuis, as a *chatterbox* surrounded by friends and *rollicking with laughter,* free to come and go, free to clown around, free to pursue her every last expectation, would she ever have written sentences so deft and so eloquent and so witty? She thought, Now maybe that's the problem in English 12—not the absence of the great subject but the presence of the lake and the tennis courts and Tanglewood. The perfect tan, the linen skirts, my emerging reputation as the Pallas Athene of Athene College—maybe that's what's doing me in. Maybe if I were locked up again in a room somewhere and fed on rotten potatoes and clothed in rags and terrified out of my wits, maybe then I could write a decent story for Mr. Lonoff!

It was only with the euphoria of *invasion fever,* with the prospect of the Allied landings and the German collapse and the coming of that golden age known around the achterhuis as *after the war,* that she was able to announce to Kitty that the diary had perhaps done more than just assuage her adolescent loneliness. After two years of honing her prose, she felt herself ready for the great undertaking: *my greatest wish is to become a journalist someday and later on a famous writer.* But that was in May of 1944, when to be famous someday seemed to her no more or less extraordinary than to be going back to school in September. Oh, that May of marvelous expectations! Never again another winter in the achterhuis. Another winter and she would have gone crazy.

The first year there it hadn't been that bad; they'd all been so busy settling in that she didn't have time to feel desperate. In fact, so diligently had they all worked to transform the attic into a *superpractical* home that her father had gotten everybody to agree to subdivide the space still further and take in another Jew. But once the Allied bombing started, the superpractical home became her torture chamber. During the day the two families squabbled over everything, and then at night she couldn't sleep, sure that the Gestapo was going to come in the dark to take them away. In bed she began to have horrifying visions of Lies, her schoolfriend, reproaching her for being safe in bed in Amsterdam and not in a concentration camp, like all her Jewish friends: *"Oh, Anne, why have you deserted me? Help, oh, help me, rescue me from this hell!"* She would see herself *in a dungeon, without Mummy and Daddy*—and worse. Right down to the final hours of 1943 she was dreaming and thinking *the most terrible things.* But then all at once it was over. Miraculously. "And what did it, Professor Lonoff? See *Anna Karenina.* See *Madame Bovary.* See half the literature of the Western world." The miracle: desire. She would be back to school in September, but she would not be returning to class the same girl. She was no longer a girl. Tears would roll down her cheeks at the thought of a naked woman. Her unpleasant menstrual periods became a source of the strangest pleasure. At night in bed she was excited by her breasts. Just these sensations—but all at once forebodings of her miserable death were replaced with a craze for life. One day she was completely recovered, and the next she was, of course, in love. Their troubles had made her her own woman, at fourteen. She began going off on private visits to the secluded corner of the topmost floor, which was occupied exclusively by Peter, the Van Daans' seventeen-year-old son. That she might be stealing him away from Margot didn't stop her, and neither did her scandalized parents: first just teatime visits, then evening assignations—then the defiant letter to the disappointed father. On May 3rd of that marvelous May: *I am young and I possess many buried qualities; I am young and strong and am living a great adventure.* And two days later, to the father who had saved her from the hell that had swallowed up Lies, to the Pim whose favorite living creature she had always longed to be, a declaration of her independence, *in mind and body,* as she bluntly put it: *I have now reached the stage that I can live entirely on my own, without Mummy's support or anyone else's for that matter . . . I don't feel in the least bit responsible to any of you . . . I don't have to give an account of my deeds to anyone but myself . . .*

Well, the strength of a woman on her own wasn't all she'd imagined it to be. Neither was the strength of a loving father. He told her it was the most unpleasant letter he'd ever received, and when she began to cry with shame for having been *too low for words,* he wept along with her. He burned the letter in the fire, the weeks passed, and she found herself growing disenchanted with Peter. In fact, by July she was wondering how it would be possible, in their circumstances, to *shake him off,* a problem resolved for her on a sunny August Friday, when in the middle of the morning, as Pim was helping Peter with his English lessons and she was off studying by herself, the Dutch Green Police arrived and dissolved forever the secret household still heedful of propriety, obedience, discretion, self-improvement, and mutual respect. The Franks, as a family, came to an end, and, fittingly enough, thought the diarist, so did her chronicle of their effort to go sensibly on as themselves, in spite of everything.

The third time she read the book through was on the way back to Stockbridge that evening. Would she ever read another book again? How, if she couldn't put this one down? On the bus she began to speculate in the most immodest way about what she had written—had "wrought." Perhaps what got her going was the rumbling, boundless, electrified, indigo sky that had been stalking the bus down the highway since Boston: outside the window the most outlandish El Greco stage effects, outside a Biblical thunderstorm complete with baroque trimmings, and inside Amy curled up with her book—and with the lingering sense of tragic grandeur she'd soaked up from the real El Grecos that afternoon in the Boston Museum of Fine Arts. And she was exhausted, which probably doesn't hurt fantastical thinking, either. Still spellbound by her first two readings of *Het Achterhuis,* she had rushed on to the Gardner and the Fogg, where, to top off the day, the self-intoxicated girl with the deep tan and the animated walk had been followed by easily a dozen Harvard Summer School students eager to learn her name. Three museums because back at Athene she preferred to tell everyone the truth, more or less, about the big day in Boston. To Mr. Lonoff she planned to speak at length about all the new exhibitions she'd gone to see at his wife's suggestion.

The storm, the paintings, her exhaustion—none of it was really necessary, however, to inspire the sort of expectations that resulted from reading her published diary three times through in the same day. Towering egotism would probably have been sufficient. Perhaps she was only a very young writer on a bus dreaming a very young writer's dreams.

All her reasoning, all her fantastical thinking about the ordained mission of her book followed from this: neither she nor her parents came through in the diary as anything like representative of religious or observant Jews. Her mother lit candles on Friday night and that was about the extent of it. As for celebrations, she had found St. Nicholas's Day, once she'd been introduced to it in hiding, much more fun than Chanukah, and along with Pim made all kinds of clever gifts and even written a Santa Claus poem to enliven the festivities. When Pim settled upon a children's Bible as her present for the holiday—so she might learn something about the New Testament—Margot hadn't approved. Margot's ambition was to be a midwife in Palestine. She was the only one of them who seemed to have given serious thought to religion. The diary that Margot kept, had it ever been found, would not have been quite so sparing as hers in curiosity about Judaism, or plans for leading a Jewish life. Certainly it was impossible for her to imagine Margot thinking, let alone writing with longing in her diary, *the time will come when we are people again, and not just Jews.*

She had written these words, to be sure, still suffering the aftereffects of a nighttime burglary in the downstairs warehouse. The burglary had seemed certain to precipitate their discovery by the police, and for days afterward everyone was weak with terror. And for her, along with the residue of fear and the dubious sense of relief, there was, of course, the guilt-tinged bafflement when she realized that, unlike Lies, she had again been spared. In the aftermath of that gruesome night, she went around and around trying to understand the meaning of their persecution, one moment writing about the misery of being Jews and only Jews to their enemies, and then in the next airily wondering if *it might even be our religion from which the world and all peoples learn good. . . . We can never become just Netherlanders,* she reminded Kitty, *we will always remain Jews, but we want to, too*—only to close out the argument with an announcement one most assuredly would not have come upon in "The Diary of Margot Frank": *I've been saved again, now my first wish after the war is that I may become Dutch! I love the Dutch, I love this country, I love the language and want to work here. And even if I have to write to the Queen myself, I will not give up until I have reached my goal.*

No, that wasn't mother's Margot talking, that was father's Anne. To London to learn English, to Paris to look at clothes and study art, to Hollywood, California, to interview the stars as someone named "Anne Franklin"—while self-sacrificing Margot delivered babies in the desert. To be truthful, while Margot was thinking about God and the homeland, the only deities she ever seemed to contemplate at any length were to be found in the mythology of Greece and Rome, which she studied all the time in hiding, and adored. To be truthful, the young girl of her diary was, compared to Margot, only dimly Jewish, though in that entirely the daughter of the father who calmed her fears by reading aloud to her at night not the Bible but Goethe in German and Dickens in English.

But that was the point—that was what gave her diary the power to make the nightmare real. To expect the great callous and indifferent world to care about the child of a pious, bearded father living under the sway of the rabbis and the rituals—that was pure folly. To the ordinary person with no great gift for tolerating even the smallest of differences the plight of that family wouldn't mean a thing. To ordinary people it probably would seem that they had invited disaster by stubbornly repudiating everything modern and European—not to say Christian. But the family of Otto Frank, that would be another matter! How could even the most obtuse of the ordinary ignore what had been done to the Jews *just for being Jews,* how could even the most benighted of the Gentiles fail to get the idea when they read in *Het Achterhuis* that once a year the Franks sang a harmless Chanukah song, said some Hebrew words, lighted some candles, exchanged some presents—a ceremony lasting about ten minutes—and that was all it took to make them the enemy. It did not even take that much. It took nothing—that was the horror. And that was the truth. And that was the power of her book. The Franks could gather together by the radio to listen to concerts of Mozart, Brahms, and Beethoven; they could entertain themselves with Goethe and Dickens and Schiller; she could look night after night through the genealogical tables of all of Europe's royal families for suitable mates for Princess Elizabeth and Princess Margaret Rose; she could write passionately in her diary of her love for Queen Wilhelmina and her desire for Holland to be her fatherland—and none of it made any difference. Europe was not theirs nor were they Europe's, not even her Europeanized family. Instead, three flights up from a pretty Amsterdam canal, they lived crammed into a hundred square feet with the Van Daans, as isolated and despised as any ghetto Jews. First expulsion, next confinement, and then, in cattle cars and camps and ovens, obliteration. And why? Because the Jewish problem to be solved, the degenerates whose contamination civilized people could no longer abide, were they themselves, Otto and Edith Frank, and their daughters, Margot and Anne.

This was the lesson that on the journey home she came to believe she had the power to teach. But only if she were believed to be dead. Were *Het Achterhuis* known to be the work of a living writer, it would never be more than it was: a young teenager's diary of her trying years in hiding during the German occupation of Holland, something boys and girls could read in bed at night along with the adventures of the Swiss Family Robinson. But dead she had something more to offer than amusement for ages 10–15; dead she had written, without meaning to or trying to, a book with the force of a masterpiece to make people finally see.

And when people had finally seen? When they had learned what she had the power to teach them, what then? Would suffering come to mean something new to them? Could she actually make them humane creatures for any longer than the few hours it would take to read her diary through? In her room at Athene—after hiding in her dresser the three copies of *Het Achterhuis*—she thought more calmly about her readers-to-be than she had while pretending to be one of them on the stirring bus ride through the lightning storm. She was not, after all, the fifteen-year-old who could, while hiding from a holocaust, tell Kitty, *I still believe that people are really good at heart.* Her youthful ideals had suffered no less than she had in the windowless freight car from Westerbork and in the barracks at Auschwitz and on the Belsen heath. She had not come to hate the human race for what it was—what could it be but what it was?—but she did not feel seemly any more singing its praises.

What would happen when people had finally seen? The only realistic answer was Nothing. To believe anything else was only to yield to longings which even she, the great longer, had a right to question by now. To keep her existence a secret from her father so as to help improve mankind . . . no, not at this late date. The improvement of the living was their business, not hers; they could improve themselves, if they should ever be so disposed; and if not, not. Her responsibility was to the dead, if to anyone—to her sister, to her mother, to all the slaughtered schoolchildren who had been her friends. There was her diary's purpose, there was her ordained mission: to restore in print their status as flesh and blood . . . for all the good that would do them. An ax was what she really wanted, not print. On the stairwell at the end of her corridor in the dormitory there was a large ax with an enormous red handle, to be used in case of fire. But what about in case of hatred—what about murderous rage? She stared at it often enough, but never found the nerve to take it down from the wall. Besides, once she had it in her hands, whose head would she split open? Whom could she kill in Stockbridge to avenge the ashes and the skulls? If she even could wield it. No, what she had been given to wield was *Het Achterhuis, van Anne Frank.* And to draw blood with it she would have to vanish again into another achterhuis, this time fatherless and all on her own.

So she renewed her belief in the power of her less than three hundred pages, and with it the resolve to keep from her father, sixty, the secret of her survival. "For them," she cried, "for them," meaning all who had met the fate that she had been spared and was now pretending to. "For Margot, for my mother, for Lies."

Now every day she went to the library to read *The New York Times.* Each week she read carefully through the newsmagazines. On Sundays she read about all the new books being published in America: novels said to be "notable" and "significant," none of which could possibly be more notable and more significant than her posthumously published diary; insipid best-sellers from which real people learned about fake people who could not exist and would not matter if they did. She read praise for historians and biographers whose books, whatever their merit, couldn't possibly be as worthy of recognition as hers. And in every column in every periodical she found in the library—American, French, German, English—she looked for her own real name. It could not end with just a few thousand Dutch readers shaking their heads and going about their business—it was too important for that! "For them, for them"—over and over, week after week, "for them"—until at last she began to wonder if having survived in the achterhuis, if having outlived the death camps, if masquerading here in New England as somebody other than herself did not make something very suspect—and a little mad—of this seething passion to "come back" as the avenging ghost. She began to fear that she was succumbing to having not succumbed.

And why should she! Who was she pretending to be but who she would have been anyway if no achterhuis and no death camps had intervened? Amy was not somebody else. The Amy who had rescued her from her memories and restored her to life—beguiling, commonsensical, brave, and realistic Amy—was herself. Who she had every right to be! Responsibility to the dead? Rhetoric for the pious! There was nothing to give the dead—they were dead. "Exactly. The importance, so-called, of this book is a morbid illusion. And playing dead is melodramatic and disgusting. And hiding from Daddy is worse. No atonement is required," said Amy to Anne. "Just get on the phone and tell Pim you're alive. He is sixty."

Her longing for him now exceeded even what it had been in childhood, when she wanted more than anything to be his only love. But she was young and strong and she was living a great adventure, and she did nothing to inform him or anyone that she was still alive; and then one day it was just too late. No one would have believed her; no one other than her father would have wanted to. Now people came every day to visit their secret hideaway and to look at the photographs of the movie stars that she'd pinned to the wall beside her bed. They came to see the tub she had bathed in and the table where she'd studied. They looked out of the loft window where Peter and she had cuddled together watching the stars. They stared at the cupboard camouflaging the door the police had come through to take them away. They looked at the open pages of her secret diary. That was her handwriting, they whispered, those are her words. They stayed to look at everything in the achterhuis that she had ever touched. The plain passageways and serviceable little rooms that she had, like a good composition student, dutifully laid out for Kitty in orderly, accurate, workaday Dutch—the superpractical achterhuis was now a holy shrine, a Wailing Wall. They went away from it in silence, as bereft as though she had been their own.

But it was they who were hers. "They wept for me," said Amy; "they pitied me; they prayed for me; they begged my forgiveness. I was the incarnation of the millions of unlived years robbed from the murdered Jews. It was too late to be alive now. I was a saint."

That was her story. And what did Lonoff think of it when she was finished? That she meant every word and that not a word was true.

After Amy had showered and dressed, she checked out of the hotel and he took her to eat some lunch. He phoned Hope from the restaurant and explained that he was bringing Amy home. She could walk in the woods, look at the foliage, sleep safely in Becky's bed; over a few days' time she would be able to collect herself, and then she could return to Cambridge. All he explained about her collapse was that she appeared to him to be suffering from exhaustion. He had promised Amy that he would say no more.

On the ride back to the Berkshires, while Amy told him what it had been like for her during the years when she was being read in twenty different languages by twenty million people, he made plans to consult Dr. Boyce. Boyce was at Riggs, the Stockbridge psychiatric hospital. Whenever a new book appeared, Dr. Boyce would send a charming note asking the author if he would kindly sign the doctor's copy, and once a year the Lonoffs were invited to the Boyces' big barbecue. At Dr. Boyce's request, Lonoff once reluctantly consented to meet with a staff study group from the hospital to discuss "the creative personality." He didn't want to offend the psychiatrist, and it might for a while pacify his wife, who liked to believe that if he got out and mixed more with people things would be better at home.

The study group turned out to have ideas about writing that were too imaginative for his taste, but he made no effort to tell them they were wrong. Nor did he think that he was necessarily right. They saw it their way, he saw it like Lonoff. Period. He had no desire to change anyone's mind. Fiction made people say all kinds of strange things—so be it.

The meeting with the psychiatrists had been underway for only an hour when Lonoff said it had been an enjoyable evening but he had to be getting home. "I have the evening's reading still ahead of me. Without my reading I'm not myself. However, you must feel free to talk about my personality when I'm gone." Boyce, smiling warmly, replied, "I hope we've amused you at least a little with our naïve speculations." "I would have liked to amuse *you*. I apologize for being boring." "No, no," said Boyce, "passivity in a man of stature has a charm and mystery all its own." "Yes?" said Lonoff. "I must tell my wife."

But an hour wasted some five years ago was hardly to the point. He trusted Boyce and knew that the psychiatrist would not betray his confidence when he went the next day to talk with him about his former student and quasi daughter, a young woman of twenty-six, who had disclosed to him that of all the Jewish writers, from Franz Kafka to E. I. Lonoff, she was the most famous. As for his own betrayal of the quasi daughter's confidence, it did not count for much as Amy elaborated further upon her consuming delusion.

"Do you know why I took this sweet name? It wasn't to protect me from my memories. I wasn't hiding the past from myself or myself from the past. I was hiding from hatred, from hating people the way people hate spiders and rats. Manny, I felt flayed. I felt as though the skin had been peeled away from half my body. Half my face had been peeled away, and everybody would stare in horror for the rest of my life. Or they would stare at the other half, at the half still intact; I could see them smiling, pretending that the flayed half wasn't there, and talking to the half that was. And I could hear myself screaming at them, I could see myself thrusting my hideous side right up into their unmarred faces to make them properly horrified. 'I was pretty! I was whole! I was a sunny, lively little girl! Look, look at what they did to me!' But whatever side they looked at, I would always be screaming, 'Look at the other! Why don't you look at the other!' That's what I thought about in the hospital at night. However they look at me, however they talk to me, however they try to comfort me, I will always be this half-flayed thing. I will never be young, I will never be kind or at peace or in love, and I will hate them all my life.

"So I took the sweet name—to impersonate everything that I wasn't. And a very good pretender I was, too. After a while I could imagine that I wasn't pretending at all, that I had become what I would have been anyway. Until the book. The package came from Amsterdam, I opened it, and there it was: my past, myself, my name, *my face intact*—and all I wanted was revenge. It wasn't for the dead—it had nothing to do with bringing back the dead or scourging the living. It wasn't corpses I was avenging—it was the motherless, fatherless, sisterless, venge-filled, hate-filled, shame-filled, half-flayed, seething thing. It was myself. I wanted tears, I wanted their Christian tears to run like Jewish blood, for me. I wanted their pity—and in the most pitiless way. And I wanted love, to be loved mercilessly and endlessly, just the way I'd been debased. I wanted my fresh life and my fresh body, cleansed and unpolluted. And it needed twenty million people for that. Twenty million ten times over.

"Oh, Manny, I want to live with you! That's what I need! The millions won't do it—it's you! I want to go home to Europe with you. Listen to me, don't say no, not yet. This summer I saw a small house for rent, a stone villa up on a hillside. It was outside Florence. It had a pink tile roof and a garden. I got the phone number and I wrote it down. I still have it. Oh, everything beautiful that I saw in Italy made me think of how happy you could be there—how happy I would be there, looking after you. I thought of the trips we'd take. I thought of the afternoons in the museums and having coffee later by the river. I thought of listening to music together at night. I thought of making your meals. I thought of wearing lovely nightgowns to bed. Oh, Manny, their Anne Frank is theirs; I want to be *your* Anne Frank. I'd like at last to be my own. Child Martyr and Holy Saint isn't a position I'm really qualified for any more. They wouldn't even have me, not as I am, longing for somebody else's husband, begging him to leave his loyal wife to run off with a girl half his age. Manny, does it matter that I'm your daughter's age and you're my father's? Of course I love the Dad-da in you, how could I not? And if you love the child in me, why shouldn't you? There's nothing strange in that—so does half the world. Love has to start somewhere, and that's where it starts in us. And as for who I am—well," said Amy, in a voice as sweet and winning as any he'd ever heard, "you've got to be somebody, don't you? There's no way around that."

At home they put her to bed. In the kitchen Lonoff sat with his wife drinking the coffee she'd made him. Every time he pictured Amy at the dentist's office reading about Otto Frank in *Time* magazine, or in the library stacks searching for her "real" name, every time he imagined her on Boston Common addressing to her writing teacher an intimate disquisition on "her" book, he wanted to let go and cry. He had never suffered so over the suffering of another human being.

Of course he told Hope nothing about who Amy thought she was. But he didn't have to, he could guess what she would say if he did: it was for him, the great writer, that Amy had chosen to become Anne Frank; that explained it all, no psychiatrist required. For him, as a consequence of her infatuation: to enchant him, to bewitch him, to break through the scrupulosity and the wisdom and the virtue into his imagination, and there, as Anne Frank, to become E. I. Lonoff's *femme fatale.*

1979

LESLIE MARMON SILKO
b. 1948

Born in Albuquerque, New Mexico, Leslie Marmon Silko believes that her work was shaped by her environment and her race. "I grew up in Laguna Pueblo," she wrote in 1974. "I am of mixed-breed ancestory, but what I know is Laguna. The place I am from is everything I am as a writer and human being." Her books include *Ceremony*

(1977), *Storyteller* (1981), and *Almanac of the Dead* (1991). She has received a MacArthur Fellowship.

The following is excerpted from *Ceremony*, a novel that blends poetry and prose. In a 1986 interview with Kim Barnes in the *Journal of Ethnic Studies*, Silko noted that "in *Ceremony* the breaks would be the parts that ideally you would rather hear than read. . . . In some ways, I feel that it's more valid to have a checklist or a discussion of what constitutes tragedy or comedy than what constitutes poetry or prose. . . . What I'm interested in is getting a feeling or an idea that's part of the story. Getting the story across. And I'm not particular how it's done. The important thing is that it goes across in a way that I want it to go."

From Ceremony

Ts'its'tsi'nako, Thought-Woman,
is sitting in her room
and whatever she thinks about
appears.

She thought of her sisters,
Nau'ts'ity'i and I'tcts'ity'i,
and together they created the Universe
this world
and the four worlds below.

Thought-Woman, the spider,
named things and
as she named them
they appeared.

She is sitting in her room
thinking of a story now

I'm telling you the story
she is thinking.

Ceremony

I will tell you something about stories,
[he said]
They aren't just entertainment.
Don't be fooled.
They are all we have, you see,
all we have to fight off
illness and death.

You don't have anything
if you don't have the stories.

Their evil is mighty
but it can't stand up to our stories.
So they try to destroy the stories
let the stories be confused or forgotten.
They would like that
They would be happy
Because we would be defenseless then.

He rubbed his belly.
I keep them here
[he said]
Here, put your hand on it
See, it is moving.
There is life here
for the people.

And in the belly of this story
the rituals and the ceremony
are still growing.

What She Said:

The only cure
I know
is a good ceremony,
that's what she said.

Sunrise.

Tayo didn't sleep well that night. He tossed in the old iron bed, and the coiled springs kept squeaking even after he lay still again, calling up humid dreams of black night and loud voices rolling him over and over again like debris caught in a flood. Tonight the singing had come first, squeaking out of the iron bed, a man singing in Spanish, the melody of a familiar love song, two words again and again, "*Y volveré.*" Sometimes the Japanese voices came first, angry and loud, pushing the song far away, and then he could hear the shift in his dreaming, like a slight afternoon wind changing its direction, coming less and less from the south, moving into the west, and the voices would become Laguna voices, and he could hear Uncle Josiah calling to him, Josiah bringing him the fever medicine when he had been sick a long time ago. But before Josiah could come, the fever voices would drift and whirl and emerge again—Japanese soldiers shouting orders to him, suffocating damp voices that drifted out in the jungle steam, and he heard the women's voices then; they faded in and out until he was frantic because he thought the Laguna words were his mother's, but when he was about to make out the meaning of the words, the voice suddenly broke into a language he could not understand; and it was then that all the voices were drowned by the music—loud, loud music from a big juke box, its flashing red and blue lights pulling the darkness closer.

He lay there early in the morning and watched the high small window above the bed; dark gray gradually became lighter until it cast a white square on the opposite wall at dawn. He watched the room grow brighter then, as the square of light grew steadily warmer, more yellow with the climbing sun. He had not been able to sleep for a long time—for as long as all things had become tied together like colts in single file when he and Josiah had taken them to the mountain, with the halter rope of one colt tied to the tail of the colt ahead of it, and the lead colt's rope tied to the wide horn on Josiah's Mexican saddle. He could still see them now—the creamy sorrel, the bright red bay, and the gray roan—their slick summer coats reflecting the sunlight as it came up from behind the yellow mesas, shining on them, strung out behind Josiah's horse like an old-time pack train. He could get no rest as long as the memories were tangled with the present, tangled up like colored threads from old Grandma's wicker sewing basket when he was a child, and he had carried them outside to play and they had spilled out of his arms into the summer weeds and rolled away in all directions, and then he had hurried to pick them up before Auntie found him. He could feel it inside his skull—the tension of little threads being pulled and how it was with tangled things, things tied together, and as he tried to pull them apart and rewind them into their places, they snagged and tangled even more. So Tayo had to sweat through those nights when thoughts became entangled; he had to sweat to think of something that wasn't unraveled or tied in knots to the past—something that existed by itself, standing alone like a deer. And if he could hold that image of the deer in his mind long enough, his stomach might shiver less and let him sleep for a while. It worked as long as the deer was alone, as long as he could keep it a gray buck on an unrecognized hill; but if he did not hold it tight, it would spin away from him and become the deer he and Rocky had hunted. That memory would unwind into the last day when they had sat together, oiling their rifles in the jungle of some nameless Pacific island. While they used up the last of the oil in Rocky's pack, they talked about the deer that Rocky had hunted, and the corporal next to them shook his head, and kept saying he had dreamed the Japs would get them that day.

The humid air turned into sweat that had run down the corporal's face while he repeated his dream to them. That was the first time Tayo had realized that the man's skin was not much different from his own. The skin. He saw the skin of the corpses again and again, in ditches on either side of the long muddy road—skin that was stretched shiny and dark over bloated hands; even white men were darker after death. There was no difference when they were swollen and covered with flies. That had become the worst thing for Tayo: they looked too familiar even when they were alive. When the sergeant told them to kill all the Japanese soldiers lined up in front of the cave with their hands on their heads, Tayo could not pull the trigger. The fever made him shiver, and the sweat was stinging his eyes and he couldn't see clearly; in that instant he saw Josiah standing there; the face was dark from the sun, and the eyes were squinting as though he were about to smile at Tayo. So Tayo stood there, stiff with nausea, while they fired at the soldiers, and he watched his uncle fall, and he *knew* it was Josiah; and even after Rocky started shaking him by the shoulders and telling him to stop crying, it was *still* Josiah lying there. They forced medicine into Tayo's mouth, and Rocky pushed him toward the corpses and told him to look, look past the blood that was already dark like the jungle mud, with only flecks of bright red still shimmering in it. Rocky made him look at the corpse and said, "Tayo, this is a *Jap!* This is a *Jap* uniform!" And then he rolled the body over with his boot and said, "Look, Tayo, look at the face," and that was when Tayo started screaming because it wasn't a Jap, it was Josiah, eyes shrinking back into the skull and all their shining black light glazed over by death.

The sergeant had called for a medic and somebody rolled up Tayo's sleeve; they told him to sleep, and the next day they all acted as though nothing had happened. They called it battle fatigue, and they said hallucinations were common with malarial fever.

Rocky had reasoned it out with him; it was impossible for the dead man to be Josiah, because Josiah was an old Laguna man, thousands of miles from the Philippine jungles and Japanese armies. "He's probably up on some mesa right now, chopping wood," Rocky said. He smiled and shook Tayo's shoulders. "Hey, I know you're homesick. But, Tayo, we're *supposed* to be here. This is what we're supposed to do."

Tayo nodded, slapped at the insects mechanically and staring straight ahead, past the smothering dampness of the green jungle leaves. He examined the facts and logic again and again, the way Rocky had explained it to him; the facts made what he had seen an impossibility. He felt the shivering then; it began at the tips of his fingers and pulsed into his arms. He shivered because all the facts, all the reasons made no difference any more; he could hear Rocky's words, and he could follow the logic of what Rocky said, but he could not feel anything except a swelling in his belly, a great swollen grief that was pushing into his throat.

He had to keep busy; he had to keep moving so that the sinews connected behind his eyes did not slip loose and spin his eyes to the interior of his skull where the scenes waited for him. He got out of the bed quickly while he could still see the square of yellow sunshine on the wall opposite the bed, and he pulled on his jeans and the scuffed brown boots he had worn before the war, and the red plaid western shirt old Grandma gave him the day he had come home after the war.

The air outside was still cool; it smelled like night dampness, faintly of rain. He washed his face in the steel-cold water of the iron trough by the windmill. The yellow striped cat purred and wrapped herself around his legs while he combed his hair. She ran ahead of him to the goat pen and shoved her head under his left arm when he knelt down to milk the black goat. He poured milk for her in the lid of an old enamel coffeepot, and then he opened the pen and let them run, greedy for the tender green shoots of tumbleweeds pushing through the sand. The kid was almost too big to nurse any more, and it knelt by the doe and hunched down to reach the tits, butting her to make the milk come faster, wiggling its tail violently until the nanny jumped away and turned on the kid, butting it away from her. The process of weaning had gone on like this for weeks, but the nanny was more intent on weeds than the lesson, and when Tayo left them, the kid goat was back at the tits, a little more careful this time.

The sun was climbing then, and it looked small in that empty morning sky. He knew he should eat, but he wasn't hungry any more. He sat down in the kitchen, at the small square table with the remains of a white candle melted to a nub on the lid of a coffee can; he wondered how long the candle had been there, he wondered if Josiah had been the one to light it last. He thought he would cry then, thinking of Josiah and how he had been here and touched all these things, sat in this chair. So he jerked his head away from the candle, and looked at the soot around the base of the coffeepot. He wouldn't waste firewood to heat up yesterday's coffee or maybe it was day-before-yesterday's coffee. He had lost track of the days there.

The drought years had returned again, as they had after the First World War and in the twenties, when he was a child and they had to haul water to the sheep in big wooden barrels in the old wagon. The windmill near the sheep camp had gone dry, so the gray mules pulled the wagon from the springs, moving slowly so that the water would not splash over the rims. He sat close to his uncle then, on the wagon seat, above the bony gray rumps of the mules. After they had dumped water for the sheep, they went to burn the spines from the cholla and prickly pear. They stood back by the wagon and watched the cows walk up to the cactus cautiously, sneezing at the smoldering ashes. The cows were patient while the scorched green pulp cooled, and then they brought out their wide spotted tongues and ate those strange remains because the hills were barren those years and only the cactus could grow.

Now there was no wagon or wooden barrels. One of the gray mules had eaten a poison weed near Acoma, and the other one was blind; it stayed close to the windmill at the ranch, grazing on the yellow rice grass that grew in the blow sand. It walked a skinny trail, winding in blind circles from the grass to the water trough, where it dipped its mouth in the water and let the water dribble out again, rinsing its mouth four or five times a day to make sure the water was still there. The dry air shrank the wooden staves of the barrels; they pulled loose, and now the rusty steel hoops were scattered on the ground behind the corral in the crazy patterns of some flashy Kiowa hoop dancer at the Gallup Ceremonials, throwing his hoops along the ground where he would hook and flip them into the air again and they would skim over his head and shoulders down to his dancing feet, like magic. Tayo stepped inside one that was half buried in the reddish blow sand; he hooked an edge with the toe of his boot, and then he let it slip into the sand again.

The wind had blown since late February and it did not stop after April. They said it had been that way for the past six years while he was gone. And all this time they had watched the sky expectantly for the rainclouds to come. Now it was late May, and when Tayo went to the outhouse he left the door open wide, facing the dry empty hills and the light blue sky. He watched the sky over the distant Black Mountains the way Josiah had many years before, because sometimes when the rain finally came, it was from the southwest.

Jungle rain had no beginning or end; it grew like foliage from the sky, branching and arching to the earth, sometimes in solid thickets entangling the islands, and, other times, in tendrils of blue mist curling out of coastal clouds. The jungle breathed an eternal green that fevered men until they dripped sweat the way rubbery jungle leaves dripped the monsoon rain. It was there that Tayo began to understand what Josiah had said. Nothing was all good or all bad either; it all depended. Jungle rain lay suspended in the air, choking their lungs as they marched; it soaked into their boots until the skin on their toes peeled away dead and wounds turned green. This was not the rain he and Josiah had prayed for, this was not the green foliage they sought out in sandy canyons as a sign of a spring. When Tayo prayed on the long muddy road to the prison camp, it was for dry air, dry as a hundred years squeezed out of yellow sand, air to dry out the oozing wounds of Rocky's leg, to let the torn flesh and broken bones breathe, to clear the sweat that filled Rocky's eyes. It was that rain which filled the tire ruts and made the mud so deep that the corporal began to slip and fall with his end of the muddy blanket that held Rocky. Tayo hated this unending rain as if it were the jungle green rain and not the miles of marching or the Japanese grenade that was killing Rocky. He would blame the rain if the Japs saw how the corporal staggered; if they saw how weak Rocky had become, and came to crush his head with the butt of a rifle, then it would be the rain and the green all around that killed him.

Tayo talked to the corporal almost incessantly, walking behind him with his end of the blanket stretcher, telling him that it wasn't much farther now, and all down hill from there. He made a story for all of them, a story to give them strength. The words of the story poured out of his mouth as if they had substance, pebbles and stone extending to hold the corporal up, to keep his knees from buckling, to keep his hands from letting go of the blanket.

The sound of the rain got louder, pounding on the leaves, splashing into the ruts; it splattered on his head, and the sound echoed inside his skull. It streamed down his face and neck like jungle flies with crawling feet. He wanted to turn loose the blanket to wipe the rain away; he wanted to let go for only a moment. But as long as the corporal was still standing, still moving, they had to keep going. Then from somewhere, within the sound of the rain falling, he could hear it approaching like a summer flash flood, the rumble still faint and distant, floodwater boiling down a narrow canyon. He could smell the foaming flood water, stagnant and ripe with the rotting debris it carried past each village, sucking up their sewage, their waste, the dead animals. He tried to hold it back, but the wind swept down from the green coastal mountains, whipping the rain into gray waves that blinded him. The corporal fell, jerking the ends of the blanket from his hands, and he felt Rocky's foot brush past his own leg. He slid to his knees, trying to find the ends of the blanket again, and he started repeating "Goddamn, goddamn!"; it flooded out of the last warm core in his chest and echoed inside his head. He damned the rain until the words were a chant, and he sang it while he crawled through the mud to find the corporal and get him up before the Japanese saw them. He wanted the words to make a cloudless blue sky, pale with a summer sun pressing across wide and empty horizons. The words gathered inside him and gave him strength. He pulled on the corporal's arm; he lifted him to his knees and all the time he could hear his own voice praying against the rain.

It was summertime
and Iktoa'ak'o'ya–Reed Woman
was always taking a bath.
She spent all day long
sitting in the river
splashing down
the summer rain.

But her sister
Corn Woman
worked hard all day
sweating in the sun
getting sore hands
in the corn field.
Corn Woman got tired of that
she got angry
she scolded
her sister
for bathing all day long.

Iktoa'ak'o'ya–Reed Woman
went away then
she went back
to the original place
down below.

And there was no more rain then.
Everything dried up
all the plants
the corn
the beans
they all dried up
and started blowing away
in the wind.

The people and the animals
were thirsty.
They were starving.

So he had prayed the rain away, and for the sixth year it was dry; the grass turned yellow and it did not grow. Wherever he looked, Tayo could see the consequences of his praying; the gray mule grew gaunt, and the goat and kid had to wander farther and farther each day to find weeds or dry shrubs to eat. In the evenings they waited for him, chewing their cuds by the shed door, and the mule stood by the gate with blind marble eyes. He threw them a little dusty hay and sprinkled some cracked corn over it. The nanny crowded the kid away from the corn. The mule whinnied and leaned against the sagging gate; Tayo reached into the coffee can and he held some corn under the quivering lips. When the corn was gone, the mule licked for the salt taste on his hand; the tongue was rough and wet, but it was also warm and precise across his fingers. Tayo looked at the long white hairs growing out of the lips like antennas, and he got the choking in his throat again, and he cried for all of them, and for what he had done.

For a long time he had been white smoke. He did not realize that until he left the hospital, because white smoke had no consciousness of itself. It faded into the white world of their bed sheets and walls; it was sucked away by the words of doctors who tried to talk to the invisible scattered smoke. He had seen outlines of gray steel tables, outlines of the food they pushed into his mouth, which was only an outline too, like all the outlines he saw. They saw his outline but they did not realize it was hollow inside. He walked down floors that smelled of old wax and disinfectant, watching the outlines of his feet; as he walked, the days and seasons disappeared into a twilight at the corner of his eyes, a twilight he could catch only with a sudden motion, jerking his head to one side for a glimpse of green leaves pressed against the bars on the window. He inhabited a gray winter fog on a distant elk mountain where hunters are lost indefinitely and their own bones mark the boundaries.

He stood outside the train depot in Los Angeles and felt the sunshine; he saw palm trees, the edges of their branches turning yellow, dead gray fronds scaling off, scattered over the ground, and at that moment his body had density again and the world was visible and he realized why he was there and he remembered Rocky and he started to cry. The red Spanish tile on the depot roof got blurry, but he did not move or wipe away the tears, because it had been a long time since he had cried for anyone. The smoke had been dense; visions and memories of the past did not penetrate there, and he had drifted in colors of smoke, where there was no pain, only pale, pale gray of the north wall by his bed. Their medicine drained memory out of his thin arms and replaced it with a twilight cloud behind his eyes. It was not possible to cry on the remote and foggy mountain. If they had not dressed him and led him to the car, he would still be there, drifting along the north wall, invisible in the gray twilight.

The new doctor asked him if he had ever been visible, and Tayo spoke to him softly and said that he was sorry but nobody was allowed to speak to an invisible one. But the new doctor persisted; he came each day, and his questions dissolved the edges of the fog, and his voice sounded louder every time he came. The sun was dissolving the fog, and one day Tayo heard a voice answering the doctor. The voice was saying, "He can't talk to you. He is invisible. His words are formed with an invisible tongue, they have no sound."

He reached into his mouth and felt his own tongue; it was dry and dead, the carcass of a tiny rodent.

"It is easy to remain invisible here, isn't it, Tayo?"

"It was, until you came. It was all white, all the color of the smoke, the fog."

"I am sending you home, Tayo; tomorrow you'll go on the train."

"He can't go. He cries all the time. Sometimes he vomits when he cries."

"Why does he cry, Tayo?"

"He cries because they are dead and everything is dying."

He could see the doctor clearly then, the dark thick hair growing on the backs of the doctor's hands as they reached out at him.

"Go ahead, Tayo, you can cry."

He wanted to scream at the doctor then, but the words choked him and he coughed up his own tears and tasted their salt in his mouth. He smelled the disinfectant then, the urine and the vomit, and he gagged. He raised his head from the sink in the corner of the room; he gripped both sides and he looked up at the doctor.

"Goddamn you," he said softly, "look what you have done."

There was a cardboard name tag on the handle of the suitcase he carried; he could feel it with the tips of his fingers. His name was on the tag and his serial number too. It had been a long time since he had thought about having a name.

The man at the ticket window told him it would be twenty-five minutes before the train left on track four; he pointed out the big doors to the tracks and told Tayo he could wait out there. Tayo felt weak, and the longer he walked the more his legs felt as though they might become invisible again; then the top part of his body would topple, and when his head was level with the ground he would be lost in smoke again, in the fog again. He breathed the air outside the doors and it smelled like trains, diesel oil, and creosote ties under the steel track. He leaned against the depot wall then; he was sweating, and sounds were becoming outlines again, vague and hollow in his ears, and he knew he was going to become invisible right there. It was too late to ask for help, and he waited to die the way smoke dies, drifting away in currents of air, twisting in thin swirls, fading until it exists no more. His last thought was how generous they had become, sending him to the L.A. depot alone, finally allowing him to die.

He lay on the concrete listening to the voices that surrounded him, voices that were either soft or distant. They spoke to him in English, and when he did not answer, there was a discussion and he heard the Japanese words vividly. He wasn't sure where he was any more, maybe back in the jungles again; he felt a sick sweat shiver over him like the shadow of the angel Auntie talked about. He fought to come to the surface, and he expected a rifle barrel to be shoved into his face when he opened his eyes. It was all worse than he had ever dreamed: to have drifted all those months in white smoke, only to wake up again in the prison camp. But he did not want to be invisible when he died, so he pulled himself loose, one last time.

The Japanese women were holding small children by the hands, and they were surrounded by bundles and suitcases. One of them was standing over him.

"Are you sick?" she asked.

He tried to answer her, but his throat made a coughing, gagging sound. He looked at her and tried to focus in on the others.

"We called for help," she said, bending over slightly, the hem of her flower-print dress swaying below her knees. A white man in a train uniform came. He looked at Tayo, and then he looked at the women and children.

"What happened to him?"

They shook their heads, and the woman said, "We saw him fall down as we were coming from our train." She moved away then, back to the group. She reached down and picked up a shopping bag in each hand; she looked at Tayo one more time. He raised himself up on one arm and watched them go; he felt a current of air from the movement of their skirts and feet and shopping bags. A child stared back at him, holding a hand but walking twisted around so that he could see Tayo. The little boy was wearing an Army hat that was too big for him, and when he saw Tayo looking he smiled; then the child disappeared through the wide depot doors.

The depot man helped him get up; he checked the tag on the suitcase.

"Should I call the Veterans' Hospital?"

Tayo shook his head; he was beginning to shiver all over.

"Those people," he said, pointing in the direction the women and children had gone, "I thought they locked them up."

"Oh, that was some years back. Right after Pearl Harbor. But now they've turned them all loose again. Sent them home. I don't guess you could keep up with news very well in the hospital."

"No." His voice sounded faint to him.

"You going to be all right now?"

He nodded and looked down the tracks. The depot man glanced at a gold pocket watch and walked away.

The swelling was pushing against his throat, and he leaned against the brick wall and vomited into the big garbage can. The smell of his own vomit and the rotting garbage filled his head, and he retched until his stomach heaved in frantic dry spasms. He could still see the face of the little boy, looking back at him, smiling, and he tried to vomit that image from his head because it was Rocky's smiling face from a long time before, when they were little kids together. He couldn't vomit any more, and the little face was still there, so he cried at how the world had come undone, how thousands of miles, high ocean waves and green jungles could not hold people in their place. Years and months had become weak, and people could push against them and wander back and forth in time. Maybe it had always been this way and he was only seeing it for the first time.

1977

E. L. DOCTOROW
b. 1931

Born in New York City, E. L. Doctorow was educated at Kenyon College and Columbia University. He began his career as a script reader for Columbia Pictures, and then became a senior editor and eventually editor-in-chief at Dial Press. He is the author of one play; a story collection, *Lives of the Poets* (1984); and eight novels, including *Welcome to Hard Times* (1960), *The Book of Daniel* (1966), *Ragtime* (1975), *Loon Lake* (1980), and *Billy Bathgate* (1989). *World's Fair* (1985) received the National Book Award, and Doctorow's novels have also received the PEN/Faulkner Award, the National Book Critics Circle Award (twice), and the William Dean Howells Medal.

As a script reader, Doctorow told *The Miami Herald* in 1975, he "had to suffer one lousy Western after another, and it occurred to me that I could lie about the West in a much more interesting way than any of these people were lying." His literary career began its historical focus with the frontier of the American West, and he continued to mine history with novels about the 1950s trial and execution of Julius and Ethel Rosenberg, early-twentieth-century New York City, the Depression, and 1930s-era New York. "What's real and what isn't?" Doctorow responded to a *Publishers Weekly* interviewer in 1975. "I used to know but I've forgotten. Let's just say that *Ragtime* is a mingling of fact and invention—a novelist's revenge on an age that celebrates nonfiction."

Of literary experimentation in general and the disjointed narrative of *Loon Lake* in particular, Doctorow said in a 1980 *New York Times Book Review* interview, "You don't know who's talking so that's one more convention out the window. That gives me pleasure, and I think it might give pleasure to readers, too. Don't underestimate them. People are smart, and they are not strangers to discontinuity. There's an immense amount of energy attached to breaking up your narrative and leaping into different voices, times, skins, and making the book happen and then letting the reader take care of himself."

"The Leather Man" first appeared in *Lives of the Poets.*

The Leather Man

They're nothing new, you can read about the Leather Man, for instance, a hundred years ago making his circuit through Westchester, Connecticut, into the Berkshires in the summer, seen sitting on the roadside, glimpsed in the woods, he had these regular stops, caves, abandoned barns, riverbanks under the iron bridges in mill towns, the Leather Man, a hulk, colossally dressed, in layers of coats and shawls and pants, all topped with a stiff hand-fashioned leather outer armor, like a knight's, and a homemade pointed hat of leather, he was ten feet tall, an apparition. Of course it's the essence of these people that they're shy, they scurry at the sign of confrontation, never hurt a soul. But it was said of this fellow that when cornered he would engage in quite rational conversation, unlearned of course, with no reference to current events, and perhaps with a singular line of association that might strike one at times as not sequential, not really reasonably sequential on first audit, but genial nonetheless, with transitions made by smile or the sincere struggle for words; even the act of talking, one assumes, is something you can lose the knack of. So there is a history. And though the country of western New England or the farmlands in the north Midwest will still find one asleep in the plains, a patch of wheat flattened in his contours, say, and although they're common enough in the big cities, living in doorways, wiping your windshields with a dirty rag for a quarter, men, or carrying their bags, smoking butts from the gutters, women, or the communities of them, living each in a private alcove underground between subway stations, in the nests of the walls alongside tracks, or down under the tracks in the hollows and nooks of the electric cable conduits, what is new is the connection they're making with each other, some kind of spontaneous communication has flashed them into awareness of each other, and hell, they may as well have applied to the national endowment as a living art form, there is someone running them but I don't know who.

I don't know who and I don't know why. Conceivably it's a harmless social phenomenon, like all the other forms of suffering, that is to say not planned for a purpose but merely a natural function of everything else going, and maybe it is heartless to look askance at suffering, to be suspicious of it, Southern church blacks, welfare recipients, jobless kids around the pool halls and so on, but that's the job, that's our role, I don't think I have to justify it. We know how danger grows, or for that matter large intangible events, spiritual events, there were five six hundred thousand, yes? at that farmer's field twenty years ago, and fifty of them were us, you remember, one part per ten thousand, like the legal chemistry for a preservative, one part per ten thousand to keep the thing from turning bad. I was there myself and enjoyed the music. My favorite was Joan C. Baez, the most conservative of musicians, ultraliberal pacifist peacenik, remember peaceniks? That was a coining we did ourselves and gave it to some columnist, in Denver I think it was, spread like wildfire. But she sang nice, early in the game, everyone stoned on sun, chemical toilets still operative . . .

We found a girl there, incidentally, who was doing these strange spastic pantomimes that drew a real crowd. Beginning with her arms over her head. Brought her elbows down over the boobs, seemed to push the elbows out, pushing at something, and then one arm went around the back of the neck, and then all these gyrations of the head, it was the weirdest thing, as if she was caught in something, a web, a net, so intense, so concentrated, the crowd, the music disappeared, and then she went down on her knees and knelt through her arms like they were some kind of jump rope, and then when her arms were behind her, that was not right, she tried to get out that way, get out, she was getting out of something, enacting the attempt, face all twisted and red to get out, you see. So we took some pictures, and then we diagrammed the action and what we came up with was very interesting, it was someone in a straitjacket, it was the classic terror enacted of someone straitjacketed and trying to break free. Now, who can you think of, the person who in fact could do that, the person who could get out of straitjackets, who was that? he said.

Houdini.

That's right, Houdini, it was one of his routines, getting out of the kind of straitjacket to break the heart.

To do hermitage, the preference for one's own company. Picture yourself in such solitude, in natural surroundings, say, the classical version. Build a hut in the woods, split your own logs, grow things, ritualize daily subsistence, listen to the wind sing, watch the treetops dance, feel the weather, feel yourself in touch with the way things are. You remember your Thoreau. There's a definite political component to avoiding all other human beings and taking on the coloration of your surroundings, invisible as the toad on the log. Whatever the spiritual content, it is the action of hiding out, you see these guys hide out. So the question is, why? It may be a normal life directed by powerful paranoidal impulses, or it may be a paranoid life that makes sense given the particular individual's background. But something has happened. If he is hiding, I want to know why.

But supposing on the other hand we all seek to impose the order we can manage, the more public the order the better we are known. Politicians are known. Artists are known. They impose public order. But say you are some hapless fellow, you can't keep a job, the wife nags, the children are vicious, the neighbors snigger. Down in your basement, though, you make nice things of wood. You make a bookshelf, you make a cabinet, sawing and planing, sanding, fitting, gluing, and you construct something very fine, you impose that order, that is the realm of your control. You make a bigger cabinet. You make a cabinet you can walk into. You build it where nobody will watch you. When it is done, you walk inside and lock the door.

Before we break for lunch, let me propose this idea. You have them walking into their boxes and locking the door behind them. Fine. But two people do that and you have a community. You see what I'm saying? You can make a revolution with people who have nothing to do with each other at the same time. There is a theory, for instance, that the universe oscillates. It is not a steady beaming thing, nor did it start with a bang. It expands and contracts, inhales and exhales, it is either growing larger than you can imagine or imploding toward a point. The crucial thing is its direction. If things come apart enough, they will have started to come together.

0001. Members of the class: feral children, hermits, street people, gamblers, prisoners, missing persons, forest-fire wardens, freaks, permanent invalids, recluses, autistics, road tramps, the sensory deprived. (See also astronauts.)

We borrowed an ordinary precinct car and went looking for one. Contact on Fourteenth Street and Avenue A, time of contact ten-thirteen P.M. Subject going east on southside Fourteenth Street. White, female, indeterminate age. Wearing WWII-issue khaki greatcoat over several dresses, gray fedora over blue watch cap, several shawls, some kind of furred shoes overlaid with galoshes. Stockings rolled to ankles over stockings. Pushing two-wheeled grocery cart stuffed with bags, sacks, rags, soft goods, broken umbrellas. Purposeful movements. Subject went directly from public trash receptacles to private trash deposits in doorways, seemed interested in anything made of cloth. Subject sat down to rest, back to fence, East Fifteenth Street. This is the site of Consolidated Edison generating plant. Subject slept several hours on sidewalk in twenty-degree weather. At four A.M. awakened by white male derelict urinating on her.

Bancroft suggests as an organizing principle we make the distinction between simple and profound dereliction. Ignore bums in the pokey and the poor slobs who shoot up. Always the snob, Bancroft. He wants only middle-class-and-above material? Still, there's something to be said: If the brain is overrun, where is the act of separation? If nothing is excluded, the meaning is lost. Interesting he designates as profound that which is incomplete.

In the city of New Rochelle, N.Y., a man was apprehended as a Peeping Tom. He'd been found in the landscaping behind the residence of Mr. and Mrs. Morris Wakefield, 19 Croft Terrace. He had the aspect of a wild man, bearded, unkempt, ragged. Reported to have been glimpsed several times over a period of months in backyards of the better neighborhoods of the city. No identification.

Slater sat up and took notice. The incident had so shocked Mrs. Morris Wakefield that she had been placed under sedation. Poor woman was in no shape. Already under severe stress as a result of the disappearance of her husband, Morris Wakefield, a partner in a bridge-construction firm, an engineer of considerable reputation in his field, no known enemies. Exemplary life. Gone. The couple was childless. They had been married twelve years. We went up there. Alone and grieving in her home, Mrs. Wakefield had prepared for bed and came downstairs in her negligee for a glass of warm milk. Two eerie eyes rolled along the rim of the windowsill. She screamed and ran upstairs and locked herself in her bedroom, where she phoned the police. I find, not infrequently, quote New Rochelle police detective Leo Kreisler, trouble breaks out in a rash, we have people in our community we have no dealings with for twenty years, and suddenly everything goes at once, someone is robbed, then hurt in a car a week later, or someone is beat up and a relative steals money, and just like that one family is in multiple crisis in the space of a few days. We asked to see him. Sure, why not, quote Detective Kreisler. Who knows, maybe he'll like you. He doesn't talk, he doesn't eat, he looks at you like he's thinking of something else.

The prisoner wore floppy chino slacks torn down one leg and belted with a piece of clothesline, dirty white Stan Smith tennis sneakers, no socks, a stained and greasy workshirt. He was not a trim person, but a person who looked formerly fat. Pants and shirt hung on him. Badly needed a haircut, and in the fluorescent light of the slammer blinked with the weak eyes and pale doughy undereyes of a person who wears glasses without his glasses. His beard white, although his matted hair reddish. He sat cross-legged on the vinyl floor. He sat with the fingers of his hands intertwined stiffly. Slater contemplated him. He was all connected, his legs crossed, his fingers laced. Under observation he raised his knees still crossed and roped, his wrists around them, his fingers still locked.

Slater: Are you in fact the owner of the property on which you were apprehended, the bridge engineer Morris Wakefield, the missing husband?

The peeper nodded yes.

An item from the files of the security department of National Dry Foods Corporation: One of their young marketing executives had been relocated from Short Hills, New Jersey, to Flint, Michigan. It was discovered sometime thereafter that in Flint he was living in domicile with a woman not his wife and two children not his children, although he represented them as such. Six months it took them to find his legal wife and two children: They were still in place in their Short Hills, New Jersey, home, living in domicile with an executive of the company who had been relocated from Flint. The two executives had been fraternity brothers at Duke University.

Slater, do you fuck around?

A long time before answering. No.

So do I. Let me tell you about the lunch I had yesterday. A very beautiful lady whom I've had my eye on for years. She and my wife are pals, they go to the galleries together. Well, we were all at this party and I make a joke, a signal joke, clearly funny if she doesn't pick up on it but a signal in case she wants to. Is that how you do it?

No, I usually come right out with it.

Well, I'm older than you are. I'm a different generation. Wit counts for me, the double entendre. So we had lunch. I could hardly hold her down. She was ready to avenge fifteen years of faithful marriage. Not only that her husband cheated on her, but that he was nasty at home. Not only that he was nasty and mean, but that he had no respect for what she did and made fun of the causes she supported. Not only that he lacked respect, but that he was infantile and went all to pieces when he cut himself shaving. And not only that, but that he spent no time with the children and complained when he had to shell out money for their school.

Slater smiled.

Oh God, it was uncanny. Like she had held up a mirror. I found myself getting defensive, wanting to argue. It finally comes down to a smile, a small kindness, a bit of good cheer, she said. Those are the important things. Your husband is a cheerful man, I said, and by this time in the conversation I didn't want to have anything more to do with her. An amiable, charming man, I said, with a good sense of humor. Oh yes, she said, so was Dr. Jekyll.

What is the essential act of the Leather Man? He makes the world foreign. He distances it. He is estranged. Our perceptions are sharpest when we're estranged. We can see the shape of things. Do you accept this as a principle? All right, then, consider something as common as philandering. I'm an old-fashioned fellow and I use old-fashioned words. After a while your marriage becomes your cover. Don't laugh, I'm quite serious. Your feelings are broken down by plurality, you don't stop, you keep moving, it becomes your true life to keep moving, to keep moving emotionally, you find finally the emotion in the movement. You are the Leather Man, totally estranged from your society, the prettiest women are rocks in the stream, flowers along the road, you have subverted your own life and live alone in the wild, your only companion your thoughts.

I think what I'm proposing is a structure, not a theory of a subversive class, but an infrastructure of layered subversion, perhaps not conspiracy at all. That something has happened like a rearrangement of molecules, and that since we are political persons here we are sensitive to the crude politics of it, we think of it as some sort of ground for antisocial action when it might not be that at all. So I'm saying the way to understand it for our particular purposes might be not the usual thing of getting inside, penetration, but distance, putting it away from us, getting as far from it as possible, to see what it really is. Because if it has gotten outside us, and we're inside and we can't see the shape of it, it comes to us as reality and it has no meaning at all.

We've got this astronaut who went bad, James C. Montgomery, who took a hero's welcome in 1966 and since then has been picked up for stock fraud, embezzlement, forgery, drunken driving—you name it, he's done it: stealing cars, assault, assault with a deadly weapon. This sometimes happens to individuals in whom history intensifies like electroshock, leaves them all scattered afterward. We've got him quiet now, but his wife keeps talking to reporters down in Florida and threatens suit.

I'll read you part of the interrogation by one of the staff psychiatrists:

> Were you ever frightened? Did anything happen on the mission you didn't report?
>
> No sir.
>
> Did anything unexpected happen?
>
> No sir.
>
> Did the idea of space hold any terror for you? Being out there so far from home?
>
> *Question repeated.*
>
> No, well, you do your job, you're busy as hell, there's no time to think, and you're always in touch, almost always in touch, control voice in the empyrean void. No, I would say not. *(pause)* You just keep your nose to the panel. Make community with the switches, little lights. Everything around you is manmade, you have that assurance. *(pause)* American-made.
>
> But then you did the landing, right?
>
> Yes sir.
>
> You walked.
>
> Yes sir.
>
> You got out of the machine and walked around.
>
> Yes sir. Oh—for a while there I was alone and miserable inside my space suit. Is that what you mean?
>
> I have the feeling you're trying to tell me what you think I want to hear.
>
> Well, shit. *(pause)* Look, the truth is I don't remember. I mean, I remember that I walked on the moon but now I can see it on television and I don't feel it, you know what I mean? I can't believe it happened. I see myself, that I did it, but I don't remember how it felt, I don't remember the experience of it.

Can I just try a quick simple experiment here? Five minutes of your time? Silence. Slater looked around the table. Someone lit a pipe. The grudging tribal assent. I'm going to give you a list of simple nouns and ask you to respond—just fill me in on what's happening. All right?

Night. Ladder. Window. Scream. Penis.

Have you been talking to my wife? someone said. Everyone laughed.

Patrol. Mud. Flare. Mortar.

All right, someone said.

President. Crowd. Bullet. Slater said, We've got thousands of people in this country whose vocation it is to let us know what our experience is. Are you telling me this is not a resource?

Slate, we're going to have a fight on our hands if you want to admit that kind of material. You don't know the minds you're dealing with. They're not going to understand, they're going to read it as source. Then you know how messy it'll get? You're going to have to interrogate these resources, the most articulate people in the land, the ones who already have their hackles up, and you're going to ask them where they got their information?

No, you're not hearing me, Slater said. We'll know where they got their information. We gave it to them.

1984

SUSAN DAITCH
b. 1954

Born in New Haven, Connecticut, Susan Daitch was educated at Barnard College and the Whitney Museum Independent Study Program. Her two novels are *L.C.* (1986) and *The Colorist* (1990). In 1996 she published a collection of stories, *Storytown.* She has taught at Bennington College and the Iowa Writers' Workshop, and since 1988 has been on the faculty of Sarah Lawrence College in Bronxville, New York. Currently she lives with her son in New York City.

"I started out as a painter, sort of," Daitch told Larry McCaffery in a 1995 *Review of Contemporary Fiction* interview. "Actually, what I was doing were more like narrative drawings than paintings, so when I began writing fiction it seemed very natural to be thinking of texts in visual terms. . . . My own position, writing these things, is by definition voyeuristic, but so much American fiction is about sentimental realism, very personal and domestic in a claustrophobic way, and that, for me, has been something to avoid."

"X≠Y" appeared in *Storytown.*

X ≠ Y

Your passport was something you needed to get on the airplane in the first place. It was blue, it meant a statistical affiliation, not something you gave a lot of thought to. The picture of George Washington, like a crucifix, or a crèche in neighbors' houses, signs you easily identified, knew all about, completely understood; but these things weren't in the house you remember. They were foreign, exiled objects. In your house bearers of different passports didn't share the neighbors' matter-of-fact, wake-up-you're-it heritage. Heritage is a word, which, like the word *leadership,* makes you uneasy. The only time you tasted Bosco or Reddi-Whip was somewhere else. The idea of nationality may be a received one, but with so many generations born in exactly the same place, it's taken for granted. A garage with a basketball hoop over a barn-red door. Your passport says you are all these things you never thought you were.

History class, 1966, *Eurasia.* All year you memorized products, imports, exports, natural resources from Ireland to Korea. You were eleven. It was called history, but this is what you commit to memory, a different country each week. What were the products of Iraq? Petroleum, that's an easy one, raw wool and dates. These are exports. Of Ireland? Live animals; imports are machinery, petroleum. The map in your textbook stopped in the middle of Europe and picked up again to the southeast. It was a book of very few dates; history was not considered to have a temporal dimension.

The men in black masks who have appeared at the front of the plane aren't interested in how you saw through your history teachers or what you say your allegiances are. You can say there is a copy of *The Eighteenth Brumaire of Louis Bonaparte* in your suitcase, but it sounds feeble. The man next to you says he thinks you will be exchanged for prisoners held in another country, but he's only guessing.

They find a place to land and, although you are sitting near a window, you can't identify the city. None of the passengers are allowed to speak.

> A spokesman for the Italian Ministry, Tanino Scelba, said Wednesday that a "terrorist multinational" existed and argued that you cannot speak of isolated groups, like the Brigata Rosa or the Red Army faction.
>
> "They are linked," he said.

The terrorist multinational does not have links to the Trilateral Commission. The syllogism falls on its face.

Airplane detritus, trays of melted ice, tiny whiskey and gin bottles roll on the floor, there will be no seconds, headphones dangle. The movie was an old one, *Greystoke,* but you didn't rent sound. Ape man swings through the jungle in utter silence. The flight attendants were asked to push the screens back up, but for some reason the movie continued and images of lianas, Tarzan's long hair and legs flash across the women's faces as they make a last trip down the aisles. You and the stranger sitting by the aisle can only look at each other. Perhaps it's just as well and saves a lot of trouble. You look for signs which will tell you what speech, in this situation, can't. Is he reading *Der Spiegel* or *People* magazine in Dutch? A newspaper whose cyrillic figures you're unable to read? When called to the front and faced with the interpreter, what story will he give? He owns things, cuff links, briefcase, tie pin, with his initials on them. You aren't in a Hitchcock movie scattered with these kinds of clues. You don't fall in love.

Hands are supposed to be raised when you want to use the bathroom. Will one of them go in with you or will you be searched before? Will speech on a limited basis creep back because, after a certain number of hours, unless people are really terrorized, they might turn into unruly children? You remember what it's like to be afraid to open your mouth. You think two of them are women.

There are passengers you saw as you boarded the plane, but you remember a few of them because they looked like the kind of people who would say anything to save themselves. It isn't clear what they might say in order to do this. After passports have been collected, some passengers are asked what they do for a living. The interpreter is a passenger who seemed to have volunteered out of the blue, although you can see from the expressions of the people around you he is viewed with suspicion. He might not know the languages in question very well and might make up answers for you. He acts a little nervous, and it's a histrionic kind of nervousness as if he's sure he has a job to do and feels himself to be on neutral ground, although perhaps only for the time being. You can see categories being assessed and wonder who's worth what to them. You stretch your neck looking for diplomats, movie stars, CIA operatives.

"Don't take me, take her."

The *Bristol Constant* doesn't have any treasure. It's on its way to the Massachusetts Bay Colony. The crew mutinies off the coast of Newfoundland. Bullets aren't wasted. Men and women are thrown overboard into the icy water. As a mutinous crew they can land in no English port and resort to piracy. One woman is kept, and she pleads to be sent back to England on the next east-sailing ship they attack. She talks of Brighton day and night. The mutineers think she's mad and leave her on the barren unpopulated shore of an island in the West Indies.

It has been two days or a day and a half. You can't really tell. You realize that even before you boarded this plane, you spent a lot of time waiting. Watch time is a form of nonsense, a form of abstract speculation because the time where you come from has no meaning. You try to remember newspaper stories of amnesty and happy endings but can recall no stories, only what the front pages of various newspapers look like. You hear someone having a hysterical conversation with themselves several rows behind you. The person is playing all the roles in the conversation, and you find it disturbing that you can't turn around and identify the speaker. You don't even know if it's a man or a woman. Everyone is awake. If rumors could circulate in silence you're not sure you would really know anything more.

a. They want four Polisarios freed from a Moroccan jail.
b. They want Italian prisoners held in "preventative detention" returned to normal life.
c. They want enough fuel to get the plane to East Berlin.
d. They want half the Vatican's treasure.

e. They want the men to sit on one side of the plane, the women on the other.
f. No one will get their passports back.

Airplane food runs out. Trays are wheeled across the tarmac. When it's distributed, the food gives no clues as to the country you've landed in. Long-thawed peas and carrots, microwaved French fries, Swiss steak, a cupcake for dessert.

There is agitation among those watching the passengers. One of the others who has been behind the curtain comes forward, and they speak in a language you can't identify. Tremendous amounts of film, videotape, and print might be generated outside the perimeters of your captivity. Mountains of lights, cameras, and extension cords approach the control tower, shredded newspapers eddy near the wheels of the plane.

In your boredom, it's easy to panic, but you have no way to demonstrate your alarm except to raise your hand to go to the bathroom. You are ignored and in your desperation turn to the stranger with monograms who has fallen asleep. Unless he secretly took some drug in the bathroom, you don't understand how he can sleep, awkwardly falling into the empty seat between you. In sleep he looks like he might be watching a movie, listening to a concert, or just having a nice dream, and you're envious of his oblivion. He has very white teeth.

They are looking at passports again, dividing them into stacks according to color. You can't see if they're looking at yours, if they've tossed it aside or will shout your name next, and it will be your turn to be questioned by the earnest interpreter. You'll walk down the aisle as slowly as you can. You've never been called on like this before and don't know exactly how to behave. Can you be sure his interpretations will correspond to your answers? He could make up your history for you; word for word will be entirely different from your recitation and you will never be aware of the discrepancy. What would happen without the translator? Two men stop to eat cupcakes and drink instant coffee.

Perhaps half the plane is asleep although it's only twilight in whatever city you're in. A vehicle moves closer to the plane, but it isn't for the purposes of rescue. The plane is refueled. Another city must be found. The sign lights up telling you to fasten your seat belt, and the plane taxis down the runway. The translator hasn't met you yet and, for the time being, your respective fictions remain separate revisions.

1988

SHERMAN ALEXIE
b. 1966

Sherman Alexie was born in Spokane, Washington. "I am a Spokane/Coeur d'Alene Indian from Wellpinit, Washington," he told an interviewer in 1993, "where I live on the Spokane Indian Reservation. Everything I do now, writing and otherwise, has its origin in that." Alexie has published six books of poetry, a book of short stories, and a novel. An additional novel, *Indian Killer,* was published in the fall of 1996. He is also working on a screenplay and has recorded a CD featuring his own lyrics.

His stories and poems were introduced in *Hanging Loose* magazine, and have since appeared widely in such publications as *Caliban, Esquire, The World, Beloit Poetry Journal, Red Dirt,* and *Story.* Awards for his writing include a National Endowment for the Arts Fellowship, Washington State Governor's Award, and a Lila Acheson Wallace–Reader's Digest grant.

"Captivity" is from *First Indian On the Moon* (1993). Alexie's "elegiac poems and stories will break your heart," Joy Harjo has written. "Watch this guy. He's making myth."

Captivity

He (my captor) gave me a biscuit, which I put in my pocket, and not daring to eat it, buried it under a log, fearing he had put something in it to make me love him.

—from the narrative of Mrs. Mary Rowlandson, who was taken captive when the Wampanoag destroyed Lancaster, Massachusetts, in 1676.

1.

When I tell you this story, remember it may change: the reservation recalls the white girl with no name or a name which refuses memory. October she filled the reservation school, this new white girl, daughter of a BIA official or doctor in the Indian Health Service Clinic. Captive, somehow afraid of the black hair and flat noses of the Indian children who rose, one by one, shouting their names aloud. She ran from the room, is still running, waving her arms wildly at real and imagined enemies. Was she looking toward the future? Was she afraid of loving all of us?

2.

All of us heard the explosion when the two cars collided on the reservation road. Five Indians died in the first car; four Indians died in the second. The only survivor was a white woman from Springdale who couldn't remember her name.

3.

I remember your name, Mary Rowlandson. I think of you now, how necessary you have become. Can you hear me, telling this story within uneasy boundaries, changing you into a woman leaning against a wall beneath a HANDICAPPED PARKING ONLY sign, arrow pointing down directly at you? Nothing changes, neither of us knows exactly where to stand and measure the beginning of our lives. Was it 1676 or 1976 or 1776 or yesterday when the Indian held you tight in his dark arms and promised you nothing but the sound of his voice? September, Mary Rowlandson, it was September when you visited the reservation grade school. The speech therapist who tore the Indian boy from his classroom, kissed him on the lips, gave him the words which echoed treaty: *He thrusts his fists against the posts but still insists he sees the ghosts.* Everything changes. Both of us force the sibilant, in the language of the enemy.

4.

Language of the enemy: *heavy lightness,* house insurance, *serious vanity,* safe-deposit box, *feather of lead,* sandwich man, *bright smoke,* second-guess, *sick health,* shell game, *still-waking sleep,* forgiveness.

5.

How much longer can we forgive each other? Let's say I am the fancydancer and every step is equal to a drum beat, this sepia photograph of you and me staring into the West of our possibilities. For now, you are wearing the calico dress that covers your ankles and wrists and I'm wearing a bone vest wrapped around a cotton shirt, my hair unbraided and unafraid. This must be 1876 but no, it is now, August, and this photograph will change the story. Remember: I am not the fancydancer, am not the fancydancer, not the fancydancer, the fancydancer, fancydancer.

6.

Fancydance through the tall grass, young man, over broken glass, past Crowshoe's Gas Station where you can buy an Indian in a Bottle. "How do you fit that beer-belly in there?" asks a white tourist. "We do it," I tell her, "piece by piece."

7.

Piece by piece, I reassemble the house where I was born, but there is a hole in the wall where there was none before. "What is this?" I ask my mother. "It's your sister," she answers. "You mean my sister made that hole?" "No," she says. "That hole in the wall is your sister." For weeks, I searched our architecture, studied the walls for imperfections. Listen: imagination is all we have as defense against capture and its inevitable changes.

8.

I have changed my mind. In this story there are words fancydancing in the in-between, between then and now, between walls in the alley behind the Tribal Cafe where Indian boys smoke old cigarettes at halftime of the all-Indian basketball game. Mary Rowlandson, it's true, isn't it? Tobacco and sugar are the best weapons.

9.

The best weapons are the stories and every time the story is told, something changes. Every time the story is retold, something changes. There are no photographs, nothing to be introduced as evidence. The 20th century overtook the reservation in 1976, but there we were, stuck in 1975. Do you remember that white boy then, who spent the summer on the reservation? I don't know how he arrived. Did his father pilot a DC-10 forced to make an emergency landing in the Trading Post parking lot? Did the BIA Forestry man find him frozen in amber? Did Irene sweep him up from the floor of a telephone booth? Lester FallsApart says he himself drank and half-swallowed the white boy out of a bottle of Annie Green Springs wine and spat him out whole into the dust. The nightwatchman at the Midnight Mine tells us he caught the white boy chewing uranium. Do you remember that white boy dove naked into Benjamin Lake? He wore the same Levi's hung low on the hips, a red bandanna wrapped around his head. He tugged at his blond hair, yes, telling us "It will grow, I promise." We beat him often, specifically. Arnold broke the white boy's nose with a snowball he had saved, frozen and hidden in the fridge since March. It was July 4th when we kidnapped him and kept him captive in a chicken coop for hours. We spat and pissed on him through the wire; Seymour shot him twice with a pellet gun. That white boy fell backward into the nests, crushed eggs, splintered wood, kicked chickens blindly. I was the first to stop laughing when the white boy started digging into dirt, shit, the past, looking for somewhere to hide. We did not make him any promises. He was all we had left.

10.

All we had left was held captive here on the reservation, Mary Rowlandson, and I saw you there chewing salmon strips in the corner, hiding from all the Indians. Did you see him, Mary Rowlandson, the Indian man who has haunted your waking for 300 years, who left you alone sipping coffee in the reservation 7-11? I saw you there, again, as I walked home from the bar, grinning to the stars, but all you could do was wave from the window and mouth the eternal question: *How?*

11.

How do you open a tin can without a sharp-edged dream? How do you sleep in your post office box using junk mail for blankets? How do you see past the iron bars someone painted on your U.S. government glasses? How do you stop a reservation tsunami before it's too late?

12.

It's too late, Mary Rowlandson, for us to sit together and dig up the past you buried under a log, salvage whatever else you had left behind. What do you want? I cannot say, "I love you. I miss you." June, Mary Rowlandson, the water is gone and my cousins are eating Lysol sandwiches. They don't need you, will never search for you in the ash after your house has burned to the ground one more time. It's over. That's all you can depend on.

13.

All we can depend on are the slow-motion replays of our lives. Frame 1: Lester reaches for the next beer. Frame 2: He pulls it to his face by memory, drinks it like a 20th century vision. Frame 3: He tells a joke, sings another song: *Well, they sent me off to boarding school and made me learn the white man's rules.*

14.

White man's rules: all of us must follow them, must remember the name of the officer who arrested us for running when the sign said DON'T WALK. It's the language of the enemy. There is no forgiveness for fancydancing on WET CEMENT. Before we move into the HUD house, we must build dreams from scratch, piece by piece, because SOME ASSEMBLY IS REQUIRED. Remember to insert CORRECT CHANGE ONLY when you choose the best weapons, the stories which measure all we have left. How do you know whether to use the IN or OUT door to escape? But it's too late to go now, our four-door visions have been towed from a NO PARKING ZONE. Leonard tells me he's waiting for the bus to the dark side of the moon, or Oz, or the interior of a drum. I load up my pockets with all my possessions and wait with him. That Greyhound leaves at 3 A.M. That's all we can depend on.

1993

JOSEPH HELLER
1923–1999

Born in the Coney Island section of Brooklyn, New York, Joseph Heller attended public school and then enlisted in the United States Army Air Force. After his discharge in 1945, he married, then pursued a university education, attending both the University of Southern California and New York University, from which he received a B.A. in 1948. While publishing short stories in *Esquire* and *The Atlantic Monthly*, he earned an M.A. from Columbia University and won a Fulbright Scholarship to Oxford University. His five novels are *Catch-22* (1961), *Something Happened* (1974), *Good as Gold* (1979), *God Knows* (1984), and *Picture This* (1988). He also authored several screenplays for film and television.

"I never thought of *Catch-22* as a comic novel," Heller told *The New York Times* in 1986. "I wanted the reader to be amused, and . . . I wanted him to be ashamed that he was amused. My literary bent . . . is more toward the morbid and the tragic. Great carnage is taking place and my idea was to use humor to make ridiculous the things that are irrational and very terrible."

From Catch-22

Chapter 9. Major Major Major Major

Major Major Major Major had had a difficult time from the start.

Like Miniver Cheevy, he had been born too late—exactly thirty-six hours too late for the physical well-being of his mother, a gentle, ailing woman who, after a full day and a half's agony in the rigors of childbirth, was depleted of all resolve to pursue further the argument over the new child's name. In the hospital corridor, her husband moved ahead with the unsmiling determination of someone who knew what he was about. Major Major's father was a towering, gaunt man in heavy shoes and a black woolen suit. He filled out the birth certificate without faltering, betraying no emotion at all as he handed the completed form to the floor nurse. The nurse took it from him without comment and padded out of sight. He watched her go, wondering what she had on underneath.

Back in the ward, he found his wife lying vanquished beneath the blankets like a desiccated old vegetable, wrinkled, dry and white, her enfeebled tissues absolutely still. Her bed was at the very end of the ward, near a cracked window thickened with grime. Rain splashed from a moiling sky and the day was dreary and cold. In other parts of the hospital chalky people with aged, blue lips were dying on time. The man stood erect beside the bed and gazed down at the woman a long time.

"I have named the boy Caleb," he announced to her finally in a soft voice. "In accordance with your wishes." The woman made no answer, and slowly the man smiled. He had planned it all perfectly, for his wife was asleep and would never know that he had lied to her as she lay on her sickbed in the poor ward of the county hospital.

From this meager beginning had sprung the ineffectual squadron commander who was now spending the better part of each working day in Pianosa forging Washington Irving's name to official documents. Major Major forged diligently with his left hand to elude identification, insulated against intrusion by his own undesired authority and camouflaged in his false mustache and dark glasses as an additional safeguard against detection by anyone chancing to peer in through the dowdy celluloid window from which some thief had carved out a slice. In between these two low points of his birth and his success lay thirty-one dismal years of loneliness and frustration.

Major Major had been born too late and too mediocre. Some men are born mediocre, some men achieve mediocrity, and some men have mediocrity thrust upon them. With Major Major it had been all three. Even among men lacking all distinction he inevitably stood out as a man lacking more distinction than all the rest, and people who met him were always impressed by how unimpressive he was.

Major Major had three strikes on him from the beginning—his mother, his father and Henry Fonda, to whom he bore a sickly resemblance almost from the moment of his birth. Long before he even suspected who Henry Fonda was, he found himself the subject of unflattering comparisons everywhere he went. Total strangers saw fit to deprecate him, with the result that he was stricken early with a guilty fear of people and an obsequious impulse to apologize to society for the fact that he was *not* Henry Fonda. It was not an easy task for him to go through life looking something like Henry Fonda, but he never once thought of quitting, having inherited his perseverance from his father, a lanky man with a good sense of humor.

Major Major's father was a sober God-fearing man whose idea of a good joke was to lie about his age. He was a long-limbed farmer, a God-fearing, freedom-loving, law-abiding rugged individualist who held that federal aid to anyone but farmers was creeping socialism. He advocated thrift and hard work and disapproved of loose women who turned him down. His specialty was alfalfa, and he made a good thing out of not growing any. The government paid him well for every bushel of alfalfa he did not grow. The more alfalfa he did not grow, the more money the government gave him, and he spent every penny he didn't earn on new land to increase the amount of alfalfa he did not produce. Major Major's father worked without rest at not growing alfalfa. On long winter evenings he remained indoors and did not mend harness, and he sprang out of bed at the crack of noon every day just to make certain that the chores would not be done. He invested in land wisely and soon was not growing more alfalfa than any other man in the county. Neighbors sought him out for advice on all subjects, for he had made much money and was therefore wise. "As ye sow, so shall ye reap," he counseled one and all, and everyone said, "Amen."

Major Major's father was an outspoken champion of economy in government, provided it did not interfere with the sacred duty of government to pay farmers as much as they could get for all the alfalfa they produced that no one else wanted or for not producing any alfalfa at all. He was a proud and independent man who was opposed to unemployment insurance and never hesitated to whine, whimper, wheedle, and extort for as much as he could get from whomever he could. He was a devout man whose pulpit was everywhere.

"The Lord gave us good farmers two strong hands so that we could take as much as we could grab with both of them," he preached with ardor on the courthouse steps or in front of the A & P as he waited for the bad-tempered gum-chewing young cashier he was after to step outside and give him a nasty look. "If the Lord didn't want us to take as much as we could get," he preached, "He wouldn't have given us two good hands to take it with." And the others murmured, "Amen."

Major Major's father had a Calvinist's faith in predestination and could perceive distinctly how everyone's misfortunes but his own were expressions of God's will. He smoked cigarettes and drank whiskey, and he thrived on good wit and stimulating intellectual conversation, particularly his own when he was lying about his age or telling that good one about God and his wife's difficulties in delivering Major Major. The good one about God and his wife's difficulties had to do with the fact that it had taken God only six days to produce the whole world, whereas his wife had spent a full day and a half in labor just to produce Major Major. A lesser man might have wavered that day in the hospital corridor, a weaker man might have compromised on such excellent substitutes as Drum Major, Minor Major, Sergeant Major, or C Sharp Major, but Major Major's father had waited fourteen years for just such an opportunity, and he was not a person to waste it. Major Major's father had a good joke about opportunity. "Opportunity only knocks once in this world," he would say. Major Major's father repeated this good joke at every opportunity.

Being born with a sickly resemblance to Henry Fonda was the first of a long series of practical jokes of which destiny was to make Major Major the unhappy victim throughout his joyless life. Being born Major Major Major was the second. The fact that he *had* been born Major Major Major was a secret known only to his father. Not until Major Major was enrolling in kindergarten was the discovery of his real name made, and then the effects were disastrous. The news killed his mother, who just lost her will to live and wasted away and died, which was just fine with his father, who had decided to marry the bad-tempered girl at the A & P if he had to and who had not been optimistic about his chances of getting his wife off the land without paying her some money or flogging her.

On Major Major himself the consequences were only slightly less severe. It was a harsh and stunning realization that was forced upon him at so tender an age, the realization that he was not, as he had always been led to believe, Caleb Major, but instead was some total stranger named Major Major Major about whom he knew absolutely nothing and about whom nobody else had ever heard before. What playmates he had withdrew from him and never returned, disposed, as they were, to distrust all strangers, especially one who had already deceived them by pretending to be someone they had known for years. Nobody would have anything to do with him. He began to drop things and to trip. He had a shy and hopeful manner in each new contact, and he was always disappointed. Because he needed a friend so desperately, he never found one. He grew awkwardly into a tall, strange, dreamy boy with fragile eyes and a very delicate mouth whose tentative, groping smile collapsed instantly into hurt disorder at every fresh rebuff.

He was polite to his elders, who disliked him. Whatever his elders told him to do, he did. They told him to look before he leaped, and he always looked before he leaped. They told him never to put off until the next day what he could do the day before, and he never did. He was told to honor his father and his mother, and he honored his father and his mother. He was told that he should not kill, and he did not kill, until he got into the Army. Then he was told to kill, and he killed. He turned the other cheek on every occasion and always did unto others exactly as he would have had others do unto him. When he gave to charity, his left hand never knew what his right hand was doing. He never once took the name of the Lord his God in vain, committed adultery or coveted his neighbor's ass. In fact, he loved his neighbor and never even bore false witness against him. Major Major's elders disliked him because he was such a flagrant nonconformist.

Since he had nothing better to do well in, he did well in school. At the state university he took his studies so seriously that he was suspected by the homosexuals of being a Communist and suspected by the Communists of being a homosexual. He majored in English history, which was a mistake.

"*English* history!" roared the silver-maned senior Senator from his state indignantly. "What's the matter with American history? American history is as good as any history in the world!"

Major Major switched immediately to American literature, but not before the F.B.I. had opened a file on him. There were six people and a Scotch terrier inhabiting the remote farmhouse Major Major called home, and five of them and the Scotch terrier turned out to be agents for the F.B.I. Soon they had enough derogatory information on Major Major to do whatever they wanted to with him. The only thing they could find to do with him, however, was take him into the Army as a private and make him a major four days later so that Congressmen with nothing else on their minds could go trotting back and forth through the streets of Washington, D.C., chanting, "Who promoted Major Major? Who promoted Major Major?"

Actually, Major Major had been promoted by an I.B.M. machine with a sense of humor almost as keen as his father's. When war broke out, he was still docile and compliant. They told him to enlist, and he enlisted. They told him to apply for aviation cadet training, and he applied for aviation cadet training, and the very next night found himself standing barefoot in icy mud at three o'clock in the morning before a tough and belligerent sergeant from the Southwest who told them he could beat hell out of any man in his outfit and was ready to prove it. The recruits in his squadron had all been shaken roughly awake only minutes before by the sergeant's corporals and told to assemble in front of the administration tent. It was still raining on Major Major. They fell into ranks in the civilian clothes they had brought into the Army with them three days before. Those who had lingered to put shoes and socks on were sent back to their cold, wet, dark tents to remove them, and they were all barefoot in the mud as the sergeant ran his stony eyes over their faces and told them he could beat hell out of any man in his outfit. No one was inclined to dispute him.

Major Major's unexpected promotion to major the next day plunged the belligerent sergeant into a bottomless gloom, for he was no longer able to boast that he could beat hell out of any man in his outfit. He brooded for hours in his tent like Saul, receiving no visitors, while his elite guard of corporals stood discouraged watch outside. At three o'clock in the morning he found his solution, and Major Major and the other recruits were again shaken roughly awake and ordered to assemble barefoot in the drizzly glare at the administration tent, where the sergeant was already waiting, his fists clenched on his hips cockily, so eager to speak that he could hardly wait for them to arrive.

"Me and Major Major," he boasted, in the same tough, clipped tones of the night before, "can beat hell out of any man in my outfit."

The officers on the base took action on the Major Major problem later that same day. How could they cope with a major like Major Major? To demean him personally would be to demean all other officers of equal or lesser rank. To treat him with courtesy, on the other hand, was unthinkable. Fortunately, Major Major had applied for aviation cadet training. Orders transferring him away were sent to the mimeograph room late in the afternoon, and at three o'clock in the morning Major Major was again shaken roughly awake, bidden Godspeed by the sergeant and placed aboard a plane heading west.

Lieutenant Scheisskopf turned white as a sheet when Major Major reported to him in California with bare feet and mud-caked toes. Major Major had taken it for granted that he was being shaken roughly awake again to stand barefoot in the mud and had left his shoes and socks in the tent. The civilian clothing in which he reported for duty to Lieutenant Scheisskopf was rumpled and dirty. Lieutenant Scheisskopf, who had not yet made his reputation as a parader, shuddered violently at the picture Major Major would make marching barefoot in his squadron that coming Sunday.

"Go to the hospital quickly," he mumbled, when he had recovered sufficiently to speak, "and tell them you're sick. Stay there until your allowance for uniforms catches up with you and you have some money to buy some clothes. And some shoes. Buy some shoes."

"Yes, sir."

"I don't think you have to call me 'sir,' sir," Lieutenant Scheisskopf pointed out. "You outrank me."

"Yes, sir. I may outrank you, sir, but you're still my commanding officer."

"Yes, sir, that's right," Lieutenant Scheisskopf agreed. "You may outrank me, sir, but I'm still your commanding officer. So you better do what I tell you, sir, or you'll get into trouble. Go to the hospital and tell them you're sick, sir. Stay there until your uniform allowance catches up with you and you have some money to buy some uniforms."

"Yes, sir."

"And some shoes, sir. Buy some shoes the first chance you get, sir."

"Yes, sir. I will, sir."

"Thank you, sir."

Life in cadet school for Major Major was no different than life had been for him all along. Whoever he was with always wanted him to be with someone else. His instructors gave him preferred treatment at every stage in order to push him along quickly and be rid of him. In almost no time he had his pilot's wings and found himself overseas, where things began suddenly to improve. All his life, Major Major had longed for but one thing, to be absorbed, and in Pianosa, for a while, he finally was. Rank meant little to the men on combat duty, and relations between officers and enlisted men were relaxed and informal. Men whose names he didn't even know said "Hi" and invited him to go swimming or play basketball. His ripest hours were spent in the day-long basketball games no one gave a damn about winning. Score was never kept, and the number of players might vary from one to thirty-five. Major Major had never played basketball or any other game before, but his great, bobbing height and rapturous enthusiasm helped make up for his innate clumsiness and lack of experience. Major Major found true happiness there on the lopsided basketball court with the officers and enlisted men who were almost his friends. If there were no winners, there were no losers, and Major Major enjoyed every gamboling moment right up till the day Colonel Cathcart roared up in his jeep after Major Duluth was killed and made it impossible for him ever to enjoy playing basketball there again.

"You're the new squadron commander," Colonel Cathcart had shouted rudely across the railroad ditch to him. "But don't think it means anything, because it doesn't. All it means is that you're the new squadron commander."

Colonel Cathcart had nursed an implacable grudge against Major Major for a long time. A superfluous major on his rolls meant an untidy table of organization and gave ammunition to the men at Twenty-seventh Air Force Headquarters who Colonel Cathcart was positive were his enemies and rivals. Colonel Cathcart had been praying for just some stroke of good luck like Major Duluth's death. He had been plagued by one extra major; he now had an opening for one major. He appointed Major Major squadron commander and roared away in his jeep as abruptly as he had come.

For Major Major, it meant the end of the game. His face flushed with discomfort, and he was rooted to the spot in disbelief as the rain clouds gathered above him again. When he turned to his teammates, he encountered a reef of curious, reflective faces all gazing at him woodenly with morose and inscrutable animosity. He shivered with shame. When the game resumed, it was not good any longer. When he dribbled, no one tried to stop him; when he called for a pass, whoever had the ball passed it; and when he missed a basket, no one raced him for the rebound. The only voice was his own. The next day was the same, and the day after that he did not come back.

Almost on cue, everyone in the squadron stopped talking to him and started staring at him. He walked through life self-consciously with downcast eyes and burning cheeks, the object of contempt, envy, suspicion, resentment and malicious innuendo everywhere he went. People who had hardly noticed his resemblance to Henry Fonda before now never ceased discussing it, and there were even those who hinted sinisterly that Major Major had been elevated to squadron commander *because* he resembled Henry Fonda. Captain Black, who had aspired to the position himself, maintained that Major Major really *was* Henry Fonda but was too chickenshit to admit it.

Major Major floundered bewilderedly from one embarrassing catastrophe to another. Without consulting him, Sergeant Towser had his belongings moved into the roomy trailer Major Duluth had occupied alone, and when Major Major came rushing breathlessly into the orderly room to report the theft of his things, the young corporal there scared him half out of his wits by leaping to his feet and shouting *"Attention!"* the moment he appeared. Major Major snapped to attention with all the rest in the orderly room, wondering what important personage had entered behind him. Minutes passed in rigid silence, and the whole lot of them might have stood there at attention till doomsday if Major Danby had not dropped by from Group to congratulate Major Major twenty minutes later and put them all at ease.

Major Major fared even more lamentably at the mess hall, where Milo, his face fluttery with smiles, was waiting to usher him proudly to a small table he had set up in front and decorated with an embroidered tablecloth and a nosegay of posies in a pink cut-glass vase. Major Major hung back with horror, but he was not bold enough to resist with all the others watching. Even Havermeyer had lifted his head from his plate to gape at him with his heavy, pendulous jaw. Major Major submitted meekly to Milo's tugging and cowered in disgrace at his private table throughout the whole meal. The food was ashes in his mouth, but he swallowed every mouthful rather than risk offending any of the men connected with its preparation. Alone with Milo later, Major Major felt protest stir for the first time and said he would prefer to continue eating with the other officers. Milo told him it wouldn't work.

"I don't see what there is to work," Major Major argued. "Nothing ever happened before."

"You were never the squadron commander before."

"Major Duluth was the squadron commander and he always ate at the same table with the rest of the men."

"It was different with Major Duluth, sir."

"In what way was it different with Major Duluth?"

"I wish you wouldn't ask me that, sir," said Milo.

"Is it because I look like Henry Fonda?" Major Major mustered the courage to demand.

"Some people say you *are* Henry Fonda," Milo answered.

"Well, I'm not Henry Fonda," Major Major exclaimed, in a voice quavering with exasperation. "And I don't look the least bit like him. And even if I do look like Henry Fonda, what difference does that make?"

"It doesn't make any difference. That's what I'm trying to tell you, sir. It's just not the same with you as it was with Major Duluth."

And it just wasn't the same, for when Major Major, at the next meal, stepped from the food counter to sit with the others at the regular tables, he was frozen in his tracks by the impenetrable wall of antagonism thrown up by their faces and stood petrified with his tray quivering in his hands until Milo glided forward wordlessly to rescue him, by leading him tamely to his private table. Major Major gave up after that and always ate at his table alone with his back to the others. He was certain they resented him because he seemed too good to eat with them now that he was squadron commander. There was never any conversation in the mess tent when Major Major was present. He was conscious that other officers tried to avoid eating at the same time, and everyone was greatly relieved when he stopped coming there altogether and began taking his meals in his trailer.

Major Major began forging Washington Irving's name to official documents the day after the first C.I.D. man showed up to interrogate him about somebody at the hospital who had been doing it and gave him the idea. He had been bored and dissatisfied in his new position. He had been made squadron commander but had no idea what he was supposed to *do* as squadron commander, unless all he was supposed to do was forge Washington Irving's name to official documents and listen to the isolated clinks and thumps of Major ——— de Coverley's horseshoes falling to the ground outside the window of his small office in the rear of the orderly-room tent. He was hounded incessantly by an impression of vital duties left unfulfilled and waited in vain for his responsibilities to overtake him. He seldom went out unless it was absolutely necessary, for he could not get used to being stared at. Occasionally, the monotony was broken by some officer or enlisted man Sergeant Towser referred to him on some matter that Major Major was unable to cope with and referred right back to Sergeant Towser for sensible disposition. Whatever he was supposed to get done as squadron commander apparently was getting done without any assistance from him. He grew moody and depressed. At times he thought seriously of going with all his sorrows to see the chaplain, but the chaplain seemed so overburdened with miseries of his own that Major Major shrank from adding to his troubles. Besides, he was not quite sure if chaplains were for squadron commanders.

He had never been quite sure about Major ——— de Coverley, either, who, when he was not away renting apartments or kidnaping foreign laborers, had nothing more pressing to do than pitch horseshoes. Major Major often paid strict attention to the horseshoes falling softly against the earth or riding down around the small steel pegs in the ground. He peeked out at Major ——— de Coverley for hours and marveled that someone so august had nothing more important to do. He was often tempted to join Major ——— de Coverley, but pitching horseshoes all day long seemed almost as dull as signing "Major Major Major" to official documents, and Major ——— de Coverley's countenance was so forbidding that Major Major was in awe of approaching him.

Major Major wondered about his relationship to Major ——— de Coverley and about Major ——— de Coverley's relationship to him. He knew that Major ——— de Coverley was his executive officer, but he did not know what that meant, and he could not decide whether in Major ——— de Coverley he was blessed with a lenient superior or cursed with a delinquent subordinate. He did not want to ask Sergeant Towser, of whom he was secretly afraid, and there was no one else he could ask, least of all Major ——— de Coverley. Few people ever dared approach Major ——— de Coverley about anything and the only officer foolish enough to pitch one of his horseshoes was stricken the very next day with the worst case of Pianosan crud that Gus or Wes or even Doc Daneeka had ever seen or even heard about. Everyone was positive the disease had been inflicted upon the poor officer in retribution by Major ——— de Coverley, although no one was sure how.

Most of the official documents that came to Major Major's desk did not concern him at all. The vast majority consisted of allusions to prior communications which Major Major had never seen or heard of. There was never any need to look them up, for the instructions were invariably to disregard. In the space of a single productive minute, therefore, he might endorse twenty separate documents each advising him to pay absolutely no attention to any of the others. From General Peckem's office on the mainland came prolix bulletins each day headed by such cheery homilies as "Procrastination is the Thief of Time" and "Cleanliness is Next to Godliness."

General Peckem's communications about cleanliness and procrastination made Major Major feel like a filthy procrastinator, and he always got those out of the way as quickly as he could. The only official documents that interested him were those occasional ones pertaining to the unfortunate second lieutenant who had been killed on the mission over Orvieto less than two hours after he arrived on Pianosa and whose partly unpacked belongings were still in Yossarian's tent. Since the unfortunate lieutenant had reported to the operations tent instead of to the orderly room, Sergeant Towser had decided that it would be safest to report him as never having reported to the squadron at all, and the occasional documents relating to him dealt with the fact that he seemed to have vanished into thin air, which, in one way, was exactly what did happen to him. In the long run, Major Major was grateful for the official documents that came to his desk, for sitting in his office signing them all day long was a lot better than sitting in his office all day long not signing them. They gave him something to do.

Inevitably, every document he signed came back with a fresh page added for a new signature by him after intervals of from two to ten days. They were always much thicker than formerly, for in between the sheet bearing his last endorsement and the sheet added for his new endorsement were the sheets bearing the most recent endorsements of all the other officers in scattered locations who were also occupied in signing their names to that same official document. Major Major grew despondent as he watched simple communications swell prodigiously into huge manuscripts. No matter how many times he signed one, it always came back for still another signature, and he began to despair of ever being free of any of them. One day—it was the day after the C.I.D. man's first visit—Major Major signed Washington Irving's name to one of the documents instead of his own, just to see how it would feel. He liked it. He liked it so much that for the rest of that afternoon he did the same with all the official documents. It was an act of impulsive frivolity and rebellion for which he knew afterward he would be punished severely. The next morning he entered his office in trepidation and waited to see what would happen. Nothing happened.

He had sinned, and it was good, for none of the documents to which he had signed Washington Irving's name ever came back! Here, at last, was progress, and Major Major threw himself into his new career with uninhibited gusto. Signing Washington Irving's name to official documents was not much of a career, perhaps, but it was less monotonous than signing "Major Major Major." When Washington Irving did grow monotonous, he could reverse the order and sign Irving Washington until that grew monotonous. And he was getting something done, for none of the documents signed with either of these names ever came back to the squadron.

What did come back, eventually, was a *second* C.I.D. man, masquerading as a pilot. The men knew he was a C.I.D. man because he confided to them he was and urged each of them not to reveal his true identity to any of the other men to whom he had already confided that he was a C.I.D. man.

"You're the only one in the squadron who knows I'm a C.I.D. man," he confided to Major Major, "and it's absolutely essential that it remain a secret so that my efficiency won't be impaired. Do you understand?"

"Sergeant Towser knows."

"Yes, I know. I had to tell him in order to get in to see you. But I know he won't tell a soul under any circumstances."

"He told me," said Major Major. "He told me there was a C.I.D. man outside to see me."

"That bastard. I'll have to throw a security check on him. I wouldn't leave any top-secret documents lying around here if I were you. At least not until I make my report."

"I don't get any top-secret documents," said Major Major.

"That's the kind I mean. Lock them in your cabinet where Sergeant Towser can't get his hands on them."

"Sergeant Towser has the only key to the cabinet."

"I'm afraid we're wasting time," said the second C.I.D. man rather stiffly. He was a brisk, pudgy, high-strung person whose movements were swift and certain. He took a number of photostats out of a large red expansion envelope he had been hiding conspicuously beneath a leather flight jacket painted garishly with pictures of airplanes flying through orange bursts of flak and with orderly rows of little bombs signifying fifty-five combat missions flown. "Have you ever seen any of these?"

Major Major looked with a blank expression at copies of personal correspondence from the hospital on which the censoring officer had written "Washington Irving" or "Irving Washington."

"No."

"How about these?"

Major Major gazed next at copies of official documents addressed to him to which he had been signing the same signatures.

"No."

"Is the man who signed these names in your squadron?"

"Which one? There are two names here."

"Either one. We figure that Washington Irving and Irving Washington are one man and that he's using two names just to throw us off the track. That's done very often, you know."

"I don't think there's a man with either of those names in my squadron."

A look of disappointment crossed the second C.I.D. man's face. "He's a lot cleverer than we thought," he observed. "He's using a third name and posing as someone else. And I think . . . yes, I think I know what the third name is." With excitement and inspiration, he held another photostat out for Major Major to study. "How about this?"

Major Major bent forward slightly and saw a copy of the piece of V mail from which Yossarian had blacked out everything but the name Mary and on which he had written, "I yearn for you tragically. A. T. Tappman, Chaplain, U. S. Army." Major Major shook his head.

"I've never seen it before."

"Do you know who A. T. Tappman is?"

"He's the group chaplain."

"That locks it up," said the second C.I.D. man. "Washington Irving is the group chaplain."

Major Major felt a twinge of alarm. "A. T. Tappman is the group chaplain," he corrected.

"Are you sure?"

"Yes."

"Why should the group chaplain write this on a letter?"

"Perhaps somebody else wrote it and forged his name."

"Why should somebody want to forge the group chaplain's name?"

"To escape detection."

"You may be right," the second C.I.D. man decided after an instant's hesitation, and smacked his lips crisply. "Maybe we're confronted with a gang, with two men working together who just happen to have opposite names. Yes, I'm sure that's it. One of them here in the squadron, one of them up at the hospital and one of them with the chaplain. That makes three men, doesn't it? Are you absolutely sure you never saw any of these official documents before?"

"I would have signed them if I had."

"With whose name?" asked the second C.I.D. man cunningly. "Yours or Washington Irving's?"

"With my own name," Major Major told him. "I don't even know Washington Irving's name."

The second C.I.D. man broke into a smile.

"Major, I'm glad you're in the clear. It means we'll be able to work together, and I'm going to need every man I can get. Somewhere in the European theater of operations is a man who's getting his hands on communications addressed to you. Have you any idea who it can be?"

"No."

"Well, I have a pretty good idea," said the second C.I.D. man, and leaned forward to whisper confidentially. "That bastard Towser. Why else would he go around shooting his mouth off about me? Now, you keep your eyes open and let me know the minute you hear anyone even talking about Washington Irving. I'll throw a security check on the chaplain and everyone else around here."

The moment he was gone, the first C.I.D. man jumped into Major Major's office through the window and wanted to know who the second C.I.D. man was. Major Major barely recognized him.

"He was a C.I.D. man," Major Major told him.

"Like hell he was," said the first C.I.D. man. "I'm the C.I.D. man around here."

Major Major barely recognized him because he was wearing a faded maroon corduroy bathrobe with open seams under both arms, linty flannel pajamas, and worn house slippers with one flapping sole. This was regulation hospital dress, Major Major recalled. The man had added about twenty pounds and seemed bursting with good health.

"I'm really a very sick man," he whined. "I caught cold in the hospital from a fighter pilot and came down with a very serious case of pneumonia."

"I'm very sorry," Major Major said.

"A lot of good that does me," the C.I.D. man sniveled. "I don't want your sympathy. I just want you to know what I'm going through. I came down to warn you that Washington Irving seems to have shifted his base of operations from the hospital to your squadron. You haven't heard anyone around here talking about Washington Irving, have you?"

"As a matter of fact, I have," Major Major answered. "That man who was just in here. He was talking about Washington Irving."

"Was he really?" the first C.I.D. man cried with delight. "This might be just what we needed to crack the case wide open! You keep him under surveillance twenty-four hours a day while I rush back to the hospital and write my superiors for further instructions." The C.I.D. man jumped out of Major Major's office through the window and was gone.

A minute later, the flap separating Major Major's office from the orderly room flew open and the second C.I.D. man was back, puffing frantically in haste. Gasping for breath, he shouted, "I just saw a man in red pajamas come jumping out of your window and go running up the road! Didn't you see him?"

"He was here talking to me," Major Major answered.

"I thought that looked mighty suspicious, a man jumping out the window in red pajamas." The man paced about the small office in vigorous circles. "At first I thought it was you, hightailing it for Mexico. But now I see it wasn't you. He didn't say anything about Washington Irving, did he?"

"As a matter of fact," said Major Major, "he did."

"He did?" cried the second C.I.D. man. "That's fine! This might be just the break we needed to crack the case wide open. Do you know where we can find him?"

"At the hospital. He's really a very sick man."

"That's great!" exclaimed the second C.I.D. man. "I'll go right up there after him. It would be best if I went incognito. I'll go explain the situation at the medical tent and have them send me there as a patient."

"They won't send me to the hospital as a patient unless I'm sick," he reported back to Major Major. "Actually, I am pretty sick. I've been meaning to turn myself in for a checkup, and this will be a good opportunity. I'll go back to the medical tent and tell them I'm sick, and I'll get sent to the hospital that way."

"Look what they did to me," he reported back to Major Major with purple gums. His distress was inconsolable. He carried his shoes and socks in his hands, and his toes had been painted with gentian-violet solution, too. "Who ever heard of a C.I.D. man with purple gums?" he moaned.

He walked away from the orderly room with his head down and tumbled into a slit trench and broke his nose. His temperature was still normal, but Gus and Wes made an exception of him and sent him to the hospital in an ambulance.

Major Major had lied, and it was good. He was not really surprised that it was good, for he had observed that people who did lie were, on the whole, more resourceful and ambitious and successful than people who did not lie. Had he told the truth to the second C.I.D. man, he would have found himself in trouble. Instead he had lied, and he was free to continue his work.

He became more circumspect in his work as a result of the visit from the second C.I.D. man. He did all his signing with his left hand and only while wearing the dark glasses and false mustache he had used unsuccessfully to help him begin playing basketball again. As an additional precaution, he made a happy switch from Washington Irving to John Milton. John Milton was supple and concise. Like Washington Irving, he could be reversed with good effect whenever he grew monotonous. Furthermore, he enabled Major Major to double his output, for John Milton was so much shorter than either his own name or Washington Irving's and took so much less time to write. John Milton proved fruitful in still one more respect. He was versatile, and Major Major soon found himself incorporating the signature in fragments of imaginary dialogues. Thus, typical endorsements on the official documents might read, "John, Milton is a sadist" or "Have you seen Milton, John?" One signature of which he was especially proud read, "Is anybody in the John, Milton?" John Milton threw open whole new vistas filled with charming, inexhaustible possibilities that promised to ward off monotony forever. Major Major went back to Washington Irving when John Milton grew monotonous.

Major Major had bought the dark glasses and false mustache in Rome in a final, futile attempt to save himself from the swampy degradation into which he was steadily sinking. First there had been the awful humiliation of the Great Loyalty Oath Crusade, when not one of the thirty or forty people circulating competitive loyalty oaths would even allow him to sign. Then, just when that was blowing over, there was the matter of Clevinger's plane disappearing so mysteriously in thin air with every member of the crew, and blame for the strange mishap centering balefully on him because he had never signed any of the loyalty oaths.

The dark glasses had large magenta rims. The false black mustache was a flamboyant organ grinder's, and he wore them both to the basketball game one day when he felt he could endure his loneliness no longer. He affected an air of jaunty familiarity as he sauntered to the court and prayed silently that he would not be recognized. The others pretended not to recognize him, and he began to have fun. Just as he finished congratulating himself on his innocent ruse he was bumped hard by one of his opponents and knocked to his knees. Soon he was bumped hard again, and it dawned on him that they did recognize him and that they were using his disguise as a license to elbow, trip and maul him. They did not want him at all. And just as he did realize this, the players on his team fused instinctively with the players on the other team into a single, howling, blood-thirsty mob that descended upon him from all sides with foul curses and swinging fists. They knocked him to the ground, kicked him while he was on the ground, attacked him again after he had struggled blindly to his feet. He covered his face with his hands and could not see. They swarmed all over each other in their frenzied compulsion to bludgeon him, kick him, gouge him, trample him. He was pummeled spinning to the edge of the ditch and sent slithering down on his head and shoulders. At the bottom he found his footing, clambered up the other wall and staggered away beneath the hail of hoots and stones with which they pelted him until he lurched into shelter around a corner of the orderly room tent. His paramount concern throughout the entire assault was to keep his dark glasses and false mustache in place so that he might continue pretending he was somebody else and be spared the dreaded necessity of having to confront them with his authority.

Back in his office, he wept; and when he finished weeping he washed the blood from his mouth and nose, scrubbed the dirt from the abrasions on his cheek and forehead, and summoned Sergeant Towser.

"From now on," he said, "I don't want anyone to come in to see me while I'm here. Is that clear?"

"Yes, sir," said Sergeant Towser. "Does that include me?"

"Yes."

"I see. Will that be all?"

"Yes."

"What shall I say to the people who do come to see you while you're here?"

"Tell them I'm in and ask them to wait."

"Yes, sir. For how long?"

"Until I've left."

"And then what shall I do with them?"

"I don't care."

"May I send them in to see you after you've left?"

"Yes."

"But you won't be here then, will you?"

"No."

"Yes, sir. Will that be all?"

"Yes."

"Yes, sir."

"From now on," Major Major said to the middle-aged enlisted man who took care of his trailer, "I don't want you to come here while I'm here to ask me if there's anything you can do for me. Is that clear?"

"Yes, sir," said the orderly. "When should I come here to find out if there's anything you want me to do for you?"

"When I'm not here."

"Yes, sir. And what should I do?"

"Whatever I tell you to."

"But you won't be here to tell me. Will you?"

"No."

"Then what should I do?"

"Whatever has to be done."

"Yes, sir."

"That will be all," said Major Major.

"Yes, sir," said the orderly. "Will that be all?"

"No," said Major Major. "Don't come in to clean, either. Don't come in for anything unless you're sure I'm not here."

"Yes, sir. But how can I always be sure?"

"If you're not sure, just assume that I am here and go away until you are sure. Is that clear?"

"Yes, sir."

"I'm sorry to have to talk to you in this way, but I have to. Goodbye."

"Goodbye, sir."

"And thank you. For everything."

"Yes, sir."

"From now on," Major Major said to Milo Minderbinder, "I'm not going to come to the mess hall any more. I'll have all my meals brought to me in my trailer."

"I think that's a good idea, sir," Milo answered. "Now I'll be able to serve you special dishes that the others will never know about. I'm sure you'll enjoy them. Colonel Cathcart always does."

"I don't want any special dishes. I want exactly what you serve all the other officers. Just have whoever brings it knock once on my door and leave the tray on the step. Is that clear?"

"Yes, sir," said Milo. "That's very clear. I've got some live Maine lobsters hidden away that I can serve you tonight with an excellent Roquefort salad and two frozen éclairs that were smuggled out of Paris only yesterday together with an important member of the French underground. Will that do for a start?"

"No."

"Yes, sir. I understand."

For dinner that night Milo served him broiled Maine lobster with excellent Roquefort salad and two frozen éclairs. Major Major was annoyed. If he sent it back, though, it would only go to waste or to somebody else, and Major Major had a weakness for broiled lobster. He ate with a guilty conscience. The next day for lunch there was terrapin Maryland with a whole quart of Dom Pérignon 1937, and Major Major gulped it down without a thought.

After Milo, there remained only the men in the orderly room, and Major Major avoided them by entering and leaving every time through the dingy celluloid window of his office. The window unbuttoned and was low and large and easy to jump through from either side. He managed the distance between the orderly room and his trailer by darting around the corner of the tent when the coast was clear, leaping down into the railroad ditch and dashing along with his head bowed until he attained the sanctuary of the forest. Abreast of his trailer, he left the ditch and wove his way speedily toward home through the dense underbrush, in which the only person he ever encountered was Captain Flume, who, drawn and ghostly, frightened him half to death one twilight by materializing without warning out of a patch of dewberry bushes to complain that Chief White Halfoat had threatened to slit his throat open from ear to ear.

"If you ever frighten me like that again," Major Major told him, *"I'll* slit your throat open from ear to ear."

Captain Flume gasped and dissolved right back into the patch of dewberry bushes, and Major Major never set eyes on him again.

When Major Major looked back on what he had accomplished, he was pleased. In the midst of a few foreign acres teeming with more than two hundred people, he had succeeded in becoming a recluse. With a little ingenuity and vision, he had made it all but impossible for anyone in the squadron to talk to him, which was just fine with everyone, he noticed, since no one wanted to talk to him anyway. No one, it turned out, but that madman Yossarian, who brought him down with a flying tackle one day as he was scooting along the bottom of the ditch to his trailer for lunch.

The last person in the squadron Major Major wanted to be brought down with a flying tackle by was Yossarian. There was something inherently disreputable about Yossarian, always carrying on so disgracefully about that dead man in his tent who wasn't even there and then taking off all his clothes after the Avignon mission and going around without them right up to the day General Dreedle stepped up to pin a medal on him for his heroism over Ferrara and found him standing in formation stark naked. No one in the world had the power to remove the dead man's disorganized effects from Yossarian's tent. Major Major had forfeited the authority when he permitted Sergeant Towser to report the lieutenant who had been killed over Orvieto less than two hours after he arrived in the squadron as never having arrived in the squadron at all. The only one with any right to remove his belongings from Yossarian's tent, it seemed to Major Major, was Yossarian himself, and Yossarian, it seemed to Major Major, had no right.

Major Major groaned after Yossarian brought him down with a flying tackle, and tried to wiggle to his feet. Yossarian wouldn't let him.

"Captain Yossarian," Yossarian said, "requests permission to speak to the major at once about a matter of life or death."

"Let me up, please," Major Major bid him in cranky discomfort. "I can't return your salute while I'm lying on my arm."

Yossarian released him. They stood up slowly. Yossarian saluted again and repeated his request.

"Let's go to my office," Major Major said. "I don't think this is the best place to talk."

"Yes, sir," answered Yossarian.

They smacked the gravel from their clothing and walked in constrained silence to the entrance of the orderly room.

"Give me a minute or two to put some mercurochrome on these cuts. Then have Sergeant Towser send you in."

"Yes, sir."

Major Major strode with dignity to the rear of the orderly room without glancing at any of the clerks and typists working at the desks and filing cabinets. He let the flap leading to his office fall closed behind him. As soon as he was alone in his office, he raced across the room to the window and jumped outside to dash away. He found Yossarian blocking his path. Yossarian was waiting at attention and saluted again.

"Captain Yossarian requests permission to speak to the major at once about a matter of life or death," he repeated determinedly.

"Permission denied," Major Major snapped.

"That won't do it."

Major Major gave in. "All right," he conceded wearily. "I'll talk to you. Please jump inside my office."

"After you."

They jumped inside the office. Major Major sat down, and Yossarian moved around in front of his desk and told him that he did not want to fly any more combat missions. *What could he do?* Major Major asked himself. All he could do was what he had been instructed to do by Colonel Korn and hope for the best.

"Why not?" he asked.

"I'm afraid."

"That's nothing to be ashamed of," Major Major counseled him kindly. "We're all afraid."

"I'm not ashamed," Yossarian said. "I'm just afraid."

"You wouldn't be normal if you were never afraid. Even the bravest men experience fear. One of the biggest jobs we all face in combat is to overcome our fear."

"Oh, come on, Major. Can't we do without that horseshit?"

Major Major lowered his gaze sheepishly and fiddled with his fingers. "What do you want me to tell you?"

"That I've flown enough missions and can go home."

"How many have you flown?"

"Fifty-one."

"You've only got four more to fly."

"He'll raise them. Every time I get close he raises them."

"Perhaps he won't this time."

"He never sends anyone home, anyway. He just keeps them around waiting for rotation orders until he doesn't have enough men left for the crews, and then raises the number of missions and throws them all back on combat status. He's been doing that ever since he got here."

"You mustn't blame Colonel Cathcart for any delay with the orders," Major Major advised. "It's Twenty-seventh Air Force's responsibility to process the orders promptly once they get them from us."

"He could still ask for replacements and send us home when the orders did come back. Anyway, I've been told that Twenty-seventh Air Force wants only forty missions and that it's only his own idea to get us to fly fifty-five."

"I wouldn't know anything about that," Major Major answered. "Colonel Cathcart is our commanding officer and we must obey him. Why don't you fly the four more missions and see what happens?"

"I don't want to."

What could you do? Major Major asked himself again. What could you do with a man who looked you squarely in the eye and said he would rather die than be killed in combat, a man who was at least as mature and intelligent as you were and who you had to pretend was not? What could you say to him?

"Suppose we let you pick your missions and fly milk runs," Major Major said. "That way you can fly the four missions and not run any risks."

"I don't want to fly milk runs. I don't want to be in the war any more."

"Would you like to see our country lose?" Major Major asked.

"We won't lose. We've got more men, more money and more material. There are ten million men in uniform who could replace me. Some people are getting killed and a lot more are making money and having fun. Let somebody else get killed."

"But suppose everybody on our side felt that way."

"Then I'd certainly be a damned fool to feel any other way. Wouldn't I?"

What could you possibly say to him? Major Major wondered forlornly. One thing he could not say was that there was nothing he could do. To say there was nothing he could do would suggest he *would* do something if he could and imply the existence of an error or injustice in Colonel Korn's policy. Colonel Korn had been most explicit about that. He must never say there was nothing he could do.

"I'm sorry," he said. "But there's nothing I can do."

1961

DAVID FOSTER WALLACE
b. 1962

David Foster Wallace was born in Ithaca, New York, the son of a philosophy professor and an English teacher. He was educated at Amherst College and the University of Arizona at Tucson and currently teaches at Illinois State University in Normal, Illinois. He is the author of one story collection, *Girl with Curious Hair* (1989); two novels, *The Broom in the System* (1990) and *Infinite Jest* (1996); and two nonfiction works, *Signifying Rappers* (1990) and *A Supposedly Fun Thing I'll Never Do Again* (1997). His stories have appeared in *Harper's, Playboy,* and *The Paris Review,* and were cited for inclusion in the *O. Henry Prize Stories* collection for 1988 and the *Best American Short Stories* collection for 1992.

In a 1996 interview for this anthology, Wallace said that he grew up, like many of his peers, in a "culture which is itself so mediated that the formation of self is both rebellion against and acquiescence to the media. . . . I attempt, whether through distortion or humor, to write about how the world interacts with people's nerve endings right now. I just want to make it seem real."

"Lyndon" appeared in *Girl with Curious Hair.*

Lyndon

"Hello down there. This is your candidate, Lyndon Johnson."
—Campaigning by helicopter for U.S. Senate, 1954

'My name is Lyndon Baines Johnson. I own the fucking floor you stand on, boy.'

There was also an aide in the office, in one corner, a skinny man with big ears, working at a long pinewood table, doing something flurried between a teletype and a stack of clipped newspapers, but Lyndon was talking to me. It was the Fifties and I was young, burned-out cool, empty. I slouched emptily where I stood, before his desk, my hands in the pockets of my topcoat, flapping the coat a little. I stood hip-shot and looked at the scarlet floor tile under my shoes. Each red square tile was decorated with a lone gold star.

He leaned over his desk at me. He looked like a big predatory bird.

'My name is Lyndon Baines *Johnson,* son. I am the Senator to the United States Senate from the state of Texas, U.S.A. I am the twenty-seventh richest personal man in the nation. I got the biggest wazoo in Washington and the wife with the prettiest name. So I don't care who your wife's Daddy knows—don't you slouch at this Senator, boy.'

The way he looked, when I looked at him, was always the same. He looked like eyes, the eyes of a small person, looking trapped from behind the lined hooked jutting face of a big bland bird of prey. His eyes are the same in pictures.

I apologized nervously. 'I'm sorry, sir. I think maybe I'm nervous. I was just sitting out there, filling out application forms, and all of a sudden here I am speaking to you, directly, sir.'

He produced a nasal inhaler and an index card. He put the inhaler to a nostril and squeezed, inhaling. He squinted at the card.

' "Every prospective part of the personnel in the office of the United States Senator from Texas shall be interviewed"—I'm reading this, boy, off this card here—"interviewed with the potential of being interviewed by *any* part of the personnel of the office he shall potentially work under." I wrote that. I don't care who your wife's Daddy's wife's internist knows—you're potentially under me, boy, and I'm interviewing you. What do you think of that?'

The big-eared aide sighted down his shears at a news clipping, making sure the cut lines were clean and square.

'A senator who interviews low-level office help?' I said. I listened to oak-muffled, far-away sounds of telephones and typewriters and teletypes. I was beginning to think I had filled out forms for an inappropriate job. I had no experience. I was young, burned out. My transcript was an amputee.

'This must be a very conscientious office,' I said.

'Goddamn right it's conscientious, boy. The president of this particular stretch of the Dirksen Building is me, Lyndon Johnson. And a president views, interviews, and reviews everything he presides over, if he's doing his job in the correct manner.' He paused. 'Say, write that down for me, boy.'

I looked to the jughead of an aide, but he was laying down long ribbons of Scotch tape along a straightedge. 'Plus "previews," ' Lyndon said. 'Stick in "previews" there at the start, son.'

Pores open, I patted at my jacket and topcoat tentatively, trying to look as if this might have been the one just-my-luck day I wasn't carrying anything connected to writing down aphorisms for inspired Senators.

But Lyndon didn't notice; he had turned his leather chair and was continuing, facing the office window, facing the regiments of autographed photos, civic awards, and the headless cattle horns, curved like pincers, those weird disconnected horns that projected from the wall behind his big desk.

Lyndon probed at his teeth with a corner of the card he'd read from, his chair's square back to me. He said:

'If there's even a pissing chicken's chance that the ass of some sorry slouching boy who can't even button up his topcoat is going to cross my path in the office of this particular United States Senator, I'm interviewing that boy's ass.'

His scalp shone, even in the Fifties. The back of his head was rimmed with a sort of terrace of hair. His head was pill-shaped, tall, with the suggestion of a huge brain cavity. His hands, treed with veins, were giant. He pointed a limb-sized finger slowly at the thin aide:

'Piesker, you keep me waiting for a news summary again and I'll kick your ass all down the hall.'

The thin aide was clipping out a complicatedly shaped newspaper article with unbelievable speed.

I cleared my throat. 'May I ask what whatever job I seem to have applied for consists of, sir.'

Lyndon remained facing the decorated wall and big window. The window had limp United States and Texas flags flanking it. Out the window was a sidewalk, a policeman, a street, some trees, a black iron fence with sharp decorative points like inverted Valentines. Beyond that was the bright green and scrubbed white of Capitol Hill.

Lyndon inhaled again from his nasal inhaler. The bottle wheezed a bit. I waited, standing, on the starred tile, while he looked through the onion-skin forms I'd completed.

'This boy's name is David Boyd. Says here you're from Connecticut. Connecticut?'

'Yes sir.'

'But your wife's Daddy is Jack Childs?'

I nodded.

'Speak up Boyd goddamnit. Black Jack Childs, of the Houston Childses? And Mrs. Childs and my own lovely wife share a internist, at the doctor's, back home, in Texas?'

'So I'm told, sir.'

He rotated his chair toward me, noiseless, still fondling the policy card he'd written, tracing his lip's outline with it as he scanned forms.

'Says here you went and dropped out of Yale Business School, does it.'

'I did that, sir, yes. I left Yale.'

'Yale is in Connecticut, also,' he said thoughtfully.

I fluttered my coat pockets. 'It is.' I paused. 'In all honesty sir I was asked to leave,' I said.

'Met Jack Childs's little girl at Yale, then? Kicked in the butt by love? Dropped them books and picked up a loved one? Admirable. Similar.' He had his boots, two big boots with sharp shining toes, up on his desk. The eyes behind that big face were looking at something far away.

'*Had* to get married did you? *Had* to leave?'

'Sir, in all honesty, I was asked to leave.'

'Yale up there in Connecticut asked you to leave?'

'Yes sir.'

He had rolled the card into a tight cylinder and had it deep inside his ear, probing at something, looking past me.

"Tomorrow will be drastically different from today."
—Speech to National Press Club, Washington, D.C., April 17, 1959

"The President is a restless man."
—Staff member, 1965

"The President is a wary man."
—Staff member, 1964

"I doubt if Lyndon Johnson ever did anything impulsive in his life, he was such a cautious, canny man."
—The Honorable Sam Rayburn, 1968

'I committed indiscretions,' I told Lyndon. 'Indiscretions were committed, and I was asked to leave.'

Lyndon was looking pointedly from Piesker to his wristwatch. Piesker, the aide, whimpered a little as he collated sheets at that very long knotty-pine table beneath a painting of scrub and dead-brown hills and a dry riverbed under a blue sky.

'I was asked by Yale to leave,' I said. 'That's why my postgraduate transcript appears as it does.'

He was always right there, but you had the sense that his side of a conversation meandered along its own course, now toward yours, now away.

'Me personally,' he said, 'I worked my ass all *through* college. I shined some shoes in a barber's. I sold pore-tightening cream door-to-door. I was a printer's devil at a newspaper. I even herded goats, for a fellow, one summer.' I saw him make that face for the first time. 'Jesus I hate the smell of a goat,' he said. 'Fucking Christ. Ever once smelled a goat, boy?'

I tried my best to shake my head regretfully. I so wish I could summon the face he made. I was laughing despite myself. The face had seemed to settle into itself like a kicked tent, his eyes rolling back. My laughter felt jagged and hysterical: I had no clue how it would be taken. But Lyndon grinned. I had not yet even been asked to sit. I stood on this great red echoing floor, separated from Lyndon and his boots by yards of spur-scuffed mahogany desktop.

'Probably heard rumors about what it smells like, though,' he mused. 'Some grapevine or other, having to do with animal smells, I'm sure I . . .'

But he sat up suddenly straight, as if he'd remembered something key and undone. The suddenness of it made Piesker drop his shears. They clattered. Lyndon looked me up and down closely.

'Shit, son, you look about twenty.'

"Remember that one of the keys to Lyndon Johnson is that he is a perfectionist—a perfectionist in the most imperfect art in the world: politics. Just remember that."
—An old associate, 1960

I finally got to sit. My back had been starting to get that sort of museum stiffness. I sat in a corner of Lyndon's broad office for four hours that cool spring day. I watched him devour Piesker's collected, clipped, and collated packet of important articles from the nation's most influential newspapers. I watched aides and advisors, together and separate, come and go. Lyndon seemed to forget I was here, in an outsized chair, in the corner, my coat puddled around my lap as I sat, watching. I watched him read, dictate, sign and initial all at once. I watched him ignore a ringing phone. I noticed how rarely such a busy man's phone seemed to ring. I watched him speak to Roy Cohn for twenty solid minutes without once answering Cohn's question about whether Everett Dirksen could be shown to be soft on those who were soft on Communism. Lyndon looked over at my corner only once, when I lit a smoke, baring his teeth until I put the long cigarette out in a low ceramic receptacle I prayed was an ashtray. I watched the Senator receive an elegantly accented Italian dignitary who wanted to talk about sales of Texas cotton to the Common Market, the two men sitting opposite on slim chairs in the waxed red floor's center, drinking dark coffee out of delicate saucer-and-spoon complexes brought in by Lyndon's personal secretary, Dora Teane, a heavily rouged, eyebrowless woman with a kind face and a girdle-roll. I watched Lyndon leave the slender spoon in his cup and reach casually down into his groin to ease his pants as he and the dignitary talked textiles, democracy, and the status of the lira.

The light in the office reddened.

I think I was drowsing. I heard a sudden: 'Yo there in my *corner.*'

'Don't just sit there with your mind in neutral, boy,' Lyndon was saying, rolling down his shirtsleeves. We were alone. 'Go and talk to Mrs. Teane out front. Go get oriented. I once see a disorientated boy on Lyndon Baines Johnson's staff, that boy's ass gets introduced to a certain sidewalk.'

'I'm hired, then? The interview's over?' I asked, standing, stiff.

Lyndon seemed not to hear. 'The man that invented specially convened sessions of the United States Senate, *that's* the man ought to be made to herd goats,' drawing his jacket on carefully, easing into it with a real grace. He fastened his cuff studs as he crossed the floor, his walk vaguely balletic, his boots clicking and jingling. I followed.

He stopped before his door and looked at his topcoat, on its coat hook. He looked to me.

The coat hook was the same ornately carved wood as the office door. I held Lyndon's coat up as he slipped back into it, snapping the lapels straight with a pop.

'May I ask what exactly I'm to be hired to do?' I asked, stepping back to give him room to rotate in front of the mirror, checking his coat.

Lyndon looked at his watch. 'You're a mailboy.'

I didn't parse. 'Isn't that a little redundant?'

'You deliver mail, boy,' he said, bearing down on the door's handle. 'You think you can deliver some mail in this office do you?' I trailed him through the noise and fluorescence of the staff's office complex. There were cubicles and desks and *Congressional Records* and gray machines. The harsh doubled overhead lights threw the range of his shadow over every desk he passed.

'The Senator places great importance on communication with citizens and constituents at all times,' Dora Teane told me. I was handed an index card.

Its heading, bold-face, read SAME DAY DIRECTIVE. 'It is an office regulation for the staff that every piece of mail the Senator receives must be answered that same day it came in.' She put her hand on my arm. I got a faint odor of luncheon meat. The card was filled with numbered instructions, the handwriting spiky and almost childish. I was sure it was not the penmanship of a secretary.

'That'—Mrs. Teane indicated the index card—'is an un*prec*edented regulation for offices of Senators.'

She showed me the Dirksen Building's basement mailroom, the mail boxes, mail bags, mail carts. Lyndon Johnson received seas of mail every day.

> "I'm a compromiser and a maneuverer. I try to *get* something. That's the way our system in the United States works."
>
> —In *The New York Times,* December 8, 1963

Margaret and I found a pleasant walk-up apartment on T Street NW. I was able to walk to the Dirksen Building. Margaret, who had gumption and drive, landed a part-time job teaching composition to remedials at Georgetown. I quickly became familiar with a good many of the huge number of young staffers who swarmed yearly from eastern colleges to the Hill. I established a regular relationship with a shy, smooth young press aide to another senior Southern Senator in the Building. Peter, who lasted four months, had a marvelous Carolinian manner and was as interested in discretion as I.

And I delivered mail. I emptied, thrice daily, gold-starred boxes, wire baskets, and dull-white sacks of mail into carts with canvas sides, trundled them over gray cellar stone into the freight elevator, and brought them up to Lyndon's maze of wooden offices and glass cubicles. I sorted mail in the sweet-smelling mimeo room. I got to know quickly what classes of mail there were and which went to whom for response. I got to know Lyndon's circle of assistants and researchers and aides and secretaries and public relations people, the whole upper-subordinate staff: Hal Ball, Dan Johnson, Walt Peltason, Jim Johnson, Coby Donagan, Lew N. Johnson, Dora Teane and her pool of typists—all pleasant, Southern, deeply tense, hard-working, dedicated to the constituency of Texas, the Democratic Party, and united in a complicated, simultaneous suspension of fear, hatred, contempt, awe, and fanatical loyalty to Lyndon Baines Johnson.

> "Every night when I go to bed I ask myself: 'What did we do today that we can point to for generations to come, to say that we laid the foundations for a better and more peaceful and more prosperous and less-suffering world?' "
>
> —Press Conference, Rose Garden
White House
April 21, 1964

> "Oh he could be a bastard. He had it in him to be a beast, and it was widely known. He'd hide paper-clips on the floor beneath his desk, to test the night custodian. He'd scream. One day he'd be as kind as you please and the next he'd be screaming and carry-

ing on and cursing you and your whole family tree, in the most vile language, in front of your public coworkers. We became accustomed to this and all stopped, gradually we stopped being embarrassed by it, because it happened to all of us at one time or another. Except Mr. Boyd. We had a policy of trying to stay out of the Vice President's peripheral vision. He would go into rages for days at a time. But they were quiet rages. But oh that only made them more frightening. He prowled the offices the way a prowling storm will prowl. You never knew when it would hit, or where, or who. Rages. It was not a working environment I enjoyed, sir. We were all terrified much of the time. Except Mr. Boyd. Mr. Boyd, sir, never received an unkind public word from the Vice President from the first day he came to work when the Vice President was still a Senator. We believed that Mr. Boyd was a close relative at the time. But I wish to say Mr. Boyd never abused his position of immunity to the rages, however. Whether as a messenger all the way up to executive assistant, oh he worked as hard as we did, sir, and was as devoted to the Vice President as one man can be devoted to another. These are only the opinions of one typist, of course."

—Former typist in the office of LBJ
November, 1963

The truth made the truth's usual quick circuit around the offices, the Building, the Hill. I was a homosexual. I had been a homosexual at Yale. In my last year before matriculating to the Business College, I met and became intimate with a Yale undergraduate, Jeffrey, a wealthy boy from Houston, Texas, who was beautiful, often considerate, wistful, but passionate, possessive, and a sufferer from periodic bouts of clinical depression so severe he had to be medicated. It was the medication, I discovered, that made him wistful.

My lover Jeffrey ran with a group of synthetic but pleasant Texas socialites, one of whom was Margaret Childs, a tall, squarely built girl who eventually claimed, from unknown motive, to be in love with me. Margaret pursued me. I declined her in every sensitive way I knew. I simply had no interest. But Jeffrey grew inflamed. He revealed that his friends did not and must not know he was a homosexual. He pushed me to avoid Margaret altogether, which was hard: Margaret, gritty, bright enough to be chronically bored, had become puzzled, suspicious, of Jeffrey's (quite unsubtle) attempts to shield me from her. She smelled potential drama, and kept up the pursuit. Jeffrey became jealous as only the manic can. In my first year in Business, while I was shopping for my father's annual Christmas golf balls, Jeffrey and Margaret had it out, publicly, dramatically, in a Beat New Haven coffeehouse. Jeffrey put his foot through a doughnut counter. Certain information became public. Bits of this public information got back to my parents, who were close to the parents of two of my housemates. My parents came to me, personally, at Yale, on campus. It was snowing. At dinner with my parents and housemates, at Morty's, Jeffrey became so upset that he had to be taken to the men's room and calmed. My father swabbed Jeffrey's forehead with moist paper towels in a cold stall. Jeffrey kept telling my father what a kind man he was.

Before my parents left—their hands literally on the handles of the station wagon's doors—my father, in the snow, asked me whether my sexual preferences were outside my own control. He asked me whether, were I to meet the right woman, I might be capable of heterosexual love, of marriage and a family and a pillar-type position in the community of my choice. These, my father explained, were his and my mother's great and only wishes for me, their one child, whom they loved without judgment. My mother did not speak. I remember a distanced interest in the steam of my own breath as I explained why I thought I could not and so would not do as my father wished, invoking Fifties' wisdom about deviancy, invoking a sort of god of glands as a shaman might blame vegetable spirits for a lost harvest. My father nodded continually throughout this whole very serious and civil conversation while my mother checked maps in the glove compartment. When I failed to present for next week's holiday, my father sent me a card, my mother a check and leftovers in foil.

I saw them only once more before my father dropped dead of something unexpected. I had left Jeffrey's company, and had been befriended in my upset by a still grimly determined Margaret Childs. Jeffrey unfortunately saw, in all this, cause to take his own life, which he did in an especially nasty way; and he left, on the table beneath the heating pipes from which he was found suspended, a note—a document—neatly typed, full enough of absolute truth concatenated with utter fiction that I was asked by the administration of the Business College to leave Yale University. Weeks after my father's wake I married Margaret Childs, under a mesquite tree, the blue stares of my mother and a Houston sky, and a system of vows, promises of strength, denial, trial, and compassion far beyond the Childs' Baptist minister's ritual prescriptions.

The truth, to which there was really no more than that, and which made its way through the Senator's staff, the Dirksen and Owen Buildings, and the Little Congress of the Hill's three-piece-suited infantry remarkably focused and unexaggerated, concluded with the fact that Margaret's father, Mr. Childs, less wealthy than outright powerful by the standards of 1958's Texas, had lines of political influence that projected all the way into the U.S. Senate, and that he, Mr. Childs, in a gesture that was both carrot and stick, slung his son-in-law on one line of that influence and had me hand-over-hand it into the offices of a risen and rising, uncouth and ingenious senior Senator, a possible Democratic candidate in the next Presidential election. Lyndon.

I categorized and delivered mail. Business mail, official mail, important or letterheaded mail was all put into the hands of one or another of Lyndon's eight closest advisors and aides. Intra-Senate mail went to one of three administrative assistants.

All envelopes addressed by hand—automatically classified as letters from constituents—were doled out by Mrs. Teane and me among secretaries, interns, typists, low-level staffers. There was often far more of this constituents' mail, these Voices of the People, full of invective or adulation or petition for redress or advantage, far, far more than the low-level personnel could handle in a physical day. I developed and got approval for a few standardized replies, form letters made to look personal, responding to some one or another major and predictable theme in some of this mail, but we were still barely ahead of the Same Day Directive's demands. Backlogs threatened. I began staying at the offices late, telephoning Margaret or Peter to release me from the evening's plans, working to finish up assembling the Senator's replies to his people's every voice. I enjoyed the night's quiet in the staff room, one lamp burning, cicadas thrilling in rhythm out on the grounds. The staffers who handled mail began to appreciate me. A typist kept bringing me loaves of banana bread. Best, I now got access to Mrs. Teane's dark and deeply bitter East Texas coffee; she'd leave me a chuckling percolator of it as she made the closing rounds, plump and clucking, turning off lights and machines. I enjoyed the offices' night.

And, most nights, Lyndon's lights would glow from the seams in his heavy office door. I could sometimes hear the muffled tinniness of the transistor radio he listened to when alone. He rarely left the building before ten, sometimes later, slinging his coat over a shoulder, sometimes speaking to someone absent, sometimes jogging toward an abrupt halt that let him slide the length of the slick staffers' floor, not a glance in my direction as I read crudely cursived letters, advancing a few to Mrs. Teane's attention, determining which of the pre-prepared responses were appropriate for which of the others, applying the Senator's signature stamp, moistening, fastening, metering, stacking, smoking.

And one night I looked up in a lean shadow to find him stopped, puzzled, before my desk in the big empty staff room, as if I were a person unknown to him. It's true we'd rarely spoken since that first interview four months ago. He stood there, cotton sportcoat over shoulder, impossibly tall, inclined slightly over me.

'What on God's green earth you doing, boy?'

'I'm finishing up on some of this mail, sir.'

He checked his wrist. 'It's twelve midnight at night, son.'

'You work yourself pretty hard, Senator Johnson.'

'Call me Mr. Johnson, boy,' Lyndon said, twirling a watchless fob that hung from his vest. 'You can just go on ahead and call me mister.'

He hit another lamp and settled tiredly behind the desk of Nunn, a summer intern from Tufts.

'This isn't your job, boy.' He gestured at the white castle of stacks I'd made. 'Do we pay you to do this?'

'Someone needs to do it, sir. And I admire the Same Day Directive.'

He nodded, pleased. 'I wrote that.'

'I think your concern with the mail is admirable, sir.'

He made that thoughtful, clicking sound with his mouth. 'Maybe not if it keeps some sorry red-eyed boy up licking all night without renumeration it isn't.'

'Someone needs to do it,' I said. Which was true.

'Words to live my life by, son,' he said, throwing a boot up onto Nunn's blotter, opening an envelope or two, scanning. 'But damned if most wives who had minds in their head would let most husbands stay out this late, leave them lonesome till twelve midnight at night.'

I looked at my own watch, then at the heavy door to Lyndon's office.

Lyndon smiled at my point. He smiled gently. 'I carry my Miss Claudia "Lady Bird" Johnson in here, boy,' he said, tapping at his chest, the spot over the scar from his recent bypass (he'd shown the whole office his scar). 'Just like my Bird carries me in her own personal heart. You give your life to other folks, you give your bodily health and your mind in your head and your intellectual concepts to serving the people, you and your wife got to carry each other inside, 'matter from how far away, or distant, or alone.' He smiled again, grimacing a little as he scratched under an arm.

I looked at him over a government postal meter.

'You and Mrs. Johnson sound like a very lucky couple, sir.'

He looked back. He put his glasses back on. His glasses had odd clear frames, water-colored, as if liquid-filled.

'My Lady Bird and me have been lucky, haven't we. We have.'

'I think you have, sir.'

'Damn right.' He looked back to the mail. 'Damn right.'

We stayed that night, answering mail, for hours, mostly silent. Though, before the air around the distant Monument got mauve and a foggy dawn lit the Hill, I found Lyndon looking at me, hunched in my loosened three-piece, staring at me, over me, somehow, nodding, saying something too low to hear.

'Excuse me, sir?'

'I was saying to keep it up, boy, is what. Keep it up. I kept it up. You keep it up.'

'Can you elaborate on that?'

'Lyndon Baines Johnson never elaborates. It's a personal rule I have found advantageous. I never elaborate. Folks distrust folks who elaborate. Write that down, boy: "Never elaborate." '

He rose slowly, using Nunn's little iron desk for support. I reached for my little notebook and pen as he shook the wrinkles out of his topcoat.

> "I never saw a man with a deeper need to be loved than LBJ."
> —Former aide, 1973

> "He hated to be alone. I mean he *really* hated it. I'd come into his office when he was sitting alone at his desk and even though you could tell it wasn't me he wanted to see, his eyes would get this relieved light . . . He carried a little pocket radio, a little transistor radio, and sometime's we'd hear it playing in his office, while he worked in there alone. He wanted a little noise. Some voice, right there, talking to him, or singing. But he wasn't a sad man. I'm not trying to give you that impression of him. Kennedy was a sad man. Johnson was just a man who *needed* a lot. For all he gave out, he needed things back for himself. And he knew it."
> —Former research aide Chip Piesker
> April, 1978

I began doing much of my quieter busywork in Lyndon's inner office, on the red floor, among the stars. I sorted and categorized and answered mail on the floor in the corner, then on the long pine table when Piesker was remanded to my desk outside to put together Lyndon's daily news summary.

I answered more and more of the personal mail. Lew N. Johnson said I lent a special, personal touch. Mrs. Teane began to forward things to my attention instead of vice versa.

Lyndon often asked me to jot things down for him—thoughts, turns of phrase, reminders. He showed, even then, a passion for rhetoric. He'd ask to see the little notebook I carried, and review it.

He did run in 1960, or rather canter, in the primaries, while still a Senator. His determination not to shirk duties in the Senate meant that he couldn't really run more than halfway. But his Dirksen Building office still tripled its staff and came to resemble a kind of military headquarters. I took orders directly from Lyndon or from Dora. Mail became more and more a priority. I did some crude 1960-era mass mailings for the campaign, working with P.R. and the weird shiny-eyed men in Demographics.

Aides and advisors and friends and rivals and colleagues came and went and came and went. Lyndon hated the telephone. Dora Teane would put only the most urgent calls through. Those who knew Lyndon well always came by personally for 'chats' that sometimes made or ended careers. They all came. Humphrey looked like the empty shell of a molted locust. Kennedy looked like an advertisement for something you ought not to want, but do. Sam Rayburn reminded me of an untended shrub. Nixon looked like a Nixon mask. John Connally and John Foster Dulles didn't look like anything at all. Chet Huntley's hair looked painted on. DeGaulle was absurd. Jesse Helms was unfailingly polite. I often brought, to whoever had to wait a few minutes, some of Mrs. Teane's dark special blend. I sometimes chatted for a few moments with the visitor. I found my new French useful with the general.

Margaret Childs Boyd, my wife of almost two years, had found undershorts of mine, in the laundry, ominously stained, she said, from the very beginning of our time on T Street. She threatened to tell Mr. Jack Childs, now of Austin, that certain elaborate and philosophical pre-nuptial arrangements seemed to have fallen through. She had entered into an ill-disguised affair with a syndicated cartoonist who drew Lyndon as a sort of hunched question mark of a man with the face of a basset. She enjoyed, besides mechanical missionary congress, drinking imported beer. She had always enjoyed the beer—the first image her name summons to me involves her holding a misted mug of something Dutch up to the New Haven light—but now she got more and more enthusiastic about it. She drank with the cartoonist, with her remedial colleagues, with other election widows. Drunk, she accused me of being in love with Lyndon Johnson. She asked whether some of my stained shorts should be tucked away for posterity. I made her some good strong East Texas blend and went to my room, where by now I frequently worked into the morning on itineraries, mail, mailings, the organization and editing of some of Lyndon's more printable observations and remarks for possible inclusion in speeches. I became, simultaneously, a paid member of Lyndon's secretarial, research, and speech-writing staffs. I drew a generous enough salary to keep my new companion, M. Duverger, a young relation to the Haitian ambassador to the United States, in a pleasant, private brownstone unit that seemed ours alone. Duverger too admired the autographed portrait of Vice President and Mrs. Johnson I had hung, with his permission, in one of our rooms.

> "So let's just don't talk, and let's just don't brag. Let's talk to our kinfolks and our uncles and our cousins and our aunts, and let's go do our duty November third and vote Democratic."
>
> —Speech to Senior Class
Chesapeake High
School,
Baltimore, Maryland
October 24, 1960

> "So you tell them what you do is just reach up there and get that lever and just say, 'All the way with LBJ.' Your Mamas and your Papas and your Grandpas, some of them are going to forget this. But I am depending on you youths who are going to have to fight our wars, and who are going to have to defend this country, and who are going to get blown up if we have a nuclear holocaust—I am depending on you to have enough interest in your future which is ahead of you to get up and prod mama and papa and make them get up early and go vote."
>
> —Speech to Fourth-grade
Class
Mansfield Elementary
School,
Mansfield, Ohio
October 31, 1964

"Boyd and Johnson? There wasn't one of us could really say we understood Dave's relationship with LBJ. None of us knew what kind of hold the boy had on Johnson. But we knew he had one."

"That's for sure."

"But it worked the other way, too, didn't it? Boyd worshipped the hell out of LBJ."

"I would've said 'worshipped' wasn't the right word."

"Loved?"

"Now let's not get off on that again, boys. Those rumors, we knew those were just rumorous lies, even at the time. There wasn't a homosexual bone in Lyndon Johnson's body. And he loved Lady Bird like an animal."

"There *was* something animalistic about LBJ, wasn't there? He confirmed animalism for me, in a way. His time in the limelight, that time seemed to confirm for the whole country that a man was nothing more than a real sad and canny animal. He could hope to be no more. It was a dark time."

"That's what those radicals hated so much about him. They were scared that all they were was animals, and that LBJ was just a cannier and more powerful animal. That's all there was to it."

"God knows what that bodes for the political future of this nation right here."

"LBJ was a genius and a gorilla at the same time."

"And Boyd liked that."

"I think Dave was certainly drawn to it, don't you all? Dave was not one bit like an animal. No way."

"Too refined to ever be animalistic, maybe."

"You could say he was refined, I suppose. But I never trusted him. Not enough of his personality or his character was ever out there for me to see for me to really call him refined. A refined what?"

"A lot of times Dave could be in a room with you and you'd never even notice him in the room."

"Almost refined right out of existence, somehow."

"Whereas a whole giant ballroom or convention hall would know if Johnson was in it. He made the whole air in a room different."

"Johnson *needed* to have people know he was in their room."

"Was that it, then? Johnson needed an audience, and Boyd was an audience that Johnson knew was just barely there? That he didn't ever even have to acknowledge or feel any responsibility to?"

"I'm still not sold on it being impossible they were involved."

"I'm sure sold on it."

"I'm sold, also. Being homosexual would have been too delicate or human for LBJ to even dream of. I doubt if LBJ even had himself any ability to even try to imagine what being homosexual was like. Being homosexual is kind of abstract, to my way of thinking, and LBJ hated abstractions. They were outside his ken."

"He hated anything outside his ken. He'd totally ignore it, or else hate it."

"Boyd lived with that third-world French nigger that wore high heels. He lived with that nigger for years."

"Johnson had to have had some kind of hold over him."

"Did LBJ ever even know, though? About Boyd and that Negro? Even as close as him and LBJ were?"

"I never knew of anybody who had any inklings as to that."

"No one knew if he knew."

"How could he not know?"

—From Dr. C. T. Peete, ed.
Dissecting a President:
Conversations with
LBJ's Inner Circle
1970

Lyndon as Vice President still kept his Dirksen Building office, the red tile with gold stars, the huge cubicled staff complex, the big window and the knotty-pine table where my new assistants sorted mail under my supervision.

'There was just one goddamned job I'd of picked up and moved that whole real carefully put-together system of offices and technology and personnel for. One goddamned job, boy,' he told me in the freezing open-air limousine on the way to his running mate's inauguration. 'And it seems like some good folks in their wisdom didn't want to give Lyndon Baines Johnson that job. So I say fuck off to all them, is what I say. Am I right Bird?' He knuckled at Claudia Johnson's ribs under her furs and taffeta.

'Now you just hush, now, Lyndon,' the lady said with a mock severity Lyndon clearly adored, a code between them. Lady Bird patted Lyndon's lined topcoat's thick arm and leaned across his red hooked profile, resting her other gloved hand on my knee.

'Now Mr. Boyd, I'm holding you responsible for making this rude and evil force of a man behave.'

'I'll try, Ma'am.'

'That's right boy, make me *behave,'* whooped the Vice President, waving to crowds he really looked at. 'I'll just tell you now, I have to blow my nose, or fart up there on that platform, I'm farting. I'm blowing my nose. Don't care how many *e*lectronic eyes are on that handsome little shit up there. Hope all this wind messes with his hair some.' He paused, looking around, surprised. 'Shoot, I *do* have to fart.'

He farted deeply into his coat and the limousine's cold hard leather seat.

'Whoo*ee.*'

'What is to be *done* with you, Lyndon?' Lady Bird laughed, cheerfully horrified, shaking her head at the crowd's waving line. I again remember white plumes of breath from everyone's mouth. It was freezing.

I first met Claudia Alta 'Lady Bird' Taylor Johnson at a summer barbecue on the banks of the Perdenales River that bordered Lyndon's ranch in Texas. Close friends and staff had been flown down to help Lyndon blow off steam and prepare for an upcoming Convention that already belonged, mathematically, to another man.

Lyndon had me shake hands with his dog.

'I'm telling Blanco to shake, not you, boy,' he reassured me. He turned to Lew N. Johnson. 'I *know* this boy will shake. Don't even have to say it to him.' Lew N. had pushed up his horn-rims and laughed.

'And this here is my unnatural wife, Mrs. Lyndon Baines Johnson,' he said, presenting to me a lovely, elegant woman with a round face and a sharp nose and a high hard hairdo. 'This is the Lady Bird, boy,' he said.

'I'm very pleased to meet you, Ma'am.'

'This pleasure is mine, Mr. Boyd,' she murmured, a soft Texan. I touched my lips to the small warm knuckles of the hand she proffered. Everyone around us could see the way Lyndon hung on the sound of his wife's voice, saw the tiny curtsies, her social motions, as though each movement of Lady Bird gently burst a layer of impediment between her and him.

'Lyndon has spoken to me of you with affection and gratitude,' she said, as Lyndon draped himself over her from behind and used his mouth to make a noise against the bare freckled shoulder just inside her gown's strap.

'Mr. Johnson is too kind,' I said, as Blanco slid against my shins and the hem of my Bermudas and then ran toward the smoking barbecue pit.

'That's *it* boy, I'm *too* kind!' Lyndon blared, knocking his head with his hand in revelation. 'Write that down for me, son: "Johnson *too* kind." ' He turned, making a bullhorn of his hands. 'Say!' he shouted. 'Is that there *band* going to play some songs, or did you boys' asses get connected onto your chairs?' A cluster of men with instruments and checked shirts and cowboy hats began to fall all over themselves rushing toward the small bandstand.

We listened, ate from paper plates. Lyndon stomped his boot in time to the band.

I felt a hand's tininess on my wrist. 'Perhaps you would do me the honor of calling to take tea and refreshment at some time.' Mrs. Johnson smiled, holding my gaze only as long as was needed to communicate something. I shivered slightly, nodding. Mrs. Johnson excused herself and moved off, turning heads and parting crowds, radiating some kind of authority that had nothing to do with power or connection or the ability to harm.

I hitched up my shorts, which tended even then to sag.

'Quit mooning around and go get you some barbecue!' Lyndon shouted in my ear, tearing at an ear of corn, stomping.

Lyndon had his second serious and first secret coronary in 1962. I was driving him home from the office, late. We moved east through Washington and toward his private ocean-side home. He began gasping in the passenger seat. He couldn't breathe properly. The nasal inhaler had no effect. His lips blued. Mr. Kutner of the Secret Service and I had a hard time of it even getting him into the house.

Lady Bird Johnson and I stripped Lyndon down and massaged his bypass-scarred chest with isopropyl alcohol. Lyndon had wheezed that this usually helped his breathing. We massaged him. He had the sort of tired, bulblike breasts old men have.

His lips continued to cyanidize. He was having his second serious coronary, he gasped. Lady Bird massaged him all over. He refused to let me ask Kutner to call an ambulance. He wanted no one to know. He said he was the Vice President. It took Lady Bird's veto finally to get him to Bethesda Naval in a black-windowed Service sedan. Kutner ignored traffic lights. It took both Lady Bird's hands to hold Lyndon's hand as he fought for breath and clutched his shoulder. He was plainly in great pain.

'Shit,' he kept saying, baring his teeth at me. 'Shit, boy. *No.*'

'Yes, *no,*' Mrs. Johnson said soothingly into his giant blue ear.

The Vice President of the United States was in Bethesda for eighteen days. For routine tests, we had Salinger tell the press. Somehow, toward the end of his stay, Lyndon persuaded a surgeon to remove his healthy appendix. Pierre talked to the media at length about the appendectomy. Lyndon showed people the appendectomy scar at every public opportunity.

'Damn appendix,' he would say.

He began to take prescribed digitalis. Lady Bird forced him to stop eating the fried pork rind he kept in his top right desk drawer alongside his silver-handled revolver. I tried hard to stop smoking in Lyndon's office.

I received a note on plain pink stationery. 'My husband and I wish to thank you for your kind and discreet attention to our needs during my husband's recent illness.' The note smelled wonderful; M. Duverger said he wanted to smell the way *L'Oiseau's* note smelled.

> "I graduated from the Johnson City High School back in Texas in a class of six. For some time I had felt that my father was not really as smart as I thought he ought to be, and I thought that I could improve on a good many of my mother's approaches to life, as well. So when I got my high school diploma I decided to follow the old philosopher Horace Greeley's advice and 'Go West, Young Man,' and seek my fortune. With twenty-six dollars in my pocket and a T-Model Ford automobile, five of my schoolmates and I started out early one morning on our way to the Golden West, the great state of California. We got there in due time, minus most of my twenty-six dollars, and I got a very well-paying job of ninety dollars a month running an elevator up and down. But I found at the end of the month, after I paid for three meals and paid for my room and my laundry that I was probably better off back there eating Mama's food than I was in California. So I went back to Texas and I got a job with the Highway Department. We didn't have to get to work until sunup, and we got to quit every night at sundown. We did have to get to work on our own time. We had to be at work at sunup, and that was usually twenty or thirty miles down the Highway, and we had to ride home on our own time after sundown. I got paid the magnificent salary of a dollar a day. After a little over a year of that at the Highway Department, I began to think that my father's advice that I should go and take some more training and not be a school drop-out—maybe he was wiser than I had thought a year before. In other words, he became a lot smarter while I was gone in California and on the Highway. And with the help of the good Lord, and with a mother persistently urging to me to go back to school and get some training, I hitchhiked fifty miles to get back into the classroom, where I spent four long years. But I have been reasonably well-employed ever since. I now have a contract that runs until January 20, 1965."
>
> —Speech to Graduating Class
> Amherst College,
> Amherst, Massachusetts
> May 25, 1963

Mother came to Washington just once in those ten years to visit; she and Margaret kept in very good touch.

The day my mother visited, Duverger cooked all morning, a crown roast, yams in cream, and Les Jeux Dieux, a Haitian dessert, a specialty, airy and painfully sweet. He fussed nervously around the kitchen all morning in only an apron and heels while I vacuumed under furniture and worked surfaces over with oil soap.

Over drinks in the spotless room redolent of spiced pork, mother talked about Margaret Childs and how mother and Jack and Sue-Bea Childs so hoped that Margaret's hospitalization for alcohol dependency would mean a new lease on life for a dear girl who'd never once done anything to hurt anybody. Duverger kept fidgeting in the sportcoat I'd lent him.

It was the only completely silent dinner party I've ever experienced. We listened to the sounds of our knives against our plates. I could hear differences in our styles of mastication.

Our housewarming gift from her was a false cluster of grapes, the grapes purple marbles on a green glass stem.

My mother did not look old.

'Elle a tort,' Duverger kept repeating, later, as he applied the gel. He had little English he was proud of; we spoke a kind of pidgin when alone.

'Elle a tort, cette salope-là. She has wrong. She has wrong.'

I asked what he meant as he spread cold gel on himself and then me. He opened me roughly, rudely. I winced into the pattern of the bed's headboard.

'About what is Mother wrong?'

'She hates me because she believes you *love* me.'

He sodomized me violently, without one thought to my comfort or pleasure, finally shuddering and falling to weep against me. I had cried out several times in pain.

'Ce n'est pas moi qui tu aimes.'

'Of course I love you. We share a life, René.'

He was having difficulty breathing. *'Ce n'est* not I.'

'Whom, then?' I asked, rolling him off. 'If you say I do not love you, whom do I love?'

'Tu m'en a besoin,' he cried, rending dark bedroom air with his nails. 'You *need* me. You feel the responsibility for me. But your love it is not for me.'

'My love is for you, Duverger. Need, responsibility: these are part of love, in this nation.'

'Elle a tort.' He turned himself away, curling fetal on his side of the bed. 'She believes we are not lonely.' I said nothing.

'Why must it be lonely?' he said. He said it as if it were a statement. He kept repeating it. I woke once, very late, to his broad brown back, moving, a rhythm, his open hand to his face, still repeating.

> "He sees life as a jungle. No matter how long a rein you think you're on, he's always got the rein in his hands."
>
> —Former associate, 1963

> "Most of his worries are of his own making. He sees troubles where none exist. He's liable to wake up in the morning and think everything's got loose during the night."
>
> —Close friend, 1963

Lyndon spent the fourteen-minute ride to Parkland Hospital on the floor of the open-air limousine's back seat, his nose jammed against the sole of Senator Yarbrough's shoe. On top of them, covering them and holding them down as they struggled, was a Secret Serviceman whose cologne alone could have caused the confused panic I saw ripple through the Dallas streets' crowds as I lay on top of them all, riding their struggle, watching from my perch three Servicemen, in the convertible ahead, restraining the First Lady as she struggled and screamed, imploring them to let her go back to the site and retrieve something I could not quite hear.

We were jammed together in that back seat, a tumble of limbs, Yalies stuffing a phone booth. Lyndon's pantcuff and white hairless ankle and low-cut dress boot waved around in front of my face as we rode. I could hear him, beneath the overpoweringly scented Serviceman, cursing Yarbrough.

The hospital was choreographed madness. Lyndon, handkerchief to his bruised nose, was besieged by cameras, microphones, doctors, Servicemen, print media, and, worst, all those Presidentially appointed officials and staffers, eyes narrowed with self-interest, who knew enough to jump hosts before the political animal they had ridden had even cooled.

I telephoned Lady Bird Johnson—Lyndon's teeth had bared at even the suggestion that he use the telephone now—to reassure her and advise her to arrange travel to Dallas as quickly as possible. I called Hal Ball to facilitate quick transportation for Mrs. Johnson. I saw Lyndon trapped by the mob in the lobby's corner, his slack cheeks flushed hot, his nose redly purple, his small person's eyes dull with shock and a dawning realization. His little eyes sought mine above the roiling coil of press and lackeys, but he could not get through, even as I waved from the phone-bank.

'You get that mike out my face or it's gonna be calling your personal ass home,' was edited from the special newscasts. Dan Rather had reeled away, pale, rubbing his crew cut.

The crowd slowly dissolved as news from doctors and Service upstairs failed to forthcome. We were able to huddle with Lyndon in a small waiting room off the lobby. The meeting was grimly efficient. An ad hoc transition team was assembled on the spot. Service had set up a line to Ball back at the office. Bunker and Califano and Salinger were filling note cards furiously. Cabinet appointments were hashed out with the kind of distanced heat reserved for arguments about golf. Lyndon said little.

I took Lyndon up to the First Lady's room. Lyndon parted the crowd around her bed. He felt her tranquilized forehead with a hand that almost covered her face. Her color was good. A flashbulb popped. I saw the First Lady's drugged eyes between Lyndon's fingers.

No one had any news even about who in the hospital might have news. We all huddled, conferred, smoked, blew the smoke away from Lyndon, waited. Lyndon was so savage to those young Bostonians who came snuffling up both to commiserate and congratulate that our group was soon left to itself. Connally, his arm in a sling, hovered pacing at the perimeter of our circle, drinking at a bottled seltzer whose volume seemed to remain somehow constant.

I called Duverger, who had been home with bronchitis, watching the news on television and out of his mind with worry. I called Mrs. Teane at her home in Arlington. I tried to call Margaret at her treatment center in Maryland and was informed that she had checked out weeks ago. My mother's line remained busy for hours.

Our huddle ended, too, long before the official word came. Everyone had a hundred things to do. The small room emptied little by little. Flanked by Pierre and me, Lyndon finally had a few minutes to slouch and reflect in his waiting-room chair. He applied the inhaler to his swollen passages. His spurs made lines on the floor as he stretched out long legs. He held his own forearm, opening and closing his fist. The skin below his eyes was faintly blue. I dispensed some digitalis and all but had to force him to swallow.

We sat. We stared for a time at the little room's white walls. Connally studied the concession machines.

'Everything,' Lyndon was murmuring.

'Excuse me sir?'

He looked out absently over his own legs. 'Boy,' he said, 'I'd give every fucking thing I have not to have to stand up there and take a job ain't mine by right or by the will of folks. Your thinking man, he avoids back doors to things. Charity. Humiliation. Distrust. Responsibility you didn't never get to get ready to expect.'

'Natural to feel that way, LB,' Connally said, feeding a candy machine coins.

Lyndon stared hard at a point I could not see, shaking his great pill of a head.

'I'd give every fucking thing I have, boy.'

Salinger shot me a look, but I had already clicked out my pen.

There was transition. Two hurried mass mailings. Boxes to be packed and taped. Burly movers to be supervised.

Duverger's health declined. He seemed unable to shake the bronchitis and the coincident infections it opened him to. He lost the strength to climb stairs and had to give up his job at the boutique. He lay in bed, listening to scratched Belafonte records and raising in our linen a daily mountain of colorful used Kleenex. He lost weight and had fevers. I learned that malaria was endemic in Haiti, and obtained quinine from Bethesda. Whether from empathy or exposure, I felt my own health getting more delicate as the time with Duverger passed. I caught every sore throat that went around the White House. I got used to having a sore throat.

The White House systems for receiving and distributing and answering mail were huge, hugely staffed, time-tested, honed to a hard edge of efficiency. Lyndon's Same Day Directive presented these quick furtive career mailboys small challenge. I became little more than a postal figurehead, responsible for drafting and updating the ten or so standardized reply letters that were printed and signature-stamped by the gross and flowed out in response to the growing number of letters and telegrams from people in every state. By 1965 the incoming mail was on the whole negative, and it was hard to prevent the formulated responses from sounding either artificial or defensive and shrill.

Duverger and I were formally married in a small civil ceremony outside a Mount Vernon suburb. The service was attended by a few close mutual friends. Peter came all the way from Charlotte. Duverger had to sit for the ceremony, dressed in mute silks that deemphasized, or maybe complemented, the sick weak gray of his complexion.

"I especially appreciate your coming here because I feel I have a rapport with you and they won't let me out of the gate so I am glad they let you in."

—To White House Tour Group
May 14, 1966

"This is not a change in purpose. It is a change in what we believe that purpose requires."

—To Young Democrats' Council
Columbia University, New York
May 21, 1966

"He seemed to get obsessed with his health. He began to seem robust in the way delicate people seem robust."

"Boyd got delicate and obsessed, too. He wore his topcoat all the time. He perspired. As if he followed LBJ's lead in everything."

"Boyd barely even had a formal function. That army of career mail-boys of Kennedy's was all over the SDD before we even got the transition over with."

"He'd just sit there holding the radio while Lyndon worked. Who knows what he did in there."

"They'd both wander around constantly. Walk around the grounds. Look out the fence."

"Sometimes just the President alone, except there wandering a ways behind him'd be Boyd, with all those Secret Service folks."

"But who knows what they walked over in that office, hour after hour."

"The radio stopped, when they were in there."

"Who knows how many decisions he was in on. Tonkin. Cambodia. The whole Great Big Society."

"We'll never know that about Lady Bird, either. She was one of those behind-the-scenes types of First Ladies. Influence impossible to gauge."

"We know Boyd helped write some of the later speeches."

"But no one even knows which ones were whose."

"They were all thick as thieves over there."

"Nobody who knows anything is even alive anymore."

"That summary-boy with the ears had that gruesome office pool going about whether Dave would outlive Lyndon."

—From *Dissecting*

"Now you folks come on and be happy, God damn it."

—Televised address
Oval Office,
White House
November 1967

Most of the stories about those last months, about Lyndon refusing sometimes ever to leave the Oval Office, are the truth. I sat in the oversized corner chair, my lap full of tissues and lozenges, and watched him urinate into the iron office wastebasket Mrs. Teane would quietly empty in the morning. Sounds in the office were hushed by thick Truman carpet, lush furnishings. The office was dark except for passing headlights and the orange flicker of the protesters' bonfire in the park across the street.

The office window facing Pennsylvania was dappled and smeared with the oil of Lyndon's nose. He stood, face touching the window, an ellipse of his breath appearing and shrinking and appearing on the glass as he whispered along with the protesters' crudely rhymed chants. Helicopters circled like gulls; fat fingers of spotlight played over the park and the White House grounds and the line of Kutner's Servicemen ranged along the black iron fence. Things were occasionally thrown at the fence, and clattered.

Lyndon applied his nasal inhaler, inhaling fiercely.

'How many kids did I kill today, boy?' he asked, turning from the window.

I sniffed deeply, swallowing. 'I think that's neither a fair nor a healthy way to think about a question like that, sir.'

'Goddamn your pale soul boy I asked you how *many.*' He pointed at a window full of yam-colored bonfire light. 'They're sure the mother-fuck asking. I think Lyndon Johnson should be allowed to ask, as well.'

'Probably between three and four hundred kids today, sir,' I said. I sneezed wetly and miserably into a tissue. 'Happy now?'

Lyndon turned back to the window. He had forgotten to rebutton his trousers.

'Happy,' he snorted. The best way to tell he'd heard you was to listen for repetition. 'You think they're happy?' he asked.

'Who?'

He twitched his big head at the bonfire, listening for the tiny loudness of the distant bullhorns and the plaintive hiss of crowds' response. He slouched, his hands on the sill for support. 'Those youths of America over across there,' he said.

'They seem pretty upset, sir.'

He hitched up his sagging pants thoughtfully. 'Boy, I get a smell of happiness off their upset, however. I think they enjoy getting outraged and vilified and unjustly ignored. That's what your leader of this here free world thinks, boy.'

'Could you elaborate on that, sir?'

Lyndon horselaughed a big misted circle onto the window, and we looked together at the big hand-lettered sign on the Oval Office wall, beside the cattle horns, behind the Presidential desk. I'd made it. It read NEVER ELABORATE.

He was shaking his head. 'I believe . . . I believe I am out of touch with the youth of America. I believe that they cannot be touched by me, or by what's right, or by intellectual concepts on what's right for a nation.'

I sneezed.

He touched, with big brown-freckled fingers, at the window, leaving more smears. 'You'll say this is easy for me to say, but I say they've had it too goddamned easy, son. These youths that are yippies and that are protesters and that use violence and public display. We gave it to them too easy, boy. I mean their Daddies. Men that I was youths with. And these youths today are pissed *off.* They ain't never once had to worry or hurt or suffer in any real way whatsoever. They do not know Great Depression and they do not know desolation.' He looked at me. 'You think that's good?'

I looked back at him.

'I think I'm gettin' to be a believer in folks' maybe needing to suffer some. You see some implications in that belief? It implies our whole agenda of domestic programs is maybe possibly bad, boy. I'm headed for thinking it's smelling bad right at the heart of the whole thing.' He inhaled nasally, watching protesters dance around. 'We're taking away folks' suffering here at home through these careful domestic programs, boy,' he said, 'without giving them nothing to replace it. Take a look at them dancing across over there, boy, shouting *fuck you* like they invented both fucking and me, their President, take a look over across, and you'll see what I see. I see some animals that need to suffer, some folks that need some suffering to even be Americans inside, boy; and if we don't give them some suffering, why, they'll just go and hunt up some for themselves. They'll take some suffering from some oriental youths who are caught in a great struggle between sides, they'll go and take those other folks' suffering and take it inside themselves. They're getting stimulation from it, son. I'm believing in the youths of America's need for some genuine stimulation. Those youths are out there making their own stimulation; they're making it from scratch off oriental youths wouldn't squat to help your Mama take a leak. We as leaders haven't given them shit. They think prosperity and leadership is dull. God bless the general patheticness of their souls.' He pressed his nose against the glass. I had a quick vision, as he stood there, of children and candy stores.

I squinted as a helicopter's passing spot brightened the Oval Office to a brief blue noon. 'So you think there's something right about what they're doing out there?'

' "Something *right,*" ' Lyndon snorted, motionless at the blue window. 'No, 'cause they got no notion of right and wrong. Listen. They got no notion whatsoever of right and wrong, boy. Listen.'

We listened to them. I sniffed quietly.

'To them, right and wrong is *words,* boy.' He came away and eased himself into his big desk chair, sitting straight, hands out before him on the unscarred presidential cherrywood. 'Right and wrong ain't words,' he said. 'They're feelings. In your guts and intestines and such. Not words. Not songs with guitars. They're what make you feel like you do. They're inside you. Your heart and digestion. Like the folks you personally love.' He felt at his forearm and clenched his fist. 'Let them sad sorry boys out across there go be *responsible* for something for a second, boy. Let them go be responsible for some folks and then come back and tell their President, me, LBJ, about right and wrong and so forth.'

We took his pulse together. We measured his pressure. There were no pains in his shoulder or side, no blue about his mouth. We reclined him for blood flow, placed his boots on the window's sill. My chest and back were soaked with perspiration. I made my way back to my chair in the corner, feeling terribly faint.

'You all right, boy?'

'Yes, sir. Thank you.'

He chuckled. 'Some pair of federal functionaries right here, I got to say.'

I coughed.

We listened, quiet, unwell, to the songs and chants and slogans and to the chop of Service helicopters and the clang and clatter of beer cans. Minutes passed in the faint bonfire glow. I asked Lyndon whether he was asleep.

'I ain't sleeping,' he said.

'Could I ask you to tell me what it feels like, then, sir.'

A silence of distant chant. Lyndon picked at his nose deeply, his eyes closed, head thrown back.

'Does what feel like?'

I cleared my throat. 'Being responsible, as you were saying, I meant. Being responsible for people. What does it feel like, if you are?'

He either chuckled or wheezed, a deep sound, almost subsonic, from the recesses of his inclined executive chair. I stared at his profile, a caricaturist's dream.

'You and Bird,' he said. 'Damned if you and my Bird don't always ask the same things of Lyndon Johnson, son. It's queer to me.' He brought himself upright to face my bit of the office's darkness. 'I done told Bird just last week how responsibility, why, it is not even like a feeling at all,' he said quietly.

'You can't feel what responsibility feels like? It numbs you?'

He administered the inhaler, played with his fob against the bad light of the window.

'I told Bird it's like the sky, boy. Is what I told her. How about if I come and ask you what does the sky *feel* like to you? The sky ain't a feeling, boy.'

We both coughed.

He pointed upward, vaguely up at the horns, nodding as if at something familiar. 'But it's there, friend. The sky is there. It's there, over your ass, every fucking day. 'Matter where you go, boy, look on up, and on top of every goddamned thing else she's there. And the day there ain't no sky . . .'

He squeezed and worked the last bits of inhalant out of his nasal inhaler. It was a hideous sound. Before long I had to help Lyndon back over to the office wastebasket full of urine. We stood there, together, on the plain white marble Presidents' floor.

> "Mr. Lyndon 'LBJ' Johnson, like all men in public service, was driven both by a great and zealous personal ambition and by a great and zealous compassion for the well-being of his fellow man. He was, like all great men, hell, like all men, a paradox of mystery. He will not and cannot ever be completely or totally understood. But for those of us gathered today under these great lone-star

skies to try and understand a man we must try to understand if we are to do him the honor he deserves, I say this. I say to go west. I say the further you go west, the nearer you get to Lyndon Baines Johnson."

—Texas State Senator Jack Childs
Eulogy on the Passing of LBJ
Austin, Texas, 1968

When I received the pink, plainly inscribed invitation to take tea and refreshment with Claudia 'Lady Bird' Johnson, I was prostrate in our big bed, down with a violent flu.

Duverger had been gone almost a week. I had come home from some mass-mailing work in New Hampshire to find him gone. He had left no word and had packed none of his several pieces of luggage. His money and several of my small black office notebooks were gone.

I can offer no better testimony to my feelings for Lyndon's career than my panic that René had either defected to or been shanghaied by some Other Side. Most of the entries in the notebooks were verbatim. One had recounted a Joint Chiefs briefing session held on sinks and hampers and the lip of a claw-footed tub while Lyndon had been moving his bowels on the commode. There was enough truth in those tiny records to embarrass Lyndon beyond repair; he had ordered that everything that was written be written. I admit, with pain, that my first day's thoughts were of Lyndon and betrayal and the masklike Republican we'd all grown to fear.

Three days of frantic searching for Duverger had taken me as far north as the New Hampshire camps of Humphrey, McCarthy, Lindsay and Percy—and that man—and as far south as the dark lounges of Chevy Chase. It left me weak beyond description, and I came down with a violent flu. Lyndon, too, had been sick, out of the office and news for a week. He had not contacted me. No one from either office or White House had called for the three days I had been home ill. And I hadn't the character to call anyone.

'Our husbands and I inquire as to whether you would do us the honor of taking tea and refreshment at our Shore home this evening,' read the note on colored stationery, without letterhead. I had become so trained to look for the letterhead first that the blankness of the First Lady's notes seemed almost high-handed.

And it was well-known scuttlebutt—scuttle, I suspected, from the butt of Margaret's old cartoonist, who had sketched me as a W.C.-Fields-nosed flower girl, holding the '68 train of Johnson as bride—that Mrs. Johnson wanted Lyndon out, and saw his office/me as the rival she'd never had in life. 'Our husbands,' then, fit what I would hear.

Too, we could never name the heady perfume that had risen from Mrs. Johnson's notes and seduced Duverger from the first. He had shopped, sniffing, for days, and had fixed the central scent as essence of bluebonnet before he had become unable to leave our home altogether.

Duverger was dying of something that was not malaria. All four of my salaries went to Bethesda, where Duverger was not covered and where the staff, like Aquinas before God, could think of nothing to do but define his decline via what it was not. The doctors between whom I had shuttled my seated, coughing husband could isolate nothing but a pattern in his susceptibility to the uncountable diseases that came and thrived in the petri dish that was Washington.

For these last many months I had lain at nighttime holding a man dying of a pattern, encircling with my white arm gray ribs that became more and more defined, feeling pulses through a wrist too wasted narrow to support the length of its long-nailed hand, watching his stomach cave and his hips flare like a woman's and his knees bulge like balls from his legs' receding meat.

'Suis fatigue. M'aimes-tu?'

'Tais-toi. Bois celui-ci.'

'M'aimes-tu?'

An ever weaker me, blinking the cornered translucence of all my connections, I saw Lyndon himself fading before a carnivorous press corps; a war as nasty and real and greenly-broadcast as it was statistical and fuzzily bordered to those of us who read and acted on the actual reports; a reversal of his presidential resolve that the government's *raison* was before all to reduce sum totals of suffering; a growing intuition of his own frailty as two more well-concealed infarctions left him gaunt and yellow and blotched, his eyes seeming to grow to fit the face that settled into itself around them.

Duverger, who hadn't the strength to leave, was gone. He had taken my notes and left none of his own. Nothing in the vase below the mantel's autographed photo and little Klee. Amid tissues and the popped aluminum shells of antinauseants, I read the finely penned note from Mrs. Johnson, hand-delivered by one of my own distant subordinates in Mail. I breathed at what rose from the note.

'Wardine has prepared some praline mix which I find to complement camomile tea very nicely, Mr. Boyd.'

'Thank you, Ma'am.'

'Thank you that will be all Wardine.'

The black servant in black stockings and a doilied apron wiped away the last of the cold cream that had masked the First Lady's round sharp face. She adjusted the pillow under Mrs. Johnson's feet and withdrew, her back always to me.

I coughed faintly. I wiped my forehead.

'My own husband is near death, child.'

I had arrived late by taxi at the Johnsons' private home, retained from his days as a Senator, a turreted post-plantation thing on the very eastern shore of the Potomac delta that pouted lip-like out into the Atlantic. I could hear ocean and see lightning bubbling over a cloud roof far out to the east's sea. A horn in a channel moaned. I felt at the glands in my throat.

'You don't look well at all yourself, Mr. Boyd.'

I looked about. 'Will the President be able to join us, Ma'am?'

She looked at me over her cup of steam. 'Lyndon is dying, child. He has had great and additional . . . trouble with the illness that has been troubling him all these years.'

'He infarcted again?'

'He has asked not to be alone on this night.'

'He's supposed to die tonight, you're saying?'

She readjusted the hem of her robe. 'It's a great trial for all of us who are close to the President.' She looked up. 'Don't you agree?'

I was wary. There were no doctors. I'd seen only the ordinary number of Kutner's men at the gate. I sniffed meatily. 'So then why aren't you with him, Ma'am, if he doesn't want to be alone?'

Lady Bird took a tiny bite of praline. She smiled the way elegant ladies smile when they chew. 'I am with Lyndon every moment of every day, dear child. As he told you. President Johnson and I are too close, we believe, to afford one another real company or comfort.' She took another little bite. 'Perhaps those come from others?'

I sipped at the sweet tea in the wafer-thin china cup. The cup was almost too delicate to hold. A wave of complete nausea went over me. I hunched and closed my eyes. My ears rang, from medicine. I wanted to tell Mrs. Johnson that I didn't believe what she, who had flown to Dallas in a *fighter-jet*, was sitting there calmly eating a cookie and telling me. I really wanted to tell her I had troubles of my own. I didn't want to tell her what they were. I wanted to talk to Lyndon.

'So I'm to go sit up with him, Ma'am?'

'Are you all right, Mr. Boyd?'

'Not exactly. But I'd be honored to sit with President Johnson.' I tried to swallow. 'But I very much doubt, with all due respect, that the President is actually dying, Ma'am. No two consecutive presidents have ever died in office, Mrs. Johnson.' I had researched this for a form letter reassuring citizens who'd written for reassurance in 1963.

Mrs. Johnson adjusted her robe under herself on the pink sofa. Everything about the room was as a First Lady's personal private parlor should be. From the mirrors with frames carved like tympana to the delicate oriental statuary to the crystal place settings spread out upright for display on white shelves to the spiraled rug whose pattern swirled into itself in a kind of arabesque between my couch and Mrs. Johnson's. I closed my eyes.

'You too, Mr. Boyd,' she said, snapping a cookie, 'seem marked for a . . . a kind of frailty by the evident love and responsibility you feel toward others.'

I heard an expensive clock tick. I decided what this was about and somehow just withdrew my thoughts from Duverger and the books. I swallowed against a hot flash. 'I'm not in love with the President,' I said.

She smiled wonderfully as what I'd said hung there. 'I beg your pardon, Mr. Boyd.'

'I'm sure it looks bad, my being sick just when he's sick,' I said. I held onto the arm of my sofa. 'I'm sure you've heard several stories about me and about how I'm supposedly in love with Mr. Johnson and follow him around like a love-starved animal and want to be intimate with him and enjoy such a close working relationship with him because I love him.' I'm afraid I retched the bit of the camomile and praline refreshment I'd taken. It hung in a dusky line of retch over my topcoat and slowly collected itself in my lap. 'Well I'm not,' I said, wiping my mouth. 'And please excuse me for retching just now.'

'Mr. Boyd,' she said. 'Dear Mr. Boyd, I have no reservations about your feelings for Lyndon. I appreciate beyond my poor power to express it your devotion to my husband, to the responsibility and tasks the Lord has seen fit to assign him. I appreciate your feelings toward my husband more than I can say. And I believe I understand what those feelings are.' She looked delicately away from my lap. 'I was speaking of *your* husband.'

I was dabbing at the puddle, swirled with praline. 'And this my-husband-your-husband business, Ma'am. I'd just ignore as much scuttlebutt as you can. Rumors are seldom all true,' I said. I stood, to facilitate my dabbing.

Mrs. Johnson's forehead furrowed and cleared. '*Your* husband, Mr. Boyd.' She produced a sort of pink index card as I stood there. 'M. Duverger,' she read, 'a Caribbean Negro with diplomatic immunity, civilly married by you in 1965.' She looked up from the card. 'He has been kind enough to provide Lyndon the company and attention he has required during his illness.'

I tried to focus on the rug. 'Duverger is here?'

'As you were north, doing what Mr. Donagan described as in*teg*ral postal work for our organization in New Hampshire,' she said, tidying the cookie tray. 'He arranged for Mr. Kutner of the Service to bring your husband to our home to be presented to the President. Who is dying.'

I sneezed. She sipped. I looked for something in her face. I had an unreasonable need to see whose script was on the index card she'd produced. These balanced off urges both to race to Duverger's side—though the Shore home was huge, and I'd never been past the rear hall—and to know how on earth Coby Donagan could have said the work I'd been north doing was important. I wanted so many different things all at once that I could not move. The First Lady sipped. 'So Mr. Johnson knows I have a husband?' I said.

'How, child, could he not know?' Lady Bird smiled kindly. 'How could he not know the heart of a young man who has emptied his life and his own heart into the life and work of Lyndon Baines Johnson?'

I began to feel for Mrs. Johnson a dislike beyond anything I'd ever felt for Margaret. She sat there, coiffed, in a robe, eating pralines. I felt simply awful. 'Is Duverger all right?' I said hoarsely. 'Where is he? Has he died? He's been dying, is the thing. Not Mr. Johnson. That's why I think I'm sick. Not Mr. Johnson.'

'They have been conversing together, Mr. Boyd.'

'René has hardly any English.'

She shrugged as at the irrelevant. 'They have had several conversations of great length, Lyndon has told me. And preserved them, as you two did.'

'How could Duverger not have said he was coming here? Is he dead?'

'M. Duverger has impressed Lyndon as a truly singular Negro, Mr. Boyd. They have discussed such issues close to Lyndon's heart as suffering, and struggles between sides, and Negroness. It was the best my husband has felt since you and Mrs. Teane finally removed him from his office, he told me.'

'Is he dead, I said,' I said.

She ate. 'Are you as privy as I to what my husband feels, David?' She looked for response. I wasn't giving any if she wasn't. 'My husband,' she continued, 'feels responsibility as you and I feel our own weight. The responsibility has eaten at him. You have watched him. You have been his sole comfort for almost a decade, child.'

'So you really are afraid he's in love with me.'

Whether from resemblance or real grief, I noticed, she answered questions as Lyndon did; she answered them as tangents, on a kind of curve that brought her now in close, now out on her own course. Now she tittered Southernly, a white hand to her mouthful of refreshment. Her hair was confined in a kind of net.

'Lyndon cannot, he insists, for the life of him understand why new generations such as your own see everything of importance in terms of love, David. As if it explained feelings lasting years, that word.'

I could see Kutner's shadow, and another, move from foyer to kitchen. I rose.

She said 'Love is simply a word. It joins separate things. Lyndon and I, though you would disagree, agree that we do not properly *love* one another anymore. Because we ceased long ago to be enough *apart* for a 'love' to span any distance. Lyndon says he shall cherish the day when *love* and *right* and *wrong* and *responsibility,* when these words, he says, are understood by you youths of America to be nothing but arrangements of distance.'

'Is that Kutner and Coby Donagan I saw going into the kitchen?'

'Please sit.'

I sat.

She leaned in. 'Lyndon is haunted by his own conception of distance, David. His hatred of being alone, physically alone, no matter atop what—the area of his hatred in which your own devoted services have been so invaluable to us—his hatred of being alone is a consequence of what his memoir will call his great intellectual concept: the distance at which we see each other, arrange each other, love. That love, he will say, is a federal highway, lines putting communities, that move and exist at great distance, in touch. My husband has stated publicly that America, too, his own America, that he loves enough to conceal deaths for, is to be understood in terms of distance.'

'So we don't even love each other, then?' I stared at her crystal place settings, arranged and never used, hot with nausea. 'Two close people can't love each other, even in a sort of Platonic way?'

'You stand in relations, my husband says. You contain one another. He says he owns the floor you stand on. He says you are the sky whose presence and meaning have become everyday.'

I coughed.

'Surely love means less?'

I realized, again, what Mrs. Johnson was talking about. I almost retched again.

'Mrs. Johnson,' I said, 'I was talking about Duverger and me.' I tried to lean as she had. 'Does Mr. Johnson know that Duverger and I love each other? That my first thoughts, when I found the notebooks and him gone, were for him? Does he know that I love?'

The shadow apart from Kutner's was Wardine, the First Lady's Negro servant, who was skilled with cold cream.

'And who wrote that card, about me, you read from?' I said.

'Someone in the room above us,' Mrs. Johnson said, not pointing, 'where the two husbands inside us have withdrawn,' not looking at me once, 'have removed themselves to positions of distance, must know that we love, child. He simply must. Don't you agree?' She inclined to the china pot, lifted its wafery lid to let Wardine check its contents. Upstairs. I was on my feet. She could tell me to sit as much as she liked.

'The President won't die, Ma'am.'

'Don't you agree?'

Wardine poured for her mistress, then came for my cup.

'Ma'am?'

She leaned, dispensing sugar, speaking to her own sharp bird's face as it trembled on the surface of her tea like the moon on water. 'I asked you, boy, whether or not you agreed.'

The smell of my soiled topcoat was the smell that came, faint, from under that door. The gently feminine clink of Lady Bird Johnson's willow-necked spoon was the masculine sound of my heavy old undergraduate ring rapping firmly against the carved panel of that great bedroom door. I rapped. A spasm passed through me, my gut, and I held until it passed. Something else moaned, businesslike, in the harbor.

The big door was silent, tonight, in November, 1968.

Forget the curved circle, for whom distance means the sheer size of what it holds inside. Build a road. Make a line. Go as far west as the limit of the country lets you—Bodega Bay, not Whittier, California—and make a line; and let the wake of the line's movement be the distance between where it starts and what it sees; and keep making that line, west, farther and farther; and the earth's circle will clutch at that line, keep it near to what it holds, like someone greedy with a praline; and the giant curve that informs straight lines will bring you around, in time, to the distant eastern point of the country behind you, that dim master bedroom on the dim far eastern shore of the Atlantic; and the circle you have made is quiet and huge, and everything the world holds is inside: the bedroom: a toppled trophy has punched a shivered star through the glass of its case, a swirling traffic-flickered carpet and massed wooden fixtures smelling of oil soap and the breath of the ill. I saw the big white Bufferin of the President's personal master bed, stripped to sheets, variously shadow-colored by the changing traffic light at the Washington and Kennedy Streets' intersection below and just outside. On the stripped bed—neatly littered with papers and cards, my notecards, a decade of stenography to Lyndon—lay my lover, curled stiff on his side, a frozen skeleton X ray, impossibly thin, fuzzily bearded, his hand outstretched with dulled nails to cover, partly, the white face beside him, the big white face attached to the long form below the tight clean sheets, motionless, the bed flanked by two Servicemen who slumped, tired, red, green. Duverger's spread cold hand partly covered that Presidential face as in an interrupted caress; it lay like a spider on the big pill of the man's head, the bland, lined, carnivore's mouth, his glasses with clear frames, his nasal inhaler on the squat bedside table, the white Hot Line blinking, mutely active, yellow in a yellow light on Kennedy. Duverger's hand was spread open over the face of the President. I saw the broad white cotton sheet, Duverger above and Johnson below, the sharp points of Johnson's old man's breasts against the sheet, the points barely moving, the chest hardly rising, the sheet pulsing, ever so faintly, like water at great distance from its source.

I wiped mucus from my lip and saw, closer, the President's personal eyes, the eyes of not that small a person, eyes yolked with a high blue film of heartfelt pain, open and staring at the bedroom's skylight through Duverger's narrow fingers. I heard lips that kissed the palm of a black man as they moved together to form words, the eyes half-focused on the alien presence of me, leaning in beside the bed.

Duverger's hand, I knew, would move that way only if the President was smiling.

'Hello up there,' he whispered.

I leaned in closer.

'Lyndon?'

1989

V Revising Tradition

On the opening page of "Dunyazadiad," the first section of John Barth's National Book Award–winning *Chimera* (1972), a critic compliments an author for the "good one you've got going, with its impostures that become authentic, its ups and downs and flights to other worlds." That this conversation is not set on an American university campus within the last decade but rather takes place between Scheherazade and Shahryar, the king who will behead her as an act of textual criticism, suggests the self-conscious inventiveness that postmodern authors have employed to transform the old stories and prose traditions into new forms. As Barth himself has written, the postmodern author knows the past, but does not carry it on his or her back; the retrospective nature of much postmodern writing is not perceived by the writers themselves as the product of a lack of originality, but rather as a celebration of the sheer volume of great narrative that is readily available to any individual residing in an age characterized by the easy and engaging flow of information of any kind. Barth's affinity for the tale of Scheherazade (as well as the luminous wit with which he retells it) reminds us that postmodern authors are not inextricably linked to projects of formal innovation that produce difficult texts, but remain mindful of the ancient art of the storyteller. Similarly, Barth's use of a new narrator—the precocious Dunyazadiad, younger sister to "Sherry"—suggests the goal underlying the postmodern retelling of any classic narrative: to discover the fallow spaces left underexplored in the original as much as to devise the new meanings for the story made possible by the passage of history. In revising traditional narratives and genres, the postmodern author pays homage to the original, but with an irreverence born of the desire to find the new story within the old.

For the most part, the selections in this section make reference to specific genres or works of literature from the nineteenth and early twentieth centuries. If not for the title, even the reader familiar with Henry James' "The Turn of the Screw" (1898) would not immediately recognize Joyce Carol Oates' "The Turn of the Screw" (1972) as a retelling of James' classic psychological ghost story. This circumstance is appropriate to Oates' vision, however: while the bifurcated text represents a formal innovation, Oates' story is not expected to stand alone, but to act as commentary (and tribute), exploring possibilities that remained latent or submerged within the original. Similarly, "I Recall My Childhood," the first chapter of Kathy Acker's *Great Expectations* (1982), begins and ends with slightly (but tellingly) altered versions of famous passages from the first chapter of Charles Dickens' *Great Expectations* (1861). In between its opening and closing paragraphs, Acker's text utilizes the shadow of Dickens' seminal coming-of-age novel to set in bas-relief her own coming-of-age novel, one that makes overt the kinds of violence and fierce emotion that the Victorian prose of the original only suggests.

Other selections refer back not to individual works, but to genres and entire prose traditions. In its dry tone and plot-staging gestures, the first chapter of Paul Auster's *City of Glass* (1985) pays homage to the hard-boiled detective fiction of the mid-century; the odd enmeshment of Auster himself within the narrative introduces a level of experimental self-consciousness that explores openly the bonds among detective, author, and reader that are made only implicitly within the novels of Dashiell Hammett, Raymond Chandler, and others. In turn, Paul Karasik and David Mazzucchelli's graphic representation of this chapter illustrates the cross-pollination of forms inherent within the variegated realm of postmodern fiction. Auster's experimental reworking of the detective novel, for instance, is itself reworked within what previous generations routinely called a comic book, and the synthesis simultaneously expands the possibilities of commercial fiction as well as commercial form.

Perhaps no other author has renewed the creative possibilities of the traditional sorcerers-and-dragons fantasy genre more than Samuel R. Delany, whose *Return to Nevèrÿon* cycle offers a fully realized primitive world where present-day political and philosophical debates provide muted but unmistakable grace notes. In "Of Dragons, Mountains, Transhumance, Sequence, and Sunken Cities, *or:* The Violence of the Letter," excerpted from *Neveryóna* (1983), Delany explores issues of naming, gender identity, and language in a manner familiar to contemporary literary scholars, but in the context of a coming-of-age story set within a vividly imagined geography of trained dragons, sunken treasures, and aged "tale-tellers." In a similar manner, Rosario Ferré's "The Youngest Doll" (1991) provides an example of how contemporary authors have discovered creative opportunities to express complex, at times radical content within the form of the traditional children's story. "The Youngest Doll" possesses the tone and diction of a fairy tale, yet its subject matter explores (without ever resolving) issues of class, vanity, artistic inspiration, and gender roles.

While the retrospective spirit of postmodernism is reflected in works that pay homage to individual texts or prose genres, that spirit is perhaps best embodied in those novels and short stories built from compelling combinations. Maxine Hong Kingston's "Trippers and Askers" (excerpted from her 1987 novel *Tripmaster Monkey*), for instance, self-consciously invokes disparate expressive traditions. Kingston's protagonist is named Wittman Ah Sing in tribute to the nineteenth-century American poet Walt Whitman, and the San Francisco in which he lives is populated and made vibrant to him by a rich and overlapping set of literary traditions ranging from William Saroyan and John Steinbeck to Jack Kerouac. Simultaneously, Wittman is patterned by Kingston after Monkey, the mythic figure who in Chinese legend brings the Buddhist scriptures from India, and his Chinese identity exists in ongoing (and often affirmative) tension with his affinity for American life and literature. Marilynne Robinson's *Housekeeping* (1980) also reflects how an individual postmodern text can draw upon and revise several separate prose traditions. Robinson's narrative about two sisters coming to terms with loss and memory in Washington State during the 1950s refers to and reimagines the traditional themes and domestic settings of earlier "sentimental" women's fiction, while also responding to the canonically American (and traditionally masculine) genres of the Horatio Alger success story and novels of rugged individualism such as *The Adventures of Huck-*

leberry Finn (1884) and *The Deerslayer* (1841). Finally, Helena María Viramontes' "The Cariboo Cafe" (1985) demonstrates how the stories of the postmodern age commingle literary styles from the past (or from other cultures) with changes in perspective that draw out new significances from those styles. The language and setting of "The Cariboo Cafe" suggest the proletarian realism of Steinbeck or Hemingway; its narrative structure suggests the Latin American fiction of Gabriel García Márquez, Isabel Allende, or even Jorge Luis Borges; but its subject matter is unfailingly attentive to the evolving Chicana culture of the Mexican-American borderlands, as well as the complex political realities that exist there.

JOYCE CAROL OATES
b. 1938

Born in Lockport, New York, Joyce Carol Oates was educated at Syracuse University and the University of Wisconsin at Madison. She published her first story in 1959, and has since then published hundreds of stories, more than twenty short-story collections, nearly thirty novels, more than forty plays, several books of nonfiction, and approximately fifteen collections of poetry. She is the most prolifically published writer of serious fiction in the United States, and she has received the National Book Award for *them* (1969), the Bobst Award for Lifetime Achievement in Fiction (1990), and the Bram Stoker Lifetime Achievement Award for horror fiction (1994). Currently she serves as Roger S. Berlind Distinguished Professor at Princeton University and coedits the literary magazine *The Ontario Review*.

Oates' work spans a number of literary genres and styles, including realism, the Gothic novel, and parodistic epics. In 1988, she took the unusual step of publishing a mystery novel, *Lives of the Twins*, under the pseudonym Rosamond Smith. "I wanted a fresh reading; I wanted to escape from my own identity," she told *The New York Times Book Review*.

"Flaubert," Oates said in a 1987 interview, "said that you should live like a bourgeois so that you can be wild and original in your writing. It's not that I follow that dictum in any conscious way, but I think our lives settle into the patterns that accommodate what we do. . . . [A]s Flannery O'Connor—another writer frequently attacked for the 'darkness and violence' of her work—has said, No writer is a pessimist; the very act of writing is an optimistic act. I think of it primarily as a gesture of sympathy."

"The Turn of the Screw" first appeared in *Marriages and Infidelities* (1972).

The Turn of the Screw

For Gloria Whalen

Tuesday, July 6.

A wide stony beach. Pebbles big as hands. Here the sky is bluer than it is at home. Got out of the hotel before anyone could say hello—need to be alone after last night. Uncle and his hacking cough! Stayed up most of the night with him. His coughing is like the noise of the earth, its insides shifting. I imagine the earth splitting to draw the old man down, his body tumbling into the crater, into Hell. . . .

(Curious about Hell: will the flames make much noise?) Had to read the Bible to him while he lay there coughing and spitting. Didn't pay attention to me. Finally he

Tuesday, July 6.

Alone here, hidden, sick at heart. Away from that horrible numerosity. The oppression of the London sky, terraces bathed in evil light, the tonnage of history, too many horizons brought up short. . . . Chimneys that mock, beckon. Stained and weathered like cheeses. . . .

The stern demanding sea. It, too, mocks. But it does not know me. *Idle now for weeks, for a month and a half.*

Dying by the sea. Wearing the same two or three sets of clothes—no need to change—anonymous slept—around five. I fell onto my bed fully dressed and slept until seven. Sleep like death. In the morning I got out fast, my head echoing with Uncle's awful noises . . . so glad to be alone! And then a strange thing happened. . . .

A mile from the hotel. Me walking fast, enjoying the air, the smell of the sea. Great gulping breaths of air. My new boots slick with mud, my eyes fixed on the ground before me . . . glancing up I saw a girl, hardly more than a child. Twelve, thirteen years old.

Staring at me!

She called out something to me, a stranger. A high wheedling voice. Words I couldn't hear. My senses rushed together, stinging. I was deaf. A pull to my insides. Pain. Ah, that girl!—not pretty but full-faced, full-bodied, her eyes gleaming slits above her coarse pinkened cheeks—eyes gleaming as if there were already a secret between us! A dress of some green material, shapeless over her full hips and thighs; her plump little feet in boots, splattered with mud; her cheeks red as if pinched, very excited, strange dark eyes gleaming. . . . A head of curls—dark blond, depths of blond and shadow, enough to make my body ache. Licking her lips. One foot extended slightly as if in a dance. Cried out to me—a question—her voice tilting upward shrilly—but the noise of the waves drowned her out, my blood drowned her out, pulsing in my ears. Her gleaming eyes. The mist seemed to thicken and cloak us both. My eyes filmed over, filmed over. . . .

gentleman dark-ringed about the eyes with failure—afraid of new arrivals at the hotel: but they are all strangers. This morning I nearly collided with the young man I had noticed last night—he and an older man, probably his father, arrived yesterday, the old man apparently quite ill—Saw him walking along the beach, alone. Rather finely dressed and yet with a look—how strange that I should feel so certain of this!—of being doubtful of his clothes, as if they belonged to someone else. A waistcoat of pale satin. Excellent boots. Hatless, dark red hair, very strong features—the eyebrows are especially dark and firm—the eyes downcast as if searching out his fate *there,* on the ground. Something heraldic about him—a figure for art—My senses stung at the sight of him—

Then I saw, standing farther up the bank, near a thicket, that poor little girl who runs loose in the town sometimes—"not right in the head"—she was beckoning to the young American. Some shy instinct made me halt, back up—what would happen? I wanted to turn and hurry away. Befuddlement everywhere about us—the crashing of the waves—the young man's agitation—His smart clothes suddenly the clothes of an actor. *I must leave, must leave!*

Flushed face—the girl's frizzy blond hair—my own strange elation—*She is putting her hand out to him, she is calling to him,* but I am too far away to hear.

He will touch her, take hold of her arm. He will approach her and touch her. The three of us stand on the beach in total silence.

Bell-like tone to her voice. I could see now the veins in her throat.

Behind her, half a mile from the beach, a building like a fortress—is it a church? A barn? Stinging film over my eyes . . . my heart is pounding violently. . . . Around us on the beach: no one. Empty. Heart pounding, temples pounding, a dense dewlike moisture on every part of my body, cold and slick as fog, my insides in pain. . . . Suddenly I thought of my uncle back in the hotel: *he might be dying.*

A thicket for us. Giant bushes, spongy ground. The pebbles fade. The girl backs away from me. Wide staring smile. Her face protruding, plump. Something about her wet mouth that is fearful . . . but I cannot stop, it is too late, I cannot stop my hand from reaching out to her . . . There! Her arm, her elbow. My fingers close about her elbow. Giggling, backing away . . . a branch catches in her hair and then snaps away again, snaps straight . . . my fingers sliding up her arm to the shoulder and she is laughing faintly, breathily, the down on her upper lip is gleaming as if with cunning, she is very young, no more than twelve or thirteen years old . . . her chest rising and falling . . . little body stumbling backward, drawing us both backward into the thicket. . . .

She gave a jump. A little scream. Jerked away from me—pointed somewhere behind me—what was it? I couldn't see anything. What? Overcome with panic—*I have made a terrible mistake. My uncle has followed me.* The girl ran away. Behind me on the beach there was Waiting.

It is too late for me to turn and hurry away—my own face flushed and dangerously heated—something churns in my brain and fixes me here to the spot—*His back is to me: what does his face show?* She is staring up into his face—she *sees*—what words are passing between them? What words are spoken at such a time?

He approaches her. His stiff back. She draws away, teasing. Giant bushes will hide them from me. Panting, dizzy. I will be sick. He has taken hold of her now—yes, he has touched her—the two of them drawing back, back, almost out of my sight—they will hide themselves from me—it is going to happen, it is going to happen—

The girl screamed suddenly. Leaped back.

Must have seen me.

I hurry up the bank, must hide. Must get out of their sight. Heart sickened with fear, panic . . . I must not stumble. . . .

Reddening terrible face.

The dowdy room I have taken: its small charms and beguilements, etched glass, lace curtains, the dust of sorrow, sorrow, sorrow. . . .

In the mirror my face surprises me. So pale, so frightened! I thought it to be, for one confused moment, the face of that young man.

nothing, no one, I stood there trembling and staring back up the beach, no, nothing, no one, and yet I had the idea that someone had been standing there watching us only a few seconds before. . . .

Not my uncle? . . .

Slick with sweat. Oh, reeking. My head is still pounding. If anyone had seen . . . if anyone. . . . Uncle would abandon me, like the rest, if he had seen. . . .

God, help me to get through each day.

Wednesday, July 7.

Papers still filled with Victoria's Jubilee. Uncle Wallace at breakfast, robust and scornful, an excellent mood. Eggs, ham, toast, marmalade, buns. Snatches up the paper to read me an item; snorts with disgust. Breakfast takes an hour and a half. The dining room has a high cavernous ceiling: everything echoes. The room is not much used, the hotel not much used. Everyone looks English except us. Cold mealy independent faces.

A woman in her early fifties at a near table . . . dull redblond hair, brusque mannish gestures . . . but her face is attractive as she glances toward me, past her husband. Uncle does not see. Reading the third newspaper, grunting, coughing up something into his napkin. . . . By the seaside windows an English family with three children—the oldest a girl about ten. A child. Alone at another table is a middle-aged man in a rough

Wednesday, July 7.

Sleepless. Preoccupied. Idle now for a month and a half. My life: turned over and over as I turn this paperweight in my hand, something to be flung down, forgotten.

Breakfast. Careful not to stare at *him.* Hot, hot tea. There is a delightful family at a window table—rather hazy light—rain today? No matter.

I will bicycle out into the isolation.

My heart has been turning inside me, tugging to one side. A leaden sickish tug. I surrender. . . . He is sitting with the old gentleman, wearing clothes that fit him splendidly. Yet somehow not *his.* I turn my paper very briskly, neatly, to draw his attention. . . . An instant of our exchanging a glance . . . perhaps he recognizes me from yesterday?

His eye wanders away from me.

tweedy jacket, too big for him, sipping tea. Reading a paper. Very British. Lifting the paper to turn it, he glances toward Uncle and me—our eyes meet—then he looks away. A large rigid face. Eyes piercing.

With Uncle at the seaside. Grunts, clearing his throat vigorously, staring out at the sea. It disappoints him. Spits something up in his handkerchief. *What if he dies?* . . . My first trip to Europe; three months of travel ahead; what if he sickens and dies and leaves me alone? No. Behind him is my father. His brother. Dying also, dying very slowly. Decades of it. In Boston they take decades. *Quarles Ltd., Dry Goods.*

Loosed, what would my body do? . . . Run from this wreck of a man. Run. Noble wreck, ruined noble face. Cascades of wrinkled shriveled flesh on his neck! Back in Boston they are frowning sourly over us—two of a kind, two failures. Uncle and nephew. When Uncle Wallace was my age he was already a father. . . . Then the children died. First the boy, then the girl. Then the wife. Now I am his son, maybe. Two failures.

Uncle in a chair below the hotel. Attendants eager to please. Cool for July, they talk of the chance of clearing by this afternoon, always squinting at the sky and making prophecies. The middle-aged lady greets us doubtfully; yes, it is cool for July, she says. I am bored, bored. In a canvas chair beside Uncle. Staring at the sea. More blue here than back home—choppy distances—I cannot stop

Close-curling red hair. Handsome, pale, American face. Sits erect at the table like a son. I imagine he is perhaps twenty-five years old, and most dreadfully bored in the company of that old man, somehow thrown in with him for a trip, yet I don't believe that they are father and son. . . .

Absurdly sad: they are leaving the dining room. Yet an elation—the prospect lies ahead of further meetings, accidental meetings. Is there a mysterious and perhaps incomprehensible alliance here?

Subdued. A solitary breakfast. The family has left the dining room now—I hear excited talk of a carriage, an excursion—two girls and a boy, beautiful children. The boy is by far the youngest and walks with a bold stride. To be a father, a father of that particular boy. . . . What would that mean? How could it be experienced, so deep and terrifying a condition? Beautiful children!

Idle. Yet a small fever begins in me, as if I were about to start work. Idle and nervous. But I see that I am not heading for my room, no, I am walking quite reasonably headlong into a kind of hush—postbreakfast solemnity in this droll old hotel, all a kind of hush, the fixtures overdone and pompous and hushed, a held breath, as in that eerie moment when something gathers or crouches in preparation for an attack. . . .

Ah, the beach. Poor helpless eyes bobbing about—from horizon to shore—there they are, seated. The thinking of that girl of yesterday, that child on the beach. My body tries to shrivel. I think of my cousin Madeline—that face of hers. Accusing me. *He said things to me! Said things!*

Like a girl of twelve herself. But she was twenty-four.

Next week I will be thirty.

Uncle clearing his throat loudly, spreading a blanket across his knees; more newspapers. Brings the edge of his fingers hard across his mustache. Someone pauses near him. Cane in hand, jaunty for a man his age, his beard trimmed to a spadelike shape. Dark. Neat. He is a gentleman but nervous—wears a polka-dot bow tie and a golfing cap. Heavyset in the thighs and torso.

Uncle Wallace and he are talking—". . . north of Boston? . . ." ". . . the Clintons, Arnold Clinton, finance . . . imports? . . ." ". . . crowds in London? . . . awful!"

My eye is drawn out to the edge of the sea.

Women: the girl of yesterday. Eyes secretive as slits. Her foot—the mud—the ankle—the pale stockings—the calf of the leg inside the stocking—the knee—the thigh—

Old men chattering: of London, of crowds, *this screaming, clumsy overdoing of a fine thing,* the man in the golfing cap says.

Ah, the cords of her little throat were taut with concentration! Cheap material of the dress drawn old man humped and tyrannical. The young man with legs crossed; white trousers, handsome high-button shoes, an air of indolence and impatience. The son of a wealthy father, certainly.

Approaching the old gentleman. His sudden raised face—querulous watery eyes—yet I introduce myself quite easily. Ah, yes, they are Americans; should I seem surprised? From Boston. It turns out that we know someone in common. I chat quite happily, quite easily with the old man. My agitation seems to have subsided. Ignore the young man's stare—it is good to hear my own voice again—too conscious of Self, too haunted, driven by Self, always Self. I must overcome myself.

Patrick Quarles II. His name.

I think of Dickens—for we are near David Copperfield's country—no, I think of Stendhal: a young man lounging idly, restlessly, ambitious and yet not strong enough to direct the progress of the story he is in. Condemned almost and never to be quite *real,* quite sympathetic. *He seems to be listening as I speak of London. . . .* He is a man marked for some strange destiny. For women? Yes, but more. He does not know what his fate will be. *Nervous, I am beginning to be nervous. . . .*

He is like a young animal: no history.

The old man contains all their family history. Draws it up into him. We chatter wonderfully, two Americans, he seems to be impressed tight across the small bosom, tight as the veins of the throat, the tense arteries of the stomach, the loins . . . blue-veined thighs, the shadowy soft insides of thighs. . . . *London defaced: an atrocious sight. Miles of unsightly scaffolding . . . a sudden, new vision of our age, an unwelcome perspective of the century that lies ahead. . . . Machinery . . . that infuriates and deflowers and destroys. . . .*

Walking slowly down the beach. Why do I want to run, run away from the chatter of old men!—a root is alive in me, stirring in me. Trembling. Ugh. I am alive and the old men are dying or are dead, if I glance over my shoulder at them I would see only two aging gentlemen—one in a canvas chair, bundled up for a cool July morning, the other with a cane thrust through his arm, words that do not matter, a flow of words that do not matter the way the pebbles of this wide wet beach matter—and behind them, in America, my own father stands like a monument, his shadow rooted to him at his base, unshakable. Can you shake them? You walk away from them.

I light a cigar.

with my denunciation of the Jubilee nonsense. Can understand best harsh abrasive words.

The young man gets to his feet suddenly, unaccountably, and strolls away. . . .

The old man is a large monument: the nephew a small mark. In a flash I see their family gravesite. Yes. I, standing here so helplessly and timidly, cane tucked through my arm, smiling and smiling, a gravestone of too fragile a substance: the wintry gusts from this sea would destroy me.

Thursday, July 8.

Was informed of a letter for me—took it from the clerk, surprised, for who would write to me?—having left home as I did—could not recognize the handwriting—walked confused out the front of the hotel, almost slipped on the steps that were wet from the morning's rain—tore open the envelope nervously—

Thursday, July 8.

Walking quickly along the shore. Unable to think. *Must think.* Not fit for company now—my face a mask of grimaces, taunts, smirks, bewilderments, small pains and pleasures, featureless as the sea. Not human now. Not human. To have dared what I did! . . . A sleepless night, palpitating heart. Absurd attempts at prayer. God-

My Dear Boy,

I am anxious for this letter to do nothing except soothe you, encourage you, insist upon the simple joy you have given me by existing so innocently and so nobly as yourself. From my timid post of observation, your future strikes me as rich and enormously open, wide as the ocean—and I beg that you do not destroy it by any impulsive act—for, you see, I was a most reluctant and helpless witness to Tuesday's small episode—or by any systematic and perhaps more wasteful surrender of your youth to another's age. Be free: I rejoice in your very being. But: Caution!

No signature.

I stumbled along the street—cobbled street—row upon row of small blank houses, shops, the tower of the church and its crumbling ivy wall—mind in a whirl—panic—must tear up this letter and get rid of it—

Went into a pub. Seated, my eyesight blotched. Din inside my head. Last night Uncle kept me awake again, reading the Bible to him. Words kept rising in my head: *Why doesn't he die!* My fear of him, my love for him. *Why don't they all die, die!* I order a small beer and drink it at once and in the instant in which I close my eyes I can see their bodies bobbing and ebbing in a tide, the bodies of the old, old men, tossed up toward an anonymous shore that is neither American nor English, just a shore, just bodies of the dead. *Why don't they die and free us from them?—free us to life?*

Spent the afternoon. Seagoing men here—retired men—noisy in their less prayer. But something, something must aid me, must beguile me out of myself . . . out of the memory of what I have done . . . memories of Father's fits of madness, the Imaginary seizing his throat, the Demon always beside him, squatting, leaping up when he did not, could not, have expected it. . . . Am I my father's son, after all?

Heroism: acquiescing to that madness.

At the bottom of my soul it squats, like that dwarf of a demon: the fear that I am mad, evil, reckless, sick, corrupting, contaminating, loosed, formless, sucking like the waves here upon the packed sand, desolate, inexhaustible, damned. . . .

Why did I write him that letter?

Yet—the joy of this morning! The utter abandoned joy of the writing, the sealing of the envelope, the very slow, slow, firm addressing of a name that suddenly seems to have been my own invention, to have been known to me all my life: *Patrick Quarles II.*

What is he? A disinherited son—so I have gathered. He has the look of a London urchin grown and clothed splendidly—an actor—a nervous flitting consciousness that no clothes can define—*I will clothe you.*

What will happen when our eyes meet? That fateful terrifying instant of our common *knowledge!* I will bow to him, I will acknowledge everything meekly. . . . Breath in ragged spurts. Aging. My best work is behind me. Now, greetings—"What ho!" they call out to each other when they meet—then fall into silence—but the silence is not awkward. Women. Moving about. They glance at me and my heart feels enormous, suffocating. One woman stares openly at me. A broad smile, straggly hairs on her forehead . . . skin not pale like Madeline's but opaque, blunt . . . *easing the stocking from her muscular leg, heavy flesh, dark hairs growing out of the flesh* . . . but I stand suddenly, hurry away. Must get back to the hotel before Uncle is angry.

I tore the letter up into small pieces and threw it away.

ahead of me, is work of another kind. . . . He is so young, he is pure instinct. The old man, the uncle, wants to suck his energy. Ignorant old man!

I am mad to have such thoughts . . . sharp pain in my chest as I climb the hotel steps, which seem suddenly steep, mountainous. . . . Is he here, waiting? The letter in his hand, waiting?

Friday, July 9.

Excursion by carriage. Out along the country roads in spite of the drizzle. Uncle's sour cough. Forgave me for leaving him yesterday: his heir.

Women. Foul and sluggish in their evil. Mud on my boots, scummy feel of my own skin. My cousin's tears and red-rimmed eyes. The woman in the tavern: the veins of her flesh would have been hidden deep inside that opaque fatty skin.

Afternoon tea: Uncle gorges himself. Buns, jam. Beer. Whisky. Coffee. Small meat pie. My duty to rise obediently as a son, to seek out more food. Which village are we in? What is its name? The map I studied is marked with names of places I had wanted to explore—Blundeston, Great Yarmouth, Bournemouth itself—but everything passes now before my eyes in a mist, my senses sting, the ma-

Friday, July 9.

Sleepless. Feverish and very happy. Three letters composed for him, and I hardly know which to select. All of them?

The chambermaid listens with her good plain worried gaze upon me. I begin explaining carefully, but end by stammering, my eyes filled with moisture—"Mr. Quarles is an extremely sensitive gentleman . . . and he would be distressed to be told that he walked off with my letters this morning . . . he quite simply picked them up by accident, when we paused to chat together. . . . I called after him, of course, but, as you may know, he doesn't hear quite so well . . . and . . . and I would actually prefer not to bring the matter up to him, and certainly I would prefer never to see the poor letters again if it were a question of . . . a question of insulting him, however indirectly. . . ." Nods in sympathy with me. Grimly. Out chinery of my brain races ahead to what, to what?—

Caution, the letter advised.

What does that mean?—why caution?—Am I about to do something I must be urged against? *Uncle's piggish grunts. The Royal Park Hotel. Will I outlive him?* Sat in the pub with him, a lonely pub. Thought of hell. Spirits brushing against us in daylight, the damned. What could they tell us about hell if they could speak?

Dutiful nephew to a sick man.

Nothing more.

of her mild gaze I think I see something growing—sharp and deadly and cunning—but no, I must be imagining it. Imagining it. She replies that it is out of her control. Only the manager, perhaps. . . . Very hard for her to know what to do. . . . But no, no, I say at once, the manager must absolutely not be bothered; I will surrender the letters—gaily I tell her this, ready to back away—She frowns, blinks slowly and stupidly at me—Suddenly she consents.

Ah, she consents! And within five minutes we are *there,* in that room! The Quarleses have taken a rather grand suite of rooms. A sitting room of really lavish proportions—excellent furniture—a carpet in much finer condition than the one in my sad little room—a balcony that stares out wonderfully at the sea and sky. There is a little old antique of a writing desk that I approach, under the chambermaid's watchful eye, for my letters would be here if Mr. Quarles had really walked off with it—and humbly, timidly I bend over the desk, in that good lady's sight, and do not touch anything on it. Only yesterday's *Times.* A letter tucked into its envelope, postmarked Boston. I shake my head—nothing here—and, with a slight questioning rise of my eyebrows, indicate that I will take just one step inside this bedroom—

Staring at me impassively. What is she thinking? Can she guess? The forbidden rises to one's face in the presence of such women, they positively draw guilt out, expose everything—But though I am nervous, extremely nervous, I smile rather bravely back at her—how she stands watching me!—

Saturday, July 10.

Three letters.

That dark demanding hand—not a lady's hand—it is someone like myself, shouting at me—trying to make me hear—

A young woman and her mother brush past me with a scent of something harsh and flowery about them—my nerves are jumping—people are beginning to notice me. An elderly man is staring quite openly at me—did he write these letters?

I walk out quickly. Must be alone.

My Dear Boy,
Understand only that I wish you well—only well!—and that I should not communicate so strangely and so secretively if other means were open to me. . . .

And so I open the door to one of the bedrooms and simply lean inside—my heart is pounding—It is *his* room.

Scent of pomade. Tobacco.

For a long icy moment I stand there—my body rigid with the necessity of showing nothing, absolutely nothing, as if the hunters and their dogs will be upon me if I flinch—I feel his strange heedless presence everywhere about me, rushing upon me. So much closer and dearer than he might ever be in his own person—

"No luck, sir?" the chambermaid calls out.

Saturday, July 10.

Another sleepless, aching night. The chambermaid's face hovering in my private darkness—witness of my folly!—this morning I will press upon her a small sum, hopefully not a bribe—or have I come to that? A gift, a sign of my gratitude for her kindness, her—

No breakfast this morning. My stomach is so weak, I am so preoccupied . . . I am terrified. . . . Must imagine *him. Him.* I stand on the balcony and think of him, envision him, only him. The sea is choppy and leaden today. Everything disappoints us that is not human.

Few people strolling out. Ladies with their long dresses, so drastically protected. Gentlemen. Hats, gloves, pipes. *Must imagine him. No freedom.* Fallen upon evil days,

The last sentence is crossed out, I can't make out anything. No signature.

My Dear Boy,
You are generous to allow me to write, knowing that it is the only manner in which I may hold you close, lay upon you—oh, so soothingly!—the most respectful of hands—I see in your face a terrible need. I fear for you. Will you stand on the shore and accept these frail words of mine, will you accept the only gift I dare give you—words, prophecies—

For a long moment I cannot think. What is happening? It is as if a secret Self—my own Self—were writing to me like this, hinting at a terrible knowledge—*prophecies:* what does that mean?—Are there spirits, ghosts? Is there a future Self—a future Patrick Quarles—gazing back upon me, seeing me, from the future—the 1900's, when we may all be free!—and reaching back to bless me—

And so I stand on the shore, yes. I accept. In this dour chilling breeze I am very happy, and I turn slowly to look back at the hotel—that monster of a hotel!

Who is watching me?

He must be gazing at me from one of the windows. But I dare not wave. What does he think? Is he there? Is there really anyone there? I stare into space, smiling.

Across the distance something passes into me, like a breath.

Lighting a cigar, I stroll down the beach and open the third letter. A sick days—signs of vastation all around me, inside me—

Ah, he is there!

Wooden steps. The boardwalk. Ah, he is reading . . . he is reading my letters. . . . He is reading what I have written to him, in such anguish!

Disgust? Shame? Or can he sense the human wish behind it, the wish to speak kindly to another soul, a solitary soul? . . .

Feverish. The wind inside my head, not cooling it. Wind. Fever. My head is swimming. He is standing there with his back to me—his figure blurs and swims in my vision—I want to cry out to him, "Must I grow old? Must I die? If you walk away from me I will die—"

No—he is turning—

His figure against the somber water. Unimagined—such splendor! He is looking toward me but I draw back at once, into the shadow of the room—my eyes brimming—

Across that space he seems to bless me. I must put my hands out against the French doors, I must steady myself or I will fling myself forward, outward, to my death—

Yes, he looks at me. It has happened. The distance between us is holy. A hush. . . . He is my living Self: I see that now. Living as I have never lived. He is magnificent. I am alive in him and dead, dead in myself, but alive in him, only in him—

letter from a friend, one who wishes me well and knows me, knows me.

My Dear Boy,
You are without history and so you must free yourself from it. But caution. Am I speaking madness? Am I offending you? Or can you understand how I should, if I dared, quite openly invite you to lean upon me as a kindly father? . . . The sense that I cannot speak to you, cannot reveal myself to you—this torments me, makes me ache at the bitterness of things. I reach out toward you—I let go—I abandon you—

More words crossed out.

Something tries to come through those X-ed out words. A command. Angry urgent words. *Utter caution.* A voice has spoken. I know there are ghosts. I understand them. I feel them in this medieval town, on all sides of me, harsh and innocent with their cold piercing eyes and their victories—their terrible victories—

I will kill him.

No. The words are not mine. I will never lay hands upon him. The mark of my hands would show upon him, it would scream out that I was his murderer—*I will suffocate him, I have been given permission to suffocate him, to destroy him*—I will not come near him, no. No. I will sit quietly at his bedside as he strangles in his own phlegm—the poison that bubbles up out of his ugly soul—

Will I sit at his bedside? Will I watch him die? Will I dare to do

In a lifetime there are few moments of such bliss.

Trembling, hiding, in the shadows of my room . . . safe. Saved. My heart lunges backward into safety. Must hide. Must remain hidden. I am growing old, yes, soon I will be as old and as ugly as his uncle—yes, and it is right, we must be pushed aside, we must die—must acquiesce to darkness—Our heirs demand the future. They demand that history be turned over to them.

In this moment of joy I am transformed.

He, *he* is myself: walking away! Free to walk away! I must strain to see him, his handsome figure about to fade into the low heathery bareness of the country, that shy purple and gold that runs nearly to the edge of the sea. . . .

A moment too deep for any utterance.

It takes me an hour to dress. I am still shaky. A little feverish. Soon I will be working again—I will work through *him.* He will possess me. I am ready to work, ready even to return to the coal-gray skies of London, that sky that encloses and entraps the mind—

He has understood my message. My love. I will live through him and he through me: born again in my writing, in something I will, must write, something I will begin soon in honor of his youth and the perfect power of his face. . . .

I hurry downstairs. I must feed the birds in the garden—I have forgotten them for days—The garden is

what those letters instruct? Will I
outlive him? Will I outlive all
these old men?

deserted, hushed. Everyone is
elsewhere. Only *he* is with me, his
presence close to me, our minds
beating with the beauty of this
somber garden and its wide gravel
paths and its pinched roses and
weathered walls—

In a lifetime there are few moments of such bliss.

1972

KATHY ACKER
1944–1997

Kathy Acker attended Brandeis University and the University of California at San Diego. After working as a file clerk, secretary, stripper, and performer in live sex shows and pornographic films, she embarked on her career as a fiction writer and screenwriter. Her novels include *Politics* (1972), *Kathy Goes to Haiti* (1978), *New York City in 1979* (1981), *Great Expectations* (1982), *Don Quixote* (1986), and *Pussy, King of the Pirates* (1996).

As she put it in a 1985 *Straits* interview, Acker saw herself "in the tradition of European novelists, post–nouveau roman." Writer and critic Elizabeth Benedict, in a 1984 *Esquire* article, called her "the best of the punk writers," with a voice that is "brash, fiesty, sexy, smart, sometimes likable." Due to Acker's radical shifts in context, Benedict also called her work "generally rough going." Acker responded that she was trying to work on "how to use language where you're not dictating to people how to think."

Her appropriations of other literary works, including Proust's *Remembrance of Things Past* and Dickens' *Great Expectations*, have also drawn critical attention. "All I can say," Acker told *Straits*, "is that, by taking these texts and just putting them there as simply as I can, and not making anything of them, not saying anything, not doing anything, I'm doing something that . . . really feels good and has joy in it."

"I Recall My Childhood" is an excerpt from *Great Expectations*, "Part 1. Plagiarism."

From Great Expectations

I Recall My Childhood

My father's name being Pirrip, and my Christian name Philip, my infant tongue could make of both names nothing longer or more explicit than Peter. So I called myself Peter, and came to be called Peter.

I give Pirrip as my father's family name on the authority of his tombstone and my sister—Mrs. Joe Gargery, who married the blacksmith.

On Christmas Eve 1978 my mother committed suicide and in September of 1979 my grandmother (on my mother's side) died. Ten days ago (it is now almost Christmas 1979) Terence told my fortune with the Tarot cards. This was not so much a fortune—whatever that means—but a fairly, it seems to me, precise psychic map of the present, therefore: the future.

I asked the cards about future boyfriends. This question involved the following thoughts: Would the guy who fucked me so well in France be in love with me? Will I have a new boyfriend? As Terence told me to do, I cut the cards into four piles: earth water fire air. We found my significator, April 18th, in the water or emotion fantasy pile. We opened up this pile. The first image was a fat purring human cat surrounded by the Empress and the Queen of Pentacles. This cluster, traveling through a series of other clusters that, like mirrors, kept defining or explained the first cluster more clearly—time is an almost recurring conical—led to the final unconscious image: during Christmas the whole world is rejecting a male and a female kid who are scum by birth. To the right of the scum is the Star. To the left is the card of that craftsmanship which due to hard work succeeds.

Terence told me that despite my present good luck my basic stability my contentedness with myself alongside these images, I have the image obsession I'm scum. This powerful image depends on the image of the Empress, the image I have of my mother. Before I was born, my mother hated me because my father left her (because she got pregnant?) and because my mother wanted to remain her mother's child rather than be my mother. My image of my mother is the source of my creativity. I prefer the word consciousness. My image of my hateful mother is blocking consciousness. To obtain a different picture of my mother, I have to forgive my mother for rejecting me and committing suicide. The picture of love, found in one of the clusters, is forgiveness that transforms need into desire.

Because I am hating my mother I am separating women into virgins or whores rather than believing I can be fertile.

I have no idea how to begin to forgive someone much less my mother. I have no idea where to begin: repression's impossible because it's stupid and I'm a materialist.

I just had the following dream:

In a large New England-ish house I am standing in a very big room on the second floor in the front of the mansion. This room is totally fascinating, but as soon as I leave it, I can't go back because it disappears. Every room in this house differs from every other room.

The day after my mother committed suicide I started to experience a frame. Within this frame time was totally circular because I was being returned to my childhood traumas totally terrifying because now these traumas are totally real: there is no buffer of memory.

There is no time; there is.

Beyond the buffers of forgetting which are our buffer to reality: there is. As the dream: there is and there is not. Call this TERROR call this TOTAL HUMAN RESPONSIBILITY. The PIG I see on the edge of the grave is the PIG me neither death nor social comment kills. This TERROR is divine because it is real and may I sink into IT.

My mother often told me: "You shouldn't care if an action is right or wrong; you should totally care if you're going to profit monetarily from it."

The helmeted bowlegged stiff-muscled soldiers trample on just-born babies swaddled in scarlet violet shawls, babies roll out of the arms of women crouched under POP's iron machine guns, a cabby shoves his fist into a goat's face, near the lake a section of the other army crosses the tracks, other soldiers in this same army leap in front of the trucks, the POP retreat up the river, a white-walled tire in front of three thorn bushes props up a male's head, the soldiers bare their chests in the shade of the mud barricades, the females lullabye kids in their tits, the sweat from the fires perfumes reinforces this stirring rocking makes their rags their skins their meat pregnant: salad oil clove henna butter indigo sulfur, at the base of this river under a shelf loaded down by burnt-out cedars barley wheat beehives graves refreshment stands garbage bags fig trees matches human-brain-splattered low-walls small-fires'-smoke-dilated orchards explode: flowers pollen grain-ears tree roots paper milk-stained cloths blood bark feathers, rising. The soldiers wake up stand up again tuck in their canvas shirttails suck in cheeks stained by tears dried by the steam from hot train rails rub their sex against the tires, the trucks go down into a dry ford mow down a few rose-bushes, the sap mixes with disemboweled teenagers' blood on their knives' metal, the soldiers' nailed boots cut down uproot nursery plants, a section of RIMA (the other army) climb onto their trucks' runningboards throw themselves on their females pull out violet rags bloody tampaxes which afterwards the females stick back in their cunts: the soldier's chest as he's raping the female crushes the baby stuck in her tits

I want: every part changes (the meaning of) every other part so there's no absolute/heroic/dictatorial/S&M meaning/part the soldier's onyx-dusted fingers touch her face orgasm makes him shoot saliva over the baby's buttery skull his formerly-erect now-softening sex rests on the shawl becomes its violet scarlet color, the trucks swallow up the RIMA soldiers, rainy winds shove the tarpaulins against their necks, they adjust their clothes, the shadows grow, their eyes gleam more and more their fingers brush their belt buckles, the wethaired-from-sweating-during-capture-at-the-edge-of-the-coals goats crouch like the rags sticking out of the cunts, a tongueless canvas-covered teenager pisses into the quart of blue enamel he's holding in his half-mutilated hand, the truck driver returns kisses the blue cross tattooed on his forehead, the teenager brings down his palm wrist where alcohol-filled veins are sticking out. These caterpillars of trucks grind down the stones the winds hurled over the train tracks, the soldiers sleep their sex rolling over their hips drips they are cattle, their truck-driver spits black a wasp sting swells up the skin under his left eye black grapes load down his pocket, an old man's white hair under-the-white-hair red burned face jumps up above the sheet metal, the driver's black saliva dries on his chin the driver's studded heel crushes as he pulls hair out the back of this head on to the sheet metal, some stones blow up

My mother is the most beautiful woman in the world. She has black hair, green eyes which turn gray or brown according to her mood or the drugs she's on at the moment, the pallor of this pink emphasizes the fullness of her lips, skin so soft the color of her cheeks is absolutely peach no abrasions no redness no white tightness. This in no way describes the delicacy of the face's bone structure. Her body is equally exquisite, but on the plump or sagging side because she doesn't do any exercise and she wears girdles. She's five feet six inches tall. She usually weighs 120 pounds even though she's always taking diet pills. Her breasts look larger and fuller than they are because they sag downwards. The nipples in them are large pale pink. In the skin around the nipples and in the tops of her legs you can easily see the varicose veins breaking through. The breast stomach and upper thigh skin is very pale white. There's lots of curly hair around her cunt.

She has a small waist hands and ankles. The main weight, the thrust, the fullness of those breasts is deceptive, is the thighs: large pockmarked flesh indicates a heavy ass extra flesh at the sides of the thighs. The flesh directly above the cunt seems paler than it has to be. So pale, it's fragile, at the edge of ugliness: the whole: the sagging but not too large breasts, the tiny waist, the huge ass are sexier MORE ABOUT PASSION than a more-tightly-muscled and fashionable body.

My mother is the person I love most. She's my sister. She plays with me. There's no one else in my world except for some kind of weird father who only partly exists part out of the shadow, and an unimportant torment I call my sister. I'm watching my mother put on her tight tawny-orange sweater. She always wears a partially lacy white bra that seems slightly dirty. As she's struggling to get into a large white panty girdle she says she doesn't like girdles. She's standing in front of her mirror and mirrored dresser. Mirrors cover every inch of all the furniture in the room except for the two double beds, my father's chair, and the TV, but they don't look sensuous. Now my mother's slipping into a tight brown wool straight skirt. She always wears tight sweaters and tight straight skirts. Her clothes are old and very glamorous. She hitches her skirt up a little and rolls on see-through stockings.

She tells me to put on my coat and white mittens because we're going outside.

Today is Christmas. Huge clean piles of snow cover the streets make the streets magical. Once we get to the park below the 59th Street Bridge I say to myself, "No foot has ever marked this snow before." My foot steps on each unmarked bit of snow. The piles are so high I can barely walk through them. I fall down laughing. My mother falls down laughing with me. My clothes especially the pants around my boots are sopping wet. I stay in this magic snow with the beautiful yellow sun beating down on me as long as I can until a voice in my head (me) or my mother says, "Now you know what this experience is, you have to leave."

My mother wants to get a strawberry soda. Today my mother's being very nice to me and I love her simply and dearly when she's being nice to me. We're both sitting on the round red vinyl turnable seats around the edge of the white counter. My mother's eating a strawberry soda with strawberry ice cream. I see her smiling. A fat middle-aged man thinks we're sisters. My mother is very young and beautiful.

At camp: males string tents up along a trench filled with muck: slush from meat refuse vomit sparkle under arching colorless weeds, the soldiers by beating them drive back the women who're trying to stick their kids in the shelter of the tents, they strike at kick punch the soldiers' kidneys while the soldiers bend over the unfolded tent canvas. Two males tie the animals to the rears of the tents, a shit-filled-assed teenager squatting over the salt-eroded weeds pants dust covers his face his head rolls vacantly around his shoulder his purple eye scrutinizes the montage of tents, a brown curly-haired soldier whose cheeks cause they're crammed full of black meat are actually touching his pock-marked earlobes crouches down next to a little girl he touches her nape his hand crawls under the rags around her throat feels her tits her armpits: the little girl closes her eyes her fingers touch the soldier's grapejuice-smeared wrist, from the shit-heaps a wind-gust lifts up the bits of film and sex mag pages the soldiers tore up while they were shitting clenched the shit burns the muscles twisted by rape. Some soldiers leaving the fire wander around the tents untie the tent thongs they crawl on the sand, the linen tent flaps brush their scabies-riddled thighs, the males the females all phosphorescent nerves huddle around the candles, no longer wanting to hear anything the teenagers chew wheat they found in the bags, the kids pick threads out of their teeth put their rags on again stick the sackcloth back over their mothers' tits lick the half-chewed flour left on their lips

My mother thinks my father is a nobody. She is despising him and lashing out at him right now she is saying while she is sitting on her white quilt-covered bed "Why don't you ever go out at night, Bud? All you do is sleep."

"Let me watch the football game, Claire. It's Sunday."

"Why don't you ever take mommy out, daddy? She never has any fun." Actually I think my mother's a bitch.

"You can't sleep all the time, Bud. It isn't good for you."

"This is my one day off, Claire. I want to watch the football game. Six days a week I work my ass off to buy you and the kids food, to keep a roof over your head. I give you everything you want."

"Daddy, you're stupid." "Daddy, you don't even know who Dostoyevsky is." "What's the matter with you, daddy?"

Daddy's drunk and he's still whining, but now he's whining nastily. He's telling my mother that he does all the work he goes to work at six in the morning and comes back after six at night (which we all know is a joke cause his job's only a sinecure: my mother's father gave him his first break, a year ago when the business was sold, part of the deal was my father'd be kept on as 'manager' under the new owners at $50,000 a year. We all know he goes to work cause there he drinks and he doesn't hear my mother's nagging). He's telling my mother he gave her her first fur coat. My father is never aggressive. My father never beats my mother up.

The father grabs a candle, the curly brownhaired soldier his red mouth rolling around the black meat takes out his knife: his hand quickly juts the red rags over his sex his pincher his grabber the curly brownhaired soldier jerks the sleepy young girl's thighs to him, she slides over the sand till she stops at the tent opening, one soldier's mutilated forehead cause he was rapping over an eagle's eggs the eagle scalped him another soldier's diseased skin-pores these two soldiers gag the father, the father throws a burning candle into their hairs, the curly brownhaired soldier takes the young girl into his arms, she sleeps she purrs her open palm on her forehead to his shudder trot, the clouded moon turns his naked arm green, his panting a gurgling that indicates rape the sweat dripping off his bare strong chest wakes the young girl up, I walked into my parents' bedroom opened their bathroom door don't know why I did it, my father was standing naked over the toilet, I've never seen him naked I'm shocked, he slams the door in my face, I'm curious I see my mother naked all the time, she closely watches inside his open cause gasping mouth the black meat still stuck to his teeth the black meat still in a ball, the curly brownhaired lifts her on to her feet lay her down on the dog-kennels' metal grating hugs her kisses her lips the ear hollows where the bloodstained wax causes whispers his hand unbuttons his sack-cloth pulls out his member, the young girl sucks out of the curly brown-haired's cheeks the black meat eyes closed hands spread over the metal grating, excited by this cheek-to-stomach muscle motion bare-headed straw-dust flying around his legs injects the devil over her scorches, the dogs waking up at the metal gratings leap out of the kennels their chains gleam treat me like a dog drag in the shit, the curly brownhaired nibbles the young girl's gums his teeth pull at the meat fibres her tongue pushes into the cracks between her teeth, the dogs howl their chains jingle against the tar of the road their paws crush down the hardened shits, the curly brownhaired's knees imprison the young girl's thighs.

My father's lying in the hospital cause he's on his third heart attack. My mother's mother at the door of my father's room so I know my father is overhearing her is saying to my mother, "You have to say he's been a good husband to you, Claire. He never left you and he gave you everything you wanted."

"Yes."

"You don't love him."

"Yes."

I know my grandmother hates my father.

I don't side with my mother rather than my father like my sister does. I don't perceive my father. My mother is adoration hatred play. My mother is the world. My mother is my baby. My mother is exactly who she wants to be.

The whole world and consciousness revolves around my mother.

I don't have any idea what my mother's like. So no matter how my mother acts, she's a monster. Everything is a monster. I hate it. I want to run away. I want to escape the Jolly Green Giant. Any other country is beautiful as long as I don't know about it. This is the dream I have: I'm running away from men who are trying to damage me permanently. I love mommy. I know she's on Dex, and when she's not on Dex she's on Librium to counteract the Dex jitters so she acts more extreme than usual. A second orgasm cools her shoulders, the young girl keeps her hands joined over the curly brown-haired's ass, the wire grating gives way, the curly brownhaired slides the young girl under him his pants are still around his knees his fingernails claw the soil his breath sucks in the young girl's cheek blows straw dust around, the mute young girls' stomach muscles weld to the curly-headed's abdominal muscles, the passing wind immediately modulates the least organic noise that's why one text must subvert (the meaning of) another text until there's only background music like reggae: the inextricability of relation-textures the organic (not meaning) recovered, stupid ugly horrible a mess pinhead abominable vomit eyes-pop-out-always-presenting-disgust-always-presenting-what-people-flee-always-wanting-to-be-lonely infect my mother my mother, blind fingernails spit the eyes wandering from the curly-headed, the curly-headed's hidden balls pour open cool down on the young girl's thigh. Under the palmtrees the RIMAS seize and drag a fainted woman under a tent, a flushing-forehead blond soldier burning coals glaze his eyes his piss stops up his sperm grasps this woman in his arms, their hands their lips touch lick the woman's clenched face while the blond soldier's greasy wine-stained arm supports her body, the young girl RECOVERED,

New York City is very peaceful and quiet, and the pale gray mists are slowly rising, to show me the world, I who have been so passive and little here, and all beyond is so unknown and great that now I am crying. My fingers touch the concrete beneath my feet and I say, "Goodbye, oh my dear, dear friend."

We don't ever have to be ashamed of feelings of tears, for feelings are the rain upon the earth's blinding dust: our own hard egotistic hearts. I feel better after I cry: more aware of who I am, more open. I need friends very much.

Thus ends the first segment of my life. I am a person of GREAT EXPECTATIONS.

1982

JOHN BARTH
b. 1930

John Barth was born in Cambridge, Maryland, and received an A.B. and an M.A. from Johns Hopkins University in Baltimore. After a twenty-year period teaching at Pennsylvania State University and the State University of New York at Buffalo, he returned to Johns Hopkins in 1973, where he taught at the Writing Seminars until his retirement in the mid-1990s. Currently he resides in Chestertown, Maryland. He is the author of more than a dozen works of fiction, including the novels *The Floating Opera* (1956), *The End of the Road* (1958), *The Sot-Weed Factor* (1960), *Tidewater Tales* (1987), and *Once Upon a Time: A Floating Opera* (1995), the story collection *Lost in the Funhouse* (1968), and the novella collection *Chimera* (1972). He has also published two collections of essays, and in 1967, he took the unusual step of publishing revised editions of his first three novels. His most recent publication is the story collection *On with the Story* (1996).

In a 1975 interview in the literary magazine *Caliban,* Barth described himself as a "concocter of comic novels." He asserted that his literary goal is to "keep a foot in two doors": to achieve originality "and, at the same time, explore especially the oldest conventions of the medium for their possible present usefulness." Because any fiction is "part of the history of fiction," Barth wrote in his first collection of essays, *The Friday Book* (1984), it "is almost always about itself."

"Dunyazadiad" first appeared as the opening novella in *Chimera,* which received the National Book Award in 1973. The three novellas of *Chimera* retell three myths and grapple with the process of disorientation and a rapprochement with the future, sharing thematic concerns with Barth's collection *Lost in the Funhouse.* Both collections, Barth wrote in an article, "Getting Oriented," in *The New York Times Book Review* in 1984, explore "the oral narrative tradition from which printed fiction evolved."

From Chimera

Dunyazadiad

1

"At this point I interrupted my sister as usual to say, 'You have a way with words, Scheherazade. This is the thousandth night I've sat at the foot of your bed while you and the King made love and you told him stories, and the one in progress holds me like a genie's gaze. I wouldn't dream of breaking in like this, just before the end, except that I hear the first rooster crowing in the east, et cetera, and the King really ought to sleep a bit before daybreak. I wish I had your talent.'

"And as usual Sherry replied, 'You're the ideal audience, Dunyazade. But this is nothing; wait till you hear the ending, tomorrow night! Always assuming this auspicious King doesn't kill me before breakfast, as he's been going to do these thirty-three and a third months.'

" 'Hmp,' said Shahryar. 'Don't take your critics for granted; I may get around to it yet. But I agree with your little sister that this is a good one you've got going, with its impostures that become authentic, its ups and downs and flights to other worlds. I don't know how in the world you dream them up.'

" 'Artists have their tricks,' Sherry replied. We three said good night then, six goodnights in all. In the morning your brother went off to court, enchanted by Sherry's story. Daddy came to the palace for the thousandth time with a shroud under his arm, expecting to be told to cut his daughter's head off; in most other respects he's as good a vizier as he ever was, but three years of suspense have driven him crackers in this one particular—and turned his hair white, I might add, and made him a widower. Sherry and I, after the first fifty nights or so, were simply relieved when Shahryar would hmp and say, 'By Allah, I won't kill her till I've heard the end of her story'; but it still took Daddy by surprise every morning. He groveled gratitude per usual; the King per usual spent the day in his durbar, bidding and forbidding between man and man, as the saying goes; I climbed in with Sherry as soon as he was gone, and per usual we spent *our* day sleeping in and making love. When we'd had enough of each other's tongues and fingers, we called in the eunuchs, maidservants, mamelukes, pet dogs and monkeys; then we finished off with Sherry's Bag of Tricks: little weighted balls from Baghdad, dildoes from the Ebony Isles and the City of Brass, et cetera. Not to break a certain vow of mine, I made do with a roc-down tickler from Bassorah, but Sherry touched all the bases. Her favorite story is about some pig of an ifrit who steals a girl away on her wedding night, puts her in a treasure-casket locked with seven steel padlocks, puts the casket in a crystal coffer, and puts the coffer on the bottom of the ocean, so that nobody except himself can have her. But whenever he brings the whole rig ashore, unlocks the locks with seven keys, and takes her out and rapes her, he falls asleep afterward on her lap; she slips out from under and cuckolds him with every man who passes by, taking their seal rings as proof; at the end of the story she has five hundred seventy-two seal rings, and the stupid ifrit still thinks he *possesses* her! In the same way, Sherry put a hundred horns a day on your brother's head: that's about a hundred thousand horns by now. And every day she saved till last the Treasure Key, which is what her story starts and ends with.

"Three and a third years ago, when King Shahryar was raping a virgin every night and killing her in the morning, and the people were praying that Allah would dump the whole dynasty, and so many parents had fled the country with their daughters that in all the Islands of India and China there was hardly a young girl fit to fuck, my sister was an undergraduate arts-and-sciences major at Banu Sasan University. Besides being Homecoming Queen, valedictorian-elect, and a four-letter varsity athlete, she had a private library of a thousand volumes and the highest average in the history of the campus. Every graduate department in the East was after her with fellowships—but she was so appalled at the state of the nation that she dropped out of school in her last semester to do full-time research on a way to stop Shahryar from killing all our sisters and wrecking the country.

"Political science, which she looked at first, got her nowhere. Shahryar's power was absolute, and by sparing the daughters of his army officers and chief ministers (like our own father) and picking his victims mainly from the families of liberal intellectuals and other minorities, he kept the military and the cabinet loyal enough to rule out a coup d'état. Revolution seemed out of the question, because his woman-hating, spectacular as it was, was reinforced more or less by all our traditions and institutions, and as long as the girls he was murdering were generally upper-caste, there was no popular base for guerrilla war. Finally, since he could count on your help from Samarkand, invasion from outside or plain assassination were bad bets too: Sherry figured your retaliation would be worse than Shahryar's virgin-a-night policy.

"So we gave up poly sci (I fetched her books and sharpened her quills and made tea and alphabetized her index cards) and tried psychology—another blind alley. Once she'd noted that *your* reaction to being cuckolded by your wife was homicidal rage followed by despair and abandonment of your kingdom, and that Shahryar's was the reverse; and established that *that* was owing to the difference in your ages and the order of revelations; and decided that whatever pathology was involved was a function of the culture and your position as absolute monarchs rather than particular hang-ups in your psyches, et cetera—what was there to say?

"She grew daily more desperate; the body-count of deflowered and decapitated Moslem girls was past nine hundred, and Daddy was just about out of candidates. Sherry didn't especially care about herself, you understand—wouldn't have even if she hadn't guessed that the King was sparing her out of respect for his vizier and her own accomplishments. But beyond the general awfulness of the situation, she was particularly concerned for my sake. From the day I was born, when Sherry was about nine, she treasured me as if I were hers; I might as well not have had parents; she and I ate from the same plate, slept in the same bed; no one could separate us; I'll bet we weren't apart for an hour in the first dozen years of my life. But I never had her good looks or her way with the world—and I was the youngest in the family besides. My breasts were growing; already I'd begun to menstruate: any day Daddy might have to sacrifice me to save Sherry.

"So when nothing else worked, as a last resort she turned to her first love, unlikely as it seemed, mythology and folklore, and studied all the riddle/puzzle/secret motifs she could dig up. 'We need a miracle, Doony,' she said (I was braiding her hair and massaging her neck as she went through her notes for the thousandth time), 'and the only genies *I've* ever met were in stories, not in Moormans'-rings and Jews'-lamps. It's in words that the magic is—Abracadabra, Open Sesame, and the rest—but the magic words in one story aren't magical in the next. The real magic is to understand which words work, and when, and for what; the trick is to learn the trick.'

"This last, as our frantic research went on, became her motto, even her obsession. As she neared the end of her supply of lore, and Shahryar his supply of virgins, she became more and more certain that her principle was correct, and desperate that in the whole world's stock of stories there was none that confirmed it, or showed us how to use it to solve the problem. 'I've read a thousand tales about treasures that nobody can find the key to,' she told me; 'we have the key and can't find the treasure.' I asked her to explain. 'It's all in here,' she declared—I couldn't tell whether she meant her inkstand or the quill she pointed toward it. I seldom understood her any more; as the crisis grew, she gave up reading for daydreaming, and used her pen less for noting instances of the Magic Key motif in world literature than for doodling the letters of our alphabet at random and idly tickling herself.

" 'Little Doony,' she said dreamily, and kissed me: 'pretend this whole situation is the plot of a story we're reading, and you and I and Daddy and the King are all fictional characters. In this story, Scheherazade finds a way to change the King's mind about women and turn him into a gentle, loving husband. It's not hard to imagine such a story, is it? Now, no matter what way she finds—whether it's a magic spell or a magic story with the answer in it or a magic anything—it comes down to particular words in the story we're reading, right? And those words are made from the letters of our alphabet: a couple-dozen squiggles we can draw with this pen. This is the key, Doony! And the treasure, too, if we can only get our hands on it! It's as if—as if the key to the treasure *is* the treasure!'

"As soon as she spoke these last words a genie appeared from nowhere right there in our library-stacks. He didn't resemble anything in Sherry's bedtime stories: for one thing, he wasn't frightening, though he was strange-looking enough: a light-skinned fellow of forty or so, smooth-shaven and bald as a roc's egg. His clothes were simple but outlandish; he was tall and healthy and pleasant enough in appearance, except for queer lenses that he wore in a frame over his eyes. He seemed as startled as we were—you should've seen Sherry drop that pen and pull her skirts together!—but he got over his alarm a lot sooner, and looked from one to the other of us and at a stubby little magic wand he held in his fingers, and smiled a friendly smile.

" 'Are you really Scheherazade?' he asked. 'I've never had a dream so clear and lifelike! And you're little Dunyazade—just as I'd imagined both of you! Don't be frightened: I can't tell you what it means to me to see and talk to you like this; even in a dream, it's a dream come true. Can you understand English? I don't have a word of Arabic. O my, I can't believe this is really happening!'

"Sherry and I looked at each other. The Genie didn't seem dangerous; we didn't know those languages he spoke of; every word he said was in *our* language, and when Sherry asked him whether he'd come from her pen or from her words, he seemed to understand the question, though he didn't know the answer. He was a writer of tales, he said—anyhow a *former* writer of tales—in a land on the other side of the world. At one time, we gathered, people in his country had been fond of reading; currently, however, the only readers of artful fiction were critics, other writers, and unwilling students who, left to themselves, preferred music and pictures to words. His own pen (that magic wand, in fact a magic quill with a fountain of ink inside) had just about run dry: but whether he had abandoned fiction or fiction him, Sherry and I couldn't make out when we reconstructed this first conversation later that night, for either in our minds or in his a number of crises seemed confused. Like Shahryar's, the Genie's life was in disorder—but so far from harboring therefore a grudge against womankind, he was distractedly in love with a brace of new mistresses, and only recently had been able to choose between them. His career, too, had reached a hiatus which he would have been pleased to call a turning-point if he could have espied any way to turn: he wished neither to repudiate nor to repeat his past performances; he aspired to go beyond them toward a future they were not attuned to and, by some magic, at the same time go back to the original springs of narrative. But how this was to be managed was as unclear to him as the answer to the Shahryar-problem was to us—the more so since he couldn't say how much of his difficulty might be owing to his own limitations, his age and stage and personal vicissitudes; how much to the general decline of letters in his time and place; and how much to the other crises with which his country (and, so he alleged, the very species) was beset—crises as desperate and problematical, he avowed, as ours, and as inimical to the single-mindedness needed to compose great works of art or the serenity to apprehend them.

"So entirely was he caught up in these problems, his work and life and all had come to a standstill. He had taken leave of his friends, his family, and his post (he was a doctor of letters), and withdrawn to a lonely retreat in the marshes, which only the most devoted of his mistresses deigned to visit.

" 'My project,' he told us, 'is to learn where to go by discovering where I am by reviewing where I've been—where we've *all* been. There's a kind of snail in the Maryland marshes—perhaps I invented him—that makes his shell as he goes along out of whatever he comes across, cementing it with his own juices, and at the same time makes his path instinctively toward the best available material for his shell; he carries his history on his back, living in it, adding new and larger spirals to it from the present as he grows. That snail's pace has become my pace—but I'm going in circles, following my own trail! I've quit reading and writing; I've lost track of who I am; my name's just a jumble of letters; so's the whole body of literature: strings of letters and empty spaces, like a code that I've lost the key to.' He pushed those odd lenses up on the bridge of his nose with his thumb—a habit that made me giggle—and grinned. 'Well, *almost* the whole body. Speaking of keys, I suspect that's how I got here.'

"By way of answer to Sherry's question then, whether he had sprung from her quill-pen or her words, he declared that his researches, like hers, had led him to an impasse; he felt that a treasure-house of new fiction lay vaguely under his hand, if he could find the key to it. Musing idly on this figure, he had added to the morass of notes he felt himself mired in, a sketch for a story about a man who comes somehow to realize that the key to the treasure he's searching for *is* the treasure. Just exactly how so (and how the story might be told despite all the problems that beset him) he had no chance to consider, for the instant he set on paper the words *The key to the treasure is the treasure,* he found himself with us—for how long, or to what end, or by what means, he had no idea, unless it was that of all the storytellers in the world, his very favorite was Scheherazade.

" 'Listen how I chatter on!' he ended happily. 'Do forgive me!'

"My sister, after some thought, ventured the opinion that the astonishing coincidence of her late reveries and his, which had led them as it were simultaneously to the same cryptic formulation, must have something to do with his translation to her library. She looked forward, she said, to experimenting whether a reverse translation could be managed, if the worst came to the worst, to spirit me out of harm's way; as for herself, she had no time or use for idle flights of fancy, however curious, from the gynocide that was ravaging her country: remarkable as it was, she saw no more relevance to her problems than to his in this bit of magic.

" 'But we know the answer's right here in our hands!' the Genie exclaimed. 'We're both storytellers: you must sense as strongly as I that it has something to do with the key to the treasure's being the treasure.'

"My sister's nostrils narrowed. 'Twice you've called me a storyteller,' she said; 'yet I've never told a story in my life except to Dunyazade, and her bedtime stories were the ones that everybody tells. The only tale I ever invented myself was this key-to-the-treasure one just now, which I scarcely understand . . .'

" 'Good lord!' the Genie cried. 'Do you mean to say that you haven't even *started* your thousand and one nights yet?'

"Sherry shook her head grimly. 'The only thousand nights I know of is the time our pig of a king has been killing the virgin daughters of the Moslems.'

"Our bespectacled visitor then grew so exhilarated that for some time he couldn't speak at all. Presently he seized my sister's hand and dumbfounded us both by declaring his lifelong adoration of her, a declaration that brought blushes to our cheeks. Years ago, he said, when he'd been a penniless student pushing book-carts through the library-stacks of his university to help pay for his education, he'd contracted a passion for Scheherazade upon first reading the tales she beguiled King Shahryar with, and had sustained that passion so powerfully ever since that his love affairs with other, 'real' women seemed to him by comparison unreal, his two-decade marriage but a prolonged infidelity to her, his own fictions mere mimicries, pallid counterfeits of the authentic treasure of her *Thousand and One Nights.*

" 'Beguiled the King with!' Sherry said. 'I've thought of that! Daddy believes that Shahryar would really like to quit what he's doing before the country falls apart, but needs an excuse to break his vow without losing face with his younger brother. I'd considered letting him make love to me and then telling him exciting stories, which I'd leave unfinished from one night to the next till he'd come to know me too well to kill me. I even thought of slipping in stories about kings who'd suffered worse hardships than he and his brother without turning vindictive; or lovers who weren't unfaithful; or husbands who loved their wives more than themselves. But it's too fanciful! Who knows which stories would work? Especially in those first few nights! I can see him sparing me for a day or two, maybe, out of relief; but then he'd react against his lapse and go back to his old policy. I gave the idea up.'

"The Genie smiled; even *I* saw what he was thinking. 'But you say you've read the book!' Sherry exclaimed. 'Then you must remember what stories are in it, and in which order!'

" 'I don't have to remember,' said the Genie. 'In all the years I've been writing stories, your book has never been off my worktable. I've made use of it a thousand times, if only by just seeing it there.'

"Sherry asked him then whether he himself had perhaps invented the stories she allegedly told, or would tell. 'How could I?' he laughed. 'I won't be born for a dozen centuries yet! You didn't invent them either, for that matter; they're those ancient ones you spoke of, that "everybody tells": Sinbad the Sailor, Aladdin's Lamp, Ali Baba and the Forty Thieves . . .'

" 'What others?' Sherry cried. 'In which order? I don't even *know* the Ali Baba story! Do you have the book with you? I'll give you everything I have for it!'

"The Genie replied that inasmuch as he'd been holding her book in his hand and thinking about her when he'd written the magic words, and it had not been translated to her library along with him, he inferred that he could not present her with a copy even if the magic were repeatable. He did however remember clearly what he called the frame-story: how Shahryar's young brother Shah Zaman had discovered his bride's adulteries, killed her, abandoned the kingdom of Samarkand, and come to live with Shahryar in the Islands of India and China; how, discovering that Shahryar's wife was equally unfaithful, the brothers had retreated to the wilderness, encountered the ifrit and the maiden, concluded that all women are deceivers, and returned to their respective kingdoms, vowing to deflower a virgin every night and kill her in the morning; how the Vizier's daughter Scheherazade, to end this massacre, had volunteered herself, much against her father's wishes, and with the aid of her sister Dunyazade—who at the crucial moment between sex and sleep asked for a story, and fed the King's suspense by interrupting the tale at daybreak, just before the climax—stayed Shahryar's hand long enough to win his heart, restore his senses, and save the country from ruin.

"I hugged my sister and begged her to let me help her in just that way. She shook her head: 'Only this Genie has read the stories I'm supposed to tell, and he doesn't remember them. What's more, he's fading already. If the key to the treasure is the treasure, we don't have it in our hands yet.'

"He had indeed begun fading away, almost disappeared; but as soon as Sherry repeated the magic sentence he came back clearly, smiling more eagerly than before, and declared he'd been thinking the same words at the same moment, just when *we'd* begun to fade and his writing-room to reappear about him. Apparently, then, he and Sherry could conjure the phenomenon at will by imagining simultaneously that the key to the treasure was the treasure: they were, presumably, the only two people in the history of the world who had imagined it. What's more, in that instant when he'd waked, as it were, to find himself back in the marshes of *America,* he'd been able to glance at the open table of contents of Volume One of the *Thousand and One Nights* book and determine that the first story after the frame-story was a compound tale called 'The Merchant and the Genie'—in which, if he remembered correctly, an outraged ifrit delays the death of an innocent merchant until certain sheiks have told their stories.

"Scheherazade thanked him, made a note of the title, and gravely put down her pen. 'You have it in your power to save my sisters and my country,' she said, 'and the King too, before his madness destroys him. All you need to do is supply me from the future with these stories from the past. But perhaps at bottom you share the King's feelings about women.'

" 'Not at all!' the Genie said warmly. 'If the key trick really works, I'll be honored to tell your stories to you. All we need to do is agree on a time of day to write the magic words together.'

"I clapped my hands—but Sherry's expression was still cool. 'You're a man,' she said; 'I imagine you expect what every man expects who has the key to any treasure a woman needs. In the nature of the case, I have to let Shahryar take me first; after that I'll cuckold him with you every day at sunset if you'll tell me the story for the night to come. Is that satisfactory?'

"I feared he'd take offense, but he only shook his head. Out of his old love for her, he gently declared, and his gratitude for the profoundest image he knew of the storyteller's situation, he would be pleased beyond words to play any role whatever in Scheherazade's story, without dreaming of further reward. His *own* policy, moreover, which he had lived by for many nights more than a thousand, was to share beds with no woman who did not reciprocate his feelings. Finally, his new young mistress—to whom he had been drawn by certain resemblances to Scheherazade—delighted him utterly, as he hoped he did her; he was no more tempted to infidelity than to incest or pederasty. His adoration of Scheherazade was as strong as ever—even stronger now that he'd met her in the lovely flesh—but it was not possessive; he desired her only as the old Greek poets their Muse, as a source of inspiration.

"Sherry tapped and fiddled with her quill. 'I don't know these poets you speak of,' she said sharply. 'Here in our country, love isn't so exclusive as all that. When I think of Shahryar's harem-full of concubines on the one hand, and the way his wife got even with him on the other, and the plots of most of the stories I know—especially the ones about older men with young mistresses—I can't help wondering whether you're not being a bit naïve, to put it kindly. Especially as I gather you've suffered your share of deceit in the past, and no doubt done your share of deceiving. Even so, it's a refreshing surprise, if a bit of a put-down, that you're not interested in taking sexual advantage of your position. Are you a eunuch?'

"I blushed again, but the Genie assured us, still unoffended, that he was normally equipped, and that his surpassing love for his young lady, while perhaps invincibly innocent, was not naïve. His experience of love gone sour only made him treasure more highly the notion of a love that time would season and improve; no sight on earth more pleased his heart, annealed as it was by his own past passions and defeats, than that rare one of two white-haired spouses who still cherished each other and their life together. If love died, it died; while it lived, let it live forever, et cetera. Some fictions, he asserted, were so much more valuable than fact that in rare instances their beauty made them real. The only Baghdad was the Baghdad of the *Nights,* where carpets flew and genies sprang from magic words; he was ours to command as one of those, and without price. Should one appear to *him* and offer him three wishes, he'd be unable to summon more than two, inasmuch as his first—to have live converse with the storyteller he'd loved best and longest—had already been granted.

"Sherry smiled now and asked him what would be the other two wishes. The second, he replied, would be that he might die before his young friend and he ceased to treasure each other as they did currently in their saltmarsh retreat. The third (what presently stood alone between him and entire contentment) would be that he not die without adding some artful trinket or two, however small, to the general treasury of civilized delights, to which no keys were needed beyond goodwill, attention, and a moderately cultivated sensibility: he meant the treasury of art, which if it could not redeem the barbarities of history or spare us the horrors of living and dying, at least sustained, refreshed, expanded, ennobled, and enriched our spirits along the painful way. Such of his scribblings as were already in print he did not presume to have that grace; should he die before he woke from his present sweet dream of Scheherazade, this third wish would go unfulfilled. But even if neither of these last was ever granted (and surely such boons were rare as treasure keys), he would die happier to have had the first.

"Hearing this, Sherry at last put by her reserve, took the stranger's writing-hand in her own, apologized for her discourtesy, and repeated her invitation, this time warmly: if he would supply her with enough of her stories to reach her goal, she was his in secret whenever he wished after her maiden night with Shahryar. Or (if deception truly had no more savor for him), when the slaughter of her sisters had ceased, let him spirit her somehow to his place and time, and she'd be his slave and concubine forever—assuming, as one was after all realistically obliged to assume, that he and his current love would by then have wearied of each other.

"The Genie laughed and kissed her hand. 'No slaves; no concubines. And my friend and I intend to love each other forever.'

" 'That will be a greater wonder than all of Sinbad's together,' Sherry said. 'I pray it may happen, Genie, and your third wish be granted too. For all one knows, you may already have done what you hope to do: time will tell. But if Dunyazade and I can find any way at all to help you with *your* tales-to-come in return for the ones you've pledged to us—and you may be sure we'll search for such a way as steadfastly as we've searched for a way to save our sex—we'll do it though we die for it.'

"She made him promise then to embrace his mistress for her, whom she vowed to love thenceforth as she loved me, and by way of a gift to her—which she prayed might translate as the precious book had not—she took from her earlobe a gold ring worked in the form of a spiral shell, of which his earlier image had reminded her. He accepted it joyfully, vowing to spin from it, if he could, as from a catherine-wheel or whirling galaxy, a golden shower of fiction. Then he kissed us both (the first male lips I'd felt except Father's, and the only such till yours) and vanished, whether by his will or another's we couldn't tell.

"Sherry and I hugged each other excitedly all that night, rehearsing every word that had passed between the Genie and ourselves. I begged her to test the magic for a week before offering herself to the King, to make sure that it—and her colleague from the future—could be relied upon. But even as we laughed and whispered, another of our sisters was being raped and murdered in the palace; Sherry offered herself to Shahryar first thing in the morning, to our father's distress; let the King lead her at nightfall into his fatal bed and fall to toying with her, then pretended to weep for being separated from me for the first time in our lives. Shahryar bid her fetch me in to sit at the foot of the bed; almost in a faint I watched him help her off with the pretty nightie I'd crocheted for her myself, place a white silk cushion under her bottom, and gently open her legs; as I'd never seen a man erect, I groaned despite myself when he opened his robe and I saw what he meant to stick her with: the hair done up in pearls, the shaft like a minaret decorated with arabesques, the head like a cobra's spread to strike. He chuckled at my alarm and climbed atop her; not to see him, Sherry fixed her welling eyes on me, closing them only to cry the cry that must be cried when there befell the mystery concerning which there is no inquiry. A moment later, as the cushion attested her late virginity and tears ran from her eye-corners to her ears, she seized the King's hair, wrapped about his waist her lovely legs, and to insure the success of her fiction, pretended a grand transport of rapture. I could neither bear to watch nor turn my eyes away. When the beast was spent and tossing fitfully (from shame and guilt, I hoped, or unease at Sherry's willingness to die), I gathered my senses as best I could and asked her to tell me a story.

" 'With pleasure,' she said, in a tone still so full of shock it broke my heart, 'if this pious and auspicious King will allow it.' Your brother grunted, and Sherry began, shakily, the tale of the Merchant and the Genie, framing in it for good measure the First Sheik's Story as her voice grew stronger. At the right moment I interrupted to praise the story and say I thought I'd heard a rooster crowing in the east; as though I'd been kept in ignorance of the King's policy, I asked whether we mightn't sleep awhile before sunrise and hear the end of the story tomorrow night—along with the one about the Three Apples, which I liked even more. 'O Doony!' Sherry pretended to scold. 'I know a dozen better than that: how about the Ebony Horse, or Julnar the Sea-Born, or the Ensorcelled Prince? But just as there's no young woman in the country worth having that the King hasn't had his fill of already, so I'm sure there's no story he hasn't heard till he's weary of it. I could no more expect to tell him a new story than show him a new way to make love.'

" 'I'll be the judge of that,' said Shahryar. So we sweated out the day in each other's arms and at sunset tried the magic key; you can imagine our relief when the Genie appeared, pushed up his eyeglasses with a grin, and recited to us the Second and Third Sheiks' Stories, which he guessed were both to be completed on that crucial second night in order, on the one hand, to demonstrate a kind of narrative inexhaustibility or profligacy (at least a generosity commensurate to that of the sheiks themselves), while, on the other hand, not compounding the suspense of unfinished tales-within-tales at a time when the King's reprieve was still highly tentative. Moreover, that the ifrit will grant the merchant's life on account of the stories ought to be evident enough by daybreak to make, without belaboring, its admonitory point. The spiral earring, he added happily, had come through intact, if anything more beautiful for the translation; his mistress was delighted with it, and would return Sherry's embrace with pleasure, he was confident, as soon as the memory of her more contemporary rivals was removed enough, and she secure enough in his love, for him to tell her the remarkable story of the magic key. Tenderly then he voiced his hope that Scheherazade had not found the loss of her maidenhood wholly repugnant to experience, or myself to witness; if the King was truly to be wooed away from his misogyny, many ardent nights lay ahead, and for the sake of Scheherazade's spirit as well as her strategy it would be well if she could take some pleasure in them.

" 'Never!' my sister declared. 'The only pleasure I'll take in that bed is the pleasure of saving my sisters and cuckolding their killer.'

"The Genie shrugged and faded; Shahryar came in, bid us good evening, kissed Sherry many times before caressing her more intimately, then laid her on the bed and worked her over playfully in as many positions as there are tales in the Trickery-of-Women series, till I couldn't tell whether her outcries were of pain, surprise, or—mad as the notion seemed—a kind of pleasure despite herself. As for me, though I was innocent of men, I had read in secret all the manuals of love and erotic stories in Sherry's library, but had thought them the wild imaginings of lonely writers in their dens, a kind of self-tickling with the quill such as Sherry herself had fallen into; for all it was my own sister I saw doing such incredible things in such odd positions, it would be many nights before I fully realized that what I witnessed were not conjured illustrations from those texts, but things truly taking place.

" 'On with the story,' Shahryar commanded when they were done. Unsteadily at first, but then in even better voice than the night before, Sherry continued the Merchant-and-Genie story, and I, mortified to find myself still moistening from what I'd seen, almost forgot to interrupt at the appropriate time. Next day, as we embraced each other, Sherry admitted that while she found the King himself as loathsome as ever, the things he did to her were no longer painful, and might even be pleasurable, as would be the things she did to him, were he a bedpartner she could treasure as our Genie treasured his. More exactly, once the alarm of her defloration and her fear of being killed in the morning began to pass, she found abhorrent not Shahryar himself—undeniably a vigorous and handsome man for his forty years, and a skillful lover—but his murderous record with our sex, which no amount of charm and tender caressing could expunge.

" 'No amount at all?' our Genie asked when he appeared again, on cue, at sunset. 'Suppose a man had been a kind and gentle fellow until some witch put a spell on him that deranged his mind and made him do atrocious things; then suppose a certain young lady has the power to cure him by loving him despite his madness. She can lift the spell because she recognizes that it *is* a spell, and not his real nature . . .'

" 'I hope that's not my tale for tonight,' Sherry said dryly, pointing out that while Shahryar may once upon a time have been a loving husband, even in those days he gave out virgin slave-girls to his friends, kept a houseful of concubines for himself, and cut his wife in half for taking a lover after twenty years of one-sided fidelity. 'And no magic can bring a thousand dead girls back to life, or unrape them. On with the story.'

" 'You're a harder critic than your lover,' the Genie complained, and recited the opening frame of the Fisherman and the Genie, the simplicity of which he felt to be a strategic change of pace for the third night—especially since it would lead, on the fourth and fifth, to a series of tales-within-tales-within-tales, a narrative complexity he described admiringly as 'Oriental.'

"So it went, month after month, year after year; at the foot of Shahryar's bed by night and in Scheherazade's by day, I learned more about the arts of making love and telling stories than I had imagined there was to know. It pleased our Genie, for example, that the tale of the Ensorcelled Prince had been framed by that of the Fisherman and the Genie, since the prince himself had been encased (in the black stone palace); also, that the resolution of the story thus enframed resolved as well the tale that framed it. This metaphorical construction he judged more artful than the 'mere plot-function' (that is, preserving our lives and restoring the King's sanity!) which Sherry's Fisherman-tale and the rest had in the story of her *own* life; but that 'mere plot-function,' in turn, was superior to the artless and arbitrary relation between most framed and framing tales. This relation (which to me seemed less important than what the stories were *about*) interested the two of them no end, just as Sherry and Shahryar were fascinated by the pacing of their nightly pleasures or the refinement of their various positions, instead of the degree and quality of their love.

"Sherry kissed me. 'That other either goes without saying,' she said, 'or it doesn't go at all. Making love and telling stories both take more than good technique—but it's only the technique that we can *talk* about.'

"The Genie agreed: 'Heartfelt ineptitude has its appeal, Dunyazade; so does heartless skill. But what you want is passionate virtuosity.' They speculated endlessly on such questions as whether a story might imaginably be framed from inside, as it were, so that the usual relation between container and contained would be reversed and paradoxically reversible—and (for my benefit, I suppose) what human state of affairs such an odd construction might usefully figure. Or whether one might go beyond the usual tale-within-a-tale, beyond even the tales-within-tales-within-tales-within-tales which our Genie had found a few instances of in that literary treasure-house he hoped one day to add to, and conceive a series of, say, *seven* concentric stories-within-stories, so arranged that the climax of the innermost would precipitate that of the next tale out, and that of the next, et cetera, like a string of firecrackers or the chains of orgasms that Shahryar could sometimes set my sister catenating.

"This last comparison—a favorite of theirs—would lead them to a dozen others between narrative and sexual art, whether in spirited disagreement or equally spirited concord. The Genie declared that in his time and place there were scientists of the passions who maintained that language itself, on the one hand, originated in 'infantile pregenital erotic exuberance, polymorphously perverse,' and that conscious attention, on the other, was a 'libidinal hypercathexis'—by which magic phrases they seemed to mean that writing and reading, or telling and listening, were literally ways of making love. Whether this was in fact the case, neither he nor Sherry cared at all; yet they liked to speak *as if it were* (their favorite words), and accounted thereby for the similarity between conventional dramatic structure—its exposition, rising action, climax, and dénouement—and the rhythm of sexual intercourse from foreplay through coitus to orgasm and release. Therefore also, they believed, the popularity of love (and combat, the darker side of the same rupee) as a theme for narrative, the lovers' embrace as its culmination, and postcoital lassitude as its natural ground: what better time for tales than at day's end, in bed after making love (or around the campfire after battle or adventure, or in the chimney corner after work), to express and heighten the community between the lovers, comrades, co-workers?

" 'The longest story in the world—' Sherry observed, '*The Ocean of Story*, seven hundred thousand distichs—was told by the god Siva to his consort Parvati as a gift for the way she made love to him one night. It would take a minstrel five hundred evenings to recite it all, but she sat in his lap and listened contentedly till he was done.'

"To this example, which delighted him, the Genie added several unfamiliar to us: a great epic called *Odyssey*, for instance, whose hero returns home after twenty years of war and wandering, makes love to his faithful wife, and recounts all his adventures to her in bed while the gods prolong the night in his behalf; another work called *Decameron*, in which ten courtly lords and ladies, taking refuge in their country houses from an urban pestilence, amuse one another at the end of each day with stories (some borrowed from Sherry herself) as a kind of *substitute* for making love—an artifice in keeping with the artificial nature of their little society. And, of course, that book about Sherry herself which he claimed to be reading from, in his opinion the best illustration of all that the very relation between teller and told was by nature erotic. The teller's role, he felt, regardless of his actual gender, was essentially masculine, the listener's or reader's feminine, and the tale was the medium of their intercourse.

" 'That makes me unnatural,' Sherry objected. 'Are you one of those vulgar men who think that women writers are homosexuals?'

" 'Not at all,' the Genie assured her. 'You and Shahryar usually make love in Position One before you tell your story, and lovers like to switch positions the second time.' More seriously, he had not meant to suggest that the 'femininity' of readership was a docile or inferior condition: a lighthouse, for example, passively sent out signals that mariners labored actively to receive and interpret; an ardent woman like his mistress was at least as energetic in his embrace as he in embracing her; a good reader of cunning tales worked in her way as busily as their author; et cetera. Narrative, in short—and here they were again in full agreement—was a love-relation, not a rape: its success depended upon the reader's consent and cooperation, which she could withhold or at any moment withdraw; also upon her own combination of experience and talent for the enterprise, and the author's ability to arouse, sustain, and satisfy her interest—an ability on which his figurative life hung as surely as Scheherazade's literal.

" 'And like all love-relations,' he added one afternoon, 'it's potentially fertile for both partners, in a way you should approve, for it goes beyond male and female. The reader is likely to find herself pregnant with new images, as you hope Shahryar will become with respect to women; but the storyteller may find himself pregnant too . . .'

"Much of their talk was over my head, but on hearing this last I hugged Sherry tight and prayed to Allah it was not another of their *as if*'s. Sure enough, on the three hundred eighth night her tale was interrupted not by me but by the birth of Ali Shar, whom despite his resemblance to Shahryar I clasped to my bosom from that hour as if I had borne instead of merely helping to deliver him. Likewise on the six hundred twenty-fourth night, when little Gharíb came lustily into the world, and the nine hundred fifty-ninth, birthday of beautiful Jamilah-Melissa. Her second name, which means 'honey-sweet' in the exotic tongues of Genie-land, we chose in honor of our friend's still-beloved mistress, whom he had announced his intention to marry despite Sherry's opinion that while women and men might in some instances come together as human beings, wives and husbands could never. The Genie argued, for his part, that no matter how total, exclusive, and permanent the commitment between two lovers might turn out to be, it lacked the dimensions of spiritual seriousness and public responsibility which only marriage, with its ancient vows and symbols, rites and risks, provided.

" 'It can't last,' Sherry said crossly. The Genie put on her finger a gift from his fiancée to her namesake's mother—a gold ring patterned with rams'-horns and conches, replicas of which she and the Genie meant to exchange on their wedding day—and replied, 'Neither did Athens. Neither did Rome. Neither did all of Jamshid's glories. But we must live as if it can and will.'

" 'Hmp,' said Sherry, who over the years had picked up a number of your brother's ways, as he had hers. But she gave them her blessing—to which I added mine without reservations or *as if*'s—and turned the ring much in the lamplight when he was gone, trying its look on different hands and fingers and musing as if upon its design.

"Thus we came to the thousandth night, the thousandth morning and afternoon, the thousandth dipping of Sherry's quill and invocation of the magic key. And for the thousand and first time, still smiling, our Genie appeared to us, his own ring on his finger as it had been for some forty evenings now—an altogether brighter-looking spirit than had materialized in the book-stacks so long past. We three embraced as always; he asked after the children's health and the King's, and my sister, as always, after his progress toward that treasury from which he claimed her stories were drawn. Less reticent on this subject than he had been since our first meeting, he declared with pleasure that thanks to the inspiration of Scheherazade and to the thousand comforts of his loving wife, he believed he had found his way out of that slough of the imagination in which he'd felt himself bogged: whatever the merits of the new work, like an ox-cart driver in monsoon season or the skipper of a grounded ship, he had gone forward by going back, to the very roots and springs of story. Using, like Scheherazade herself, for entirely present ends, materials received from narrative antiquity and methods older than the alphabet, in the time since Sherry's defloration he had set down two-thirds of a projected series of three *novellas*, longish tales which would take their sense from one another in several of the ways he and Sherry had discussed, and, if they were successful (here he smiled at me), manage to be seriously, even passionately, *about* some things as well.

" 'The two I've finished have to do with mythic heroes, true and false,' he concluded. 'The third I'm just in the middle of. How good or bad they are I can't say yet, but I'm sure they're *right*. You know what I mean, Scheherazade.'

"She did; I felt as if I did also, and we happily re-embraced. Then Sherry remarked, apropos of middles, that she'd be winding up the story of Ma'aruf the Cobbler that night and needed at least the beginning of whatever tale was to follow it.

"The Genie shook his head. 'My dear, there are no more. You've told them all.' He seemed cruelly undisturbed by a prospect that made the harem spin before my eyes and brought me near to swooning.

" 'No more!' I cried. 'What will she do?'

" 'If she doesn't want to risk Shahryar's killing her and turning to you,' he said calmly, 'I guess she'll have to invent something that's not in the book.'

" 'I don't invent,' Sherry reminded him. Her voice was no less steady than his, but her expression—when I got hold of my senses enough to see it—was grave. 'I only recount.'

" 'Borrow something from that treasury!' I implored him. 'What will the children do without their mother?' The harem began to spin again; I gathered all my courage and said: 'Don't desert us, friend; give Sherry that story you're working on now, and you may do anything you like with me. I'll raise your children if you have any; I'll wash your Melissa's feet. Anything.'

"The Genie smiled and said to Sherry, 'Our little Dunyazade is a woman.' Thanking me then for my offer as courteously as he had once Scheherazade, he declined it, not only for the same reasons that had moved him before, but also because he was confident that the only tales left in the treasury of the sort King Shahryar was likely to be entertained by were the hundred mimicries and retellings of Sherry's own.

" 'Then my thousand nights and a night are ended,' Sherry said. 'Don't be ungrateful to our friend, Doony; everything ends.'

"I agreed, but tearfully wished myself—and Ali Shar, Gharíb, and little Melissa, whom-all I loved as dearly as I loved my sister—out of a world where the only *happy* endings were in stories.

"The Genie touched my shoulder. 'Let's not forget,' he said, 'that from my point of view—a tiresome technical one, I'll admit—it *is* a story that we're coming to the end of. All these tales your sister has told the King are simply the middle of her own story—hers and yours, I mean, and Shahryar's, and his young brother Shah Zaman's.'

"I didn't understand—but Sherry did, and squeezing my other shoulder, asked him quietly whether, that being the tiresome technical case, it followed that a happy ending might be invented for the framing-story.

" 'The author of *The Thousand and One Nights* doesn't invent,' the Genie reminded her; 'he only recounts how, after she finished the tale of Ma'aruf the Cobbler, Scheherazade rose from the King's bed, kissed ground before him, and made bold to ask a favor in return for the thousand and one nights' entertainment. "Ask, Scheherazade," the King answers in the story—whereupon you send Dunyazade to fetch the children in, and plead for your life on their behalf, so that they won't grow up motherless.'

"My heart sprang up; Sherry sat silent. 'I notice you don't ask on behalf of the stories themselves,' the Genie remarked, 'or on behalf of your love for Shahryar and his for you. That's a pretty touch: it leaves him free to *grant* your wish, if he chooses to, on those other grounds. I also admire your tact in asking only for your life; that gives him the moral initiative to repent his policy and marry you. I don't think I'd have thought of that.'

" 'Hmp,' said Sherry.

" 'Then there's the nice formal symmetry—'

" 'Never *mind* the symmetry!' I cried. 'Does it work or not?' I saw in his expression then that it did, and in Sherry's that this plan was not news to her. I hugged them both, weeping enough for joy to make our ink run, so the Genie said, and begged Sherry to promise me that I could stay with her and the children after their wedding as I had before, and sit at the foot of her bed forever.

" 'Not so fast, Doony,' she said. 'I haven't decided yet whether or not I care to end the story that way.'

" 'Not care to?' I looked with fresh terror to the Genie. 'Doesn't she *have* to, if it's in the book?'

"He too appeared troubled now, and searched Sherry's face, and admitted that not everything he'd seen of our situation in these visions or dreams of his corresponded exactly to the story as it came to him through the centuries, lands, and languages that separated us in waking hours. In his translation, for example, all three children were male and nameless; and while there was no mention of Scheherazade's *loving* Shahryar by the end of the book, there was surely none of her despising him, or cuckolding him, more or less, with me and the rest. Most significantly, it went without saying that he himself was altogether absent from the plot—which, however, he prayed my sister to end as it ended in his version: with the double marriage of herself to your brother and me to you, and our living happily together until overtaken by the Destroyer of Delights and Severer of Societies, et cetera.

"While I tried to assimilate this astonishing news about myself, Sherry asked with a smile whether by 'his version' the Genie meant that copy of the *Nights* from which he'd been assisting us or the story he himself was in midst of inventing; for she liked to imagine, and profoundly hoped it so, that our connection had not been to her advantage only: that one way or another, she and I and our situation were among those 'ancient narrative materials' which he had found useful for his present purposes. How did *his* version end?

"The Genie closed his eyes for a moment, pushed back his glasses with his thumb, and repeated that he was still in the middle of that third novella in the series, and so far from drafting the climax and dénouement, had yet even to plot them in outline. Turning then to me, to my great surprise he announced that the title of the story was *Dunyazadiad;* that its central character was not my sister but myself, the image of whose circumstances, on my 'wedding-night-to-come,' he found as arresting for taletellers of his particular place and time as was my sister's for the estate of narrative artists in general.

" 'All those nights at the foot of that bed, Dunyazade!' he exclaimed. 'You've had the whole literary tradition transmitted to you—and the whole erotic tradition, too! There's no story you haven't heard; there's no way of making love that you haven't seen again and again. I think of you, little sister, a virgin in both respects: All that innocence! All that sophistication! And now it's *your* turn: Shahryar has told young Shah Zaman about his wonderful mistress, how he loves her as much for herself as for her stories—*which he also passes on;* the two brothers marry the two sisters; it's your wedding night, Dunyazade . . . But wait! Look here! Shahryar deflowered and killed a virgin a night for a thousand and one nights before he met Scheherazade; Shah Zaman has been doing the same thing, but it's only now, a thousand nights and a night later, that *he* learns about Scheherazade—that means he's had two thousand and two young women at the least since he killed his wife, and not one has pleased him enough to move him to spend a second night with her, much less spare her life! What are you going to do to entertain *him,* little sister? Make love in exciting new ways? There are none! Tell him stories, like Scheherazade? He's heard them all! Dunyazade, Dunyazade! Who can tell your story?'

"More dead than alive with fright, I clung to my sister, who begged the Genie please to stop alarming me. All apologies, he assured us that what he was describing was not *The Thousand and One Nights* frame-story (which ended happily without mention of these terrors), but his own novella, a pure fiction—to which also he would endeavor with all his heart to find some conclusion in keeping with his affection for me. Sherry further eased my anxiety by adding that she too had given long thought to my position as the Genie described it, and was not without certain plans with respect to our wedding night; these, as a final favor to our friend, she had made written note of in the hope that whether or not they succeeded, he might find them useful for his story; but she would prefer to withhold them from me for the present.

" 'You sense as I do, then,' the Genie said thoughtfully, 'that we won't be seeing each other again.'

"Sherry nodded. 'You have other stories to tell. I've told mine.'

"Already he'd begun to fade. 'My best,' he said, 'will be less than your least. And I'll always love you, Scheherazade! Dunyazade, I'm your brother! Good night, sisters! Fare well!'

"We kissed; he disappeared with Sherry's letter; Shahryar sent for us; still shaken, I sat at the bed-foot while he and Sherry did a combination from the latter pages of *Ananga Ranga* and *Kama Sutra* and she finished the tale of Ma'aruf the Cobbler. Then she rose as the Genie had instructed her, kissed ground, begged boon; I fetched in Ali Shar, walking by himself now, Gharíb crawling, Jamilah-Melissa suckling at my milkless breast as if it were her mother's. Sherry made her plea; Shahryar wept, hugged the children, told her he'd pardoned her long since, having found in her the refutation of all his disenchantment, and praised Allah for having appointed her the savior of her sex. Then he sent for Daddy to draft the marriage contract and for you to hear the news of Scheherazade and her stories; when you proposed to marry me, Sherry countered with Part Two of our plan (of whose Part Three I was still ignorant): that in order for her and me never to be parted, you must abandon Samarkand and live with us, sharing your brother's throne and passing yours to our father in reparation for his three-years' anguish. I found you handsomer than Shahryar and more terrifying, and begged my sister to say what lay ahead for me.

" 'Why, a fine wedding-feast, silly Doony!' she teased. 'The eunuchs will perfume our Hammam-bath with rose- and willow-flower water, musk-pods, eagle-wood, ambergris; we'll wash and clip our hair; they'll dress me like the sun and you the moon, and we'll dance in seven different dresses to excite our bridegrooms. By the end of the wine and music they'll scarcely be able to contain their desire; each of us will kiss the other three good night, twelve goodnights in all, and our husbands will hurry us off toward our separate bridal-chambers—'

" 'O Sherry!'

" '*Then,*' she went on, no tease in her voice now, 'on the very threshold of their pleasures I'll stop, kiss ground, and say to my lord and master: "O King of the Sun and the Moon and the Rising Tide, et cetera, thanks for marrying me at last after sleeping with me for a thousand and one nights and begetting three children on me and listening while I amused you with proverbs and parables, chronicles and pleasantries, quips and jests and admonitory instances, stories and anecdotes, dialogues and histories and elegies and satires and Allah alone knows what else! Thanks too for giving my precious little sister to your brute of a brother, and the kingdom of Samarkand to our father, whose own gratitude we'll hope may partially restore his sanity! And thanks above all for kindly ceasing to rape and murder a virgin every night, and for persuading Shah Zaman to cease also! I have no right to ask anything further of you at all, but should be overjoyed to serve your sexual and other interests humbly until the day you tire of me and either have me killed or put me by for other, younger women—and indeed I *am* prepared to do just that, as Dunyazade surely is also for Shah Zaman. Yet in view of your boundless magnanimity Q.E.D., I make bold to ask a final favor." If we're lucky, Shahryar will be so mad to get me into bed that he'll say "Name it"—whereupon I point out to him that a happy occasion is about to bring to pass what a thousand ill ones didn't, your separation from me till morning. Knowing my husband, I expect he'll propose a little something *à quatre,* at which I'll blush appropriately and declare that I'm resigned after all to the notion of losing you for a few hours, and wish merely thirty minutes or so of private conversation with you before you and your bridegroom retire, to tell you a few things that every virgin bride should know. "What on earth is there in that line that she hasn't seen us do a hundred times?" your delicate brother-in-law will inquire. "Seeing isn't doing," I'll reply: "I myself have pretty intensive sexual experience, for example, but of one man only, and would be shy as any virgin with another than yourself; Shah Zaman has the widest carnal acquaintance in the world, I suppose, but no long and deep knowledge of any one woman; among the four of us, only you, King of the Age, et cetera, can boast both sorts of experience, having humped your way through twenty years of marriage, a thousand and one one-nighters, and thirty-three and a third months with me, not to mention odd hours with all the concubines in your stable. But little Dunyazade has no experience at all, except vicariously." That master of the quick retort will say "Hmp" and turn the matter over to Shah Zaman, who after bringing to it the full weight of his perspicacity will say, in effect, "Okay. But make it short." They'll withdraw, with the grandest erections you and I have ever shuddered at—and *then* I'll tell you what to do in Part Three. After which we'll kiss good night, go in to our husbands, and do it. Got that?'

" 'Do *what?*' I cried—but she'd say no more till all had fallen out as she described: our wedding-feast and dance; the retirement toward our chambers; her interruption and request; your permission and stipulation that the conference be brief, inasmuch as you were more excited by me than you'd been by any of the two thousand unfortunates whose maidenheads and lives you'd done away with in the five and a half years past. You two withdrew, your robes thrust out before; the moment your bedroom doors closed, Sherry spat in your tracks, took my head between her hands, and said: 'If ever you've listened carefully, little sister, listen now. For all his good intentions, our Genie of the Key is either a liar or a fool when he says that any man and woman can treasure each other until death—unless their lifetimes are as brief as our murdered sisters'! Three thousand and three, Doony—dead! What have you and I and all that fiction accomplished, except to spare another thousand from a quick end to their misery? What are they saved for, if not a more protracted violation, at the hands of fathers, husbands, lovers? For the present, it's our masters' pleasure to soften their policy; the patriarchy isn't changed: I believe it will persist even to our Genie's time and place. Suppose his relation to his precious Melissa were truly as he describes it, and not merely as he wishes and imagines it: it would only be the exception that proves the wretched rule. So here we stand, and there you're about to lie, and spread your legs and take it like the rest of us! Thanks be to Allah you can't be snared as I was in the trap of *novelty,* and think to win some victory for our sex by diverting our persecutors with naughty stunts and stories! There *is* no victory, Doony, only unequal retaliation; it's time we turned from tricks to trickery, tales to lies. Go in to your lusty husband now, as I shall to mine; let him kiss and fondle and undress you, paw and pinch and slaver, lay you on the bed; but when he makes to stick you, slip out from under and whisper in his ear that for all his vast experience of sex, there remains one way of making love, most delicious of all, that both he and Shahryar are innocent of, inasmuch as a Genie revealed it to us only last night when we prayed Allah for a way to please such extraordinary husbands. So marvelous is this Position of the Genie, as we'll call it, that even a man who's gone through virgins like breakfast-eggs will think himself newly laid, et cetera. What's more, it's a position in which the woman does everything, her master nothing—except submit himself to a more excruciating pleasure than he's ever known or dreamed of. No more is required of him than that he spread-eagle himself on the bed and suffer his wrists and ankles to be bound to its posts with silken cords, lest by a spasm of early joy he abort its heavenly culmination, et cetera. Then, little sister, then, when you have him stripped and bound supine and salivating, take from the left pocket of your seventh gown the razor I've hid there, as I shall mine from mine—and geld the monster! Cut his bloody engine off and choke him on it, as I'll do to Shahryar! Then we'll lay our own throats open, to spare ourselves their sex's worse revenge. Adieu, my Doony! May we wake together in a world that knows nothing of *he* and *she!* Good night.'

"I moved my mouth to answer; couldn't; came to you as if entranced; and while you kissed me, found the cold blade in my pocket. I let you undress me as in a dream, touch my body where no man has before, lay me down and mount to take me; as in a dream I heard me bid you stay for a rarer pleasure, coax you into the Position of the Genie, and with this edge in hand and voice, rehearse the history of your present bondage. Your brother's docked; my sister's dead; it's time we joined them."

2

"That's the end of your story?"

Dunyazade nodded.

Shah Zaman looked narrowly at his bride, standing naked beside the bed with her trembling razor, and cleared his throat. "If you really mean to use that, kindly kill me with it first. A good hard slice across the Adam's apple should do the trick."

The girl shuddered, shook her head. As best he could, so bound, the young man shrugged.

"At least answer one question: Why in the world did you tell me this extraordinary tale?"

Her eyes still averted, Dunyazade explained in a dull voice that one aspect of her sister's revenge was this reversal not only of the genders of teller and told (as conceived by the Genie), but of their circumstances, the latter now being at the former's mercy.

"Then have some!" urged the King. "For yourself!" Dunyazade looked up. Despite his position, Shah Zaman smiled like the Genie through his pearly beard and declared that Scheherazade was right to think love ephemeral. But life itself was scarcely less so, and both were sweet for just that reason—sweeter yet when enjoyed as if they might endure. For all the inequity of woman's lot, he went on, thousands of women found love as precious as did their lovers: one needed look no farther than Scheherazade's stories for proof of that. If a condemned man—which is what he counted himself, since once emasculate he'd end his life as soon as he could lay hands on his sword—might be granted a last request, such as even *he* used to grant his nightly victims in the morning, his would be to teach his fair executioner the joys of sex before she unsexed him.

"Nonsense," Dunyazade said crossly. "I've seen all that."

"Seeing's not feeling."

She glared at him. "I'll learn when I choose, then, from a less bloody teacher: someone I love, no matter how foolishly." She turned her head. "If I ever meet such a man. Which I won't." Vexed, she slipped into her gown, holding the razor awkwardly in her left hand while she fastened the hooks.

"What a lucky fellow! You don't love me then, little wife?"

"Of course not! I'll admit you're not the monster I'd imagined—in appearance, I mean. But you're a total stranger to me, and the thought of what you did to all those girls makes me retch. Don't waste your last words in silly flirting; you won't change my mind. You'd do better to prepare yourself to die."

"I'm quite prepared, Dunyazade," Shah Zaman replied calmly. "I have been from the beginning. Why else do you suppose I haven't called my guards in to kill you? I'm sure my brother's long since done for Scheherazade, if she really tried to do what she put you up to doing. Shahryar and I would have been great fools not to anticipate this sort of thing from the very first night, six years ago."

"I don't believe you."

The King shrugged his eyebrows and whistled through his teeth; two husky mamelukes stepped at once from behind a tapestry depicting Jamshid's seven-ringed cup, seized Dunyazade by the wrists, covered her mouth, and took the open razor from her hand.

"Fair or not," Shah Zaman said conversationally as she struggled, "your only power at present is what I choose to give you. And fair or not, I choose to give it." He smiled. "Let her have the razor, my friends, and take the rest of the night off. If you don't believe that I deliberately put myself in your hands from the first, Dunyazade, you can't deny I'm doing so now. All I ask is leave to tell you a story, in exchange for the one you've told me; when I'm finished you may do as you please."

The mamelukes reluctantly let her go, but left the room only when Shah Zaman, still stripped and bound, repeated his order. Dunyazade sat exhausted on a hassock, rubbed her wrists, pinned up her fallen hair, drew the gown more closely about her.

"I'm not impressed," she said. "If I pick up the razor, they'll put an arrow through me."

"That hadn't occurred to me," Shah Zaman admitted. "You'll have to trust me a little, then, as I'm trusting you. Do pick it up. I insist."

"You insist!" Dunyazade said bitterly. She took up the razor, let her hand fall passively beside the hassock, began to weep.

"Let's see, now," mused the King. "How can we give you the absolute advantage? They're very fast, those guards, and loyal; if they really *are* standing by, what I fear is that they'll misconstrue some innocent movement of yours and shoot."

"What difference does it make?" Dunyazade said miserably. "Poor Sherry!"

"I have it! Come sit here beside me. Please, do as I say! Now lay that razor's edge exactly where you were going to put it before; then you can make your move before any marksman can draw and release. You'll have to hold me in your other hand; I've gone limp with alarm."

Dunyazade wept.

"Come," the King insisted: "it's the only way you'll be convinced I'm serious. No, I mean right up against it, so that you could do your trick in half a second. Whew, that gooseflesh isn't faked! What a situation! Now look here: even this advantage gripes you, I suppose, since it was given instead of taken: the male still leading the female, et cetera. No help for that just now. Besides, between any two people, you know—what I mean, it's not the patriarchy that makes you take the passive role with your sister, for example. Never mind that. See me sweat! Now, then: I agree with that Genie of yours in the matter of priorities, and I entreat you not only to permit me to tell you a story, but to make love with me first."

Dunyazade shut her eyes and whipped her head from side to side.

"As you wish," said the King. "I'd never force you, as you'll understand if you'll hear my story. Shall I tell it?"

Dunyazade moved her head indifferently.

"More tightly. Careful with that razor!"

"Can't you make it go down?" the girl asked thickly. "It's obscene. And distracting. I think I'm going to be sick."

"Not more distracting than your little breasts, or your little fingers . . . No, please, I insist you keep hold of your advantage! My story's short, I promise, and I'm at your mercy. So:

"Six years ago I thought myself the happiest man alive. I'd had a royal childhood; my college years were a joy; my career had gone brilliantly; at twenty-five I ruled a kingdom almost as prosperous as Shahryar's at forty. I was popular with my subjects; I kept the government reasonably honest, the various power groups reasonably in hand, et cetera. Like every king I kept a harem of concubines for the sake of my public image, but as a rule they were reserved for state visitors. For myself I wanted nobody except my bride, never mind her name, whom after a whole year of marriage I still loved more than any woman I'd ever known. After a day's work in the durbar, bidding and forbidding et cetera, I'd rush in to dinner, and we'd play all night like two kittens in a basket. No trick of love we didn't turn together; no myth of gods and nymphs we didn't mimic. The harem girls, when I used them, only reminded me of how much I preferred my wife; often as not I'd dismiss them in mid-clip and call her in for the finish.

"When my brother summoned me here to visit that first time, much as I longed to see him it was all I could do to leave my bride behind; we made our first goodbyes; then I was as overjoyed as I imagined she'd be when I discovered that I'd forgotten a diamond necklace I'd meant to present to Shahryar's queen. I rushed back to the palace myself instead of sending after it, so that we could make love once again before I left—and I found her in our bed, riding astride the chief cook! Her last words were 'Next time invite *me*'; I cut them both in two, four halves in all, not to seem a wittol; came here and found my sister-in-law cuckolding my brother with the blackamoor Sa'ad al-Din Saood, who swung from trees, slavered and gibbered, and sported a yard that made mine look like your little finger. Kings no more, Shahryar and I left together by the postern gate, resolved to kill ourselves as the most wretched fools on earth if our misery was particular. One day as we were wandering in the marshes, far from the paths of men, devouring our own souls, we saw what we thought was a waterspout coming up the bay, and climbed a loblolly pine for safety. It turned out to be that famous ifrit of your sister's story: he took the steel coffer out of its casket, unlocked the seven locks with seven keys, fetched out and futtered the girl he'd stolen on her wedding night, and fell asleep in her lap; she signaled us to come down and ordered us both to cuckold the ifrit with her then and there. Who says a man can't be forced? We did our best, and she added our seal rings to the five hundred seventy she'd already collected. We understood then that no woman on earth who wants a rogering will go unrogered, though she be sealed up in a tower of brass.

"So. When I'd first told my brother of my own cuckolding, he'd vowed that in my position he'd not have rested till he'd killed a thousand women: now we went back to his palace; he put to death his queen and all his concubines and their lovers, and we took a solemn oath to rape and kill a virgin a night, so as never again to be deceived. I came home to Samarkand, wondering at the turns of our despair: how a private apocalypse can infect the state and bring about one more general, et cetera. With this latter motive, more than for revenge on womankind, I resolved to hold to our dreadful policy until my kingdom fell to ruin or an outraged populace rose up and slew me.

"But unlike Shahryar, I said nothing at first to my vizier, only told him to fetch me a beautiful virgin for the night. Not knowing that I meant to kill her in the morning, he brought me his own daughter, a girl I knew well and had long admired, Samarkand's equivalent of Scheherazade. I assumed he was pandering to his own advancement, and smiled at the thought of putting them to death together; I soon learned, however, from the woman herself, that it was her own idea to come to me—and her motive, unlike your sister's, was simple love. I undressed and fell to toying with her; she wept; I asked what ailed her: it was not being separated from her sister, but being alone at last with me, the fulfillment of her lifelong dream. I found myself much touched by this and, to my surprise, impotent. Stalling for time, I remarked that such dreams could turn out to be nightmares. She embraced me timidly and replied that she deplored my murdering my wife and her paramour, both of whom she'd known and rather liked, for though in a general way she sympathized with my disenchanted outrage, she believed she understood as well my wife's motives for cuckolding me, which in her view were not all that different, essentially, from the ifrit's maiden's in the story. Despite my anger, she went on bravely to declare that she herself took what she called the Tragic View of Sex and Temperament: to wit, that while perfect equality between men and women was the only defensible value in that line, she was not at all certain it was attainable; even to pursue it ardently, against the grain of things as they were, was in all likelihood to spoil one's chances for happiness in love; *not* to pursue it, on the other hand, once one had seen it clearly to be the ideal, no doubt had the same effect. For herself, though she deplored injustice whether in individuals or in institutions, and gently affirmed equality as the goal that lovers lovingly should strive for, however far short of it their histories and temperaments made them fall, yet she knew herself personally to be unsuited for independence, formed by her nature and upbringing to be happy only in the shadow of a man whom she admired and respected more than herself. She was anything but blind to my faults and my own blindness to them, she declared, but so adored me withal that if I could love her even for a night she'd think her life complete, and wish nothing further unless maybe a little Shah Zaman to devote the rest of her years to raising. Or if my disillusionment with women were so extreme (as she seemed uncannily to guess from my expression) that I had brought her to my bed not to marry her or even add her to my harem, but merely to take her virginity and her life, I was welcome to both; she only prayed I might be gentle in their taking.

"This last remark dismayed me the more because it echoed something my late wife had said on our wedding night: that even death at my hands would be sweeter to her than life at another's. How I despised, resented, missed her! As if it were I who was cut in two, I longed to hold her as in nights gone by, yet would have halved her bloody halves if she'd been restored to me. There lay my new woman on the bed, naked and still now; I stood on my knees between hers, weeping so for her predecessor's beauty and deceit, my own blindness and cruelty—and the wretched state of affairs between man and womankind that made love a will-o'-the-wisp, jealousy and boredom and resentment the rule—that I could neither function nor dissemble. I told her of all that had taken place between my departure from Samarkand and my return, the oath I'd sworn with my brother, and my resolve to keep it lest I seem chicken-hearted and a fool.

" 'Lest you *seem!'* the girl cried out. 'Harems, homicides—everything for the sake of seeming!' She commanded me then, full of irony for all her fears, to *keep* my vow if I meant to keep it, or else cut out her tongue before I cut off her head; for if I sent her to the block without deflowering her first, she would declare to any present, even if only her executioner, that I was a man in seeming merely, not in fact, and offer her maidenhead as proof. Her courage astonished me as much as her words. 'By Allah,' I vowed to her, 'I won't kill you if I can't get it up for you first.' But that miserable fellow in your left hand, which had never once failed me before, and which stands up now like an idiot soldier in enemy country, as if eager to be cut down, deserted me utterly. I tried every trick I knew, in vain, though my victim willingly complied with my instructions. I could of course have killed her myself, then and there, but I had no wish to seem a hypocrite even for a moment in her eyes; nor, for that matter, to let her die a virgin—nor, I admitted finally to myself, to let her die at all before she was overtaken like the rest of us by the Destroyer of Delights et cetera. For seven nights we tossed and tumbled, fondled and kissed and played, she reaching such heats of unaccustomed joy as to cry out, no longer sarcastically, that if only I would stick her first with my carnal sword, she'd bare her neck without complaint to my steel. On the seventh night, as we lay panting in a sweat of frustration, I gave her my dagger and invited her to do me and Samarkand the kindness of killing me at once, for I'd rather die than seem unable to keep my vow.

" 'You *are* unable to keep it,' she told me softly: 'not because you're naturally impotent, but because you're *not* naturally cruel. If you'd tell your brother that after thinking it over you've simply come to a conclusion different from his, you'd be cured as if by magic.' And in fact, as if by magic indeed, what she said was so true that at her very words the weight was lifted from heart and tool together; they rose as one. Gratefully, tenderly, I went into her at last; we cried for joy, came at once, fell asleep in each other's arms.

"No question after that of following Shahryar's lead; on the other hand, I found myself in the morning not yet man enough after all to send word to him of my change of heart and urge him to change his. Neither was I, after all, in love enough with the Vizier's daughter to risk again the estate of marriage, which she herself considered problematical at best.

" 'I never expected you to marry me,' she told me when I told her these things, 'though I'd be dishonest if I didn't say I dreamed and prayed you might. All I ever really hoped for was a love affair with you, and a baby to remember it by. Even if I don't have the baby, I've had the affair: you truly loved me last night.'

"I did, and for many nights after—but not enough to make the final step. What your Genie said concerning marriage could have come from my own mouth if I had the gift of words: to anyone of moral imagination who's known it, no other relation between men and women has true seriousness; yet that same imagination kept me from it. And I dreaded the day my brother would get word of my weakness. I grew glum and cross; my mistress, intuitive as ever, guessed the reason at once. 'You can neither keep your vow nor break it,' she told me: 'Perhaps you'd better do both for a while, till you find your way.' I asked her how such a contradiction was possible. 'By the magic words *as if,*' she replied, 'which, to a person satisfied with seeming, are more potent than all the genii in the tales.'

"She then set forth a remarkable proposal: legend had it that far to the west of Samarkand was a country peopled entirely with women, adjoining another wholly male: for two months every spring they mated freely with each other on neutral ground, the women returning home as they found themselves pregnant, giving their male children to the neighboring tribe and raising the girls as members of their own. Whether or not such a community in fact existed, she thought it a desirable alternative to the present state of affairs, and unquestionably preferable to death; since I couldn't treasure her as she treasured me (and not for a moment did she *blame* me for that incapacity), she proposed to establish such an alternative society herself, with my assistance. I was to proclaim my brother's policy as my own, take to bed a virgin every night and declare her executed in the morning; but instead of actually raping and killing them I would tell them of her alternative society and send them secretly from Samarkand, in groups of a hundred or so, to organize and populate it. If, knowing their destiny, they chose to spend their last night in Samarkand making love with me, that was their affair; none, she imagined, would choose death over emigration, and any who found their new way of life not to their liking could return to Samarkand if and when I changed my policy, or migrate elsewhere in the meanwhile. In any case they'd be alive and free; or, if the pioneers were captured and made slaves of by barbarians before the new society was established, they'd be no worse off than the millions of their sisters already in that condition. On the other hand, separate societies of men and women, mingling freely at their own wills as equals on neutral ground, might just make possible a true society of the future in which the separation was no longer necessary. And in the meantime, of course, for better or worse, it would be as if I'd kept my dreadful vow.

"At first hearing, the plan struck me as absurd; after a few nights it seemed less so, perhaps even feasible; by the end of a week of examining passionately with her all the alternatives, it seemed no less unreasonable than they. My angel herself, in keeping with her Tragic View, didn't expect the new society to *work* in the naïve sense: what human institutions ever did? It would have the vices of its virtues; if not nipped in the bud by marauding rapists, it would grow and change and rigidify in forms and values quite different from its founders'—codifying, institutionalizing, and perverting its original spirit. No help for that.

"Was there ever such a woman? I kissed her respectfully, then ardently a final time. After one last love-making in the morning, while my hand lingered on her left breast, she declared calmly her intention, upon arriving at her virgin kingdom, to amputate that same breast for symbolic reasons and urge her companions to do the same, as a kind of initiation rite. 'We'll make up a practical excuse for it,' she said: ' "The better to draw our bows," et cetera. But the real point will be that in one aspect we're all woman, in another all warrior. Maybe we'll call ourselves The Breastless Ones.'

" 'That seems extreme,' I remarked. She replied that a certain extremism was necessary to the survival of anything radically innovative. Later generations, she assumed, established and effete, would find the ancestral custom barbaric and honor its symbolism, if at all, with a correspondingly symbolic mammectomy—a decorative scar, perhaps, or cosmetic mark. No matter; everything passed.

"So did our connection: with a thousand thanks to her for opening my eyes, a thousand good wishes for the success of her daring enterprise, and many thousands of dinars to support it (which for portability and security she converted into a phial of diamonds and carried intravaginally), I declared her dead, let her father the Vizier in on our secret, and sent her off secretly to one of my country castles on a distant lake, where she prepared for the expedition westward while her companions, the ostensible victims of my new policy, accumulated about her. Perhaps a third, apprised of their fate, chose to remain virginal, whether indignantly, ruefully, or gratefully; on the other two-thirds who in whatever spirit elected to go hymenless to the new society, I bestowed similar phials of jewels. Somewhat less than fifty per cent of this number found themselves impregnated by our night together, and so when the first detachment of two hundred pioneers set out across the western wastes, their actual number was about two hundred sixty. Since I pursued this policy for nearly two thousand nights, the number of pilgrims and unborn children sent west from Samarkand must have totaled about twenty-six hundred; corrected for a normal male birth rate of somewhat over fifty per cent, a rather higher than normal rate of spontaneous abortion, and infant as well as maternal mortality owing to the rigors of traveling and of settling a new territory, and ignoring—as one must to retain one's reason—the possibility of mass enslavement, rape, massacre, or natural catastrophe, the number of pioneers to the Country of the Breastless must be at least equal to the number of nights until Shahryar's message concerning your sister arrived from the Islands of India and China.

"Of the success or failure of those founding mothers I know nothing; kept myself ignorant deliberately, lest I learn that I was sending them after all to the Destroyer of Delights and Severer of Societies. The folk of Samarkand never rose against me; nor did my vizier, like Shahryar's, have difficulty enlisting sacrificial virgins; even at the end, though my official toll was twice my brother's, about half the girls were volunteers—from all which, I infer that their actual fate was an open secret. For all I know, my original mistress never truly intended to found her gynocracy; the whole proposal was perhaps a ruse; perhaps they all slipped back into the country with their phials of gems for dowry, married and lived openly under my nose. No matter: night after night I brought them to bed, set forth their options, then either glumly stripped and pronged them or spent the night in chaste sleep and conversation. Tall and short, dark and fair, lean and plump, cold and ardent, bold and timid, clever and stupid, comely and plain—I bedded them all, spoke with them all, possessed them all, but was myself possessed by nothing but despair. Though I took many, with their consent, I wanted none of them. Novelty lost its charm, then even its novelty. Unfamiliarity I came to loathe: the foreign body in the dark, the alien touch and voice, the endless *exposition.* All I craved was someone with whom to get on with the story of my life, which was to say, of our life together: a loving friend; a loving wife; a treasurable wife; a wife, a wife.

"My brother's second message, when it came, seemed a miraculous reprise of that fatal first, six years before: I turned the kingdom over to my vizier and set out at once, resolved to meet this Scheherazade who had so wooed and yarned him back to the ways of life that he meant to wed her. 'Perhaps she has a younger sister,' I said to myself; if she does, I'll make no inquiries, demand no stories, set no conditions, but humbly put my life in her hands, tell her the whole tale of the two thousand and two nights that led me to her, and bid her end that story as she will—whether with the last goodnight of all or (what I can just dimly envision, like dawn in another world) some clear and fine and fresh good morning."

Dunyazade yawned and shivered. "I can't imagine what you're talking about. Am I expected to believe that preposterous business of Breastless Pilgrims and Tragic Views?"

"Yes!" cried Shah Zaman, then let his head fall back to the pillow. "They're too important to be lies. Fictions, maybe—but truer than fact."

Dunyazade covered her eyes with her razor-hand. "What do you expect me to do? Forgive you? Love you?"

"Yes!" the King cried again, his eyes flashing. "Let's end the dark night! All that passion and hate between men and women; all that confusion of inequality and difference! Let's take the truly tragic view of love! Maybe it *is* a fiction, but it's the profoundest and best of all! Treasure me, Dunyazade, as I'll treasure you!"

"For pity's sake stop!"

But Shah Zaman urged ardently: "Let's embrace; let's forbear; let's love as long as we can, Dunyazade—then embrace again, forbear and love again!"

"It won't work."

"Nothing *works!* But the enterprise is noble; it's full of joy and life, and the other ways are deathy. Let's make love like passionate equals!"

"You mean *as if* we were equals," Dunyazade said. "You know we're not. What you want is impossible."

"Despite your heart's feelings?" pressed the King. "Let it be *as if!* Let's make a philosophy of that *as if!*"

Dunyazade wailed: "I want my sister!"

"She may be alive; my brother, too." More quietly, Shah Zaman explained that Shahryar had been made acquainted with his brother's recent history and opinions, and had vowed that should Scheherazade ever attempt his life, he'd manage himself somewhat similarly: that is (as he was twenty years older, and more conservative), not exactly granting his wife the power to kill him, but disarming and declining to kill *her,* and within the bounds of good public relations, permitting her a freedom comparable to his own. The harem was a royal tradition, necessarily public; Scheherazade could take what lovers she would, but of necessity in private. Et cetera.

"Did you really imagine your sister *fooled* Shahryar for a thousand nights with her mamelukes and dildoes?" Shah Zaman laughed. "A man couldn't stay king very long if he didn't even know what was going on in the harem! And why do you suppose he permitted it, if not that he loved her too much, and was too sick of his other policy, to kill her? She changed his mind, all right, but she never fooled him: he used to believe that all women were unfaithful, and that the only way to spare himself the pain of infidelity was to deflower and kill them; now he believes that all *people* are unfaithful, and that the way to spare oneself the pain of infidelity is to love and not to care. He chooses equal promiscuity; I choose equal fidelity. Let's treasure each other, Dunyazade!"

She shook her head angrily, or desperately. "It's absurd. You're only trying to talk your way out of a bad spot."

"Of course I am! And of course it's absurd! Treasure me!"

"I'm exhausted. I should use the razor on both of us, and be done with it."

"Treasure me, Dunyazade!"

"We've talked all night; I hear the cocks; it's getting light."

"Good morning, then! Good morning!"

3

Alf Laylah Wa Laylah, The Book of the Thousand Nights and a Night, is not the story of Scheherazade, but the story of the story of her stories, which in effect begins: "There is a book called *The Thousand and One Nights,* in which it is said that once upon a time a king had two sons, Shahryar and Shah Zaman," et cetera; it ends when a king long after Shahryar discovers in his treasury the thirty volumes of *The Stories of the Thousand Nights and a Night,* at the end of the last of which the royal couples—Shahryar and Scheherazade, Shah Zaman and Dunyazade—emerge from their bridal chambers after the wedding night, greet one another with warm good mornings (eight in all), bestow Samarkand on the brides' long-suffering father, and set down for all posterity *The Thousand Nights and a Night.*

If I could invent a story as beautiful, it should be about little Dunyazade and her bridegroom, who pass a thousand nights in one dark night and in the morning embrace each other; they make love side by side, their faces close, and go out to greet sister and brother in the forenoon of a new life. Dunyazade's story begins in the middle; in the middle of my own, I can't conclude it—but it must end in the night that all good mornings come to. The Arab storytellers understood this; they ended their stories not "happily ever after," but specifically "until there took them the Destroyer of Delights and Desolator of Dwelling-places, and they were translated to the ruth of Almighty Allah, and their houses fell waste and their palaces lay in ruins, and the Kings inherited their riches." And no man knows it better than Shah Zaman, to whom therefore the second half of his life will be sweeter than the first.

To be joyous in the full acceptance of this dénouement is surely to possess a treasure, the key to which is the understanding that Key and Treasure are the same. There (with a kiss, little sister) is the sense of our story, Dunyazade: The key to the treasure is the treasure.

1972

PAUL AUSTER
b. 1947

Born in Newark, New Jersey, Paul Auster was educated at Columbia University, where he received both a B.A. and an M.A. A translator, critic, poet, screenwriter, and novelist, he first worked as a merchant seaman, a census taker, and a tutor. His book publications include poetry collections, screenplays, nonfiction and novels including *The Invention of Solitude* (1982); *In the Country of Last Things* (1987); *The New York Trilogy,* which is comprised of *City of Glass* (1985), *Ghosts* (1986), and *The Locked Room* (1987); *Leviathan* (1992); *Mr. Vertigo* (1994); and *Timbuktu* (1999).

In a 1989 *Publishers Weekly* interview, Auster acknowledged that "there's a certain reflexiveness about the activity of writing in the books" he has produced. *City of Glass,* excerpted here, was nominated for an Edgar Award for best mystery novel, although Auster said it was not intended to be read as a mystery. "It's simply a novel that uses genre conventions." The writer Toby Olson, in *The New York Times Book Review* (1985), remarked on "the descent of a writer into a labyrinth in which fact and fiction become increasingly difficult to separate."

From City of Glass

1

It was a wrong number that started it, the telephone ringing three times in the dead of night, and the voice on the other end asking for someone he was not. Much later, when he was able to think about the things that happened to him, he would conclude that nothing was real except chance. But that was much later. In the beginning, there was simply the event and its consequences. Whether it might have turned out differently, or whether it was all predetermined with the first word that came from the stranger's mouth, is not the question. The question is the story itself, and whether or not it means something is not for the story to tell.

As for Quinn, there is little that need detain us. Who he was, where he came from, and what he did are of no great importance. We know, for example, that he was thirty-five years old. We know that he had once been married, had once been a father, and that both his wife and son were now dead. We also know that he wrote books. To be precise, we know that he wrote mystery novels. These works were written under the name of William Wilson, and he produced them at the rate of about one a year, which brought in enough money for him to live modestly in a small New York apartment. Because he spent no more than five or six months on a novel, for the rest of the year he was free to do as he wished. He read many books, he looked at paintings, he went to the movies. In the summer he watched baseball on television; in the winter he went to the opera. More than anything else, however, what he liked to do was walk. Nearly every day, rain or shine, hot or cold, he would leave his apartment to walk through the city—never really going anywhere, but simply going wherever his legs happened to take him.

New York was an inexhaustible space, a labyrinth of endless steps, and no matter how far he walked, no matter how well he came to know its neighborhoods and streets, it always left him with the feeling of being lost. Lost, not only in the city, but within himself as well. Each time he took a walk, he felt as though he were leaving himself behind, and by giving himself up to the movement of the streets, by reducing himself to a seeing eye, he was able to escape the obligation to think, and this, more than anything else, brought him a measure of peace, a salutary emptiness within. The world was outside of him, around him, before him, and the speed with which it kept changing made it impossible for him to dwell on any one thing for very long. Motion was of the essence, the act of putting one foot in front of the other and allowing himself to follow the drift of his own body. By wandering aimlessly, all places became equal, and it no longer mattered where he was. On his best walks, he was able to feel that he was nowhere. And this, finally, was all he ever asked of things: to be nowhere. New York was the nowhere he had built around himself, and he realized that he had no intention of ever leaving it again.

In the past, Quinn had been more ambitious. As a young man he had published several books of poetry, had written plays, critical essays, and had worked on a number of long translations. But quite abruptly, he had given up all that. A part of him had died, he told his friends, and he did not want it coming back to haunt him. It was then that he had taken on the name of William Wilson. Quinn was no longer that part of him that could write books, and although in many ways Quinn continued to exist, he no longer existed for anyone but himself.

He had continued to write because it was the only thing he felt he could do. Mystery novels seemed a reasonable solution. He had little trouble inventing the intricate stories they required, and he wrote well, often in spite of himself, as if without having to make an effort. Because he did not consider himself to be the author of what he wrote, he did not feel responsible for it and therefore was not compelled to defend it in his heart. William Wilson, after all, was an invention, and even though he had been born within Quinn himself, he now led an independent life. Quinn treated him with deference, at times even admiration, but he never went so far as to believe that he and William Wilson were the same man. It was for this reason that he did not emerge from behind the mask of his pseudonym. He had an agent, but they had never met. Their contacts were confined to the mail, for which purpose Quinn had rented a numbered box at the post office. The same was true of the publisher, who paid all fees, monies, and royalties to Quinn through the agent. No book by William Wilson ever included an author's photograph or biographical note. William Wilson was not listed in any writers' directory, he did not give interviews, and all the letters he received were answered by his agent's secretary. As far as Quinn could tell, no one knew his secret. In the beginning, when his friends learned that he had given up writing, they would ask him how he was planning to live. He told them all the same thing: that he had inherited a trust fund from his wife. But the fact was that his wife had never had any money. And the fact was that he no longer had any friends.

It had been more than five years now. He did not think about his son very much anymore, and only recently he had removed the photograph of his wife from the wall. Every once in a while, he would suddenly feel what it had been like to hold the three-year-old boy in his arms—but that was not exactly thinking, nor was it even remembering. It was a physical sensation, an imprint of the past that had been left in his body, and he had no control over it. These moments came less often now, and for the most part it seemed as though things had begun to change for him. He no longer wished to be dead. At the same time, it cannot be said that he was glad to be alive. But at least he did not resent it. He was alive, and the stubbornness of this fact had little by little begun to fascinate him—as if he had managed to outlive himself, as if he were somehow living a posthumous life. He did not sleep with the lamp on anymore, and for many months now he had not remembered any of his dreams.

It was night. Quinn lay in bed smoking a cigarette, listening to the rain beat against the window. He wondered when it would stop and whether he would feel like taking a long walk or a short walk in the morning. An open copy of Marco Polo's *Travels* lay face down on the pillow beside him. Since finishing the latest William Wilson novel two weeks earlier, he had been languishing. His private-eye narrator, Max Work, had solved an elaborate series of crimes, had suffered through a number of beatings and narrow escapes, and Quinn was feeling somewhat exhausted by his efforts. Over the years, Work had become very close to Quinn. Whereas William Wilson remained an abstract figure for him, Work had increasingly come to life. In the triad of selves that Quinn had become, Wilson served as a kind of ventriloquist, Quinn himself was the dummy, and Work was the animated voice that gave purpose to the enterprise. If Wilson was an illusion, he nevertheless justified the lives of the other two. If Wilson did not exist, he nevertheless was the bridge that allowed Quinn to pass from himself into Work. And little by little, Work had become a presence in Quinn's life, his interior brother, his comrade in solitude.

Quinn picked up the Marco Polo and started reading the first page again. "We will set down things seen as seen, things heard as heard, so that our book may be an accurate record, free from any sort of fabrication. And all who read this book or hear it may do so with full confidence, because it contains nothing but the truth." Just as Quinn was beginning to ponder the meaning of these sentences, to turn their crisp assurances over in his mind, the telephone rang. Much later, when he was able to reconstruct the events of that night, he would remember looking at the clock, seeing that it was past twelve, and wondering why someone should be calling him at that hour. More than likely, he thought, it was bad news. He climbed out of bed, walked naked to the telephone, and picked up the receiver on the second ring.

"Yes?"

There was a long pause on the other end, and for a moment Quinn thought the caller had hung up. Then, as if from a great distance, there came the sound of a voice unlike any he had ever heard. It was at once mechanical and filled with feeling, hardly more than a whisper and yet perfectly audible, and so even in tone that he was unable to tell if it belonged to a man or a woman.

"Hello?" said the voice.

"Who is this?" asked Quinn.

"Hello?" said the voice again.

"I'm listening," said Quinn. "Who is this?"

"Is this Paul Auster?" asked the voice. "I would like to speak to Mr. Paul Auster."

"There's no one here by that name."

"Paul Auster. Of the Auster Detective Agency."

"I'm sorry," said Quinn. "You must have the wrong number."

"This is a matter of utmost urgency," said the voice.

"There's nothing I can do for you," said Quinn. "There is no Paul Auster here."

"You don't understand," said the voice. "Time is running out."

"Then I suggest you dial again. This is not a detective agency."

Quinn hung up the phone. He stood there on the cold floor, looking down at his feet, his knees, his limp penis. For a brief moment he regretted having been so abrupt with the caller. It might have been interesting, he thought, to have played along with him a little. Perhaps he could have found out something about the case—perhaps even have helped in some way. "I must learn to think more quickly on my feet," he said to himself.

Like most people, Quinn knew almost nothing about crime. He had never murdered anyone, had never stolen anything, and he did not know anyone who had. He had never been inside a police station, had never met a private detective, had never spoken to a criminal. Whatever he knew about these things, he had learned from books, films, and newspapers. He did not, however, consider this to be a handicap. What interested him about the stories he wrote was not their relation to the world but their relation to other stories. Even before he became William Wilson, Quinn had been a devoted reader of mystery novels. He knew that most of them were poorly written, that most could not stand up to even the vaguest sort of examination, but still, it was the form that appealed to him, and it was the rare, unspeakably bad mystery that he would refuse to read. Whereas his taste in other books was rigorous, demanding to the point of narrow-mindedness, with these works he showed almost no discrimination whatsoever. When he was in the right mood, he had little trouble reading ten or twelve of them in a row. It was a kind of hunger that took hold of him, a craving for a special food, and he would not stop until he had eaten his fill.

What he liked about these books was their sense of plenitude and economy. In the good mystery there is nothing wasted, no sentence, no word that is not significant. And even if it is not significant, it has the potential to be so—which amounts to the same thing. The world of the book comes to life, seething with possibilities, with secrets and contradictions. Since everything seen or said, even the slightest, most trivial thing, can bear a connection to the outcome of the story, nothing must be overlooked. Everything becomes essence; the center of the book shifts with each event that propels it forward. The center, then, is everywhere, and no circumference can be drawn until the book has come to its end.

The detective is one who looks, who listens, who moves through this morass of objects and events in search of the thought, the idea that will pull all these things together and make sense of them. In effect, the writer and the detective are interchangeable. The reader sees the world through the detective's eyes, experiencing the proliferation of its details as if for the first time. He has become awake to the things around him, as if they might speak to him, as if, because of the attentiveness he now brings to them, they might begin to carry a meaning other than the simple fact of their existence. Private eye. The term held a triple meaning for Quinn. Not only was it the letter "i," standing for "investigator," it was "I" in the upper case, the tiny life-bud buried in the body of the breathing self. At the same time, it was also the physical eye of the writer, the eye of the man who looks out from himself into the world and demands that the world reveal itself to him. For five years now, Quinn had been living in the grip of this pun.

He had, of course, long ago stopped thinking of himself as real. If he lived now in the world at all, it was only at one remove, through the imaginary person of Max Work. His detective necessarily had to be real. The nature of the books demanded it. If Quinn had allowed himself to vanish, to withdraw into the confines of a strange and hermetic life, Work continued to live in the world of others, and the more Quinn seemed to vanish, the more persistent Work's presence in that world became. Whereas Quinn tended to feel out of place in his own skin, Work was aggressive, quick-tongued, at home in whatever spot he happened to find himself. The very things that caused problems for Quinn, Work took for granted, and he walked through the mayhem of his adventures with an ease and indifference that never failed to impress his creator. It was not precisely that Quinn wanted to be Work, or even to be like him, but it reassured him to pretend to be Work as he was writing his books, to know that he had it in him to be Work if he ever chose to be, even if only in his mind.

That night, as he at last drifted off to sleep, Quinn tried to imagine what Work would have said to the stranger on the phone. In his dream, which he later forgot, he found himself alone in a room, firing a pistol into a bare white wall.

The following night, Quinn was caught off guard. He had thought the incident was over and was not expecting the stranger to call again. As it happened, he was sitting on the toilet, in the act of expelling a turd, when the telephone rang. It was somewhat later than the previous night, perhaps ten or twelve minutes before one. Quinn had just reached the chapter that tells of Marco Polo's journey from Peking to Amoy, and the book was open on his lap as he went about his business in the tiny bathroom. The ringing of the telephone came as a distinct irritation. To answer it promptly would mean getting up without wiping himself, and he was loath to walk across the apartment in that state. On the other hand, if he finished what he was doing at his normal speed, he would not make it to the phone in time. In spite of this, Quinn found himself reluctant to move. The telephone was not his favorite object, and more than once he had considered getting rid of his. What he disliked most of all was its tyranny. Not only did it have the power to interrupt him against his will, but inevitably he would give in to its command. This time, he decided to resist. By the third ring, his bowels were empty. By the fourth ring, he had succeeded in wiping himself. By the fifth ring, he had pulled up his pants, left the bathroom, and was walking calmly across the apartment. He answered the phone on the sixth ring, but there was no one at the other end. The caller had hung up.

The next night, he was ready. Sprawled out on his bed, perusing the pages of *The Sporting News,* he waited for the stranger to call a third time. Every now and then, when his nerves got the better of him, he would stand up and pace about the apartment. He put on a record—Haydn's opera *Il Mondo della Luna*—and listened to it from start to finish. He waited and waited. At two-thirty, he finally gave up and went to sleep.

He waited the next night, and the night after that as well. Just as he was about to abandon his scheme, realizing that he had been wrong in all his assumptions, the telephone rang again. It was May nineteenth. He would remember the date because it was his parents' anniversary—or would have been, had his parents been alive—and his mother had once told him that he had been conceived on her wedding night. This fact had always appealed to him—being able to pinpoint the first moment of his existence—and over the years he had privately celebrated his birthday on that day. This time it was somewhat earlier than on the other two nights—not yet eleven o'clock—and as he reached for the phone he assumed it was someone else.

"Hello?" he said.

Again, there was a silence on the other end. Quinn knew at once that it was the stranger.

"Hello?" he said again. "What can I do for you?"

"Yes," said the voice at last. The same mechanical whisper, the same desperate tone. "Yes. It is needed now. Without delay."

"What is needed?"

"To speak. Right now. To speak right now. Yes."

"And who do you want to speak to?"

"Always the same man. Auster. The one who calls himself Paul Auster."

This time Quinn did not hesitate. He knew what he was going to do, and now that the time had come, he did it.

"Speaking," he said. "This is Auster speaking."

"At last. At last I've found you." He could hear the relief in the voice, the tangible calm that suddenly seemed to overtake it.

"That's right," said Quinn. "At last." He paused for a moment to let the words sink in, as much for himself as for the other. "What can I do for you?"

"I need help," said the voice. "There is great danger. They say you are the best one to do these things."

"It depends on what things you mean."

"I mean death. I mean death and murder."

"That's not exactly my line," said Quinn. "I don't go around killing people."

"No," said the voice petulantly. "I mean the reverse."

"Someone is going to kill you?"

"Yes, kill me. That's right. I am going to be murdered."

"And you want me to protect you?"

"To protect me, yes. And to find the man who is going to do it."

"You don't know who it is?"

"I know, yes. Of course I know. But I don't know where he is."

"Can you tell me about it?"

"Not now. Not on the phone. There is great danger. You must come here."

"How about tomorrow?"

"Good. Tomorrow. Early tomorrow. In the morning."

"Ten o'clock?"

"Good. Ten o'clock." The voice gave an address on East 69th Street. "Don't forget, Mr. Auster. You must come."

"Don't worry," said Quinn. "I'll be there."

1985

PAUL KARASIK
b. 1956

DAVID MAZZUCCHELLI
b. 1960

David Mazzucchelli's art and stories regularly appear in his self-published, award-winning magazine, *Rubber Blanket.* His credits include both a Batman book for D.C. Comics and a regular series of covers and drawings for *The New Yorker.* The script and the original panel-by-panel breakdown for *Paul Auster's* CITY OF GLASS were created by Paul Karasik. A former contributing editor to *Raw,* Karasik is currently a schoolteacher in Cape Cod, Massachusetts. A longtime admirer of Auster's work, Karasik had the beginnings of a script for CITY OF GLASS in his notebooks before this project was even imagined by its publishers.

From Paul Auster's CITY OF GLASS

...THE TELEPHONE RINGING THREE TIMES IN THE DEAD OF NIGHT...

...AND THE VOICE ON THE OTHER END...

...ASKING FOR SOMEONE HE WAS NOT.

MUCH LATER, HE WOULD CONCLUDE...

RRING

...THAT NOTHING WAS REAL...

DIRECTORY
...EXCEPT CHANCE.

WHETHER IT MIGHT HAVE TURNED OUT DIFFERENTLY OR WAS PREDETERMINED IS NOT THE QUESTION.

THE QUESTION IS THE STORY ITSELF...

...AND WHETHER OR NOT IT MEANS SOMETHING IS NOT FOR THE STORY TO TELL.

AS FOR QUINN, HE WAS THIRTY-FIVE AND BOTH HIS WIFE AND SON WERE DEAD.

AS A YOUNG MAN, HE HAD WRITTEN POETRY, PLAYS AND ESSAYS.
Wilson Clam Up
Good Guy/BAD GUY WILSON
Deceit WILLIAM WILSON
UNDERCOVER
WILSON DEAD MAN'S TALE
Suicide Squeeze

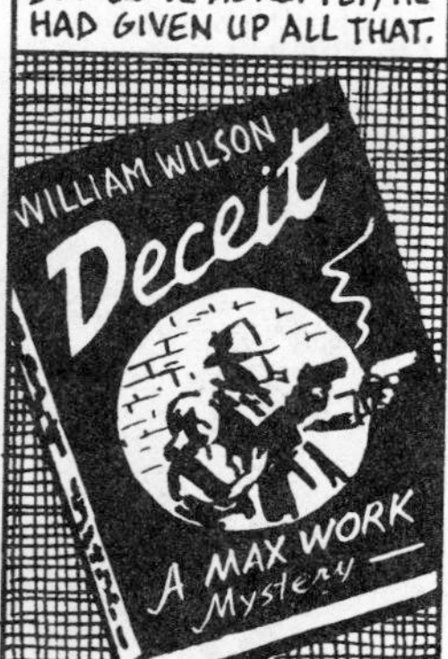
BUT QUITE ABRUPTLY, HE HAD GIVEN UP ALL THAT.
WILLIAM WILSON
Deceit
A MAX WORK Mystery

A PART OF HIM HAD DIED AND HE DID NOT WANT IT HAUNTING HIM.

HE NOW WROTE MYSTERY NOVELS UNDER THE NAME OF WILLIAM WILSON.

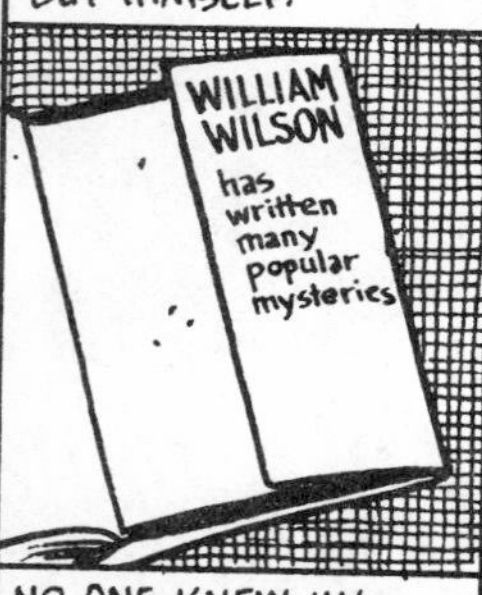
QUINN NO LONGER EXISTED FOR ANYONE BUT HIMSELF.
WILLIAM WILSON has written many popular mysteries
NO ONE KNEW HIS SECRET.

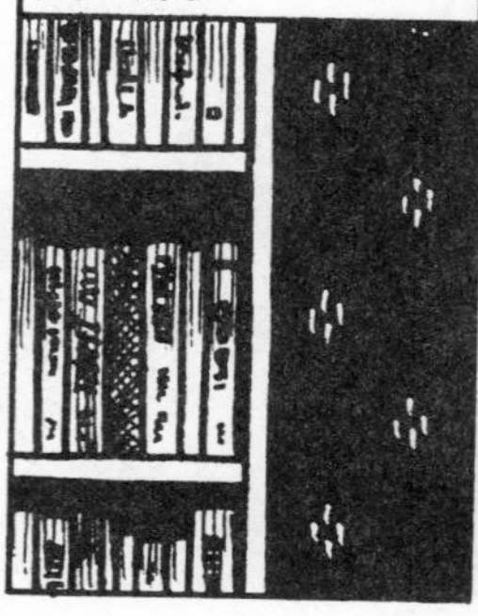
HE TOLD HIS FRIENDS THAT HE HAD INHERITED A TRUST FUND FROM HIS WIFE.

BUT THE FACT WAS THAT HIS WIFE HAD NEVER HAD ANY MONEY.

AND THE FACT WAS THAT HE NO LONGER HAD ANY FRIENDS.

MORE THAN ANYTHING ELSE, WHAT QUINN LIKED TO DO WAS WALK.
NEW YORK WAS A LABYRINTH OF ENDLESS STEPS...
...AND NO MATTER HOW FAR HE WALKED, IT ALWAYS LEFT HIM WITH THE FEELING OF BEING LOST.
EACH TIME HE TOOK A WALK, HE FELT HE WAS LEAVING HIMSELF BEHIND.
BY GIVING HIMSELF UP TO THE STREETS, BY REDUCING HIMSELF TO A SEEING EYE, HE WAS ABLE TO ESCAPE THINKING.
ALL PLACES BECAME EQUAL, AND ON HIS BEST WALKS, HE WAS ABLE TO FEEL THAT HE WAS NOWHERE.
THIS WAS ALL HE EVER ASKED OF THINGS: TO BE NOWHERE.
NEW YORK WAS THE NOWHERE HE HAD BUILT AROUND HIMSELF...
...AND HE HAD NO INTENTION OF EVER LEAVING IT AGAIN.

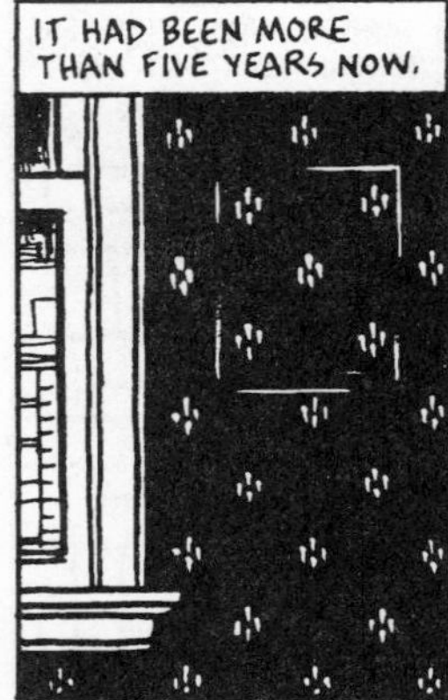
IT HAD BEEN MORE THAN FIVE YEARS NOW.

HE DID NOT THINK ABOUT IT VERY MUCH ANYMORE.

EVERY ONCE IN A WHILE, HE WOULD SUDDENLY FEEL WHAT IT HAD BEEN LIKE...

...TO HOLD THE THREE-YEAR-OLD BOY IN HIS ARMS,

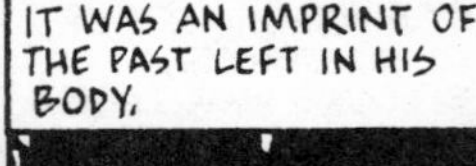
IT WAS AN IMPRINT OF THE PAST LEFT IN HIS BODY.

BUT THESE MOMENTS CAME LESS OFTEN NOW.

HE HAD CONTINUED TO WRITE BECAUSE IT WAS THE ONLY THING HE FELT HE COULD DO.
RRIN—

YES?
THERE WAS A LONG PAUSE.

HELLO?

WHO IS THIS?
HELLO?
I'M LISTENING. WHO IS THIS?

IS THIS PAUL AUSTER? I WOULD LIKE TO SPEAK TO PAUL AUSTER.
THERE'S NO ONE HERE BY THAT NAME.

PAUL AUSTER. OF THE AUSTER DETECTIVE AGENCY.
THERE IS NO PAUL AUSTER HERE.

YOU DON'T UNDERSTAND. THIS IS A MATTER OF UTMOST URGENCY.
THEN I SUGGEST YOU DIAL AGAIN. THIS IS NOT A DETECTIVE AGENCY.

CLIK

QUINN HAD LONG AGO STOPPED THINKING OF HIMSELF AS REAL.
WHO'S ASKIN'?
IF HE LIVED NOW IN THE WORLD AT ALL, IT WAS THROUGH THE IMAGINARY PERSON OF MAX WORK, THE PRIVATE-EYE NARRATOR OF WILLIAM WILSON'S NOVELS.

WHAT QUINN LIKED ABOUT MYSTERIES WAS THEIR ECONOMY.

THERE IS NO SENTENCE, NO WORD THAT IS NOT SIGNIFICANT.

AND EVEN IF IT IS NOT, IT HAS THE POTENTIAL TO BE SO.

EVERYTHING BECOMES ESSENCE: THE CENTER OF THE BOOK SHIFTS, IS EVERYWHERE...

...AND NO CIRCUMFERENCE CAN BE DRAWN UNTIL THE END.

OVER THE YEARS, WORK HAD BECOME VERY CLOSE TO QUINN.
Daniel Quin
WRITER
MAX WORK
PRIVATE INVESTIGATOR
WHEREAS WILLIAM WILSON REMAINED AN ABSTRACT FIGURE, WORK HAD INCREASINGLY COME TO LIFE.
MAX WO
VATE INVE
IN THE TRIAD OF SELVES, WILSON SERVED AS A KIND OF VENTRILOQUIST...
...QUINN HIMSELF WAS THE DUMMY...
...AND WORK WAS THE VOICE THAT GAVE PURPOSE TO THE ENTERPRISE.
LITTLE BY LITTLE, WORK HAD BECOME A PRESENCE IN QUINN'S LIFE...
...HIS COMRADE IN SOLITUDE.

MAXINE HONG KINGSTON
b. 1940

Maxine Hong Kingston was born in Stockton, California. Educated at the University of California at Berkeley, she went on to teach high school English and mathematics in California and Hawaii. Her four books include three works of general nonfiction—*The Woman Warrior: Memoirs of a Girlhood among Ghosts* (1976), *China Men* (1980), *Hawaii One Summer* (1987)—and the novel *Tripmaster Monkey: His Fake Book* (1987). Kingston received the National Book Critics Circle Award for general nonfiction for *Woman Warrior* and the American Book Award for general nonfiction for *China Men.*

In a 1989 *New Republic* article, the writer Anne Tyler calls *Tripmaster Monkey,* excerpted here, "a great, huge sprawling beast of a novel, over 400 pages densely packed with the rantings and ravings and pranks and high jinks of one Wittman Ah Sing." During the 1960s, as Kingston said in a 1989 *New York Times Magazine* interview, "men had more fun than women. . . . Women were still wearing black sweaters and white lipstick and being cool and silent. However, the careful reader will see that the omniscient narrator is a woman. Definitely a female voice. She's always kicking Wittman around and telling him to do this and that and making fun of him. She always understands the woman characters. She's Kuan Yin, goddess of mercy."

From Tripmaster Monkey: His Fake Book

From *Trippers and Askers*

* * *

Though they walked through the land of the wasted, no Malte sights popped out to hurt him, she dispelling them. By day, the neon was not coursing through its glass veins. The dancing girl in spangles and feathers had flown out of her cage, which hung empty over the street. Nobody barked and hustled at the doorways to acts and shows. The day-folks, wheeling babies, wheeling grandpas, holding children by the hand, were shopping for dinner at the grocery stores and the bakery, dropping by the shoe repair. Oh, the smell of the focaccia ovens—O Home. A florist with white moustachios jaywalked through traffic with armsful of leonine football chrysanthemums. Behind glass, at the all-day-all-night place on the pie-wedge corner, poets, one to a table, were eating breakfast. The Co-Existence Bagel Shop was gone. The old guys, *Seventh Seal* knights, had played chess with Death and lost. The Bagel Shop, Miss Smith's Tea Room, Blabbermouth Night at The Place—all of a gone time. Out from the open door of La Bodega, a folksy guitar sweetened the air. The guitar was being passed around, and each played the tune he knew. You should have been there the night Segovia dropped by and played flamenco. Wittman musefully sang as if to himself a Mose Allison riff.

A young ma-a-an
ain't nothin' in this world today.

Because the ol' men's
got all the money.

The air of the City is so filled with poems, you have to fight becoming imbued with the general romanza. Nanci's long black hair and long black skirt skirled with the afternoon breezes. The leather of her shoulder bag strapped a breast. Her arms and outstretching legs were also long and black; she wore a leotard and tights like an old-fashioned Beat chick but, honestly, a dancer, dance togs for a good reason. Here he was: Wittman Ah Sing profiling down the street with a beautiful almost-girlfriend, clipping along, alongside, keeping up with him, the two of them making the scene on the Beach, like cruising in the gone Kerouac time of yore.

He ducked into the bookstore. She followed right on in. She stood beside him, browsing the rack of quarterlies, quite a few brave Volume I Number Ones. There were homemade books too, mimeo jobs, stencils, and small-press poetry that fit neat in the hand. On the top rack—right inside the door at eye level for all to see coming in or going out—was: an artistic avant-garde far-out new magazine that had published—in print—a scene from his play-in-progress—the lead-off piece—with his byline—right inside the front cover. He could reach over and hand it to her, but it would be more perfect if she happened to pick it out herself, come upon his premiere on her own, and be impressed. (F. Scott Fitzgerald, trying to impress Sheilah Graham, had driven to every bookstore in L.A., but could not find a copy of any of his books.)

Wittman went downstairs to the cool basement, where among the bookshelves were chairs and tables with ashtrays. He had first come to this place when he was a high-school kid on one of his escapes from Sacramento, Second City to Big City. No *No Free Reading* sign. No *No Smoking*. You didn't have to buy a book; you could read for nothing. You had a hangout where you didn't have to spend money. Quiet. All the radios in Chinatown blaring out the ball game, but here, we don't care about the World Series. He hadn't known the City Lights Pocket Book Shop was famous until the *Howl* trial, which he had cut school to attend. "Shig" Shigeyoshi Murao was the one charged with selling an obscene book. The muster of famous poets had blown Wittman away—everybody friends with everybody else, a gang of poets. He, poor monkey, was yet looking for others of his kind.

There had been a Chinese-American guy who rode with Jack and Neal. His name was Victor Wong, and he was a painter and an actor. Wittman had maybe seen him, or someone Chinese with the asymmetrical face of a character actor; he wore a white t-shirt with paint streaks and "hand-tooled leather shoes." Victor Wong, who went to the cabin in Bixby Canyon with Jack Duluoz and Neal/Cody. All this written up in *Big Sur,* where Jack calls Victor Wong Arthur Ma ("Little Chinese buddy Arthur Ma." Shit.), and flips out of his gourd walking in the moonless night above the wild ocean that rants for his life. Jack hangs on to the side of the mountain and listens and shouts back and sings. "Mien Mo Big Sur killer mountain for singing madly in." It would have been better if Victor/Arthur had been a writing man like the rest of them, but anyway he talked a lot and was good at hallucinations. "Little Arthur Ma [yet again "little"!] who never goes anywhere without his drawing paper and his Yellowjacket felt tips of all colors, red, blue, yellow, green, black, he draws marvelous subconscious glurbs and can also do excellent objective scenes or anything he wants on to cartoons—." They stay up all night, and Arthur Ma keeps making it up; he's not one of those storytellers who has to rehearse in the bathroom. Wittman had not gone up to the man with the character actor's face—one eye big, one eye small—and grabbed him by the arm and introduced himself. The poets at Big Sur fall asleep but not Arthur, who stays awake with Jack, the two of them yelling till dawn. ". . . and Arthur Ma suddenly yells: 'Hold still you buncha bastards, I got a hole in my eye.' "

It would be nice were Nanci to walk down the pine-slab steps and say, "Oh, you're published. Why didn't you tell me? Will you autograph a copy for me?" Holding his words to her bosom.

Girls in my native land. May the loveliest of you on an afternoon in summer in the darkened library find herself the little book that Jan des Tournes printed in 1556. May she take the cooling, glossy volume out with her into the murmurous orchard, or yonder to the phlox, in whose oversweet fragrance there lies a sediment of sheer sweetness.

She was two aisles away browsing through the French and German shelves. The Europeans made books with creme linen paper; the soft covers were not illustrated except for a sharp line of vermillion trim. When you slice the pages open with your paperknife, the book will have flossy raggedy edges. You feel like owning books like that. Remember Phoebe Weatherfield Caulfield asking Holden to name one thing he liked a lot? "Name one thing." "One thing I like a lot, or one thing I just like?" "You like a lot." Wittman liked a lot this poky hole in the San Francisco underground earth. He will not point out to Nanci what's so good about it. Spoil it to make a big deal. She had to take a liking of her own accord. He took his own sweet time, testing her scanning and skimming of foreign lit.

But the next time he looked her way, she was talking to a couple of Black guys, laughing, carrying on in French. Maybe they had met before, or maybe she let herself be picked up. There was something Black about her too, come to think of it; it was in a fullness of the mouth, and a wildness in her clothes, and something about her dry hair. "Très joli. Ahh, très joli. Oo-la-la, très joli." So, people really do say "Oo-la-la." She and they were mutually delighting in something. These black French must have lately arrived from one of those colonial places. Their faces were not chary and wary; they were not "friendly," or "bad," or "loose." Their long hands and fingers wafted through a gentler atmosphere. Give them a few more weeks among the Amerikans; we'll show them how far très joli manners get them, and how much respect with *Saturday Review* tucked under the arm. They'll tighten up their act. Turn complicated. He squeezed past them; they easily stepped aside, gave him no trouble. Let's go already, Nanci. Wittman gave a jerk of his head—¡Vamos! ¡Andalay!—and, surprisingly, she said her adieux and followed him up the stairs. You would think only homely girls obey like that.

"Wait," she called. "I'll be right with you." She paid for a book. "See?" she said. "Beckett."

"Ah, Bik Giht," he said, Chinatown having a pronunciation because of Beckett Street and not because of absurdity. Of course not.

"I'm looking for audition pieces," said Nanci as they walked along. "The speeches of just about any Beckett man make sense—more sense—coming from a woman. A minority woman. It doesn't matter what a Beckett character looks like. I won't play an oriental prostitute, and I won't speak broken English. No matter what. I can't. I won't. I'll be too old to play an ingenue? I'm a leading lady. I am the leading-lady type. No ching-chong chinaman for me."

What did she say? She said "ching-chong chinaman." She can bear to say that. God, she's tough. He had to get tougher. His head and bod were going through contortions from merely hearing that. Did I hear wrong? Hallucinating again? She mean me? Who you talking to? You talking to me, girl? You talking *about* me? Am I too paranoid, or what? She hadn't called me a name, had she? Someone called her that? Who called her that? Who she quoting? Was he hearing English wrong like any greenhorn F.O.B.? Now he was laughing nervously—the Chinese laugh—the giggle—lest it be a joke—that please-let-it-be-a-joke giggle. That betraying Chinese giggle trebled out of him. Where he'd almost gone deaf, she had said, "No ching-chong chinaman for me." She meant she refused to read a grotesque whose bucktoof mouth can't make intelligent American sounds. As if this language didn't belong to us. Well, the ugly is ugly no matter whose beautiful mouth it comes out of. She shouldn't wreck her mouth, and her voice, and her face, and her soul by repeating scurrilities.

"For my classical, I'll do Rosalind or Portia. Then when I'm older, anybody can be the queen." Anybody. Her. A leading lady. Why not? Who has more in common with a Shakespeare queen—a country-fair beauty starlet or Leontyne Price? Medea and Cleopatra and Clytemnestra and the statue lady from *Winter's Tale* are not blondies. Nor, it so happened, were any of the people walking by them on the street, nor are most people in the world.

"I don't like *Flower Drum Song*," she said. Wittman didn't either—a bunch of A.J.A.s and "Eurasians" playing weird Chinese. Not that Chinese have to play Chinese. Chineseness does not come to an actor through genetic memory. The well-trained actor observes humanity and the text.

"Oh, I'm so sorry," said Nanci, "that I took my grandmother to see *The World of Suzie Wong* for the scenes of Hong Kong. I'm so sorry. Wittman? I've been to New York and Hollywood. I look a bit dark. They're overt, you know? They say, 'You don't *look* oriental.' I walk in, they can tell about me. They read me, then they say, 'You don't sound right. You don't sound the way you look. You don't look the way you talk. Too distracting.' I'm wearing my high heels, and walking elegant, you know? The a.d. hands me the script, and tells me I have to take my shoes off. It's a cold reading, but I know what my part will be—an oriental peasant. You only need high heels for the part of the oriental prostitute. A good-looking talented actor, who's gotten his callback, who's been cast maybe, says my cue, which is 'Hey, there, mama-san.' And I have to say, I have to say, you know, something stupid. I have to speak in a way I've worked hard not to speak like. I stand there barefoot saying a line like—like that. And the director says, 'Can't you act more oriental? Act oriental.' I haven't been making rounds for a while." Oh, no, Nanci, don't lose the will to audition.

Wittman, now's your chance to whip out your Rilke, and give her his sympathy: *Let us be honest about it, then; we have no theatre, any more than we have God: for this, community is needed. . . . Had we a theatre, would you, tragic one, stand there again and again and again—so slight, so bare, so without pretext of a role. . . .*

"Wittman?" she said, laying a hand on his arm. "I performed twice as a crowd member. Once in a movie, and once on t.v. While the make-up lady was shading my nose, she said, 'I'm going to give you a cute Irish nose.' I'm tilted back in the chair, and holding my face steady. I don't reply. I don't want to get her mad so she makes me up ugly. And I wanted to see what I'd look like with my nose upturned. She shadowed the nostrils, and put white make-up down the length, ending with a diamond on the tip. The other show I was in, we had a male make-up artist—bitchy gay?—who finished my face without talking to me. Then he says, 'There's just so much we can do about those eyes.' " Those eyes were now downcast with mortification and tears. Oh, baby, what can I do to defend you against—cosmetologists. "They were trying to give me advice? For my own good? They didn't mean to hurt me."

"Yes, they did. They hurt you."

"Yes. I should have done my own make-up."

"It's no fair," said Wittman, who would not put his arm around her shoulder or waist. This called for a higher level of comforting. Help her out by thinking up a piece for her to do without insult. He ought to tell her that her face was perfectly lovely. But he was annoyed at her for talking about her face so much. Her nickname in college had been The Face. "How about the girl in *The Seven Year Itch?*" he suggested. "Yeah, that's what the script says—The Girl. Not The White Girl. The Girl. She's just a girl in New York on her own. No family from the old country camping in her apartment."

"I hate *The Seven Year Itch.* I loathe it."

"Just testing. I was testing you. You passed." Therefore, thou art mine, sought and found.

"But you're right. She could very well look like me. There isn't any reason why she shouldn't look like me. Wittman?" She had his sleeve in her fingers, and pulled at it for them to stop walking so fast. "I was thinking of *Krapp's Last Tape.* I could do it by myself, no other face up there to compare mine to. A director doesn't have to match me. My lost love who's beside me in the boat could be a male nurse. 'We lay there without moving but under us all moved, and moved us, gently, up and down, and from side to side.' When Krapp says, 'Let me in,' I, a woman, could mean: Open your eyes, and let me into your eyes."

Why hadn't he thought of that? She must think him ill-read and a dried-up intellectual not to have seen the sensuality in Beckett. "You're resorting to Krapp, Nanci, because of being left out of the Hogan Tyrone Loman Big Daddy family. And whatever the names of those families were in *Seven Brides for Seven Brothers.* Seven white brides for seven white brothers. They took a perfectly good pro-miscegenation legend and wrote fourteen principal parts for Caucasians. I know legends about seven Chinese brothers named Juan; they were part of a nation of one hundred and eight heroes and heroines. What I'm going to do, I've got to wrest the theater back for you. Those Juans were hermanos chinos.

"I understand your agony, Nanci," he said. "The most important tradition in my high school was the senior play. My year they did *The Barretts of Wimpole Street.* The student who won the most Willie Awards was supposed to play the lead. In the U.K., 'willie' means 'weenie'; in Sacramento, it means 'talent.' I was the man of a thousand faces and got my Willies for winning talent shows. Robert Browning, tall, thin, sensitive, dark, melancholy—that's me, let me count the ways. But the drama coach held auditions. Then he told me, I'm the emcee for the evening, the 'host'; I warm up the audience, talk to them entr'acte, do my stand-up shtick, whatever I like, do my magic act, my ventriloquist act, throw my voice, 'Help. Help. Let me out.' I'd be featured. Very special, my spot. The way they staged *The Barretts of Wimpole Street* was Wilderesque, with an important *Our Town* stage manager character played by me. I look like Frank Craven, who had Chinese eyes and a viewpoint from the outskirts of Grover's Corners, U.S.A. I did my medley of soliloquies, Hamlet, Richard III, Macbeth, Romeo. No Juliet. I did my bearded Americans, Walt Whitman and John Muir, guys with a lot of facial hair to cover up my face and my race. Mark Twain: '. . . a white to make a body sick, a white to make a body's flesh crawl—a tree-toad white, a fish-belly white.' Between *Barretts,* I also did great movie lines. 'Philip. Give me the letter, Philip.' 'Last night I dreamt I went to Manderley again.' 'As God is my witness, I'll never be hungry again. Chomp chomp.' 'The calla lilies are in bloom. Such a strange flowah.' "

Nanci guessed the actress whom each of those lines belonged to. " 'Maybe you found someone you like betta,' " she said. "Mae Clarke before James Cagney shoves the grapefruit in her kisser. 'I'd rather have his one arm around me than be in the two arms of another man.' "

"I know. I know. That movie where Linda Darnell and the British flyer and Tab Hunter are marooned on an island of desire. The British flyer has one arm, and Tab Hunter has the two arms but doesn't get the girl."

"No. Thelma Ritter says it to Marilyn Monroe in *The Misfits.*"

"Nanci, I think we're on to something. That line is so meaningful, they've used it in two movies. It's what you call a perennial favorite. Women have all the good lines. I almost turned into a Mei Lan Fan androgyne doing those lines single-handed. I'm ruined for ensemble work. I haven't been on the stage since."

Grant Avenue, or Du Pont Gai—they/we call it Du Pont Gai—changed from North Beach to Chinatown. That factory which baked the Beatnik fortune cookies for the Actor's Workshop benefit should be situated at this border. You can't pick out just exactly which Italian store or Chinese store or red or red-white-and-green festooning it is that demarcates the change, but suddenly or gradually—depending on how closely you're keeping a lookout—you are in the flak and flash of Chinatown. Autumn was here: A red banner strung above the street announced the Double Ten parade and its sponsors, the Chinese-American Anti-Communist League and the Six Companies. They'll leave the banner up there all this month before Double Ten and afterwards into winter. To show Immigration and HUAC that we Chinese-Americans, super Americans, we too better dead than red-hot communists. Neither Wittman nor Nanci had plans to observe Double Ten. They had no idea how you go about doing that since nobody they knew showed much interest. It seemed like a fake holiday. A woody station wagon with Ohio plates drove slowly by. Painted across it was: "North Beach or Bust." Poor bastards. Too late. They had crossed the country to join the Beatniks.

"I'm writing a play for you, Nanci," said Wittman. Wait for me while I write for you a theater; I will plant and grow for you a pear garden. Then she did look at him—he's wonderful. She stopped in her tracks to look up at him. She took his upper arm with her two hands. "I'll write you a part," he said, "where the audience learns to fall in love with you for your ochery skin and round nose and flat profile and slanty eyes, and your bit of an accent."

She made a pouty mouth. They walked on, she still holding his arm with both hands. Nanci, as a matter of fact, had a pointy nose with a bridge, where her dark glasses had a place to sit. Even Marilyn Monroe, blonde, dead, had not been able to get away with a round nose. Rhinoplasty. Nanci looked good. When the directors tell her, "You don't look Chinese," they mean: too pretty for a Chinese. She had represented Cal at the intercollegiate (Chinese) beauty-personality-good-grades contest at U.C.L.A.

What theater do we have besides beauty contests? Do we have a culture that's not these knickknacks we sell to the bok gwai? If Chinese-American cutlure is not knickknackatory—look at it—backscratcher swizzle sticks, pointed chopsticks for the hair, Jade East aftershave in a Buddha-shape bottle, the head screws off and you pour lotion out of its neck—then what is it? No other people sell out their streets like this. Tourists can't buy up J-town. Wait a goddamn minute. *We* don't make Jade East. It's one of your hakujin products by Swank. Would we do that to you? Make Jesus-on-the-cross bottles, so every morning, all over the country, hairy men twist his head off, and pour this green stuff out of his neck? So what do we have in the way of a culture besides Chinese hand laundries? You might make a joke on that—something about 'What's the difference between a Chinese hand laundry and a French laundry?' Where's our jazz? Where's our blues? Where's our ain't-taking-no-shit-from-nobody street-strutting language? I want so bad to be the first bad-jazz China Man bluesman of America. Of all the music on the airwaves, there's one syllable that sounds like ours. It's in that song by the Coasters. "It'll take an ocean of calamine lotion. Poison iv-ee-eeee-ee." No, not the ivy part. It's where they sing, "Aro-ou-ound-aaaaa-ah." Right there, that's a Chinese opera run. A Coaster must have been among those Black guys you see at the Chinese movies and at dojos seeking kung fu power.

Wittman and Nanci toned down any show-off in their walks. Chinese like for young people to look soo-mun or see-mun. Proper. Well turned out. Decorous. Kempt. The Ivy League look is soo-mun. Clean-cut all-American. For girls: sprayed, fixed hair—hair helmet—and they should have a jade heart at their throat always. Wittman was glad Nanci was wearing a defiant black leotard. If they were Japanese and walking through J-town in their grubbies, the Issei, who have a word for every social condition, would call them "yogore." (Zato-Ichi the Blind Swordsman, who flicked his snot into the haw-haw-haw mouth of a villain, is yogore. He'd be rolling the snotball all the time he's pretending to be putting up with their taunts.) Wittman went up Jackson Street (Dik-son Gai), sort of herding Nanci, turned her at the corner, guided her across the street by leaning toward her or leading away. Strange the way a man has to walk with a woman. She follows his lead like they're dancing, she wasn't even a wife or girlfriend. Did you hear what Jack Kennedy said to his media advisers, who told him that in pictures Jackie isn't walking beside him enough? He said, "She will just have to walk faster." (It is not a Chinese custom for women to walk behind men. That's a base stereotype.) No, Wittman didn't want to slow down for anybody either, become an inclining, compliant owned man. Husbands walk differently from single guys. He unlocked the door of his building, having to reach in through the security bars for a somewhat hidden lock. Nanci went right on in. They climbed the many steps and landings, she ahead, and he behind thinking, "Pomegranates." They didn't run into anybody in the hallways, all decent people at work, their doors shut, rows of jailhouse-green doors.

"My ah-pok-mun," he said, opening the door wide to his roomland, switching on the overhead light, which also switched on the desk lamp. "Come in. Come in," turning his desk chair around for his guest. "Welcome to my pok-mun. Sit. Sit." He dumped the fullness of his ashtray into the trash and set the ashtray next to his mattress on the floor. "For sitting furniture, I don't have but the one chair." She hung her suede jacket over the back of it, and sat down. Sweeping open his invisible magician's cape, he presented: his roomland, his boxes of papers, his table, which was desk and dining table, his hotplate on a crate, which was a cupboard for foodstuffs such as instant coffee and Campbell's Soup, edible out of the can. (Cook like a Mexicano: Put the tortilla directly on the burner, flipflop, ready to eat. So you get burner rings on your tortilla, but fast and nongreasy.) He quoted to her some Beat advice: " 'How many things do you own?' 'Fifteen.' 'Too many.' " No rug here. No sofa here. Never own a rug or a sofa. And thus be free. " 'What's the use of living if I can't make paradise in my own roomland?' " Peter Orlovsky was another one good at how to live. She laughed but did not give him the next lines, which are: "For this drop of time upon my eyes / like the endurance of a red star on a cigarette / makes me feel life splits faster than scissors."

Good thing the typewriter crouched, ready, on the table—his grand piano—that faces the window, where you look out at another pok-mun. If he was going to bring people up here, he ought to have been a painter. Painters have something to show for their work—an easel with the painting they're working on like a billboard all sunny under the skylight, their food composed into still-lifes, their favorite colors everywhere. They get to wear their palette on their grey sweatshirts, and spatters and swipes on their blue jeans. He sat down on the mattress, straightened out his sleeping bag, bed made.

"So this is where you live," Nanci said, looking down into one of his cartons, not touching the poems, just looking.

"See that trunk over there?" He pointed at it with the toe of his boot. Books, papers, his coffee cup sat on its lid; a person could sit on it too, and it became a second chair.

"That's the trunk I told you about. Proof, huh? Evidence. It exists. It *became* a theatrical trunk; it used to be a Gold Mountain trunk." It was big enough for crossing oceans, all right. It would take a huge man to hoist it onto his back. The hasps and clasps were rusty (with salt sea air), and the leather straps were worn. Big enough to carry all you own to a new land and never come back, enough stuff to settle the Far West with. And big enough to hold all the costumes for the seventy-two transformations of the King of the Monkeys in a long run of *The Journey to the West* in its entirety. "My great-great-grandfather came to America with that trunk."

"Yes," said Nanci, "I recognize it." Every family has a Gold Mountain trunk in their attic or basement.

"I can't die until I fill it with poems and play-acts," said Wittman.

"Would you like to read me a poem?" asked Nanci.

Oh, yes. Yes, I would. My name is Wittman Ah Sing, but you may call me Bold. When you get to know me better, you may call me Bolder, and I'll show you like Emily Dickinson secret poems in the false bottom of my Gold Mountain theater trunk. Oh, too guest-happy.

He rummaged through a carton for a poem that had made him feel like a genius when he made it. "New poems. New green poems. Haven't gone over this batch. Too green. Need one or two more drafts, make fair copies." Oh, shut up. Take one up at random. Any old poem.

Remember when everyone you fell in love with read poems and listened to poems? Love poetry has gone. And thou? Where went thou?

He put on his intellectual's glasses with the heavy black rims, scowled, made no eye contact. Oh, no—a poem—nah, a paragraph—that had been forced on speed, and coffee jacking the bennies up higher, then grass to smooth out the jaw-grinding jangles—does it show? A poem on beanie weenies, when he was a frijoles head—from his Making a Living series, a cycle of useful poetry—well, prose poems, actually—Gig Poems. Wishing he had a chance to re-do it, explain, he read aloud to Nanci something like this: Should a window-washing poet climb over the edge of a skyscraper, one leg at a time, onto his swing, and unclutch the ropes, may the tilted City hold still. Don't look down those paned streets. In view of the typing pools, he makes a noose, and tests the slide of it, and the dingle dangle of it. Yes? Yes? No? No? Yes? No? Hey, look—sky doggies. Up here—a stampede of longhorns. Point the rope like a wand, whirl a Möbius strip, outline a buffalo. Shoot la riata sideways over the street, overhead at the helicopters, jump in and out of it, and lass*oo* one of those steers. It drags the poet right off the plank—but the harness holds! Hey, you pretty girls of the typing pool, give me a big pantomime hand. Can't hear the clap-clap, but it's applause, and it's mine. Kisses blow through glass. Their impact knocks me off again, falling far down, and down as the pulley runs, and brakes. I vow: I will make of my scaffold, a stage.

The poet—the one in real life, not the one in the poem—wouldn't mind, when the poem ends, if his listening lady were to pay him a compliment. Such as agreeing, yes, let's transfigure every surface of the City with theater. Such as saying, "Did you on purpose make the line that tells about the tilted City bevel upsettingly—the verb fulcrumming a lot more phrases on one end than the other?" He'd love her for such particular appreciation. At least, praise him on the utilitarian level. From out of my head into the world. The window-washer was using newspapers and water, the chemicals in newsprint as good as Windex spray. Also, you can get rich by contracting with the owners of buildings for window-washing services a year in advance. Charge thousands, but pay the window-washers minimum wage by the hour. The kind of men you hire, whatever you pay them, they think it's a lot.

Nanci made no move to show that she heard that the poem was over. Give her a love story, Wittman. He ought to have read her the one about how this broken-hearted guy had long ago stashed in his *Physicians' Desk Reference* the last letter, unread, from the ex–love of his life, written upon taking her leave of him. A lifetime later, an envelope falls out of the *P.D.R.* . . . (No, he wasn't a doctor. Each head had his own *P.D.R.* to identify street pills, and their effects and side effects, that is, trips and side trips.)

"Want to hear another one?" he asked.

"Okay," she said.

He reached into the poem box beside the black curve of her calf. His arm could graze its black length. But a true poet can't love up a woman who doesn't get that he's a poet. He can't touch her until she feels his poetry. Japanese have a custom where the host leaves a piece of art about, and the guest may notice it. The carton was labeled The International Nut Corporation, 100 Phoenix Ave., Lowell, Mass. His soul chick would notice it, and say, "Did you make a pilgrimage to Kerouac's town and his city?" Then he grabs her leg.

"What do you want to hear? How about one of my railroad cantos? A land chantey, the worker-poet as chanteyman? How's about a dueling sequence? 'The Dueling Mammy,' ha ha. Loss poems? You need a revenge sonnet? I've got twenty-eight sonnets now. I have one hundred and twenty-six sonnets to go to catch up with Shakespeare, who finished everything at the age of forty-five. I'm twenty-three. You too, right?"

She nodded, crossing one of those legs over the other. She folded her arms under her breasts.

He read to her about the ineluctable goingness of railroad tracks. Then he gave her the poet's intense stare, holding her eyes until she spoke. "Lovely," she said. "Sweet."

But he did not want to be sweet and lovely.

He dug deeper into the poem box, letting the ashes of his cigarette fall right on in. He took hold of a bane poem. Standing up, as if on platform, he read to her about mongoloids. " 'What's wrong with the baby, doctor?!' 'Is it deformed!?' 'Is it Chinese?!' Interbang?! Interbang!? 'But *we're* Chinese.' 'He's *supposed* to look like that!?' 'How can you tell if it's defective or if it's Chinese?!' 'Look at its little eyes.' 'Its tongue's too long.' 'Yellow skin *and* yellow jaundice?!' 'It's mongoloid?!' 'It's mongoloid!' 'It's an idiot?!' 'It's a mongolian idiot!' 'They're affectionate.' 'No, they bite.' 'Do they drool?!' 'All babies drool.' 'Can they be house-broken?!' 'Let's put it in a home.' The chorus goes like this: 'Gabble gobble. One of us. One of us.' " Wittman opened his eyes as wide as they got and looked into Nanci's—epicanthic eyes meeting epicanthic eyes. Fingers wiggling to communicate. " 'Look at it cry!' 'Is that a cleft palate in there? And a giraffe tongue?!' 'It's got a wee penis.' 'All babies have a small penis.' 'Unlike apes, mongoloids do not turn dangerous to their keepers at puberty.' " Wittman played like he was sitting with the other mongoloid children on the go-around in the playground at the home. Their arms and chins hang over the top railing, a head lolls. A club foot gives the earth a kick, and they go around and around and around. Reading in the manner of Charles Laughton as the Hunchback of Notre Dame (who grunted and snorted in some scenes, and in others discoursed fluently on the nature of man) and like Helen Keller, he stuttered out, " 'Wa-wa-wa-water? Gabble gobble, one of us.' "

No coward, Wittman asked Nanci, "How do you like my work?" Straight out. Asking for it. I can take it.

"You sound black," she said. "I mean like a Black poet. Jive. Slang. Like LeRoi Jones. Like . . . like Black."

He slammed his hand—a fist with a poem in it—down on the desk—fistful of poem. He spit in his genuine brass China Man spittoon, and jumped up on top of the desk, squatted there, scratching. "Monkey see, monkey do?" he said. "Huh? Monkey see, monkey do?" Which sounds much uglier if you know Chinese. "Monkey shit, monkey belly." "A lot you know," he said. "A lot you know about us monkeys." She got up and stood behind her chair. He sprang from the desk onto the chair, and from the chair to the mattress, and from the mattress up to the desk again, dragging his long arms and heavy knuckles. His head turned from side to side like a quick questioning monkey, then slower, like an Indian in a squat, waggling his head meaning yes-and-no. He picked a flea from behind an ear—is this a flea?—or is it the magic pole in its toothpick state that the King of the Monkeys keeps hidden behind his ear? He bit it. "Monkey see. Monkey do. What you do in fleaman's pok-mun?" She didn't answer him. He picked up loose papers with one hand and looked at them, scratched his genitals with the other hand, smelled hands and pages, nibbled the pages. " 'Black?' " he hatefully imitated her. " 'Jive.' " He let drop the papers, nudged one farther with his toe, and wiped his fingers on his moustache. "That bad, huh?" He lifted a page and turned it, examined it back and front. Upside down and sideways. " 'LeRoi Jones?!' " He recoiled from it, dropped it over the edge of the desk, and leaned way over to watch it fall. Keeping an eye on it, he picked up another sheet and sniffed it. "Too Black. If you can't say something nice, don't say anything at all. That's my motto." He wadded it up and threw it over his shoulder. He jumped on top of the trunk, scrunching and scattering the whole shit pile, then pounced on a page, and returned with it to the desk. "This is it! Here's one you'll like. That is, likee. Guarantee. Ah. I mean, aiya. 'Wokking on da Waywoad. Centing da dollahs buck home to why-foo and biby. No booty-full Ah-mei-li-can gal-low fo me. Aiya. Aiya.' " He wiped his eyes with the paper, crushed it, and pitched the wad at the window, which was shut. Sorting papers into two piles, he said, "Goot po-yum. Goot. Goot. No goot. No goot. Goot. No goot." He tasted one, grimaced. "No goot." Breaking character, he said, "Now, if I were speaking in a French accent, you would think it charming. Honk-honk-ho-onk." He did the Maurice Chevalier laugh, which isn't really a laugh, is it? He started new piles. "Angry po-yum." "Sad po-yum." "Goot and angry." "Angry." "Angry." "Imitation of Blacks." He threw some to the floor. "Angry too muchee. Sad. Angry sad. No goot. Angry no goot. Sad. Sad. Sad."

"Please don't freak out," Nanci requested, standing behind the chair.

"I am not freaking out," Wittman said. "I've got to tell you the real truth.

No lie. Listen, Lois. Underneath these glasses"—ripping the glasses off, wiping them on his sleeve, which he pulled out over his hand, so it looked like one hand was missing—"I am really: the present-day U.S.A. incarnation of the King of the Monkeys." He unbuttoned his blue chambray workshirt, which he wore on top of his black turtleneck. "Promise me you won't blab this all over the front page of the *Chron.* You'd like a scoop, I know, but I'm trusting you to keep our secret. For the sake of the world."

Now, if Nanci were the right girl for him, she would have said, "Dear monkey. Dear, dear old monkey. Poor monkey." She could scratch his head and under his chin, laugh at his antics, saying, "Poor dear monkey, what's to become of you?" and have him eating out of her hand. "Dear monkey. Poor poor monkey. You do have such an endearing Chinese giggle."

But who could be the right consoling girl for him? Nanci was getting into her jacket and finding her purse. How fucked up he is.

She hurried for the door, and got it open. She turned in the doorway, and said, "An actress says other people's words. I'm an actress; I know about saying other people's words. You scare me. A poet saying his own words. I don't like watching." She held up her hand, "Ciao," closed her fingers, and shut the door.

Alone, Wittman jumped off the table to the mattress, trampolined off that to the Gold Mountain trunk and onto the chair. Keep up the mood, not in liege to her. Elongating his chimp-like torso, he stretched for a look at himself in the built-in mirror on the door. He ruffled out his hair. Sao mang mang mang-key maw-lau. Skinny skinny monkey. "Bee-e-een!" he yelled, loud enough for her to hear. "Bee-e-een!" which is what Monkey yells when he changes. He whipped around and began to type like mad. Action. At work again.

And again whammed into the block question: Does he announce now that the author is—Chinese? Or, rather, Chinese-American? And be forced into autobiographical confession. Stop the music—I have to butt in and introduce myself and my race. "Dear reader, all these characters whom you've been identifying with—Bill, Brooke, and Annie—are Chinese—and *I* am too." The fiction is spoiled. You who read have been suckered along, identifying like hell, only to find out that you'd been getting a peculiar, colored, slanted p.o.v. "Call me Ishmael." See? You pictured a white guy, didn't you? If Ishmael were described—ochery ecru amber umber skin—you picture a *tan* white guy. Wittman wanted to spoil all those stories coming out of and set in New England Back East—to blacken and to yellow Bill, Brooke, and Annie. A new rule for the imagination: The common man has Chinese looks. From now on, whenever you read about those people with no surnames, color them with black skin or yellow skin. Wittman made an end run, evaded the block. By writing a play, he didn't need descriptions that racinated anybody. The actors will walk out on stage and their looks will be self-evident. They will speak dialects and accents, which the audience will get upon hearing. No need for an unreadable orthography such as Mark Twain's insultingly dumb dis and dat misspelling and apostrophying. Yes, the play's the thing.

It is ridiculous. Here I sit in my little room, I, Brigge, who have grown to be 28 years old and of whom no one knows. I sit here and am nothing. And nevertheless this nothing begins to think and think, five flights up, on a grey Parisian afternoon, these thoughts: . . .

A long time ago, before the blackbottom, a band of ancestors with talent left their music house, which was the largest hut in Ancient Wells, a place, and sailed a music boat a-roving the rivers of China. They beat the big drum hard, which vibrated in stomachs and diaphragms for miles around. An audience gathered on the riverbank, and saw the red swan boat come floating on strains of mandolin and flute. Between red wings, got up in the style of putting-on-a-show, rode the players. To the knocking of the wood fish drums—dok-dok-dok—the singer lifted his skylark voice over water and fields. He threw out ropes, and their audience pulled them to shore. Party time again. Let musicians rule. Play a—what kind of music?—how does it go?—and make the world spin in the palm of your hand.

Our Wittman is going to work on his play for the rest of the night. If you want to see whether he will get that play up, and how a poor monkey makes a living so he can afford to spend the weekday afternoon drinking coffee and hanging out, go on to the next chapter.

1987

SAMUEL R. DELANY
b. 1942

Samuel R. Delany was born in New York City and attended the City College there. He is the author of several short-story collections and more than thirty novels, including *The Jewels of Aptor* (1962), *Babel-17* (1966), *The Einstein Intersection* (1967), *Dhalgren* (1975), *Tales of Nevèrÿon* (1979), and *They Fly at Çiron* (1992). He has twice received a Nebula Award for best novel, and has also received a Hugo Award for best short story and a Pilgrim Award.

In an interview in *Alive and Writing: Interviews with American Authors of the 1980s* (1987), Delany said, "The aesthetic bias I share with a lot of others is that you can't propagandize directly in fiction. You have to present politics by indirection, by way of allegory—and complex allegory at that. You have to resort to figurative means. When you just break out and start preaching, however right your sermon might be, it's still propaganda and hence awkward art."

The following chapter is excerpted from *Neveryóna; or, The Tale of Signs and Cities* (1983), the second of four novels in the "Return to Nevèrÿon" series.

From Neveryóna

1. Of Dragons, Mountains, Transhumance, Sequence, and Sunken Cities, or: *The Violence of the Letter*

. . . the modality of novelistic enunciation is *inferential*: it is a process within which the subject of the novelistic utterance affirms a sequence, as *conclusion to the inference,* based on other sequences (referential—hence narrative, or textual—hence citational), which are the *premises of the inference* and, as such, considered to be true.

JULIA KRISTEVA, *Desire in Language*

She was fifteen and she flew.

Her name was pryn—because she knew something of writing but not of capital letters.

She shrieked at clouds, knees clutching scaly flanks, head flung forward. Another peak floated back under veined wings around whose flexing joints her knees bent.

The dragon turned a beaked head in air, jerking reins—vines pryn had twisted in a brown cord before making a bridle to string on the dragon's clay-colored muzzle. (Several times *un*twisted vines had broken—fortunately before take-off.) Shrieking and joyful, pryn looked up at clouds and down on streams, off toward returning lines of geese, at sheep crowding through a rocky rift between one green level and another. The dragon jerked her head, which meant the beast was reaching for her glide's height . . .

On the ground a bitter, old, energetic woman sat in her shack and mumbled over pondered insults and recalled slights, scratching in ash that had spilled from her fireplace with a stick. That bitter woman, pryn's great-aunt, had never flown a dragon, nor did she know her great-niece flew one now. What she had done, many years before, was to take into her home an itinerant, drunken barbarian, who'd come wandering through the town market. For nearly five months the soused old reprobate had slept on the young woman's hearth. When he was not sleeping or incoherent with drink, the two of them had talked; and talked; and talked; and taken long walks together, still talking; then gone back to the shack and talked more. Those talks, the older woman would have assured her great-niece, were as wonderful as any flight.

One of the things the barbarian had done was help her build a wooden rack on which stretched fibers might be woven together. She'd hoped to make some kind of useful covering. But the funny and fanciful notions, the tales and terrifying insights, the world lighted and shadowed by the analytic and synthetic richness the two of them could generate between them—that was the thing!

One evening the barbarian had up and wandered off again to another mountain hold—for no particular reason; nor was the aunt worried. They were the kind of friends who frequently went separate ways—for days, even weeks. But after a month rumor came back that, while out staggering about one winter's night, he'd fallen down a cliff, broken both legs, and died some time over the next three days from injury and exposure.

The rack had not worked right away.

The marshpool fluff that pryn's great-aunt had tried to stretch out was too weak to make real fabric, and the sheared fleece from the winter coats of mountain nannies and billies made a fuzzy stuff that was certainly warm but that tore with any violent body movement. Still, the aunt believed in the 'loom' (her word for it in that long-ago distant language) and in the barbarian, whose memory she defended against all vilification. For hadn't he also designed and supervised the construction of the fountains in the Vanar Hold, one of the three great houses around which fabled Ellamon had grown up? And hadn't the Suzerain of Vanar himself used to nod to him on the street when they'd passed, and hadn't the Suzerain even taken him into his house—for a while—as had she? While her friends in other shacks and huts and cottages felt sorry for the young woman so alone now with her memories, it occurred to the aunt, as she sat before her fireplace on a dim winter's afternoon, watching smoke spiral from the embers: Why not *twist* the fibers first before stringing them on the rack? The (also her word) 'thread' she twisted made a far smoother, stronger, and—finally!—functional fabric. And the loom, which had been a tolerated embarrassment among those friends to whom she was always showing it, was suddenly being rebuilt all over Ellamon. Women twisted. Women wove. Many women did nothing *but* twist thread for the weavers, who soon included men. That summer the aunt chipped two holes in a flat stone, wrapped the first few inches of twisted fibers through them, then set the stone to spin, helped on by a foot or a hand, thus using the torque to twist thread ten to twenty times as fast as you could with just your fingers. But with the invention of the spindle (not the aunt's word, but an amused neighbor's term for it), a strange thing happened. People began to suggest that neither she nor the long-dead barbarian were really the loom's inventors; and certainly she could not have thought up thread twisting by herself. And when it became known that there were other towns and other counties throughout Nevèrÿon where weaving and spinning had been going on for years—as it had, by now, been going on for years at fabled Ellamon—then all the aunt's claims to authorship became a kind of local joke. Even her invention of the spindle was suddenly suspect. And though he never claimed it for himself, the neighbor who'd named it was often credited with at least as much input into *that* discovery as the barbarian about whom the aunt was always going on must have had into the loom. For the barbarian turned out to have been quite a famous and fabled person all along, at least outside of Ellamon. And the spindle? Surely it was something she had seen somewhere. It was too useful, too simple, and just not the kind of thing you 'thought up' all alone. The aunt spun. The aunt wove. The aunt took in abandoned children, now of a younger cousin, now of a wayward niece, and, several years later, the grandson of a nephew. For wasn't her shack the warmest in the village? When she had made it, she had filled every chink of it with a mixture of oil and mud, into which she had blown hundreds and hundreds of small air bubbles through a hollow reed; it would hold both warm air and cool air for more than twenty-four hours. (She had told the barbarian—whose name had been Belham—about her insulation method that first day in the market; and wasn't that *why* he had consented to stay with her when the Suzerain of Vanar had put him out?) From all the looms of fabled Ellamon bolts of goats' wool and dogs' hair cloth and sheep wool rolled out, slower than smoke spiraling over winter embers. The great-aunt spoke little with her neighbors, loved her little cousins and great-nieces (and her great-nephew—seven years older than pryn—who had recently become a baker), and grew more bitter. What mountain pasturage there was about the High Hold was slowly given over to sheep, already prized for their thin but nourishing milk. (Sheep wool clearly made the strongest, warmest cloth. But that, alas, was not among the aunt's particular discoveries.) And more and more milkless, fleeceless dragons leapt from the pastures' ledges and cliffs, with their creaking honks, to tear their wings on treetops and brambles decently out of sight.

Because the slopes around Ellamon sported more rockweed than grass, the local shepherds never could raise the best sheep: Ellamon's fabrics were never particularly fabled.

Today pryn's great-aunt was over eighty.

The barbarian had slipped drunkenly down the cliff more than fifty years ago.

Bound to the sky by vines twisted the same way her great-aunt still twisted goats' fleece and marshpool fluff and dogs' hair into thread that bound that bitter, old, energetic woman to the earth, pryn flew!

Flying, she saw the crazily tilting mountains rise by her, the turning clouds above her, the rocking green, the green-licked rock. Somewhere below, sheep, bleating, wandered over another rocky rise. Wind rushed pryn's ears to catch in the cartilages and turn around in them, cackling like a maiden turning from her shuttle to laugh at a companion's scabrous joke. Air battered her eye sockets, as a wild girl pounds the wall of the room where she has been shut in by a mother terrified her child might, in her wildness, run loose and be taken by slavers. Air rushed pryn's toes; her toes flexed up, then curled in the joy, in the terror of flight. Wind looped coolly about pryn's arms, pushed cold palms against her kneecaps.

They glided.

And much of the space between pryn and the ground had gone.

She had launched from a ledge and, through common sense, had expected to land on one. How else to take off once more? Somehow, though, she'd assumed the dragon knew this too.

Trees a-slant the slope rose.

She pulled on the reins, hard. Wings flopped, fluttered, flapped behind her knees; pryn leaned back in wind, searching for ledges in the mountains that were now all around.

She glanced down to see the clearing—without a ledge any side! Treetops veered, neared.

That was where they were going to land . . . ? Leaves a-top a tall tree slapped her toes, stinging. She yanked vines. Dragon wings rose, which meant those green membranes between the long bones would not tear on the branches. But they were falling—no, still gliding. She swallowed air. The dragon tilted, beating back against her own flight—pryn rocked against the bony neck. Reins tight, she knuckled scales. Dragon muscle moved under her legs. A moment's floating, when she managed to push back and blink. And blinked again—

—because they jarred, stopping, on pebbles and scrub.

A lurch: the dragon stepped forward.

Another lurch: another step.

She pulled on the reins again. The slow creature lurched *another* step and . . . halted.

She craned to see the trees behind her. Above them, rock—

'Hello!'

The dragon took another step; pryn swung forward.

The woman, cross-legged across the clearing by the fireplace, uncrossed and pushed to one knee. 'Hello, there!' She stood, putting a hand on the provision cart's rail. 'That your dragon?' The ox bent to tear up ragged rockweed; the cart rumbled for inches. The rail slipped under the woman's palm.

Swinging her leg over the dragon's neck, pryn slid down scales, feeling her leather skirt roll up the backs of her thighs. On rough ground she landed on two feet and a fist—'Yes . . . !'—and came erect in time to duck the wing that opened, beat once, then folded. 'I mean—I *rode* it . . .'

The woman was middle-aged, some red left in her hair. Her face was sunburned and freckled.

With suspicion and curiosity, pryn blinked. Then, because she had flown, pryn laughed. It was the full, foaming laugh of a loud brown fifteen-year-old with bushy hair. It broke up fear, exploded curiosity, and seemed—to the woman, at any rate—to make the heavy, short girl one with the pine needles and shale chips and long, long clouds pulled sheer enough to see blue through.

That was why the woman laughed too.

The dragon swung her head, opened her beak, and hissed over stained, near-useless teeth, tiny in mottled gum.

The girl stepped up on a mossy rock. 'Who are you?'

'Norema the tale-teller,' the woman said. She put both hands in the pocket of her leggings and took a long step across the burnt-out fireplace. 'Who are you?'

'I am pryn, the . . . adventurer, pryn the warrior, pryn the thief!' said pryn, who had never stolen anything in her life other than a ground oaten cake from the lip of her cousin's baking oven three weeks before—she'd felt guilty for days!

'You're going to have trouble getting that dragon to take off again.'

The girl's face moved from leftover laugh to scowl. 'Don't I know it!'

The ox took another step. The cart's plank wheels made brief noises among themselves and on small stones. The ox blinked at the dragon, which stood now, one foreclaw raised.

Dragons sometimes stood like that a long time.

'You're not one of the regular dragon grooms—the little girls they keep in the corrals above Ellamon . . . ?'

The ox tore up more rockweed.

The girl shook her head. 'But I live in Ellamon—just outside Ellamon, actually. With my great-aunt. I've seen them, though, flying their dragons with their trainers and guards for the tourists who go out to the hill to watch. They're all bad girls, you know. Girls who've struck their mothers or disobeyed their fathers, stolen things, sometimes even killed people. They've been brought from all over Nevèrÿon—'

'. . . adventurers, warriors,' Norema suggested, 'thieves?'

The girl looked at the ground, turning her bare foot on sand. 'You're a foreigner. You probably don't know much about dragons, or the bad girls who ride them.'

'Oh,' Norema said, 'one hears fables. Also, I've been through this strange and . . . well, this strange land before. What were you doing on that dragon?'

'Flying,' pryn answered, then wondered if that sounded disingenuous. She bent to brush a dusty hand against a dusty knee. 'It's something I've always wanted to do. And I'm growing—everyone always tells me how much I'm growing. So I thought: soon I shall be too tall or too fat. I'd better do it now. The girls they use for riders up in the dragon corrals are half starved anyway, till they're thin as twigs. They're all twelve and thirteen years old—forever, it seems like.' She smoothed her overblouse down her waistless stomach. 'I'm short. But I'm not thin.'

'True,' Norema said, 'You're not. But you look strong. And I like your laugh.'

'I don't know how strong I am either,' pryn said, 'but I caught a wild dragon, bridled her, and led her to a ledge.'

'That seems strong enough.'

'You've been here before . . . ?' It sounded more suspicious than pryn meant. But suspicion was a habit of tongue picked up from her aunt more than a habit of mind; and, anyway, her laugh belied it. 'What are you doing here now?'

'Looking for a friend,' Norema said. 'A friend of mine. Years ago she used to be a guard at the dragon corrals and told me all about those . . . bad girls. My friend wore blue stone beads in her hair and a black rag mask across her eyes; and she killed with a double-bladed sword. We were companions and traveled together several years.'

'What happened to her?' pryn asked.

'Oh,' Norema said. 'I told her tales—long, marvelous, fascinating tales. Sometimes I wasn't sure if they were tales told to me when I was a child, or tales I'd made up. I told her tales, and after a while my masked friend grew more interested in the tales than she was in me. One night, sitting on her side of the campfire, cleaning her double blade, she told me she was going off the next morning to see if one particular tale I told were true. The next day when I woke, she and her bedroll were gone—along with her double-bladed sword. Nor was I worried. We were the kind of friends who frequently went separate ways—for days, even weeks. But weeks became months; and I did not run across my friend's campfire on the rim of the Menyat canyon, nor did I hear any word of her tramping along the northernmost Faltha escarpments, nor did I meet her taking shade in one of the Makalata caves at the rim of the western desert, nor did I hear rumor of her lean-to set up a mile further down the beach at Sarness.'

Squatting, pryn picked up a stick. 'So what did you do?' She scratched at spilled ash.

'I decided to take my cart and go look for her. I've looked many places; no doubt I'll look many more. But I've come to Ellamon because my friend once worked here and was happy.'

'Mmm,' pryn said, suspiciously.

The woman looked down to see what pryn had been scratching. ' "Pyre," ' she read. ' "Ynn." Pyre-ynn?'

' ". . . pryn",' pryn said. *'That* is my name. In writing.'

The woman stepped around the figures and squatted too. 'Here.' She took the stick and added a line above the two syllabics the girl had etched in ash. 'You, "pryn". *That's* your name. In writing. That line there means you squish the two sounds together into one. Otherwise you'll have people mispronouncing it every which way.'

In late sunlight pryn squinted at the woman. 'How do you know?'

'Actually—' the woman looked back at pryn with a moment's uncertainty—'because I invented it.'

The girl frowned. 'Invented what?'

'Writing. A long time ago. I must have been about your age—now I don't mean I invented *every* kind of writing. I just added the idea of making written signs stand for particular words, so you could *say* them. Till then, you know, written signs stood for animals, foods, amounts, tasks, instructions, ideas, even people, even *kinds* of people—whole complexes of notions. But written words—that's *my* innovation.'

'You did that?' The girl blinked.

The woman nodded. 'When I was a girl. I lived on an island—that's where I invented my system. I taught it to my island friends, many of whom were fishers and sailors. Years later, when I came to Nevèrÿon, I found my writing system had preceded me. With changes, of course. But most of the signs were quite recognizably the ones I had made up when I was a child.'

'Everyone says this kind of writing came across the sea from the Ulvayns.' Looking at the tall, middle-aged woman, pryn thought of her own, short, bitter aunt. 'You invented . . . my name?'

'Only the way to write it. Believe me, it comes in very handy if you're a tale-teller. But you know—' The woman was apparently not as comfortable squatting as pryn, so she put one leather legging's knee on the ground. She scratched the name again, this time above what pryn had written. '—I've made some changes in my system. About names, for instance. Today I always write a name with a slightly larger version of the initial sign; and I put a little squiggle down under it, like that—' She added another scratch. 'That way, if I'm reading it aloud, I can always glance ahead and see a name coming. You speak names differently from the way you speak other words. You mean them differently, too. The size of the initial sign stands for the way you speak it. The squiggle stands for what names mean that's different. So everything is indicated. These days, you have to indicate *every*thing, or nobody understands.'

The girl looked down at her name's new version, below and above the old one she herself had glyphed.

'Really, it's quite useful,' Norema went on. 'My friend, for example, was called Raven. Now there are ravens that caw and fly—much more efficiently than dragons. And there's my friend, Raven. Since she left, I find that now, more and more, both will enter my stories. The distinction marks a certain convenience, a sort of stability. Besides, I like distinguishing people from things in and of the land. It makes tale-telling make a lot more sense.'

The girl grinned at the woman. 'I like that!' She took the stick and traced the syllabics, first the larger with the mark beneath, then the smaller, and last the eliding diacritic.

She read it.

Then Pryn laughed again.

It was much the same laugh she had laughed when she'd dismounted; but it sounded richer—to Pryn, at any rate. Indeed, it sounded almost as rich and wild to Pryn as it had before to Norema—almost as though the mountain, with its foaming falls and piled needles and scattered shale chips (all named 'Pryn' by the signs now inscribed thrice on its ashy surface, twice with capitals, enclosing the miniscule version), had itself laughed.

And that *is* my name, Pryn thought. 'What tales did you tell?'

'Would you like to hear one?'

'Yes,' Pryn said.

'Well, then sit here. Oh, don't worry. It won't be that long.'

Pryn, feeling very differently about herself, sat.

Norema, who had taken the stick, stood, stepped from the fireplace, turned her back, and lowered her head, as though listening to leaves and dragon's breath and her ox's chewing and some stream's plashing just beyond the brush, as though they all were whispering to the tale-teller the story she was about to tell. Pryn listened too. Then Norema turned and announced, 'Once upon a time . . .' or its equivalent in that long-ago distant language. And Pryn jumped: the words interrupted that unheard flow of natural speech as sharply as a written sign found on a stretch of dust till then marred only by wind and rolling pebbles.

'Once upon a time there was a beautiful young queen—just about your age. Your height, too. And your size.'

'People say I'm clever, that I'm young, and that I'm growing,' Pryn said. 'They *don't* say I'm beautiful.'

'At this particular time,' Norema explained, 'young queens who looked like you were all thought to be ravishing. Standards of beauty change. And this happened many years back. Once upon—'

'Was your friend my age?'

Norema chuckled. 'No. She was closer to my age. But it's part of the story, you see, to say the queen was the age of the hearer. Believe me, I told it the same way to my friend.'

'Oh.'

'Once upon a time there was a beautiful queen, about your age and your size. Her name was Olin, and she was queen of all Nevèrÿon—at least she was supposed to be. Her empire extended from the desert to the mountains, from the jungles to the sea. Unfortunately, however, she had an unhappy childhood. Some evil priests shut Olin, her family, and her twenty-three servants in an old monastery on the Garth peninsula, practically from the time she was born until she was, well . . .' The woman questioned Pryn with narrowed eyes. 'Fifteen?'

Pryn nodded.

'When she was fifteen years old, for arcane political reasons, the evil priests decided to kill her outright. But they were afraid to do it themselves—for more political reasons, equally arcane. They couldn't get any of her family to do it, so they tried to hire her own servants, one after the other, all twenty-three. But the first servant was the queen's nurse, an old woman who loved the girl and came to her young mistress and told her what the priests intended.

' "What shall I do?" the queen cried.

' "You can be afraid," said the old servant. "But don't be terrified. That's first. You see, I have a plan, though it's a sad and sorrowful one. I've made a bargain with the preists, which they'll respect because they think me a great magician. I've told them I will betray you *if* they will pay me one gold piece. And I have also made them promise that if I fail, they will hire the next servant to do the same deed for *two* gold pieces—twice what they have paid me. And if that servant fails, they will hire the next one to do the deed for four gold pieces, twice again the amount paid the former. And if he fails, the next will be hired for twice the amount paid to the previous one. And so on." The old woman produced from the folds of her gown a single gold coin—and a knife. "Take my pay and hide it. Then take this knife—and strike me in the heart! For only my death will corroborate my failure."

' "*Kill* you?" demanded the queen.

' "It's the only way."

'The queen wept and cried and protested. "You are my beloved friend, my faithful bondswoman, and my dear nurse as well. You are closer to me than my own mother!" But the old woman put her arms around the girl and stroked her hair. "Let me explain some of the more arcane politics behind this whole nasty business. These are brutal and barbaric times, and it is either you or I—for even if I *do* kill you, the wicked priests plan to dispense with me as soon as I stab you. They cannot suffer the murderer of a queen to live, even the murderer of a queen they hate as much as they hate you. If you do what I say, you will have the gold coin as well as your life, whereas I shall lose *my* life in any case."

'And so, after more along the same lines, the queen took the coin, and the knife—which she thrust into her old nurse's heart.

'Not so many days later, a second servant came to Queen Olin. "Here are two gold coins and a rope with which I am to garrote you. Take the coins and hide them; then take the rope and strangle me—if you yourself would live. For *my* life is over in any case." Again the queen protested, but again the servant prevailed. So the young queen took the rope and strangled him. A few days later a third servant came with four gold pieces and a great rock to smash in the queen's head. After that a fourth came with eight gold pieces and a draught of corrosive poison. The fifth had sixteen gold pieces. The sixth had thirty-two coins. The next—'

Pryn suddenly laughed. 'But I've heard this story before! Or one just like it—only it was about grains of sand piled on the squares of a gaming board. I don't remember how many squares there were, but by the end, I remember, all the sand in the world was used up. Am I right about the ending? At the end of the twenty-three servants, she had all the money in the world . . . ?'

Norema smiled. 'She certainly had all the money in the monastery. And at that particular time, all the money in the monastery was pretty much all the money in Nevèrÿon.'

'That *is* an old story. I know, because I've heard it before. The version about the sand grains, that is.'

'That part of the story is old. But there are some new parts too. For example, after she had killed all her servants, the beautiful young queen felt very differently about herself.'

Pryn frowned. 'How do you mean?'

'Well,' Norema said, 'for one thing, in less than a year she had stabbed, strangled, bashed out the brains, poisoned, beheaded, and done even worse to twenty-two of her most faithful bondsmen and bondswomen, who were also the closest things she'd had to friends. After that she began to act very strangely and behave quite oddly. On and off, she behaved oddly the rest of her life—even for a queen. And in those days queens were expected to be eccentric. Often, after that, she was known as Mad Olin.'

'I thought you said there were twenty-*three* servants.'

'There were. But the last survived. He was not only a servant, but also her maternal uncle—though, alas, I can't remember his family name. And there're reasons to remember it, too, but for the life of me I can't recall what they are. Anyway. Years before, he had fallen on bad times and had indentured himself to the queen's mother, which was why he was with Olin in the first place. But he had always set himself apart. Along about the queen's murderings of the nineteenth, twentieth, and twenty-first servants—all particularly gruesome—the evil priests were, financially speaking, in rather bad shape. Olin was by then quite well off—though mentally she was a bit shaky. Her maternal uncle, who, like the first servant, was also something of a magician, had, with the help of the rest of the family, managed to engineer an escape for the queen. It took a good deal of the money; and Olin took the rest—to hide lest the wicked priests manage to trick it back, even as her first wise and faithful servant had tricked it from the priests.' Norema sighed. 'Raven and I once visited that monastery—it's still there today. And there are still priests—at least there were when we went. Now, I'm not sure. Anyway, you could certainly tell that the place had seen better times. Clearly they hadn't gotten their money back.'

'Are the priests still wicked?'

Reddish brows lowered. 'Well, I doubt if either my friend or I would ever stop there again—unless we absolutely had to.'

'What about Olin's escape?'

'Ah, the exciting part!' Norema said. 'Her uncle spirited her away from the monastery in the middle of the night, with the money in a caravan of six great wagons, each pulled by six horses. It was a lot of money, you see, and took more than one wagon to carry. Also, there was a lot more than gold coins in it by now—jewels and iron trinkets and all sorts of precious and semi-precious stones. The uncle took her to his family home, there in the south, and that evening he went with her up into a tall tower—at least that's how one version of the story goes. In another version, he took her up on a high rocky slope—'

'Shouldn't you choose one or the other for the sake of the telling?' Pryn asked.

'For the sake of the story,' Norema answered, 'I tell both and let my hearer make her choices.'

'Oh,' Pryn said.

'In the stone chamber at the tower top—or in the rocky cell at the top of the rocky slope—the uncle began to read her the sequence by which the gold coins had come to her: one, two, four, eight, sixteen, thirty-two, sixty-four, one hundred twenty-eight, two hundred fifty-six, five hundred twelve, one thousand twenty-four, two thousand forty-eight, four thousand ninety-six—'

'I *see* how fast it goes up!' Pryn exclaimed. 'That's just halfway through them, and it's already almost five thousand gold pieces. Two more, and it'll be over twenty thousand. Twenty thousand gold pieces must be close to all the money in the world!'

'That's what you see.' Norema smiled. 'What the young queen saw, however, was a city.'

Pryn blinked.

Norema said: 'The queen blinked.'

'What city?' Pryn asked. 'Where did she see it?'

'Precisely what the queen wondered too—for she blinked again . . . It was gone! Through the stone columns at the stone rail, the queen looked down from the tower—or down to the foot of the slope—and saw only some marshy water, an open inlet, rippling out between the hills to the sea. But the queen *had* seen a city, there among the ripples, as clearly as she now saw the hills on either side of the inlet, or, indeed, as clearly as she saw the swampy growths that splotched the waters where they came in to the land. When she told her uncle what she had seen, immediately he stopped reading the numbers and showed her all sorts of magic wonders, including a circle full of different stars, which he gave her to keep. Then he took her down from the tower—or down from the rocks—to a great dinner that had been prepared for her, where they talked of more magic things. Then he did something terrible.'

'What?' Pryn asked. 'So far, this story sounds more confusing than exciting.'

'To the proper hearer,' Norema said, 'precisely what seems confusing will *be* the exciting part. When the queen came back from a stroll in the garden between courses, the uncle gave her a goblet of poison, which she, unknowing, drank.'

Norema was silent a long time.

Finally Pryn asked: 'Was that the end of the queen? I'm sure her uncle probably wanted the money for himself. This doesn't sound like a real story to me. What about the "circle of different stars?" I don't even know what that is! I mean, it doesn't *seem* like a story, because it . . . doesn't really end.'

'It certainly doesn't end there,' Norema said. 'It goes on for quite a while, yet. But that always seemed to me an exciting place for a pause.'

'What *did* happen, then?'

'See, you *are* caught up in the excitement, the action, the suspense! You want to know the outcome—I think it's very important to alert your listeners to the progress of their own reactions. I can foresee a time, after lots more tales have been told, when that won't be necessary. But for now it's a must. Well, the poison *didn't* kill the queen. It put her in a trance—and when she woke, if indeed she wasn't dreaming, she was on a rocky ledge. It was night, and as she pushed herself up on her hands and looked around, she saw she was lying between two white stones, one taller than the other—now here, again, there's another version that says the queen woke up in a boat which sailed in to a strange shore that morning, and on the shore she found the white stones—one higher than the other; at noon on the longest day of summer, this version says, one stone casts a shadow three times as long as—'

'But in this version—' Pryn tried to blot the image of sun and glaring sand that had itself blotted her image of darkness, full moon, and cool air—'it was night?'

'Yes,' Norema said. 'And the full moon was up.'

Pryn started to ask, *But how did you know?*, then decided that if she were going to hear the end, she'd best stop interrupting. Besides, it was the teller's tale; the teller ought to know what happened in it, for all her multiple versions.

'The remaining money was in huge piles beside the queen, in heaps and bags and bundles, and the circle of different stars lay on the rock near her knee. Down the ledge from her, the water was covered with fog. The moon looked ghastly, a yellow disk hanging over a fuming inlet. Water flickered beneath mists. Olin sat on the rock, hugging her knees in the chill light, biting her inner lip, her chin on her kneecaps. A bird woke up and screeched! The queen looked to see green wings starting from the branches of a pecan tree. She got to her feet unsteadily, still groggy from the poison. She stood on the ledge and cried out across the waters, just as if someone had told her what to say (though none of the versions I know says who): "I am Olin, and I have come to warn the Worm of the Sea of the Northern Eagle's evil gaze!" Then she took a step back and put her wrist up to her mouth as if she were afraid she had said something blasphemous. She stepped to the ledge's edge again and looked down toward the foggy water. The mists were a-broil, and now and again splashes geysered up hot silver.

'There was a rumbling, as of some vast engine, not only from the water, but from the ground. Trees trembled; small stones shook loose to roll down into fog. Below swirling fumes waves swirled even faster.

'Water surged, now into the land, now away. At each surge away, water lowered; and lowered.

'Olin saw the first broken building tops cleave mist and waves—three towers and a bridge between, dripping. Waves broke higher than fog; foam fell back, roaring, into the sea. More buildings emerged. Water poured from their roofs. Through fog, water erupted from stone windows. Fog rolled and roiled off. Green and white water lapped away through mud and weeds and clotted alleys. Water rushed from a street where pillars still stood. Water carried weed and mud from patterned blue flags; other pillars were broken. One lay across its square pedestal. At the same time she saw the cleared street, she saw other avenues still silted, dark, and wet. Shapes that might have been buildings were mounded over with mud, glistening, black, and green. To the earth's rumblings and the water's ragings, the city rose.

'The young queen, half running, half falling down the slope, only just managed to get her feet under her—when she plunged shin deep in muck. She staggered on, arms flailing, till she reached the first cracked paving—nowhere near as clean as it had looked from the ledge. Mud clung to the walls beside her. Weeds in windows hung down dripping stones. Fallen masonry, scattered shells, and soaked branches made her progress by the carved pillars almost as slow as it had been in the mud. Dirty-footed, wet-handed, scratches on her shoulders and legs, the young queen pushed between stones and driftwood, making her way by broken walls, their carvings veiled in sea moss.

'What movement down what alley made her stop, the queen was never sure. Off in the wet green filling another street, something dark as excrement flexed, shifted, slid. The building beside her was heaped over with runnelled mud. That moved too, quivered, rose—not mud at all, but some immense tarpaulin. The sheet shook itself loose.

'Olin looked up.

'The moon lit yellow fogs which shifted over roofs. Through them, over them, the wing rose—not a soft, feathered, birdlike wing, but a taut, spined, reptilian wing, sheer enough to let moonlight through its skin, here and there darkened by spine or vein.

'That wing blotted a fifth the sky!

'Wind touched the queen's cheek, her wrist. A second wing, as huge, rose from where it had lain over buildings at the street's far side. Ahead, beyond the pillars, something slid forward, pulled back.

'To the extent she had seen it at all, she'd thought it was a toppled carving, a sculpted demon's head, big as a house and fallen on its chin. A gold and black eye opened; and opened; and opened, wider than the wide moon. Then, perhaps fifteen feet away, from under a rising lid, the other eye appeared. A lip lifted from teeth longer and thicker than the queen's legs. The head, still wet, rose on its thick neck, clearing the near roofs, rising over the towers, spiring between the wings.

'The dragon—a giant dragon, a sea dragon many times the size of her mountain cousins—was coiled through the streets. She'd slept with the city beneath the water. But now, as the city rose, the dragon rose above it, to stare down at the young queen with black and gold eyes.

'Again Olin cried out, loud enough to hurt her throat: "Oh great Gauine—" for that was the dragon's name, though I don't know where she learned it—"I have come to hide my treasure with you and warn you of the Eagle's antics—" '

Squinting silvery eyes in the sun, the ordinary mountain dragon just then put her foot down and hissed at the ox; the ox shied, backing up five steps. The cart trundled and creaked. Norema turned to grab it.

Pryn pushed up to her feet and snatched at the dragon's swinging reins. Green wings flapped futilely.

Norema calmed her ox. Pryn led her dragon to a tree and lashed it. Norema came over to give her a hand, then walked with Pryn back to the fireplace. Pryn rubbed her hands together. Her palms were sore where the reins, first in landing, then in tethering, had jerked through. 'The story you were telling?' Pryn asked. 'What happened next?'

'Not much,' Norema said. 'Using the magic circle of different stars as a guide, Olin and Gauine hid the money in the city. Then Gauine settled down on top of it to guard it—just in time, too. For water began to roll back through the streets. Once more the city began to sink. The queen clambered up the slope to the ledge, barely managing to escape drowning. And the moon was down.'

Pryn frowned.

'Oh, Gauine was a very exceptional dragon,' Norema explained.

They stopped by the cart; the ox nipped more weed.

'But then, if she hadn't been,' Norema went on, 'I doubt the queen would have entrusted the treasure into her keeping. The next day, wandering half dazed along the beach, Olin was found by a troop of traveling mummers. Fortunately, over the night she'd been gone, the rest of her relatives had managed to defeat the evil priests. The young queen was taken to Kolhari, capital of all Nevèrÿon, where she was crowned queen for real. From all reports, she was never popular and led a horrid life. She went through several kings and a number of children, most of whom ended up frightfully. But she managed to make several arcane political decisions which have always been considered praiseworthy, at least by people who count such things important.'

'Queen Olin,' Pryn mused. 'I've heard other stories about her, here in Ellamon. She was the queen who set up the dragon corrals and decided that bad little girls would be condemned to work there.'

'One of the more interesting fables,' Norema said. 'Well, she was always fond of the animal, since it was a giant sea dragon that guarded her sunken treasure on which her power rested.'

'That was the story your friend set out to find was true or not?'

Norema nodded.

'She wanted to find Mad Queen Olin's treasure in the sunken city guarded by the dragon Gauine?'

'That's what she said.'

Suddenly Pryn turned around and looked off at her own winged mount swaying at its tree. 'Brainless, stupid beast! I thought I'd fly you away from home to excitement and adventure—or at least to a ledge from which I could return. But here—' she turned back to Norema— 'she has landed in this silly clearing and can't take off again!'

'You want to leave home for good,' Norema said seriously.

'Yes,' Pryn said. 'And *don't* tell me not to!'

'You aren't afraid of slavers?'

Pryn shook her head. 'You're traveling alone, and *you're* still a free woman.'

'True,' Norema said. 'And I intend to stay one.' She considered a moment. 'Let me give you two more gifts—besides my tale.'

Pryn looked perplexed. She hadn't thought much of the story. It had stopped and started, leaving her anxious and expectant precisely where she had wanted answers and explanations.

'You can be frightened,' Norema said. 'But don't be terrified. That's first.'

'I'm *not* terrified,' Pryn said.

'I know,' Norema said. 'But that's the way with advice. The part you can accept is the part you always already know.'

'I'm not afraid either,' Pryn said. Then she frowned again. 'No, I *am* afraid. But it doesn't matter, because I made my mind up to it a long time ago.'

'Good.' Norema smiled. 'I wasn't going to argue. One of my gifts, then, is a packet of food; that I'll give you out of my provisions cart. The other is some geographical information about the real world over which you've just so cavalierly flown—both are things one cannot trust tales to provide. Oh, yes, and another piece of advice: Untie your dragon and let her wander into the mountains where she belongs. Left to herself, she'll find the ledges she needs, as you must too—but you can't be tied down with dragons that won't fly where you want to go, no matter how much fun the notion of flight. Through those trees, maybe a hundred yards on, you'll find the junction of two roads, giving you a choice of four directions. The one going—' Norema glanced at the sun— 'toward the sunset will take you, with three days' walk, to a white desert with dangerous tribes who sew copper wire up the rims of their ears. Take the road leading in the opposite direction, down between the mountain hills, and with four days' walk you'll reach the coast and a brave village of rough-handed men and women who live from the sea. Take the road running to your right as you approach the crossroads, and you'll be back at the High Hold of fabled Ellamon in no more than three hours. Take the path that runs away from the junction to your left, and seven days' hike will finally bring you to the grand port of Kolhari, capital city of all Nevèrÿon—like in my story.' Norema smiled. (That so famous city had not played much of a part in the tale, Pryn thought; though certainly she knew enough of Kolhari by other reports.) 'Along with my tale, I think my gifts should stand a young woman like you, off to see the world, in good stead.'

'Thank you,' Pryn said, because her aunt, for all her bitterness, had taught her to be polite.

Some hours later, when Pryn was several miles along her chosen route, she stopped a minute. Of all the day's marvels it was neither her own flight, nor the tale of the dragon and the sunken city, nor the food pack tied on her back—with twisted vines—which held her thoughts. She picked up a stick from the highway's shoulder and scratched her name in its dust, new capital and eliding mark. She put the stick down. Again she read over her name, which seemed so new and wondrous and right.

Then she walked on.

An hour later a dead branch, blown out on the road by a mountain gust, obscured it beyond reading.

1983

ROSARIO FERRÉ
b. 1942

Rosario Ferré was born in Ponce, Puerto Rico, and received her Ph.D. at the University of Maryland. She is the founder and director of *Zona de carga y descarga,* a Latin American journal devoted to new Puerto Rican literature. Her books include *Papeles de Pandora* (1976) and its English translation, *The Youngest Doll* (1991); *Sweet Diamond Dust* (1988); and *House on the Lagoon* (1995).

Growing up in Puerto Rico, she attended the School of the Sacred Heart, where she was instructed "that women were hidden from view and should never appear in public." In her essay "The Writer's Kitchen" (1988), Ferré claims that imagination is "irreverence towards the establishment," that it is "always subversive." Many of her stories culminate in death, she said in *Interviews with Latin American Writers* (1989), because "that feeling of violence is an expression of the current situation in Puerto Rico, which has one of the highest crime rates anywhere in the world."

Ferré does not write directly in English, but has translated her work into English after completing it in Spanish. "The word is extremely important. As a writer, it is my means for self-definition, the tool to express my idiosyncracies, my personality. I write . . . because I want to know how I think."

"Characters have a life of their own—it is not that they fight against me, but rather that they do what they want," she said in the 1989 interview. "I very much believe in the influence of magic and the subconscious on the literary process."

The Youngest Doll

Early in the morning the maiden aunt had taken her rocking chair out onto the porch facing the canefields, as she always did whenever she woke up with the urge to make a doll. As a young woman, she had often bathed in the river, but one day when the heavy rains had fed the dragontail current, she had a soft feeling of melting snow in the marrow of her bones. With her head nestled among the black rock's reverberations she could hear the slamming of salty foam on the beach mingled with the sound of the waves, and she suddenly thought that her hair had poured out to sea at last. At that very moment, she felt a sharp bite in her calf. Screaming, she was pulled out of the water, and, writhing in pain, was taken home in a stretcher.

The doctor who examined her assured her it was nothing, that she had probably been bitten by an angry river prawn. But the days passed and the scab would not heal. A month later, the doctor concluded that the prawn had worked its way into the soft flesh of her calf and had nestled there to grow. He prescribed a mustard plaster so that the heat would force it out. The aunt spent a whole week with her leg covered with mustard from thigh to ankle, but when the treatment was over, they found that the ulcer had grown even larger and that it was covered with a slimy, stonelike substance that couldn't be removed without endangering the whole leg. She then resigned herself to living with the prawn permanently curled up in her calf.

She had been very beautiful, but the prawn hidden under the long, gauzy folds of her skirt stripped her of all vanity. She locked herself up in her house, refusing to see any suitors. At first she devoted herself entirely to bringing up her sister's children, dragging her monstrous leg around the house quite nimbly. In those days, the family was nearly ruined; they lived surrounded by a past that was breaking up around them with the same impassive musicality with which the crystal chandelier crumbled on the frayed embroidered linen cloth of the dining-room table. Her nieces adored her. She would comb their hair, bathe and feed them, and when she read them stories, they would sit around her and furtively lift the starched ruffle of her skirt so as to sniff the aroma of ripe sweetsop that oozed from her leg when it was at rest.

As the girls grew up, the aunt devoted herself to making dolls for them to play with. At first they were just plain dolls, with cottony stuffing from the gourd tree in the garden and stray buttons sewn on for eyes. As time passed, though, she began to refine her craft more and more, thus earning the respect and admiration of the whole family. The birth of a new doll was always cause for a ritual celebration, which explains why it never occurred to the aunt to sell them for a profit, even when the girls had grown up and the family was beginning to fall into need. The aunt continued to increase the size of the dolls so that their height and other measurements conformed to those of each of the girls. There were nine of them, and the aunt would make one doll for each per year, so it became necessary to set aside a room for the dolls alone in the house. When the eldest girl turned eighteen, there were one hundred and twenty-six dolls of all ages in the room. Opening the door gave you the impression of entering a dovecote, or the ballroom in the czarina's palace, or a warehouse in which someone had spread out a row of tobacco leaves to dry. But the aunt didn't enter the room for any of these pleasures. Instead, she would unlatch the door and gently pick up each doll, murmuring a lullaby as she rocked it: "This is how you were when you were a year old, this is you at two, and like this at three," measuring out each year of their lives against the hollow they had left in her arms.

The day the eldest turned ten, the aunt sat down in her rocking chair facing the canefields and hardly ever got up again. She would rock away entire days on the porch, watching the patterns of rain shift like watercolor over the canefields, and coming out of her stupor only when the doctor would pay her a visit, or she awoke with the desire to make a doll. Then she would call out so that everyone in the house would come and help her. On that day, one could see the hired help making repeated trips to town like cheerful Inca messengers, bringing wax, porcelain clay, needles, spools of thread of every shade and color. While these preparations were taking place, the aunt would call the niece she had dreamt about the night before into her bedroom and take her measurements. Then she would make a wax mask of the child's face, covering it with plaster on both sides, like a living face sheathed in two dead ones. Then she would draw out an endless flaxen thread of melted wax through a pinpoint on her chin. The porcelain of the hands and face was always translucent; it had an ivory tint to it that formed a great contrast with the curdled whiteness of the bisque faces. For the body, the aunt would always send out to the garden for twenty glossy gourds. She would hold them in one hand and, with an expert twist of her knife, would slice them up and lean them against the railing of the balcony, so that the sun and wind would dry the cottony guano brains out. After a few days, she would scrape off the dried fluff with a teaspoon and, with infinite patience, feed it into the doll's mouth.

The only items the aunt would agree to use in the birth of a doll that were not made by her with whatever materials came to her from the land, were the glass eyeballs. They were mailed to her directly from Europe in all colors, but the aunt considered them useless until she had left them submerged at the bottom of the stream for a few days, so that they would learn to recognize the slightest stirring of the prawn's antennae. Only then would she carefully rinse them in ammonia water and place them, glossy as gems and nestled in a bed of cotton, at the bottom of one of her Dutch cookie tins. The dolls were always outfitted in the same way, even though the girls were growing up. She would dress the younger ones in Swiss embroidery and the older ones in silk guipure, and on each of their heads she would tie the same bow, wide and white and trembling like the breast of a dove.

The girls began to marry and leave home. On their wedding day, the aunt would give each of them their last doll, kissing them on the forehead and telling them with a smile, "Here is your Easter Sunday." She would reassure the grooms by explaining to them that the doll was merely a sentimental ornament, of the kind that people used to place on the lid of grand pianos in the old days. From the porch, the aunt would watch the girls walk down the fanlike staircase for the last time. They would carry a modest checkered cardboard suitcase in one hand, the other hand slipped around the waist of the exuberant doll made in their image and likeness, still wearing the same old-fashioned kid slippers and gloves, and with Valenciennes bloomers barely showing under their snowy, embroidered skirts. But the hands and faces of these new dolls looked less transparent than those of the old: they had the consistency of skim milk. This difference concealed a more subtle one: the wedding doll was never stuffed with cotton but was filled with honey.

All the girls had married, and only the youngest niece was left at home when the doctor paid his monthly visit to the aunt, bringing his son along this time, who had just returned from studying medicine up north. The young man lifted the starched ruffle of the aunt's skirt and looked intently at the huge ulcer which oozed a perfumed sperm from the tip of its greenish scales. He pulled out his stethoscope and listened to it carefully. The aunt thought he was listening for the prawn's breathing, to see if it was still alive, and so she fondly lifted his hand and placed it on the spot where he could feel the constant movement of the creature's antennae. The young man released the ruffle and looked fixedly at his father. "You could have cured this from the start," he told him. "That's true," his father answered, "but I just wanted you to come and see the prawn that has been paying for your education these twenty years."

From then on it was the young doctor who visited the old aunt every month. His interest in the youngest niece was evident from the start, so that the aunt was able to begin her last doll in plenty of time. He would always show up for the visit wearing a pair of brightly polished shoes, a starched collar, and an ostentatious tiepin of extravagant poor taste. After examining the aunt he would sit in the parlor, leaning his paper silhouette against the oval frame of the chair, and each time would hand the youngest an identical bouquet of purple forget-me-nots. She would offer him ginger cookies and would hold the bouquet with the tip of her fingers, as if she were holding a purple sea urchin turned inside out. She made up her mind to marry him because she was intrigued by his drowsy profile, and also because she was deathly curious to find out what dolphin flesh was like.

On her wedding day, as she was about to leave the house, the youngest was surprised to find that the doll the aunt had given her as a wedding present was warm. As she slipped her arm around her waist, she examined her attentively, but quickly forgot about it, so amazed was she at the excellence of the craft. The doll's face and hands were made of the most delicate Mikado porcelain, and in her half-open and slightly sad smile she recognized her full set of baby teeth. There was also another notable detail: the aunt had embedded her diamond eardrops in the doll's pupils.

The young doctor took off to live in town, in a square house that made one think of a cement block. Each day he made his wife sit out on the balcony, so that passersby would be sure to see that he had married into society. Motionless inside her cubicle of heat, the youngest began to suspect that it wasn't just her husband's silhouette that was made of paper, but his soul as well. Her suspicions were soon confirmed. One day he pried out the doll's eyes with the tip of his scalpel and pawned them for a fancy gold pocket watch with a long, embossed chain. From then on the doll remained seated as always on the lid of the grand piano, but with her gaze modestly lowered.

A few months later the doctor noticed the doll was missing from her usual place and asked the youngest what she'd done with it. A sisterhood of pious ladies had offered him a healthy sum for the porcelain hands and face, which they thought would be perfect for the image of the Veronica in the next Lenten procession. The youngest answered him that the ants had at last discovered the doll was filled with honey and, streaming over the piano, had devoured it in a single night. "Since the hands and face were made of Mikado porcelain and were as delicate as sugar," she said, "the ants have probably taken them to some underground burrow and at this very moment are probably wearing down their teeth, gnawing furiously at fingers and eyelids to no avail." That night the doctor dug up all the ground around the house, but could not find the doll.

As the years passed the doctor became a millionaire. He had slowly acquired the whole town as his clientele, people who didn't mind paying exorbitant fees in order to see a genuine member of the extinct sugarcane aristocracy up close. The youngest went on sitting in her chair out on the balcony, motionless in her muslin and lace, and always with lowered eyelids. Whenever her husband's patients, draped in necklaces and feathers and carrying elaborate handbags and canes, would sit beside her, perhaps coughing or sneezing, or shaking their doleful rolls of flesh with a jingling of coins, they would notice a strange scent that would involuntarily make them think of a slowly oozing sweetsop. They would then feel an uncontrollable urge to rub their hands together as if they were paws.

There was only one thing missing from the doctor's otherwise-perfect happiness. He noticed that, although he was aging naturally, the youngest still kept the same firm, porcelained skin she had had, when he had called on her at the big house on the plantation. One night he decided to go into her bedroom, to watch her as she slept. He noticed that her chest wasn't moving. He gently placed his stethoscope over her heart and heard a distant swish of water. Then the doll lifted up her eyelids, and out of the empty sockets of her eyes came the frenzied antennae of all those prawns.

Translated by Rosario Ferré and Diana Vélez
1991

MARILYNNE ROBINSON
b. 1944

Born in Sandpoint, Idaho, Marilynne Robinson was educated at Brown University and the University of Washington, where she received a Ph.D. Her first book of fiction, *Housekeeping* (1980), received the Ernest Hemingway Foundation Award for best first novel from PEN American Center, and the Richard and Hinda Rosenthal Award from the American Academy and Institute of Arts and Letters. In 1989, Robinson published a book of nonfiction entitled *Mother Country*. Currently, she is on the permanent faculty at the University of Iowa Writers' Workshop, where she is working on a new novel.

"It's very hard for me to describe how I think about *Housekeeping* in terms of gender," Robinson noted in a 1993 Iowa Writers' Workshop newsletter interview. "One reason all the characters are female is because I think of them as being intrinsically one character, which is female. One of the reasons those characters, or that character, is female is because I was writing about a Western landscape, which people from the outside have always imagined as being deeply masculine in its essence. I didn't experience it that way at all, growing up there. If you were to evoke the emotional tenor of that landscape it would be female, not male." As to whether she enjoyed writing fiction or nonfiction more, she responded: "Well, fiction is much more interesting to write. In writing nonfiction you defer to certain constraints. You are dependent on what you can believe."

From Housekeeping

From *Chapter 8*

Sylvie made up a lunch that night after supper and we set the alarm clock for five and went to sleep early, with our clothes on. Nevertheless, Sylvie had to tease me awake. She pinched my cheek and pulled my ear. Then she set my feet on the floor and pulled me up by the hands. I sat down on the bed again and fell over onto the pillow, and she laughed. "Get up!"

"In a minute."

"Now! Breakfast is ready!"

I crouched on the covers, hoarding warmth and sleep, while they passed off me like a mist. "Wake up, wake up, wake up," Sylvie said. She picked up my hand, patted it, toyed with my fingers. When I was no longer warm enough or quite asleep, I sat up. "Good girl," Sylvie said. The room was dark. When Sylvie put the light on, it still seemed sullen and full of sleep. There were cries of birds, sharp and rudimentary, that stung like sparks or hail. And even in the house I could smell how raw the wind was. That sort of wind brought out a musk in the fir trees and spread the cold breath of the lake everywhere. There was nothing out there—no smell of wood smoke or oatmeal—to hint at human comfort, and when I went outside I would be miserable. It was almost November and long before dawn, and I did not want to leave my bed.

"Come, Ruthie," Sylvie said, and pulled me by both hands toward the door.

"My shoes," I said. She stopped, still holding my hands, and I stepped into them, but she did not wait for me to tie the laces.

"Come on, come on. Down the stairs, now."

"Do we have to hurry?"

"Yes. Yes. We have to hurry." She opened the trapdoor and went down the stairs ahead of me, still pulling me by one hand. In the kitchen she stopped to scoop an egg out of the frying pan and set it on a piece of bread. "There's your breakfast," she said. "You can eat it while we walk."

"I have to tie my shoes," I said to her back as she walked out to the porch. "Wait!" but the screen door slammed behind her. I tied my shoes and found my coat and pulled it on, and ran out the door after her.

The grass was blue with frost. The road was so cold it rang as I stepped on it, and the houses and trees and sky were one flat black. A bird sang with a sound like someone scraping a pot, and was silent. I had given up all sensation to the discomforts of cold and haste and hunger, and crouched far inside myself, still sleeping. Finally, Sylvie was in front of me, and I put my hands in my pockets, and tilted my head, and strode, as she did, and it was as if I were her shadow, and moved after her only because she moved and not because I willed this pace, this pocketing of the hands, this tilt of the head. Following her required neither will nor effort. I did it in my sleep.

I walked after Sylvie down the shore, all at peace, and at ease, and I thought, We are the same. She could as well be my mother. I crouched and slept in her very shape like an unborn child.

"Wait here," Sylvie said when we came to the shore. She walked down to a place where trees grew near the water. After a few minutes she came back. "The boat is not where I left it!" she said. "Well, we'll have to look for it. I'll find it. Sometimes it takes a while, but I always find it." She climbed up onto a rock that stood out from the hillside, almost to the water, and looked up and down the shore. "I'll bet it's over there." She climbed down from the rock and began walking south. "See those trees? I found it once before, in a place just like that, all covered with branches."

"Someone was trying to hide it," I suggested.

"Can you imagine? I always put it right back where I find it. I don't care if someone else uses it. You know, so long as they don't damage it."

We walked down to where a stand of birch and aspen trees sheltered a little inlet. "This would be a perfect place for it," Sylvie said, but it was not there. "Don't be discouraged," she said. "We're so early. No one could have got to it first. Wait." She walked up into the woods. Behind a fallen log, and behind a clump of fat, low-growing pines, was a heap of pine boughs with poplar branches and brown needles and leaves. Here and there an edge or a corner of tarpaulin showed. "Look at that," Sylvie said. "Someone went to a lot of trouble." She kicked away the branches until on one side the tarpaulin and the shape of the rowboat were exposed. Then she lifted the side of the boat until it fell over upright on the heap of branches. She pulled at the tarpaulin that had been spread under the boat until she found the oars. She stuck them under the seat. The boat made a thick, warm sound as we pushed it through the pine needles. It scraped dully across some big rocks, then dragged through the sand. We pushed it into the water. "Get in," Sylvie said. "Hurry." I climbed in and sat down on a narrow, splintery plank, facing the shore. "There's a man yelling at us," I said.

"Oh, I know!" Sylvie pushed the boat out in two long strides, and then, with a hand on each gunwale, half leaped and half pulled herself into it. The boat wallowed alarmingly. "I have to sit in that seat," she said. She stood up and turned around and stooped to hold the gunwales, and I crawled under her body and out between her legs. A stone splashed the water inches from my face, and another rattled into the bottom of the boat. Sylvie swung an oar over my head, settled it into the lock, crouched, and pulled us strongly away from the shore. A stone flew past my arm. I looked back and saw a burly man in knee boots and black pants and a red plaid jacket. I could see that he was wearing one of those shapeless felt hats that fishermen there decorate with preposterous small gleams and plumes and violent hooks. His voice was full of rage. "Just ignore him," Sylvie said. She pulled again, and we were beyond reach. The man had followed us into the water until he was up to his boot tops in it. "Lady!" he bawled. "Ignore him," Sylvie said. "He always acts like that. If he thinks someone's watching him, he just carries on more."

I turned around and watched Sylvie. Her handling of the boat was strong and easy. When we were about one hundred yards from the shore she turned the boat toward the north. The man, now back on the beach, was still yelling and dancing his wrath and pitching stones after us. "It's pitiful," Sylvie said. "He's going to have a heart attack someday."

"It must be his boat," I suggested.

Sylvie shrugged. "Or he might just be some sort of lunatic," she said. "I'm certainly not going to go back and find out." She was unperturbed by our bare escape and by her drenched loafers and the soggy skirts of her coat. I found myself wondering if this was why she came home with fish in her pockets.

"Aren't you cold, Sylvie?"

"The sun's coming up," she said. The sky above Fingerbone was a floral yellow. A few spindled clouds smoldered and glowed a most unfiery pink. And then the sun flung a long shaft over the mountain, and another, like a long-legged insect bracing itself out of its chrysalis, and then it showed above the black crest, bristly and red and improbable. In an hour it would be the ordinary sun, spreading modest and impersonal light on an ordinary world, and that thought relieved me. Sylvie continued to pull, strongly and slowly.

"You wouldn't believe how many people live out here on the islands and up in the hills," Sylvie said. "I bet there are a hundred. Or more. Sometimes you'll see a little smoke in the woods. There might be a cabin there with ten children in it."

"They just hunt and fish?"

"Mostly."

"Have you ever seen any of them?"

"I think I have," Sylvie said. "Sometimes if I think I see smoke I go walking toward it, and now and then I'm sure there are children around me. I can practically hear them."

"Oh."

"That's one reason I keep crackers in my pockets."

"I see."

Sylvie rowed on through the gilded water, smiling to herself.

"I'll tell you something. You'll probably think I'm crazy. I tried to catch one once." She laughed. "Not, you know, trap it, but lure it out with marshmallows so I could see it. What would I do with another child?"

"So you did see someone."

"I just stuck marshmallows on the twigs of one of the apple trees, almost every day for a couple of weeks. Then I sat sort of out of sight—there's still a doorstep there with lilacs growing on both sides of it. The house itself fell into the cellar hole years ago, of course. I just sat there and waited, but it never came. I was a little bit relieved," she said. "A child like that might claw or bite. But I did want to look at it."

"This was at the place we're going to now."

Sylvie smiled and nodded. "Now you're in on my secret. Maybe you'll have better luck. And at least we don't have to hurry. It was so hard to get home in time for you and Lucille."

Sylvie pulled and then pulled, and we slid heavily through the slosh and jostle of the water. Sylvie looked at the sky and said no more. I peered over the side now and then, into the murky transparencies of the upper waters, which were clouded and crude as agate. I saw gulls' feathers and the black shapes of fish. The fragmented image of jonquil sky spilled from top to top of the rounding waves as the shine spills on silk, and gulls sailed up into the very height of the sky, still stark white when they could just be seen. To the east the mountains were eclipsed. To the west they stood in balmy light. Dawn and its excesses always reminded me of heaven, a place where I have always known I would not be comfortable. They reminded me of my grandfather's paintings, which I have always taken to be his vision of heaven. And it was he who brought us here, to this bitter, moon-pulled lake, trailing us after him unborn, like the infants he had painted on the dresser drawers, whose garments swam in some ethereal current, perhaps the rim of the vortex that would drag them down out of that enameled sky, stripped and screaming. Sylvie's oars set off vortices. She swamped some leaves and spun a feather on its curl. The current that made us sidle a little toward the center of the lake was the draw of the river, and no vortex, though my grandfather's last migration had settled him on the lake floor. It seemed that Sylvie's boat slipped down the west side of every wave. We would make a circle, and never reach a shore at all, if there were a vortex, I thought, and we would be drawn down into the darker world, where other sounds would pour into our ears until we seemed to find songs in them, and the sight of water would invade our eyes, and the taste of water would invade our bowels and unstring our bones, and we would know the seasons and customs of the place as if there were no others. Imagine my grandfather reclined how many years in his Pullman berth, regarding the morning through a small blue window. He might see us and think he was dreaming again of flushed but weightless spirits in a painted sky, buoyant in an impalpable element. And when our shadow had passed he might see the daylit moon, a jawless, socketed shard, and take it for his image in the glass. Of course he was miles away, miles south, at the foot of the bridge.

At last she pulled us toward a broad point that lay out into the lake. I could see that the mountain standing behind and against the one from which the point extended had a broken side. Stone showed pink as a scar on a dog's ear. "You can see where it is from here," Sylvie said. "They built right beside those cliffs." She brought us up against the shore and we climbed out of the boat and dragged it up on the beach. I followed Sylvie inland along the side of the point.

The mountains that walled the valley were too close, the one upon the other. The rampages of glaciers in their eons of slow violence had left the landscape in a great disorder. Out from the cleft or valley the mountains made spilled a lap of spongy earth, overgrown with brush. We walked up it along the deep, pebbly bed left by the run-off and the rain, and there we came upon the place Sylvie had told me about, stunted orchard and lilacs and stone doorstep and fallen house, all white with a brine of frost. Sylvie smiled at me. "Pretty, isn't it?"

"It's pretty, but I don't know how anyone could have wanted to *live* here."

"It's really pretty in the sunlight. You'll see in a little while."

"Well, let's not wait here, though. It's too cold."

Sylvie glanced at me, a little surprised. "But you'll want to watch for the children."

"Yes. All right."

"Well, I think you better just stay in one place and be very quiet."

"Yes, but it's too cold here."

Sylvie shrugged. "It's still early." We walked back down to the shore, and found some rocks against which we could sit, out of the wind, facing the sun. Sylvie crossed her ankles and folded her arms. She appeared to fall asleep.

After a while I said, "Sylvie?"

She smiled. "Shhh."

"Where's our lunch?"

"Still in the boat. You're probably right. It would be good if they saw you eating."

I found a bag of marshmallows among the odds and ends that Sylvie had bundled into a checkered tablecloth and brought along for lunch—a black banana, a lump of salami with a knife through it, a single yellow chicken wing like an elegant, small gesture of defeat, the bottom fifth of a bag of potato chips. I ripped the cellophane and took out marshmallows to fill my pockets. Then I sat down by Sylvie and made a small fire of driftwood and skewered one through its soft belly with a stick and held it in the flame until it caught fire. I let it burn until it was as black as a lump of coal, then I pulled off the weightless husk with my fingers and ate it, and held the creamy part that still clung to the stick in the flame until it caught fire; and so the morning passed.

Sylvie stood up and stretched, and nodded at the sun, which was a small, white, wintery sun and stood askant the zenith although it was surely noon. "We can go up there now," she said. I followed her up into the valley again and found it much changed. It was as if the light had coaxed a flowering from the frost, which before seemed barren and parched as salt. The grass shone with petal colors, and water drops spilled from all the trees as innumerably as petals. "I told you it was nice," Sylvie said.

Imagine a Carthage sown with salt, and all the sowers gone, and the seeds lain however long in the earth, till there rose finally in vegetable profusion leaves and trees of rime and brine. What flowering would there be in such a garden? Light would force each salt calyx to open in prisms, and to fruit heavily with bright globes of water—peaches and grapes are little more than that, and where the world was salt there would be greater need of slaking. For need can blossom into all the compensations it requires. To crave and to have are as like as a thing and its shadow. For when does a berry break upon the tongue as sweetly as when one longs to taste it, and when is the taste refracted into so many hues and savors of ripeness and earth, and when do our senses know any thing so utterly as when we lack it? And here again is a foreshadowing—the world will be made whole. For to wish for a hand on one's hair is all but to feel it. So whatever we may lose, very craving gives it back to us again. Though we dream and hardly know it, longing, like an angel, fosters us, smooths our hair, and brings us wild strawberries.

Sylvie was gone. She had left without a word, or a sound. I thought she must be teasing, perhaps watching me from the woods. I pretended not to know I was alone. I could see why Sylvie thought children might come here. Any child who saw once how the gleaming water spilled to the tips of branches, and rounded and dropped and pocked the softening shadows of frost at the foot of each tree, would come to see it again.

If there had been snow I would have made a statue, a woman to stand along the path, among the trees. The children would have come close, to look at her. Lot's wife was salt and barren, because she was full of loss and mourning, and looked back. But here rare flowers would gleam in her hair, and on her breast, and in her hands, and there would be children all around her, to love and marvel at her for her beauty, and to laugh at her extravagant adornments, as if they had set the flowers in her hair and thrown down all the flowers at her feet, and they would forgive her, eagerly and lavishly, for turning away, though she never asked to be forgiven. Though her hands were ice and did not touch them, she would be more than mother to them, she so calm, so still, and they such wild and orphan things.

I walked out of the valley and down the little apron of earth at its entrance. The shore was empty and, after its manner, silent. Sylvie must be up at the point, I thought. I imagined her hiding the boat more securely. That would be a reasonable precaution for her to take, convinced as she was that these woods were peopled. I sat on a log and whistled and tossed stones at the toe of my shoe. I knew why Sylvie felt there were children in the woods. I felt so, too, though I did not think so. I sat on the log pelting my shoe, because I knew that if I turned however quickly to look behind me the consciousness behind me would not still be there, and would only come closer when I turned away again. Even if it spoke just at my ear, as it seemed often at the point of doing, when I turned there would be nothing there. In that way it was persistent and teasing and ungentle, the way half-wild, lonely children are. This was something Lucille and I together would ignore, and I had been avoiding the shore all that fall, because when I was by myself and obviously lonely, too, the teasing would be much more difficult to disregard. Having a sister or a friend is like sitting at night in a lighted house. Those outside can watch you if they want, but you need not see them. You simply say, "Here are the perimeters of our attention. If you prowl around under the windows till the crickets go silent, we will pull the shades. If you wish us to suffer your envious curiosity, you must permit us not to notice it." Anyone with one solid human bond is that smug, and it is the smugness as much as the comfort and safety that lonely people covet and admire. I had been, so to speak, turned out of the house now long enough to have observed this in myself. Now there was neither threshold nor sill between me and these cold, solitary children who almost breathed against my cheek and almost touched my hair. I decided to go back up and wait for Sylvie by the cellar hole, where she could not help but find me.

Daylight had moved up the eastern wall of the valley and shone warmly on the ragged and precipitious stands of black old trees that grew at those altitudes. Down below there was only shadow and a wind that swept along toward the lake just at the level of my knees. The lilacs rattled. The stone step was too cold to be sat upon. It seemed at first that there was no comfort for me here at all, so I jammed my hands in my pockets, pressed my elbows to my sides, and cursed Sylvie in my heart, and that was a relief because it gave me something to think about besides the woods. With effort, I began to think of other things. If I went down into the cellar hole, out of the wind, I could build a fire and be warm. This could not be done easily since the cellar had received the ruins of the old house.

Someone had scavenged there. Most of the shingles had been stripped from the roof, and all in all, the poles and planks that remained seemed much less than the makings of a house. The ridgepole had snapped, no doubt under the weight of snow. That was probably the beginning of the catastrophe, which might then have continued over weeks or years. I had heard of a family who lived some distance to the north of the lake who had been snowed in up to the eaves and whose house began to fall. They upended the kitchen table to prop the ridgepole in the middle, but the roof had pried loose from the walls at either end, admitting the wind, and the walls sagged the window frames out of square so that all the panes broke. They had only snow to stanch all these openings. They hardly dared make the fire in the stove hot enough to warm drinking water, they said, for fear that the snow, which was all that held the house up, would sodden and shift and pull it down. There were reputed to have been seventeen in that family. They were said to have survived by stacking themselves like firewood at night under nineteen quilts and as many hooked rugs. The mother was said to have kept a stew on the stove of water and vinegar, into which she put the tongues of all their shoes, as well as the trimmings of their hair and beards and fingernails, and pine pitch and a pair of antlers and a long-handled shoehorn—and they had lived on the pot liquor, poured over snow to stretch it. But that is a part of the world where people tend to boast of discomfort and hardship, having little else worthy of mention.

The houses in the mountains of Fingerbone were generally built as this one had been, of planks nailed to a frame vertically, and strips of wood perhaps two inches wide nailed on at each seam to close the chinks. If the house began to lean, the chinking sprang loose and the pine knots popped out and as often as not the windowpanes fell and the door could only be opened with increasing effort, until finally it could not be closed. I imagine that this kind of building was a habit acquired in a milder climate. I do not know why it was persisted in, for it turned people out of house with a frequency to startle even Fingerbone. And if the way to the next shelter was impassable because of snow, the family would not be seen again until the snow melted. The woods were full of such stories. There were so many stories, in fact, that there must have been at some time a massive exodus or depopulation, for now there were very few families in the woods, even near town—too few by far to account for such an enormous tribe of ancestors—even ancestors given, as these seem to have been, to occasional wholesale obliteration.

Abandoned homesteads like this one were rare, however, so perhaps all the tales of perished settlers were at root one tale, carried off in every direction the way one cry of alarm is carried among birds through the whole of the woods and even the sky. It might have been this house that peopled all these mountains. When it broke it might have cast them invisibly into the wind, like spores, thousands from one drab husk, or millions, for there was no reason to believe that anyone ever had heard all the tales of unsheltered folk that were in these mountains, or that anyone ever would. And that is perhaps why, when they saw me alone, they would practically tug at my sleeve. You may have noticed that people in bus stations, if they know you also are alone, will glance at you sidelong, with a look that is both piercing and intimate, and if you let them sit beside you, they will tell you long lies about numerous children who are all gone now, and mothers who were beautiful and cruel, and in every case they will tell you that they were abandoned, disappointed, or betrayed—that they should not be alone, that only remarkable events, of the kind one reads in books, could have made their condition so extreme. And that is why, even if the things they say are true, they have the quick eyes and active hands and the passion for meticulous elaboration of people who know they are lying. Because, once alone, it is impossible to believe that one could ever have been otherwise. Loneliness is an absolute discovery. When one looks from inside at a lighted window, or looks from above at the lake, one sees the image of oneself in a lighted room, the image of oneself among trees and sky—the deception is obvious, but flattering all the same. When one looks from the darkness into the light, however, one sees all the difference between here and there, this and that. Perhaps all unsheltered people are angry in their hearts, and would like to break the roof, spine, and ribs, and smash the windows and flood the floor and spindle the curtains and bloat the couch.

I began pulling loose planks out of the cellar hole, the right corner at the front. They were splintery and full of snaggled nails, but I pulled them out and tossed them onto the ground behind me, for all the world as if I had some real purpose or intention. It was difficult work, but I have often noticed that it is almost intolerable to be looked at, to be watched, when one is idle. When one is idle and alone, the embarrassments of loneliness are almost endlessly compounded. So I worked till my hair was damp and my hands were galled and tender, with what must have seemed wild hope, or desperation. I began to imagine myself a rescuer. Children had been sleeping in this fallen house. Soon I would uncover the rain-stiffened hems of their nightshirts, and their small, bone feet, the toes all fallen like petals. Perhaps it was already too late to help. They had lain under the snow through far too many winters, and that was the pity. But to cease to hope would be the final betrayal.

I imagined myself in their place—it was not hard to do this, for the appearance of relative solidity in my grandmother's house was deceptive. It was an impression created by the piano, and the scrolled couch, and the bookcases full of almanacs and Kipling and Defoe. For all the appearance these things gave of substance and solidity, they might better be considered a dangerous weight on a frail structure. I could easily imagine the piano crashing to the cellar floor with a thrum of all its strings. And then, too, our house should not have had a second story, for, if it fell while we were sleeping, we would plummet disastrously through the dark, knowing no more perhaps than that our dreams were suddenly terrible and suddenly gone. A small house was better. It broke gracefully, like some ripe pod or shell. And despite the stories I made up to myself, I knew there were no children trapped in this meager ruin. They were light and spare and thoroughly used to the cold, and it was almost a joke to them to be cast out into the woods, even if their eyes were gone and their feet were broken. It is better to have nothing, for at last even our bones will fall. It is better to have nothing.

I sat down on the grass, which was stiff with the cold, and I put my hands over my face, and I let my skin tighten, and let the chills run in ripples, like breezy water, between my shoulder blades and up my neck. I let the numbing grass touch my ankles. I thought, Sylvie is nowhere, and sometime it will be dark. I thought, Let them come unhouse me of this flesh, and pry this house apart. It was no shelter now, it only kept me here alone, and I would rather be with them, if only to see them, even if they turned away from me. If I could see my mother, it would not have to be her eyes, her hair. I would not need to touch her sleeve. There was no more the stoop of her high shoulders. The lake had taken that, I knew. It was so very long since the dark had swum her hair, and there was nothing more to dream of, but often she almost slipped through any door I saw from the side of my eye, and it was she, and not changed, and not perished. She was a music I no longer heard, that rang in my mind, itself and nothing else, lost to all sense, but not perished, not perished.

* * *

1980

HELENA MARÍA VIRAMONTES
b. 1954

Helena María Viramontes was born in East Los Angeles, California, and received her B.A. in English literature from Immaculate Heart College and her M.F.A. in creative writing from the University of California at Irvine. Her first short-story collection, *The Moths and Other Stories,* was published in 1985, and her most recent publication is the novel *Under the Feet of Jesus* (1995). She is also coeditor of *Chicana Creativity and Criticism: Charting New Frontiers in American Literature* (1987).

"The Cariboo Cafe" was written in 1984. In her personal journal at the time, Viramontes wondered how "we can sit here peacefully when we know that our tax dollars are supporting the death squads in Central America. It is no secret. Just a matter of politics. . . . And our silence is our submission. Can you sleep at night?"

The Cariboo Cafe

I

They arrived in the secrecy of night, as displaced people often do, stopping over for a week, a month, eventually staying a lifetime. The plan was simple. Mother would work, too, until they saved enough to move into a finer future where the toilet was one's own and the children needn't be frightened. In the meantime, they played in the back alleys, among the broken glass, wise to the ways of the streets. Rule one: never talk to strangers, not even the neighbor who paced up and down the hallways talking to himself. Rule two: the police, or "polie" as Sonya's popi pronounced the word, was La Migra in disguise and thus should always be avoided. Rule three: keep your key with you at all times—the four walls of the apartment were the only protection against the streets until Popi returned home.

Sonya considered her key a guardian saint and she wore it around her neck as such until this afternoon. Gone was the string with the big knot. Gone was the key. She hadn't noticed its disappearance until she picked up Macky from Mrs. Avila's house and walked home. She remembered playing with it as Amá walked her to school. But lunch break came, and Lalo wrestled her down so that he could see her underwear, and it probably fell somewhere between the iron rings and sandbox. Sitting on the front steps of the apartment building, she considered how to explain the missing key without having to reveal what Lalo had seen, for she wasn't quite sure which offense carried the worse penalty.

She watched people piling in and spilling out of the buses, watched an old man asleep on the bus bench across the street. He resembled a crumbled ball of paper, huddled up in the security of a tattered coat. She became aware of their mutual loneliness and she rested her head against her knees blackened by the soot of the playground asphalt.

The old man eventually awoke, yawned like a lion's roar, unfolded his limbs and staggered to the alley where he urinated between two trash bins. (She wanted to peek, but it was Macky who turned to look.) He zipped up, drank from a paper bag, and she watched him until he disappeared around the corner. As time passed, buses came less frequently, and every other person seemed to resemble Popi. Macky became bored. He picked through the trash barrel; later, and to Sonya's fright, he ran into the street after a pigeon. She understood his restlessness, for waiting was as relentless as long lines to the bathroom. When a small boy walked by, licking away at a scoop of vanilla ice cream, Macky ran after him. In his haste to outrun Sonya's grasp, he fell and tore the knee of his denim jeans. He began to cry, wiping snot against his sweater sleeve.

"See?" she asked, dragging him back to the porch steps by his wrist. "See? God punished you!" It was a thing she always said because it seemed to work. Terrified by the scrawny tortured man on the cross, Macky wanted to avoid his wrath as much as possible. She sat him on the steps in one gruff jerk. Seeing his torn jeans and her own scraped knees, she wanted to join in his sorrow and cry. Instead, she snuggled so close to him she could hear his stomach growling.

"Coke," he said. Mrs. Avila gave him an afternoon snack which usually held him over until dinner. But sometimes Macky got lost in the midst of her own six children and . . .

Mrs. Avila! It took Sonya a few moments to realize the depth of her idea. They could wait there, at Mrs. Avila's. And she'd probably have a stack of flour tortillas, fresh off the comal, ready to eat with butter and salt. She grabbed his hand. "Mrs. Avila has Coke."

"Coke!" He jumped up to follow his sister. "Coke," he cooed.

At the major intersection, Sonya quietly calculated their next move while the scores of adults hurried to their own destinations. She scratched one knee as she tried retracing her journey home in the labyrinth of her memory. Things never looked the same when backwards and she searched for familiar scenes. She looked for the newspaperman who sat in a little house with a little T.V. on and sold magazines with naked girls holding beach balls. But he was gone. What remained was a little closet-like shed with chains and locks, and she wondered what happened to him, for she thought he lived there with the naked ladies.

They finally crossed the street at a cautious pace, the colors of the street lights brighter as darkness descended, a stereo store blaring music from two huge, blasting speakers. She thought it was the disco store she passed, but she didn't remember if the sign was green or red. And she didn't remember it flashing like it was now. Studying the neon light, she bumped into a tall, lanky dark man. Maybe it was Raoul's Popi. Raoul was a dark boy in her class that she felt sorry for because everyone called him spongehead. Maybe she could ask Raoul's Popi where Mrs. Avila lived, but before she could think it all out, red sirens flashed in their faces and she shielded her eyes to see the polie.

The polie is men in black who get kids and send them to Tijuana, says Popi. Whenever you see them, run, because they hate you, says Popi. She grabs Macky by his sleeve and they crawl under a table of bargain cassettes. Macky's nose is running, and when he sniffles, she puts her finger to her lips. She peeks from behind the poster of Vincente Fernandez to see Raoul's father putting keys and stuff from his pockets onto the hood of the polie car. And it's true, they're putting him in the car and taking him to Tijuana. Popi, she murmured to herself. Mamá.

"Coke." Macky whispered, as if she had failed to remember.

"Ssssh. Mi'jo, when I say run, you run, okay?" She waited for the tires to turn out, and as the black and white drove off, she whispered "Now," and they scurried out from under the table and ran across the street, oblivous to the horns.

They entered a maze of alleys and dead ends, the long, abandoned warehouses shadowing any light. Macky stumbled and she continued to drag him until his crying, his untied sneakers, and his raspy breathing finally forced her to stop. She scanned the boarded-up boxcars, the rows of rusted rails to make sure the polie wasn't following them. Tired, her heart bursting, she leaned him against a tall chain-link fence. Except for the rambling of some railcars, silence prevailed, and she could hear Macky sniffling in the darkness. Her mouth was parched and she swallowed to rid herself of the metallic taste of fear. The shadows stalked them, hovering like nightmares. Across the tracks, in the distance, was a room with a yellow glow, like a beacon light at the end of a dark sea. She pinched Macky's nose with the corner of her dress, took hold of his sleeve. At least the shadows will be gone, she concluded, at the zero-zero place.

II

Don't look at me. I didn't give it the name. It was passed on. Didn't even know what it meant until I looked it up in some library dictionary. But I kinda liked the name. It's, well, romantic, almost like the name of a song, you know, so I kept it. That was before JoJo turned fourteen even. But now if you take a look at the sign, the paint's peeled off 'cept for the two O's. The double zero cafe. Story of my life. But who cares, right? As long as everyone 'round the factories knows I run an honest business.

The place is clean. That's more than I can say for some people who walk through that door. And I offer the best prices on double-burger deluxes this side of Main Street. Okay, so it's not pure beef. Big deal, most meat markets do the same. But I make no bones 'bout it. I tell them up front, 'yeah, it ain't dogmeat, but it ain't sirloin either.' Cause that's the sort of guy I am. Honest.

That's the trouble. It never pays to be honest. I tried scrubbing the stains off the floor, so that my customers won't be reminded of what happened. But they keep walking as if my cafe ain't fit for lepers. And that's the thanks I get for being a fair guy.

Not once did I hang up all those stupid signs. You know, like 'We reserve the right to refuse service to anyone,' or 'No shirt, no shoes, no service.' To tell you the truth—which is what I always do though it don't pay—I wouldn't have nobody walking through that door. The streets are full of scum, but scum gotta eat too is the way I see it. Now, listen. I ain't talking 'bout out-of-luckers, weirdos, whores, you know. I'm talking 'bout five-to-lifers out of some tech. I'm talking Paulie.

I swear Paulie is thirty-five, or six. JoJo's age if he were still alive, but he don't look a day over ninety. Maybe why I let him hang out is 'cause he's JoJo's age. Shit, he's okay as long as he don't bring his wigged-out friends whose voices sound like a record at low speed. Paulie's got too many stories and they all get jammed up in his mouth so I can't make out what he's saying. He scares the other customers, too, acting like he is shadow boxing, or like a monkey hopping on a frying pan. You know, nervous, jumpy, his jaw all falling and his eyes bulgy and dirt-yellow. I give him the last booth, coffee, and yesterday's donut holes to keep him quiet. After a few minutes, out he goes, before lunch. I'm too old, you know, too busy making ends meet to be nursing the kid. And so is Delia.

That Delia's got these unique titties. One is bigger than the other. Like an orange and grapefruit. I kid you not. They're like that on account of when she was real young she had some babies, and they all sucked only one favorite tittie. So one is bigger than the other, and when she used to walk in with Paulie, huggy-huggy and wearing those tight leotard blouses that show the nipple dots, you could see the difference. You could tell right off that Paulie was proud of them, the way he'd hang his arm over her shoulder and squeeze the grapefruit. They kill me, her knockers. She'd come in real queen-like, smacking gum and chewing the fat with the illegals who work in that garment warehouse. They come in real queen-like, too, sitting in the best booth near the window, and order cokes. That's all. Cokes. Hey, but I'm a nice guy, so what if they mess up my table, bring their own lunches and only order small cokes, leaving a dime as tip? So sometimes the place ain't crawling with people, you comprende, buddy? A dime's a dime as long as it's in my pocket.

Like I gotta pay my bills, too. I gotta eat. So like I serve anybody who's got the greens, including that crazy lady and the two kids that started all the trouble. If only I had closed early. But I had to wash the dinner dishes on account of I can't afford a dishwasher. I was scraping off some birdshit glue stuck to this plate, see, when I hear the bells jingle against the door. I hate those fucking bells. That was Nell's idea. Nell's my wife; my ex-wife. So people won't sneak up on you, says my ex. Anyway, I'm standing behind the counter staring at this short woman. Already I know that she's bad news because she looks street to me. Round face, burnt-toast color, black hair that hangs like straight ropes. Weirdo, I've had enough to last me a lifetime. She's wearing a shawl and a dirty slip is hanging out. Shit if I have to dish out a free meal. Funny thing, but I didn't see the two kids 'til I got to the booth. All of a sudden I see these big eyes looking over the table's edge at me. It shook me up, the way they kinda appeared. Aw, maybe they were there all the time.

The boy's a sweetheart. Short Order don't look nothing like his mom. He's got dried snot all over his dirty cheeks and his hair ain't seen a comb for years. She can't take care of herself, much less him or the doggie of a sister. But he's a tough one, and I pinch his nose 'cause he's a real sweetheart like JoJo. You know, my boy.

It's his sister I don't like. She's got these poking eyes that follow you 'round 'cause she don't trust no one. Like when I reach for Short Order, she flinches like I'm 'bout to tear his nose off, gives me a nasty, squinty look. She's maybe five, maybe six, I don't know, and she acts like she owns him. Even when I bring the burgers, she doesn't let go of his hand. Finally, the fellow bites it and I wink at him. A real sweetheart.

In the next booth, I'm twisting the black crud off the top of the ketchup bottle when I hear the lady saying something in Spanish. Right off I know she's illegal, which explains why she looks like a weirdo. Anyway, she says something nice to them 'cause it's in the same tone that Nell used when I'd rest my head on her lap. I'm surprised the illegal's got a fiver to pay, but she and her tail leave no tip. I see Short Order's small bites on the bun.

You know, a cafe's the kinda business that moves. You get some regulars but most of them are on the move, so I don't pay much attention to them. But this lady's face sticks like egg yolk on a plate. It ain't 'til I open a beer and sit in front of the B & W to check out the wrestling matches that I see this news bulletin 'bout two missing kids. I recognize the mugs right away. Short Order and his doggie sister. And all of a sudden her face is out of my mind. Aw, fuck, I say, and put my beer down so hard that the foam spills onto last month's Hustler. Aw, fuck.

See, if Nell was here, she'd know what to do: call the cops. But I don't know. Cops ain't exactly my friends, and all I need is for bacon to be crawling all over my place. And seeing how her face is vague now, I decide to wait 'til the late news. Short Order don't look right neither. I'll have another beer and wait for the late news.

The alarm rings at four and I have this headache, see, from the sixpack, and I gotta get up. I was supposed to do something, but I got all suck-faced and forgot. Turn off the T.V., take a shower, but that don't help my memory any.

Hear sirens near the railroad tracks. Cops. I'm supposed to call the cops. I'll do it after I make the coffee, put away the eggs, get the donuts out. But Paulie strolls in looking partied out. We actually talk 'bout last night's wrestling match between BoBo Brazil and the Crusher. I slept through it, you see. Paulie orders an O.J. on account of he's catching a cold. I open up my big mouth and ask about De. Drinks the rest of his O.J., says real calm-like, that he caught her eaglespread with the vegetable fatso down the block. Then, very polite-like, Paulie excuses himself. That's one thing I gotta say about Paulie. He may be one big Fuck-Up, but he's got manners. Juice gave him shit cramps, he says.

Well, leave it to Paulie. Good ole Mr. Fuck-Up himself to help me with the cops. The prick O.D.'s in my crapper; vomits and shits are all over—I mean all over the fuckin' walls. That's the thanks I get for being Mr. Nice Guy. I had the cops looking up my ass for the stash. Says one, the one wearing a mortician's suit, We'll be back, we'll be back when you ain't looking. If I was pushing, would I be burning my goddamn balls off with spitting grease? So fuck 'em, I think. I ain't gonna tell you nothing 'bout the lady. Fuck you, I say to them as they drive away. Fuck your mother.

That's why Nell was good to have 'round. She could be a pain in the ass, you know, like making me hang those stupid bells, but mostly she knew what to do. See, I go bananas. Like my mind fries with the potatoes and by the end of the day, I'm deader than dogshit. Let me tell you what I mean. A few hours later, after I swore I wouldn't give the fuckin' pigs the time of day, the green vans roll up across the street. While I'm stirring the chili con carne I see all these illegals running out of the factory to hide, like roaches when the lightswitch goes on. I taste the chile, but I really can't taste nothing on account of I've lost my appetite after cleaning out the crapper, when three of them run into the Cariboo. They look at me as if I'm gonna stop them, but when I go on stirring the chile, they run to the bathroom. Now look, I'm a nice guy, but I don't like to be used, you know? Just 'cause they're regulars don't mean jackshit. I run an honest business. And that's what I told them agents. See, by that time, my stomach being all dizzy, and the cops all over the place, and the three illegals running in here, I was all confused, you know. That's how it was, and well, I haven't seen Nell for years, and I guess that's why I pointed to the bathroom.

I don't know. I didn't expect handcuffs and them agents putting their hands up and down their thighs. When they walked passed me, they didn't look at me. That is the two young ones. The older one, the one that looked silly in the handcuffs on account of she's old enough to be my grandma's grandma, looks straight at my face with the same eyes Short Order's sister gave me yesterday. What a day. Then, to top off the potatoes with the gravy, the bells jingle against the door and in enters the lady again with the two kids.

III

He's got lice. Probably from living in the detainers. Those are the rooms where they round up the children and make them work for their food. I saw them from the window. Their eyes are cut glass, and no one looks for sympathy. They take turns, sorting out the arms from the legs, heads from the torsos. Is that one your mother? one guard asks, holding a mummified head with eyes shut tighter than coffins. But the children no longer cry. They just continue sorting as if they were salvaging cans from a heap of trash. They do this until time is up and they drift into a tunnel, back to the womb of sleep, while a new group comes in. It is all very organized. I bite my fist to keep from retching. Please, God, please don't let Geraldo be there.

For you see, they took Geraldo. By mistake, of course. It was my fault. I shouldn't have sent him out to fetch me a mango. But it was just to the corner. I didn't even bother to put his sweater on. I hear his sandals flapping against the gravel. I follow him with my eyes, see him scratching his buttocks when the wind picks up swiftly, as it often does at such unstable times, and I have to close the door.

The darkness becomes a serpent's tongue, swallowing us whole. It is the night of La Llorona. The women come up from the depths of sorrow to search for their children. I join them, frantic, desperate, and our eyes become scrutinizers, our bodies opiated with the scent of their smiles. Descending from door to door, the wind whips our faces. I hear the wailing of the women and know it to be my own. Geraldo is nowhere to be found.

Dawn is not welcomed. It is a drunkard wavering between consciousness and sleep. My life is fleeing, moving south towards the sea. My tears are now hushed and faint.

The boy, barely a few years older than Geraldo, lights a cigarette, rests it on the edge of his desk, next to all the other cigarette burns. The blinds are down to keep the room cool. Above him hangs a single bulb that shades and shadows his face in such a way as to mask his expressions. He is not to be trusted. He fills in the information, for I cannot write. Statements delivered, we discuss motives.

"Spies," says he, flicking a long burning ash from the cigarette onto the floor, then wolfing the smoke in as if his lungs had an unquenchable thirst for nicotine. "We arrest spies. Criminals." He says this with cigarette smoke spurting out from his nostrils like a nosebleed.

"Spies? Criminal?" My shawl falls to the ground. "He is only five and a half years old." I plead for logic with my hands. "What kind of crimes could a five-year-old commit?"

"Anyone who so willfully supports the Contras in any form must be arrested and punished without delay." He knows the line by heart. I think about moths and their stupidity. Always attracted by light, they fly into fires, or singe their wings with the heat of the single bulb and fall on his desk, writhing in pain. I don't understand why nature has been so cruel as to prevent them from feeling warmth. He dismisses them with a sweep of a hand. "This," he continues, "is what we plan to do with the Contras and those who aid them." He inhales again.

"But, Señor, he's just a baby."

"Contras are tricksters. They exploit the ignorance of people like you. Perhaps they convinced your son to circulate pamphlets. You should be talking to them, not us." The cigarette is down to his yellow finger tips, to where he can no longer continue to hold it without burning himself. He throws the stub on the floor, crushes it under his boot. "This," he says, screwing his boot into the ground, "is what the Contras do to people like you."

"Señor. I am a washerwoman. You yourself see I cannot read or write. There is my X. Do you think my son can read?" How can I explain to this man that we are poor, that we live as best we can? "If such a thing has happened, perhaps he wanted to make a few centavos for his mamá. He's just a baby."

"So you are admitting his guilt?"

"So you are admitting he is here?" I promise, once I see him, hold him in my arms again, I will never, never scold him for wanting more than I can give. "You see, he needs his sweater . . ." The sweater lies limp on my lap.

"Your assumption is incorrect."

"May I check the detainers for myself?"

"In time."

"And what about my Geraldo?"

"In time." He dismisses me, placing the forms in a big envelope crinkled by the day's humidity.

"When?" I am wringing the sweater with my hands.

"Don't be foolish, woman. Now off with your nonsense. We will try to locate your Pedro."

"Geraldo."

Maria came by today with a bowl of hot soup. She reports, in her usual excited way, that the soldiers are now eating the brains of their victims. It is unlike her to be so scandalous. So insane. Geraldo must be cold without his sweater.

"Why?" I ask as the soup gets cold. I will write Tavo tonight.

At the plaza a group of people are whispering. They are quiet when I pass, turn to one another and put their finger to their lips to cage their voices. They continue as I reach the church steps. To be associated with me is condemnation.

Today I felt like killing myself, Lord. But I am too much of a coward. I am a washerwoman, Lord. My mother was one, and hers, too. We have lived as best we can, washing other people's laundry, rinsing off other people's dirt until our hands crust and chap. When my son wanted to hold my hand, I held soap instead. When he wanted to play, my feet were in pools of water. It takes such little courage, being a washerwoman. Give me strength, Lord.

What have I done to deserve this, Lord? Raising a child is like building a kite. You must bend the twigs enough, but not too much, for you might break them. You must find paper that is delicate and light enough to wave on the breath of the wind, yet must withstand the ravages of a storm. You must tie the strings gently but firmly so that it may not fall apart. You must let the string go, eventually, so that the kite will stretch its ambition. It is such delicate work, Lord, being a mother. This I understand, Lord, because I am. But you have snapped the cord, Lord. It was only a matter of minutes and my life is lost somewhere in the clouds. I don't know, I don't know what games you play, Lord.

These four walls are no longer my house; the earth beneath it, no longer my home. Weeds have replaced all good crops. The irrigation ditches are clodded with bodies. No matter where we turn, there are rumors facing us and we try to live as best we can under the rule of men who rape women then rip their fetuses from their bellies. Is this our home? Is this our country? I ask Maria. Don't these men have mothers, lovers, babies, sisters? Don't they see what they are doing? Later, Maria says, these men are babes farted out from the Devil's ass. We check to make sure no one has heard her say this.

Without Geraldo, this is not my home; the earth beneath it, not my country. This is why I have to leave. Maria begins to cry. Not because I am going, but because she is staying.

Tavo. Sweet Tavo. He has sold his car to send me the money. He has just married and he sold his car for me. Thank you, Tavo. Not just for the money. But also for making me believe in the goodness of people again . . . The money is enough to buy off the border soldiers. The rest will come from the can. I have saved for Geraldo's schooling and it is enough for a bus ticket to Juarez. I am to wait for Tavo there.

I spit. I do not turn back.

Perhaps I am wrong in coming. I worry that Geraldo will not have a home to return to, no mother to cradle his nightmares away, soothe the scars, stop the hemorrhaging of his heart. Tavo is happy I am here, but it is crowded with the three of us, and I hear them arguing behind their closed door. There is only so much a nephew can provide. I must find work. I have two hands willing to work. But the heart. The heart wills only to watch the children playing in the street.

The machines, their speed and dust, make me ill. But I can clean. I clean toilets, dump trash cans, sweep. Disinfect the sinks. I will gladly do whatever is necessary to repay Tavo. The baby is due any time and money is tight. I volunteer for odd hours, weekends, since I really have very little to do. When the baby comes I know Tavo's wife will not let me hold it, for she thinks I am a bad omen. I know it.

Why would God play such a cruel joke, if he isn't my son? I jumped the curb, dashed out into the street, but the street is becoming wider and wider. I've lost him once and can't lose him again and to hell with the screeching tires and the horns and the headlights barely touching my hips. I can't take my eyes off him because, you see, they are swift and cunning and can take your life with a snap of a finger. But God is a just man and His mistakes can be undone.

My heart pounds in my head like a sledgehammer against the asphalt. What if it isn't Geraldo? What if he is still in the detainer waiting for me? A million questions, one answer: Yes. Geraldo, yes. I want to touch his hand first, have it disappear in my own because it is so small. His eyes look at me in total bewilderment. I grab him because the earth is crumbling beneath us and I must save him. We both fall to the ground.

A hot meal is in store. A festival. The cook, a man with shrunken cheeks and the hands of a car mechanic, takes a liking to Geraldo. It's like birthing you again, mi'jo. My baby.

I bathe him. He flutters in excitement, the water gray around him. I scrub his head with lye to kill off the lice, comb his hair out with a fine-tooth comb. I wash his rubbery penis, wrap him in a towel, and he stands in front of the window, shriveling and sucking milk from a carton, his hair shiny from the dampness.

He finally sleeps. So easily, she thinks. On her bed next to the open window he coos in the night. Below, the sounds of the city become as monotonous as the ocean waves. She rubs his back with warm oil, each stroke making up for the days of his absence. She hums to him softly so that her breath brushes against his face, tunes that are rusted and crack in her throat. The hotel neon shines on his back and she covers him.

All the while the young girl watches her brother sleeping. She removes her sneakers, climbs into the bed, snuggles up to her brother, and soon her breathing is raspy, her arms under her stomach.

The couch is her bed tonight. Before switching the light off, she checks once more to make sure this is not a joke. Tomorrow she will make arrangements to go home. Maria will be the same, the mango stand on the corner next to the church plaza will be the same. It will all be the way it was before. But enough excitement. For the first time in years, her mind is quiet of all noise and she has the desire to sleep.

The bells jingle when the screen door slaps shut behind them. The cook wrings his hands in his apron, looking at them. Geraldo is in the middle, and they sit in the booth farthest away from the window, near the hall where the toilets are, and right away the small boy, his hair now neatly combed and split to the side like an adult, wrinkles his nose at the peculiar smell. The cook wipes perspiration off his forehead with the corner of his apron, finally comes over to the table.

She looks so different, so young. Her hair is combed slick back into one thick braid and her earrings hang like baskets of golden pears on her finely sculptured ears. He can't believe how different she looks. Almost beautiful. She points to what she wants on the menu with a white, clean fingernail. Although confused, the cook is sure of one thing—it's Short Order all right, pointing to him with a commanding finger, saying his only English word: coke.

His hands tremble as he slaps the meat on the grill; the patties hiss instantly. He feels like vomiting. The chile overboils and singes the fires, deep red trail of chile crawling to the floor and puddling there. He grabs the handles, burns himself, drops the pot on the wooden racks of the floor. He sucks his fingers, the patties blackening and sputtering grease. He flips them, and the burgers hiss anew. In some strange way he hopes they have disappeared, and he takes a quick look only to see Short Order's sister, still in the same dress, still holding her brother's hand. She is craning her neck to peek at what is going on in the kitchen.

Aw, fuck, he says, in a fog of smoke, his eyes burning tears. He can't believe it, but he's crying. For the first time since JoJo's death, he's crying. He becomes angry at the lady for returning. At JoJo. At Nell for leaving him. He wishes Nell here, but doesn't know where she's at or what part of Vietnam JoJo is all crumbled up in. Children gotta be with their parents, family gotta be together, he thinks. It's only right. The emergency line is ringing.

Two black and whites roll up and skid the front tires against the curb. The flashing lights carousel inside the cafe. She sees them opening the screen door, their guns taut and cold like steel erections. Something is wrong, and she looks to the cowering cook. She has been betrayed, and her heart is pounding like footsteps running, faster, louder, faster, and she can't hear what they are saying to her. She jumps up from the table, grabs Geraldo by the wrist, his sister dragged along because, like her, she refuses to release his hand. Their lips are mouthing words she can't hear, can't comprehend. Run, Run is all she can think of to do, Run through the hallway, out to the alley, Run because they will never take him away again.

But her legs are heavy and she crushes Geraldo against her, so tight, as if she wants to conceal him in her body again, return him to her belly so that they will not castrate him and hang his small blue penis on her door, not crush his face so that he is unrecognizable, not bury him among the heaps of bones, and ears, and teeth, and jaws, because no one but she cared to know that he cried. For years he cried and she could hear him day and night. Screaming, howling, sobbing, shriveling and crying because he is only five years old, and all she wanted was a mango.

But the crying begins all over again. In the distance, she hears crying.

She refuses to let go. For they will have to cut her arms off to take him, rip her mouth off to keep her from screaming for help. Without thinking, she reaches over to where two pots of coffee are brewing and throws the streaming coffee into their faces. Outside, people begin to gather, pressing their faces against the window glass to get a good view. The cook huddles behind the counter, frightened, trembling. Their faces become distorted and she doesn't see the huge hand that takes hold of Geraldo and she begins screaming all over again, screaming so that the walls shake, screaming enough for all the women of murdered children, screaming, pleading for help from the people outside, and she pushes an open hand against an officer's nose, because no one will stop them and he pushes the gun barrel to her face.

And I laugh at his ignorance. How stupid of him to think that I will let them take my Geraldo away, just because he waves that gun like a flag. Well, to hell with you, you pieces of shit, do you hear me? Stupid, cruel pigs. To hell with you all, because you can no longer frighten me. I will fight you for my son until I have no hands left to hold a knife. I will fight you all because you're all farted out of the Devil's ass, and you'll not take us with you. I am laughing, howling at their stupidity. Because they should know by now that I will never let my son go and then I hear something crunching like broken glass against my forehead and I am blinded by the liquid darkness. But I hold onto his hand. That I can feel, you see, I'll never let go. Because we are going home. My son and I.

1985

VI Technoculture

"Technoculture" in postmodern American fiction takes a myriad of forms. In the age of television, the automobile, the telephone, and the computer, the fascination of contemporary fiction writers with technology might be considered social realism. Novels such as Don DeLillo's *White Noise* (1985) and Douglas Coupland's *Generation X* (1991), for instance, are set within familiar, even traditional settings, but deal explicitly with the effects of increasingly complex technologies within those venues. "Technoculture" in literature can also describe a new proximity between the author and technology. From the computer code that accompanies the text of Laurie Anderson's *Stories from the Nerve Bible* (1994; see pp. 216–25), to the metaphors of binary computer logic used by Thomas Pynchon in *The Crying of Lot 49* (1966; see pp. 4–15), to the full partnership of computer and authorship represented by hypertext fiction, many recent developments in literature suggest a paradigm shift, linking the act of creativity with the telecommunications machines that now facilitate—and mediate—human contact. In addition, "technoculture" in literature encompasses the resuscitation of science fiction as an experimental literary genre, one that has for three decades produced compelling dystopian visions, social allegories, and innovative variations on traditional fantasy forms. Taken together, these three aspects of "technoculture" describe a new and powerful engagement among American authors with technology as a social and creative force.

The selections in this section illustrate each of these aspects of technoculture. Don DeLillo's *White Noise* is a comic but disturbing exploration of the dark side of the technologies that permeate our everyday lives. The novel's narrative power emerges from eerie dissonances between the mundane domesticity of family life and the ominous intrusions of "airborne toxic events" and mysterious, untraceable environmental hazards in public school buildings; between the banality of everyday conversation and the fragments of television discourse that indiscriminately mix news of disaster with marketing "data"; and between the determined good cheer and community of supermarket and mall shopping and the underlying fear of isolation and death they serve to forestall.

While the dangers of our technologies are great, so are their possibilities. The critic Donna Haraway suggests that present-day technologies might be used by women and other historically disenfranchised groups as "tools [to] embody and enforce new social relations." In "Feral Lasers" (1991), Gerald Vizenor's crossblood trickster technician Almost Browne appropriates first-world technology to produce holographic laser lightshows that project the ghosts of the past over the landscapes of the Quidnunc reservation and urban Detroit. And as Almost Browne asserts the cause of "light rights" in the courtroom where he is being tried for "causing a public disturbance," people inspired by him deploy the lasers "to revise histories, to hold their memories, and to create a new wilderness over the interstates."

Science fiction has always provided imaginative extrapolations of present-day phenomena, and we see in numerous postmodern works of science fiction the thoughtful projection forward of contemporary medical practices such as organ transplants, genetic engineering, and artificial insemination, or evolving social changes such as the rise of the suburb and the growing disparity between rich and poor. Octavia Butler's *Imago* (1989), from the Xenogenesis Trilogy, extends the traditional science fiction figure of the cyborg—part human, part machine—to encompass human/alien combinations that complicate the self/other distinction and destabilize binary notions of sex. Neal Stephenson's *Snow Crash* (1992) is an exemplar of "cyberpunk" science fiction, with its depiction of an ever-expanding, thoroughly commercialized "virtual" cyberspace universe complemented by a "real" America fragmented into burbclaves, private city-states where four major industries drive the national economy: music, movies, microcode, and high-speed pizza delivery.

While cyberpunk represents a fast-forward vision of the present, contemporary science fiction is also often the site for a peculiarly postmodern technological retrospection. William Gibson, whose 1984 cyberpunk novel *Neuromancer* is widely regarded as one of the most influential futuristic visions in American literary history, is here represented by such a backward glance. In "The Gernsback Continuum" (1981), a present-day photographer is haunted by hallucinations of an alternate America, the modernist utopia of 1930s pulp sci-fi magazines; the story's closing dialogue, in which the narrator is asked, " 'Hell of a world we live in, huh?' " and responds that it could be worse—" 'it could be perfect' "—can stand as the paradigmatic postmodern response to modernism's grand ambitions. Douglas Coupland too utilizes the utopian visions of past generations of science fiction to measure the tenor of contemporary life. "Shopping is Not Creating," from Coupland's best-seller *Generation X,* invokes the clichés of handsome astronauts and distant planets, but in an allegory suggesting the depth of alienation, nostalgia, and diminished expectations of both the story's teller and its audience. "Schrödinger's Cat" (1988), Ursula K. Le Guin's wistful meditation on the strange new reality of relativity, quantum mechanics, and Heisenbergian uncertainty, is suffused with a nostalgic longing for the lost certainties of the Newtonian universe.

The parallel or alternative universes imagined by quantum physicists are adopted by Joanna Russ for her 1975 feminist exploration of gender, *The Female Man.* In the first part, excerpted here, we encounter three of the four "J"s, identical genotypes but quite different women, the product of radically different times and worlds (though all are Earth): Janet Evason is an emissary to the present from "Whileaway," an all-female "Earth ten centuries from now, but not *our* Earth, if you follow me"; Jeannine, an inhabitant of an alternate present in which there was no Hitler, the Great Depression never ended, and the Women's Liberation Movement never happened; and Joanna, from a present quite similar to our own and on a collision course with the other versions of Earth's present and future that will illuminate and change forever the relations between the sexes. In "She Unnames Them" (1988), Ursula K. Le Guin, who in her distinguished literary career has written many works of socially conscious science fiction and fantasy, creates a wayward Eve who unnames all the animals and finally herself, thus undoing the age-old order of language and society, so that "the hunter could not be told from the hunted, nor the eater from the food." In a coda that speaks for all of the postmodern reimaginings of this section, Eve reflects on the new world she has made possible: "I could not chatter away as I used to do, taking it all for granted. My words now must be as slow, as new, as single, as tentative as the steps I took going down the path away from the house."

In some circumstances, technology offers a more assertive realignment of the relationship between reader and writer. For many observers, including such "traditional postmodernists" as Robert Coover, the advent of electronic textual forms represents a potentially historic transformation of literature, one where the reader's self-guided tour through a series of linked and interrelated "lexias" (or blocks of text) departs sharply from the model of a single, linear narrative compelled by the printed page. Michael Joyce's *afternoon, a story* (1990) has been celebrated both for the gracefulness of its prose and for its realization of the possibilities of hypertext narrative. Using the interconnected and random properties of the hypertext reading experience to simulate the tangles of memory, *afternoon* explores the consciousness of a writer named Peter, who is drawn into premonitions of loss and tragedy that—depending upon the paths through the text the reader chooses—lead toward different and often ambiguous outcomes. J. Yellowlees Douglas's "I Have Said Nothing" (1993) represents a particularly self-conscious investigation into how traditional narrative is transformed by hypertext. Also treating issues of loss and memory, "I Have Said Nothing" illustrates how the power of suggestion often found in realist fiction can be reconstructed and enhanced using the fragmentation and chance inherent in hypertext forms.

WILLIAM GIBSON
b. 1948

William Gibson was born in Conway, South Carolina, and, after dropping out of high school and journeying to Canada, received his B.A. from the University of British Columbia. "A lot of my friends were becoming lawyers and librarians," he told the *Chicago Tribune* in 1988, "things that filled me with horror." He began writing science fiction, despite the fact that, he reported in *Rolling Stone* in 1989, "it seemed like such a goofy, unhip thing to do," while his wife supported the family as a teacher. By the early 1980s, his work was appearing frequently in *Omni* magazine. *Neuromancer* (1984), his first novel, became the first book ever to sweep the major prizes for science fiction—the Hugo, Nebula, and Philip K. Dick Awards. Today that novel, *Count Zero* (1986), and *Mona Lisa Overdrive* (1988) form his "Cyberspace" trilogy. In *The Difference Engine* (1991), cowritten with Bruce Sterling, he departed from cyberpunk fiction to conjure a Victorian fantasy. His most recent novel is *Idoru* (1996).

Growing up in a small town on the edge of the Appalachian Mountains influenced Gibson's taste in fiction from the outset. "It was a boring, culturally deprived environment," he recalled in a 1988 interview in the *Sacramento Union*. "The library burned down in 1910, and nobody bothered to rebuild it." And as he told *Interview* magazine in 1989, "Science-fiction books were the only source I had for subversive information." As a writer, he reported in the *Mississippi Review* (1988), he developed a grim vision of the future influenced by artificial intelligence, including the cyberspace concept that "there's some kind of actual *space* behind the screen." "I thought I was on this literary kamikaze mission," he told *Rolling Stone*. "I thought my work was so disturbing it would be dismissed and ignored by all but a few people."

"The Gernsback Continuum," first published in *Universe II* in 1981, was reprinted in the collection *Burning Chrome* (1986).

The Gernsback Continuum

Mercifully, the whole thing is starting to fade, to become an episode. When I do still catch the odd glimpse, it's peripheral; mere fragments of mad-doctor chrome, confining themselves to the corner of the eye. There was that flying-wing liner over San Francisco last week, but it was almost translucent. And the shark-fin roadsters have gotten scarcer, and freeways discreetly avoid unfolding themselves into the gleaming eighty-lane monsters I was forced to drive last month in my rented Toyota. And I know that none of it will follow me to New York; my vision is narrowing to a single wavelength of probability. I've worked hard for that. Television helped a lot.

I suppose it started in London, in that bogus Greek taverna in Battersea Park Road, with lunch on Cohen's corporate tab. Dead steam-table food and it took them thirty minutes to find an ice bucket for the retsina. Cohen works for Barris-Watford, who publish big, trendy "trade" paperbacks: illustrated histories of the neon sign, the pinball machine, the windup toys of Occupied Japan. I'd gone over to shoot a series of shoe ads; California girls with tanned legs and frisky Day-Glo jogging shoes had capered for me down the escalators of St. John's Wood and across the platforms of Tooting Bec. A lean and hungry young agency had decided that the mystery of London Transport would sell waffle-tread nylon runners. They decide; I shoot. And Cohen, whom I knew vaguely from the old days in New York, had invited me to lunch the day before I was due out of Heathrow. He brought along a very fashionably dressed young woman named Dialta Downes, who was virtually chinless and evidently a noted pop-art historian. In retrospect, I see her walking in beside Cohen under a floating neon sign that flashes THIS WAY LIES MADNESS in huge sans-serif capitals.

Cohen introduced us and explained that Dialta was the prime mover behind the latest Barris-Watford project, an illustrated history of what she called "American Streamlined Moderne." Cohen called it "raygun Gothic." Their working title was *The Airstream Futuropolis: The Tomorrow That Never Was.*

There's a British obsession with the more baroque elements of American pop culture, something like the weird cowboys-and-Indians fetish of the West Germans or the aberrant French hunger for old Jerry Lewis films. In Dialta Downes this manifested itself in a mania for a uniquely American form of architecture that most Americans are scarcely aware of. At first I wasn't sure what she was talking about, but gradually it began to dawn on me. I found myself remembering Sunday morning television in the Fifties.

Sometimes they'd run old eroded newsreels as filler on the local station. You'd sit there with a peanut butter sandwich and a glass of milk, and a static-ridden Hollywood baritone would tell you that there was A Flying Car in Your Future. And three Detroit engineers would putter around with this big old Nash with wings, and you'd see it rumbling furiously down some deserted Michigan runway. You never actually saw it take off, but it flew away to Dialta Downes's never-never land, true home of a generation of completely uninhibited technophiles. She was talking about those odds and ends of "futuristic" Thirties and Forties architecture you pass daily in American cities without noticing; the movie marquees ribbed to radiate some mysterious energy, the dime stores faced with fluted aluminum, the chrome-tube chairs gathering dust in the lobbies of transient hotels. She saw these things as segments of a dreamworld, abandoned in the uncaring present; she wanted me to photograph them for her.

The Thirties had seen the first generation of American industrial designers; until the Thirties, all pencil sharpeners had looked like pencil sharpeners—your basic Victorian mechanism, perhaps with a curlicue of decorative trim. After the advent of the designers, some pencil sharpeners looked as though they'd been put together in wind tunnels. For the most part, the change was only skin-deep; under the streamlined chrome shell, you'd find the same Victorian mechanism. Which made a certain kind of sense, because the most successful American designers had been recruited from the ranks of Broadway theater designers. It was all a stage set, a series of elaborate props for playing at living in the future.

Over coffee, Cohen produced a fat manila envelope full of glossies. I saw the winged statues that guard the Hoover Dam, forty-foot concrete hood ornaments leaning steadfastly into an imaginary hurricane. I saw a dozen shots of Frank Lloyd Wright's Johnson's Wax Building, juxtaposed with the covers of old *Amazing Stories* pulps, by an artist named Frank R. Paul; the employees of Johnson's Wax must have felt as though they were walking into one of Paul's spray-paint pulp utopias. Wright's building looked as though it had been designed for people who wore white togas and Lucite sandals. I hesitated over one sketch of a particularly grandiose prop-driven airliner, all wing, like a fat symmetrical boomerang with windows in unlikely places. Labeled arrows indicated the locations of the grand ballroom and two squash courts. It was dated 1936.

"This thing couldn't have flown . . . ?" I looked at Dialta Downes.

"Oh, no, quite impossible, even with those twelve giant props; but they loved the look, don't you see? New York to London in less than two days, first-class dining rooms, private cabins, sun decks, dancing to jazz in the evening . . . The designers were populists, you see; they were trying to give the public what it wanted. What the public wanted was the future."

I'd been in Burbank for three days, trying to suffuse a really dull-looking rocker with charisma, when I got the package from Cohen. It is possible to photograph what isn't there; it's damned hard to do, and consequently a very marketable talent. While I'm not bad at it, I'm not exactly the best, either, and this poor guy strained my Nikon's credibility. I got out, depressed because I do like to do a good job, but not totally depressed, because I did make sure I'd gotten the check for the job, and I decided to restore myself with the sublime artiness of the Barris-Watford assignment. Cohen had sent me some books on Thirties design, more photos of streamlined buildings, and a list of Dialta Downes's fifty favorite examples of the style in California.

Architectural photography can involve a lot of waiting; the building becomes a kind of sundial, while you wait for a shadow to crawl away from a detail you want, or for the mass and balance of the structure to reveal itself in a certain way. While I was waiting, I thought myself in Dialta Downes's America. When I isolated a few of the factory buildings on the ground glass of the Hasselblad, they came across with a kind of sinister totalitarian dignity, like the stadiums Albert Speer built for Hitler. But the rest of it was relentlessly tacky: ephemeral stuff extruded by the collective American subconscious of the Thirties, tending mostly to survive along depressing strips lined with dusty motels, mattress wholesalers, and small used-car lots. I went for the gas stations in a big way.

During the high point of the Downes Age, they put Ming the Merciless in charge of designing California gas stations. Favoring the architecture of his native Mongo, he cruised up and down the coast erecting raygun emplacements in white stucco. Lots of them featured superfluous central towers ringed with those strange radiator flanges that were a signature motif of the style, and made them look as though they might generate potent bursts of raw technological enthusiasm, if you could only find the switch that turned them on. I shot one in San Jose an hour before the bulldozers arrived and drove right through the structural truth of plaster and lathing and cheap concrete.

"Think of it," Dialta Downes had said, "as a kind of alternate America: a 1980 that never happened. An architecture of broken dreams."

And that was my frame of mind as I made the stations of her convoluted socioarchitectural cross in my red Toyota—as I gradually tuned in to her image of a shadowy America-that-wasn't, of Coca-Cola plants like beached submarines, and fifth-run movie houses like the temples of some lost sect that had worshiped blue mirrors and geometry. And as I moved among these secret ruins, I found myself wondering what the inhabitants of that lost future would think of the world I lived in. The Thirties dreamed white marble and slipstream chrome, immortal crystal and burnished bronze, but the rockets on the covers of the Gernsback pulps had fallen on London in the dead of night, screaming. After the war, everyone had a car—no wings for it—and the promised superhighway to drive it down, so that the sky itself darkened, and the fumes ate the marble and pitted the miracle crystal. . . .

And one day, on the outskirts of Bolinas, when I was setting up to shoot a particularly lavish example of Ming's martial architecture, I penetrated a fine membrane, a membrane of probability. . . .

Ever so gently, I went over the Edge—

And looked up to see a twelve-engined thing like a bloated boomerang, all wing, thrumming its way east with an elephantine grace, so low that I could count the rivets in its dull silver skin, and hear—maybe—the echo of jazz.

I took it to Kihn.

Merv Kihn, free-lance journalist with an extensive line in Texas pterodactyls, redneck UFO contactees, bush-league Loch Ness monsters, and the Top Ten conspiracy theories in the loonier reaches of the American mass mind.

"It's good," said Kihn, polishing his yellow Polaroid shooting glasses on the hem of his Hawaiian shirt, "but it's not *mental;* lacks the true quill."

"But I saw it, Mervyn." We were seated poolside in brilliant Arizona sunlight. He was in Tucson waiting for a group of retired Las Vegas civil servants whose leader received messages from Them on her microwave oven. I'd driven all night and was feeling it.

"Of course you did. Of course you saw it. You've read my stuff; haven't you grasped my blanket solution to the UFO problem? It's simple, plain and country simple: people"—he settled the glasses carefully on his long hawk nose and fixed me with his best basilisk glare—"*see* . . . things. People see things. Nothing's there, but people *see* them anyway. Because they need to, probably. You've read Jung, you should know the score. . . . In your case, it's so obvious: You admit you were thinking about this crackpot architecture, having fantasies. . . . Look, I'm sure you've taken your share of drugs, right? How many people survived the Sixties in California without having the odd hallucination? All those nights when you discovered that whole armies of Disney technicians had been employed to weave animated holograms of Egyptian hieroglyphs into the fabric of your jeans, say, or the times when—"

"But it wasn't like that."

"Of course not. It wasn't like that at all; it was 'in a setting of clear reality,' right? Everything normal, and then there's the monster, the mandala, the neon cigar. In your case, a giant Tom Swift airplane. It happens *all the time.* You aren't even crazy. You know that, don't you?" He fished a beer out of the battered foam cooler beside his deck chair.

"Last week I was in Virginia. Grayson County. I interviewed a sixteen-year-old girl who'd been assaulted by a *bar hade.*"

"A what?"

"A bear head. The severed head of a bear. This *bar hade,* see, was floating around on its own little flying saucer, looked kind of like the hubcaps on cousin Wayne's vintage Caddy. Had red, glowing eyes like two cigar stubs and telescoping chrome antennas poking up behind its ears." He burped.

"It assaulted her? How?"

"You don't want to know; you're obviously impressionable. 'It was cold' "—he lapsed into his bad southern accent—" 'and metallic.' It made electronic noises. Now that is the real thing, the straight goods from the mass unconscious, friend; that little girl is a witch. There's just no place for her to function in this society. She'd have seen the devil, if she hadn't been brought up on 'The Bionic Man' and all those 'Star Trek' reruns. She is clued into the main vein. And she knows that it happened to her. I got out ten minutes before the heavy UFO boys showed up with the polygraph."

I must have looked pained, because he set his beer down carefully beside the cooler and sat up.

"If you want a classier explanation, I'd say you saw a semiotic ghost. All these contactee stories, for instance, are framed in a kind of sci-fi imagery that permeates our culture. I could buy aliens, but not aliens that look like Fifties' comic art. They're semiotic phantoms, bits of deep cultural imagery that have split off and taken on a life of their own, like the Jules Verne airships that those old Kansas farmers were always seeing. But you saw a different kind of ghost, that's all. That plane was part of the mass unconscious, once. You picked up on that, somehow. The important thing is not to worry about it."

I did worry about it, though.

Kihn combed his thinning blond hair and went off to hear what They had had to say over the radar range lately, and I drew the curtains in my room and lay down in air-conditioned darkness to worry about it. I was still worrying about it when I woke up. Kihn had left a note on my door; he was flying up north in a chartered plane to check out a cattle-mutilation rumor ("muties," he called them; another of his journalistic specialties).

I had a meal, showered, took a crumbling diet pill that had been kicking around in the bottom of my shaving kit for three years, and headed back to Los Angeles.

The speed limited my vision to the tunnel of the Toyota's headlights. The body could drive, I told myself, while the mind maintained. Maintained and stayed away from the weird peripheral window dressing of amphetamine and exhaustion, the spectral, luminous vegetation that grows out of the corners of the mind's eye along late-night highways. But the mind had its own ideas, and Kihn's opinion of what I was already thinking of as my "sighting" rattled endlessly through my head in a tight, lopsided orbit. Semiotic ghosts. Fragments of the Mass Dream, whirling past in the wind of my passage. Somehow this feedback-loop aggravated the diet pill, and the speed-vegetation along the road began to assume the colors of infrared satellite images, glowing shreds blown apart in the Toyota's slipstream.

I pulled over, then, and a half-dozen aluminum beer cans winked goodnight as I killed the headlights. I wondered what time it was in London, and tried to imagine Dialta Downes having breakfast in her Hampstead flat, surrounded by streamlined chrome figurines and books on American culture.

Desert nights in that country are enormous; the moon is closer. I watched the moon for a long time and decided that Kihn was right. The main thing was not to worry. All across the continent, daily, people who were more normal than I'd ever aspired to be saw giant birds, Bigfeet, flying oil refineries; they kept Kihn busy and solvent. Why should I be upset by a glimpse of the 1930s pop imagination loose over Bolinas? I decided to go to sleep, with nothing worse to worry about than rattlesnakes and cannibal hippies, safe amid the friendly roadside garbage of my own familiar continuum. In the morning I'd drive down to Nogales and photograph the old brothels, something I'd intended to do for years. The diet pill had given up.

The light woke me, and then the voices.

The light came from somewhere behind me and threw shifting shadows inside the car. The voices were calm, indistinct, male and female, engaged in conversation.

My neck was stiff and my eyeballs felt gritty in their sockets. My leg had gone to sleep, pressed against the steering wheel. I fumbled for my glasses in the pocket of my work shirt and finally got them on.

Then I looked behind me and saw the city.

The books on Thirties design were in the trunk; one of them contained sketches of an idealized city that drew on *Metropolis* and *Things to Come,* but squared everything, soaring up through an architect's perfect clouds to zeppelin docks and mad neon spires. That city was a scale model of the one that rose behind me. Spire stood on spire in gleaming ziggurat steps that climbed to a central golden temple tower ringed with the crazy radiator flanges of the Mongo gas stations. You could hide the Empire State Building in the smallest of those towers. Roads of crystal soared between the spires, crossed and recrossed by smooth silver shapes like beads of running mercury. The air was thick with ships: giant wing-liners, little darting silver things (sometimes one of the quicksilver shapes from the sky bridges rose gracefully into the air and flew up to join the dance), mile-long blimps, hovering dragonfly things that were gyrocopters . . .

I closed my eyes tight and swung around in the seat. When I opened them, I willed myself to see the mileage meter, the pale road dust on the black plastic dashboard, the overflowing ashtray.

"Amphetamine psychosis," I said. I opened my eyes. The dash was still there, the dust, the crushed filtertips. Very carefully, without moving my head, I turned the headlights on.

And saw them.

They were blond. They were standing beside their car, an aluminum avocado with a central shark-fin rudder jutting up from its spine and smooth black tires like a child's toy. He had his arm around her waist and was gesturing toward the city. They were both in white: loose clothing, bare legs, spotless white sun shoes. Neither of them seemed aware of the beams of my headlights. He was saying something wise and strong, and she was nodding, and suddenly I was frightened, frightened in an entirely different way. Sanity had ceased to be an issue; I knew, somehow, that the city behind me was Tucson—a dream Tucson thrown up out of the collective yearning of an era. That it was real, entirely real. But the couple in front of me lived in it, and they frightened me.

They were the children of Dialta Downes's '80-that-wasn't; they were Heirs to the Dream. They were white, blond, and they probably had blue eyes. They were American. Dialta had said that the Future had come to America first, but had finally passed it by. But not here, in the heart of the Dream. Here, we'd gone on and on, in a dream logic that knew nothing of pollution, the finite bounds of fossil fuel, or foreign wars it was possible to lose. They were smug, happy, and utterly content with themselves and their world. And in the Dream, it was *their* world.

Behind me, the illuminated city: Searchlights swept the sky for the sheer joy of it. I imagined them thronging the plazas of white marble, orderly and alert, their bright eyes shining with enthusiasm for their floodlit avenues and silver cars.

It had all the sinister fruitiness of Hitler Youth propaganda.

I put the car in gear and drove forward slowly, until the bumper was within three feet of them. They still hadn't seen me. I rolled the window down and listened to what the man was saying. His words were bright and hollow as the pitch in some Chamber of Commerce brochure, and I knew that he believed in them absolutely.

"John," I heard the woman say, "we've forgotten to take our food pills." She clicked two bright wafers from a thing on her belt and passed one to him. I backed onto the highway and headed for Los Angeles, wincing and shaking my head.

I phoned Kihn from a gas station. A new one, in bad Spanish Modern. He was back from his expedition and didn't seem to mind the call.

"Yeah, that is a weird one. Did you try to get any pictures? Not that they ever come out, but it adds an interesting *frisson* to your story, not having the pictures turn out. . . ."

But what should I do?

"Watch lots of television, particularly game shows and soaps. Go to porn movies. Ever see *Nazi Love Motel*? They've got it on cable, here. Really awful. Just what you need."

What was he talking about?

"Quit yelling and listen to me. I'm letting you in on a trade secret: Really bad media can exorcise your semiotic ghosts. If it keeps the saucer people off my back, it can keep these Art Deco futuroids off yours. Try it. What have you got to lose?"

Then he begged off, pleading an early-morning date with the Elect.

"The who?"

"These oldsters from Vegas; the ones with the microwaves."

I considered putting a collect call through to London, getting Cohen at Barris-Watford and telling him his photographer was checked out for a protracted season in the Twilight Zone. In the end, I let a machine mix me a really impossible cup of black coffee and climbed back into the Toyota for the haul to Los Angeles.

Los Angeles was a bad idea, and I spent two weeks there. It was prime

Downes country; too much of the Dream there, and too many fragments of the Dream waiting to snare me. I nearly wrecked the car on a stretch of overpass near Disneyland, when the road fanned out like an origami trick and left me swerving through a dozen minilanes of whizzing chrome teardrops with shark fins. Even worse, Hollywood was full of people who looked too much like the couple I'd seen in Arizona. I hired an Italian director who was making ends meet doing darkroom work and installing patio decks around swimming pools until his ship came in; he made prints of all the negatives I'd accumulated on the Downes job. I didn't want to look at the stuff myself. It didn't seem to bother Leonardo, though, and when he was finished I checked the prints, riffling through them like a deck of cards, sealed them up, and sent them air freight to London. Then I took a taxi to a theater that was showing *Nazi Love Motel,* and kept my eyes shut all the way.

Cohen's congratulatory wire was forwarded to me in San Francisco a week later. Dialta had loved the pictures. He admired the way I'd "really gotten into it," and looked forward to working with me again. That afternoon I spotted a flying wing over Castro Street, but there was something tenuous about it, as though it were only half there. I rushed into the nearest newsstand and gathered up as much as I could find on the petroleum crisis and the nuclear energy hazard. I'd just decided to buy a plane ticket for New York.

"Hell of a world we live in, huh?" The proprietor was a thin black man with bad teeth and an obvious wig. I nodded, fishing in my jeans for change, anxious to find a park bench where I could submerge myself in hard evidence of the human near-dystopia we live in. "But it could be worse, huh?"

"That's right," I said, "or even worse, it could be perfect."

He watched me as I headed down the street with my little bundle of condensed catastrophe.

1986

URSULA K. LE GUIN
b. 1929

Born in Berkeley, California, Ursula K. Le Guin was educated at Radcliffe College and Columbia University. She has published over twenty novels, many children's books, and several volumes of short fiction and poetry. Her novel *The Left Hand of Darkness* (1969), her novella *The Word for World Is Forest* (1973), and her short story "The Ones Who Walk Away from Omelas" (1974) each received the Hugo Award in its genre; and she has received Nebula, Jupiter, Jules Verne, and National Book Awards for her writing.

Le Guin's work spans many genres and forms, and its setting is sometimes Earth, sometimes other planets. "Some of my fiction is 'science fiction,' " she said in a 1989 interview, "some of it is 'fantasy,' some of it is 'realist,' some of it is 'magical realism.' " In a 1989 *Los Angeles Times* article, author Theodore Sturgeon attempted to pinpoint a common denominator: "A cautionary fear of the development of democracy into dictatorship. Celebrations of courage, endurance, risk. Language, not only loved and shaped, but investigated in all its aspects; call that, perhaps, communication. But above all, in almost unearthly terms Ursula Le Guin examines, attacks, unbuttons, takes down and exposes our notions of reality."

"Schrödinger's Cat" was published in *Universe 5* (1974), and "She Unnames Them" first appeared in *The New Yorker* (1985). Both stories were collected in *Buffalo Gals and Other Animal Presences* (1988).

Schrödinger's Cat

As things appear to be coming to some sort of climax, I have withdrawn to this place. It is cooler here, and nothing moves fast.

On the way here I met a married couple who were coming apart. She had pretty well gone to pieces, but he seemed, at first glance, quite hearty. While he was telling me that he had no hormones of any kind, she pulled herself together, and by supporting her head in the crook of her right knee and hopping on the toes of the right foot, approached us shouting, "Well what's *wrong* with a person trying to express themselves?" The left leg, the arms, and the trunk, which had remained lying in the heap, twitched and jerked in sympathy. "Great legs," the husband pointed out, looking at the slim ankle. "My wife has great legs."

A cat has arrived, interrupting my narrative. It is a striped yellow tom with white chest and paws. He has long whiskers and yellow eyes. I never noticed before that cats had whiskers about their eyes; is that normal? There is no way to tell. As he has gone to sleep on my knee, I shall proceed.

Where?

Nowhere, evidently. Yet the impulse to narrate remains. Many things are not worth doing, but almost anything is worth telling. In any case, I have a severe congenital case of Ethica laboris puritanica, or Adam's Disease. It is incurable except by total decapitation. I even like to dream when asleep, and to try and recall my dreams: it assures me that I haven't wasted seven or eight hours just lying there. Now here I am, lying here. Hard at it.

Well, the couple I was telling you about finally broke up. The pieces of him trotted around bouncing and cheeping, like little chicks, but she was finally reduced to nothing but a mass of nerves: rather like fine chicken-wire, in fact, but hopelessly tangled.

So I came on, placing one foot carefully in front of the other, and grieving. This grief is with me still. I fear it is part of me, like foot or loin or eye, or may even be myself: for I seem to have no other self, nothing further, nothing that lies outside the borders of grief.

Yet I don't know what I grieve for: my wife? my husband? my children, or myself? I can't remember. Most dreams are forgotten, try as one will to remember. Yet later music strikes the note and the harmonic rings along the mandolin-strings of the mind, and we find tears in our eyes. Some note keeps playing that makes me want to cry; but what for? I am not certain.

The yellow cat, who may have belonged to the couple that broke up, is dreaming. His paws twitch now and then, and once he makes a small, suppressed remark with his mouth shut. I wonder what a cat dreams of, and to whom he was speaking just then. Cats seldom waste words. They are quiet beasts. They keep their counsel, they reflect. They reflect all day, and at night their eyes reflect. Overbred Siamese cats may be as noisy as little dogs, and then people say, "They're talking," but the noise is farther from speech than is the deep silence of the hound or the tabby. All this cat can say is meow, but maybe in his silences he will suggest to me what it is that I have lost, what I am grieving for. I have a feeling that he knows. That's why he came here. Cats look out for Number One.

It was getting awfully hot. I mean, you could touch less and less. The stove-burners, for instance; now I know that stove-burners always used to get hot, that was their final cause, they existed in order to get hot. But they began to get hot without having been turned on. Electric units or gas rings, there they'd be when you came into the kitchen for breakfast, all four of them glaring away, the air above them shaking like clear jelly with the heat-waves. It did no good to turn them off, because they weren't on in the first place. Besides, the knobs and dials were also hot, uncomfortable to the touch.

Some people tried hard to cool them off. The favorite technique was to turn them on. It worked sometimes, but you could not count on it. Others investigated the phenomenon, tried to get at the root of it, the cause. They were probably the most frightened ones, but man is most human at his most frightened. In the face of the hot stove-burners they acted with exemplary coolness. They studied, they observed. They were like the fellow in Michelangelo's *Last Judgment,* who has clapped his hands over his face in horror as the devils drag him down to Hell—but only over one eye, the other eye is busy looking. It's all he can do, but he does it. He observes. Indeed, one wonders if Hell would exist, if he did not look at it. However, neither he, nor the people I am talking about, had enough time to do much about it. And then finally of course there were the people who did not try to do or think anything about it at all.

When the water came out of the cold-water taps hot one morning, however, even people who had blamed it all on the Democrats began to feel a more profound unease. Before long forks and pencils and wrenches were too hot to handle without gloves; and cars were really terrible. It was like opening the door of an oven going full blast, to open the door of your car. And by then, other people almost scorched your fingers off. A kiss was like a branding iron. Your child's hair flowed along your hand like fire.

Here, as I said, it is cooler; and, as a matter of fact, this animal is cool. A real cool cat. No wonder it's pleasant to pet his fur. Also he moves slowly, at least for the most part, which is all the slowness one can reasonably expect of a cat. He hasn't that frenetic quality most creatures acquired—all they did was ZAP and gone. They lacked presence. I suppose birds always tended to be that way, but even the hummingbird used to halt for a second in the very center of his metabolic frenzy, and hang, still as a hub, present, above the fuchsias—then gone again, but you knew something was there besides the blurring brightness. But it got so that even robins and pigeons, the heavy impudent birds, were a blur; and as for swallows, they cracked the sound barrier. You knew of swallows only by the small, curved sonic booms that looped about the eaves of old houses in the evening.

Worms shot like subway trains through the dirt of gardens, among the writhing roots of roses.

You could scarcely lay a hand on children, by then: too fast to catch, too hot to hold. They grew up before your eyes.

But then, maybe that's always been true.

I was interrupted by the cat, who woke and said meow once, then jumped down from my lap and leaned against my legs diligently. This is a cat who knows how to get fed. He also knows how to jump. There was a lazy fluidity to his leap, as if gravity affected him less than it does other creatures. As a matter of fact there were some localized cases, just before I left, of the failure of gravity; but this quality in the cat's leap was something quite else. I am not yet in such a state of confusion that I can be alarmed by grace. Indeed, I found it reassuring. While I was opening a can of sardines, a person arrived.

Hearing the knock, I thought it might be the mailman. I miss mail very much, so I hurried to the door and said, "Is it the mail?" A voice replied, "Yah!" I opened the door. He came in, almost pushing me aside in his haste. He dumped down an enormous knapsack he had been carrying, straightened up, massaged his shoulders, and said, "Wow!"

"How did you get here?"

He stared at me and repeated, "How?"

At this my thoughts concerning human and animal speech recurred to me, and I decided that this was probably not a man, but a small dog. (Large dogs seldom go yah, wow, how, unless it is appropriate to do so.)

"Come on, fella," I coaxed him. "Come, come on, that's a boy, good doggie!" I opened a can of pork and beans for him at once, for he looked half starved. He ate voraciously, gulping and lapping. When it was gone he said "Wow!" several times. I was just about to scratch him behind the ears when he stiffened, his hackles bristling, and growled deep in his throat. He had noticed the cat.

The cat had noticed him some time before, without interest, and was now sitting on a copy of *The Well-Tempered Clavier* washing sardine oil off its whiskers. "Wow!" the dog, whom I had thought of calling Rover, barked. "Wow! Do you know what that is? *That's Schrödinger's Cat!*"

"No it's not; not any more; it's my cat," I said, unreasonably offended.

"Oh, well, Schrödinger's dead, of course, but it's his cat. I've seen hundreds of picture of it. Erwin Schrödinger, the great physicist, you know. Oh, wow! To think of finding it here!"

The cat looked coldly at him for a moment, and began to wash its left shoulder with negligent energy. An almost religious expression had come into Rover's face. "It was meant," he said in a low, impressive tone. "Yah. It was *meant.* It can't be a mere coincidence. It's too improbable. Me, with the box; you, with the cat; to meet—here—now." He looked up at me, his eyes shining with happy fervor. "Isn't it wonderful?" he said. "I'll get the box set up right away." And he started to tear open his huge knapsack.

While the cat washed its front paws, Rover unpacked. While the cat washed its tail and belly, regions hard to reach gracefully, Rover put together what he had unpacked, a complex task. When he and the cat finished their operations simultaneously and looked at me, I was impressed. They had come out even, to the very second. Indeed it seemed that something more than chance was involved. I hoped it was not myself.

"What's that?" I asked, pointing to a protuberance on the outside of the box. I did not ask what the box was as it was quite clearly a box.

"The gun," Rover said with excited pride.

"The gun?"

"To shoot the cat."

"To shoot the cat?"

"Or to *not shoot* the cat. Depending on the photon."

"The photon?"

"Yah! It's Schrödinger's great Gedankenexperiment. You see, there's a little emitter here. At Zero Time, five seconds after the lid of the box is closed, it will emit one photon. The photon will strike a half-silvered mirror. The quantum mechanical probability of the photon passing through the mirror is exactly one-half, isn't it? So! If the photon passes through, the trigger will be activated and the gun will fire. If the photon is deflected, the trigger will not be activated and the gun will not fire. Now, you put the cat in. The cat is in the box. You close the lid. You go away! You stay away! What happens?" Rover's eyes were bright.

"The cat gets hungry?"

"The cat gets shot—or not shot," he said, seizing my arm, though not, fortunately, in his teeth. "But the gun is silent, perfectly silent. The box is soundproof. There is no way to know whether or not the cat has been shot, until you lift the lid of the box. There is NO way! Do you see how central this is to the whole of quantum theory? Before Zero Time the whole system, on the quantum level or on our level, is nice and simple. But after Zero Time the whole system can be represented only by a linear combination of two waves. We cannot predict the behavior of the photon, and thus, once it has behaved, we cannot predict the state of the system it has determined. We cannot predict it! God plays dice with the world! So it is beautifully demonstrated that if you desire certainty, any certainty, you must create it yourself!"

"How?"

"By lifting the lid of the box, of course," Rover said, looking at me with sudden disappointment, perhaps a touch of suspicion, like a Baptist who finds he has been talking church matters not to another Baptist as he thought, but a Methodist, or even, God forbid, an Episcopalian. "To find out whether the cat is dead or not."

"Do you mean," I said carefully, "that until you lift the lid of the box, the cat has neither been shot nor not been shot?"

"Yah!" Rover said, radiant with relief, welcoming me back to the fold. "Or maybe, you know, both."

"But why does opening the box and looking reduce the system back to one probability, either live cat or dead cat? Why don't we get included in the system when we lift the lid of the box?"

There was a pause. "How?" Rover barked, distrustfully.

"Well, we would involve ourselves in the system, you see, the superposition of two waves. There's no reason why it should only exist *inside* an open box, is there? so when we came to look, there we would be, you and I, both looking at a live cat, and both looking at a dead cat. You see?"

A dark cloud lowered on Rover's eyes and brow. He barked twice in a subdued, harsh voice, and walked away. With his back turned to me he said in a firm, sad tone, "You must not complicate the issue. It is complicated enough."

"Are you sure?"

He nodded. Turning, he spoke pleadingly. "Listen. It's all we have—the box. Truly it is. The box. And the cat. And they're here. The box, the cat, at last. Put the cat in the box. Will you? Will you let me put the cat in the box?"

"No," I said, shocked.

"Please. Please. Just for a minute. Just for half a minute! Please let me put the cat in the box!"

"Why?"

"I can't stand this terrible uncertainty," he said, and burst into tears.

I stood some while indecisive. Though I felt sorry for the poor son of a bitch, I was about to tell him, gently, No; when a curious thing happened. The cat walked over to the box, sniffed around it, lifted his tail and sprayed a corner to mark his territory, and then lightly, with that marvelous fluid ease, leapt into it. His yellow tail just flicked the edge of the lid as he jumped, and it closed, falling into place with a soft, decisive click.

"The cat is in the box," I said.

"The cat is in the box," Rover repeated in a whisper, falling to his knees. "Oh, wow. Oh, wow. Oh, wow."

There was silence then: deep silence. We both gazed, I afoot, Rover kneeling, at the box. No sound. Nothing happened. Nothing would happen. Nothing would ever happen, until we lifted the lid of the box.

"Like Pandora," I said in a weak whisper. I could not quite recall Pandora's legend. She had let all the plagues and evils out of the box, of course, but there had been something else, too. After all the devils were let loose, something quite different, quite unexpected, had been left. What had it been? Hope? A dead cat? I could not remember.

Impatience welled up in me. I turned on Rover, glaring. He returned the look with expressive brown eyes. You can't tell me dogs haven't got souls.

"Just exactly what are you trying to prove?" I demanded.

"That the cat will be dead, or not dead," he murmured submissively. "Certainty. All I want is certainty. To know for *sure* that God *does* play dice with the world!"

I looked at him for a while with fascinated incredulity. "Whether he does, or doesn't," I said, "do you think he's going to leave you a note about it in the box?" I went to the box, and with a rather dramatic gesture, flung the lid back. Rover staggered up from his knees, gasping, to look. The cat was, of course, not there.

Rover neither barked, nor fainted, nor cursed, nor wept. He really took it very well.

"Where is the cat?" he asked at last.

"Where is the box?"

"Here."

"Where's here?"

"Here is now."

"We used to think so," I said, "but really we could use larger boxes."

He gazed about him in mute bewilderment, and did not flinch even when the roof of the house was lifted off just like the lid of a box, letting in the unconscionable, inordinate light of the stars. He had just time to breathe, "Oh, wow!"

I have identified the note that keeps sounding. I checked it on the mandolin before the glue melted. It is the note A, the one that drove the composer Schumann mad. It is a beautiful, clear tone, much clearer now that the stars are visible. I shall miss the cat. I wonder if he found what it was we lost.

1988

She Unnames Them

Most of them accepted namelessness with the perfect indifference with which they had so long accepted and ignored their names. Whales and dolphins, seals and sea otters consented with particular grace and alacrity, sliding into anonymity as into their element. A faction of yaks, however, protested. They said that "yak" sounded right, and that almost everyone who knew they existed called them that. Unlike the ubiquitous creatures such as rats or fleas who had been called by hundreds or thousands of different names since Babel, the yaks could truly say, they said, that they had *a name*. They discussed the matter all summer. The councils of the elderly females finally agreed that though the name might be useful to others, it was so redundant from the yak point of view that they never spoke it themselves, and hence might as well dispense with it. After they presented the argument in this light to their bulls, a full consensus was delayed only by the onset of severe early blizzards. Soon after the beginning of the thaw their agreement was reached and the designation "yak" was returned to the donor.

Among the domestic animals, few horses had cared what anybody called them since the failure of Dean Swift's attempt to name them from their own vocabulary. Cattle, sheep, swine, asses, mules, and goats, along with chickens, geese, and turkeys, all agreed enthusiastically to give their names back to the people to whom—as they put it—they belonged.

A couple of problems did come up with pets. The cats of course steadfastly denied ever having had any name other than those self-given, unspoken, effanineffably personal names which, as the poet named Eliot said, they spend long hours daily contemplating—though none of the contemplators has ever admitted that what they contemplate is in fact their name, and some onlookers have wondered if the object of that meditative gaze might not in fact be the Perfect, or Platonic, Mouse. In any case it is a moot point now. It was with the dogs, and with some parrots, lovebirds, ravens, and mynahs that the trouble arose. These verbally talented individuals insisted that their names were important to them, and flatly refused to part with them. But as soon as they understood that the issue was precisely one of individual choice, and that anybody who wanted to be called Rover, or Froufrou, or Polly, or even Birdie in the personal sense, was perfectly free to do so, not one of them had the least objection to parting with the lower case (or, as regards German creatures, uppercase) generic appellations poodle, parrot, dog, or bird, and all the Linnaean qualifiers that had trailed along behind them for two hundred years like tin cans tied to a tail.

The insects parted with their names in vast clouds and swarms of ephemeral syllables buzzing and stinging and humming and flitting and crawling and tunneling away.

As for the fish of the sea, their names dispersed from them in silence throughout the oceans like faint, dark blurs of cuttlefish ink, and drifted off on the currents without a trace.

None were left now to unname, and yet how close I felt to them when I saw one of them swim or fly or trot or crawl across my way or over my skin, or stalk me in the night, or go along beside me for a while in the day. They seemed far closer than when their names had stood between myself and them like a clear barrier: so close that my fear of them and their fear of me became one same fear. And the attraction that many of us felt, the desire to smell one another's smells, feel or rub or caress one another's scales or skin or feathers or fur, taste one another's blood or flesh, keep one another warm,—that attraction was now all one with the fear, and the hunter could not be told from the hunted, nor the eater from the food.

This was more or less the effect I had been after. It was somewhat more powerful than I had anticipated, but I could not now, in all conscience, make an exception for myself. I resolutely put anxiety away, went to Adam, and said, "You and your father lent me this—gave it to me, actually. It's been really useful, but it doesn't exactly seem to fit very well lately. But thanks very much! It's really been very useful."

It is hard to give back a gift without sounding peevish or ungrateful, and I did not want to leave him with that impression of me. He was not paying much attention, as it happened, and said only, "Put it down over there, OK?" and went on with what he was doing.

One of my reasons for doing what I did was that talk was getting us nowhere; but all the same I felt a little let down. I had been prepared to defend my decision. And I thought that perhaps when he did notice he might be upset and want to talk. I put some things away and fiddled around a little, but he continued to do what he was doing and to take no notice of anything else. At last I said, "Well, goodbye, dear. I hope the garden key turns up."

He was fitting parts together, and said without looking around, "OK, fine, dear. When's dinner?"

"I'm not sure," I said. "I'm going now. With the—" I hesitated, and finally said, "With them, you know," and went on. In fact I had only just then realized how hard it would have been to explain myself. I could not chatter away as I used to do, taking it all for granted. My words now must be as slow, as new, as single, as tentative as the steps I took going down the path away from the house, between the dark-branched, tall dancers motionless against the winter shining.

1988

DON DELILLO

b. 1936

Born in Bronx, New York, Don DeLillo attended Fordham University. Beyond that, he is reluctant to share details of his personal history. An interviewer who tracked him down in Athens, Greece, in 1979, was handed a business card engraved with DeLillo's name and "I don't want to talk about it." His literary history includes ten novels, among them *Americana* (1971), *Great Jones Street* (1973), *Ratner's Star* (1976), *The Names* (1982), *White Noise* (1985), *Libra* (1988), and *Mao II* (1991).

"My work doesn't offer the comforts of other kinds of fiction," DeLillo told *The Paris Review* in 1993, "work that suggests that our lives and our problems and our perceptions are no different today than they were fifty or sixty years ago. I don't offer comforts except those that lurk in comedy and in structure and in language. . . . Before history and politics, there's language. And it's language, the sheer pleasure of making it and bending it and seeing it form on the page and hearing it whistle in my head—this is the thing that makes my work go. . . . What I try to do is create complex human beings, ordinary-extraordinary men and women who live in the particular skin of the late twentieth century. I try to record what I see and hear and sense around me—what I feel in the currents, the electric stuff of the culture. I think these are American forces and energies. And they belong to our time."

White Noise, excerpted here, was nominated for the National Book Critics Circle Award and received the American Book Award in fiction. "In *White Noise,*" DeLillo said, "there is less language and more human dread. There's a certain equation at work. As technology advances in complexity and scope, fear becomes more primitive."

From White Noise

7

Two nights a week Babette goes to the Congregational church at the other end of town and lectures to adults in the basement on correct posture. Basically she is teaching them how to stand, sit and walk. Most of her students are old. It isn't clear to me why they want to improve their posture. We seem to believe it is possible to ward off death by following rules of good grooming. Sometimes I go with my wife to the church basement and watch her stand, turn, assume various heroic poses, gesture gracefully. She makes references to yoga, kendo, trance-walking. She talks of Sufi dervishes, Sherpa mountaineers. The old folks nod and listen. Nothing is foreign, nothing too remote to apply. I am always surprised at their acceptance and trust, the sweetness of their belief. Nothing is too doubtful to be of use to them as they seek to redeem their bodies from a lifetime of bad posture. It is the end of skepticism.

We walked home under a marigold moon. Our house looked old and wan at the end of the street, the porch light shining on a molded plastic tricycle, a stack of three-hour colored-flame sawdust and wax logs. Denise was doing her homework in the kitchen, keeping an eye on Wilder, who had wandered downstairs to sit on the floor and stare through the oven window. Silence in the halls, shadows on the sloping lawn. We closed the door and disrobed. The bed was a mess. Magazines, curtain rods, a child's sooty sock. Babette hummed something from a Broadway show, putting the rods in a corner. We embraced, fell sideways to the bed in a controlled way, then repositioned ourselves, bathing in each other's flesh, trying to kick the sheets off our ankles. Her body had a number of long hollows, places the hand might stop to solve in the dark, tempo-slowing places.

We believed something lived in the basement.

"What do you want to do?" she said.

"Whatever you want to do."

"I want to do whatever's best for you."

"What's best for me is to please you," I said.

"I want to make you happy, Jack."

"I'm happy when I'm pleasing you."

"I just want to do what you want to do."

"I want to do whatever's best for you."

"But you please me by letting me please you," she said.

"As the male partner I think it's my responsibility to please."

"I'm not sure whether that's a sensitive caring statement or a sexist remark."

"Is it wrong for the man to be considerate toward his partner?"

"I'm your partner when we play tennis, which we ought to start doing again, by the way. Otherwise I'm your wife. Do you want me to read to you?"

"First-rate."

"I know you like me to read sexy stuff."

"I thought you liked it too."

"Isn't it basically the person being read to who derives the benefit and the satisfaction? When I read to Old Man Treadwell, it's not because I find those tabloids stimulating."

"Treadwell's blind, I'm not. I thought you liked to read erotic passages."

"If it pleases you, then I like to do it."

"But it has to please you too, Baba. Otherwise how would I feel?"

"It pleases me that you enjoy my reading."

"I get the feeling a burden is being shifted back and forth. The burden of being the one who is pleased."

"I want to read, Jack. Honestly."

"Are you totally and completely sure? Because if you're not, we absolutely won't."

Someone turned on the TV set at the end of the hall, and a woman's voice said: "If it breaks easily into pieces, it is called shale. When wet, it smells like clay."

We listened to the gently plummeting stream of nighttime traffic.

I said, "Pick your century. Do you want to read about Etruscan slave girls, Georgian rakes? I think we have some literature on flagellation brothels. What about the Middle Ages? We have incubi and succubi. Nuns galore."

"Whatever's best for you."

"I want you to choose. It's sexier that way."

"One person chooses, the other reads. Don't we want a balance, a sort of give-and-take? Isn't that what makes it sexy?"

"A tautness, a suspense. First-rate. I will choose."

"I will read," she said. "But I don't want you to choose anything that has men inside women, quote-quote, or men entering women. 'I entered her.' 'He entered me.' We're not lobbies or elevators. 'I wanted him inside me,' as if he could crawl completely in, sign the register, sleep, eat, so forth. Can we agree on that? I don't care what these people do as long as they don't enter or get entered."

"Agreed."

"I entered her and began to thrust."

"I'm in total agreement," I said.

" 'Enter me, enter me, yes, yes.' "

"Silly usage, absolutely."

" 'Insert yourself, Rex. I want you inside me, entering hard, entering deep, yes, now, oh.' "

I began to feel an erection stirring. How stupid and out of context. Babette laughed at her own lines. The TV said: "Until Florida surgeons attached an artificial flipper."

Babette and I tell each other everything. I have told everything, such as it was at the time, to each of my wives. There is more to tell, of course, as marriages accumulate. But when I say I believe in complete disclosure I don't mean it cheaply, as anecdotal sport or shallow revelation. It is a form of self-renewal and a gesture of custodial trust. Love helps us develop an identity secure enough to allow itself to be placed in another's care and protection. Babette and I have turned our lives for each other's thoughtful regard, turned them in the moonlight in our pale hands, spoken deep into the night about fathers and mothers, childhood, friendships, awakenings, old loves, old fears (except fear of death). No detail must be left out, not even a dog with ticks or a neighbor's boy who ate an insect on a dare. The smell of pantries, the sense of empty afternoons, the feel of things as they rained across our skin, things as facts and passions, the feel of pain, loss, disappointment, breathless delight. In these night recitations we create a space between things as we felt them at the time and as we speak them now. This is the space reserved for irony, sympathy and fond amusement, the means by which we rescue ourselves from the past.

I decided on the twentieth century. I put on my bathrobe and went down the hall to Heinrich's room to find a trashy magazine Babette might read from, the type that features letters from readers detailing their sexual experiences. This struck me as one of the few things the modern imagination has contributed to the history of erotic practices. There is a double fantasy at work in such letters. People write down imagined episodes and then see them published in a national magazine. Which is the greater stimulation?

Wilder was in there watching Heinrich do a physics experiment with steel balls and a salad bowl. Heinrich wore a terry cloth robe, a towel around his neck, another towel on his head. He told me to look downstairs.

In a stack of material I found some family photo albums, one or two of them at least fifty years old. I took them up to the bedroom. We spent hours going through them, sitting up in bed. Children wincing in the sun, women in sun hats, men shading their eyes from the glare as if the past possessed some quality of light we no longer experience, a Sunday dazzle that caused people in their churchgoing clothes to tighten their faces and stand at an angle to the future, somewhat averted it seemed, wearing fixed and fine-drawn smiles, skeptical of something in the nature of the box camera.

Who will die first?

9

They had to evacuate the grade school on Tuesday. Kids were getting headaches and eye irritations, tasting metal in their mouths. A teacher rolled on the floor and spoke foreign languages. No one knew what was wrong. Investigators said it could be the ventilating system, the paint or varnish, the foam insulation, the electrical insulation, the cafeteria food, the rays emitted by microcomputers, the asbestos fireproofing, the adhesive on shipping containers, the fumes from the chlorinated pool, or perhaps something deeper, finer-grained, more closely woven into the basic state of things.

Denise and Steffie stayed home that week as men in Mylex suits and respirator masks made systematic sweeps of the building with infrared detecting and measuring equipment. Because Mylex is itself a suspect material, the results tended to be ambiguous and a second round of more rigorous detection had to be scheduled.

The two girls and Babette, Wilder and I went to the supermarket. Minutes after we entered, we ran into Murray. This was the fourth or fifth time I'd seen him in the supermarket, which was roughly the number of times I'd seen him on campus. He clutched Babette by the left bicep and sidled around her, appearing to smell her hair.

"A lovely dinner," he said, standing directly behind her. "I like to cook myself, which doubles my appreciation of someone who does it well."

"Come any time," she said, turning in an effort to find him.

We moved together into the ultra-cool interior. Wilder sat in the shopping cart trying to grab items off the shelves as we went by. It occurred to me that he was too old and too big to be sitting in supermarket carts. I also wondered why his vocabulary seemed to be stalled at twenty-five words.

"I'm happy to be here," Murray said.

"In Blacksmith?"

"In Blacksmith, in the supermarket, in the rooming house, on the Hill. I feel I'm learning important things every day. Death, disease, afterlife, outer space. It's all much clearer here. I can think and see."

We moved into the generic food area and Murray paused with his plastic basket to probe among the white cartons and jars. I wasn't sure I understood what he was talking about. What did he mean, much clearer? He could think and see what?

Steffie took my hand and we walked past the fruit bins, an area that extended about forty-five yards along one wall. The bins were arranged diagonally and backed by mirrors that people accidentally punched when reaching for fruit in the upper rows. A voice on the loudspeaker said: "Kleenex Softique, your truck's blocking the entrance." Apples and lemons tumbled in twos and threes to the floor when someone took a fruit from certain places in the stacked array. There were six kinds of apples, there were exotic melons in several pastels. Everything seemed to be in season, sprayed, burnished, bright. People tore filmy bags off racks and tried to figure out which end opened. I realized the place was awash in noise. The toneless systems, the jangle and skid of carts, the loudspeaker and coffee-making machines, the cries of children. And over it all, or under it all, a dull and unlocatable roar, as of some form of swarming life just outside the range of human apprehension.

"Did you tell Denise you were sorry?"

"Maybe later," Steffie said. "Remind me."

"She's a sweet girl and she wants to be your older sister and your friend if you'll let her."

"I don't know about friend. She's a little bossy, don't you think?"

"Aside from telling her you're sorry, be sure to give her back her *Physicians' Desk Reference.*"

"She reads that thing all the time. Don't you think that's weird?"

"At least she reads something."

"Sure, lists of drugs and medicines. And do you want to know why?"

"Why?"

"Because she's trying to find out the side effects of the stuff that Baba uses."

"What does Baba use?"

"Don't ask me. Ask Denise."

"How do you know she uses anything?"

"Ask Denise."

"Why don't I ask Baba?"

"Ask Baba," she said.

Murray came out of an aisle and walked alongside Babette, just ahead of us. He took a twin roll of paper towels out of her cart and smelled it. Denise had found some friends and they went up front to look at the paperback books in spindly racks, the books with shiny metallic print, raised letters, vivid illustrations of cult violence and windswept romance. Denise was wearing a green visor. I heard Babette tell Murray she'd been wearing it fourteen hours a day for three weeks now. She would not go out without it, would not even leave her room. She wore it in school, when there was school, wore it to the toilet, the dentist's chair, the dinner table. Something about the visor seemed to speak to her, to offer wholeness and identity.

"It's her interface with the world," Murray said.

He helped Babette push her loaded cart. I heard him say to her, "Tibetans believe there is a transitional state between death and rebirth. Death is a waiting period, basically. Soon a fresh womb will receive the soul. In the meantime the soul restores to itself some of the divinity lost at birth." He studied her profile as if to detect a reaction. "That's what I think of whenever I come in here. This place recharges us spiritually, it prepares us, it's a gateway or pathway. Look how bright. It's full of psychic data."

My wife smiled at him.

"Everything is concealed in symbolism, hidden by veils of mystery and layers of cultural material. But it is psychic data, absolutely. The large doors slide open, they close unbidden. Energy waves, incident radiation. All the letters and numbers are here, all the colors of the spectrum, all the voices and sounds, all the code words and ceremonial phrases. It is just a question of deciphering, rearranging, peeling off the layers of unspeakability. Not that we would want to, not that any useful purpose would be served. This is not Tibet. Even Tibet is not Tibet anymore."

He studied her profile. She put some yogurt in her cart.

"Tibetans try to see death for what it is. It is the end of attachment to things. This simple truth is hard to fathom. But once we stop denying death, we can proceed calmly to die and then go on to experience uterine rebirth or Judeo-Christian afterlife or out-of-body experience or a trip on a UFO or whatever we wish to call it. We can do so with clear vision, without awe or terror. We don't have to cling to life artificially, or to death for that matter. We simply walk toward the sliding doors. Waves and radiation. Look how well-lighted everything is. The place is sealed off, self-contained. It is timeless. Another reason why I think of Tibet. Dying is an art in Tibet. A priest walks in, sits down, tells the weeping relatives to get out and has the room sealed. Doors, windows sealed. He has serious business to see to. Chants, numerology, horoscopes, recitations. Here we don't die, we shop. But the difference is less marked than you think."

He was almost whispering now and I tried to get up closer without ramming my cart into Babette's. I wanted to hear everything.

"Supermarkets this large and clean and modern are a revelation to me. I spent my life in small steamy delicatessens with slanted display cabinets full of trays that hold soft wet lumpy matter in pale colors. High enough cabinets so you had to stand on tiptoes to give your order. Shouts, accents. In cities no one notices specific dying. Dying is a quality of the air. It's everywhere and nowhere. Men shout as they die, to be noticed, remembered for a second or two. To die in an apartment instead of a house can depress the soul, I would imagine, for several lives to come. In a town there are houses, plants in bay windows. People notice dying better. The dead have faces, automobiles. If you don't know a name, you know a street name, a dog's name. 'He drove an orange Mazda.' You know a couple of useless things about a person that become major facts of identification and cosmic placement when he dies suddenly, after a short illness, in his own bed, with a comforter and matching pillows, on a rainy Wednesday afternoon, feverish, a little congested in the sinuses and chest, thinking about his dry cleaning."

Babette said, "Where is Wilder?" and turned to stare at me in a way that suggested ten minutes had passed since she'd last seen him. Other looks, less pensive and less guilty, indicated greater time spans, deeper seas of inattention. Like: *"I didn't know whales were mammals."* The greater the time span, the blanker the look, the more dangerous the situation. It was as if guilt were a luxury she allowed herself only when the danger was minimal.

"How could he get out of the cart without my noticing?"

The three adults each stood at the head of an aisle and peered into the traffic of carts and gliding bodies. Then we did three more aisles, heads set forward, weaving slightly as we changed our sightlines. I kept seeing colored spots off to the right but when I turned there was nothing there. I'd been seeing colored spots for years but never so many, so gaily animated. Murray saw Wilder in another woman's cart. The woman waved at Babette and headed toward us. She lived on our street with a teenage daughter and an Asian baby, Chun Duc. Everyone referred to the baby by name, almost in a tone of proud proprietorship, but no one knew who Chun belonged to or where he or she had come from.

"Kleenex Softique, Kleenex Softique."

Steffie was holding my hand in a way I'd come to realize, over a period of time, was not meant to be gently possessive, as I'd thought at first, but reassuring. I was a little astonished. A firm grip that would help me restore confidence in myself, keep me from becoming resigned to whatever melancholy moods she thought she detected hovering about my person.

Before Murray went to the express line he invited us to dinner, a week from Saturday.

"You don't have to let me know till the last minute."

"We'll be there," Babette said.

"I'm not preparing anything major, so just call beforehand and tell me if something else came up. You don't even have to call. If you don't show up, I'll know that something came up and you couldn't let me know."

"Murray, we'll be there."

"Bring the kids."

"No."

"Great. But if you decide to bring them, no problem. I don't want you to feel I'm holding you to something. Don't feel you've made an ironclad commitment. You'll show up or you won't. I have to eat anyway, so there's no major catastrophe if something comes up and you have to cancel. I just want you to know I'll be there if you decide to drop by, with or without kids. We have till next May or June to do this thing so there's no special mystique about a week from Saturday."

"Are you coming back next semester?" I said.

"They want me to teach a course in the cinema of car crashes."

"Do it."

"I will."

I rubbed against Babette in the checkout line. She backed into me and I reached around her and put my hands on her breasts. She rotated her hips and I nuzzled her hair and murmured, "Dirty blond." People wrote checks, tall boys bagged the merchandise. Not everyone spoke English at the cash terminals, or near the fruit bins and frozen foods, or out among the cars in the lot. More and more I heard languages I could not identify much less understand, although the tall boys were American-born and the checkout women as well, short, fattish in blue tunics, wearing stretch slacks and tiny white espadrilles. I tried to fit my hands into Babette's skirt, over her belly, as the slowly moving line edged toward the last purchase point, the breath mints and nasal inhalers.

It was out in the parking lot that we heard the first of the rumors about a man dying during the inspection of the grade school, one of the masked and Mylex-suited men, heavy-booted and bulky. Collapsed and died, went the story that was going around, in a classroom on the second floor.

17

Babette said to me in bed one night, "Isn't it great having all these kids around?"

"There'll be one more soon."

"Who?"

"Bee is coming in a couple of days."

"Good. Who else can we get?"

The next day Denise decided to confront her mother directly about the medication she was or was not taking, hoping to trick Babette into a confession, an admission or some minimal kind of flustered response. This was not a tactic the girl and I had discussed but I couldn't help admiring the boldness of her timing. All six of us were jammed into the car on our way to the Mid-Village Mall and Denise simply waited for a natural break in the conversation, directing her question toward the back of Babette's head, in a voice drained of inference.

"What do you know about Dylar?"

"Is that the black girl who's staying with the Stovers?"

"That's Dakar," Steffie said.

"Dakar isn't her name, it's where she's from," Denise said. "It's a country on the ivory coast of Africa."

"The capital is Lagos," Babette said. "I know that because of a surfer movie I saw once where they travel all over the world."

"The Perfect Wave," Heinrich said. "I saw it on TV."

"But what's the girl's name?" Steffie said.

"I don't know," Babette said, "but the movie wasn't called *The Perfect Wave.* The perfect wave is what they were looking for."

"They go to Hawaii," Denise told Steffie, "and wait for these tidal waves to come from Japan. They're called origamis."

"And the movie was called *The Long Hot Summer,"* her mother said.

"The Long Hot Summer," Heinrich said, "happens to be a play by Tennessee Ernie Williams."

"It doesn't matter," Babette said, "because you can't copyright titles anyway."

"If she's an African," Steffie said, "I wonder if she ever rode a camel."

"Try an Audi Turbo."

"Try a Toyota Supra."

"What is it camels store in their humps?" Babette said. "Food or water? I could never get that straight."

"There are one-hump camels and two-hump camels," Heinrich told her. "So it depends which kind you're talking about."

"Are you telling me a two-hump camel stores food in one hump and water in the other?"

"The important thing about camels," he said, "is that camel meat is considered a delicacy."

"I thought that was alligator meat," Denise said.

"Who introduced the camel to America?" Babette said. "They had them out west for a while to carry supplies to coolies who were building the great railroads that met at Ogden, Utah. I remember my history exams."

"Are you sure you're not talking about llamas?" Heinrich said.

"The llama stayed in Peru," Denise said. "Peru has the llama, the vicuña and one other animal. Bolivia has tin. Chile has copper and iron."

"I'll give anyone in this car five dollars," Heinrich said, "if they can name the population of Bolivia."

"Bolivians," my daughter said.

The family is the cradle of the world's misinformation. There must be something in family life that generates factual error. Overcloseness, the noise and heat of being. Perhaps something even deeper, like the need to survive. Murray says we are fragile creatures surrounded by a world of hostile facts. Facts threaten our happiness and security. The deeper we delve into the nature of things, the looser our structure may seem to become.

The family process works toward sealing off the world. Small errors grow heads, fictions proliferate. I tell Murray that ignorance and confusion can't possibly be the driving forces behind family solidarity. What an idea, what a subversion. He asks me why the strongest family units exist in the least developed societies. Not to know is a weapon of survival, he says. Magic and superstition become entrenched as the powerful orthodoxy of the clan. The family is strongest where objective reality is most likely to be misinterpreted. What a heartless theory, I say. But Murray insists it's true.

In a huge hardware store at the mall I saw Eric Massingale, a former microchip sales engineer who changed his life by coming out here to join the teaching staff of the computer center at the Hill. He was slim and pale, with a dangerous grin.

"You're not wearing dark glasses, Jack."

"I only wear them on campus."

"I get it."

We went our separate ways into the store's deep interior. A great echoing din, as of the extinction of a species of beast, filled the vast space. People bought twenty-two-foot ladders, six kinds of sandpaper, power saws that could fell trees. The aisles were long and bright, filled with oversized brooms, massive sacks of peat and dung, huge Rubbermaid garbage cans. Rope hung like tropical fruit, beautifully braided strands, thick, brown, strong. What a great thing a coil of rope is to look at and feel. I bought fifty feet of Manila hemp just to have it around, show it to my son, talk about where it comes from, how it's made. People spoke English, Hindi, Vietnamese, related tongues.

I ran into Massingale again at the cash terminals.

"I've never seen you off campus, Jack. You look different without your glasses and gown. Where did you get that sweater? Is that a Turkish army sweater? Mail order, right?"

He looked me over, felt the material of the water-repellent jacket I was carrying draped across my arm. Then he backed up, altering his perspective, nodding a little, his grin beginning to take on a self-satisfied look, reflecting some inner calculation.

"I think I know those shoes," he said.

What did he mean, he knew these shoes?

"You're a different person altogether."

"Different in what way, Eric?"

"You won't take offense?" he said, the grin turning lascivious, rich with secret meaning.

"Of course not. Why would I?"

"Promise you won't take offense."

"I won't take offense."

"You look so harmless, Jack. A big, harmless, aging, indistinct sort of guy."

"Why would I take offense?" I said, paying for my rope and hurrying out the door.

The encounter put me in the mood to shop. I found the others and we walked across two parking lots to the main structure in the Mid-Village Mall, a ten-story building arranged around a center court of waterfalls, promenades and gardens. Babette and the kids followed me into the elevator, into the shops set along the tiers, through the emporiums and department stores, puzzled but excited by my desire to buy. When I could not decide between two shirts, they encouraged me to buy both. When I said I was hungry, they fed me pretzels, beer, souvlaki. The two girls scouted ahead, spotting things they thought I might want or need, running back to get me, to clutch my arms, plead with me to follow. They were my guides to endless well-being. People swarmed through the boutiques and gourmet shops. Organ music rose from the great court. We smelled chocolate, popcorn, cologne; we smelled rugs and furs, hanging salamis and deathly vinyl. My family gloried in the event. I was one of them, shopping, at last. They gave me advice, badgered clerks on my behalf. I kept seeing myself unexpectedly in some reflecting surface. We moved from store to store, rejecting not only items in certain departments, not only entire departments but whole stores, mammoth corporations that did not strike our fancy for one reason or another. There was always another store, three floors, eight floors, basement full of cheese graters and paring knives. I shopped with reckless abandon. I shopped for immediate needs and distant contingencies. I shopped for its own sake, looking and touching, inspecting merchandise I had no intention of buying, then buying it. I sent clerks into their fabric books and pattern books to search for elusive designs. I began to grow in value and self-regard. I filled myself out, found new aspects of myself, located a person I'd forgotten existed. Brightness settled around me. We crossed from furniture to men's wear, walking through cosmetics. Our images appeared on mirrored columns, in glassware and chrome, on TV monitors in security rooms. I traded money for goods. The more money I spent, the less important it seemed. I was bigger than these sums. These sums poured off my skin like so much rain. These sums in fact came back to me in the form of existential credit. I felt expansive, inclined to be sweepingly generous, and told the kids to pick out their Christmas gifts here and now. I gestured in what I felt was an expansive manner. I could tell they were impressed. They fanned out across the area, each of them suddenly inclined to be private, shadowy, even secretive. Periodically one of them would return to register the name of an item with Babette, careful not to let the others know what it was. I myself was not to be bothered with tedious details. I was the benefactor, the one who dispenses gifts, bonuses, bribes, *baksheesh*. The children knew it was the nature of such things that I could not be expected to engage in technical discussions about the gifts themselves. We ate another meal. A band played live Muzak. Voices rose ten stories from the gardens and promenades, a roar that echoed and swirled through the vast gallery, mixing with noises from the tiers, with shuffling feet and chiming bells, the hum of escalators, the sound of people eating, the human buzz of some vivid and happy transaction.

We drove home in silence. We went to our respective rooms, wishing to be alone. A little later I watched Steffie in front of the TV set. She moved her lips, attempting to match the words as they were spoken.

1985

JOANNA RUSS
b. 1937

Born in New York City, Joanna Russ was educated at Cornell University and Yale University. Her fifteen books include the novels *Picnic on Paradise* (1968) and *The Female Man* (1975) and the short-story collection *The Hidden Side of the Moon* (1988). Her novella *Souls* (1982) received both a Nebula Award and a Hugo Award. Currently she is professor of English at the University of Washington in Seattle.

In general, as she told *The New York Times Book Review* in 1988, Russ considers much of her work to be "experiments in fiction." While she has "created my subjects to suit female readers," her overall objective is to offer a "showcase of different approaches and techniques."

With *The Female Man*, excerpted here, Russ admits, "I tried to find out how to do propaganda in fiction." She adds, "Feminism is threatening and difficult for some people to handle, because people with the edge have something very concrete to lose." Russ notes that "there is a huge tradition of literature by women writers that's been lost," and that this tradition "has been thoroughly swept under the rug and will probably never be recovered."

From The Female Man

Part One

I

I was born on a farm on Whileaway. When I was five I was sent to a school on South Continent (like everybody else) and when I turned twelve I rejoined my family. My mother's name was Eva, my other mother's name Alicia; I am Janet Evason. When I was thirteen I stalked and killed a wolf, alone, on North Continent above the forty-eighth parallel, using only a rifle. I made a travois for the head and paws, then abandoned the head, and finally got home with one paw, proof enough (I thought). I've worked in the mines, on the radio network, on a milk farm, a vegetable farm, and for six weeks as a librarian after I broke my leg. At thirty I bore Yuriko Janetson; when she was taken away to a school five years later (and I never saw a child protest so much) I decided to take time off and see if I could find my family's old home—for they had moved away after I had married and relocated near Mine City in South Continent. The place was unrecognizable, however; our rural areas are always changing. I could find nothing but the tripods of the computer beacons everywhere, some strange crops in the fields that I had never seen before, and a band of wandering children. They were heading North to visit the polar station and offered to lend me a sleeping bag for the night, but I declined and stayed with the resident family; in the morning I started home. Since then I have been Safety Officer for the county, that is S & P (Safety and Peace), a position I have held now for six years. My Stanford-Binet corrected score (in your terms) is 187, my wife's 205 and my daughter's 193. Yuki goes through the ceiling on the verbal test. I've supervised the digging of fire trails, delivered babies, fixed machinery, and milked more moo-cows than I wish I knew existed. But Yuki is crazy about ice-cream. I love my daughter. I love my family (there are nineteen of us). I love my wife (Vittoria). I've fought four duels. I've killed four times.

II

Jeannine Dadier (DADE-yer) worked as a librarian in New York City three days a week for the W.P.A. She worked at the Tompkins Square Branch in the Young Adult section. She wondered sometimes if it was so lucky that Herr Shicklgruber had died in 1936 (the library had books about this). On the third Monday in March of 1969 she saw the first headlines about Janet Evason but paid no attention to them; she spent the day stamping Out books for the Young Adults and checking the lines around her eyes in her pocket mirror (*I'm only twenty-nine!*). Twice she had had to tuck her skirt above her knees and climb the ladder to the higher-up books; once she had to move the ladder over Mrs. Allison and the new gentleman assistant, who were standing below soberly discussing the possibility of war with Japan. There was an article in *The Saturday Evening Post.*

"I don't believe it," said Jeannine Nancy Dadier softly. Mrs. Allison was a Negro. It was an unusually warm, hazy day with a little green showing in the park: imaginary green, perhaps, as if the world had taken an odd turning and were bowling down Spring in a dim by-street somewhere, clouds of imagination around the trees.

"I don't believe it," repeated Jeannine Dadier, not knowing what they were talking about. "You'd better believe it!" said Mrs. Allison sharply. Jeannine balanced on one foot. (Nice girls don't do that.) She climbed down the ladder with her books and put them on the reserve table. Mrs. Allison didn't like W.P.A. girls. Jeannine saw the headlines again, on Mrs. Allison's newspaper.

WOMAN APPEARS FROM NOWHERE ON
BROADWAY, POLICEMAN VANISHES

"I don't—" (*I have my cat, I have my room, I have my hot plate and my window and the ailanthus tree.*)

Out of the corner of her eye she saw Cal outside in the street; he was walking bouncily and his hat was tipped forward; he was going to have some silly thing or other to say about being a reporter, little blond hatchet face and serious blue eyes; "I'll make it some day, baby." Jeannine slipped into the stacks, hiding behind Mrs. Allison's *P.M.-Post:* Woman Appears from Nowhere on Broadway, Policeman Vanishes. She daydreamed about buying fruit at the free market, though her hands always sweated so when she bought things outside the government store and she couldn't bargain. She would get cat food and feed Mr. Frosty the first thing she got to her room; he ate out of an old china saucer. Jeannine imagined Mr. Frosty rubbing against her legs, his tail waving. Mr. Frosty was marked black-and-white all over. With her eyes closed, Jeannine saw him jump up on the mantelpiece and walk among her things: her sea shells and miniatures. "No, no, *no!*" she said. The cat jumped off, knocking over one of her Japanese dolls. After dinner Jeannine took him out; then she washed the dishes and tried to mend some of her old clothing. She'd go over the ration books. When it got dark she'd turn on the radio for the evening program or she'd read, maybe call up from the drugstore and find out about the boarding house in New Jersey. She might call her brother. She would certainly plant the orange seeds and water them. She thought of Mr. Frosty stalking a bath-robe tail among the miniature orange trees; he'd look like a tiger. If she could get empty cans at the government store.

"Hey, baby?" It was a horrid shock. It was Cal.

"No," said Jeannine hastily. "I haven't got time."

"Baby?" He was pulling her arm. Come for a cup of coffee. But she couldn't. She had to learn Greek (the book was in the reserve desk). There was too much to do. He was frowning and pleading. She could feel the pillow under her back already, and Mr. Frosty stalking around them, looking at her with his strange blue eyes, walking widdershins around the lovers. He was part Siamese; Cal called him The Blotchy Skinny Cat. Cal always wanted to do experiments with him, dropping him from the back of a chair, putting things in his way, hiding from him. Mr. Frosty just spat at him now.

"Later," said Jeannine desperately. Cal leaned over her and whispered into her ear; it made her want to cry. He rocked back and forth on his heels. Then he said, "I'll wait." He sat on Jeannine's stack chair, picking up the newspaper, and added:

"The vanishing woman. That's you." She closed her eyes and daydreamed about Mr. Frosty curled up on the mantel, peacefully asleep, all felinity in one circle. Such a spoiled cat.

"Baby?" said Cal.

"Oh, all right," said Jeannine hopelessly, "all right."

I'll watch the ailanthus tree.

III

Janet Evason appeared on Broadway at two o'clock in the afternoon in her underwear. She didn't lose her head. Though the nerves try to keep going in the previous track, she went into evasive position the second after she arrived (good for her) with her fair, dirty hair flying and her khaki shorts and shirt stained with sweat. When a policeman tried to take her arm, she threatened him with le savate, but he vanished. She seemed to regard the crowds around her with a special horror. The policeman reappeared in the same spot an hour later with no memory of the interval, but Janet Evason had returned to her sleeping bag in the New Forest only a few moments after her arrival. A few words of Pan-Russian and she was gone. The last of them waked her bedmate in the New Forest.

"Go to sleep," said the anonymous friend-for-the-night, a nose, a brow, and a coil of dark hair in the dappled moonlight.

"But who has been mucking about with my head!" said Janet Evason.

IV

When Janet Evason returned to the New Forest and the experimenters at the Pole Station were laughing their heads off (for it was not a dream) I sat in a cocktail party in mid-Manhattan. I had just changed into a man, me, Joanna. I mean a female man, of course; my body and soul were exactly the same.

So there's me also.

V

The first man to set foot on Whileaway appeared in a field of turnips on North Continent. He was wearing a blue suit like a hiker's and a blue cap. The farm people had been notified. One, seeing the blip on the tractor's infrared scan, came to get him; the man in blue saw a flying machine with no wings but a skirt of dust and air. The county's repair shed for farm machinery was nearby that week, so the tractor-driver led him there; he was not saying anything intelligible. He saw a translucent dome, the surface undulating slightly. There was an exhaust fan set in one side. Within the dome was a wilderness of machines: dead, on their sides, some turned inside out, their guts spilling on to the grass. From an extended framework under the roof swung hands as big as three men. One of these picked up a car and dropped it. The sides of the car fell off. Littler hands sprang up from the grass.

"Hey, hey!" said the tractor-driver, knocking on a solid piece set into the wall. "It fell, it passed out!"

"Send it back," said an operator, climbing out from under the induction helmet at the far end of the shed. Four others came and stood around the man in the blue suit.

"Is he of steady mind?" said one.

"We don't know."

"Is he ill?"

"Hypnotize him and send him back."

The man in blue—if he had seen them—would have found them very odd: smooth-faced, smooth-skinned, too small and too plump, their coveralls heavy in the seat. They wore coveralls because you couldn't always fix things with the mechanical hands; sometimes you had to use your own. One was old and had white hair; one was very young; one wore the long hair sometimes affected by the youth of Whileaway, "to while away the time." Six pairs of steady curious eyes studied the man in the blue suit.

"That, *mes enfants,*" said the tractor-driver at last, "is a man.

"That is a real Earth man."

VI

Sometimes you bend down to tie your shoe, and then you either tie your shoe or you don't; you either straighten up instantly or maybe you don't. Every choice begets at least two worlds of possibility, that is, one in which you do and one in which you don't; or very likely many more, one in which you do quickly, one in which you do slowly, one in which you don't, but hesitate, one in which you hesitate and frown, one in which you hesitate and sneeze, and so on. To carry this line of argument further, there must be an infinite number of possible universes (such is the fecundity of God) for there is no reason to imagine Nature as prejudiced in favor of human action. Every displacement of every molecule, every change in orbit of every electron, every quantum of light that strikes here and not there—each of these must somewhere have its alternative. It's possible, too, that there is no such thing as one clear line or strand of probability, and that we live on a sort of twisted braid, blurring from one to the other without even knowing it, as long as we keep within the limits of a set of variations that really make no difference to us. Thus the paradox of time travel ceases to exist, for the Past one visits is never one's own Past but always somebody else's; or rather, one's visit to the Past instantly creates another Present (one in which the visit has already happened) and what you visit is the Past belonging to that Present—an entirely different matter from your own Past. And with each decision you make (back there in the Past) that new probable universe itself branches, creating simultaneously a new Past and a new Present, or to put it plainly, a new universe. And when you come back to your own Present, you alone know what the other Past was like and what you did there.

Thus it is probable that Whileaway—a name for the Earth ten centuries from now, but not *our* Earth, if you follow me—will find itself not at all affected by this sortie into somebody else's past. And vice versa, of course. The two might as well be independent worlds.

Whileaway, you may gather, is in the future.

But not *our* future.

VII

I saw Jeannine shortly afterward, in a cocktail lounge where I had gone to watch Janet Evason on television (I don't have a set). Jeannine looked very much out of place; I sat next to her and she confided in me: "I don't belong here." I can't imagine how she got there, except by accident. She looked as if she were dressed up for a costume film, sitting in the shadow with her snood and her wedgies, a long-limbed, coltish girl in clothes a little too small for her. Fashion (it seems) is recovering very leisurely from the Great Depression. Not here and now, of course. "I don't belong here!" whispered Jeannine Dadier again, rather anxiously. She was fidgeting. She said, "I don't *like* places like this." She poked the red, tufted leather on the seat.

"What?" I said.

"I went hiking last vacation," she said big-eyed. "That's what I like. It's healthy."

I know it's supposed to be virtuous to run healthily through fields of flowers, but I like bars, hotels, air-conditioning, good restaurants, and jet transport, and I told her so.

"Jet?" she said.

Janet Evason came on the television. It was only a still picture. Then we had the news from Cambodia, Laos, Michigan State, Lake Canandaigua (pollution), and the spinning globe of the world in full color with its seventeen man-made satellites going around it. The color was awful. I've been inside a television studio before: the gallery running around the sides of the barn, every inch of the roof covered with lights, so that the little woman-child with the wee voice can pout over an oven or a sink. Then Janet Evason came on with that blobby look people have on the tube. She moved carefully and looked at everything with interest. She was well dressed (in a suit). The host or M.C. or whatever-you-call-him shook hands with her and then everybody shook hands with everybody else, like a French wedding or an early silent movie. *He* was dressed in a suit. Someone guided her to a seat and she smiled and nodded in the exaggerated way you do when you're not sure of doing the right thing. She looked around and shaded her eyes against the lights. Then she spoke.

(The first thing said by the second man ever to visit Whileaway was, "Where are all the men?" Janet Evason, appearing in the Pentagon, hands in her pockets, feet planted far apart, said, "Where the dickens are all the women?")

The sound in the television set conked out for a moment and then Jeannine Dadier was gone; she didn't disappear, she just wasn't there anymore. Janet Evason got up, shook hands again, looking around her, questioned with her eyes, pantomimed comprehension, nodded, and walked out of camera range. They never did show you the government guards.

I heard it another time and this is how it went:

MC: How do you like it here, Miss Evason?
JE (looks around the studio, confused): It's too hot.
MC: I mean how do you like it on—well, on Earth?
JE: But I live on the earth. (Her attention is a little strained here.)
MC: Perhaps you had better explain what you mean by that—I mean the existence of different probabilities and so on—you were talking about that before.
JE: It's in the newspapers.
MC: But Miss Evason, if you could, please explain it for the people who are watching the program.
JE: Let them read. Can't they read?
(There was a moment's silence. Then the M.C. spoke.)
MC: Our social scientists as well as our physicists tell us they've had to revise a great deal of theory in light of the information brought by our fair visitor from another world. There have been no men on Whileaway for at least eight centuries—I don't mean no human beings, of course, but no men—and this society, run entirely by women, has naturally attracted a great deal of attention since the appearance last week of its representative and its first ambassador, the lady on my left here. Janet Evason, can you tell us how you think your society on Whileaway will react to the reappearance of men from Earth—I mean our present-day Earth, of course—after an isolation of eight hundred years?
JE (She jumped at this one; probably because it was the first one she could understand): Nine hundred years. What men?
MC: What men? Surely you expect men from our society to visit Whileaway.
JE: Why?
MC: For information, trade, ah—cultural contact, surely. (laughter) I'm afraid you're making it rather difficult for me, Miss Evason. When the—ah—the plague you spoke of killed the men on Whileaway, weren't they missed? Weren't families broken up? Didn't the whole pattern of life change?
JE (slowly): I suppose people always miss what they are used to. Yes, they were missed. Even a whole set of words, like "he," "man" and so on—these

are banned. Then the second generation, they use them to be daring, among themselves, and the third generation doesn't, to be polite, and by the fourth, who cares? Who remembers?
MC: But surely—that is—
JE: Excuse me, perhaps I'm mistaking what you intend to say as this language we're speaking is only a hobby of mine, I am not as fluent as I would wish. What we speak is a pan-Russian even the Russians would not understand; it would be like Middle English to you, only vice-versa.
MC: I see. But to get back to the question—
JE: Yes.
MC (A hard position to be in, between the authorities and this strange personage who is wrapped in ignorance like a savage chief: expressionless, attentive, possibly civilized, completely unknowing. He finally said): Don't you want men to return to Whileaway, Miss Evason?
JE: Why?
MC: One sex is half a species, Miss Evason. I am quoting (and he cited a famous anthropologist). Do you want to banish sex from Whileaway?
JE (with massive dignity and complete naturalness): Huh?
MC: I said: Do you want to banish sex from Whileaway? Sex, family, love, erotic attraction—call it what you like—we all know that your people are competent and intelligent individuals, but do you think that's enough? Surely you have the intellectual knowledge of biology in other species to know what I'm talking about.
JE: I'm married. I have two children. What the devil do you mean?
MC: I—Miss Evason—we—well, we know you form what you call marriages, Miss Evason, that you reckon the descent of your children through both partners and that you even have "tribes"—I'm calling them what Sir ——— calls them; I know the translation isn't perfect—and we know that these marriages or tribes form very good institutions for the economic support of the children and for some sort of genetic mixing, though I confess you're way beyond us in the biological sciences. But, Miss Evason, I am not talking about economic institutions or even affectionate ones. Of course the mothers of Whileaway love their children; nobody doubts that. And of course they have affection for each other; nobody doubts that, either. But there is more, much, much more—I am talking about sexual love.
JE (enlightened): Oh! You mean copulation.
MC: Yes.
JE: And you say we don't have that?
MC: Yes.
JE: How foolish of you. Of course we do.
MC: Ah? (He wants to say, "Don't tell me.")
JE: With each other. Allow me to explain.

She was cut off instantly by a commercial poetically describing the joys of unsliced bread. They shrugged (out of camera range). It wouldn't even have gotten that far if Janet had not insisted on attaching a touch-me-not to the replay system. It was a live broadcast, four seconds' lag. I begin to like her more and more. She said, "If you expect me to observe your taboos, I think you will have to be more precise as to exactly what they are." In Jeannine Dadier's world, she was (would be) asked by a lady commentator:

How do the women of Whileaway do their hair?

JE: They hack it off with clam shells.

VIII

"Humanity is unnatural!" exclaimed the philosopher Dunyasha Bernadetteson (A.C. 344–426) who suffered all her life from the slip of a genetic surgeon's hand which had given her one mother's jaw and the other mother's teeth—orthodontia is hardly ever necessary on Whileaway. Her daughter's teeth, however, were perfect. Plague came to Whileaway in P.C. 17 (Preceding Catastrophe) and ended in A.C. 03, with half the population dead; it had started so slowly that no one knew about it until it was too late. It attacked males only. Earth had been completely re-formed during the Golden Age (P.C. 300–ca. P.C. 180) and natural conditions presented considerably less difficulty than they might have during a similar catastrophe a millennium or so earlier. At the time of The Despair (as it was popularly called), Whileaway had two continents, called simply North and South Continents, and a great many ideal bays or anchorages in the coastline. Severe climatic conditions did not prevail below 72° S and 68° N latitude. Conventional water traffic, at the time of the Catastrophe, was employed almost exclusively for freight, passenger traffic using the smaller and more flexibly routed hovercraft. Houses were self-contained, with portable power sources, fuel-alcohol motors or solar cells replacing the earlier centralized power. The later invention of practical matter-antimatter reactors (K. Ansky, A.C. 239) produced great optimism for a decade or so, but these devices proved to be too bulky for private use. Katharina Lucyson Ansky (A.C. 201–282) was also responsible for the principles that made genetic surgery possible. (The merging of ova had been practiced for the previous century and a half.) Animal life had become so scarce before the Golden Age that many species were re-invented by enthusiasts of the Ansky Period; in A.C. 280 there was an outbreak of coneys in Newland (an island off the neck of North Continent), a pandemic not without historical precedent. By A.C. 492, through the brilliant agitation of the great Betty Bettinason Murano (A.C. 453–A.C. 502) Terran colonies were re-established on Mars, Ganymede, and in the Asteroids, the Selenic League assisting according to the Treaty of Mare Tenebrum (A.C. 240). Asked what she expected to find in space, Betty Murano made the immortal quip, "Nothing." By the third century A.C. intelligence was a controllable, heritable factor, though aptitudes and interests continued to elude the surgeons and intelligence itself could be raised only grossly. By the fifth century, clan organization had reached its present complex state and the re-cycling of phosphorus was almost completely successful: by the seventh century Jovian mining made it possible to replace a largely glass-and-ceramics technology with some metals (which were also re-cycled) and for the third time in four hundred years (fashions are sometimes cyclic too) duelling became a serious social nuisance. Several local Guilds Councils voted that a successful duellist must undergo the penalty of an accidental murderer and bear a child to replace the life lost, but the solution was too simple-minded to become popular. There was the age of both parties to consider, for example. By the beginning of the ninth century A.C. the induction helmet was a practical possibility, industry was being drastically altered, and the Selenic League had finally outproduced South Continent in kg protein/person/annum. In 913 A.C. an obscure and discontented descendant of Katy Ansky put together various items of mathematical knowledge and thus discovered—or invented—probability mechanics.

In the time of Jesus of Nazareth, dear reader, there were no motor-cars. I still walk, though, sometimes.

That is, a prudent ecologist makes things work as nearly perfectly as they can by themselves, but you also keep the kerosene lantern in the barn just in case, and usually a debate about keeping a horse ends up with the decision that it's too much trouble, so you let the horse go; but the Conservation Point at La Jolla keeps horses. We wouldn't recognize them. The induction helmet makes it possible for one workwoman to have not only the brute force but also the flexibility and control of thousands; it's turning Whileawayan industry upside down. Most people walk on Whileaway (of course, their feet are perfect). They make haste in odd ways sometimes. In the early days it was enough just to keep alive and keep the children coming. Now they say "When the re-industrialization's complete," and they still walk. Maybe they like it. Probability mechanics offers the possibility—by looping into another continuum, exactly chosen—of teleportation. Chilia Ysayeson Belin lives in Italian ruins (I think this is part of the Vittore Emmanuele monument, though I don't know how it got to Newland) and she's sentimental about it; how can one add indoor plumbing discreetly without an unconscionable amount of work? Her mother, Ysaye, lives in a cave (the Ysaye who put together the theory of probability mechanics). Pre-fabs take only two days to get and no time at all to set up. There are eighteen Belins and twenty-three Moujkis (Ysaye's family; I stayed with both). Whileaway doesn't have true cities. And of course, the tail of a culture is several centuries behind the head. Whileaway is so pastoral that at times one wonders whether the ultimate sophistication may not take us all back to a kind of pre-Paleolithic dawn age, a garden without any artifacts except for what we would call miracles. A Moujki invented non-disposable food containers in her spare time in A.C. 904 because the idea fascinated her; people have been killed for less.

Meanwhile, the ecological housekeeping is enormous.

IX

JE: I bore my child at thirty; we all do. It's a vacation. Almost five years. The baby rooms are full of people reading, painting, singing, as much as they can, to the children, with the children, over the children. . . . Like the ancient Chinese custom of the three-years' mourning, an hiatus at just the right time. There has been no leisure at all before and there will be so little after—anything I do, you understand, I mean really do—I must ground thoroughly in those five years. One works with feverish haste. . . . At sixty I will get a sedentary job and have some time for myself again.

COMMENTATOR: And this is considered enough, in Whileaway?

JE: My God, no.

X

Jeannine dawdles. She always hates to get out of bed. She would lie on her side and look at the ailanthus tree until her back began to ache; then she would turn over, hidden in the veils of the leaves, and fall asleep. Tag-ends of dreams till she lay in bed like a puddle and the cat would climb over her. On workdays Jeannine got up early in a kind of waking nightmare: feeling horrid, stumbling to the hall bathroom with sleep all over her. Coffee made her sick. She couldn't sit in the armchair, or drop her slippers, or bend, or lean, or lie down. Mr. Frosty, perambulating on the window sill, walked back and forth in front of the ailanthus tree: Tiger on Frond. The museum. The zoo. The bus to Chinatown. Jeannine sank into the tree gracefully, like a mermaid, bearing with her a tea-cosy to give to the young man who had a huge muffin trembling over his collar where his face ought to have been. Trembling with emotion.

The cat spoke.

She jerked awake. *I'll feed you, Mr. Frosty.*

Mrrrr.

Cal couldn't afford to take her anywhere, really. She had been traveling on the public buses so long that she knew all the routes. Yawning horribly, she ran the water into Mr. Frosty's cat food and put the dish on the floor. He ate in a dignified way; she remembered how when she had taken him to her brother's, they had fed him a real raw fish, just caught in the pond by one of the boys, and how Mr. Frosty had pounced on it, bolting it, he was so eager. They really do like fish. Now he played with the saucer, batting it from side to side, even though he was grown up. Cats were really much happier after you . . . after you . . . (she yawned) Oh, it was Chinese Festival Day.

If I had the money, if I could get my hair done. . . . He comes into the library; he's a college professor; no, he's a playboy. "Who's that girl?" Talks to Mrs. Allison, slyly flattering her. "This is Jeannine." She casts her eyes down, rich in feminine power. Had my nails done today. And these are good clothes, they have taste, my own individuality, my beauty. "There's something about her," he says. "Will you go out with me?" Later on the roof garden, drinking champagne, "Jeannine, will you—"

Mr. Frosty, unsatisfied and jealous, puts his claw into her leg. "All right!" she says, choking on the sound of her own voice. *Get dressed quick.*

I do (thought Jeannine, looking in the precious full-length mirror inexplicably left by the previous tenant on the back of the closet door) *I do look a little bit like . . . if I tilt my face. Oh! Cal will be SO—MAD*—and flying back to the bed, she strips off her pajamas and snatches at the underwear she always leaves out on the bureau the night before. Jeannine the Water Nymph. *I dreamed about a young man somewhere.* She doesn't quite believe in cards or omens, that's totally idiotic, but sometimes she giggles and thinks it would be nice. *I have big eyes. You are going to meet a tall, dark—*

Placing Mr. Frosty firmly on the bed, she pulls on her sweater and skirt, then brushes her hair, counting strokes under her breath. Her coat is so old. Just a little bit of make-up, lip pomade and powder. (She forgot again and got powder on her coat.) If she got out early, she wouldn't have to meet Cal in the room; he would play with the cat (down on his hands and knees) and then want to Make Love; this way's better. The bus to Chinatown. She stumbled down the stairs in her haste, catching at the banister. Little Miss Spry, the old lady on the bottom floor, opened her door just in time to catch Miss Dadier flying through the hall. Jeannine saw a small, wrinkled, worried, old face, wispy white hair, and a body like a flour sack done up in a black shapeless dress. One spotted, veined hand round the edge of the door.

"How do, Jeannine. Going out?"

Doubling up in a fit of hysterics, Miss Dadier escaped. *Ooh! To look like that!*

There was Cal, passing the bus station.

XI

Etsuko Belin, stretched cruciform on a glider, shifted her weight and went into a slow turn, seeing fifteen hundred feet below her the rising sun of Whileaway reflected in the glacial-scaur lakes of Mount Strom. She flipped the glider over, and sailing on her back, passed a hawk.

XII

Six months ago at the Chinese New Year, Jeannine had stood in the cold, holding her mittens over her ears to keep out the awful sound of firecrackers. Cal, next to her, watched the dragon dance around in the street.

XIII

I met Janet Evason on Broadway, standing to the side of the parade given in her honor (I was). She leaned out of the limousine and beckoned me in. Surrounded by Secret Service agents. "That one," she said.

Eventually we will all come together.

XIV

Jeannine, out of place, puts her hands over her ears and shuts her eyes on a farm on Whileaway, sitting at the trestle-table under the trees where everybody is eating. *I'm not here. I'm not here.* Chilia Ysayeson's youngest has taken a fancy to the newcomer; Jeannine sees big eyes, big breasts, big shoulders, thick lips, all that grossness. Mr. Frosty is being spoilt, petted and fed by eighteen Belins. *I'm not here.*

XV

JE: Evason is not "son" but "daughter." This is *your* translation.

XVI

And here we are.

1975

GERALD VIZENOR
b. 1934

Gerald Vizenor was born in Minneapolis, Minnesota, and educated at New York University, the University of Minnesota, and Harvard University. He has published nine books of poetry and four novels, including *Darkness in Saint Louis Bearheart* (1973) and *Griever: An American Monkey King in China* (1987), which received an American Book Award. His other books of prose include the short-story collections *Earthdivers: Tribal Narratives on Mixed Descent* (1981) and *Landfill Meditations* (1991). A collection of fiction and essays, *Shadow Distance: A Gerald Vizenor Reader,* was published in 1994.

"I was conceived on a cold night in a kerosene heated tenement near downtown Minneapolis," Vizenor wrote in *Interior Landscapes: Autobiographical Myths and Metaphors* (1990). "President Franklin Delano Roosevelt had been inaugurated the year before, at the depth of the Great Depression. He told the nation, 'The only thing we have to fear is fear itself.' My mother and millions of other women stranded in cold rooms, heard the new president, listened to their new men, and were roused to remember the movies; elected politicians turned economies, but the bright lights in the Depression came from the romantic and glamorous screen stars."

"Feral Lasers" is from *Landfill Meditations.*

Feral Lasers

Almost Browne was born twice, the sublime measure of a crossblood trickster. His parents, a tribal father and a white mother, had been in the cities and ran out of gas on the way back to deliver their first son on the White Earth Reservation in Minnesota.

Almost earned his nickname in the back seat of a seventeen-year-old hatchback. The leaves had turned, the wind was cold. Two crows bounced on the road, an auspicious chorus near the tribal border.

Father Browne pushed the car to a small town; there, closer to the reservation, he borrowed two gallons of gas from a station manager and hurried to the hospital at White Earth.

Wolfie Wight, the reservation doctor, an enormous woman, opened the hatchback; her wide head, hard grin, and cold hands menaced the child. "Almost brown," the doctor shouted. Later, she printed that name on the reservation birth certificate, with a flourish.

Almost was concerned with creations; his untraditional birth and perinatal name would explain, to some, his brute dedication to trickster simulations. No one, not even his parents, could remember much about his childhood. He was alone, but not lonesome, a dreamer who traveled in trickster stories. He learned to read in back seats and matured in seven abandoned cars, his sanctuaries and private mansions on the reservation. Station wagons were his beds, closets, hospitals, libraries; and in other cars he conversed with mongrels, counted his contradictions, and overturned what he heard from the elders. He lived in the ruins of civilization and shouted at trees, screamed into panic holes; he was, in his own words, "a natural polyvinyl chloride partisan."

Almost started a new tribal world with the creation of a winter woman, an icewoman as enormous as the reservation doctor; she saluted and laughed at men. Hundreds of people drove from the cities and other reservations to hear the icewoman laugh, to watch her move her arms. The sound of her cold voice shivered into summer, into rash rumors that ran down the trickster. He was secure in the blood, a bold protester, an eminent romancer, but censure was a cold tribal hand.

Almost was never a failure in the tribal sense; he resisted institutions and honored chance but never conclusions or termination. His imagination overcame last words in education; he never missed a turn at machines, even those dead in the weeds.

Once, when he applied for work, he told the reservation president that he had earned a "chance doctorate" at the Manifest Destiny Graduate School in California. The president was impressed and hired the trickster as a tribal computer consultant. "Chance," he boasted later, was a "back seat degree." He wired the reservation with enough computer power to launch it into outer space.

Theories never interested the trickster, but he was a genius at new schemes and practices, and the mechanical transanimation of instincts. He saw memories and dreams as three dimensional, colors and motion, and used that to understand race and laser holograms. "Theories," he said, "come from institutions, from the sacred and lonesome, from people who fear the realities of their parents." Theories, he said, were "rush hours."

Almost never said much; he worked on computers and held hands with a teacher at the government school. Em Wheeler lived in the woods with two gray mongrels; she was lonesome, thin at the shoulders, and she listened to tricksters. He told her that "creations were obvious, a rope burn, a boil on the nose, warm water, and much better than theories." He mussed theories and harnessed instincts, natural responses. For instance, the icewoman was animated by a caged mongrel wired to a solenoid, the source of electromotivation. When the mongrel moved, when his heartbeat leaped, the icewoman saluted. The wires, gears, and pulleys, hidden beneath chicken mesh and wire, were powered by solar batteries. "There you have it, sun, snow, and a cold sleight of hand," he mocked, "considerate winter moves." The mongrels barked, and the icewoman laughed and laughed at the visitors.

The trickster was an instinctive mechanician; communal sentiments and machines were his best teachers. He was a bear, a crow in a birch, a mongrel, and he reached in imagination to a postbiological world. Cold robotics and his communion with bears caused the same suspicious solicitude on the reservation. He practiced seven bear poses under a whole moon. Much later, when he was on trial in tribal court, he said he was a shaman, a bear shaman selenographer. "Tricksters have the bear power to enchant women with the moon." He persuaded seven women, three tribal and four white, to bare their bottoms to the moon each month.

The icewoman, snow machines that saluted, bears, and moon studies, however, were not cited as the main reasons for his banishment late that summer. He was responsible for those postshamanic laser holotropes that hovered over the reservation; lucent presidents from old peace medals and other figures danced, transformed the lakes and meadows, and terrified tribal families.

Almost was tried and removed to the cities because he studied electromagnetism, luminescence, and spectral memories; more than that, he deconstructed biological time and paraded western explorers in laser holograms. The pale figures loomed over the mission pond and blemished the clear summer nights on the reservation.

The Quidnunc Council, dominated by several mixed femagogues, gathered to consider the grimmest gossip about the trickster and his laser holotropes: the ghosts of white men returned to steal tribal land, harvest wild rice, and net fish. Sixgun, a detached stump puller, said he saw a white monster sprout six heads and suck up the lake six times. "Sucker Lake is down six feet from last year."

The best stories on the reservation would contain some technologies, the electromagnetic visuals of the trickster mechanism. The femagogues, in the end, told the tribal court to settle for the terror he had caused on the reservation with his laser holograms. The court convened in the preschool classroom; the trickster, the judge, other court officials, and witnesses were perched on little chairs.

"Almost, some say you are a wicked shaman, not with us the whole time," said the tribal judge. He leaned back on the little chair. His stomach rolled over his belt. His feet were wide. His thumbs were stained and churned when he listened. "Your dad and me go back a long time, we hunted together, so what is this business about six white heads sucking off a lake?"

"Lasers, nothing more," said Almost.

"Who are they?"

"Nobody," he said. "Laser light shows."

"Whose lights?"

"Laser holotropes."

"Indian?" asked the judge. "Where's he from then?"

"Nowhere, laser is a light."

"Laser, what's his last name again?"

"Holotropes, but that's not a real name."

"Does he shine on our reservation?"

"Laser is an image."

"Not when he shines our deer," said the judge.

"Listen," said the trickster. "Let me show you." Almost drew some pictures on a chalkboard and talked about reflections, northern lights, and natural luminescence, but not enough to understand laser holotropes. His mother told him that a real healer, a trickster with a vision, "must hold back some secrets." The tribal court, wise elders but not healers, would not believe a chalk and talk show in a preschool classroom. The tribal judge ordered the crossblood to demonstrate his laser holotropes that night over the mission pond at White Earth.

The court order reached tribal communities more than a hundred miles from the reservation. The loons wailed at the tribunal on the pond; mosquitoes whined in the moist weeds; fireflies traced the wide shore; bats wheeled and turned over the black water.

Christopher Columbus arose from the white pine, he saluted with a flourish, turned his head, circled the pond once, twice, three times, and then posed on the water tower. The school windows shimmered, blue and green light swarmed the building. Then, bright scuds carried the explorer to the center of the pond; there, his parts—an arm, hands, his loose head—protruded from the lucent scuds. Tribal families, the casual juries that night, gathered on the shore and cheered the dismemberment; later, when the explorer was put back together again and walked on water, most families retreated to the woods. One femagogue shouted that she could smell white diseases, the crotch of Christopher Columbus.

Almost Browne never revealed how he created the postshamanic laser holograms over the mission pond, but he told the tribal court that white men and diseases were not the same as electroluminations. "Columbus was here on a laser and withered with a wave of my hand," he said. "Laser holograms created the white man, but we set the memories and the skin colors."

"Not on your life," said a crossblood.

"Darker on the inside," the trickster countered.

"Never," she shouted.

"The laser is the new trickster."

"Not on this reservation, not a chance," said the tribal judge. Almost was held accountable for accidents, diseases, and death on the reservation that summer. He was shamed as a shaman and ordered to remove his machines and laser demons from the reservation; he was the first tribal member to be removed to the cities, a wild reversal of colonial histories. The trickster moved no one but the preschool teacher who held his hand and nurtured his imagination.

Em Wheeler had lived on the reservation for nineteen years, nine months, seventeen nights. She counted lonesome nights, and she held a calendar of contradictions and denials. The trial was held in her classroom; she listened, turned morose, and threatened to leave the reservation if the crossblood was removed.

Em and Almost lived in a camper van with two mongrels and a songbird in a bamboo cage. She smiled behind the wheel, liberated by a light show; he laughed, ate corn chips, and read newspaper stories out loud about their trickster laser shows. He was a natural at interviews. "Name the cities and we'll be there before winter," he told a television reporter. "We're on laser relocation." The reporter nodded and told him to repeat what he had said for a sound check. "Back on the reservation we presented holograms, white men over ponds and meadows," the trickster continued, "but in the cities we launched wild animals, tribal warriors, and presidents over the interstates."

"Will lasers replace traditions?"

"We need three lasers to create our light bears out there," he told the reporter, "so we bought two junkers with sun roofs and parked them in strategic places."

"How does it work?"

"Which one?"

"The bear over the interstate."

"Can't tell you," said the trickster.

"How about the presidents?"

"Peace medals."

"Show me your best president," she said to the camera.

"The nudes?"

"The police said your presidents are obscene."

"Light is no erection."

"Show me," the reporter teased.

"Lasers undress the peace presidents."

"Show me," she insisted.

"Lasers substantiate memories, dreams, with no obverse, no other, no shadows," he said. The trickster turned to the camera and pounced at the words; then he moved his mouth, saying in silence, "Lasers are the real world."

Hologramic warriors and wild animals over urban ponds were natural amusements, but when the trickster chased a bear and three moose over a rise on the interstate, no one on the road was pleased. Late traffic was slowed down for several miles; the bear was too close to the dividers and scared hundreds of drivers. Later, several people were interviewed on television and complained about the wild animals.

"That's why we spent billions for interstates," said a retired fireman, "to keep wild animals where they belong, in the woods, and out of harm's way in traffic."

"But the animals are light shows," said an interviewer.

"Right, but this guy ought to keep his lights to himself, his creation is not for me on the road," said the fireman. "Indians should know that much by now."

Almost and Em stopped traffic in several cities between Minneapolis and Detroit. The laser tricksters were cursed on the interstates, but he was celebrated on television talk shows and late night radio. Instant referenda revealed that native tribal people had natural rights to create animals over the cities; these rights, one woman insisted, were part of the treaties.

"These people have suffered enough," said a librarian, a caller on late night radio. "We took their land and resources; the least we can do now is be amused with their little light shows and metamorphoses."

"We watched in bed through our skylight," said another night talker. "Wild men, wild neighborhoods in the sky, me on my back, the tribes above, the whole thing is turned around somehow."

"We drove into the wilderness," a man whispered.

"Next thing you know we'll need a hunting license to drive home from work at night," said a woman on a television talk show. She was a trucker who drove cattle to market.

The trickster and the schoolteacher were precious minutes from arrest in most cities. At last, the two were located by the military, a special surveillance plane used to track drug smugglers, and cornered on a dead end road at a construction site in downtown Milwaukee.

The police impounded their lasers and ordered them to appear in court later that week. They were charged with causing a public disturbance, endangerment on an interstate, and amusements without a license.

Editorial columnists and media interviewers defended their tribal rights to the air, where there were no legal differences between light and sound. "Indians show, we sound; our rights are the same," a constitutional lawyer said on public radio.

The prosecutor, however, argued in court that the "two laser shiners" should be tried "because a light show is neither speech nor art, and is not protected by current copyright laws."

"The prosecutor is a racist," said a student.

"The creator in this case is a digital code, not a tribal artist," said the prominent prosecutor. "Furthermore, bright lights like loud music are a public nuisance and put basic transportation at risk."

Almost and Em represented themselves at the hearing. "Your honor, my chest is white but my heart is tribal," she said. The judge, on loan from a northern rural district, smiled, and others laughed in the crowded courtroom. "Remember when you were a child, silhouettes on the bedroom wall at night?"

"Make your point," said the judge.

"Well, lasers heal in three dimensions, a real silhouette, and besides, an animal of the light has a natural tribal right to the night, more so than a trucker with higher beams," said Em.

"You have a point there."

"Your honor, our presentation is procedural," pleaded the prosecutor. "This is not the proper forum for a lecture on candlepower." He pinched his chin, a measure of his pleasure over his last phrase. "We are prepared for trial."

"Christopher Columbus," shouted the trickster.

"Your witness?"

"Would you hold the right to his image over the road?" Almost pounded his chest several times, a filmic gesture, and then posed at the prow of the polished bench. "Columbus is our precedence."

"New World indeed, but the issue here is an interstate, not a novel port for the Niña, Pinta, Santa Maria," the prosecutor lectured. "Real bears and laser simulations have no legal voice in our courts, your honor. Their beams are not protected, not even in tribal courts."

"Then cut the lights."

"What?"

"Plead in the dark," said the trickster.

"Your honor, please. . . ."

"Then we have a right to be tried with our light."

"Your honor, please, the accused was removed from the reservation for the same cause, the perilous light that comes before this court," said the prosecutor. "Their new cause is not sacred but postbiological as we read Hans Moravec in *Mind Children,* and this world 'will host a great range of individuals constituted from libraries of accumulated knowledge.' "

"Can the lard," said the judge.

"Christopher Columbus is all over the place," the trickster continued, "in lights, kites, trailers on planes, but his image is no more important than a warrior, a bear over the road at night."

"What is the cause here?"

"Light, light," lauded the trickster, "is a tribal right."

"First Amendment lights?"

"First and Sixth," shouted Em, "lights and rights."

"Due process?"

"Feral lasers," said the trickster, and then the lights were turned out. Lucent animals, superconductors on the dark, appeared as defendants. Then the spectators chanted two words, feral laser, feral laser, faster and faster. The trickster lasers created a wild Mount Rushmore National Memorial. George Washington, Jefferson, Lincoln, and Theodore Roosevelt beamed over the bench; however, tribal warriors eclipsed the presidents in a new tribunal.

Meanwhile, in old and troubled cities across the nation, people by the thousands bought lasers to revise histories, to hold their memories, and to create a new wilderness over the interstates. The cities came alive with laser holograms, a communal light show, a right to come together in the night. Lights danced over the cities; lonesome figures returned to their lost houses.

"The laser is a tribal pen, a light brush in the wild air," the judge pronounced, overcome with light amusement, "and these warriors are new creations, an interior landscape, memories to be sure, an instance of communal rights and free expression." The judge ruled in favor of light rights and dismissed the case; he appeared that night with the animals over seven cities.

Antoine de la Mothe Cadillac, tribal mummers in the new fur trade, peace medal presidents, bears, and crows appeared with Almost Browne and Em Wheeler in a comic opera, trickster lasers on a summer night over the Renaissance Center in Detroit.

1991

OCTAVIA BUTLER
b. 1947

Born in Pasadena, California, Octavia Butler was educated at Pasadena City College, California State University at Los Angeles, and the University of California at Los Angeles. In 1969 she enrolled in the Clarion Science Fiction Writers' Workshop in western Pennsylvania, a "science fiction boot camp"—as she called it in a 1993 *Publishers Weekly* interview—and for five years struggled at menial jobs while developing her writing. Her ten novels include four books set in the human hierarchical "Patternist" world, beginning with *Patternmaster* (1976); *Kindred* (1979); three books set in the alien-human hybrid world of "Xenogenesis," beginning with *Dawn* (1987); and *The Parable of the Sower* (1993). In 1984 she received a Hugo Award for her short story "Speech Sounds," and in 1985 she received Hugo, Nebula, Locus, *Science Fiction Chronicle Reader*, and Science Fiction Writers of America Awards for her novelette, "Bloodchild."

In the *Publishers Weekly* interview, Butler noted that for her "the greatest influences were the early pulp magazine writers," and she cited Ray Bradbury among them. "To write science fiction," she said, "you do have to be kind of a loner, live in your head, and, at the same time, have a love for talking. . . . I write about things that interest me, and I'm not the most unique person on earth. So I figure what will interest me will interest other people."

The following excerpt is from *Imago* (1989), the last book of the Xenogenesis trilogy. "I started the series at a time when Reagan was saying we could have winnable nuclear wars and how we'd all be safer if we had more nuclear weapons," Butler recalled. "I thought if people believed this, then there must be something wrong with us as human beings."

From Imago

1

I slipped into my first metamorphosis so quietly that no one noticed. Metamorphoses were not supposed to begin that way. Most people begin with small, obvious, physical changes—the loss of fingers and toes, for instance, or the budding of new fingers and toes of a different design.

I wish my experience had been that normal, that safe.

For several days, I changed without attracting attention. Early stages of metamorphosis didn't normally last for days without bringing on deep sleep, but mine did. My first changes were sensory. Tastes, scents, all sensations suddenly became complex, confusing, yet unexpectedly seductive.

I had to relearn everything. River water, for instance: when I swam in it, I noticed that it had two distinctive major flavors—hydrogen and oxygen?—and many minor flavors. I could separate out and savor each one individually. In fact, I couldn't help separating them. But I learned them quickly and accepted them in their new complexity so that only occasional changes in minor flavors demanded my attention.

Our river water at Lo always came to us clouded with sediment. "Rich," the Oankali called it. "Muddy," the Humans said, and filtered it or let the silt settle to the bottom before they drank it. "Just water," we constructs said, and shrugged. We had never known any other water.

As quickly as I could, I learned again to understand and accept my sensory impressions of the people and things around me. The experience absorbed so much of my attention that I didn't understand how my family could fail to see that something unusual was happening to me. But beyond mentioning that I was daydreaming too much, even my parents missed the signs.

They were, after all, the wrong signs. No one was expecting them, so no one noticed when they appeared.

All five of my parents were old when I was born. They didn't look any older than my adult sisters and brothers, but they had helped with the founding of Lo. They had grandchildren who were old. I don't think I had ever surprised them before. I wasn't sure I liked surprising them now. I didn't want to tell them. I especially didn't want to tell Tino, my Human father. He was supposed to stay with me through my metamorphosis—since he was my same-sex Human parent. But I did not feel drawn to him as I should have. Nor did I feel drawn to Lilith, my birth mother. She was Human, too, and what was happening to me was definitely not a Human thing. Strangely I didn't want to go to my Oankali father, Dichaan, either, and he was my logical choice after Tino. My Oankali mother, Ahajas, would have talked to one of my fathers for me. She had done that for two of my brothers who had been afraid of metamorphosis—afraid they would change too much, lose all signs of their Humanity. That could happen to me, though I had never worried about it. Ahajas would have talked to me and for me, no matter what my problem was. Of all my parents, she was the easiest to talk to. I would have gone to her if the thought of doing so had been more appealing—or if I had understood why it was so unappealing. What was wrong with me? I wasn't shy or afraid, but when I thought of going to her, I felt first drawn, then . . . almost repelled.

Finally there was my ooloi parent, Nikanj.

It would tell me to go to one of my same-sex parents—one of my fathers. What else could it say? I knew well enough that I was in metamorphosis, and that that was one of the few things ooloi parents could not help with. There were still some Humans who insisted on seeing the ooloi as some kind of male-female combination, but the ooloi were no such thing. They were themselves—a different sex altogether.

So I went to Nikanj only hoping to enjoy its company for a while. Eventually it would notice what was happening to me and send me to my fathers. Until it did, I would rest near it. I was tired, sleepy. Metamorphosis was mostly sleep.

I found Nikanj inside the family house, talking to a pair of Human strangers. The Humans were standing back from Nikanj. The female was almost sheltering behind the male, and the male was making a painful effort to appear courageous. Both looked alarmed when they saw me open a wall and step through into the room. Then, as they got a look at me, they seemed to relax a little. I looked very Human—especially if they compared me to Nikanj, who wasn't Human at all.

The Humans smelled most obviously of sweat and adrenaline, food and sex. I sat down on the floor and let myself work out the complex combinations of scents. My new awareness wouldn't allow me to do anything else. By the time I was finished, I thought I would be able to track those two Humans through anything.

Nikanj paid no attention to me except to notice me when I came in. It was used to its children coming and going as they chose, used to all of us spending time with it, learning whatever it was willing to teach us.

It has an incredibly complex scent because it was ooloi. It had collected within itself not only the reproductive material of other members of the family but cells of other plant and animal species that it had dealt with recently. These it would study, memorize, then either consume or store. It consumed the ones it knew it could re-create from memory, using its own DNA. It kept the others alive in a kind of stasis until they were needed.

Its most noticeable underscent was Kaal, the kin group it was born into. I had never met its parents, but I knew the Kaal scent from other members of the Kaal kin group. Somehow, though, I had never noticed that scent on Nikanj, never separated it out this way.

The main scent was Lo, of course. It had mated with Oankali of the Lo kin group, and on mating, it had altered its own scent as an ooloi must. The word "ooloi" could not be translated directly into English because its meaning was as complex as Nikanj's scent. "Treasured stranger." "Bridge." "Life trader." "Weaver." "Magnet."

Magnet, my birth mother says. People are drawn to ooloi and can't escape. She couldn't, certainly. But then, neither could Nikanj escape her or any of its mates. The Oankali said the chemical bonds of mating were as difficult to break as the habit of breathing.

Scents . . . The two visiting Humans were longtime mates and smelled of each other.

"We don't know yet whether we want to emigrate," the female was saying. "We've come to see for ourselves and for our people."

"You'll be shown everything," Nikanj told them. "There are no secrets about the Mars colony or travel to it. But right now the shuttles allotted to emigration are all in use. We have a guest area where Humans can wait."

The two Humans looked at one another. They still smelled frightened, but now both were making an effort to look brave. Their faces were almost expressionless.

"We don't want to stay here," the male said. "We'll come back when there's a ship."

Nikanj stood up—unfolded, as Humans say. "I can't tell you when there'll be a ship," it said. "They arrive when they arrive. Let me show you the guest area. It isn't like this house. Humans built it of cut wood."

The pair stumbled back from Nikanj.

Nikanj's sensory tentacles flattened against its body in amusement. It sat down again. "There are other Humans waiting in the guest area," it told them gently. "They're like you. They want their own all-Human world. They'll be traveling with you when you go." It paused, looked at me. "Eka, why don't you show them?"

I wanted to stay with it now more than ever, but I could see that the two Humans were relieved to be turned over to someone who at least looked Human. I stood up and faced them.

"This is Jodahs," Nikanj told them, "one of my younger children."

The female gave me a look that I had seen too often not to recognize. She said, "But I thought . . ."

"No," I said to her, and smiled. "I'm not Human. I'm a Human-born construct. Come out this way. The guest area isn't far."

They did not want to follow me through the wall I opened until it was fully open—as though they thought the wall might close on them, as though it would hurt them if it did.

"It would be like being grasped gently by a big hand," I told them when we were all outside.

"What?" the male asked.

"If the wall shut on you. It couldn't hurt you because you're alive. It might eat your clothing, though."

"No, thanks!"

I laughed. "I've never seen that happen, but I've heard it can."

"What's your name?" the female asked.

"All of it?" She looked interested in me—smelled sexually attracted, which made her interesting to me. Human females did tend to like me as long as I kept my few body tentacles covered by clothing and my few head tentacles hidden in my hair. The sensory spots on my face and arms looked like ordinary skin, though they didn't feel ordinary.

"Your Human name," the female said. "I already know . . . Eka and Jodahs, but I'm not sure which to call you."

"Eka is just a term of endearment for young children," I told her, "like lelka for married children and Chka between mates. Jodahs is my personal name. The Human version of my whole name is Jodahs Iyapo Leal Kaalnikanjlo. My name, the surnames of my birth mother and Human father, and Nikanj's name beginning with the kin group it was born into and ending with the kin group of its Oankali mates. If I were Oankali-born or if I gave you the Oankali version of my name, it would be a lot longer and more complicated."

"I've heard some of them," the female said. "You'll probably drop them eventually."

"No. We'll change them to suit our needs, but we won't drop them. They give very useful information, especially when people are looking for mates."

"Jodahs doesn't sound like any name I've heard before," the male said.

"Oankali name. An Oankali named Jodahs died helping with the emigration. My birth mother said he should be remembered. The Oankali don't have a tradition of remembering people by naming kids after them, but my birth mother insisted. She does that sometimes—insists on keeping Human customs."

"You look very Human," the female said softly.

I smiled. "I'm a child. I just look unfinished."

"How old are you?"

"Twenty-nine."

"Good God! When will you be considered an adult?"

"After metamorphosis." I smiled to myself. Soon. "I have a brother who went through it at twenty-one, and a sister who didn't reach it until she was thirty-three. People change when their bodies are ready, not at some specific age."

She was silent for some time. We reached the last of the true houses of Lo—the houses that had been grown from the living substance of the Lo entity. Humans without Oankali mates could not open walls or raise table, bed, or chair platforms in such houses. Left alone in our houses, these Humans were prisoners until some construct, Oankali, or mated Human freed them. Thus, they had been given first a guest house, then a guest area. In that area they had built their dead houses of cut wood and woven thatch. They used fire for light and cooking and occasionally they burned down one of their houses. Houses that did not burn became infested with rodents and insects which ate the Human's food and bit or stung the Humans themselves. Periodically Oankali went in and drove the non-Human life out. It always came back. It had been feeding on Humans, eating their food, and living in their buildings since long before the Oankali arrived. Still the guest area was reasonably comfortable. Guests ate from trees and plants that were not what they appeared to be. They were extensions of the Lo entity. They had been induced to synthesize fruits and vegetables in shapes, flowers, and textures that Humans recognized. The foods grew from what appeared to be their proper trees and plants. Lo took care of the Humans' wastes, keeping their area clean, though they tended to be careless about where they threw or dumped things in this temporary place.

"There's an empty house there," I said, pointing.

The female stared at my hand rather than at where I pointed. I had, from a Human point of view, too many fingers and toes. Seven per. Since they were part of distinctly Human-looking hands and feet, Humans didn't usually notice them at once.

I held my hand open, palm up so that she could see it, and her expression flickered from curiosity and surprise through embarrassment back to curiosity.

"Will you change much in metamorphosis?" she asked.

"Probably. The Human-born get more Oankali and the Oankali-born get more Human. I'm first-generation. If you want to see the future, take a look at some of the third- and fourth-generations constructs. They're a lot more uniform from start to finish."

"That's not our future," the male said.

"Your choice," I said.

The male walked away toward the empty house. The female hesitated. "What do you think of our emigration?" she asked.

I looked at her, liking her, not wanting to answer. But such questions should be answered. Why, though, were the Human females who insisted on asking them so often small, weak people? The Martian environment they were headed for was harsher than any they had known. We would see that they had the best possible chance to survive. Many would live to bear children on their new world. But they would suffer so. And in the end, it would all be for nothing. Their own genetic conflict had betrayed and destroyed them once. It would do so again.

"You should stay," I told the female. "You should join us."

"Why?"

I wanted very much not to look at her, to go away from her. Instead I continued to face her. "I understand that Humans must be free to go," I said softly. "I'm Human enough for my body to understand that. But I'm Oankali enough to know that you will eventually destroy yourselves again."

She frowned, marring her smooth forehead. "You mean another war?"

"Perhaps. Or maybe you'll find some other way to do it. You were working on several ways before your war."

"You don't know anything about it. You're too young."

"You should stay and mate with constructs or with Oankali," I said. "The children we construct are free of inherent flaws. What we build will last."

"You're just a child, repeating what you've been told!"

I shook my head. "I perceive what I perceive. No one had to tell me how to use my senses any more than they had to tell you how to see or hear. There is a lethal genetic conflict in Humanity, and you know it."

"All we know is what the Oankali have told us." The male had come back. He put his arm around the female, drawing her away from me as though I had offered some threat. "They could be lying for their own reasons."

I shifted my attention to him. "You know they're not," I said softly. "Your own history tells you. Your people are intelligent, and that's good. The Oankali say you're potentially one of the most intelligent species they've found. But you're also hierarchical—you and your nearest animal relatives and your most distant animal ancestors. Intelligence is relatively new to life on Earth, but your hierarchical tendencies are ancient. The new was too often put at the service of the old. It will be again. You're bright enough to learn to live on your new world, but you're so hierarchical you'll destroy yourselves trying to dominate it and each other. You might last a long time, but in the end, you'll destroy yourselves."

"We could last a thousand years," the male said. "We did all right on Earth until the war."

"You could. Your new world will be difficult. It will demand most of your attention, perhaps occupy your hierarchical tendencies safely for a while."

"We'll be free—us, our children, their children."

"Perhaps."

"We'll be fully Human and free. That's enough. We might even get into space again on our own someday. Your people might be dead wrong about us."

"No." He couldn't read the gene combinations as I could. It was as though he were about to walk off a cliff simply because he could not see it—or because he, or rather his descendants, would not hit the rocks below for a long time. And what were we doing, we who knew the truth? Helping him reach the cliff. Ferrying him to it.

"We might outlast your people here on Earth," he said.

"I hope so," I told him. His expression said he didn't believe me, but I meant it. We would not be here—the Earth he knew would not be here—for more than a few centuries. We, Oankali and construct, were spacegoing people, as curious about other life and as acquisitive of it as Humans were hierarchical. Eventually we would have to begin the long, long search for a new species to combine with to construct new life-forms. Much of Oankali existence was spent in such searches. We would leave this solar system in perhaps three centuries. I would live to see the leave-taking myself. And when we broke and scattered, we would leave behind a lump of stripped rock more like the moon than like his blue Earth. He did not know that. He would never know it. To tell him would be a cruelty.

"Do you ever think of yourself or your kind as Human?" the female asked. "Some of you look so Human."

"We feel our Humanity. It helps us to understand both you and the Oankali. Oankali alone could never have let you have your Mars colony."

"I heard they were helping!" the male said. "Your . . . your parent said they were helping!"

"They help because of what we constructs tell them: that you should be allowed to go even though you'll eventually destroy yourselves. The Oankali believe . . . the Oankali *know to the bone* that it's wrong to help the Human species regenerate unchanged because it *will* destroy itself again. To them it's like deliberately causing the conception of a child who is so defective that it must die in infancy."

"They're wrong. Someday we'll show them how wrong."

It was a threat. It was meaningless, but it gave him some slight satisfaction. "The other Humans here will show you where to gather food," I said. "If you need anything else, ask one of us." I turned to go.

"So goddamn patronizing," the male muttered.

I turned back without thinking. "Am I really?"

The male frowned, muttered a curse, and went back into the house. I understood then that he was just angry. It bothered me that I sometimes made them angry. I never intended to.

The female stepped to me, touched my face, examined a little of my hair. Humans who hadn't mated among us never really learned to touch us. At best, they annoyed us by rubbing their hands over sensory spots, and once their hands found the spots they never liked them.

The female jerked her hand back when her fingers discovered the one below my left ear.

"They're a little like eyes that can't close to protect themselves," I said. "It doesn't exactly hurt us when you touch them, but we don't like you to."

"So what? You have to teach people how to touch you?"

I smiled and took her hand between my own. "Hands are always safe," I said. I left her standing there, watching me. I could see her through sensory tentacles in my hair. She stood there until the male came out and drew her inside.

1989

NEAL STEPHENSON
b. 1959

Born in Fort Meade, Maryland, Neal Stephenson was educated at Boston University, where he served as a teaching assistant in the physics department. He has also worked as a researcher for the U.S. Department of Energy and for Boston's Corporation for a Cleaner Commonwealth, and he is a former computer programmer. His four novels are *The Big U* (1984), *Zodiac* (1988), *Snow Crash* (1992), and *The Diamond Age* (1995).

Snow Crash was originally intended as an interactive multimedia program, cocreated with the artist Tony Sheeder. But, as Stephenson explained in *The New York Times* in 1994, "We figured that . . . wasn't going to work because we would have had to have mastered TV and film and sound production. In a sense it was a lot easier for me to just sit down and write the thing."

From Snow Crash

1

The Deliverator belongs to an elite order, a hallowed subcategory. He's got esprit up to here. Right now, he is preparing to carry out his third mission of the night. His uniform is black as activated charcoal, filtering the very light out of the air. A bullet will bounce off its arachnofiber weave like a wren hitting a patio door, but excess perspiration wafts through it like a breeze through a freshly napalmed forest. Where his body has bony extremities, the suit has sintered armorgel: feels like gritty jello, protects like a stack of telephone books.

When they gave him the job, they gave him a gun. The Deliverator never deals in cash, but someone might come after him anyway—might want his car, or his cargo. The gun is tiny, aero-styled, lightweight, the kind of a gun a fashion designer would carry; it fires teensy darts that fly at five times the velocity of an SR-71 spy plane, and when you get done using it, you have to plug it into the cigarette lighter, because it runs on electricity.

The Deliverator never pulled that gun in anger, or in fear. He pulled it once in Gila Highlands. Some punks in Gila Highlands, a fancy Burbclave, wanted themselves a delivery, and they didn't want to pay for it. Thought they would impress the Deliverator with a baseball bat. The Deliverator took out his gun, centered its laser doohickey on that poised Louisville Slugger, fired it. The recoil was immense, as though the weapon had blown up in his hand. The middle third of the baseball bat turned into a column of burning sawdust accelerating in all directions like a bursting star. Punk ended up holding this bat handle with milky smoke pouring out the end. Stupid look on his face. Didn't get nothing but trouble from the Deliverator.

Since then the Deliverator has kept the gun in the glove compartment and relied, instead, on a matched set of samurai swords, which have always been his weapon of choice anyhow. The punks in Gila Highlands weren't afraid of the gun, so the Deliverator was forced to use it. But swords need no demonstrations.

The Deliverator's car has enough potential energy packed into its batteries to fire a pound of bacon into the Asteroid Belt. Unlike a bimbo box or a Burb beater, the Deliverator's car unloads that power through gaping, gleaming, polished sphincters. When the Deliverator puts the hammer down, shit happens. You want to talk contact patches? Your car's tires have tiny contact patches, talk to the asphalt in four places the size of your tongue. The Deliverator's car has big sticky tires with contact patches the size of a fat lady's thighs. The Deliverator is in touch with the road, starts like a bad day, stops on a peseta.

Why is the Deliverator so equipped? Because people rely on him. He is a roll model. This is America. People do whatever the fuck they feel like doing, you got a problem with that? Because they have a right to. And because they have guns and no one can fucking stop them. As a result, this country has one of the worst economies in the world. When it gets down to it—talking trade balances here—once we've brain-drained all our technology into other countries, once things have evened out, they're making cars in Bolivia and microwave ovens in Tadzhikistan and selling them here—once our edge in natural resources has been made irrelevant by giant Hong Kong ships and dirigibles that can ship North Dakota all the way to New Zealand for a nickel—once the Invisible Hand has taken all those historical inequities and smeared them out into a broad global layer of what a Pakistani brickmaker would consider to be prosperity—y'know what? There's only four things we do better than anyone else

music
movies
microcode (software)
high-speed pizza delivery

The Deliverator used to make software. Still does, sometimes. But if life were a mellow elementary school run by well-meaning education Ph.D.s, the Deliverator's report card would say: "Hiro is *so* bright and creative but needs to work harder on his cooperation skills."

So now he has this other job. No brightness or creativity involved—but no cooperation either. Just a single principle: The Deliverator stands tall, your pie in thirty minutes or you can have it free, shoot the driver, take his car, file a class-action suit. The Deliverator has been working this job for six months, a rich and lengthy tenure by his standards, and has never delivered a pizza in more than twenty-one minutes.

Oh, they used to argue over times, many corporate driver-years lost to it: homeowners, red-faced and sweaty with their own lies, stinking of Old Spice and job-related stress, standing in their glowing yellow doorways brandishing their Seikos and waving at the clock over the kitchen sink, I swear, can't you guys tell time?

Didn't happen anymore. Pizza delivery is a major industry. A managed industry. People went to CosaNostra Pizza University four years just to learn it. Came in its doors unable to write an English sentence, from Abkhazia, Rwanda, Guanajuato, South Jersey, and came out knowing more about pizza than a Bedouin knows about sand. And they had studied this problem. Graphed the frequency of doorway delivery-time disputes. Wired the early Deliverators to record, then analyze, the debating tactics, the voice-stress histograms, the distinctive grammatical structures employed by white middle-class Type A Burbclave occupants who against all logic had decided that this was the place to take their personal Custerian stand against all that was stale and deadening in their lives: they were going to lie, or delude themselves, about the time of their phone call and get themselves a free pizza; no, they deserved a free pizza along with their life, liberty, and pursuit of whatever, it was fucking inalienable. Sent psychologists out to these people's houses, gave them a free TV set to submit to an anonymous interview, hooked them to polygraphs, studied their brain waves as they showed them choppy, inexplicable movies of porn queens and late-night car crashes and Sammy Davis, Jr., put them in sweet-smelling, mauve-walled rooms and asked them questions about Ethics so perplexing that even a Jesuit couldn't respond without committing a venial sin.

The analysts at CosaNostra Pizza University concluded that it was just human nature and you couldn't fix it, and so they went for a quick cheap technical fix: smart boxes. The pizza box is a plastic carapace now, corrugated for stiffness, a little LED readout glowing on the side, telling the Deliverator how many trade imbalance–producing minutes have ticked away since the fateful phone call. There are chips and stuff in there. The pizzas rest, a short stack of them, in slots behind the Deliverator's head. Each pizza glides into a slot like a circuit board into a computer, clicks into place as the smart box interfaces with the onboard system of the Deliverator's car. The address of the caller has already been inferred from his phone number and poured into the smart box's built-in RAM. From there it is communicated to the car, which computes and projects the optimal route on a heads-up display, a glowing colored map traced out against the windshield so that the Deliverator does not even have to glance down.

If the thirty-minute deadline expires, news of the disaster is flashed to CosaNostra Pizza Headquarters and relayed from there to Uncle Enzo himself—the Sicilian Colonel Sanders, the Andy Griffith of Bensonhurst, the straight razor–swinging figment of many a Deliverator's nightmares, the Capo and prime figurehead of CosaNostra Pizza, Incorporated—who will be on the phone to the customer within five minutes, apologizing profusely. The next day, Uncle Enzo will land on the customer's yard in a jet helicopter and apologize some more and give him a free trip to Italy—all he has to do is sign a bunch of releases that make him a public figure and spokesperson for CosaNostra Pizza and basically end his private life as he knows it. He will come away from the whole thing feeling that, somehow, he owes the Mafia a favor.

The Deliverator does not know for sure what happens to the driver in such cases, but he has heard some rumors. Most pizza deliveries happen in the evening hours, which Uncle Enzo considers to be his private time. And how would you feel if you had to interrupt dinner with your family in order to call some obstreperous dork in a Burbclave and grovel for a late fucking pizza? Uncle Enzo has not put in fifty years serving his family and his country so that, at the age when most are playing golf and bobbling their granddaughters, he can get out of the bathtub dripping wet and lie down and kiss the feet of some sixteen-year-old skate punk whose pepperoni was thirty-one minutes in coming. Oh, God. It makes the Deliverator breathe a little shallower just to think of the idea.

But he wouldn't drive for CosaNostra Pizza any other way. You know why? Because there's something about having your life on the line. It's like being a kamikaze pilot. Your mind is clear. Other people—store clerks, burger flippers, software engineers, the whole vocabulary of meaningless jobs that make up Life in America—other people just rely on plain old competition. Better flip your burgers or debug your subroutines faster and better than your high school classmate two blocks down the strip is flipping or debugging, because we're in competition with those guys, and people notice these things.

What a fucking rat race that is. CosaNostra Pizza doesn't have any competition. Competition goes against the Mafia ethic. You don't work harder because you're competing against some identical operation down the street. You work harder because everything is on the line. Your name, your honor, your family, your life. Those burger flippers might have a better life expectancy—but what kind of life is it anyway, you have to ask yourself. That's why nobody, not even the Nipponese, can move pizzas faster than CosaNostra. The Deliverator is proud to wear the uniform, proud to drive the car, proud to march up the front walks of innumerable Burbclave homes, a grim vision in ninja black, a pizza on his shoulder, red LED digits blazing proud numbers into the night: 12:32 or 15:15 or the occasional 20:43.

The Deliverator is assigned to CosaNostra Pizza #3569 in the Valley. Southern California doesn't know whether to bustle or just strangle itself on the spot. Not enough roads for the number of people. Fairlanes, Inc. is laying new ones all the time. Have to bulldoze lots of neighborhoods to do it, but those seventies and eighties developments exist to be bulldozed, right? No sidewalks, no schools, no nothing. Don't have their own police force—no immigration control—undesirables can walk right in without being frisked or even harassed. Now a Burbclave, that's the place to live. A city-state with its own constitution, a border, laws, cops, everything.

The Deliverator was a corporal in the Farms of Merryvale State Security Force for a while once. Got himself fired for pulling a sword on an acknowledged perp. Slid it right through the fabric of the perp's shirt, gliding the flat of the blade along the base of his neck, and pinned him to a warped and bubbled expanse of vinyl siding on the wall of the house that the perp was trying to break into. Thought it was a pretty righteous bust. But they fired him anyway because the perp turned out to be the son of the vice-chancellor of the Farms of Merryvale. Oh, the weasels had an excuse: said that a thirty-six-inch samurai sword was not on their Weapons Protocol. Said that he had violated the SPAC, the Suspected Perpetrator Apprehension Code. Said that the perp had suffered psychological trauma. He was afraid of butter knives now; he had to spread his jelly with the back of a teaspoon. They said that he had exposed them to liability.

The Deliverator had to borrow some money to pay for it. Had to borrow it from the Mafia, in fact. So he's in their database now—retinal patterns, DNA, voice graph, fingerprints, footprints, palm prints, wrist prints, every fucking part of the body that had wrinkles on it—almost—those bastards rolled in ink and made a print and digitized it into their computer. But it's their money—sure they're careful about loaning it out. And when he applied for the Deliverator job they were happy to take him, because they knew him. When he got the loan, he had to deal personally with the assistant vice-capo of the Valley, who later recommended him for the Deliverator job. So it was like being in a family. A really scary, twisted, abusive family.

CosaNostra Pizza #3569 is on Vista Road just down from Kings Park Mall. Vista Road used to belong to the State of California and now is called Fairlanes, Inc. Rte. CSV-5. Its main competition used to be a U.S. highway and is now called Cruiseways, Inc. Rte. Cal-12. Farther up the Valley, the two competing highways actually cross. Once there had been bitter disputes, the intersection closed by sporadic sniper fire. Finally, a big developer bought the entire intersection and turned it into a drive-through mall. Now the roads just feed into a parking system—not a lot, not a ramp, but a system—and lose their identity. Getting through the intersection involves tracing paths through the parking system, many braided filaments of direction like the Ho Chi Minh trail. CSV-5 has better throughput, but Cal-12 has better pavement. That is typical—Fairlanes roads emphasize getting you there, for Type A drivers, and Cruiseways emphasize the enjoyment of the ride, for Type B drivers.

The Deliverator is a Type A driver with rabies. He is zeroing in on his home base, CosaNostra Pizza #3569, cranking up the left lane of CSV-5 at a hundred and twenty kilometers. His car is an invisible black lozenge, just a dark place that reflects the tunnel of franchise signs—the loglo. A row of orange lights burbles and churns across the front, where the grille would be if this were an air-breathing car. The orange light looks like a gasoline fire. It comes in through people's rear windows, bounces off their rearview mirrors, projects a fiery mask across their eyes, reaches into their subconscious, and unearths terrible fears of being pinned, fully conscious, under a detonating gas tank, makes them want to pull over and let the Deliverator overtake them in his black chariot of pepperoni fire.

The loglo, overhead, marking out CSV-5 in twin contrails, is a body of electrical light made of innumerable cells, each cell designed in Manhattan by imageers who make more for designing a single logo than a Deliverator will make in his entire lifetime. Despite their efforts to stand out, they all smear together, especially at a hundred and twenty kilometers per hour. Still, it is easy to see CosaNostra Pizza #3569 because of the billboard, which is wide and tall even by current inflated standards. In fact, the squat franchise itself looks like nothing more than a low-slung base for the great aramid fiber pillars that thrust the billboard up into the trademark firmament. Marca Registrada, baby.

The billboard is a classic, a chestnut, not a figment of some fleeting Mafia promotional campaign. It is a statement, a monument built to endure. Simple and dignified. It shows Uncle Enzo in one of his spiffy Italian suits. The pinstripes glint and flex like sinews. The pocket square is luminous. His hair is perfect, slicked back with something that never comes off, each strand cut off straight and square at the end by Uncle Enzo's cousin, Art the Barber, who runs the second-largest chain of low-end haircutting establishments in the world. Uncle Enzo is standing there, not exactly smiling, an avuncular glint in his eye for sure, not posing like a model but standing there like your uncle would, and it says

The Mafia
you've got a friend in The Family!
paid for by the Our Thing Foundation

The billboard serves as the Deliverator's polestar. He knows that when he gets to the place on CSV-5 where the bottom corner of the billboard is obscured by the pseudo-Gothic stained-glass arches of the local Reverend Wayne's Pearly Gates franchise, it's time for him to get over into the right lanes where the retards and the bimbo boxes poke along, random, indecisive, looking at each passing franchise's driveway like they don't know if it's a promise or a threat.

He cuts off a bimbo box—a family minivan—veers past the Buy 'n' Fly that is next door, and pulls into CosaNostra Pizza #3569. Those big fat contact patches complain, squeal a little bit, but they hold on to the patented Fairlanes, Inc. high-traction pavement and guide him into the chute. No other Deliverators are waiting in the chute. That is good, that means high turnover for him, fast action, keep moving that 'za. As he scrunches to a stop, the electromechanical hatch on the flank of his car is already opening to reveal his empty pizza slots, the door clicking and folding back in on itself like the wing of a beetle. The slots are waiting. Waiting for hot pizza.

And waiting. The Deliverator honks his horn. This is not a nominal outcome.

Window slides open. That should never happen. You can look at the three-ring binder from CosaNostra Pizza University, cross-reference the citation for *window, chute, dispatcher's,* and it will give you all the procedures for that window—and it should never be opened. Unless something has gone wrong.

The window slides open and—you sitting down?—*smoke* comes out of it. The Deliverator hears a discordant beetling over the metal hurricane of his sound system and realizes that it is a smoke alarm, coming from inside the franchise.

Mute button on the stereo. Oppressive silence—his eardrums uncringe—the window is buzzing with the cry of the smoke alarm. The car idles, waiting. The hatch has been open too long, atmospheric pollutants are congealing on the electrical contacts in the back of the pizza slots, he'll have to clean them ahead of schedule, everything is going exactly the way it shouldn't go in the three-ring binder that spells out all the rhythms of the pizza universe.

Inside, a football-shaped Abkhazian man is running to and fro, holding a three-ring binder open, using his spare tire as a ledge to keep it from collapsing shut; he runs with the gait of a man carrying an egg on a spoon. He is shouting in the Abkhazian dialect; all the people who run CosaNostra pizza franchises in this part of the Valley are Abkhazian immigrants.

It does not look like a serious fire. The Deliverator saw a real fire once, at the Farms of Merryvale, and you couldn't see anything for the smoke. That's all it was: smoke, burbling out of nowhere, occasional flashes of orange light down at the bottom, like heat lightning in tall clouds. This is not that kind of fire. It is the kind of fire that just barely puts out enough smoke to detonate the smoke alarms. And he is losing time for this shit.

The Deliverator holds the horn button down. The Abkhazian manager comes to the window. He is supposed to use the intercom to talk to drivers, he could say anything he wanted and it would be piped straight into the Deliverator's car, but no, he has to talk face to face, like the Deliverator is some kind of fucking ox cart driver. He is red-faced, sweating, his eyes roll as he tries to think of the English words.

"A fire, a little one," he says.

The Deliverator says nothing. Because he knows that all of this is going onto videotape. The tape is being pipelined, as it happens, to CosaNostra Pizza University, where it will be analyzed in a pizza management science laboratory. It will be shown to Pizza University students, perhaps to the very students who will replace this man when he gets fired, as a textbook example of how to screw up your life.

"New employee—put his dinner in the microwave—had foil in it—boom!" the manager says.

Abkhazia had been part of the Soviet fucking Union. A new immigrant from Abkhazia trying to operate a microwave was like a deep-sea tube worm doing brain surgery. Where did they get these guys? Weren't there any Americans who could bake a fucking pizza?

"Just give me one pie," the Deliverator says.

Talking about pies snaps the guy into the current century. He gets a grip. He slams the window shut, strangling the relentless keening of the smoke alarm.

A Nipponese robot arm shoves the pizza out and into the top slot. The hatch folds shut to protect it.

As the Deliverator is pulling out of the chute, building up speed, checking the address that is flashed across his windshield, deciding whether to turn right or left, it happens. His stereo cuts out again—on command of the onboard system. The cockpit lights go red. *Red.* A repetitive buzzer begins to sound. The LED readout on his windshield, which echoes the one on the pizza box, flashes up: 20:00.

They have just given the Deliverator a twenty-minute-old pizza. He checks the address; it is twelve miles away.

1992

DOUGLAS COUPLAND
b. 1961

Born on a Canadian military base in Baden-Sollingen, Germany, Douglas Coupland was educated at the Emily Carr College of Art and Design in Vancouver, Canada. Upon graduation, he pursued a two-year course in Japanese business science in Hawaii ("I don't know what that was all about," he admitted to *Maclean's* in 1992). Currently he lives in Vancouver. "Yes, I'm Canadian by birth," Coupland wrote in a 1996 e-mail correspondence for this anthology. "I've lived in Honolulu and Los Angeles for a good part of the 1980s. I identify myself more as a citizen of the West Coast than as anything else—the intellectual 'Chile' that spans from Anchorage right down to San Diego; Juneau, Vancouver, Victoria, Seattle, Portland, San Francisco, and Los Angeles."

Coupland's novels include *Generation X: Tales for an Accelerated Culture* (1991), *Shampoo Planet* (1992), *Life After God* (1994), *Microserfs* (1995), and *Polaroids from the Dead* (1996). He was quickly anointed as spokesman for the generation he described in his first book. "With *Generation X,* what started out as characters in a book became representatives of a broad layer of people, and of changing times," he told *Maclean's.* "Still, they were just characters in a novel." And while the so-called Generation X is generally thought of as a class of young people with little hope—and little reason to hope—Coupland asserted, "I'm not Pollyannaish, but I'm optimistic about the future."

From Generation X

Shopping Is Not Creating

The dogs are already pooped from the heat and lying in the shadow of the Saab, chasing dream bunnies with twitching back legs. Dag and I, both being in a carbohydrate coma, aren't far behind and are in a good listening mood as Claire begins her story of the day. ¶"It's a Texlahoma story," she says, much to our pleasure, for Texlahoma is a mythic world we created in which to set many of our stories. It's a sad Everyplace, where citizens are always getting fired from their jobs at 7-Eleven and where the kids do drugs and practice the latest dance crazes at the local lake, where they also fantasize about being adult and pulling welfare-check scams as they inspect each other's skin for chemical burns from the lake water. Texlahomans shoplift cheap imitation perfumes from dime stores and shoot each other over Thanksgiving dinners every year. And about the only good thing that happens there is the cultivation of cold, unglamorous wheat in which Texlahomans take a justifiable pride; by law, all citizens must put bumper stickers on their cars saying: NO FARMERS: NO FOOD. ¶Life is boring there, but there are some thrills to be had: all the adults keep large quantities of cheaply sewn scarlet sex garments in their chests of drawers. These are panties and ticklers rocketed in from Korea—and I say rocketed in because Texlahoma is an asteroid orbiting the earth, where the year is permanently 1974, the year after the oil shock and the year starting from which real wages in the U.S. never grew ever again. The atmosphere contains oxygen, wheat chaff, and A.M. radio transmissions. It's a fun place to spend one day, and then you just want to get the hell out of there.

Anyhow, now that you know the setting, let's jump into Claire's story.

"This is a story about an astronaut named Buck. One afternoon, Buck the Astronaut had a problem with his spaceship and was forced to land in Texlahoma—in the suburban backyard of the Monroe family. The problem with Buck's spacecraft was that it wasn't programmed to deal with Texlahoma's gravity—the people back on earth had forgotten to tell him that Texlahoma even existed!

" 'That always happens,' said Mrs. Monroe, as she led Buck away from the ship and past the swing set in the backyard toward the house, 'Cape Canaveral just plum forgets that we're here.'

"Being the middle of the day, Mrs. Monroe offered Buck a hot nutritious lunch of cream of mushroom soup meatballs and canned niblet corn. She was glad to have company: her three daughters were at work, and her husband was out on the thresher.

"Then, after lunch, she invited Buck into the parlor to watch TV game shows with her. 'Normally I'd be out in the garage working on my inventory of aloe products that I represent, but business is kind of slow right now.'

"Buck nodded his concurrence.

" 'You ever thought of being a rep for aloe products after you retire from being an astronaut, Buck?'

" 'No ma'am,' said Buck, 'I hadn't.'

" 'Give it a thought. All you have to do is get a chain of reps working under you, and before you know it, you don't have to work at all—just sit back and skim the profit.'

" 'Well, I'll be darned,' said Buck, who also complimented Mrs. Monroe on her collection of souvenir matchbooks placed in an oversized brandy snifter on the parlor table.

"But suddenly something went wrong. Right before Mrs. Monroe's eyes, Buck began to turn pale green, and his head began to turn boxy and veined, like Frankenstein's. Buck raced to look at a little budgie mirror, the only mirror available, and knew instantly what had happened: he had developed space poisoning. He would start to look like a monster, and shortly, he would fall into an almost permanent sleep.

"Mrs. Monroe immediately assumed, however, that her cream of mushroom soup meatballs had been tainted and that as a result of her culinary shortcomings, she had ruined Buck's adorable astronaut's good looks, and possibly his career. She offered to take him to the local clinic, but Buck deferred.

" 'That's probably for the best,' said Mrs. Monroe, 'considering that all there is at the clinic is peritonitis vaccinations and a jaws of life.'

LEGISLATED NOSTALGIA: To force a body of people to have memories they do not actually possess: *"How can I be a part of the 1960s generation when I don't even remember any of it?"*

NOW DENIAL: To tell oneself that the only time worth living in is the past and that the only time that may ever be interesting again is the future.

" 'Just show me a place where I can fall down to sleep,' Buck said, 'I've come down with space poisoning, and within minutes I'll be out cold. And it looks like you'll have to nurse me for a while. You promise to do that?'

" 'Of course,' replied Mrs. Monroe, eager to be let off the hook of food contamination, and he was quickly shown to the cool basement room with half-finished wall covered with simulated wood grain particle board. There were also bookshelves bearing Mr. Monroe's bonspiel trophies and the toys belonging to the three daughters: an array of Snoopy plush toys, Jem dolls, Easy Bake ovens, and Nancy Drew mystery novels. And the bed Buck was given to sleep in was smallish—a child's bed—covered with ruffled pink Fortrel sheets that smelled like they'd been sitting in a Goodwill shop for years. On the headboard there were scuffed up Holly Hobby, Veronica Lodge, and Betty Cooper stickers that had been stuck and halfheartedly peeled away. The room was obviously never used and pretty well forgotten, but Buck didn't mind. All he wanted to do was fall into a deep deep sleep. And so he did.

"Now, as you can imagine, the Monroe daughters were most excited indeed at having an astronaut/monster hibernating in their guest room. One by one the three daughters, Arleen, Darleen, and Serena came down to the room to stare at Buck, now sleeping in their old bed amid the clutter of their childhood. Mrs. Monroe wouldn't let her daughters peek long, still being fractionally convinced of her implication in Buck's illness, and shooed them away, wanting him to get better.

"Anyhow, life returned more or less to normal. Darleen and Serena went to work at the perfume counter of the local dime store, Mrs. Monroe's aloe product business picked up a bit, taking her out of the house, Mr. Monroe was out on his thresher, leaving only Arleen, the eldest daughter, who had recently been fired from the 7-Eleven, to take care of Buck.

" 'Make sure he gets lots to eat!' shouted Mrs. Monroe from her salt-rusted blue Bonneville sedan as she screeched out of the driveway, to which Arleen waved and then rushed inside to the bathroom where she brushed her blond feathered hair, applied alluring cosmetics, and then dashed down to the kitchen to whip up a special lunchtime treat for Buck, who, owing to his space poisoning, would only awaken once a day at noon, and then only for a half hour. She made a platter of Vienna franks appended to toothpicks and accessorized by little blocks of orange cheese. These she prettily arranged on a platter in a shape reminiscent of the local shopping mall logo, the Crestwood Mall letter *C*, angled heavily to the right. *'Facing the future'* as the local newspaper had phrased it upon the mall's opening several hundred years previously when it was still 1974, even back then, since, as I have said, it has *al*ways been 1974 in Texlahoma. As far back as records go. Shopping malls, for instance, a recent innovation on Earth, have been supplying Texlahomans with running shoes, brass knickknacks, and whimsical greeting cards for untold millennia.

"Anyway, Arleen raced down to the basement with the food platter and pulled a chair up to the bed and pretended to read a book. When Buck woke up at one second past noon, the first thing he glimpsed was her reading, and he thought she looked ideal. As for Arleen, well, her heart had a romantic little arrhythmia right on the spot, even in spite of Buck's looking like a Frankenstein monster.

" 'I'm hungry,' Buck said to Arleen, to which she replied, 'Won't you please please have some of these Vienna frank-and-cheese kebabs. I made them myself. They were most popular indeed at Uncle Clem's wake last year.'

" 'Wake?' asked Buck.

" 'Oh, yes. His combine overturned during the harvest, and he was trapped inside for two hours while he waited for the jaws of life to arrive. He wrote his will out in blood on the cab ceiling.'

"From that moment on, a conversational rapport developed between the two, and before long, love bloomed, but there was a problem with their love, for Buck would always fall back asleep almost as soon as he would awaken, owing to his space poisoning. This grieved Arleen.

"Finally one noon, just as Buck awoke, he said to Arleen, 'Arleen, I love you very much. Do you love *me*?' And, of course, Arleen replied, 'yes,' to which Buck said, 'Would you be willing to take a big risk and help me? We could be together always and I could help you leave Texlahoma.'

"Arleen was thrilled at both thoughts and said, 'Yes, yes,' and then Buck told her what she would have to do. Apparently, the radiation waves emitted by a woman in love are of just the right frequency to boost the rocket ship's engines and help it to lift off. And if Arleen would just come with him in the ship, they could leave, and Buck could get a cure for his space poisoning at the moon base. 'Will you help me, Arleen?'

" 'Of course, Buck.'

" 'There's just *one* catch.'

" 'Oh?' Arleen froze.

" 'You see, once we take off, there's only enough air in the ship for one person, and I'm afraid that after takeoff, you'd have to die. Sorry. But, of course, once we got to the moon, I'd have the right machines to revive you. There's really no problem.'

"Arleen stared at Buck, and a tear came down her cheek, dripped over her lip and onto her tongue, where it tasted salty, like urine. 'I'm sorry, Buck, but I can't do that,' she said, adding that things would probably be for the best if she no longer took care of him. Heartbroken but unsurprised, Buck fell back asleep and Arleen went upstairs.

"Fortunately, Darleen, the youngest daughter, got fired from her perfume sales job that day and was able to take care of Buck next, while Arleen got hired at a fried chicken outlet and was no longer around to cast gloomy feelings on Buck.

"But with Buck's being on the rebound and Darleen's having too much free time on her hands, it was only a matter of minutes, practically, before love again blossomed. Days later, Buck was making the same plea for help to Darleen that he had made to Arleen, 'Won't you please help me, Darleen, I love you so much?'

"But when Buck's plea came to the part about Darleen's having to die, like her sister before her, she froze. 'I'm sorry, Buck, but I can't do that,' she, too, said, adding that things would probably be for the best if she no longer took care of him. Again heartbroken but again unsurprised, Buck fell back to sleep and Darleen went upstairs.

"Need I say it, but history repeated itself *again.* Darleen got hired at the local roadside steak house, and Serena, the middle child, got fired from Woolworth's scent counter and so was put in charge of taking care of Buck, who had ceased being a novelty in the basement and had become instead, kind of a grudge—of the same caliber of grudge as, say, a pet dog that the children argue over whose turn it is to feed. And when Serena appeared at noon with lunch one day, all Buck could bring himself to say was, 'God, did *another* one of you Monroe girls get fired? Can't any of you hold a job?'

"This just bounced right off of Serena. 'They're just small jobs,' she said. 'I'm learning how to paint and one of these days I'm going to become so good that Mr. Leo Castelli of the Leo Castelli art galleries of New York City is going to send a rescue party up to get me off of this God forsaken asteroid. Here,' she said, jabbing a plate of crudité celery and carrot in his chest, 'eat these celery sticks and shut up. You look like you need fiber.'

"Well. If Buck thought he had been in love before, he realized now that those were merely mirages and that Serena was indeed his real True Love. He spent his waking time for the next few weeks, savoring his half hours which he spent telling Serena of the views of the heavens as seen from outer space, and listening to Serena talk of how she would paint the planets if only she could see what they looked like.

" 'I can show you the heavens, and I can help you leave Texlahoma, too—if you're willing to come with me, Serena my love,' said Buck, who outlined his escape plans. And when he explained that Serena would have to die, she simply said, 'I understand.'

"The next day at noon when Buck awoke, Serena lifted him out of the bed and carried him out of the basement and up the stairs, where his feet knocked down framed family portraits taken years and years ago. 'Don't stop,' said Buck. 'Keep moving—we're running out of time.'

"It was a cold gray afternoon outside as Serena carried Buck across the yellowed autumn lawn and into the spaceship. Once inside, they sat down, closed the doors, and Buck used his last energies to turn the ignition and kiss Serena. True to his word, the love waves from her heart boosted the engine, and the ship took off, high into the sky and out of the gravitational field of Texlahoma. And before Serena passed out and then died from a lack of oxygen, the last sights she got to see were Buck's face shedding its pale green Frankenstein skin in lizardy chunks onto the dashboard, thus revealing the dashing pink young astronaut beneath, and outside she saw the glistening pale blue marble of earth against the black heavens that the stars had stained like spilled milk.

"Below on Texlahoma, Arleen and Darleen, meanwhile, were both returning home from their jobs, from which they both been fired, just in time to see the rocket fire off and their sister vanish into the stratosphere in a long, colonic, and fading white line. They sat on the swing set, unable to go back into the house, thinking and staring at the point where the jet's trail became nothing, listening to the creak of chains and the prairie wind.

" 'You realize,' said Arleen, 'that that whole business of Buck being able to bring us back to life was total horseshit.'

" 'Oh, I knew *that,*' said Darleen. 'But it doesn't change the fact that I feel jealous.'

" 'No, it doesn't, does it?'

"And together the two sisters sat into the night, silhouetted by the luminescing earth, having a contest with each other to see who could swing their swing the highest."

1991

J. YELLOWLEES DOUGLAS
b. 1962

J. Yellowlees Douglas received a B.A. and an M.A. from the University of Michigan and a Ph.D. from New York University. Formerly director of the Program in Professional Writing at Lehman College, the City University of New York, Douglas is now director of the Center for Written and Oral Communication at the University of Florida, where she is also assistant professor of English. Her critical work on hypertext has appeared in journals and collections in the United States, the United Kingdom, and Australia, focusing on the applicability of literary theory, narratology, and aesthetics to hypertext environments.

"I see hypertext as something that returns us to the notions of intention and narrative more strongly even than print does," Douglas said in a 1996 interview for this anthology. "My problem with the aesthetics of print is that it has all the restrictions real life has: all these intricate scenarios and variables converge and you only get to discover a single outcome."

An electronic selection from "I Have Said Nothing" is available at the Norton Website: http://www.wwnorton.com

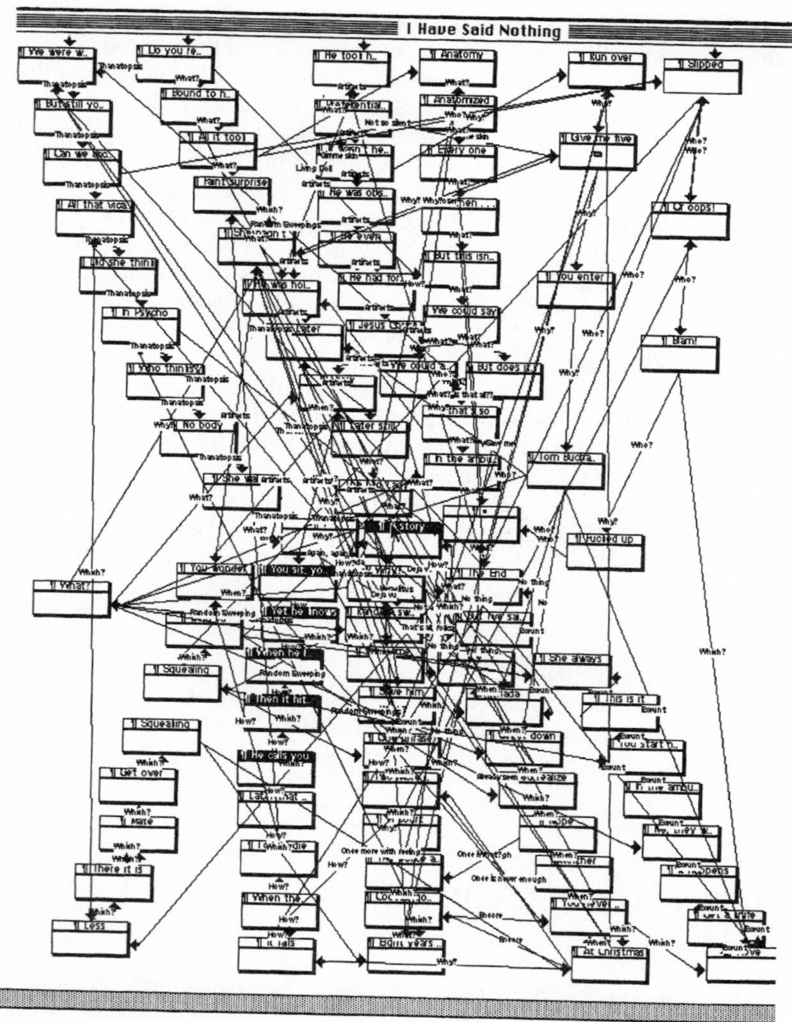

An overview of the structure and links of "I Have Said Nothing."

From I Have Said Nothing

He calls you

on New Year's Eve. There's such a long silence on the phone after you pick it up that you assume automatically it's an obscene call and you get ready to slam the phone down at the first hint of audible breathing. It's an unusually silent pause, though, with just a hint of rushing white noise at the back of it that suggests, maybe, a trans-continental phone call, so you hang on.

"I think Jake's flipped," he says, finally.

Jule's father can't speak—he's hooked up to a respirator and he's in traction—but he can scratch out messages on a little slate strapped to the side of the bed. When Luke went to see him, he'd struggled to chalk out a message.

I think I'll go take a walk and get my paper, he'd written.

"He's cracking up," Luke says.

Then it hits you

—he's not going to pieces: he's trying to make a joke. But Luke can't see it.

That's because when Jake looks at Luke, he sees his daughter's boyfriend looking hollow-eyed, slumped over in the visitor's chair, the kind of morose, hang-dog type nearly always in need of a bit of cheering up.

He can't even begin to imagine what Luke sees when he looks across at him. When Luke looks at Jake, he doesn't see someone who will never walk again. What he sees is a man who hasn't yet realized that the two daughters he saw on Christmas day are now two tidy piles of ashes lying in two gold foil boxes, stowed in a rented house somewhere in North Hollywood.

When he looks at Jake

he realizes the utter impossibility of his ever having the words to tell him this.

He has no inkling of what they would even sound like.

Yet he knows

that the only person in the world who is going to break the news to Jake is sitting in his chair.

Last night, in the parking lot, a guy with a shitty Saturday Night Special had jumped him. When he found Luke didn't have a shred of fucking paper on him—nothing, nada—he was so disgusted he didn't even try to pistol-whip him. Now, looking at Jake's lips curling up around the tube in an attempt at a smile, he wishes the guy had fucking bashed his skull to kingdom come. Given him retrograde amnesia. Tossed the coroner another stiff for the fridge. Three foil boxes back at the goddamned house.

Through the jungle of IV's and feeding tubes and snarl of catheter and ventilator, Jake's fingers are scrabbling at the slate.

They give you far too much to eat in here, he writes.

You sit, you think

You sit and think for a while, maybe forty-five minutes solid, about the ugliness of your primary urge—which is to write all of this down. Somewhere inside you, through all the tears and the gastric juices churning away in your stomach, and the faint, sour taste of vomit you can't seem to rinse completely out of your mouth, somewhere, through all of this, your brain is ticking away like a metronome.

This goes just before the climax, you're thinking. And, when your brother breathes audibly down the line for a moment or two, then says clearly:

"I wish to Christ it'd been you. Why the fuck wasn't it you instead?"

You know you've really got a story. This is simply the grain that irritates. You hear it. And then again you don't.

A story

It's all just a story, something you can spin into a plot with memorable characters and a few good lines that'll stick in the craw and maybe even something approximating real closure, if you play your cards right.

Then it'll be something tangible, something solid that exists Out There and maybe even gives somebody a few minutes' distraction from, say, riding the Lexington Avenue local at rush hour zippered into the cars like sardines in a can, or the pitch of the high-powered whine of the dentist's drill—heard piercing the dreadful quiet of the waiting room just before your name is called.

In short, something that has fucking nothing whatever to do with you. It's all just fiction.

Tell me a goddamned story.

1993

MICHAEL JOYCE
b. 1945

Born in Lackawanna, New York, Michael Joyce was educated at Canisius College and received an M.F.A. from the University of Iowa Writers' Workshop. Currently he is Randolph Visiting Distinguished Professor of English and the Library at Vassar College. His writings include the novel *The War Outside Ireland* (1982), the interactive novel *afternoon, a story* (1990), and the collection of essays *Of Two Minds: Hypertext Pedagogy and Poetics* (1995).

In a 1996 interview, Joyce reported that after publishing his first novel, he decided that he "wanted, quite simply, to write a novel that would change in successive readings, and to make those changing versions according to the connections which I had for some time naturally discovered in the process of writing, and which I wanted my readers to share. . . . It seemed to me that if I, as author, could use a computer to move paragraphs about, it wouldn't take much to let readers do so according to some scheme I had predetermined and which they could shape." His determination led to the development of Storyspace, a hypertext program. "Storyspace," Joyce continued, "enabled me to write a hyperfiction, *afternoon, a story,* which changes every time you read it and which in some sense defined the beginning of a new literature (albeit a transitory one in an uncertain medium)."

More information about how to read *afternoon* can be found in Terry Harpold"s essay "Conclusions" (p. 637). An electronic selection from *afternoon* is available at the Norton Website: http://www. wwnorton.com

From afternoon, a story

a hypertext

The story exists at several levels and changes according to decisions you make. A text you have seen previously may be followed by something new, according to a choice you make or already have made during any given reading.

read at depth

I haven't indicated what words yield, but they are usually ones which have texture, as well as character names and pronouns.

There are more such words early on in the story, but there are almost always options in any sequence of texts.

The lack of clear signals isn't an attempt to vex you, rather an invitation to read either inquisitively or playfully and also at depth. Click on words that interest or invite you.

in my mind

In my mind the story, as it has formed, takes on margins. Each margin will yield to the impatient, or wary, reader. You can answer yes at the beginning and page through on a wave of Returns, or page through directly—again using Returns—without that first interaction.

These are not versions, but the story itself in long lines. Otherwise, however, the center is all—Thoreau or Brer Rabbit, each preferred the bramble. I've discovered more there too, and the real interaction, if that is possible, is in pursuit of texture.

There we match minds.

work in progress

Closure is, as in any fiction, a suspect quality, although here it is made manifest. When the story no longer progresses, or when it cycles, or when you tire of the paths, the experience of reading ends. Even so, there are likely to be more opportunities than you think there are at first. A word which doesn't yield the first time you read a section may take you elsewhere if you choose it when you encounter the section again; and sometimes what seems a loop, like memory, heads off again in another direction.

There is no simple way to say this.

There are sixteen choices which can follow for the new reader who encounters the opening screen of afternoon. *For a reader who encounters this screen again during an extended reading there are another three choices which the story itself makes depending on the screens that reader has read thus far.*

Begin

I try to recall winter. < As if it were yesterday? > she says, but I do not signify one way or another.

By five the sun sets and the afternoon melt freezes again across the blacktop into crystal octopi and palms of ice—rivers and continents beset by fear, and we walk out to the car, the snow moaning beneath our boots and the oaks exploding in series along the fenceline on the horizon, the shrapnel settling like relics, the echoing thundering off far ice. This was the essence of wood, these fragments say. And this darkness is air. < Poetry > she says, without emotion, one way or another.

Do you want to hear about it?

This first screen allows a yes/no choice. If the reader chooses "yes" she reads:

yes

She had been a client of Wert's wife for some time. Nothing serious, nothing awful, merely general unhappiness and the need of a woman so strong to have friends.

It was all very messy, really. For they did become friends, Lolly and Nausicaa, a very early eighties kind of thing when you think of it, appropriately post-feminist and oddly ambiguous. Therapist and client—Lolly's not so scrupulous professional bounds already stretched by herbal tea after each and every session, each and every client—easily became friend and friend when someone, they are neither sure who, suggested they stretch a five p.m. post-session tea to supper.

< Vegetables doubtlessly > Wert smirked, telling me, stressing each syllable in his approximation of the german.

However if the reader chooses "no" she reads:

no

I understand how you feel. Nothing is more empty than heat. Seen so starkly the world holds wonder only in the expanses of clover where the bees work.

Elsewhere it is sheer shimmer, like the skim of hallucination which holds above roads in summer. We have been spoiled by air conditioned automobiles to think we can transcend the blankness. It is as if paper were never invented.

No wonder. Says it exactly. And I am taken by the medievalism of Hours, to think of the day so. In this season the day has only two long hours. Mornings, when I walk, I pass through zones of odors: chemical fertilizer, cigar smoke, lingering exhaust fumes, an occasional talcum scent when an infant has been ferried from the car to home or vice-versa.

For the reader who chooses neither "yes" nor "no" nor any of the other "words that yield" but who rather chooses to "turn the page", the text continues with:

I want to say

I want to say I may have seen my son die this morning.

And the reader who chooses the word "die" here reads:

die?

I felt certain it was them, I recognized her car from that distance, not more than a hundred yards off along the road to the left where she would turn if she were taking him to the Country Day School.

Two men stood near the rear of the grey buick and a woman in a white dress sprawled on the wide lawn before them, two other men crouching near her. Another, smaller body beyond.

In the distance, coming toward them and the road along which I passed, there were the insistent blue lights of a sheriff's cruiser and a glimpse of what I thought to be the synchronized red lights of the emergency wagon.

It was like something from a film: Blowup or the Red Desert.

While the reader who chooses to "turn the page" enters what seems to be another story that will before long loop back on any of the stories begun above:

I want 1

This would be too dramatic for me, although not for Werther.

He enjoys death in the abstract; for instance, how, when he drives this Japanese truck of his, sometimes his eyes will turn steely and he will grip the wheel in a definite line, resisting road and emotion both, hardly breathing, eyes to the vanishing point along the road crest, practicing—he says—unveering.

< Lest sometime an animal cause an accident. I drive through imaginary beasts: raccoons, muskrat, deer, snakes and crows.

<It is a sort of insurance. > He laughs.

1990

VII A Casebook of Postmodern Theory

The relationship between postmodern theory and postmodern fiction is shifting and ambiguous. When Samuel R. Delany quotes Julia Kristeva in the epigraph of his *Neveryóna,* he signals that authors and theorists sometimes read and acknowledge each other's work. Oppositely, the literary scholars who have argued that Jean Baudrillard's theories regarding information and simulation are fully realized in Don DeLillo's *White Noise* appear to suggest that theorists and authors share the same cultural ethos, often expressing many of the same ideas without evident contact with one another. Yet, as Toni Morrison's comments in a 1981 interview with *The New Republic* make clear, many authors maintain an open antipathy toward a realm of literary theory where authors have become author-functions, works have become texts, and critics have become something more than unobtrusive intermediaries between writers and readers. In this context, the role of a casebook of postmodern theory in an anthology of postmodern fiction must be viewed as essential but not dominant, symbiotic without being consensual. Taken together, the essays and book excerpts collected in this section address the question of what constitutes postmodernism and postmodernity from a variety of demographic, historical, and theoretical perspectives. As important, they also provide a conceptual backdrop against which the fiction of the postmodern era can be understood in relation to history and to other fields of intellectual conduct.

Several essays offer holistic definitions of postmodernity, or particularly vivid if truncated histories of postmodernism as a movement. In "Postmodernism, Irony, the Enjoyable," an essay collected in *Postscript to* The Name of the Rose (1984), Umberto Eco emphasizes the role of ironic distance in postmodern fiction, and further insists upon the centrality of play and pleasure in postmodern aesthetics. Invoking cultural references ranging from Terry Eagleton to Arnold Schwarzenegger, Michael Bérubé provides in "Just the Fax, Ma'am: Or, Postmodernism's Journey to Decenter" (1994) a chronological and thematic map of the ongoing breakdown of the boundary between popular and high culture. Ihab Hassan's "Toward a Concept of Postmodernism" (1987) contains one of the most thorough and widely cited descriptions of the relationship between modernism and postmodernism in contemporary critical literature.

Other essays illuminate implicitly or explicitly the work of authors who appear in the fiction sections of this anthology. In "A Cyborg Manifesto: Science, Technology, and Socialist-Feminism in the Late Twentieth Century" (1991), Donna Haraway, a historian of science, examines how science fiction authors such as Joanna Russ, Octavia Butler, and William Gibson employ the figure of the cyborg as a way of coming to terms with the "crucial boundary breakdowns" of the postmodern world. "Cyborg imagery," she argues, "can suggest a way out of the maze of dualisms"—man and machine, body and mind, nature and culture, master and slave—that limit our ability to understand and respond to the political, economic, and social dislocations of contemporary existence. Similarly, Trinh T. Minh-ha's discussions (excerpted from *Woman, Native, Other* [1989]) of Leslie Marmon Silko, Maxine Hong Kingston, Gloria Anzaldúa, and Theresa Hak Kyung Cha provide direct insight into the works of those authors. Her broader discussions of individual identity ("I am not i"), female and postcolonial identity, and history and storytelling, however, all reverberate within the many fictions collected here that examine the cultural constructedness of the individual, as well as the creative instability of the boundary between fact and fiction. Exploring issues such as narrative closure, navigation, and chance, Terry Harpold's "Conclusions" (1994) introduces conventionally trained readers to the new metaphorical framework for literary communication that hypertext both inspires and requires. Additionally, "Conclusions" provides a reading of Michael Joyce's *afternoon, a story,* as well as substantial references to the work of J. Yellowlees Douglas, both featured in the electronic component of this anthology.

Other essays describe the historical and theoretical phenomena that provide the general background for postmodern fiction. In "Postmodern Blackness" (1990), bell hooks provides an anecdotal and theoretical outline of the ambivalent relationship between African-American intellectual culture and mainstream postmodern theory. Asking "Where is she?", French feminist Hélène Cixous in "Sorties" (1975) explores how gender distinctions are coded into the canonical oppositions (e.g., "Sun/Moon," "Culture/Nature") that have dominated Western literary history and philosophy. Further, she argues that "[w]e are living in an age . . . never known before," where such radical inquiries create "historic" opportunities to retell "all the history, all the stories." Excerpts from Jean Baudrillard's *Simulacra and Simulation* (1981) elucidate the disappearance of the real behind the image—what Baudrillard calls the "simulacrum"—and introduce Disneyland as the archetypal example of a new American landscape of the inauthentic. Finally, "Postmodernism and Consumer Society" (1983) provides an overview of Fredric Jameson's ideas regarding pastiche, schizophrenia, the disappearance of history, the cooptation of resistance, and the "logic of consumer capitalism" as determining characteristics of the postmodern era.

HÉLÈNE CIXOUS
b. 1937

Born in Algeria, Hélène Cixous is currently head of the Center of Research in Feminine Studies, in Paris. Since the publication of *La Jeune née* in France in 1975, she has been considered a leading theoretician of the French feminist intellectual movement. Her books have been translated into Danish, German, and English, and her most recent play was performed by the Théâtre du Soleil.

From Sorties: Out and Out: Attacks/Ways Out/Forays

Where is she?
Activity/passivity
Sun/Moon
Culture/Nature
Day/Night

Father/Mother
Head/Heart
Intelligible/Palpable
Logos/Pathos.
Form, convex, step, advance, semen, progress.
Matter, concave, ground—where steps are taken, holding- and dumping-ground.

$\frac{\text{Man}}{\text{Woman}}$

Always the same metaphor: we follow it, it carries us, beneath all its figures, wherever discourse is organized. If we read or speak, the same thread or double braid is leading us throughout literature, philosophy, criticism, centuries of representation and reflection.

Thought has always worked through opposition,
Speaking/Writing
Parole/Écriture
High/Low

Through dual, hierarchical oppositions. Superior/Inferior. Myths, legends, books. Philosophical systems. Everywhere (where) ordering intervenes, where a law organizes what is thinkable by oppositions (dual, irreconcilable; or sublatable, dialectical). And all these pairs of oppositions are *couples.* Does that mean something? Is the fact that Logocentrism subjects thought—all concepts, codes and values—to a binary system, related to "the" couple, man/woman?

Nature/History
Nature/Art
Nature/Mind
Passion/Action

Theory of culture, theory of society, symbolic systems in general—art, religion, family, language—it is all developed while bringing the same schemes to light. And the movement whereby each opposition is set up to make sense is the movement through which the couple is destroyed. A universal battlefield. Each time, a war is let loose. Death is always at work.

Father/son Relations of authority, privilege, force.
The Word/Writing Relations: opposition, conflict, sublation, return.
Master/slave Violence. Repression.

We see that "victory" always comes down to the same thing: things get hierarchical. Organization by hierarchy makes all conceptual organization subject to man. Male privilege, shown in the opposition between *activity* and *passivity,* which he uses to sustain himself. Traditionally, the question of sexual difference is treated by coupling it with the opposition: activity/passivity.

There are repercussions. Consulting the history of philosophy—since philosophical discourse both orders and reproduces all thought—one notices[1] that it is marked by an absolute *constant* which orders values and which is precisely this opposition, activity/passivity.

Moreover, woman is always associated with passivity in philosophy. Whenever it is a question of woman, when one examines kinship structures, when a family model is brought into play. In fact, as soon as the question of ontology raises its head, as soon as one asks oneself "what is it?," as soon as there is intended meaning. Intention: desire, authority—examine them and you are led right back . . . to the father. It is even possible not to notice that there is no place whatsoever for woman in the calculations. Ultimately the world of "being" can function while precluding the mother. No need for a mother, as long as there is some motherliness: and it is the father, then, who acts the part, who is the mother. Either woman is passive or she does not exist. What is left of her is unthinkable, unthought. Which certainly means that she is not thought, that she does not enter into the oppositions, that she does not make a couple with the father (who makes a couple with the son).

There is Mallarmé's tragic dream,[2] that father's lamentation on the mystery of paternity, that wrenches from the poet *the* mourning, the mourning of mournings, the death of the cherished son: this dream of marriage between father and son.—And there's no mother then. A man's dream when faced with death. Which always threatens him differently than it threatens a woman.

"a union
a marriage, splendid
—and with life
still in me
I shall use it
for . . .
so not mother then?"

And dreams of filiation
that is masculine, dreams
of God the father
issuing from himself
in his son—and
no mother then

She does not exist, she can not-be; but there has to be something of her. He keeps, then, of the woman on whom he is no longer dependent, only this space, always virginal, as matter to be subjected to the desire he wishes to impart.

And if we consult literary history, it is the same story. It all comes back to man—to *his* torment, his desire to be (at) the origin. Back to the father. There is an intrinsic connection between the philosophical and the literary (to the extent that it conveys meaning, literature is under the command of the philosophical) and the phallocentric. Philosophy is constructed on the premise of woman's abasement. Subordination of the feminine to the masculine order, which gives the appearance of being the condition for the machinery's functioning.

Now it has become rather urgent to question this solidarity between logocentrism and phallocentrism—bringing to light the fate dealt to woman, her burial—to threaten the stability of the masculine structure that passed itself off as eternal-natural, by conjuring up from femininity the reflections and hypotheses that are necessarily ruinous for the stronghold still in possession of authority. What would happen to logocentrism, to the great philosophical systems, to the order of the world in general if the rock upon which they founded this church should crumble?

If some fine day it suddenly came out that the logocentric plan had always, inadmissibly, been to create a foundation for (to found and fund) phallocentrism, to guarantee the masculine order a rationale equal to history itself.

So all the history, all the stories would be there to retell differently; the future would be incalculable; the historic forces would and will change hands and change body—another thought which is yet unthinkable—will transform the functioning of all society. We are living in an age where the conceptual foundation of an ancient culture is in the process of being undermined by millions of a species of mole (Topoi, ground mines) never known before.

When they wake up from among the dead, from among words, from among laws.

Once upon a time . . .

Notes

1. All Derrida's work traversing-detecting the history of philosophy is devoted to bringing this to light. In Plato, Hegel, and Nietzsche, the same process continues: repression, repudiation, distancing of woman; a murder that is mixed up with history as the manifestation and representation of masculine power.
2. "For Anatole's Tomb" (Seuil, p. 138). This is the tomb in which Mallarmé keeps his son from death and watches over him as his mother.

1975 (trans. 1986)

IHAB HASSAN

b. 1925

Ihab Hassan was born in Cairo, Egypt, and emigrated to the United States in 1946. Currently he is Vilas Research Professor at the University of Wisconsin in Milwaukee. His writings include *Radical Innocence: The Contemporary American Novel* (1961), *The Dismemberment of Orpheus: Toward a Postmodern Literature* (1971), and *The Postmodern Turn: Essays in Postmodern Theory and Culture* (1987).

Toward a Concept of Postmodernism

The strains of silence in literature, from Sade to Beckett, convey complexities of language, culture, and consciousness as these contest themselves and one another. Such eerie music may yield an experience, an intuition, of postmodernism but no concept or definition of it. Perhaps I can move here toward such a concept by putting forth certain queries. I begin with the most obvious: can we really perceive a phenomenon, in Western societies generally and in their literatures particularly, that needs to be distinguished from modernism, needs to be named? If so, will the provisional rubric 'postmodernism' serve? Can we then—or even should we at this time—construct of this phenomenon some probative scheme, both chronological and typological, that may account for its various trends and counter-trends, its artistic, epistemic, and social character? And how would this phenomenon—let us call it postmodernism—relate itself to such earlier modes of change as turn-of-the-century avant-gardes or the high modernism of the twenties? Finally, what difficulties would inhere in any such act of definition, such a tentative heuristic scheme?

I am not certain that I can wholly satisfy my own questions, though I can assay some answers that may help to focus the larger problem. History, I take it, moves in measures both continuous and discontinuous. Thus the prevalence of postmodernism today, if indeed it prevails, does not suggest that ideas or institutions of the past cease to shape the present. Rather, traditions develop, and even types suffer a seachange. Certainly, the powerful cultural assumptions generated by, say, Darwin, Marx, Baudelaire, Nietzsche, Cézanne, Debussy, Freud, and Einstein still pervade the Western mind. Certainly those assumptions have been reconceived, not once but many times—else history would repeat itself, forever the same. In this perspective postmodernism may appear as a significant revision, if not an original *épistémè*, of twentieth-century Western societies.

Some names, piled here pell-mell, may serve to adumbrate postmodernism, or at least suggest its range of assumptions: Jacques Derrida, Jean-François Lyotard (philosophy), Michel Foucault, Hayden White (history), Jacques Lacan, Gilles Deleuze, R. D. Laing, Norman O. Brown (psychoanalysis), Herbert Marcuse, Jean Baudrillard, Jürgen Habermas (political philosophy), Thomas Kuhn, Paul Feyerabend (philosophy of science), Roland Barthes, Julia Kristeva, Wolfgang Iser, the 'Yale Critics' (literary theory), Merce Cunningham, Alwin Nikolais, Meredith Monk (dance), John Cage, Karlheinz Stockhausen, Pierre Boulez (music), Robert Rauschenberg, Jean Tinguely, Joseph Beuys (art), Robert Venturi, Charles Jencks, Brent Bolin (architecture), and various authors from Samuel Beckett, Eugène Ionesco, Jorge Luis Borges, Max Bense, and Vladimir Nabokov to Harold Pinter, B. S. Johnson, Rayner Heppenstall, Christine Brooke-Rose, Helmut Heissenbüttel, Jürgen Becker, Peter Handke, Thomas Bernhardt, Ernst Jandl, Gabriel García Márquez, Julio Cortázar, Alain Robbe-Grillet, Michel Butor, Maurice Roche, Philippe Sollers, and in America, John Barth, William Burroughs, Thomas Pynchon, Donald Barthelme, Walter Abish, John Ashbery, David Antin, Sam Shepard, and Robert Wilson. Indubitably, these names are far too heterogeneous to form a movement, paradigm, or school. Still, they may evoke a number of related cultural tendencies, a constellation of values, a repertoire of procedures and attitudes. These we call *postmodernism.*

Whence this term? Its origin remains uncertain, though we know that Federico de Onís used the word *postmodernismo* in his *Antología de la poesía española e hispanoamericana* (1882–1932), published in Madrid in 1934; and Dudley Fitts picked it up again in his *Anthology of Contemporary Latin-American Poetry* of 1942.[1] Both meant thus to indicate a minor reaction to modernism already latent within it, reverting to the early twentieth century. The term also appeared in Arnold Toynbee's *A Study of History* as early as D. C. Somervell's first-volume abridgement in 1947. For Toynbee, Post-Modernism designated a new historical cycle in Western civilization, starting around 1875, which we now scarcely begin to discern. Somewhat later, during the fifties, Charles Olson often spoke of postmodernism with more sweep than lapidary definition.

But prophets and poets enjoy an ample sense of time, which few literary scholars seem to afford. In 1959 and 1960, Irving Howe and Harry Levin wrote of postmodernism rather disconsolately as a falling off from the great modernist movement.[2] It remained for Leslie Fiedler and myself, among others, to employ the term during the sixties with premature approbation, and even with a touch of bravado.[3] Fiedler had it in mind to challenge the elitism of the high-modernist tradition in the name of popular culture. I wanted to explore the impulse of self-unmaking which is part of the literary tradition of silence. Pop and silence, or mass culture and deconstructing, or Superman and Godot—or as I shall later argue, immanence and indeterminacy—may all be aspects of the postmodern universe. But all this must wait upon more patient analysis, longer history.

Yet the history of literary terms serves only to confirm the irrational genius of language. We come closer to the question of postmodernism itself by acknowledging the psychopolitics, if not the psychopathology, of academic life. Let us admit it: there is a will to power in nomenclature, as well as in people or texts. A new term opens for its proponents a space in language. A critical concept or system is a 'poor' poem of the intellectual imagination. The battle of the books is also an ontic battle against death. That may be why Max Planck believed that one never manages to convince one's opponents—not even in theoretical physics—one simply tries to outlive them. William James described the process in less morbid terms: novelties are first repudiated as nonsense, then declared obvious, then appropriated by former adversaries as their own discoveries.

I do not mean to take my stand with the postmoderns against the (ancient) moderns. In an age of frantic intellectual fashions, values can be too recklessly voided, and tomorrow can quickly preempt today or yesteryear. Nor is it merely a matter of fashions; for the sense of supervention may express some cultural urgency that partakes less of hope than fear. This much we recall: Lionel Trilling entitled one of his most thoughtful works *Beyond Culture* (1965); Kenneth Boulding argued that 'postcivilization' is an essential part of *The Meaning of the 20th Century* (1964); and George Steiner could have subtitled his essay *In Bluebeard's Castle* (1971) 'Notes toward the definition of postculture'. Before them, Roderick Seidenberg published his *Post-Historic Man* exactly in mid-century; and most recently, I have myself speculated, in *The Right Promethean Fire* (1980), about the advent of a posthumanist era. As Daniel Bell put it: 'It used to be that the great literary modifier was the word *beyond*. . . . But we seem to have exhausted the beyond, and today the sociological modifier is *post*.'[4]

My point here is double: in the question of postmodernism, there is a will and counter-will to intellectual power, an imperial desire of the mind, but this will and desire are themselves caught in a historical moment of supervention, if not exactly of obsolescence. The reception or denial of postmodernism thus remains contingent on the psychopolitics of academic life—including the various dispositions of people and power in our universities, of critical factions and personal frictions, of boundaries that arbitrarily include or exclude—no less than on the imperatives of the culture at large. This much, reflexivity seems to demand from us at the start.

But reflection demands also that we address a number of conceptual problems that both conceal and constitute postmodernism itself. I shall try to isolate ten of these, commencing with the simpler, moving toward the more intractable.

1. The word postmodernism sounds not only awkward, uncouth; it evokes what it wishes to surpass or suppress, modernism itself. The term thus contains its enemy within, as the terms romanticism and classicism, baroque and rococo, do not. Moreover, it denotes temporal linearity and connotes belatedness, even decadence, to which no postmodernist would admit. But what better name have we to give this curious age? The Atomic, or Space, or Television, Age? These technological tags lack theoretical definition. Or shall we call it the Age of Indetermanence (indeterminacy + immanence) as I have half-antically proposed?[5] Or better still, shall we simply live and let others live to call us what they may?

2. Like other categorical terms—say poststructuralism, or modernism, or romanticism for that matter—postmodernism suffers from a certain *semantic* instability: that is, no clear consensus about its meaning exists among scholars. The general difficulty is compounded in this case by two factors: (a) the relative youth, indeed brash adolescence, of the term postmodernism and (b) its semantic kinship to more current terms, themselves equally unstable. Thus some critics mean by postmodernism what others call avant-gardism or even neo-avant-gardism, while still others would call the same phenomenon simply modernism. This can make for inspired debates.[6]

3. A related difficulty concerns the *historical* instability of many literary concepts, their openness to change. Who, in this epoch of fierce misprisions, would dare to claim that romanticism is apprehended by Coleridge, Pater, Lovejoy, Abrams, Peckham, and Bloom in quite the same way? There is already some evidence that postmodernism, and modernism even more, are beginning to slip and slide in time, threatening to make any diacritical distinction between them desperate.[7] But perhaps the phenomenon, akin to

Hubble's 'red shift' in astronomy, may someday serve to measure the historical velocity of literary concepts.

4. Modernism and postmodernism are not separated by an Iron Curtain or a Chinese Wall; for history is a palimpsest, and culture is permeable to time past, time present, and time future. We are all, I suspect, a little Victorian, Modern, and Postmodern, at once. And an author may, in his or her own lifetime, easily write both a modernist and postmodernist work. (Contrast Joyce's *Portrait of the Artist as a Young Man* with his *Finnegans Wake.*) More generally, on a certain level of narrative abstraction, modernism itself may be rightly assimilated to romanticism, romanticism related to the Enlightenment, the latter to the Renaissance, and so back, if not to the Olduvai Gorge, then certainly to ancient Greece.

5. This means that a 'period', as I have already intimated, must be perceived in terms of *both* continuity *and* discontinuity, the two perspectives being complementary and partial. The Apollonian view, rangy and abstract, discerns only historical conjunctions; the Dionysian feeling, sensuous though nearly purblind, touches only the disjunctive moment. Thus postmodernism, by invoking two divinities at once, engages a double view. Sameness and difference, unity and rupture, filiation and revolt, all must be honored if we are to attend to history, apprehend (perceive, understand) change both as a spatial, mental structure and as a temporal, physical process, both as pattern and as unique event.

6. Thus a 'period' is generally not a period at all; it is rather both a diachronic and synchronic construct. Postmodernism, again like modernism or romanticism, is no exception; it requires *both* historical *and* theoretical definition. We would not seriously claim an inaugural 'date' for it as Virginia Woolf pertly did for modernism, though we may sometimes woefully imagine that postmodernism began 'in or about September 1939'. Thus we continually discover 'antecedents' of postmodernism—in Sterne, Sade, Blake, Lautréamont, Rimbaud, Jarry, Tzara, Hofmannsthal, Gertrude Stein, the later Joyce, the later Pound, Duchamp, Artaud, Roussel, Bataille, Broch, Queneau, and Kafka. What this really indicates is that we have created in our mind a model of postmodernism, a particular typology of culture and imagination, and have proceeded to 'rediscover' the affinities of various authors and different moments with that model. We have, that is, reinvented our ancestors—and always shall. Consequently, 'older' authors can be postmodern—Kafka, Beckett, Borges, Nabokov, Gombrowicz—while 'younger' authors need not be so—Styron, Updike, Capote, Irving, Doctorow, Gardner.

7. As we have seen, any definition of postmodernism calls upon a fourfold vision of complementarities, embracing continuity and discontinuity, diachrony and synchrony. But a definition of the concept also requires a dialectical vision, for defining traits are often antithetical, and to ignore this tendency of historical reality is to lapse into single vision and Newton's sleep. Defining traits are dialectical and also plural; to elect a single trait as an absolute criterion of postmodern grace is to make of all other writers

preterites.[8] Thus we can not simply rest—as I have sometimes done—on the assumption that postmodernism is antiformal, anarchic, or decreative; for though it is indeed all these, and despite its fanatic will to unmaking, it also contains the need to discover a 'unitary sensibility' (Sontag), to 'cross the border and close the gap' (Fiedler), and to attain, as I have suggested, an immanence of discourse, an expanded noetic intervention, a 'neo-gnostic immediacy of mind'.[9]

8. All this leads to the prior problem of periodization itself, which is also that of literary history conceived as a particular apprehension of change. Indeed, the concept of postmodernism implies some theory of innovation, renovation, novation, or simply change. But which one? Heraclitean? Viconian? Darwinian? Marxist? Freudian? Kuhnian? Derridean? Eclectic?[1] Or is a 'theory of change' itself an oxymoron best suited to ideologues intolerant of the ambiguities of time? Should postmodernism, then, be left—at least for the moment—unconceptualized, a kind of literary-historical 'difference' or 'trace'?[2]

9. Postmodernism can expand into a still larger problem: is it only an artistic tendency or also a social phenomenon, perhaps even a mutation in Western humanism? If so, how are the various aspects of this phenomenon—psychological, philosophical, economic, political—joined or disjoined? In short, can we understand postmodernism in literature without some attempt to perceive the lineaments of a postmodern society, a Toynbeean postmodernity, or future Foucauldian *épistémè*, of which the literary tendency I have been discussing is but a single, elitist strain?[3]

10. Finally, though not least vexing, is postmodernism an honorific term, used insidiously to valorize writers, however disparate, whom we otherwise esteem, to hail trends, however discordant, which we somehow approve? Or is it, on the contrary, a term of opprobrium and objurgation? In short, is postmodernism a descriptive as well as evaluative or normative category of literary thought? Or does it belong, as Charles Altieri notes, to that category of 'essentially contested concepts' in philosophy that never wholly exhaust their constitutive confusions?[4]

No doubt, other conceptual problems lurk in the matter of postmodernism. Such problems, however, cannot finally inhibit the intellectual imagination, the desire to apprehend our historical presence in noetic constructs that reveal our being to ourselves. I move, therefore, to propose a provisional scheme that the literature of silence, from Sade to Beckett, seems to envisage, and do so by distinguishing, tentatively, between three modes of artistic change in the last hundred years. I call these avant-garde, modern, and postmodern, though I realize that all three have conspired together to create that 'tradition of the new' that since Baudelaire, brought 'into being an art whose history, regardless of the credos of its practitioners, has consisted of leaps from vanguard to vanguard, and political mass movements whose aim has been the total renovation not only of social institutions but of man himself'.[5]

By avant-garde, I mean those movements that agitated the earlier part of our century, including 'Pataphysics, Cubism, Futurism, Dadaism, Surrealism, Suprematism, Constructivism, Merzism, de Stijl. Anarchic, these assaulted the bourgeoisie with their art, their manifestoes, their antics. But their activism could also turn inward, becoming suicidal—as happened later to some postmodernists like Rudolf Schwartzkogler. Once full of brio and bravura, these movements have all but vanished now, leaving only their story, at once fugacious and exemplary. Modernism, however, proved more stable, aloof, hieratic, like the French Symbolism from which it derived; even its experiments now seen Olympian. Enacted by such 'individual talents' as Valéry, Proust, and Gide, the early Joyce, Yeats, and Lawrence, Rilke, Mann, and Musil, the early Pound, Eliot, and Faulkner, it commanded high authority, leading Delmore Schwartz to chant in *Shenandoah:* 'Let us consider where the great men are/Who will obsess the child when he can read . . .'. But if much of modernism appears hieratic, hypotactical, and formalist, postmodernism strikes us by contrast as playful, paratactical, and deconstructionist. In this it recalls the irreverent spirit of the avant-garde, and so carries sometimes the label of neo-avant-garde. Yet postmodernism remains 'cooler', in McLuhan's sense, than older vanguards—cooler, less cliquish, and far less aversive to the pop, electronic society of which it is a part, and so hospitable to kitsch.

Can we distinguish postmodernism further? Perhaps certain schematic differences from modernism will provide a start.

↕ Modernism	↔ Postmodernism
Romanticism/Symbolism	'Pataphysics/Dadaism
Form (conjunctive, closed)	Antiform (disjunctive, open)
Purpose	Play
Design	Chance
Hierarchy	Anarchy
Mastery/Logos	Exhaustion/Silence
Art Object/Finished Work	Process/Performance/Happening
Distance	Participation
Creation/Totalization	Decreation/Deconstruction
Synthesis	Antithesis
Presence	Absence
Centering	Dispersal
Genre/Boundary	Text/Intertext
Semantics	Rhetoric
Paradigm	Syntagm
Hypotaxis	Parataxis
Metaphor	Metonymy
Selection	Combination
Root/Depth	Rhizome/Surface
Interpretation/Reading	Against Interpretation/Misreading
Signified	Signifier
Lisible (Readerly)	*Scriptible* (Writerly)
Narrative/*Grande Histoire*	Anti-narrative/*Petite Histoire*

Master Code	Idiolect
Symptom	Desire
Type	Mutant
Genital/Phallic	Polymorphous/Androgynous
Paranoia	Schizophrenia
Origin/Cause	Difference-Differance/Trace
God the Father	The Holy Ghost
Metaphysics	Irony
Determinacy	Indeterminacy
Transcendence	Immanence

The preceding table draws on ideas in many fields—rhetoric, linguistics, literary theory, philosophy, anthropology, psychoanalysis, political science, even theology—and draws on many authors—European and American—aligned with diverse movements, groups, and views. Yet the dichotomies this table represents remain insecure, equivocal. For differences shift, defer, even collapse; concepts in any one vertical column are not all equivalent; and inversions and exceptions, in both modernism and postmodernism, abound. Still, I would submit that rubrics in the right column point to the postmodern tendency, the tendency of indetermanence, and so may bring us closer to its historical and theoretical definition.

The time has come, however, to explain a little that neologism: 'indetermanence'. I have used that term to designate two central, constitutive tendencies in postmodernism: one of indeterminacy, the other of immanence. The two tendencies are not dialectical; for they are not exactly antithetical; nor do they lead to a synthesis. Each contains its own contradictions, and alludes to elements of the other. Their interplay suggests the action of a 'polylectic', pervading postmodernism. Since I have discussed this topic at some length earlier, I can advert to it here briefly.[6]

By indeterminacy, or better still, *indeterminacies*, I mean a complex referent that these diverse concepts help to delineate: ambiguity, discontinuity, heterodoxy, pluralism, randomness, revolt, perversion, deformation. The latter alone subsumes a dozen current terms of unmaking: decreation, disintegration, deconstruction, decenterment, displacement, difference, discontinuity, disjunction, disappearance, decomposition, de-definition, demystification, detotalization, delegitimization—let alone more technical terms referring to the rhetoric of irony, rupture, silence. Through all these signs moves a vast will to unmaking, affecting the body politic, the body cognitive, the erotic body, the individual psyche—the entire realm of discourse in the West. In literature alone our ideas of author, audience, reading, writing, book, genre, critical theory, and of literature itself, have all suddenly become questionable. And in criticism? Roland Barthes speaks of literature as 'loss', 'perversion', 'dissolution'; Wolfgang Iser formulates a theory of reading based on textual 'blanks'; Paul de Man conceives rhetoric—that is, literature—as a force that 'radically suspends logic and opens up vertiginous possibilities of referential aberration'; and Geoffrey Hartman affirms that 'contemporary criticism aims at the hermeneutics of indeterminacy'.[7]

Such uncertain diffractions make for vast dispersals. Thus I call the second major tendency of postmodernism *immanences*, a term that I employ without religious echo to designate the capacity of mind to generalize itself in symbols, intervene more and more into nature, act upon itself through its own abstractions and so become, increasingly, im-mediately, its own environment. This noetic tendency may be evoked further by such sundry concepts as diffusion, dissemination, pulsion, interplay, communication, interdependence, which all derive from the emergence of human beings as language animals, *Homo pictor* or *Homo significans*, gnostic creatures constituting themselves, and determinedly their universe, by symbols of their own making. Is 'this not the sign that the whole of this configuration is about to topple, and that man is in the process of perishing as the being of language continues to shine ever brighter upon our horizon?' Foucault famously asks.[8] Meanwhile, the public world dissolves as fact and fiction blend, history becomes derealized by media into a happening, science takes its own models as the only accessible reality, cybernetics confronts us with the enigma of artificial intelligence, and technologies project our perceptions to the edge of the receding universe or into the ghostly interstices of matter.[9] Everywhere—even deep in Lacan's 'lettered unconscious', more dense than a black hole in space—everywhere we encounter that immanence called Language, with all its literary ambiguities, epistemic conundrums, and political distractions.[1]

No doubt these tendencies may seem less rife in England, say, than in America or France, where the term postmodernism, reversing the recent direction of poststructuralist flow, has now come into use.[2] But the fact in most developed societies remains: as an artistic, philosophical, and social phenomenon, postmodernism veers toward open, playful, optative, provisional (open in time as well as in structure or space), disjunctive, or indeterminate forms, a discourse of ironies and fragments, a 'white ideology' of absences and fractures, a desire of diffractions, an invocation of complex, articulate silences. Postmodernism veers toward all these yet implies a different, if not antithetical, movement toward pervasive procedures, ubiquitous interactions, immanent codes, media, languages. Thus our earth seems caught in the process of planetization, transhumanization, even as it breaks up into sects, tribes, factions of every kind. Thus, too, terrorism and totalitarianism, schism and ecumenicism, summon one another, and authorities decreate themselves even as societies search for new grounds of authority. One may well wonder: is some decisive historical mutation—involving art and science, high and low culture, the male and female principles, parts and wholes, involving the One and the Many, as pre-Socratics used to say—active in our midst? Or does the dismemberment of Orpheus prove no more than the mind's need to make but one more construction of life's mutabilities and human mortality?

And what construction lies beyond, behind, within, that construction?

Notes

1. For the best history of the term *postmodernism* see Michael Köhler, ' "Postmodernismus": Ein begriffsgeschichtlicher Überblick', 1977, 8–18. That same issue contains other excellent discussions and bibliographies on the term; see particularly Gerhard Hoffmann, Alfred Hornung, and Rüdiger Kunow, ' "Modern", "postmodern", and "contemporary" as criteria for the analysis of 20th century literature'.

2. Irving Howe, 'Mass society and postmodern fiction', 1959, 420–36, reprinted in his *Decline of the New,* New York, 1970, pp. 190–207; and Harry Levin, 'What was modernism?', *Massachusetts Review,* 1, 4 (1960), reprinted in *Refractions,* New York, 1966, pp. 271–95.
3. Leslie Fiedler, 'The new mutants', 1965, reprinted in his *Collected Essays,* vol. 2, New York, 1971, pp. 379–400; and Ihab Hassan, 'Frontiers of criticism: Metaphors of silence', *Virginia Quarterly,* 46, 1 (1970). In earlier essays I had also used the term 'anti-literature' and 'the literature of silence' in a proximate sense; see, for instance, Ihab Hassan, 'The literature of silence', *Encounter,* 28, 1 (1967).
4. Daniel Bell, *The Coming of Post-Industrial Society,* 1973, p. 53.
5. See I. Hassan, *The Postmodern Turn,* 1987, pp. 46–83.
6. Matei Calinescu, for instance, tends to assimilate 'postmodern' to 'neo-avant-garde' and sometimes to 'avant-garde', in *Faces of Modernity: Avant-garde, decadence, kitsch,* 1977, though later he discriminates between these terms thoughtfully, in 'Avant-garde, neo-avant-garde, and post-modernism', unpublished manuscript. Miklos Szabolcsi would identify 'modern' with 'avant-garde' and call 'postmodern' the 'neo-avant-garde', in 'Avant-garde, neo-avant-garde, modernism: Questions and suggestions', *New Literary History,* 3, 1 (1971); while Paul de Man would call 'modern' the innovative element, the perpetual 'moment of crisis' in the literature of every period, in 'Literary history and literary modernity', in *Blindness and Insight,* New York, 1971, ch. 8; in a similar vein, William V. Spanos employs the term 'postmodernism' to indicate 'not fundamentally a chronological event, but rather a permanent mode of human understanding', in 'De-struction and the question of postmodern literature: Towards a definition', *Par Rapport,* 2, 2 (1979), 107. And even John Barth, as inward as any writer with postmodernism, now argues that postmodernism is a synthesis yet to come, and what we had assumed to be postmodernism all along was only late modernism, in 'The literature of replenishment: Postmodernist fiction', 1980, 65–71.
7. In my own earlier and later essays on the subject I can discern such a slight shift. See 'POSTmodernISM', *New Literary History,* 3, 1 (1971), 5–30, 'Joyce, Beckett, and the Postmodern imagination', *TriQuarterly,* 34 (1975), and 'Culture, indeterminacy, and immanence', in *The Postmodern Turn,* pp. 46–83.
8. Though some critics have argued that postmodernism is primarily 'temporal' and others that it is mainly 'spatial', it is in the particular relation between these single categories that postmodernism probably reveals itself. See the two seemingly contradictory views of William V. Spanos, 'The detective at the boundary', in *Existentialism* 2, ed. William V. Spanos (New York, 1976), pp. 163–89; and Jürgen Peper, 'Postmodernismus: Unitary sensibility', 1977, 65–89.
9. Susan Sontag, 'One culture and the new sensibility', in *Against Interpretation,* 1967, pp. 293–304; Leslie Fiedler, 'Cross the border—close that gap', in *Collected Essays,* vol. 2, New York, 1971, pp. 461–85; and Ihab Hassan, 'The new gnosticism', *Paracriticisms: Seven speculations of the times,* Urbana, IL, 1975, ch. 6.

1. For some views of this, see Ihab Hassan and Sally Hassan, eds, *Innovation/Renovation: Recent trends and reconceptions in Western culture,* 1983.
2. At stake here is the idea of literary periodicity, challenged by current French thought. For other views of literacy and historical change, including 'hierarchic organization' of time, see Leonard Meyer, *Music, the Arts, and Ideas,* Chicago, 1967, pp. 93, 102; Calinescu, *Faces of Modernity,* pp. 147 ff; Ralph Cohen, 'Innovation and variation: Literary change and Georgic poetry', in Ralph Cohen and Murray Krieger, *Literature and History,* Los Angeles, 1974; and my *Paracriticisms,* ch. 7. A harder question is one Geoffrey Hartman asks: 'With so much historical knowledge, how can we avoid historicism, or the staging of history as a drama in which epiphanic raptures are replaced by epistemic ruptures?' Or, again, how can we 'formulate a theory of reading that would be historical rather than historicist'? *Saving the Text: Literature/Derrida/philosophy,* Baltimore, MD, 1981, p. xx.
3. Writers as different as Marshall McLuhan and Leslie Fiedler have explored the media and pop aspects of postmodernism for two decades, though their efforts are now out of fashion in some critical circles. The difference between postmodernism, as a contemporary artistic tendency, and postmodernity, as a cultural phenomenon, perhaps even an era of history, is discussed by Richard E. Palmer in 'Postmodernity and hermeneutics', 1977, 363–93.
4. Charles Altieri, 'Postmodernism: A question of definition', *Par Rapport,* 2, (1979), 90. This leads Altieri to conclude: 'The best one can do who believes himself post-modern . . . is to articulate spaces of mind in which the confusions can not paralyze because one enjoys the energies and glimpses of our condition which they produce', p. 99.
5. Harold Rosenberg, *The Tradition of the New,* New York, 1961, p. 9.
6. See I. Hassan, *The Postmodern Turn,* pp. 65–72. Also, my 'Innovation/renovation: Toward a cultural theory of change', *Innovation/Renovation,* ch. 1.

7. See, for instance, Roland Barthes and Maurice Nadeau, *Sur la littérature,* Paris, 1980, pp. 7, 16, 19f., 41; Wolfgang Iser, *The Act of Reading,* Baltimore, MD, 1978, *passim;* Paul de Man, *Allegories of Reading,* New Haven, CT, 1979, p. 10; and Geoffrey H. Hartman, *Criticism in the Wilderness,* New Haven, CT, 1980, p. 41.
8. Michel Foucault, *The Order of Things,* New York, 1970, p. 386.
9. 'Just as Pascal sought to throw dice with God . . . so do the decisions theorists, and the new intellectual technology, seek their own *tableau entier*—the compass of rationality itself,' Daniel Bell remarks in 'Technology, nature, and society', in *Technology and the Frontiers of Knowledge,* Garden City, NY, 1975, p. 53. See also the more acute analysis of *'l'informatique'* by Jean-François Lyotard, *La Condition postmoderne,* 1979, *passim.*
1. This tendency also makes for the abstract, conceptual, and irrealist character of so much postmodern art. See Suzi Gablik, *Progress in Art,* New York, 1977, whose argument was prefigured by Ortega y Gasset, *The Dehumanization of Art,* Princeton, NJ, 1968. Note also that Ortega presaged the gnostic or noetic tendency to which I refer here in 1925: 'Man humanizes the world, injects it, impregnates it with his own ideal substance and is finally entitled to imagine that one day or another, in the far depths of time, this terrible outer world will become so saturated with man that our descendants will be able to travel through it as today we mentally travel through our own inmost selves—he finally imagines that the world, without ceasing to be like the world, will one day be changed into something like a materialized soul, and, as in Shakespeare's *Tempest,* the winds will blow at the bidding of Ariel, the spirit of ideas', p. 184.
2. Though postmodernism and poststructuralism can not be identified, they clearly reveal many affinities. Thus in the course of one brief essay, Julia Kristeva comments on both immanence and indeterminacy in terms of her own: 'postmodernism is that literature which writes itself with the more or less conscious intention of expanding the signifiable, and thus human, realm'; and again: 'At this degree of singularity, we are faced with ideolects, proliferating uncontrollably.' Julia Kristeva, 'Postmodernism?', in *Romanticism, Modernism, Postmodernism,* ed. Harry R. Garvin, 1980, pp. 137, 141.

1987

MICHAEL BÉRUBÉ
b. 1961

Michael Bérubé is professor of English and a member of the Unit for Criticism and Interpretive Theory at the University of Illinois at Urbana-Champaign. His books include *Public Access: Literary Theory and American Cultural Politics* (1994), *Life As We Know It: A Father, a Family, and an Exceptional Child* (1996), and *Higher Education Under Fire: Politics, Economics, and the Crisis of the Humanities* (1995, coedited with Cary Nelson).

From Public Access

From *Just the Fax, Ma'am: Or, Postmodernism's Journey to Decenter*

In the waning moments of the 1970s, *Eraserhead* was playing at the Waverly in the West Village, and David Lynch, its director, was not exactly a household name, though he did find some kindred spirits who'd always known there were puffy-cheeked women singing under the radiator. When he was given a TV series in the spring of 1990, eyebrows went up nationwide, and everyone waited to see whether the Apocalypse would follow from the historic encounter between David Lynch and prime-time network TV. But Lynch's relentlessly strange and provocative *Twin Peaks* became so widely acknowledged a critical success that it wound up being explained to—and defended from—the uncomprehending masses by none other than the house organ of the uncomprehending masses, *USA Today*, whose *Life* section loudly protested the show's hiatuses and eventual cancellation by ABC. *Soap Opera Weekly* checked in from time to time with astute, sympathetic, and theoretically sophisticated assessments of the show's development, and large segments of middle America were served up Lynch's hallucinogenic Northwest, along with a side of pie, for over a year.

Meanwhile, back in the late 1970s, a few miles north of the Waverly, Kool DJ Herc and Grandmaster Flash were busy recycling vinyl cultural products in some strange new ways. A mere decade or so later, 'rap', aka hip-hop, has become the single largest music on the block—*any* block. On the technical tip, hip-hop's dazzling blends of traditional and electronic musical forms, together with its dexterous pillaging of various recent cultural archives, have launched (among other things) a thorough, multimedia examination of blackness and the technological means of cultural reproduction. And in the space of a few years, hip-hop has made its way from turntables to TV ads for cola, throat lozenges and kids' breakfast cereals, all the way from the Bronx to Bel Air—surviving its many co-optations and crossovers at every little step. Not even Hammer and Vanilla Fro-Yo have frozen out Ice-T and Ice Cube; and while black radio in Philly and elsewhere keeps trumpeting its new 'no-rap' programming, grain-fed American youth can *still* hear the latest singles from L. L. Cool J and Monie Love on central Illinois' best mix of yesterday and today. Hip-hop has become a national music whether it likes it or not, our most politically important music *despite* (or in addition to) its gradual citation-and-absorption by fast-food chains and *People* magazine.

Hip-hop and David Lynch have little else in common, but between them they do go to show that postmodernism isn't merely a 'style' located somewhere in cultural products; at a much greater reach, it involves new configurations of cultural transmission, the means by which artifacts (and 'copies' thereof) circulate in the general culture. It isn't that pomo gives you 30 percent more modernism for your money (more uncertainty, more fragmentation, more playful self-consciousness), and it's not that postmodernism is modernism's evil dwarf twin, hell-bent on knocking down everything modernism took such a long time to build. Instead, what's going on involves a more subtle and elusive cultural shift, in which it's getting harder (and more challenging) to determine what it means for ostensibly 'avant-garde' cultural works to be available in so many media instantaneously.

These disseminations, these 'new configurations', are by no means limited to the work of our contemporary 'avant-gardes'; on the contrary, they include the retransmission of what was once the modernist avant-garde—which has, in the past fifty years, gotten itself distributed in such a way that it is now more likely to show up on the walls of corporate offices than in cafés or garrets. Yet when we try to gauge the relation between mo and pomo, it doesn't help to ask yet again what modernism was, because (as we'll see later on) even that question is a distinctively modernist question. Rather, what pomo wants to ask is this: How do we understand modernism's circuitous route into our general culture, whereby *The Waste Land* wound up in every classroom and *faux* Piet Mondrian wound up in the packaging design of L'Oreal mousse and hair spray? And does the transmission of Eliot and Mondrian involve the same processes by which Lynch and hip-hop became part of our cultural lingua franca?

Of course, it's easy to claim that postmodernism simply entails the corporate co-optation of everything in sight, since postmodernism seems to follow from (and accelerate) modernism's own absorption into the general culture. As *New German Critique* editor Andreas Huyssen puts it in *After the Great Divide,* the irony here is that 'the first time the US had something resembling an "institution art" in the emphatic European sense, it was modernism itself, the kind of art whose purpose had always been to resist institutionalization.'[1] Why then should we be mourning the passing of the modernist avant-garde in the first place? In the 1990s, when you can't tell anymore where the *garde* is, it's a fair bet that you don't know whether you're *avant* of it or not. And as a result, 'avant-gardism', even in these troubled times, has come to seem gestural if not downright reactionary.

This is what Huyssen means when he calls ours a 'post-avant-garde' society. For Huyssen, as for a legion of younger cultural critics, it no longer makes any sense for artists or critics to claim positions on the 'margin' or in the 'center' of the culture, because the contemporary cultural landscape resists precisely such static confrontations between margins and centers. And if there are no margins and centers, then there's no vanguard; and if there's no vanguard, then there's no site of authentic, unsullied, 'pure' cultural production, immune to the technologies of economic and cultural *re*production.

Them's fighting words, you know, to people who continue to see themselves as 'avant-garde'. Yet even if there were a bona fide, certified-authentic vanguard out there, who's to say that its cultural work would be more important than—or even distinguishable from—the kinds of stuff we find in what we still call 'mainstream' media? It may yet come to pass that thirty years from now, when we look back at how the 1980s replayed the 1950s with a knowing but deceptive wink, we will care less about the 'media image' photographs of Cindy Sherman than about Nick at Nite's relentlessly campy promotions for its reruns of *The Donna Reed Show,* which fill your late-night TV screen with a graphic style composed of equal parts early *Jetsons* and late John Waters.[2] Besides, who needs artists and writers to 'lay bare the device' of contemporary culture, when laying bare the device has become standard business practice anyway? As Kirk Vardenoe and Adam Gopnik, the directors of *High & Low: Modern Art and Popular Culture,* have written, 'in the age of Joe Isuzu, a hardened knowingness about the value-emptied amorality of media culture was, far from being the preserve of a small cadre of vanguard thinkers, the sour, commonplace cynicism of the whole commercial culture.'[3] The *High & Low* show itself was brought to you by the folks at AT&T, who urge you to reach out and touch someone by giving the gift of modern art, the gift that keeps on giving.

How did we get into this strange party? Who's responsible for these lousy hors d'oeuvres? Uh—can we come in again?

Sure, we can *always* come in again; postmodernism means never having to say you've been here before. In fact the word 'postmodern' has just hurtled into its fifth decade, bandied about since the 1950s by art critics as by *Spy* magazine, real estate agents and *TV Guide,* and in the process of going through a few demigenerational changes, it's become a strange kind of 'essentially contested' term that many people are just tired of contesting. Even Ihab Hassan, who had been using the word since way back in the 1960s when John Barth was Prince of Pomo and everybody was talking about the 'literature of exhaustion'—even Hassan recently dropped his pen in fatigue, writing, 'I have already written enough of these matters, and . . . I would let postmodernism rest.'[4] (Thud. Snore.)

Well, who wouldn't be tired, confronted with all these postmodernisms, this L=A=N=G=U=A=G=E writing, MTV, ACT UP, e-mail, junk bonds, Madonna, smart bombs, poststructuralism, Reaganism, terrorism, colorization, Houstonization and, if you order right away, much, much more? And as if this profusion weren't enough, we now have a number of constituencies for whom the adjective 'postmodern' signifies little more than a new brand name, as in the case of *Postmodern MTV*, a seemingly redundant phrase of the late 1980s–early 1990s that, as one of my students suggested in a seminar on postmodernism (itself a postmodern artifact), merely denoted 'things that sound like Morrissey'.

However, we do have some idea of why a unified field theory of 'postmodernism' is neither possible nor desirable, and before I get to my own concerns about postmodernism and history, I want to suggest two reasons why postmodernism remains a cultural field distinguished by internal dissensus.

For one thing, one man's postmodernism is another woman's poison. In some ways, all of post-1960s feminism is postmodern, because it's destabilized 'universal' languages, questioned gender and subjectivity, and rewritten our dominant historical narratives. But then again, not every feminism *wants* to be postmodern, since the suspicion remains that pomo will dissolve all possibility for political resistance in a bubbling vat of textuality and ironic self-parody. In 1983, in an essay entitled 'The Discourse of Others: Feminists and Postmodernism', the late Craig Owens convincingly charged his fellow theorists with a systematic neglect of feminism's role in pomo, practice and theory; but six years later, in *The Politics of Postmodernism,* Linda Hutcheon claimed that postmodernism lacks any theory of agency, without which feminism is impossible.[5] So either the question is whether pomo should acknowledge the feminists in its midst, or whether feminism should acknowledge the postmodernism sitting next to it on the bus and mumbling to itself about Max Headroom and identity politics. Does one of these isms bracket the other? You tell me.

Thing number two has to do with 'facts'. To wit, it's hard to determine the relevant facts and features of pomo when so much of pomo has questioned how 'facticity' is constructed. David Byrne opened the 1980s by intoning, in 'Crosseyed and Painless', that 'Facts don't do what I want them to / Facts just twist the truth around.' Ronald Reagan, having been reportedly 'brutalized' by facts before a 1984 debate with Walter Mondale, closed the decade by stammering, 'Facts are stupid things.'[6] In the meantime, we switched over painlessly to a government by the photo op, of the photo op, and for the photo op, and the neofascist Institute for Historical Review offered $50,000 to anyone who could disprove its claim that the Holocaust never happened. In what may have been facticity's last stand, in 1985 the IHR was defeated in court by a Holocaust survivor, Mel Mermelstein; nonetheless, the IHR's director, Tom Marcellus (a man apparently immune to fact), replied that the defeat was 'the best outcome we could have had', since 'we did not have to compromise any of our positions.'[7]

On another front altogether, fifty years of anti-positivism from people as diverse as Ludwig Wittgenstein, Thomas Kuhn, and Michel Foucault have led the cultural left to argue that objects of knowledge are locally and historically specific, and that they become available for human understanding only within certain 'language-games', 'paradigms', and 'discursive formations' (not that these are three names for the same thing, either). So we have multiple histories of postmodernism, which are themselves licensed by postmodernism's multiplicity. And they're also a result of pomo's propensity for searching out and destroying unitary, linear historical narratives, the kind that serve up clear origins and straightforward plot-development (whether of rise or decline). This 'anti-foundationalist' aspect of postmodernism has sometimes been taken to be a potentially liberating intellectual tool, since it suggests that our beliefs and practices are culturally 'contingent', subject to ongoing revision, bound to no historical determinism. And by the same token, we've found that 'proof' is a more slippery thing than we'd thought—something that depends more on rhetoric, power, persuasion and consensus than on 'incontrovertible fact'.

It's not that there are no 'facts' in pomo, or that anything goes so long as everybody's happy; rather, it's that pomo has paid acute attention to how various human communities go about deciding what will count as 'facts'. As Kuhn argued in *The Structure of Scientific Revolutions* (1962), revolutionary 'paradigm-shifts' occur when one dominant theory supersedes another, but the new paradigm doesn't simply 'falsify' or 'disprove' the older model. Instead, writes Kuhn, paradigm-shifts are matters in which 'neither proof nor error is at issue', because different scientific communities were simply seeing different 'facts' even when they were looking at what we now think are the same phenomena: 'theories, of course, do "fit the facts", but only by transforming previously accessible information into facts that, for the preceding paradigm, had not existed at all.'[8]

But while pomo's encounters with anti-foundationalism and feminism have rendered us unable to conceive of a single, monolithic thing called 'History', postmodernism has been acquiring a history of its own. And this alone should provoke us into some historical reflection, because as far as I can see, the recent history of pomo's shifting definitions can be charted largely in terms of how people have determined pomo's relation to history. Perhaps nothing has been so widely misunderstood about pomo as this; indeed, in some cases, the postmodernism we thought to be lamely ahistorical has now been judged by some recent histories of pomo to be nothing less than the very spur to revisionary historicism. To put matters another way: although postmodern historicism flaunts its inability to capture the past 'the way it really was', it has also quite effectively exploded the claims of other historicisms (such as marxisms) to be able to do so either.

OK, I know this one takes some explaining, so let me back up a second and fill in the details.

For much of the first half of the 1980s, critics from left and right spent a good deal of their time forming two neat, separate lines to take turns bashing postmodernism. On the left, Terry Eagleton found pomo to be facetious, pointlessly playful and possessed by an attitude toward history not unlike that of *Bill and Ted's Excellent Adventure;* on the right, Hilton Kramer found pomo to be facetious, pointlessly playful and possessed by an attitude toward history not unlike that of *Total Recall.* Ageless modernist torch-bearer Denis Donoghue complained that 'postmodernism is content to let a thousand discrepancies bloom', because in pomo, 'no artist's desire reaches out for spontaneity or an original relation to the world'; and the earl of Duke, Marxist critic Fredric Jameson, proposed that postmodernism and late capitalism had bequeathed us 'a world in which stylistic innovation is no longer possible, all that is left is to imitate dead styles.'[9] Donoghue and Jameson? Kramer and Eagleton? Golly, it finally looked as if *something* had gotten these boys to stop fighting and play nicely—and that something was pomo. It was a happy time, and soon, 'rock' musicians stopped suggesting that they wanted to die before they became old enough to do 25th Anniversary Reunion Tours, and started singing instead that they were working out 'most every day, and watching what they eat.

Just as it was getting hip to be square, squares were getting hip to whimsical Left-Banker Jean Baudrillard's notion (first advanced in 1983) that our era is distinguished by what he called 'the precession of simulacra'. In the era of the simulacrum, Baudrillard declared, when 'the map engenders the territory' and everything is a twentieth-generation copy of everything else, we find a suspiciously compensatory cultural reflex—'a proliferation of myths of origin and signs of reality . . . a panic-stricken production of the real and referential.'[1] This Baudrillard calls the 'hyperreal', and no doubt it's here to stay, since we hear so frequently that real people purchase real food for real people and drink beer that's as real as it gets, 'cause you can't beat the real thing. Except maybe if you have two hundred Elvis impersonator impersonators ringed around a replica of the Statue of Liberty.[2]

Baudrillard's essay has now become something of a postmodern classic, so much so that it's been invoked to explain everything from the art of Jeff Koons to the Iran-Contra hearings; simulacra of roadside kitsch, simulacra of parliamentary 'justice'. And in an appropriately Baudrillardian way, 'The Precession of Simulacra' has itself had a significant impact on postmodern writers and artists whose work Baudrillard's theories are then called upon to explain, in a rather circular fashion.

Yet I think Baudrillard's essay—and its influence—may be remembered less as a definitive description of postmodernism than as an index of what the pomo debate looked like in the mid 1980s. For it wasn't hard to see, even seven or eight long years ago, that what people feared or celebrated about postmodernism had to do with issues of tangibility and thinginess. Hence all the apocalyptic rhetoric about the disappearance of the referent, the death of Man, the end of philosophy, the death of the author, the dissolution of the subject and the impossibility of apocalyptic rhetoric. In a 1986 lecture, Jameson opined almost off the cuff that word processors were to postmodernism what the typewriter was to modernism: that is, in the breaking-point between mechanical reproduction (keys, ink, hammers, machinery, industrial economies, sweaty Socialist Realist men in overalls) and electronic transmission (laser printing, modems, microchips, information economies, Steve Jobs on the cover of *USA Today*) lay the distinction between mo and pomo.[3] Sort of like the difference between pinball and video, and who *wouldn't* be nostalgic for the days when pinball games had no microchips, no sound effects, and a top score of 99,999?

The only problem was that while the right hated pomo for fairly obvious reasons (having never even learned to play pinball, the right naturally figured that 'Space Invaders' was the death knell of reflective thought), the left—including Baudrillard—seemed paralyzed by dreams of days when things were better, days when things were *thingy*. You know, when the proletariat and the haute-bourgeoisie wore recognizable uniforms, and sat down facing each other at heavy, wooden tables arguing about *real* wages—silver dollars, doubloons and florins. None of this 'simulacra' nonsense, none of these credit rollovers and reinvested pension funds, and most of all, none of these dang teleconferences.

Of course, not all of the left felt this way. But perhaps it was only the repeated interventions of women, ethnic minorities and variously queer theorists that finally shattered the pernicious sense of nostalgia to which so many men on the postmodernist *and* anti-postmodernist left fell victim. Or perhaps it wasn't until pomo began to come to grips with the various social liberation movements of the past generation that it began to take stock of what it might mean to retheorize recent history from the vantage point of *plural*, discontinuous, multiply constituted 'public spheres'. Surely, it is hard to imagine a group other than white male intellectuals who would be in the position to tell stories about exhausted literature, or about our decline and fall from the Golden Age of the public intellectual; and in this sense, 'history' simply wasn't available for postmodern scrutiny until the disenfranchised showed up and put it on the table. As Barbara Ehrenreich has recently said, one reason we shouldn't make the mistake of confusing 'multiculturalism' with the left is that 'the left is not sufficiently multicultural to deserve being confused with multiculturalism, at least not yet.'[4]

Either way, in the past few years, it seems that only a few pointed words from people like Nancy Fraser, Gayatri Spivak, Douglas Crimp and Cornel West have gotten most of what remains of the left to check its books and think again about the project of going back to the future. As for the rest of the erstwhile anti-pomo 'left', the mugged-liberal crowd who thought social justice was a good thing so long as they didn't have to get their own coffee, live in bad neighborhoods, or put up with men kissing each other in public . . . well, the less said about that bunch the better.

I don't mean to replay the notorious false dichotomy between postmodernism and the left. My point is simply that the left has had a number of misgivings about pomo's alleged erasure of materiality and about its relation to history. If, for instance, postmodernism has troubled the distinction between consumption and production (as it certainly has), then the left has some reason to say that pomo is no different in this respect from consumer capitalism, in which consumption has itself become a kind of 'production' (and notoriously so in the merger-mad 1980s). Obviously, the same can be said for much of recent literary and cultural theory, especially 'reception theory', which, in its more interesting formulations, maintains that cultural artifacts are 'produced' only by means of their continued consumption.

But pomo isn't just consumerism with a veneer of theory—not in hip-hop (which 'consumed' late 1970s disco only to spit it back out in scratching and sampling), and not in the work of artists like Hans Haacke. When Haacke foregrounds the means of cultural transmission, he doesn't do so in order to glorify consumption; on the contrary, Haacke's work rigorously interrogates the socioeconomic conditions of art's 'ownership' and contests the corporate reprivatization of public expression. From the perspective of Haacke's left postmodernism, then, you could say that what makes Philip Johnson's famous AT&T building postmodern is not its Chippendale top but its tax-abatement 'plaza', which, as Herbert Schiller noted in *Culture Inc.* (1989), is marked by a revealing sign of the times:

> PUBLIC SPACE
> Owned and Maintained by A. T. & T.
> 550 Madison Ave., N.Y.C.

In AT&T's 'public space', as in the critical reception of Haacke and hip-hop, we find that postmodernism isn't without enemies in its reconfiguration of the means of cultural transmission. Even as pomo culture spans the globe and appears in your living room, the global culture of 'free market' capitalism is doing its best, often (and paradoxically) enough, to *restrict* circulation, to *reprivatize* culture, to *recapture* public spheres, museums, airwaves and Xerox machines, and to *reinforce* the laws of copyright, ownership, and authorship.[5] In pomo's future tenses, right and left will very likely duke it out over the availability of 'public' information; and postmodernism's politics will be a struggle for control—not over the means of production, but over the means of *replication*. Who cares about the funny Chippendale top? Not me.

* * *

Notes*

1. Andreas Huyssen, *After the Great Divide: Modernism, Mass Culture, Postmodernism* (Bloomington, Ind.: Indiana University Press, 1986), p. 193. * * *
2. Here I originally meant to oppose Cindy Sherman to *The Donna Reed Show* along high/mass culture lines: the one as an 'avant-garde' artist about whom many academics have written in relation to feminism and postmodernism, the other as a piece of TV schlock whose reruns are brought to you by a tongue-in-cheek cable network claiming to 'preserve our television heritage'. Yet little did I imagine in 1991 (despite this essay's insistence that cultural products circulate too widely and rapidly to allow for the possibility of 'avant-gardism') that Cindy Sherman herself would soon be available in 'mainstream' media. * * * See Cathy Hainer, 'For Cindy Sherman, Art Has Many Guises', *USA Today,* 18 November 1993, p. 6D. * * *
3. Kirk Vardenoe and Adam Gopnik, *High and Low: Modern Art and Popular Culture* (New York: The Museum of Modern Art, 1990), p. 375. According to the authors, Gopnik was the principal author of 'Contemporary Reflections', the chapter in which this passage appears.
4. Ihab Hassan, 'On the Problem of the Postmodern', *New Literary History,* vol. 20, no. 1 (1988), p. 22.
5. Craig Owens, 'The Discourse of Others: Feminists and Postmodernism', in Hal Foster, ed., *The Anti-Aesthetic: Essays on Postmodern Culture* (Port Townshend, Wash.: Bay Press, 1983), pp. 57–82; Linda Hutcheon, *The Politics of Postmodernism* (New York: Routledge, 1989), p. 168.
6. See Paul Laxalt's account of Reagan's performance in his first debate with Mondale, as quoted in Steven R. Weisman, 'President Says He Needed to Relax before Debating', *New York Times,* 12 October 1984, p. B8; for a transcript of Reagan's speech at the 1988 Re-

*Some of the author's notes have been abridged.—Eds.

publican convention, at which he stumbled over the refrain, 'facts are stubborn things' and said 'facts are stupid things—stubborn things, I should say', see 'Reagan's Address: Hailing Fruits of the Party's Dream of 1980', *New York Times,* 16 August 1988, p. A20.

7. Quoted in a UPI story, 'Lawsuit over Proof of Holocaust Ends with Payment to a Survivor', *New York Times,* 25 July 1985, p. A12. For more substantial news coverage of the case, see Myrna Oliver, 'Holocaust Doubters Settle Auschwitz Survivor's Suit', *Los Angeles Times,* 25 July 1985, pp. 1, 26.
8. Thomas S. Kuhn, *The Structure of Scientific Revolutions* (Chicago: University of Chicago Press, 1962), pp. 151, 141. * * *
9. Denis Donoghue, 'The Promiscuous Cool of Postmodernism', *New York Times Book Review,* 22 June 1986, p. 1. Fredric Jameson, 'Postmodernism and Consumer Society', in Hal Foster, ed., *The Anti-Aesthetic,* p. 115. * * *

1. Jean Baudrillard, *Simulations,* Paul Foss, Paul Patton and Philip Beitchman, trans. (New York: Semiotext(e), 1983), pp. 2, 12–13.
2. The conundrum here has been nicely phrased by T. V. Reed in a book that appeared after this essay was first composed: 'anyone who posits postmodernism as a discourse about a world in which the "real" can no longer be found must deal with the irony that to do so is to posit this "reallessness" as our real state of affairs.' T. V. Reed, *Fifteen Jugglers, Five Believers: Literary Politics and the Poetics of American Social Movements* (Berkeley, Calif.: University of California Press, 1992), pp. 20–21.
3. Jameson's typewriter/ word processor analogy was an aside he apparently appended to, but did not incorporate into, the paper that eventually became the chapter, 'Surrealism without the Unconscious' in *Postmodernism, or the Cultural Logic of Late Capitalism* (Durham, N.C.: Duke University Press, 1991).
4. Barbara Ehrenreich, 'The Challenge for the Left', rpt. in Berman, ed., *Debating P.C.*, pp. 336–7.
5. For Schiller's argument on the corporate recapture of public space, see *Culture, Inc.: The Corporate Takeover of Public Expression* (New York: Oxford University Press, 1989), esp. pp. 89–110. For an analysis of the postmodern politics of global electronic transmission, see Schiller, pp. 111–34, and Constance Penley's and Andrew Ross's 'Introduction' to *Technoculture,* Penley and Ross, eds (Minneapolis: University of Minnesota Press, 1991), pp. viii–xvii.

1994

DONNA HARAWAY
b. 1944

Donna Haraway holds a Ph.D. in biology from Yale University and teaches in the History of Consciousness Program at the University of California at Santa Cruz. Her books include *Primate Visions: Gender, Race, and Nature in the World of Modern Science* (1989) and *Simians, Cyborgs, and Women: The Reinvention of Nature* (1991).

From A Cyborg Manifesto: Science, Technology, and Socialist-Feminism in the Late Twentieth Century[1]

An Ironic Dream of a Common Language for Women in the Integrated Circuit

This chapter is an effort to build an ironic political myth faithful to feminism, socialism, and materialism. Perhaps more faithful as blasphemy is faithful, than as reverent worship and identification. Blasphemy has always seemed to require taking things very seriously. I know no better stance to adopt from within the secular-religious, evangelical traditions of United

States politics, including the politics of socialist feminism. Blasphemy protects one from the moral majority within, while still insisting on the need for community. Blasphemy is not apostasy. Irony is about contradictions that do not resolve into larger wholes, even dialectically, about the tension of holding incompatible things together because both or all are necessary and true. Irony is about humour and serious play. It is also a rhetorical strategy and a political method, one I would like to see more honoured within socialist-feminism. At the centre of my ironic faith, my blasphemy, is the image of the cyborg.

A cyborg is a cybernetic organism, a hybrid of machine and organism, a creature of social reality as well as a creature of fiction. Social reality is lived social relations, our most important political construction, a world-changing fiction. The international women's movements have constructed 'women's experience', as well as uncovered or discovered this crucial collective object. This experience is a fiction and fact of the most crucial, political kind. Liberation rests on the construction of the consciousness, the imaginative apprehension, of oppression, and so of possibility. The cyborg is a matter of fiction and lived experience that changes what counts as women's experience in the late twentieth century. This is a struggle over life and death, but the boundary between science fiction and social reality is an optical illusion.

Contemporary science fiction is full of cyborgs—creatures simultaneously animal and machine, who populate worlds ambiguously natural and crafted. Modern medicine is also full of cyborgs, of couplings between organism and machine, each conceived as coded devices, in an intimacy and with a power that was not generated in the history of sexuality. Cyborg 'sex' restores some of the lovely replicative baroque of ferns and invertebrates (such nice organic prophylactics against heterosexism). Cyborg replication is uncoupled from organic reproduction. Modern production seems like a dream of cyborg colonization work, a dream that makes the nightmare of Taylorism seem idyllic. And modern war is a cyborg orgy, coded by C^3I, command-control-communication-intelligence, an $84 billion item in 1984's US defence budget. I am making an argument for the cyborg as a fiction mapping our social and bodily reality and as an imaginative resource suggesting some very fruitful couplings. Michael Foucault's biopolitics is a flaccid premonition of cyborg politics, a very open field.

By the late twentieth century, our time, a mythic time, we are all chimeras, theorized and fabricated hybrids of machine and organism; in short, we are cyborgs. The cyborg is our ontology; it gives us our politics. The cyborg is a condensed image of both imagination and material reality, the two joined centres structuring any possibility of historical transformation. In the traditions of 'Western' science and politics—the tradition of racist, male-dominant capitalism; the tradition of progress; the tradition of the appropriation of nature as resource for the productions of culture; the tradition of reproduction of the self from the reflections of the other—the relation between organism and machine has been a border war. The stakes in the border war have been the territories of production, reproduction, and imagination. This chapter is an argument for *pleasure* in the confusion of boundaries and for *responsibility* in their construction. It is also an effort to contribute to socialist-feminist culture and theory in a postmodernist, non-naturalist mode and in the utopian tradition of imagining a world without gender, which is perhaps a world without genesis, but maybe also a world without end. The cyborg incarnation is outside salvation history. Nor does it mark time on an oedipal calendar, attempting to heal the terrible cleavages of gender in an oral symbiotic utopia or post-oedipal apocalypse. As Zoe Sofoulis argues in her unpublished manuscript on Jacques Lacan, Melanie Klein, and nuclear culture, *Lacklein,* the most terrible and perhaps the most promising monsters in cyborg worlds are embodied in non-oedipal narratives with a different logic of repression, which we need to understand for our survival.

The cyborg is a creature in a post-gender world; it has no truck with bisexuality, pre-oedipal symbiosis, unalienated labour, or other seductions to organic wholeness through a final appropriation of all the powers of the parts into a higher unity. In a sense, the cyborg has no origin story in the Western sense—a 'final' irony since the cyborg is also the awful apocalyptic *telos* of the 'West's' escalating dominations of abstract individuation, an ultimate self untied at last from all dependency, a man in space. An origin story in the 'Western', humanist sense depends on the myth of original unity, fullness, bliss and terror, represented by the phallic mother from whom all humans must separate, the task of individual development and of history, the twin potent myths inscribed most powerfully for us in psychoanalysis and Marxism. Hilary Klein has argued that both Marxism and psychoanalysis, in their concepts of labour and of individuation and gender formation, depend on the plot of original unity out of which difference must be produced and enlisted in a drama of escalating domination of woman/nature. The cyborg skips the step of original unity, of identification with nature in the Western sense. This is its illegitimate promise that might lead to subversion of its teleology as star wars.

The cyborg is resolutely committed to partiality, irony, intimacy, and perversity. It is oppositional, utopian, and completely without innocence. No longer structured by the polarity of public and private, the cyborg defines a technological polis based partly on a revolution of social relations in the *oikos,* the household. Nature and culture are reworked; the one can no longer be the resource for appropriation or incorporation by the other. The relationships for forming wholes from parts, including those of polarity and hierarchical domination, are at issue in the cyborg world. Unlike the hopes of Frankenstein's monster, the cyborg does not expect its father to save it through a restoration of the garden; that is, through the fabrication of a heterosexual mate, through its completion in a finished whole, a city and cosmos. The cyborg does not dream of community on the model of the organic family, this time without the oedipal project. The cyborg would n[illegible] nize the Garden of Eden; it is not made of mud and cannot drea[illegible] turning to dust. Perhaps that is why I want to see if cyborgs can su[illegible] apocalypse of returning to nuclear dust in the manic compulsion [illegible] the Enemy. Cyborgs are not reverent; they do not re-member the cosmos. They are wary of holism, but needy for connection—they seem to have a natural feel for united front politics, but without the vanguard party. The main trouble with cyborgs, of course, is that they are the illegitimate offspring of militarism and patriarchal capitalism, not to mention state socialism. But illegitimate offspring are often exceedingly unfaithful to their origins. Their fathers, after all, are inessential.

I will return to the science fiction of cyborgs at the end of this chapter, but now I want to signal three crucial boundary breakdowns that make the following political-fictional (political-scientific) analysis possible. By the late twentieth century in United States scientific culture, the boundary between human and animal is thoroughly breached. The last beachheads of uniqueness have been polluted if not turned into amusement parks—language, tool use, social behaviour, mental events, nothing really convincingly settles the separation of human and animal. And many people no longer feel the need for such a separation; indeed, many branches of feminist culture affirm the pleasure of connection of human and other living creatures. Movements for animal rights are not irrational denials of human uniqueness; they are a clear-sighted recognition of connection across the discredited breach of nature and culture. Biology and evolutionary theory over the last two centuries have simultaneously produced modern organisms as ob- [illegible] wledge and reduced the line between humans and animals to a [illegible] -etched in ideological struggle or professional disputes between [illegible] al science. Within this framework, teaching modern Christian [illegible] should be fought as a form of child abuse.

Biological-determinist ideology is only one position opened up in scientific culture for arguing the meanings of human animality. There is much room for radical political people to contest the meanings of the breached boundary.[2] The cyborg appears in myth precisely where the boundary between human and animal is transgressed. Far from signalling a walling off of people from other living beings, cyborgs signal disturbingly and pleasurably tight coupling. Bestiality has a new status in this cycle of marriage exchange.

The second leaky distinction is between animal-human (organism) and machine. Pre-cybernetic machines could be haunted; there was always the spectre of the ghost in the machine. This dualism structured the dialogue between materialism and idealism that was settled by a dialectical progeny, called spirit or history, according to taste. But basically machines were not self-moving, self-designing, autonomous. They could not achieve man's dream, only mock it. They were not man, an author to himself, but only a caricature of that masculinist reproductive dream. To think they were otherwise was paranoid. Now we are not so sure. Late twentieth-century machines have made thoroughly ambiguous the difference between natural and artificial, mind and body, self-developing and externally designed, and many other distinctions that used to apply to organisms and machines. Our machines are disturbingly lively, and we ourselves frighteningly inert.

Technological determination is only one ideological space opened up by the reconceptions of machine and organism as coded texts through which we engage in the play of writing and reading the world.[3] 'Textualization' of everything in poststructuralist, postmodernist theory has been damned by Marxists and socialist feminists for its utopian disregard for the lived relations of domination that ground the 'play' of arbitrary reading.[4] It is certainly true that postmodernist strategies, like my cyborg myth, subvert myriad organic wholes (for example, the poem, the primitive culture, the biological organism). In short, the certainty of what counts as nature—a source of insight and promise of innocence—is undermined, probably fatally. The transcendent authorization of interpretation is lost, and with it the ontology grounding 'Western' epistemology. But the alternative is not cynicism or faithlessness, that is, some version of abstract existence, like the accounts of technological determinism destroying 'man' by the 'machine' or 'meaningful political action' by the 'text'. Who cyborgs will be is a radical question; the answers are a matter of survival. Both chimpanzees and artefacts have politics, so why shouldn't we (de Waal, 1982; Winner, 1980)?

The third distinction is a subset of the second: the boundary between physical and non-physical is very imprecise for us. Pop physics books on the consequences of quantum theory and the indeterminacy principle are a kind of popular scientific equivalent to Harlequin romances as a marker of radical change in American white heterosexuality: they get it wrong, but they are on the right subject. Modern machines are quintessentially microelectronic devices: they are everywhere and they are invisible. Modern machinery is an irreverent upstart god, mocking the Father's ubiquity and spirituality. The silicon chip is a surface for writing; it is etched in molecular scales disturbed only by atomic noise, the ultimate interference for nuclear scores. Writing, power, and technology are old partners in Western stories of the origin of civilization, but miniaturization has changed our experience of mechanism. Miniaturization has turned out to be about power; small is not so much beautiful as pre-eminently dangerous, as in cruise missiles. Contrast the TV sets of the 1950s or the news cameras of the 1970s with the TV wrist bands or hand-sized video cameras now advertised. Our best machines are made of sunshine; they are all light and clean because they are nothing but signals, electromagnetic waves, a section of a spectrum, and these machines are eminently portable, mobile—a matter of immense human pain in Detroit and Singapore. People are nowhere near so fluid, being both material and opaque. Cyborgs are ether, quintessence.

The ubiquity and invisibility of cyborgs is precisely why these sunshine-belt machines are so deadly. They are as hard to see politically as materially. They are about consciousness—or its simulation.[5] They are floating signifiers moving in pickup trucks across Europe, blocked more effectively by the witch-weavings of the displaced and so unnatural Greenham women, who read the cyborg webs of power so very well, than by the militant labour of older masculinist politics, whose natural constituency needs defence jobs. Ultimately the 'hardest' science is about the realm of greatest boundary confusion, the realm of pure number, pure spirit, C^3I, cryptography, and the preservation of potent secrets. The new machines are so clean and light. Their engineers are sun-worshippers mediating a new scientific revolution associated with the night dream of post-industrial society. The diseases evoked by these clean machines are 'no more' than the minuscule coding changes of an antigen in the immune system, 'no more' than the experience of stress. The nimble fingers of 'Oriental' women, the old fascination of little Anglo-Saxon Victorian girls with doll's houses, women's enforced attention to the small take on quite new dimensions in this world.

There might be a cyborg Alice taking account of these new dimensions. Ironically, it might be the unnatural cyborg women making chips in Asia and spiral dancing in Santa Rita jail* whose constructed unities will guide effective oppositional strategies.

[illegible] n is about transgressed boundaries, potent fusions, and [illegible] es which progressive people might explore as one part [illegible] work. One of my premises is that most American so- [illegible] see deepened dualisms of mind and body, animal and machine, idealism and materialism in the social practices, symbolic formulations, and physical artefacts associated with 'high technology' and scientific culture. From *One-Dimensional Man* (Marcuse, 1964) to *The Death of Nature* (Merchant, 1980), the analytic resources developed by progressives have insisted on the necessary domination of technics and recalled us to an imagined organic body to integrate our resistance. Another of my premises is that the need for unity of people trying to resist world-wide intensification of domination has never been more acute. But a slightly perverse shift of perspective might better enable us to contest for meanings, as well as for other forms of power and pleasure in technologically mediated societies.

From one perspective, a cyborg world is about the final imposition of a grid of control on the planet, about the final abstraction embodied in a Star Wars apocalypse waged in the name of defence, about the final appropriation of women's bodies in a masculinist orgy of war (Sofia, 1984). From another perspective, a cyborg world might be about lived social and bodily realities in which people are not afraid of their joint kinship with animals and machines, not afraid of permanently partial identities and contradictory standpoints. The political struggle is to see from both perspectives at once because each reveals both dominations and possibilities unimaginable from the other vantage point. Single vision produces worse illusions than double vision or many-headed monsters. Cyborg unities are monstrous and illegitimate; in our present political circumstances, we could hardly hope for more potent myths for resistance and recoupling. I like to imagine LAG, the Livermore Action Group, as a kind of cyborg society, dedicated to realistically converting the laboratories that most fiercely embody and spew out the tools of technological apocalypse, and committed to building a political form that actually manages to hold together witches, engineers, elders, perverts, Christians, mothers, and Leninists long enough to disarm the state. Fission Impossible is the name of the affinity group in my town. (Affinity: related not by blood but by choice, the appeal of one chemical nuclear group for another, avidity.)[6]

The Informatics of Domination

In this attempt at an epistemological and political position, I would like to sketch a picture of possible unity, a picture indebted to socialist and feminist principles of design. The frame for my sketch is set by the extent and importance of rearrangements in world-wide social relations tied to science

*A practice at once both spiritual and political that linked guards and arrested anti-nuclear demonstrators in the Alameda County jail in California in the early 1980s.

and technology. I argue for a politics rooted in claims about fundamental changes in the nature of class, race, and gender in an emerging system of world order analogous in its novelty and scope to that created by industrial capitalism; we are living through a movement from an organic, industrial society to a polymorphous, information system—from all work to all play, a deadly game. Simultaneously material and ideological, the dichotomies may be expressed in the following chart of transitions from the comfortable old hierarchical dominations to the scary new networks I have called the informatics of domination:

Representation	Simulation
Bourgeois novel, realism	Science fiction, postmodernism
Organism	Biotic component
Depth, integrity	Surface, boundary
Heat	Noise
Biology as clinical practice	Biology as inscription
Physiology	Communications engineering
Small group	Subsystem
Perfection	Optimization
Eugenics	Population Control
Decadence, *Magic Mountain*	Obsolescence, *Future Shock*
Hygiene	Stress Management
Microbiology, tuberculosis	Immunology, AIDS
Organic division of labour	Ergonomics / cybernetics of labour
Functional specialization	Modular construction
Reproduction	Replication
Organic sex role specialization	Optimal genetic strategies
Biological determinism	Evolutionary inertia, constraints
Community ecology	Ecosystem
Racial chain of being	Neo-imperialism, United Nations humanism
Scientific management in home / factory	Global factory / Electronic cottage
Family / Market / Factory	Women in the Integrated Circuit
Family wage	Comparable worth
Public / Private	Cyborg citizenship
Nature / Culture	Fields of difference
Co-operation	Communications enhancement
Freud	Lacan
Sex	Genetic engineering
Labour	Robotics
Mind	Artificial Intelligence
Second World War	Star Wars
White Capitalist Patriarchy	Informatics of Domination

This list suggests several interesting things.[7] First, the objects on the right-hand side cannot be coded as 'natural', a realization that subverts naturalistic coding for the left-hand side as well. We cannot go back ideologically or materially. It's not just that 'god' is dead; so is the 'goddess'. Or both are revivified in the worlds charged with microelectronic and biotechnological politics. In relation to objects like biotic components, one must think not in terms of essential properties, but in terms of design, boundary constraints, rates of flows, systems logics, costs of lowering constraints. Sexual reproduction is one kind of reproductive strategy among many, with costs and benefits as a function of the system environment. Ideologies of sexual reproduction can no longer reasonably call on notions of sex and sex role as organic aspects in natural objects like organisms and families. Such reasoning will be unmasked as irrational, and ironically corporate executives reading *Playboy* and anti-porn radical feminists will make strange bedfellows in jointly unmasking the irrationalism.

[illegible] or race, ideologies about human diversity have to be formu- [illegible] of frequencies of parameters, like blood groups or intelligence [illegible] rrational' to invoke concepts like primitive and civilized. For liberals and radicals, the search for integrated social systems gives way to a new practice called 'experimental ethnography' in which an organic object dissipates in attention to the play of writing. At the level of ideology, we see translations of racism and colonialism into languages of development and under-development, rates and constraints of modernization. Any objects or persons can be reasonably thought of in terms of disassembly and reassembly; no 'natural' architectures constrain system design. The financial districts in all the world's cities, as well as the export-processing and free-trade zones, proclaim this elementary fact of 'late capitalism'. The entire universe of objects that can be known scientifically must be formulated as problems in communications engineering (for the managers) or theories of the next (for those who would resist). Both are cyborg semiologies.

One should expect control strategies to concentrate on boundary conditions and interfaces, on rates of flow across boundaries—and not on the integrity of natural objects. 'Integrity' or 'sincerity' of the Western self gives way to decision procedures and expert systems. For example, control strategies applied to women's capacities to give birth to new human beings will be developed in the languages of population control and maximization of goal achievement for individual decision-makers. Control strategies will be formulated in terms of rates, costs of constraints, degrees of freedom. Human beings, like any other component or subsystem, must be localized in a system architecture whose basic modes of operation are probabilistic, statistical. No objects, spaces, or bodies are sacred in themselves; any component can be interfaced with any other if the proper standard, the proper code, can be constructed for processing signals in a common language. Exchange in this world transcends the universal translation effected by capitalist markets that Marx analysed so well. The privileged pathology affecting all kinds of components in this universe is stress—communications breakdown (Hogness, 1983). The cyborg is not subject to Foucault's biopolitics; the cyborg simulates politics, a much more potent field of operations.

This kind of analysis of scientific and cultural objects of knowledge which have appeared historically since the Second World War prepares us to notice some important inadequacies in feminist analysis which has proceeded as if the organic, hierarchical dualisms ordering discourse in 'the West' since Aristotle still ruled. They have been cannibalized, or as Zoe Sofia (Sofoulis) might put it, they have been 'techno-digested'. The dichotomies between mind and body, animal and human, organism and machine, public and private, nature and culture, men and women, primitive and civilized are all in question ideologically. The actual situation of women is their integration/exploitation into a world system of production/reproduction and communication called the informatics of domination. The home, workplace, market, public arena, the body itself—all can be dispersed and interfaced in nearly infinite, polymorphous ways, with large consequences for women and others—consequences that themselves are very different for different people and which make potent oppositional international movements difficult to imagine and essential for survival. One important route for reconstructing socialist-feminist politics is through theory and practice addressed to the social relations of science and technology, including crucially the systems of myth and meanings structuring our imaginations. The cyborg is a kind of disassembled and reassembled, postmodern collective and personal self. This is the self feminists must code.

Communications technologies and biotechnologies are the crucial tools recrafting our bodies. These tools embody and enforce new social relations for women world-wide. Technologies and scientific discourses can be partially understood as formalizations, i.e., as frozen moments, of the fluid social interactions constituting them, but they should also be viewed as instruments for enforcing meanings. The boundary is permeable between tool and myth, instrument and concept, historical systems of social relations and historical anatomies of possible bodies, including objects of knowledge. Indeed, myth and tool mutually constitute each other.

Furthermore, communications sciences and modern biologies are constructed by a common move—*the translation of the world into a problem of coding*, a search for a common language in which all resistance to instrumental control disappears and all heterogeneity can be submitted to disassembly, reassembly, investment, and exchange.

In communications sciences, the translation of the world into a problem in coding can be illustrated by looking at cybernetic (feedback-controlled) systems theories applied to telephone technology, computer design, weapons deployment, or data base construction and maintenance. In each case, solution to the key questions rests on a theory of language and control; the key operation is determining the rates, directions, and probabilities of flow of a quantity called information. The world is subdivided by boundaries differentially permeable to information. Information is just that kind of quantifiable element (unit, basis of unity) which allows universal translation, and so unhindered instrumental power (called effective communication). The biggest threat to such power is interruption of communication. Any system breakdown is a function of stress. The fundamentals of this technology can be condensed into the metaphor C^3I, command-control-communication-intelligence, the military's symbol for its operations theory.

In modern biologies, the translation of the world into a problem in coding can be illustrated by molecular genetics, ecology, sociobiological evolutionary theory, and immunobiology. The organism has been translated into problems of genetic coding and read-out. Biotechnology, a writing technology, informs research broadly.[8] In a sense, organisms have ceased to exist as objects of knowledge, giving way to biotic components, i.e., special kinds of information-processing devices. The analogous moves in ecology could be examined by probing the history and utility of the concept of the ecosystem. Immunobiology and associated medical practices are rich exemplars of the privilege of coding and recognition systems as objects of knowledge, as constructions of bodily reality for us. Biology here is a kind of cryptography. Research is necessarily a kind of intelligence activity. Ironies abound. A stressed system goes awry; its communication processes break down; it fails to recognize the difference between self and other. Human babies with baboon hearts evoke national ethical perplexity—for animal rights activists at least as much as for the guardians of human purity. In the US gay men and intravenous drug users are the 'privileged' victims of an awful immune system disease that marks (inscribes on the body) confusion of boundaries and moral pollution (Treichler, 1987).

But these excursions into communications sciences and biology have been at a rarefied level; there is a mundane, largely economic reality to support my claim that these sciences and technologies indicate fundamental transformations in the structure of the world for us. Communications technologies depend on electronics. Modern states, multinational corporations, military power, welfare state apparatuses, satellite systems, political processes, fabrication of our imaginations, labour-control systems, medical constructions of our bodies, commercial pornography, the international division of labour, and religious evangelism depend intimately upon electronics. Microelectronics is the technical basis of simulacra; that is, of copies without originals.

Microelectronics mediates the translations of labour into robotics and word processing, sex into genetic engineering and reproductive technologies, and mind into artificial intelligence and decision procedures. The new biotechnologies concern more than human reproduction. Biology as a powerful engineering science for redesigning materials and processes has revolutionary implications for industry, perhaps most obvious today in areas of fermentation, agriculture, and energy. Communications sciences and biology are constructions of natural-technical objects of knowledge in which the difference between machine and organism is thoroughly blurred; mind, body, and tool are on very intimate terms. The 'multinational' material organization of the production and reproduction of daily life and the symbolic organization of the production and reproduction of culture and imagination seem equally implicated. The boundary-maintaining images of base and superstructure, public and private, or material and ideal never seemed more feeble.

* * *

Women in the Integrated Circuit

Let me summarize the picture of women's historical locations in advanced industrial societies, as these positions have been restructured partly through the social relations of science and technology. If it was ever possible ideologically to characterize women's lives by the distinction of public and private domains—suggested by images of the division of working-class life into factory and home, of bourgeois life into market and home, and of gender existence into personal and political realms—it is now a totally misleading ideology, even to show how both terms of these dichotomies construct each other in practice and in theory. I prefer a network ideological image, suggesting the profusion of spaces and identities and the permeability of boundaries in the personal body and in the body politic. 'Networking' is both a feminist practice and a multinational corporate strategy—weaving is for oppositional cyborgs.

So let me return to the earlier image of the informatics of domination and trace one vision of women's 'place' in the integrated circuit, touching only a few idealized social locations seen primarily from the point of view of advanced capitalist societies: Home, Market, Paid Work Place, State, School, Clinic-Hospital, and Church. Each of these idealized spaces is logically and practically implied in every other locus, perhaps analogous to a holographic photograph. I want to suggest the impact of the social relations mediated and enforced by the new technologies in order to help formulate needed analysis and practical work. However, there is no 'place' for women in these networks, only geometrics of difference and contradiction crucial to women's cyborg identities. If we learn how to read these webs of power and social life, we might learn new couplings, new coalitions. There is no way to read the following list from a standpoint of 'identification', of a unitary self. The issue is dispersion. The task is to survive in the diaspora.

Home: Women-headed households, serial monogamy, flight of men, old women alone, technology of domestic work, paid homework, reemergence of home sweat-shops, home-based businesses and telecommuting, electronic cottage, urban homelessness, migration, module architecture, reinforced (simulated) nuclear family, intense domestic violence.

Market: Women's continuing consumption work, newly targeted to buy the profusion of new production from the new technologies (especially as the competitive race among industrialized and industrializing nations to avoid dangerous mass unemployment necessitates finding ever bigger new markets for ever less clearly needed commodities); bimodal buying power, coupled with advertising targeting of the numerous affluent groups and neglect of the previous mass markets; growing importance of informal markets in labour and commodities parallel to high-tech, affluent market structures; surveillance systems through electronic funds transfer; intensified market abstraction (commodification) of experience, resulting in ineffective utopian or equivalent cynical theories of community; extreme mobility (abstraction) of marketing/financing systems; interpenetration of sexual and labour markets; intensified sexualization of abstracted and alienated consumption.

Paid Work Place: Continued intense sexual and racial division of labour, but considerable growth of membership in privileged occupational categories for many white women and people of colour; impact of new technologies on women's work in clerical, service, manufacturing (especially textiles), agriculture, electronics; international restructuring of the working classes; development of new time arrangements to facilitate the homework economy (flex time, part time, over time, no time); homework and out work; increased pressures for two-tiered wage structures; significant numbers of people in cash-dependent populations world-wide with no experience or no further hope of stable employment; most labour 'marginal' or 'feminized'.

State: Continued erosion of the welfare state; decentralizations with increased surveillance and control; citizenship by telematics; imperialism and political power broadly in the form of information rich/information poor differentiation; increased high-tech militarization increasingly opposed by many social groups; reduction of civil service jobs as a result of the growing capital intensification of office work, with implications for occupational mobility for women of colour; growing privatization of material and ideological life and culture; close integration of privatization and militarization, the high-tech forms of bourgeois capitalist personal and public life; invisibility of different social groups to each other, linked to psychological mechanisms of belief in abstract enemies.

School: Deepening coupling of high-tech capital needs and public education at all levels, differentiated by race, class, and gender; managerial classes involved in educational reform and refunding at the cost of remaining progressive educational democratic structures for children and teachers; education for mass ignorance and repression in technocratic and militarized culture; growing anti-science mystery cults in dissenting and radical political movements; continued relative scientific illiteracy among white women and people of colour; growing industrial direction of education (especially higher education) by science-based multinationals (particularly in electronics- and biotechnology-dependent companies); highly educated, numerous élites in a progressively bimodal society.

Clinic-hospital: Intensified machine-body relations; renegotiations of public metaphors which channel personal experience of the body, particularly in relation to reproduction, immune system functions, and 'stress' phenomena; intensification of reproductive politics in response to world historical implications of women's unrealized, potential control of their relation to reproduction; emergence of new, historically specific diseases; struggles over meanings and means of health in environments pervaded by high technology products and processes; continuing feminization of health work; intensified struggle over state responsibility for health; continued ideological role of popular health movements as a major form of American politics.

Church: Electronic fundamentalist 'super-saver' preachers solemnizing the union of electronic capital and automated fetish gods; intensified importance of churches in resisting the militarized state; central struggle over women's meanings and authority in religion; continued relevance of spirituality, intertwined with sex and health, in political struggle.

The only way to characterize the informatics of domination is as a massive intensification of insecurity and cultural impoverishment, with common failure of subsistence networks for the most vulnerable. Since much of this picture interweaves with the social relations of science and technology, the urgency of a socialist-feminist politics addressed to science and technology is plain. There is much now being done, and the grounds for political work are rich. For example, the efforts to develop forms of collective struggle for women in paid work, like SEIU's District 925,* should be a high priority for all of us. These efforts are profoundly tied to technical restructuring of labour processes and reformations of working classes. These efforts also are providing understanding of a more comprehensive kind of labour organization, involving community, sexuality, and family issues never privileged in the largely white male industrial unions.

The structural rearrangements related to the social relations of science and technology evoke strong ambivalence. But it is not necessary to be ultimately depressed by the implications of late twentieth-century women's relation to all aspects of work, culture, production of knowledge, sexuality, and reproduction. For excellent reasons, most Marxisms see domination best and have trouble understanding what can only look like false consciousness and people's complicity in their own domination in late capitalism. It is crucial to remember that what is lost, perhaps especially from women's points of view, is often virulent forms of oppression, nostalgically naturalized in the face of current violation. Ambivalence towards the disrupted unities mediated by high-tech culture requires not sorting consciousness into categories of 'clear-sighted critique grounding a solid political epistemology' versus 'manipulated false consciousness', but subtle understanding of emerging pleasures, experiences, and powers with serious potential for changing the rules of the game.

There are grounds for hope in the emerging bases for new kinds of unity across race, gender, and class, as these elementary units of socialist-feminist analysis themselves suffer protean transformations. Intensifications of hardship experienced world-wide in connection with the social relations of science and technology are severe. But what people are experiencing is not transparently clear, and we lack sufficiently subtle connections for collectively building effective theories of experience. Present efforts—Marxist, psychoanalytic, feminist, anthropological—to clarify even 'our' experience are rudimentary.

I am conscious of the odd perspective provided by my historical position—a PhD in biology for an Irish Catholic girl was made possible by Sputnik's impact on US national science-education policy. I have a body and mind as much constructed by the post–Second World War arms race and cold war as by the women's movements. There are more grounds for hope in focusing on the contradictory effects of politics designed to produce loyal American technocrats, which also produced large numbers of dissidents, than in focusing on the present defeats.

The permanent partiality of feminist points of view has consequences for our expectations of forms of political organization and participation. We do not need a totality in order to work well. The feminist dream of a common language, like all dreams for a perfectly true language, of perfectly faithful naming of experience, is a totalizing and imperialist one. In that sense, di-

*Service Employees International Union's office workers' organization in the US.

alectics too is a dream language, longing to resolve contradiction. Perhaps, ironically, we can learn from our fusions with animals and machines how not to be Man, the embodiment of Western logos. From the point of view of pleasure in these potent and taboo fusions, made inevitable by the social relations of science and technology, there might indeed be a feminist science.

Cyborgs: A Myth of Political Identity

I want to conclude with a myth about identity and boundaries which might inform late twentieth-century political imaginations [. . .]. I am indebted in this story to writers like Joanna Russ, Samuel R. Delany, John Varley, James Tiptree, Jr, Octavia Butler, Monique Wittig, and Vonda McIntyre.[9] These are our story-tellers exploring what it means to be embodied in high-tech worlds. They are theorists for cyborgs. Exploring conceptions of bodily boundaries and social order, the anthropologist Mary Douglas (1966, 1970) should be credited with helping us to consciousness about how fundamental body imagery is to world view, and so to political language. French feminists like Luce Irigaray and Monique Wittig, for all their differences, know how to write the body; how to weave eroticism, cosmology, and politics from imagery of embodiment, and especially for Wittig, from imagery of fragmentation and reconstitution of bodies.[1]

American radical feminists like Susan Griffin, Audre Lorde, and Adrienne Rich have profoundly affected our political imaginations—and perhaps restricted too much what we allow as a friendly body and political language.[2] They insist on the organic, opposing it to the technological. But their symbolic systems and the related positions of ecofeminism and feminist paganism, replete with organicisms, can only be understood in Sandoval's terms as oppositional ideologies fitting the late twentieth century. They would simply bewilder anyone not preoccupied with the machines and consciousness of late capitalism. In that sense they are part of the cyborg world. But there are also great riches for feminists in explicitly embracing the possibilities inherent in the breakdown of clean distinctions between organism and machine and similar distinctions structuring the Western self. It is the simultaneity of breakdowns that cracks the matrices of domination and opens geometric possibilities. What might be learned from personal and political 'technological' pollution? I look briefly at two overlapping groups of texts for their insight into the construction of a potentially helpful cyborg myth: constructions of women of colour and monstrous selves in feminist science fiction.

Earlier I suggested that 'women of colour' might be understood as a cyborg identity, a potent subjectivity synthesized from fusions of outsider identities and in the complex political-historical layerings of her 'biomythography', *Zami* (Lorde, 1982; King, 1987a, 1987b). There are material and cultural grids mapping this potential; Audre Lorde (1984) captures the tone in the title of her *Sister Outsider.* In my political myth, Sister Outsider is the offshore woman, whom US workers, female and feminized, are supposed to regard as the enemy preventing their solidarity, threatening their security. Onshore, inside the boundary of the United States, Sister Outsider is a potential amidst the races and ethnic identities of women manipulated for division, competition, and exploitation in the same industries. 'Women of colour' are the preferred labour force for the science-based industries, the real women for whom the world-wide sexual market, labour market, and politics of reproduction kaleidoscope into daily life. Young Korean women hired in the sex industry and in electronics assembly are recruited from high schools, educated for the integrated circuit. Literacy, especially in English, distinguishes the 'cheap' female labour so attractive to the multinationals.

Contrary to orientalist stereotypes of the 'oral primitive', literacy is a special mark of women of colour, acquired by US black women as well as men through a history of risking death to learn and to teach reading and writing. Writing has a special significance for all colonized groups. Writing has been crucial to the Western myth of the distinction between oral and written cultures, primitive and civilized mentalities, and more recently to the erosion of that distinction in 'postmodernist' theories attacking the phallogocentrism of the West, with its worship of the monotheistic, phallic, authoritative, and singular work, the unique and perfect name.[3] Contests for the meanings of writing are a major form of contemporary political struggle. Releasing the play of writing is deadly serious. The poetry and stories of US women of colour are repeatedly about writing, about access to the power to signify; but this time that power must be neither phallic nor innocent. Cyborg writing must not be about the Fall, the imagination of a once-upon-a-time wholeness before language, before writing, before Man. Cyborg writing is about the power to survive, not on the basis of original innocence, but on the basis of seizing the tools to mark the world that marked them as other.

The tools are often stories, retold stories, versions that reverse and displace the hierarchical dualisms of naturalized identities. In retelling origin stories, cyborg authors subvert the central myths of origin of Western culture. We have all been colonized by those origin myths, with their longing for fulfilment in apocalypse. The phallogocentric origin stories most crucial for feminist cyborgs are built into the literal technologies—technologies that write the world, biotechnology and microelectronics—that have recently textualized our bodies as code problems on the grid of C^3I. Feminist cyborg stories have the task of recoding communication and intelligence to subvert command and control.

Figuratively and literally, language politics pervade the struggles of women of colour; and stories about language have a special power in the rich contemporary writing by US women of colour. For example, retellings of the story of the indigenous woman Malinche, mother of the mestizo 'bastard' race of the new world, master of languages, and mistress of Cortés, carry special meaning for Chicana constructions of identity. Cherríe Moraga (1983) in *Loving in the War Years* explores the themes of identity when one never possessed the original language, never told the original story, never resided in the harmony of legitimate heterosexuality in the garden of culture, and so cannot base identity on a myth or a fall from innocence and right to natural names, mother's or father's.[4] Moraga's writing, her superb literacy, is presented in her poetry as the same kind of violation as Malinche's mastery of the conqueror's language—a violation, an illegitimate production, that allows survival. Moraga's language is not 'whole'; it is self-consciously spliced, a chimera of English and Spanish, both conqueror's languages. But it is this chimeric monster, without claim to an original language before violation, that crafts the erotic, competent, potent identities of women of colour. Sister Outsider hints at the possibility of world survival not because of her innocence, but because of her ability to live on the boundaries, to write without the founding myth of original wholeness, with its inescapable apocalypse of final return to a deathly oneness that Man has imagined to be the innocent and all-powerful Mother, freed at the End from another spiral of appropriation by her son. Writing marks Moraga's body, affirms it as the body of a woman of colour, against the possibility of passing into the unmarked category of the Anglo father or into the orientalist myth of 'original illiteracy' of a mother that never was. Malinche was mother here, not Eve before eating the forbidden fruit. Writing affirms Sister Outsider, not the Woman-before-the-Fall-into-Writing needed by the phallogocentric Family of Man.

Writing is pre-eminently the technology of cyborgs, etched surfaces of the late twentieth century. Cyborg politics is the struggle for language and the struggle against perfect communication, against the one code that translates all meaning perfectly, the central dogma of phallogocentrism. That is why cyborg politics insist on noise and advocate pollution, rejoicing in the illegitimate fusions of animal and machine. These are the couplings which make Man and Woman so problematic, subverting the structure of desire, the force imagined to generate language and gender, and so subverting the structure and modes of reproduction of 'Western' identity, of nature and culture, of mirror and eye, slave and master, body and mind. 'We' did not originally choose to be cyborgs, but choice grounds a liberal politics and epistemology that imagines the reproduction of individuals before the wider replications of 'texts'.

From the perspective of cyborgs, freed of the need to ground politics in 'our' privileged position of the oppression that incorporates all other dominations, the innocence of the merely violated, the ground of those closer to nature, we can see powerful possibilities. Feminisms and Marxisms have run aground on Western epistemological imperatives to construct a revolutionary subject from the perspective of a hierarchy of oppressions and/or a latent position of moral superiority, innocence, and greater closeness to nature. With no available original dream of a common language or original symbiosis promising protection from hostile 'masculine' separation, but written into the play of a text that has no finally privileged reading or salvation history, to recognize 'oneself' as fully implicated in the world, frees us of the need to root politics in identification, vanguard parties, purity, and mothering. Stripped of identity, the bastard race teaches about the power of the margins and the importance of a mother like Malinche. Women of colour have transformed her from the evil mother of masculinist fear into the originally literate mother who teaches survival.

This is not just literary deconstruction, but liminal transformation. Every story that begins with original innocence and privileges the return to wholeness imagines the drama of life to be individuation, separation, the birth of the self, the tragedy of autonomy, the fall into writing, alienation; that is, war, tempered by imaginary respite in the bosom of the Other. These plots are ruled by a reproductive politics—rebirth without flaw, perfection, abstraction. In this plot women are imagined either better or worse off, but all agree they have less selfhood, weaker individuation, more fusion to the oral, to Mother, less at stake in masculine autonomy. But there is another route to having less at stake in masculine autonomy, a route that does not pass through Woman, Primitive, Zero, the Mirror Stage and its imaginary. It passes through women and other present-tense, illegitimate cyborgs, not of Woman born, who refuse the ideological resources of victimization so as to have a real life. These cyborgs are the people who refuse to disappear on cue, no matter how many times a 'Western' commentator remarks on the sad passing of another primitive, another organic group done in by 'Western' technology, by writing.[5] These real-life cyborgs (for example, the Southeast Asian village women workers in Japanese and US electronics firms described by Aihwa Ong) are actively rewriting the texts of their bodies and societies. Survival is the stakes in this play of readings.

To recapitulate, certain dualisms have been persistent in Western traditions; they have all been systemic to the logics and practices of domination of women, people of colour, nature, workers, animals—in short, domination of all constituted as others, whose task is to mirror the self. Chief among these troubling dualisms are self/other, mind/body, culture/nature, male/female, civilized/primitive, reality/appearance, whole/part, agent/resource, maker/made, active/passive, right/wrong, truth/illusion, total/partial, God/man. The self is the One who is not dominated, who knows that by the service of the other, the other is the one who holds the future, who knows that by the experience of domination, which gives the lie to the autonomy of the self. To be One is to be autonomous, to be powerful, to be God; but to be One is to be an illusion, and so to be involved in a dialectic of apocalypse with the other. Yet to be other is to be multiple, without clear boundary, frayed, insubstantial. One is too few, but two are too many.

High-tech culture challenges these dualisms in intriguing ways. It is not clear who makes and who is made in the relation between human and machine. It is not clear what is mind and what body in machines that resolve into coding practices. In so far as we know ourselves in both formal discourse (for example, biology) and in daily practice (for example, the homework economy in the integrated circuit), we find ourselves to be cyborgs, hybrids, mosaics, chimeras. Biological organisms have become biotic systems, communications devices like others. There is no fundamental, ontological separation in our formal knowledge of machine and organism, of technical and organic. * * *

* * *

Monsters have always defined the limits of community in Western imaginations. The Centaurs and Amazons of ancient Greece established the limits of the centred polis of the Greek male human by their disruption of marriage and boundary pollutions of the warrior with animality and woman. Unseparated twins and hermaphrodites were the confused human material in early modern France who grounded discourse on the natural and supernatural, medical and legal, portents and diseases—all crucial to establishing modern identity.[6] The evolutionary and behavioural sciences of monkeys and apes have marked the multiple boundaries of late twentieth-century industrial identities. Cyborg monsters in feminist science fiction define quite different political possibilities and limits from those proposed by the mundane fiction of Man and Woman.

There are several consequences to taking seriously the imagery of cyborgs as other than our enemies. Our bodies, ourselves; bodies are maps of power and identity. Cyborgs are no exception. A cyborg body is not innocent; it was not born in a garden; it does not seek unitary identity and so generate antagonistic dualisms without end (or until the world ends); it takes irony for granted. One is too few, and two is only one possibility. Intense pleasure in skill, machine skill, ceases to be a sin, but an aspect of embodiment. The machine is not an *it* to be animated, worshipped, and dominated. The machine is us, our processes, an aspect of our embodiment. We can be responsible for machines; *they* do not dominate or threaten us. We are responsible for boundaries; we are they. Up till now (once upon a time), female embodiment seemed to be given, organic, necessary; and female embodiment seemed to mean skill in mothering and its metaphoric extensions. Only by being out of place could we take intense pleasure in machines, and then with excuses that this was organic activity after all, appropriate to females. Cyborgs might consider more seriously the partial, fluid, sometimes aspect of sex and sexual embodiment. Gender might not be global identity after all, even if it has profound historical breadth and depth.

The ideologically charged question of what counts as daily activity, as experience, can be approached by exploiting the cyborg image. Feminists have recently claimed that women are given to dailiness, that women more than men somehow sustain daily life, and so have a privileged epistemological position potentially. There is a compelling aspect to this claim, one that makes visible unvalued female activity and names it as the ground of life. But *the* ground of life? What about all the ignorance of women, all the exclusions and failures of knowledge and skill? What about men's access to daily competence, to knowing how to build things, to take them apart, to play? What about other embodiments? Cyborg gender is a local possibility taking a global vengeance. Race, gender, and capital require a cyborg theory of wholes and parts. There is no drive in cyborgs to produce total theory, but there is an intimate experience of boundaries, their construction and deconstruction. There is a myth system waiting to become a political language to ground one way of looking at science and technology and challenging the informatics of domination—in order to act potently.

One last image: organisms and organismic, holistic politics depend on metaphors of rebirth and invariably call on the resources of reproductive sex. I would suggest that cyborgs have more to do with regeneration and are suspicious of the reproductive matrix and of most birthing. For salamanders, regeneration after injury, such as the loss of a limb, involves regrowth of structure and restoration of function with the constant possibility of twinning or other odd topographical productions at the site of former injury. The regrown limb can be monstrous, duplicated, potent. We have all been injured, profoundly. We require regeneration, not rebirth, and the possibilities for our reconstitution include the utopian dream of the hope for a monstrous world without gender.

Cyborg imagery can help express two crucial arguments in this essay: first, the production of universal, totalizing theory is a major mistake that misses most of reality, probably always, but certainly now; and second, taking responsibility for the social relations of science and technology means refusing an anti-science metaphysics, a demonology of technology, and so means embracing the skilful task of reconstructing the boundaries of daily life, in partial connection with others, in communication with all of our parts. It is not just that science and technology are possible means of great human satisfaction, as well as a matrix of complex dominations. Cyborg imagery can suggest a way out of the maze of dualisms in which we have explained our bodies and our tools to ourselves. This is a dream not of a common language, but of a powerful infidel heteroglossia. It is an imagination of a feminist speaking in tongues to strike fear into the circuits of the supersavers of the new right. It means both building and destroying machines, identities, categories, relationships, space stories. Though both are bound in the spiral dance, I would rather be a cyborg than a goddess.

[Notes*]

1. Research was funded by an Academic Senate Faculty Research Grant from the University of California, Santa Cruz. An earlier version of the paper on genetic engineering appeared as 'Lieber Kyborg als Göttin: für eine sozialistisch-feministische Unterwanderung der Gentechnologie', in Bernd-Peter Lange and Anna Marie Stuby, eds, Berlin: Argument-Sonderband 105, 1984, pp 66–84. The cyborg manifesto grew from my 'New machines, new bodies, new communities: political dilemmas of a cyborg feminist', 'The Scholar and the Feminist X: The Question of Technology', Conference, Barnard College, April 1983. * * *
2. Useful references to left and/or feminist radical science movements and theory and to biological/biotechnical issues include: Bleier (1984, 1986), Harding (1986), Fausto-Sterling (1985), Gould (1981), Hubbard *et al.* (1982), Keller (1985), Lewontin *et al.* (1984), *Radical Science Journal* (became *Science as Culture* in 1987), 26 Freegrove Road, London N7 9RQ; *Science for the People,* 897 Main St, Cambridge, MA 02139.
3. Starting points for left and/or feminist approaches to technology and politics include: Cowan (1983), Rothschild (1983), Traweek (1988), Young and Levidow (1981, 1985), Weizenbaum (1976), Winner (1977, 1986), Zimmerman (1983), Athanasiou (1987), Cohn (1987a, 1987b), Winograd and Flores (1986), Edwards (1985). * * *
4. A provocative, comprehensive argument about the politics and theories of 'postmodernism' is made by Fredric Jameson (1984), who argues that postmodernism is not an option, a style among others, but a cultural dominant requiring radical reinvention of left politics from within; there is no longer any place from without that gives meaning to the comforting fiction of critical distance. Jameson also makes clear why one cannot be for or against postmodernism, an essentially moralist move. My position is that feminists (and others) need continuous cultural reinvention, postmodernist critique, and historical materialism; only a cyborg would have a chance. * * *
5. Baudrillard (1983). Jameson (1984, p. 66) points out that Plato's definition of the simulacrum is the copy for which there is no original, i.e., the world of advanced capitalism, of pure exchange. See *Discourse* 9 (Spring/Summer 1987) for a special issue on technology (cybernetics, ecology, and the postmodern imagination).
6. For ethnographic accounts and political evaluations, see Epstein (forthcoming), Sturgeon (1986). * * *
7. This chart was published in 1985. My previous efforts to understand biology as a cybernetic command-control discourse and organisms as 'natural-technical objects of knowledge' were Haraway (1979, 1983, 1984). * * * The differences indicate shifts in argument.

*Some of the author's notes have been abridged.—Eds.

8. For progressive analyses and action on the biotechnology debates: *GeneWatch, a Bulletin of the Committee for Responsible Genetics,* 5 Doane St, 4th Floor, Boston, MA 02109; Genetic Screening Study Group (formerly the Sociobiology Study Group of Science for the People), Cambridge, MA; Wright (1982, 1986); Yoxen (1983).
9. King (1984). An abbreviated list of feminist science fiction underlying themes of this essay: Octavia Butler, *Wild Seed, Mind of My Mind, Kindred, Survivor;* Suzy McKee Charnas, *Motherliness;* Samuel R. Delany, the Nevèrÿon series; Anne McCaffery, *The Ship Who Sang, Dinosaur Planet;* Vonda McIntyre, *Superluminal, Dreamsnake;* Joanna Russ, *Adventures of Alix, The Female Man;* James Tiptree, Jr, *Star Songs of an Old Primate, Up the Walls of the World;* John Varley, *Titan, Wizard, Demon.*
1. French feminisms contribute to cyborg heteroglossia. Burke (1981); Irigaray (1977, 1979); Marks and de Courtivron (1980); *Signs* (Autumn 1981); Wittig (1973); Duchen (1986). For English translation of some currents of francophone feminism see *Feminist Issues: A Journal of Feminist Social and Political Theory,* 1980.
2. But all these poets are very complex, not least in their treatment of themes of lying and erotic, decentred collective and personal identities. Griffin (1978), Lorde (1984), Rich (1978).
3. Derrida (1976, especially part II); Lévi-Strauss (1961, especially 'The Writing Lesson'); Gates (1985); Kahn and Neumaier (1985); Ong (1982); Kramarae and Treichler (1985).
4. The sharp relation of women of colour to writing as theme and politics can be approached through: Program for 'The Black Woman and the Diaspora: Hidden Connections and Extended Acknowledgments', An International Literary Conference, Michigan State University, October 1985; Evans (1984); Christian (1985); Carby (1987); Fisher (1980); *Frontiers* (1980, 1983); Kingston (1977); Lerner (1973); Giddings (1985); Moraga and Anzaldúa (1981); Morgan (1984). Anglophone European and Euro-American women have also crafted special relations to their writing as a potent sign: Gilbert and Gubar (1979), Russ (1983).
5. The convention of ideologically taming militarized high technology by publicizing its applications to speech and motion problems of the disabled/differently abled takes on a special irony in monotheistic, patriarchal, and frequently anti-semitic culture when computer-generated speech allows a boy with no voice to chant the Haftorah at his bar mitzvah. See Sussman (1986). Making the always context-relative social definitions of 'ableness' particularly clear, military high-tech has a way of making human beings disabled by definition, a perverse aspect of much automated battlefield and Star Wars R&D. See Welford (1 July 1986).
6. DuBois (1982), Daston and Park (n.d.), Park and Daston (1981). The noun *monster* shares its root with the verb *to demonstrate.*

1991

UMBERTO ECO
b. 1932

Born in Alessandria, Italy, Umberto Eco is both a scholar and a novelist, whose *The Name of the Rose* (1980) has sold more than one million copies worldwide. Currently he is professor of semiotics at the University of Bologna in Italy. His writings include *A Theory of Semiotics* (1976), *Semiotics and the Philosophy of Language* (1984), and *The Limits of Interpretation* (1991).

From Postscript to *The Name of the Rose*

From *Postmodernism, Irony, the Enjoyable*

* * *

* * * The postmodern reply to the modern consists of recognising that the past, since it cannot really be destroyed, because its destruction leads to silence, must be revisited; but with irony, not innocently. I think of the postmodern attitude as that of a man who loves a very cultivated woman and

knows he cannot say to her, 'I love you madly,' because he knows that she knows (and that she knows that he knows) that these words have already been written by Barbara Cartland. Still, there is a solution. He can say, 'As Barbara Cartland would put it, I love you madly.' At this point, having avoided false innocence, having said clearly that it is no longer possible to speak innocently, he will nevertheless have said what he wanted to say to the woman: that he loves her, but loves her in an age of lost innocence. If the woman goes along with this she will have received a declaration of love all the same. Neither of the two speakers will feel innocent, both will have accepted the challenge of the past, of the already said, which cannot be eliminated; both will consciously and with pleasure play the game of irony . . . But both will have succeeded, once again, in speaking of love.

Irony, metalinguistic play, enunciation squared. Thus, with the modern, anyone who does not understand the game can only reject it, but with the postmodern, it is possible not to understand the game and yet to take it seriously. Which is, after all, the quality (the risk) of irony. There is always someone who takes ironic discourse seriously. I think that the collages of Picasso, Juan Gris, and Braque were modern: this is why normal people would not accept them. On the other hand, the collages of Max Ernst, who pasted together bits of nineteenth-century engravings, were postmodern: they can be read as fantastic stories, as the telling of dreams, without any awareness that they amount to a discussion of the nature of engraving, and perhaps even of collage. If 'postmodern' means this, it is clear why Sterne and Rabelais were postmodern, why Borges surely is, and why in the same artist the modern moment and the postmodern moment can coexist, or alternate, or follow each other closely. Look at Joyce. The *Portrait* is the story of an attempt at the Modern. *Dubliners,* even if comes before, is more modern than *Portrait. Ulysses* is on the borderline. *Finnegans Wake* is already postmodern, or at least it initiates the postmodern discourses: it demands, in order to be understood, not the negation of the already said, but its ironic rethinking.

On the subject of the postmodern nearly everything has been said (namely, in essays like 'The Literature of Exhaustion' by John Barth, which dates from 1967). Not that I am entirely in agreement with the grades that the theoreticians of postmodernism (Barth included) give to writers and artists, establishing who is postmodern and who has not yet made it. But I am interested in the theorem that the trend's theoreticians derive from their premises:

> My ideal postmodernist author neither merely repudiates nor merely imitates either his twentieth-century modernist parents or his nineteenth-century premodernist grandparents. He has the first half of our century under his belt, but not on his back . . . He may not hope to reach and move the devotees of James Michener and Irving Wallace—not to mention the lobotomised mass-media illiterates. But he *should* hope to reach and delight, at least part of the time, beyond the circle of what Mann used to call the Early Christians: professional devotees of high art . . . The ideal postmodernist novel will somehow rise above the quarrel between realism and irrealism, formalism and 'contentism', pure and committed literature, coterie fiction and junk fiction . . . My own analogy would be with good jazz or classical music:

> one finds much on successive listenings or close examination of the score that one didn't catch the first time through; but the first time through should be so ravishing—and not just to specialists—that one delights in the replay.

This is what Barth wrote in 1980, resuming the discussion, but this time under the title 'The Literature of Replenisment: Postmodernist Fiction'. Naturally, the subject can be discussed further, with greater taste for paradox; and this is what Leslie Fiedler does. In 1980 *Salmagundi* (no. 50–51) published a debate between Fiedler and other American authors. Fiedler, obviously, is out to provoke. He praises *The Last of the Mohicans,* adventure stories, Gothic novels, junk scorned by critics that was nevertheless able to create myths and capture the imagination of more than one generation. He wonders if something like *Uncle Tom's Cabin* will ever appear again, a book that can be read with equal passion in the kitchen, the living room, and the nursery. He includes Shakespeare among those who knew how to amuse, along with *Gone with the Wind.* We all know he is too keen a critic to believe these things. He simply wants to break down the barrier that has been erected between art and enjoyability. He feels that today reaching a vast public and capturing its dreams perhaps means acting as the avant garde, and he still leaves us free to say that capturing readers' dreams does not necessarily mean encouraging escape: it can also mean haunting them.

1984

BELL HOOKS
b. 1955

bell hooks (née Gloria Watkins) is a social critic, an educator, and currently assistant professor of Afro-American Studies and English at Yale University. Her writings include *Talking Back: Thinking Feminist, Thinking Black* (1979), *Ain't I a Woman: Black Women and Feminism* (1981), *Yearning: Race, Gender and Cultural Politics* (1990), and *Sisters of the Yam: Black Women and Self Recovery* (1992).

Postmodern Blackness

Postmodernist discourses are often exclusionary even as they call attention to, appropriate even, the experience of "difference" and "Otherness" to provide oppositional political meaning, legitimacy, and immediacy when they are accused of lacking concrete relevance. Very few African-American intellectuals have talked or written about postmodernism. At a dinner party I talked about trying to grapple with the significance of postmodernism for contemporary black experience. It was one of those social gatherings where only one other black person was present. The setting quickly became a field of contestation. I was told by the other black person that I was wasting my time, that "this stuff does not relate in any way to what's happening with black people." Speaking in the presence of a group of white onlookers, staring at us as though this encounter were staged for their benefit, we engaged in a passionate discussion about black experience. Apparently, no one sympathized with my insistence that racism is perpetuated when blackness is associated solely with concrete gut level experience conceived as either opposing or having no connection to abstract thinking and the production of critical theory. The idea that there is no meaningful connection between black experience and critical thinking about aesthetics or culture must be continually interrogated.

My defense of postmodernism and its relevance to black folks sounded good, but I worried that I lacked conviction, largely because I approach the subject cautiously and with suspicion.

Disturbed not so much by the "sense" of postmodernism but by the conventional language used when it is written or talked about and by those who speak it, I find myself on the outside of the discourse looking in. As a discursive practice it is dominated primarily by the voices of white male intellectuals and/or academic elites who speak to and about one another with coded familiarity. Reading and studying their writing to understand postmodernism in its multiple manifestations, I appreciate it but feel little inclination to ally myself with the academic hierarchy and exclusivity pervasive in the movement today.

Critical of most writing on postmodernism, I perhaps am more conscious of the way in which the focus on "Otherness and difference" that is often alluded to in these works seems to have little concrete impact as an analysis or standpoint that might change the nature and direction of postmodernist theory. Since much of this theory has been constructed in reaction to and against high modernism, there is seldom any mention of black experience or writings by black people in this work, specifically black women (though in more recent work one may see a reference to Cornel West, the black male scholar who has most engaged postmodernist discourse). Even if an aspect of black culture is the subject of postmodern critical writing, the works cited will usually be those of black men. A work that comes immediately to mind is Andrew Ross's chapter "Hip, and the Long Front of Color" in *No Respect: Intellectuals and Popular Culture;* while it is an interesting reading, it constructs black culture as though black women have had no role in black cultural production. At the end of Meaghan Morris' discussion of postmodernism in her collection of essays *The Pirate's Fiance: Feminism and Postmodernism,* she provides a bibliography of works by women, identifying them as important contributions to a discourse on postmodernism that offer new insight as well as challenging male theoretical hegemony. Even though many of the works do not directly address postmodernism, they address similar concerns. There are no references to works by black women.

The failure to recognize a critical black presence in the culture and in most scholarship and writing on postmodernism compels a black reader, particularly a black female reader, to interrogate her interest in a subject where those who discuss and write about it seem not to know black women exist or even to consider the possibility that we might be somewhere writing or saying something that should be listened to, or producing art that should be seen, heard, approached with intellectual seriousness. This is especially the case with works that go on and on about the way in which postmodernist discourse has opened up a theoretical terrain where "difference and Otherness" can be considered legitimate issues in the academy. Confronting both the absence of recognition of black female presence that much postmodernist theory re-inscribes and the resistance on the part of most black folks to hearing about real connection between postmodernism and black experience, I enter a discourse, a practice, where there may be no ready audience for my words, no clear listener, uncertain then, that my voice can or will be heard.

During the sixties, black power movement was influenced by perspectives that could easily be labeled modernist. Certainly many of the ways black folks addressed issues of identity conformed to a modernist universalizing agenda. There was little critique of patriarchy as a master narrative among black militants. Despite the fact that black power ideology reflected a modernist sensibility, these elements were soon rendered irrelevant as militant protest was stifled by a powerful, repressive postmodern state. The period directly after the black power movement was a time when major news magazines carried articles with cocky headlines like "Whatever Happened to Black America?" This response was an ironic reply to the aggressive, unmet demand by decentered, marginalized black subjects who had at least momentarily successfully demanded a hearing, who had made it possible for black liberation to be on the national political agenda. In the wake of the black power movement, after so many rebels were slaughtered and lost, many of these voices were silenced by a repressive state; others became inarticulate. It has become necessary to find new avenues to transmit the messages of black liberation struggle, new ways to talk about racism and other politics of domination. Radical postmodernist practice, most powerfully conceptualized as a "politics of difference," should incorporate the voices of displaced, marginalized, exploited, and oppressed black people. It is sadly ironic that the contemporary discourse which talks the most about heterogeneity, the decentered subject, declaring breakthroughs that allow recognition of Otherness, still directs its critical voice primarily to a specialized audience that shares a common language rooted in the very master narratives it claims to challenge. If radical postmodernist thinking is to have a transformative impact, then a critical break with the notion of "authority" as "mastery over" must not simply be a rhetorical device. It must be reflected in habits of being, including styles of writing as well as chosen subject matter. Third world nationals, elites, and white critics who passively absorb white supremacist thinking, and therefore never notice or look at black people on the streets or at their jobs, who render us invisible with their gaze in all areas of daily life, are not likely to produce liberatory theory that will challenge racist domination, or promote a breakdown in traditional ways of seeing and thinking about reality, ways of constructing aesthetic theory and practice. From a different standpoint, Robert Storr makes a similar critique in the global issue of *Art in America* when he asserts:

> To be sure, much postmodernist critical inquiry has centered precisely on the issues of "difference" and "Otherness." On the purely theoretical plane the exploration of these concepts has produced some important results, but in the absence of any sustained research into what

> artists of color and others outside the mainstream might be up to, such discussions become rootless instead of radical. Endless second guessing about the latent imperialism of intruding upon other cultures only compounded matters, preventing or excusing these theorists from investigating what black, Hispanic, Asian and Native American artists were actually doing.

Without adequate concrete knowledge of and contact with the nonwhite "Other," white theorists may move in discursive theoretical directions that are threatening and potentially disruptive of that critical practice which would support radical liberation struggle.

The postmodern critique of "identity," though relevant for renewed black liberation struggle, is often posed in ways that are problematic. Given a pervasive politic of white supremacy which seeks to prevent the formation of radical black subjectivity, we cannot cavalierly dismiss a concern with identity politics. Any critic exploring the radical potential of postmodernism as it relates to racial difference and racial domination would need to consider the implications of a critique of identity for oppressed groups. Many of us are struggling to find new strategies of resistance. We must engage decolonization as a critical practice if we are to have meaningful chances of survival even as we must simultaneously cope with the loss of political grounding which made radical activism more possible. I am thinking here about the postmodernist critique of essentialism as it pertains to the construction of "identity" as one example.

Postmodern theory that is not seeking to simply appropriate the experience of "Otherness" to enhance the discourse or to be radically chic should not separate the "politics of difference" from the politics of racism. To take racism seriously one must consider the plight of underclass people of color, a vast majority of whom are black. For African-Americans our collective condition prior to the advent of postmodernism and perhaps more tragically expressed under current postmodern conditions has been and is characterized by continued displacement, profound alienation, and despair. Writing about blacks and postmodernism, Cornel West describes our collective plight:

> There is increasing class division and differentiation, creating on the one hand a significant black middle-class, highly anxiety-ridden, insecure, willing to be co-opted and incorporated into the powers that be, concerned with racism to the degree that it poses contraints on upward social mobility; and, on the other, a vast and growing black underclass, an underclass that embodies a kind of walking nihilism of pervasive drug addiction, pervasive alcoholism, pervasive homicide, and an exponential rise in suicide. Now because of the deindustrialization, we also have a devastated black industrial working class. We are talking here about tremendous hopelessness.

This hopelessness creates longing for insight and strategies for change that can renew spirits and reconstruct grounds for collective black liberation struggle. The overall impact of postmodernism is that many other groups now share with black folks a sense of deep alienation, despair, uncertainty, loss of a sense of grounding even if it is not informed by shared circumstance. Radical postmodernism calls attention to those shared sensibilities which cross the boundaries of class, gender, race, etc., that could be fertile ground for the construction of empathy—ties that would promote recognition of common commitments, and serve as a base for solidarity and coalition.

Yearning is the word that best describes a common psychological state shared by many of us, cutting across boundaries of race, class, gender, and sexual practice. Specifically, in relation to the post-modernist deconstruction of "master" narratives, the yearning that wells in the hearts and minds of those whom such narratives have silenced is the longing for critical voice. It is no accident that "rap" has usurped the primary position of rhythm and blues music among young black folks as the most desired sound or that it began as a form of "testimony" for the underclass. It has enabled underclass black youth to develop a critical voice, as a group of young black men told me, a "common literacy." Rap projects a critical voice, explaining, demanding, urging. Working with this insight in his essay "Putting the Pop Back into Postmodernism," Lawrence Grossberg comments:

> The postmodern sensibility appropriates practices as boasts that announce their own—and consequently our own—existence, like a rap song boasting of the imaginary (or real—it makes no difference) accomplishments of the rapper. They offer forms of empowerment not only in the face of nihilism but precisely through the forms of nihilism itself: an empowering nihilism, a moment of positivity through the production and structuring of affective relations.

Considering that it is as subject one comes to voice, then the postmodernist focus on the critique of identity appears at first glance to threaten and close down the possibility that this discourse and practice will allow those who have suffered the crippling effects of colonization and domination to gain or regain a hearing. Even if this sense of threat and the fear it evokes are based on a misunderstanding of the postmodernist political project, they nevertheless shape responses. It never surprises me when black folks respond to the critique of essentialism, especially when it denies the validity of identity politics by saying, "Yeah, it's easy to give up identity, when you got one." Should we not be suspicious of postmodern critiques of the "subject" when they surface at a historical moment when many subjugated people feel themselves coming to voice for the first time. Though an apt and oftentimes appropriate comeback, it does not really intervene in the discourse in a way that alters and transforms.

Criticisms of directions in postmodern thinking should not obscure insights it may offer that open up our understanding of African-American experience. The critique of essentialism encouraged by postmodernist thought is useful for African-Americans concerned with reformulating outmoded notions of identity. We have too long had imposed upon us from both the outside and the inside a narrow, constricting notion of blackness. Postmodern critiques of essentialism which challenge notions of universality and static over-determined identity within mass culture and mass consciousness can open up new possibilities for the construction of self and the assertion of agency.

Employing a critique of essentialism allows African-Americans to acknowledge the way in which class mobility has altered collective black experience so that racism does not necessarily have the same impact on our lives. Such a critique allows us to affirm multiple black identities, varied black experience. It also challenges colonial imperialist paradigms of black identity which represent blackness one-dimensionally in ways that reinforce and sustain white supremacy. This discourse created the idea of the "primitive" and promoted the notion of an "authentic" experience, seeing as "natural" those expressions of black life which conformed to a pre-existing pattern or stereotype. Abandoning essentialist notions would be a serious challenge to racism. Contemporary African-American resistance struggle must be rooted in a process of decolonization that continually opposes re-inscribing notions of "authentic" black identity. This critique should not be made synonymous with a dismissal of the struggle of oppressed and exploited peoples to make ourselves subjects. Nor should it deny that in certain circumstances this experience affords us a privileged critical location from which to speak. This is not a re-inscription of modernist master narratives of authority which privilege some voices by denying voice to others. Part of our struggle for radical black subjectivity is the quest to find ways to construct self and identity that are oppositional and liberatory. The unwillingness to critique essentialism on the part of many African-Americans is rooted in the fear that it will cause folks to lose sight of the specific history and experience of African-Americans and the unique sensibilities and culture that arise from that experience. An adequate response to this concern is to critique essentialism while emphasizing the significance of "the authority of experience." There is a radical difference between a repudiation of the idea that there is a black "essence" and recognition of the way black identity has been specifically constituted in the experience of exile and struggle.

When black folks critique essentialism, we are empowered to recognize multiple experiences of black identity that are the lived conditions which make diverse cultural productions possible. When this diversity is ignored, it is easy to see black folks as falling into two categories: nationalist or assimilationist, black-identified or white-identified. Coming to terms with the impact of postmodernism for black experience, particularly as it changes our sense of identity, means that we must and can rearticulate the basis for collective bonding. Given the various crises facing African-Americans (economic, spiritual, escalating racial violence, etc.), we are compelled by circumstance to reassess our relationship to popular culture and resistance struggle. Many of us are as reluctant to face this task as many non-black postmodern thinkers who focus theoretically on the issue of "difference" are to confront the issue of race and racism.

Music is the cultural product created by African-Americans that has most attracted postmodern theorists. It is rarely acknowledged that there is far greater censorship and restriction of other forms of cultural production by black folks—literary, critical writing, etc. Attempts on the part of editors and publishing houses to control and manipulate the representation of black culture, as well as the desire to promote the creation of products that will attract the widest audience, limit in a crippling and stifling way the kind of work many black folks feel we can do and still receive recognition. Using myself as an example, that creative writing I do which I consider to be most reflective of a postmodern oppositional sensibility, work that is abstract, fragmented, non-linear narrative, is constantly rejected by editors and publishers. It does not conform to the type of writing they think black women should be doing or the type of writing they believe will sell. Certainly I do not think I am the only black person engaged in forms of cultural production, especially experimental ones, who is constrained by the lack of an audience for certain kinds of work. It is important for postmodern thinkers and theorists to constitute themselves as an audience for such work. To do this they must assert power and privilege within the space of critical writing to open up the field so that it will be more inclusive. To change the exclusionary practice of postmodern critical discourse is to enact a postmodernism of resistance. Part of this intervention entails black intellectual participation in the discourse.

In his essay "Postmodernism and Black America," Cornel West suggests that black intellectuals "are marginal—usually languishing at the interface of Black and white cultures or thoroughly ensconced in Euro-American settings." He cannot see this group as potential producers of radical postmodernist thought. While I generally agree with this assessment, black intellectuals must proceed with the understanding that we are not condemned to the margins. The way we work and what we do can determine whether or not what we produce will be meaningful to a wider audience, one that includes all classes of black people. West suggests that black intellectuals lack "any organic link with most of Black life" and that this "diminishes their value to Black resistance." This statement bears traces of essentialism. Perhaps we need to focus more on those black intellectuals, however rare our presence, who do not feel this lack and whose work is primarily directed towards the enhancement of black critical consciousness and the strengthening of our collective capacity to engage in meaningful resistance struggle. Theoretical ideas and critical thinking need not be transmitted solely in written work or solely in the academy. While I work in a predominantly white institution, I remain intimately and passionately engaged with black community. It's not like I'm going to talk about writing and thinking about postmodernism with other academics and/or intellectuals and not discuss these ideas with underclass non-academic black folks who are family, friends, and comrades. Since I have not broken the ties that bind me to underclass poor black community, I have seen that knowledge, especially that which enhances daily life and strengthens our capacity to survive, can be shared. It means that critics, writers, and academics have to give the same critical attention to nurturing and cultivating our ties to black community that we give to writing articles, teaching, and lecturing. Here again I am really talking about cultivating habits of being that reinforce awareness that knowledge can be disseminated and shared on a number of fronts. The extent to which knowledge is made available, accessible, etc. depends on the nature of one's political commitments.

Postmodern culture with its decentered subject can be the space where ties are severed or it can provide the occasion for new and varied forms of bonding. To some extent, ruptures, surfaces, contextuality, and a host of other happenings create gaps that make space for oppositional practices which no longer require intellectuals to be confined by narrow separate spheres with no meaningful connection to the world of the everyday. Much postmodern engagement with culture emerges from the yearning to do intellectual work that connects with habits of being, forms of artistic expression, and aesthetics that inform the daily life of writers and scholars as well as a mass population. On the terrain of culture, one can participate in critical dialogue with the uneducated poor, the black underclass who are thinking about aesthetics. One can talk about what we are seeing, thinking, or listening to; a space is there for critical exchange. It's exciting to think, write, talk about, and create art that reflects passionate engagement with popular culture, because this may very well be "the" central future location of resistance struggle, a meeting place where new and radical happenings can occur.

1990

JEAN BAUDRILLARD
b. 1929

Jean Baudrillard is a French sociologist and philosopher. His books include *The System of Objects* (1968), *Consumer Society* (1970), and *For a Critique of the Political Economy of the Sign* (1972). *America* (1986) portrayed his travels across the United States as he cataloged various manifestations of his theories of postmodernism.

From Simulacra and Simulation

From *The Precession of Simulacra*

The simulacrum is never what hides the truth—it is truth that hides the fact that there is none.

The simulacrum is true.

—Ecclesiastes

If once we were able to view the Borges fable in which the cartographers of the Empire draw up a map so detailed that it ends up covering the territory exactly (the decline of the Empire witnesses the fraying of this map, little by little, and its fall into ruins, though some shreds are still discernible in the deserts—the metaphysical beauty of this ruined abstraction testifying to a pride equal to the Empire and rotting like a carcass, returning to the substance of the soil, a bit as the double ends by being confused with the real through aging)—as the most beautiful allegory of simulation, this fable has now come full circle for us, and possesses nothing but the discrete charm of second-order simulacra.[1]

Today abstraction is no longer that of the map, the double, the mirror, or the concept. Simulation is no longer that of a territory, a referential being, or a substance. It is the generation by models of a real without origin or reality: a hyperreal. The territory no longer precedes the map, nor does it survive it. It is nevertheless the map that precedes the territory—*precession of simulacra*—that engenders the territory, and if one must return to the fable, today it is the territory whose shreds slowly rot across the extent of the map. It is the real, and not the map, whose vestiges persist here and there in the deserts that are no longer those of the Empire, but ours. *The desert of the real itself.*

In fact, even inverted, Borges's fable is unusable. Only the allegory of the Empire, perhaps, remains. Because it is with this same imperialism that present-day simulators attempt to make the real, all of the real, coincide with their models of simulation. But it is no longer a question of either maps or territories. Something has disappeared: the sovereign difference, between one and the other, that constituted the charm of abstraction. Because it is difference that constitutes the poetry of the map and the charm of the territory, the magic of the concept and the charm of the real. This imaginary of representation, which simultaneously culminates in and is engulfed by the cartographer's mad project of the ideal coextensivity of map and territory, disappears in the simulation whose operation is nuclear and genetic, no longer at all specular or discursive. It is all of metaphysics that is lost. No more mirror of being and appearances, of the real and its concept. No more imaginary coextensivity: it is genetic miniaturization that is the dimension of simulation. The real is produced from miniaturized cells, matrices, and memory banks, models of control—and it can be reproduced an indefinite number of times from these. It no longer needs to be rational, because it no longer measures itself against either an ideal or negative instance. It is no longer anything but operational. In fact, it is no longer really the real, because no imaginary envelops it anymore. It is a hyperreal, produced from a radiating syn[illegible] combinatory models in a hyperspace without atmosphere.

[illegible]ssing into a space whose curvature is no longer that of the real, nor [illegible]th, the era of simulation is inaugurated by a liquidation of all referentials—worse: with their artificial resurrection in the systems of signs, a material more malleable than meaning, in that it lends itself to all systems of equivalences, to all binary oppositions, to all combinatory algebra. It is no longer a question of imitation, nor duplication, nor even parody. It is a question of substituting the signs of the real for the real, that is to say of an operation of deterring every real process via its operational double, a programmatic, metastable, perfectly descriptive machine that offers all the signs of the real and short-circuits all its vicissitudes. Never again will the real have the chance to produce itself—such is the vital function of the model in a system of death, or rather of anticipated resurrection, that no longer even gives the event of death a chance. A hyperreal henceforth sheltered from the imaginary, and from any distinction between the real and the imaginary, leaving room only for the orbital recurrence of models and for the simulated generation of differences.

The Divine Irreference of Images

To dissimulate is to pretend not to have what one has. To simulate is to feign to have what one doesn't have. One implies a presence, the other an absence. But it is more complicated than that because simulating is not pretending: "Whoever fakes an illness can simply stay in bed and make everyone believe he is ill. Whoever simulates an illness produces in himself some of the symptoms" (Littré). Therefore, pretending, or dissimulating, leaves the principle of reality intact: the difference is always clear, it is simply masked, whereas simulation threatens the difference between the "true" and the "false," the "real" and the "imaginary." Is the simulator sick or not, given that he produces "true" symptoms? Objectively one cannot treat him as being either ill or not ill. Psychology and medicine stop at this point, forestalled by the illness's henceforth undiscoverable truth. For if any symptom can be "produced," and can no longer be taken as a fact of nature, then every illness can be considered as simulatable and simulated, and medicine loses its meaning since it only knows how to treat "real" illnesses according to their objective causes. Psychosomatics evolves in a dubious manner at the borders of the principle of illness. As to psychoanalysis, it transfers the symptom of the organic order to the unconscious order: the latter is new and taken for "real" more real than the other—but why would simulation be at the gates of the unconscious? Why couldn't the "work" of the unconscious be "produced" in the same way as any old symptom of classical medicine? Dreams already are.

Certainly, the psychiatrist purports that "for every form of mental alienation there is a particular order in the succession of symptoms of which the simulator is ignorant and in the absence of which the psychiatrist would not be deceived." This (which dates from 1865) in order to safeguard the principle of a truth at all costs and to escape the interrogation posed by simulation—the knowledge that truth, reference, objective cause have ceased to exist. Now, what can medicine do with what floats on either side of illness, on either side of health, with the duplication of illness in a discourse that is no longer either true or false? What can psychoanalysis do with the duplication of the discourse of the unconscious in the discourse of simulation that can never again be unmasked, since it is not false either?[2]

What can the army do about simulators? Traditionally it unmasks them and punishes them, according to a clear principle of identification. Today it can discharge a very good simulator as exactly equivalent to a "real" homosexual, a heart patient, or a madman. Even military psychology draws back from Cartesian certainties and hesitates to make the distinction between true and false, between the "produced" and the authentic symptom. "If he is this good at acting crazy, it's because he is." Nor is military psychology mistaken in this regard: in this sense, all crazy people simulate, and this lack of distinction is the worst kind of subversion. It is against this lack of distinction that classical reason armed itself in all its categories. But it is what today again outflanks them, submerging the principle of truth.

Beyond medicine and the army, favored terrains of simulation, the question returns to religion and the simulacrum of divinity: "I forbade that there be any simulacra in the temples because the divinity that animates nature can never be represented." Indeed it can be. But what becomes of the divinity when it reveals itself in icons, when it is multiplied in simulacra? Does it remain the supreme power that is simply incarnated in images as a visible theology? Or does it volatilize itself in the simulacra that, alone, deploy their power and pomp of fascination—the visible machinery of icons substituted for the pure and intelligible Idea of God? This is precisely what was feared by Iconoclasts, whose millennial quarrel is still with us today.[3] This is precisely because they predicted this omnipotence of simulacra, the faculty simulacra have of effacing God from the conscience of man, and the destructive, annihilating truth that they allow to appear—that deep down God never existed, that only the simulacrum ever existed, even that God himself was never anything but his own simulacrum—from this came their urge to destroy the images. If they could have believed that these images only obfuscated or masked the Platonic Idea of God, there would have been no reason to destroy them. One can live with the idea of distorted truth. But their metaphysical despair came from the idea that the image didn't conceal anything at all, and that these images were in essence not images, such as an original model would have made them, but perfect simulacra, forever radiant with their own fascination. Thus this death of the divine referential must be exorcised at all costs.

One can see that the iconoclasts, whom one accuses of disdaining and negating images, were those who accorded them their true value, in contrast to the iconolaters who only saw reflections in them and were content to venerate a filigree God. On the other hand, one can say that the icon worshipers were the most modern minds, the most adventurous, because, in the guise of having God become apparent in the mirror of images, they were already enacting his death and his disappearance in the epiphany of his representations (which, perhaps, they already knew no longer represented anything, that they were purely a game, but that it was therein the great game lay—knowing also that it is dangerous to unmask images, since they dissimulate the fact that there is nothing behind them).

This was the approach of the Jesuits, who founded their politics on the virtual disappearance of God and on the worldly and spectacular manipulation of consciences—the evanescence of God in the epiphany of power—the end of transcendence, which now only serves as an alibi for a strategy altogether free of influences and signs. Behind the baroqueness of images hides the éminence grise of politics.

This way the stake will always have been the murderous power of images, murderers of the real, murderers of their own model, as the Byzantine icons could be those of divine identity. To this murderous power is opposed that of representations as a dialectical power, the visible and intelligible mediation of the Real. All Western faith and good faith became engaged in this wager on representation: that a sign could refer to the depth of meaning, that a sign could be exchanged for meaning and that something could guarantee this exchange—God of course. But what if God himself can be simulated, that is to say can be reduced to the signs that constitute faith? Then the whole system becomes weightless, it is no longer itself anything but a gigantic simulacrum—not unreal, but a simulacrum, that is to say never exchanged for the real, but exchanged for itself, in an uninterrupted circuit without reference or circumference.

Such is simulation, insofar as it is opposed to representation. Representation stems from the principle of the equivalence of the sign and of the real (even if this equivalence is utopian, it is a fundamental axiom). Simulation, on the contrary, stems from the utopia of the principle of equivalence, *from the radical negation of the sign as value,* from the sign as the reversion and death sentence of every reference. Whereas representation attempts to absorb simulation by interpreting it as a false representation, simulation envelops the whole edifice of representation itself as a simulacrum.

Such would be the successive phases of the image:

it is the reflection of a profound reality;
it masks and denatures a profound reality;
it masks the *absence* of a profound reality;
it has no relation to any reality whatsoever: it is its own pure simulacrum.

In the first case, the image is a *good* appearance—representation is of the sacramental order. In the second, it is an evil appearance—it is of the order of maleficence. In the third, it plays at being an appearance—it is of the order of sorcery. In the fourth, it is no longer of the order of appearances, but of simulation.

The transition from signs that dissimulate something to signs that dissimulate that there is nothing marks a decisive turning point. The first reflects a theology of truth and secrecy (to which the notion of ideology still belongs). The second inaugurates the era of simulacra and of simulation, in which there is no longer a God to recognize his own, no longer a Last Judgment to separate the false from the true, the real from its artificial resurrection, as everything is already dead and resurrected in advance.

When the real is no longer what it was, nostalgia assumes its full meaning. There is a plethora of myths of origin and of signs of reality—a plethora of truth, of secondary objectivity, and authenticity. Escalation of the true, of lived experience, resurrection of the figurative where the object and substance have disappeared. Panic-stricken production of the real and of the referential, parallel to and greater than the panic of material production: this is how simulation appears in the phase that concerns us—a strategy of the real, of the neoreal and the hyperreal that everywhere is the double of a strategy of deterrence.

* * *

The Hyperreal and the Imaginary

Disneyland is a perfect model of all the entangled orders of simulacra. It is first of all a play of illusions and phantasms: the Pirates, the Frontier, the Future World, etc. This imaginary world is supposed to ensure the success of the operation. But what attracts the crowds the most is without a doubt the social microcosm, the *religious,* miniaturized pleasure of real America, of its constraints and joys. One parks outside and stands in line inside, one is altogether abandoned at the exit. The only phantasmagoria in this imaginary world lies in the tenderness and warmth of the crowd, and in the sufficient and excessive number of gadgets necessary to create the multitudinous effect. The contrast with the absolute solitude of the parking lot—a veritable concentration camp—is total. Or, rather: inside, a whole panoply of gadgets magnetizes the crowd in directed flows—outside, solitude is directed at a single gadget: the automobile. By an extraordinary coincidence (but this derives without a doubt from the enchantment inherent to this universe), this frozen, childlike world is found to have been conceived and realized by a man who is himself now cryogenized: Walt Disney, who awaits his resurrection through an increase of 180 degrees centigrade.

Thus, everywhere in Disneyland the objective profile of America, down to the morphology of individuals and of the crowd, is drawn. All its values are exalted by the miniature and the comic strip. Embalmed and pacified. Whence the possibility of an ideological analysis of Disneyland (L. Marin did it very well in *Utopiques, jeux d'espace* [Utopias, play of space]): digest of the American way of life, panegyric of American values, idealized transposition of a contradictory reality. Certainly. But this masks something else and this "ideological" blanket functions as a cover for a *simulation of the third order:* Disneyland exists in order to hide that it is the "real" country, [illegible] erica that *is* Disneyland (a bit like prisons are there to hide [illegible] ial in its entirety, in its banal omnipresence, that is carceral). [illegible] resented as imaginary in order to make us believe that the [illegible] ereas all of Los Angeles and the America that surrounds it are no longer real, but belong to the hyperreal order and to the order of simulation. It is no longer a question of a false representation of reality (ideology) but of concealing the fact that the real is no longer real, and thus of saving the reality principle.

The imaginary of Disneyland is neither true nor false, it is a deterrence machine set up in order to rejuvenate the fiction of the real in the opposite camp. Whence the debility of this imaginary, its infantile degeneration. This world wants to be childish in order to make us believe that the adults are elsewhere, in the "real" world, and to conceal the fact that true childishness is everywhere—that it is that of the adults themselves who come here to act the child in order to foster illusions as to their real childishness.

Disneyland is not the only one, however. Enchanted Village, Magic Mountain, Marine World: Los Angeles is surrounded by these imaginary stations that feed reality, the energy of the real to a city whose mystery is precisely that of no longer being anything but a network of incessant, unreal circulation—a city of incredible proportions but without space, without dimension. As much as electrical and atomic power stations, as much as cinema studios, this city, which is no longer anything but an immense scenario and a perpetual pan shot, needs this old imaginary like a sympathetic nervous system made up of childhood signals and faked phantasms.

Disneyland: a space of the regeneration of the imaginary as waste-treatment plants are elsewhere, and even here. Everywhere today one must recycle waste, and the dreams, the phantasms, the historical, fairylike, legendary imaginary of children and adults is a waste product, the first great toxic excrement of a hyperreal civilization. On a mental level, Disneyland is the prototype of this new function. But all the sexual, psychic, somatic recycling institutes, which proliferate in California, belong to the same order. People no longer look at each other, but there are institutes for that. They no longer touch each other, but there is contactotherapy. They no longer walk, but they go jogging, etc. Everywhere one recycles lost faculties, or lost bodies, or lost sociality, or the lost taste for food. One reinvents penury, asceticism, vanished savage naturalness: natural food, health food, yoga. Marshall Sahlins's idea that it is the economy of the market, and not of nature at all, that secretes penury, is verified, but at a secondary level: here, in the sophisticated confines of a triumphal market economy is reinvented a penury/sign, a penury/simulacrum, a simulated behavior of the underdeveloped (including the adoption of Marxist tenets) that, in the guise of ecology, of energy crises and the critique of capital, adds a final esoteric aureole to the triumph of an esoteric culture. Nevertheless, maybe a mental catastrophe, a mental implosion and involution without precedent lies in wait for a system of this kind, whose visible signs would be those of this strange obesity, or the incredible coexistence of the most bizarre theories and practices, which correspond to the improbable coalition of luxury, heaven, and money, to the improbable luxurious materialization of life and to undiscoverable contradictions.

Notes

1. Cf. J. Baudrillard, "L'ordre des simulacres" (The order of simulacra), in *L'échange symbolique et la mort* (Symbolic exchange and death) (Paris: Gallimard, 1976).
2. A discourse that is itself not susceptible to being resolved in transference. It is the entanglement of these two discourses that renders psychoanalysis interminable.
3. Cf. M. Perniola, *Icônes, visions, simulacres* (Icons, visions, simulacra), 39.

Translated by Sheila Faria Glaser
1981

TERRY HARPOLD
b. 1959

Terry Harpold is assistant professor of literature, communication, and culture at the Georgia Institute of Technology. He is the author of *Links and Their Vicissitudes: Essays on Hypertext* (1998).

Conclusions

In conclusion

"I want to say," says a character named Peter, somewhere in the course of Michael Joyce's hypertext fiction, *afternoon, a story,* "I want to say I may have seen my son die this morning" {I want to say}.[1] The problem is, he isn't sure; he doesn't want to be sure; he can't be sure. Like many hypertexts, *afternoon* appears to begin *in medias res,* sometime after a pivotal encounter. On his way to work, Peter has witnessed a fatal automobile accident that might have involved his former wife and their son. But the apparent false start is a trick of the genre: *afternoon* is bound to a different model of narrative closure than the epic mode from which it borrows the cast of its opening lines.[2] Starting in the middle of a hypertext does not mean that there is an "earlier" beginning to which you may be able to return, even if making sense of everything else in the narrative depends upon it. The 539 lexias in *afternoon* include no description of the accident or of Peter's reaction as he drives by it. We have only his troubled memory of the scene that might have been and the complex trajectory of his efforts to discover—or avoid—what it is that he has seen, what it is that he remembers. When he returns to the site of the accident sometime later (when, exactly, is not clear, as the "before" and "after" of the moment are entangled by his inability to recall now what it was that he saw then), there are only the skid marks of a crashing car, the cigarette butts and footprints left by onlookers, and a shifting pile of newspapers, candy wrappers, and children's homework.

> Most of the papers are old and waterstained, dried by the sun into yellowing things. There is a fresh white paper with my son's name upon it, and red markings from a teacher. It is a report on Louis Quattorze [*sic*], and his looping handwriting makes me weep.
>
> It begins: "I am the Sun King," said Louis the Fourteenth of France. (*afternoon,* {Fenceline})

The school report might be evidence that Peter's son was in the accident; it might simply have been dropped, with the other flotsam and jetsam trailed by his classmates on their journey home. You can work your way through *afternoon* a half-dozen times without learning any more. There is more to say about the accident—we will return to this scene of failed memory—but the thing that impresses you on the second or third reading of *afternoon* is that coming to a conclusion about what might have happened, while still appearing to be possible, seems as unlikely as it did on the first reading. What you make of what you read is confined to the interval in Peter's recollection that divides his account of what he has seen from his desire to make it actual, present, real. You have only scraps of paper, the traces of departed observers, the evidence of lexias reviewed repeatedly, the familiar shapes of darkened pixels against the blank field of the screen, suggesting with each recurrence that there is something more to be said. You could spend a long time deciphering the looping traces of this misremembered history.

Saying this, I concede, is not saying much more than: *afternoon* is a narrative, albeit a very fragmentary and unruly one (at least by the standards of printed texts), and narratives are always *told,* after the fact. We can only conjecture the existence of things before they were folded into the shroud of language: speech divides us from its objects, even as it makes them known to us. Saying that our readings of *afternoon* are divided in this way is saying that it thus resembles other artifacts of language: diverted from their objective (the re-presentation of the thing, so spoken) by the insufficiencies of the instrument (language) used to attain that goal—though this disjunction between the thing and the sign will be constituted or sustained differently within different species of discourse. *Afternoon* is a digital text and thus disposed to formulate this missed encounter in ways that would be impossible or unlikely in printed texts.

Afternoon was published as a Readingspace, a read-only format for Storyspace, the hypertext application in which the text was composed. A Readingspace hypertext displays one lexia on the screen at a time, in a single, fixed window (Figure 1). The user switches between lexias by clicking on buttons of a "toolbar" that floats over the window, or by double-clicking on words within a lexia or typing the same words in a text field, or by pressing

fenceline

Here there is a catch place, a low wire fence along a ditch which snatches what the wind wafts. Among candy wrappers, newspaper pages, and oak leaves, there are children's schoolpapers, evidently blown free from the knapsacks and backpacks of the children from the County Day School, some who walk along this road on their way home.

Most of the papers are old and waterstained, dried by the sun into yellowing things. There is a fresh white paper with my son's name upon it, and red markings from a teacher. It is a report on Louis Quattorze, and his looping handwriting makes me weep.

It begins: "I am the Sun King," said King Louis the Fourteenth of France.

Figure 1 {Fenceline}
(From afternoon, *©1990 Michael Joyce. Published by Eastgate Systems, Inc. Used by permission.)*

the Return key. There are four buttons on the toolbar: a left arrow, which takes you to the previously-viewed lexia; a "Browse" button, resembling a book, that opens a dialog listing available "paths" (collections of links with shared labels) from the current lexia; and "Y[es]" and "N[o]" buttons. The "Yes" and "No" buttons are used to respond to questions ("Do you want to hear about it?" asks the first lexia of the text, called {Begin}), or to change the current lexia, though no indication is given of where one or the other response will lead. Pressing the Return key is the same as clicking on the "Yes" button. The list of paths displayed by clicking on the Browse button is less informative than it might at first appear, as only the names of paths and the lexias they connect are listed. These are often cryptic or repetitive, and seldom suggest much about the content of the target lexia (Figure 2).

Words within lexias that lead to other lexias (Joyce calls them "words that yield") are not identified by any distinguishing style or symbol.[3] There may be more than one such word in a lexia, and different yield words in the same lexia sometimes lead to one target lexia. In some cases, where a yield word leads depends on the sequence of lexias that have previously been visited. *Afternoon* makes heavy use of Storyspace's "guard" function, which places hidden restrictions on the reader's movements, making it impossible to visit some lexias until a specified sequence of other lexias has been followed. Jane Yellowlees Douglas has calculated that *afternoon*'s use of guards makes it unlikely that most readers will, in only one or two readings, visit more than 10% of the lexias in the text ("Print Pathways," ch. 3).

Superficially, *afternoon* resembles the sword-and-sorcery, gumshoe detective, Star Trekking recreations that have heretofore dominated the field of interactive gaming. What distinguishes Joyce's novel from that crowd is its sly resistance to readers' efforts to draw inferences from what they have

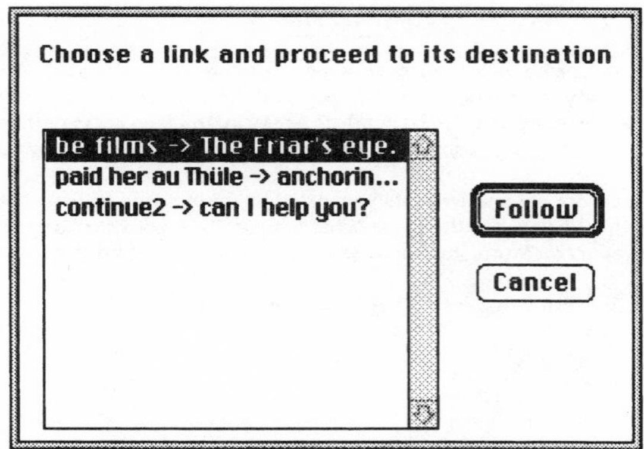

Figure 2 The Storyspace Browser
(From afternoon, *©1990 Michael Joyce. Published by Eastgate Systems, Inc. Used by permission.)*

read before. As Stuart Moulthrop observes, the suppleness of the yield mechanism makes all the difference:

> With this system in operation, *afternoon* resembles an automated railway in which the points keep switching of their own accord. Since the story is heavily recursive, readers may find themselves frequently returning to the same textual locales; but a yield word that took them from "son" to "Sun King" on the first iteration may now lead somewhere else entirely. ("Hypertext and 'the Hyperreal'," 263)

Reading the text, you move between episodes along paths that are not always marked. You make decisions, you choose directions and form conclusions, finding the next time through that they may lead you somewhere else. You may, very nearly, read differently every time you open the document. The cunning of a text like *afternoon* lies in the limit of that "very nearly": each reading can't be unique—the 539 lexias and 950-odd links define a finite domain—except in a "citable" or "iterable" sense (to invoke Derrida's use of those terms) that has less to do with singularity than with a loss of originality. Very nearly: it is possible to saturate the field of readings, at least in a serviceable, quotidian sense; and so you may repeat a reading, hoping to find the path between lexias that will close a question left open by a prior reading. But the possibilities need not be endless to be exhausting; your patience or your curiosity may not be a match for the text's erratic calculus, and the principle of contingent repeatability is sufficient in and of itself to block some conclusions.

Douglas has, for example, identified four independent constellations of lexias in *afternoon;* it is possible to read the fiction from within each of these constellations and not be aware of the position or significance of a given lexia in the other constellations ("Print Pathways," ch. 5). Moulthrop's *Victory Garden* includes nearly a thousand lexias and twenty-eight hundred links; it is possible to follow paths in that fiction for dozens of lexias, to independent closures, without coming across evidence that the text supports completely different paths joining the same lexias. That you might *not* discover what you are looking for means that familiar strategies of discovery may always prove unreliable, and you might have to try again. "*afternoon* is a 'mystery,' " says Moulthrop, "only in the older sense of that word, the sense of ritual or hieratic procedure" ("Hypertext and 'the Hyperreal,' " 262).

In other words, in a text like *afternoon* it is possible only to arrive at a *contingent* conclusion. Any ending will be marked by the punctuality of interruption. (Thus the purest paradigm of a hypertext ending: you can just stop reading, decide that you have had enough, get up from the computer and walk away.) But you can't come to a definitive ending *within the universe of the text.* "Closure is, as in any fiction, a suspect quality," says an unnamed voice in a lexia of *afternoon* entitled {Work in Progress},

> although here it is made manifest. When the story no longer progresses, or when it cycles, or when you tire of the paths, the experience of reading it ends. Even so, there are likely to be more opportunities than you think there are at first. A word which doesn't yield the first time you read a section may take you elsewhere if you choose it when you encounter the section again; and sometimes what seems a loop, like memory, heads off again in another direction.

The excess of possible trajectories means that you cannot quite be sure of where you are going, just as you may never be sure of where you have been. Readings of hypertexts are always subject to misadventure: the possibility that you might end up at a different destination from the one you intended overdetermines every turn you take. The presumed directionality of a hypertext link—instrument, signpost, and phylactery of the reading-as-navigation model—is always supplemented by the link's potential for *misdirection;* the chance encounters of reading always *may* redefine the route you thought you were following; narrative turns between lexias (however many times you revisit them) may be indeterminate or inconsistent . . .

This general possibility of an alternative is, paradoxically, contradicted by the consistency of the text's presentation. The interface of a hypertext suggests a metanarrative frame of purposiveness and utility, the possibility that the terrain traversed by our readings can be mapped, can be modeled by software and replayed in successive visits to a window, a menubar, a button. Jakob Nielsen, a leading theorist of hypertext usability, has observed that hypertexts are widely understood to describe underlying "belief networks": if two lexias are linked, then we believe that they must be related in some way (*Hypertext and Hypermedia,* 140). Virginia M. Doland has noted that the expectation on the part of readers that links *should* represent well-founded semantic relations may, when paired with implicit ideological content in a hypertext, have a deterministic effect on their abilities to discern which kind of connection is to be made: "All connections are critical/ideological statements of value, importance, relationship. Thus, it is not possible to create a critically neutral set of linkages because the act of linking involves an assertion of relationship and meaning" ("Hypermedia as an Interpretive Act," 17).

Like readings of other kinds of texts, readings of hypertexts are sustained by a pledge of meaningful resolution that appears to be anchored in the artifact (in its reference) or in its commerce (the conversation between an other and the reader). This is the contractual obligation presupposed by all narratives: an implicit question from the reader is directed to an other in possession of some thing presumed to guarantee the convergence of the narrative's substance and signification.[4] Moving onward, you have faith that you will return to a conclusion, guided by the voice of one who remembers where you have been and where you are going. By recognizing yourself as the potential addressee of the reply from the absent other who would spell out the text's truth, you seal your subordination to the other's demand that you engage it in the conversation upon which its authority rests. The question "Do you want to hear about it?" will always elicit a response; whether you elect to answer yes or no, you must recognize the other's authority in the first place to demand that you respond. In *afternoon,* choosing "Yes" to the first query takes you to a lexia entitled "Yes"; choosing "No" takes you to another entitled "No." Neither choice frees you from the burden of deciding what to do next, or from the consequences of your enforced response.

You must come to a conclusion, even though the text's possible productivity, its memory of events that might have happened or might yet occur, will not be exhausted.

> In my mind, the story, as it has formed, takes on margins. Each margin will yield to the impatient, or wary reader. You can answer yes at the beginning and page through on a wave of Returns, or page through directly—again using Returns—without that first interaction.
>
> There are not versions, but the story itself in long lines. Otherwise, however, the center is all—Thoreau or Brer Rabbit, each preferred the bramble. I've discovered more there too, and the real interaction, if that is possible, is in the pursuit of texture. (*afternoon,* {In my mind})

Going no place

. . . One of the conspicuous traits of hypertextual form is the absence of clear structural cues distinguishing a "primary" text from secondary or peripheral texts—the elements (footnotes, chapter titles, page numbers, marginal scribbles) that frame a printed text and describe its limits. Most hypertext applications allow you to open multiple windows on different sections of a document, or on different documents. Though typically only one window reacts to the keyboard or mouse at any one time, all or part of every window is visible at the same time.[5] Moreover, most hypertexts use a browser or similar navigational tool to display document structure in an outline, "overview," or "map" format; you can use the browser to switch between lexias that otherwise lack navigational links or cues. The increased immediacy and variety of movement within hypertexts, in comparison to printed texts, introduces a qualitative as well as quantitative change in the perceptual plane of reading: interrupting a sequence of lexias with the click of a mouse or the press of a key does not *feel* the same as flipping to the table of contents or to the back of a volume to find a note or check an index entry. The suddenness of the transition suppresses your awareness that you have moved between blocks of text that would on paper be inches, pages, or shelves apart, as opposed to, say, only a paragraph, or a turned page away. The possibility of an interactive shuffling of lexias within a narrative forces you to change another expectation learned from printed texts: the order of the lexias (which in a hypertext may be subject to unpredictable variety) is no longer a reliable indicator of hierarchies of argument or plot development.

Distinctions between textual registers that are meaningful in print collapse into a single measure: the pause between lexias, more a function of program efficiency or microprocessor speed than of the "distance" between destinations. The link (the place or moment of a turn) marks a boundary between lexias in two ways: at the level of the interface, it is the irreducible, concrete signature of a pause; it is as really "there" as the letters on the screen "really" describe the textual fields they represent. Phenomenologically, it traces a pure interval, spatiality deferred in time, displacement as dis-place-ment. Reading across the link introduces a discontinuity that cannot be accounted for in spatial models of the text's narrative structure, a point of singularity where everything that came "before" is changed in ways that cannot be predicted prior to that rupture. The passage between lexias marks a "pure act," in Slavoj Zizek's sense of that term:

> The act differs from an active intervention (action) in that it radically transforms its bearer (agent): the act is not simply something I "accomplish"—after the act I'm literally "not the same as before." . . . The act is defined by the irreducible *risk:* in its most fundamental dimension, it is always *negative,* i.e., an act of annihilation, of wiping out—we not only don't know what will come out of it, its final outcome is ultimately even insignificant, strictly secondary in relation to the NO! of the pure act . . . With an act, *stricto sensu,* we can therefore never fully foresee its consequences, i.e., the way it will transform the existing symbolic space: the act is a rupture after which "nothing remains the same." Which is why, although History can always be explained, accounted for, afterward, we can never, as its agents, caught in its flow, foresee its course in advance: we cannot do it insofar as it is not an "objective process" but a process continuously interrupted by the scansion of acts. (*Enjoy Your Symptom!,* 44–46)

The link assumes its conventional function as a marker of the lexial intersection only insofar as it concretizes (fixes, petrifies) the disjunctions between lexias. It measures their retrospective interpretation and anchors the reader's position in relation to the promise of closure—naming the memorable "where" of the irreducible "when" of the break. "Here is the truth," begins a lexia in Joyce's *WOE: A memory of what will be,*

> though you will never know this for certain: all day long this window you now read stood empty (open for awhile with the [Macintosh II] cx on, then sleeping in some data structure when it seemed there would be thunderstorms, before the haze burned off and the jungle heat of Michigan overcame me—it is Sunday June 17, 1990, Father's Day as we've already noted, yesterday the second number of the first volume of *Writing on the Edge* arrived in the mail, I do not own issue one, though I have cited Stuart's article from it, and this story itself somehow grows from that commissioned work which, if all goes well, you read now in some future number (there was talk of 5) of *WOE* [that last the name I've given this document temporarily on the cx] <History is hard to bracket at the depth it requires>)}].

Shandean digressions of this sort are common in hypertext writing. You cannot write or read in this environment without ending up writing or reading to the moment. And the more you consider the temporality of the moment, the tighter the recursion of your memory of it. Closure is always fixed afterward, *après-coup, Nachträglichkeit.* The historicity of digital narrative is hard to bracket because the disjunctive rhythms of its signifiers can easily mislead you about the when of writing and reading. And the irreducible slices of deferral between the lexias, stretching in a series of cuts from a beginning (after the fact) to an ending (possibly before you get to a conclusion) will always claim their portion from you, always demand a certainty that you may never possess . . .

I want to say

Let's finish by returning to *afternoon.* As I noted earlier, you can move through the lexias of *afternoon* by pressing the Return key at each new screen of text, that is, by responding with the default "yes" to the implicit question posed by the opening of each lexia, the repetition of the explicit question of the initial lexia, "Do you want to hear about it?" Doing this takes you through 36 lexias (and the beginning of Peter's efforts to remember what he saw on the way to work or to discover some evidence that will help him to remember), before dead-ending in a lexia entitled, {I call}, where Peter decides not to begin phoning local hospitals but rather to call someone named Lolly. You know the path ends here because pressing the Return key does not take you anywhere else, and the computer stubbornly beeps at you every time you try to move onward.

You do not, however, know who Lolly is, and you do not know much about anyone else who has made an appearance in this, the most restricted sequence of lexias in the text. You could stop reading here, refusing after a single audience the text's promise that it has more to say. Or, you could go back to the beginning and start again. And, perhaps, several times after that, or at least until your patience or curiosity is exhausted, each time varying your responses—choosing "No" instead of "Yes" or clicking on different words that seem likely to yield. (*Every* click yields, so you cannot be sure that the word you clicked, rather than the lexia as a whole, was linked to the click's destination.) Subsequent readings will appear to reveal more about the characters of the fiction and the sequence of events on the morning and afternoon of the day Peter calls Lolly, who is, you may discover, a sometimes therapist married to Peter's boss. It is precisely because each reading *may* disclose some new particle of information that will appear to saturate the text with meaning, to guarantee the possibility of coming to a conclusion, that the reader feels compelled to return. Douglas's report of her experience of reading *afternoon* is instructive in this regard:

> Instead of narrowing the margins of the narrative the farther I read, *afternoon* considerably broadens them. Where the number of probable and plausible narrative outcomes conventionally progressively [*sic*] dwindles in print narratives the nearer we approach their ending, the more of the narrative we read in interactive narratives the more these

> seem to multiply . . . In one version [of *afternoon*] the accident seems not to have occurred; in another, Wert [Peter's boss] distracts Peter from his fears about the fates of ex-wife and child with bawdy suggestions. In one scenario, only Peter is having an affair with Nausicaa [a co-worker]; in another, Wert knows both that he and Peter are having an affair with Nausicaa and that Peter is blissfully ignorant of Nausicaa's involvement with him. In one version of the scene, Wert idly wonders aloud how Peter would react if he, Wert, were sleeping with Peter's ex-wife; in another, Wert is testing the extent of Peter's ignorance of his involvement with Peter's ex-wife. While my readings of all these versions are physically possible, I cannot accept all of them simultaneously in my final understanding of the events described in *afternoon*. ("Print Pathways," ch. 5)

Douglas records spending three years reading and re-reading Joyce's text and coming to a conclusion about what happened the morning of the afternoon of the phone call ("Understanding the Act of Reading: The *WOE* Beginner's Guide to Dissection," 117). She extracts from her readings four (sometimes contradictory) versions of the story told in *afternoon*. The fourth and conclusive version depends on her discovery of three lexias linked to {I call}, entitled {1/}, {2/}, and {white afternoon} (Figure 3). These suggest that (1) Peter is concerned for the whereabouts of his ex-wife and son *before* he drives to work; (2) while driving to work, he may have seen them riding with Wert, and the shock of recognizing that his boss's offhand comment about having an affair with his ex-wife may not have been in jest causes Peter to briefly lose control of his car, resulting in another car crashing to avoid his; (3) the car that crashes is the one in which his ex-wife and son were riding: Peter may have been responsible for the death of his ex-wife and son. Douglas asks,

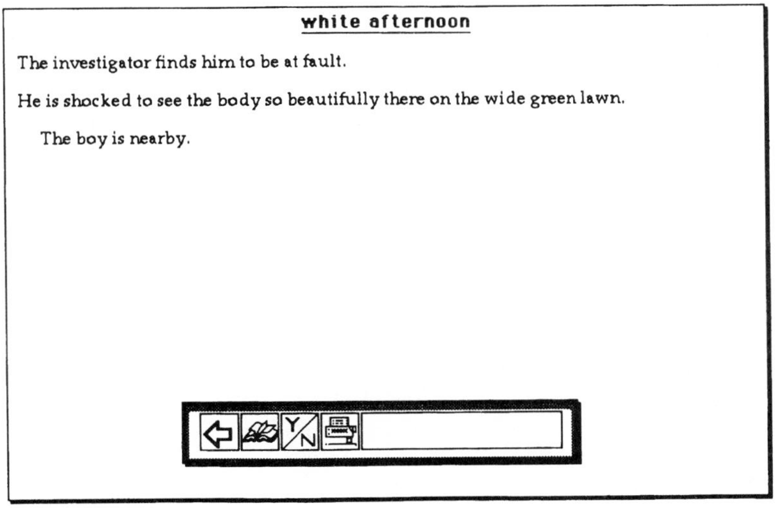

white afternoon

The investigator finds him to be at fault.

He is shocked to see the body so beautifully there on the wide green lawn.

The boy is nearby.

Figure 3 *White afternoon*
(From afternoon, *©1990 Michael Joyce. Published by Eastgate Systems, Inc. Used by permission.)*

> What, precisely, triggered my sense of having come to some sort of closure, my sense that I did not need to continue reading *afternoon*? Most obviously, I became conscious of my readings having satisfied one of the primary quests outlined in the narrative: what has happened to Peter's ex-wife and child? Although my discovery that Peter has caused the accident is not entirely congruent with his desire to learn of their condition, it does short-circuit Peter's quest. Since Peter himself has caused the accident, clearly, he knows whether the pair is unharmed, fatally injured, or already dead. The language in the place {white afternoon} suggests the last possibility may be the most valid: "The investigator finds him to be at fault. He is shocked to see the body . . . on the wide green lawn. The boy is nearby." The word "body" may signify that the woman Peter sees is lifeless, but it could also refer to the fact that she is unconscious, inert, quantifiable as an accident victim. ("Print Pathways," ch. 5)

On the contrary, I would suggest that the key to the apparent conclusiveness of the {white afternoon} reading is not that it represents, to use Douglas's terms, "a resolution which accounts for the greatest number of ambiguities in the narrative" or "the most *plausible* conclusion to the narrative's network of mysteries and tensions" (ch. 5). *It is rather the raw, irreducible inertness of the woman's body that establishes closure in the {white afternoon} reading.* The body and the discarded report on Louis Quatorze (which Douglas takes as evidence of the boy's death) represent the missing thing that appears to bring the story to an end. They mark the literal dead end of the narrative, an appalling fragment broken off from its fabric: the position of the stupid, real object at the focus of the reader's pursuit of closure. As such, they appear to confirm the promise of fullness and saturability (within the fiction of *prosopopoeia*) invoked by our first response to the opening question: "Do you want to hear about it?"

With regard to this object, Peter's phone call to Lolly assumes a specific value of corroboration. In the reading from evidence, the call can be interpreted, as Douglas suggests, as an effort to find someone who can help Peter remember and help relieve him of his feelings of guilt—Lolly is a therapist. Or, I would counter, it can be read more generally, as a call to the other to recognize the value of the reader's (of Peter's) sacrifice, and thus to guarantee the closure for which that sacrifice is offered. Peter calls Lolly as if to ask, "Is this the thing I want to find? Is this the thing I want to say? *Is this the thing you want me to say?*" The appeal to Lolly's guarantee can only lead nowhere, returning Peter (and the reader) to the immovable kernel of impossible closure. Could there be a more fitting signifier for the pure object-cause of desire than the idiotic beep of the computer that sounds every time you press the Return key? Is this not exactly what you were looking for when you replied "Yes, tell me about it" in the first place?

The idiotic beep has another function as well, on the level of interface: it is the purest signal that our response to the question, "Do you want to hear about it?" can have meaning; it is a recognition from the other that there is an anchor in the Symbolic to which we may tie our desire to have read the text. As such, it corresponds in inverted form to what Zizek calls, in an allusion to Hitchcock, the "MacGuffin" of our relation to the other:

"its meaning is purely self-referential, it amounts to the fact that the subjects involved in the narrative ascribe a meaning to it" ("I doubt," 47n14). Strictly speaking, the Hitchcockian MacGuffin gets the story going, it is the hook upon which the characters hang their (mis)understanding of what has taken place before the story begins—as Peter hangs his search in *afternoon* on the uncanny evidence of bodies witnessed briefly from a passing car window. For the reader, the narrative dead end can have the same effect, though it comes at the apparent end of the story: the purely arbitrary, reflexive signifier that is the beep sanctions the belief that meaning is possible, that a story *has been told.* This is, finally, where we locate the sense of an ending: in a point of no-sense, nonsense—a rude object that occupies the gap in the text we fill with sense.

The sordid secret of (hypertextual) dialogue with the other is that the Other itself ("big O", the field of the Symbolic) is inconsistent, lacking, capable of being held accountable. The rude object of an ending covers a gap, the awful spectacle of no end at all. The one who promises to know the truth of narrative is, as Zizek says, purely an impostor (*Enjoy Your Symptom!,* 103.) The link purports to be the index of the other's saturation (there is a story here, to be told to its conclusion); but it represents more correctly the blemish of the other's lack (there is a story here, but no guarantee that you will ever be satisfied that you have come to its conclusion.) *I want . . . to say.* A concealed copula joins the halves of the invocatory phrase that begins a story, soldering the irreducibility of lack to the divagation of narration, or, in another formulation, to the repeated act of beginning to read a narrative, of calling on it to fulfill its promise. Asking what it is you want to say is, in the end, asking the same of the other, who always *may not* be able to give you the answer you are nonetheless compelled to pursue: "tell me a story," you say. "Tell me what you want." "Tell me the thing you are *wanting.*"

Notes

1. For extended readings of *afternoon,* see Jay David Bolter, *Writing Space,* 123–30, George P. Landow, *Hypertext,* 113–19, and Jane Yellowlees Douglas, "Print Pathways," ch. 5. I am indebted to Douglas for generously sharing her reading notes.
2. *Afternoon* does not begin, in the usual sense of the term, with Peter's hesitant declaration. The first lexias that one encounters after opening *afternoon* make no mention of the accident, which enters the foreground of the narrative(s) only after about a dozen lexias have been viewed. My reasons for focusing on this "accidental" thread of *afternoon* should become clearer as this essay progresses, but I do not mean to suggest that this is the "central," "most important," or even "symptomatic" thread of the text—it is, in fact, because *afternoon* is a *hyper*text that such distinctions are highly problematic. There are other threads in *afternoon* that are arguably as significant to the progress and conclusion of the reader's interaction with the text; "what makes [an] event important," observes Bolter, "is that it is a structural crossroads: the intersection of many narrative paths" (*Writing Space,* 125). That most readers of *afternoon* are likely to conclude that it is mostly "about" the accident (I offer this observation based on anecdotal evidence, the comments of those with whom I have discussed Joyce's work) is, I suspect, a consequence of how *the accidental thread thematizes the disjunctions of its structure.* Other factors may come into play here: the affective value of the event (a father may have witnessed his son's death), or its mythic character (a *father,* his *son's* death, etc.)
3. Storyspace is unusual among hypertext authoring systems in that it does not force authors to mark the presence of links with special symbols or typefaces. The user's manual for the

program encourages the author to "choose [her] own approach" as to the appearance of links (Jay David Bolter, *et al., Getting Started with Storyspace,* 39), and Storyspace authors commonly leave links unmarked. Joyce's role in the development of Storyspace and his decision to not mark the links in *afternoon,* the *Ur*-text of the hypertext fiction boom of recent years, suggest that his preference for unmarked links has been decisive for the school of hypertext fiction that favors this method. The invisibility of links in *afternoon* is a crucial element in the coerciveness of the text's yield mechanism, in that it implicitly founds the field of authority of an other to whom the links are *not* invisible. This is reinforced by the interface gesture that permits the Storyspace user to see very briefly the location of links in the current lexia by holding down the Command and Option keys simultaneously (links are framed in gray rectangles as long as the keys are held down.) Peeking into the secret system of the text's narrative structure is another form of the petition to the other to guarantee eventual closure—though, significantly, the Page Reader format does not make links visible in this way.

4. Paul de Man identifies this implicit contract with the classical rhetorical figure of *prosopopoeia:* speech directed to an absent or deceased entity that elicits a reply, and confers an identity upon the absent interlocutor ("Autobiography as Defacement," 926) See Derrida's discussion of *prosopopoeia* in *Mémoires for Paul de Man,* where he explicitly situates it within the scene of narrative promise that I am evoking here: "Every reading finds itself caught, engaged precisely by the promise of saying the truth, by a promise which will have taken place with the very first word, within a scene of signature which is a scene of writing" (99).
5. *Afternoon's* single-window interface is unusual. Joyce's choice of the Page Reader format may have been determined by a decision to push a familiar compositional model—in the typographic sense of the term—to its extremes. He began writing *afternoon* as a test of the features of Storyspace when the program was in the first stages of development (Douglas, "Print Pathways," ch. 3), and the Readingspace format in which the text was published by Eastgate Press in 1987 used a late beta version of software. More recent complex fictions written in Storyspace (Joyce's *WOE,* Guyer and Petry's *Izme Pass,* Moulthrop's *Victory Garden*) have relied primarily on the program's multiple-window, topographically-organized readers.

Bibliography

Bolter, Jay David. *Writing Space: The Computer, Hypertext, and the History of Writing.* Hillsdale, NJ: Lawrence Erlbaum, 1991.

Bolter, Jay David, *et al. Getting Started with Storyspace.* Cambridge, MA: Eastgate Systems, Inc., 1993.

De Man, Paul. "Autobiography as De-facement." *MLN* 94 (1979): 919–30.

Derrida, Jacques. *Mémoires for Paul de Man.* Trans. Cecile Lindsay, Jonathan Culler, and Eduardo Cadava. New York: Columbia University Press, 1986.

Doland, Virginia M. "Hypermedia as an Interpretive Act." *Hypermedia* 1 (1989): 6–19.

Douglas, Jane Yellowlees. "Gaps, Maps and Perception: What Hypertext Readers (Don't) Do." *Perforations* 3 (1992).

———. "Print Pathways and Interactive Labyrinths: How Hypertext Narratives Affect the Act of Reading." Diss. New York University, 1992.

———. "Understanding the Act of Reading: The *WOE* Beginner's Guide to Dissection." *Writing on the Edge* 2.2 (1991): 112–25.

Guyer, Carolyn, and Martha Petry. *Izme Pass. Writing on the Edge* 2.2 (1991).

Joyce, Michael. *afternoon, a story.* Version 1.0. Cambridge, MA: Eastgate Systems, 1990.

———. "A Feel for Prose: Interstitial Links and the Contours of Hypertext." *Writing on the Edge* 4.1 (1992): 83–101.

———. *WOE: A memory of what will be. Writing on the Edge* 2.2 (1991).

Moulthrop, Stuart. "Hypertext and 'the Hyperreal'." *Hypertext '89.* Pittsburgh, PA: Association for Computing Machinery, 1989. 259–67.

———. *Victory Garden.* Version 1.0. Cambridge, MA: Eastgate Systems, 1991.

Nielsen, Jakob. *Hypertext and Hypermedia.* San Diego, CA: Academic Press, 1990.

Zizek, Slavoj. *Enjoy Your Symptom!* New York: Routledge, 1992.

———. " 'I Doubt, Therefore I am,' or, the Precipitous Identification." *Newsletter of the Freudian Field* 6.1–2 (1994): 34–48.

1994, rev. 1996

TRINH T. MINH-HA
b. 1952

Trinh T. Minh-ha is a filmmaker, composer, social theorist, and writer. Her work includes the book *Woman, Native, Other: Writing Postcoloniality and Feminism* (1989) and the films *Reassemblage* (1982), *Naked Spaces—Living is Round* (1985), and *Surname Viet, Given Name Nam* (1989). Currently she teaches at San Francisco State University.

From Woman, Native, Other

Infinite layers: I am not i can be you and me

A critical difference from myself means that I am not i, am within and without i. I/i can be I or i, you and me both involved. We (with capital W) sometimes include(s), other times exclude(s) me. You and I are close, we intertwine; you may stand on the other side of the hill once in a while, but you may also be me, while remaining what you are and what i am not. The differences made *between* entities comprehended as absolute presences—hence the notions of *pure origin* and *true* self—are an outgrowth of a dualistic system of thought peculiar to the Occident (the "onto-theology" which characterizes Western metaphysics). They should be distinguished from the differences grasped *both between* and *within* entities, each of these being understood as multiple presence.[1] Not One, not two either. "I" is, therefore, not a unified subject, a fixed identity, or that solid mass covered with layers of superficialities one has gradually to peel off before one can see its true face. "I" is, itself, *infinite layers.* Its complexity can hardly be conveyed through such typographic conventions as I, i, or I/i. Thus, I/i am compelled by the will to say/unsay, to resort to the entire gamut of personal pronouns to stay near this fleeing *and* static essence of Not-I. Whether I accept it or not, the natures of *I, i, you, s/he, We, we, they,* and *wo/man* constantly overlap. They all display a necessary ambivalence, for the line dividing *I* and *Not-I, us* and *them,* or *him* and *her* is not (cannot) always (be) as clear as we would like it to be. Despite our desperate, eternal attempt to separate, contain, and mend, categories always leak. Of all the layers that form the open (never finite) totality of "I," which is to be filtered out as superfluous, fake, corrupt, and which is to be called pure, true, real, genuine, original, authentic? Which, indeed, since all interchange, revolving in an endless process? (According to the context in which they operate, the superfluous can become the real; the authentic can prove fake; and so on.) *Authenticity* as a need to rely on an "undisputed origin," is prey to an obsessive *fear:* that of *losing a connection.* Everything must hold together. In my craving for a logic of being, I cannot help but loathe the threats of interruptions, disseminations, and suspensions. To begin, to develop to a climax, then, to end. To fill, to join, to unify. The order and the links create an illusion of continuity, which I highly prize for fear of nonsense and emptiness. Thus, a clear origin will give me a connection back through time, and I shall, by all means, search for that genuine layer of myself to which I can always cling. To abolish it in such a perspective is to remove the basis, the prop, the overture, or the finale—giving thereby free rein to indeterminancy: the result, forefeared, is either an anarchic succession of climaxes or a de(inex)pressive, uninterrupted monotony—and to enter into the limitless process of interactions and changes that nothing will stop, not even death. In other words, things may be said to be what they are, not exclusively in relation to what was and what will be (they should not solely be seen as clusters chained together by the temporal sequence of cause and effect), but also in relation to each other's immediate presences and to themselves as non/presences. The *real,* nothing else than a *code of representation,* does not (cannot) coincide with the lived or the performed. This is what Vine Deloria, Jr. accounts for when he exclaims: "Not even Indians can relate themselves to this type of creature who, to anthropologists, is the 'real' Indian."[2] A realistic identification with such a code has, therefore, no reality whatsoever: it is like "stopping the ear while trying to steal the bell" (Chinese saying).

* * *

The female identity enclosure

Difference as uniqueness or special identity is both limiting and deceiving. If identity refers to the whole pattern of sameness within a human life, the style of a continuing me that permeates all the changes undergone, then difference remains within the boundary of that which distinguishes one identity from another. This means that *at heart,* X must be X, Y must be Y, and X *cannot* be Y. Those who run around yelling that X is not X and X *can* be Y usually land in a hospital, a "rehabilitation" center, a concentration camp, or a res-er-va-tion. All deviations from the dominant stream of thought, that is to say, the belief in a permanent essence of wo/man and in an invariant but fragile identity, whose "loss" is considered to be a "specifically human danger," can easily fit into the categories of the "mentally ill" or the "mentally underdeveloped." It is probably difficult for a "normal," probing mind to recognize that to seek is to lose, for seeking presupposes a separation between the seeker and the sought, the continuing me and the changes it undergoes. What if the popularized story of the identity crisis proves to be only a story and nothing else? Can identity, indeed, be viewed other than as a by-product of a "manhandling" of life, one that, in fact, refers no more to a consistent "pattern of sameness" than to an inconsequential process of otherness? How am I to lose, maintain, or gain an (fe/male) identity when it is impossible to me to take up a position outside this identity from which I presumably reach in and feel for it? Perhaps a way to portray it is to borrow these verses from the *Cheng-tao-ke:*

> You cannot take hold of it,
> But you cannot lose it.
> In not being able to get it, you get it.
> When you are silent, it speaks;
> When you speak, it is silent.[3]

Difference in such an insituable context is *that which undermines the very idea of identity*, deferring to infinity the layers whose totality forms "I." It subverts the foundations of any affirmation or vindication of value and cannot, thereby, ever bear in itself an absolute value. The difference (within) between *difference* itself and *identity* has so often been ignored and the use of the two terms so readily confused, that claiming a female/ethnic identity/difference is commonly tantamount to reviving a kind of naïve "male-tinted" romanticism. If feminism is set forth as a demystifying force, then it will have to question thoroughly the belief in its own identity. To suppose, like Judith Kegan Gardiner, that "the concept of female identity provides a key to understanding the *special qualities* of contemporary writing by women . . ., the diverse ways in which writing by women *differs* from writing by men," and to "propose the preliminary metaphor 'female identity is a process' for the most fundamental of these differences" does not, obviously, allow us to radically depart from the master's logic. Such a formulation endeavors to "reach a theory of female identity . . . that *varies from the male model*," and to demonstrate that:

> primary identity for women is more flexible and relational *than for men*. Female gender identity is *more* stable *than male gender identity*. Female infantile identifications are *less* predictable *than male ones* . . . the *female counterpart* of the male identity crisis may occur more diffusely, at a different stage, or not at all. (my italics)

It seems quite content with reforms that, at best, contribute to the improvement and/or enlargement of the identity enclosure, but do not, in any way, attempt to remove its fence. The constant need to refer to the "male model" for comparisons unavoidably maintains the subject under tutelage. For the point is not to carve one's space in "identity theories that ignore women" and describe some of the faces of female identity, saying, like Gardiner: "I picture female identity as typically less fixed, less unitary, and more flexible than male individuality, both in its primary core and in the entire maturational complex developed from this core,"[4] but patiently to dismantle the very notion of core (be it static or not) and identity.

Woman can never be defined. Bat, dog, chick, mutton, tart. Queen, madam, lady of pleasure. MISTRESS. *Belle-de-nuit*, woman of the streets, fruitwoman, fallen woman. Cow, vixen, bitch. Call girl, joy girl, working girl. Lady and whore are both bred to please. The old Woman image-repertoire says She is a Womb, a mere baby's pouch, or "nothing but sexuality." She is a passive substance, a parasite, an enigma whose mystery proves to be a snare and a delusion. She wallows in night, disorder, and immanence and is at the same time the "disturbing factor (between men)" and the key to the beyond. The further the repertoire unfolds its images, the more entangled it gets in its attempts at capturing Her. "Truth, Beauty, Poetry—she is All: once more all under the form of the Other. All except herself,"[5] Simone De Beauvoir wrote. Yet, even with or because of Her capacity to embody All, Woman is the lesser man, and among male athletes, to be called a woman is still resented as the worst of insults. "Wo-" appended to "man" in sexist contexts is not unlike "Third World," "Third," "minority," or *"color"* affixed to *woman* in pseudo-feminist contexts. Yearning for universality, the generic "woman," like its counterpart, the generic "man," tends to efface difference within itself. Not every female is "a real woman," one knows this through hearsay . . . Just as "man" provides an example of how the part played by women has been ignored, undervalued, distorted, or omitted through the use of terminology presumed to be generic, "woman" more often than not reflects the subtle power of linguistic exclusion, for its set of referents rarely includes those relevant to Third World "female persons." "All the Women Are White, All the Blacks are Men, But Some of Us Are Brave" is the title given to an anthology edited by Gloria T. Hull, Patricia Bell Scott, and Barbara Smith. It is, indeed, somehow devious to think that WOMAN also encompasses the Chinese with bound feet, the genitally mutilated Africans, and the one thousand Indians who committed *suttee* for one royal male. Sister Cinderella's foot is also enviably tiny but never crooked! And, European witches were also burnt to purify the body of Christ, but they do not pretend to "self-immolation." "Third World," therefore, belongs to a category apart, a "special" one that is meant to be both complimentary and complementary, for First and Second went out of fashion, leaving a serious Lack behind to be filled.

* * *

IV. Grandma's Story

> *See all things howsoever they flourish*
> *Return to the root from which they grew*
> *This return to the root is called Quietness*
> —Lao Tzu, *Tao-te-ching*, 16 (tr. A. Waley)

Truth and fact: story and history

Let me tell you a story. For all I have is a story. Story passed on from generation to generation, named Joy. Told for the joy it gives the storyteller and the listener. Joy inherent in the process of storytelling. Whoever understands it also understands that a story, as distressing as it can be in its joy, never takes anything away from anybody. Its name, remember, is Joy. Its double, Woe Morrow Show.

> Let the one who is diseuse, one who is mother who waits nine days and nine nights be found. Restore memory. Let the one who is diseuse, one who is daughter restore spring with her each appearance from beneath the earth. The ink spills thickest before it runs dry before it stops writing at all. (Theresa Hak Kyung Cha)[6]

Something must be said. Must be said that has not been *and* has been said before. "It will take a long time, but the story must be told. There must not be any lies" (Leslie Marmon Silko). It will take a long time for living cannot be told, not merely told: living is not livable. Understanding, however, is creating, and living, such an immense gift that thousands of people benefit from each past or present life being lived. The story depends upon every one of us to come into being. It needs us all, needs our remembering, understanding, and creating what we have heard together to keep on coming into being. The story of a people. Of us, peoples. Story, history, literature (or religion, philosophy, natural science, ethics)—all in one. They call it the tool of primitive man, the simplest vehicle of truth. When history separated itself from story, it started indulging in accumulation and facts. Or it thought it could. It thought it could build up to History because the Past, unrelated to the Present and the Future, is lying there in its entirety, waiting to be revealed and related. The act of revealing bears in itself a magical (not factual) quality—inherited undoubtedly from "primitive" storytelling—for the Past perceived as such is a well-organized past whose organization is already given. Managing to identify with History, history (with a small letter h) thus manages to oppose the factual to the fictional (turning a blind eye to the "magicality" of its claims); the story-writer—the historian—to the storyteller. As long as the transformation, manipulations, or redistributions inherent in the collecting of events are overlooked, the division continues its course, as sure of its itinerary as it certainly dreams to be. Story-writing becomes history-writing, and history quickly sets itself apart, consigning story to the realm of tale, legend, myth, fiction, literature. Then, since fictional and factual have come to a point where they mutually exclude each other, fiction, not infrequently, means lies, and fact, truth. DID IT REALLY HAPPEN? IS IT A TRUE STORY?

> I don't want to listen to any more of your stories [Maxine Hong Kingston screamed at her champion-story-talker mother]; they have no logic. They scramble me up. You lie with stories. You won't tell me a story and then say, "This is a true story," or "This is just a story." I can't tell the difference. I don't even know what your real names are. I can't tell what's real and what you made up.[7]

Which truth? the question unavoidably arises. The story has been defined as "a free narration, not necessarily factual but truthful in character. . . . [It] gives us human nature in its bold outlines; history, in its individual details."[8] Truth. Not one but two: truth and fact, just like in the old times when queens were born and kings were made in Egypt. (Queens and princesses were then "Royal Mothers" from birth, whereas the king wore the crown of high priest and did not receive the Horus-name until his coronation.) Poetry, Aristotle said, is truer than history. Storytelling as literature (narrative poetry) must then be truer than history. If we rely on history to tell us what happened at a specific time and place, we can rely on the story to tell us not only what might have happened, but also what is happening at an unspecified time and place. No wonder that in old tales storytellers are very often women, witches, and prophets. The African griot and griotte are well known for being poet, storyteller, historian, musician, and magician—all at once. But why truth at all? Why this battle for truth and on behalf of truth? I do not remember having asked grand mother once whether the story she was telling me was true or not. Neither do I recall her asking me whether the story I was reading her was true or not. We knew we could make each other cry, laugh, or fear, but we never thought of saying to each other, "This is just a story." A story is a story. There was no need for clarification—a need many adults considered "natural" or imperative among children—for there was no such thing as "a blind acceptance of the story as literally true." Perhaps the story has become *just* a story when I have become adept at consuming truth as fact. Imagination is thus equated with falsification, and I am made to believe that if, accordingly, I am not told or do not establish in so many words what is true and what is false, I or the listener may no longer be able to differentiate fancy from fact (sic). Literature and history once were/still are stories: this does not necessarily mean that the space they form is undifferentiated, but that this space can articulate on a different set of principles, one which may be said to stand outside the hierarchical realm of facts. On the one hand, each society has its own politics of truth; on the other hand, being truthful is being in the in-between of all regimes of truth. Outside specific time, outside specialized space: "Truth embraces with it all other abstentions other than itself" (T. Hak Kyung Cha).

Notes

1. I have discussed at length the notions of non-dualistic thinking and of multiple presence in Trinh T. Minh-ha, *Un Art sans oeuvre. L'Anonymat dans les arts contemporains* (Troy, Mich.: International Books Pubs., 1981).
2. Vine Deloria, Jr., *Custer Died for Your Sins* (New York: Avon Books, 1969), p. 86.
3. Quoted in Alan W. Watts, *Nature, Man, and Woman* (1958, rpt. New York: Vintage Books, 1970), p. 121.
4. "On Female Identity and Writing by Women," *Critical Inquiry* 8 (Special Issue on *Writing and Sexual Difference,* ed. E. Abel), no. 2 (1981), pp. 348–49, 354, 353.
5. Simone De Beauvoir, *The Second Sex* (1952, rpt. New York: Bantam, 1970), p. 223.
6. Theresa Hak Kyung Cha, *Dictée* (New York: Tanam Press, 1982), p. 133.
7. Maxine Hong Kingston, *The Woman Warrior* (1975, rpt. New York: Vintage Books, 1977), p. 235.
8. Herman Harrell Horne, *Story-telling, Questioning and Studying* (New York: Macmillan, 1917), pp. 23–24.

1989

FREDRIC JAMESON
b. 1934

A leading Marxist critic and literary theorist, Fredric Jameson is William A. Lane, Jr., Professor of Comparative Literature and Director of the Graduate Program in Literature and the Duke Center for Critical Theory at Duke University. His books include *Sartre: The Origins of a Style* (1961), *Marxism and Form: Twentieth Century Dialectical Theories of Literature* (1971), *The Prison-House of Language* (1972), *The Political Unconscious: Narrative as a Socially Symbolic Act* (1981), and *Postmodernism, or, The Cultural Logic of Late Capitalism* (1991).

From Postmodernism and Consumer Society

The concept of postmodernism is not widely accepted or even understood today. Some of the resistance to it may come from the unfamiliarity of the works it covers, which can be found in all the arts: the poetry of John Ashbery, for instance, but also the much simpler talk poetry that came out of the reaction against complex, ironic, academic modernist poetry in the '60s; the reaction against modern architecture and in particular against the monumental buildings of the International Style, the pop buildings and decorated sheds celebrated by Robert Venturi in his manifesto, *Learning from Las Vegas;* Andy Warhol and Pop art, but also the more recent Photorealism; in music, the moment of John Cage but also the later synthesis of classical and "popular" styles found in composers like Philip Glass and Terry Riley, and also punk and new-wave rock with such groups as the Clash, the Talking Heads and the Gang of Four; in film, everything that comes out of Godard—contemporary vanguard film and video—but also a whole new style of commercial or fiction films, which has its equivalent in contemporary novels as well, where the works of William Burroughs, Thomas Pynchon and Ishmael Reed on the one hand, and the French new novel on the other, are also to be numbered among the varieties of what can be called postmodernism.

This list would seem to make two things clear at once: first, most of the postmodernisms mentioned above emerge as specific reactions against the established forms of high modernism, against this or that dominant high modernism which conquered the university, the museum, the art gallery network, and the foundations. Those formerly subversive and embattled styles—Abstract Expressionism; the great modernist poetry of Pound, Eliot or Wallace Stevens; the International Style (Le Corbusier, Frank Lloyd Wright, Mies); Stravinsky; Joyce, Proust and Mann—felt to be scandalous or shocking by our grandparents are, for the generation which arrives at the gate in the 1960s, felt to be the establishment and the enemy—dead, stifling, canonical, the reified monuments one has to destroy to do anything new. This means that there will be as many different forms of postmodernism as there were high modernisms in place, since the former are at least initially specific and local reactions *against* those models. That obviously does not make the job of describing postmodernism as a coherent thing any easier, since the unity of this new impulse—if it has one—is given not in itself but in the very modernism it seeks to displace.

The second feature of this list of postmodernisms is the effacement in it of some key boundaries or separations, most notably the erosion of the older distinction between high culture and so-called mass or popular culture. This is perhaps the most distressing development of all from an academic standpoint, which has traditionally had a vested interest in preserving a realm of high or elite culture against the surrounding environment of philistinism, of schlock and kitsch, of TV series and *Reader's Digest* culture, and in transmitting difficult and complex skills of reading, listening and seeing to its initiates. But many of the newer postmodernisms have been fascinated precisely by that whole landscape of advertising and motels, of the Las Vegas strip, of the late show and Grade-B Hollywood film, of so-called paraliterature with its airport paperback categories of the gothic and the romance, the popular biography, the murder mystery and the science fiction or fantasy novel. They no longer "quote" such "texts" as a Joyce might have done, or a Mahler; they incorporate them, to the point where the line between high art and commercial forms seems increasingly difficult to draw.

A rather different indication of this effacement of the older categories of genre and discourse can be found in what is sometimes called contemporary theory. A generation ago there was still a technical discourse of professional philosophy—the great systems of Sartre or the phenomenologists, the work of Wittgenstein or analytical or common language philosophy—alongside which one could still distinguish that quite different discourse of the other academic disciplines—of political science, for example, or sociology or literary criticism. Today, increasingly, we have a kind of writing simply called "theory" which is all or none of those things at once. This new kind of discourse, generally associated with France and so-called French theory, is becoming widespread and marks the end of philosophy as such. Is the work of Michel Foucault, for example, to be called philosophy, history, social theory or political science? It's undecidable, as they say nowadays; and I will suggest that such "theoretical discourse" is also to be numbered among the manifestations of postmodernism.

Now I must say a word about the proper use of this concept: it is not just another word for the description of a particular style. It is also, at least in my use, a periodizing concept whose function is to correlate the emergence of new formal features in culture with the emergence of a new type of social life and a new economic order—what is often euphemistically called modernization, postindustrial or consumer society, the society of the media or the spectacle, or multinational capitalism. This new moment of capitalism can be dated from the postwar boom in the United States in the late 1940s and early '50s or, in France, from the establishment of the Fifth Republic in 1958. The 1960s are in many ways the key transitional period, a period in which the new international order (neocolonialism, the Green Revolution, computerization and electronic information) is at one and the same time set in place and is swept and shaken by its own internal contradictions and by external resistance. I want here to sketch a few of the ways in which the new postmodernism expresses the inner truth of that newly emergent social order of late capitalism, but will have to limit the description to only two of its significant features, which I will call pastiche and schizophrenia: they will give us a chance to sense the specificity of the postmodernist experience of space and time respectively.

One of the most significant features or practices in postmodernism today is pastiche. I must first explain this term, which people generally tend to confuse with or assimilate to that related verbal phenomenon called parody. Both pastiche and parody involve the imitation or, better still, the mimicry of other styles and particularly of the mannerisms and stylistic twitches of other styles. It is obvious that modern literature in general offers a very rich field for parody, since the great modern writers have all been defined by the invention or production of rather unique styles: think of the Faulknerian long sentence or of D.H. Lawrence's characteristic nature imagery; think of Wallace Stevens's peculiar way of using abstractions; think also of the mannerisms of the philosophers, of Heidegger for example, or Sartre; think of the musical styles of Mahler or Prokofiev. All of these styles, however different from each other, are comparable in this: each is quite unmistakable; once one is learned, it is not likely to be confused with something else.

Now parody capitalizes on the uniqueness of these styles and seizes on their idiosyncrasies and eccentricities to produce an imitation which mocks the original. I won't say that the satiric impulse is conscious in all forms of parody. In any case, a good or great parodist has to have some secret sympathy for the original, just as a great mimic has to have the capacity to put himself/herself in the place of the person imitated. Still, the general effect of parody is—whether in sympathy or with malice—to cast ridicule on the private nature of these stylistic mannerisms and their excessiveness and eccentricity with respect to the way people normally speak or write. So there remains somewhere behind all parody the feeling that there is a linguistic norm in contrast to which the styles of the great modernists can be mocked.

But what would happen if one no longer believed in the existence of normal language, of ordinary speech, of the linguistic norm (the kind of clarity and communicative power celebrated by Orwell in his famous essay, say)? One could think of it in this way: perhaps the immense fragmentation and privatization of modern literature—its explosion into a host of distinct private styles and mannerisms—foreshadows deeper and more general tendencies in social life as a whole. Supposing that modern art and modernism—far from being a kind of specialized aesthetic curiosity—actually anticipated social developments along these lines; supposing that in the decades since the emergence of the great modern styles society has itself begun to fragment in this way, each group coming to speak a curious private language of its own, each profession developing its private code or idiolect, and finally each individual coming to be a kind of linguistic island, separated from everyone else? But then in that case, the very possibility of any linguistic norm in terms of which one could ridicule private languages and idiosyncratic styles would vanish, and we would have nothing but stylistic diversity and heterogeneity.

That is the moment at which pastiche appears and parody has become impossible. Pastiche is, like parody, the imitation of a peculiar or unique style, the wearing of a stylistic mask, speech in a dead language: but it is a neutral practice of such mimicry, without parody's ulterior motive, without the satirical impulse, without laughter, without that still latent feeling that there exists something *normal* compared to which what is being imitated is rather comic. Pastiche is blank parody, parody that has lost its sense of humor: pastiche is to parody what that curious thing, the modern practice of a kind of blank irony, is to what Wayne Booth calls the stable and comic ironies of, say, the 18th century.

But now we need to introduce a new piece into this puzzle, which may help explain why classical modernism is a thing of the past and why postmodernism should have taken its place. This new component is what is generally called the "death of the subject" or, to say it in more conventional language, the end of individualism as such. The great modernisms were, as we have said, predicated on the invention of a personal, private style, as unmistakable as your fingerprint, as incomparable as your own body. But this means that the modernist aesthetic is in some way organically linked to the conception of a unique self and private identity, a unique personality and individuality, which can be expected to generate its own unique vision of the world and to forge its own unique, unmistakable style.

Yet today, from any number of distinct perspectives, the social theorists, the psychoanalysts, even the linguists, not to speak of those of us who work in the area of culture and cultural and formal change, are all exploring the notion that that kind of individualism and personal identity is a thing of the past; that the old individual or individualist subject is "dead"; and that one might even describe the concept of the unique individual and the theoretical basis of individualism as ideological. There are in fact two positions on all this, one of which is more radical than the other. The first one is content to say: yes, once upon a time, in the classic age of competitive capitalism, in the heyday of the nuclear family and the emergence of the bourgeoisie as the hegemonic social class, there was such a thing as individualism, as individual subjects. But today, in the age of corporate capitalism, of the so-called organization man, of bureaucracies in business as well as in the state, of demographic explosion—today, that older bourgeois individual subject no longer exists.

Then there is a second position, the more radical of the two, what one might call the poststructuralist position. It adds: not only is the bourgeois individual subject a thing of the past, it is also a myth; it *never* really existed in the first place; there have never been autonomous subjects of that type. Rather, this construct is merely a philosophical and cultural mystification which sought to persuade people that they "had" individual subjects and possessed this unique personal identity.

For our purposes, it is not particularly important to decide which of these positions is correct (or rather, which is more interesting and productive). What we have to retain from all this is rather an aesthetic dilemma: because if the experience and the ideology of the unique self, an experience and ideology which informed the stylistic practice of classical modernism, is over and done with, then it is no longer clear what the artists and writers of the present period are supposed to be doing. What is clear is merely that the older models—Picasso, Proust, T.S. Eliot—do not work any more (or are positively harmful), since nobody has that kind of unique private world and style to express any longer. And this is perhaps not merely a "psychological" matter: we also have to take into account the immense weight of seventy or eighty years of classical modernism itself. There is another sense in which the writers and artists of the present day will no longer be able to invent new styles and worlds—they've already been invented; only a limited number of combinations are possible; the most unique ones have been thought of already. So the weight of the whole modernist aesthetic tradition—now dead—also "weighs like a nightmare on the brains of the living," as Marx said in another context.

Hence, once again, pastiche: in a world in which stylistic innovation is no longer possible, all that is left is to imitate dead styles, to speak through the masks and with the voices of the styles in the imaginary museum. But this means that contemporary or postmodernist art is going to be about art itself in a new kind of way; even more, it means that one of its essential messages will involve the necessary failure of art and the aesthetic, the failure of the new, the imprisonment in the past.

Modernism has individuality

POMO, not necessarily

As this may seem very abstract, I want to give a few examples, one of which is so omnipresent that we rarely link it with the kinds of developments in high art discussed here. This particular practice of pastiche is not high-cultural but very much within mass culture, and it is generally known as the "nostalgia film" (what the French neatly call *la mode rétro*—retrospective styling). We must conceive of this category in the broadest way: narrowly, no doubt, it consists merely of films about the past and about specific generational moments of that past. Thus, one of the inaugural films in this new "genre" (if that's what it is) was Lucas's *American Graffiti,* which in 1973 set out to recapture all the atmosphere and stylistic peculiarities of the 1950s United States, the United States of the Eisenhower era. Polanski's great film *Chinatown* does something similar for the 1930s, as does Bertolucci's *The Conformist* for the Italian and European context of the same period, the fascist era in Italy; and so forth. We could go on listing these films for some time: why call them pastiche? Are they not rather work in the more traditional genre known as the historical film—work which can more simply be theorized by extrapolating that other well-known form which is the historical novel?

I have my reasons for thinking that we need new categories for such films. But let me first add some anomalies: supposing I suggested that *Star Wars* is also a nostalgia film. What could that mean? I presume we can agree that this is not a historical film about our own intergalactic past. Let me put it somewhat differently: one of the most important cultural experiences of the generations that grew up from the '30s to the '50s was the Saturday afternoon serial of the Buck Rogers type—alien villains, true American heroes, heroines in distress, the death ray or the doomsday box, and the cliffhanger at the end whose miraculous resolution was to be witnessed next Saturday afternoon. *Star Wars* reinvents this experience in the form of a pastiche: that is, there is no longer any point to a parody of such serials since they are long extinct. *Star Wars,* far from being a pointless satire of such now dead forms, satisfies a deep (might I even say repressed?) longing to experience them again: it is a complex object in which on some first level children and adolescents can take the adventures straight, while the adult public is able to gratify a deeper and more properly nostalgic desire to return to that older period and to live its strange old aesthetic artifacts through once again. This film is thus *metonymically* a historical or nostalgia film: unlike *American Graffiti,* it does not reinvent a picture of the past in its lived totality; rather, by reinventing the feel and shape of characteristic art objects of an older period (the serials), it seeks to reawaken a sense of the past associated with those objects. *Raiders of the Lost Ark,* meanwhile, occupies an intermediary position here: on some level it is *about* the '30s and '40s, but in reality it too conveys that period metonymically through its own characteristic adventure stories (which are no longer ours).

Now let me discuss another interesting anomaly which may take us further towards understanding nostalgia film in particular and pastiche generally. This one involves a recent film called *Body Heat,* which, as has abundantly been pointed out by the critics, is a kind of distant remake of *The Postman Always Rings Twice* or *Double Indemnity.* (The allusive and elusive plagiarism of older plots is, of course, also a feature of pastiche.) Now *Body Heat* is technically not a nostalgia film, since it takes place in a contemporary setting, in a little Florida village near Miami. On the other hand, this technical contemporaneity is most ambiguous indeed: the credits—always our first cue—are lettered and scripted in a '30s Art-Deco style which cannot but trigger nostalgic reactions (first to *Chinatown,* no doubt, and then beyond it to some more historical referent). Then the very style of the hero himself is ambiguous: William Hurt is a new star but has nothing of the distinctive style of the preceding generation of male superstars like Steve McQueen or even Jack Nicholson, or rather, his persona here is a kind of mix of their characteristics with an older role of the type generally associated with Clark Gable. So here too there is a faintly archaic feel to all this. The spectator begins to wonder why this story, which could have been situated anywhere, is set in a small Florida town, in spite of its contemporary reference. One begins to realize after a while that the small town setting has a crucial strategic function: it allows the film to do without most of the signals and references which we might associate with the contemporary world, with consumer society—the appliances and artifacts, the high rises, the object world of late capitalism. Technically, then, its objects (its cars, for instance) are 1980s products, but everything in the film conspires to blur that immediate contemporary reference and to make it possible to receive this too as nostalgia work—as a narrative set in some indefinable nostalgic past, an eternal '30s, say, beyond history. It seems to me exceedingly symptomatic to find the very style of nostalgia films invading and colonizing even those movies today which have contemporary settings: as though, for some reason, we were unable today to focus our own present, as though we have become incapable of achieving aesthetic representations of our own current experience. But if that is so, then it is a terrible indictment of consumer capitalism itself—or at the very least, an alarming and pathological symptom of a society that has become incapable of dealing with time and history.

So now we come back to the question of why nostalgia film or pastiche is to be considered different from the older historical novel or film (I should also include in this discussion the major literary example of all this, to my mind the novels of E.L. Doctorow—*Ragtime,* with its turn-of-the-century atmosphere, and *Loon Lake,* for the most part about our 1930s. But these are, to my mind, historical novels in appearance only. Doctorow is a serious artist and one of the few genuinely Left or radical novelists at work today. It is no disservice to him, however, to suggest that his narratives do not represent our historical past so much as they represent our ideas or cultural stereotypes about that past.) Cultural production has been driven back inside the mind, within the monadic subject: it can no longer look directly out of its eyes at the real world for the referent but must, as in Plato's cave, trace its mental images of the world on its confining walls. If there is any realism left here, it is a "realism" which springs from the shock of grasping that confinement and of realizing that, for whatever peculiar reasons, we seem condemned to seek the historical past through our own pop images and stereotypes about that past, which itself remains forever out of reach.

* * *

Now I must try very rapidly in conclusion to characterize the relationship of cultural production of this kind to social life in this country today. This will also be the moment to address the principal objection to concepts of postmodernism of the type I have sketched here: namely that all the features we have enumerated are not new at all but abundantly characterized modernism proper or what I call high-modernism. Was not Thomas Mann, after all, interested in the idea of pastiche, and are not certain chapters of *Ulysses* its most obvious realization? Did we not mention Flaubert, Mallarmé and Gertrude Stein in our account of postmodernist temporality? What is so new about all of this? Do we really need the concept of a *post*-modernism?

One kind of answer to this question would raise the whole issue of periodization and of how a historian (literary or other) posits a radical break between two henceforth distinct periods. I must limit myself to the suggestion that radical breaks between periods do not generally involve complete changes of content but rather the restructuration of a certain number of elements already given: features that in an earlier period or system were subordinate now become dominant, and features that had been dominant again become secondary. In this sense, everything we have described here can be found in earlier periods and most notably within modernism proper: my point is that until the present day those things have been secondary or minor features of modernist art, marginal rather than central, and that we have something new when they become the central features of cultural production.

But I can argue this more concretely by turning to the relationship between cultural production and social life generally. The older or classical modernism was an oppositional art; it emerged within the business society of the gilded age as scandalous and offensive to the middle-class public—ugly, dissonant, bohemian, sexually shocking. It was something to make fun of (when the police were not called in to seize the books or close the exhibitions): an offense to good taste and to common sense, or, as Freud and Marcuse would have put it, a provocative challenge to the reigning reality- and performance-principles of early 20th-century middle-class society. Modernism in general did not go well with overstuffed Victorian furniture, with Victorian moral taboos, or with the conventions of polite society. This is to say that whatever the explicit political content of the great high modernisms, the latter were always in some mostly implicit ways dangerous and explosive, subversive within the established order.

If then we suddenly return to the present day, we can measure the immensity of the cultural changes that have taken place. Not only are Joyce and Picasso no longer weird and repulsive, they have become classics and now look rather realistic to us. Meanwhile, there is very little in either the form or the content of contemporary art that contemporary society finds intolerable and scandalous. The most offensive forms of this art—punk rock, say, or what is called sexually explicit material—are all taken in stride by society, and they are commercially successful, unlike the productions of the older high modernism. But this means that even if contemporary art has all the same formal features as the older modernism, it has still shifted its position fundamentally within our culture. For one thing, commodity production and in particular our clothing, furniture, buildings and other artifacts are now intimately tied in with styling changes which derive from artistic experimentation; our advertising, for example, is fed by postmodernism in all the arts and inconceivable without it. For another, the classics of high modernism are now part of the so-called canon and are taught in schools and universities—which at once empties them of any of their older subversive power. Indeed, one way of marking the break between the periods and of dating the emergence of postmodernism is precisely to be found there: in the moment (the early 1960s, one would think) in which the position of high modernism and its dominant aesthetics become established in the academy and are henceforth felt to be academic by a whole new generation of poets, painters and musicians.

But one can also come at the break from the other side, and describe it in terms of periods of recent social life. As I have suggested, non-Marxists and Marxists alike have come around to the general feeling that at some point following World War II a new kind of society began to emerge (variously described as postindustrial society, multinational capitalism, consumer society, media society and so forth). New types of consumption; planned obsolescence; an ever more rapid rhythm of fashion and styling changes; the penetration of advertising, television and the media generally to a hitherto unparalleled degree throughout society; the replacement of the old tension between city and country, center and province, by the suburb and by universal standardization; the growth of the great networks of superhighways and the arrival of automobile culture—these are some of the features which would seem to mark a radical break with that older prewar society in which high modernism was still an underground force.

I believe that the emergence of postmodernism is closely related to the emergence of this new moment of late, consumer or multinational capitalism. I believe also that its formal features in many ways express the deeper logic of that particular social system. I will only be able, however, to show this for one major theme: namely the disappearance of a sense of history, the way in which our entire contemporary social system has little by little begun to lose its capacity to retain its own past, has begun to live in a perpetual present and in a perpetual change that obliterates traditions of the kind which all earlier social formations have had in one way or another to preserve. Think only of the media exhaustion of news: of how Nixon and, even more so, Kennedy are figures from a now distant past. One is tempted to say that the very function of the news media is to relegate such recent historical experiences as rapidly as possible into the past. The informational function of the media would thus be to help us forget, to serve as the very agents and mechanisms for our historical amnesia.

But in that case the two features of postmodernism on which I have dwelt here—the transformation of reality into images, the fragmentation of time into a series of perpetual presents—are both extraordinarily consonant with this process. My own conclusion here must take the form of a question about the critical value of the newer art. There is some agreement that the older modernism functioned against its society in ways which are variously described as critical, negative, contestatory, subversive, oppositional and the like. Can anything of the sort be affirmed about postmodernism and its social moment? We have seen that there is a way in which postmodernism replicates or reproduces—reinforces—the logic of consumer capitalism; the more significant question is whether there is also a way in which it resists that logic. But that is a question we must leave open.

1983

Permissions Acknowledgments

Walter Abish, "Ardor/Awe/Atrocity," from IN THE FUTURE PERFECT. Copyright © 1977 by Walter Abish. Reprinted by permission of New Directions Publishing Corp.

Kathy Acker, "I Recall My Childhood," from GREAT EXPECTATIONS. Copyright © 1982 by Kathy Acker. Used by permission of Grove/Atlantic, Inc.

Sherman Alexie, "Captivity," from FIRST INDIAN ON THE MOON. Copyright © 1993 by Sherman Alexie. Reprinted by permission of Hanging Loose Press.

Laurie Anderson, materials reproduced from STORIES FROM THE NERVE BIBLE by Laurie Anderson. Reproduced with the permission of the author. Copyright © 1994 Laurie Anderson.

Gloria Anzaldúa, "The Path of the Red and Black Ink," from BORDERLANDS/LA FRONTERA: THE NEW MESTIZA. Copyright © 1987 by Gloria Anzaldúa.

Paul Auster, excerpt, CITY OF GLASS. Copyright © 1985 by Paul Auster. Reprinted with permission of Sun & Moon Publishers, and the author.

Lynda Barry, excerpts from COME OVER COME OVER. Copyright © 1990 Lynda Barry.

John Barth, "Dunyazadiad," from CHIMERA. Copyright © 1972 by John Barth, reprinted by permission of The Wylie Agency, Inc.

Donald Barthelme, "See the Moon?" Copyright © 1964 by Donald Barthelme, reprinted by permission of The Wylie Agency, Inc.

Donald Barthelme, "Sentence." Reprinted by permission of The Putnam Publishing Group from FORTY STORIES by Donald Barthelme. Copyright © 1988 by Donald Barthelme.

Jean Baudrillard, excerpts from SIMULACRA AND SIMULATION. Used by permission of the University of Michigan Press.

Michael Bérubé, excerpt, "Just the Fax, Ma'am: Or, Postmodernism's Journey to Decenter," from PUBLIC ACCESS. Reprinted by kind permission of the publisher Verso.

Richard Brautigan, "The Cover for Trout Fishing in America" and "Trout Death by Port Wine," from TROUT FISHING IN AMERICA. Copyright © 1967 by Richard Brautigan. Reprinted by permission of Ianthe Brautigan Swensen.

William S. Burroughs, "Crab Nebula," from NOVA EXPRESS. Copyright © 1964 by William S. Burroughs. Reprinted by permission of Grove/Atlantic, Inc.

Octavia Butler, chapter 1, pp. 3–17, from IMAGO. Copyright © 1989 by Octavia E. Butler. Reprinted by permission of Warner Books, Inc.

Jay Cantor, "Our Town" and "The Gadget," from KRAZY KAT. Reprinted by the permission of Russell & Volkening as agents for the author. Copyright © 1987 by Jay Cantor.

Truman Capote, pp. 67–90 from IN COLD BLOOD. Reprinted by permission of Random House, Inc. Copyright © 1965 by Truman Capote and renewed 1993 by Alan U. Swartz.

Theresa Hak Kyung Cha, "Clio History," from DICTEE. Used by permission of the University Art Museum, University of California, Berkeley.

Hélène Cixous, excerpt from "Sorties," in THE NEWLY BORN WOMAN, with Catherine Clément, translated by Betsy Wing. Original, French language, edition copyright © 1975 by Union Générale d'Éditions, Paris. English translation copyright © 1986 by the University of Minnesota.

Robert Coover, "The Phantom of the Movie Palace," from A NIGHT AT THE MOVIES, OR YOU MUST REMEMBER THIS. Copyright © 1987 by Robert Coover. Reprinted by permission of Georges Borchardt, Inc. for the author.

Douglas Coupland, "Shopping Is Not Creating," from GENERATION X. Copyright © 1991 by Douglas Coupland. St. Martin's Press, Inc., New York, NY.

Ricardo Cortez Cruz, "Welcome to the Ghetto," from PREMATURE AUTOPSIES. Copyright © 1997 by Ricardo Cortez Cruz. First published in THE IOWA REVIEW. Reprinted by permission of the author.

Susan Daitch, "X≠Y." Reprinted with permission from Dalkey Archive Press and the author.

Samuel R. Delany, "Of Dragons, Mountains, Transhumance, Sequence, and Sunken Cities, *or:* The Violence of the Letter," from NEVERYÓNA, OR: THE TALE OF SIGNS AND CITIES. By permission of the University Press of New England.

Don DeLillo, from WHITE NOISE. Copyright © 1984, 1985 by Don DeLillo. Used by permission of Viking Penguin, a division of Penguin Books, USA Inc.

E. L. Doctorow, from LIVES OF THE POETS by E. L. Doctorow. Copyright © 1984 by E. L. Doctorow. Reprinted by permission of Random House.

J. Yellowlees Douglas, excerpt from "I Have Said Nothing," a hypertext published by Eastgate Systems, Inc. © Copyright 1993–4 by Eastgate Systems, Inc. All Rights Reserved.

Umberto Eco, excerpt from "Postmodernism, Irony, the Enjoyable," in POSTSCRIPT TO *THE NAME OF THE ROSE*, copyright © 1983 by Umberto Eco, English translation copyright © 1984 by Harcourt Brace & Company, reprinted by permission of the publisher.

Rosario Ferré, "The Youngest Doll," pp. 1–6 from THE YOUNGEST DOLL. Copyright © 1976, 1991 by Rosario Ferré. Reprinted with permission from University of Nebraska Press.

William Gass, "In the Heart of the Heart of the Country." Copyright © 1968 by William Gass. Used by permission of International Creative Management, Inc.

William Gibson, "The Gernsback Continuum." Copyright © 1986 by William Gibson. By permission of William Morrow & Company, Inc.

Barry Gifford, from WILD AT HEART by Barry Gifford. Copyright © 1990 by Barry Gifford. Used by permission of Grove/Atlantic, Inc.

Donna Haraway, excerpts from "A Cyborg Manifesto: Science, Technology, and Socialist-Feminism in the Late Twentieth Century." Reprinted from SIMIANS, CYBORGS, AND WOMEN: THE REINVENTION OF NATURE, by Donna Haraway, copyright © 1991, with permission of the publisher, Routledge, New York.

Terry Harpold, excerpt from "Conclusions," in HYPER/TEXT/THEORY, edited by George Landow, pp. 189–213. Copyright © 1994. Used by permission of Johns Hopkins University Press.

Ihab Hassan, "Toward A Concept of Postmodernism," from THE DISMEMBERMENT OF ORPHEUS: TOWARD A POSTMODERN LITERATURE. Copyright © 1971, 1982. Reprinted by permission of the University of Wisconsin Press.

Joseph Heller, from CATCH-22. Reprinted by permission of Simon and Schuster. Copyright © 1955, 1961 by Joseph Heller.

George Herriman, "Krazy Kat" cartoon (1921). Reprinted by special permission of King Features Syndicate.

bell hooks, "Postmodern Blackness." Reprinted from bell hooks' YEARNING: RACE, GENDER, AND CULTURAL POLITICS, with permission from the publisher, South End Press, 116 Saint Botolph Street, Boston, MA 02115.

Fredric Jameson, "Postmodernism and Consumer Society," from THE ANTI-AESTHETIC, ed. Hal Foster. Used by permission of Fredric Jameson.

Michael Joyce, excerpt from "afternoon, a story," a hypertext published by Eastgate Systems, Inc. © Copyright 1990 by Michael Joyce. All Rights Reserved.

Paul Karasik and David Mazzucchelli, pp. 1–8 from PAUL AUSTER'S CITY OF GLASS. Copyright © 1994. Reprinted by permission of Bob Callahan Studios and the authors.

Maxine Hong Kingston, from TRIPMASTER MONKEY by Maxine Hong Kingston. Copyright © 1987, 1988, 1989 by Maxine Hong Kingston. Reprinted by permission of Alfred A. Knopf Inc.

Ursula K. Le Guin, "Schrödinger's Cat" and "She Unnames Them," from BUFFALO GALS AND OTHER ANIMAL PRESENCES. "Schrödinger's Cat" first appeared in UNIVERSE 5, edited by Terry Carr, copyright © 1974 by Ursula K. Le Guin. "She Unnames Them" first appeared in THE NEW YORKER, copyright © 1985 by Ursula K. Le Guin. Reprinted by permission of the author and her agent, Virginia Kidd.

Mark Leyner, "The Making of TOOTH IMPRINTS ON A CORN DOG," from TOOTH IMPRINTS ON A CORN DOG. Copyright © 1995 by Mark Leyner. Reprinted by permission of Harmony Books, a division of Crown Publisher, Inc.

Audre Lorde, chapter 4, pp. 34–42, from ZAMI: A NEW SPELLING OF MY NAME. Copyright © 1982 by Audre Lorde. Reprinted by permission of The Crossing Press, Freedom, CA.

Norman Mailer, "The Historian," The Citizen," from THE ARMIES OF THE NIGHT. Copyright © 1968 by Norman Mailer. Used by permission of Dutton Signet, a division of Penguin Books USA Inc.

Carole Maso, from THE AMERICAN WOMAN IN THE CHINESE HAT. Copyright © 1994 by Carole Maso. Reprinted by permission of Dalkey Archive Press.

Leslie Marmom Silko, pp. 1–18 from CEREMONY. Copyright © 1977 by Leslie Silko. Used by permission of Viking Penguin, a division of Penguin Books USA Inc.

Art Spiegelman, pp. 86–91 from MAUS: A SURVIVOR'S TALE I: MY FATHER BLEEDS HISTORY. Copyright © 1973, 1980, 1981, 1982, 1983, 1984, 1985, 1986 by Art Spiegelman. Reprinted by permission of Pantheon Books, a division of Random House, Inc.

Neal Stephenson, chapter 1 from SNOW CRASH. Copyright © 1992 by Neal Stephenson. Reprinted by permission of Bantam Books, a division of Bantam Doubleday Dell Publishing Group, Inc.

Lynne Tillman, "Living with Contradictions," from ABSENCE MAKES THE HEART. Copyright © Lynne Tillman, with permission from Serpent's Tail.

Gerald Vizenor, "Feral Lasers," from LANDFILL MEDITATIONS: CROSSBLOOD STORIES. Copyright © 1991 by Gerald Vizenor, Wesleyan University Press by permission of University Press of New England.

Helena María Viramontes, "The Cariboo Cafe," from THE MOTHS AND OTHER STORIES. Copyright © 1985 by Helena María Viramontes. Reprinted with permission from Arte Publico Press, University of Houston.

William T. Vollmann1, "A Note on the Truth of the Tales" and "The Visible Spectrum," from THE RAINBOW STORIES (1992). Used by permission of Andrew Deutsch Ltd.

Kurt Vonnegut, preface and chapter 1 (p. 1–16) from BREAKFAST OF CHAMPIONS. Copyright © 1973 by Kurt Vonnegut. Reprinted by permission of Delacorte Press/Seymour Lawrence, a division of Bantam Doubleday Dell Publishing Group, Inc.

David Foster Wallace, "Lyndon," from GIRL WITH CURIOUS HAIR. Copyright © 1989 by David Foster Wallace. Reprinted by permission of W. W. Norton & Company, Inc.

Curtis White, "Combat," from MEMORIES OF MY FATHER WATCHING T.V. First published by THE IOWA REVIEW. Reprinted with permission of Dalkey Archive Press and the author.

Index